Catherine Cookson

Catherine Cookson

The Round Tower
The Fifteen Streets
A Grand Man
Feathers in the Fire
The Blind Miller

Heinemann/Octopus

The Round Tower first published in Great Britain in 1968
by Macdonald & Janes (Publishers) Ltd
The Fifteen Streets first published in Great Britain in 1952
by Macdonald & Janes (Publishers) Ltd
A Grand Man first published in Great Britain in 1954
by Macdonald & Janes (Publishers) Ltd
Feathers in the Fire first published in Great Britain in 1971
by Macdonald & Janes (Publishers) Ltd
The Blind Miller first published in Great Britain in 1963
by Macdonald & Janes (Publishers) Ltd

This edition first published in Great Britain in 1978
jointly by

William Heinemann Limited
10 Upper Grosvenor Street
London W1

Secker & Warburg Limited
54 Poland Street
London W1

and
Octopus Books Limited
59 Grosvenor Street
London W1

ISBN 0 905712 27 7

Printed in the United States of America

Contents

The Round Tower

The Round Tower

To
John Foster White
My publisher for many years
and always my friend

I have you fast in my fortress,
And will not let you depart,
But put you down into the dungeon,
In the round tower of my heart.

And there will I keep you for ever,
Yes, for ever and a day,
Till the walls shall crumble to ruin,
And moulder in dust away!

HENRY WADSWORTH LONGFELLOW

Bower Place

The four heads were almost wedged together as they looked out of the small open window of the fitting shop and leered at the uniformed schoolgirls walking down the public pathway that ran between the railings cutting off Affleck and Tate's Engineering Works, on one side, and the firm's playing fields on the other.

'There's a new one there the day; I haven't seen her afore.'

'Coo! haven't you? Why, that's God-Almighty's daughter.'

'No kiddin'.'

'Aye, it is. They usually send the Bentley to the Convent for her.'

'They're not gona let on the day.'

'Let them get by and when they think we're not gona say nowt I bet yer life they'll squint round.'

'There! What did I tell you.'

As one of the four girls slanted her glance backwards towards the men, the tallest of them shouted, 'What yer gona be when yer grow up? . . . Oh! a tart, are you?' He shook is head, 'Eeh! that's nice. Let me know when you're done an' I'll come an' have a nibble at yer.' When the girl's head jerked upwards, the man's voice, louder now, called, 'How about a bit of homework first?'

'Never mind bloody homework, see to the dayshift!' The voice brought the heads from the window, and three of the men returned sheepishly to their benches, but the fourth one who had been doing most of the talking rubbed his greasy hands through his hair and remarked nonchalantly, 'Oh, aye.'

'None of your lip, Taggart; don't come the smart Aleck with me. Now get back to your bench, and bloody quick.'

As the man moved away he said as if to himself, 'All right, Gussie?' then, 'Oh, pardon–' he looked sideways–'or should I say Mr Cotton?'

Angus Cotton let out a string of oaths, then went to close the windows. The girls, farther along the path now, were looking back, and he stared at them for a second before banging the window closed. He now glanced round at the bowed heads of the ten men of whom he was in charge, then walked to the end of the shop where, on a bench, lay a large sheet of paper on which was a square and a compass, and his teeth began grating together as he continued to work out measurements on the paper.

About five minutes later he took a rough sketch to a bench to the right of him, where stood an oldish man. 'Can you follow that, Danny?' he asked. 'Or will I take it along to the drawing-office and have it polished up?'

Danny Fuller surveyed the drawing, then said, 'I'll have a shot.' His casual reply meant that his hand would make the work as accurate as any machine could. He was studying the drawing when he said, 'There'll be trouble if you don't do something with that big head. Every day they're at those lasses. One of these times they'll go home and tell their folks what's been said in passin', and then there'll be sparks flying. Taggart comes out with some red rivets I'm tellin' you. An' if I was you I'd make it me business to be in the shop around this time when they're leaving school, 'cos I'm tellin' you, lad, they come out with things. The day was nothin'.'

'I don't suppose they say anythin' that those daisies haven't heard afore.'

'They're at the Convent, lad.'

Angus Cotton turned a humorous glance on the old man. 'And you think that's any protection the day? Their real education can start when they turn the telly on.'

'Oh, I don't suppose those lassies are allowed to look at the telly much.'

Angus now thrust out his hand and pushed Danny, saying, 'You're fifty years behind it, Danny. I bet you if you heard them talkin' among themselves your last three hairs would rise.' He flicked the thin fringe of white hanging over the collar of the old man's coat, then returned to his bench.

But as he worked he thought, 'He's right about Taggart. I'll bloody well have to sew his mouth up if it's the last thing I do; it's stretching too wide for peace.' Yet he knew he'd have to get Taggart for something else other than chatting up the lasses. The fellows in this shop had always chatted the lasses. Any lass that came along that path expected it, and some could give as much as they got, but, as Danny said, those were Convent school kids.

It was thirty minutes later when Mr Wilton caused an uneasy stir by marching through the shop, calling, 'Cotton! Cotton!'

'Aye. You want me?' Angus came from under a machine, straightened his back and stood wiping his hands on a rag as he looked into the infuriated face of a man who had to be reckoned with in Affleck and Tate. Mr Jonathan Ratcliffe might be the manager but it was his second in command whom the employees had to answer to usually. But Angus never let Wilton, or anybody else for that matter, think he could intimidate him. As he waited for the assistant manager to speak he said again, 'You want me?'

Mr Wilton now seemed to find difficulty in getting out his words. 'What's been going on here?' He flung his head from one side to the other, swallowed deeply, then added, 'Can't you control these louts?'

'Control these . . . ?' Angus didn't repeat the word. There was only one lout in this shop, and even he wouldn't thank anybody for putting a name to him. He said stiffly, 'I don't know what you're gettin' at.'

'You'll know soon enough when the boss is finished with you. He's at white heat; he's had two parents phone him within the last ten minutes because their daughters cannot pass down the Cut without filth being strewn over them.'

'Oh . . . Oh!' Angus nodded his head.

'You know then?'

'I know nowt about filth; I know the lads have a crack now and again.'

'A crack? What are you talking about, man? These are schoolgirls from the Convent, and one, for your information, happens to be Mr Ratcliffe's daughter.'

Angus felt his body stiffen. He hadn't noticed Van there; she never came this way.

'You'd better get along, and sharp; he wants to see you. And there'll be some sweeping out of this shop if I have anything to do with it.'

Angus turned a cool eye on Mr Wilton. He liked Wilton as much as he did God-Almighty Ratcliffe. Perhaps he liked Wilton less because he had more to do with him. He walked past him now and took off his overall and hung it on a nail; then, looking into the narrow, pale face of the assistant manager, he said, 'There are lots of places looking out for sweepings these days, Mr Wilton. One should bear that in mind.'

He heard a sound that could have been a chuckle coming from the direction of Danny Fuller's bench; then he went out of the shop, through the sheds, across the car park and into the building that housed the offices.

He took the lift to the third floor and stepped out into the panelled hall, looked about him for a second, then crossed to a door which bore the name 'Jonathan Ratcliffe' on a gilt-lettered board. He didn't bother to knock on the door because he knew he would have to pass the secretary before he could get into the holy of holies.

Miss Morley raised her eyes and looked at the burly shock-haired workman. She didn't ask what his business was, she knew. 'Wait a minute,' she said stiffly.

As she went towards a far door Mr Wilton came panting into the room, and he checked her, saying, 'I'll see to this,' and went swiftly through the door, closing it after him, and Miss Morley turned and favoured this Angus Cotton with a glance that told him plainly what she thought about him and all his kin: Dirty-mouthed individuals.

It was on the point of his tongue to say, 'Now look here you, get this straight,' when the door opened and Mr Wilton said crisply, 'This way, Cotton.'

Angus was a second before moving, and then his step was slow, and as he passed Mr Wilton he looked him straight in the face before turning his attention to the man sitting behind the big black desk at the end of the long room.

Although this was only the second time that Angus had been in the boss's office, he guessed he knew more about this man than did any of the thousand employees in the firm.

He had been eight years old when his mother first went to work at the Ratcliffe's house, as a daily. That was all they could afford in those days, because although Jonathan Ratcliffe was a draughtsman and earning good money, both he and his missus thought big, and spent big. As his mother said, they knew what they were doing right from the start, for the guests they wined and dined were always people of influence. And it had paid off. Oh aye, it had paid off for Mr Ratcliffe, for he was the big noise of the town now.

All you needed was a little bit of brain, a good bit of influence and a cart load of luck, not to mention the art of sucking up. It was the sucking up that had pushed him over Mr Brett's head. If anybody should be sitting in that chair now it was Mr Brett, and everybody in the place knew it, but Mr Brett was still in the drawing office.

'Remember the last time you were in this office, Cotton?'

Neither the tone nor the words startled him as they were meant to.

'I remember, sir.'

'You were then doing rough work in number one shop, and out of regard for your mother's long service with my family I wanted to help her, so I didn't only have you transferred to number three, I put you in charge of number three.'

Angus drew in a deep breath that pushed out his waistcoat, and he let it out again before he said, 'You put me in number three, sir, on the recommendation of Mr Brett, who had seen some of my drawings and thought I should be given a chance to develop.'

Jonathan Ratcliffe brought his fist firmly down on the blotting pad, and he thrust his face forward slightly as he said below his breath, 'Mr Brett's recommendations would have counted as nothing unless I gave the word; surely you have the sense to understand that. And let me tell you, I was criticised from a number of quarters for going over other recommendations and pushing you up. Such chances don't often come the way of men from the floor in number one, not at your age anyway, and with your slight experience, . . .'

'Did you have me here, sir, just to tell me this? Because if you did then I've got me answers ready for you. The first is, I'm doing a good job along there, a damn fine one, Mr Brett says. . . .'

'Be quiet! How dare you! You're forgetting yourself, Cotton. You take advantage because of your mother. But since you ask, no, I didn't bring you here to remind you why you were promoted but to tell you that in my opinion–no matter what Mr Brett might say–you are not making a damn fine job of running number three because you cannot control the men under you. It is coming to something when parents demand to speak to me on the phone because their daughters are insulted every time they pass the works: schoolgirls having filth hurled at them, bar-room chatter, obscenities, and you allow it to happen.'

'I allow nothing of the sort.'

'You were present.'

'I was WHAT!'

'One of the girls said so, she even described you. Big, fair hair. . . .'

'Well, she's a bloody liar, that's all I can say.'

'Will you moderate your language, Cotton. I think you forget who you are, and where you are.'

'I don't forget either, sir; an' I say, if she says I was there she's a bloody liar. I heard the lads at the window and I went and stopped them and shut the window. . . . But anyway–' he lifted his hand airily–'what's all the fuss about? You know yourself, sir, that all along the east side of the building where the Cut is the men have always chipped the lasses.'

'These are not lasses, these are Convent school girls, young ladies.'

'Huh!' Angus's head jerked backwards, and the sound infuriated Jonathan Ratcliffe further. The one desire he had at the moment was to get rid of this fellow for good and all, to say, 'Get out! You're finished.' But there were two simple reasons why he couldn't put his desire into action. The Union was one, and the second had even much more bearing, his wife. If he were to sack young Cotton they would lose Emily's services. Now, when they had the money to employ four servants, even with the wages they demanded today, they were quite impossible to come by. Helps came and went by the week in the house; only Emily was constant. Even if her blunt manner was as big a trial to his wife as was her son's I'm-as-good-as-you attitude, nothing must happen to cause Emily to give in her notice. That would be disastrous; especially at the present time with Susan's wedding in the offing and the Braintrees likely to drop in at any time.

He made a great effort to mollify his tone, but he could not look at the fellow as he said, 'Well, I'll overlook it this time–not that the parents concerned will, I can assure you–but should it occur again,' he now raised his eyes without lifting his head, 'I will be forced to take very strong measures. By the way, who are the men concerned?'

'Does it matter?'

'Of course it matters.' He was barking again.

'Roland, Weekes, Naylor . . . and Taggart.'

'I'll get Mr Wilton to deal with them, but,' his finger wagged now accompanying each word, 'I'm holding you responsible, Cotton. Remember that. That's what you're paid for, responsibility. That's all.'

He watched the big figure turn slowly about, and when the door closed on him he drew his lips tightly in between his teeth and muttered to himself, 'Insolent swine! . . . Trash.'

Jonathan Ratcliffe left his office at six o'clock. Miss Morley was still working, as was Mr Wilton, but the rest of the works seemed entirely deserted. There were only three cars standing in the car park and it was with a sense of deep irritation that he noticed a man with his head under the bonnet of a Volkswagen. As he unlocked his car door he asked, 'Something wrong, Arthur?'

Arthur Brett straightened himself and smiled grimly, saying, 'Third time in a week it's packed up on me. I'll have to get the garage to come and fetch it.'

There was nothing for Jonathan Ratcliffe but to say, 'Well, hop in.'

As he drove his Bentley through the gates that the watchman held open for him, he remarked casually, 'You want to change it.'

'Yes . . . yes, I know that.'

'Well, can't you?' He cast a swift glance towards the man whom he had lived next door to for the past eighteen years, the man who made him feel uneasy when in his presence, the man whose head he had jumped over, which jump had enabled him to take another two jumps into dead men's shoes, men who had died apparently long before their time. Well, as he had told himself often before, some were destined to move upwards and some to remain stationary. Arthur Brett had remained stationary because he had no push, no initiative; he was a plodder. What was more, he'd never had to strive for anything in his young days, he'd had it on a plate from when he was born. It wasn't good to have things too easy when you were young, not if you wanted to go places.

When he stopped at the traffic lights he stared ahead as he said, 'I've been having trouble with Cotton.'

'You mean Angus?'

'Who else? There's only one Cotton on the books as far as I know.'

'What's he done?'

'Spewing filth from the shop window at the Convent school girls.'

'Angus! I can't believe it. He's a rough customer, but his roughness doesn't take that form, I'd lay my life.'

'He's your golden-headed boy, isn't he Arthur?'

'No, he's no golden-headed boy of mine, but he's got ideas. Given the chance, he'll do things. Pity he hadn't had more schooling though. But he's no fool. . . . No, he's no fool.' His voice had sunk on the last words and there was a silence as they drove along the embankment, round the park and up Brampton Hill, until Jonathan Ratcliffe said, 'The trouble is he can't control the fellows under him. Apparently, they are at this every day.'

'You can't hold him responsible for that.'

'Oh, can't I?' Jonathan cast a glance sideways. 'That I can. If his men are hanging out of the windows, they're not working. I'm going to put a stop to it.'

Halfway up the hill the car turned right down a wooded lane and came to a stop at the end of the line of arches, and as Arthur Brett went to get out of the car he said, 'Thanks, Jonathan.' Then standing on the kerb he bent down and, looking through the window, said slyly. 'Whatever you do to Angus will react on Emily; I don't think Jane would be pleased if Emily went, do you?'

For answer Jonathan slammed in the gears and drove past the remaining larches, past the blue sitka trees that marked his boundary, through the imposing iron gate and up the dull pink composition drive that led to his equally imposing-looking house.

Bower Place, as he had named his house, was both a source of pleasure and irritation to him. Pleasure, because he had designed it himself. Its situation was one of the best in the town and its value had risen phenomenally in the last five years. He had paid old Brett five hundred pounds for two acres in 1949, and it had cost him four thousand to build the house. Now he wouldn't take a penny less than twenty thousand for the place, not with the money he had spent on it lately, and if only his ground had access to the river that would put another five thousand on it.

This was the irritation, the fact that Arthur Brett, with all that river frontage, wouldn't sell him a yard of it. He was as stubborn as his old man had been. There he was, without a penny to bless himself with–it took all his salary to keep his place going–yet he wouldn't part with one of his six acres.

It was sheer spite, that's what it was; Arthur was jealous of him because he had got the post he thought should have been his by rights.

At times he became so angry that he thought he'd sell his place to a speculator and let him run up a twenty-storey block of flats. That would fix Brett. And it could be done. Oh yes, it could be done. At other times he could see the council confiscating some of Brett's six acres, and running up council houses. What did he want with six acres anyway? He never touched his land, it was like an African jungle.

He entered the house and marched through the hall, throwing his hat on to the marble and gilt hallstand, then went into the lounge where his wife and two daughters were seated. They all looked at him, and his wife spoke first. She said briefly, 'Well, what have you done about it?'

'I spoke to him.'

'Who?'

'Cotton, of course.'

She rose to her feet. 'It was him then?'

'Well, not by what he makes out. He said it was some other fellows in the shop. But he's in charge. What did happen?' He turned now towards his younger daughter, where she was sitting on the couch, one leg curled under her.

'Nothing as far as I'm concerned.'

'Nothing as far as you're concerned!' His thick greying eyebrows were beetling. 'Well, well! this is news. The other three were concerned; their parents were concerned. I suppose what shocked their girls didn't shock you.'

'I didn't hear anything, Father.'

'You were with them, weren't you?'

'Yes, of course.'

'And you didn't hear anything?'

'I was thinking. I didn't even know the boys were at the window.'

'Boys! Boys! They were men, and they were throwing filth down on you and you tell me you didn't hear them?'

The girl turned her head on to her shoulder and closed her eyes, and her mother said sharply, 'Vanessa! Now don't take that attitude, your father is talking to you.'

Vanessa Ratcliffe unwound herself from the couch and stood up straight and looked at her father. She was almost as tall as he, and a good three inches taller than her mother. Her hair was a dark chestnut and fell straight on to her shoulders at the front, but tapered to a point in the middle of her back. Her eyes were brown and round, and the skin over her cheekbones spread to her lower lids without making the slightest hollow. Overall, her face was long and thin, but her lips were full, and when she smiled the corners of her mouth looked square. Her body was unformed and flat. In appearance, she took after neither her mother nor father, nor did she hold any resemblance to her elder sister, Susan, because Susan was a replica of their mother; with Ray, a ten-year-old brother, who had been sent out of the room a few minutes earlier, she had one thing in common, the colour of her hair.

Vanessa was sixteen years old and she was at the turbulent, unrestful stage of adolescence. For weeks now she had been irritated by her family, her girl friends, and everyone about her; what was more, she was experiencing a feeling that both frightened and intrigued her. She knew what it was all about but she could do nothing about it. They talked about it at school, but that didn't help, only tended to make it worse.

'I asked you a question.'

'I've told you, Father. I don't remember hearing anything, only the boys . . . men shouting. Anyway,' she shrugged her shoulders, 'they always shout down at the girls, and that's why they go along that path. They needn't, you know.'

'Do you mean to tell me that they go along there . . . ?'

'Yes, Father, I do. Lucy Fulton goes that way every day just to egg them on.'

Jonathan Ratcliffe swallowed deeply, then said, 'Well, the Fultons didn't phone me, but Mrs Herring did, and Kathy Young's mother. Was this the first time they'd been that way?'

'I don't know because I don't usually go home with them. But anyway, why should those two make such a fuss? You should hear how they talk.'

'Be quiet!' Jonathan Ratcliffe looked as if he were about to burst. 'What are things coming to? Been attending the Convent school since they could walk and you telling me they. . . .' His indignation wouldn't allow him to go on.

'Well they do. And after all,' she gave a little laugh, 'we're not infants you know, Father; I'm sixteen and a half and Kathy Young is seventeen. . . .'

'Be quiet, girl! I don't care if you're twenty-six and a half, I wouldn't expect you to listen unmoved to the spewing of the fitting-shop louts. The trouble with you, girl, is you've no sense of dignity. The Convent has failed lamentably there. Don't you realize that you're the daughter of one of the leading families of this town.' He almost said 'THE leading family'. 'And what are people going to think if you take such talk casually, while other girls are squirming. . . . Where are you going?'

'Upstairs to do my prep.'

'Well, get that defiant look off your face; and bang that door after you if you dare.'

When the door was not closed at all Jane Ratcliffe hurried down the room and shut it; then returning to the fireplace and looking at her husband, she said in her prim, thin voice, 'Now you'll understand when I tell you what I've got to put up with; she's getting more difficult every day. I never had this with Susan.' She looked at her elder daughter. 'She's getting worse.'

'It's a phase; it'll pass.' Susan smiled at her mother knowingly. She had no great love for her sister–they had always been at loggerheads–but since her engagement she had felt much more kindly disposed towards her. She knew what was wrong with Vanessa; she was suffering from the same complaint herself, but soon that feeling would be alleviated; only four months and she would be married. She wished it was four weeks . . . four days . . . four minutes. Yes, four minutes. Oh, she knew what was the matter with Vanessa all right. And if her mother had any sense she'd understand too. But sex was a taboo subject in this household. Her mother would have you believe that babies came by kissing. 'Mind, Susan; if a boy should try to kiss you keep your lips closed. Mind, now; keep your lips closed.' That was the sex instruction she'd had. When she had children she'd tell them the whole caboodle at ten. Yes, ten. Ten wasn't too young; just look at Ray. He didn't need any sex training that little devil; you could see the knowledge in his eyes. Give him another five or six years and her father would really know what trouble meant, she was sure of that. But she was getting out of it, and oh, Lord! wasn't she thankful. No more church twice on Sundays. Brian's connections might be county and titled, but she felt sure of one thing, they were as godless as they came.

When her mother said to her father, 'I told Emily,' Susan rose to her feet; she just couldn't sit and listen to another debate on Emily.

'Do you think that was wise?' Jonathan Ratcliffe looked at his wife under gathered brows.

'Yes, I do. You see, she took the call from Mavis Herring, and as usual she had her ears cocked, and when Mavis said point blank that her Rona had stated that Angus Cotton was one of the men, well, I inadvertently repeated the name Angus Cotton. I said, just like that, Angus Cotton? Are you sure? And there was Emily standing at the kitchen door all eyes and ears, so I just had to tell her. But, as I said, I think it was best; she has heard our side of it now, and when she gets home and hears Angus ranting off because he was called over the coals she'll understand why. Oh!' She pursed her lips and her left eye twitched in a nervous fashion. 'It's all so annoying. Why do we have to be bothered with such things at a time like this when I've so much on my mind and Brian's people coming at the week-end? By the way, you didn't really go for Angus, did you?'

Jonathan Ratcliffe now bent his head forward and hunched his shoulders up, and the action told her that he was deeply irritated, and this came over clearly in his voice as he snapped, 'Yes, I went for him. But not as much as I would have liked to. It maddens me to think that I have to put up with that ignorant upstart's attitude simply because we cannot do without his mother. . . . Look, Jane.' He now stabbed his finger towards her. 'I'm sure if you put yourself out and went around the agencies you'd come across someone.'

'Don't talk nonsense, Jonathan.' Jane Ratcliffe drew herself up to the limit of her five feet four inches. 'You know for a fact that I need another two in the house and can't get them.'

'Well, you should do what Irene is doing.' He jerked his head backwards in the direction of the Brett house. 'Take an au pair girl.'

Jane Ratcliffe turned her head towards the french windows and focused her eyes on a white-painted, wrought-iron chair standing on the terrace, and she surveyed it for almost a minute before she said, 'We've had all that out before. I'm not having any more foreigners in the house; I'm not going through that again and I think it very tactless of you, to say the least, to re-open the subject.'

Oh, my God! Jonathan Ratcliffe almost said the words aloud but his

Chapel training prevented it. He could blaspheme and swear in his mind. but not even his wife's finickiness. not her narrow outlook with regard to pretty Swedish girls would permit him to take the Lord's name openly in vain. He turned and left her without further words. and as he reached the top of the broad shallow stairs he saw his younger daughter coming out of her bedroom. She turned her head in his direction for a moment. then turned it away again. There was something defiant in the action; there was something defiant in the way she walked to the bathroom; her whole body was expressing defiance. He wasn't startled when the desire came to him that he wished it were possible to take a horse whip to her. Fifty years ago he could have done it. He remembered his mother saying that her father had horsewhipped her because she had committed the deadly sin of entering a theatre. It didn't matter if the play was Uncle Tom's Cabin. she had disobeyed his wishes. and she carried one of the marks of his anger visible on her neck for the rest of her life. He had never felt sorry that his mother should be so treated; he had been in entire agreement with his grandfather's attitude. A man had to stand by his principles. he had to be master in his own house. It might be considered an old-fashioned adage. but he thanked God that it still held true in some families.

As the bathroom door closed and he opened his bedroom door he thought. 'Yes. one of these days I will chastise you. madam.' But as he took off his coat he remembered her saying she was sixteen and a half years old. Soon she'd be beyond the age of open chastisement. Well. he would see. he would see.

24 Ryder's Row

Looking down on Ryder's Row from the embankment you could well imagine you were viewing the efforts of a model railway enthusiast who had stuck a short row of houses next to the goods yard at the foot of the embankment to give a natural touch to his lay-out.

The cottages were surrounded on three sides by the accoutrements of the railway company. the embankment. the goods yard. and the cleaning sheds; the end of the row fronted the main road that ran between Fellburn and Newcastle.

Over the years the occupants of the Row had become immune to the clanking and clashing of wagons, to the hissing of steam, and now the thunder of diesel engines. Some of them had been born amid the noise. and Emily Cotton was one of these.

The Cottons had always considered themselves fortunate that they lived in the last house because their back yard was twice the size of any other in the Row, and they had only one wall through which could permeate their neighbours' conversation and their own loud interchange.

Saturday morning was usually the time when their interchange was at its loudest and most penetrating, for on a Saturday morning neither Angus Cotton nor his sister, Rose, nor Emily was at work. But on this particular Saturday morning the intermittent exchange between Angus and Rosie had been comparatively quiet. Although neither of them would admit it openly, they thought the house dead when their mother wasn't in it. Without her, there was no incentive to have a bust-up, or a cracking laugh. They sometimes said, 'Coo! itn't it peaceful without her'; then they would look at the clock and wish the hours away until she burst in on them.

'She's late, isn't she?' Angus put his head into the narrow scullery and looked at Rosie where she was emptying two tins of soup at once into a pan.

'I bet she's gone to the jumble on the way back; trust her not to miss that.'

'Workin' Saturday mornin'! They'll have her there on Sunday after this. Why the hell doesn't she give it up! There's no need for her to stay on there; she's done enough, she's past it.'

'Don't you tell her that.' Rosie jerked her black hair out of her eyes. 'She'd scalp you.'

'Well, let's face it. She can't do it all. Just look at this place. It's like a pig-sty; she's had enough by the time she gets in, and she doesn't need the money now. I'm goin' to have it out with her.'

'Don't be so bloomin' daft, our Angus, and use your loaf. You know old Ratcliffe would wangle you out of the shop if Mam left there. . . . You know it.'

'I bloody well know nowt of the sort.' Angus thrust his square chin aggressively towards her. 'That's what I'm wantin' to put to the test. What do you think I feel like, being carried on her shoulders . . . at least that's what they think. But let me tell you, I got into that shop through my ability. Mark you that, through my ability.'

'All right; don't bawl your head off. I can hear you.'

The clank, clank, clank of shunting wagons filled the silence between them, until Rosie said, 'Here she is.'

As the back gate opened there came the sound of a train whistle and it seemed to pipe Emily Cotton into the house. She came in backwards, thrusting her thick, firm buttocks against the door and from her arms she dropped on to the table an assortment of garments, exclaiming 'There! What do you think of that lot?'

'Oh, Mam! Look at the bread.' Rosie retrieved the loaf from underneath the clothes, then swiftly began picking up one article after another. Holding a jumper up in front of her, she said, 'Oh, this is all right. What did you give for it?'

'Threepence.'

'Here, I got you a couple of shirts; they'll do for work for you.' Emily threw two garments towards her son and he caught them, and without looking at them he threw them on to a chair, saying, 'I've told you, Mam, I don't like wearin' other blokes' gear.'

'You were bloody glad to wear other blokes' gear, let me tell you, once on a time.'

'Well, I'm not any more, Mam; so don't get them for me.'

'God!' Emily Cotton lowered herself into a straight-backed chair and lifting one foot slowly up on to her knee she stroked her swollen ankle vigorously, and it was to it she addressed her remarks as she said, 'Talk about out of the frying-pan into the fire, I've spent most of my bloody life with upstarts. That lot along there; their noses in the bloody air so much they have to have their necks massaged. And now I come to me own house and me son tells me that he's got too damned big to wear another bloke's shirts. Let me tell you,' she lifted her head to him, 'you'll never be able to buy shirts of that quality in your lifetime. Let me tell you that.'

Angus stared at his mother for a moment. Then, the corner of his mouth moving upwards, he went towards her and, leaning forward, put his big hands on her shoulders and brought his face down within an inch of hers and said, 'Emily Cotton, that's where you're wrong. One of these days I'm goin' out and I'm goin' to buy six of the best bloodiest silk shirts in all this bloody town, and I'm goin' to wear them for work just to let them see.'

As Rosie's laugh burst forth Emily put her hands up and grabbed handfuls of her son's hair and, shaking his head none too gently, she grinned widely back into his face, saying, 'Aye. An' you will an' all.' Then giving him a push, she ended, 'But in the meantime, you'll bloody well wear these shirts for work else I'll know the reason why.'

The three of them were laughing unrestrainedly now, Angus with his hand covering his face, Rosie leaning over the table, her forearms buried in the pile of old clothes, while Emily, her head back, her mouth open, thumped her broad knees with her clenched fists; then, wiping the back of her hand across her nose and mouth, she exclaimed, 'Well, this won't do. We don't get paid for laughin'. Get that clobber off the table and let's get somethin' to eat. What you got ready?'

Rosie lifted up the assortment of clothes and threw them into an old armchair, saying, 'Soup, and fish and chips. They'll be soggy by now; I got them nearly an hour ago. An' some Ambrosia rice. By the way, what did you pay for that lot?'

'Four and six.'

'Go on! There's three dresses and two skirts there.'

'I paid four and six, I tell you, I didn't pinch them.'

'That's because you didn't get a chance. Who was on the counter?' Angus cast his eyes sideways at his mother, and she said, 'Old fat arse Flanagan. Nobody's going to pinch much when she's around; although I saw Alice Brownlow stuff somethin' in her bag. Eeh! she's barefaced, that one. Did you hear that Millie Taylor was caught again yesterday in the supermarket? She'll go along the line as sure as life this time. This must be her tenth nap. Well, it serves her right; you can be too greedy.'

'Oh, aye. Well, you remember that, Mrs Cotton, when your fingers start to itch . . . now remember.' As Angus turned to go out of the kitchen Emily threw an old woollen tea cosy at his head, saying, 'Snotty young bugger!'

A few minutes later, when they sat down to their meal at the small square table in the middle of the kitchen, Rosie remarked, on a laugh, 'You know,

Mam, I've often wondered how you manage not to come out with something up there.'

'Oh, you have, have you? Well, I'll tell you, Rosie.' Emily's voice took on a pseudo-refined note. 'It's because I know how to pass meself. I always suit me language to the company I'm in–when in Rome they say–an' I'm tellin' you there's nobody can act more refined than meself when I like.'

As Angus drew his hand slowly down his face her voice suddenly changed and she bellowed at him, 'You take the bloody micky, me lad, and I'll skite you out of that door.'

'Who's taking the micky?' His brown eyes were dancing as he looked at her. 'Of course you can pass yourself. You wouldn't have survived so long up there if you hadn't been able to. But, you know, there's somethin' I've often wondered an' all, Mam; I've wondered what effect a real good mouthful of yours would have on them.'

Once more they were laughing, spluttering over their soup. When the laughter subsided Angus asked, 'Did you hear anything more about yesterday's business?'

'Not much,' said Emily. 'Only she informed me that the master was very vexed at the whole affair.' She inclined her head deeply towards Angus, and he inclined his back and said, 'Oh, aye.'

'She was at her most buttery this mornin'. She impressed on me that the master didn't hold you responsible; it was them awful common fellows that you work with.'

'What did you say to that?'

'Nothin', I kept me silence. I find it pays with her. Say nowt and speed the work up and she gets into a tizzy. Oh, don't you worry, I can manage her all right. You don't live with somebody five days a week for eighteen years and not know them inside out. I've been along of her more than I've been with either of you.' She nodded from one to the other. 'That's strange to say, isn't it?'

'And you don't like her?'

Emily looked at her son and said slowly, 'I don't dislike her. I sort of understand her. She's a damned upstart, but she's got it from him, because he's a sactimonious, hymn-singing, big-headed nowt. An' that's only half of it, because he's deep and calculating into the bargain. An' that Susan takes after him. An' I'm another one that'll be delighted when the wedding comes off, for then she'll be away from under me feet.'

'Have you seen much of her fellow?' asked Rosie.

'Oh, he's been in twice this week. He's not a bad sort. . . . I'll tell you somethin'. He's not got one quarter of the side they have. Although he has one uncle a lord and one an admiral, he acts just like any other fellow. 'Hello, Emily', he says. 'How goes it?''

'He doesn't; you're kiddin'.' Rosie flapped her hand at her mother.

'I'm not kiddin'. An' don't you start mickying either. That's what he said. He came into the kitchen when I was gettin' lunch, and that's what he said. 'Hello, Emily. How goes it? What you hashin' up?''

'He did?'

'Aye, he did. An' I'll tell you something else. He said I was a fine cook. An' that's more than me family's ever said to me.'

'But your family never tastes your cookin', so how are we to judge? I ask you. How are we to judge?' Angus spread his hand out, palm upwards, giving emphasis to the question, and he expected her to laugh or come out with a mouthful at him. But when she dropped her fork, which was halfway to her mouth, back on to her plate and, looking at it, said dully, 'I'm sorry I've neglected you,' his face showed utter dismay.

'In the name of God, woman!' He scraped his chair back. 'Don't be so bloody soft. You know I was only pulling your leg. If you don't cook at the week-end it's our fault because we won't let you. Isn't it, Rosie?'

'Aye, Mam. Look.' Rosie put out her hand gently on her mother's thick arm. 'You're tired, that's what it is. He was only pullin' your leg. You neglect us! As Angus says, don't talk so dippy; where do you think we'd have been if it hadn't been for you goin' out to work. We've never wanted for anything in our lives, an' it's thanks to you.'

Emily bowed her head and closed her eyelids tightly, and as the tears welled up they came one to each side of her. Their concern making them tender, they put their hands about her shoulders.

'Look,' said Angus; 'You're in need of a holiday, a break . . . a long one.'

'I'm in need of no holiday.' Emily's voice was quiet.

'Well, you want a change, Mam.' Rosie stroked the blatantly dyed black hair. 'What about going to the club the night; you haven't been for weeks. That's an idea, isn't it?' She looked up at Angus. 'I'll get Stan to come along. We were going to the pictures, but he doesn't mind where he goes as long as he can have his slap and tickle.' She pressed her lips together and giggled, then said, 'What about it, eh Angus, the club?'

'I'm game. It should be a good night. We'll have a knees-up, eh?' He brought his face down to his mother's, and she blinked rapidly and sniffed, then smiled and said, 'Aye, that'll do me good, a knees-up, even if I can't get me feet off the floor.' She looked at her swollen legs. 'Anyway, I think I'll go and put them up for an hour now.' She rose stiffly to her feet, and Rosie went with her along the narrow passage and watched her mount the stairs before returning to the kitchen. There she looked at Angus and said, 'Funny, I've not seen her like that afore.'

'She's tired.' Angus's voice was low. 'I'm tellin' you, she's tired, she's worn out.'

'But she's not old,' said Rosie sadly; 'she's just fifty odd.'

'Well she's had enough in the last twenty years to make her feel eighty. I wonder she hasn't cracked up afore now.'

'But I've always thought she was as strong as a horse.'

'Horses get old. Don't you know that? Even horses get old and tired. . . . Go on up and see how she is.'

When Rosie entered her mother's room Emily was lying on the bed, her stockinged feet showing the prominent hump of bunions. Her stomach was pressing up a hillock under her skirt band and her square, heavy face looked pallid in contrast to the colour of her hair.

'You all right, Mam?'

'Oh aye, lass; just a bit tired.'

Rosie sat on the edge of the bed. 'Anything worryin' you?'

'Aye.' Emily stared at her daughter for a full minute before saying. 'Yes, there's somethin' worryin' me.'

'What then?'

'Angus.'

'Angus? Why you worrying about him? He's all right. He's fine and fixed.'

'Aye, he's fine, but he's not really fixed, not securely fixed. Do you know something?' Emily pulled herself up on the pillows and, supporting herself on her elbow, she leant towards her daughter and whispered, 'If I was to leave up there the morrow he would have Angus out of that shop afore you could blink.'

'Mr Ratcliffe! He couldn't do that, Mam. He'd have to have a reason. If he sacked him for nothing he'd have the whole shop out, the whole place out. You remember last year when they came out because of John Petrick. They were out three weeks but they got him reinstated in the end. They couldn't do anything to Angus.'

'There's ways and means, lass. An' I bet you what you like he'd have put the whole blame for yesterday's business on him if they weren't frightened of losin' me.'

'Well, I can understand them not wanting to lose you, Mam, because they won't get anybody like you in a hurry.' Rosie patted her mother's hand, and Emily said firmly, but without bumptiousness, 'I know that, an' they know that, and the missus knows if it wasn't for Angus I'd have left there two or three years back.' Her voice suddenly dropped and she said, 'I'm tired, Rosie.' Then she put in quickly, 'I'm not bad, I'm just tired. Tired, lass, tired of working for other folks. I want to stay in me own house and get it shipshape an' have the meals ready for you both when you come in . . . Aw, I know you won't be here much longer, you'll be gettin' married. And Angus an' all, he'll find somebody to his likin' afore long, if he doesn't take May, and then likely I'll be wishin' I had a job. But I can always get a job. Aw, that doesn't worry me, but in the meantime I want a space, not just a week off, or even a fortnight–she's promised me a fortnight–I want a month, two, three, a year.'

'Oh, Mam!' Rosie dropped sideways and laid her head against her mother's shoulder and her voice had a broken sound as she said again, 'Aw, Mam.'

'There, there, don't upset yourself. And mind,' she pushed her daughter's head away from her, 'now don't you bloody well go downstairs and tell him. Now mind you.'

'I'm not daft, Mam. But I can tell you this. He could get a job anywhere. There's dozens of places he could start the morrow, on Monday at any rate.' She gave a little laugh now.

'Yes, I know that, but not with the prospects there are at Affleck's. Mr Brett recommended him to chargehand and he can recommend him further. I want to see him be something, lass, not just a workman like his dad and my dad and their dads afore them. I want to see our Angus rise, and he can, given half a chance. You know it was only because of the set-up in this house that he left school when he did to help look after your dad, an' him being bad so long. You see,' she swung her legs over the edge of the bed until she was sitting side by side with Rosie, and she started to pull the knuckle of each finger in turn as she went on, 'you need education to rise, not so much brains. Ratcliffe hasn't any more brains than a louse to my mind but he had education. An' look where it got him. A grammar school education and a few kicks in the backside and he's at the top of the tree now. Aye, you need education and our Angus hasn't it, not the kind he needs to push him on, so he's got to get there in some other way.'

'But where do you expect him to get, Mam? He's in charge of his shop; he'll not get much higher than that in Affleck's.'

Emily turned her face towards her daughter and the words came under her breath, but they were weighty as she said, 'He could get himself into the drawin' office where the draughtsmen are. That's why he's been goin' to evening classes on the quiet. He doesn't know that I know he's been goin'. Did you know owt about it?'

'No, Mam. Evening classes! Our Angus?'

'Aye, our Angus.'

'He's twenty-four!'

'Twenty-four or not, he's goin'. But mind you–' she poked her finger into Rosie's chest–'don't you let on for God's sake, else he'll stop. You know what his temper's like. If he wants us to know he'll tell us in his own good time. Now go on downstairs afore he comes up an' tell him I'm all right.'

When Rosie entered the kitchen again Angus asked, 'How is she?' and Rosie replied, 'She's all right. She's goin' to have a nap.'

'All right. All right. She's not all right. An' I know why she won't leave up there, she thinks it'll affect me. I know, and she's a bloody old fool. He can do nothing to me and he knows it. You know something?' He turned round and looked at Rosie across the table. 'That man Ratcliffe has hated my guts since I was a nipper?'

'But why?'

'I think I know; in a sort of way I know.' He went and looked out of the window and down the narrow back yard. Then he said musingly, 'It was him that stopped me playing with Van. I remember the day. It was just after Dad died. Me Aunt Mary had you, an' me mam told me to go up there after school and she'd slip me a bit to eat. She was workin' late because they were havin' a dinner or somethin'–they gave dinners when they couldn't meet their grocery bills. Anyway, this day I was keeping out of the way round the back when Van comes on me. She was about five at the time. Well, there happened to be a garden barrer on the back path, you know one of those wooden ones, an' I put her in it and started to wheel her up and down. An' she laughed so much I thought she would burst. It must have been her laughin' that brought his lordship round, and he bellowed so loudly that he startled me and I nearly upset the barrer and her an' all. After he had ordered her in he stood looking at me with a look on his face that he sometimes has now, as if he considers me so much slime that should be washed down the drain. Yet even on that day he didn't go for Mam and tear her off a strip. But I never got the chance to play with Van again. Anyway, I've worked out his theory about Ratcliffe's attitude to me. It's just this. He can show his dislike for me and nothin' comes of it, but if he did it to Mam she would leave, and knowing this he not only hates me guts but her's an' all.'

'Go on. You're just imagining things. They think the world of her.'

'Think the world of her! Why? They think the world of her because she's necessary to them. They won't get a woman like Mam the day. Who they goin' to get to work from eight till five for five quid a week, turning her hand to anything from cooking to waiting on the 'At Home' do's and their blasted dinners? Think the world of her! If she died the morrow they wouldn't come to her funeral.'

'Oh, you're too bitter against them, our Angus.'

'Not me, I've just got them taped, him most of all. He'd like to kick her backside out of the door. You see she doesn't kowtow to him, she answers him straight–without the bloodies of course.'

They both laughed softly now, and Rosie said, 'Eeh! I wonder what they'd think if they heard her going on sometimes?'

'Do them good. God! wouldn't I like to hear her let rip at them.' He boxed the air and Rosie said, 'Well, that reminds me. When you're gettin' it out of your system why aren't you at the match the day? Is your back still hurting?'

'I've left.' He was still punching the air, dancing round the table now, boxer-fashion, on his toes.

'You've left?' Her exclamation was high.

'Aye.'

'Are you barmy altogether? You broke your neck to get in, and it was an honour.'

He stopped abruptly and repeated, 'An honour? From who?'

'Well.' Rosie tossed her head. 'With Callow, the solicitor, playin', and that young Brownlow in the accountant's office.'

'To hell! Who's Callow, the solicitor, and Brownlow? Don't forget Ted Robson's the star player, and he's a bricklayer. And Andy Thompson, what does he do? He carts ballast. If they had to depend on the white collar bods they wouldn't have a team at all. Honour!'

'Well it was,' Rosie persisted. 'It isn't everybody who is asked to join the Rugby team in this town. You must be barmy leaving it.'

'Well, I have left.'

'Does me mam know?'

'No, she doesn't.'

'When did this happen?'

'Two weeks ago, if you want to know.'

'When you hurt your back?'

'Yes, when I hurt me back; when somebody hurt me back, jumping on it with both feet. For the last year I've been asking meself what it's all about. Why get half-killed every week? I've had me ribs nearly kicked in, me shins torn. There was one time last year I nearly had me neck broke. And so I asked meself why I was doing it? And then when you're playin' away, the drink. Swimming in it. I don't mind a drink, you know I like a drink, but oh, God! the stupid things they get up to, the way they carry on. I used to an' all. I did me share, but I happened to be solid and sober one night when I went along to the Bull late. They had been at it a couple of hours, and aw, it turned me stomach over. They had put a nappie on Bill Webster. That's all he had on, a nappie, an' there he was sittin' in the middle of the floor sucking his thumb and slobberin', and Alec Turner was playin' the mother. I tell you, Rosie, I nearly spewed.'

'Well, it's only a bit of fun.'

'Well, it's not my kind of fun.' He nodded his head at her.

'You know what, our Angus?' She pursed her lips and grinned. 'I think you're goin' through a bad time. It can't be adolescence, so it must be an early change. I should warn May.'

The old tea cosy flew through the air again and she ran into the scullery laughing, and he was laughing as he went into the front room, which was his room.

The front room was twelve feet by nine. In it was a single divan bed, a new acquisition, an old chest of drawers, a hanging wardrobe, a small table in the corner near the window, and a gas fire in front of an open grate. The floor was covered with blue-and-white check linoleum and there were blue cotton curtains at the windows. The room was tidy and, if not bright, it was clean. No matter what condition the rest of the house got into Emily saw to this room.

Early change. He grinned to himself and jerked his head, then pulled a straight-backed chair up to the table on which were a number of books and some drawing paper, but he didn't start to work. He rested his elbow on the table and supported his chin on his hand, and he gazed through the narrow aperture of the curtains, across the street to the high, faceless wall of the railway sheds. An early change. Well, he might not be going through an early change but there was something wrong with him. He didn't know what, except, as he put it, he was at sixes and sevens with himself. He knew this much though. If it wasn't for his mam he would pack up the morrow and clear out, he would that. Ratcliffe, Afflecks, the lot would go to hell. . . . What about May? Oh, May an' all for that matter.

The Larches

As they went out of the door it began to rain and Rosie said, 'Oh lor! me hair'll be flat. Why the devil can't we have a car, our Angus? Nearly everybody else in the street's got one 'cept us.'

'Aye; and look at them.' He thumbed a derelict looking specimen they were passing. 'I'll get a car when I can afford one, not one from the scrap.'

'You'll get no car at all,' said Emily, 'if you want to stay alive. Remember Sammy Cullen afore Christmas. I bet where he is the night he wishes he had never seen a car.'

'His was an old wreck, Mam,' said Rosie. 'You can get a nearly new one for a couple of hundred from Hallows.'

'Listen her!' exclaimed Angus. 'A couple of hundred! Why don't you get Stan to fork out and buy you a car?'

'He will an' all. That's what he's goin' to do if he wins the talent spot next week, goin' to put it down on one.'

Angus gave a ha-ha of a laugh; then nudging his mother, he said, 'Why don't we go in for the talent spot, Mam, eh? You could do your bit poetry, you know.

'Between the dark and the daylight,
When the night is beginning to lower,
Comes a pause in the day's occupations
That is known as the children's hour.
I hear in the chamber above me
The patter of little feet. . . .'

He was pushed into the gutter. 'You'll hear the crack of me hand across your lug, me lad, if you don't stop takin' the micky. I'll tell you one thing, they learnt you poetry in my day. Aye, at a council school at that.'

'Eeh! The Children's Hour.' Rosie shook her head. 'It used to petrify me, that, Mam, when you used to say it to me.

'I have you fast in my fortress
And will not let you depart
But put you down in the dungeon
In the round tower of my heart.'

You used to say it to me to send me to sleep but it always sent me into nightmares; I was always cryin' to get out of dungeons.'

They were laughing hilariously as they boarded the bus. They were still laughing and talking, and all at once, when they alighted in the main street, and they were a few yards from the club entrance and passing a tobacconist's, when Angus said, 'You go on in, I'm goin' to get some baccy.'

'Baccy? You?' Rosie had hold of his arm.

'Aye, baccy, me. I've decided to smoke a pipe. Better for your lungs, they tell you.'

Their laughter vied with the noise of the traffic, and as they parted he tried to control his face before entering the shop.

Carsons was a big shop, the best in the town. A number of people were inside, and he did not notice the young girl until she moved a step to allow a man to pass her, and then he said, 'Why, hello, Van.' He had almost said Miss Van. It was just a habit, the Miss. Sometimes he added it to her name and sometimes he didn't.

'Oh, hello, Angus.' Her face, which had been solemn in repose, brightened.

He bent his head down to her. 'You takin' to smokin'?'

'No.' She smiled widely at him. 'It's father's birthday on Monday.'

He looked her up and down, then whispered, 'I didn't recognise you without your school rig; you know, it's the first time I've seen you out of school uniform in years.' He jerked his head. 'You look different.'

She stretched her face slightly up to his and whispered back, 'And you know something, Angus? I feel different.'

They both chuckled, then moved a step forward as another customer left the counter. They were silent for a moment, he staring ahead towards the cigarette-laden shelves; then turning to her again, he whispered under his breath, 'Don't often see you down this way,' and she answered as softly, 'I don't often get down this way; I've been let out.' And they exchanged an understanding smile.

When her turn came to be served she asked for a box of cigars and paid over thirty shillings for them. As she turned from the counter he said, 'Be seeing you, Van.' And she nodded at him and answered, 'Yes. Be seeing you, Angus.'

A minute or so later, when he left the shop, she was standing in the shelter of the doorway and she turned to him and said, 'What a night! I'm going to wait here until the bus comes across the road and then make a dive for it.'

He peered at her in the dim light, saying, 'This is one time when I wish I had a car. We were just talking about a car when we left the house, me Mother and Rosie. They said I should have a car.'

'Are they here?' She nodded towards the street.

'They're in the club; we're goin' to make a night of it.' The corner of his mouth moved characteristically upwards.

She looked into his face, hers unsmiling now, and she said, 'You do enjoy yourselves, don't you? I mean Emily and Rosie and you, you do enjoy yourselves.'

'Oh, I don't know, not more than anybody else. Life's very dull at times.' In his mind he was talking to a very young girl, a girl who had everything, yet whom he was sorry for in a way, whom he had always been sorry for in a way. He said now, 'It's about time you splashed out at dances, isn't it? Country balls an' that?'

'The school dance is as far as I've got so far, Angus; but I'll likely start in the autumn.'

'Well, that's something to look forward to.' He paused and stretched his thick neck upwards out of his collar before saying, 'By the way, Van, there's something I'd like you to get clear.' He now rubbed the side of his forefinger across his chin. 'It's about yesterday's business. You know I wouldn't have let that happen if I could have helped it, but the lads—'

Her gloved fingers lightly flicked his sleeve. 'Look, Angus, forget it. All that fuss. They ask for what they get, I know that.'

'Yes, but nevertheless, the fellows should mind their tongues . . . I didn't know you came along that way?'

'I don't as a rule, but I was going to my friend's house and apparently she uses it as a short cut,' her lips pressed together for a moment, 'because she likes to egg them on.'

He stood looking down at her. She was wise in a way was Van. He'd always felt that. Different from the rest, inside as well as in appearance. She was turning into a lovely looking lass, and she would get lovelier. With startling suddenness there came into his chest, just below the ribs, a strange feeling, and for a moment he felt he had been cut off from life; he felt empty, sort of lost. The feeling so enveloped him that he didn't notice a car drawing up to the kerb. When a man got out and came into the shop doorway, Vanessa said, 'Oh, hello, Brett,' and the man answered on a surprised note, 'Why! Vanessa.' Then he looked at Angus and added, 'Hello there, Angus.' He didn't show any surprise that Angus Cotton, one of the floor men, should be standing in a doorway talking to the manager's daughter. But, on the other hand, Angus showed a great deal of embarrassment.

'Hello, Mr Brett,' he said; then added quickly, 'Van . . . Miss Van here got caught in the rain. She's waitin' for a bus.'

'Waiting for a bus? Well, it's a good job I came along. I won't be a minute, Vanessa. Go on in the car; Irene's there'

'Oh thanks. That's fine. Good-bye, Angus.' She smiled at him.

'Good-bye, Van.' They were alone again for a moment. 'Be seeing you.'

'Yes. Be seeing you, Angus.'

As she got into the back of the car she said, 'Hello Irene,' and Irene Brett turned round in her seat and said, 'Hello, Vanessa. A beastly night, isn't it?' Then after a slight pause she added, 'Wasn't that Emily's son you were talking to?'

'Yes, Irene. I just met him in the shop a minute ago.'

Vanessa always thought of the woman she had known from a small child as Irene Brett, not Auntie Irene. Susan called her Auntie, but she herself had stubbornly refused to call their neighbour Auntie, or her husband Uncle. She had even amazed her parents by going so far as to address Arthur Brett by his surname. When she was asked why, she said she didn't like the name Arthur, she liked Brett, and so he had been Brett to her ever since.

This familiarity had always incensed Irene Brett. She now sat looking at the rain-smeared windscreen, and she was again feeling annoyed that she could find nothing to say to this girl. She had always considered Vanessa a deep, withdrawn type of girl, and she felt now that she was indeed right about her being deep. She didn't believe for a moment that she had met Angus Cotton by accident. This wasn't the first time she had seen them together; a fortnight ago she had seen them both standing talking outside the Technical School. Now what would she want outside the Technical School? It was miles away from the Convent, and from Brampton Hill. She had felt for a long time that Jonathan and Jane were going to have trouble with this one. They weren't going to be able to plan her life as they had done Susan's. Anyway, perhaps they'd be satisfied in wangling one daughter into the fringes of the titled set. They'd never let up, those two, get there or die.

Her thoughts, touching on the second main grievance of her life, gathered momentum and she became lost in her hate, and she started as the door opened and her husband took his seat, saying over his shoulder, 'Don't often see you in the town, Vanessa.'

'No, I don't often come down. But it's Father's birthday. I was getting him a present.'

'It's his birthday is it?'

'Yes, he'll be fifty on Monday.'

'Fifty! Well, well. Yes . . . yes, he will be fifty.' He was talking as if to himself. When he got the car going he added, 'Time doesn't stand still; no, time doesn't stand still.'

There wasn't another word spoken until they turned from Brampton Hill into the side road; then Vanessa said, 'Just drop me at your gate, Brett, that'll be all right.'

'No, I'll take you along.'

'No, please. It's eased off.'

'All right, just as you say.'

When she got out of the car she said. 'Thanks for the lift, Brett. Good-night, Irene.'

They both said together, 'Good-night, Vanessa.'

A few minutes later they went up the steps, through the glass-covered lobby and into the dark, panelled hall, and there, as Irene Brett took off her hat and coat, she remarked casually, 'Well, what do you think of that?'

'What?'

'Her standing talking to that Angus Cotton.'

He hadn't looked at her before, but now he turned round and faced her. Then after staring at her for a moment, he said, 'Angus Cotton and Vanessa? Well, why shouldn't she talk to him? They've known each other all their lives. I remember them playing together.'

She threw up her head, closed her eyes and turned from him, and as she went into the high-ceilinged, old-fashioned looking drawing-room, she said, 'Your simplicity makes me want to scream. It must be all of ten years or more since Jonathan put a stop to that. But of course you wouldn't remember anything so mundane.'

She turned round now and watched him coming slowly into the room, and when he came near her she said, 'I saw them together outside the Technical School only a few days ago. And that's not the only time.'

Arthur Brett surveyed his wife. There were times when he had to screw his eyes up to get her into focus, when he had to remind himself that he had lived with this woman for twenty-five years, that she wasn't a stranger whom he didn't know. He said quietly to her, 'What are you trying to make of it?'

'What am I trying to make of it?' She stressed the I. 'I'm only making a statement. What do you think would be Jonathan's reaction if he knew that she was talking to that fellow in the main street?'

'I don't know, Irene; and I don't care very much what Jonathan would think. But I would think it strange if those two met in the street and passed each other. And whether Jonathan stopped them playing together years ago or not, I can recall when Angus was a big lump of a lad and Vanessa was seven or eight or more seeing them together in the garden.'

'Well, you've seen something that nobody else saw, because if either Jonathan or Jane had known there'd have been an abrupt stop put to it. And I think a stop should be put to this if they don't want consequences . . . That fellow! He's like a great big Irish navvy. I think at least Jane should know about it.'

'And I think,' there was a hardness in Arthur Brett's usually soft, lazy-sounding voice now, 'I think you should mind your own business and not take it out of Jane through Vanessa.'

'Take it out of . . . ! What are you talking about? What are you insinuating?'

'Just that you're not too pleased, are you, that Jane is getting Susan married into the Braintrees. But you can't do much about that so you intend to make her uneasy through Vanessa. That's it, isn't it?'

'How dare you! How dare you suggest such a thing. You're making me out to be a vile, mischief-making . . .'

'I'm not making you out to be anything but what you are, Irene.' As he turned from her she hissed at him under her breath, 'Don't leave me like that, Arthur. Listen. Listen to me. Do you hear?'

Not until he was at the room door did he turn, and then he said quietly, 'I'm not going to listen to you, Irene; I don't happen to be a member of one of your committees, not a fellow councillor whom you are rating, nor yet a delinquent up before you on the bench. There are a number of things you can't make me do, Irene, and that's one of them; listen to you.'

When he closed the door behind him and she was alone she stood with her two hands pressed tightly over her thin lips. She could understand why women committed murder. He hadn't the gumption he was born with, yet he was inflexible about what he considered his ideals, his principles. Oh, God, how had she of all people got stuck with someone like him! She knew the answer to this, but she had long refused to think about it.

She now walked to the couch, and with her hands still in the same position she sat herself down. She did not lean back against the couch for support, her thin body remained erect. She had a good figure and she looked after it, as she did her complexion and her hair. She was looked upon as a smart woman, but no one had ever said she was good-looking or pretty . . . or charming, but she was often referred to as clever and business-like. She was a committee woman and could get things done, at least outside her own house and family.

After a moment she lowered her hands to her lap and her eyes moved slowly around the room. She almost hated this room, this whole house, as much as she did its owner. The place had never been redecorated inside or out for years, yet he had only to sell two or three acres of land and the whole place could be renovated. Even if he could have been persuaded to sell some of the furniture, some of these ugly monstrosities, this would have gone a long way towards lightening and refurnishing the house.

There was a Queen Anne secretaire on the landing for which he had been offered three hundred pounds, and in a corner, over there, in the recess that hardly saw the light of day, was a William and Mary side-table. There was a very old mahogany commode in Colin's bedroom that would be worth a small fortune at Sotheby's. There were French chairs dotted all over the house, the tapestry so threadbare the wadding was sticking through, and there was no hope of having them re-covered; he wouldn't even allow her to put loose-covers on them. There wasn't one of the twelve rooms in the house that didn't hold a piece of furniture that would bring in hundreds, but because his grandfather had furnished this house for his bride in 1892 he thought that was sufficient reason why it should remain as it was for his life. She knew that he had even made a will to the effect that all the furniture couldn't be sold on his death; certain pieces he had willed to the three boys with a request that they would think twice before parting with them. He had dared to tell her that he was going to do this. Spite. Spite, that's what it was, and all because she wouldn't supply him with his needs. His needs indeed! If he came into her room again she would tear his face off. Only last week he had dared to try to get into bed with her. Why? Why? When he cared as little for her as she did for him. She had warded him off for years with the excuse that she didn't want any more children, and nothing was safe. . . . And nothing was safe. Michael, her youngest son, was only six years old. Fancy, on the verge of forty having become pregnant again! The shame of it almost killed her. She had hardly been able to face the boys. . . . Boys? Colin had been almost a man then: eighteen, and Paul thirteen.

And last night he had dared to try it on again, even knowing how she felt about him. Again she had to ask herself, Why?

Upstairs in his room, Arthur Brett was asking himself the same question. Why? Why, when their love was dead, so dead you forgot when it had died, did you re-visit the corpse? Why did you want to put your arms around it, put your mouth on its mouth, press your body into it, work over it, struggle with it, even knowing it wouldn't move? It never had moved during all the years of their married life. The act had been an act of sufferance on her side and had brought him humiliation; yet he suffered humiliation a thousandfold in going to her and begging for his body's easement. Why? Why didn't he go down to Bog's End. He could find ease in Bog's End. He could reel off the names of at least eight men he knew on his floor who visited Bog's End regularly. He had just to say one word to Will Hobson and he'd be fixed up. The times he had made up his mind to say that word to Will. He would be determined when he had left the house in the morning that the first thing he'd do would be to see Will and put an end to this torment. He always got as far as seeing Will but he never mentioned Bog's End. Again why?

Perhaps it was because at these moments he would remember that but for his grandfather's taste for high living, and his father's easy going-ness and lack of business sense, he might today be Will Hodson's employer, because the firm of Affleck and Tate had once belonged to the Bretts. His grandmother's name was Affleck. She had brought the business–much smaller than it was now admittedly, but nevertheless a thriving concern–she had brought it to one Arthur Brett, a handsome, loving, carefree individual, who had a taste for good furniture, good wine, entertaining, and horses, which tastes he indulged right up to the middle of the thirties. He died at the table drinking wine; he actually died in toasting his white-haired and still beautiful wife. It was all very romantic.

He could remember the night his grandfather died as if it was yesterday. It was a beautiful summer evening, and he was home from boarding-school. He was sitting at his grandmother's right hand and he was looking at her profile as she gazed down the table towards her big, corpulent, but still handsome husband. When he fell forward over the table she gave a thin high scream and then became quite still. Three days later she herself died. His father said that was as it should be; they both had enjoyed life and one couldn't exist without the other.

His own father had almost repeated the pattern in his approach to life and way of living. It wasn't until Arthur himself was seventeen that he realized that Affleck and Tate was no longer their firm, that the shares had been sold gradually until their holdings were now non-existent, and that all that remained of the once-affluent Afflecks was the house and land; and of course, the furniture, the furniture which his father wouldn't part with even to keep up some kind of appearance in the town.

He was nineteen when he met Irene Bailey, and she was a year older than him, and he hadn't thought he was deceiving her by not explaining the financial position in which his parents stood. After all, thinking socially, she was of little consequence in town. Her father was a schoolteacher, elementary. She was attractive and vivacious, and he had fallen deeply in love with her, besides which he was full of admiration of her. She hadn't got to the high school, but she had supplemented her elementary education by going to night school. She could talk intelligently; she only had to have a smattering of any subject and she could give the impression of knowledge.

He knew she was flattered by his attention; also that she was impressed by the big house, and the fact that he was the only son of the Bretts, and that they were Affleck and Tate.

He had told her casually before they were married that they were no longer Affleck and Tate, and he imagined at the time that it had meant nothing to her, but he knew now that she married him because she thought she could do something with him, restore him to the lost eminence of his grandfather, if not in the works, then along other lines.

But he was not cut out for other lines; except perhaps he could have been manager of Affleck and Tate. Oh yes, yes, he could have been manager, and he should have been manager because, after all, Affleck and Tate was in his blood so to speak. Yet all this had been forgotten when a certain Jonathan Ratcliffe, whom incidentally he had befriended when he first came into the drawing-office, inveigled himself into the good books of the board, by what method he had never been able to find out, and he had been too proud to enquire. Of course there had been the usual tittle-tattle about sucking up; but any move upwards brought this reaction. Anyway, Jonathan had gone from the drawing-office to the building across the yard, and there had become assistant to the under-manager, Rowland. Yet he must be fair. That was likely as far as he would have got if both Bowden, who was manager at the time, and Rowland, who took his place, hadn't died within the next five years.

Life was odd. He went to the window and looked out through the leafless trees. There, in the distance, he could see Jonathan's house. It was lit up. They were entertaining again, likely Susan's fiancé's people. He liked entertaining did Jonathan; it was a mark of his power. They were rarely asked next door, because he embarrassed Jonathan. He also knew he angered him. He had still things Jonathan wanted, the river frontage, for instance, and the land, all of it. The land. Oh, yes, all of the land.

He turned from the window and went out of the room and was crossing the landing when his eldest son, Colin, came up the stairs. They blinked at each other over the distance and Colin's look said, "You two been at it again?"

Arthur knew that his eldest son saw him through the eyes of his mother. This didn't boost one's morale. Still he had the consolation of Paul. Paul was different. Paul was the replica of himself, quiet, easy going; clever in a way. But what was the use of being clever in a way, you had to be clever in all ways. He doubted somehow if Paul would be any different from himself in this way either. He had no push. He wanted to meander through life like they both used to meander at night through the wood, then sit in the old summerhouse looking at the river and talk, or be silent, and sometimes laugh. Paul was the only real companion he'd had in his life. Irene had made certain of Colin and was making certain of Michael, but she could do nothing with Paul. Paul had stuck to him as if he was his own sweat.

Irene had made no fuss about Paul going to college. He knew that she had welcomed the fact that the other part of her husband would be out of the house. She was at her worst during the holidays, but the holidays were the only thing he lived for. And this year they would be short, at least for him, because Paul was going abroad on a walking tour. He had wanted him to go along, and if there had only been the two of them he would have jumped at the chance, but he couldn't see himself being one of a party of four exuberant youths.

After his bath he went straight to bed. This wouldn't interfere with the routine of the house; he rarely had anything to eat after teatime. Later on, when they had all retired, he might go down to the kitchen and make himself a hot drink and sit by the stove. He liked sitting by the stove. He had sat a lot in the kitchen when he was a boy; it had been a different stove then. The old one had exploded one day and the cook had fainted. She had been a big old Irish woman, and when she came round the first thing she said was, "Oh God, have I been blown into heaven?" And they had all laughed and laughed. They had laughed a lot in this house at one time. Everybody in it had been compatible; there had been no in-law trouble when he was young. His mother and father had lived all their married life with his grandfather and grandmother, and he himself had brought his bride to live with his mother and father. It was from then that the laughter had eased off.

It was around ten o'clock when he heard Irene come upstairs and go to her room. She did not look in on him. That, too, had ceased a long time ago. He lay for a time, his book lying on top of the quilt, his two hands flat on the open pages, and he staring down at them as he asked himself questions to which there were no answers. When eleven o'clock struck he switched the light off and got up and opened the curtains. He was surprised to see the moon shining brightly. The rain had stopped and the tangled garden below him and the long stretch of wood beyond looked like an enchanted forest. He pulled his dressing-gown about him and sat on the broad windowsill, with his knees up under his chin. He could still do that for he wasn't pot-bellied. There was no movement outside, no wind; March was in but she was withholding her signs. It could have been a June evening except that it would be cold out. He had always wanted to write poetry; there seemed such a lot of poetry locked up inside of him. He envied people who could write. There must be great easement in writing, pouring out your feelings and being able to read them back to yourself. Not only must it be alleviative, but also satisfactory. That's why he missed Paul so much. Paul, in a way, had been his form of release, his outlet.

As he stared at the treetops his eyes were caught by a movement down below to the left of him. There was a shadow crossing the open space, which was the north side of the Ratcliffe's garden. There were no open spaces in his garden. It took gardeners to create open spaces, and he himself was no gardener for the simple reason he hated to cut anything down, even weeds. Killing in any way was abhorrent to him, but he didn't give this reason for the neglect of his garden. He just said that he was no gardener, also that he was innately lazy.

The shadow disappeared, then reappeared again in a patch of moonlight. It was making for the gate in his boundary fence, the gate which allowed the Ratcliffes' access to the river bank, his river bank. He had had the gate made when Jonathan first built the house. A second before the figure disappeared again into the shadows he recognized Vanessa. Now what would Vanessa be doing out at this time of night? He turned and glanced at the clock. Ten minutes to twelve. He now turned his gaze towards the Ratcliffes' house. The lights were all out.

Once more he focused his gaze in the direction of the gate. It was impossible to see if she had come into the wood. But she had been making for the gate. When, five minutes later, he had not seen her return up the garden, the reason for her midnight stroll came to him as he remembered what Irene had said earlier in the evening, and he muttered aloud, "Oh no! No!"

It was one thing Angus Cotton speaking to her in the street, but it was entirely another thing meeting her secretly, and at this time of night. The wire fencing at the bottom of the wood was broken in several places where it bordered the side road. The children were always coming in for cob nuts or bluebells. Angus could easily come in that way and walk along by the river bank to the summerhouse.

God! No! He liked Angus. He was a good, honest fellow, and he had brains of a sort, but to start anything with Vanessa! He began swiftly to pull his trousers on. One thing was certain. If there was anything in this, Jonathan would blame him for giving the fellow ideas above his station. He had already used that very term.

He got into his coat, took his shoes in his hand, then opened the door softly, and, crossing the landing, he went down the back stairs that led directly into the kitchen, then let himself out at the side door.

The night air made him shiver. As he took the side path around what had once been the rose garden he asked himself what he would say to them. Well, he could just be taking a stroll. That was it. He couldn't sleep and had come out for some air. Then he would get Angus on one side and let him have it. Oh yes, he'd let him have it. This kind of thing couldn't go on. It wasn't only because Jonathan would blame him, it was because a girl like Vanessa mustn't get herself mixed up with a fellow like Angus. No matter how decent he was, it just wouldn't work out. He liked reading mythology and tales of princesses and plough boys, but these were only to entertain that section of the mind that remained for ever in youth. The fate of the princess and the plough boy in real life could only spell disaster. In a sort of way his own romance had been like the prince and the beggar maid. Not that Irene would thank him for placing her in that category.

The path was well worn, and last year's leaves had been trodden into mush by his own feet. He entered the wood, and although he was in deep shadow he found his way unerringly between the great oak tree which dominated the top of the wood and the forked group of three birch trunks that stood to the right of it; then through a thicket of spidery hazel trees, and on to a pathway again. He was careful to keep to the path so as not to tread on to the carpet of wood anemones and the sprouting daffodils and narcissus. In another week or so the wood would be a picture of white and gold with a sprinkling of blue, and when the blue took over he would think again the sky had fallen. He now turned sharp right to the gate that gave access to the wood. It was open, pushed back on its rusty hinge. He left it like that, then walked quickly in the direction of the river and the summerhouse.

He paused by the landing stage and looked along the bank and up the rise to where the summerhouse stood. The moon was lighting up the scene as if it was daylight. He strained his ears but could hear no sound of voices. God, but this was going to be awkward. Yet she might not be there at all, she might have gone back. No, she would have closed the gate after her if she had gone back. They always closed the gate so that Michael's puppy wouldn't again get through into Jonathan's garden and play havoc among the formal beds. No, somehow he had no doubt but that she was still here, and in the summerhouse. Well–he squared his shoulders–he couldn't stay out all night, he'd better get it over with. His feet made no sound on the grass bank as he approached the wooden structure that had a disintegrating veranda and a thatched roof in a similar state. Three steps along the veranda took him to the door. To his surprise it was open and, further to his surprise, there was Vanessa, her hand held tightly against her cheek, sitting on the slatted form staring at him.

'Vanessa!'

'Oh, Brett. Oh!' She put her other hand up to her face and closed her eyes.

'Oh, you did give me a start.' She swallowed deeply now as she gazed up at him. 'I . . . I nearly had a fit.'

He was blacking out the moonlight, and in the shadow of himself he could only see the dark gleam of her eyes, their brown now appearing like pieces of jet. 'What on earth are you doing here, on your own?'

'Oh, well.' She rose to her feet, then dropped her head and said again, 'Oh, you did give me a fright, Brett.'

'You're shaking.' He had hold of her arm. 'Sit down. I . . . I didn't mean to frighten you. But why are you out here at this time of night?'

'Oh, I often come down. I hope you don't mind, Brett.'

'Mind? Of course not. But why?'

'Well, I suppose it's because I'm restless, I can't sleep. This is only the second time I've been here this year; it's a bit cold yet.' She shrugged her shoulders upwards around her chin. 'I started to come down last summer. I could have sat in our garden but it wasn't the same, I wanted to look at the river. You really don't mind?'

'Don't be silly.' He turned his head away from her. Then looking at her quickly again, he asked, 'You're . . . you're not in trouble of any sort?'

'No. No, of course not, Brett. Trouble? What trouble could I be in?' This was followed by an embarrassed silence. She was sixteen and a half, as she had informed her father, and she knew what trouble she could be in, but she didn't think Brett was referring to that kind of trouble. Cecilia Tomache had had to leave school last year because of a similar trouble, but she was well over seventeen. She said airily now, 'Well, it's now my turn to ask why you are out at this hour?'

'That's easy to answer. I saw you coming down, and I may as well tell you I wondered what you were up to.'

'Oh, Brett, you didn't!'

'I did, young woman, I did.'

They were laughing softly together. 'Who did you expect to find me with?'

'Well now.' It would never do to tell her the truth, so he stroked his chin and pretended to think deeply before he said, 'Seeing that Susan might well one day be Lady Braintrees I thought you would at least be hobnobbing with a count.' He looked at her. 'Yes, a count, Italian. But on second thought, no. Italian counts are two-a-penny, and it would have to be someone exclusive for you, a prince. Yes. . . . Now who are the eligible princes? There's not many left. Now let's see. . . .'

'Oh, Brett, you are funny.' She pushed him. 'I'll settle for something less than a prince.'

'Well, don't do too low. Now mind, I'm telling you.' He wagged his finger at her. 'Aim high. Aim high, young woman.'

The moonlight was falling across their faces, just below their eyes, but he could see the expression in hers as she said, 'Who are you thinking about, Brett, when you say I should aim high? Me, or mother and father?'

It was a sobering question, and the bantering went out of his voice as he answered, 'I wasn't thinking of them, I was merely being funny. When the time comes, high or low, you'll know.'

He said to her, high or low, yet a few minutes ago he had been worried stiff in case she had given her young freshness to someone like Angus Cotton. People never said what they meant. He was no exception.

She was looking out of the door now down the slope on to the moonlight water and she said, 'I want to get married some time, Brett, but I . . . I don't want it manoeuvred, like Susan's. Brian's young, but if he had been as old as father I think she would have been manoeuvred into it, and she herself would have wanted to be manoeuvred into it, she's got a thing about titles. She's as bad as mother.' She turned her head sharply towards him. 'People make me sick, Brett.'

'People make me sick too, Vanessa.' He laughed tolerantly.

'Yes, I should imagine they do, Brett, because you've had what is known as a dirty deal, haven't you?'

His eyes widened as he stared at her. Then he said, 'How did you come by that impression?'

'Oh!' She shook her head quickly. 'Father, Mother, the things they say. Father's guilt complex. He feels awfully guilty about you. I know he does; that's why he blusters.'

'Nonsense, nonsense, Vanessa. Good gracious, child, you do have queer ideas about some things.'

'I haven't, Brett. You know I haven't. And I'm not a child, I'm going on seventeen and I'm very, very worldly.' She bowed her head in a deep obeisance towards him, and he threw back his head and laughed aloud, only to check it quickly as he whispered, 'I could be heard from the road, and if the night patrol was passing he'd be in here like a shot. And what would he think, finding us here at this time of night, eh?'

'He'd think the worst, Brett.'

'Vanessa!' There was astonishment in his voice, yet he was still laughing.

'I told you I'm very worldly.'

He looked at her with his head on one side. 'You're very sweet, Van. I used to call you that when you were young but your father didn't like it. Vanessa is her name, Vanessa she must be called. . . . Come on, I think we'd both better be making for indoors.' He rose to his feet and put out his hand and pulled her upwards, and as they went out on to the veranda she said, 'Paul will soon be home; you'll be happy then, Brett, won't you?'

He stopped dead and stared at her. 'What makes you think I'm unhappy without Paul, Vanessa?'

'Oh, I don't know, just the way you look, sad like, lost. Yet you never look like that when you're with Paul. You know when you were together at Christmas, you remember at the party, I thought to myself you were like twins.'

'Oh, my dear, that's the best compliment I've had in my life. Thank you, Vanessa, thank you.' He bowed deeply from the waist.

'I mean it.' She turned from him and went down the steps on to the greasy slope, saying over her shoulder, 'I like Paul, I like Paul better than anybody I know, except you.' She was laughing widely as she turned her glance back towards him.

He laughed back at her, then said, 'I am deeply honoured, ma'am, deeply honoured.' And he added, 'Seriously, I am.'

'I am looking forward to Paul coming. He's good fun.'

'You like Paul, really like him?'

'Yes, yes, I do. Would you like me to marry Paul, Brett?'

'Vanessa, what's got into you tonight? It must be the moon.'

'Yes, I think it is the moon because I'm being very forward, aren't I? I'm not usually like this, am I? They say I don't talk enough. They think I'm reserved. Sulky, Father calls it. But I've always talked with you, and I can feel forward with you and know you'll not tick me off.'

Again they were laughing, smothered laughter.

'But would you, would you like me to marry Paul, Brett?'

'Since you ask, Vanessa, I would. It would make me very happy if you married Paul. But that's up to you and Paul.'

'Yes, that's up to me and Paul, and Paul doesn't even know I exist.'

'Nonsense, Paul's very fond of you. I know that.'

'Yes, as the kid next door.'

'Well, you know,' he said thoughtfully, 'up till last summer, even up till Christmas, even up to yesterday, you did appear like the kid next door, but not any longer.' He held up his hand warningly against her attack, and they were laughing softly again as they entered the shadows of the trees. He whispered to her now, 'Keep your voice down,' and they said nothing further until they reached the gate, and there, looking up at him, she murmured below her breath, 'I feel better, better than I've done for weeks. There was a dinner tonight, and, oh, it was boring.'

'You were down for dinner?'

'Yes, of course. Don't you know that I'm a young lady and must be initiated into society?' The bantering tone left her voice and she said. 'You know, sometimes, Brett, I think I'm in one of Jane Austen's novels; the pattern in our house is just like that. Mother talks about "getting one ready". In this day and age, "getting one ready"! I ask you. When they are already talking of school children getting married and going back to school. It's true, it was on the telly. She's still living in her youth, even in her own mother's youth. There's no fun, Brett. You know, down on the main street where I was tonight, you know when I was talking to Angus, there's a club. They were going, his sister and Emily, and they would be laughing and singing and enjoying themselves up till midnight. It made me feel sad, forgotten somehow. Not that I want to go to clubs, but some of the girls from school, younger than me, they go out on a Saturday night to dances. The Golf Club have a wonderful dance once a month. But what happends to me? I'm allowed down to dinner to be "got ready". Got ready for what, Brett? Not to get married, not really, you don't really need to be got ready to get married, do you? I should imagine that comes, naturally, doesn't it?'

'Well.' He was stumped, he was stumped by the whole train of her conversation.

'I know what I'm being got ready for, Brett. I'm being got ready to hook someone in the Braintree set. Oh, I know all about it, and it makes me furious inside.'

'Take it slowly, dear,' he said gently. 'I know how you feel, I really do, and when Paul comes home you'll go off to a dance together. It'll be arranged in some way.'

She sighed deeply. 'It won't be arranged, it can't. Father will see to that, and in any case I wouldn't want to go to a dance with Paul because it would be on sufferance.'

'Don't talk nonsense, he'd be delighted to take you, because, you know, you're a very, very attractive young lady. In fact, I could say truthfully you're a very beautiful young lady when you're not scowling, and if I'm not mistaken you're going to cause some havoc in the male world before you're much older.'

'Do you think so, Brett?' Her voice was eager. 'Really? You're not just being soothing?'

'No, I'm not just being soothing. It's a prophesy, and all my prophesies come true.' He raised his hand, and again they were laughing gently. Now he pushed her through the gateway, saying, 'How do you get in?'

'Up the fire escape, on to the second landing, and once I'm there and anyone should open their door I'm just coming from the bathroom.'

'You're a minx.'

'How did you get out?'

'Down the back stairway.' Again he pushed her. 'Go on, sleep well. See you tomorrow.'

She moved a step from him, then turned swiftly towards him and, reaching up, she kissed him on the chin, saying, 'You are the nicest man I know, the very nicest.'

He stood perfectly still until he imagined she had reached the side of the house where the fire escape was, then he moved slowly up through the wood, his head bent on his chest, and when he re-entered his room again he switched on the light and looked at himself closely in the mirror. Then he held his hand a few inches from his face as if he was cupping the face that had kissed his.

As he went to sleep he thought, 'And I went out to tear a strip off Angus Cotton!'

BOOK ONE

Chapter One

Vanessa just managed to board the train with the assistance of a lift and an, 'In you go!' from a porter. She stumbled over the feet of the second-class passengers and excused herself; then she went out into the corridor and down the train towards the few first-class compartments. She was passing the last compartment in the corridor when the sight of the sole occupant of it brought her to a halt and she said, 'Why! hello, Angus.'

'Oh, hello.' Angus got hastily to his feet, dropping the paper to the floor as he did so. He retrieved it and threw it on to the seat before saying, 'Fancy meeting you here.'

'Yes.' She nodded and smiled at him.

'Lookin' for a seat?' He looked down at her.

She hesitated just a moment, and his chin jerked up as he said, 'Oh, you're going down to the first. I'm sorry.'

'Don't be silly.' She moved into the compartment and sat down; immediately he sat opposite to her, saying, 'You're not at school the day? That's a daft question, but I mean. . . .'

'I've been to the dentist.'

'In Newcastle?' His thick, sandy, well-defined eyebrows moved upwards. I thought we had an overflow of them in Fellburn.'

'I had to see a specialist. I'm getting an extra ration.' She pressed the corner of her mouth back and upwards to reveal a small tooth jutting out between the roots of two others.

'Good lord! Cutting your milk teeth again? Aw,' his smile widened, 'in your case it would be a wisdom tooth.'

She laughed. 'Wisdom, huh! Wisdom. By the way, while we're explaining why we aren't at our particular jobs, why aren't you at work?'

'Oh.' He leant back. 'I've been to a funeral.'

'A funeral?

'Yes; me uncle's. We haven't seen him for years, ten or more, but me mother thought somebody should go. It wasn't decent like,' He mimicked Emily's words 'to let him be put away and not one of the family near him.'

'But why didn't she . . . ?' Her voice trailed off and she ended lamely, 'Oh yes. Oh yes, the company.'

He nodded at her slowly and repeated, 'Yes, the company.'

'But if she had asked mother, I'm sure it could have been arranged.'

He stared at her. He didn't say she did ask mother, but that mother said it would be very inconvenient, and wouldn't it be simpler for Rosie to attend the funeral? No, Rosie was just a lass and, what was more, she couldn't abide funerals. Then it must be arranged that Angus should have the day off; she would see the master. And she had seen the master, and here he was.

His silence and his intent look implied the facts of the case to Vanessa and she thought, 'Oh, Mother!' Then merely for something to say she said naïvely, 'But how are they managing in your shop without you?'

His bellow of a laugh could have been heard above the noise of the train and he wiped his eyes and said, 'You know, it's funny but I've never been able to make out how the firm managed to carry on afore I got into the shop. An' you know something else?' He now leant forward and rested his elbows on his knees and brought his face level with hers. 'I bet there's twice as much work done in that shop that day, because, you see, I've got a friend, oh a very dear friend.' He stretched his upper lip well over his teeth and pulled a face before he continued, 'One, Jim Taggart. He likes me so much that he'll get his blokes to work twice as hard when I'm out of the way and he'll say to me the morrow, "What do you think of that, Angus? We didn't slack, eh?" but what he's really sayin' is, "I can get twice as much work out of the . . . out of them than you, boy."'

'He sounds a horrible individual.'

'He's not really, he's just ambitious; it's funny what ambition can do to you. It made me hate his guts; it's also made me take up evening classes just to show him that I'm goin' places.'

'You're going to evening classes, Angus?'

'Yes, the Tech. You know; I met you outside.'

'Oh, I thought you were just passing, I didn't realize.'

The eyes looking into his were full of interest; her smile was sweet. She was slim and long and beautiful. He gazed at her. Who would have thought she would have grown into this? And there was more to come. She would be a stunner in a few years' time. She could get anybody . . . anybody. Bye, she looked lovely. And she was lovely, because besides everything else she had a nice nature. As his mother always said, she'd been nice right from a bairn. And to think that he once used to put his arms around her and hump her up on to his bike or lift her into the barrow. She would have forgotten all that but he never would. If he had been brought up differently perhaps he would have had a girl like her, beautiful and untouched. Aye, she looked untouched, not like the paw-patterned misses that got in the club and thereabouts. Not like May . . . funny about May. He had thought he loved her until the other night she had told him she had been with two other blokes. She felt she had to tell him, she said, because she loved him. He had been with her himself more times than he could remember, but he had intended to marry her, so it was different. But from then he just couldn't. He had scudded away like a frightened rabbit; or a better description in his case, with his bulk, would be like a shying buffalo. He knew his attitude was unreasonable, oh aye, he knew that, but it was different for a man. A fellow had to have it; it was as necessary as a morning cuppa, or the evening pint; but with a lass . . . well, it was different. Oh yes, he had worked that out an' all. If they all preserved their virginity it would be pretty hard on the males in general. But there would always be lasses who wanted it and no responsibility, no marriage ties, they wanted it for the cash they could get out of it . . . Yet May hadn't wanted cash. Give May her due, the only thing May had wanted was him. He felt bad about May, but there it was. He had this kink in him, and he couldn't do anything about it. If and when he married he'd like to make sure he was the first buyer at that particular stall, but as things went the day she'd have to be pretty young or so bloody ugly that nobody would have wanted to try their luck. He laughed inwardly, and it brought a quirk to his lips, and Vanessa asked, 'What's tickling you, Angus?'

'Oh!' he straightened up. 'I was just thinking about something.' He leant back against the seat. 'What are you going to do when you leave school?'

She, too, leant her head back against the seat then she turned it towards the window and looked out on to a stretch of green countryside that lay between the towns as she said musingly, 'I don't know. Sometimes I think one thing, and then another, I just don't know.'

'What do your people want you to be?'

'Oh.' She was looking at him again, her face stretched, her brown eyes wide, the thick lashes on her lower lids forming dark circles on her high cheekbones. 'A duchess. A countess. Queen of the Outer Isles.'

They were laughing together and he brought his head forward as he said, 'You've got them weighed up, Vanessa.'

Her face suddenly became straight. Yes, she had her people weighed up, but she knew it wasn't right to discuss them with Angus Cotton, nor have him laugh at them. With Brett, yes, but not Angus for, after all, his mother was their daily.

Oh lord! lord, stop it! It was as if she was being reprimanded by an elder self. You're talking like Susan. He's right, I've got them weighed up; he's got them weighed up; and Emily's got them weighed up. They know as much about us as we do ourselves, more, in fact, being lookers-on. She was fond of Emily, very fond of her, and not in the way her mother was either. Her mother kept saying, 'What would I do without Emily?' but she wasn't thinking of Emily, she was thinking of herself and the difficulty in getting staff. Emily was a common woman; she talked common and she acted common, yet there was something lovable about her. She was the only one who had cuddled her. She used to do it on the quiet in the kitchen. She could never remember her mother cuddling her. Angus was like his mother. He, too, was what you would call common; but he was nice for all that. There was something about Angus that she liked. It was odd when she came to think about it but there were only two men with whom she could really talk without stopping to think of every word she said. Angus was one, and Brett the other. They seemed alike in some way. Yet they were as far apart as the poles; Brett with his soft, cultured way of speaking, against Angus with his hard, thick, North-country intonation and his appalling lack of grammar.

She said seriously now, 'Emily's feet are badly swollen.'

'Aye, yes; I've noticed that.' His tone matched his cynical look.

'She should rest more. I mean when she gets home.'

He stared at her for a full minute before saying quickly, 'She's got a house to look after besides yours, you know. She's got me coming in at night, tearing hungry, and Rosie. She needs to eat an' all.'

'Oh, I'm sorry, I really am, Angus. I didn't think.'

'It's all right, oh, it's all right. But I know you're right, she should rest. I might as well tell you, I've been at her to leave your place for a long time now.'

Her hand went instinctively to her lips and her face showed dismay. 'No, Angus! Oh, the house wouldn't be the same without her. As for mother, well, she'd go round the bend. The people we've had over the last three years, part-time dailies, au-pairs, gentlewomen,' she poked her face towards him on the last title, 'the lot. But whoever came or went, Emily was there. I think Mother would really go potty if Emily left. And she knows it's hard on her, Angus; and she does try to get help for her. She's even offered them factory wages, but they just won't do housework.'

'Can you blame them?' The question was soft.

'What? Oh! Well, I suppose not.'

'Have you ever done housework?'

'I do my own room at times.'

He stared at her again without speaking, then laughed gently as he said, 'And why should you do housework or do your own room when you're going to be a duchess, or a countess, or Queen of the Outer Isles?'

'Oh, Angus, you're making fun of me.'

'No, I'm not. No, honest, 'cos I could see you carryin' any of those positions off right to the tee.'

'I couldn't, Angus. Susan could, but not me. And I would get bored.'

'Bored? Not you. Wait till you get going and you'll enjoy yourself, you'll be belle of the ball, top of the pops, the lot.'

Her face was bright with laughter again. 'You're very comforting, Angus. You know, you always were. I'm so glad I ran into you. I was feeling down in the dumps, and this,' she pointed to the offending tooth, 'this has been giving me gyp for days. Look, we're running in. Hasn't the time flown?'

He stood up. 'Yes, that's the quickest half-hour I've known for a long while. I wish the time went like that at work.'

They went into the corridor and walked to the end of the coach, and when the train stopped he got out and gallantly helped her down the high step on to the platform. As they went through the barrier together a young man standing among a group waiting to get on to the platform said, 'Hello there, Vanessa.'

She turned her head and answered on a high note, 'Oh, hello there, Colin. You going into town?'

'Yes.'

'I've just been.'

He nodded at her, then looked to the side where stood Angus Cotton; then he nodded again. 'Good-bye,' he said.

'Good-bye, Colin. Be seeing you.'

'That was Colin Brett.' She looked at Angus as they went out into the station yard and he said, 'Aye, I know.'

'Oh!' Her voice was hesitant now. 'I thought perhaps you mightn't know him; he doesn't work in the yard, he's an accountant in Forrester's.'

Oh, aye, an accountant in Forrester's, was he? By the look he had given him you'd think he was God Almighty in paradise. He knew Colin Brett all right; they were both of the same age. He had played with him once or twice when he had gone up to the house, but Colin Brett wasn't the kind who would remember that. Oh no, he was an accountant in Forrester's. He'd likely be a member of the Conservative Club and the Golf Club. Had he been a member of the Rugby Club he would have spoken to him in the dressing-room, he would have drunk with him in the pub afterwards, but he would hardly have recognized him in the street, particularly if he was with any of his women folk. Oh, aye, they were living in an age of social equality. Social equality, his backside!

'I'm gettin' the bus here,' he said abruptly. 'Been nice seein' you.'

'It was nice seeing you, Angus. I'll tell Emily I came down with you.'

'Do.' He nodded at her, then turned on his heel and crossed the road to the bus station; and she walked some distance behind him wondering at his sudden change of manner. She had to get the bus, too, not the same one as he was getting but the one next to it; he could have walked across the road with her, he had walked out of the station with her. But all of a sudden he had looked grim and bad-tempered, like Emily did when something upset her. Had she upset him? Had she said anything? Oh, bust and botheration. That was people. Everybody seemed at sixes and sevens lately.

When she boarded her bus she saw him standing on the pavement opposite his; he was talking to a girl. She was of medium height and a blonde. Her skirt was well above her knees; she was wearing a short, hairy coat like imitation fur. She looked common.

As she took her seat in the bus she did not retract her use of the word this time for the girl did look common, cheap. Well, she supposed that was the kind of girl Angus would go for. Men usually went for blondes, they said, some time or other.

As the bus turned out of the square it came to her with a kind of shock that Angus was a man. He was no longer a youth or a young fellow, he was a man. A big, virile, rough, coarse man, yet she had chatted to him in the train as if there was no difference between them with regard to age. Somehow she didn't think she'd ever chat to him again like that.

The house was quiet when she entered, it seemed empty. She looked into the lounge but no one was there. In the dining-room the table was set for dinner. There were eight places. This was the second time the Braintrees had been here within the last three weeks. The table looked nice, all gold and silver, the gold being the daffodil heads her mother had arranged in a flowing line down the centre of the table. She used to cringe when, as a child, she saw her mother wiring the heads for a flower display. Her mother was very clever at arranging flowers.

When she went into the kitchen Emily was at the stove. 'Oh, hello there. You back? Did it hurt?' she said.

'No, not at all. Well, he didn't do much. I've got to go again next week. By the way, guess who I came home with on the train?'

'The Lord Mayor.' Emily closed the oven door and added, 'Would you like a cup of tea?'

'Oh, yes, Emily, if there's any going . . . Where's Mother?' Her voice had dropped on the question and Emily answered as quietly, 'Upstairs, having a nap afore the fray. She's jiggered.'

As Emily took down two cups and saucers from the cupboard Vanessa looked at the back of her legs. There was no shape in them; her ankles were the same width as her broad calves.

'What are you looking at? Oh, me feet? Oh, they're giving me gyp the day; I feel they're going to bust any minute.' She put the cups and saucers on the table. 'I'm gonna put them in some epsom salts as soon as I get home.'

'After you've made the dinner for Angus and Rosie?'

'What's that you say?' Emily held her head to one side and screwed up her eyes.

'I came back in the train with Angus.'

'Aw, you did, did you?' Emily now took the kettle from the Aga plate and mashed the tea. 'And he told you that I'm a poor soul who has to go home and cook for the family, eh?'

'No, no, he didn't, not like that, but he said he'd been trying to get you to leave us.'

'Oh, that! You don't want to listen to him. And look, Miss Van.' She turned quickly. 'Don't you go scaring your ma. Well, what I mean is the missus has got enough on her plate without worrying about being left high and dry. By the way.' She leant against the rail of the stove and a smile spread over her broad, flat face. 'That one that came for interview this mornin', she took one look at the place and skited out of the gate as it we had turned a hose on her.'

'She wouldn't even give it a try.'

'Give it a try? You should have heard what she said. An' what she wanted. Double time for waiting on dinner at night. I said to the missus she should have asked her if she thought this was a factory. I tell you, they don't want work, Miss Van; they won't work the day.'

As Emily again turned to the stove and lifted the teapot Vanessa once more let her gaze drop to the feet encased in a pair of old leather slippers that had once belonged to her father. Her father had big feet, he took size ten, yet the slippers, stretched as they were, were still too small for Emily's feet.

'You should put your feet up in the afternoon, Emily. You know, Mother told you to.'

'Well, I've had them up. I've just got off me . . . I just got out of the chair a minute or so afore you got in. I haven't done a hand's turn since half-past two.'

'What's happening tonight?'

Emily handed Vanessa a cup of tea, then said, 'Oh, I'm slipping home for an hour, then coming back.'

'It wouldn't surprise me if Angus doesn't let you.'

Emily now turned fully about and surveyed the only member of this household for whom she had any liking, and she said tersely, 'Since when did Angus Cotton tell me what and what not to do? It's all arranged. Miss Susan's dropping me off in the car at half-past five and picking me up an hour later, and let Angus have anything to say on the matter and he'll get a mouth . . . I'll tell him somethin' that he won't forget in a hurry. Because he can boss the men under him at the works it doesn't say he can do the same at home. An' I've told him.' She jerked her head. The statement carried pride that her son was in the position to boss men, and this fact was not lost on Vanessa.

'Have a piece of cake?' Emily asked the question with a conspiratorial air. 'Walnut cream sponge.'

'Oh, yes, Emily, please.'

Emily went to the pantry and returned with a large shive of cake and, placing it before Vanessa, said, 'Get it down you in case we should have visitors.'

It was a rule that 'the children' weren't to eat in the kitchen, and Emily had always seen that Susan complied with it and also Master Ray. Oh yes, she kept firmly to the order where that young demon was concerned. She spoke of Ray now, saying, 'Oh, by the way, we had some high jinks here just afore lunch. His nibs climbed the spout and got stuck on the roof near the garret. How, in the name of God, he got up there nobody knows. He got up but he couldn't come down.' Her body began to shake with laughter now.

'What happened?' Vanessa, too, was laughing quietly.

'They had to phone the works for extra ladders.'

'No! Never.'

'I's the truth I'm tellin' you. They brought a lorry and two blokes, and one of them went up and got him. Oh, you should have heard the master.'

'Where's Ray now?'

'In his room . . . It'll be nice when the holidays are over, peaceful like. Thank God for schools, I say.'

Vanessa was laughing openly with her hand over her mouth to still the sound; then rising and taking the plate to the sink, she said, 'Thanks, Emily; that was lovely.'

'Leave those, I'll see to them.'

'No, no, I'll rinse them.'

'Leave them and go on your way. Go on.'

Vanessa rinsed the plate and cup and saucer under the hot tap; then turning and bowing her head stiffly towards Emily, she said, 'There.' It was as if she had assisted her with some major household task, and the look on Emily's face seemed to bear this out as she said, 'You always were stubborn, Miss Van. But get along with you; you don't want your mother to come down and find you here. Go on now.'

As Vanessa ran lightly up the stairs she thought again of Emily's feet, and the thought took her into the bathroom that she shared with Susan, and there, from her own particular cupboard, she took a plastic bag and filled it almost to the top with a proprietary brand of bath salts that promised to relieve all the aches and pains the body harboured.

Downstairs again, she went hurriedly into the kitchen where Emily was sitting down now and, putting the bag in her lap, said under her breath, 'These are very special salts. Bathe your feet with them, they're bound to do them good.'

'Aw, lass, aw, that's real thoughtful of you, Miss Van. Ah, that is. Thanks.'

Vanessa stood for a moment looking down into the smiling face; then she ran out of the kitchen and up the stairs again with a strange feeling of happiness inside her. There was something in what you learned at church, she supposed. Kindness had its own reward. She felt very good.

The dinner was over. Emily, her feet encased in black shoes, had brought the coffee into the drawing-room and now Susan and Brian were going to run her home. They had just gone out of the room together. They looked happy and self-satisfied. Vanessa thought perhaps Susan, too, was feeling the rewards of charity. The conversation over the last fifteen minutes had been between her mother, Mrs Braintree and Susan, and it concerned Emily. Their mother said, as always, she didn't know how she would exist without Emily. She spoke of Emily as if she was a very old family retainer. She said as much without actually using the term. Mrs Braintree said how lucky she was to have such a faithful servant, yet such service could only have been maintained through kindness. Susan put in with deceptive casualness that she was in the habit of running Emily to and from her home. Her mother said it was all a matter of consideration.

The Braintrees had brought their younger son with them. He was eighteen years old and pimply. His name was Alan and he talked big about cars. He was standing now, talking to her father. She watched her mother rise from her chair and come towards her. She was smiling. She still smiled as she bent over her and said under her breath, 'What is the matter with you, Vanessa? Have you gone dumb all of a sudden? Why can't you talk to Alan?'

'Because he wants to talk, you can't get a word in.' Vanessa's face looked sulky.

'Don't be difficult, child. Your father's noticed it. You're being difficult. You don't want to make him angry, do you? Now you get up and go and talk to Alan.'

As she looked back into her mother's face Vanessa almost said, 'He's no good wasting time on, he'll never come into the title, not unless Brian dies,' but what she said was, 'I'd like to go upstairs.'

'You'll do nothing of the kind. You'll stay here until they go.'

As she turned away she was smiling again.

After a while Vanessa rose to her feet and gradually made her way towards Alan Braintree, but he took no notice of her; he continued to talk cars to her father. Cars were his only interest, the only thing he could talk about. What was more he did not want to be left alone with Vanessa Ratcliffe. She made him uneasy. She was one of those clever sticks of girls, and he had no time for clever sticks.

Half an hour later, when Susan and Brian returned, they all sat down to a game of bridge. It was a comparatively short game and the guests left at half-past eleven. At twelve o'clock all the lights in the house were out, and at five past twelve Vanessa went down the fire escape and into the garden. It was moonlight again, but tonight the clouds were scudding across the sky and the wind was high.

It was nearly four weeks since Brett had found her in the summerhouse, and she had been down there at least half-a-dozen times since. Twice when it was black dark. She had been a bit scared those times, yet excited. The first time she had gone into the woods after that particular night she had half expected Brett to appear again, and on each occasion since she had hoped she might see him. He was nice, was Brett. But tonight she didn't expect to see him. It was too late; the whole world was asleep.

She could have fallen asleep at any time during the dinner or after, particularly during the bridge, but now she felt wide awake. She had never felt so wide awake and so filled with unrest. She felt unhappy. Was it because Susan was so happy? Was she jealous of Susan? Yes, she supposed she was. She wasn't jealous of her having Brian, or marrying into the Braintrees, but she was jealous of her getting married. She was nodding at herself as she went through the gate and into the deep shadow. One had to be honest with oneself.

Perhaps if she had a boy she would feel different. But boys didn't make for her. Look at Alan tonight. Not that she'd wanted anyone like him, the spotty oaf. But still, he hadn't been attracted to her at all. Boys didn't seem to be attracted to her; what was wrong with her? Rona and Kathy, they'd had boys since they were fourteen. Of course, their mothers hadn't known, but Rona's mother knew now, and Kathy took Harold Blackett home. And neither Rona nor Kathy were good-looking. She considered she was better looking than either of them; she wasn't being conceited. No, because she knew she wasn't as good-looking as Lucy Fulton, because Lucy was beautiful. But she wasn't bad-looking; she had nice hair and eyes. So, what was wrong with her? It was the same when she went to a party. Look at the parties last Christmas. All the necking that went on, but the boy that was with her just sat and played with her fingers. There must be something wrong with her somewhere. It must be something inside that boys sensed.

Further on, the wind lashed a branch against her face and she covered her cheek and bent her head against the pain of it. When she looked up again she saw the figure crossing a dappled moonlit space. First of all her heart seemed to stop still in fright because it didn't look like Brett, not as tall; then she realized he was walking with his head down. Before he was aware of her she called softly, 'Brett! Is that you, Brett?' She watched him stand motionless, looking in her direction, and when she reached him she said, 'You gave me a start again, I didn't think it was you. What would have happened if it hadn't been you?'

He didn't speak, he just stared into her face, which was illuminated in moving patterns of moonlight.

'What's the matter, Brett? Are you sick?'

'No, no. I had the beast of a headache, I had to come out. But . . . but why are you out at this time? It's well past midnight.'

'I couldn't sleep.' She turned away from him, walking in the direction of the river. 'I felt all het up inside. Oh, I don't know.' She turned again, expecting to find him by her side, but when she looked back he was still standing in the same place, and she retraced a few steps and said anxiously, 'There's something wrong, Brett. What is it? What's the matter? You . . . There's nothing happened to Paul?'

'Oh, no, no; he's all right.'

'You've heard from him?'

'Yes, we had a letter yesterday.'

'Is he having a good time?'

'By all accounts, the time of his life.'

'You're missing him, aren't you? Going off like that the second day of his holiday. You . . . You didn't expect it.'

'Oh, yes. Yes, I did.'

'No, not until the summer, and remember,' she gave a little laugh, 'he was going to take me to dances. You promised.' She took hold of his arm and shook it. She was endeavouring in her own way to lighten whatever depression had fallen on him, because even in this light she could see that his face was almost the colour of chalk. He never had much colour but she had never seen him looking so pale.

'Come on,' she coaxed. 'Come on down to the summerhouse and let's talk.'

'No, not at this hour. You'd best get back indoors. What if they should miss you?' His voice was stiff.

'They won't miss me.'

'I'm going up, Vanessa; it's late.'

'All right then.' She made her voice sound a little huffy. 'You go on up and I'll go and sit in the summerhouse and muse.'

She had gone half-a-dozen steps towards the river again when he joined her. He had his head bent once more, and he muttered something that she couldn't hear above the wind, but she didn't question what he had said. She suddenly felt gay and excited. It must be the wind and the moonlight and the fact that she–and Brett–must be the only people in Fellburn to be walking in a wood at this time of night.

When she slipped her hand into his arm she brought him to a stop again and he turned his face to hers, pleading with her now. 'Van, be a good girl, come on back.'

'Look, we're there.' She pointed across the clearing to the summerhouse, then tugged him forward.

They sat on the step and she pulled the rush mat from the middle of the floor to make the seat more comfortable, and then, joining her hands round her knees, she said, 'There.' She had the same feeling now as when she had taken Emily the bath salts, she felt good. What she was doing she felt was good for Brett. He was lonely. She knew that he didn't get on with Irene. She had gauged that much from snatches of conversation she had overheard between her mother and father, and latterly between her mother and Susan.

'What is it, Brett?' she said now. 'You're worried. You can tell me. Is it about the yard?'

He was about to say no, but he said, 'Yes.' He'd have to tell her something. 'Your father gave me the chance to go to Holland, Germany and round and about. You know Mr Cribber is in hospital and likely to be there for the next two or three months. He's the representative. Your father wanted me to take his place. Temporary, that is . . .'

'And you're going to?'

'No. No, I turned it down.'

'But why? Why, Brett? It would be a kind of holiday for you.'

'Oh, for a number of reasons. But the main one, I think, was I'd have to be away from here for weeks on end. You know I've never been away from this place for longer than three weeks in my life, and even after a week I long to be back.'

'You are funny, Brett.'

'Yes, I suppose so.'

Their faces were turned to each other, and she nodded slowly at him as she said, 'But I can understand. I can understand how you feel. It's the trees and the river and the house, and it's yours. Yes, I can understand. I often wish we had a bit of woodland. Oh. Oh,' she put her hand on his arm again, 'I don't mean that you should sell it to father. I would say don't sell it to father, hang on to it. I would if it were mine. But I would like a garden with trees in it. Ours is so formal, you feel you're in the park. I wouldn't be surprised any day to see some women coming through the gate pushing prams.' She laughed, but he didn't laugh with her.

She said now, 'Are you worried because you refused? I mean, did it upset Father? He hates doing anything without getting loud applause.'

'Oh, Vanessa!' Now he was laughing a little.

'Oh, I know I shouldn't talk like that, but you see I know him. I've said that before to you, haven't I, that I know him?' She joined her hands once more round her knees and began to sway a little back and forwards as she asked, 'Why isn't love a sort of natural thing like growing hair or cutting your second teeth, I mean loving your parents. You're theirs and they've brought you up, and you should just love them out of gratitude if for nothing else. It worries me.' She stopped swaying and turned her face towards him again and repeated, 'It worries me. Can you understand that, Brett? I don't love them and it worries me.'

He nodded, then said thickly, 'You can't love to order, even your parents.'

'I think about it a lot, Brett, I mean loving people. I . . . I can't even like them. There are so few people I really like. I thought I used to like Rona and Kathy and Lucy, but I don't any more. I used to have a thing about Kathy when I was fourteen and now I think she's silly and I was stupid for having a pash on her. And, I . . . I don't like Susan, Brett. Fancy me saying that about my own sister, but I don't like her. And Ray. At times I loathe Ray. You know the only person I like in our house is Emily. She's fat and at times doesn't look overclean, and she's common. I mean . . . Well, Mother says she's common, they all say she's common. They need her services but behind her back they say she's common. And she is, but I like her. Why should I like her better than Susan or Mother or Father?'

'I can't answer you that one, Vanessa; perhaps because she's more natural, hasn't got so many skins.'

'Do you dislike people, Brett?'

'No, not really. I find it hard to dislike people.'

'Even Father?'

'Yes. Yes, even Jonathan.'

'As you get older will it become easier to love people?'

'In your case perhaps.' He smiled tenderly at her. 'You'll find somebody that stirs you, makes you feel warm, somebody that you can't bear to live without seeing every minute of the day and night; you'll love like that one day, then everything will be ironed out. You're going through a difficult period; it happens to us all.'

She said now, 'You know I was thinking today there were only two men I could talk to, Angus and . . . and you. I could love you, Brett.'

She didn't know why she had said it, perhaps because he needed comfort. When she leant her head on his shoulder and put her hand through his arm, the result of her action surprised and frightened her for a moment; she felt his whole body quivering, and then to her dismay she saw his head droop over his knees, and she watched him cover his face and his hands.

'Brett! Brett! What is it? Oh, Brett, don't. Don't. What have I done? What have I said?' She put her arms round his shoulders, and when her hand covered his it became wet with his tears. 'Oh, Brett, Brett. Dear Brett.' She pulled him round to her. His head drooped on to her shoulder; his wet face was buried in her neck. When she heard him murmur, 'Oh God! Oh God' as if he was in pain, she held him more tightly to her, stroking his hair, patting him, soothing him. When, a few minutes later, she held his tear-stained face between her hands and looked into his eyes she became consumed with pity and love, a first love, a love that expected no future, a love that consumed itself in its very creation, a love that was made up of curiosity and desire.

When, locked together, they dropped sideways on to the wooden floor, he hoisted her farther into the summerhouse, and when his hands moved over her she could not have stopped him if she had wanted to for the gentle Brett had vanished and a strange man was tearing her apart, choking her with his tongue and rending her in two with his body.

Her curiosity was being satisfied.

Chapter Two

'It's the beer talking,' said Emily.

'Now, Mam, it isn't the beer. I haven't passed me quota; I've had me six and that's all.'

'You can't kid me.'

'No, I can't kid you, Mam.' Angus bent over the back of the chair where Emily was sitting with her feet up on a cracket, and he nipped one of her sagging chins as he repeated dramatically, 'No, I can't kid you. I'll have to confess, I've had a drop of hard.'

'I knew it, else you wouldn't be talkin' so damn soft. You know you can't carry it. As for this hair-brained scheme of joining up with Fred Singleton, you can forget it. You're not leaving the yard. Head of a shop at your age and wantin' to give it up. And for what? To start a one-man . . . all right, a two-men, haulage business when the neighbourhood is infested with haulage businesses.'

'I know that, Mam, the big bods. But . . . but the big bods can't carry all the work they've got in. That's what I've been tellin' you. They sub-contract, you know, let it out.'

'I know all about it.' Emily now brought her feet from the cracket. 'And I'm tellin' you this, you're not puttin' your bit of money into any bloody racket Fred Singleton can think up.'

'Fred's a good lad.'

'Then why hasn't he made his fortune afore now?'

'For the simple reason he didn't have enough to start with; he's just got one lorry and he's on his own. Now if he had two or three . . .'

'Bought with your money like.'

'Aye, bought with my money like, then we would be in clover.'

'Do you know where the most clover grows, Angus Cotton? In the Bankruptcy Court. You big gowk, I'll talk to you in the mornin' when you're sober.'

Angus was standing with his hand to his brow and his eyes closed when the door opened and Rosie came in, accompanied by Stan, and before they had time to close the door Emily cried at them, 'You want to hear what this 'n is on about now; he's talkin' of puttin' his bit in with Fred Singleton and startin' a haulage business. Haulage, I ask you. Bloody silly bugger.'

Rosie looked from Angus where he was sitting at the end of the table now, his head resting on one hand, an oily smile covering his face and his lips moving back and forward over each other, and she laughed outright. Their

Angus always looked funny when he was carrying a drop; he was never bad-tempered, like some. Wanting to rouse her mother still further and wanting a laugh, she said, 'Well I don't think it's a bad idea, not really. I mean if you put five thousand down and pay the rest in instalments.'

Angus let out a roar of a laugh and cried, 'Aw, Rosie! Aw, Rosie! That's good. Trust you.'

'I don't see anythin' to laugh at.' Emily was glaring at Rosie now. 'He's serious, it isn't a joke. He started this afore he went out an' he was solid and sober then.' She turned to Stan now and demanded, 'What do you think, Stan? You're on the factory side of cement, you should have your ear to the ground about this kind of thing, haulage.'

'Well.' Stan walked to the table and took a seat opposite Angus. Then looking at Emily, he said, 'If you had a few hundred about you, and the strength of a bull an' plenty of nerve you could get through.'

'There you are. There you are.' Angus's arm was extended high above his head. 'Nerve, he said. And the strength of a bull; and a few hundred. Is anybody more qualified than me?' He got to his feet and banged his chest with his clenched fists. 'Oo! Oo! . . . Oo! Oo!'

The Tarzan call was too much for Emily. She joined in the laughter and she laughed till the tears ran down her face . . .

But Emily didn't laugh the following morning when Angus informed her he was going to have a run out with Fred Singleton. But she did not go for him either, she pleaded with him.

'Look, lad,' she said. 'It's only three hundred and seventy-five but it's taken a bit of gettin'. Don't be a bloody fool, lad.'

'Listen, Mam.' He was speaking as quietly as she was. 'I'm not bein' any kind of a bloody fool, I'm not committing meself, I'm just goin' out to see this lorry.'

'If Fred Singleton thinks he's on a good thing why can't he buy another lorry?'

Angus sighed. 'Aw, Mum, he's got a wife and six kids and his widowed mother living with him. It takes every penny. But he tells me at times he can turn forty a week, not all the time, but pretty often. But with a couple of lorries running and the prospect of more there's no reason why it shouldn't be forty every week.'

'As long as it lasts, lad; these buildings won't be goin' up for ever.'

'You heard Stan last night, Mam. They've got plans out for along the river that'll take another ten years.'

'Listen. Listen to me. I don't want you to leave the yard. There's a sort of, well, call it status, or prestige or whatever you like, but you're chargehand of your shop an' you've got it.'

'God, Mam.' His tone was scathing. 'Chargehands an' foremen, they're two a penny. As for prestige, that went down the sink years ago. You're living in the past, Mam. Men don't look up to them a step above them these days, they spit in their eye. You should hear Jim Taggart at me.'

'What's Jim Taggart? Scum. Scum, that's all he is.'

'Well, there's a lot of scum about and you find that out once you've been put over them. Anyway, Mam, I've got a fancy for being me own boss.'

'Well, what about all this evening-class business you've been goin' at?'

'Oh that'll come in handy, nothin's ever lost.'

'And what if you want to get married and your money goes down the drain?'

'If I want to get married, Mam! Who's talking of gettin' married?'

She turned from him and went into the scullery, and from there she shouted, 'May was round here last night. She had been to the club lookin' for you.'

'Oh, aye.'

'You're not playin' fair by May, Angus.'

'That's my business, Mam.'

'It can be your business but I still say you're not playing fair by her. Three years you've known her; you should be married now, with a bairn.'

'Oh, for God's sake! Look, Mam, you can stick your finger in any pie that I'm eatin', but with regard to May, or any other piece, that's my business. Now, I'm tellin' you.' He walked towards the scullery door and addressed her back. 'I'll marry when I think fit, May or anybody else I want to, but it'll be when I want to. Now understand that.'

He went out without saying good-bye, but the frame of his mind was conveyed to her as he banged the door, and she hurried into the front-room and watched him go down the street. He was a fine figure of a man, and he was as well put on as any gentleman in the town. He knew how to dress did her Angus. The cut of his overcoat suited his broad shoulders. He was wearing one of those new velour sporty hats. She shook her head. It was a motion of pride, but as she turned from the window she exclaimed aloud, 'The stubborn bugger.'

Angus went with Fred Singleton in his old car to Morpeth. He saw the lorry that was for sale, but thought they were asking about twice what it was worth, and so they returned the way they had gone, nothing settled.

On the return journey they stopped just before closing time and had a drink and discussed the situation for the twentieth time. 'I'm not going to jump into anything, Fred; I've got a good job as you know, an' what's more I've got me mam to consider. As I say there's plenty of time.'

'There's not, you know, Angus; there's not. There's other fellows borrowing money to start up.'

'Well, why don't you borrow to get another lorry?'

'Well, as I've told you, I'd have to take on another bloke. What I want is a partner, somebody who'll carry his weight, like you. Tough, with a level head on him. And, I don't mind admitting this to you Angus, somebody who'll be able to do the correspondence like, the writin' and bargainin'. I'm not much good at it. If I did things in writin' I would get further, but everythin' is by word of mouth, you know.'

Angus nodded, then said, 'I'm sorry, Fred, but I'm gonna leave it for the time being. Not too long; no, not too long, but just for a week or so. I've got to consider, you see.'

It started to rain as they left the pub and when they were about two miles outside of Fellburn and taking a side road that was bordered by the open fell, Angus suddenly said, 'Hold your hand a minute, Fred, stop her!'

'What!'

'Stop the car. Stop her a minute.'

When the car had stopped Angus swung round in his seat and looked out of the rear window. Then, leaning across Fred, he said, 'Pull the window down a minute, I want to see over there.'

Over there was a young girl walking by herself. She had a raincoat on with a collar turned up and a scarf round her head. She was walking with her hands in her pockets and her shoulders hunched.

'Who is it? Somebody you know?'

'Aye.' Angus nodded his head. 'I wonder what she's doin' out up here on her own, in the rain. Hang on a minute, will you?'

Fred grinned and said, 'Oh aye; I've all the time in the world.'

Angus got out of the car and went up the bank on to the fell. The girl had her back to him now, but there was no mistaking Vanessa. He would have picked out her walk and her style from a hundred; but he didn't call her name until he came abreast of her, about six yards distant, and then she turned and looked at him and he said, 'I thought it was you. What you doin' up here in the wet? You lost?'

She stared at him, her mouth slightly open; then she said, 'Oh, hello, Angus.'

'You lost? I mean it's pourin''. Do you like being out in the wet?'

'I don't mind. I wanted to have a long walk.'

'Do you want a lift back?' He nodded over towards the car. 'There's another two miles to go, three to your place.'

She followed his gaze, then said, 'No. No, thanks.'

He was now standing in front of her and he peered at her through the driving rain for a moment before saying, 'You all right?'

'Yes, yes.'

'You look peaked.'

'Oh, I'm all right.'

'Look.' He came close to her. 'You're not tellin' the truth, are you? You're not all right. What's up?'

'Nothing, nothing.'

'Mam said you'd been off colour and had a cold, tummy upset; you'd been off school for a week or two.'

'Yes, I have. I've had a cold but it's better now.'

'Well, you don't look better. And you won't stay better long in this. Come on, get into the car.' He put out his hand towards her but she shrank back, saying, 'No, no; I want to walk.'

He continued to look at her for some minutes before he said, 'All right,' then turned abruptly away and went toward the car. And there, bending down to Fred, who was sitting smoking, he said, 'Do you mind finishin' on your own? I feel I'd better see her home.'

'Oh, aye. But you're not goin' to enjoy yourself very much, it beltin' like this.'

'Oh, it's nothing like that, man.' Angus put his fist against Fred's shoulder. 'She's the daughter, you know, where Mam works. She's been ill and I think she still is. She looks odd to me; I think I'd better see to her.'

'Please yourself. But . . . but you'll think about the other, won't you?'

'Aye. Yes, I promise, Fred, I'll think about it. And I'll let you know one way or the other in a week or two. All right?'

'All right.' Fred's face looked crestfallen as he moved off, and Angus, turning, went on to the fell again. Vanessa was some distance farther away now and he had to hurry to catch up with her. When he came to her side he said, 'Well now, which is the shortest way home?'

She stopped and again she looked at him with her mouth open. Then lowering her head and moving it from side to side, she said, 'Look, Angus, I'm all right, really I am.'

'Well, if you're all right, it's a poor look-out for the bad 'uns. It strikes me you should be in bed. You look as white as lint and you're shiverin'.' He put his hand on her arm. 'Come on. An' I'm standing no nonsense; if we're going to walk we're going to do it briskly. And you want to get home and get into bed. You shouldn't pick days like this to take a tramp; although,' he remarked as if to himself, 'it wasn't so bad earlier on. But this is our summer, flaming June. Look, we'll cross over the top,' he pointed into the distance, 'an' go down by the river and over the stepping stones. That'll cut almost a mile off and bring us to the end of Mr Brett's wood.'

When her body jerked he thought she had stumbled, and he put out his other hand to steady her.

They walked some distance in silence, until it became embarrassing to him and he said, 'Mam tells me you're leaving school at the end of this term.'

'Yes.'

'I thought you were staying on until you were seventeen next year?'

'I'm seventeen in August.' For the first time she turned and looked at him. 'In exactly six weeks and two days I'll be seventeen.'

He was slightly nonplussed by both her voice and her manner but he said airily, 'Well, it's plain to be seen you've got it worked out to the hour.'

'Yes, to the hour.'

What was wrong with her? There was something amiss. He hadn't seen her for some time, not since that day they had travelled up from Newcastle and he had got himself narked by the way young Brett had looked at him, and he had left her abruptly. Surely, she in her turn hadn't been narked about his manner. . . . Could be, could be. What did she expect him to do? Bow and scrape. He said, 'Haven't seen you for some time, not since that day when we came up on the train together. I . . . I had to leave you rather sharp, there was somebody I wanted to see.'

She was looking at him again. She didn't for the moment know what he was talking about; and then she remembered him walking away and talking to a cheap-looking girl.

CHEAP LOOKING. CHEAP LOOKING. CHEAP LOOKING.

The words were re-echoing in her mind, as words were doing a lot lately. Significant words such as cheap, consequences, retribution, sin, scandal, death, suicide, water. Yes, water. But she would never drown, she was too good a swimmer; and they hadn't gas in the house, only electricity and the Aga. This only left the asprins, there were all kinnds of aspirins in the bathroom cupboard. If only Brett would come back. If he knew he would do something about it. He would take her away. She hadn't a doubt but that he would take her away.

For days after it happened she hadn't been able to think of him without wanting to be sick. For days and days after, she could feel his body on hers; she could see his part naked flesh as he rolled off her exhausted, finished. When she had finally come to herself she had for the first time experienced loathing, loathing of herself and him. But it was too late, the thing was done, the beastly horrible slimy thing was accomplished.

Some parts of the episode had faded from her mind and there was only a feeling left about them, but she still remembered the sound and sight of his crying. He had started to cry again, he had cried as he had kissed her all over; he had cried until she had kicked herself free from him and run through the wood in panic. And the panic was still with her, and only his presence could ease it.

If she could only hide her panic until he came back then it would be all right, they would go away. He would get a divorce and they would marry. That's how things were done.

'What? I'm sorry I wasn't paying attention.'

'I said, had you decided on anything, a job or anything?'

'No. That is Mother and Father want me to go to France to stay with a family; my French is weak.' She tried to put a smile to her words but it wouldn't come.

He helped her across the stepping stones; then they went up the bank and along the towpath that ran by the side of the river, and fifteen minutes later they came out into the lane where the wire fence that bordered the Brett ground ran down into the river. She had her head down as she walked up the narrow lane towards the road. They were about half-way along the lane, and silent once more, when her name being called brought them both to a startled halt. There were two voices calling 'Hi, Vanessa! Hi, Vanessa!' and the voices appeared to be coming out of the air.

She looked up into the trees, and Angus's gaze followed hers and he said, 'There's somebody up there in the trees.'

She was walking on again. 'It's Ray,' she said, 'and Michael Brett. They've built a platform in the oak.'

'Good for them. But it gave me a bit of a gliff hearin' your name being called out of the sky.' He was looking at her profile, waiting for her to say something, but she didn't, and when they came to the end of the lane he stopped and said, 'Well, here's the parting of the ways. Now you take my advice and go to bed; you look as if you're sickenin' for something. Have you had the doctor?'

'No; I'm all right really and. . . . Thanks.' Her voice trailed off, and he added with a smile, 'For forcing meself on you? But me mam would never have forgiven me if I'd left you up there in the rain all by yourself. You looked lost.' He leant his head slightly to the side. 'If you go on this way you'll be losin' your looks, you know, an' you don't want that to happen, do you? What's the duke or the count goin' to say?'

When she swung away from him without a word of goodbye he stood gazing after her until she disappeared into her own gateway; then he turned towards home. . . .

Emily was having her Sunday afternoon rest when he arrived, and he went straight upstairs and into her room. She was sitting up in bed with a cup of tea in her hand and she said 'Oh, so you're back. Well, what's happened?'

'Enough of that after.' He sat down heavily on the foot of the bed and began: 'Look, Mam, when we were comin' down the fell lane about two miles out, Fred and me in the car, I saw Van meandering across the fells in the rain and I got out and asked if she would like a lift, but she wouldn't come, and she was in such a state that I let Fred go on and I brought her back.'

'Here?' Emily straightened herself up.

'No, no. Don't get yourself agitated. I mean home; we came the river way. She was in a state, Mam. She looks bad.'

Emily lay back and closed her eyes for a moment before saying 'Oh, she's been like that for a week or two. The missus hasn't known what to do with her, nor me for that matter. We used to have a crack at one time but I've not been able to get a word out of her, not for days. It's exam nerves, that's what the missus says.'

'Exam nerves? Good God, is that what it is?'

'Yes, they all get it when they're sitting for 'O' levels; sick, tummy upsets, the lot.'

'Christ!' He banged his forehead with his double fist. 'Me thinking she was going into the old-fashioned decline or some-thin'. Well, I'll be jiggered. You know, she hardly opened her mouth all the way, and when she did she was so bloomin' dramatic you'd think she was rehearsing for a play. Once or twice I could have laughed, but then she looked so bad.'

'Oh, they take it seriously.' Emily nodded. 'I remember Miss Susan and her 'O' levels. She was sick, an' in the night an' all, and the lazy little beggar wouldn't get up. I remember that bed I had to tackle the next mornin'. Well now, tell me what happened about Singleton.'

'Oh, they were asking too much, far too much. I told them when they came down to practically half I'd think about it.'

'What did Fred say?'

'I told him that I'd give him me answer one way or the other in a few weeks' time.'

'Well, it'll be the other if I've got anything to do with it.'

He stood up, then poked his head down to her and said, 'Yes, Mam. Yes, Mam.'

'Go on with you.'

'Where's Rosie?'

'She's in her room. There should be some tea in the pot.'

'I'm not havin' your leavings, I'm going' to make fresh.'

'You don't need to make fresh, it's just been made.'

As he went out of the room he said to her over his shoulder, 'Don't be so stingy; you'd think you bought it. I like making fresh pots of God Almighty Ratcliffe's tea. Anyway, I brought his daughter home out of the wet.' He pushed his head back round the door towards her. 'That's a good 'un. It's the title of a story: Out of the Wet.'

'You're not just wet, lad, you're drippin'.' Emily lay back and gurgled at her own joke; then she emptied her cup, saying to herself, 'Thank God. But he's got sense, our Angus. I needn't have worried.'

Chapter Three

'You're mad. You must be mad.'

'Yes, we're all slightly mad, Mrs Ratcliffe.'

'But you are.' She checked herself from adding, 'or drunk.' It was a well-known fact that he was a tippler; hadn't Mrs Carey objected to his breath when he visited her? She would change; she had been thinking about it for a long time.

The doctor seemed to read her thoughts, and he buttoned up his coat briskly as he said, 'Mad, drunk, or daft, Mrs Ratcliffe, your daughter is pregnant.'

There was the word again; it hadn't really registered the first time. Pregnant. PREGNANT. Oh, no, no! This couldn't happen to them. Not only was he mad, she was going mad. The wedding in six weeks' time. Their position. Oh, Jonathan! He would go insane. This would drive him insane. Jonathan couldn't stand things like this. When they happened to other people's daughters he condemned them out of hand; but to his daughter! Where? How? What had they done to deserve this? WHAT? The question was spiralling in her head. She heard the doctor say, 'Come along now, sit down. It isn't the end of the world; these things are happening every day.'

Every day. Every day. Every day. The words carried her into a dead faint.

Doctor Carr went to the drawing-room door and in no small voice yelled, 'Emily! Emily!'

'Aye, doctor. What is it?' Emily came scurrying across the hall. It was one of the quirks of the social set-up that Doctor Carr should also be her doctor.

'Your mistress has fainted.'

'God God! What caused it?' She was hurrying past him to the couch.

'She's had a bit of a shock.'

'About . . . about Miss Van?' She was loosening the front of Jane

Ratcliffe's dress as she spoke, and she turned her shrewd glance up at the doctor.

'Yes, about Miss Van.'

'Has she caught something? Infectious or something? She'll go mad,' she nodded down towards the prostrate figure, 'if anything happens to put a spoke in the weddin'.'

'This will put the spoke in a number of things, Emily, if I'm not mistaken. Look, go and make a cup of tea. And be quick about it.'

Emily straightened up and was in the act of hurrying away when she turned and looked at him and said, 'God Almighty! You don't mean . . .?'

'Yes, I do mean.' He nodded at her. 'And go on and get that tea made.'

Oh no! No! What's the world comin' to? NO! Not Miss Van. God in Heaven! She went into the kitchen and stood gripping the edge of the table. That's what had been wrong with her all these weeks. But who would have suspected Miss Van! Examination nerves, everybody said. Aw, no! No! She just wouldn't believe it. She rammed the kettle on to the top of the hot plate. But the doctor . . . the doctor had just examined her. The missus had insisted on him coming because Van wouldn't get up out of bed to go to school. She kept saying she wasn't feeling well, and begod, she wouldn't be feeling well . . . But who? . . . Who did the child know? Child? She was a child no longer, she was nearly seventeen. She herself had been married a week after her seventeenth birthday. But in this class, this house, it was different; they were still children at that age. Aw, she answered herself, there were no children these days. But, in any case, God strike them down dead the one who had brought it about. It would be Van this would happen to, the nicest of the bunch; it always happened to the nice ones. 'Hurry up you!' She scraped the kettle backwards and forwards on the hot plate.

The master? Oh, God Almighty! There'd be high jinks the night. When he got wind of this they'd have to tie him down, because he was a sanctimonious prig, was Jonathan Ratcliffe. He went to the most fashionable church in town and subscribed handsomely to the fashionable charities, but let a fellow come to the door and ask for a bit, as they used to years ago–not now; they didn't need to now–and he showed them what charity was. Oh, there'd be hell to pay the night in this house.

When she took the tray of tea into the room Jane Ratcliffe was sitting up, her head supported in the wing of the couch, and as Emily held the cup to her lips Doctor Carr said, 'I think your husband should be here. May I use your phone?'

For answer Jane Ratcliffe just raised her eyes.

It took some minutes to convince Jonathan Ratcliffe's secretary that the doctor had no intention of leaving a message and that he intended to speak to Mr Ratcliffe.

'Yes?' Jonathan's voice was abrupt, and Doctor Carr's matched it as he said, 'This is Carr speaking. I think it would be wise if you came home for a while.'

'Home? What on earth for? What's the matter? Something happened?'

'Yes, something's happened, Mr Ratcliffe.'

Doctor Carr's words were clipped. 'Your wife has collapsed.'

'My wife! But . . . but I thought you were calling to see Vanessa.'

'I have seen Vanessa.'

'What's the matter with her?'

'I don't think we can go into this on the phone; you'd better come home. I can't stay; I have another call to make, I'm late already.' On this he banged down the phone, returned to the drawing-room and said quietly, 'He'll be here shortly. Now just take it calmly. I'm leaving you some tablets. If you need me give me a ring.'

Jane Ratcliffe didn't speak, she didn't even move her head; she was in a state of shock.

At the door Doctor Carr motioned Emily towards him, and as he picked his bag up from the hall table he said under his breath, 'The one upstairs could do with a drink too, Emily.'

'Aye, Doctor, aye. I'll see to it.'

But Emily didn't get the chance to take a tray upstairs until fifteen minutes later, because her missus kept hanging on to her hand, staring up into her face while not uttering a word. That was, until the master walked into the room, and then she released Emily and whimpered, 'Oh, Jonathan.'

Emily hurried out of the room with the tea tray in her hand and, standing in the hall for a minute, she wondered whether she could get a cup upstairs in time to fortify the lass before he started on her.

A few seconds later she knocked gently on Vanessa's door, then went in.

Vanessa was sitting on the side of the bed in her dressing gown. To Emily she looked all eyes, teeth and hair. She said softly, 'You could do with a cup, lass?'

'Emily.'

Emily looked at the quivering face, and she said, 'Aye. What is it, hinny?' She was no longer talking to Miss Vanessa, only to a lass, who, like many another, and better, before her, had been laid down.

'Oh, Emily!'

'Now, now, now, don't take on. Drink this up. You'll be havin' visitors in a minute; your father's downstairs.'

The cup rattled on the saucer and Emily had to steady it. 'Come on now, drink it up.'

Before Vanessa had drunk half the cup of tea there came the sound of quick muted footsteps across the landing; then the door was thrust open.

Jonathan Ratcliffe stood aside to allow Emily to leave the room, and he allowed his wife to pass in; then he closed the door quietly, which spoke of the control he had put himself under. But when he looked at his daughter sitting with bowed head on the side of the bed his control vanished, and he almost sprang towards her.

'Look at me!'

Her head remained bowed until his hand shot out and jerked her chin up. He did not say, 'Is this true?' but 'You dirty, dirty little slut! You filthy little slut!' There were dobbles of saliva spurting from between his clenched teeth. 'Who was it?'

Petrified, she stared up into his face. This is what she had been afraid of, this moment, in case her fear of him would cause her to betray Brett. She knew she must do nothing until Brett came and he would do the telling. He would stand up to her father. This once he would stand up to her father.

'Answer me, girl.'

When the only answer he got was the wide stare from her eyes it was too much. He struck her once, twice, three times before she fell backwards over the bed.

Jane Ratcliffe was clinging to him now crying, 'Jonathan! Jonathan, no! Not that.' She forced him back. Afraid herself now of the wild stare in his eyes which he kept fixed on his daughter. Using all her strength, she led him out of the room.

On the landing, he stood, his eyes unblinking as he fought the desire to return to the room and tear every stitch off her and flay her until she cried out for mercy. He should have done it. He glared at his wife for a full minute; then, taking a handkerchief, he rubbed the sweat and saliva from around his mouth.

'What's to be done? What's to be done?' Jane was whimpering now.

He moved down the landing, still wiping his mouth; then ground out through his handkerchief, 'She'll have it taken away.'

'Taken away? But Jonathan, that's illegal.'

'Don't be stupid, woman!' He turned on her 'Nothing's illegal if you can pay well enough for it. But one thing is certain; there's going to be no baby born on the side in this house. And think, just think what this will mean if the Braintrees get wind of it; it could ruin everything. Their outlook might be modern but they're narrow underneath. Remember the other night? Remember when he was on about cleaning up certain quarters of the town?' He put his hand to his head, then turned and looked towards Vanessa's room again and asked, 'Who? Who? That's what I want to know.' When he brought his infuriated gaze round to her he demanded, 'Have you no idea?'

She shook her head in bewilderment. 'I can't think I don't know . . . anyone.'

'Well, you should know, woman. It's your duty to know. There's a man somewhere, boy or man; she can't be having a baby through auto-suggestion.'

As they went down the stairs Ray came from the narrow passage that led to the second bathroom and he watched his parents' heads disappear before turning and looking towards Vanessa's door. Vanessa was going to have a baby. He knew how people had babies; Clive at school, had told him. He had shown him how it was done in the lavatories. . . . He bit on his lip. Vanessa was going to have a baby. He was grinning as he went out down the back staircase to Michael's tree house. He would whistle to Michael, he should be back from school now. He would tell him Vanessa was going to have a baby.

Emily stood at the table and looked at Angus where he was standing with his coat in his hand. He had taken it off but he hadn't hung it up. She said, 'I wanted to tell you afore Rosie got in. I promised him faithfully I wouldn't utter a word. He got me in the study and made me swear I wouldn't let on. They're goin' to have it taken away as far as I can gather . . . Don't look like that, lad, but I know how you feel. I've never got such a gliff in me life. Honest to God, I was floored.'

'Can't be true.' Angus's voice was rumbling in his throat. 'Van? No, not her. She's only a kid and—'

'Look, lad, you know as well as me, they're hardly out of the cradle afore they're fallin' with bairns these days. You haven't to go any further than three doors down. Fourteen years old.'

'Oh, I know, I know.' His voice was suddenly high and harsh. 'But you don't judge the world on Betty Halliday, do you? We're talking about Vanessa Ratcliffe. . . . How did it happen? Was she raped?'

'Oh, lad!' Emily put her hand to her head, swinging it from side to side. 'You're askin' me, and they're askin' her, and they can't get one word out of her. And they don't know any fellow she's been with. She doesn't go round with fellows; she hasn't even got a boy friend. There were three lasses, Lucy Fulton, Kathy Young, and that Rona girl. They come to the house for tea. Those are all she ever sees. At least, that's what everybody thought. . . . And then they nearly had another casualty on their hands. I thought Susan was going to go clean up the pole. She went up the stairs and I heard her screaming from down in the kitchen. The missus had to go up an' stop her. You know, it could put a spoke in that one's wheel, a scandal like this.' Emily sighed now and ended, 'Well, there's nowt we can do about it, so go and have a wash, and by that time your tea'll be ready.'

He went towards the scullery, saying, 'I've got no appetite the night, I'll just have a cup of tea for now.'

'You'll eat your tea. I've cooked it.' She was barking at him.

In the scullery he stripped off his shirt and went to the sink and began to wash himself, pausing every now and again to stare at the wall. He felt sick, actually sick, like he did sometimes on a Sunday morning when he had gone over his quota on a Saturday night, and he knew this was only the beginning. Later on tonight, when he was in bed and could think quietly, it would be worse.

As he dried himself he stood looking out of the window on to the back yard, and he did not think, 'Poor kid. What luck!' but aggressively, 'Why had she to do it? Her! She had been a kind of symbol to him, the queen who smiled at the shoemaker, the princess who touched the hand of the swine herd.' He had likened her to the characters in the books that had once been Susan's and hers and had been passed on to Rosie. She had been in his mind something so aloof that even when he thought of her he had to look upwards. She was, he realized at this moment with a mixture of astonishment and scorn at himself for being such a fool, the reason why he had cooled off May when she let on about having the other fellows. He had indeed been a bloody fool. He didn't like feeling a bloody fool. He turned to the kitchen door and said, 'She could have been attacked or somethin'.'

'I don't think so, lad,' said Emily flatly. 'If that had happened she would have come home in a state at the time. Lasses don't keep things like that to themselves. No, it was no rape to my way of thinkin'. But whoever it is, she's keepin' mum about him. But, oh, the look on her face as she sat on the side of that bed when I took a cup of tea up to her. That is afore he saw her. She looked like all the lost souls in the Bible; all eyes she was and them full of fear. Oh, I can't explain how she looked. And them gettin' the doctor for exam nerves. That's the only funny part about it.'

He turned back into the scullery. Funny part . . . exam nerves. By aye. She had exam nerves all right. That is why she had been wandering around the fells in the rain and he had taken her home as if she was a little bairn who had lost her way. Oh, she must have been laughing up her sleeve at him. God, but wasn't he the bloodiest of bloody fools. He recalled how he felt as he walked by her side, proud, sort of humble and grateful, all mixed up together. He had always felt grateful to her because she spoke to him. But all the while they had walked over the fells she was pregnant. She had been with a fellow. She knew all about it.

He wondered how many times she had done it, and who with. Likely some pimply groping grammar-school twirp, some sixth former; a boy at school, but a man when he got out of the gates and stuffed his school cap in his pocket.

'Come an' get your tea.'

He went into the kitchen and, looking down at the two chops bordered by fried potatoes and tomatoes, he said, 'I couldn't stomach it.'

Emily glared at him for a moment; then, wagging her head, she said flatly, 'All right, we'll say nothin' more about it. I'll warm it up after for you. Go and yet yourself changed and have a pint; you'll feel better.'

Yes, he'd get himself changed and have a pint. But he wouldn't feel better; he'd only feel more of a so and so fool because the beer would unlock the secret places in himself, that only it and dreams had the power to do; places in which he would wander as he had done on the fells the other day and hold conversations with her. He didn't just talk at these times, he conversed, speaking correctly. He always spoke correctly in the secret places; there was nothing about himself to be ashamed of in the secret places. He had no need to be aggressive in the secret places for there he had an ease of mind and a demeanour that could only elicit admiration–and from the one person he wanted, had always wanted, admiration. . . .

He returned at eleven o'clock. He had been on the hard, and Emily had to put him to bed and she was dismayed. She had always known he was fond of Miss Vanessa, right from she was a bairn, but not all that fond. You see, you thought you knew everything, but there were things you didn't know, even about your own.

In the kitchen Rosie asked, 'What's brought this on in the middle of the week?' and Emily replied, 'Miss Van; he's cut up.'

'Huh!' said Rosie. 'What the hell for! That's rich, that is. He wants to tell that to May.'

'Now, now,' said Emily. 'You can be sorry for her.'

'Sorry for her, me backside. She had everything, an' she wanted that an' all; she couldn't wait. She's asked for it, an' boy, she's got it. Sorry for her!

You're askin' something, aren't you? She always got on my wick.'

What Rosie was saying was that she had sense enough to be jealous of the advantages that had fallen to the lot of Vanessa Ratcliffe and she was now feeling a little compensation for the gaucheness that she experienced whenever she was in Vanessa's company. That Vanessa was nearly three years younger than herself made no difference, it was her manner that created the disadvantage.

Chapter Four

Irene Brett hadn't been so happy for years. She couldn't wait to go next door to offer her condolences.

She had made her son repeat again and again what Ray had said to him, and she linked this with having seen Doctor Carr driving in next door when she was coming home not more than two hours ago. She wished her patience would allow her to wait until the day after tomorrow when Arthur would be home. Not that he would feel as she did because in a way he had been fond of Vanessa, always taking her part; but he would be bound to feel some satisfaction over this calamity falling on Jonatham. As great as the difference was between her and Arthur, she could, she told herself, joy with him in this. How are the mighty fallen. Ah, yes, that saying was applicable to their neighbour. It was another Jonathan in the Bible it was said of. She would have to look it up so that she could quote it pat to Arthur when she told him; and she would also point out to him that she had been justified in her suspicions. She could almost say she had been expecting this outcome; she had always known that, beneath that reserve, Vanessa was a cheap little piece. Her choice of a partner had proved that; she couldn't have picked much lower. Really, really, when you came to think about it.

She looked at the clock; it was turned seven. She would go next door now. . . .

Susan opened the door to her and her manner indicated the state of her mind for she stammered and said, 'Oh, hel-lo, Auntie;' then added, 'Mother's resting.'

'Yes, I expect she is, Susan, but I just want to see her for a minute.' She slipped into the hall and turned and faced Susan, who was slowly closing the door. Then bending towards her, she whispered, 'I . . . I don't know whether to believe it or not, children carry such tales, but if it isn't true, your mother should do something with Ray.'

'Ray!' Susan moved her head in small jerks. 'What's . . . what's Ray done?'

'It's not what Ray's done, it's what he's said. Look, Susan; is your mother in the lounge?' She turned and walked across the hall, and Susan, after a moments hesitation, followed her almost at a run and pushed open the door, saying, 'It's Aunt Irene, Mother.'

Jane Ratcliffe turned sharply round. Her face was pale and her eyes red, and on the sight of Irene Brett she turned as sharply away again, saying, 'Oh, Irene, I've got a headache.'

'Yes, dear, I expect you have. I . . . I was just saying to Susan. I thought I had better come over, It's about Vanessa.'

Jane Ratcliffe looked as if she had been frozen into stillness. Her body slightly twisted, she stood gaping at Irene Brett, then she almost whimpered 'Vanessa?'

'Yes.' Irene's voice was low and sympathetic. 'Ray has told Michael something utterly fantastic and I think you should speak to him.' She looked now from Jane to Susan, and unmercifully she went on, 'He said that . . . well, I really don't know how to put it, but he said that . . . well, the fact is he said that she is going to have a baby.' Her voice faded away as if in shock, and for the second time that day Jane Ratcliffe almost fainted. She groped backwards at a chair and sat down; then looked up at her daughter, and Susan turned away and walked towards the fireplace.

'Oh, I am sorry, Jane. Oh, I am. It's appalling. What can I say? What a terrible thing to happen. I . . . I didn't believe it, but, well, if it's true he should be horse-whipped, or put in jail. If I had him up before me, oh I would give him enough time to cool him down I can assure you. It's a pity the birch has gone. I say that again and again.'

Both Susan and her mother were staring at Irene now.

'You know who . . . who it is?' It was Susan asking the question, and Irene looked at her and her eyebrows moved slowly upward as she asked on a high, surprised note that sounded genuine, 'Don't you?'

Susan turned her gaze on her mother, and Jane Ratcliffe, calling to her aid all the dignity of which she was capable, straightened her back and said, 'Who do you imagine has done this thing to Vanessa, Irene?' She asked the question as if she herself already knew the name of the perpetrator.

'Well,' Irene shook her head as if in perplexity. 'I mean. . . . Well, I thought. Well, it's no use beating about the bush. I've told Arthur about the number of times I've seen them together, and Michael saw them last Sunday from up in the tree house. He saw them coming across the river. He was with Ray; they shouted to them.'

'They shouted to them! Who? Who was with her?'

'Why Angus, Emily's Angus. Didn't you know?'

Jane's hand went slowly to her throat. She told herself that she mustn't faint, not again. She had thought that nothing worse could happen, but it had, and the consequences were terrifying. Angus Cotton . . . Emily's Angus. NO. She could never have degraded herself with Angus Cotton; he must have taken advantage of her. That was the only thing; he had taken advantage of her. Yes! Yes! That was it, and she was frightened to say anything, knowing how they all valued Emily's services. . . . Emily's services? Oh, no! Oh, no! This would mean she would lose Emily. It was too awful. What would Jonathan say? What was more to the point, what would he do? In anger Jonathan could be terrible. Oh, why had this come upon them? Why? And Irene Brett standing there gloating. She got to her feet, saying, 'If you'll excuse me, Irene. I'm sure you understand. . . .'

'Yes, yes, of course, Jane; I understand. And if there's anything I can do, anything at all, I'll only be too—'

'Thank you. Show Irene out, Susan.' She didn't say Aunt Irene, and the tone she used and the words themselves were in the form of an insult, as she meant them to be; and of this Irene Brett was aware, but she continued to smile her sympathetic smile, and she touched Susan's hand at the door as she said, 'Good-bye, Susan dear. And I wouldn't let it upset any of your plans.'

'Cat! Mean, narrow-faced cat!' Susan was speaking aloud as she re-entered the lounge, and going straight to her mother she stood before her and cried, 'Angus Cotton. No wonder she wouldn't say anything. Angus Cotton. Dear Lord! Can you believe it, Mother? Angus Cotton!'

Jane Ratcliffe could believe it; yes, she could believe it. Vanessa had always been fond of Emily's Angus. But she knew she must never voice this. She looked up at Susan and said, 'He must have forced her.'

Susan was scornful. 'She's not a child.'

'She'd be a child in his hands; he's a great big bulky individual.'

Susan turned away, her face screwed up in distaste, saying, 'Bulky. Horrible. The big oaf!' Then swinging round again, she demanded, 'What am I going to do? It's out now; it'll be all over the town tomorrow. I could murder that boy.' She clenched her fists, then ended, 'Why did you have to talk in front of him?'

'Don't be silly,' said Jane Ratcliffe wearily. 'As if we would have said anything if we had known he was about. He must have been outside the door or somewhere when we were upstairs.' She put her hands to her head as she added, 'And when your father comes in I just daren't think what will happen. I just daren't think.'

'I can see something even worse than that. Just think what will happen when you confront Emily with this tomorrow morning. Have you thought of that?'

Yes, in a way she had thought of it. Not what Emily's reactions would be, but that Emily would now leave her. The thing she feared had come upon her.

Emily stood for a full minute without speaking; then she startled her mistress by yelling, 'You're a bloody liar! And she is an' all if she says it's him.'

'Emily! You're forgetting yourself.' Jane Ratcliffe's pale, pained countenance flushed.

'Forgettin' meself? You stand there and accuse my Angus of puttin' her in the family way. Miss Van who he thinks about as a child still, an' you tell me I'm forgettin' meself.'

'Well, there's no need for language.'

'No need you say, no need? Begod! you'll hear somethin' more than this afore you're finished. Wait till he gets wind of it. Just wait till Angus gets wind of this. Anyway, who said this? Did she say it was him?'

'No, but . . . but deducing from what we know it can only be him. She's been seen a number of times with him lately.'

'Where, might I ask?'

'Well, they were seen coming across the river last Sunday. And they've been seen in the town together. . . . She doesn't know anyone else, Emily–she hasn't any boyfriends–he can be the only one. . . .'

'Listen to her.' Emily banged her head with her fist. 'You're talkin' through the fat of your neck, woman.' Gone was the cultivated servile manner of years. Her mistress was now just a woman who was accusing her son of taking down a girl. She could have been May's mother, or that of any lass in Ryder's Row. 'There must be thirty thousand blokes in this town altogether,' she flung one arm wide, 'and you're pickin' on him because they were seen talkin' together. He's always talked to her. Or I could say, she's talked to him. She's never passed him in the street like the rest of you.' She turned her glare on Susan, who was standing gripping the back of a chair. 'Let me tell you, I know my Angus, and he would as soon have broken into the Convent and raped one of the nuns as he would have done that lass up there.' She thumbed the ceiling. 'Well now. Well now.' She was tearing off her apron. 'This is the end. I've stood you, the lot of you, for years, but this has put paid to it. But afore I go I'm havin' a word with your daughter.'

'You're not to go upstairs.'

'I'm goin' to see her and you're not goin' to stop me.' Emily glared into Jane Ratcliffe's face.

'She'll only say to you what she said to us, that it wasn't him. She's maintaining that because she doesn't want to cause further trouble.'

'Further trouble!' Emily brought her chin into her neck. 'You don't know anythin' about it yet. Wait till my Angus hears of it, then you'll know what trouble means.'

As she marched out of the room and across the hall Jonathan Ratcliffe came down the stairs, and he stood in an advantageous position on the bottom step and looked down at her with open loathing on his face; and she glared back at him as she said, 'I want to see your daughter.'

His teeth moved tightly across each other and he ground through them, 'After I have seen your son. And if you know what's good for both of you, you won't go yelling your head off about this.'

'Huh!' She gave a mirthless laugh. 'I've just told her.' She nodded back towards the drawing-room door where Jane Ratcliffe was standing. 'I've just told her you don't know what you're in for when he gets wind of it. . . . Yelling me head off. Huh!'

'I know what I'm in for.' His voice was deadly calm now. 'But as yet your son doesn't. He's the one you should worry about. Now I presume you're going; well do, and as quickly as possible.'

She was nonplussed for a moment by his manner. She looked up into his thin, bony face, then she turned her gaze on the woman for whom she had worked for years, and her lip curled upwards from her teeth and, squaring her shoulders, she walked from them with exaggerated dignity.

In the kitchen she grabbed her hat and coat from behind the scullery door, screwed her feet into her outdoor shoes, tore her aprons out of a drawer, then went to a cupboard to find a piece of paper with which to wrap them, and as she pulled it out she saw a tarnished silver milk jug and sugar basin. They were among other oddments that her mistress had pushed away in this cupboard from time to time to save cleaning. With a swift movement she grabbed them up and put them in the middle of her aprons. She had worked for these, and much more, they were only Elkington A1 silver, not solid, but they would fetch something. Aye, by God she had worked for them; she wasn't going out empty-handed. And if she had only thought of it at the time she would have asked for a week's money in lieu of notice, but she had been paid last night.

Without a backward glance she walked out of the kitchen, banging the door behind her, but when she left the drive and entered the road she had to stop and lean against the railings for a moment because her whole body was shaking. What should she do now? His lordship there would go to the office within the next half-hour and send for Angus, and if he threw it at him the same way as the missus had thrown it at herself then only the Lord knew what would happen. She had better go to the works and warn him. But how she was going to put it she didn't know. . . .

It was a bus ride and twenty minutes later when she came to the gates of Affleck and Tate and told the gate man she wanted to see her son.

'Oh!' he said. 'Angus Cotton? Oh well, look. Just follow the road straight on, take the first turning right across the open space, and anybody there will tell you where his shop is.'

Another seven minutes and she saw him coming towards her and her throat swelled and her body began to shake again.

'What is it?' He was holding her arm. 'Something happened to Rosie?'

She shook her head. 'Is there any place I can sit down for a minute?'

He looked about him. There was a wooden cask lying on its side, and with a heave he righted it and pushed it against the wall, then led her to it. 'What is it?' he said again anxiously.

She looked up into his big, rugged face, tender at the moment with his concern for her. She wetted her lips, but she couldn't speak because she was realizing that he would now lose his job. In some way or another Ratcliffe would get rid of him; if not altogether, because of the Union, he'd knock him to the bottom again.

'Look. Look, what's happened? Why aren't you at work?'

She grabbed hold of his hands. 'Listen to what I'm gona tell you, an' don't go mad, don't shout.' She looked about her at the different men moving about the yard. 'I . . . I went in this mornin' like . . . like ordinary, you know, an' . . . an' she sent for me. Susan come and said–I'd just got me hat and coat off and me shoes changed–and she said her mother wanted to speak to me. I went in never thinkin', and then–' She tightened the pressure on his hands, swallowed again and shook her head before muttering, 'Now, Angus, please, please, for God's sake don't go mad, but,' she had to close her eyes as she whispered it, 'they're blamin' you for Vanessa.'

When there was no movement of his hands within hers, when there was no yell or volley of oaths, she opened her eyes and looked up into his face, and then she realized he hadn't taken it in; or, if he had thought it was funny. He was actually smiling. And then he took his hands from hers and, going to the wall, put his forearm on it and dropped his head against his wrist, and his shoulders began to shake. But he made no sound. Then turning, he looked at her and said, 'They're blaming me for dropping Van?'

She nodded at him.

'You mean,' his voice was louder now, 'you mean they're blaming me?' He dug his fingers hard into his chest, making a metallic sound. 'Christ! You're joking, aren't you?'

'No son, I'm not jokin'. I came straightaway 'cos when he gets in,' she jerked her head upwards, 'he'll likely be sendin' for you.'

'Huh!' His sandy brows knit together and again he said, 'Huh!' It was the beginning of a deep laugh that never materialised. He looked up at the high façade of the shops; then looking down at her again he said, "Well, they must be bloody well hard up to pin it on somebody when they've picked on me. But why me?'

'Because you're the only one who she's been seen with. That's what they said.'

'What did she say?'

'I didn't see her; they wouldn't let me. But the missus said they had faced her with it but she kept denying it because she–she didn't want to cause trouble.'

'Cause trouble did you say?' He was bending over her, his look full of mock enquiry. Then straightening himself, he said, 'God Almighty! Mam, it's bloody well fantastic, isn't it? Me an' her!'

'You've said it, lad, fantastic. What'll you say when he sends for you?' She was breathing more evenly; she was relieved beyond measure that he had so far taken it sort of calm like.

'What'll I say?' he said. 'Now, you leave it to me. Oh, just leave it to me. But you're wrong, Mam, about one thing. He won't send for me here, not about that he won't. He won't want the whole place to know about that, not if I know Mr Ratcliffe. He'll want it hushed and he'll hush me up an' all one way or another. You'll see I'll either be pushed out, or,' he bent his head towards her again, 'I'll be pushed up.'

'Pushed up?'

'Aye, Mam, pushed up, to keep me quiet.' He jerked his head slightly.

She now stood up, and they looked at each other. Then she said grimly, 'Knowin' you, an' your kind of reaction, it'll be the out not the up you'll get.'

'True, true, Mam, but just you wait. He'll try it on, you'll see. That's if the lady concerned doesn't name the right man and straighten things out, and herself into the bargain.' His voice now ended on a bitter note. He put out his hand and said grimly, 'Come on; I'll take you to the bus, an' you get home and put your feet up. There's one thing.' His voice lightened just the slightest. 'You'll be able to have your house clean again and the meal on the table when we come in. It's odd how things happen . . . I've had to become a dad-dy,' he drew the word out, 'before I could get you to leave your job, Mrs Cotton.'

He put her on the bus outside the works gates, and he left her with a smile. But it disappeared immediately he re-entered the gates. His reactions now were becoming normal to him. His temper was beginning to boil. His thoughts, bitter and cynical, made his face hard and ugly, yet there was among them a feeling he couldn't pin down. It would be later in the day when he would realize that he was flattered that the Ratcliffes should even think he had given their daughter a baby . . .

It was an uneasy morning in the shop, uneasy for all the workers; even old Danny Fuller enquired what had got into him. 'Don't bark me head off, lad,' he said. 'If you want me to do anythin' just ask me, but don't bark me head off.'

It was round half-past eleven when the call came.

'You're wanted up top,' said the messenger boy. 'Boss's office.'

But when he got up top, his body stiff with tension, he was confronted by Mr Wilton.

Mr Ratcliffe, Mr Wilton said, was indisposed. He wanted these papers immediately and he wanted him, Angus Cotton, to deliver them. Why this should be, Mr Wilton didn't know. But, it wasn't altogether unexpected. Brett had been trying for a long time to give Cotton another push up. But he was no favourite of the boss, nor of himself. He didn't like the fellow, or the idea of him getting any status.

He handed Angus the envelope, and Angus looked at it and all he said was 'Thanks'; then turned on his heel and walked out.

Jane Ratcliffe herself opened the door to him as Susan had refused to do this office. After barely glancing at him she inclined her head to indicate that he should enter the house, then she led the way to her husband's study where she opened the door and again indicated by a movement of her head that Angus should enter the room.

Jonathan Ratcliffe was in a place of authority behind his desk, which was set in a corner of the room with a window to the side of it so that the light fell fully on anyone who was sitting on the chair in front of him.

But Jonathan Ratcliffe did not ask Angus to be seated. He himself sat, his hands gripping the arms of the revolving chair, and stared at the figure confronting him. He had disliked many people in his life, he had hated a few, but the combined hate he had ever experienced was nothing compared to the feeling he had for the man opposite to him. He had sat here for the last half-an-hour thinking about this man, his thoughts taking him right back, back to the day he had first seen him, when he had disliked him on sight. Even as a boy there had been something about Emily Cotton's son that caused him to grit his teeth, and as the years mounted so did his dislike. He saw Angus Cotton as a brash, utterly common individual; added to this he was powerfully built, making his own thin frame appear like a reed, which did not improve matters.

He glared up at him now. This was the man who had dared to handle his daughter. Her loud screams and protests had only convinced him more firmly that it was nobody else but this obnoxious individual who had brought her low.

He was preparing himself to speak, to say one word, 'WELL?' but before he could utter it Angus threw the envelope on to the blotting pad, remarking caustically, 'You wanted that. Or did you?'

It was with something akin to a feeling of triumph that he saw Ratcliffe's jaws tighten until the cheekbones shone white through his skin. He could get this man on the raw; he had always known it. He, too, had his memories from a boy. Perhaps his determination not to knuckle under to him right from the start was the reaction to hearing his mother saying, 'Yes, ma'am,' and 'Yes, sir.' His mother wasn't made for knuckling under either, but she'd had to do it. They'd had to eat.

Ratcliffe picked up the envelope and slapped it on the table as if it were a cane, saying as he did so, 'You know the real reason why I sent for you.'

'Aye!' The words sounded casual. 'I understand I'm giving your daughter a baby.'

'You dirty . . .!'

'Hold it. Hold it.' The careless attitude was gone. Angus was leaning over the desk, his hands flat on it. 'I'm warning you. Don't use any of those terms on me.'

Jonathan Ratcliffe had to swing his chair round before he could rise. Then when he was on his feet he said, 'You've taken advantage of a young girl of good family; you've taken advantage of the fact that your mother . . .'

'I'll take advantage of the fact that we're alone here without witnesses and bust your mouth open for you, MR RATCLIFFE, and then I'll bloody well take you to Court. How would you like that? Justice is impartial. That's what they say. Well, I would see that it was impartial in this case.'

For a second Jonathan Ratcliffe knew a moment's fear. It was two-pronged. It was a fear of being physically handled, also the fear that he had made a mistake. But this reasoning was quick to reassure him on the latter point. Last night they had gone over everybody she knew; there was not one boy they could name that she had seen more than once in the last six months. They had gone over her movements for weeks past. She had been in the house most evenings doing her homework. When she went to the pictures it was with Kathy, or Rona, and, he, himself, had picked them up in the car, having insisted on this because the High Street was usually full of hooligans at night. The only person she had been seen with was this man here. He had made it his business this morning to go next door and have a word with Irene Brett. She said she had seen them together at least four times during the past few weeks. She told him of the night she had seen them standing in the shop doorway together, and Arthur had insisted on bringing her home. She also remembered to tell him of the time Colin had seen them coming off the train together.

Added to this was the tale his son had gone over for him yet again, of how he had seen his sister being helped over the stepping stones in the river by Angus. They had come from over the fells and they had come up the road and stood talking near the railings. He had shouted to them and then Angus had gone away.

He said grimly, 'Threatening won't help you any, Cotton. We may be in Court together yet, but I'll give you a guess as to who will be on trial, and what is more I haven't to guess why you have done this.' He leaned forward again. 'You wanted to inveigle yourself in, didn't you? You were determined to get up into the drawing-office by whatever means in your power. You couldn't get there owing to your lack of education and limited brains so you used . . .'

Angus's arm flashed upwards, his fist doubled and looking like a huge hammer head, but whether it was the width of the table beween them and the fact that Jonathan Ratcliffe stumbled back against the wall, or that in the nick of time he realized what he was about to do, his fist dropped with a crash on to the oak desk, the force lifting up a cut-glass inkwell from its brass stand, and as it shuddered back into place again he bent his head deeply over his chest and drew the air into his lungs. After a moment he lifted his eyes to where Jonathan Ratcliffe was still standing against the wall, his face looking like a piece of new lint, and he muttered thickly, 'You and your bloody job! You can stick it. Right from this minute, you can stick it. Do you hear? I'm finished. As for brains I've got more in me little finger than you've got in your whole body. The whole works, the whole town knows how you got into the top office, by leap-frogging poor Mr Brett . . . Sucking up. Do you know what your nickname is in the yard, and around? Do you know it?' He was yelling now. 'It's Tit Ratcliffe. That doesn't need much working out, does it? Tit Ratcliffe, the biggest sucker-up in the game an' the biggest upstart into the bargain, because your father was no better than any of ours. A little huckster grocer's shop, that's what he had. But he scraped and saved and sent you to college, and what did you learn there? To suck up, Mr Ratcliffe!' He gave an imitation of spitting. Then straightening himself, he ended. 'There's one thing I want afore I go, an' you'll not get me out of this house unless you do it. You'll bring her in here, and she'll face me, and she'll tell you if it was me or not.' There was a long pause before he said, 'Well, get going an' ring your bell.'

And Jonathan Ratcliffe did just that. He rang the bell. He was shivering with rage and humiliation; the only thing he wanted now was to get this man out of his sight. There was part of him wishing that the position was reversed, at least physically, that he was broad and tough and had fists like hammers because with them he would batter Angus Cotton to a pulp. Tit Ratcliffe! How dare he! . . . How dare THEY!

When the door opened he did not look at his wife but muttered in a voice that she did not recognize, 'Bring her down.'

During the time they waited Ratcliffe sat down before his desk again and Angus stood facing the door, and when she came in he hardly recognized her. Not only were her eyes swollen but her whole face was swollen, and there was a dark patch on her cheekbone as if she'd had a blow. She looked even younger than when he had last seen her walking on the fells in the rain, and . . . she looked frightened.

After a moment's hesitation she came straight to him and, standing in front of him, she looked up into his face and said, 'I . . . I'm sorry, Angus. I told them. I've told them but they still won't believe me. I'm sorry. Oh, I am sorry.'

Her words, instead of convincing her father and mother, only proved to them still further that this was the man, and that because of her fear she was frightened to name him; fear of what might happen to him at the works, and through that how Emily would be affected, because they knew she had always been very fond of Emily too.

Angus, now looking down at her, asked quietly but stiffly, 'Have I ever touched you?'

For answer she lowered her head and shook it slowly.

'Have I ever made any improper suggestion to you, or said anything out of place?'

Again there was a shake of her head.

'They say you're goin' to have a baby and I'm the father.'

Her head went further down and still kept shaking.

'If they're right then I should marry you, shouldn't I?'

He had never intended to say any such thing and his words came as a shock to her and brought her head up with a jerk. 'But . . . but you won't. I mean, you're not . . .' the look on her face made him sick; the prospect had terrified her.

She turned frantically now and looked from her mother to her father, and she said again, 'He's not! He's not!' she cupped her face with her hands and began to rock herself and Jonathan Ratcliffe cried sternly, 'That's enough!' then nodded to his wife, and she came forward and took hold of Vanessa's arm and led her from the room.

But before she passed through the door Vanessa turned and looked over her shoulder at Angus and whimpered again, 'I'm sorry, Angus. I'm sorry.'

Now Angus moved towards the door, but he, too, turned before he reached it and he asked tersely but rather flatly now, 'Well, does that convince you?'

Jonathan Ratcliffe wanted to bawl a loud 'No!' but what he wanted above all things at the moment was to be rid of this man, and so he remained silent.

A few minutes after the front door banged Jane Ratcliffe came into the study and, moving slowly towards her husband, she said, 'He wouldn't admit it?'

'No; but it's him all right. I'm more convinced than ever now. Did you see how she went? "I'm sorry Angus. I'm sorry Angus. I'm sorry." She'll be sorrier before she finishes.' He gulped in his throat. Then nervously moving papers about on his desk, he said, 'I'm going into Newcastle to see Muxlington again. I'm sure he could do it, but he won't. But he'll arrange about London. You can say she's going to visit relatives, anything. When she comes back and there's no sign of it, it'll give the lie to Irene's tongue.'

'People will still think . . .'

'Yes, they'll think,' he said bitterly, 'And they'll always think. And they'll know, but she won't have any baby.' He turned on her. 'Understand Jane. She's not going to have any baby.'

'Doctor Carr?'

'I'll settle with Doctor Carr. He can't do anything. She'll have a miscarriage. Anybody can have a miscarriage. And if he knows what's good for him he'll keep his tongue quiet, else he'll find himself and his bottle out of practice. He's not fit to be on the books anyway. Now go up and tell her what's arranged. And stand no nonsense. Tell her from me, if she knows what's good for her she'll comply . . . and quietly.'

But Vanessa didn't comply, and quietly. She wasn't going to London, she said; she wasn't going to have the baby taken away.

Then what, asked her mother, did she intend to do?

Vanessa could give no answer to this question until tomorrow. Brett would be here tomorrow, and when he knew what had happened everything would be smoothed out. There would be trouble. Oh yes, there would be more trouble. But they would be away from it all. Tomorrow night she would go down to the summerhouse as soon as it was dark, and he would be there because Irene would certainly put him in the picture the minute he got indoors. She would have her cases packed ready and they would go off. They would go through the wood, out into the main road that way. She could see it all plainly.

'You're not to think of seeing him again. Do you hear me, Vanessa?'

'What. . . . You mean, Angus?'

Jane Ratcliffe bit on her lip. Her daughter wasn't stupid, far from it, she was much brighter than Susan, yet her responses were those of some dim child. 'Who do you think I mean, girl? And don't take that attitude with me. There's only one person responsible for your condition . . . at least I hope so.' The implication startled even herself, together with the fact that she had voiced it. 'Now I've told you. Your father is arranging for you to go to London. You'll go into a nursing home, and when it's all over you'll go to Great-Aunt Jean's and stay there until your father considers it fit for you to come home again.'

'Oh no, I won't. I won't go to Great-Aunt Jean's.' Vanessa was startled into protest. 'You're not going to shut me away with Great-Aunt Jean, out in the wilds in Scotland, so don't think you are.'

She was about to protest further when she reminded herself there was no need. Great-Aunt Jean who lived in a cottage on a hill six miles from a town, surrounded by her hens, dogs and goats, with her Bible-reading and hymn-singing–the only form of entertainment she allowed–Great-Aunt Jean wouldn't see her, whatever happened, she would die first. But there would be no need for that. She must be quiet and just let them think she was going to go along with them. She turned from her mother and sat down and looked out of the window, and Jane Ratcliffe, taking her change of attitude for acceptance of the situation, said firmly, 'There now, let's hear no more protests. The time is past for that attitude. It's all settled.' Then she went downstairs to tell her husband.

Vanessa spent the following day cleaning her room, and Susan's. Since, her mother said, she had been the means of depriving them of Emily's services she would have to learn to do things for herself in future. She also delegated to her the cleaning of the two bathrooms, and she ordered her to have her meals in the kitchen because her father couldnt' bear to sit at table with her. . . .

By six o'clock she knew that Brett was home. Ray brought the information into the house. She heard him call, 'Did you know Uncle Brett was home, Mammy? He's brought Michael a cowboy outfit with a gun. Not a real one but pretty like it. It shoots pellets. It's in a holster.'

That evening was the longest she had spent in her life. She sat looking out of the window in the direction of the larches. She could see part of the side of the house through the trees, but she wouldn't be able to see him until he came right to the fence that divided the grounds. And he didn't come. He wouldn't come out until it was dark and they were all in bed.

She herself was in bed pretending to be asleep when her mother looked in before going to her room. She felt her standing staring towards the bed, then the door clicked shut. She waited a full half hour before she went down the fire escape. She didn't take her cases with her; he mightn't be able to get away immediately, he would have to to go the bank for money tomorrow. She had thought about all this. But she'd take them and hide them in the wood when the arrangements were made.

There was a moon due but it wasn't up yet, but she had a torch with her. She was trembling from head to foot as she neared the river. She wondered what he would look like. Remembering him over the past weeks he had seemed to get younger and younger until she imagined he was almost her own age.

She knew he was in the summerhouse before she reached it. She stood below the steps and played the light through the open doorway, and there he stood. His face was brown, for he had been in the sun for the last three weeks, yet it was an odd kind of brown, and he didn't look young, not even youngish; he looked old, very old . . . and different.

She whispered softly, 'Brett!' but he didn't answer her, he just stared into the light.

She couldn't bear the look on his face; it looked all twisted and misshapen. She switched off the light and said, 'Say something. Say something to me, Brett.'

For answer he reached out and pulled her to him and pressed his lips to her forehead, and she clung to him for a moment before bursting into tears. He still held her as he led her the few steps to the wooden seat and they sat down together. He did not say, 'There, there, don't cry'; he uttered no word of comfort, and after a while his silence told on her and she pulled herself from his arms and peered at him in the darkness. 'It's been awful, Brett,' she said. She heard him gulping in his throat before he spoke. Then his words sounded ordinary and not suited to the occasion. 'Yes,' he said, 'it must have been.'

'I haven't told them, or anyone. No one knows, Brett.'

'Thank you, my dear.' He could have been giving thanks for someone offering him bread and butter, and his peculiar attitude eventually got through to her and she exclaimed on a high note, 'Brett, I'm going to have a baby!'

She thought he said, 'Oh, Christ!' Then he was holding her hand and talking. 'I'm sorry. I'm sorry Vanessa. You'll never live long enough to know how sorry I am. I didn't stay away because of this. You understand? I stayed away because I couldn't bear to see you. I didn't know this had happened. I thought it might, but again I dismissed the idea. Most . . . most women don't at their. . . .' She felt the movement of his body as he swung his head widely on his shoulders. 'It was just that I wanted to pull myself together. When . . . when I finished the firm's business I got in touch with your father and asked him if I could stay on for my holiday. I wanted time, time, and . . .' he almost added, 'enough satisfaction for my body's needs to keep me away from you.' And he had certainly done his best in that direction during the past three weeks. No man could have done more.

She put in breathlessly now. 'What are we going to do, Brett?' She felt she must give him a lead because she wanted to be reassured quickly that he was going to take her away, but when after a moment he asked flatly, 'What can we do, child?' she was stunned into silence. And now he was asking her, 'What did they say? What do they intend to do?'

'They . . . they want to send me to London to have it taken away.'

'Well . . . well, that's the best thing, dear.'

'But Brett! Brett!' Her voice sounded full of terror. 'I can't. I won't. I won't have one of those operations. It showed about them on television. People die.'

'Hush, dear. Hush. It won't be that kind of operation. They'll send you to a clinic, to a good man. Those girls who die, they go to old women in back streets, ignorant people. You'll be all right. And when you come back. . . .'

She withdrew her hands slowly from his. She was no longer peering at him. Her eyes were wide, staring out of her head into the blackness, and her voice sounded like that of a child's who had been told that they weren't going on holiday after all. 'But . . . but I thought you would take me away, Brett. I thought we would go away. You don't love Irene. You said you didn't. You said that night you had never loved her for years; she was cold and hard. You said she was. You said if only you could take me away–' 'Fly away with you, my princess,' were the words he had used–'you could get a divorce and . . . and we could be married. I . . . I want to have the baby, I really do, Brett, I do. I feel I would like a baby, but . . . but not unless I'm married. I want to be married, Brett.' Her voice, filled with pleading and fear, was like a thin whistle coming up from her bowels.

When he groped over her knees for her hands she felt herself shrinking inwardly, yet she allowed him to bring them to his chest and press them there as he said, 'Oh, my darling, Vanessa, if only we could. If only we could. But it's impossible, child. There's so many things against it. You see, it would be difficult, almost impossible, for me to get started again at my time of life. And I haven't any money by me, and we'd have to live some place. What is more, Irene would never divorce me, never. I know that. And there's. . . .' He stopped abruptly. It was impossible to say to her, 'And there's this house and the wood. I couldn't live long away from either.' What was more he couldn't bear the thought of starting a family again. He had no real love for children, which was likely why his own sons, with the exception of Paul, had never responded to him. You only got back what you gave out. He was well aware of that. When he heard her catch her breath on a sob he wondered if he would have been kinder to lie and tell her they were going away, say tomorrow or the day after–but in the long run that would only make things harder for her.

From five minutes after he had entered the house this afternoon he knew exactly what he was going to do. As he listened to Irene pouring out her spleen, openly gloating over what had befallen Vanessa, he knew then what he must do, and now, holding the child's hands, his decision was firmer than ever. If only he had the courage to take her away. But he hadn't. He hadn't the courage to start all over again, to face up to the responsibilities that would attend such an action. Yet at the same time he hadn't the courage to live without her. He was a weak man and he knew it. Life had been pretty bleak before the night he had come down into the wood to send Angus Cotton packing; but since then it had been sheer hell.

When she withdrew her hands from his he said, 'It's going to be all right, Vanessa. Everything is going to be all right. It wouldn't work with you and me. In a year's time, even in a few weeks' time, you would regret having tied yourself to me. You're young; you haven't started to live yet. I've done you a great injustice, a great harm, but . . . but do what they advise and it will be all right. You can start again, and tomorrow morning,' he coughed here, 'you can tell your mother and father just how it happened and they'll understand.'

'You mean . . . you mean I'm to tell them, not you?'

'Yes, my dear. They must have kept at you to know.'

'Yes, yes, they have.' Her voice sounded far away. 'But they think it's Angus, Angus Cotton.'

'What!' He was on his feet. He seemed to have come alive for the first time since their meeting. 'You mean . . .? Have they tackled him with it?'

'Yes. Father . . . Father brought him to the house yesterday. Emily . . . Emily's left. She was in a state.'

'And you let them think this.'

'No, no! I told them flatly that it wasn't him but they wouldn't believe me. You see, Irene came over and told Mother that she had seen us together a number of times . . . and then Ray and Michael had seen us too.'

'Irene came and. . . .' His voice trailed away.

'Yes, and from what I understand she seemed very pleased about it all.' There was a sound of bitterness in Vanessa's voice now. 'She's never liked me and she's jealous of Susan marrying well. I think she hopes that this will, in some way, put a stop to it. Mother and Father are afraid of the same thing. I've to be got out of the way, hushed up. They're going to send me to Great-Aunt Jean's, up in the wilds of Scotland, after I come back from London.' She was talking dully now as if she was accepting what had been arranged for her.

He asked quietly, 'Have you seen Angus?'

'Only yesterday morning in the study. He was very angry.'
Brett made no comment on this but, putting his hand out blindly until he found her arm, he drew her to her feet, saying, 'Come along, dear. Come along. And believe me, it's going to be all right. Tomorrow you can explain everything. It'll be all right.'

'What . . . what about you? What will happen to you?'

'Don't worry about me, dear, everything will work out tomorrow. You'll see.' He led her up the bank and through the wood, and at the gate they stopped and he drew her into his arms and, putting his lips against her brow, he held them there tightly for a moment, then said thickly, 'I just want you to remember one thing. No matter what happens remember this. I love you. I've loved you for a long time, but I've only been aware of it in the past few months. Thank you, dear.' When he pressed her away from him she muttered, 'Will I see you tomorrow?' She was crying bitterly now.

'Yes, you'll see me tomorrow.'

He stood on the same spot for almost ten minutes after she was gone, then he walked slowly up through the trees. He let himself in by the side door and went upstairs; but he didn't go to his own room, he went to his wife's.

After he had switched on the light he stood with his back to the door. Irene, blinking, pulled herself up in the bed and said, 'Yes, yes. What is it? . . . Oh!' She focused him through narrowed lids, then asked, 'Is it Michael? Is he sick?'

'No, it's not Michael.' He moved slowly towards the bed, and by the time he had reached the foot she had pulled the coverlet up under her chin. The action was a defensive one that a timid woman might take, but there was no timidity about her voice when she said, 'We've had all this out. No, do you hear, no.'

He stood staring at her, not speaking. He watched her thin mouth form into a button that aged her.

She was hissing at him now. 'You're not back five minutes and this starts again. I thought you would have learned more sense.'

'Do you know something?' His voice was quiet, even gentle. 'I wouldn't want to take you, Irene, if you were stark naked doing a fandango. I saw a naked woman doing that dance when I was abroad. She was fat and ugly and her skin was greasy. Moreover, she smelt. But you know something? Given the choice, I'd take her any day in the week rather than touch you with my little finger. . . . Does that surprise you, Irene?'

Her mouth had slackened. It was slightly agape. 'You've been drinking,' she said under her breath. 'You could never carry your drink.'

'No, I haven't been drinking, and you know it. I'm solid and sober and I'm going to talk to you. We've never talked for years, and this will be the last time I'll talk to you, and for that I'm grateful.' He paused, and they stared unblinkingly at each other, until he said, 'Do you know what you are, Irene? Fundamentally, you're a mean, narrow-minded bitch. You're a woman who has fought her way into positions in this town on my name, on my father's name, and his father's name. You're uneducated, unintelligent and without the slightest scrap of breeding. You've had a shot at imitating these various qualities, and you've hoodwinked a few into believing they are your own, but they're only a few. Besides which, Irene, you're cruel. It's a hobby with you, cruelty.'

Her lips trembled before she put in, 'Are . . . are you quite finished?'

'No, not by a long chalk. I'm coming to our neighbours now. Jonathan did me a dirty turn some years ago, but what happened was my own fault. Jonathan got the post over my head because he was ambitious. I'm not. And you've never forgiven him or his, not, let me stress, because of me but because of how it affected you. You saw yourself as the wife of the manager of Affleck and Tate's. You would have carried it off with a high hand, but not half as successfully as Jane has done. She's a snob of the first water, she's a social climber, but, unlike you, she came from a decent family.'

'Get out!'

'I'm not going out until I'm ready, Irene. As I said, we're going to talk. I'm going to talk. Now you, in a way, are on a par with Jonathan. You both came originally from the gutters of Fellburn. Your father was an elementary schoolteacher; his father had been a little grocer and his grandfather. . . . You didn't know I knew this, but his grandfather, together with your great-grandfather were well known taggereen men in Bog's End. They both had donkeys and flat carts and they gathered scrap. A couple of Steptoes, but not quite so famous I should say.'

Her hair was pulled tight back in curlers held in place by an invisible net, and the skin at her temples now showed the veins standing up like pieces of thick blue string.

As he paused again they held each other's glance, hers wide, bitter, full of hatred, his scornful, sad, and bitter too. He moved from one foot to the other before going on. 'Your chagrin gave you sleepless nights when Susan burst into the titled set, didn't it? So you looked around for something to spoil, something to smash, and you found it, didn't you? You found it when you saw Vanessa talking to Angus Cotton. Your mean little mind put two and two together and made a dozen. They couldn't be talking unless they were up to something, and so what did you do? You flew next door and named the man, the father of Vanessa's child, didn't you? . . . DIDN'T YOU?' His voice had suddenly exploded in a shout and she leant towards him, gritting out between her teeth, 'Stop it! Stop it! Do you want to raise the house?'

'Yes. Yes, I would like to raise the house. I have something very interesting to say.' There was a considerable silence now and his voice had dropped when he spoke again. 'First, I want to ask you. Do you really, in your heart of hearts, think Vanessa was having an affair with Angus Cotton?'

'There was no need to think,' her voice was thin, low and bitter, 'there's enough proof. And I've seen them together again and again. And the children—'

'Yes, I know all about that. The children saw them together. But . . . but he's not the father of her child.'

'How do you know? What do you know about it? You've been away for weeks, and you took your time in coming—'

'Yes, I took my time in coming back, because I was afraid to face up to my responsibilities. I still am.'

'What are you talking about?'

'If you weren't so dull, woman, you'd realize without me having to put it into words. . . . I'm the father of Vanessa's child.'

Slowly she leant back against the bed head. She thought for a moment she was going to have a seizure of some sort. She had to wait seconds, minutes, before her heart stopped racing. Then she muttered, 'You're mad. You're sex mad. It's because you wanted her. I don't doubt but that you wanted her. You've thought of nothing but sex for years. But you, you, wouldn't have dared. . . . You. . . .'

'Well, I did dare. I had one short amazingly glorious moment of living down in the summerhouse.'

Her eyes were like pieces of flint piercing him. 'I–I don't believe you; you're just making it up. Wishful thinking, that's what it is, wishful thinking. I deal with people like you every week in the courts, people who say they've done things because they want to do them but are afraid to. I don't doubt but you wanted one glorious moment, but you would never have dared, never.'

'Well, I tell you I did dare, Irene. And Vanessa has been waiting for me coming back before she's spoke. She's been very, very brave. She wanted me to take her away. And oh, I would have dearly loved to have done just that. And I would if I'd been younger, and with more nerve and some money behind me. Yet if I could have done this she wouldn't have been happy. She's made for someone young, and she'll get someone young. A girl like her must be made happy, because you know why? She's kind, and kind people, even if they're the biggest rogues or scamps in the world, they're happy, they're made happy in some way. I've seen it again and again. . . . Of course there are exceptions. I was kind to you, Irene. And my people were kind to you. But my mother's last years were made miserable through you, and all my married years have been made miserable through you. . . . Well, it's finished. Or nearly so. By the way, I'd better tell you I made another will some time ago. Funny, but I must have known this was coming. I've made a stipulation in it that the land and house, when it is sold, mustn't be divided, and it must be sold as one and the money that it brings is to go into trust until Michael is twenty-one. Then it is to be divided between the three boys. I've also left special pieces of furniture to Paul alone. You, my dear, will have the interest on the money until Michael comes of age. After that you are at the mercy of your three sons.

She was unable to speak. Her whole body was shaking as if with an ague. When he said, 'Good-bye, Irene,' and turned slowly from her she knew what he was going to do. The only thing she didn't know was how he was going to do it. But she didn't get out of bed or say one word to stop him.

Chapter Five

Vanessa had sat by her bedroom window until almost two o'clock in the morning, and when she eventually did go to bed she didn't sleep, at least for a long time. When she heard her mother's voice saying stiffly, 'Vanessa! Vanessa! It's almost eight o'clock. Come along,' she imagined she had been asleep only a few minutes.

At half-past eight she went downstairs and into the morning room. She had stopped being sick these last two or three mornings and had felt hungry, yet at the same time she thought it wasn't right somehow that she should eat at all.

She had the morning room to herself; her father had already had his breakfast and would now be in his study where he would stay until after nine. There was some bacon under cover on an electrically heated plate, and as she served herself she thought, 'I can't eat, I can't'; yet she ate the bacon and had two cups of coffee and some toast and marmalade.

The sun was shining full into the room and she looked about it, seeming to see it for the first time. It was a beautiful room. Pale grey walls, thick pink satin curtains, two large mushroom-coloured rugs on the polished parquet floor. The sideboard with its gleaming silver, most of which was now going to be put away, and the period dining chairs with their seats and backs upholstered in rose. This had always been her favourite room, and perhaps after today, or tomorrow, or the next day she wouldn't see it any more. After she had told them about Brett–and how she was going to deliver this bombshell she didn't really know–she was going to tell them something else. She was going to tell them she meant to get a job of some kind, any kind, and, what was more, she was going to have the baby because the prospect of having the baby in six months' time was less frightening to her than having it taken away now. She knew that when she told them what she intended to do her father would bring his authority to bear, and if he couldn't force her to go to London he would send her somewhere. It wouldn't matter much to him where she went during the next few weeks as long as she was out of his sight, and not an embarrassment to them all until the wedding was over.

But she was fully aware that she couldn't stand up to her father on her own regarding the baby, particularly when he knew it was Brett's. He would be madder then ever at this disclosure. He would see it as a personal affront, and she daren't think of his reaction. She would need a higher authority to fall back on and she knew she would find that authority in Doctor Carr. She would go to Doctor Carr and say, 'I want to have this baby, I don't want it to be taken away.' And she could hear him now exclaiming loudly, 'If you want to have it, you have it; you're strong and healthy. Don't let me hear any talk of you having it taken away.' After that, let her father try and send her to London. Abortions were illegal and people could go to prison for doing them, or aiding them.

One minute her chin was jerking upwards in support of her thoughts, the next she had her face buried in her hands biting on the pad of her thumb to stop herself crying. She wished she had someone she could talk to. She felt dreadful inside, lonely, lost, all mixed up and confused.

She sat now, telling herself that she didn't know her own mind from one day to the next, because this time yesterday she was just longing to see Brett, knowing that he would take her away, and last night when she knew that he was going to do no such thing she had been sick. Even when she saw him as a timid, vicillating old man, she had still been sick with disappointment, and fear of what was going to happen to her. Yet this morning, when her mother had wakened her, she was filled with relief that they hadn't gone away together, that she wasn't going to marry him.

It was as she sat wishing that the day was over and shuddering inwardly at the repercussion her news would have on the two households that she heard the screaming. It was quite near, it seemed to be in the garden.

When she hastily pulled open the french windows and stood on the paved terrace the screaming filled the air. She saw her mother come to the drawing-room window, then her father come round by the side of the house. He looked along towards her, then her mother came through the morning room and on to the terrace beside her and she asked, 'What is it? Who is it?'

'Next door.' Jonathan Ratcliffe moved down the garden, saying over his shoulder. 'It sounds like Michael.'

The screaming now seemed to come from the top of the trees, and when her mother followed her father she followed them both, and then they were all standing by the gate looking into the wood, looking at Irene and Colin Brett. Irene was standing with one clenched fist pressed against her cheek, she was looking upwards into the tree house. Colin, too, was looking upwards. He was calling, 'Michael! Michael! Do you hear. Come down. I'll only have to come and fetch you. Come down.'

'What is it? What's the matter?' They all went through the gate and into the wood, Vanessa still walking a few yards behind her parents. As another series of screams came from the tree, Colin mounted the rickety ladder.

'What is it, Irene? What is it? What's upset him?'

Irene Brett turned and looked at Jonathan Ratcliffe, then she looked at Jane, and she gulped and moved her head twice before she said in a strangely controlled voice, 'He . . . he found his father in the cellar. Arthur . . . Arthur's hanged himself.'

No one moved for a moment. Then Jonathan said, 'Oh no! No!' And Jane put her two hands up and covered her cheeks, a characteristic gesture when she was without words. Then they both went to Irene's side, and they murmured over her. But she did not look at them, she looked straight between them and to their daughter, and she said again, 'Arthur hanged himself in the cellar. Do you hear?'

Both Jonathan and Jane Ratcliffe imagined she was repeating herself in this way because she was distraught, but Vanessa was aware that she was telling her she knew why her husband had hanged himself. It was in the hate in her eyes, and she was sending it like an arrow into her. Turning, she flew back through the wood and up the garden, and her parents made no comment on her actions because they knew their daughter had been very fond of Arthur Brett.

Back in her room, Arthur's death was having a strange effect on Vanessa; she was experiencing both anger and resentment against him. Her reasoning told her that resentment towards Brett should have taken effect weeks ago when she knew he had given her a baby. Yet her condition had evoked no such feeling. But his deliberate death had.

She saw him in this moment as Irene had seen him, and she hated him. She told herself that she should have known when he cried that he had no guts, gumption, nothing. He had used his tears to gain her sympathy, to get her to touch him, to hold him. She was glad he was dead, she was, she was. She stood in front of the long mirror and nodded at herself, nodded at her long white face, at her long, thin, leggy body, nodded at her stomach which was showing a slight fullness beneath her dress.

When she lay on top of the bed and buried her face in the pillow she asked herself what she was going to do now. Would she tell them, or would she leave it to Irene? He had told Irene. The thought brought her upwards. He must have told Irene last night after he had left her. She knew what would happen now. When her parents took Irene back to the house she would tell them why her husband had committed suicide, it was all because of their daughter. Oh dear Lord, dear Lord. Like her mother, she was holding her face in her hands.

It was nearly an hour later when her parents returned to the house. She was glad she was alone to meet them. Susan was staying with Brian's people for a week. She didn't think she could have borne to see Susan's face when she knew who it was who had given her the child. Her scorn and distaste would have been too much, even worse when she had thought it was Angus, for after all Angus was young.

She was standing waiting for them when they came into the lounge. She watched her father go and sit down in the big chair to the side of the fireplace. She watched her mother sit down on the couch. And she looked at them and waited, but neither of them looked at her. Then her mother said to her father, 'What on earth could have made him do it? The trip was successful wasn't it? Nothing went wrong there?'

'No, nothing went wrong there, the stuff sells itself. He got the orders. He was only going to be out there six weeks, which was more than ample, but when I knew Cribber wouldn't be able to start again for at least another six months I phoned and asked him if he would like to go on to Germany and Italy. He seemed quite pleased about it. Then just before he was due to come back he phoned me and said he was going to take his holiday out there, was it all right?'

'Do you think something could have happened on his holiday?'

'How should I know?' He got to his feet. 'She says she doesn't know anything, yet I feel she knows something, that look on her face. She's a bitter pill, is Irene. They've never hit it off for years. I could have understood him doing it if he had been at home for weeks and they'd been having one of their periodical rows, but he just came back yesterday. . . . Ah well, I'll have to get to the office. You'd better keep looking in,' he nodded at his wife, 'she's going to need all the help she can get. As for that boy, this'll leave a mark on him for life.'

He went out into the hall, and after a moment Jane Ratcliffe followed him, at least as far as the lounge door, and there she seemed to become aware for the first time that Vanessa was in the room and she turned to her and said, 'You can dust the drawing-room and dining-room. I've got a woman coming for interview at half-past eleven, put her in the morning-room and should I happen to be next door ring me.'

She wasn't going to tell. Irene Brett wasn't going to tell. She stood gaping towards the closed door. What should she do? If she didn't tell the truth they would still blame Angus, but if she told the truth now they would blame her for Brett committing suicide. She couldn't stand that on top of everything else. And it looked as if Irene didn't want it known. Yes, it looked like that because she'd had plenty of time to tell them. What must she do? She'd have to think.

Five days later Arthur Brett was buried. At the inquest they had brought in a verdict of death while the balance of his mind was disturbed. On the day of the funeral, at which all the professional people in the town were at least represented, the local evening newspaper gave the event full-page coverage. It said that Arthur Brett was a descendant of one of the oldest families in the county. There had been Bretts in Fellburn for the last two hundred and fifty years and that the early Bretts had once occupied the Moat House and owned considerable stretches of land on the outskirts of the town. It went on to say that the late Mr Brett's grandfather had married one Alice Affleck whose family had started the engineering firm of Affleck and Tate.

After reading the report Jonathan Ratcliffe handed it to his wife, and after she had read it she laid the paper down before saying, 'It sounds all very fine, but she is left practically penniless. Fancy him making a will like that; he must have hated her.'

'Well, you haven't had to wait all this time to realize that, have you?' he said tartly. 'But, you know he wasn't only hitting at her when he made that will.' His lips were in a tight thin line now and his voice was bitter. 'He was hitting at me. By what I gather from Colin the land is tied up tighter than ever. It cannot be sold without the house.'

'Would you buy it if it was up?'

'Of course I'd buy it. That's a silly question to ask. But I don't want the house. I'd pull the place down, it's dropping to bits anyway.'

'Did Colin say there was anything against their selling?'

'No; but he'll have Paul to deal with there because he's as daft about the place as Arthur was?'

'Are you going to give her a pension?'

'Yes, she'll get the usual, what he had paid in for.'

'Nothing more?'

'I have little say in that. Any suggestion like that would have to go before the board. And anyway,' he turned his face fully towards her, 'the more she has the longer she's likely to stay there. She likes prestige, does Irene, as you know. But,' he rose to his feet, 'we'll talk about that later. There's plenty of time to deal with that. At present we've enough difficulties of our own. Have you told her?'

'Yes.'

'And she's ready?'

'She didn't say anything.'

'You've got her packed?'

'Yes. . . . Jonathan.'

'Yes, what is it?'

'I'm worried about this. At least I'm worried about what Doctor Carr might do. You know she said. . . .'

'It doesn't for one single moment matter what she said. And I don't believe she went to Carr. Why didn't he get in touch with me, eh?'

'Well, he hasn't had much time, it was only yesterday.'

'If she had been to him at all he'd have been on that phone before now. And I was ready for him. I know a thing or two about Carr that will check his tongue. . . . By the way, have you written to your Aunt Jean?'

'Yes . . . I've asked her to answer by return.'

'Well, that'll be settled. She'll go there straight from the clinic.'

'She says she won't.'

'Oh, does she?' His mouth formed a straight line again. 'Well, it's your business to see that she does. You'll be up there, and you'll take her yourself. And you can tell her that if she knows what's good for her she'll do what she's told.' He paused; then looking upwards, he added, 'It might make a deeper impression if I tell her myself. Go and fetch her down.'

As his wife moved towards the door he said, 'By the way, you didn't leave her in alone? This afternoon, I mean.'

She turned towards him. 'No, of course not,' she said; 'Susan was here.'

He nodded; then said under his breath, 'I wouldn't put it past her to try and sneak out to meet that oaf. If she got what she deserves I'd make him marry her. That would be an object lesson all right. . . . Go on, bring her.'

He had taken up his stand with his back to the fire, his arms crossed, and he looked towards the door as his wife re-entered the room again. She had one hand cupping her face, in the other she held a letter. She held it out to him without a word, and he met her halfway across the room and snatched it from her and read:

'Dear Mother and Father,

I am not going to London, I am going to have the baby. Doctor Carr said I should. I told you last night but you didn't believe me. What I didn't tell you was he said if you force me to go to a clinic he'll take the matter up. I'm going to get work as I told you. I have taken my bank book. I don't want you to worry about me so I'll write you every week. I'll be all right, I've arranged to stay with a friend. I am sorry I've caused you all this trouble. Tell Susan I am sorry and I hope the wedding goes off all right and she's very happy. Please believe I am very, very sorry that I have upset you.

Vanessa.'

It was too much, he actually took the Lord's name in vain. 'God!' He held his head. 'Where? How long? Ask Susan!' He was yelling now.

'How can I, she's out with Brian?'

'God!' he repeated again as he walked up and down; then smoothing out the letter that he had crumpled in his fist he said aloud, 'I am staying with a friend'; rounding on his wife now he cried, 'A friend! Which friend has she that'll take her? Which friend knows about her condition? One friend, Cotton.'

'No, no, Jonathan, she would never go to Emily . . . I mean to him.'

'Then tell me which friend she has gone to?' He nearly knocked her on to her back as he turned and marched out of the room, and she ran after him, crying, 'Where are you going, Jonathan?'

He was at the door which led into the garage from the kitchen when he barked, 'Where do you think? I'll break her neck . . . and his . . . We'll be the laughing-stock of the town one daughter marrying into the county, the other into Bog's End, and her pregnant!'

'Jonathan!' Her voice was loud now and stern. 'Don't publicise us, not in that quarter. Keep your temper.'

He got into the car and from there he looked at her. Drawing in a deep breath, he bowed his head. 'Yes,' his voice was low now, 'yes, you're right. Keep my temper. But wait till I get her back here, just wait. I'll flay her. God! See if I don't.'

Three times he had blasphemed aloud, which proved to his wife the extent of the depth to which he was moved.

Ryder's Row wasn't new to Jonathan Ratcliffe. He had once or twice, in the early days, brought Emily home after a late session of washing-up from a dinner party, but now, when he drove up the narrow street and he had to edge the Bently into the space between the railway wall and a dilapidated Rover the rage within him increased. People owning cars in this street!

He knocked twice on the door, the second time banging with his fist. He heard someone shouting, 'Turn that down will you! There's somebody at the front door.' The music of either the wireless or television was lowered as the door opened and in the light of the dim passage bulb he saw the towering bulk of Angus Cotton in his shirt sleeves, neck open showing a dark growth of hair on his chest, and his rage was inflamed still further. This was the man who had dared to touch something that belonged to him, something that was part of him. Again the wish came that he could change places with him physically, just for one minute.

'I've come for my daughter.' He had to thrust the words out of his mouth.

'You've what? What the hell are you on about now! Look, what d'you want here?'

'Don't ask the road; you know. Where is she?'

'God Almighty! You must be bonkers, man.'

'Who is it? Who is it, Angus?' Emily came into the dim light. Then seeing the visitor she exclaimed, 'Why sir!' only to have her words cut off by Angus crying, 'Sir, be damned! Do you know what he's here for? He's here to take his daughter home.'

'Van?'

'Aye, Van. He thinks she's here. I ask you! They won't be told, will they?' Angus turned from his mother and, glaring at Ratcliffe, shouted, 'You won't be told. You won't believe the truth.'

'Keep your voice down.' Emily's own voice was low and harsh. 'You don't want the street to know.'

'It doesn't matter a bloody damn to me who knows. I'm not afraid of anythin', or ashamed either. Has she run away then?'

When no answer came from Ratcliffe, Angus cried, 'Good for her. Good for her.'

For a moment Jonathan Ratcliffe stood bewildered. He hadn't the smallest doubt in his mind but that he would find her here. He didn't believe that Cotton had nothing to do with Vanessa's condition, but he did believe him when he said she wasn't here. So when Emily said, 'Come in and see for yourself, if that will satisfy you,' he turned on his heel and walked to his car. And Angus moved on to the step and watched him, his whole body quivering the while. He stood there until the lights of the car disappeared from the street. Then returning to the kitchen, where Emily stood waiting for him, he asked her grimly, 'Well, what do you say to that?'

Emily sighed and shook her head. Sitting down heavily, she said, 'All I can say, lad, is they're dead sure it's you.'

'You know somethin', Mam?' He leant towards her. 'If I knew as much a few months ago as I do now, it would have been.'

'Don't say that, Angus.'

'I'm sayin' it, Mam, and you can believe me. God! I stuck that girl on a pedestal from when she was that high.' He pointed down to the level of his knee. 'You know I did. As hard bitten as I am I was still under the impression–because I wanted to be under the impression. Oh aye, because I wanted to be under the impression–that there were some virgins left, and she was top of the list . . . top of the pops. Aye, top of the pops. An' all the time she was messing about with some pimply schoolboy.'

'How do you know that it was a schoolboy?'

'I don't know, but ask yourself. She was at the Convent school, wasn't she? If she had been goin' out with a fellow regular, I mean like one of the Braintree set, they would have named him surely, but she was seen with nobody but me. She's likely met the bloke on her way from school; there's plenty of lanes between the Convent and Brampton Hill. There's also the golf course and Poulter's Wood.'

'Oh, Angus, don't say that.'

'Well, it wasn't another bloody immaculate conception, was it?'

'Oh!' Emily rested her face on her hands and muttered, 'I don't want to laugh, it's no laughin' matter.'

'No begod, it's no laughin' matter.' He, too, sat down, and after a moment he spoke as if to himself, saying, 'I wonder where she's gone.'

'They'll find her. They'll put the polis on her.'

'I wonder.'

'Of course they will.' Emily's voice was high. 'She's only sixteen, well seventeen in a day or so. But she's nothin' but a bairn.'

Nothing but a bairn. Huh! Angus got to his feet now and walked out of the kitchen and into his room and sat down in the wooden chair opposite the little table. His forearms resting on the table, taking the weight of his slumped shoulders, he stared down at the drawing paper and pencils, and his aggressiveness seeped from him. After a while his eyes lifted to the hanging shelf attached to the wall. His hand went up and he pulled one of the books down and looked at the title. It read 'The King's English, by H. W. Fowler and S. G. Fowler.' It was her who had made him buy that book, her and the fact of being put in charge of the fitting shop. Not that he needed grammar in the fitting shop, he had all the language necessary for the fitting shop, but he knew he wasn't going to stay in the fitting shop. Yet that wasn't the real reason why he bought the book; it was because of how she talked. It had happened he had met her on her way to school one afternoon last year. She was carrying a great armful of flowers, white and pink, and he had admired them and asked their name, and she had said they were called Esther Reads. They were quite a common flower really, she said, at least the white ones were, and she had pointed through the park railings and said, 'Look! There they are, those are they.' It had been that last bit, 'those are they.' It sounded all wrong. Surely it should have been 'those are them'. He knew his grammar was bad, but he felt he was right about that bit, for whoever said those are they. It was like saying 'was you?' So, he had gone and bought this book. But far from helping him it had only confused him further; he hadn't been able to find out from it if 'those are they' was right or not. One thing the book did bring home to him was the fact that he'd never be able to understand grammar. He had never heard of gerunds. What were gerunds anyway? And compound possessives? One thing only came out of buying the book, and that was begrudging admiration for those who did speak correctly. He thought that they must have had their work cut out to learn, and understand, all these two fellows said was necessary to speak English properly.

He recalled feeling a bit down and browned off for a few days after buying the book but it had soon passed. He had a home-spun philosophy of his own: If you couldn't do one thing then try something else.

He could draw, he was a good drawer. But now the chance to draw had been whipped away from him. The drawing office, any drawing office, was now as far from his reach as the moon, that was unless he did the thing properly and went every evening to a technical school, and it was too late for that. Anyway, he had burnt his boats. He was committed now for good or ill to cartage; he had gone in with Fred Singleton. Tomorrow he was to collect his lorry and start. And all this had come about through Van Ratcliffe.

Where was she? Where had she gone? Certainly not to any of the family friends else he wouldn't have come tearing around here. The bloody nerve of the man. He was sure, wasn't he? He was so sure. He picked up the book and rammed it back on to the hanging shelf. Je-hov-ah he would like to get even with that bloke. Wouldn't he just. He'd give half his life, or sell his soul, to get even with him. But what chance had he of that, apart from going and shooting him? And he could understand now why blokes got shot. Yes, he could that!'

The door opened and Rosie put her head into the room. 'I hear you've had a visitor,' she said.

He got to his feet and smiled wryly, saying, 'Aye. You missed it; you shouldn't have gone to the pictures.'

'Mam's brewed up. Come on, have a cupper.' She moved towards him, smiling now and adding, 'because, you know, this is the last night of Angus Cotton, Fitter; from the-morrow mornin', boy, you'll be Angus Cotton of Cotton and Singleton, Haulage Contractors. Just think of that, lad.' She pushed him hard in the chest, and he, punching her back playfully on the jaw, said, 'Aye, just think of that.'

'Come on.' She pulled him towards the door. 'I bet you what you like you'll remember this night. Won't he, Ma?' she called to Emily who was sitting with her feet on a modern oxidised kerb fronting the old-fashioned grate. 'When he's got his big house and his Rolls won't he look back to the night and say, "Remember?" you know, like they do on the telly where the poor lad makes good and buys out the lord of the manor, together with his mama and his papa.' She was giggling. 'That sounded funny, Mam and Papa.'

'Funny or not,' Emily's voice was flat and there was no smile on her face as she said, 'there's many a true word spoken in joke, and I know this much, he'll see his day yet with that bugger.'

On this prophecy Angus jerked his head, whether hopefully or hopelessly it was hard to tell.

A few minutes later, when Rosie had poured out the tea and they were sitting at the table amid an unusual silence, she remarked, 'I wonder where she's got to? She's going to find it chilly out there in the big, big world is Miss Vanessa. It'll be like being thrown in from the deep end.'

Aye, thought Angus, just like that, being thrown in from the deep end.

Chapter Six

Susan's wedding was over. It had been a big affair; half the county had been there. Vanessa's absence had not been remarked upon. One thing education did, it enabled one to be tactful, at least before the parties concerned.

Jane Ratcliffe explained her daughter's absence by saying that she was on the Continent touring with friends. It was rather an inopportune time for her to be away from home, but one of the party had dropped out and Vanessa had been so anxious to go. She was very adventurous was Vanessa. And she wrote every week, such interesting letters.

The recipients of this information smiled and nodded and said how nice for Vanessa, it was what every young girl should do, travel and have experience.

Jane Ratcliffe wondered if there was a double meaning behind these smiling replies. She also wondered where her daughter was. Two postmarks had said London, another Brighton, another Eastbourne, one as far away as Torquay. She had been forced to show Vanessa's note and her first letter to Doctor Carr because he had become difficult. He had acted as if they had done away with her. She had become very frightened about his attitude, but Jonathan had taken care of him and they had changed their doctor.

Jonathan said he had washed his hands of Vanessa once and for all, he never wanted to see her again. She herself wasn't so adamant; after all, she was her daughter and she was so young. She still felt the matter should be placed in the hands of the police, but Jonathan went almost mad if she brought up the subject. Perhaps it was because Rowland, the Chief Constable, was a member of his club, and Jonathan thought a lot about his status in his club, yet it would reflect badly on them if Vanessa had the baby in some charity home and the fact was discovered. But she couldn't make Jonathan see this. She was at the other end of the country, he said, and let her stay there. Far better that than under their noses and consorting with that lout; at least she'd had the sense to break away from him.

The house seemed very empty now without Susan, and when Ray started boarding-school–another decision of Jonathan's–she wouldn't know what to do with herself. She would have to take up some charity work to fill in her time. The house was no great concern now, for she had been fortunate enough to get a woman equally as good as Emily, if not better. She had thought for years that the world would come to an end if ever she lost Emily, but, you see, everybody could be done without. This had proved it.

BOOK TWO

Chapter One

It was Rosie who first found out where Vanessa was. It happened while she and Stan were in Newcastle. They had arrived at three o'clock with the intention of looking round before going to the cinema, but they were back in Fellburn by five o'clock.

Angus was in the house but he hadn't yet changed. He had finished work at twelve and spent the hours since going over his lorry in the shed that Singleton rented as a garage. He had bought it cheap and it was acting cheap. In the last three months he had learned a great deal about the mechanics of an engine. He'd had to or go bust, for during the first week the lorry had broken down four times. He knew he had been done over his purchase, and he put it down to experience; it would all add up to knowledge when next he went lorry hunting, but by the look of things at present, he was telling himself, that would be some time ahead. Forty quid a week they could make each, Fred had said. The highest he had touched was thirty. Last week he was down to twenty-four. They both worked all the hours that God sent, but their lorries were not big enough or good enough. The business that had passed them by in the last four weeks made him literally sick, yet he knew that even with new lorries two men on their own weren't going to get very far. He wanted half-a-dozen lorries at least, and the same number of men to go with them. He also told himself he wanted the moon. At the rate he was saving now it would take him a year to buy one lorry and that second-hand. he could have got one on the never-never but he didn't want to start that. He was against hire purchase because he had seen too many of the swabs coming claiming the stuff back around the doors; no, he wanted to pay on the nail. It might be frustrating waiting, but that was what he'd have to put up with. There was another thing. Once he started the never-never business Fred would keep him at it. He was finding he had to be firm with Fred; he was too slap-dash, too easy going.

He was looking dolefully down at the exercise book in which he did his accounts when the door opened and Rosie came in, still in her out-door things. 'What do you think,' she said, excitedly. 'I've seen her.'

'You've seen who?' She could have been meaning anyone at the moment.

'Miss Van, of course.'

His face was straight as he asked, 'Where?'

'In Newcastle. Come on, come into the kitchen, I'm not going to tell it twice.' She turned about and left him, and he followed, but slowly.

'Well, go on,' said Emily. 'Where . . . where did you see her? Stop muckin' about an' tell us.'

'You'll never guess, not in a thousand years. Not her. Would they, Stan?' She looked from Stan to Angus, but Angus didn't speak, he just waited. And then she looked at her mother again and said almost gleefully, 'Servin' in a greengrocer's. A potty, dirty little greengrocer's. Wasn't she, Stan?'

'Not Miss Van, no!'

'Aye, Mam, MISS VAN. It was her, Stan, wasn't it? She looked at Stan for confirmation, and Stan nodded. 'You said it was.'

'It was.' She looked from one to the other. 'We had just got out of the bus station and gone round by the pig market. Stan wanted to have a look at the river and I wanted to go and have a look at the flats, you know where Kyle Street used to be. We were wandering about there, and then we came to some of the streets that hadn't been pulled down yet, old mucky places you know, worse than anything round here.'

'Go on, get on with it,' said Emily impatiently.

'I am, Mam, I am. I'm just tellin' you, I'm givin, you the settin'. Well, we saw this little greengrocer's, you know, that sells everything; candles, firewood, the lot, a real huckster shop. There was some pomegranates in a box outside and Stan here says he wants one and I said I'd like one an' all. It would be like being a kid again eatin, pomegranates in the street. Well, Stan went to the door where there was an old woman servin', and there was a lass inside serving somebody else, an' it was as I stood by the window that I recognized her. It was Miss Van.'

'Couldn't be. She could get a job anywhere. She wouldn't want to go into a huckster shop; she would go into one of the big stores. . . .'

'Mam,' said Rosie slowly and patiently, 'she couldn't go into one of the big stores an' she wouldn't get a job any place, not lookin' like she does . . . she's big.'

'God in heaven! Did you speak to her?'

'No, course not, I kept out of the way, she didn't know Stan. You know I've never cottoned to her but I felt sorry for her for a minute servin' in that bruised apple dump.'

She looked at Angus as he said, 'You could have made a mistake.'

'I'm not daft, our Angus; I know her as well as you do.'

'Where did you say the shop was?'

'I told you, where they haven't started pullin' down yet. I don't know what the name of the street was. Do you, Stan?'

Stan shook his head, then said, 'No; but I remember that it was near Murphy Street and it was the end one. There was a big open space filled with rubble behind it.' He added, 'I've heard a lot about her but I'd never seen her afore. She's a good-lookin' piece, even if she's—'

'Watch it! Watch it!' Rosie dug him hard in the ribs and they both laughed; but Emily and Angus didn't join in.

'You goin' to the club, our Angus?' Rosie now asked, and he answered,

'Aye, I might as well. But I'm goin, down to the baths first.'

'You were there last night.' Rosie's voice was high.

'Aye, well. And I'm goin' the night again.' His tone said, 'What you trying to make of it?' He stared at her for a minute before he turned away and went into his room, and Emily, now bending towards Rosie, whispered thickly, 'You shouldn't have let on.'

'Let on?' She screwed up her face at her mother. 'What do you mean?'

Her voice lower still, Emily said, 'Don't be a stupid bugger; about Miss Van.'

'Why not for?' Rosie was whispering back.

'Because it's ten to one if she's in a plight he'll do somethin'.'

'Don't be so daft, Mam.' Rosie pulled her chin to her neck, 'And him being accused of droppin' her. He's not barmy altogether.'

'You don't know him like I do, and he is barmy about some things. If he wasn't barmy he would have married May years ago.'

Rosie now turned her head slowly and looked towards the front-room door and she asked under her breath, 'You mean . . . you mean he's been struck with her?' Her tone was incredulous, and her mother whispered sharply, 'I mean no such thing, he knows his place, but, as I said, if she was in a fix he could be sorry for her an' want to do somethin'. He's not barmy you say, an' I say he's bloody well barmy in some ways.'

During the next week Angus came home every night about the usual time. He would have a wash in the sink or take his soap and towel and go down to the public baths three streets away. It all depended on what he had been loading during the day. Monday night he stayed indoors; Tuesday night he went to the club–Stan gave Rosie this information the following day–Wednesday night he stayed at home again; Thursday night he went to the pictures, and on Friday night he was going to the dogs. But on Friday afternoon he took his lorry into Newcastle.

He found Murphy Street and parked the lorry near a mound of rubble. Dusting down his coat and adjusting his cap he went up the first street and found the huckster shop. There were pomegranates in a box outside, and onions and soft tomatoes. He looked through the window but could see only an oldish woman. He bit tight on his lip before he entered the shop and the oldish woman said, 'What can I get you?'

'I'll have a pound of apples, please.'

As she went to weight the apples he looked towards the little back shop but could see or hear no one. 'You've got a young lady helping you?' he asked.

Her eyes narrowed and she peered up at him without speaking, and he said, 'Haven't you?'

'What business is it of yours?'

'It happens that I know her. Can I have a word with her?' He looked towards the back shop again, and she said, 'She's not here, she's off bad.'

'Bad?'

'Aye, that's what I said, bad.'

'You . . . you mean the baby, it's. . . .'

'No, I don't mean the baby, its not due yet. You know about that, but I don't suppose. . . .' She looked him up and down and didn't finish, but he finished for her. 'That it could be me. That's what you mean, isn't it?'

'I didn't say nowt of the sort.'

'You didn't need to. Where's she livin'?'

'Why should I tell you that?'

He stared at her and decided to tell her the truth, for her sort could keep mum and he'd have had his journey for nothing, and another night of thinking ahead of him. 'Well you see the truth is me mother used to work for her family and she's been worried since she ran away.'

'And so you want to go back and tell her where she's living so she can carry it to the lass's folks?'

'Nothin' of the sort. Me mother doesn't work for them any more and she's no intention of letting on about her. I just want to see her and have a word with her.'

The woman stared at him again, then said, 'It's funny you findin' her; her people haven't done much searchin'. I don't know what kind of folks they are to let her be on her own, an' her in her state. She's nowt more than a bairn herself and no more fit to be left on her own than a new bride in a barracks.'

He hadn't heard that one before. He must remember that one–A new bride in a barracks.

'It's a good job she stumbled on Nell Crawford's house when looking for a room; if she had got in some places I could speak of, even in her condition, she'd have been eaten alive. But Nell's is all right, an' clean.'

'Where's this Nell Crawford's?' he said.

The woman moved her head impatiently. He had only to go out into the street, she said, and ask to be directed to Nell Crawford's and anybody in this district would show him the way. It's 132 Batterby Bay Road,' she said.

Batterby Bay Road! God! Of all the places she could have landed in she had to land in Batterby Bay Road. Nell Crawford, whoever she was, might run a clean house but, if she was in Batterby Bay Road, he'd like to bet his life it was the only one there. He said 'Thanks' and turned on his heel, and when she said, 'You haven't paid for the apples,' he said, 'Oh, I'm sorry. How much?'

'One and fourpence.'

He gave her the money and went out of the shop and he sat in the cab of his lorry for a few minutes biting on his lip. Batterby Bay Road! Good God! They made them in Batterby Bay Road; it was a training school for them. He'd first walked down Batterby Bay Road when he was fifteen. It was on a Saturday night, and he and three mates had come into Newcastle and had dared each other to go down the road.

They had gone down it, but they had come out the other end quicker than they had entered it. They had thought they were great guys to go down Batterby Bay Road and had bragged about it for weeks afterwards, but each one of them had been scared stiff by the tarts. Tarts of all types, tall and short, young, middle-aged and old 'uns. Not one of them had started yet. Talked about it never-ending, but never got down to it, and, all the opportunity in the world offered them, they didn't that night either.

He took the lorry right to the door of number 132. It was a tall, double-fronted terraced house. It had undoubtedly at one time been the home of a middle-class family. Now its ten rooms had ten separate occupants. Their names were on dirty pieces of paper pinned on a board inside the dim hallway; even the paper bearing the name V, Ratcliffe was thumb-marked. There was a glass door leading out of the lobby, but he found it locked. Looking to the side he saw a bell. He did not hear it ring, but after a few minutes there came the sound of footsteps on the other side of the door, and as it was opened a voice said, 'Haven't you got your key?'

The woman stared up at Angus and added, 'Oh, what do you want? I'm full up.'

'I've come to see a Miss Ratcliffe.'

She was now looking at him in the same way as the woman in the greengrocer's shop. Then she said, 'Ee'. You have, have ya. And what would you be wantin' with her?'

'That's my business.' He stepped towards the door with the intention of entering, but her thin arms checked him with a force that was surprising.

'Don't rush it, lad. Don't rush it. And let me tell you somethin'. If you're after anythin' you've come to the wrong shop.'

He closed his eyes for a second and turned his head to the side, then said, 'Look Missus, what I want is to have a word with Miss Ratcliffe. I happen to know her. Will you tell her that Angus Cotton is here?'

She wagged her head in small movements and her lids blinked over her round black eyes; then she said, 'I'm not deaf. Stay where you are.'

As she mounted the stairs he watched her, and when she was half up them she turned and looked down at him, scrutinizing him from head to foot as if she couldn't make him out. Then she continued on her way.

It was a full five minutes before she returned and her manner was unchanged. She said briefly, 'It's the top floor, number eight. And you'd better mind your head on the ceiling on the top flight.'

He was glad she had warned him about the ceiling. The third flight of stairs was dark and he had almost to grope his way up them. The top landing was lit by a fanlight in the roof and the door to the left of him was marked number eight.

He was again nipping his lip as he knocked on the door. After a moment it was opened and she was standing looking at him. She was wearing a loose kind of dressing-gown and he reckoned she must have just got out of bed. Her face, as his mother had once described it, looked all eyes and teeth. He had always thought he had never seen hair the colour of hers, a real chestnut with a gleam of dark red in it. There was no gleam in it today, it was dull and lank. When her lips began to tremble he said, 'Hello, Van.'

'He-llo, Angus.' She gulped on his name. Then standing aside, she said, 'Wo . . . n't you come in?'

He walked into the attic room and tried not to notice how it looked, but his immediate impression made him compare it with the home she had left, and he thought, it's unbelievable! His own home left a lot to be desired, but it was

Buckingham Palace compared to this. There was a narrow iron bed under the sloping roof, there was one chair and a small square deal table; there was a hanging wardrobe attached to the ceiling at its highest point near the little four-paned window, and beside a much-battered chest of drawers there stood on the floor a tin tray, on which was a gas-ring and a kettle. When he turned and looked at her she dropped her head and said below her breath, 'Don't say it, Angus. Don't say it.' Then her head still bowed, she said, 'Won't you sit down?' She motioned towards the chair; at the same time she sat down on the foot of the bed.

When he was seated he dropped his hands between his knees and tried to think of something to say, but found it impossible. Of the two, she seemed more in control of the situation. 'How is Emily?' she asked.

Even now he couldn't answer her right away; then after a moment he said, 'Oh, she's fine.'

'Has . . . has she got a new job?'

'No, no. I don't want her to go out any more; she's done enough.'

'Yes, of course.'

There was silence between them again, and in the silence the smell of the place filled his nostrils. The air was dank, dirty, thick. He imagined that the walls were impregnated with muck. He longed to turn round and throw the window open, but the room was chilly. His eyes moved about, looking for a means of heating, and then he saw a tiny gas-fire by the wall at the head of the bed.

When they both broke the silence together he smiled and nodded at her, giving her place, and she said, 'I was going to ask where you are working now.'

'Oh.' He straightened his back against the chair, 'I'm on me own, I'm me own boss. I'm in partnership with a fellow called Singleton. Haulage, you know, contracting. It's working out fine.' He wanted to assure her about that at least.

'Oh, I'm glad, Angus.' Her head drooped for a moment before she raised her eyes to his again and said, 'I'm . . . I'm sorry, Angus, about the trouble I brought on you and the others.'

'Oh, you've got no need to worry about that. If that's all you're worried about you can put your mind at rest. It did us both a good turn. I mean me mam and me. It set me up on me own, and Mam's a new woman now she's had a rest.'

'I'm glad.' she said again.

Now his face became straight and he stared at her blankly for a moment before asking, 'And what about you?'

When she made no reply he leant slightly forward and said under his breath, 'This is no place for you, Van. Why don't you go home?'

'No! I'll never do that, Angus.'

'But why? They're your people.'

She looked at him for a time before saying, 'Yes, they're my people. And if I'd gone on the streets they couldn't have treated me worse. They were terrified, really terrified, about me having the baby. Not because of what it might do to me, but because of the effect it would have on their prestige. You see . . . father was determined that I got rid of it, and, and I didn't want to.' There was a firmness in her voice that hadn't been there before.

'Well, you know I think he was right. I do. I don't hold with a damn thing he's ever done or said, in fact I might as well tell you I hate his guts, but on that score I think he was right. You could have started again.' She was looking downwards, and he stumbled on, 'You know what I mean. You're young, you would have forgotten all about this, and they would have stood by you and seen you all right.'

She was gazing into his face now and there was a deep bitterness in her voice as she said, 'They would have stood by me, but how? They intended that after I came out of the clinic in London I should stay indefinitely with a great-aunt in Scotland. She lives miles and miles off the beaten track. She has an old couple who look after her. They are over seventy. There's nobody young within miles. The minister visits them on Sunday and they have prayers. He's made a special journey out to her for years hoping that when she dies he'll be taken care of. They haven't a car. There's one taxi down in the village, and that's miles away. I was there last year for a week. . . .Mother, too, wants to be remembered in her will.' Her tone was cynical now. 'So I was packed off there as a sort of insurance premium to be raked off later. After two days I thought I would go mad.'

As Angus listened to her talking in a way that surprised him he realized that, although she still looked very young, the girl he had known was gone. But then that was to be expected; the girl would have ceased to be when she started the bairn. It was as his mother said, he was barmy in some ways. Into the silence that had fallen on them he said, 'You've been bad, I mean ill?' and she answered, 'I caught a chill. The shop is rather draughty where I work.'

'Yes, I know.' He nodded at her.

'How . . . how did you find out?' she asked.

'I didn't, it was Rosie. They passed the place last Saturday and saw you.'

'Will . . . will she talk? What I mean is, Angus, I . . . I don't want anyone to know I'm here. You see, I write home every week and my letters go from as far away as London, Devon, and places like that. I give them to Mr Noakes. He's . . . he's in number nine.' She nodded towards the door. 'He's a long-distance lorry driver. He, he posts them in London for me, and gets one of his work mates to post them some other place.'

A long-distance lorry driver, Mr Noakes. And what did Mr Noakes expect for his kind service? Long-distance lorry drivers who picked up any slimy piece that thumbed them from the gutter. She didn't know what she was askin' for. Doubtless Mr Noakes would one day inform her. After the bairn was born likely, if not afore; it all depended on how desperate was his need.

She seemed to sense his reaction to what she had just told him and she said, 'He's a very nice man, kind, oldish.' When she shuddered he said, 'You're cold, I'm keepin' you out of bed. Can't . . . can't you light the fire?'

'Oh, yes. I have it on most of the time but it got a little too hot and I put it out.'

He didn't believe her, but he didn't go and light it. Instead, he said, 'Where do you eat?'

'I usually have my lunch in a café in the town and bring something in for an evening meal. I manage all right.'

'Van.' He got to his feet. 'I've got to be going now, I've got a load waiting for me,' he nodded towards the window, 'but I'd like to come and see you again. Can I?'

She shook her head slowly, then said, 'No, Angus. I don't think it would be right. If they ever found out you know what they'd say; they would put—'

'Aye, I know what they'd say, and what they would put together. Well, they would be bloody well wrong, wouldn't they?' He lowered his head and said, 'I'm sorry.' When he looked at her she was smiling slightly, the first time the muscles of her face had moved upwards since he saw her, and she said quietly, 'Don't apologize; I've enlarged my vocabulary quite a bit in the last few months. It, it isn't that I don't want to see you, Angus, it's been wonderful seeing you but, but I don't want to cause any more trouble, and you know it would only lead to—'

'Well,' he said briskly, 'let me deal with the trouble and whatever it leads to. Now look. You get back into bed and I'll call later on and bring something back for you to eat. And in the meantime you tell that one downstairs that my intentions are honourable.' He felt he had said the wrong thing, and he blustered, 'Well, I've got to go. There'll be so much ballast waitin' at yon end they'll have me scalped. I'll be seein' you. Now get back into bed. I can't say what time, after six though. Aye, it'll be well after six.'

She was standing at the foot of the bed holding the iron rail with both hands, and she said softly, 'Good-bye, Angus.'

He forgot about the ceiling as he went down the stairs and cursed as he hit his head; then he took the other flights two at a time.

He had already lost two loads but he finished early, parked the lorry in the garage, then went straight to the baths, where he hired a towel and soap. He reached home at five-thirty, and sat down immediately to his tea.

'Aren't you going to have a wash?' said Emily.

'Don't I look clean?' He turned his head towards her. 'I had a bath afore I came in.'

Ten minutes later when the room door closed on him, Rosie said, 'Him and his baths, he'll wash himself away! In the end it would be cheaper to put one in the washhouse. He said that years ago, didn't he?'

'Where's he off to in this rush?' asked Emily under her breath. 'The dogs don't start afore eight.'

'Why don't you ask him?'

Ten minutes later, when he came out of the room, Emily did ask him. Casually she said, 'Where you off to, lad?' and he answered without blinking, 'I'm goin' along to see a fellow about a lorry. This one's drivin' me up the wall; it only goes when it's pushed.'

'A lorry?' Emily's brows gathered suspiciously. 'You never mentioned it afore.'

'I couldn't, I only heard of it this afternoon. A fellow on the site told me I might pick up one cheap.'

'The other one was cheap, and look what it's brought you.'

'Well, I've got me eyes open this time. Be seein' you.' As he went out of the front door he knew that they would both be looking at each other and wondering. Well, he would let them wonder for a little while until he knew what he was going to do. He'd have to do something, but what he wasn't sure. Well, not really.

Chapter Two

This was his sixth visit to number 132 Batterby Bay Road, and he brought with him, on this occasion, two bags of fish and chips, two half-pint bottles of pale ale, a sliced loaf, a half-pound of Danish butter, and half a pound of cheese. It was Monday and she had started work today.

He knocked on the door and entered when she said, 'Come in.' He hadn't seen her since Friday night and he had worked late on Saturday to make up for lost time, and then to allay his mother's suspicions he had gone to the club as usual; and yesterday he had made himself lie in, after which he had followed the usual Sunday routine. He had gone along to the pub for a couple of pints with Stan, and they had come back, had their dinner and, when his mother had gone upstairs to put her feet up, he had left the kitchen to Rosie and Stan and gone and lain down on his bed; and in the evening they had all gone to the club again, for as his mother had said it was often better on a Sunday night than it was on a Saturday. But here he was, here he was where his thoughts had been every minute during this last week and all the week-end.

He stared at her. She was looking different. She was no longer wearing the slack dressing-gown thing but had on a brown woollen dress that hadn't been cut for maternity.

It was evident that she hadn't expected him so soon, because when he entered the room she was going towards the wardrobe, and he watched her take the dressing-gown from it. When she was about to put it on he said quietly, 'Leave that off.' She turned a surprised look towards him, and as he dropped his purchases upon the table he added, 'You don't have to hide yourself.'

When he turned towards her she was standing in much the same attitude as her mother was wont to do, she was cupping her cheeks with her hands, 'Oh, Angus!' she said, and to this he replied brusquely, 'Never mind "oh Angus"! Get those plates out and let's have this while it's hot. I got skate. I don't know whether you like skate or not, I like it.'

She had never tasted skate; she couldn't remember having it at home, but she said, 'Yes, I like skate.' So deep was her gratitude to him that if he had brought in fried dog she would have eaten it. She brought a dinner-plate and a tea-plate to the table; the smaller one she set before herself, and he said, 'You'll have to sport another meal-size plate, eh?'

'Yes, I must get another plate. She doesn't provide for visitors.'

'She doesn't provide for boarders, if you ask me.' He looked disdainfully round the room.

'It's better than some, Angus.'

He paused with a chip to his mouth, saying, 'You're kiddin'.'

'No, I'm not. There was a place farther down the street. It was terrible, dreadful. And at least the people in this house work.'

'Well, didn't the people in that house?' He was quizzing her.

'Yes.' She had her eyes cast downwards. 'Yes, I suppose so, work of a kind.'

'Aye, of a kind,' he repeated. Then turning the conversation abruptly, he added, 'We're goin' out.'

'What!'

'You heard what I said.' He poked his big face towards her. 'We're goin' out.'

'No, Angus, no. What if we were seen together?'

'You frightened?' He placed his knife and fork down on the table, and she was quick to assure him, 'Oh, not that way, Angus. Not what you mean, no, but I'm frightened that someone might see us and tell Father, and if he saw us together then nothing on earth would convince him but that—'

'Look, Van. Get it into your head he's convinced already. God Almighty steppin' out of heaven wouldn't convince him otherwise. I told you he came to the house when you ran off, and although he believed you weren't there at that minute he believed that I knew where you were. I'm sure of it.'

'Well, I don't want to prove him right, Angus.'

'Now let's get this straight, Van. You can't stay in this place for ever, you can't come from that stinkin' little shop and bury yourself under this roof seven nights a week until the bairn's born. And that's another point. We've got to talk about this. . . .It's no use sticking your head in the sand.' He looked at her downcast face. 'What's going to happen when it's born? You goin' to have it adopted?' He waited, and after a while she said, 'I . . . I suppose I should, yet I don't know. I keep thinking first one way then another. It seems stupid having gone through all this then letting it be adopted. If that's what I'm going to do I think it would have been simpler to have done what they wanted in the first place. . . .'

'Aye, it would,' he put in. 'As I said, that's one thing him and me agree on, it would. It would have saved you a lot of trouble and worry, because as it is, you know yourself, you can't keep it. Now where could you keep a bairn here? You could hump him along to the shop and put him in a basket out at the back. That's easy fixed, it's been done afore. I spent me early years in a clothes bbasket in people's wash-houses when me mother went out doin' a day's washin'; under the table in different kitchens when she went out cleanin'; and once, she tells me, I spent three weeks in a hen cree. The old dear she worked for couldn't stand bairns, and there was an empty hen cree at the bottom of the garden, and there me mother used to dump me.' He was smiling now. 'So you see you could manage that part, that would be easy. But this here house is the problem. You'd have to hump up water from the next landing, and take it down again and empty it. And, you must remember, a bairn needs a lot of water.' He almost added, 'And makes a lot an' all,' but refrained. 'You've got some thinkin' to do about this, Van.'

She kept her head lowered as she said, 'I do nothing else but think.'

'Is there nobody you could go to? I mean, none of your relations or friends?'

'Not one of them who wouldn't be embarrassed to see me and who wouldn't immediately get in touch with Father.' Now she raised her eyes to his and said quietly, 'But I'll manage. I've got this far and I'll manage.'

'Manage be damned!' He jerked his head–he had ceased to apologize to her for swearing. 'You're only at the beginning of it, an' what's more you know nothin' about bairns. By the way, have you made arrangements about having it?'

'Yes, yes, I've done that.'

'Do you go to a clinic, or one of them places?'

'No, I went once, but there were so many people there I . . . was afraid someone might see me.'

'But you can't hide away for ever.'

'I . . . I'm not going to. It's just till it's born, and then the thing will be done and he can't do anything about it.'

'Only press you to get it adopted. That's the tack he'll take then.'

'No, I don't think he would do that. I don't think he ever wants to see me again. I think he'd show me the door if I did go home.'

'How did your mother react to it?'

'She is guided by Father, she always has been.'

He rose from the chair and walked down the middle of the attic. He had to keep in the middle to prevent bumping his head. And he walked the length of the room twice before he spoke again, and then he had his back to her as he asked, 'The fellow. Couldn't he marry you?'

He waited for her to answer, and when none was forthcoming he turned and looked at her. She was sitting staring down at her hands resting on the mound of her stomach, and he went to her now and, dropping on his hunkers before her, he put his hand under her chin and pushed it upwards and asked again, 'Couldn't he?'

'No.' She shook her head.

'Why?'

'It's . . . it's impossible.'

'Nothing's impossible.'

'That is.'

They stared at each other for a moment. Then he rose to his feet and, drawing in a deep breath, said flatly, 'Well, you can't go on like this, you just can't.'

'Other girls do. They survive.'

'Aye, but other girls aren't like you.'

'You'd be surprised. I've seen girls at the clinic. The look in their eyes.

You can tell us. Oh, you'd be surprised.'

'Nothin' surprises me, Van. And anyway, I'm not concerned what happens to other girls, I'm just concerned at the moment at what's gonna happen to you.'

She was staring up at him, and slowly her face crumpled; then her body bent forward and she was sobbing into her hands.

When his arms went about her and his hands felt her shoulder blades under her dress his own body stiffened against the touch of her. But only for a moment; then he was clasping her tightly and saying, 'There now, there now. It's all right.' But the more he soothed her the more she cried. 'Look.' He brought her damp hair from her brow and face. 'Don't carry on like that, it'll only upset you. An' the bairn as well. Come on, come on, stop it. Give over. Look, give over.'

But she couldn't stop, she couldn't give over. She had cried before, she had cried night after night when she had first come to this room, but it wasn't this kind of crying. This was a deluge of weeping; the force of it was a hurricane shaking her body. He became worried, not only for her, but that at any moment one of them across the landing would come to the door. That bloke Noakes, whom he had met once and whose age and manner had allayed any suspicions he had had of him, but who in his turn might be thinking her visitor was up to something. He implored her now, 'Van! Van! Don't. Aw, don't.'

He led her to the edge of the bed and, pressing her backwards, he said, 'There, there, lie down.'

She was lying on her side now, her face covered with her hands, and he knelt by the bed and held her wrists, and he wished his mother was here–his mother would have known what to do. If she went on like this she'd really be ill. She wasn't only crying, it was more like hysteria. The cure for hysteria, he had read, was a good slap along the lug; well, he couldn't administer that kind of shock treatment, but he could give her a shock. Aye, it was one way to do it.

He had wondered all the week-end how he would put it over and what her reaction would be. Well, now was the opportune time to try it out. He pulled her hands roughly from her face and putting his own down close to hers he said firmly, 'Listen, Van. Listen to what I'm going to say to you. Now listen . . . Will you marry me?'

It worked. After a few minutes her sobs turned to intermittent shudders, and then she was staring at him. Her breath still coming in gasps, her eyes puckered, she was staring into his face. Then stammering, she asked, 'W . . . what did you s . . . say?'

'You heard what I said all right, but I'll say it again. Will you marry me? Under ordinary circumstances this could never have happened, you know it, and I know it, but you're not livin' under ordinary circumstances, are you? That's not sayin' what I've got to offer you is a piece of cake, God knows it's far from it, but . . . but it would get you out of this. And I'll have you off me mind sort of, not worrin' every hour of the day what's happening to you in this warren of pimps and whores. Our house is not a palace, you might think it's a slum, but God, it's better than this, and you'll have me mum to see to you. What about it?'

'Oh, Angus, Angus.' Her face crumpled again, and he shook her hands roughly, saying harshly under his breath, 'Now don't start that again, you'll make yourself bad.'

She was biting down on her lip as he said, 'Think about it. I don't want yes or no now, just think about it. But as I see it, when you're drowning in the deep sea you don't turn your nose up at a floating plank.'

She tugged her hands from his and again her face was covered, and again she was crying, but quietly, and he stood up now and walked to the table, and from there, with his back to her, he said, 'I know it'll be a big comedown for you. I might be looked on as a bit of a catch round our quarter, but from the place where you're standin' I'm less than the dust beneath thy chariot wheels, sort of, an' if you did decide to come to our place,' he didn't say 'to marry me,' now, 'you'd have to stand the racket. And it would hit you from a good many sides. You'd be livin' atween the devil and the deep sea. Your own folks wouldn't own you ever again, so you've got to think on that, and my kind would be suspicious. So I'm warnin' you, do a bit of thinkin' about it. I'll be back the morrow night. But mind, don't think I'm blackmailing you or anything like that, for if you do say no you haven't seen the last of me.'

When he turned to her, she was sitting up, leaning wearily against the iron rails of the bed. He came and looked down at her and he put out his hand and lightly took the hair from behind one ear, and as he touched her the tears welled in her eyes again, and he said brusquely. 'Now, now, stop it. I'm off. Well, you have it. Chew on it. I'll see you the morrow night.' As he reached the door her turned to her and said, 'Think hard; it's usually for life.'

When he reached the bottom of the stairs he stood in the darkness and wiped the sweat from his face. God! Where in hell's name had he got the nerve from. And if she said no, what then? Aye, what then? He knew what then. His self-esteem would never rise to the surface again. He would shout louder, bluster more and belly laugh at every opportunity, but under his skin he'd be grovelling in the deep, deep chasm that held his self-disdain.

He didn't go straight home but called in a pub and had a double whisky. When he reached the house there was only his mother in and he was glad of this.

She greeted him rather tersely as he threw off his hat and coat, and when he took his seat opposite her at the side of the fireplace she looked at him and waited. In a way she knew what was coming, but still wouldn't believe it.

'I've been to see Van, Mum,' he said.

'Tell me somethin' I don't know,' she answered; then went on looking at a magazine she had been reading.

'Now, look!' He pointed his index finger at her as if it was a gun. 'Don't you start.'

'You're a bloody fool.' She was on her feet, and he cried back at her, 'Aye, I know I'm a bloody fool. But I'm not the first, an' I won't be the last. Are you going to listen to me or not?'

She walked over to the dresser and snatched up a cup and saucer from the rack; then coming to the fire and lifting up a brown teapot that had been standing on the hob for the past hour she returned to the table and poured herself out a cup of tea that looked like tar.

'I'm askin' you.' He, too, was standing now, leaning on the table looking down at her, 'Are you goin' to listen me out?'

'I haven't much choice, have I? I have to listen you out apparently whether I like it or not.'

He bowed his head and fought to control his temper. Then his voice deep in his throat, he said, 'She's in a frightful state, Mam. Rosie saw where she's workin'. That's bad enough. But if you saw the house where she's livin', you wouldn't believe it; you just wouldn't, Mam.'

'Whose fault is that?'

'We're not talkin' about faults or blame or anythin' else. By the way, I thought you liked her; I thought you liked her the best of the bunch.'

'Aye, I liked her, but I don't like the idea of you gettin' yourself mixed up with her. You got blamed for somethin' you didn't do, and now you're walkin' right into their hands. Do you think anybody would believe that you're not the father now?'

'Do you know somethin'?' His voice was deceptively low. 'I don't care a monkey's cuss what anybody believes. They'll believe what they like in any case, no matter what you say, or I say, or God Almighty says, but I would have thought that you might have had a different attitude, especially under the circumstances.'

'What did you expect? The old family retainer with the heart of gold? . . . Well,' she leant towards him and thumbed her chest, 'that isn't a picture of me. Charity begins at home. What charity I have is needed here. As for her, she should be in her own home, an' gettin' charity there.'

'Well, she thinks different, Mam. And so do I.'

'You do, do you?'

'Aye, I do.'

'And what can you do about it, do you think, except make a bloody fool of yourself?'

'It isn't what I can do about it, Mam, it's what I'm goin' to do. Bloody fool or not.'

She stared fixedly at him before she asked, 'You're goin' to live with her then?'

'Live with her!' He sounded slightly shocked. 'No I'm not going to live with her, I'm going to marry her.' He didn't add now, 'If she'll have me.'

'Christ Almighty!' Slowly she subsided back into her chair. After all, she hadn't expected this. She had expected him to say he was going to look after her or some such damn silly thing. She had even expected him to ask if she could come here to be looked after. Aye, that's what she had expected. But, marry her! Her son, Angus Cotton, marry the daughter of Affleck and Tate's manager! Jonathan Ratcliffe's daughter. He was stark, staring, bloody mad, and she said that to him. 'You're stark, staring, bloody mad. You don't know what you're talkin' about. You! You goin' to marry Miss Vanessa Ratcliffe? Aw, lad!' she shook her head slowly at him while she smiled mirthlessly.

'Not so much of the aw lad. What's wronge with me, anyway? Oh, I know I haven't had an education to match hers, but who's fault is that? It isn't mine. But it's not too late. An' what the hell does education matter after all? It's money that counts, money that sets you up. When you have money you get things, an' they change you. I've seen it.'

'Shut up.' Her voice was quiet.

'Look!' He almost pounced on her. 'Don't tell me to shut up, Mam. An' listen to me. I'm goin' to make money, I'm goin' to change—'

'So can a leopard.' She was scornful.

'My God!' He was standing straight now, taut. 'That's what you think of me, worse than them, and you me own, with the scorn drippin' from your lips.'

She looked at him pityingly now. 'Aye, that's what I think of you, lad, when you're aimin' at her. I wanted you to rise, I wanted you to rise in Affleck's. I stayed on up there for years just so that it would give you the chance. But I knew how far you could go. You see, I'm of two worlds meself. I've lived up there the best part of eighteen year. You could say it hasn't brushed off on me, an' you'd be right, yet inside I know what's what; I know that oil an' water don't mix. And you and she are oil an' water. And I'm goin' to tell you frankly to your face, lad, that if she's marryin' you she must be pretty desperate.'

He swallowed the truth hard. He gulped on it. His lips worked one over the other until there was no saliva left on them. And then he said quietly, 'That's it, Mam; she's pretty desperate. You've said it. You've said a mouthful, haven't you? But look you here.' His voice was almost gentle now and his movements, when he bent towards her, had no aggressiveness about them, he was just making a plain statement. 'I'll surprise you one day. I'll let you see. I'll let you see as well as the rest. From you up to Ratcliffe, I'll let you see. That's a promise, and whatever else I do, or don't do, you know once given I keep me word.'

She reached out and picked up the cup of black tea again and as she stirred it she said, her voice as quiet as his now, 'There'll be nobody more pleased than me, lad, if you bring it off.'

'If I bring it off! But I haven't got a chance in hell. That's what you're thinkin', isn't it?'

She looked at him and her voice still quiet, she asked, 'Where do you intend to live?'

'Here. Where else? Here.'

'Aw no! No!' Her voice was a roar. 'You couldn't. Where do you think she's goin' to live in here?'

'There's my room; it's big enough for two.'

'But, lad . . . Aw,' she was pleading with him now, 'what do you think my life is goin' to be like? If you and her are oil and water don't forget I'm on the same side as you. You'll leave her in the mornin' and I'll have her all day. No, no.' She shook her head slowly, slowly and widely as she gazed at him standing silent now. And she waited for him to speak; and when he did he said, 'And where else could I take her? I can't run two houses, and I'm not leavin' you. As bloody bitchy as you've been, I'm not leavin' you, Mam. You know I wouldn't.'

'Look.' She waved her hand at him. 'You can leave me any day you like, lad. I can fend for meself; I've still got a pair of hands.'

'Aye, and a pair of feet that won't carry you much longer.' He looked down at her still swollen legs. 'Anyway, I'm not taking her anywhere else, I'm bringin' her here.' His voice was gritty again. 'An' she's stayin' here until I can make other arrangements, arrangements that's goin' to suit both you and her, and me.' He thumbed his chest on the 'me'. 'Then we'll talk about it.' As he turned from her she said helplessly, 'Have you thought about our Rosie? She'll go mad. She never cared for her.'

He stood in the kitchen doorway and, looking back at her, said, 'That's a pity for Rosie. Anyway, she's got Stan. It's about time she was married.'

As he turned to go into his room she flung one last missile at him. 'What about May?' she cried. 'What about May?'

He turned again to her and said deeply and bitterly, 'To hell with May. To hell with her and everybody else.'

When his door banged she cried at it, 'You've played her dirty. She served your purpose for years and you've played her dirty. You'll pay for it, lad, you'll pay for it; you can't get away with those things.' Then turning to the fire, she raised her hands and gripped the high mantelpiece and stood staring down on to the flickering coals. Her world had been shattered into smithereens. She wished she was dead.

Chapter Three

It was three days later that Angus went to see Doctor Carr. He was the only person he knew who was in sympathy with Vanessa and who might be able to advise him on how to go about getting married legally without her parents' consent.

He had been to the reference library and looked up books on Common Law, but had found nothing to enlighten him about a matter of this kind, and he didn't want to go to a minister until he knew where he stood. He would, he told himself, feel embarrassed as it was going to a parson, as he'd never put his foot inside a church since he was christened.

Doctor Carr's eyes were whisky hazed as he looked across his desk at Angus, but nevertheless he listened intently to him. His interest had been caught from the moment the young fellow had mentioned the Ratcliffe girl, and he was both astonished and absolutely tickled pink when he heard what he intended to do. Lord, but wouldn't this hit Jonathan Ratcliffe where it hurt most. The feeling gave him a feeling of glee never engendered by the whisky, without which he was finding, more and more, he was unable to get through a day's work. But before he advised the young fellow what to do he would ask him a question. He asked it bluntly. 'You the father of her child?' he said.

'No, I'm not.' The answer was equally blunt.

'Oh, well, you know you'll get the blame for it when you marry her?'

'That doesn't matter to me.'

Doctor Carr surveyed Emily Cotton's son. He was a good-looking fellow in a way, well made, tough looking, but working class written all over him. It was a pity he wasn't her type. He said, 'I think it's like this. You'd have to have their consent to a register office marriage, but if your banns are called three times at your parish church and nobody raises any objection the marriage can go ahead, and it's legal. I think that's one set-up. It's a bit tricky but it's been done. Anyway there's always the court. You present him with that alternative and if I know Ratcliffe he'll soon sign because in her condition the verdict would be a foregone conclusion. Which parish are you in?' He asked the question of himself. 'Oh, you must be in St Edward's. You frequent any church?'

'No.'

'Have you ever?'

'No.'

'Where were you christened?'

'I think it was St Edward's. I don't know but my mother will.'

'Well now, if I know anything about St Edward's, it's dying on its feet, and but for a few old dears that go there the place is almost empty. I don't think the name Ratcliffe will have any significance for them. It's worth trying. I advise you to go and see the minister. He's like his church, very old, and he mumbles, which is another good thing in your favour. Take her along with you. You'll both look like an ordinary couple doing the usual thing.' He got to his feet and came round the desk, and when he was confronting Angus, he said, 'And good luck to you.' He didn't add 'You'll need it'; that went without saying.

The following evening Angus brought Vanessa in the lorry to the vicarage, and in a musty, dim lit room he asked that the banns for their marriage should be put up. The old man repeated her name twice. 'Ratcliffe. Ratcliffe,' then he peered at her and said, 'Hm! Hm! You will want your birth certificate and your parents' consent.' They couldn't be sure if he recognised her or not. Angus had the idea that he might not be as old and doddery as he looked.

When they came out Vanessa had her head buried deep in her coat collar. She seemed afraid to look up; or, he wondered, was she ashamed to. He hoisted her up into the cab and then he drove her home to Ryder's Row.

Again there was only Emily in the house. Rosie had refused point-blank to meet her future sister-in-law; there was nobody going to look down her nose at her, not if she could help it. Although Emily had said far better stay and get it over, she had replied, 'Not me. You might have to, but not me.' And now Emily stood self-consciously in her own kitchen looking at the girl she had practically brought up, and she saw her as a stranger. Physically she was changed. Her body naturally had filled out, not only her stomach but her face, and also naturally she looked older. Emily also saw that the girl had entirely gone. Here was a lass, a lass in a jam, and the jam had made her calculating. That was how she saw Vanessa now, and in consequence the feeling she gave out was one of resentment.

'Well, Mam; here we are.' Angus looked at Emily, then turned to Vanessa and said, 'Sit down, sit yourself down.' But Vanessa did not sit down, she stared back at Emily and said softly, 'Hello, Emily.'

'Hello.' There was no Miss Van now, not even Van.

Angus sensed that the situation was going to be more awkward than he had bargained for, and the best thing he could do was to leave them alone for a while, so loudly he exclaimed, 'Look. I'm as hungry as a hunter; I'll slip along to get some fish. All right?' He cast his glance down at Vanessa, and she nodded at him and tried to smile, for he was, she knew, doing his best to help matters along.

They sat silent for a long time after the door had banged, before Vanessa said softly. 'I'm sorry, Emily.'

'Aye. An' you've reason to be; you've brought a lot of trouble on a lot of people.' She moved about the kitchen before she went on, 'And if he isn't the father why are you marryin' him?'

'Be . . . because I like Angus and because he wanted me to marry him.'

'You like him!' Emily stopped and, turning, faced Vanessa. 'Lots of people like him. Likin' him isn't enough, it'll be for life. You know likin' isn't enough if he's goin' to look after your bairn and give you some of his own. You don't get by just on likin'. But you've got a thousand and one obstacles in your way; I suppose you know that?'

'Yes, Emily; I know that.'

'Look round you. Look round you, lass.' She was bending towards her. 'This is where we live. This is where he lives. Come here.' She pulled Vanessa towards the front room and, thrusting open the door and switching on the light, she said, 'This is his room. That will be your room. Look at it.'

Vanessa looked. Compared to the one she had just left it could be termed a palace.

'We're cramped for space as it is, but just imagine, with you and the bairn here . . . And there's another thing I'll tell you.' She turned her about and, pulling her almost roughly into the middle of the kitchen again and pointing to another door, said. 'That's the scullery in there. Talk about swinging a cat. Two of us can only just get in together. And beyond that is the door leading into the yard, and at the bottom is the lav. Not the loo here, the lav. Sick or well, wet or fine, you go down the yard to the lav, or do it in your room and have it under the bed. This is the way some folks still have to live.'

Vanessa closed her eyes and Emily, letting go of her arm, thrust herself around and said, 'I'm puttin' it plainly to you; I'm lettin' you see what you're in for. You were brought up with carpets in the lavatories, carpets in the bathrooms, powders and scents and creams, bath sprays, the lot. You're goin' to find this very different.'

Vanessa could say nothing in her own defence; there was nothing really to say; she only knew that she wanted to placate Emily. 'I've been living without all these things for some months now, Emily,' she said. 'I'll . . . I'll be quite pleased to live here if . . . if you'll have me.'

'If I'll have you?' Emily's voice was flat now and her face held a dead expression as she turned and looked at Vanessa again, 'I haven't much choice, lass, have I? I know it's my house; my name appears on the rent book, but Angus has always been the head of it since his dad died, even before, because my man was sick for years. And although I keep sayin' I can look after meself I've been on me feet too long.' She slapped her legs. 'They're lettin' me down an' they're not going to get any better. I know that. It's water. They'll get worse. All the doctor's medicine won't cure what I've got. I stood in your mother's kitchen for years just for one thing, so that your father would push my lad on. And now see where it's got me. Do you know something?' Again she bent towards Vanessa. 'I just can't believe this is happenin'; I think I'm in a sort of a dream, or at the pictures. Daughter of influential man marries fitter . . . Daughter of influential man marries cook's son . . . Daughter of influential man lives in slum. An' that's what the papers 'll say when they get hold of it. At least the local one will, unless your father plonks down on them, 'cos he's got shares in that company, hasn't he?'

Vanessa said nothing. She was trying her hardest not to cry, because she knew that if she cried Angus would blame Emily. She sat down abruptly on a wooden chair near the table and, supporting her face with her hands, she muttered brokenly, 'Emily, I said I'm sorry and I am, but . . . but I'm very tired, I'm sort of lost. When . . . when Angus came that day to my room the first time, I was . . . I was thinking about finishing it all. I'd lain in that awful place for three days and the only person I'd seen was my landlady, and then only once. I wanted to die. If I'd had enough aspirins or tablets, I would have taken them. Angus was the first person who had spoken a kind word to me in weeks, except the woman whom I worked for in the greengrocer's shop; and then she was a very brusque kind of person.' She lifted her eyes and looked at Emily. She could have added, 'Just like you.'

There was silence between them again, and Emily turned to the fire and stared into it. Then after a moment she gave a deep sigh and said flatly, 'Well, what's done's done, I suppose. But it's no use sayin', lass, that I'm goin' to welcome you with open arms because I can't. And then there's our Rosie. You're goin' to put Rosie at a disadvantage.'

'Oh, no. No. I won't, Emily; I–I've always got on with Rosie.'

'You've spoken to her kindly, but she's always been tongue-tied in your presence. Think back. Has Rosie ever chatted with you like Angus has? No. There's as big a difference between Rosie and you as between him and you. Only he's got sex on his side. Oh! Oh!' She raised her hand. 'He's a man. That breaks down barriers of a sort, but not atween women, not atween lasses. You've got every advantage over my Rosie; and Rosie's no fool, she knows it.' She came now to the table and, bending down quite close to Vanessa, she asked quietly, 'It isn't his, is it?'

'No, Emily, no.'

'Well, why didn't you say who it was and get him to marry you?'

They were staring at each other, and then Vanessa said, 'I couldn't do that, Emily.'

'Does he know who it is?'

'No.'

'Do you think that's fair to him?'

Vanessa turned her gaze away, then said, 'Fair or not, I can't ever tell him.'

Emily straightened up, then walked away, saying, 'Well, you're not out of the wood yet. You know what'll happen if your father gets wind of this? He'll come storming along here again. . . .'

'I don't think so, Emily. He'll close his eyes to it. I'm quite dead to them, at least him. I'm sure of that. I've realized lately that he's always disliked me.'

At this point the door was thrust open and Angus came in carrying three paper bags, and the kitchen reeked with the smell of fish and chips.

'Haven't you got the plates warmed?' He looked at his mother. 'What you been up to?' His voice was loud, covering the embarrassment that pervaded the three of them.

'Put them in the oven a minute,' said Emily, 'the plates won't take a tick.'

A few minutes later they were sitting at the table eating the fish and chips. At least Emily made an attempt to, but all of a sudden she got to her feet and, taking her plate and thrusting it back in the oven, she said, 'It's not ten minutes ago I had me tea, I'll have them after. I'll make a drink.' And on this she went into the scullery.

Angus looked up at Vanessa under his eyelids. She had stopped eating. He put his hand out and pressed hers; then silently he mouthed the words, 'It'll be all right.'

Fifteen minutes later they left the house, and on the journey back to Newcastle they hardly exchanged a word, and not until they were standing in her room did he ask, 'How did she take it?'

'Not very well, Angus.'

'She'll get over it; she'll come round; I know me mam.'

'It isn't fair to her. I . . . we could get a room somewhere . . .'

'We're getting no rooms anywhere, Vanessa. If you're marrying me, as I said you're comin' home; I'm not leaving her to God and good neighbours. There's too many does that the day. Round our place it's littered with old folks livin' alone. Well, she's had it hard enough. And I'm not being easy on her now; I know that, but I'm not making it worse by walking out on her. I explained it all to you. . . .'

'Oh, I know, Angus, I know. I'm sorry, but I've been thinking. Is it wise to . . .?' She stared into his eyes, and after a moment he said, 'You're going to marry me. It's settled, so just take things as they come, one at a time. The next hurdle you've got to get over is our Rosie. She won't be as easy as me mam, so prepare yourself. . . . Well now, I'd better be gettin' back; I've got to get up early in the mornin'. I'll see you the morrow night, same time.'

He made no move towards her; all he said was, 'Tarah!' and he smiled at her and went out. And she went and sat on the side of the bed, and slowly her head dropped in her hands and as the tears fell through her fingers she muttered, 'Oh, God! Oh, God! What am I doing? It isn't fair to him, it isn't. Oh, Brett. . . . You! You!' Her thoughts ground to a standstill on her clenched teeth, and she rocked herself back and forward, much the same as Emily would have done.

Chapter Four

Jonathan Ratcliffe heard of the banns being called in St Edward's through Mr Wilton. Mr Wilton was standing at the other side of the desk, his face showing deep concern as he explained how he had come by the knowledge. One of the men in the fitting shop had a mother who attended St Edward's. She had heard the names being called and had put two and two together. Mr Wilton thought Mr Ratcliffe should know.

Jonathan Ratcliffe looked at his subordinate and was unable to speak; then after a moment he thanked him and nodded his dismissal. As Mr Wilton went out of the door he was about to call him back and tell him to keep this knowledge to himself when he realized that Wilton would be the last but one in the whole works who had remained in ignorance of the situation between his daughter and Cotton.

He picked up a steel ruler and endeavoured to break it between his clenched fists. The slut! The low, low slut! The scheming little hussy. It was only three or four days ago that she had written to her mother thanking her for sending her birth certificate, the birth certificate that was supposed to be required by an employer. It has never dawned on them for a moment why she wanted her birth certificate. My God! And she was in the town. But that last letter had been postmarked Islington. . . . Islington. She could never have been in Islington; you had to reside at least three weeks in the parish where you were to be married. The scheming . . .! The treacherous . . .! words failed him. He rang his secretary and told her to get his wife on the phone.

All Jane Ratcliffe could say to her husband's information was, 'Oh, no! Oh, no! But how?' and again 'Oh, no! Oh, no!' Then she asked, 'What are you going to do?'

'I'll tell you when I get in,' he answered and rammed the phone down. . . .

And he told her immediately he entered the house, even before he had taken his coat off. After asking, 'Is anyone in?' and getting her answer 'No,' he said, 'Can you believe it?'

She shook her head. 'No, I can't make it out,' she said. 'How did she send the letters from those various places?'

'He likely manoeuvred that for her.' And he hit on part of the truth by saying, 'Lorry driver. Long-distance lorry drivers. That could be it. Taking her letters down there. . . . And to think you sent that birth certificate and it was picked up and returned to this very town.'

'How was I to know? What are we going to do?'

'I'm going to put a stop to it. Anyway he can't do it without our consent, but by God he's likely forged that. I know what he's up to. Once he's married her he thinks I'll come round, and there'll be a place for him well up the ladder at Affleck's. He was never more mistaken in his life.'

'Do you really think that's his intention?' Her question was tentative and conveyed her doubts and brought him barking, 'Of course, woman! I know him and all his type. He thinks I won't be able to bear them being in this town together, not her living in that quarter and us up here. And he's right. But his plans are going a little awry.' He now beat his fist into the palm of his hand as he cried, 'That girl! she must have a defective streak in her. That's it.' He nodded at his wife as if he had discovered the root of the trouble, then went on, 'I'll straighten that out when I get her home. I'll have her put in care. I will. I will.'

'You're going to fetch her home?'

'Just that. And then we're taking her to your Aunt Jean's, and we're taking her ourselves, every step of the road. And then you're staying with her for as long as is necessary.'

'Oh, Jonathan! I . . . I can't do that. How are you going to . . .?'

'Look, woman. Put first things first. I'll manage and see to Ray.'

It was as if by speaking his son's name he had conjured the boy up, for he turned his eyes slightly to the side towards the passage leading to the kitchen, and there he saw his son standing. This was a thing that annoyed him about the boy; he was always standing in dark corners listening. He yelled at him, 'Come out of that!'

When Ray walked slowly into the hall he said angrily, 'You've been listening again.'

'Not really. Not really, Father; I was just coming out of the kitchen.'

'I've told you about it, haven't I?'

'Yes, Father.'

'What did you hear?'

The boy glanced at his mother, then back to his father again and said, 'About Vanessa going to marry Angus Cotton.'

As Jonathan Ratcliffe ground his teeth his wife said, 'It can't do any harm now, no matter what he hears.'

As her husband stalked into the drawing-room she took hold of the boy and drew him into the kitchen, and there she said to him, 'Now mind, Ray, I'm warning you, don't discuss this with Michael. Remember, Michael is only a little boy; you shouldn't talk to him about things that happen in the house. I've told you, haven't I?'

'Yes, Mother.' He stared fixedly at her. He wasn't afraid of his mother; he wasn't really afraid of his father; well, just a little bit. He knew something he would like to tell his father just to see him go red in the face and nearly choke, like he did when he was in a temper. He had forgotten about it for a long time now, but hearing his father talking about Vanessa going to marry Angus had brought it back to his mind. He liked to be able to surprise people. He knew he would have spoken about it before if Uncle Arthur hadn't killed himself, yet he knew that this knowledge was somehow connected with Uncle Arthur killing himself.

The next best thing to surprising his father was to surprise his mother. He said to her now under his breath, 'I didn't think Vanessa would marry Angus, I thought she would marry Uncle Arthur.'

'What did you say?'

'I said I thought Vanessa would marry Uncle Arthur, that he'd give up Aunt Irene and marry her, Vanessa, like they do after a divorce. There were three boys in our form whose parents were divorced.'

Jane Ratcliffe was sitting down now. She had hold of her son's shoulders and was staring into his face. Her lips were moving, but no words issued from them for some time. And then she whispered, 'Ray, what are you saying? Come along, tell me what you know. What makes you think Vanessa should have married Uncle Arthur?'

'Well,' he shrugged his thin shoulders and moved his dark, satanic eyebrows upwards, 'they used to kiss and slop.'

She was doing now what she had never done before, she was shaking her son as if he was a rat, and for the first time in his short life he himself was really frightened. When her hands were still again but still gripping his shoulders, she muttered thickly, 'Tell me, boy, tell me everything. Everything mind.'

His head seemed to be still wobbling and he jerked it once before he said, 'Well, I saw them kissing.'

'You saw them . . .?' She swallowed deeply, 'Yes, go on.'

'I used to go out at night down the drainpipe, and one night I saw her go down the wood and when she came back Uncle Arthur was with her, and they stood by the gate talking, and he kissed her. I was up in the tree house.'

'Go on.'

'And another time I followed her and she and Uncle Brett were in the summerhouse.'

His mother was gripping his shoulders so hard that he hunched them up against his head, and when she relaxed her hold and again said, 'Go on,' he continued, 'Well I saw them sitting on the steps. Uncle Arthur was talking and then they were kissing and things.'

He was surprised the way his mother started calling on God. He had never heard anybody say things like that, except Emily.

There was a long silence now before she said, 'Why didn't you tell me this before?'

'Well–well, I didn't want to give Vanessa away; I–I knew she would get wrong. And then Uncle went away and I forgot about it until he came back.'

'What happened when he came back?'

He bowed his head, then said, 'She went into the wood, but–but I didn't follow her; I was waiting for Michael. He had promised to sneak out and I thought he would be frightened if I wasn't there and go indoors again. We were going to sleep there all night.'

'Yes, yes, go on.'

'Well I saw Uncle and Vanessa at the gate, the wood gate, and she was crying and he kissed her.'

He was now looking down right on to the crown of his mother's head. He looked at it for a long time before she straightened herself up and said to him in a funny voice, 'Come on.'

When they entered the dining-room she checked what her husband was about to say in a voice that caught his attention. 'Ray's got something to tell you,' she said.

He looked at her face for a moment longer, then turned to his son and said, 'Yes, what is it?'

'I think you'd better sit down.'

He stared at her hard again, but sat down, and she pushed Ray towards him, saying, 'Tell you father what you've just told me . . . all of it.'

Jonathan Ratcliffe said not one word as his son talked haltingly, but when the boy was finished speaking he rose from the chair, pushed his son to one side and walked out of the room, across the hall and into his study. A moment later Jane Ratcliffe joined him, and at the first sight of him she was afraid of what might happen. He looked as if he was on the point of a seizure. His complexion was both red and grey, and the greyness around his mouth had paled to a sickly white. She dared not speak in case she said the wrong thing and incited him more.

When he spoke he surprised her because he didn't speak immediately of his daughter but of Arthur Brett, and not about what Arthur had done to Vanessa but what Arthur had done to him. 'You see,' he said; 'you see why he did it? To spite me. He planned it; he planned it every step of the road; he did it to get his own back. I always knew he'd do something one day. He took it too quietly years ago, too smoothly. He must have been boiling against me all this time; behind that quiet smile of his he was hatching this. He wanted some way to bring me low, and he knew exactly how to do it. And he timed it, he timed it that the balloon would go up before the wedding. Don't you see? DON'T YOU SEE?'

No, she didn't see, not quite the way he was seeing it. For once she saw a situation in its true light, an older man, an unhappy man, playing on the sensitive nerves of a young girl at her most impressionable age. She dared to say now, 'No, don't look at it like that, Jonathan; I'm sure he—'

'You're sure of nothing, woman. I know, I know. Everything fits. He had refused my offer to send him abroad in the first place. Then he got cold feet and thought he'd better get out of the way. The swine. The dirty swine. He expected the balloon to burst while he was away, when she found out she was pregnant . . . and he hoped she would be. You mark my words.' He was stabbing his finger towards her. 'That's what he was aiming at, her pregnancy. Then he would come back and gloat.'

'But,' she felt she had to reason with him. 'but he took his life, Jonathan. He didn't gloat, he took his life.'

'Yes, to spite me, so that people who didn't know the real facts would say he had done it out of frustration. He had done it because I had walked over his head; that's what they would say. He had been brooding over the injustices for years; that's what they did say.'

She knew it wasn't any good trying to combat at the moment his irrational way of thinking, nor in fact in the future; Jonathan was a law unto himself; he would think what he wanted to think; but she voiced now what had been in her mind from the moment Ray had spoken. 'And we accused Angus,' she said.

He stared at her, trying to collect his whirling thoughts, Angus, Angus Cotton. And he was going to marry her. Well, this only confirmed what he had known all along–that slob was determined to rise. Ten minutes ago he was determined to put his spoke in his wheel, but now, no, no, he'd let him get on with it, because one thing was utterly vital: not a breath of this latest development must come to light.

It was evident that she hadn't told Cotton who the father was and he was taking her on trust, on trust that he thought was going to pay off a good dividend later on. Oh yes, Cotton's type did nothing for nothing; he was ambitious, he was a climber. Being one himself, he thought he recognized the same traits when he met them in another man.

She said now, 'What are you going to do about them? I mean about them marrying?'

He hadn't enough cool nerve to go on looking at her as he said, 'Let them get on with it.'

'You mean, you're not going to do anything?' she was addressing his back.

'Just that.' He turned to her again. 'I'd even give them consent, for this thing mustn't leak out. Do you hear? Fetch that boy in. He's got to understand that he must never mention this to a soul. If she's kept quiet we can keep quiet. We've got to. I–we'd be the laughing stock of the town if it leaked out. The past scandal would be nothing compared to what it would be if it was known that Brett,' he ground his teeth, 'the dirty, dirty swine had given her the child.'

'You don't think they know, they guessed? I mean next door? Irene and Colin and Paul?'

'Don't be stupid, woman.' His voice was filled with scorn. 'Do you think that Irene would have kept that to herself? And did we guess?'

'No. But knowing Irene. Yes, I think she would have kept it to herself if she had known.'

'Nonsense! Nonsense! That kind of a woman couldn't keep anything to herself. Go on and bring the boy in. And one more thing. Don't breathe a word to Susan about this, mind. Do you hear me?'

'I hear you; you've got no need to stress the point,' she said.

She did not go immediately into the lounge but stood in the hall trying to collect herself. For weeks now her feelings had been softening towards her errant daughter. She imagined her travelling from one job to another, from one place to another, and the baby's birth getting nearer and nearer, but now her duplicity had wiped away any lingering tenderness. Granted she had been taken advantage of by an older man, but that was no reason why she should now resort to marrying a person like Angus Cotton, someone who was the antithesis of all she had been brought up to expect in a man and a gentleman. She could see herself now accepting the child knowing it was Arthur's, because after all Arthur had been a gentleman; but Emily's Angus! Well, he was nothing more than an uncouth, gauche, ignorant individual, and in marrying him her daughter was indeed sinking to the depths. And there, as Jonathan had implied, she must be allowed to wallow.

It was, after all, a comfort to her that she saw eye to eye with her husband over this unhappy affair.

Chapter Five

They were married at ten o'clock on a Saturday morning. Emily wasn't present, nor was Rosie, but Stan acted as Angus's best man and the verger made the other witness. When the short service was over Vanessa couldn't believe that she was now married, and to Angus Cotton.

As she stood in the vestry she had an overpowering desire to turn and fly out of the church, fly out of the town, to put as much space between herself and him as possible. But she liked Angus, for he was the only one who had been kind to her, the only one who had stood by her; the only one who had accepted her condition and hadn't asked questions, at least after the night he asked her to marry him. And now she was married to him and the enormity of the step she had taken loomed over her like a dark canopy.

Yet she felt she could live with Angus and know a modicum of happiness if it was possible for them to be alone. But she was going back to that tiny little house which was filled with Emily . . . and Rosie, and she was frightened, frightened of them both.

She had lodged with Stan's mother for the past three weeks, so fulfilling the requirements of living in the parish during the calling of the banns. Stan's mother was a quiet woman who asked no questions and talked mostly about the weather, and her Stan. She wished they were going back there, or that, things being as they were, they were returning straight home–she thought of it now as home–so that she would get the meeting with her new mother-in- law and sister-in-law over. But Angus had arranged that they would spend the day in Newcastle. She didn't wonder why this was; she knew it had to do with Emily and Rosie.

And it had, it definitely had. Angus thanked Stan and said rather sheepishly they would have a drink later–which term gave no indication of time. Then he bade him good-bye, and Stan, after awkwardly shaking hands with Vanessa, wished her, ironically, the best of luck, following which he took his departure with unconcealed haste.

At this moment, more than at any time in his life, Angus wanted company, lots of company. If someone had told him years ago that one day he could have Aladdin's lamp and three wishes, he would have used all three to wish that he could some day marry a lass like Vanessa Ratcliffe; and now

Aladdin's lamp had been rubbed and he had married, not an imitation of Vanessa Ratcliffe, but Vanessa Ratcliffe herself, and the fact had stilled his tongue, made him self-conscious, yet elated, and at the same time sad, sad because his mother had refused to come to the church.

Last night there had been hell to pay. 'You still goin' through with it?' she had said. 'God Almighty, Mam!' he had bawled back at her. 'Haven't you got it into your head yet? I'm marryin' her the morrow. Come hell-fire or high water, I'm marrying her the morrow.' And to this she had said quietly, which made it all the worse, 'Aye, well, I hope you don't live to regret it.'

Then May had come in. One or other of them had used May as a last straw. Neither of them had like May; May was common. Aye, there were grades below 24 Ryder's Row.

May was standing at the kitchen table when he came out of the room ready to go and meet Vanessa, and she had said, 'Hello there, Angus.' And he grinned sheepishly and replied, 'Oh hello, there, May. How you keepin'?' To which she had replied. 'How do you think?' She would never had made this answer, not within those four walls, if she hadn't had his mother and Rosie behind her.

Rosie and his mam had gone upstairs and left them alone and May said to him, 'Is it right that you're gettin' married the morrow?' and he had answered quietly, 'Yes, May. I'm sorry an' all that, but it's right.' And to this, and with her voice as quiet as his, she had said. 'You know what you are, Angus Cotton; you're a lousy, rotten twister, you're nothin' but a stinking bugger. I've been good enough for you on an' off for years; I've served your purpose, haven't I? Every time I made a break from you an' got a decent fellow, up you'd pop again and wag your little finger and expect me to come runnin'. And being the bloody fool that I am, I came runnin'. And now this. But don't think you'll get off with it; you'll get paid out one way or the other.'

At this point he had asked her had she quite finished, and she had replied, 'Not by a long chalk. You'd have been married already, and to me, wouldn't you, if I hadn't been such a bloody fool as to tell you the truth?' Her voice was weighed now with bitterness. 'You can do it every night in the week and with as many as you like, can't you? But because I was honest and told you of the other two you cooled off. Like a parson at a strip-tease, you melted away.'

When he hadn't answered her she moved towards the door and from there she said. 'Well, I wish you joy of her, and from what I hear you'll need it. She'll make you feel like a worm, that's after she gets rid of the bairn. Once she's had the bairn she won't be scared out of her wits any more. She won't want a life-belt then. It makes a difference having a bairn. I should know, shouldn't I? And when she wakes up and see the big galoot that she's married she'll ask herself is she was clean barmy, because she will wake up. Oh aye, she will, an' then you can look out, Mr Bloody Big-Head.'

What had upset him more than anything she had said was when she looked around the room and put her head back and laughed mirthlessly, saying, 'And you're bringing her back to this? God Almighty! Even I wouldn't have stood for that. I'm going' to wish you luck, big boy, because you're goin' to need it. And how! . . . Who put the overalls in Mrs Murphy's chowder.' She ended on a saying that she usually fitted to situations that puzzled or were beyond her. It had always made him want to belly laugh. May had had the knack of making him belly laugh. Vanessa would never have that kind of knack.

They were sitting in the bus now and he turned to her and asked, 'All right?' She smiled faintly at him as she answered, 'Yes, Angus.' After a moment he said, 'We're going to have a spot of lunch, then have a look round.' He paused. 'Is there anything you would like?'

'Like? What do you mean?'

'Something for yourself.' He was smiling into her eyes now. 'Wedding present, sort of.'

'No Angus, thank you very much.'

'Nothing?' The smile had gone from his face.

'Well,' she lowered her head and shook it slightly, 'I haven't thought; perhaps later.'

'Yes, aye.' He looked ahead again.

They had lunch, then they went to the cinema. They sat side by side and he didn't take her hand. He hadn't touched her in any way except to put the ring on her finger. He hadn't even kissed her at the service, and the minister had made no comment on it. What he would do later on the night, he didn't know. The separate beds would help.

That had been another hell-raising moment when the other single bed had been delivered at the house. On this occasion his mother had bawled at him, 'Well you are marryin' her, aren't you? Look . . . if you want my advice you'll start the way you mean to go on. There's a sayin': You've made your bed and you must lie on it, but there's another sayin': If you don't make your bed the first night, whether it's through being sozzled or not havin' it in you, then there's little chance you'll do any better the second, or the third.'

She was a coarse old bitch when all was said and done, and he had told her so. But she had replied that he was already trying to jump the fence to Van's side where nothing was looked at squarely because it wasn't the thing to do, but he wasn't cut out for politeness, and he would soon find that it was choking him. Her words stirred a tiny fear that she might be right.

It was around seven when they came out of the pictures, and there was a cold drizzle falling, and as they stood under a lamp he said, 'What about a bit to eat, eh?'

She pulled her coat collar up under his chin, and she looked up at him for a moment before she answered. 'I'd rather go home, Angus.'

He smiled broadly. 'Good idea. Good idea.'

He had wanted to put the going home off to the very last minute when he hoped both Emily and Rosie would be in bed. Tomorrow morning everything would look different; everybody would take a different slant at each other; but now she had said she would rather go home, and in a way he knew she was right. Far better get it over with. Anyway, they would likely be out at the club. One thing was certain, Rosie wouldn't be in; Stan would see to that. Stan was a good fellow at bottom.

It took much longer to get from Newcastle to Felburn by train than it did by lorry, and then they caught a bus from the station to the end of the street. It was pouring with rain when they alighted and he took her by the arm and ran her across the road, and he kept her in the shelter of the railway wall until they were almost opposite the door. But as he made to cross over to the pavement he stopped. He had heard the singing farther up the street but he hadn't thought it was coming from their house. The Conways usually had their wireless blazing away at all hours, but this wasn't the wireless or telly, it was singing, voices singing. There was a difference.

When he pushed open the front door the sound hit them like a backwash of a huge wave. The voices were all raised on the last line of a dated song: 'Now is the Hour.' His hold tightened on Vanessa's arm as he stared along the dimly lit passage. God! She had got company in, which told him one thing even before he saw her, she was bottled. She wasn't the one for having neighbours in. Only twice before in his life had he known her do this, and on both occasions she had been burnt up inside with anger.

He stood in the kitchen doorway almost in front of Vanessa looking at the company. He was surprised to see Stan there, but the look that Stan gave him said, 'I couldn't do anything with them,' and he could see that for himself, because Rosie had had a skinful too.

There was Alf Piggot and his missus from down the street, and Bill Wilson and his missus from next door. Bill had his old concertina on his knee; they weren't relying on the television or the wireless the night. His mother always said she hated the sound of Bill's concertina, but she was singing to it now. As the song ended on different notes, the visitors all turned and greeted him, saying in different ways, 'Congratulations, lad.' They didn't say anything to the bride; they just looked at her, and not at her face but at her distended shape, and grinned.

What Emily said was, 'Well, it's a weddin', isn't it?' She stared across the room at her son, but even her glance did not take in Vanessa. 'Come on.' She got to her feet. 'Some of the old 'uns, Bill. Cock-o-doodle. Play Cock-o-doodle. If you don't I'll bloody well do me poetry piece again:

'I hear in the chamber above me the patter of little feet. Da-da, de-da, de-da.

Do you think, O blue-eyed banditti,
Because you have scaled the wall,
Such an old moustache as I am
Is not a match for you all?'

'Cock-o-doodle, for God's sake!' cried Rosie, and after a moment's hesitation Bill was playing 'Cock-o-doodle' and Emily and the others were singing. But Emily's voice was louder than the rest.

'Cock-o-doodle, cock-o-doodle,
I'm the cock of the North.
Cock-o-doodle, cock-o-doodle,

I'm the cock of the North.
Me faather went out on a Saturda' night
After giving me ma a bairn;
He filled up with rum
And came doddering back
And tried to give her mairn.'

With the quickness of a freak wave, anger rose in him. Grabbing hold of Vanessa, he pushed her past Alf Taggart's chair, then in front of Stan, and to his room door, and, thrusting it open, he went inside with her, saying grimly under his breath, 'It'll be all right. Stay there.' When he returned to the kitchen his mother was singing,

'He killed five thousand Irishmen
In the battle of the boiling water.'

Over and over again he had told her that it wasn't the boiling water, it was the Boyne Water, but now he was boiling. He yelled at her, 'Stop it! Do you hear me? Stop it!'

'What! It's a weddin', isn't it? It's a weddin'. Everybody's merry at a weddin'. What do you say, Bill? What do you say, Rosie? We know it's a weddin', don't we? She punched her daughter on the shoulder, and Rosie punched her back, crying,

'You wouldn't take your mother's device,
You wouldn't take your faather's device,
But you took Barney Rooney's device,
And now you've got your belly full of Barney Rooney.'

As the company, with the exception of Stan, howled their appreciation of this quip, Angus's hand drew back above his sister's head. It was only Stan catching at his arm and crying, 'Steady on! Steady on, Angus,' that checked the blow.

'Get out! Do you hear me?' Angus now swept the Piggotts and Wilsons with a look that brought them swiftly to their feet, and when he added, 'Quick, the bloody lot of you!' the male in Mr Piggott rose and he turned on Angus and shouted, 'Now look here, lad, don't try any of your big—'

'OUT!'

'Whose house do you think this is, eh?' Emily grabbed at the back of Angus's coat, and he swung swiftly round, almost sending her to the floor as he said, 'Shut your mouth, you!' Then he turned his attention to his sister who was standing by the table blinking at him. 'Get up the stairs. Go on now.'

'By damn, you won't tell me what to—'

Stan, now pulling Rosie to the door, said, 'Give over. Give over. Look, go on up. Do as he says. I'll see you the morrow.'

'You're as bad as him. Why, you bugger, you're as bad as him!'

'Go on.' Stan pushed her into the passage and towards the stairs. 'Go on now.'

There was only Angus and Emily left in the kitchen, but the walls seemed to be pressing outwards with the bitterness between them. Emily was sitting by the table, her forearms on it; she was staring at her hands and her head was moving in small, pathetic jerks. He stared down at her, love, compassion and understanding all fighting for a place in his thoughts, fighting against the words of recrimination he wanted to pour on her, fighting against his hate of her. Bending his big head down to hers, be gritted out below his breath. 'That was a bloody dirty trick to play.'

Slowly she lifted her eyes to his and her fuddled gaze swept over his face before she brought out thickly, 'I take after me son, playin' bloody dirty tricks.' He straightened up and her eyes were still holding his when he said, 'I'll talk to you in the mornin' when you're sober.'

She rose unsteadily to her feet; her eyes had never moved from his face and she took two unsteady steps away from him as she muttered, 'I might be sober in the mornin', lad, an' in me right senses, but not you; things'll happen to you from now on like as if you'd taken to drugs. Mark my words. You think she's taken your name but she hasn't, lad; you've taken hers, and you're going to break your bloody neck tryin' to keep up with her. Well, you can go on breakin' it, I'll leave you to it.'

She shambled past him and he said nothing, but he turned and watched her go out of the passage and up the stairs. He watched her until he saw her grotesquely swollen feet and ankles disappear from view through the stair railings; then turning to the fire he stood staring down into it, until, with a swift movement, he brought his clenched fist hard against his forehead. The action caused him to screw up his eyes tightly and he held his fist motionless for some minutes before he dropped his hand.

The house was quiet now and he looked towards his room door. Then the habit of years taking over, he followed the nightly pattern and went down to the bottom of the yard.

When he returned to the kitchen he stood confounded for a moment as to how he was going to tell her to do the same. How different it would have been with May; there would have been no feeling of delicacy in mentioning a lavatory to May; rather it would have evoked laughter. He went into the room.

Vanessa had not even taken her outdoor things off. She was sitting on his chair near the little table; her bag was on her knee and her cases were standing near the wall, where he had left them last night. He went to her and said softly, 'It's all right; she'd had a drop.' He refrained from saying that it was rarely she did anything like this, it would only have worsened matters. He made his lips move into a smile as he added, 'She'll be herself in the mornin'.'

'She won't, Angus.'

'What do you mean?'

'You know what I mean . . . We couldn't . . . ?'

'No, we couldn't, Van.' He bent his head down until his face was on a level with hers. 'We've had this out. I've got to look after her; not only with money, you understand. Oh, I dare say she would get along with supplementary and one thing and another, but she needs me here; she's always needed me. I explained it all to you about me father. I've been the man in her life, if you can put it like that. She's had nobody else, and she's just lived for me. Whatever happens now I'm stuck with her, whether I like it or not. Sometimes I like it fine, other times, like the night, I don't like it one bit.'

Vanessa sat looking at him. She was sick and weary, weary in her mind and body. She wondered vaguely why this should be happening to her, why she had ever let herself be talked into marrying him. She was finding things out about him all the time, things that repulsed her secretly; the depths of his crudity, the depths of his ignorance; yet there were other depths, such as his depths of loyalty, the feeling of responsibility he had towards Emily, which feeling she imagined outweighed all others in his life, even his love for her.

Intuitively, because he had never put it into words, she knew that he was in love with her, that he had always been in love with her, and that although he had found her when she was at rock bottom, he was nevertheless flattered that she should consent to marry him. But he covered this up with his off-hand and casual attitude towards her. She also knew that she was afraid of him, afraid of his body and what it might do to her.

'Come on.' He held out his hand, pulling her up. 'You're tired. It's been a day. Get ready for bed.'

Perhaps it was the small jerk of her fingers within his grasp that made him say brusquely, 'Oh, it's all right, don't worry. There,' he pointed to the opposite corner from where his bed stood, 'That's yours. At least for the time being.' He did not add 'until the bairn comes'. Although why he was considering the bairn he didn't know; they said it thrived on a little action, and women liked it at this time; brought them a sort of comfort. Well maybe. And that was all right if they had been at it from the beginning, but to take her now, no, he couldn't. He looked at her blankly for a moment. She looked neither Vanessa Ratcliffe, Miss Van, nor Vanessa Cotton. She was a girl with a protruding stomach and a weary face, and eyes with a sadness in them that seemed to be drawn from the very pit of her.

When he turned from her and said, 'By the way, if you want it, it's down at the bottom of the yard,' her head drooped and she went towards the door, pulling off her head scarf as she did so. It was this act that brought a deep embarrassment to them both, for as she flicked the scarf downwards it caught at one of the little ornaments on the mantelpiece and she was only just in time to save it. The ornament was of blue Venetian glass; it was six inches high and stood in a base of silver, so tarnished now as hardly to be recognizable as such. From its narrow base the vase mounted outwards to a fluted top, and as her fingers gripped the scalloped edge she remembered that her mother had always considered it a nice little vase for roses; they didn't topple out. The vase's disappearance had been noted after one of the dailies had left. Over the years the household had come to look on dailies as members of a pilfering gang, for always, after their departure, something was missing, and, as Emily had said to her mother, 'It's not a bit of use going after them, they've likely sold it, and you'd have to pin it on them anyway.'

She placed the vase slowly back on the mantelpiece among the bric-a-brac. When she lifted her head Angus was looking at her.

'God blast her!' He had forgotten about all her perks, because she hadn't brought home anything of value for some time as there hadn't been anybody to pin the blame on; not that she would have let them stand the racket if there had been any possibility of them being caught. She was thoughtful that way. But the house was dotted with bits an pieces from up there. Why the hell hadn't he thought about it! If she had thought she had purposely done nothing about it! She hadn't thoroughly cleaned this room for weeks now; all she had done was to lick a duster over it. But he himself should have remembered and got rid of the things. There was that silver teapot and jug in the chiffonier in the kitchen. He'd put that in the dustbin first thing in the morning. God! What more could happen?

He went to the door and watched Vanessa walking across the kitchen, and when she went out into the yard he followed into the scullery and put the kettle on. A cup of coffee might help. After making it he put the cups on a tray and took it back into the room; then he waited. It was after he had been waiting ten minutes that it suddenly came to him that she had been a long time. The back door! She could have gone out the back door. He almost leaped across the kitchen, and when he opened the scullery door and saw her standing there about to enter he leaned against the stanchion for a moment and closed his eyes. It took him a few seconds to pull himself together, and then he said, 'Are you all right?'

'Yes. Yes, I'm all right.' She smiled faintly at him.

'I've made a drink.' He led the way into the room and closed the door.

As they drank their coffee he made several light remarks in order to cover up the awkwardness that lay between them. It was an awkwardness that had nothing to do with sex; it was the awkwardness of two diverse personalities thrown into close proximity. After a while he rose and hung his coat up on the back of the door, saying, 'It won't look so bad when you titivate it up a bit, new curtains and things. She didn't do anything to it because she thought you'd like to have it your own way.'

She, too, rose to her feet. She felt better, quieter inside. She thought the hot coffee must have done her good. She stared at him as he turned towards her. He looked bigger without his coat. The muscles of his arms bulged through his shirt sleeves–his arms looked long and powerful, as did his hands and shoulders; an Irish navvy, one of them had called him. Well, she supposed he did look like an Irish navvy, but he was being kind and thoughtful and she was grateful for any kindness. When he stood in front of her, saying, 'Don't worry; it'll be different in the morning. I mean,' and jerked his head towards the ceiling, she didn't answer, but on an impulse similar to that which had brought her lips to Brett's cheek with the result that she was now married to Angus Cotton, she leaned forward and placed her lips lightly against the corner of his mouth.

It was the first time their faces had come into contact, and the effect was electrifying. The next minute he had her pressed tightly to him. Her body slightly askew, he held her in a vice as his mouth covered hers. But within a minute they were standing apart again and she was gasping for breath while he wiped the sweat from his face with the back of his hand.

'You shouldn't have done that,' he said. 'It was all right until you did that. Asking for trouble, aren't you? what do you think I am, eh? Well,' he strained his neck up out of his collar, 'when I want you I'll take you, in me own time. Get that. In me own time.'

She was unable to speak; all she could do was to stare at him. She had only meant it to be a sort of thank you for all he had done. She had never really thanked him; he made it so hard. She watched him go to the switch and put the light out. Then his voice came out of the darkness, saying, 'Get to bed.' And she got to bed. Like a child who had been whipped and was afraid of the lesson being repeated, she scrambled out of her clothes, and because she hadn't unpacked anything she got into her petticoat again, and, groping at the bedclothes, she slid down between the sheets and lay stiff and taut, listening to her heart as its beat thumped in her ears. It was so loud that it shut out the sound of Angus's breathing.

But six feet away Angus listened to her breathing as he lay on his back staring upwards. His mother had been right; he had been a blasted fool, he should have got a double bed. He needn't have touched her; she could have just lain by his side and he could have held her hand. Aw, God, he was kiddin' himself, wasn't he? Lying by her side and holding her hand, when that peck she gave him set him off like a starter gun! But, nevertheless, his mother had something.

Into the silence now there permeated a sound that didn't come from the bed to the left of him but from the ceiling at which his eyes were directed. It was a sound that he hadn't heard for many years, not since the night his dad had died; it was the sound of his mother crying. With a heave he turned on his side and pulled the clothes over his head. Had there ever been a wedding night like this, ever? No. He bet his damned life there never had.

Chapter Six

Why no one liked the month of November had always, up to now, puzzled Vanessa. She had said once to Susan that it was just a different kind of weather, and all weather was nice. She liked walking in the rain, she liked wind, she liked to lie in bed and hear it whine and moan through the tall chimneys. She particularly liked November, December and January because she associated them with roaring open fires both in the drawing-room and dining-room. She had always had more time to read in the winter. After she had done her homework she would curl up before the fire, preferably in a room which she had to herself, and munch crisps and chew caramels–she didn't care for chocolates.

Now, again, it was November, and she was seeing it as most people saw it; a month of rain, fog, cold, sleet, snow flurries and half light that bore you down.

At ten o'clock on this particular Wednesday morning she stood in the middle of the kitchen and thought, not for the first time by any means, 'I'll go mad, I'll go insane and they'll put me away.' She had been married just over three weeks and, mentally, she had gone through more torment during this period than during all the weeks since the night in the summer-house with Brett. She was learning that there were different kinds of torment. There was the torment of this tiny house, where every word you said above your breath could be heard upstairs, and vice versa, where five steps one way and four the other were all you could do in the privacy of your room.

She knew every square inch of the ground floor of this house, but she didn't know anything about upstairs. Even when she was alone in the house, and that was pretty often, she didn't venture upstairs; upstairs was Emily's and Rosie's rooms, and she didn't want to get any nearer to them than she must. Their resentment of her filled the air when they were indoors, and it stayed with her long after they left the house in the morning, because now Emily was again going to work.

For the first week after Angus had brought her here she was, most of the time, alone with Emily, and Emily would speak to her only when it was necessary. 'Well, aren't you goin' to get him his tea ready?' she had said to her on the first Monday.

'I–I don't know what he likes; I'll leave it to you, Emily.'

'Oh no, begod, you won't, lass. You're his wife; you've got to cook for him.'

She had felt an anger rising in her against Emily, but she had tried to control it. Yet in spite of her effort her voice took on a slight hauteur as she said, 'You know for a fact I can't cook, Emily.'

'You should have thought of that afore. And don't use that tone to me; I'm not up at the house now.'

'I'm not using any tone to you, Emily.' Vanessa was beseeching now. 'I just want you to help me, show me how to cook.'

'I'm sorry; I'll have no time for that, I'm going after a job the morrow,' said Emily flatly.

Vanessa had groaned inwardly. That's what Angus feared she would do, go after another job.

But this was only the beginning. There were the evenings when Angus came in and she put before him what she had cooked, and he rarely ate it; but he soon went through the things she hadn't cooked, such as fish and chips, or peas and pies. She said to him, 'I'll go to cookery classes once it's over,' and he had nodded and smiled at her but hadn't said, 'You'll have other things to do besides cookery classes once it's over.'

As much in an effort to make conversation as to find out his tastes, she had said to him, 'What is your favourite dish?' and when he replied, 'Steak and kidney pudding,' she had said, 'Oh!' There was as much chance of her making a steak and kidney pudding as there was of her making crepe suzette, in fact she might have had more success with the latter as she had tried her hand at pancakes.

On Monday of this week she had bought a cookery book only to find that there wasn't an ingredient in the house that was stated in any of the recipes. So yesterday she had ventured into the centre of the town to buy what was necessary, for she didn't like going into the little shops near the house, because the looks she received said plainly, 'So this is who all the trouble's about.'

It was while she was waiting for a bus in the main street that she became aware of two women in a car, held up in a line of traffic, almost at the same time as they became aware of her. They were Mrs Herring and Mrs Young, the mothers of Kathie and Rona. She had been entertained in their homes countless times, and they had always been charming to her, but now they were surveying her with hard, blank stares. Their eyes, in a way, looked sightless, as if they weren't really seeing her.

She looked away, and it was all she could do not to run away from the bus queue. She had never felt a 'bad girl' before, but she did now. She wanted to sink down through the earth.

It was unfortunate that this incident should have followed so closely on a row between Angus and Emily the night before.

'Where you goin'?' Angus had asked his mother.

'Out,' Emily had replied.

'You've taken to goin' out a lot of late, haven't you?'

'It's my life, lad. You do what you like with yours, I do what I like with mine. Is there any reason why I shouldn't go out?'

'Aye,' he had yelled at her; 'every bloody reason under the sun, you awkward old bitch you.'

'Don't you call me an awkward old bitch else I'll brain you. As sure as God's me judge, I'll brain you.'

'Try it on then. Try it on.'

Vanessa had stood in their room, her face held between her two hands, and like a child she had prayed: Dear Lord, make them stop. She was dazed by the yelling and shouting that went on in the house. What should be ordinary conversation was conducted in a tone that would have been used only for deep anger in her own home, and she had rarely heard it until she herself had evoked it. At one point when the swearing was filling the house she thrust her fingers into her ears, and when she extracted them it was to hear Angus yelling, 'You've no bloody need to go out workin'. You know you haven't. And Emily's reply, 'You're goin' to break stones with a bloody great stick, aren't you? Sixteen pounds! You'd get more sweepin' roads. Your own boss, me backside.'

'It was a bad week. I told you . . . in between contracts. Anyway, what the hell has it got to do with you what I make and what I don't make? I pay the rent and every other bloody commitment in the house, so what are you talking about?'

As the door banged before he had finished speaking, Rosie's voice took over from her mother's. 'You should be bloody well ashamed of yourself, our Angus, speakin' to her like that.'

'Now you, YOU keep your trap shut. I'm standin' none of it from you, because you've turned out to be nothin' more than a damned little upstart. That's what you are. And you've got nothing to be uppish about.'

'There you're wrong; I have got something to be uppish about. And I'm going to remain uppish. I'm not like some people I know gettin' me belly filled at the first opportun—'

When the sound of the blow came to her, Vanessa threw herself on the bed and buried her face in the pillow. A few minutes later when she raised her head she expected to hear Rosie crying, but Rosie's voice, as strident as ever, was yelling, 'You great, big, soft nowt. Don't think you'll frighten me. And you lift your hand again and, begod, I'll do what me mam threatened, I'll brain you. Now mind, I'm warnin' you.'

She had sat on the edge of the bed gripping her hands on the dome of her stomach. She felt dazed by it all. She knew she'd never, never get used to it, at the same time she was amazed by the fact that this was how people lived, had gone on living for years and years. Emily and Rosie and Angus hadn't just started shouting at each other since she had come into the house. Everybody in this neighbourhood seemed to shout. They shouted greetings across the narrow streets as if they were miles away; even the tenants in the new block of flats round the corner in the main street, they shouted from their upper windows down to the children in the play yards. Life here was one big shout, when it should have been a whisper, because there was hardly space to breathe. Perhaps it was because they lived in such close proximity to each other that made them want to shout, to break out.

It had been nearly fifteen minutes later when Angus came into the room, and after looking at her face he said, 'Don't look so worried; there's nobody been murdered.'

'You surprise me.'

He had turned swiftly on her. This was a tone, she knew, she must never use to him. It was the tone she had used to Emily, the tone of her class, slightly haughty, supercilious, condescending, and he reacted to it as such. 'Look, this is our way.' He was yelling at her now. 'It means nothing, well, not all that. It'll work out. I keep telling you it'll work out. I know her.' His voice dropped.

'And Rosie?'

'Aw, Rosie. She's jealous of you, that's what's the matter with Rosie. I always had a soft spot for her. She's jealous of you.'

Following this he had gone to the little table in the corner and sat down with his exercise books, working out figures, and she had taken up her knitting. She was knitting a baby coat; she could knit and sew quite well. They had taught her something in the Convent. It would have been better if they had taught her Domestic Science, but they only taught that to those who wanted to go in for it. There had been no need for her to study Domestic Science. Somewhere inside she was laughing derisively. She had taken languages, German and French, instead of a meat pudding. She would have given all her knowledge, however limited, to be able to make a meat pudding.

They had been sitting in silence for some time when he turned to her abruptly and said, 'What I want is another couple of lorries, besides two new ones to replace the crates we've got. I missed a job the day because we weren't big enough; a fellow said it would take six lorries but he'd stretch a point if I had four.'

She had no interest in his business or the lorries that he had or hadn't got, but she said, 'Can't you go to the bank and get the money?'

'Oh my God, Van.' He smiled pityingly. 'I'm down to one hundred and twenty-five quid. I don't have a bank account; our dealings are strictly cash. It helps with the tax man an' all. But go to the bank you say. You're talkin, daft.'

She suddenly put down her knitting and straightened her back, and her tone changed again, not to the one that would anger him, but to one filled with protest as she said, 'I'm not a fool altogether, Angus.'

'Look honey, I didn't say you were.' He was leaning over the back of the chair towards her. 'But it's just that you've got a different slant on things.'

'I haven't got a different slant on things, not with reference to the bank. What I meant was, couldn't you go to the bank and raise a loan? I know you've got no money in the bank.'

He pulled a chair round until he was facing her, his knees almost touching hers, and he said, 'Oh, I see. But I ask you; what have I got as security? We don't own this place, not that that would mean very much if we did. I've got nothing as security except a broken-down lorry, the other one is Fred's.'

'Has he no security?'

'Insecurity; a wife and six bairns.'

She said, 'You mentioned an insurance some time ago.'

'Oh, that. It isn't due for another eight years. And then what is it? Three hundred pounds.'

'How long was it for?'

'Fifteen years. I've paid seven.'

'Wouldn't they take that as part security?'

'And me not paid half yet? I don't know about that. But.' he jerked his head, 'I could see. It's an idea. You've given me an idea.' His smile widened and he leant nearer to her and asked now softly, in the voice that he kept for her alone, 'How you feelin'?' These were the only words that his tenderness seemed to supply him with: 'How you feelin'?'

'All right,' she said.

'You always say you're all right. If you were peggin' out you would say you were all right, wouldn't you, because it's the thing to say?'

'But I am feeling all right.'

'No, you're not; you're feeling bloody miserable. There I go.' He wagged his head. 'I told you I was goin' to stop swearing in front of you.'

'It doesn't matter.'

'But it does. If I said I was going to stop swearin' I should stop swearin'; at least in front of you.'

She wanted to say, 'The more you try the more it will emphasise the difference. Don't change yourself; it'll be better that way.'

He looked down at his hands, the nails all broken, the finger tips as hard as pieces of dried leather, and he said, 'You're having it pretty rough, but believe me once it's over everything will be all right, you'll see. And we'll go out; we'll start going places; I'll take you round; we'll enjoy ourselves . . . Oh,' he wagged his hand at her, 'she'll look after the bairn; she'll be in her seventh heaven havin, a bairn to see to. You'll see. I'm tellin' you. And by that time business will have bucked up, and I'll bet what you like we'll have a car. Not a new one, oh no, not yet, because every penny I make I want to push into the business. It's going to be big, I'm tellin' you.' He turned his head almost on to his shoulder and nodded it as if she was contradicting him, and he said again, 'I'm telling you. It's a prophecy if ever there was one, it's going to be big. I mean it to be big. I generally get what I want.' He brought his head slowly towards her again and his hand went out and touched hers.

She always shivered when he touched her. She wasn't repulsed by him, but nevertheless she couldn't stop her limbs shivering when her flesh made contact with his, and each time he was aware of this. She knew it angered him, but he endeavoured not to show it.

He had left the house at seven o'clock this morning, before either Emily or Rosie had come downstairs, and when they did come down she heard them talking. They intended she should.

She felt sick and ill this morning, not only in her body but in her mind. A dark depression had fallen on her. Her thoughts were going round in circles, she couldn't see ahead, yet when she looked back into the past all was brightness. She had had a wonderful home, wonderful parents; she even saw her father as kindly and good, and her mother as sympathetic. She had been going to wear the most gorgeous dress as bridesmaid to Susan. There would have been marvellous people at the wedding. Never before had she thought of Susan's friends or the Braintrees as marvellous, but now, in retrospect, they were all charming and kindly; and none of them raised their voices when speaking. What had segregated her from this wonderful past? It was Brett. He should have known that would happen. But she mustn't blame Brett, at least not all the way. She had liked Brett; she could say she had loved Brett. He was a gentleman, except when . . . Her mind shut out the picture of the moments during which Brett had ceased to be a gentleman.

Emily's voice penetrated the fog of her depression as she called to Rosie, 'Times have changed, lass, times have changed. I was goin' at it scrubbin' for nine hours a day up till twenty-four hours afore you were born, not sittin' on me arse all day. Aye, times have changed.'

When finally the door banged for the second time and she had the house to herself she got up and dressed. She knew what she was going to do, and she knew that she should have done it sooner. She should have done it instead of marrying Angus. She had brought trouble on him and parted him from his family. As Rosie had made it plain a number of times, they had been a happy family once.

She got dressed and went to the little shop around the corner. They hadn't any large packets of aspirins, only strips. She asked for four. At the next shop she bought a box holding twenty-five, and now she was standing in the kitchen and the aspirins were on the table before her.

She knew she must leave some word for Angus, so she went into the room and looked for a piece of drawing paper on which to write, but there was none on the table. There was a piece of paper sticking between two books and she pulled it out, and with it Fowler's 'King' English.' She had been surprised to find that on the bookshelf. Angus and Fowler's 'King's English.' She smiled a pitying smile. He tried, did Angus, he tried. Perhaps she could have helped him here. No, he would never have allowed her to help him with his grammar because that would have meant facing the fact that he needed help in that direction. There was a pride in him that mustn't be hurt. She took the piece of paper and a pencil into the kitchen and she wrote on it: 'I'm sorry, Angus. It was a great mistake; I should never have let you do it. Emily was right. It would never have worked out. Thank you for all the kindness you have shown me. You have nothing to regret, believe me, because you're the only one who has given me a kind word during all these awful months. Thank you, Angus. Vanessa.' She read what she had written and felt that she hadn't expressed herself clearly, hadn't thanked him enough, then she went into the scullery and brought back a glass of water, and, opening the aspirins, she dropped thirty into the water and slowly stirred them. They took a long time to dissolve, and as she waited she thought, I wonder if I'll see Brett. Odd, us both going out the same way; but I could never have hanged myself. When eventually the liquid was a milky mass of whirling particles she raised the glass to her lips. Her hand began to tremble now; then her body; and she knew if she hesitated for one moment longer she wouldn't do it.

When the glass was empty she shuddered and gritted her teeth against the taste; then she put her forearms on the table and sat gazing down at the letter she had written and she wondered how long it would be before the aspirins took effect.

Chapter Seven

They were at break in the canteen. Rosie, Freda Armstrong, her pal and fellow machinist, and two other girls. They were seated at their usual table in the corner and Freda was pouring sympathy over Rosie. The expression of her sympathy was questionable but nevertheless sincere. 'You look awful, Rosie girl,' she was saying. 'Cor! your face is green. I've never seen you as bad as this; it makes you look fifty. You should go home, shouldn't she?'

One of the other girls nodded and said 'Aye. I would tell the boss, Rosie. Tell her you can't stick it, she's all right. She has it herself.' There was a giggle at this which turned into a laugh when Freda added seriously, 'Now you ain't got no proof of that, now have you? Her sex's been in question afore the day.'

Rosie did not join her laughter to the others but said, 'I wouldn't have come in this mornin' but it meant stayin' at home with that 'un. God, what a life it is now. You've no idea.'

'Does she still put it on?' One of the girls asked, and Rosie replied, 'No, by God, she doesn't put it on with me. I'd swipe her mouth for her if she did. She knows better. She keeps out of me way. Our Angus. Of all the bloody fools, our Angus . . . Oh, my God, I do feel sick.'

'If you don't do it for free like you should get married, Rosie, that's what you should do. They say it clears up once you start.'

'It all goes into the first bairn,' said the other girl.

'Aw, shut your traps,' said Rosie, straightening herself up. 'Married, bairns; I'm livin' with it. I don't want to hear any more about marriage, or bairns, so shut up.'

There was silence at the table until the pain in Rosie's stomach brought her bending again, and after a moment she stood up, saying, 'I'm goin' to be sick.'

Ten minutes later Rosie went to the forewoman and told her that she'd have to go home. And fifteen minutes later, when she entered the house, she was still in pain and still feeling sick, but the moment she opened the kitchen door and saw Vanessa sitting at the table with a glazed look on her face and the table strewn with the covers of numerous aspirins she forgot about how she herself was feeling. 'God Almighty!' She put her hand across her mouth; then diving across the room she cried, 'What you done?'

Vanessa's lips moved but no sound came from them, and slowly her head sank on to her arm.

'Oh, God! God Almighty!' The words seemed to issue out of the top of Rosie's head. Then pulling Vanessa upwards, she shook her and cried, 'You bloody young fool you! You bloody young fool. What have you done, Oh, my God!' She let Vanessa's head and shoulders drop to the table again; then she grabbed the letter and scanned the first few lines, before throwing it down and crying, 'Mam! Mam!' She was running between the scullery door and the passage like someone demented. Her mother was at her job. Mrs Wilson next door? No, no, she was a big mouth; there would be trouble. She'd have to get the doctor, and her mother, but if she left her she could die. You made them sick. Yes, that's what you did, you made them sick. What did you make them sick with? Oh, my God! She pulled Vanessa up again and shook her. 'Get up, Van,' she implored as she unconsciously used her name. 'Van! Van! Do you hear me? Come on. Come on.' She was in tears now as she pleaded.

Salt water. Aye, salt water. She dashed to the cupboard and, getting a packet of salt, poured a third of it into a mug and filled it with warm water from the kettle standing on the hob. She was talking and crying and swearing as she worked. 'Bloody fool! I knew something like this would happen. Our Angus, you should be battered. That's what you should be, battered. You should never have brought her here. She can't stand it, she's not made for it. God! if she dies. Come on. Come on.' She grabbed hold of Vanessa's shoulder, but when her head still lolled forward she gripped her hair and pulled her head up and, leaning her back in the chair, she whispered, 'Get this down you. It's going to make you sick. Can you hear me?'

Half the liquid ran over Vanessa's face, but some went down her throat as she gasped and gulped.

Now Rosie tried to get her to her feet but it was impossible, and once more she slumped across the table.

There was nothing for it, Rosie knew, but to get her mother and the doctor. She had her mother's phone number. If she could get a taxi she could be here in ten minutes. She looked once more at the inert figure, then flew out of the house and down to the corner of the street and across the road to where there was a telephone kiosk. When a strange voice answered her ring she asked if she could speak to Mrs Cotton, it was very important.

When her mother came to the phone, she said quickly, 'Mam, you've got to come. Listen. She's tried to do herself in. Get a taxi, do you hear?'

There was no answer from the other end and she yelled, 'Do you hear me, Mam?' and she thought she heard her mother say, 'Aye, I heard you,' before the click of the phone came to her. She was gasping herself now, and on the point of being actually sick as she phoned Doctor Carr. Fortunately, he was still in his surgery and she began by saying, 'Doctor Carr?' and when he answered 'Yes,' she said, 'Do–do you remember Vanessa Ratcliffe? She–she married my brother, Angus.'

When again he said, 'Yes, yes I remember,' she said 'Well she's tried to do herself in, in our house.'

'What with?' he asked sharply now.

'With aspirins.'

'What have you done?'

'I've given her salt and water; that's all I could think of.'

'I'll be with you in a minute.'

'Ta, thanks doctor.'

She ran out of the box, across the road again, just missing being run down by a bus, down the street and into the house. It was very quiet and she stood for a moment looking down at the relaxed figure lying across the table, and she put her double fists over her mouth and whispered to her, 'Don't die. For God's sake, don't die.'

She continued to stare at her, not knowing what to do. She couldn't get her to her feet on her own, so perhaps it was better just to leave her there.

Emily was the first to arrive. It couldn't have been five minutes since she got the phone call. She must have walked straight out of the house, for she was without hat or coat and was wearing a blue print dress with a big white bibbed apron over it. She, like Rosie, stood just within the door and gazed for a moment at the inert figure. Her face looked bleached. Then she whispered in much the same way as Rosie had done, 'Oh, God Almighty! . . . Did you do anything?' Her lips were quivering as she asked the question.

'I–I gave her salt water to make her sick, but it hasn't.'

'Get at the other side of her. Hoist her up. Keep her walking. That's what we must do, keep her walking. Did you get the doctor?'

'Yes, he's comin'. He should be here any minute.'

It was as much as they could do between them to support Vanessa. They pulled her arms around their shoulders and Emily thrust her arm around Vanessa's waist, and they managed to walk her up and down the kitchen twice. And then they could go no further. As they sat her in the chair again her body heaved and out of her mouth frothed the salt water and some of the liquid she had swallowed earlier.

'That's it, get it up, lass. Get it up.' Emily now started to rub her back with a large circling movement, talking in a coaxing, wheedling voice as she did so. 'Come on, come on, have another try. Doesn't matter about the floor.' It was as if Vanessa had pointed out that she was being sick all over the floor. 'If that's all we've got to worry about then we're all right. Come on, lass, get it up.'

'Hoist her again,' she said to Rosie, and as they were about to resume the walk the door opened and the doctor came in.

'Has she got it up?' he asked abruptly.

'Just a bit, Doctor,' said Emily.

'How many has she taken?'

'There's the papers.' She pointed to the table. 'Twenty, thirty. I don't know.'

He opened his bag quickly and filled a syringe. Then baring Vanessa's arm, he pressed the needle in gently. 'Get a bowl or something,' he said without turning his head.

It was Rosie who ran to the kitchen for a bowl and placed it at Vanessa's feet.

'Shall we walk her again, Doctor?' asked Emily.

'No, she'll be sick in a minute . . . I hope.' He slanted a bleary glance towards Emily, asking now, 'What's brought this to a head?'

Emily's eyes were cast down and she muttered something, and he repeated scathingly, 'You couldn't say? You couldn't say?'

Emily's head jerked up quickly in the old aggressive manner, only to turn sideways, and, her face averted, she said, 'It's been difficult all round, Doctor; the blame isn't all mine.'

'No, I dare say not, but you could have helped.' He was patting Vanessa's cheeks now, first one and then the other, keeping her head up the while. 'By all accounts, you've been giving her hell.'

Again Emily's head swung upwards; then after a pause she said, 'You've had your ear to the ground, haven't you?'

'I didn't have to put it that far to hear what she's been going through. Angus did a decent thing, if you could use an old phrase, a noble thing, not that it was purely altruistic on his part; nevertheless, he did what many another wouldn't have done, no matter what his feelings. But you've done your best to spoil it Emily.'

'Begod, look here—'

'Don't shout; I should think you've done enough of that.'

'What do you know about it?' Emily turned her back on him, and he said, 'Quite a bit; we've all got crosses to bear. And if I hadn't had my ear to the ground, I would still have known your reaction to the present set-up. You seem to forget I've known you for the last twenty-five years.'

It was in her mind to say, 'And me you, you drunken slob,' but this wasn't the time for retaliation. Perhaps she had retaliated too much. Aye, what he said was true, but who was he to say it, anyway?

The sound of Vanessa retching brought her swiftly round and as she saw the volume of water spurt from the girl's mouth she said deep within her, 'Thank God. Oh, thank God.'

'Oh de-ar, oh de-ar, oh de-ar me,' Vanessa groaned, and Doctor Carr said, 'You're all right.' He was now holding her head against her breast, and as she moaned again he stroked the hair back from her head. 'There now, it's all over. You'll feel better soon.'

She opened her eyes dazedly and muttered, 'I'm sick.'

'Yes. It's all to the good; it's all to the good.' He nodded towards Emily now and said, 'We'll get her to bed.'

Emily and Rosie between them undressed her. Rosie supported her as Emily pulled off her clothes. Neither of them spoke until the doctor, standing at the foot of the bed, said, 'Where's Angus working?'

'He's on haulage. He's with Fred Singleton; they're running a sideline on their own.'

'Can you get him?'

Emily looked at Rosie, and Rosie said, 'They're under contract to Farrer's.'

'Well, I would phone Farrer's and get him here. I think he should see this.'

'Yes, Doctor.' Rosie ran out of the room. She had forgotten entirely about the pain in her stomach and her own sickness.

Emily, now standing close to the doctor at the foot of the bed, asked under her breath, 'Will it harm the bairn?' and he raised his eyebrows and said, 'That's to be seen. It could bring it on. . . . Has she been going to the clinic?'

'No, not that I know.'

'Well, you should have seen to it, woman.' He poked his face towards her, and his attitude now brought no feeling of retaliation to her because her conscience was working against her. What she said was, 'Aye, I suppose I should. I should have done many things, but bein' meself I didn't.'

'Being yourself, you're a stubborn, ignorant individual. You know that, don't you?'

'Yes, I know it, Doctor, and I don't need you to rub it in; it takes every man to look to his own house.' They stared at each other; then she added more calmly, 'How was I to know she was working up to this?'

His voice, too, was calmer now as he said, 'You've known her for years. You knew her background, soft, easy, filled with refinements. Your own sense should have told you what this set-up would do to her.' He jerked his chin twice as he looked round the room.

'She seemed to be fallin' in. I thought she was settlin', makin' the best of a bad job. She doesn't show things very much. How was I to know?'

'You, with your experience of people, should know that there are greater conflicts fought beneath the skin than in any open battle. She couldn't get rid of her inhibitions by yelling and shouting; it isn't done in her quarter. You know that, Emily. Their battles are fought quietly, secretly, not like round here.' Again his chin jerked twice. 'You should know that it's a saving grace to be able to bawl your head off. There's very few suicides in this quarter, whereas in the Brampton Hill area there were four last year, one a close neighbour of hers. If any of them from that quarter had one such row as you have on a Saturday night, say, it would break up the entire family for ever. She's from a different world, Emily. You should have realized that. . . . But it's not too late.'

Vanessa moaned now and Doctor Carr went to her side, and when he touched her forehead she muttered, 'Angus. I'm sorry, Angus.'

'Don't worry. Don't talk any more. Go to sleep; you're all right.'

She opened her eyes, then shook her head slightly and whispered, 'Doctor Carr.'

'Go to sleep.'

Rosie came back into the room now. She was panting, and she said, 'They're goin' to tell him when he comes back for his next load.'

The doctor walked into the kitchen and Emily, about to follow him, said to Rosie, 'Stay with her a minute, will you?' Then she pulled the door closed before she asked, 'What are you goin' to do about it? Will you have to report it?'

'I should, yes.'

'But must you?' She was staring hard at him.

And he returned her stare for a full minute before he asked, 'Does anybody else know?'

'I'll find out.' She went into the bedroom and came out within a minute, saying, 'No. Rosie's got her head screwed on right. She phoned for me; she didn't even go next door. They'll think it's a miscarriage coming.'

He was nodding at her. 'What did she tell them when she got on the phone to Angus?'

Once more Emily went into the room, and when she came back she said, 'She told them to tell him that Vanessa had been taken bad, that's all.'

Again they were staring hard at each other; then he said, 'There's a possibility she might make a second attempt, and the next time when she's found she'll likely to be too far gone to be sick.'

'No such thing, no such thing,' said Emily. 'She won't do it again; I'll see to that. I'm staying here. I'll see to her; I promise you.'

'Well, we'll see.' He sighed; then went to his bag, closed it, picked up his coat from a chair, put it on, and, going towards the door, said, 'I'll be in my surgery around one-thirty. Send Angus along to see me then.'

'Yes, Doctor.' She came close to him again and muttered softly, 'Thanks. I promise you things'll be different. I'll see to her.'

'You've nearly been too late, remember that.'

She closed her eyes and shook her head, as she said, 'Don't worry. It's somethin' I won't forget in a hurry.'

Half-an-hour later the lorry stopped at the door, and Angus burst into the house. 'What is it?' he demanded. 'What's happened her?'

'She's all right,' said Emily from the other side of the table. 'Don't go in for a minute; Rosie's in there with her. You'd better read this.' She handed him Vanessa's letter. It was no use with-holding it from him because Vanessa would ask him if he had got it when she came round.

His mouth was agape when he stopped reading and he put his hand up and ran it slowly through his rough hair. He did it a second time before he muttered, 'Aw, no. No.'

Emily, her lips compressed to stop them trembling, stared at her son. The dark stubble round his chin was standing out against the dead whiteness of his face. There was a grey dust on his hair and shoulders. He looked all white and grey. She dreaded his onslaught; she dreaded to hear the truth from him that she was to blame for this; and she waited silently. And to her surprise he didn't break the silence, but moved slowly across the room and opened the door.

Rosie was sitting by the head of the bed. She had her hands clasped tightly between her knees; she looked like a very young girl, and she, too, was evidently waiting for the onslaught. She stared at her brother and rose to her feet as he came to the bed. She tried to say something but couldn't. He didn't look at her, and after a moment she went out into the kitchen.

Angus stared down on the long pale face. Her hair was scattered over the pillow. It looked dank and tousy. She looked almost dead. He couldn't take it in that she had tried to die. His mind seemed to have got stuck for he was still repeating to himself 'Aw, no. No.' Then slowly he began to tell himself things and ask himself questions. He should have realized she was at this pitch. But how could he have told? She had been so quiet; she didn't talk much, and when she did she gave no indication of how she was feeling.

He was a thick-headed numbskull; he had been mad to marry her in the first place; but having done so he should never have brought her back here. Yet what could he have done? AYE, WHAT COULD HE HAVE DONE?; Not married her at all; just been friendly to her until she had got on her feet. He had rushed her, taken advantage of the fix she was in.

He knelt down by the bed and, enclosing her thin hands between his two hard dirt-covered ones, he whispered, 'Van! Aw, Van!' He had the desire to lay his head down on her chest and cry.

When she neither moved nor spoke he realized she was asleep, and after a moment he got to his feet and went into the kitchen.

They were waiting for him, standing stiffly within arm's length of each other looking towards the door. He knew they were expecting him to blow them sky high, but he couldn't, he didn't feel that he had a shout or a bawl left in him. He had the sensation of being winded. Moreover, he knew it would achieve nothing to blame his mother now. She couldn't have acted differently if she had tried; she had acted according to her nature, as he himself had, as Rosie had. As he walked towards the table he asked, 'Who found her?'

The moderation of his tongue loosened Rosie's tongue, and she said, 'Me. I–I had to come home, I had the cramp, and when I got in she was sittin' there.' She pointed to the chair. ' I–I nearly went mad meself.' She shook her head. 'I rung me mam–' she nodded towards Emily, who was staring at her son, and then she ended, 'And I rang the doctor.'

'What did he say?' He was addressing his mother, and Emily moved her tongue over her lips for a moment. She wasn't going to repeat what the doctor said, she wasn't a fool; anyway, he'd likely open his mouth to him when he went along. And that's what she told him. 'He says you've got to go and see him about half-past one.'

'Does–does he think it'll affect the bairn?'

Emily glanced down for a moment. 'It might, he says; we've got to wait and see.'

He dropped suddenly on to a chair and he looked downwards as he asked, 'Have you got anythin' in, a drop of hard anywhere?'

She shook her head. 'No, but Rosie will slip along and get you somethin', won't you, Rosie?'

'Aye; it won't take a minute.'

They were both openly eager in their placating of him.

'It doesn't matter,' he said. 'Coffee will do, black.' He put his elbow on the table and rested his head in his hands. After a time he got to his feet as quickly as he had sat down and, going to the fireplace, stared into the fire as he said quietly, 'There's got to be a change, Mam.'

It was some seconds before she answered, and then briefly. 'Aye,' she said.

'I've got to get her away from here.'

'It would be best,' she said.

'I–I can't do it at once, not straightaway; I'll have to look for something.'

'I understand that.' She was supporting herself against the edge of the table, the nails of one hand digging into the underside of the wood. 'But until you do,' she said, 'I'll see to things. I'll see she's all right.'

He turned and looked at her squarely but didn't speak, and she said, 'I'm gettin' Rosie to phone Mrs McVeigh. I never liked working for her anyway; she's a mean scrub. I'll be glad to be back home.'

He surprised and broke her down at the same time by saying, 'Thanks, Mam.'

'Don't,' she turned from him, her voice harsh, her manner almost back to normal, 'Don't heap coals of fire on me head; you know in your heart you're blamin' me for what's happened the day and . . . and, although I don't blame you, I'll remind you that I didn't start this. However,' she turned on him quickly before he had any time to reply, 'it's done and I'm not very proud of me share in it, but as I've said, as long as she's here I'll see to her.'

Rosie came in from the scullery, a cup of coffee in one hand and a sugar basin in the other, and she stood mutely before him while he ladled three spoonfuls of sugar into the cup. She wanted to say, 'I'm sorry,' but you didn't say you were sorry, not openly; you didn't ask for forgiveness, although you might crave it badly to take the fear away from you, the fear that told you that if Vanessa had died you yourself would have been more than a little to blame, for, to use her own words, she had been a bloody stinker.

Her tone when she said quietly, 'I made it strong,' was in itself a plea for forgiveness, and when he answered quietly, 'Ta. Ta, Rosie,' the words were a form of absolution.

They were all sitting quiet now, still somewhat stunned but united, and all three were strangely at peace.

It was as he had been telling Van all the while, things would work out, but when the thought came to him how nearly they hadn't he had to get up quickly and go down the yard.

Chapter Eight

Three weeks later Vanessa lost her baby. Doctor Carr ordered her into hospital on the Friday night and the baby was taken away on the Sunday afternoon. It was eight days later when she returned home. Angus brought her in a taxi, and as soon as she entered the house she noticed a difference, particularly in their room. There were new curtains at the windows; the furniture had been polished and there was a cherry-coloured wall-to-wall carpet covering the floor. The room had been papered in a plain grey paper and the old pictures hadn't been re-hung. The single beds were still there, but they both had new candlewick spreads. She paused in the doorway, then looked at Angus and smiled weakly as she said, 'It's nice, lovely. Thank you.'

He wished she didn't always thank him, not in that polite way anyhow. He said, 'Rosie picked the colours; I wasn't any good at it, and me mam not much better.' He turned and looked at Rosie where she was standing well back in the kitchen, and Vanessa turned towards her, too, and across the distance she again spoke her thanks, in that quiet, polite, courteous way, which would have befitted an elderly woman but sounded strange coming from this young girl.

Rosie nodded and smiled self-consciously. She couldn't see herself ever liking her sister-in-law; you never really liked anybody who always seemed to put you at a disadvantage; yet she no longer detested the sight of her. She took a step forward, saying, 'I thought the cherry and grey would go nice together.'

'It does. It looks lovely,' Vanessa moved into the room and to a coffee table on which was now set tea for two peole. There were two cups and saucers and a milk jug and sugar basin to match, a plate of bread and butter and another of small cakes. She looked down at it; then turned and looked at Emily, and Emily said, 'I thought you'd like to eat in here.'

'No, Emily, no.' There was a firmness about the shake of her head that silenced the three people looking at her, until Angus said, 'It's all arranged, don't worry; we'll eat here.'

'No, Angus.' She looked straight into his face for a moment, then turned to Emily and said again, 'No, Emily. We eat as before.'

'Oh, then have it your own way.' Angus was tossing his head. It was as if he was giving in reluctantly to some outrageous demand, but what the three women knew in their different ways was, he was pleased and relieved at her decision.

The pattern now was different. The atmosphere in the house was light, even gay, but whereas before Angus had felt that his marriage, for good or ill, was an established fact, he no longer had this feeling of security concerning it, for as each day passed and Vanessa returned to full health, he felt that she could walk out on him any minute; there was nothing to hold her. She wasn't dependent on him to look after her and her child; she could go any place and get a job. She had the looks and figure that models were made out of; she was almost eighteen and she hadn't begun to live; she didn't know yet what it was all about.

Each night when he came back from work he felt sick, until he saw she was still there. He felt that there was one solution to it all; he had to put her in a position similar to the one she had just got out of, and everything would be as it was before.

'Go gently with her,' Doctor Carr he told him. 'She's of a different calibre to you. You've got to realize that. Modern, swingin', or what-have-you, as brash as they are today, early environment counts.' He hadn't minced his words had Doctor Carr. 'You're mother's been an old swine to her,' he said. Then he waved his hand and silenced him by adding, 'I've got three hundred patients in your quarter and four of them are in your street, one next door. You cannot stop people talking.' And then he had ended, 'I'm telling you, go gently with her. It'll pay off in the long run."

Well he had gone gently for two months, he was burnt up inside. There was no May to go to now to relieve the pressure, and he wasn't picking anybody up. He thought too much of his skin for that; he didn't want to catch anything.

So, like a man who proposed to seduce the girl of his fancy, he planned in his mind how he would take her. They would go out the morrow night, it being Saturday; he would take her to some posh restaurant and they'd have a good dinner and a bottle of wine, and then later . . . well, that was up to him.

As he had been doing every week for the past two months, he called in at the estate agents' office to ask if they had found anything in the way of a flat for him, and today Reg Walker, who incidentally had at once time lived in Ryder's Row, greeted him with, 'No, there's nothing in the way of a flat, Angus, but I wonder you don't go in for a house, or a bungalow.'

'Oh, that's in the far future for me. What I want before a house or a bungalow is a couple of lorries.'

'It's a pity,' said Reg Walker; 'a bungalow came on my books yesterday and it's a snip. It's on the outskirts. Bit out for most people. An old couple had it and they died within a month of each other and their only son is in Australia, and he's given us the O.K. to sell it. Do you remember Arthur

Ridley? You know, they had the little hardware shop at the corner of Wolf Lane.''

'Yes,' nodded Angus. 'Yes, I remember them.'

'Well, it's him. I mean his people. He wrote me from Australia and asked me to get rid of the bungalow and furniture; they hadn't any money except a small insurance that paid for the funeral. He's cagey is Arthur Ridley. He once had a huge bill in from a solicitor for something and he's never dealt with them since. That's how I've come to be handling it.'

'Aye.' Angus jerked his head. 'What you askin' for it?'

'Well, it's in need of decoration inside and repair outside, and the gardens overgrown. If it was all done up it would bring anybody's four thousand, and then it would be cheap.'

'Oh, aye.' Again Angus jerked his head, laughing now.

'I'm on the level, Angus.' Reg Walker nodded at him. 'I stated a price of two thousand five hundred and Arthur Ridley agreed, so it'll go for that. And I'm telling you, these days it's an absolute snip. And there's nearly three quarters of an acre of land with it, and you know what land is the day.'

Again Angus said, 'Oh, aye,' but now he neither shook his head nor laughed. He hadn't been doing too badly these last few weeks, in fact he and Fred had split seventy pounds for each of the last five weeks. Of course there was tax off that; but then there were the Saturday runs he did and the three Sunday mornings. They had been for cash and had brought in over eighty pounds. Things were looking up, but he could do nothing big until he got more lorries, and he wanted those more than a house, but he said, ''Have you put it in the paper?'

'Yes; it'll be out the morrow.'

Angus bit on his lip. 'When could I see it?'

'Any time you like. Run you out now if you like.'

'Well, there's no time like the present.'

And so Angus went to see the bungalow, and he immediately agreed with Reg that it was a good buy, an excellent buy. It had six rooms, bathroom and garage, and it overlooked the river and fine stretch of country. He stood in the road looking back over the tangled garden towards the roof of the bungalow. This was the answer, but it would mean good-bye to the lorries for some time to come because he would still have to help his mother. And taking the bungalow was only the beginning. There would be the repayments, rates, electricity . . . and a phone, not to mention furnishing the whole place. He said to Reg Walker, 'Will you give me until five o'clock?'

'Aye,' said Reg. 'And I won't mention it to anybody in the meantime. But mind, you'll have to make you your mind then. I can't hold it, and I dare say after it comes out the morrow it'll be gone by Monday.'

'I'll let you know by five,' said Angus.

He didn't get into the house until half-past six. Emily had the tea set waiting. 'You're late,' she said; 'I thought you must have run into Van.'

'Run into Van?' He looked towards the room door. 'She's not in?'

'No, she went out early this afternoon; she was going to do a bit of shoppin' or somethin'."

As he moved slowly towards their room she said, 'Now don't go in there on that carpet with your boots on. I've told you,' and he stopped and looked down at the floor for a moment, then sat down by the side of the fireplace and took off his heavy boots and put on a pair of slippers that were resting on the fender. 'Get your wash . . . You're not goin' to the baths the night?'

'No . . . She's never been out at this time.'

'She could have gone to Newcastle.' Emily was bending down to the oven.

'What would she want in Newcastle, there's plenty of shops here? What was she after, do you know?'

Emily lifted a pie from the oven. Its top was brown and there was a pattern of pastry leaves around the edges. It could have been cooked for the table at Bower Place. She said now, 'Stop your worryin'. Surely she can go out for five minutes . . . .'

'It isn't five minutes if she went out this afternoon.'

'Well, anyway, you're not very early yourself; you're nearly an hour past your time. Where've you been?'

He got to his feet and went into the scullery and, stripping to the waist, he started to wash himself before he called out to her, 'I've been after a bungalow.'

She was at the scullery door, looking at him. 'A bungalow?' Her voice was high.

'Aye. Reg Walker had a snip on his books; he offered it to me. I had to make up me mind for five o'clock; it was as quick as that.'

'How much?'

'Two thousand five hundred.'

'Oh, my God!'

'It's worth four thousand, even as it stands. It wants doing up.'

'That'll take some payin' for. What'll happen to the lorries you were goin' after?'

'They'll have to wait. First things first.'

As he reached for a towel he paused and looked at her and said, 'You'll be all right . . . I'll see to you.'

'Now look.' Her voice was high and held the old aggressive quality. 'Don't you bother about me, lad; I can take care of meself. And there's always supplementary. I don't see why I shouldn't get it; every other bugger in the street's on it. You look after yourself . . . and her. Anyway, if Stan and Rosie marry, an' they're bound to, they'll come in with me, so don't let anythin' at this end put you off.'

He nodded at her.

A few minutes later, back in the kitchen, he said 'Hold it for another ten minutes or so until I get changed; she'll likely be in by then.'

In the room the fire was burning brightly; it looked comfortable and cheery. Inwardly he was delighted at the change in the room, but it was still small, and to her it must appear like a box.

Where was she? Had she gone? He brought his forefinger to his teeth and bit the end completely off his nail. It would be just like the thing, wouldn't it, him getting the bungalow and her going off all in the same day. What would he do without her? How could he go on without her? How did he go on before he had her? And yet he'd never had her in that sense. He had lived in this room with her for weeks on end and he'd never had her. It was all going to happen tomorrow night. He was barmy, mad. Be nice to her, gentle, Doctor Carr had said. Gentle be damned. He should have taken his rights weeks ago; that would have settled it. She would likely have been well on the way now with another. God it was as his mother had said, he was soft, barmy, a blasted fool. He had worked his guts out these last few weeks to get the money to put down for the lorries and now what had he done with it? Given Reg Walker fifty poinds in advance, and promised him another two hundred and fifty the morrow. That would take every penny of his capital and push him back a year, two years; in fact he might never get on his feet again. Well, it served him right . . . And wouldn't there be some laughter round the doors when they knew she had left him high and dry. They had been waiting for it, betting on it . . . Aw, he knew them.

He went to the narrow mantelpiece and, leaning his forearms along it, he dropped his head on to them and groaned inwardly.

When he heard his mother's voice saying, 'Hello, we thought you had got lost,' he almost sprang to the little table in the corner of the room, and when she opened the door he was emptying his back trouser pocket of notes and silver.

'Hello, there.' He smiled at her. 'You look froze. Where've you been?' He continued to smile at her as he walked towards her.

'I went into Newcastle.'

'Oh. Mam thought you might.' He was nodding at her.

She was taking off her hat and coat. 'It's raw,' she said, 'bitter; it's nice to see a fire.' She bent forward and held her hands down to the blaze and, looking over her shoulder, said, 'You were late, too?'

'Yes. Yes, I've been doing a bit of business . . . What have you been up to? Shoppin'?'

She turned and hunched her shoulders up over her long neck, then smoothed down her mauve woollen dress over her flat stomach before saying, 'I've been after a job.'

When he made no comment on this she said, 'Don't be vexed.'

'Vexed! Me? I'm not vexed. What kind of a job?'

'In one of the stores, Daintrees.'

'Oh. It's a classy shop that.'

'Yes.' She nodded. 'Quite nice. You don't mind?'

If he didn't know what he was going to do tomorrow night, or tonight for that matter, he would have said, 'Mind? You're bloody well right, I do mind. If you can't fill your time in then I'll have to give you something to fill it in with, won't I?' but what he said was, 'I've got a surprise for you an' all.'

'You have?' She waited.

'How would you like a bungalow?'

'Bungalow!' She brought her head forward, her smile widening her large mouth.

'Aye, I've bought one.'

She moved a step towards him. 'You've bought a bungalow? What . . . what kind?' She didn't say, 'You bought a bungalow without me seeing it? I mightn't even like it.'

'Big one. Six rooms. The lot. There was no time to let you know. I had to make up me mind by five o'clock. It's a snip. I'll run you out first thing in the mornin' to see it.'

'Where is it?' Her face was bright and eager.

'Oh, it's a bit outside. Collier Road way, on a rise. You can see the river from the windows.'

The river. Her throat constricted just the slightest; the smile was fading from her face when she brought it back again and said, 'Oh, that sounds lovely. Is it going to cost a lot?'

'No. As I said, it's a snip. Two thousand five hundred. It's worth four, even as it stands. Get it put into shape and you can add another two on to that.'

She glanced towards the door, then said under her breath, 'But, Emily.'

'She knows; she's glad.'

'Are you goin' to let this get spoilt?' Emily's voice, coming from the other room, made them both grimace, then laugh gently, and he pushed her towards the door, saying, 'I'll be there in a tick.'

As Vanessa entered the kitchen Rosie came down the stairs, and she asked immediately, under her breath, 'Did you get it?' and Vanessa nodded and said, 'Yes.'

'What they payin' you?'

'Six pounds ten.'

Rosie shrugged her shoulders. 'That isn't very much; in fact it's nowt. And then you've got your fares to pay.'

'That's only to start with, sort of training period. I'll get commission on sales after two months.'

'What did he say?' Rosie jerked her head backwards.

'Oh, he doesn't mind.'

'Coo!' Rosie again jerked her head; 'that's a surprise.'

'What's a surprise?' Angus came into the room, buttoning his shirt up, and Rosie said, 'It's none of your business.'

'Have you told her?' He looked from his mother to Vanessa, and when Vanessa shook her head and his mother said 'No, I've not had time, she's just come down,' he turned to Rosie and said, 'I've got a bungalow.'

'A bungalow? You come into some money or summat? A bungalow? When did this all happen?'

When they sat down to their meal he explained briefly how it had all happened, and then Rosie voiced what was in the back of his mind all the time. 'Well, that's put paid to you're gettin' any more lorries, at least for some time,' she said, ''cos you'll need furniture and things. Good job you started work.' She nodded at Vanessa, and Vanessa, after a moment, said, 'Yes. Yes, it is.' She herself had forgotten about the lorries for the moment, and yet they hadn't been out of her mind for weeks past; the job she had got today was in a way connected with the lorries.

It was as they finished the meal that Angus, suddenly determining in his mind to push personal matters forward a little, said, 'What about us all goin' to the club to celebrate? Friday night's a good night.'

Neither Emily nor Rosie made any rejoinder, but after a moment's pause Vanessa said, 'Yes. Yes, that's a good idea.'

'Oh, I don't feel like it,' said Emily sitting back in the chair. 'Me feet's killin' me.'

It wouldn't have taxed Emily's feet very much in visiting the club. She would have loved to have gone along tonight and had a bit of a sing-song. It was what she needed, to be in a crowd and yell her head off, but the last time they had gone to the club altogether it hadn't been a success. It was Vanessa's initiation, so to speak, into their kind of entertainment and she had smiled all the while, even laughed at some of the turns, but Emily hadn't seen her almost since she was a bairn not to know that it was a façade covering her real feelings. She knew that even if Vanessa had been challenged she wouldn't have admitted to her opinion of the company, of the drinking, singing, rocketing company, where, although the men were well put on and the women wore dresses that were a good imitation of the Bower Place lot, they acted as they had always done. It would have taken somebody like Miss Susan to say outright, 'Common individuals!'

Rosie wanted Vanessa to accompany them to the club no more than her mother, so she said brightly, 'Why the club? Look, our Angus, why don't you take Van along to some place like Donovan's? Now, that would be a night out, sort of celebration for her getting her job.'

'Donovan's.' Angus cocked his chin in the air and repeated, 'Donovan's. Aye.' He looked at Vanessa. 'Would you like to go to Donovan's?'

'I've never been, I don't know what it's like.' She glanced at Rosie, and Rosie said, 'Oh, it's posh is Donovan's. That's where all the Rugby players get on a Saturday night. Angus used to go, didn't you?'

'Oh, well.' He moved his head from side to side. 'I've been a couple of times, but–' he turned to Vanessa–'I wouldn't take you there on a Saturday night.' Then bending towards her he added jocularly, 'But this is Friday. We'll go to Donovan's, eh?'

'Is it . . . is it evening dress or . . .?'

'No anything,' he answered.

'Your blue one,' Rosie put in, 'that he bought you for Christmas. That would do. It's smart and warm and it's your colour. You look smashing in it.'

Vanessa smiled at Rosie. When Rosie was kind to her, as now, she ceased to think, 'If only you had been like this from the beginning I wouldn't have done it.'

The shame of trying to take her own life was still with her. She felt that her action had been the admission of utter failure. She was like Brett. Brett had given her the child, then had taken his life because he couldn't face up to the consequences. They were a pair, weak; nice, but weak. His weakness had created the child and her weakness had killed it. No matter what Doctor Carr said to the contrary, she would always feel that it was through her attempted suicide that the child had died. It had been shocked into death when on the point of coming alive.

'You're for it, aren't you?' Angus's question brought her mind quickly to the present, and she answered eagerly, 'Yes, yes, of course. I'd love it. That's if we're not too late. I've got to get ready and it's after seven.'

'Oh, places like those don't get going until nine or ten.'

'Well, don't sit there,' said Emily, energetically now. 'An' don't you go on stuffing yourself.' She nodded at Angus. 'Else what's the good you payin' for a meal?'

As he got to his feet he bent towards her, saying, 'I bet you a shilling that no matter what we pay it won't be half as good as this.' He was trying to please her in all ways these days. She was all right was his mam; he had always known it . . .

Half-an-hour later they were both ready, and Emily, looking at them as they stood side by side in the kitchen, thought that whatever difference there was underneath it didn't show much when they were dressed up. She was proud of the way Angus was turned out; nothing flashy about him; he could have come from Brampton Hill itself. He knew how to dress, did Angus, and how to carry himself. He had been to Donovan's before and mixed with them lot. Oh, she had no fear of how he would carry himself in that swell place.

'Bye-bye,' said Vanessa, looking from Emily to Rosie; and they didn't answer as was usual with them, saying, 'Ta-rah,' but said, 'Bye-bye . . . And enjoy yourselves,' they both added.

'Don't wait up mind.' Angus turned from the door and Emily answered robustly, 'Wait up for you? What would I wait up for you for? Go on, get yourself away.'

As they stood waiting at the corner of the street for a bus he looked at Vanessa and said, 'There's one thing missing.'

'What's that?'

'A car. People don't go by bus to Donovan's. You can't get near it for cars.'

'Well, we can get off at the stop before and pretend we've left ours parked at the end of the road.'

He dug her gently in the ribs and jerked his head as he said, 'You've got something.'

He was happy as he had never been happy before. The happiness banked down on that corner of his mind where were piled his worries.

In the bus she asked, with excitement in her voice, 'Is there a place to dance?'

'Aye, a bit of floor, but . . .' He drooped his head to the side to look full into her face. 'Do you dance? Funny, I've never asked you; do you dance?'

'I've had lessons.' Her brows moved upwards.

'But you've never been on a dance floor?' He felt superior. This he could teach her, anyway, because he was a good dancer. Heavily made as he was, he was light on his feet.

'Once,' she said.

'Once!' His look and tone ridiculed her single effort; then he added, 'If you stand on me toes I'll yell the place down mind.'

When she laughed and looked down at his size ten shoes his happiness moved in all directions through his body; it made him want to grab her to him and hold her tightly, not do anything, just hold her tightly, like his Uncle Dick used to do to his Aunt Ann. They had been married for twenty years but he used to get hold of her and hug her, and she used to laugh up into his face. She was a little woman, round and fat, but there was something between them, a sort of something. He remembered it when he went to his funeral, that day he had met Van in the train. Lord, that seemed ten years ago. Did he ever think then that . . .? Blimey? He would have asked them to cart him away if he had even dreamed of it.

They got off the bus, and when they reached the hotel car park where the cars were spilling over on to the drive it looked as if it was a busy night after all.

'We . . . we mightn't get a table.' His voice was flat. 'I should have had the sense to slip out and phone when I got the idea.'

'I don't suppose it would have made much difference; you likely have to book up a day or so ahead. Anyway, we can always try.' She smiled consolingly at him, and her eyes lingered on his face. She wasn't ashamed to be out with him; that was something she was grateful for. Another thing she was grateful for was, he didn't raise his voice outside. He could bawl and shout in the house; even in their room he shouted to her in ordinary conversation as if she was at the end of the street, but outside his manner was different. He tried, did Angus. Oh yes, he tried very hard. She wished he would let her help him. She had learned a lot over the past weeks about the man she had married. She knew, for instance, that he was in constant fear that she would leave him now that there was nothing to hold her, only a marriage that could be dissolved quite easily, it never having been consummated. She knew that he didn't want her to go to work in case she would meet someone else. She was getting to understand all his little ways, his moods, but this did not alleviate the fear in which she held him, the fear that would be strengthened or erased completely when he began to make demands of her; and the time for that was very near. She knew it; she felt it; it was very near.

Having left their outer things in the cloakroom they walked side by side past the open cocktail bar, past the main bar, across the deeply carpeted lounge that was studded with small tables and groups of people, and towards the dining-room. When they were almost there he stopped and said, 'Would you like a drink first?' He motioned towards one of the tables, and without looking at them she said, 'No. No, I would rather not.' She felt excited; nervous, and strangely more ill at ease than he was.

'Good evening, sir. Good evening, madam. You have a table reserved?'

'No, I'm sorry,' said Angus. 'We just came on speck.' His voice sounded airy.

'Ah!' The head waiter looked straight into Angus's face, and Angus said, 'I'd be obliged if you could find us a table.' The words were a promise and the head waiter said, 'Well, sir, you're lucky, there's been a cancellation . . .

and a very nice table. It's in the alcove. Come this way. This way, madam.'

The table was indeed a nice table. It was screened from part of the main room by an ornamental partition, and the head waiter pulled out a chair that backed on to the partition for Vanessa, giving her a view over part of the dining-room towards the space allotted for dancing and to the small platform where four musicians were seated.

When they were alone for a moment Angus drew in a deep breath and adjusted his coat, then said, 'Nice?'

'Lovely.' She nodded across the table at him.

As the band struck up the wine waiter came to the table and handed Angus the wine list.

'Well now.' He looked at it, then across at her and asked, 'What do you fancy?'

'I'll have a sherry,' she said.

'Dry or sweet, madam?' asked the waiter.

'Dry, please.'

Angus, after a pause said, 'Make it two.'

'And for later, sir; you'd like a little wine with the meal?'

'Yes. Oh, yes.' Angus looked at the wine list again. He knew nothing about wines. He could name any make of beer in the country, even the brands that were popular in the South, but of wines he was completely ignorant. He felt the heat of embarrassment creeping up his neck. He saved it getting further by looking over the list and saying to Vanessa, 'Have you any particular fancy?'

Intuitively she knew he needed help and she answered, 'I would like,' she paused as she was about to say, 'a white wine.' Instead she named it. 'A Graves Supèriur or a Liebfraumilch.' She looked at Angus, and the waiter looked at Angus, waiting for the final word. And Angus, taking a deep breath, gave him the final word, and he pronounced it almost as Vanessa had done. 'Graves Supèriur,' he said, nodding once. He couldn't have attempted to pronounce the other tongue-twister.

'Very good, sir. Very good.'

When they were alone again, he stared at her, without speaking now. She knew about wines. The space between them was marked again.

She leaned forward and said to him now, under her breath, and as if she had read his thoughts, 'I only know about them because father used to discuss them with mother when people were coming for a meal.' Her voice trailed away. She knew she had said the wrong thing. As far as she could remember it was the first time she had spoken her father's name to him since they were married. This could spoil everything. She said quickly, 'I'm sorry.'

'What you sorry for? No need to be sorry because you know the name of a wine.' He flapped his hand lightly at her, and ignored the fact that she had mentioned her father.

Then they were ordering dinner. He knew his way about here. This was safer ground; it wasn't the first time he had ordered dinner. That was until he looked at the menu. 'What about a shrimp cocktail to start with?' He was bending towards her.

And she answered, 'Lovely.'

'Two shrimp cocktails.'

'And the main course, sir?'

Again Angus looked at her. She was looking at the menu. It was mostly in French.

He too looked at the menu. He looked at it for quite a while; then he raised his eyes to the waiter and said coolly, 'A steak for me, medium rare.'

'Very good, sir. Very good, and you, madam?'

She did not say Chicken sauté à la Marengo but fried chicken in sauce, please.

When that was over they both relaxed for different reasons.

There were couples dancing on the floor now, and when she began to tap her fingers to the tune he said laughingly, 'Now you're not going to get up there and show them until you've had something to eat.'

She laughed softly across at him. They both looked across the room when a roar of laughter came from the direction of the cocktail bar, and as the band struck up a number of couples came through from the lounge and began to dance.

Angus, still looking across the room, said, 'I didn't think that was allowed; I thought the dancing space was only for the diners.' He had the air of a regular patron.

As the noise and the laughter rose above the music, Angus commented, 'They're all high. Looks like a Saturday night after all.'

'You used to come here on a Saturday night?'

'Once or twice after we finished the game.'

'I never knew you played Rugby until tonight.'

There was a twisted smile on his face and he looked at her for a full minute before saying, 'There's lots of things you don't know about me, Van.'

When she lowered her gaze from his he turned it quickly into a joke. 'I've got a medal for live-savin',' he said; 'I once dived into four feet of water and got a bairn up in the baths.' When she gave a little splutter he said, 'It's a fact. There was a gang of lads together and someone shouted that their Willie or some such was drownin' and I ran along and dived in, and it was nearly fifteen minutes later when I came round; I'd hit me head on the bottom.'

'Was anyone drowned?'

'I don't know, I've never found out to this day.' They were laughing openly now. 'And that's not all,' he said. 'You should have seen what I got for doing a good deed.' He lifted the quiff of his sandy hair from his brow. 'Have you noticed that?'

She looked at the scar and said, 'Yes, I had noticed it, and I wondered how you got it.'

'Oh, that was the payment for doing the good deed. I was on top of a bus and a woman was going to go down the stairs. She had a basket of groceries, a huge basket, an' she was hanging on to the top rail. The bus was going round a corner so I said, 'Give it here, missis; I'll take it down for you.' I was a big brawny fellow of fifteen and she said, "Thanks, lad," and she went down the stairs and me after her. Only I tripped, and it was the iron rail you know the rail you hang on to, that stopped me falling into the road and, boy, I've never seen a basket of groceries go so far in me life. Talk about the three loaves and the five fishes.'

He had her laughing now, really laughing. Her shoulders were hunched and she had her hand across her mouth, and when she murmured, 'Oh, Angus, don't,' he warmed to his theme. He was entertaining her; she was happy; it was the first time he had seen her really laugh. He said, 'That's nothing. I could fill a book. Every time I've done a good turn in me life I've got it slapped back straight in me face.' Somewhere in the back of his mind he knew this was a tactless remark, and at the same time some part of him was praying that this was one time in his life that he wouldn't have his good deed slapped right back into his face, that life would go on from here and that she would never leave him.

'There was Mrs Halliday's fire,' he said. 'You know Mrs Halliday, five doors down. I was comin' down the street one day and there was smoke comin' out of her window, and she came out yellin' that her gas stove had caught fire, and in dashed brave Angus Cotton. I couldn't get near the stove. "Have you got any salt?" I yelled. Mam was always douching our fire with salt when the chimney caught ablaze, you know, and Mrs Halliday yelled back at me, "What!" and I yelled, "Salt!" She was a very methodical woman was Mrs Halliday and she kept a good supply of stuff in the house–everybody used to go and borrow from her. Anyway, when she pointed I picked up the jar of salt, only it wasn't salt it was sugar, and I threw it on the fire. Believe me we were nearly blown over the railway wall.'

Her head was down, her hands were joined tightly in her lap, her eyes were wet; she looked up at him from under her thick short lashes and asked, 'What was the end to that?'

'The fire brigade. Her whole kitchen was burnt down. Lord, I daren't pass her door for months after that.'

Again she said, 'Oh, Angus.' He was nice. She had always known he was nice. He was trying to make her happy. Oh, if only he could . . .

The steak came medium rare, the chicken and its sauce were delicious. They ate everything on their plates, and then made their choice from a trolley of assorted sweets. Finally there was coffee.

'Will you have it here or in the lounge, sir?'

They decided to have it in the lounge. They walked around the outskirts of the dancing couples, past the head waiter, whom Angus thanked for an excellent meal and supplemented his thanks with a piece of folded paper, and they were again escorted to their seats.

Over the coffee Angus looked at her and asked, 'Enjoying it?'

'It's lovely, Angus, wonderful. Do you know,' she twisted round to him, 'this is the first time I've ever been out to dinner. I've never enjoyed myself like this before, never in my life.'

His eyes ranged over her face. All the tenseness had gone from it; she looked soft and warm and beautiful. There was nobody in here who could hold a candle to her; and she had to develop yet. In two or three years' time she'd be a stunner; a little more flesh on her and she'd be something. Did she know that? Was she aware of how she looked to other people? He must keep her. By fair means or foul he must keep her. He knew now that all his life he had wanted her, and he had got her, but when she came awake could he keep her? Because the raw fact was, she wasn't awakened yet, not to anything. She'd had a bairn but it hadn't really touched her.

He got abruptly to his feet now and, buttoning up his coat, said, 'We're going into the fray, it's a quick-step. Have you ever done a quick-step?'

She shook her head. 'I've done the twist. I can do the twist.' She sounded confident.

'Aw, the twist! That went out with the first programme of 'Top of the Pops'. Quick-step's back, á la ballroom dancin'; it's all back. I even saw a young lad on the telly the other night in "Top of the Pops" put his arm round a girl's waist when they were dancing. Do you know somethin'?' He shook his head at her. 'It looked quite indecent, it did really.'

He had her laughing again when they reached the dance floor. And there he put his arm around her and walked her gently backwards and forwards.

She had a lightness and rhythm all her own, and soon they were moving in motion together and she smiled up at him, pleased that this was so. Two or three times they were bumped into, and occasionally he had to excuse himself for bumping into someone else; the small floor was packed even before the company from the cocktail bar came on to it again.

It was when they were almost knocked off their balance by a stumbling, laughing couple that Angus said somewhat angrily, 'Here, steady on,' and, balancing Vanessa, he glared at the back of the man who had bumped into them, and who was evidently far from sober for he had his head on his partner's neck as he shook with laughter. But Angus's tone piercing his mirth, brought him round and he stared from one to the other. Then, his mouth widening, he said, 'Ah, Good Lord! Cotton . . . And you!' His eyebrows moved upwards as he continued to stare at Vanessa. Then on a hic of a laugh, he said, 'Why; would you believe it? Vanessa Ratcliffe!' He poked his head towards her. 'You know me. You remember at Susan's do? Brian Cornell. Fancy seeing you here.'

'Yes, fancy,' said Angus flatly, putting his arm round Vanessa once more and moving away into the dance.

Within a minute Cornell was at their shoulder again, shouting above the music and the noise, 'We'll have to get together, eh?'

Angus made no reply, and a few minutes later he walked Vanessa back to the lounge.

'You know him?'

She screwed up her face as if trying to remember. 'Yes, yes, I've seen him before. He came to a party of Susan's. And you . . . you know him, too?'

'He was in the Rugby team. Still is for all I know.' He didn't add that Cornell was one of those individuals who would speak to you if he must in the dressing-room, or when he was drunk, as now, but would ignore you flat in the street when he was with his women folk. And they said there was no class distinction these days. God! That was funny. He remembered thinking along the same lines the day he met Colin Brett in the station. 'Have another coffee?' he asked her.

'Yes, I think I will.'

He leaned towards her. 'What about a liqueur? Would you like a liqueur?'

'No.' It was a firm no. 'And stop throwing your money about.' She was smiling gently at him. 'You'll need all you can get from now on.'

'Yes,' he said, 'I know. But this is a night apart.'

They were looking at each other; then her head drooped and she moved the spoon around in her cup as she said, 'I'm glad I've got a job, Angus; it'll help, won't it?'

He didn't answer her for a moment; and then he said, 'I don't want you to go to work, Van. You know that, don't you?'

'But I can't stay at home all day, Angus; there's nothing to do.'

'There will be once you get into the bungalow. There'll be more than you can tackle.'

Once more their gaze held until he exclaimed. 'Aw, don't let's talk about that now. Drink your coffee and then I'll let you stand on me toes again.'

She had just put her cup down when there loomed over them the tall, heavy figure of Brian Cornell. 'Ha-ha!' He put out a hand on each of their shoulders. 'I've caught you.'

There was the thing about getting to your feet, Angus knew, when another man came to a table when a woman was present, but he remained seated, his head to one side, staring up into the grinning countenance.

'Spare her a minute?' Cornell's voice was thick and fuddled, and his glance merely touched on Angus as he made his request. But it rested heavily on Vanessa as he said briefly, 'Dance?'

'She's not dancing any more.'

'What!' Cornell straightened himself. 'Now, now. Come on, Cotton; don't play the heavy husband. You should have got over that by now. What is it? Four months? six months? Anyway, I knew her before you did.' He laughed as he punched Angus not too gently on the back.

'You do remember me, don't you?' He was leaning over Vanessa, his face close to hers. 'Susan's party. You know something? I remember thinking then that you'd beat Susan to a frazzle. Come on, give me this dance?' He caught hold of her arm, but she remained seated.

'Leave go of her!' Angus was now on his feet.

'What! Aw, Cotton, be your age.' Cornell thrust his arm backwards across Angus's chest. 'Don't come the heavy husband, man. You're out of your depths; they don't act like that where she comes from.'

His raised voice had attracted the other occupants of the lounge. There was a man sitting to the right of them who had turned completely round and was listening intently to all that was going on.

'I–I don't want to dance, thank you,' Vanessa said; then looking from Cornell to Angus she added quickly, 'It's about time we were going.'

The look she bent on Angus said plainly, 'Please, please don't make a scene,' and he obeyed it. His jaw stiff, his fists clenched tight, he waited for

Cornell to leave them. But Cornell had no intention of leaving them. Sidling down on to the wall seat to the left of Vanessa, he mumbled thickly, 'S'prised to see you; didn't think they would let you up out of the ghetto.'

The next second Brian Cornell was up on his feet again, brought there by Angus's hands gripping the lapels of his coat.

'Come on outside.'

'Go to the devil!' Cornell tugged himself from Angus's hold; then surveyed him with disdain.

'Are you coming outside?'

'You'd better go.' The words came from the man who had taken an interest in the proceedings. He was a youngish forty, dapper looking, small.

'Oh, you, Fowler.' Cornell turned towards the man. 'Well, you keep out of this.'

'Are you coming outside or have I to give it to you here?'

'Have it anyway you like, chum, only don't forget you asked for it.' Cornell's mouth curled upwards.

As they went through the lounge, Cornell shouted 'Arthur! Tony!' but when Arthur and Tony came from the cocktail bar counter they were stayed by the man Cornell had called Fowler. 'Hold your hand!' he said. 'They'll have it out on their own.'

'What the hell is it all about?'

'You can ask Cornell when it's over.'

It was quickly all over. Out in the open near the car park they squared up to each other.

If Cornell had been sober he would have been a match for Angus, but in his present condition his blows were aimed wildly; not so Angus's. A blow with the right hand to the stomach was immediately followed by a quick left-right to the face. When Cornell stumbled against the wall, his body bent over double, Angus stood back gasping.

There was a small crowd around them now, all men, with the exception of Vanessa, and as she moved to Angus's side he pushed her roughly away muttering, 'Go and get your things on.'

After a moment's pause she turned to obey him, and it was then she saw one of Cornell's friends, with his fist at shoulder level, making for Angus from behind, but he never reached him, for experiencing a feeling of anger that was quite new to her she sprang forward crying, 'Stop it, you drunken beast you.' Whether it was the push she gave the man, or the surprise of being attacked by a girl, he stumbled backwards, and those around sniggered. But the sound died swiftly away as Brian Cornell raised himself up and leant against the wall for support. There was blood running from the corner of his mouth and one eye was already swelling.

Another man, going to Cornell's aid, turned and confronted Angus, crying, 'You should be damned well ashamed of yourself. If there was a policeman about I'd hand you over. They're never here when they're wanted.'

The quiet voice interrupted again, saying, 'You're talking to the wrong fellow; he didn't start it.'

'I saw what he started; I was in the lounge. He attacked him first.'

'Under provocation.'

'Come on.' Angus pushed Vanessa past the men and into the hotel again, where the manager was waiting in the foyer, his face no longer smiling. His voice stiff, he said, 'This is a very unfortunate incident, sir.'

'You should be more particular who you let in then, shouldn't you? And you shouldn't keep on serving drink to drunks.'

'Angus!' There was deep appeal in Vanessa's voice and he turned to her and, biting on his lip, said harshly, 'All right, all right. Get your things.'

She wasn't a minute collecting her coat and hat, and when she returned to the hall Angus was talking to the dapper man; at least, the dapper man was talking to Angus. He turned to Vanessa and said, 'Now don't let this little incident worry you. I was just telling your husband that should anything come of it he can call on me to say my piece.'

'Thank you.' She inclined her head towards him, and, looking intently at her, he smiled and said, 'You don't know me but I know of you. I happen to be Brian Braintree's half-cousin.' Perhaps it was because he felt that both of them stiffened that he added quickly, 'But on the poor side. Brian's father and mine are full cousins but they're not on speaking terms; we weren't invited to the wedding.' He brought his head forward as he pulled a face. 'I recognised you right away. You were at the Taylor's house about three years ago when I was there. You haven't changed much. My name's Fowler, Andrew Fowler.'

All she could say was 'Oh.' Her face was flushed. She knew he was trying to be nice, smooth things over, but she wished he wouldn't. She felt sure that the very mention of him being connected in any way with her family, or the one into which Susan had married, would make Angus angry. But Angus showed no actual resentment towards the man; in fact, he bade him good-night quite civilly, and when he turned towards the door the man turned with them, saying, 'I'm off too.' And on the steps of the hotel he left them, adding 'Good-bye. And don't let it worry you. Cornell's been asking for that for a long time.'

They walked across the drive and round by the car park and to the bus stop almost in silence. It was as they were standing there that Andrew Fowler passed them in the car. Drawing up sharply and backing towards them, he asked, 'Can I give you a lift?'

Angus hesitated for a moment, then said, 'Thanks,' and opened the door and helped Vanessa in.

'Where can I drop you.'

'Oh, anywhere near Caxton Bridge,' said Angus in an off-hand manner.

They had gone a little way when Fowler dropped his head backwards as he said, 'You're in the contracting business, aren't you?'

'Yes. How did you know?'

'Oh, I'm an architect. I remember seeing you down at Ralstons, in the office or somewhere, and somebody happened to remark that you had started up.'

Yes, thought Angus to himself; I bet they did. And I bet they added,

'That's him that got old Ratcliffe's daughter into trouble.' Only the term wouldn't have been as polite as that.

'How's business going?'

'Oh, not too bad. Could be better though.'

'How many are you running . . . lorries?'

'Just the two at the moment.' He was talking as if the concern was his own.

'Hmm!' There was a silence after this for a while until Andrew Fowler remarked, 'You really need more than two, unless you're always going to be dependent on the big firms.'

As if he didn't know that.

When they reached the bridge, and the car stopped, Andrew Fowler turned to Angus and, handing him his card, said, 'You may want to get in touch with me if they stir anything up about tonight. As I said, I'll vouch for you being provoked. Cornell's a nasty piece of work; I think you'd better know that.'

'I already know it; I've met him afore. We were in the Rugby team together.'

'Oh.'

'But thanks. Thanks all the same. And thanks for the lift. Good-night.'

'Good-night,' said Vanessa. 'And thank you.'

He nodded to them both and said, 'Good-night,' and drove off.

They walked down the main road and over the traffic lights, past the railway bridge and up the street, and just before they reached the door he pulled her to a stop and, peering at her in the dimness, said, 'I'm sorry. It . . . it was such a grand night, but . . . it wasn't really my fault.'

'Oh, I know, Angus, I know. He was a horrible beast, and I'm glad that you hit him.' There was a vehemence in her voice that he hadn't heard before, and he smiled slightly and said with some surprise, 'You are?'

'Yes. I wanted to hit him myself.' She, too, was smiling weakly now. 'I pushed that other man.' She put her hand up to her face as she added, 'I've never done that before in my life; but . . . but I wished I'd had a stick or something.'

He put his hand out swiftly and grasped her round the shoulders and pressed her to him for a moment; then they went into the house.

Emily was in; so too were Rosie and Stan; and Emily turned and looked at them in surprise, saying, 'Well! you're back early.'

'No good?' asked Rosie.

'Very good,' said Vanessa. 'Very good indeed.' She looked from one to the other; then slowly she started to laugh. Leaning against the table she laughed and laughed.

They had never heard her laugh like this; they had never seen her mouth stretch in real laughter. They watched her put her arm around her waist as her laughter grew. It was almost touching on hysteria and they became infected by it. Angus sat heavily down on a chair, and threw his head back. Emily was laughing, as was Rosie and Stan, although they didn't know what they were laughing about.

'What is it? Tell us the joke,' Rosie spluttered, and when Vanessa, gasping and holding her chin tightly, said, 'He . . . Angus had a fight,' Emily's laughter suddenly ceased and she cried, 'MY God! You didn't. Not at the Donovan?'

Vanessa was nodding her head when Rosie, who had also stopped laughing, said, 'Oh, our Angus. You had a fight in the Donovan? Trust you to show yourself up.'

Vanessa was still gasping, and the tears were running down her face, and she tried to check her mirth as she said to Rosie, 'But he didn't, he didn't. There was a man and he was bothering me and he wouldn't stop and,' she glanced at Angus, and the laughter bubbled in her again, 'he–he made him go outside and blacked his eyes.' Her long thin body drooped and she collapsed into a chair.

'Oh, my God!' Emily was no longer amused. Staring at Angus now, she asked, 'Who was he? Anybody important?'

'Oh, Mam!' He too had stopped laughing. 'Important? Who's important? Yes, I suppose you could say he was important. It was Brian Cornell.'

'Cornell? You mean the shop Cornell; him who's got the chain stores?'

'Yes, him who's got the chain stores.'

'Well mind, you picked on somebody to hit, didn't you?'

'Aye, I picked on somebody to hit, Mam; and I'll hit him again if I meet up with him.'

'Good for you,' said Stan. 'I know a bit about Cornell. Beer and bawd Cornell, they call him, and it isn't spelt b,o,a,r,d. He's no good.'

'We agree on that, Stan,' said Angus, nodding across the table.

'Aw dear, dear me,' said Emily, getting to her feet. 'Trust you to get into trouble. I don't know when you have gone out of this house that something hasn't happened to you.'

'We had a lovely dinner,' said Vanessa now.

'Aye, what did you have?' asked Stan, aiming to change the subject.

And Vanessa told them, and in detail, and she ended, 'We had Liebfraumilch with it.' They hadn't, but it sounded better than Graves Supèrier.

'Lieb–what? What in the name of goodness is that when you're out?' asked Rosie.

'It's a wine. Angus chose it.'

Both Rosie and Emily were looking at Angus as if they had never seen him before. They didn't ask what he knew about this lieb-frau or whatever it was, they just looked at him, and he laughed openly at them. He was suddenly happy again, very happy. She was with him; she had said he had picked that wine. He bent forward now and, pointing his finger at his mother, said, 'And there's something more you won't believe. She hit a fellow.' He thumbed in the direction of Vanessa; and now they were all looking at Vanessa, and Emily said in a shocked tone, 'You didn't, did you?'

'Yes.' She nodded her head in small jerks, smiling widely.

'You must be spiffy,' said Rosie.

'No, no; I only had a sherry and two glasses of—' she paused–'Leibfraumilch.' She brought her head into deep obeisance as she said it again, and Emily said, 'Well, I've heard everything. Was it this fellow, this Cornell fellow?'

'No. I don't know who it was, but after Angus had finished with Brian Cornell this man was going to hit him on the back of the head. I could see it coming, and so I pushed him as hard as I could.'

After a few seconds of silence the kitchen was suddenly filled with gales and gales of laughter. It mounted and mounted. Rosie leant her head helplessly against her mother's flabby breast and they rocked together. Stan shook, and Angus shook, and Vanessa laid her head on her arms, so helpless had she become with laughing.

Never before in her life had Vanessa experienced this exhilarating feeling of laughter. They had never laughed at home, not really. Smiled; oh yes, all the time. But they had never really laughed. She couldn't remember hearing her father laugh out loud. She had seen him chuckle. Even Susan never laughed outright. It wouldn't be the done thing for Susan. And Ray? Ray made noises of glee but he didn't laugh. Nobody laughed like these people, the people to whom she had linked herself, and in this moment she loved them. And it was in this moment that her love for Angus was born.

It was almost an hour later when they went into their room and there, doubling his fist, he said, 'I didn't realize it before but my knuckles are hurting.'

'I bet his face is hurting more.'

They were standing looking at each other on the hearth rug in front of the dead fire, and after a moment he put out his hand and touched her cheek and said under his breath, 'You've been grand the night, grand.'

She looked down; then turned away, saying, 'You'd think I'd been in the fight, I feel so tired.'

It had been his practice to put the light out when they were about to get undressed. He knew this was a daft idea right from the beginning, but once he had started it, it became a habit. But tonight he didn't put it out. He took off his coat and loosened his tie, then reached for his pyjamas that were underneath the pillow.

Vanessa had her back to him. She had taken off her dress and was standing in her slip. Then he was surprised to see her pull her night-dress over her head and do some wriggling motions under it. When her slip and panties dropped to the floor he thought, 'Well! Well!'

He had no tent under which to undress, nor did he need one. As he stripped off his clothes and got into his pyjamas she was getting into bed and she didn't look at him until he came and sat by her side. His weight brought the edge of the divan right down, and she rolled a little towards him. As they stared at each other the sound of Emily's and Rosie's laughter came to them from the rooms above, and, without taking his eyes from hers, he said, 'They're happy.'

She nodded at him.

'They think you're the tops.'

She could say nothing to this. They hadn't always thought her the tops; perhaps it was because they thought she had come down to their level that they had changed their opinion of her.

He said, 'It's been a strange night; a lot has happened.'

She nodded again; she was unable to speak.

'We could have some good times together, Van.' His hand came out and stroked her cheek, then moved down her neck on to the top of her breasts. Her flesh was trembling but she didn't shrink openly from him. Yet she couldn't look at him. He said softly, 'Van! Van!' When she didn't answer or look at him, he was about to say, 'All right, we'll leave it,' but he asked himself was he daft altogether. Lie there half the night awake, his innards churning as if they were filled with boiling oil? The time had passed for words. They were no longer necessary. Get on with it. That's what he had to do, get on with it. He had made up his mind, hadn't he that it was the night or the morrow night. If this stillness of hers put him off now it would put him off the morrow, and all the morrows.

As he rose quickly from the bed her eyes sprang wide and she was staring at him as he crossed the room and put the light out; then he was throwing back her bedclothes and the next minute she was in his arms and his mouth was on hers and his hands were over her; and it was quite different from what it had been with Brett.

Chapter Nine

'You're not taken with it?'

She turned from him and looked about her once more. 'Yes, yes; it's very nice.' What she wanted to say was 'It's wonderful,' and it would be wonderful, she thought, decorating it. She was sure she could do it herself, at least inside. And then there was the garden. Angus could dig it and she would plant it with roses and shrubs and perennials. . . . Yes, she could have said 'It's wonderful,' but instead she said coolly, 'It's very nice.'

'What's the matter with it? I know it's all brown paint; I don't think it's been painted inside since it was built; but that'll come off. And I'm telling you, if it was done up we wouldn't be getting it for this price.'

'That's the point.' She turned towards him again. 'We can't afford it.'

'Now look!' He spread his fingers wide, almost in front of her face. 'You leave that to me. I'll manage. Things aren't going to stay as they are; I'm going on and up. You'll see.' He jerked his head at her in his characteristic fashion.

She was staring at him in a way she wouldn't have done this time yesterday. There was a confidence about her, an assurance that hadn't been there then. Had it come about because she had defended him last night? Because she had pushed his assailant? Or because she had taken the strain out of her body in loud hilarious laughter? Or had the difference been created because he had made love to her for the first time and she hadn't shrunk from him. Not that she had enjoyed the process. And when afterwards she had lain in his arms and he had fallen asleep, his flesh still pressed against hers, she had asked herself what all the fuss was about, why people craved for this thing, and she remembered her curiosity concerning it that had kept her awake at nights, made her irritable and a willing victim of Brett's.

She also thought that the gigantic consequences of the act was the most illogical, even diabolical, happening nature could have thought up. A second of unison and you filled your body with a child. And then the further illogicality was that the goodness or the badness of the act was decided by a ceremony, during which a man said you are now married and gave you a piece of paper to that effect. She hadn't got to sleep for a long time.

But whatever it was that had changed her, she was undoubtedly different, and Angus naturally put it down to his love-making.

She said to him now, 'How much would you have to pay for a second-hand lorry?'

He screwed up his eyes at her. 'Seven hundred; anything less would be like what I've got, held up by paper and string. But . . . but what are you getting at?'

'Take the money that you're going to put down on this and put it on a lorry. You can pay it off by instalments, just as if you were buying this.'

He came and stood close to her, his bulging chest almost touching her. 'You'd give up this so's I could get a lorry?'

The look in his eyes embarrassed her and she turned her glance away as she said lightly, 'Perhaps I'm after something bigger, and the only way to get it is for you to get more business.'

He pulled her round squarely to him. 'It could mean staying in number twenty-four for God knows how long, you realise that, don't you?'

'Yes.'

'And you don't mind?'

The question was silly and he knew it, but when she answered truthfully, 'Not as much as I used to,' he nodded at her, and after a moment during which his gaze burrowed deep into hers, said, 'You'll do.' It was a compliment. Then stepping back from her, he ended, 'You know, if I give it up I'll lose fifty quid.'

Her reaction was immediate. 'Oh no! He'll give it back to you.'

'I can't see him doing it.'

'But I thought you knew him.'

'Oh, aye, I know him; but business is business.'

'I'll go with you; I'll help to explain.'

His head went back and he laughed. Then looking at her again he said, 'I think you would an' all.'

'Well,' she began walking down the narrow hall towards the front door, 'you can tell him that when, one day, we go after a bigger place we'll put the business in his hands.'

She found herself swung round, and the next minute her breath was taken away with his kisses, which covered her mouth, her eyes, her neck, and she became filled with panic when she thought where his frenzy of loving might lead: daylight would hold no obstacle, they were alone in this house. She managed to press herself from him and to say between gasps, and in an airy fashion, 'Come one, come on; there's fifty pounds at stake.'

He looked at her, at her flushed skin, which was like tinted cream, and he swallowed deeply; then with a rumbling laugh he pulled her arm tightly against his side, and he held it there as he locked the door. Then they walked down the path, but before they went through the gate he drew her to a stop and, leaning his face close to hers, he said, 'I'm so happy I could bust.'

The summons came on the Wednesday afternoon. It was served by a policeman.

In the usual way Angus wouldn't have been in the house on a Wednesday afternoon, but he had wanted to show Vanessa the lorry; after all, it was she who had really got things moving.

Reg Walker had given him back his deposit without much demur–a five-pound note had eased the situation here–and on the Saturday afternoon he and Fred Singleton had gone lorry hunting and had found one, but Angus hadn't been able to pick it up until an hour ago, when the owners use for it had come to an end.

Vanessa and Emily had stood on the pavement and admired the new acquisition, which showed up to disadvantage Fred's lorry. They were both on their way to a job, but now they returned to the kitchen and the cups of tea Emily had poured out for them, also to continue the discussion of hiring another man for the old lorry. Angus was eager for this move, but Fred seemed reluctant. Angus was wondering about Fred. There was, he put it to himself, something up with him these days. He hadn't the interest in the business he once had, yet he had started it. It was his missis, Angus thought; she was a nagger. She didn't belong to these parts and had never settled. Doncaster was her home.

Angus was saying, in answer to Fred's statement that it was risky engaging another driver, 'You've got to take a risk, man; I've put me lot into that out there,' when the knock came on the front door.

Emily returned to the kitchen. She stared at Angus for a full minute before she said, 'It's for you. It's the polis.'

'The polis?' He looked puzzled, he had forgotten about Friday night. Then under his breath he muttered in horror, 'It must have been nicked, the lorry.'

Emily shook her head, then stood aside as he thrust himself into the passage. And now she looked at Vanessa, who had come to her side, and whispered, ''Tisn't the lorry.'

Vanessa knew what it was before Angus returned to the room. He walked past them and to the table, and there he flung down the sheet of paper, then put his fist on it and looked first at Emily then at Vanessa. He looked at her for quite a while before he turned his gaze to Fred, and it was to him he spoke. 'That bugger, Cornell, that I told you about; he's summonsing me.' He always tried to curtail his swearing in front of Vanessa, but his good intentions went by the board at this moment. 'The bastard, summonsing me for assault. I told you, Fred, he started all this. He's a good three inches taller than me and could give me a stone any day, and if one of his blows had contacted, as drunk as he was, I don't suppose I'd have stood much of a chance. He's got fists and feet on him as hard as a bull. I've felt them on the field many a time when we've been in the scrum, and he's summonsing me!'

'Aw, Angus, you don't want nowt like that at this time.' Fred pushed his cap on the back of his head. 'Summonsing means money, a solicitor. And then there'll be a fine; as likely as not you'll get fined.'

'I'll not, you know.' Angus rounded on him. 'I'll not you know. I'll tell them exactly what happened. And you will an' all, won't you, Van?' He was glaring at her.

'Yes, yes, of course, Angus.' Her voice was low but firm.

'There; he'll not get his own way in this. By God, no!'

'What does the charge say?' It was the first time Emily had spoken, and he picked up the paper and after a moment read, 'Assault occasioning actual bodily harm.'

Emily said nothing for a while, but her colour faded. Then she sat down and muttered, as if to herself, 'That's bad . . . You'll have to get help.'

'I'll get help all right, don't you worry.' He looked at the summons again and said scornfully, 'Actual bodily harm!'

'Don't you think you should go an see that Mr Fowler?'

He stared at Vanessa; then said, 'Aye. Fowler . . .' His voice was high now. 'Aye, yes, you've got something there, Van. Funny, he thought something might come of it. He said if I should need him he'd speak up for me, but by damned I never dreamed I would. It just shows you, doesn't it? It was a little punch up, clean, nothing dirty.' He was speaking to Fred again. 'And that was that. Finished as far as I was concerned. And now this.' He swiped the paper aside; then looking at Vanessa, said, 'I've got to go through the town, I'll drop in and see him if he's there.'

'I'll come with you.'

'Oh, there's no need; not yet, anyway.'

'I'd like to come.'

'Aye, let her go along of you,' said Emily, and Angus shrugged his shoulders. It looked an indifferent, nonchalant movement, and it covered up the fact that he was glad she was coming. He turned to Fred. 'I shouldn't be more than fifteen minutes behind you, all right?'

'All right,' said Fred. 'You be as long as you like.'

'Time's money and it looks as if I'm going to need it, doesn't it?' He nodded from one to the other.

Andrew Fowler's office was a surprise to both of them. It stood in a new block of buildings. There was a secretary in the outer office, and she asked if they had an appointment.

'No,' said Angus, 'but Mr Fowler told me to look him up.'

The secretary spoke into the phone, and listened, and she'd hardly replaced the phone and said, 'Will you wait a moment?' when Andrew Fowler appeared at the connecting door. He looked pleased to see them. 'Hello,' he said; then, 'I'm going to give a guess. He didn't waste much time.'

'You're right there.' Angus smiled and nodded towards him, as he handed him the summons.

'Come in.' He stood aside and allowed them to walk into the inner office; and pushing a seat towards Vanessa, he said, 'Do sit down.' And he motioned to another for Angus to be seated. He did not go round the desk and sit in his chair but perched himself on the corner of the desk, and after reading the summons he looked from one to the other and said, 'Well, I'm not at all surprised. He's a vindictive beggar, Cornell, nasty piece of work. But assault occasioning actual bodily harm, that's laying it on. And he'll likely have a good solicitor. You'll have to be well prepared. Have you a solicitor?'

'No, and I don't feel like paying for one. I'll do my own defending. I can only speak the truth, and my wife here will tell exactly what happened. And . . . and then there's you.'

'Oh well, you can rely on me. I'll put them in the picture.' He laughed now, adding, 'And as much as I'd like to hear you defending your own case I think it would be wise to get a solicitor.'

'How much would that cost?'

'Oh, it all depends. Fifteen, twenty guineas. If you lose you'll have to pay the costs. And then the fine can be pretty stiff for what's stated here, I think.'

'How much?'

'Oh, I'm not sure, fifty I'd say.'

They both looked at Vanessa because she had groaned, and she, looking at Fowler, said with a weak smile, 'And this morning he bought a new lorry.'

'You did?' He looked at Angus with interest, then asked, 'You've got another man?'

Angus moved his tongue quickly around his upper lip and after a pause said, 'No, not yet; but I've got the promise of a fellow.' And he added, 'It looks as if I'm going to need half-a-dozen lorries, and the blokes to go with them, afore I'm finished.'

'Oh, I don't think it'll be as bad as that. A lot depends on who's on the Bench and how they're feeling.'

'And . . . and you don't mind speaking up for me?'

Andrew Fowler looked at the big fellow before him He looked rough, he walked rough, but there was something about him that attracted one. It had certainly attracted the daughter of Jonathan Ratcliffe. He would like to know the real ins and outs of how it came about, and he would through time. In the meantime he liked the idea of giving the fellow a hand.

Andrew Fowler was honest enough, as he always was with himself, to see the philanthropic gesture to Cotton as a roundabout way of getting his own back for past slights received from distant relatives. Who knew, but if this rough diamond rose he might come to be an embarrassment to the combined families of Ratcliffe and Braintree. As it was, he must be something of an embarrassment to the Ratcliffes, for had he not stormed the citadel of the mighty and snatched their convent-bred lily white chick from under their noses? Indeed, yes. And from the little he had seen of her the chick was adapting herself to her changed circumstances. She was out to push this rough man of hers. He would like to bet it was she who reminded him about coming here this morning; it was she who certainly had brought up the subject of the lorries again. They said she was seventeen. She looked older, nineteen at the least. Having a child likely did that; and, of course, being under the tuition of Mr Angus Cotton.

He chuckled. Andrew Fowler in his puckish way liked people. He liked these two, and no matter how it worked out he would enjoy giving them a lift. And he wouldn't lose anything by it, of that he was sure. Not if young Cotton got some lorries going, he wouldn't. He nodded inwardly and said, 'By the way, I'm going to look at a site yon side of Durham some time this week. Plastows have got the contract for excavating. He's not all that big and I know that he's often very glad of an extra lorry or two when any of his fellows are laid off, and this can happen, especially after a long run and they get a bit tired and want a break, a couple of weeks' holiday or something. Will I mention your name?'

'Aye, yes. Thank you very much.'

'How are you fixed now?'

'Oh, I'm set for the next month up at the quarry, Peterson's.'

'Well, look me up before that . . . Oh, I forgot; we're most certainly sure to meet before then, aren't we?' He slid off the edge of the table, saying, 'And don't worry too much about this. If I were you I'd go and have a talk with a solicitor. Millard's a good chap. Millard and Fogerty, you know, in the Market Square.'

'Thanks, I'll think about it.'

Angus waited until they reached the outer door, and there, turning to Andrew Fowler, he said, 'Thanks again for everything.'

'A pleasure.' Fowler nodded his head. 'And don't be afraid to pop in any time.'

'I won't. Good-bye.'

'Good-bye, Mrs Cotton.' Andrew Fowler inclined his head towards Vanessa, and she answered, 'Good-bye, Mr Fowler.' She wanted to thank him, but she refrained; Angus had done that.

In the lorry, Angus turned towards home, and presently he said, 'It isn't often you meet blokes like that, is it?'

'No. I think he's very nice; and–and he could be a great help to you.'

He glanced quickly towards her; then back to the wheel again before saying, 'Do you think so?'

'Yes, yes, I do indeed.'

Angus was quiet now. All of a sudden he was wondering why this stranger was going out of his way to help him. Or was he aiming to help himself to something that didn't belong to him? You could never trust blokes and she would catch anybody's eye; and that fellow had a discerning one. Yes, he could say that. He didn't look at her as he asked, 'Is he married?'

Vanessa bit on her bottom lip and with a great effort she did not smile or laugh but answered, 'I don't know.'

'But you had met him before; he said you had.'

'Well, if I did I don't remember.' Then she added a little comfort. 'He's not the kind of man one would remember, is he?' She was learning quickly.

After a while he said, 'When we're down this far I'll drop in at the station yard and see if some spares have arrived; those bits I sent for out of the catalogue, you know. You don't mind waiting a minute?'

She smiled and said, 'No, of course not.'

In the station yard he got out of the cab, saying, 'I won't be a tick,' and she answered, 'Don't hurry. I want a magazine; I'll get it from the stall.'

'Well, come on then.' He held up his arms and gripped her waist and lifted her down. Whenever he touched her now he wanted to kiss her, and his hands stayed on her longer than was necessary. Her face had been smiling when he used to lift her into the garden barrow. Now, as on the very last time he had done this, he saw her expression change, and for the same reason.

She was looking over his shoulder, and he turned round and saw Jonathan Ratcliffe and his wife passing at a distance of not more than six yards, and in spite of his toughness his heart began to bounce and he was filled with apprehension, as if she'd be snatched away from him.

Vanessa's heart, too, was bouncing; she had an almost irresistible urge to run forward. She knew that her mother would have stopped if her father hadn't been there. It was he who had caught sight of her first, and the look he had sent across the distance told her that he didn't know her, nor did he want to.

She stood watching them until they reached the car, then she turned away and was quite unable to check the flood of tears that rained down her face.

'Get up.' His voice was rough and he almost pushed her back into the cab. He revved up the engine as if he were at the start of a race, and he drove out of the yard ahead of Jonathan Ratcliffe's car. 'Bloody nowts!' He was muttering under his breath, swearing with every other word; but she remained silent until they reached the house. And when they entered the kitchen Emily asked, 'What's happened now?' She moved towards Vanessa, then looking quickly at Angus said, 'What is it?'

'I dropped in at the station, and she saw them . . . From up there. And she could have been a mongrel dog for all the notice they took of her.'

When Vanessa sat down at the table and dropped her head on to her arms it was Emily who went to her and said comfortingly, 'Never mind, lass. Never mind. Time heals everything.'

'My–my mother would have stopped. I–I think she would.' She raised her head and looked up at Emily. 'I'm sure she would.'

'Aye, I'm sure she would, lass. But it's him. Men are like that. But one of these days you'll come across your mother on her own and then you can have a crack. You'll see; the opportunity'll present itself, it always does.'

Vanessa now looked towards Angus. His face was hard and tight, and she said, 'I'm not really dying to see them, or anything like that. It's the truth. I would never go back even if I had the chance; but it was just, just coming on them like that.'

'Aye,' he said. Then turning abruptly, he added, 'I'm off.'

She got up hastily and followed him into the passage, and at the door she said quietly, 'After all, Angus, they are my people. You,' her voice dropped to a whisper, 'you–you would defend Emily to the last gasp. You know you would.'

'Aye,' he said again, 'but not if she let me down when I most needed her. That would have finished me. But it's all right.' He put out his hand and tapped her cheek. 'See you later.'

When she returned to the kitchen, Emily said brusquely, 'Take no notice of him. Men look at things differently. Of course you would be upset seein' them; you would have been unnatural if you hadn't. Now go an' wash your face, and I'll make a cup of tea. And then I'm goin' to do a bit of bakin'. I'll show you how; it's about time you learned. You can try your hand at a lemon pie and a fruit loaf; he's fond of both. Go on now.'

Vanessa went into the scullery, and as she sluiced her face under the tap she asked herself why had she to run into her parents at this time. She knew that there was always a possibility of meeting up with her mother, or Susan; her father she was less likely to meet as he was in the works all day. She had often pictured meeting her mother, and she always imagined them talking; there would be an interval filled with embarrassment and then they would come together, and talk, because her mother, although narrow, wasn't as hard grained as her father.

But that she should see both her mother and father on this particular day, and when she was with Angus, was most unfortunate. He had enough to think about with the summons. And that was another thing. They had more than likely heard of the fight; such kind of news travelled fast. In their estimation, she would have now sunk even further, if that were possible.

As she swilled the water around the shallow sink there returned to her a momentary longing for the material comforts of her home, the bathroom in particular, and on this thought came regret that she had turned down the bungalow. Oh, she was tired of it all. She had made a mess of her life, if anyone had.

As despondency flooded over her she gazed at herself in the small mirror on the wall to the side of the sink. Her face looked longer; she looked white and miserable. This was how she looked, and felt, before she took the pills. She stepped back from the mirror as if frightened of what she saw. There must be no more of that; she had caused enough trouble to so many people. Her parents might not want to have anything to do with her; nor anyone from her own class; and she was not unaware she was merely living under kindly toleration from the class she was in now, even from Emily and Rosie; but there was one person who did want her, one person all along who had stood by her, and who needed her. And not only sexually. In an odd sort of way she knew that to him she was the equivalent of a gold medal at the Olympic Games, or of a knighthood; in short, she was an honour. Men needed honour, recognition of having done something, acquired something, something that caused other men to look up to them or hate them as Angus did her father.

Angus and her father were opposed in every way. Yet oddly their aims were the same, both were ambitious for recognition.

She thought it strange that she had this knowledge of them while they hadn't it of themselves.

Chapter Ten

The case was due to be heard on Thursday, a day over three weeks since the summons had been issued.

The tension in the house had been mounting over the last few days, and as Rosie had remarked, on a laugh, last night, the case was causing nearly as much interest in the town as a Cup Final. The lasses in the factory were betting on it, as were the people roundabout the doors. Would Cornell, with his money and influence, win by a length? Or would Cotton, who was defending his wife from insults, romp home? It was anybody's guess.

Vanessa herself was very uneasy. Up till two o'clock on the Wednesday afternoon when she returned home–it was half-day closing–she had made her concern centre around the size of the fine that would be imposed on Angus; she wouldn't allow herself to think of an alternative. But once she entered the house the suppressed dread that Angus could be sent to prison burst into the open and she was forced to face it.

She had just got in the door when Emily, turning to her, said, 'Aw, there you are, lass. You've just missed him by about five minutes. He came in over the moon. He thought old Cargill and Howard were goin' to be on the Bench the morrow, but old Cargill's laid up, and he hears that Mrs Brett's takin' his place; so he'll be all right . . . What's the matter? You feelin' funny?'

'Just a bit. I . . . I felt a bit sick in the train.'

'It's an empty stomach; that's what's the matter with you. Get somethin' down you and you'll be all right.' She walked towards the oven. 'And you're worryin' about the morrow. But you can rest your mind easy; everythin' will go smoothly now. It's ten to one she'll say 'Case Dismissed', like that.' She turned and snapped her fingers towards Vanessa before stooping down and bringing a dish from the bottom shelf. 'Mr Brett thought a lot of our Angus. It was a bad day for him and everybody else when he went. . . . What is it, lass?' She looked towards Vanessa where she was hurrying into the scullery. Then going to the door she said, 'Well, it's better up, whatever it is.'

A few minutes later Vanessa, returning to the kitchen, said, 'Do you mind if I lie down for a minute, Emily? I couldn't eat anything yet.'

'Go on, lass, go on. Put your feet up. I'll bring you a cup of tea in. But try an' get over it afore teatime, for he plans takin' you out somewhere, the pictures, or some place in Newcastle, because, as he says, if we sit here the night we'll be jabberin' about nothin' else but the morrow. He should be home early, he says; there was only a few more loads and they'll be finished up at the quarry. They're not startin' on a new lot until Monday. Go on now.'

In the room Vanessa stood with her back to the door and pressed her hand tightly across her mouth, as if to prevent from escaping the groan that was straining up through her body. Irene Brett being kind to Angus!

The charge was assault occasioning actual bodily harm. They had never put it into words in the house but they all knew that men were sent to prison every day in the week on that charge.

And Irene Brett was to be Angus's judge! Irene knew that Brett was the father of her child. She had seen the knowledge in her eyes the morning Brett died; her look had been full of bleak hate, and it had found its target.

But Irene had said nothing. Why hadn't she come to the house and openly accused her of stealing her husband? Of causing his death? She had asked the question of herself at the time, but now she asked herself no longer for she knew the reason why Irene Brett had remained silent. It had been gall to a woman of her calibre that she should lose anything she considered hers, especially to a young, unformed girl, and one of no particular ability; she had kept silent because she couldn't bear the public ignominy of having been passed over.

But at ten o'clock tomorrow morning she would have her revenge. She'd pay her out through Angus, and it would be the maximum sentence she would give. She could almost see his face stretching in surprise that Mrs Brett should do this to him.

When Emily brought her in the cup of tea she was sitting in the chair by the fire, and Emily said, 'Now why don't you take your shoes off and put your feet up?'

'No; it's passing off a little; I'm all right now.'

'You don't look it. You never had much colour, but you're as white as a sheet. It's the morrow you're worrying about, I know by meself. Me stomach's been as sick as a dog's, but since he was in and told me about Mrs Brett I feel better. She does a lot of good work, does Mrs Brett; she gets things done. Some don't like her. But there it is; if you get things done people don't like you, do they? Now drink that up, and do as I say and put your feet up for a while.'

When she was alone again Vanessa joined her hands tightly between her knees and began to rock herself slightly; then, taking off her shoes, she got to her feet and began to walk from one side of the small room to the other . . . She had to do something. She stopped in her pacing. She would go and see her. NO. NO. That would mean going to Brampton Hill and she couldn't bear to go so near her old home. Would she be able to find her in one of the offices in the Town Hall? But wasn't there some rule about getting at the jury? She shook her head. But she wasn't a jury, she was a magistrate. Well, it might still hold good. And what would she say when she did see her? . . . What could she say? 'Will you please be lenient with Angus?' No, no; that wasn't the line to take with Irene Brett. She picked up the cup of tea from the low table, and although it was still hot she drank it almost at once; and as she put the cup down again she knew what she was going to do.

A few minutes later, when she again entered the kitchen with her coat on, Emily turned to her in surprise, saying, 'Where you off to? What's up?' But all she said was, 'You don't have any stamps, do you?' knowing full well that Emily never had any stamps.

'No. What would I do with stamps, lass?'

'I've run out and I want to write a letter. And Angus will be needing some; there's two letters he must get off tonight.'

'You don't look fit to go out; I'll go along for you.'

'No, no, Emily; the walk will do me good, give me something to do. And when I come back I'll have my dinner.'

'Please yourself. Please yourself.' There was the old tart note in Emily's voice, but Vanessa was used to it now. As Angus said, it meant nothing.

She hurried down to the bottom of the street, walked along the main road to the pedestrian crossing, crossed over and walked a little further up the far pavement to the telephone kiosk. She knew the number; her mother had at one time frequently phoned next door. She stared down at the phone for a full minute before she picked it up. Then she inserted the coins and dialled Fellburn 538506. She knew it wasn't likely that either Colin or Paul would answer the phone; and if the house was running as it had done for some time past there would be no woman there in the afternoon–Irene had no au pair girl now but a daily who came twice a week in the mornings; so it would be Irene or silence.

When she heard Irene Brett's voice her lips moved but she couldn't speak.

'Hello. This is Fellburn 538506.'

'Mrs Brett?' She did not say Auntie Irene, nor yet Irene.

'Yes.' There was a pause. 'Who . . . who's speaking?'

'Vanessa . . . Cotton.' She had almost said Ratcliffe. There was no sound on the line now, and Vanessa said quickly, 'Are you there?'

'What do you want?'

'I just want to tell you something; and . . . and it isn't that Brett was the father of my baby because you already know that, don't you?'

The line seemed to be dead, but Vanessa knew that Irene Brett was still at the other end, and she swallowed and went on, 'What I want to tell you is, that if you take out your spite on me through Angus I'll stand up in Court and shout out the reason why you're doing it. If you send Angus to prison he'll come out again, but you'll never be able to come out from where this town will put you. You'll be fin—' There was no longer anyone on the other end of the line, the receiver had been banged down.

She leant against the dust-covered side of the kiosk and closed her eyes for a second. Would she do what she had said she would if Angus received a prison sentence? Would she stand up and cry 'She's only doing this for spite because her husband gave me a baby?' She didn't know; she wouldn't know until the moment came. She had already made a name for herself in this town, but if she did that her mother and father, the whole family, and she imagined, the family that Susan had married into would be bent low with embarrassment. And once sentence was passed, would it help Angus? Perhaps not; the only thing it would do would be to show him that she cared what happened to him. But again, would Angus thank her for publicly naming the father of her child? He had never pressed her to know who it was, but at times she felt his curiosity. How would he respond when he knew it was 'Mr Brett', the man he admired who had done this to her?

Well, whatever she would do tomorrow morning, the main thing was, she felt, she had convinced Irene Brett that she was quite capable of acting on her word.

She came out of the box and walked farther along the road, until she was opposite the little sub post office. And there she waited for an opportunity to cross . . .

As Vanessa had come out of the kiosk Angus had passed her in the lorry. It was impossible in the traffic to attract her attention, but he went round the island and came back up the other side of the road, and as he parked he saw her going into the post office.

He was waiting for her when she came out, and the first thing she said was, 'How long have you been here?'

'Oh, only a minute. I . . . I saw you as I was passing.' He did not mention seeing her coming out of the phone box, although he wondered who she was phoning; but he said quickly, 'Mam all right?'

Yes, yes, of course. Why shouldn't she be? You were in at dinner time?'

'Oh, aye.' He stared at her. She looked paler than usual, her eyes larger.

'You all right?' he asked.

'I felt a bit sick when I came in. It was the train; it was packed, being Wednesday; I had to stand all the way. Are you finished for the day?'

'Yes,' he answered; 'but I've picked up another bit of business that'll keep Fred and me busy until the start of the quarry again. Come on, get in; I can't leave her parked here. And I'll have a cuppa before I put her away.'

Seated next to her, he said, 'Where to, modam?'

Taking his cue, she replied, 'Twenty-four Ryder's Row, Cotton.'

'Very good, modam.'

He had to drive to the next side turning, back into it, and come down the main road again before he could enter the street, and as he drove he thought, 'Why hasn't she said who she was phoning?'

When they entered the house Emily greeted them with, 'Oh, there you are. Going out in ones and coming in in twos. I suppose you want a cuppa.'

'That's the idea.' He nodded at her.

Then she said to him, 'I think you should see she goes and lies down; she's out of sorts.' She jerked her head towards Vanessa.

'Now, does she ever take notice of anything I say?' He was keeping things light.

Vanessa went into the room and took her coat off, and a few minutes later he joined her. He had a cup of tea in his hand and, sitting down and crossing his legs, he looked at her and asked casually, 'Who were you phoning?'

He watched her mouth open and close again and her expression changed, her face becoming even paler; and he uncrossed his legs and said, 'Well, who were you? I saw you coming out of the box.'

She was so taken aback that she hadn't a lie on her lips. He got to his feet and moved slowly towards her, the cup of tea still in his hand, and after surveying her for a moment he asked thickly, 'What's the mystery?'

'There's no mystery.'

'All right then,' he inclined his head towards her patiently, 'who were you phoning? It's as simple as that. Give me a straight answer. Who were you phoning?'

When she didn't answer at all but made to turn from him he put the cup down noisily on the table, grabbing her arm at the same time. Then pulling her round to him, he looked deep into her face as he said, 'You weren't in the telephone box to rob it, were you? And you weren't in there to do wilful damage, were you? You were in there to phone . . . Who were you phoning?'

'A–a girl in the shop.'

'But the shop's closed this afternoon,'' His voice was very low and ominously quiet.

'I know the shop's closed this afternoon. I–I phoned at her home.'

'What's her name?'

This was easy. 'Teresa Bumpstead.''

'And her number?'

Could she think of a number? Of all the thousands, the millions of numbers in all the directories in the country she couldn't think of one number. All she could remember was that all Newcastle numbers began with 53, and she stammered 'Five, three . . .'

'Don't think too hard,' he said. Then, his voice rising slightly, he added, 'Are you going to tell me the truth?'

If she said 'I was phoning Mrs Brett,' he would say, 'what the hell did you want to do that for? She's on my side.' And he would believe this until tomorrow, when he found she wasn't.

'You were phoning your house, weren't you?'

'Oh, no! No, Angus.' Her voice was high with relief. 'No, I wouldn't do that.' She watched his face relax for a moment, then tighten again as he said, 'Well then, it was some bloke . . . Fowler. You were phoning Fowler?'

'Oh, Angus!' She closed her eyes and put her hand to her cheek and smiled faintly. 'Why would I want to phone Mr Fowler?'

'Because he's breaking his neck to help me, and all the while I'm wondering why; and I tell meself I haven't far to look for the reason. Why would he want to help me if it wasn't for you being a sort of distant family connection? . . . And mind,' he stabbed his finger at her, 'I'm being kind when I think along those lines, because he's got an eye wide open, he has.'

'Don't be silly.' Her voice was harsh now; it was a woman's voice showing impatience with an unreasonable man.

'All right.' He turned and walked to the fireplace. 'If it wasn't Fowler, then tell me who it was. Look.' He swung round and glared at her fiercely. 'It's as easy as that. Just tell me who you were phoning, because I'll not let up on you until I know. I'm made like that. It'll niggle and niggle at me mind, getting bigger and bigger every minute. I've got a mind that makes mountains out of molehills where you're concerned. You know that already, don't you, and you're playing on it?'

'I'm not, Angus. That's unfair; I'm not. I don't play on people's emotions.'

Dropping down into the chair, he said, 'All right, I'll be reasonable. Let's start from the beginning, eh? You went to the phone; I saw you coming out. You must have gone to phone somebody. I've asked you a simple question and you can't give me a simple answer. Now this is how I look at it. If you've nothing to hide why can't you tell me truthfully who you were phoning?'

She stared down into his face; then said slowly, 'All right, Angus; I'll tell you who I was phoning . . . tomorrow dinnertime.'

He screwed up his eyes at her. 'After the case you mean? Is it to do with the case?'

'Yes and no. There's more to it than that.'

'But why did you . . .? Who did you get in touch with? Look. I'll be all right; you've got no need to worry.' He got to his feet and gripped her arms. 'If you're worrying about me, stop it. I've got a good solicitor. And there's our Mr Fowler.' He smiled a tight smile and made a deep obeisance with his head. 'And above all, I've got somebody on the right side of the Bench, Mrs Brett.'

She lowered her head slightly and she kept her eyes shadowed with her lashes as she said, 'I'll tell you tomorrow. Have patience with me, Angus. As I said, there's more in it than that, I mean the case. I–I promise you I'll tell you tomorrow.'

After staring at her bent head for a moment his grip on her arms tightened and he shook her once before grinding out below his breath, 'You're not going to walk out on me, are you? That's not what you're going to tell me?'

She was looking at him, half-smiling now, as she said quietly, 'No, Angus, that's not what I'm going to tell you.'

He drew in a deep, shivering breath, and after a moment he said, 'Reprieved. For a while at any rate. But one of these days you will, won't you, Van? You'll say to me; I've had enough, I'm going back . . . And you know what I'll do on that day . . . do you? Do you know what I'll do? I'll kill you. I mean it.' He nodded his head at her.

She gave a little huh of a laugh and unwittingly her smile held derison as she said, 'Well, I won't have to tell you, will I, because now I want to stay alive at least a little longer.'

He couldn't stand being laughed at, or taken lightly. He turned away and punched his fist into the palm of one hand, then went to the little table in the corner and sat down, and, picking up the letters that had come that morning, he read them once more. One was a request for his estimate on clearing a building site. It had been sent to him direct, and not to Fred–although Fred always passed any correspondence on to him–and he felt he had Andrew Fowler to thank for it. A lot might depend, he knew, not only on his estimate, but how he got it out and also on the accompanying letter.

He put his hand slowly up to the little bookcase and lifted down Fowler's 'King's English,' and opened it at a page on which the heading read: 'On sustained metaphor'. A page of Egyptian hieroglyphics would have posed no greater problem, and he did at this odd moment what he had been wanting to do for weeks, but had been too proud to voice his need. 'Will you take me through this?' he said. He lifted up the book to shoulder height but did not turn round, and when she did not answer he moved his head slowly until he had her in the corner of his eye. Then he said, 'It'll be a laugh for you. I've made so many bloomers you could fill a book. 'Those are them' won't be in it. I've got some prize ones.'

She was standing by the side of the table now, and she looked into his face, saying softly, 'Don't, Angus.'

'Don't what?'

She did not add, 'You know what I mean,' and he pushed it no further.

Taking the book from his hand, she looked at it, saying softly, 'I'd love to help you, you know that. There's a lot I don't know, although English was my best subject. We,' she glanced down at him, 'we could learn together.'

He covered her hand on the book, pressing it hard, saying, 'You know, this is only another ruse to keep you, you know that, don't you? Everything I do is aimed at keeping you.' He was looking at her in a way he sometimes did, like a small boy who was asking to be needed, and loved. But he wasn't a small boy, he was a man, a rough, arrogant, bumptious man, who would, as he said, kill her if he thought she was going to leave him.

The issue seemed to have moved away from the telephone box to the region of raw emotions, but she could cope with this. And so she turned from him, saying, 'Go and put the lorry away. I haven't had any lunch yet; I'll get it, and then we'll go out.' She half turned her head. 'You were thinking of going out, weren't you?'

'Who told you that? Oh, me mam. She can't keep her mouth shut, that one.' He rose swiftly and stalked out of the room, and she heard him crying to Emily, 'You and your big mouth, Ma Cotton; you can't even let me spring a little surprise on me own.'

He was covering up the things that hurt and embarrassed him. During the past half hour he had been the questioning jealous husband, the young man pleading for education, two kinds of small boy, one loving, one rough, loud-mouthed, but threading all his attitudes was a man with a deep need.

There came, in the region of her heart, a restricted feeling that turned into an ache. The ache spread until her body was filled with it. If he went to prison, what would she do? She'd be lost. Yes, without him she'd be lost. She–she was in love with him. No; not just in love, she loved him. How had it come about that she should love Angus Cotton because he was . . .? She didn't tell herself all the things he was, but she went over all the things he wasn't. Was, or wasn't, it didn't matter; what did matter was that if he went to prison she wouldn't live until he came out again. She loved him.

They shouted to Angus as he and Vanessa went down the street the following morning: 'Good luck, lad.' It was as if they had been waiting behind their doors for him. One wit cracked, 'See you at the assizes, Angus,' and Angus turned a laughing face towards the man and shouted, 'And I wouldn't be surprised at that an' all, Jim.'

'Ten years' hard, you'll get, Angus, ten years, not a day less. You might as well have been in the train robbery.'

'Aye, Mrs Grant, you're right there; I might as well.'

When they were on the bus he turned to her and said, 'They were enjoying themselves, weren't they?' There was a kind of pain in the back of his eyes, and she answered softly, 'I don't think they meant to be unkind.'

'Huh!' He jerked his chin up. 'You defending 'me ain folk'? Oh, I know them, I know them all like the back of me hand. They'll all come round and help you when you're in trouble, but that doesn't stop them being happy that you are in trouble, somebody else is getting it, not them . . . Do you follow me?'

Yes, in a way she did follow him, and she was surprised at the depth of his knowledge concerning his . . . ain folk, as he called them.

He kept on talking. 'Human nature all over, that is. If you move away from the street you're a nowt, an upstart; if you stay in the street you're a stick-in-the-mud, you've got no gumption. You can never be right. I used to worry about it at one time.' He turned his face fully towards her. 'Can't imagine me worrying, can you?'

'Yes, Angus, yes, I can imagine you worrying.' She had a desire to take his hand; he was worrying now. He had been worrying since he got up. He had never stopped talking, which was proof that he was worrying.

'I used to worry because I couldn't get Mam into a better house. I used to worry because I hadn't got a decent job; then when I got promoted I used to worry in case I got demoted. Still do. And the more I worry the louder I yell.' His mouth was wide now and his smile cynical. 'I've been yelling since I got up, haven't I.''

She wanted to laugh, she wanted to cry. She touched his fingers and found her hand grasped painfully tight.

They got out at the market square and walked across the open space which, tomorrow, would be packed with stalls, and went through the iron gates that guarded the flower-decked space in front of the Town Hall where the Court was being held, and at the bottom of the steps he said, 'Are you sure you want to come in?'

'Yes, yes, I want to be there.'

'You've a stronger stomach than me Mam. Funny isn't it, she just couldn't stand to come and hear it. You'd think I was going to get the long drop. Oh, there they are,' he said under his breath, as he saw the solicitor standing in the distance talking to Andrew Fowler. And he added, 'I hope they look as happy when it's all over.'

The two men were laughing together as Angus and Vanessa came up to them, but they stopped immediately, and when Angus introduced Vanessa to the solicitor, he inclined his head deeply and said, 'How do you do, Mrs Cotton?'

She always felt it strange to be addressed as Mrs Cotton.

'Our–our opponents are already seated,' said Andrew Fowler to Angus, 'and our Mr Cornell's face is still showing signs of the fray.' He slanted his glance sideways at Angus. 'It's a good job old Cargill's indisposed and you have Mrs Brett to deal with.'

'Yes, indeed, indeed,' said the solicitor. 'Although when I saw her upstairs a few minutes ago she looked as if it was a murder charge she had on her hands. Likely suffering from indigestion. But usually she's fair, except for desertion or maintenance, and then, oh dear, does she jump on them. But as you're up for neither,' he glanced with a thin smile at Vanessa, 'I think we're fairly certain of having her on our side.'

His tone changing, he now spoke directly to Angus, saying, 'The main issue as I see it is: you were protecting your wife; he was making a nuisance of himself and did it repeatedly . . . not once, but repeatedly. You had warned him, but he would take no heed. You know the line to take. You were protecting your wife from being annoyed. Mr Fowler, here, will vouch for all that; we have been all over it. Ah, here we go.' He answered the summons of a policeman standing before two double doors at the far end of the hall and he went forward. Angus followed, walking at one side of Vanessa, while Andrew Fowler walked at the other. And so they entered the Court.

Half-an-hour later they re-entered the hall and they stood in a circle, and looked at each other; then Mr Millard said almost angrily, 'It's preposterous, ridiculous. She was utterly bitchy.' He looked from Andrew Fowler to Vanessa, and then to Angus again, and repeated, 'Utterly, absolutely bitchy. Old Cargill wouldn't have made it anything near as stiff as that even at his worst. It was the maximum.'

Angus said nothing. He felt stunned. He was remembering how Mrs Brett had looked at him as she said, 'You're lucky I am not passing a prison sentence on you. I am dealing with you leniently this time, but should you come before this Court again on a similar charge then there'll be no option of a fine, I can assure you of that. This town can do without your sort. Too long we have put up with big heads and bruisers: it has got to stop. Decent people can't have an evening out, or approach an old friend, but they are punched in the face. Their teeth are knocked out . . .'

It was as if she had got the wrong fellow. All she had said to him she should have said to Cornell. And he wasn't the only one who thought so; the whole Court seemed confused. Even Cornell was surprised. Pleased; oh aye, pleased, but nevertheless he was surprised . . . Mrs Brett! Angus couldn't understand it. He had spoken to her numbers of times since he was a lad; and it was her husband who had pushed him on. He just couldn't understand it. It was as if she had hated his guts. One hundred pounds and costs! It was unbelievable. And besides that, she could have sent him along the line for six months. She had said so. What was the matter with him anyway? Everything was hitting him. It was coming at him from all sides.

He looked along the hall now to where his solicitor and Cornell's were chatting amiably together, quietly and amiably together. Somehow he thought that shouldn't be. Yet they did it on the telly, try to cut each other's throats in the courtroom and pat each other on the back when they came out of it, like 'The Defenders'.

He wanted to get home out of this; he wanted to think. He felt he had been dealt a dirty deal somehow. He thought again: Mrs Brett! Mrs Brett! All right, she could have fined him, but to slam into him in front of everybody like that as if he was one of the local tearaways, why? Why? He said abruptly to Vanessa, 'Come on, out of this.'

'Just a minute.' It was Andrew Fowler touching him on the arm. 'I know you're puzzled,' he said soothingly. 'So am I. So are they all. But it's over and done with . . . Listen, did you get a letter this morning from Fenwick?'

'Fenwick!' Angus had to think, and Vanessa put in quietly, 'Yes, Yes, about estimates.'

'Oh aye, I've got a letter.'

'Well, it'll be O.K.,' said Andrew Fowler; 'I'll see to it. Make yourself a good margin. You might have to hire a couple more lorries and more men. Pop in tomorrow and we'll have a word'

'Aye, all right. Thanks.' He spoke as if in a daze, and his 'Thanks' was desultory, and Vanessa, looking at Andrew Fowler, said firmly, 'Thank you, Mr Fowler.'

'It's a pleasure.'

He watched them going down the steps. The smile had gone from his face now and he was nipping his lip. There was something fishy here. Why had Mrs Brett flayed him like that? Evidently he didn't know, he had looked flabbergasted. Cotton had counted on her being on the Bench–her husband had apparently been a kind benefactor to him when he worked at Affleck and Tate's. Had she taken that attitude because her neighbour's daughter had stepped over the rails? But that was nothing to her, surely. There was something here he would like to get to the bottom of. He liked to get to the bottom of things. Knowledge was power even if you didn't use it. He wondered how he could go about finding out. Well, something would happen that would give him a lead; it usually did.

Three days later not only had he a lead but the whole reason why Irene Brett had come down like a ton of bricks on Angus Cotton.

Chapter Eleven

'It's a bloody shame!' everybody said. They called to him across the main road; 'Just heard, Angus. It's a bloody shame.' They said it in the street: 'A hundred quid and costs! It's a bloody shame, Angus.'

Emily said it standing behind the kitchen table. 'She didn't!' she said. 'Mrs Brett? No. One hundred pounds and costs? Oh, no! lad.

'She did. But that's not all, Mam. You should have heard her. I mean, if she had gone for Cornell in the same way I could have understood it, everybody could have understood it, couldn't they, Van?' He turned towards Vanessa, but all Vanessa did was nod her head. 'She flayed me in front of everybody, talked to me as if I was a tough, running scatty, knocking people on the head in the main street, telling me what she would do if I came afore her again? You know what I feel like doing? . . . Going along there and asking her why, I do, honest to God, Mam.'

Vanessa went into the room, took off her coat and stood waiting. In a short while he would get over this shock to some extent, and then he would say, 'Ah now, time's up. You're going to tell me who you phoned yesterday.' So she wouldn't wait for that, she'd come straight to the point.

When he entered the room she turned stiffly towards him and, looking him straight in the face, said, 'I can tell you, Angus, why she did it.'

'You?' He moved near to her. 'You mean you know why she got at me?'

'Yes . . . You–you wanted to know who I phoned yesterday. Well–well it was her.'

'Mrs Brett?' His eyes were screwed up tightly at the corners.

'Yes; I–I phoned her because I knew that when you came up before her this morning she would get at me through you; I was afraid she would give you a prison sentence. I threatened that if she did I would shout it out in the Court.'

'Shout what out? What are you talking about, girl? You all right?'

'YES! YES!'' She had almost yelled. Then clamping her hand over her mouth, she bowed her head and said, 'She hates me because . . . because she knows who was the father of the baby.' Her head bent lower and her voice was hardly audible as she ended, 'It was Brett, her husband.'

From underneath her lowered lids she could see his body up to the waist, and it was perfectly still. Then his silence forced her to raise her head and the expression on his face turned her cold. It had in it the essence of incredulity, but something more, a surprising quality for him to show towards her, disgust. His lips moved well back from his upper teeth before he said, 'Mister Brett and you!'

Her head was moving down again and her voice was a whimper. 'It just happened. He–he was very sad, lonely, unhappy . . .'

'Christ!' The exclamation was like a crack of a whip. 'Aren't all old married men unhappy, lonely, sad? But that doesn't mean you've got to lie with them . . . You and Brett! He was as old as your father . . . Brett!'

As he continued to stare at her he remembered that he had always liked Mr Brett, that Mr Brett had been kind to him, but he also remembered, and with a sense of deep shock, that when he wondered who had given her a bairn he had imagined it to be a lad of her own age. He had imagined him carried away on the first real wave of emotion and being borne under with the pressure of it. He had imagined them both fumbling at the act without enjoying it; then the boy skulking away and keeping his tongue quiet while she carried the can. He had even admired her for not revealing who the young fellow was . . . But she had been under the hands of no young fellow, she had been with a man old enough to be her grandfather; aye, he could have been her grandfather.

He had the urge now to take her by the neck and choke her. He had been made a fool of. She had let everybody blame him while she could have put a stop to it, a real stop to it, by naming the fellow next door . . . But there hadn't been any fellow next door had there when the balloon went up? No, he had skedadled, gone touring, supposedly getting orders for the firm; and when he came back and found what happened to her, what did he do? He hanged himself. It was a pity he hadn't done it earlier. How often had he had her?

There was a strange feeling in him now. He didn't want to go near her, or touch her. When she said, 'Angus, I'm sorry. Don't look like that. It–it was a sort of accident; it only happened . . .' he put in quickly, 'I don't want to hear.' He curled his lip at her. 'But you know something. I'll tell you something. I thought you had been let down by a young lad, and I could understand that and I could put up with it, but not when it was a bloke like Brett, with a son as old as me, and two others.'

He walked towards the door, then turned to her and said in a tone that was frightening because for him it was quiet, 'You're no better than the rest. You know something? I wouldn't marry May because I found she'd been with other blokes. Bit illogical you might say, when I've had my whack, but I'm made that way. I stomached what happened to you because, as I said, I though it was a slip between two young 'uns, not a calculated get-together, as it must have been atween you and him, because a man of Brett's age wouldn't jump in feet first, he'd know he'd have to tread warily until he was sure of his ground. And he was sure, wasn't he?'

She was so stunned by his attitude that she could make no reply. All her mother and father had said, the treatment she had received from her friends, nothing she had gone through, affected her like Angus's reaction.

When he went out of the room he didn't band the door behind him. Presently she head the murmur of his voice coming from the scullery. He would be telling Emily.

He had no need to tell Emily, she already knew. She had picked enough up from standing at the kitchen door to put two and two together, and now she was looking at her son and saying bitterly, 'What are you going to do?'

'Nothing.' He looked out of the scullery window. 'Damn all. What's the good of raking up muck, you only get more smells, and at the present moment me nose is full of them. I couldn't stand any more.'

'I thought it must have been a young lad.'

'Aye.' He turned and looked at her. 'Aye, that's what I thought an' all; and I took the rap because of that. But do you think for a moment if I'd guessed it had been Brett I would have? As sorry as I was for her, I would have seen her in hell first.'

'Mr Brett. MR BRETT. He was a quiet, refined, gentlemanly . . .'

'Oh, Mam, for God's sake come off it. Gentlemanly. They do it an' all; even royalty has to be born. What's maddening me is that I've been made the scapegoat and that bitch on the bench finished it the day. She's right about one thing though . . .' He jerked his head back towards the room. 'It's ten to one if she hadn't got on the phone yesterday and threatened what she might do I might quite easily be along the line at this minute.'

Emily shuddered. She knew that what he said was true; he could easily have been along the line. That lot! That lot! Look what they had done to her lad. Turned him into a lorry driver when he should have been in the drawing office. Then fining him a hundred pounds and blamin' him for the bairn, when all the time it was Mr Brett.

She was working herself up into a fury when Angus said, 'I'm going.'

'Where? Where you off to?'

'To get the lorries ready.'

'What time will you be back?'

'I don't know.' His voice was flat.

She followed him to the yard door and, her voice a low murmur in case someone was sitting in the lavatory beyond the wall, their ears' cocked, she said, 'Don't go and get sozzled; that won't solve matters.'

He turned and looked at her once, then moved away down the back lane; and she returned to the scullery, and as she stood gripping her forearms with each hand her anger mounted into a white blaze, strangely not against Vanessa, but against her parents, and the Bretts, the whole family of Bretts, those two grown-up sons who must have been stone blind not to guess what their father was up to.

She was thinking along similar lines to Angus. This thing couldn't have happened like the snap of your fingers. There must have been some outward sign somewhere, to show that Brett–she did not now think of him as Mr Brett–had his sights on the young lass next door. And next door? Had they been stone blind an' all? God-Almighty Ratcliffe and his missus? And the things they said. Aye. She was recalling practically every word they had said to her regarding Angus, and the manner in which they had said it.

Her anger seemed to lend wings to her feet now and she was upstairs donning her hat and coat and downstairs again within a few minutes. Opening a cupboard, she grabbed up her handbag, looked in it to see if she had enough for the fare, then went out of the house, taking the well-known road towards Brampton Hill again.

Chapter Twelve

Irene Brett was pouring tea in the drawing-room. It was seldom she had tea in this room; except when there were visitors, and they were few and far between. But today she was serving tea in the drawing-room because Paul was home. It was the first day of the Easter vac and tomorrow he would be off on another of his walking tours. She had little time to impress him, and her future lay very much in his hands; in fact, how long she could remain in this house depended on him.

If everything had gone to Colin, as it should have done, he being the eldest son, she would have known a sense of security, whereas now she felt she was dealing with a younger edition of her husband. She had urged Colin to contest the will, but for some reason or other he wouldn't. This was another thing that irked her; although the brothers were as different in character as chalk from cheese there was an affinity between them that she had no part of.

Her object now was to persuade Paul to sell some of the mouldering antiques in order that she might have the ground floor, at least, redecorated. When she had broached the subject at Christmas he had said neither yes nor no to the matter. He was like his father there, a ditherer . . . His father! When she thought of his father she knew she wouldn't live long enough to erase the hate of him that burned in her. She had always known she was capable of strong emotions, but she had never imagined that a man like Arthur, a weak, vacillating creature such as he could have aroused in her this unrelenting feeling of hate and resentment. And then there was that girl . . . Her thoughts sank into the depths and dragged up adjectives, and it was as much as she could do not to voice them. She had a picture of Vanessa sitting in Court staring at her, daring her to do what she most desired, send Angus Cotton down. She wished now she had defied her threat and done it. Oh, if only she had.

'Been a busy day for you?'

She brought her face round to her son, whom she couldn't look at without seeing his father, and she made herself say lightly, 'So-so, rather upsetting; some cases tend to be upsetting.'

'You take it all too seriously.'

'Perhaps.'

'You should have a holiday.'

'You know I can't have a holiday, Paul.'

He was silent, and the feeling of guilt that he always had now when he was with her mounted. He knew that within a few minutes she would bring up the subject again about selling the furniture. He supposed he would have to give in; although he would like to keep things intact as his father had done. But times were changing. Sooner or later the whole place would have to go, house, land, the lot. It was too big anyway for any one family these days. It had been too big for years. He wished he could feel more sympathy towards her but somehow he couldn't. He had never been able to understand the driving force that animated her thin body. There was too much of his father in him, he supposed. Poor Dad. When his thoughts were touched with pity he always addressed his father in his mind as Dad. He had wanted so little, and that's what he got, so little. He wished that tomorrow was here and he could get away. The house wasn't the same. Nothing was the same. Perhaps he had grown up suddenly, or perhaps it was the events that had happened in the last year. Whatever it was, life didn't appear bright and starry any more.

When the ring came on the bell he rose and said, 'I'll take it'; and when he opened the front door there stood Emily Cotton. After a moment's pause he said, 'Emily! Oh, hello, Emily.'

'You mother in?' No 'Master Paul' now.

'Mother? Yes, Yes. You want to see her?'

'Yes, I want to see her.'

There was something wrong here; Emily was in fighting mood. He said, 'Come in a minute,' and when she'd walked past him and stood in the hall he closed the door and went quickly towards the drawing-room door, which he pushed behind him but not closed before he went to his mother and said softly, 'It's Emily, Emily Cotton, you know.'

He watched the cold blue of her eyes turn to a steely grey and her narrow jaws tighten.

'Will I bring her in?'

'No, I'll see her in the hall . . . Stay here.'

When she entered the hall she closed the drawing-room door behind her, then looked at the cheaply dressed, unshapely woman, and, aiming to take command of the situation, she said, 'Yes, Emily. What can I do for you?'

'Don't you come that tone with me, Mrs Brett; you know what you can do for me. By! you've got a nerve. You know what you are?' Emily advanced two steps. 'You're a vindicative bitch, that's what you are.'

'How dare you! And stop shouting, woman. You forget yourself.'

'I'm tellin' you not to come that line with me. I'm not forgettin' meself; you're the one, Mrs Magistrate, who forgot yourself when you were up on that bench this mornin'. You forgot why you were put there. You were put there for justice, not to dish out personal spite. An' that's what you did, didn't you? If it hadn't been for Vanessa phoning you and threatenin' you yesterday that she would broadcast who was the father of her bairn if you sent my Angus along the line, you would have done just that, wouldn't you. You would have sent him up for six months, just to get back at her.'

'Be quiet, woman! And get out.' Irene was hissing at her now.

But Emily had no intention of being quiet or of leaving until she had had her say, and she said it even louder now.

'Be quiet, you say. When I'm ready an' not afore. I tell you again you're a bloody, vindictive bitch, and that's swearing to it. Your man took a young lass down, a schoolgirl, and then he took his life because he couldn't face it. An' you knew about it; you knew this all the time my lad was being blamed for givin' her this bairn, but you let it go on. Councillor Mrs Irene Brett, Magistrate, Chairman of this an' God knows what else, couldn't stand the racket of being shown up . . .'

'Get out! Do you hear me. GET OUT.'

'Aye, I'll get out, but I'm not goin' very far, just to your neighbours . . .'

'You wouldn't dare!'

'I wouldn't what?' Emily was bawling now. 'You tell me what I wouldn't dare?'

'I forbid you, woman.' They were standing close to each other now, Irene's words spitting between her teeth. 'Do you hear. I forbid you. This is between her and me . . . Vanessa.'

'Aw, but that's where you've made a mistake. It's not atween you and Vanessa, it's atween you and my lad. His name's been blackened all over this town, and beyont. He had dared to step over the white line and have an affair with one of his betters, that's what was said. A few years ago they would have had him flogged. Old Ratcliffe would have taken a horsewhip to him. Something similar was done to one of the grooms from Brampton Manor, an' that was in the thirties, not so very long ago. But times have changed, except on the bench, where there's upstarts like you . . . An' don't you call me woman . . .' She thrust her lower jaw outwards. 'I'm clearin' me lad's name.

If it's the last thing I do I'll do that, an' people won't have to guess why he got it hot and hard from you this mornin'.'

'It will be you who'll be in Court next if you're not careful.' Irene's voice was trembling now, as was her whole body.

'All right, summons me, but you'll have to give me a summons for telling the truth. That's how you'll have to word it. Emily Cotton accused of telling the truth, the suppressed truth.'

Emily's eyes were brought for a moment from Irene Brett's bleached face to the open drawing-room door, where stood Paul, so changed that she thought for a moment she was looking at his father.

She turned now and walked towards the front door, and after she had opened it she jerked her head round to give one parting shot, but checked it as she saw Irene Brett and her son staring at each other. She had said enough, she was satisfied, in this quarter anyway. Mrs Magistrate had her son to deal with, and from the looks of him she was going to have her work cut out.

Her body was still quivering with indignation, she marched down the drive along the road, through the open gates and to the house in which, as she herself had said, she had spent a greater length of time over the past eighteen years than she had in her own home. She did not take the tradesman's path to the back door but made for the front door, and as she looked at the car standing on the drive she thought, 'Good. Madam Susan's here.' Then she pressed the bell with her thumb, holding it tight for some seconds.

The door was opened by a young woman who was wearing a small frilled apron over an ordinary housedress, which in itself told Emily that there was company. 'Yes?' said the woman, looking her up and down.

'Your missus in?'

'What do you want?'

'You tell Mrs Ratcliffe that Emily's here and wants to see her. Just say that.' Then she put her hand out quickly, adding. 'You needn't close the door; I'm not goin' to pinch anything; I worked here when you were still in nappies. Go and tell her.'

The young woman's eyes were wide, but she made no further protest; she had heard of Emily Cotton. Emily followed her slowly and stood in the hall, and as she waited her eyes roamed around, and she noted, with some chagrin, that everything looked as usual. When the lounge door opened the maid came out alone and said to her, 'The mistress will see you in a minute.' Then she went on into the kitchen, and Emily waited. She waited a full three minutes before her late mistress made her appearance.

Jane Ratcliffe closed the lounge door carefully behind her; then, coming slowly forward, she said unsmilingly, 'Good-afternoon, Emily.'

Emily did not return the greeting but said, 'Do you know why I'm here . . .?' she had almost said ma'am but checked herself in time.

'No, Emily, I don't know why you're here.'

'I've come for an apology.'

'For what?'

'You heard, for an apology.'

'Come–come into the morning-room, please.'

'No, I'm not goin' into any morning-room, missus; what I've got to say I'll say here, where there's ears cocked at the doors, an' they'll be my witnesses . . . Is he in?'

'If you're referring to the master, no, he's not, Emily.' Jane Ratcliffe's voice was trembling.

'That's a pity. That is a pity, because it's him I want to see more than you; but you can pass on what I've got to say. I suppose you know about my lad being up afore the Bench this mornin'. He was up there because he was defending your daughter–for the second time mind–against a man who was pestering her, and what did he get? He gets fined one hundred pounds an' costs. And, you know, he was lucky to just get fined. If it hadn't been for Van phonin' next door yesterday an' tellin' Madam Councillor, Mrs Irene Brett, that she would stand up in Court this mornin' and yell the truth at her if she dared send my Angus along the line, he would have been along the line at this minute.'

'Emily! Emily, please, come into the morning-room.'

'I'm not goin' into any mornin'-room; you can save your breath. And I haven't finished yet. You know what Van was goin' to shout at Mrs Brett, do you?' She bent her body almost double. 'She was goin' to shout out the name of the man who gave her the bairn, an' the name was Mr Brett. Your esteemed neighbour . . . Mr Brett! That's who gave her the bairn. And his wife knew it, she knew it; an' she knew it was because of that he committed suicide . . . Aye,' her voice dropped a tone lower as she looked at Jane Ratcliffe supporting herself by the banister. 'I thought you would need some support. But you didn't think me or me lad needed any support, did you? You made him out to be the scum of the earth. He was accused of takin' Van down because he had been seen talkin' to her once or twice, and all the time under your very noses a man old enough to be her grandfather was having his fun with her; an' you knew nowt about it. Of course, of course.' Her voice changed. 'You could trust people like Mr Brett; he was a gentleman. The same goes for Mr Brian Cornell, another gentleman. He can say what he likes and gets off with it, but because my lad had neither money or position he didn't stand a chance.'

'Will you please go, Emily!' Jane Ratcliffe's voice had a far-away sound to it. She was standing stiffly upright now staring straight ahead, and Emily said, 'Aye, I'll go when I say this. My Angus is a bloody fool, that's what he is, for, knowin' that he was playing into your hands, he goes an' marries her. He marries her out of sympathy 'cos he finds her living in a filthy dump in Newcastle. Do you know Batterby Bay Road? No. I don't suppose you do. But your husband will. Oh, aye, there's not a man in this county who doesn't know of Batterby Bay Road. It's where the prostitutes hang out, an' that's where he found her. And he brought her from there an' married her, and he hadn't,' she paused, 'he hadn't given her the bairn . . .'

The lounge door was pulled sharply open at this stage and it checked Emily's spate, and she watched Susan Ratcliffe, or Braintree as she now was, going quickly towards her mother, saying, 'Come along, dear. Come along.'

As Susan put her arms round her mother she turned and looked at Emily and said, 'I think you'd better go. You've had your say, now get out.'

The young man standing in the doorway didn't speak, but he looked at Emily for a full minute and she at him before she said, 'Aye, I'll go. But I haven't finished me say yet; this town's goin' to hear the truth. Your lot's treated my lad as if he was a Geordie lout, an' there's not one of you fit to wipe his boots. Well, now we'll see what the town thinks and how the so-called gentleman from next door'll stand up against Angus Cotton.'

There were two reactions to Emily's outburst. The one in Bower Place was that Jonathan Ratcliffe refused to listen to his wife's pleas to move. Angus Cotton wasn't putting him on the run. All right, let the town know, let them talk, but he wasn't going to be frightened out of his home by that young slob.

He was still fighting Angus Cotton, more so now than ever, because Angus Cotton had got the better of him. He was in the right and the town would be laughing. Oh yes, behind their hands they would be laughing. Young Cotton had taken the blame of giving Ratcliffe's daughter a child just so that he could marry her and get his foot in.

Jonathan Ratcliffe was still convinced that Angus Cotton's motive in marrying Vanessa was to inveigle himself into her family's good books.

The other reaction took place in the kitchen in No. 24 between Emily and Angus. He had been utterly astounded when she told him where she had been. For a moment he could say nothing, then his wrath poured over her. She was a bloody, silly old cow, an interfering, stupid old swine. Why the hell couldn't she mind her own business! Hadn't there been enough talk and tittle-tattle without her going stirring things up? All right, all right, he knew he had been wrongly accused, nobody knew better, but that was his business.

'Thanks!' Emily screamed. 'Thanks! That's what I get. You're a bloody, ungrateful sod. Your name's been mud in this place for months now, aye, even round the doors. They said you had a nerve, and it was a dirty trick to take a young lass down like that an' her still at school, and a convent into the bargain. Virgin huntin' in the right place, they said. Taking advantage of his mother being up there, they said. Well then, I was determined they weren't goin' to say that no longer; they were going to know the truth an' this is what I get.'

'You haven't got half of it yet. For two pins I'd slap yer mouth for you.'

'Begod you would!' She thrust her hand back and grabbed up a large sauce bottle from the dresser; but at this moment Vanessa came out of the room. She stood in the doorway and, her voice louder than it had ever been raised in this house or anywhere before, she cried, 'Stop it! Stop it! I'm sick of you, do you hear, the both of you. I'm sick of your shouting and fighting. You're like wild animals, the pair of you. That's all you are, wild animals.'

Perhaps it was surprise that silenced them, for they both turned towards her and made no reply; they just looked at her. Her hair was tangled as if she had been running her hands through it; her clothes looked dishevelled as if she had been lying in them; her face was bloated with crying; she looked tired and weary, but above all she looked an angry woman. 'All right!' she said. 'I'm the cause of all this, but I'm going to end it, I'm leaving.' She was looking at Angus directly now, 'Do you hear me? I'm leaving?' When he still made no comment she went into the room and banged the door.

There was now exchanged between Emily and Angus a shame-faced look before he went slowly across the kitchen and into the room. With his back to the door he stood for a moment watching her pulling her dresses from the hanging wardrobe in the corner, and when she had put them in the case he approached her and said grimly, 'What d'you think you're doing?'

She glanced up at him with a look that was new, because it was defiant. She was looking at him as May might have looked at him when she was on the point of telling him to go to hell.

When he put his hand out and caught hers as she went to close the case, she jerked it away, and he said flatly, 'You're not leaving. Make up your mind to that; you're not leaving.'

'You can't stop me. If I don't go now I'll go once you leave the house; you can't keep watch over me all the time.' She was staring straight into his face, and he held her eyes with an unblinking stare as he said, 'You know what I said I'd do to you the other night if ever you left me. Well, you might have thought it was a joke, but it wasn't. If you walk out I'll drop everything till I find you, and I'll bring you back. Every time you go off I'll find you and I'll haul you back again. I mean it.'

She stepped back from him as she asked, 'Why? Why do you want to keep me here? Yesterday I thought I knew, but not now, because you were disgusted when I told you the truth. You were, you were disgusted. Just because it was Brett who was the father you were disgusted. You had already accepted the situation because you thought I had been with a boy. Why, I could have been with a boy twenty times, fifty times and nothing could have happened and you wouldn't have known anything about it, but because this happened with Brett once, just once, your whole attitude towards me changes. It was as if you had suddenly heard that I'd had a baby; or, if you thought it was yours, then found out it was Brett's, you couldn't have reacted worse. I–I can't understand you.'

'You can't understand me! That's rich. But then I can't understand meself. I don't know why in hell I bother about you, but I do, so there's a pair of us who can't understand me. But you think it's odd I was disgusted when I heard it was Brett, an' I was disgusted, that's the right word; and it wasn't only because he was an old man, oldish anyway,' he flung his head upwards, 'but because, well, I liked him. I'd always liked him, and was fool enough to look up to him, thinking he represented something big, something fine, even great.' His voice dropped. 'I looked up to him the same as I looked up to you . . .'

It was his last words that took all the fight out of her. She turned from him and, going to the little table, sat before it and dropping her head on to her arms began to cry, painful, quiet crying.

He remained where he was, looking at her. The defiant woman was gone, and he saw a young girl again. Once, she said. She had only been with him once. He thought back and tried to remember when Brett had gone abroad. It must have been pretty near when it happened, for it was three months later when he came back, at the time when they were looking for somebody to pin it on. He must have known that there was a chance she might fall and he had scurried away like a frightened rabbit, jumped at the opportunity to get away, because he now recalled that when Mr Cribber went into hospital, Mr Bindley was going to get the chance of going out abroad to fill in. He knew this because he often had a word with him at the Tech, where he did spare teaching at nights, but then Brett had gone instead.

She had been left high and dry by them all: Brett, her own family, and now, it must appear to her, that he was another one of them. Quite suddenly it didn't matter any longer who had been the father of her bairn; it was a thing that was over and done with. He went to the case and, lifting the lid, took out her dresses, one by one, and put them over his arm. Then going to her, he said, 'Hang these up.'

She raised her tear-streaked face and looked at him for a moment before, getting to her feet, and saying, quietly, 'No, no, Angus, it's not going to be like that. I don't care what you say, or what you do, I'm . . . I'm going. I'm not living in sufferance any longer.'

'Sufferance? What do you mean?'

'Just what I say. You married me because you were sorry for me. I–I thought you loved me; I imagined that you needed me; but now I know that was all girlish imagination. Another reason why you married me was so that you could cock your snoot at my folks. Oh, I know, I know.' She flapped her hand in front of her face. 'You'll deny it, but it's true. You were letting them see, father in particular, that you could marry anyone you liked, that you were as good as they were. So you married me, but you've never said one endearing word to me in all the months since then. Oh, yes,' her voice was scornful now, 'you can kiss me and hug me until I can hardly breathe; you can show me how strong you are, what a man you are; but you've never once said you've cared for me. I could have been that May woman you used to know.' The impetus went out of her voice and she ended, 'You don't really care for me, Angus, so why do you want to keep me? Just to hold me up and say, "Look what I've got; someone from Brampton Hill"?'

He was shaking his head slowly at her, bewilderment showing in every feature of his face, and, his voice humble now, he said low in his throat, 'You've got it all wrong, Van, you've got it all wrong. Admittedly I was shaken when I knew it was Brett, but the feeling's past, it's over. But about the other, how I feel about you, you've got it all wrong. You want fancy words. Well, I'm not up to it. It's almost impossible for me to express how I feel about you in words, but I thought I was showing it in a thousand and one other ways. If it means anything to you, I live in dread every day of you walking out, and that bit about what I would do if ever you left me, about bringing you back, and even polishing you off, it's just talk, wind, the big fellow bellowing . . . Look, if you go out of that door now, Van, I won't try to stop you. I'll know you're going because you can't stand the set-up or me any longer. And don't worry, I won't even ask you to come back, because who in their right senses would want to come back to this?' He flung one arm wide. 'Not even an ordinary lass from around the doors would have put up with what you've put up with. I know all this, and I've tried to tell you I know it, but I'm no hand at expressing meself that way. The only thing I can say now, and I've never said it afore, not in so many words is . . . I love you, that I've loved you since you were a nipper, and I'll go on loving you to the end of me days. That's not saying, if you leave me I won't take anybody else. I'm a man, I need somebody, but that isn't love. It's you I love, an' it's you I want. If you go, you go, but if you stay . . . well . . .'

All this time he had been holding her dresses over one arm, and now he went and put them on top of her case again, and when he turned round she was standing near him. But he did not touch her, not even when her hands went up to her face in distress and her fingers pressed so tightly across her mouth that her nose was pushed out of shape did he touch her, not until, her body leaning forward, she drooped her head against his shoulder did his arms go around her. And then his face, falling into her hair at the back of her neck, he muttered, 'Aw, Van. Van. God, don't you know how I feel about you?'

Her body began to shake again with her sobbing, and, his own voice thick and broken now, he said, 'It's a new start; we'll go on from here, no more looking back. I love you, love you, love you. Do you hear that? Always have and always will. It goes past lovin' what I feel for you. I need words now. I adore you, Van. Aye. I do. I adore you. Teach me words, Van. Teach me words so as I can tell you just how much I adore you . . . But there's one thing I don't need fancy words for, an' it's this.' He held her from him and looked deep into her tear-blinded eyes as he ended. 'I'm going to make you a promise and I'll carry it through by fair means or foul. I mean to put you back where you belong afore I'm finished. Brampton Hill, or even beyond. Now that's a solemn promise.'

When the shaking of her body increased with her sobbing he took it as a sign that she was pleased with the prospect. He was quite mistaken.

BOOK THREE

Chapter One

It was a week before Christmas, almost eighteen months from the day Angus had left Afflecks. Two things of import had happened to him and Vanessa since that day. First, and most important, was that Vanessa was going to have another baby, and it was due any time now. The second thing, and hardly of less importance, was that Angus Cotton was now a haulage contractor with his own name on ten lorries, and a respectable bank balance, together with a less respectable but equally important horde of five-pound notes in a cavity under the floor boards.

Angus's rise in the contracting world had been swift, even taking into account the many men who had made quick piles in this line of business. His success had really started when he thought he was finished altogether. It was on the day Fred Singleton asked him if he would buy his lorry because he was moving–the wife wanted to get back to her people in Doncaster.

Fred had thrown this bombshell on the very day Angus had secured a sub-contract to clear the rubble from a complete street of demolished houses. He had come by the contract through the help of Andrew Fowler, and it was to him he went to say that he couldn't go on with it; one man and one lorry couldn't do the job and he hadn't any cash at the moment to buy Fred Singleton's lorry. It was at this point that Andrew Fowler said 'Why don't you strike out on your own? Take a chance, borrow the money. Hire a couple of men and take a chance.'

Where, asked Angus, could he borrow the money without any security behind him?

'From me,' Andrew Fowler had answered; 'at five per cent. I won't be over-charging you or under-charging you. I'm willing to take a chance if you are, and, as you've seen, I can push a lot your way. If you take this chance I think you'll find it very much worth your while–and mine too.' He had nodded his head slowly. 'We can come to an agreement.'

Angus didn't know then whether Andrew Fowler was a bit of a sharp-shooter or not, and even now he didn't know; but what he did know at this present time was that if he kept going ahead during the next two or three years at the rate he had done these past months he would be set fair for the top. And tonight's little transaction would undoubtedly help it along.

'Move over, love,' he said. He dropped on to his knees on the hearth rug as he spoke; and as Vanessa rose to her feet he didn't immediately pull the mat back but, putting his arms around her waist, he pressed his face against the bulge of her stomach, and shouted, 'Hurry up, you in there. Hurry up. Do you hear me?'

Vanessa gave a contented laugh, saying, 'Angus don't. Look, you'll have me over.'

''Bout time too,' he said; ''bout time.' Then poking her stomach again gently he said in a lowered tone, 'Get a move on, d'you hear? Somebody else has got claims as well as you, you know.'

She turned away, biting on her lip, her head slightly lowered. He was raw, uncouth in many ways, and she doubted if he would ever change. Definitely, the English lessons and selected reading had made no notable impression on him; but it didn't seem to matter, she loved him; she loved him as she hadn't imagined loving anybody. She had never imagined what it would be like to love like she loved him; it was a consuming feeling. Yet she wasn't happy.

She turned now and looked on his bent head as he put a knife down between the two floor boards and prised them upwards, then lifted a metal box on to the mat, from which he began counting out five-pound notes.

When he had counted to eight she said in some surprise, 'What are you going to give him?'

'A hundred.'

'A hundred pounds, Angus?'

'Aye.'

'But–but will he take all that from you?'

'Take me hand off for it an' all.' He grinned up at her with slanted glance.

He now replaced the box under the floor boards, and after straightening the mat and putting the chair back on it he counted the money again before putting it in an envelope.

When he looked at Vanessa she shook her head and said, 'I can never believe that he takes it.'

'You can believe it all right.' His head was bouncing up and down. 'That's how these blokes get rich, that's how all blokes get rich. You never find a rich honest business man. I mean, not one sticking to the books, everything down in black and white. Such men make a profit but they don't get stinkin' rich. And our kind friend, Mr Fowler, intends to get . . . stinkin' rich. And he should do with all the pies he's got his fingers in.'

'But he helped you at first without taking anything.'

'Aye, aye, you're right he did; but he had his eye on the future, and I soon picked things up. I know which side me bread is buttered.' He jerked his head at her.

'What if you hadn't given him any money on the side?'

'What do you think? I'd have been dropped. I'd have managed a one-man little business, just keeping afloat but nothing like where I am now, and where Stan is. It would appear we all took a chance and it paid off. Do you know how much Stan picked up last week? Forty-seven quid. Mind you, he had to work for it. And there's our Rosie going on about him coming home late. She doesn't say that when she goes and spends a small fortune on her clothes on a Saturday afternoon. She wants her ears scudded, that one.'

Vanessa said now, 'How long will you be? They're coming round tonight.'

'Oh, about an hour I should say. We'll just have a drink together and a natter . . . and a little exchange.'

'Why doesn't he transact the business in the office?'

'Not this kind of business, honey.' He leant towards her and tickled her chin. 'He's a very wise guy, is Mr Andrew Fowler. He's got a secretary there and secretaries have ears and noses. As he said himself, the walls have ears. No, he's cunning and cute, yet likeable. You know, I like him. You can't help liking him because, in a way, he's sort of honest about it. "Come for a walk along the river bank," he'll say, and there we go out of the office and along the river bank, and he'll say to me something like he did a month ago, like this. "Threadgill's are putting out a tender. They're opening up the land beyond Dark Town. It's just a sort of pilot scheme; your ten lorries could manage it. There's a fellow called Richardson there; he's got a lot of influence, but he's got a weakness for presents–a television, or a crate or two, or something like that. I said "Wines?" and he said, "No. His taste runs to something a bit stronger, whisky."'

'But you got that contract, didn't you. I wrote—'

'Yes. Yes, I got the contract. Of course I did. That's what's been pulling it in these past few weeks.'

'And . . . and did you send him a . . . present?'

'Aye. Aye, I did. I didn't tell you about it at the time because I felt a bit chipped about doing it, sort of, well, half-ashamed like.'

She came and stood close to him and looked into his face, 'A television set?'

'No; nor whisky. You'd never believe in a month of Sundays what I sent him. Go on have a guess.'

'A wrist watch?'

He shook his head.

'Gold cuff links?'

Again he shook his head.

'Was it something for himself?'

'Not exactly.'

'I give up.'

'A donkey.'

'A what!' Her face was spread wide with laughter. 'A donkey?'

'For his daughter; a very good donkey an' all. Now who would suspect anyone of doing a graft through a donkey? Sixty-two quid it cost me, that donkey. And it's not a donkey really, it's a pony, and a spanker.'

'Oh, Angus! Oh, Angus!' She leant against him sideways and they both began to laugh. 'And you know something else?' They were still laughing. 'I heard yesterday from Fowler that he's looking for a little go-cart, what they used to call a governess trap, you know. I haven't seen one in me life, and Fowler can't remember seeing one either, but that's what Mr. Richardson's looking for, so Mr Angus Cotton is going to enquire if anybody's got a governess trap hanging about their back yard that they don't want.' They were holding on to each other shaking. When he released her she wiped her eyes, then held her hands on her high stomach as she asked, 'But what's the hundred pounds for?'

'I'm not sure meself yet.' He turned his head slowly towards her again. 'But if it means what I think it's going to mean that'll be the first of a few hundred I'll be dishing out . . . Now, now.' He put his hand up to her cheek. 'You don't have to worry; this is how business is done. Your big, ignorant slob of a man has learned a lot in the last few months, and he's got a lot to learn yet. But whatever he learns he's going to make it pay, because–because he's promised his wife something.' He took her chin firmly in the palm of his hand and squeezed it. 'I'll never rest until I fulfil that promise.'

'There's no need, Angus. Please, I've told you. I–I would rather you got the work in the ordinary way, I would, believe me, Angus, rather than run risks.'

'Risks? Oh! Oh! Now you're on the wrong track. There's no risk. I told you. Fowler walks me along the river bank; I buy a donkey for Mr Richardson's daughter. Why do I buy a donkey for Mr Richardson's daughter? Because Mr Richardson's daughter tells me that she is looking out for a donkey and I happen to see one going reasonable and I go and buy it. Does Mr Richardson pay me for it? Of course he does . . . That would be the way it would go if anybody said anything. There's no risk.' His face suddenly becoming straight, his jocular manner disappearing and his eyes hardening, he said, 'No risk, only the feeling you want to kick somebody up the backside every time they give you a hint a backhander is required if you want the job. When I see tenders put out it makes me laugh–grimly.'

There now came to them the sound of a door opening and Rosie's voice high and excited coming from the kitchen. The next minute both she and Emily were in the room, and Emily cried, 'What do you think? Rosie says Old Davis has died at the corner.'

'Aye?' Angus looked from one to the other. Then addressing Rosie, he said, 'What do you expect me to do? Send him a wreath? I've hardly seen him for years.'

'Don't be so daft, man.' Rosie pushed her hand out towards him. 'The house. He's been living there by himself since his wife died. The house; it'll be empty.'

'Oh, aye, aye.' He nodded at her. 'You've got something there, our Rosie. You don't miss much, do you?'

They both flapped their hands at each other; then Vanessa, coming forward, said, 'But there'll be a waiting list.'

'Not for these places,' said Rosie scornfully. 'They're all up for comin' down. Five years is the limit. Well don't stand there, our Angus; go and do somethin'. If we hadn't got that place last month I'd have been after it like a shot.'

'When did he die?' asked Angus, picking up his coat and going towards the door.

'About half-an-hour ago I should say. I saw Mrs Green coming out of the house. She's just washed him.'

'God! He's hardly cold.'

'Warm or cold, it doesn't matter to him now,' cried Emily. 'Go on, get yourself away. It'll be a godsend, that house especially, 'cos there's a bath in it.'

'Oh yes.' Angus turned quickly towards Vanessa. 'I forgot about the bath. There was quite a to-do in the street when he put it in. I'm off . . . Wait a minute.' He went back into the room towards the small table and, opening a drawer, took out three pounds, saying, 'I want more than this. Have you got any loose?'

Vanessa went to a chest of drawers to the right of the fire place and took her bag from the top, saying, 'How much do you want?'

'Oh, give me what you've got. A fiver should help get me into that bath. If not, it can be doubled.'

As he was passing Emily he gripped her wrinkled face tightly between his fists and, bending towards her, he quoted,

'Between the dark and the daylight,
When the night is beginning to lower,
Comes a pause in the day's occupation
That is known as the Children's Hour.'

He ended on a deep note, thumbing towards Vanessa, 'Hurry that Children's Hour up, will you, 'cos I can't stand much more. If I have another night like last night I'll never live to see him. I was twisted up with cramp.'

Emily jerked her head from his grasp and pushed him through the kitchen, crying, 'Go on. Go on, you great big gowk.' But when they reached the front door the laughter went from his face and his bantering tone vanished as he said under his breath, 'See to her, won't you? Don't leave her?'

'Look,' said Emily, 'bairns have been born afore, and they'll be born again. This is just one of millions.'

'Aw, no, aw no.' He jerked his head at her. 'One in a million, that's what you mean. One in a million. Now do as I tell you, stay with her, don't leave her for a minute. You won't go out, will you?'

'I'm not barmy, lad, or in me dotage. Go on, get on with your job an' I'll get on with mine; and she'll get on with hers. What's the matter with you? Gone soft all of a sudden? Go on an' get the contract. An' get that house. And anything else you can lay hands on.'

He nodded at her; then said slyly, 'Will do, Mrs Cotton. Will do.' Then he stepped across the narrow pavement and into his car, a ten-year-old Rover, which he had chosen, because it was the remains of a good thing. That was to be his policy, he told himself, all the way up: he'd rather have the remains of a good thing until he could get the good thing. No shoddy tin-pot new stuff, not for him or his.

Vanessa, Rosie, Emily and Stan waited in the kitchen for him coming back. He had said to Vanessa he would be an hour, but taking into account his visit to the rent agent they gave him another hour. That should have brought him back into the house at eight o'clock. At nine, he hadn't returned, and at half-past nine Vanessa's pains began; and Emily began to swear. He was a thoughtless, ignorant swine, that's what he was. In some pub likely, or fancy hotel, stuffing himself. There was the supper spoilt and them all starving. He thought of nobody but himself. He was a selfish swine, he always had been and always would be. Damn him.

At ten o'clock they began to get worried. At half-past ten Vanessa was sitting in her coat with her bag packed waiting to be taken to the hospital in Angus's car.

'If he comes in sodden,' said Emily, 'I'll brain him. We won't see him till closing time, you'll see. The night of all nights.'

Rosie, pacing the kitchen, stopped at this point and looked at Stan and said, 'If you did this to me, Stan, you'd have your eyeballs served up to you the next day, and I'm tellin' you.'

Stan grinned sheepishly at her, and then said, 'Somethin's keepin' him. You know for a fact he's as worried as if he was going to have it himself.'

Nobody said there could have been an accident, only the thought was constant in Vanessa's mind. Over the last half-hour she had resorted to prayer. It was as if she was back in the convent listening to the nuns: 'Hail Mary, full of grace, the Lord is with thee . . . Blessed Michael, the Archangel, defend us in the day of battle; be our safe-guard against the wickedness and snares of the devil; rebuke him, we humbly pray . . . Angus, Angus, hurry up. Please come home. Hail Mary, full of grace, the Lord is with thee. Let him come now, please.'

Her last prayer seemed to receive a lightning answer, for there came the sound of a car drawing up outside. The next minute Angus was in the room. He wasn't drunk, as they all expected, but he wasn't rightly sober. He stood in the doorway and raised his hands for silence, crying, 'Now all of you, all of you don't say it. I'm telling you, don't say it.' He didn't seem to take in the fact that Vanessa was sitting in her coat. 'I've done it. A treble up . . . Mrs Cotton Junior, Mrs Cotton Senior, Mrs Rosie Barrett, Mr Stanley Barrett, you see before you a successful business man, a man who's going up and up. I've pulled off the Henson quarry deal, two years' work. I've got the whole contract. Twenty lorries I'll need. Twenty lorries and twenty men, Stan. And,' he moved slowly towards Vanessa, 'you're moving, Mrs Cotton Junior, to a house with a bathroom. But it's only temporary; this is only the beginning.' He wagged his finger down into her pale but smiling face. 'And now for the last news, the top of the treble.' He turned to his mother, where Emily was standing at the far end of the table, her fists thrust into her hips, her face grim. 'Mrs Cotton Senior, your son has had an honour bestowed on him. You always said it would happen. Give the lad a chance, you said and it'll happen. And it has.' He leant across the table towards her. 'I've been put forward as a member of the Round Table. Now what do you think of that?' He straightened up and looked from one to the other. There was both pride and scorn on his face. 'Me, Angus Cotton, asked to represent the contractors of this town in the Round Table, because you know,' he shook his head widely, 'only one man can be in there representing one profession. Profession mind; I said, profession.'

Whatever Emily felt at her son's success, at this moment what she said was, 'You big, gormless gowk, shut up. Shut your trap a minute if you can. What do you think's been happenin' while you've been swillin' beer? She's had her pains all night since you left, an' we've been waitin' for you. She wouldn't let Stan get a taxi. She's a fool; she wanted her husband to take her, an' she's been hangin' on. Now, pick up that case, that's if you're able to carry it, an' get goin'."

Angus was deaf to Emily's bawling. He was looking down at Vanessa and she up at him, and he said softly, 'Aw, honey.'

His voice was cut off by Rosie saying airily, 'Well, you should have known what was happenin'. Didn't you have your pains?' On this, both she and Stan began to laugh heartily. Then their laughter was checked abruptly by Vanessa's body doubling forward.

'Look!' cried Emily. 'Get her into the car as quick as you can.'

'No . . . o. No . . . o.' Vanessa refused to move from the chair. She was gripping Angus's hands, her fingers digging into his flesh.

After a few minutes, when the pain didn't subside, Emily looked from one to the other and said, 'God, no!'

But it was God, yes.

When Angus tried to get Vanessa to her feet she slumped down his legs on to the mat, saying between gasps, 'Get . . . get the doctor.'

While Stan flew for Doctor Carr they all tried in various ways to get Vanessa to her feet and into the bedroom, and when Angus put his arms under to lift her up she cried out in agony, 'No! No!'

It was Rosie who said, 'Get an eiderdown and sheets to put under her.'

They managed to do this, and it was only fifteen minutes later when, on the mat in front of the fire, in the kitchen of the house where he himself had been born, Angus saw, to his horrified gaze, the head of his son coming into the world.

When Doctor Carr hurried into the room and took over, Angus went down the yard and was violently sick; and when he returned his mother was holding a screaming child in her arms. He did not look at it but went and knelt at Vanessa's side.

Vanessa looked at him. She was smiling. 'It's–it's a boy,' she said.

He nodded at her, unable to speak.

'It's been a day.'

He nodded again.

'You know something?' Her voice was faint. 'I want to laugh.'

'You can laugh the morrow.' His voice was shaking. 'What you want to do now is to go to sleep. Here's the doctor.' He moved aside and stood bewildered at what was going on around him. Rosie was gathering some pieces of linen from the floor and his mother was saying, 'Put them in soak and get me a dish of hot water. And here,' she turned to him, 'this belongs to you, so hold him until I find some place to put him. Make yourself useful for once.'

He took into his arms the thing he had created. It looked old and wrinkled, mummified, but it was his son, the beginnings of a man. He had been born on a mat in a condemned house. That shouldn't have happened; it was his fault. But he would remedy that. Oh aye, by God he would. His son would have education, the best money could buy, boarding school, public school, the lot. He'd have no memories of Ryder's Row, number twenty-four or number two. Angus Cotton's son would be a gentleman . . . He'd show them.

Chapter Two

The Rover 2000 swerved expertly into the car park and to the corner opposite the side door of the club. Angus got out, and after adjusting his Aquascutum overcoat he went towards the building, not to the side door, but around to the main entrance of Ransome's Club.

Ransome's had first been established in 1864; it said so on a brass plate discreetly embedded in an alcove in the lobby. It was, supposedly, a non-political club, but it was rarely you found any well-known member of the Labour Party registered on its books. But there was one thing necessary to become a member of Ransome's . . . money.

The name of Mr Angus Frederick Cotton had been on the books now for over six months now. He wasn't a frequent visitor, sometimes a fortnight would go by and he wouldn't look in, but whenever he did visit the club he came dressed in his best.

On the admission of Mr Angus Frederick Cotton to Ransome's it had lost one distinguished member. Mr Jonathan Ratcliffe had met Mr Cotton in the lobby, and Mr Ratcliffe's reactions had been apoplectic, and the town had something else to chuckle over.

The town was very interested in the situation that existed between the house of Angus Cotton–still after five years at the corner of Ryder's Row–and the house of Mr Jonathan Ratcliffe of Bower Place, Brampton Hill. It was said over both pints of beer and sherry before dinner that there was nothing against people getting on, but they shouldn't forget themselves and play God Almighty. The definition over the sherry might be reduced merely to God, but it meant the same thing: Jonathan Ratcliffe had become too high-handed, too uppish for the forthright, outspoken, down-to-earth citizens of Fellburn.

Now young Angus Cotton: there was a lad who had got on but who hadn't forgotten himself. This was almost entirely the view of the beer drinkers. He knew where he was going right from the start did Cotton. Not only did he take on Jonathan Ratcliffe's girl when she was going to have a bairn–and not by him mind, and that was the telling point, and it hadn't come out till after. Oh aye, that was a great telling point, to take on somebody else's bairn; it showed what a man was made of. Well, not only had he done that, but he had gone into business as a one-lorry man, and whether he had begged, borrowed or stolen the money, nobody knew, but in next to no time he had got two lorries, then four, then six, and seemingly overnight he had a fleet because you couldn't walk yards in the town without seeing one of Cotton's lorries. But he hadn't forgotten himself, had Angus Cotton.

At least, not yet, said the sherry drinkers. They were watching him very closely. He still lived in the same street as his mother, and although his wife was turned out in the best, as were his two bairns, Ryder's Row wasn't an address for a member of Ransome's.

Yes, both quarters of the town were very interested in the doings of Angus Cotton. And he knew it, and thrived on it.

He left his hat and coat in the cloakroom, looked at himself in the mirror above the wash-basin, rubbed his hands lightly over his discreetly oiled hair, opened his mouth wide and brought his fingers down tightly against each cheek to make sure there was no stubble, then straightened his tie and adjusted his coat and walked quietly out and into the hallway. Here he looked about him for a moment before saying to a passing waiter, 'Mr Fowler about?'

'Yes, sir; he went into the Brown Room just a minute ago.'

'Thanks.'

The Brown Room had an ornate high ceiling. Its walls were covered with faded red wallpaper on which was hung portraits of past distinguished members of the club. There were deep leather armchairs and down cushioned settees. In an armchair in a far corner sat Andrew Fowler. And he raised his hand as Angus entered the room.

'Hello, there.' Angus took his seat opposite Fowler, then said, 'I'm sorry I couldn't make it yesterday; I had to go down to Lessington; they are taking it too easy in that quarter.'

Andrew Fowler smiled, nodded, then said. 'What are you having?'

'Oh, a brandy.' He would have preferred a beer, but beer wasn't drunk in this room; he had learned that early.

Andrew Fowler hailed a waiter who was bringing drinks to other occupants of the room. Having given his order, he settled back and said, still with a smile on his face, 'Served you right if you had missed it.'

'Missed what?'

'Oh.' Fowler jerked his head to the side. 'Just something I thought you should know about.'

'Well, let's have it,' said Angus. 'You're just bursting at the seams . . . Don't tell me they're going to pull the new Town Hall down in Newcastle and they want me to salvage it?'

They both laughed a little; then Fowler said, 'How would you like to live on Brampton Hill?'

'What!'

'You heard me. How would you like to live on Brampton Hill?'

Angus's face was straight, his eyes hard. 'It all depends which part. Brampton Hill's a long hill and there's all kinds of houses on it. I don't know whether I'd like to live there or not.' He lay back in his chair and stretched his neck out of his collar. 'It's not the place it was; a lot of the big houses are in flats now.' He surveyed Fowler. He was giving nothing away to him, not about Brampton Hill, he wasn't. There were things about Fowler he couldn't understand. Sometimes he thought he was playing him like a puppet. He didn't like the idea.

'The Larches is to be put up for sale.'

Angus felt a wave of heat cover him. It was as if he'd had an injection straight into an artery. His head seemed to be swelling and he knew his face was a deep red. The Larches. Brett's place. The house next to Jonathan Ratcliffe's. There was a tightness in his jaws that was painful. He drew in a long, steady breath. Was this it? Was this what he had been waiting for? Striving for? He had promised her he'd put her back where she belonged, even on the hill, but he'd never dreamed of anything on the scale of The Larches. The Larches up for sale. And all that land. God, yes. He screwed his buttocks farther back against the soft leather of the chair. This was it. This was what he had been waiting for. He'd put her in The Larches.

'What are they asking?' he said.

'I don't rightly know; the bills aren't out yet. And then most likely it'll be put up for auction. But it'll fetch money, big money, because of the land. Six acres all with river frontage; that'll bring money.'

'Oh,' Angus moved his head deprecatingly, 'not as much as all that; it's controlled, isn't it? No building there.'

'Not for a while. But they're pulling off the controls everywhere. Anybody getting it could hang on for a few years and then they'd be in clover, no matter what they had to pay for it now.'

'Have you any idea what it will go for?'

Andrew Fowler pushed his head back into the chair and looked upwards for a moment before saying, 'Well, the house needs a lot of doing to it, both inside and out, I understand. I would say anything up to fifteen thousand. That's playing up the supposition that you'll never be able to do anything with the land, only as a garden. But if there's a breeze of a whisper that it could be used for building land in a few years' time when we have a change of Government,' he pulled his nose at Angus, 'the price will soar; it could go as far as thirty.'

Angus gave a low whistle, then said, 'Who's got the business?'

'Pearson.'

'You know Pearson.'

'Yes, I know Pearson.'

'Could you do anything?'

'I might.'

Suddenly Angus tossed his head from one side to the other and gritted his teeth and muttered under his breath, 'For God's sake, don't stall, Andrew. I hate this cat and mouse business. Could you?'

Andrew Fowler's expression took on a slightly cold look now and he said, 'You get too agitated, Angus. That's your trouble. Play it cool; it pays off in the long run. I've got something else to tell you. It isn't only money you've got to worry about, Ratcliffe's after it. He's been at Pearson already; it could be sold privately before the sale.'

Angus didn't ask why Ratcliffe didn't go next door to the Bretts and do a deal straight-away; he guessed there had likely been no interchange between those two houses since the morning his mother had visited them both.

Do you know what he's offering?'

'Sixteen thousand. But here's another thing. He's not doing it himself, he's working through a third party. Crafty, very crafty.'

Angus took a drink from his glass, then bent towards Fowler saying, 'I'll go seventeen,'

'Won't that be rocking your boat?'

'Aye, I suppose it will. But if it means twenty-seven and it almost sinks me, I mean to get that house . . . And another thing, tell Pearson I'll see him all right.'

'What would you suggest? It might be steep.'

'Five hundred?'

'Five hundred, it is.'

They both drew in deep breaths, and then Fowler said, 'There's another thing I'd like to talk over with you, Angus, while we're on the subject.'

'Aye, come on, let's have it; I thought we weren't finished.'

'Well, you know me.'

'Nobody better, Andrew.' Angus's lip was up at the corner.

Fowler ignored the implication and went on: 'As long as you buy the house and use it as a habitation, well and good, but should you sell the land for building . . . well, then I think there should be a little agreement on that.'

Angus stared at his mentor for a moment before saying, 'Fair enough, fair enough. Do you want it in writing?'

'Yes, I think that would be wise, Angus.'

'What per cent?'

'Well, don't let's be greedy, say trade price.' He smiled. 'Thirty three and a third.'

'Let's drink to it.'

Andrew Fowler raised his glass, and after they had drunk he got to his feet and added, 'Now we can have our dinner in peace. By the way, how's Vanessa and the children?'

'Fine, grand.'

'What's she going to say when you tell her about this latest venture?'

'I'm not going to tell her.'

'What! you're not . . . ?'

'No. At least until it's all signed and sealed. How long will it take?'

'Oh, don't gallop, Angus; I've got to put the wheels in motion first. And then it can be a slow business: solicitors, Land Registry, one thing and another, they take time. Once we get going two months should see it all cleared up.'

'Two months! As long as that?' He bit on his lip and his step quickened unconsciously as he left the room, and he thought, 'I'll not sleep for two months, I'll not know a minute's peace until it's mine, MINE . . .'

And Angus's sleep was fitful for the next eight days, during which time the price of The Larches rocketed from seventeen thousand to twenty-three thousand, but on the eighth day he wrote out a cheque for five per cent of twenty-three thousand pounds to be paid to James Pearson Esq., Estate Agents, being the deposit required to purchase The Larches from the joint owners, Colin, Paul and Michael Brett.

Now Angus was bursting to tell Vanessa, but a wariness in him warned him to keep quiet until the whole thing was legally settled. He believed if he were to tell her now she'd put a spanner in the smooth-running works, she'd bring up the excuse it was too close to her people. But once the thing was settled and he'd saddled himself with a liability of twenty-three thousand pounds she couldn't do much else but accept the house with a good grace, and oh, to see her ensconced next to the folks who had thrown her off as if she were a dirty clout. Parents or no parents, she was bound to feel one up on them, if only for his sake, because he had done as he said, and in a short time at that, and put her back where she belonged.

And he had no doubt in his own mind where Vanessa belonged. She didn't belong in Ryder's Row, and if she lived to be a thousand she would never fit in there. She stuck out like a sore thumb; she was as great an embarrassment to those around her as he would be, God helping him, to Jonathan Ratcliffe.

Although he constantly told himself he wanted the house for Vanessa he knew that, with even more intensity, he wanted that house for Angus Cotton. Oh, to come out of that drive in the morning in a Bentley. Aye, the next car he would get would be a Bentley. And which Bentley would make way for which when they met in the road? He couldn't wait to find out. And another thing, he'd have his mother with him. Aye, that would be a feather in his cap, and in hers. She'd be going back to Brampton Hill, and not as a skivvy. No, she'd be going into the kitchen only to give her orders. He didn't conjure up what part Vanessa was going to play in this arrangement, but told himself he'd employ a couple of maids and a gardener; he'd have The Larches the show-place of the town. And one more thing, his bairns, they were going to be educated . . . Private school for Andrew, and then public school. God, aye, he'd see to that. There'd be no Ryder's Row for his family. He'd let Ratcliffe see how Angus Cotton did things. Angus Cotton, the contractor, who, but for being blamed for giving his daughter a bairn, might be still Angus Cotton the foreman. When he came to think of it he had something to thank God-Almighty Ratcliffe for after all, and he would thank him one day . . . Aye, but spitting in his eye. And the first spit would be when he moved into The Larches. Hurry up, hurry up, the days, the weeks; he couldn't wait.

Feeling as he did he had to tell somebody, so he told Emily.

Emily had just finished soaking her feet in a tin dish before the fire and he sat on his hunkers on the edge of the mat and told her, and she was so thunderstruck by his news that she let him go on talking. The water got cold and her legs began to turn blue and shiny, and when he said, 'Well, say something, say something. Don't sit there looking like a stuffed duck with your feet in the water. Say something, woman,' she closed her eyes, heaved a deep sigh, then, taking up a towel where it had been warming on the fender, she put it on the hearth rug and lifted her feet on to it before she turned and looked at him and said. 'You're bloody-well stark, staring mad, lad.'

There was a short silence before he brought his body upwards in a bound, saying, 'Aw, for crying out loud, Mam! Have you heard what I've been saying to you? I've bought The Larches. Me, Angus Cotton, I've bought The Larches in Brampton Hill, and all you can bloody well say is that I'm mad. Do you know what this means? We're all going to live on Brampton Hill.'

'Who? Me?' She dug her thumb into the hollow of her neck. 'Oh, no, lad. Now, you can count me out of your scheme. Me live on Brampton Hill? Now get this into that great, big, swollen head of yours, the only time you'll get me up Brampton Hill again is if they take the hearse up that way. But that's not even likely as it's the long way round to the cemetery.'

'Well, we can't go and live up there and leave you down here, woman.'

'Look. Look.' She stood up now and walked to the edge of the towel, which brought her close to him. 'You're not my keeper. You're married, you've got a wife and family. You see to them an' that'll take you all your time, but what I do is my business. This is my home and until they pull it down I'm stayin' here. And then I'll go into whatever they provide. But I'm not livin' with you and Van on Brampton Hill, or any other bloody hill. Now get that . . . And here's somethin' else I'll give you to think about. You said you haven't told her, you're keepin' it a secret; well, if I'm any judge, you're in for one great, bloody, shock. And it wouldn't surprise me if you haven't got a twenty-three thousand-pound white elephant on your hands. What you still don't understand, lad, after five years is you've married somebody quite different to yoursel'.'

'Oh, for God's sake, Mam, don't talk bloody tripe. I know what I married, nobody better.'

'But you don't, lad, you don't. 'Cos if you think she's goin' to go on livin' next door to her folks just like that, then you don't. She's a highly sensitive lass. Some folk call it breeding. Anyway, she's different, an' I can't see her lettin' you push her up there right on to their doorstep. She couldn't stand it. You know.' she stabbed her finger at him and smiled a tight smile, 'I know why you're doin' this. I know why you've bought Brett's place, an' I don't blame you. Oh, I don't blame you. And I'd be laughin' up me sleeve if you were takin' anybody else up there but his daughter. In fact, if your wife wasn't any connection of his I'd go up there on a Saturday night and have me knees up in the garden just to show him an' all.' Her voice dropped to a sad note as she ended, 'But you did marry his daughter, and if I know anythin' about your Van she's not going to like your little surprise, 'cos to say the least, it's sort of tactless like.'

'Tactless be-buggered. Look, Mam, don't give me the jitters. Twenty-three thousand I've spent. Do you realize, twenty-three thousand! I'm going up fast, but twenty-three thousand takes some finding. And that's not all. With the side lines I've had to keep going to get the damned place I'll be lucky if I get away with twenty-five thousand when I'm finished.'

Emily's voice was still quiet, but had a touch of laughter in it now and her smile was smirky as she said, 'It should be a nice experiment for you playing with thousands. Now who would have thought that the snotty-nosed, shock-headed, ugly mug, Angus Cotton, whose mam was the Ratcliffe's daily for years, can now talk in thousands, twenty-five thousands, when up to a few years ago twenty-five shillings spare would have been a Godsend to him. It's a credit to you, lad, and it's your mother that's saying it. Go on, lash out with your thousands, but don't think,' her voice rose sharply, 'that you're goin' to push me around, or that you're goin' to make your wife do somethin' that will be against every grain in her body.' She thrust out her hand and thumped him on the shoulder, her voice barking now as she finished, 'If you want my advice, you'll spend the next few weeks preparing yourself for a disappointment, sort of building yourself up, if you get what I mean, 'cos your big-head is goin' to have a puncture.'

'Aw, to hell with you!'

As he stalked out of the kitchen she bawled after him, 'An' to hell with you. And if you see me there, don't you open your mouth to me because I'm particular about the company I keep. I've no room for upstarts. You're goin' the same road as the man you're fightin'.'

When the door banged she quickly padded into the front room, and, standing to the side of the window, watched her son marching down the street. A big, well-dressed, prosperous-looking man, who had just been in this little box of a house talking about spending twenty-five thousand pounds as if they were shillings. Life was strange. Would he persuade Van to go and live in a house next to her parents? He persuaded her to do most things. It was always a mystery to her what Vanessa saw in her son; that she herself should know his worth was a different matter altogether. She knew him to be a good man, big-headed, bumptious, argumentative, all the qualities that went to make a rough northerner; he took after herself, and she knew what she was all right, nobody better, and him being the flesh of her flesh she could appreciate him; but how did it come that a girl like Vanessa could appreciate him? What did she see in him? She didn't talk much ever, never opened up, and she didn't seem to have any life of her own. She was his wife, the mother of his children; his secretary, aye, an' his teacher, she had been learning him for years to speak properly, grammer an' that. She had seen his efforts on his desk but she hadn't remarked on them; she knew better. She didn't want to spoil a good thing. Yet he showed no evidence of improvement when he was talking to her. No, he was the same old ha'-penny dodger. But that lass; everything she did was for him, and what did she get out of it? Damn little that she could see. He could have got her into a decent house long afore this but he had put it off and put it off, partly, she had thought, because he didn't want to move away from herself. But now she saw the real reason for him staying put. He had been after big game all along, no modern bungalow or imitation Regency house for him; it had to be on Brampton Hill, and not only on Brampton Hill, it had to be one of the biggest houses; and not only one of the biggest, but the place that had the most land left. He was going too fast; he was rising too high; he'd blow himself up unless something, or somebody, put the brakes on him.

Chapter Three

It was in the afternoon that she went down the street to the end house. She knew Vanessa's routine. It being after four o'clock Andrew and Annabella would be out with Mary Ridley in the park, and Vanessa would be preparing the evening meal.

She found her in the kitchen, a small, modern, well-equipped kitchen, and she said, 'Oh, hello, lass. Isn't it close? And it's going to pour afore the day's out; I can tell by me feet.'

'Aren't they any better?' Vanessa looked down at the swollen ankles bulging over the top of black-laced shoes.

'No, lass; an' they won't be until I'm in me coffin. And I bet you what you like, the swellin'll go down immediately then. Enough to make you kick yourself.'

'Oh, Emily!' Vanessa was laughing. She always got a laugh and felt happy when Emily was about. It was a different kind of happiness from that which she experienced with Angus; that happiness was a taut, high-tensioned feeling. She said now, 'Rosie popped in. She's just gone along to Stodart's; she'll be back in a short while. She was coming down to you.'

'Stodart's! For more shoes? She's always buyin' shoes. How many pairs is that she's got?'

'At the last count,' said Vanessa, breaking an egg into some flour, 'eighteen.'

'God above! Eighteen pairs of shoes. She would have to be a centipede to get her wear out of them.'

Vanessa was laughing again. 'She likes shoes.'

'She likes too many things, that one. The money's gone to her head; she's never done spendin'. Have they got owt in the bank? She won't tell me; she says it's none of my business.'

'Oh, I think they're all right, Emily. Stan's sensible where money is concerned.'

'It would take him to be. She'd have him on the rocks else . . . Van.'

'Yes, Emily?' Vanessa turned her head round, but still kept beating the egg and flour together.

'Can you stop a minute? I want a word with you, serious like.'

Serious? Vanessa laid down the fork and wiped her hands and turned about, and Emily, going into the living-room, said, 'Come an' sit down a minute; I want to get it over afore our Rosie comes in. This is atween you and me, understand?'

When they were seated Emily bent forward and repeated, 'Mind, lass; this is just atween you and me. I want your word on it.'

'Something's wrong, Emily . . . Angus?'

'Aye, Angus. Oh, it's all right. Don't look like that; it's not that kind of wrong.' She reached out and roughly pulled Vanessa's hand away from her mouth and, holding on to it, she said, 'Now listen, lass. Have you noticed any difference in him lately, the last week or so?'

Vanessa considered a minute, then said, 'Well, yes. He's not sleeping. He seems excited about something; bursting out singing one minute, and gloomy the next. Yes. Yes, I've noticed it.'

'But you didn't say nothing?'

'No, Emily.'

'Well, I can tell you he is excited an' all, because he's keeping somethin' back from you. He's done somethin' an' he's not tellin' you until the matter is clinched. An' when it is it'll be too late to alter things; or so he thinks. You know, he's your husband, Van, but I don't think he really knows you. I feel I know you a damn sight better than him; but then, of course I've known you longer, haven't I?' she smiled.

'What's it all about, Emily?' Vanessa's voice was quiet; her whole demeanour was quiet. She had grown into a rather reserved young woman. She was very seldom gay, unless she was with her children, and then she had to be alone with them before she could let herself go. She added now, 'Tell me. Tell me quickly, please, because Rosie might be back at any minute. And Angus himself will be in shortly.'

'Well, hold on to your seat there, lass. Here it comes . . . He's buying the Bretts' place, The Larches.'

Emily watched the colour drain completely from Vanessa's face. She thought for a moment she was going to collapse, and she said, 'Now steady on, lass. Steady on. Don't let go. This is not the time for lettin' go; you've got to put your thinkin' cap on.'

'The Larches? He's buying The Larches for us?' Vanessa's voice came as the smallest whisper.

'For you. He's goin' to give you the surprise of your life. He gave me the surprise of mine when he out with it. He was bustin' at the seams, like a bairn with a new toy. I've never stopped worryin' since. I told him he was mad . . . You don't want to go an' live in The Larches, do you?'

'Oh, Emily. Me! Live in The Larches? In Brett's house? O-Oh!' The last word came as a groan. 'I couldn't. I couldn't live there even . . . even if it wasn't next door to home.' She still thought of Bower Place as home. 'And just think what it would do to mother and father. They wouldn't stand for it; they would leave.'

'Aye, aye, I'd thought of that.'

'And . . . and they love that place. Oh. Oh, how could he, Emily? How could he?'

'He could because he's barmy; he thinks that because you came from there you want to go back there. It's no use tellin' him. But that's not the only reason he bought the place; the other is he's wantin' to get one back on your father. That's at the bottom of it; he wants to show him.'

'I'll never go there, Emily.'

'I know that, lass.'

'He'll just have to sell it again.'

'An' that'll knock the spunk out of him if anythin' will. And I'd hate to see it happen, 'cos he's mine, and I know how he'll feel. But as I see it there's nothing else for it. I thought I'd better tell you because if he sprung it on you and you hadn't time to think there might be a flare-up. And it's like this.' She smiled now. 'Him an' me, an' our lot, we can flare up and threaten to murder each other one minute, an' we'll be shakin' hands the next, but if you had a flare-up you wouldn't get over it easily. Would you now?'

Vanessa looked from the dyed-hair to the prematurely wrinkled face of her mother-in-law, and she thought: She's right. She's always right. But what was she going to do about this, this latest venture, which must appear to him as the summit of his aims? This is what he had been waiting for, working for, striving for, wearing himself out for, to give her this. Her refusal must be made in such a way that a flare-up, when it came, would not burn him out, burn them both out. Their marriage, as she saw it, was a precarious union, resting as it were on a knife's edge, and this in spite of love and two children.

At this moment they heard Rosie coming pitter-pattering up the stairs on her high heels and, after looking hard at each other, they went quickly out of the room, and Emily greeted her daughter with, 'You want you lugs scudded, buying more shoes.'

'Shoes are made for walking,' Rosie sang, as she pranced round the table in her latest acquisition. Then stopping suddenly, she looked at Vanessa and said, 'Oh, by the way. What's going with our Angus these days? Stan says he's like a dog with two tails.'

Vanessa and Emily refrained from exchanging glances; then Rosie exclaimed, 'You're not,' she shook her head before adding, 'again?'

'No, Rosie. I'm not again.' Vanessa smiled.

'Well; what is it?'

'Oh,' Vanessa turned towards the fireplace, 'I suppose it's because things are going well.'

'Oh, it isn't only that. Stan says they've been going well for a long time, and he wasn't like this. Stan says he's all keyed-up, just as if he was going to take off by parachute.'

'Very likely is,' said Emily now, going towards the door. 'You never know what he's goin' to do next. The only thing is, I hope he doesn't forget to pull the strings afore he hits the ground.'

On this enigmatic comment, enigmatic at least to Rosie, Emily left them.

Life seemed to follow the usual pattern until almost a week later. It was in the evening. Angus was late and Vanessa had just got the children to bed, promising them that their father would come and see them immediately he entered the house. But they were sound asleep by the time he did get in.

He looked tired tonight, and somewhat strained, and so she let him have his meal and cleared away before she said, 'I want to talk to you, Angus.'

'Talk?' He cast a sidelong glance at her. 'Well, fire ahead.'

She swallowed deeply and walked the length of the sitting-room and back to him before she said, 'I understand you are buying me a house?'

She watched his head turn from her and swing from side to side, and when his fist crashed on to the table she said, 'She had to tell me.'

'The big-mouthed-old-bitch!' He spaced each word. 'That's all she is, a great, big, loose-mouthed, old bitch.' His head stopped its swinging, his fists relaxed, and then slowly he turned and looked at her and asked in an entirely different voice, in which she detected a plea, 'Well, what do you think? Go on, tell me what you think?'

'I . . . I think it's wonderful that you could pay so much money for the place.'

'Is that all?' His shoulders stiffened. 'Aren't you excited? You know what place I've bought, don't you? Brett's. Now. Now.' He thrust his hand swiftly out towards her and jerked it back and forwards. 'Don't get me wrong. It isn't animosity; nothing like that; not against Brett; it's just that I wanted you to be back on the Hill, where you belong.'

'I–I understand, Angus.'

'Do you? Aw,' his head was swinging again, 'I don't think you do really.'

'Yes, yes, I do; and I think it's marvellous. There's only one thing.'

'Aye, one thing. Well, what is it?' His face looked grim now, for he expected her answer to be, 'I can't live there.' But it wasn't. What she said was, 'Would you do something more for me?'

'Anything.' His voice was full of relief. The tension went out of his body; he grabbed her hands, saying softly, 'Anything in the wide world. You know that. I don't have to tell you.'

'But this is something big, different; you–mightn't be able to understand why I'm asking it.'

'Well, I won't,' he smiled at her, 'not until you tell me.'

She dropped her eyes down to their joined hands, and then said softly, 'Would you have the house put in my name, not jointly, in–in my name?'

This request was the last thing in the world he imagined her making. It sounded utterly preposterous. He wanted to think he hadn't heard her aright, but he had. Put the house in her name? He wanted it for her but it was to be his property. He wanted to own The Larches, his name on the title deeds. That was one of the things he was living for, to see Angus Cotton written on the deeds of The Larches.

'Why? Tell me why?' he said flatly. 'Jointly, aye; but why do you want it in your name?'

She raised her lashes but didn't look at him; she looked beyond him as she said, 'It's–it's just a whim, I suppose.'

He stared at her. Just a whim, she said. If he didn't satisfy her whim what then? She'd think him mean. All his life she'd consider him mean, and it would raise a barrier between them. Another one to be broken down. He spent his life breaking down barriers. The one that stood between Brampton Hill and Ryder's Row was about to fall, but if he didn't comply with her wish in this, even when the barrier was down, wouldn't she in some way, like a woman, hold it against him? He was always saying that everything he did was for her, now he'd have to prove it by giving her the house.

She was at the window looking down into the street. She was standing very still. She could do that, stand still with no muscle moving. He stared at her long, straight back. Even the lines of her could churn up his stomach any time of the day, and that after nearly six years. Aw, to hell! Who was to know whose name was on the deed? The house would be known as Angus Cotton's place, and Van wasn't the kind of woman to go loud-mouthing it round the town that it was in her name. She wasn't like his mother. Wait till he got his tongue around that one. She had knocked all the guts out of his plans. The excitement of driving Van up there when the thing was signed and sealed and saying, 'This is yours. I've bought it for you. Didn't I say I'd put you back where you belong?'

He said now, 'Well, if that's how you want it, that's how you'll have it. It'll be in your name.'

She turned round. 'Thanks, Angus,' she said. 'Thanks.'

That was all, just, 'Thanks, Angus.' No throwing her arms around his neck and hugging him and telling him that he was the most generous man on earth, that it was wonderful the things he had achieved in so short a time. Nothing like that. Just, 'Thanks, Angus.' Aye, well; that's how things went. Coolly. That was part of her makeup, coolness. If he ever could hate her it would be when she was cool.

'How long will it be before everything is settled?' she had her face averted as she asked the question, and he said, 'Oh, a few weeks. The solictor will have to make a few more alterations now, but the papers haven't gone up to the Land Registry yet. It won't be too long. A month; five weeks perhaps.' His voice sounded flat as if he had lost interest in the whole project and turning away, he added, 'I think I'll go down to the club.'

There was a pause before she answered, 'Yes. Yes, I would do that; it will relax you.'

'I don't need relaxing.' His voice was brittle as he turned and faced her again, and there was about his face an explosive look, and she combated it by saying quietly, 'All right, you don't need to relax. But you need a change. Go on; you'll feel better when you get back.'

He stared at her. There was something here he couldn't get to the bottom of. She should be a bit elated that she was having a twenty-three thousand pound house as a gift. She should be acting differently, not sending him out casually to a club, as if it was an ordinary night in an ordinary week–as if he was an ordinary bloke . . . Aye, as if he was just an ordinary bloke who hadn't one penny to rub against another. He had a feeling inside that things weren't right, the kind of feeling he had years ago when everything was going against him. He wanted to talk, to get to the bottom of it, but he couldn't do any probing with Van, not with the cool mood on her. But there was someone he could talk to, that loud-mouthed old bitch down there. He'd go down and blow her sky high.

He was in the street before he decided against visiting Emily; the mood he was in he'd want to bawl her down, and she didn't seem able these days to stand up to him as she used to. He cursed deep in his throat, got into his car and drove to the club. It was something when he had to go to Ransome's to be appreciated.

When the house door banged Vanessa, sitting down suddenly on a chair, closed her eyes and thought, 'This is just the beginning. He'll want to kill me when he finds out.'

Chapter Four

The day was dull and chilly. It had started with rain, which had slowed to a drizzle, and this in turn had developed into a wet mist. The streets were greasy. The town traffic bustled through the heavy greyness as if making for more pleasant scenes beyond.

Vanessa made her way down to the main street to Tiller's Garage and asked for a taxi, and when she was seated in it she held her large handbag upright on her knees and tightly between her hands. In her handbag were the deeds of The Larches. She'd had them in her possession since eleven o'clock when the solicitor has smilingly handed them to her and she had surprised both him and Angus by saying, 'I want to keep them with me for today.'

'Look; what's up with you? They're yours,' Angus had said. 'Let Mr Black hold them with all the other stuff.'

'Just for today,' she had repeated; and he had shaken his head and said, 'All right, all right, have it your own way.'

He had an appointment at half-past eleven but he was coming back about one for her and they were going up to . . . their house. It was a blind date, he said, because he had never seen inside The Larches. Fancy that, buying a place without looking it over. Had she ever heard of anyone doing that?'

When she said to the taxi-driver, 'Brampton Hill, Bower Place, please,' she shivered. She was going home. For the first time in years she was going home. Deep down in her there was a suppressed longing to visit her old home, to see her mother and Susan, and . . . even her father. Knowing her father's temperament, she was well aware that if it lay with him she would never see the inside of her old home again, and that already, under the circumstances, he would be preparing to leave the house he had built, the house he loved; and this also he would have chalked up against her. She was aware that she was about to do something extraordinary, and something that would likely drive Angus mad, for the time being anyway. But as things stood, no word of hers would convince him that she would find it impossible to live next door to her people, and, in particular, in Brett's house. Angus wasn't insensitive, on the contrary, but he was totally blind in some instances to what was right and proper.

She was still shivering when the taxi drew up outside the gates of Bower place. She had asked the driver not to go into the drive, and she paid him off for she did not know how long she would be.

She timed her visit. They would just be sitting down to lunch; they wouldn't be able to say he wasn't in.

It was strange to ring the doorbell. She could never remember ringing the doorbell. She wondered what kind of a maid they had at the moment.

When the door opened, Susan confronted her, a plumper, older Susan, Susan with her mouth open and her eyes popping out of her head.

'Hello, Susan.'

Susan was unable to speak. She turned her head and cast a glance quickly back across the hall, then said on a high whisper, 'Vanessa.' She looked her up and down for a moment. Her younger sister was now a woman, a tall, beautiful woman, very well dressed. She knew a moment's keen envy of her. She didn't ask her to come in but stood staring at her, until Vanessa said, 'Are they in?'

'Yes. At–at lunch.'

'Will you tell them I'm here? I'd like to see them.'

'Vanessa,' Susan shook her head, 'he's in a dreadful state. You've . . . your . . .'

'I know, I know; me and mine. It's that I want to see him about. Things will be different from now on.' She smiled reassuringly down on her sister. She felt older, oh so much older than Susan at this moment. Susan looked dowdy, harassed, surprisingly commonplace. This fact made her slightly more at ease, but it didn't stop her body trembling.

'I–I put you . . . I mean, you'd better go into the morning-room. I'll–I'll break it to them.'

'All right, Susan.' She looked about the hall for a moment before crossing to the morning-room door. It was as if the years had rolled away and all in them was but a dream and she was back home once more. The morning-room was the same, except that there was not so much silver dotted about. She stood looking out of the window waiting. And she waited . . . and waited. And then her mother came in alone.

They looked at each other across the length of the room until Vanessa moved slowly forward, saying, 'Hello, Mother.'

Jane Ratcliffe nipped at her lower lip and gulped gently in her throat before saying, 'Hello, Vanessa.' The words came out on a hoarse whisper as if she had a cold.

'How are you, Mother?'

'Quite–quite well, thank you.' She did not ask her daughter to sit down; she just stared at her, because she was surprised at what she saw. She had caught a glimpse of her now again in the town; once with her children; once a few years ago coming out of a store laden with shopping bags. But this woman before her was no relation to the girls she had known. She had never seen her before. This woman who had been associating with the common people for years was poised and dignified and looked sure of herself. She said stiffly now, 'Why have you come? Haven't you wrought enough havoc on us?'

It was some seconds before Vanessa answered: 'The reason for my visit is to try and rectify that in some small way. I would like to see Father.'

Jane Ratcliffe closed her eyes and said, 'That's impossible; he won't see you.'

'But I mean to see him. I must see him. I don't suppose it's news to you that Angus has bought The Larches.' She looked back into her mother's unblinking eyes, then went on. 'He has given it to me. It's in my name and I can do entirely what I like with it. I–I propose to sell it to father for what it cost Angus. He's always wanted the land, and I know he would have bought it only Angus went over his head. Well, that's why I'm here.'

Jane Ratcliffe blinked now. Then, after a moment, she exclaimed on a relieved note, 'That's very kind of you, Vanessa, very kind. I'll go and tell him.'

Again Vanessa waited, but not so long this time. And when the door opened again her father entered, and her mother was behind him.

She hadn't seen her father since that morning in the station yard. He had looked no different then from how he had always looked, but now there was a difference. Although he was only in his middle fifties he looked an old man, a bitter, tight-faced old man. She forced herself to speak, to break the tension-filled silence in the room. 'Hello, Father,' she said.

He did not answer for a moment, and then his thin lips scarcely moving he said thickly, 'Feeling triumphant, aren't you? Having dragged yourself up from the gutter you come to show off, bearing a gift, I understand, from your husband. Well,' his bony lower jaw jutted outwards, bringing his lower lip overlapping his upper one, and he went on in a spate of scarcely controlled fury, 'you can take his gift back to him and tell him he's dealing with the same man that used to be his master. You can tell him that. I've never accepted gifts from menials and scum and I'm not starting now.'

She choked as the words rushed from her, her anger almost matching his now. 'He knows nothing about it. He didn't send me to you; he wouldn't because he loathes you. But I knew you couldn't stand us living next door. And what is more, I don't want to live next door to you. It was my own idea to offer you the house, because you've always coveted the land, but he knows nothing about it. As for being scum, don't you dare call him scum. He's worth more—'

His voice cracked at her like a whip, breaking off her words, 'I didn't ask you into this house. If I'd had my way you wouldn't have been allowed through the door. Now get out! You made your choice years ago when you went to live in the gutter, and I repeat gutter, with your upstart.' He moved two steps towards her, his head poked forward. 'You think because he's making money that he can buy himself into a decent society. Well, wherever he goes he'll be like a pig in a parlour and an object of derision.'

'You would like to think so, wouldn't you?' She was glaring back at him. 'You hate him; you've always hated him, and you wish that all the things you're saying were true. But they're not. He's getting on, rising fast, and he is accepted. Because he's himself, he's accepted. You called him an upstart. I–I wonder if you know what people call you.'

'Vanessa!' It was her mother speaking. 'Would you please go now.'

'No. No, I won't until I've had my say.' She kept her eyes on her father as she answered, 'If there's anybody you should have hated it should have been Brett, but even knowing what he did you wouldn't have hated him, because you had felt guilty about him for so long. You had done him out of his job, his rightful job.'

'Vanessa! Do you hear me? Leave the house this minute.'

Vanessa now took three steps along the side of the breakfast table. It was a long way round to the door and she talked as she moved. 'Brett never stood up to you. He hadn't the spunk to stand up to you, not as my Angus'–she stressed the 'my'–'stood up to you when he was just Emily's son . . . and scum, as you have so kindly called him. And there's something I've learned over the years, and it's being proved at this moment, for even if he were still scum he'd be twice the man that you are, and he'll be a name in this town when you're forgotten, like you forgot your own people, my grandfather Ratcliffe.'

'GET OUT!' Jonathan Ratcliffe's hand moved towards the sideboard and groped blindly for something to grip, to throw, to hurl, while his eyes remained fastened on his daughter; and Jane Ratcliffe, rushing in front of him, cried at Vanessa, 'Go, will you! Go!'

It was Susan who, coming into the room, grabbed her sister's arm and pulled her into the hall and to the front door, and almost pushed her through it as she cried, 'You were mad to come here. You know he'll never forgive you. You've only made things worse. And if you were actually aiming to get him to leave this house you've achieved it.'

It was because she knew every inch of the curved drive that she could walk down it with her hand covering her eyes. It was as she turned out of the drive into the main road that a car raced towards her and pulled up with a skidding of brakes, and Angus shot out and stood confronting her, his face livid with an anger that had bleached his rugged complexion white and which had the power to frighten her as her father's anger had not done.

'YOU! YOU!' The spittle sprayed from his lips, and when she bent her head and fell against him, muttering his name, his body remained rigid, and he growled, 'Don't you bloody-well "Oh Angus" me. I'm going in there and getting that deed, if it means I do life for it.'

She was gripping his coat as she sobbed, 'He . . . he hasn't got it. It's here.' She lifted her arm, from which hung the bag, and he snatched it from her and, tearing it open, looked at the long, thick envelope that was wedged inside. He brought the air into his body so quickly that it sent him coughing and spluttering, and he turned from her and leant against the car.

He hadn't been able to take it in when his mother had told him where she had gone. She'd said she'd better tell him in order to break his fall. To break his fall! He had worked for years to get even with that bastard of a Ratcliffe and to see Vanessa installed in her rightful sphere, and what does she do? She takes all his efforts, his early strivings, his sixteen to eighteen hours a day, running, scurrying, planning, aye, and cheating, cheating other men out of contracts with the help of Andrew Fowler, and hands it to the one man he'd like to hang.

His mother had dared to tell him that Vanessa had asked to have the house in her name precisely in order to be able to go to her father and sell it to him, and at the same price. Not only had she tricked him but she had got his mother on to her side an' all, because the old bitch had bawled at him that no man in his right senses would expect his wife to go and live next door to her people after the way they had treated her, and that his wife wasn't out for revenge, only him. And he had bawled back at her that Vanessa would live in that house if he had to tie her in it, and let anybody get in his way to try and stop him getting that deed back from Ratcliffe, and they wouldn't live to tell the tale. And that went for her an' all!

And here he was within a few yards of his new home and his wife crying as if he had knocked her teeth in. And that's what he'd like to do at this very minute. He gripped her by the arm and pushed her into the car. Then, taking his seat, he turned the car swiftly about, drove down the the next gate and into the drive of The Larches.

Vanessa had been sobbing so much that she didn't realize where she was until the car stopped and she looked out of the window. Then she blinked upwards and turned to him and whimpered. 'Oh, no! No, Angus.'

'Get out!' He reached down and pulled her on to the gravel. Then taking firm hold of her, he mounted the steps, put the key in the lock, turned it, and pushed her before him into the house.

They stood in the hall, Vanessa with her head down, he with his up looking about him. He was in Arthur Brett's house. No, no; he was in Angus Cotton's house; but what he saw didn't please him. The hall was big and dark; the panelling browning to black; the twisted rails of the stairs gave them an old-fashioned appearance. This was an old house; it would take thousands to modernise it. He left her and moved towards a door and looked into a room with an ornate and very high ceiling and windows at the far end looking out on a tangle of undergrowth. He passed her once more and looked in another room. It was smaller and the walls looked as if they hadn't been prepared or the woodwork painted since the place had been built, and his knowing eye detected the bulge of dry rot in the two-foot high skirting board to the side of the fireplace.

Vanessa stood perfectly still all the while he looked round the ground floor, and when he stood before her again he said quietly, 'It'll be all right when it's done up.'

Now she looked straight into his face. 'I'll never live here, Angus,' she said. 'You can't make me.'

'Then why did you let me go on and buy the bloody place?' He was bawling now in a restrained way.

'Because I knew I couldn't stop you. You had to buy it. You had to do something to get even with father. Well, now you've got even with him. When I asked you to put it in my name I saw it was a way of getting the hatred out of your system and making up for what I had done to them, because I don't hoodwink myself about that point, Angus. What I did shook the foundations of their life. It might be narrow; they might be mean-spirited, they are mean-spirited; so what I did had a greater effect on them than it would have had it happened to parents more generous-minded. Their whole aim in life was social prestige, and I tore the foundations of it from under their feet. I . . . I might as well tell you now, I've wanted to go back for years; I've wanted to see them, not because I loved them, but, well, I can't really explain, ties, blood, kinship, what you will, but I've wanted to see them; I wanted to know if I was forgiven; and I've found out . . . They'll never forgive me. My father will live and die hating me. I knew he'd rather be crucified than be under the slightest obligation to either of us, and–and it saddens me to the very soul. I can't help it. That's how it is.'

The mighty wind was being taken out of his sails. A deflating calm was settling on him. He fought it by saying, 'We could pull it down and build.'

'No, no, Angus; it wouldn't make any difference. You see, I couldn't bear to live near them. And anyway, they wouldn't allow it, they'd move.'

'That's what I was hoping.' There was iron in his voice again. 'To put them on the move; to let them see that he isn't the only one that can crack the whip and see men jump.'

'And what would that achieve? He would move to a bigger and better place. He could raise the money; his name is good.'

'Meaning mine isn't?'

'You know I don't mean that.'

'Look, I don't mind telling you now that I've had to do some twisting and bribing to get this piece of land. The house doesn't matter; it's the land. Yet all the while I've seen you here in this house, where you belong.'

'I don't belong in this house, Angus. What is more, I've never liked this house. I belong,' she paused, 'I belong where you belong; but you don't belong here. Face it; you don't belong here.'

He turned from her, the colour rushing into his face, and she said softly now, 'I realized a long time ago that I never belonged here either. I was the odd one out. I couldn't help being born here no more than you could being born in Ryder's Row.'

She watched him walk away from her and open the doors that led on to the overgrown terrace, and slowly she followed him. Her heart beating rapidly she followed him down the steps and along the narrow path that led into the wood, and all the while she knew what he was thinking. Somewhere in here they used to meet, him and her. She had known all along; at least since she had learned he had bought the place, that this moment would come, but she prayed now he wouldn't make his way down to the river and the summerhouse.

He stopped under an oak tree, almost on the spot where Brett had kissed her good-bye on that last night before he died, and standing dumbly before him she returned his look, his questioning, probing look; then, her voice breaking, she said, 'Come away from here, Angus, please. Please. I'm asking, you, begging you. Please.'

He turned and walked silently up into the house, through it and to the car.

His jaw was stiff and his eyes hard.

When they reached the bottom of Brampton Hill she broke the silence by saying, 'Would . . . would you like to drive me out to the quarry, Angus?'

He cast a quick glance at her; then, his eyes on the road again, he growled, 'Why the quarry?'

'I . . . I would like to show you something.'

'At the quarry?' His mouth was square.

'Yes, YES, ANGUS.' She shouted the last two words, and when again he glanced at her she was looking out through the windscreen and she said, quite loudly still. 'You don't seem to take anything in unless it's bawled at you.' Another time this would have made him smile, even laugh, but his expression didn't change; yet when they came to the roundabout he didn't go back into town but went straight ahead.

Fifteen minutes later he drew the car up in yellow mud beside a great hole; and when he alighted he didn't open the door for her to get out but stood by the bonnet waiting, silent and tense. She came now and stood beside him, her hands resting on the bonnet as she asked, 'How much would you have to pay for it, I mean the quarry itself and the bit of hill beyond?' She nodded into the distance.

'Pay for it? You mean buy it?' He screwed up his face at her.

'Yes.'

'In the name of God what for? Why should I buy a hole? There's nothing more I can get out of it, it's finished.'

She walked away from him on to flat ground, stepping on hard surfaces where she could find them, and made her way past stone outhouses that were the only remains of a country house that had once stood where the sandpit was now. She climbed a slope, not looking back to see if he was following, and at the top she stood and looked about her.

Angus stopped when he was a yard or so from her. He didn't want to go near her at the moment. If she had been May or someone like May he would have skelped her lugs long afore this, and likely given her a black eye into the bargain. Making a blasted fool of him. But she wasn't May, or someone like May. Funny, he should think of May now; she hadn't crossed his mind for years. He supposed he had thought of her, because she was the kind who wouldn't have thwarted him; his word would have been law to her. She wouldn't have wanted to have brought him down to pocket size.

Vanessa was pointing now. 'Look,' she said; 'down there. There's the river. It's like a scaly snake going round the town, isn't it? And over there.' She pointed to the right. 'You can see for miles and miles, open countryside.' She came towards him and put her hands on his thick, broad chest before she said, 'I'd like you to build our house here, Angus.'

He strained back from her, his face all creased up, his head moving slowly. Then with a jerk he was free from her hands, and he kicked the earth as he said, 'Here! You must be bloody well barmy, woman.'

'I'd–I'd like it built here, Angus.' She was smiling now. 'I can see it. I came out last week and measured.'

'You what!' His shout resounded down the valley.

'That's it, shout.' She nodded at him. 'You'll hear the echo of it from up here.'

He spoke a few tones lower now as he said, 'You came up here and measured . . . ?'

She stared at him. She thought he was going to choke. She felt strangely calm now, at peace, and, more strangely still, in control of the situation . . . and him.

'Yes, I came up here and measured. I want it long and low, and spreading, with a paved terrace all about it. And that,' she swung round and pointed to the quarry, 'that'll be a lake with a boat on it. Two boats; and a diving board just there.' She pointed farther away to the side.

'Christ Almighty!' He had his head bowed now, holding his brow.

'How much land is there altogether, including . . . the hole?'

'You're not serious?'

'I was never more serious. That's a trite phrase.' She smiled tightly. 'What I should have said was, I'm doing something on my own for the first time in my life . . . besides having babies.' Her smile widened. 'How much land is there?' she repeated.

'About four acres.'

'Very nice.' She put her head on one side. 'There used to be heather on this part of the fell at one time, and not so very long ago because I can remember it. We'll have heather again, a heather garden, and shrubs, rhododendrons and azaleas. And the house on the rise here.' She spread an arm wide. 'And the gardens running down to the road on that side, and down to the lake on that.'

She was walking away from him now, down the slope towards the stone buildings. The door of the first one was half ajar and she went in and looked about her. The place had three rooms. One had been used as an office, the other two as a storage place for tools. She saw Emily living here, near Angus, yet still independent. She said so as soon as he came through the door.

He stood staring at her again. She looked different, more beautiful, more of a woman at this moment than she had ever been before; even after having the bairns. She was stately, mature, classy; aye, that was the word, classy. He was still furious inside at her, at the position she had put him in; at the way she had brought his castle tumbling down as if she had barraged it with a twelve-pounder, and now she was asking for favours. . . . No, she wasn't asking, she was demanding. She had her plans all made, and he knew that when he had time to simmer down and think he would realize that she was right about building above the hole. He knew that she had what he would never have, vision. And she had thought of his mother an' all. He would remember that, aye.

She had her back to him and she startled him now by saying, 'You don't have to buy me anymore, Angus.'

'WHAT!'

'You heard what I said. You still think you have to buy me; you've got to give me something to keep me with you. I've so many clothes I don't know where to put them, and jewellery that I never wear. You know. Angus, your imagination is limited, even to your own capabilities and attraction. Oh yes, you're always yelling about what you can do, but inside you're always fearful of not being able to accomplish it. It's true, isn't it?' She waited, and when he didn't answer she went on, 'I've never really talked to you, shown you my real feelings, and you've been aware of this all the while, but I'd like you to know something now. It's just this, that whether I knew it or not I loved you when I married you, and now I can't love you any more . . . I mean,' she moved her head hastily, 'I can't love you any more than I do; I'll never be able to love you any more than I do at this moment. If you gave me everything in the world it wouldn't make any difference. As to yourself, I don't want you to change, no matter what you think. I know that only with you, and through you, can I be happy. . . . There's been a sort of vacant spot in me for a long time. You didn't fill it, and the children didn't fill it, so I thought it was the miss of my people, and my venture today was as much to see them and find out to make things right in other ways. But now I know that we're cut off for good and all, the void, in a strange way, is filled, and . . . and I'm not unhappy about it now. One thing I know is that I want to start a life of my own, on my own plane, on our own plane, neither lower-class nor middle-class, but our class. Your mother and Rosie have ceased to stress how different I am from them by every look and word, yet they still look upon me in the same way as they did when I first came into their lives. Beneath the surface we haven't mixed. But you and I are different, Angus; we've rubbed off on each other.' Her voice was trembling as she finished, 'I love you, Angus; and–and not just out of gratitude, as you've always thought.'

Her whole body trembled as he came towards her, and when he held her face between his rough hands she put hers up and cupped his. Slowly now he dropped his head forward on to her shoulder and muttered thickly, 'Thanks, Van. Thanks.' Then after a moment he added, haltingly, 'I love you so much I'd go crazy without you. You know that, don't you?' Her heart beats were sending the blood flowing fast through her veins and she was about to answer, 'You'll never have to be without me, darling, never.' But that was a reply she could have made to Arthur Brett had she married him. It was a formal, acceptable, reply. What she wanted was a reply to fit the plane on which they were going to live from now on. If Emily had ever been called upon to reply to such a statement undoubtedly she would have said, 'You might go crazy without me, lad, but there's an even chance you'll go bloody well stark staring mad with me.' But she wasn't Emily, and she couldn't bring herself to swear to be amusing. Yet she wanted him to laugh as Emily could; she wanted to bring him back to normality; she wanted to set the pattern for the future, and so she ventured, in a good imitation of her mother-in-law's voice, 'Aye, I do, an' I'll Emily Cotton well see that you never get the chance to be without me, lad.'

The result was even more successful than she had anticipated. His head came up and he stared at her blankly for a moment; then he dropped it back on his shoulders and let out a roar of deep laughter, such laughter as she hadn't heard from him for a long time. It seemed to sweep away the obsession of his years of striving, and, as he picked her up, as if she were a child, and swung her around, she laughed loudly too.

When they were standing still again, he gathered her into his arms and he looked into her face before he said, with a self-conscious shyness that was new, 'Remember Mam's bit of poetry? Well, I'm always saying it in me mind to you:

'I have you fast in my fortress,
And will not let you depart,
But put you down into the dungeon
In the round tower of my heart.

And there will I keep you for ever,
Yes, for ever and a day,
Till the walls shall crumble to ruin,
And moulder in dust away.'

'Oh, Angus. Angus.' For the first time in their joint lives her mouth dropped fiercely on to his.

Bower Place and Ryder's Row were merging.

The Fifteen Streets

The Fifteen Streets

Author's note

The characters in this book are entirely fictitious and have no relation to any living person.

Although the setting is Tyneside and several place names have been used, 'The Fifteen Streets' are imaginary.

Owing to difficulty in comprehension by the uninitiated, I have not adhered to the Tyneside dialect.

Chapter One

The Brothers

'Hannah, drop that an' come an' see. The O'Briens are at it again . . . blue murder! Come on. Come upstairs, you can see better from our top window.'

Wiping the soap suds from her arms. Hannah Kelly hastily lifted the lid of the wash-house boiler, scooped off the grey scum with an enamel mug, dabbed the contents of the boiler with a stick, then ran out of the wash-house and across the back-yard, thinking as she did so, 'Eeh, I haven't got time for this. . . . And our Joe warned me.'

She caught up with her neighbour as she was opening the stair door.

'Who is it this time? The old man?'

'Yes.'

'Who's he at? Dominic?'

'Aye.'

'Are they drunk?'

'Are they ever owt else!'

They scurried across the kitchen to the front room, and automatically took up their stations, one at each side of the window, bodies close to the wall, heads held slightly to the side against the mesh of the Nottingham lace curtains, their arms wound tightly in their aprons.

'My God, what a mess, Bella!'

'He must have thrown them two pictures out since I came down for you.'

'Eeh, God Almighty! It's a shame. Just as Mary Ellen was getting things pulled together again.'

'Look'–there was glee in Bella's voice–'there they are at the window throttling each other. Christ!' she exclaimed as something came hurtling through the window into the street, 'which one missed that, I wonder?'

'Eeh! he's thrown the pot through the window. Oh, Bella, that'll bring the pollis. God Almighty, it's awful! It's enough to bring on the bairn . . . she's at the worst time, on eight months.'

'Best thing that could happen. Who wants a bairn at forty-five, I ask you? She should have been more cute. Anyway, she wouldn't listen to me. I told her I could get her a bottle of white mixture from our Harry's Emma, who scrubs the wards up at the grubber; the nurses would have given it to her. It would have skited everything out of her.'

'Well, you know she wouldn't do that, she's a Catholic, Bella.'

'Catholic, be damned! They tell 'em to have bairns, but do they bloody well keep them? I'd like to see any priest tell me I must have bairns. Do you know what I'd say?'

Hannah chuckled. 'I've a pretty good idea. . . . Look, there she is, there's Mary Ellen. She looks like death.'

They both became silent and watched the woman below picking up the two picture frames from the road. The loose glass splintered about her feet as she shook the frames, and as she shooed some children away from the broken chamber, Hannah remarked, regretfully, 'Pity about that. It was a boody one, too.'

Unblinkingly they watched the woman edge her way indoors, with neither a glance upwards nor to the right or left, although as they knew, she was fully aware of the watchers. Only the children were on the street, staring silently until the door closed, when they drew nearer, and some daring spirits, braving the glass, hitched themselves up on to the high window sill to get their faces level with the hole. But as they did so the blind was dropped, and Hannah exclaimed, clicking her tongue. 'She shouldn't have done that–dropping the blind right down before dark–it's the sign of a death. It'll be the bairn, likely.'

'Damn good job too. Better if it was her old man though, in case he lands her with another.'

They turned slowly from the window, and Hannah said, 'By, that wouldn't have happened if John had been in; he'd have put a stop to that. . . . Funny, isn't it, Bella, that the old man doesn't go for John.'

'Not funny a bit. He's afraid of him, if the truth was known. Old O'Brien and Dominic are both alike, full of wind and water. That's why they fight. . . . By God! I wish I was in Mary Ellen's place for five minutes. I'd lay those two sods out with the poker! She's soft, that's what she is, soft as clarts. . . . Are you going to stay for a cup of tea?' she added. 'I'll put the kettle on, it won't be a minute.'

'No, lass, I'm not half through, and it's getting on for dark.'

Bella glanced sideways at Hannah. 'Should you come across Mary Ellen–you see her more than I do–and she tells you what it was all about, knock up.'

'Aye, I will. But there's small chance. She's close, is Mary Ellen. You know that.'

'I know she doesn't like me. Thinks I can't mind me own business.'

And she's right there, thought Hannah.

'And anyway, I'm not the same colour as them,' went on Bella nodding her long horse-face. 'Me St Patrick's Day's colour's blue. Wait until next Thursday week when Dominic's wearing his shamrock. There'll be skull and hair flying then. The fifteen streets won't hold him. . . . My God, remember last St Patrick's Day? That was a do, eh?' She laughed at the memory.

'Eeh, Bella, I must be off.' Hannah unwrapped her mottled arms, and banged out the creases in her coarse apron.

'Well don't forget to knock up if you hear owt.'

'I won't.'

Hannah went down the stairs, walking sideways in case she slipped, as the stairs were too narrow for her feet encased in an old pair of men's boots. By the time she reached the bottom she had also reached a decision: she wouldn't tell Bella Bradley what she heard, if she heard owt at all. Too nosey was Bella, by half. She'd rather keep in with Mary Ellen, narrow as she was. At least, she minded her own business. And her Joe warned her only last night against Bella Bradley. He said he'd bash her face in if he found her upstairs again–he was nettled after hearing what she said about their Nancy not being all there. He knew Nancy wasn't all there, but it maddened him to hear any one say it. More so now that Nancy was growing up. . . . Hannah sighed. What would become of Nancy? She didn't know. And anyway, there was no time to think now, the washing had to be finished.

Across the road, in number 10 Fadden Street, Mary Ellen O'Brien worked in the semi-darkness behind the drawn blind. She adjusted the block of wood under the chest of drawers–the leg had been kicked off during the last row–and screwed in the knob of the top drawer. She picked up the grey blanket and patchwork quilt from the floor and spread them again over the lumpy bare mattress on the iron bed. She pushed the wicker table back into the centre of the room, and stood leaning on its weak support, breathing heavily. Her eyes, dry with the pricking dryness of sand, looked round the walls. They were quite bare. . . . Well, they would remain so. The only two pictures in the house were now gone. Never again would she try to build up. She had told herself, if they went this time it would be the last.

She looked towards the closed door, which led into the kitchen. She knew that beyond, on either side of the fireplace, they'd be sitting, spent. Their rage and passion flown, they would be like the two halves of one body, accepting each other now that the conflict was over for a time.

She lifted her apron and wiped the sweat from her forehead. If only they weren't so big . . . like giants. She hadn't dared go between them this time because of the bairn. . . . She put her hand on the raised globe of her stomach and felt a movement. It brought no sense of feeling to her other than that of apprehension. Why, oh why was she to have this all over again? Hadn't she been through enough in her time? During the twenty-six years of her married life she had given birth to eleven bairns, and only five were alive, for which she thanked God. What she would have done with thirteen in these three rooms only the Almighty knew.

A pain through her breast made her gasp, and she covered it with her hand, lifting up its weight. Last year this time they'd been flat . . . flat for all time she'd thought, for it was ten years since Katie was born. Practically every year since she was married she'd been dropped, but from Katie there'd been nothing. The pain shot through her again, and she remembered such a pain from the past. It was before John was born. She was as strong as a horse then, as small as she was, and she enjoyed the feeling of the pain, anticipating the tugging of the young mouth on the nipples . . . if it lived. It did live, and it was John . . . John, who had never given her any trouble. Oh, if they were all like John, and, at the other end of the scale, Katie. Funny that these two should be alike and the others so different from them. Dominic was different from the day he was born, the year after John. She had always been slightly afraid of Dominic, even when he was a child. It wasn't that he alone suffered from the O'Brien rages, for they all did, except Katie. It was rather that there was something fiendish about Dominic. It showed in everything he did, in his teasing, in his laughter, and especially in his good-looking face. Like John and Mick, he took after his da for his looks. But although they all took after their da Dominic and Mick were better looking than John. When she looked at her eldest son she had the feeling that the features which made the other two good looking made him ugly, and in some strange way this pleased her. To her mind it separated him entirely from them. It was his nose that made the difference, she supposed, with that funny little nob on the side of the nostril. He got that when he climbed the dock wall to get some coal that bad winter. He slipped and his nose was cut on the broken glass set in the top of the wall. The cut did not join properly and gave his face a quaint look from the side. But it wasn't only his nose; John's eyes were different from the others. They were large and brown too, but a different brown . . . dark and kind. That was it, they were kind, like Katie's.

She sighed and rubbed her hand gently round and round her breast. Then, hearing a shout coming through the kitchen from the back-yard, she moved her head impatiently–she never thought of Molly unless the girl made herself felt by sight or sound. Molly was . . . well, she couldn't place Molly. She was of a too apparent mixture of them all, and so had no individuality of her own. She was swayed, first one way and then the other; even her rages could be deflected by a stronger will. No, Molly would be no heartache, for she aroused no feeling.

Mary Ellen straightened her shoulders and refastened the top button of her blouse over her straining breasts before walking towards the kitchen door. It was no use standing here thinking; thinking got you nowhere. It was close on five o'clock, and John would be in at half past. She'd have to get on with the tea. . . . Thank God they fought in here and not in the kitchen. They might have knocked the pan of broth off the hob, and there was nearly fourpennorth of vegetables in besides a twopenny scrag end. . . . Well, if you searched hard enough there was always something to be thankful for.

As she expected, her husband and son were sitting one each side of the fireplace, their brows puckered over half-closed eyes. Shane's grey hair was standing up straight in tufts; there was blood on the hair near his temple, and his high cheek bones were showing blue under the tightened skin. At the first glance she saw that his rage wasn't entirely spent, for the muscle was moving in his cheek as he clenched and unclenched his teeth, and his limbs, as always, were jerking with the nerve tick. His knees, in their reddened moleskin trousers, were wide apart, and his feet were crossed below his hands, which were gripping the seat of the wooden armchair. His body looked as if it was still ready to spring. . . . No, his rage wasn't spent yet, because he was sober. He'd had only two shifts in this week and had tipped the money up. But Dominic had a full week. For three weeks now he'd worked full weeks. Not that it made much difference to her–she was lucky if she got ten shillings out of him. She often had to meet him at the dock gates to get even that . . . or send Katie. But Dominic's rage was spent because he was drunk and happy.

She took Dominic by the shoulder and shook him. 'Here! Get yourself to bed.'

He lifted his head and smiled crookedly at her, cracking the dried blood on his mouth as he did so. He looked at her out of one merry, brown eye, the other being hidden behind a curling lock of light brown, youthful hair.

'All right, old girl.'

He rose obediently to his feet, and some detached part of her marvelled for the countless time at his docility towards her when he was in drink. Why was it she could manage him when he was drunk? She even found herself liking him in this state. She had no fear of him in drink, when he spoke civilly to her, often with a touch of affection. But it was strange that even in drink she could have any affection for him now, for she remembered the look in his eyes during these past weeks when they lit on her stomach . . . ridicule, scorn, and something else . . . a something for which she could find no word. She pushed him before her into the bedroom, her head coming just to the bottom of his shoulder blades. She always wondered, when close to them, how she gave birth to such great men.

Dominic sat down with a plop on the side of his bed and began to laugh. 'If he wasn't my old man I'd have knocked him stiff. But I'll break his bloody neck the next time he interferes with me. I didn't ask to be set on the ore boat–they want the young 'uns down the holds.'

He fell back on the bed and lifted up his legs, and Mary Ellen immediately swung them down again. She took off his boots and loosened his belt, then unbuttoned his trousers and tugged them off his legs, leaving these looking particularly ludicrous in their tight long pants. Never in all the many times she had pulled trousers off them had she yet been able to conquer the feeling of revulsion. Husband or son, it was the same.

She heaved him up by the shirt front and dragged off his coat. Then she let him fall back on to the bed. She threw the quilt over him and put his coat on top of it, and lifting his trousers quietly from the floor, she put them across her arm and went out, through the kitchen, past her husband, who now sat hunched up over the fire, and into the front room, where she turned out the contents of the trousers pockets on to the table.

There was a half-sovereign, two two-shilling pieces, and four pennies. The half-sovereign he would have to stump up for his board, so she put that back into the pocket again, together with a two-shilling piece. The other two-shilling piece and the coppers went into a little cloth bag that dangled from a pin fastened to the inside of her skirt. It already held tenpence. She had taken to this device of the bag when Shane came back from the Boer War, because he lifted every penny he could get his fingers on for drink.

She went back to the bedroom and quietly placed the trousers over the bed rail, and as she returned to the kitchen the window was darkened by a distorted bulk, and a gentle tap-tap came on the door.

Mary Ellen sighed. As inevitably as the calm which followed the storm would come this tap-tap on the door after any disturbance in the house. She often thanked God for an upstairs neighbour such as Peggy Flaherty. Many a one, placed as she was above the noise and fighting that was almost part of the weekly routine, would have done more than object, she would have brought the pollis; and after a number of such visits they would have been in court and likely turned out of the house. Peggy was a bit queer; still, as God knew, there were worse states than being queer. But today, Mary Ellen felt tired, and even Peggy's well-meant sympathy was an irritant. She opened the door, and would have smiled, if she could, at the quaint tact of this fat, dirty woman.

'I was after warming meself up with a mouthful of stew, Mary Ellen, an' I said to meself, "I'll take a drop below, it'll stick to Mary Ellen's ribs."' She proffered the basin, full of a lead-coloured liquid, with darker pieces of matter floating about on its surface. 'Are you all right, lass?' She peered at Mary Ellen through her short-sighted eyes, looking for a black eye or other evidence of the fight.

'Yes, I'm all right, Peggy. And thanks for the soup.'

'Oh, that's all right, Mary Ellen. . . . You'll drink it, now, won't you?'

'Yes, yes,' Mary Ellen hastily assured her, wondering whether Peggy was suspicious of the fate of her proffered balms. She would have to be very hungry, she thought, before she ate anything made by Peggy's hands in that menagerie upstairs. Before he died, Charlie Flaherty earned his living in many ways. At one time, he worked for himself as a tally man, and when payment was not forthcoming, took the equivalent in kind; so two of the three rooms upstairs were stacked from floor to ceiling with an odd assortment of things, not one of which Peggy would part with, ranging from a stuffed baby crocodile to a collection of books, out of which Peggy was wont to say 'she got the extinsive iducation' she possessed. She spread more false knowledge round the fifteen streets than it was possible to imagine. Many of the inhabitants would have sworn that Henry VIII was Queen Elizabeth's husband, and that England once belonged to the Irish before William the Conqueror came over and took it from them. For the sum of a penny she would write a letter; for a little more, give advice on how to deal with a summons, or a case of defamation of character, or assault. Often this advice, if faithfully carried out, would have got the worried seeker a sojourn in jail. It was strange, that although she was said to be odd and barmy, her advice was still sought. Perhaps it was because it was known that on these pennies she mainly relied for her existence. There was an unspoken feeling in these streets, which, if translated, would have implied . . . you save someone the workhouse and you'll never land there yourself.

'God and His Holy Mother preserve us this day, the trials we have! Is there anything more I can do for you, Mary Ellen?' went on Peggy.

'No, I'm all right, Peggy, thanks.' Mary Ellen looked at the basin in her hands, hoping to convey a hint that she would like to go in and make a start on the soup.

But Peggy did not notice this move; or if she did, she refused to take the hint; for she had something weighty to say. Leaning forward, she whispered,

'Did I ever tell you, Mary Ellen, Mr Flaherty's cure for all this?' She nodded towards the closed scullery door.

Mary Ellen, suppressing another sigh, said, 'No, Peggy.'

'Iducation! No man would fight, he said, once he had iducation. And he knew what he was talking about, for he got about among the gentry, you know, Mary Ellen. It was his theory that once a man got iducation he wouldn't raise a hand to his wife. He might, being a human being, get a bit irritated and say, "Retire to your room before I kick your backside!" or some such thing, but to lift his hand . . . no!'

'There may be something in it.' Mary Ellen again looked at the basin. 'Sure you haven't left yourself short, Peggy?'

'Not at all. Not at all. Away you go now inside, and don't talk anymore; and get that down you, it'll put a lining on your stomach. And remember, if you want any advice you know where to come.'

She shuffled away, and Mary Ellen closed the door. . . . Don't talk anymore, and, Retire to your room before I kick your backside! If there was a laugh left in her she would have laughed; but she would remember them, and some night by the fire she would tell them to John, and they would laugh together.

John came in at half-past five. He hung his cap and coat, together with his black neckerchief on the back of the kitchen door, then sat down on a box in the tiny square of scullery and loosened the yorks that bound his trousers below the knee. Before washing his hands in the tin dish that was standing on another box he looked into the lighted kitchen and smiled towards the three children sitting at the table. Only Katie returned his smile, her round, blue eyes sending him a greeting.

Mick called, 'Got anything, John? Any bananas or anything?'

And he answered, 'Not tonight; we're still on the grain boat.'

When John came to the table, his mother set a plate of broth before him, out of which a series of bare ribs stuck up, like the skeleton of a hulk. The smell was appetizing, and the eyes of the three children focused on the plate.

Mary Ellen exclaimed harshly, 'Get on with your bread and dripping!' and almost simultaneously each bit into his own inch-thick slice of bread.

She placed another plate on the table and said to her husband, 'Your tea's out.'

Shane turned from the fire and stared at the plate, and from there to his son and the other three. His body started to jerk, first his head, then his arms, and lastly his right leg. His words too, when they came, were spasmodic and heavy with bitterness: 'Served last now, am I? It's a difference when you're not bringing it in. You've got to work or you don't eat . . . not till everybody else is finished.'

John put his spoon down and stared at his father: 'I'll wait until you're done.'

His mother signalled wildly to him from behind her husband, and pointed to the bedroom. John read her signal, but continued to stare at his father, until Shane's eyes dropped away and he growled, 'It's them young 'uns–I was never set down before me father.'

His head jerked to one side as if he was straining at a bit, and Mary Ellen said quietly, 'Don't be a fool! Get your tea.'

'You want to start, you do!' Shane sprang up from his chair, kicking it to one side as he did so. 'It only needs you to start. Belittling me before the bairns! That's a new tack.' He towered like a swaying mountain of rage over the short unwieldy figure of his wife.

Mary Ellen took no notice, but went on cutting bread on the corner of the oil cloth which covered the table, and the children continued to eat, their eyes fixed on their plates. Only John kept his eyes on his father, and Shane lifted his bloodshot gaze from the top of his wife's head to meet John's again. He stared at his son for a moment, his compressed lips moving in and out. Then he swung round, grabbed his cap from the back of the door and went to go out: but as he reached the back door he paused and cast his infuriated glance back into the kitchen again: 'The next bloody thing'll be: There's the door. . . . Get out!'

He kicked savagely at the box holding the dish of water. There was a clatter and a splash; the door opened and banged, and only the clink of his heel plates becoming fainter down the yard broke the silence in the kitchen.

When they could be heard no more, Mary Ellen moved. She went into the scullery and, bending down with difficulty, began to sop up the water from the hollowed stones.

Dimly, with a mixture of pity and understanding, her thoughts followed her husband . . . Dominic getting drunk on his earnings . . . John coming in from work. Both of them on full time, and him with only two shifts in. He was getting on and he couldn't work like he used to, and the gaffer picked the young and strong 'uns. His strength was failing–she'd noticed that. Drink and hard work and wet clothes that were often frozen to his skin were at last taking their toll. He seemed to retain his strength for one thing alone . . . if only that would slacken with the rest. It must sometime. Then God, let it be soon.

'I'll help you, ma.' Katie was on her knees by the side of her mother.

'No! Get up out of that. That's the only clean pinny you've got!'

'Well I haven't got to go to school the morrer.'

'Doesn't matter. Get up out of that.'

'Here!'–John stood above her–'let's have it.' He held out his hand for the cloth.

'Oh get out of me road, the both of you!' Her voice pushed them back into the kitchen, and she went on bending and wringing out the cloth. Who did they think did all the other work, the washing, the cooking, the scouring, the humping of the coal, bucket by bucket from the back lane into the coal house because now she couldn't throw the shovelfuls through the hatch?

She partly soothed her irritation by saying to herself: 'You know John's always telling you to leave the coal until he comes in. Yes, but how can I'–her irritation refused to be soothed–'with people waiting to get their washing out!' She flung the cloth into the bucket. Oh, she felt so tired. If only she could see a way out of all this . . . if only the bairn was born! Yes, that was the main stumbling block. Once that was over everything would be all right; she would cope, as always.

She went into the kitchen again and said to Mick, 'Go and empty the bucket and wash it out, and bring some clean water. . . . See you wash it out, mind!'

Mick's mouth dropped, and he muttered, 'Aw! Why can't she do it?'

He dug Molly in the side, and she cried, 'Look at him, ma! Stop it, our Mick!'

John took the rib of bones from his mouth: 'Your mother spoke to you.'

'Me ear's bad'–Mick placed his hand over the side of his head–'it's been running all day.'

'You going out to play the night?' John asked.

'Yes.' Mick scowled at the table.

'Then empty the bucket.'

John went on picking his bone, and Mick clattered from the table, while Molly sniggered into her pinny.

'You'll laugh the other side of your face in a minute, my girl,' said Mary Ellen. 'Get those dishes washed.'

'Then can I go out to play?'

'Who you going out to play with in the dark, you're not going to run the streets?'

'We're going in Annie Kelly's wash-house; her ma's had the pot on, and it's warm. Annie has some bits of candle, and we're going to put them in bottles and play houses and dress up.'

'Play houses and dress up,' Mary Ellen muttered to herself. Aloud, she said, 'And burn yourselves to death! . . . Well, and only half an hour, mind. And you can take Katie with you.'

'I don't want to go, ma; I've got to do some homework.'

'What!' the mother and John lifted their heads and stared at Katie.

'You got your sums wrong?' asked John, in surprise.

'No.' Katie shook her head and tried to repress a smile, but her eyes grew rounder and her dimples deeper as she looked at their straight faces.

'Then why have you to do homework?' John asked; 'you never have before.'

'I've got to learn something. Miss Llewellyn asked me to . . .'

'She's Miss Llewellyn's pet, everybody says she is. . . . I hated Miss Llewellyn. I was glad when I was moved up.' Molly wet the tip of her finger on her tongue, and in this way she secured a number of crumbs from the table. When she had put them in her mouth, she swung round on Katie, saying, 'You didn't tell me ma Miss Llewellyn gave you a penny the day for learning your poetry first, did you? Nelly Crane told me . . . so!'

The smile vanished from Katie's face, and Mary Ellen looked down on her daughter in surprise, the daughter who was the only one of the family to take after her. She could see this child, as she herself once was, plump and bonnie and open-handed. It was unusual for Katie to keep anything.

'Did she give you a penny?' she asked.

Katie neither moved nor spoke, but her eyes, as they looked back into her mother's, became glazed, and she cried out within herself, 'Oh, our Molly! Our Molly!' Now it was all spoilt–the wonderful, wonderful thing she was going to do was spoilt. The Easter egg . . . the real Easter egg in a real box, tied up with a real silk ribbon, was lying in fragments about her! And the picture of herself handing it to Miss Llewellyn was lying with it.

That penny had brought her secret hoard to fivepence. For three weeks she had kept John's Saturday penny and the two halfpennies her mother had given her. Today's surprise penny had meant such a lot, for she had only another month or so during which to get the remainder of the shilling.

Her mother became blotted out by a mist; then she felt John's big hands drawing her to him and pressing her against his knees.

When he bent and whispered in her ear, 'Are you saving up to buy a present?' she experienced the feeling she had felt before that John was in some way connected with God and the priests, because he knew everything.

She nodded her head against the bottom of his waistcoat, and he whispered again, 'Your teacher?'

At this she gasped and pressed her face tightly against him. John exchanged a glance with his mother, and a smile flickered for an instant across her face.

'I think you must be the cleverest lass in the school,' John went on.

Katie brought her head up swiftly and stared at him. 'Why, that's what Miss Llewellyn says! She says . . . she says I'm advanced and I must work at nights and . . . and read a lot.'

'There you are. There you are. Miss Llewellyn knows. She knows when she's on a good thing. What have you got to learn the night?'

'Oh, I already know some of it, the end bit,' she laughed. 'Listen. A man named Shakespeare did it.' She stood back from his knee, threw her long black plaits over her shoulder, joined her hands behind her back, and said:

'There take an inventory of all I have,
To the last penny; 'tis the king's: my role,
And my integrity to heaven is all
I dare now call my own. O Cromwell, Cromwell!
Had I but serv'd my God with half the zeal
I serv'd my king, he would not in mine age
Have left me naked to mine enemies.'

John stared down on her face, which was illuminated by the feel of the strange words on her tongue, and Mary Ellen stared at the back of her dark head. Then their eyes met, reflecting the glow of her words, which were unintelligible to both of them. . . . But Katie had said them . . . their Katie . . . the only one of them who had ever wanted to learn. With a swoop, John lifted her up and held her on his upstretched hands. Her head was within a few inches of the ceiling, and he laughed up at her: 'Will I push you through to Mrs Flaherty?'

'Eeh! No, John. Eeh, our John, let me down.'

She wriggled on his hands, anxious to get away from the ceiling and the proximity of Mrs Flaherty and her weird house.

As he lowered her to the floor John laughed, 'You'll soon be cleverer than Mrs Flaherty, and then everybody will be coming here and saying, "Please, Katie O'Brien, will you write me a letter?' and you'll say, 'Yes, if you give me sixpence."'

'Oh, our John, I wouldn't! I wouldn't ask for sixpence.'

He bent down to her and whispered hoarsely, 'Oh yes you would, if it would get your teacher a present.'

She slapped his knee playfully, then turned her face away to hide the telltale glow.

Molly banged the mugs into the cupboard; she banged the door as she went out; then her voice came through the keyhole:

'Miss Llewellyn has a swellin',
An' I'm not tellin'
Where Miss Llewellyn
Has a swellin'.'

John turned quickly away from Katie's outraged face, rubbing his hand across his mouth. But he could not rub the laughter from his eyes, and Katie turned on him, her voice full of hurt surprise: 'Oh, our John, you're laughing! Our Molly's awful. . . . Miss Llewellyn hasn't got a . . . She's lovely, she's beautiful. She wears a lovely white blouse with a frill at her neck, and her hair's brown and shines all over the place. And Mr Culbert's after her. Cathleen Pearson says he wants to marry her.' Katie's voice broke: 'She's beautiful . . . she's beautiful.'

John sat down by the fire and pulled her on to his knee, cradling her in his arms and soothing her: 'Of course she's beautiful, of course she is. And who's Mr Culbert when he's out?'

'He's . . . he's a teacher at St Jude's.'

'Is he? Is he? Well, he can be the Prime Minister for all I care. But you know what I'm going to do? I'm going to this Mr Culbert, and I'm going to say, "You going to marry Miss Llewellyn and take her way from teaching our Katie? You are . . . like panhacklety!!"'

'Oh, our John, you're awful!'

Laughing, she scrambled up and stood on his knees and flung her arms about his neck, endeavouring to strangle him with her small strength.

'Here! hold on.'

'Eeeh!'–she drew her face back from his–'you haven't got to say that.'

'What, hold on?'

'Yes. Miss Llewellyn says you've got to say, "Wait a moment," or, "Stop a moment."'

'Do you hear that, ma?' He winked at his mother, who was now sitting at the other side of the hearth mending a pair of moleskin trousers.

She gave a flicker of a smile and went on adjusting a patch. What was it about these two bairns of hers that brought her such strange joy? To see them playing together like they were now seemed to make up for all the heart scolds of life. She still thought of John as her bairn, although he was twenty-two and six foot one. He would always be her bairn, her first bairn. There were some who said you loved all you gave birth to. Fools! You couldn't love even two alike. Even those two opposite, she loved one more than the other, but she couldn't tell which.

Her mind returned to concrete things, and she said without looking up, 'The front window's out.'

John did not reply, but after a moment put Katie on the floor and, taking a box of matches from his pocket, went to the front room.

Katie was about to follow him, when Mary Ellen said, 'Get on with your homework, hinny.'

It was some time before John returned, and still he said nothing. He sat down on his chair again and took off his boots and put his stockinged feet on the fender, and sat staring at the kettle singing on the side of the hob. Presently he took a loose Woodbine from his pocket and lit it. . . . Would it never end? Would life go on like this for her until she died?

He cast a glance at her bent head. The hair was grey, yet coarse and strong, springing from the centre parting and refusing to be drawn flat into the knob behind; but the face beneath was deeply marked with lines. They ran in puckered furrows across her forehead and bit deep from her nose to the corners of her mouth. The mouth in repose, as it was now, looked despondent, without hope. Could you wonder at it! And there was this other thing to happen. And her so little, not much bigger than a bairn herself.

He shifted suddenly in his chair. What could he do? He was helpless. If only he had a decent job, if only he hadn't been pushed into the docks. Well, where else could he have gone? If a lad wanted to make money at fourteen he had to give up all idea of being apprenticed to a trade. It was the same in all the places: Palmer's shipyard, the steel works, the chemical works. Now he'd be a dock labourer for the rest of his life; and he would never earn enough money to make any noticeable difference to her life. Did his father ever feel like this, feel this sense of frustration and helplessness? That's why he drank as he did. And Dominic? Ugh–he made an involuntary gesture with his hand as if wiping his brother away–that swiller!

He lifted his feet up to the side of the pan hob and sank deeper into his chair. Drink was a funny thing once it got you. He was drunk only once, and could still remember isolated parts of the feeling. It happened the first week he was on capstan work. He had been promoted from hatching at two-and-six a shift and now felt a man. After being paid off, he was walking out of the dock gates with the men when one of them, nodding towards the line of public houses filling the street opposite, said, 'Comin' over?'

He felt flattered, and went with them into The Grapes. He remembered the feeling of his stomach swelling and the continual belching of wind, and his mouth becoming fixed open in a wide grin. It was this grin that was partly the reason why he did not touch the drink again, for he brought the picture of himself over into his sober consciousness, and in it he saw the face of his father when in drink, as he had seen it since he was a child, with the large full-lipped mouth stretched wide, conveying not the impression of geniality but of imbecility. And his cure was completed by knowing, on waking up in bed undressed, that his mother had done for him what she did for his father. It was some time before he could entirely rid himself of the feeling of shame and humiliation when he thought of himself being undressed by her.

There were times when he wanted a drink badly–like today, when his throat felt clogged tight with dust–unloading grain was a dry job. He had gone across to the horse trough outside the gates and filled the iron cup four times. Some of his mates called, 'Cheap that, John.' 'Aye, and no headache the morrow,' he replied. They no longer asked him to join them.

A crescendo of snores came from the bedroom, and he shifted his position again. There was something he wanted more than a drink, and that was a mattress. Could he put it to her now? He looked towards his mother. She'd had enough for one day, he told himself, without anything more to worry about. But when a series of spluttering coughs terminated the snores, he said, 'There's a pitch boat due in shortly; if I get on her, it'll mean extra. Could you . . . get me a mattress with it?'

'A mattress!' Mary Ellen stopped sewing and looked at him. 'A mattress?'

He turned his head to the fire again. 'I want you to put Mich in the bed; I'll sleep in the cupboard.'

'Oh lad'–she joined her hands together over the patch–'you can't sleep on the floor. And anyway, the cupboard isn't big enough, it barely holds Mick.'

'I can leave the door open.'

The sadness seemed to sink from her eyes into her body, shrinking it still further. She turned her gaze to the fire, and her hands lay idle. . . . There was no way of getting another bed into the room, even if they could get one. And for John to lie in the cupboard! She shook her head, not knowing she did so.

The cupboard in the bedroom ran under Mrs Flaherty's front stairs; its total length was five feet, and he wanted to sleep in that! If the door was open, it was cold and draughty, even in the summer; if it was closed, it was naturally airless. She often worried about Mick having to lie there . . . but John! And his feet would extend over any mattress–they did through the red rails, both his and Dominic's. But that wasn't the floor.

She looked at him and saw by the way his face was set that he meant to do it, and if she didn't get him the mattress he'd lie in the cupboard in any case, on Mick's bag of straw. She sighed, and her hands began to work again.

There was no sound in the kitchen except the sound of Katie's pencil and Dominic's muffled snores, until Molly rushed in the back door, crying, 'Ma! do you know what?'

'Make less noise!' Mary Ellen said.

'But ma, there's somebody moving in next door the morrer.'

'Wash yourself and get ready for bed. . . . Who told you that?' Mary Ellen asked.

'Mrs Bradley told Annie Kelly's ma, and Annie Kelly told me.'

'Then if Mrs Bradley said so, it must be right.' Mary Ellen rose, pulled the table to one side to get at the wooden couch beyond, and began to make up the girls' beds, one at each end.

'Get your things off, hinny,' she said over her shoulder to Katie.

The two girls undressed in the scullery, all except their boots and stockings. These they took off, sitting on crackets before the fire, chatting to each other now quite friendly. Katie sat next to John, her bare feet on the fender sticking out from under her patched, flannelette nightie.

John's fingers moved slowly through her hair. And when the bedroom door opened and Dominic lurched into the kitchen he didn't lift his eyes from the paper he was reading.

Dominic stood near the table, blinking in the gaslight. He yawned, running both his hands over his head; then pulled his belt tighter before coming to the fire. He shivered and sat down in the seat vacated by Mary Ellen, growling to Molly as he did so, 'Move your carcass!' He ran his tongue round his dry lips, shook his head in an endeavour to throw off the muzziness, and stretched out his hands to the fire.

'Any grub?' he asked, without turning his head.

'There's broth,' his mother answered from her bent position over the couch.

Katie looked past Molly to her brother's face. It looked huge and frightening, with the dark stubble around his chin and up the sides of his cheeks, and the darker marks of the dried blood standing out around his mouth. When he hawked in his throat and spat at the bars, she drew her feet sharply beneath her nightie, nearly falling off the cracket as she did so. John's hand, still on her head, steadied her, but he did not take his eyes from the paper.

Dominic saw her frightened glance, and a twisted grin spread slowly over his face. He leaned back in his chair, and after a while Katie's toes came from beneath her nightie again. Her feet were cold, for the steel fender was well below the bottom red bar of the fire. She lifted one foot up above those of Molly, to wriggle her toes in front of the lower bar. There was a hiss, a splatter, and Dominic's yellow saliva was running over her foot.

As she hid her face from the sight and pressed her mouth to stop herself from being sick, she felt John springing away from her. His chair was kicked back, and she flung herself to the floor by the bottom of the fender, lying along its length, pressing close to its brass bars to keep clear of the pounding feet. Molly had sprung to the couch, where she now sat huddled. And before Mary Ellen could reach them John's fist swung out and Dominic reeled backwards and crashed into the cupboard door.

Mary Ellen flung herself on John, crying, 'Lad! lad!' She beat his chest with her fists in an endeavour to push him back: 'John lad! John lad! For God's sake!'

John did not look at her, but gathered her flaying hands in one of his, and tried to push her aside. But she kept in front of him by pressing her body against his, calling beseechingly up to him, 'Lad! Lad! John, lad!'

His face was bereft of colour; his lips were drawn back from his teeth, and his eyes were like black marble. Through her body she could feel the waves of anger running through his; her breast was pressed against his stomach, which shook with the elemental forces demanding release.

'Holy Mary, Mother of God, Mother of God!' she cried. 'No more the day, lad!' She took no heed of her other son, standing with his fists at the ready behind her; Dominic, she knew, wouldn't fight John unless he had to, for in John he had more than his match. No, it was John she must stop. 'John, lad–John! I can't stand any more this day. Oh, Jesus, Mary and Joseph, you know I can't stand no more the day.'

She felt a great intake of breath coming into his lungs and the rumbling thunder of the words as they were released from his throat: 'I warned you what would happen if you did that again!'

Relief swept through her; he had spoken; she could manage him if he spoke.

He spoke again, and his words now brought a faintness over her; the child in her womb seemed to stop breathing. The words fell into her innerconsciousness, to be remembered as would those spoken by a prophet have been, for, like Katie, she felt that John was near the priests and God, for what he said was mostly true. And he said now to his brother, 'One of these days I'll kill you.'

There was no threat in the words, only a quiet certainty.

Chapter Two

A Day of Bonny Lasses

Poverty is comparative. There were those who did not live in the fifteen streets who considered the people living there to be of one stratum, the lowest stratum; but the people inside this stratum knew that there were three different levels, the upper, the middle, and the lower. All lived in 'houses' either upstairs or down; but in the lower end each house had only two small rooms, and upstairs or down the conditions were the same–the plaster on the walls was alive with bugs. These might appear only at night, to drop on the huddled sleepers, but that strange odour, which was peculiarly their own, wafted through the houses all the time, stamping them as buggy. No one went to live in the lower end unless he was forced. To the middle and upper fifteen streets the bottom end was only one step removed from the workhouse, for its inhabitants were usually those whose furniture had been distrained or who had been ejected from their former houses for non-payment of rent.

There were three nightmares in the lives of the occupants of the middle and upper fifteen streets. And these were linked together: they were the bums, the lower end, and the workhouse.

In the middle houses there were four rooms . . . boxes, generally, but boxes that were divided, giving privacy of a sort to one or two extra beings. The upper end had only three rooms to each house, and these were either up or down. Here, water was not carried from the central tap in the back lane but from a tap at the bottom of each yard. This stamped the area as selective, automatically making it the best end.

But even into this stratum of the fifteen streets no one had ever been known to arrive with their furniture in a van. A flat lorry, yes, or a coal cart; at worst, a hand barrow, after dark. These were the three general modes of removal. But a van! a proper one, bearing the words 'Raglan, Furniture Removers, Jarrow-on-Tyne', never.

The street was out to watch with as much interest as if it were a wedding, or a funeral, or, what was more common, a fight. The three O'Brien children had a grandstand view: they stood in a row beneath their front window sill, and behind them, in the room, were the elders, Mary Ellen, Shane, Dominic and John. The sons stood one at each side of their mother and father. They were standing together as a family for once, joined by the common interest, watching in silent wonder as each piece of furniture was carried into the house next door. They had not seen furniture like this before. There was the big, bright, round table, with the thick single leg and bunchy feet like claws; there was the suite of patterned plush, with ball fringe all round the bottom of the couch and chairs; there was the big clock, nearly six feet high; and there was the bed, a wooden one painted white, with pictures on the panels; there were two other beds, but these were of brass. Yet these were outstanding too, for they were neither chipped nor battered. That was not all. There were carpets, two of them, besides a load of rugs one man could hardly shoulder. And the road was strewn with all kinds of things that rent Mary Ellen through with envy; a feeling she thought she was past this many a year. But then, she had never seen owt like this before in the fifteen streets . . . or anywhere else: the mahogany plant stand, with its looped chains, the large china flower pots, the clothes basket full of coloured china, and the little mangle, which looked like a toy but which she knew wasn't. Who were these folks who could own such things, yet had come to live here? It didn't make sense somehow.

She glanced up at John to see what effect all this was having on him, and here eyes left him quickly and travelled down his gaze to the street again. He was looking at a lass who had just come out of the house. May Ellen wasn't sure if she was a child, a lass, or a woman.

John, staring at the girl over the brown paper that covered the hole in the window, was being puzzled in much the same way; the girl on the pavement was as shapeless in form as Katie, showing no evidence of either hips or bust. Judged on her figure, she could be a child; and her face too had something of the immaturity of the child in it. Yet it was old. No, not old–he rejected the word–wise, that was it . . . and bonnie too. Yes, she was bonnie, that pale skin against the dark hair. The hair was unusual in that it hung loose about her head. Cut short, boyish fashion, it was like a dark halo. He was curious to see more of her, and, as she turned to speak to the old man with the white hair, who was directing the unloading, he unconsciously bent forward.

Whatever she said brought a smile from the long, serious face of the man, and she smiled in return: and John knew them to be related; it was as if the same light shone from them. It illuminated their faces, and seemed to convey a ray of light even to himself, for he found his face relaxing into a smile as he watched them. He wondered who they could be. Was the man her da, or her grandda? And the little lad running to and fro was evidently one of them, for he had the same pale skin and dark hair.

As John considered the fine furniture and their fine clothes, his smile faded. The old man was wearing a suit and a collar and tie, as though got up for a do, and the girl, a blue woollen dress with a little woollen coat of the same colour. It looked neat and trim and was as unlike anything the lasses of the fifteen streets wore as John could possibly imagine.

The two removal men were struggling to get a chest of drawers through the front door. It was the biggest chest John had seen in his life; it was taller than himself. He could see only one of the men, who was bearing the weight of the bottom end and was stepping backwards and forwards under the other's directions. John knew what had happened. The front door did not lead directly into the front room, but into a tiny square of passage. The other man had got his end stuck in this passage.

The old man's assistance was to no avail; and John watched the girl glance about her at the dark, huddled figures blocking the doorways. Then her eyes came to the window and met his. For a second they looked at each other, and he noted the surprise and curiosity in her glance, and realized in a flash that to her he must appear as if he was standing on something to look over the brown paper. Humorously he thought: I'd better show her it's me all the way. I'll give them a hand with those drawers . . . and damn the tongues! He turned, to find Dominic, who was nearer the front door, looking at him with eyes full of mirthless laughter. Dominic slowly hitched up his trousers, buttoned his coat, then went out into the street.

With a feeling of frustration mixed with anger, John watched Dominic speak to the girl, and saw her look sharply from Dominic's face to the window as if to reassure herself there were two of them. Then she smiled on Dominic, and he bent his broad back under the chest, taking the weight off the men, and in a few minutes they all moved into the house.

John and Mary Ellen turned from the window and went to the kitchen. Nothing had escaped Mary Ellen; she had followed the desire of her son and felt Dominic interpret John's thought and use it against him. She said, 'Come and finish your dinner, lad, it'll be kissened up to cork.'

Taking three plates out of the oven, she called to her husband. Shane, looking mystified and his head jerking, came to the table. 'Must be bloody millionaires,' he said. 'Know who they are?'

'No,' she answered. 'I know nowt about them.'

The meal was eaten in silence. Once or twice Mary Ellen glanced at John, but his face was closed, telling her nothing. She got up to clear the table, and muttered impatiently when a face was pressed against the window and a voice called, 'Can I come in, Mrs O'Brien?'

Mary Ellen's brows knit together, but she answered pleasantly, 'Oh, it's you, Nancy. Yes, come in.'

A girl of sixteen sidled into the room. Her face was flat, almost concave, and her nose and eyes seemed to be lost in its centre, as though a force were sucking them in. The expression was serious and earnest, like that of a child struggling to be impressive. She began with quaint ceremony, 'Hallo, Mrs O'Brien.'

And Mary Ellen answered kindly, 'Hallo, Nancy.'

'Hallo, John.'

John turned from the table and said, 'Hallo, there, Nancy.'

'Hallo, Mr O'Brien.'

Shane growled something, keeping his eyes directed towards his plate. And Mary Ellen, thanking God that the rest of the family weren't in to lengthen Nancy's usual formal greeting, said, 'Sit yourself down, Nancy.'

Nancy sat down, and John said to her, 'Still like your place, Nancy?'

'Yes, John,' she answered; 'I've nearly been there a month now.' It was a curious defect of her speech that her mouth never closed; her lips refused to meet, so her voice sounded nasal, like that of someone with a hare lip.

John answered tolerantly, 'Yes, you have, Nancy,' knowing that the time she had scrubbed and cleaned in the Fitzsimmons's outdoor beershop was nearer to four years than four weeks–time had no place in Nancy's mind. Her body gave the impression of uncontrolled strength; her long arms hung out from the short sleeves of her coat, a brown, faded thing, and her boots looked too small for her big feet.

John said kindly, 'You look very nice the day, Nancy.'

She smiled at him, stretching her face; then, preening herself and dusting down the front of her coat with her red hands, she said, 'This is a new coat. Me ma bought it. And these boots too. And I've got a silk dress, with a sash. And I'm going to get a hat with a feather in.'

Shane's chair scraped back and he went to the front room. Mary Ellen looked after him for a moment–he never could stand the senseless prattle of Nancy. She went into the scullery to wash the dishes, glad that John was in to cope with Nancy should she start laughing. . . . Oh, Nancy's laughter! Mary Ellen shuddered. She thought she was afraid of nothing on earth as she was of Nancy Kelly's laughter–it put the fear of God in her. But John could manage her–he always had; he made her think she was like other lasses. She could sense John's pity for Nancy; it was like her own, but without the strain of fear that ran through hers.

She heard Dominic coming up the backyard, whistling. He was pleased with himself for outwitting John, she supposed. She hoped to God he did nothing more to aggravate John's feelings; the sick premonition of last night was still partly with her. She was more afraid of John's rages than of either Shane's or Dominic's, for his were stronger, being made more fierce through sober justification.

Dominic came in and surprised her by closing the scullery door and so shutting them off from the kitchen. He stood near her as she bent over the dish, and said softly, 'Any chance of you lending me the money to get me clothes out?'

She looked up at him, her hands still in the water. 'I've only got the rent. You put your suit in, you'll have to get it out.'

'I'll give it to you back next week.'

'I haven't got it; I only have a few coppers left for the gas over the week-end.'

Dominic's suit had been in pawn for more than a month, and he had made no effort to get it out, even on his full shifts. Without it he was tied to the house and spent his Sundays in bed, for by some unwritten law no one went out of doors on a Sunday dressed in their working clothes. Even if a man possessed a shilling to 'get a set in', he never showed his face inside a public house unless he was 'tidy'.

Strangely enough, Mary Ellen realized it wasn't tomorrow Dominic was thinking of, but tonight, and that new lass next door; although how he'd had the nerve to ask such as her out, she didn't know. . . . But then she did. Dominic had the nerve for anything if he wanted it badly enough. She said cuttingly, 'Why don't you ask one of your cronies for it?'

He cast her a sidelong glance, in which she saw the sharp, questioning look–he wondered how much she knew. She knew more than he thought she did, to her sorrow. There was a certain woman of the docks, Lady Pansy, so-called because of her style in her heyday when she entertained nothing less than a chief engineer. But times had changed, and with them Lady Pansy's figure and face. Although she couldn't claim big money now she still liked her man young and strong, and Mary Ellen knew that all the money from Dominic's full shifts was not spent on drink–the thought made her sick–and the woman was as old as she was, if not older!

If Mary Ellen's refusal dampened Dominic's spirits, he hid it successfully, for in the kitchen he was extra hearty, forestalling Nancy's greeting by giving an imitation of herself.

'Hal-lo, Nan-cy!'

'Hallo, Dominic.' Nancy wriggled on her chair.

Dominic went and stood over her: 'What's this I'm hearing about you, Nancy? They tell me you're courtin'.'

'Eeh! who told you that?' The girl wriggled in agitation. 'Eeh! I'm not . . . am I, John?'

John said nothing, but left the table and took a seat by the fire. He knew where Dominic's teasing would lead.

'Well, that's what I heard,' Dominic went on; 'I thought you were goin' to wait for me. Nice one, you are.' He pulled his belt tighter in feigned annoyance.

'Eeh, Dominic! I haven't got a lad, I haven't. I don't let them come near me. If they touch me, I yells I do.' Her face gathered itself into a troubled pucker.

John thrust the poker between the bars and raked savagely–he knew that Dominic's tactics were more to madden him than to tease Nancy.

Dominic laughed, and went on, with mock seriousness, 'Let's get this settled. When are me and you goin' out for a walk, eh?'

Mary Ellen came hurriedly into the kitchen: 'I think you'd better be going home now, Nancy, your ma will be wondering where you are.'

As Nancy stood up, Dominic said softly, 'I'll get another lass, mind.'

And Mary Ellen cried, 'That's enough of that! Get away home now, Nancy.' She turned to the girl and led her, trembling, to the door; but before they reached it, it opened, and Hannah Kelly herself stood there.

'Oh, this is where you are'–she looked unsmilingly at her daughter–'I guessed as much. Go on, get yourself over home.'

Nancy slid by her mother, and Hannah came in and closed the door. Her manner was conspiratorial. 'Well, what d'yer think, eh? D'ye know who ye've got next door, Mary Ellen?'

Mary Ellen shook her head.

'My God! Ye'd never believe. They call this the Irish quarter, but what with the Jews and the ranters . . . and now this! Well, my God, I ask ye!'

'What are they?' asked Mary Ellen bluntly.

'Spooks!' Hannah's head came forward, impressing the word.

'What!'

'Spooks. He's called The Spook in Jarrow and Howden and round there. Remember a bit back when the Irish navvies burnt a hut down and the pollis had to get the man away? Well, that was him. He was givin' a service or somethin'.'

Mary Ellen turned and looked from one to the other of her sons, who were now both listening to Hannah Kelly with interest.

'Dorrie Clark knew who he was the minute she set eyes on him, and she was tellin' Bella Bradley that when she was delivering once in Jarrow, he came in and wanted to lay his hands on the woman. That's what she said . . . lay his hands on her! Did ye ever hear owt like it? To ease her labour, he said, because she'd been in it four days.'

Mary Ellen looked distinctly shocked. 'Did she let him?'

'Did she hell! Ye know old Dorrie. She said she kicked his arse out of the door. And she would an' all, full of gin or not. But my God, there'll be the divil's figarties around these doors before long! Mark my words; ye'll see.'

Mary Ellen was evidently disturbed. She looked from one to the other; then she addressed John, 'What d'you make of it?'

John turned away, and went to the bedroom, saying, 'I don't know; they looked all right to me.'

Hannah laughed and called after John, 'Mind yerself, John lad, that she don't lay hands on you. They say the lass is as bad as the old man.' Then turning to Dominic, she said, 'And you there, ye've soon got yer leg in.'

Ignoring her jibe, Dominic asked: 'D'you know what the old man works at?'

'Now that's another funny thing'–Hannah pointed her finger at him–'he's the Mr Bracken that has the boot shop in Jarrow.'

The three of them looked from one to the other, and the same question was running through their minds: 'Why did a man who owned a boot shop come to live in the fifteen streets?'

In the bedroom, John pulled the wooden box from beneath the bed and took out his suit. It was too creased to wear, so he knew it hadn't been in the pawn; had it been in his mother would have pressed it ready for him. Taking a dirty raincoat from the back of the door, he stood pondering a moment whether he should change his black neckerchief for a white muffler, but decided against doing so. He would keep it for tonight, when he would be going to the Shields to have a look round the market and perhaps go to the second-house somewhere. Now, he was just going for a walk.

He did not bother to change his working boots, but went into the kitchen and finding his mother alone, asked, 'Will you put an iron over my suit?'

'Yes, lad,' she replied. 'Are you off for a walk?'

He nodded. 'Where's Katie?'

'Here she is, coming up the yard,' said Mary Ellen.

'Want to come?' he asked her.

'Oh yes, John. Yes! Yes!' In her excitement, Katie hopped from one foot to the other.

'Not with hands and face like that,' he said. 'What have you been up to?'

'Playing shops. . . . I won't be a tick; wait for me.'

Mary Ellen was already pouring the water into the dish; and after a few minutes Katie, her face shining and a round draw hat lying straight on the top of her head, was walking down the yard with John.

He took her hand, and they went along the cobbled back lane to the main road.

'Where shall we go?' he asked her.

'Oh, the country, John. Up the country!'

'Simonside?'

'Yes. Oh yes, Simonside!'

The day was cold and clear, with the wind blowing straight in from the sea. The sky was high above the housetops and above the towering cranes, which reared up inside the stone wall edging the road opposite the fifteen streets.

John looked up at the white tufted clouds moving swiftly across the sky, and said, 'Look up there. They look like a fleet of white brakes off for a day's outing, don't they? I bet they're off to the country, too–Morpeth or some place.'

Katie chuckled. This was one of the many reasons why she loved going walks with John–he made up stories about everything. She glanced up at him, her eyes twinkling: 'I bet when they come back they'll be singing, like the people do on the brake trips:

"Aam', back to canny auld Jarrer,
A hip, a hip hooray."'

She giggled, and John tilted her hat over her eyes, saying 'Saucy piece!'

They walked by the side of the wall for some way, until they came to the chemical works and the tram sheds. Then, further on, as they passed a narrow cut, bordered on one side by the end of the chemical works and on the other by the railings which fence in part of the Jarrow slacks, John asked her, 'Do you want to go down the slipway?'

Katie shook her head quickly and shuddered.

'What are you frightened of?'

'It's that black mud–it's deep, and if you fell in you'd never get out.'

'But the tide's up now, and there might be a little boat moored there. . . . All right, all right,' he laughed when Katie shuddered again; 'but you never used to be afraid of the slipway.'

She didn't say that Mick had dragged her down there and pretended he was going to push her in. He had held her over the stone coping, and she had gazed, petrified, at the silvery black, slimy mud sloping away from just below her face to the narrow stream of water at the bottom, running slowly beneath its shot-coloured oily surface. She didn't dare tell her mother in case John got to know, for then he would have gone for Mick.

They came to the Jarrow slacks at the point where they were open to the road. The water was lapping just below the bank, a few feet from the edge of the pavement. The large, square stretch of water was covered with timbers, roped together in batches, right up to the gut.

There was a permanent way, starting below the pavement and reaching to the gut, running through the middle of them. It consisted of logs, a foot wide, lashed end to end and to each side of posts driven in at intervals over the stretch. In parts, the logs were black and rotten and looked as safe for foothold as a loose rock on the edge of a precipice. But children were playing on them with happy unconcern, jumping from them to the roped timbers. Some children were far away over the timbers, laying flat along the edges, trying to rake in pieces of wood that were floating by. And the sight of them brought back the past vividly to John. How many times had he perilously stood on the end timbers, near the edge of the gut, and waited for the tide to come in, bringing with it its drift wood. Often, for weeks on end, this wood was their only source of warmth, but often again, they had to do without the warmth whilst he hawked the sack of wood around, trying to sell it for twopence. He seldom succeeded; coke was the best sell. If he followed the coke carts from Jarrow right into Shields he could pick up as much as two bucketfuls each trip. Pieces would roll off the cart as it jogged along, especially when it crossed the tram lines. He'd get twopence for the coke, and if he could follow the cart three times, that meant sixpence. But he rarely completed the third journey, for his legs became so tired. He remembered the melancholy feeling that would settle on him as he followed the carts. It seemed to be worse when the sun was shining. . . . That was an odd thing he hadn't entirely grown out of–he didn't like the sunshine. For years this feeling vaguely puzzled him. Then one day the reason was made known to him. The sunshine, he discovered, showed up his surroundings. It brought a queer kind of pain to him. On a dull day, the docks, the coal dust, the houses, the rattling trams, and the people all seemed to merge into one background; but when the sun shone, there they all were, standing out in relief, dirty, stark, tired; and in some odd way it hurt him. . . . The feeling was coming on him now, and he tried to ignore it, for it always made him start thinking; and when he thought, he got mad at things. As his mother said, thinking got you nowhere.

Katie plunged him further into the trough by exclaiming, 'You know, when I grow up, John, I'm going to be a teacher.'

He squeezed her hand and said, 'I bet you will too . . . headmistress!'

A teacher! Would Katie's dreams ever be fulfilled? He couldn't see it happening. She would go into a place at fourteen like the other lasses, and the bright eagerness would die. Her dreams, like his own when a lad, would be lost in the fight for food. . . . It was funny, but that was all life amounted to . . . working life out to keep it in–working for food and warmth; and when the futility of this was made evident, blotting it out with drink. What did it all mean, anyway? What was living for?

When in this state of mind he always asked this question. The priests had one answer; but that had long ago ceased to satisfy him. Now he was asking himself another question: Had he to stay round these quarters until he died? He wasn't happy around here, yet when he moved out of this quarter, as he was doing now, up into Simonside, the lonely feeling became intensified and he felt lost, and some part of him wanted to get back again into the fifteen streets, into the docks, anywhere but near these grand houses that stood back from the Simonside bank, with their drives and large gardens. He couldn't understand why his sense of loneliness should be greater away from the life that was irking him.

He was being daft, he told himself–just daft. He should get himself a lass. That's what he needed. He was twenty-two and he'd never had a lass. He had never kissed a lass, not even in a bit of fun. Katie was the only one he kissed. He knew there were one or two in the fifteen streets who would come at his nod, but he hadn't nodded. His flingings and tossings in bed at night had equalled Dominic's, and many a time he promised himself to ask Jenny Carey or Lily McDonald to go out on a Saturday night; but with the light of day he forgot about them.

Lately, Dominic hadn't tossed so much. And once or twice John had been tempted to seek his cure; but then again, the temptation vanished with the light.

'Look, John,' said Katie; 'there's Father Bailey.'

The priest was coming down the drive of one of the big houses, and he waved to them, calling, 'Hallo, there.'

John stopped and said, 'Hallo, Father.'

He wouldn't have stopped had it been Father O'Malley; but then, Father O'Malley wouldn't have called 'Hallo, there.' At best, he would have inclined his head slightly. Not even if he knew you hadn't been to mass would he speak to you on the street; he would wait till he had you indoors, then raise the roof on you. But Father Bailey was different. Even when he was chastising you for not going to mass he was nice about it.

'Are you going for a walk, the pair of you?' The priest smiled, first up at John then down on Katie; and not waiting for an answer, went on, 'It's just the day for it. You know, John'–he took a step backwards–'I believe you get taller.'

'It's the clothes, Father; they've shrunk.'

'Well, there may be something in that, but I've always had the idea I came up to your shoulder. It must have been just an idea.'

He turned to Katie. 'And now, Katie O'Brien, what honours have you been gathering on your head this week? Do you know we have a clever girl here, John? Every week I hear something about Katie O'Brien. She's the top of her class for this, that, and the other. It'll be teaching the teachers she'll be in the end.'

'Oh, Father!' Katie O'Brien lowered her head and blinked at her boots.

The priest patted her straw hat. 'I'm just on my way up to the fifteen streets; I'll look in on your mother. How is she, John?'

'Oh, just middling, Father.'

'And your da, and Dominic?' There was a question in the priest's eyes.

They held John's, and he replied gruffly, 'Things don't change.'

'Oh, you're wrong there, John; every minute of the day they're changing.'

'Yes? Well I haven't noticed it.'

Father Bailey patted Katie's hat again, but still addressing John said, 'We never do. But look ahead, John. . . . Shall I be seeing you at mass to-morrow?'

'I don't think so, Father.'

'Oh! This'll never do. Not at all, at all! I'll have to come and have a crack with you soon. But I must be off now. Enjoy your walk, both of you. Good-bye. Good-bye.'

'Good-bye, Father.' 'Good-bye, Father,' they said, and continued their way up the Simonside bank, past the little school and into what was termed the country, a few fields with hedged lanes between. If you didn't turn round and look back you could imagine there were no docks, no pits, no drab grey streets; and if you could stretch your imagination you could visualize these fields with their straight rows of tender green going on for ever.

'Shall we walk to the Robin Hood?' Katie asked.

'It'll be too far for you,' said John.

'No, it won't. I could walk miles and miles.'

She skipped on ahead of him, leaving him with his thoughts–thoughts of the priest; of this lonely feeling; and of the lass next door. His mind dwelt on the lass: Would he like to take her out? Good God! he'd never have the nerve to ask the likes of her, even if she were free–she was different somehow. . . . Then why was she living next door? . . . There was no answer to this. And Dominic, he wouldn't be backward in asking her. But no! surely he wouldn't have the cheek, the state he was in with drink, and that woman. Yet why did he go out and give them a hand? It wasn't with any idea of helping, but to speak to the lass. . . . Anyway, why was he thinking about all these things that didn't matter a damn! Hadn't he other things to think about? His mother in her trouble; and the house with hardly a whole stick standing.

But the sun and the wind were changing his mood–he didn't want to think, he only wanted to wander here in this quiet road.

He took off his cap and let the wind play through his hair. He ran his hand through it, and felt the freedom of being uncovered out of doors. It was such a relief to walk with his cap off, and no one would see him here so it didn't matter, for it was another unwritten law that a woman did not go out without a hat or shawl covering her head, nor a man a cap.

Katie came running back to him, exclaiming, 'Oh, John, your hair looks just like Miss Llewellyn's with the sun shining on it! It's all brown and shiny.'

'What!' he exclaimed. 'Miss— Don't be silly.' He ruffled it more.

'It is though.'

'Go on with you!' He took her hand and pulled her to his side, and they walked on until they came within sight of the Robin Hood, then turned towards Simonside again. Katie sang hymns, school songs, and rhymes, one following on the other without pause, while John walked along in strange contentment, listening to her.

They were nearing the top of the bank, where it dipped to the docks, when her singing ended abruptly and he felt her hand tugging on his. He looked down on her upturned face. It was alight with pleased surprise–her eyes were wide, sending him a mute message. Wondering, he followed her gaze, and saw a woman coming towards them, a young woman. She was taller than average, and wore a brown cloth coat with a full skirt. It was nipped in at the waist and gave emphasis to her bust. She carried her head high, and her hat, which was green and had a brown feather curling round its brim, appeared like a crown set on the top of her head.

As she came nearer, John became aware of her hair. It fell over her ears in soft folds, and when he noticed the colour, he connected it with Katie's excitement and thrust his cap on his head. Good God! Miss Llewellyn–and she not much more than a lass. And he'd thought she was getting on . . . well, in her thirties. She was looking directly at Katie and smiling.

He looked beyond her, but to his horror she stopped as she came abreast of them and said, 'Hallo, Katie.'

'Hallo, Miss Llewellyn.'

John felt Katie's fingers opening and shutting within his palm.

'You are a long way from home.'

'Yes, Miss Llewellyn.' Katie was breathless.

John gave a sidelong glance at the bent head–he could dare this because she wasn't looking at him. He had never before been so close to such a face. Katie said she was lovely. Katie wasn't far wrong. The skin of her cheeks was a soft, creamy pink, the nose was short, and in striking contrast the mouth was wide and laughing.

When she turned her eyes on him, he switched his away; and he fumbled in the pocket of his coat for his red handkerchief as she said, 'You're John, aren't you?'

He felt his eyes forced back to her, to look her full in the face, and for no reason he could understand he began to tremble inside–almost, he felt, like the jerking of his father's limbs, only invisible. He was painfully conscious of the cap on his tousled hair, of his dirty raincoat, of his neckerchief, and of his big boots, with their leather laces showing numerous knots. His Adam's apple moved swiftly, and he swallowed, but no words came.

And she went on, 'I've heard such a lot about you.'

Her voice, too, was like none he had heard before. Like her face, there was laughter playing around it. Was she laughing at him? Very likely.

He knew she was, and though he felt it was kindly laughter the hot colour flooded his face when she said, 'I don't suppose you know, but you are a combination of Prince Charming and God to a certain young lady.'

He thought quickly, as he found himself doing at times, and spoke before he could stop himself: 'Neither of them would be flattered. And if the last one hears of it there's not much chance of me getting up there.'

Her laugh rang out, joyous and infectious, and to his utter surprise he found himself laughing with her.

Katie stood looking up from one to the other. She did not join in with their laughter, her happiness was too profound–Miss Llewellyn laughing with their John!

When he thought of it later, he was surprised at her next remark–and her a Catholic and a teacher too–for she said, 'I don't suppose that will worry you very much. I should take the heaven you're sure of.' Her words seemed to confuse her slightly and the tinge of pink grew deeper in her cheeks.

He made no answer, thinking that if this life was her idea of heaven he'd bet on the one up there. The wind swirled about them, and she turned her back to it, leaning slightly back and holding her hat on with both hands. Then she terminated the meeting by saying, 'Well, I'll see you on Monday morning, Katie,' and to John, 'I'm glad I've met you in the flesh, for now when I listen to your sayings being recorded I'll be able to place them. Good-bye. Good-bye, Katie.'

'Good-bye, Miss Llewellyn.'

'Good-bye.' John did not turn immediately away, but watched her bending against the wind, the coat pressed against her legs. And he saw that she wore shoes and that her ankles were thin. He turned away, and Katie, walking close by his side, sighed. They looked at each other and smiled secretly, then walked on in silence, until John asked, 'You don't tell her all I say, do you?'

'No. Oh, no!' Katie lied firmly. And in the next breath she exclaimed, 'Isn't she lovely!'

He stopped and looked towards the docks, and Katie went on, 'And isn't it a lovely day!'

'Grand.' The word seemed to answer both her questions.

Far away in the distance he could see the masts of the ships, disembodied things, seemingly borne on air. He looked up at the sun, and for the first time in his life felt glad to be out and under it. He thought of the lass next door and of the lovely lass just gone, and he said, more to himself than to Katie, 'Yes, it's a lovely day; a day of clean wind and far mast-heads, and bonnie lasses.'

Katie stared up at him. 'Oh, their John was wonderful, the things he said! A day of clean wind and far mast-heads, and bonnie lassies! It was like . . . well, not like the poetry she learnt at school . . . and yet it was. Oh, and Miss Llewellyn had seen him! She had seen how wonderful he was.'

Mary Llewellyn, walking briskly away in the opposite direction, was smiling no longer. Her face was thoughtful, and her eyes sad. So that was John. Poor soul! Poor soul!

Chapter Three

St Patrick's Day

Mick led the Catholics, not because he was the eldest but because he was the biggest. At the top corner of Fadden and Blacket Streets he marshalled his gang, twenty-five in all, and saw that they were supplied with weapons. He made sure that the innocent-looking paper balls dangling from lengths of rope or string each had a good-sized stone in its centre. About twenty yards away, at the corner of Whitley Street, the Protestants were gathering, and their leaders were doing much the same as Mick. This was to be the climax to the day's badgering and cornering of individuals and isolated groups, of swinging the paper balls round the heads of victims, whether Catholic or Protestant, and asking the terrifying question, 'Are you blue or green?' Pity help the individual who had the courage to defend his colour to the opposite clan, for he was often hit until he was sick or rescued by some indignant passer-by.

Mick's gang were protesting loudly that it wasn't fair, for the ranters had three separate gangs–the churchies, the chapelies, and the odds, the latter group consisting of Jews, Salvationists, and a Quaker.

Mick exclaimed loudly that three lots were nowt, for they'd bash all their bleeding heads in. Adroitly he spread out his men in the form of an arrow, placing the bigger boys at the head.

He took a long time over this, for he was enjoying his momentary power and the admiration of the younger children swarming on the top of the stackyard wall that hemmed in the ends of the fifteen streets.

Someone began to sing the hymn:

'Oh glorious St Patrick, dear Saint of our Isle,'

and all the children on the wall took it up:

'On us, thy dear children, bestow a sweet smile;
And now thou art high in the mansions above,
Oh glorious St Patrick look down in thy love.'

The ending was the signal for the advance, both sides moving slowly towards each other. Then, with a rush, there was a swirling of balls, and there were screams and cries of 'Long live Ireland!' 'Up the shamrock!' in which were mingled 'England for ever!' and 'God save the King!'

Hard blows were struck by the arrow heads. But they had learned no lesson from last year; so their balls became entwined, and many combatants had to stop and free them, and whilst doing so a number of them laughed, especially if their enemy happened to be a pal on the other three hundred and sixty-four days of the year. And so the fight became spasmodic, lacking the ferocity of the earlier battles; it became a melee of half-hearted punches and pushes. And the jeering from the mixed supporters on the wall became derisive.

Mick realized there was something lacking. He fell back with his side and engaged in a battle of vituperation!

'Protestant, Protestant, you dirty lot,
Yer backside's blue and yer nose all snot!'

to which the Protestants replied:

'Catholic, Catholic, ring the bell,
When you die you'll go to hell.'

It was all very half-hearted–the excitement seemed to have died in the completion of the preparations.

Mick felt a definite sense of disappointment and feared the flatness of the fight might be put down to his leadership, and that Big Geordie Flannagan might be picked to take his place. He looked round for some sign that would be the means of leading him fresh applause. And like manna from heaven he found it. Standing solitary at the top end of his own back lane was the boy from next door . . . the spook's lad.

The boy was looking from one group to the other with evident curiosity. His face looked all eyes, and Mick was quick to detect a gleam of fear in them. With the true instinct of a leader, he first of all planned to cut off the enemy's retreat. So he called three of his best men to him, and in a few words told them what he intended doing, and dispatched them down Fadden Street with orders to come up the back lane. A few more whispered words to other members of his gang, and they stopped yelling and stood looking towards the boy.

As soon as Mick saw the three outriders coming up the back lane he called out loudly, 'Look! There's the spook!'

After a moment's hesitation the word was taken up, 'The spook! The spook!' Those on the other side stopped their abuse and they too turned towards the boy, whose face had blanched. He did not turn and try to escape down the back lane, for he knew, from the laughs behind him, that escape was cut off. Instead he tried to think of what his grandfather had told him to do when confronted with hostile thought, but terror swamped any thinking.

Fascinated, he watched the two opposing sides converging on each other and the children swarming down from the wall. They began to form a solid mass before him, and he listened to shouts that weren't new to his ears:

'His da's a spook!'

'Me ma says he's a divil.'

'Me ma says if you bless yersel' when you pass him he can't do you any harm.'

'Me da says the priest put a curse on him an' he was kicked out of Jarrer, an' he'll wither away.'

'Mr Roberts, our minister, says they're evil and we mustn't have any truck with 'em.'

On and on it went, not loudly or angrily, but steadily and defiantly, and in some faint way the boy detected fear of himself in their voices. Yet he knew what that fear would make them do. It wasn't the first time he had been in a similar situation, but he found that repetition did not make him more brave.

Mick too was aware of the fear. The crowd of them would do nothing, he thought, just call the spook names and perhaps throw a stone or two, until some woman came out from her backyard and scattered the lot of them. He wanted a chase, some life in the proceedings.

Again he gave instructions to others of his gang, who sped away to block the ends of the streets, all but the last one. Then he yelled out to the crowd, proclaiming himself leader and a man of fair play, 'Give him a chance. . . . Let him away! Give him a start!'

Molly, who was standing near him, whispered, 'Were you goner chase him?'

'The gut,' he whispered back without looking at her, for his eyes were now fixed on those of the boy.

The boy was shivering in stark terror; he knew what this chance meant; it meant running, running, running until his whole body sobbed and his trousers became wet. And he knew that long after the fear would have passed the feeling of his wet trousers would remain. But it was either running or being stoned here.

A gap appeared in the crowd and Mick's voice yelled, 'Come on, spooky! We'll give you a start.' He was leading them all now, the Catholics, the Protestants, the Chapelies and the others. He kept yelling, 'Let him through! . . . Come on, spook. We'll give you ten for a start when you're through.'

There was a whirling in Mick's blood when he saw the boy begin to move, and a stream of saliva trickled from the corner of his mouth. The boy, his face the colour of dirty dough and his eyes stretching the skin, came abreast of Mick. He would never reach the gut, Mick thought–he was too small. They would drag him there.

Suddenly he threw his arms out wide, a signal that no one must move and shouted, 'One!'

At the sound the boy became galvanized. He shot away, and Mick, when he noted the speed with which the boy ran, quickened his counting, almost choking with suppressed glee when he saw the boy's maddened terror on realizing the exits of the streets and back lanes were blocked.

'Ten!' was a scream in Mick's throat. He was off, ahead of the milling, screeching children. They stumbled into each other, kicking and pushing to get a clear road. Some left the main chase and ran down the streets, knowing that this would be the quickest way and that they would pick up the chase again on the main road, the word had been passed, 'To the gut! To the gut!'

Among those who diverted was Molly. She sped down her own street, her hair and legs flying. And she almost cried with vexation when she saw her mother step from their front door.

'Here!' Mary Ellen caught at Molly's arm, almost unbalancing herself. 'Have you gone mad? What's all the screeching for?'

'Aw! ma, let go.'

'Get inside!' said Mary Ellen.

'Aw! ma, I'm goin' with our Mick.'

'With Mick? What's he doin'?'

'He's . . . he's . . . They're chasin' the lad next door to the gut.'

Mary Ellen brought her hand across her daughter's ear with a crack. 'Get yersel inside–I'll gut you! A big lass like you running mad with a lot of lads!' She pushed Molly before her through the front room, calling, 'John!'

John came out of the bedroom asking, 'What is it?'

'It's our Mick . . . he's chasing the lad next door to the gut. There's dozens of them running mad!'

'Are you sure it's Mick?'

'Ask her.' Mary Ellen pointed to the snivelling Molly.

When John looked at Molly she hung her head, and Mary Ellen said, 'Go and see what he's up to, lad; for if the pollis catches him at anything down there they won't give him another chance, after catching him loosening the timbers that time.'

'Why are they chasing the lad next door, are they playing at something?' John asked Molly.

'No,' Molly muttered into her chest. 'It's because he's a spook.'

John hastily put on his coat and left the house; and as he went out into the back lane he bumped into the girl from next door. She was running, and gasped, 'I'm sorry.' She smiled faintly at him and ran on again.

He did not speak, but hurried after her. He guessed where she was going . . . someone must have told her. Children were straggled along the road; most of them, frightened by the thought of the gut, especially as it was getting dark, had given up the chase.

One bold spirit addressed John: 'Your Mick's goin' to push the spook into the gut, Mr O'Brien.'

John knew that between Mick and Dominic there was only the difference in years; the cruelty was already fully matured in Mick, and he was quite capable of doing what this boy said. He set off at a run and caught up with the girl before she reached the short cut leading to the gut. Shortening his step to suit hers, he said, 'Are you looking for your brother?'

She nodded, but did not speak; and John again had the impression of age. There was a similarity, he noticed, between her expression and that which was more often than not on his mother's face. . . . This wasn't the first time she'd gone to her brother's aid–by God, he'd break that young rat's neck!

'You go back, and I'll see to them,' he said to her. But she shook her head.

As they turned down the cut, the shouting came to them, and John sprang away from the girl and ran on ahead.

With the intuition of the young, his coming was noted and the boys crowding round the disused boathouse on the edge of the gut gave the cry, 'Look out! Scatter!'

The size of John looming out of the gathering dusk and the fear of being caught and held responsible gave aid to their legs. They made for the opening near the boathouse, and like dots of vapour they disappeared across the disused ground adjoining the slacks.

John pulled up at the slipway. There was no sign of the boy. Likely, he had taken refuge on the wall round the corner. The wall supporting the slipway turned sharply at right angles, bordering the gut for a considerable distance, and ended abruptly where the gut was deepest, for the swirling tides had by slow degrees loosened its large granite stones, and many of these now made only a row of pin-points in the mud. The wall was just above ground level and was eighteen inches wide on the top, but from its back edge arose a six-foot fence of stout sleepers.

John walked sideways along the wall, pressing his back against the sleepers, and as he turned the corner he saw the boy and Mick.

The boy was standing up against the last sleeper of the fence, Mick was lying flat along the wall; and there was no sound from either of them, except the whack of the stick as Mick hit at the boy's legs, trying to dislodge him into the black, oozing mud. So lost was Mick in the relish of the moment that he did not hear John's approach. The first he knew was the sound of harsh breathing over him; then he was whipped to his feet and for one sickening second he was hanging in mid-air over the mud. John brought him to his feet and shook him until his head rolled on his shoulders.

'Get home and stay there! If you're not in when I get back it'll mean twice as much when I find you.'

Mick clutched at the sleepers to steady himself, and growled, 'You hit me and I'll tell me da.' Then he retreated hastily along the wall, and John went on to the boy.

In the dim light the white face shone at him, and he said soothingly, 'It's all right, sonny, it's all right.'

The boy did not answer, and John said, 'Come on, give me your hand.'

But the boy still did not move; he seemed petrified into dumbness, and his fingers held on to the sleeper as if glued to it. The wall ended directly below this sleeper, and the rising tide was already creeping towards its fallen stones.

As John unbent the boy's fingers he saw that they were bleeding, and he wished for the moment he would have Mick under his hands. When he picked him up the boy lay stiff across his arms like something frozen hard. The girl was standing at the corner, her face as white as her brother's, and she clutched at them both, saying, 'Is he all right? Oh, David, are you all right?'

'Steady!' John said. 'Let's get off here.' And she went before them along the wall to where it met the ground.

As John put the boy down she drew David into her arms, crying, 'Oh, my dear, what have they done?'

The boy shuddered, and his body fell against hers, and she soothed him, saying, 'There! There! . . . We'll go home–Grandfather will soon be in and everything will be all right.'

But when she took his hand to walk him up the bank his legs gave way beneath him, and he fell forward. John picked him up again, saying, 'You better get him to bed.'

As he strode up the road with the girl trotting by his side and holding on to her brother's ankle, he thanked God that most of the people were indoors having their tea and that the corners of the streets were deserted by their usual batches of men, for he felt self-conscious in doing this rescue act.

The door was open and the house lighted just as she had left it; and as John passed through the front room and into the kitchen he had the impression that his home next door was a hundred miles away. He became conscious of his big, dirty boots on the carpet, and when he laid the boy in the chair, drawn up to the fire, the comfort of it was conveyed to him by his hands sinking beneath the boy into the upholstery.

The girl ran into the bedroom, and returned with something in a glass. David drank it, then asked, in a thin, small voice, 'How long will Grandfather be?'

'Not long, darling.'

The girl was kneeling by the chair, and John, looking down on her, repeated to himself. 'Not long, darling.' Never before had he heard the word spoken, except in derision. How strange these people were.

He was turning to go, saying, 'I hope he'll be all right. My brother will be dealt with,' when the girl sprang to her feet.

'What are you going to do to your brother?' she asked. 'Thrash him?'

'What else?'

'Oh please!' her words tumbled over one another–'Please, don't do that! It won't do a bit of good . . . not the slightest, just the opposite.'

John frowned down on her in perplexity: 'What do you expect me to do? Let him off? He might have killed the lad there—' He nodded towards the chair.

Her eyes, set deep in her white face, looked black and enormous, and she began to plead with him as if her life depended on it: 'But he didn't! You must talk to him, point out where he was wrong. . . . Will you? . . . Please. But don't thrash him; you'll only thrash it into him.'

'Thrash what into him?' John's brows drew closer together.

'The fears, the inhibitions . . . all the things that drove him to do what he did.'

John stared at her. What was she getting at? Was this part of the spook religion? She was strange, not in sayings alone, but in her looks; her curveless body, like a lad's, was as attractive as any bulging bust and wobbling hips.

He turned away from her and went towards the kitchen door, but she hastily blocked his exit: 'Please! . . . Oh!'–she closed her eyes and moved her head from side to side–'if only Grandfather was in he'd explain so much better than me. . . . But you mustn't thrash him.'

Looking down into her strained face, John saw that for the moment, the thought of Mick being thrashed had entirely eliminated the worry for her brother–she was like no one he had met before . . . she was really in earnest that Mick should be let off. But he knew Mick, and she didn't, so he said, 'Do you think he would understand a talking to? No. The only thing Mick and his like understand is the thick end of the belt across their . . .' Somehow he couldn't say 'arses' in front of her, so he ended lamely, 'You see, you don't know them.'

'Oh, but I do,' she said, smiling faintly, trying to override his last remark; 'I've known dozens of Micks. Look—' She put out her hands and caught hold of the lapels of his coat. The gesture was almost childish in its naturalness, and he looked down at her hands, then at her face close beneath his own; and an odd sensation passed over him. . . . Hannah Kelly said, 'Mind she doesn't lay hands on you, lad.' But this wasn't the kind of laying on she was referring to. If a lass of the fifteen streets laid hold of him, there would be a particular meaning to it; they would lark about a lot before she did this though, and afterwards his arms would go round her. He had seen the process enacted at the corner ends and in dark places in the back lanes. Often, when a lad, he watched the climax with an envy that dissolved into loneliness. And now here was this lass with her hands on him, and the sensation he was experiencing was almost one of reverence, similar to that which he at one time felt for the Virgin. . . . But he didn't want to feel reverence for her, or any other lass. She was fetching and he wanted . . . He lifted his hand and covered one of hers–it wasn't much bigger than Katie's, but it was different. His blood began to warm with the feel of her, and he smiled slowly. Her soft, curving mouth was just below his, and as he watched it move, it fascinated him. He wasn't fully aware of the words it was forming until she stepped away from him, taking her hand from his and saying, 'If you had to treat a dirty wound, you wouldn't rub more dirt into it, would you?'

Still on about Mick. . . . He came to himself, and said thickly, 'I'm sorry; I'll have to deal with him as I think fit.' A feeling of bewilderment and frustration, mixed with annoyance was filling him; and he passed her, saying gruffly, 'He'll have to take what's coming to him.'

It was with relief he entered his own kitchen. Here were people and things he could understand . . . and manage. Going straight to the wall by the fireplace he unhooked the razor strop.

'Is the lad all right?' Mary Ellen asked.

'Just,' John answered briefly. 'Come on'–he motioned with his head to Mick.

'I'm not comin'. I'll tell me da!'

'Go canny, lad,' Mary Ellen said to John.

Go canny. Here was another one. 'Go canny!' he rapped out at her with unusual irritation. 'Do you know he nearly killed the lad! As it is he's practically sent him out of his mind. It's as well for you you got hold of Molly when you did, or you'd have something more than a thrashing on your plate the night. Go canny!' He flung round from her and pointed to the door.

Mick began to snivel and cried, 'Ma! Ma, don't let him!'

Mary Ellen turned from Mick to the fire, and John seized him by the collar and pulled him to the door, there to meet Dominic coming in.

Dominic looked from one to the other before eyeing John through narrowed lids: 'What you at? Playin' boss of the house again?'

'You mind your own damn business. If you'd had a little more of it there might have been an improvement in you!'

Mary Ellen hastily broke in, addressing herself to Dominic, 'He's nearly killed the little lad next door.'

After a moment, during which he glanced from one to the other, Dominic stepped aside, and John pushed Mick before him down the yard and into the wash-house.

Mary Ellen found herself staring at Dominic; she couldn't quite take it in; he was sober, solid and sober; and it St Patrick's Day! And added to this surprise was another; for when he took his cap off she saw that he'd had a haircut . . . a proper one; his thick, brown, curling hair was neatly trimmed up the sides, making him, even with the dust of the ore on him, look more attractive. He hadn't come in to tea and she imagined him to be in the bars; but he must have been having a haircut!

She went to the oven to take out his tea, a plate of finnan haddock, but he said, 'I don't want that yet.'

With further amazement she saw him wash himself quickly, take off his yorks and change his coat. He was banging the dust from his trousers as he hurried past her to the front room.

'Where you off to?' she asked.

Dominic paused a moment, and the expression she hated, a mixture of scorn, cocksuredness and craft, came over his face. His eyes flicked over her, and her throat contracted with dislike of him. He said heavily, 'Where d'yer think?'

She stood still, listening to him going out of the front door, and between Mick's howls out in the backyard, she heard the knocker of the next door banging. Her fingers moved nervously back and forth across her lips. . . . How would it work out? Candidly she wouldn't care if Dominic left home tomorrow and she never set eyes on him again, but there was no such luck as that happening; he was here and he was going after that lass. It would have been bad enough had she been a Protestant–that was something you could lay your finger on–but what these people next door were was something beyond her ken, something dark and mysterious, something not far removed from the devil; for whoever heard anyone connected with God daring to say they could cure people! Even the priests wouldn't dare. And then another strong point proving their ungodliness was all their fine things. God didn't shower gifts on those He loved–He pointed out the road of poverty to them. Father O'Malley could be hard, but he was right in some things; if you got your reward here, then you could make sure it wasn't from God.

From last Saturday, when they moved in, she had made up her mind to have no truck with them. At odd times she had stopped working and found herself listening to the girl singing. The first time she had heard her she was shocked; she felt it was indecent somehow, almost as bad as if she had seen her walking naked, for it wasn't like a woman singing to a bairn, nor yet over her poss-tub, but was high and clear and without restraint. And the morning she heard the singing before breakfast she was bewildered; for even if you had something to sing about you wouldn't do it before breakfast, unless you were prepared to cry your eyes out before supper. . . . No, she wanted no truck with them. Yet here was John saving the lad and braying their Mick, and Dominic in next door pouring sympathy over the lass in his best manner. And he had a best manner, Mary Ellen knew; but she also knew it was an impossibility for him to keep it up. Well–she again fastened the errant button of her blouse and momentarily lifted the weight of her body–that was as far as things were going, if she could help it . . . not one of them would darken this door!

She crossed herself swiftly and murmured, 'May the Lord bless us and preserve us from all evil, and bring us to life everlasting. Amen.'

Chapter Four

The Conflict

Mary Ellen's temper was fraying thin. The weather was bad enough with the rain pelting down and the wind howling as if it was December, but to have them all in the house except Mick and Molly, who were at school, was too much. Neither John nor Dominic had been set on this morning; a mail boat had come in with a cargo of fruit, but the gaffer had given the work to the men who had not been set on the recent boats. It was bad enough that they were off work, but to have them all stuck round her like this was too much of a good thing. And what was more, she was feeling a little sick with the heat of the oven and the smell of the dirty working clothes put to dry all round the kitchen. . . . If only this other business were over. She was tired of it all–her body was so bairn-weary. She was feeling now that things were getting beyond her.

Even Katie could draw no kind word from her, and she pushed her to one side to get to the oven, saying, 'Get out of me way, bairn.'

Katie was home from school because her boots leaked; and her eyes were streaming, not only as the result of a cold but with crying. She hated to be off school, more so now than ever, for Miss Llewellyn had said that if she worked hard she could sit for an examination, which might be the first step on the road to her becoming a teacher. She had tried to tell her mother, but Mary Ellen snapped at her, and even John did not seem interested.

She looked towards him now. He was sitting in the corner on the far side of the fireplace mending her boots. He had put odd pieces of leather on the soles and was now cutting up an old boot to get enough leather to sew across the slits. She returned to her book, the only one she possessed, a Grimm's Fairy Tale, and she knew each word by heart.

The front-door knocker was suddenly banged, and without waiting she went to answer it. It had been knocked twice already this afternoon, once by a tally man and once by a man begging. The beggar wasn't pleased when she brought him a slice of bread. He bent it up and put it in his pocket, and her mouth watered, for it was new bread from a flat cake just out of the oven; it was a long time till tea-time, and she had got out of the habit of asking for bread between meals for she remembered times when they all had bread at tea-time except her mother, and she was frightened that this would happen again.

It was Mrs Bradley at the door, and she asked, 'Is yer ma in?'

Katie said, 'Yes.'

'Then tell her we're gathering for poor Mrs Patton's wreath. . . . Here, take her the paper.'

Katie took the paper and went into the scullery to her mother. 'It's Mrs Bradley–she's gathering for flowers, ma.'

Mary Ellen's lips set in a tight line as she read down one side of the list and half-way down the other . . . shillings, sixpences . . . only two or three threepences. She gave a sigh, and lifting up her skirt took fourpence from the little bag and handed it to Katie, together with the list.

As Katie passed John he asked, 'What's that for?'

But before she could reply, Mary Ellen called, 'Go on, you, Katie,' and Katie went on to the front door. Mary Ellen knew that John didn't hold with gathering for wreaths, but what could she do . . . and that Bella Bradley collecting!

John knew what he would have done . . . the gathering for wreaths had always irked him. They would collect as much as two pounds and spend the whole lot on flowers, when the widow, if it was a man who had died, was more often than not destitute, and within a week the bairns would be crying for bread. They knew this only too well, the women who took it on themselves to gather, yet they still bought flowers to show respect for the dead. He snorted and banged the hammer on the last, sending a pain through his knee. It made him mad! He knew that, even if there was no insurance money, besides collecting for the flowers they would collect for cabs, to make the dead look decent. They didn't collect for the hearse. No, that could be ticked, to be paid off at so much a week. But the undertakers weren't so ready to tick cabs. And if it was for one of the Irish, the relatives would pawn, beg, borrow or steal, but they would have a bit of a wake. It was all crazy! And yet he understood from his mother that the funerals were nothing like they used to be, for in her young days, she told him, she longed for the Irish to die so she could go to the wake with her mother and have a good feed.

What had she put on the list, he wondered. Whatever it was, by this time next week they would be glad of it; for if they were not set on there wouldn't be a penny in the house.

Many things were beginning to make him wild. And on a day like this, tied to the house, he had nothing else to do but think. Lately he had been feeling the desire for someone to talk to, someone who could answer questions. Once or twice he tried to talk to Father Bailey, and endeavoured to have the material in his mind formed into concrete questions; but when he was with the priest he found it was no use–he knew what he wanted to say but couldn't get it out.

His mother was always saying thinking got you nowhere; you must have faith and rely on that. Faith! He looked at her now, pounding a great piece of dough, the second batch of bread she had baked today. What had faith done for her? She could hardly get her arms into the bowl for the roundness of her stomach. He took his eyes from her. Where would they put the bairn when it came? He'd have to try and rig up something out of boxes–the clothes basket that had served them all as a cradle was done long since. He pulled his legs up hastily as Dominic made to pass him on his way to the bedroom.

Mary Ellen called after Dominic, 'Don't lie on that bed with those boots on, mind!' but the only answer she received was the banging of the door.

John settled himself back against the wall: he always felt easier when Dominic was out of the room. He had finished one boot and was preparing the thread by rubbing it with tallow for patching the other when he heard his mother give a startled mutter. She was looking out through the kitchen window, and she exclaimed, 'I don't want them in here!'

As she rubbed the dough off her hands, there came a knock on the kitchen door. Katie was about to open it, but Mary Ellen said, 'Hold on. I'll see to it.' When she opened the door, there stood the old man and the girl.

'Good afternoon, Mrs O'Brien.' It was the old man who spoke, and his voice was as kindly as his smile; but Mary Ellen would not allow it to make any impression on her. She didn't reply, but stared at them fixedly, the door held firmly in her hand, while he went on, 'I thought we would just come round and get acquainted. And also ask you to thank your son for helping my boy last night.'

Mary Ellen's eyes darted to the girl. She was wearing a waterproof coat with a hood attached, and from under it she smiled at Mary Ellen, like a child who was asking to be liked. They were barmy, Mary Ellen thought. Their Mick had nearly done for the lad, and here they were, coming to thank John! They weren't all there, either of them–they couldn't be. She wanted no truck with them. She was aware that the old man was becoming drenched, but that was his look-out; they weren't crossing the doorstep.

She was saying abruptly, 'That's all right. It was our Mick's fault, anyway,' when she felt her hand taken from the door, and John stood there, saying, 'Won't you come in?' It wasn't often she got angry with John, but now it took her all her time not to turn on him.

The old man said, 'Thank you. Thank you. Are you by any chance the Mr O'Brien I owe so much to?'

Pushing two chairs forward John said, 'Take a seat.' He did not look at the girl, but went on, 'It's us should be doing the thanking. Not many people would be taking it like this.' Then he turned to Shane: 'This is my father.'

Shane reluctantly took the proffered hand and muttered something, and his head, which had been still, began to jerk.

The old man, seeming not to notice the lack of cordiality, said, 'My name's Peter Bracken. And this is my grand-daughter, Christine.'

Shane nodded, and after a short silence that was broken only by the scraping of chairs, he turned to Mary Ellen, now vigorously pounding the dough, and said, 'I'm off to see if there's anything in.' He pulled his steaming coat off the rod that ran under the mantleshelf, and with a final nod towards Mr Bracken, he went out.

Mary Ellen watched his huge figure slumping down the yard. Off to see if there's anything in at this time of the day! It was just to get out of the way; he hated to talk to strangers at any time. There was a faint wreath of steam still hovering about the shoulders of his coat as he disappeared into the back lane. It brought a tightness to her breast, and she murmured to herself, 'Shane, Shane,' as she was wont to do years ago when her pity was mixed with love. And the feeling made her more resentful towards the pair sitting behind her. Now he'd be wet to the skin, and his twitching would go on all night.

She knew she was being very bad mannered standing with her back to them, but she couldn't help it; yet she found herself listening to the girl talking to Katie. They were talking about the book, Katie's voice sounding broad in comparison with the girl's, which was quiet and even and without dialect. And then she found herself listening to John. He was talking more than she had heard him do so before. He was talking to the old fellow about the docks and the kind of boats that came in and what they brought . . . iron ore from Bilbao, black fine ore from Benisaf, the heavy ore from Sweden that made the steel, esparto grass for paper, prop boats from Russia, with the cargo stacked from one end of the boat to the other to make the tonnage. As if the old fellow would want to know all that! She had never heard him talk so much about the docks before. He went on to speak of the unloading as if he had been down the holds all his life, instead of just two years. What had come over him? Perhaps he was doing it because she was offhand with them. Well, he knew she wanted no truck with them; and they were a thick-skinned pair to sit there knowing, as they must know, that they weren't wanted.

'I suppose you are always kept busy, Mrs O'Brien?'

She started, and was forced to half turn her body and look at the old man, and to answer him civilly: 'Yes, most of the time I'm at it.'

'You must find it very hard looking after such a big family. And I mean big,' he laughed.

'Well, you've got to take what God sends.' Immediately she felt she had said the wrong thing, giving him an opening to start his ranting, but to her surprise he didn't take it.

He stood up, saying, 'Well, we mustn't delay you–I just felt I would like to make your acquaintance, Mrs O'Brien.'

Mary Ellen turned from the dish, again forced to respond, this time with a smile. It was funny, but they seemed all right. Was this spook business just an idle rumour? People were in the habit of making a lot out of nowt.

She returned the girl's smile too, but when she saw John, silent now, looking at the lass, the smile froze on her face. She didn't want any of that kind of truck, not for John she didn't. . . . Dominic could do what he liked.

There was another knock on the front door, and this time she had to tell Katie, who was hanging on to the girl's hand, to go and open it.

Christine spoke directly to Mary Ellen for the first time, 'Will you let Katie come in to tea, Mrs O'Brien? It's rather a special occasion, it's Grandfather's birthday.'

She cast a smile, full of light, on the old man, and he said, 'Sh!'

She answered, 'No, I won't. Do you know how old he is?' She was speaking to John now, looking up into his face.

John's eyes twinkled, and he answered seriously. 'Twenty-six.'

They all laughed, except Mary Ellen.

'You're just sixty years out!' said the girl.

'You're not eighty-six!' Amazement brought the words out of Mary Ellen.

'Yes, that's what I am, Mrs O'Brien.'

Mary Ellen stared at the straight, lean body of Peter Bracken, at his unlined face and deep-set eyes, shining like black coals. The only sign of real age was the white hair, and he was eighty-six. Fear of him overcame her again. You didn't reach eighty-six and be like that, not naturally you didn't. Shane was fifty-seven, and he was old. She had known men live to eighty, but they ended their days in bed, or on sticks. No, her instinct had been right at first . . . there was something funny about them, something beyond her understanding; and she wanted no truck with them.

She was brought from her fear by the sound of footsteps accompanying Katie's through the front room. Who on earth could Katie have let in now!

The small, black-clad figure standing in the open doorway soon informed her. She gasped at the sight of Father O'Malley. His presence always meant a rating for something or other. Today it would be Katie off school and Mick being kept from Mass last Sunday. Oh, she'd had enough for one day! And there were these two still standing there, not smiling now but staring at the priest as if they were struck.

'Good afternoon, Father. Will you take a seat? It's dreadful weather; you must be wet.' Mary Ellen was doing her duty. At the same time, she noticed the half-inch thick soles on the priest's stout boots, and chided herself for thinking: It'll take some water to get through them.

John spoke next: 'Good afternoon, Father.'

'Good afternoon,' said Father O'Malley, in his thin, tight voice; but he looked neither at Mary Ellen nor at John, for his eyes were fixed on those of Peter Bracken.

Noting this, John said, 'Mr Bracken's a new neighbour of ours, Father.'

The priest did not answer, and Peter Bracken said, quietly, 'Father O'Malley and I already know one another.'

'What is this man doing in your house?'

Mary Ellen knew the priest was addressing her, although he did not look at her. She shivered and said hesitantly 'Well Father . . .'

'Order him to leave at once! And forbid him the door in future.'

Mary Ellen twisted the corner of her apron and turned towards Mr Bracken and the girl. But before she could get the words out, John broke in sharply, 'Hold your hand a minute! Me da's not in, and next to him I'm head of this house, such as it is, and I'm telling no one to get out, Father.'

The priest swung round on him, his eyes almost lost behind their narrowed lids and the double lenses of his glasses: 'So you are head of the house, are you? And you will take the responsibility on your soul for associating with this man?'

'I know nothing against the man.' John's face was as set as the priest's.

'You don't?' Father O'Malley raised his eyebrows. 'Then you're about the only one in these parts who doesn't. I will enlighten you. This man is an enemy of the Catholic Church. . . .'

'That is not true! I'm an enemy of no church. . . .'

Father O'Malley cut short Peter Bracken's protest, and went on: 'Why, I ask you, is a man of his standing living in a quarter like this? Because he makes it his business to live among Catholics so he can turn them against the Church.'

'I live wherever there is fear and poverty, and try to ease it.' The old man's face was no longer placid; it was alight with a force and energy that gave the impression he was towering above them all.

'Do you know what this man has dared to say? Only that he has a power equal to that of Christ!' Father O'Malley's eyes bored into Mary Ellen's and then into John's. 'In fact, he says he is a Christ!'

John, his eyes wide and questioning now, looked to Mr Bracken for denial. But none came.

'You know you are twisting my words!' cried the old man. 'What I maintain is we all have the power to be Christs. If we are made in God's image and likeness, then it stands to reason we are part of Him; our spirit is pure God material. The only difference between my spirit and God's is the size of it–the quality is exactly the same. That is what I preach. And the more I become aware of my spirit, the more I get in touch with it, the more God-like things I can do. . . . And I have done God-like things—' Mr Bracken pointed at the priest: 'You know I have! And it is this very proof that upsets your slavish doctrine.'

'Silence!' Father O'Malley's voice was like deep and terrible thunder.

Mary Ellen clutched at the neck of her blouse, and Katie hid her face in the folds of her mother's skirt; the bedroom door opened and Dominic came into the kitchen, but no one took any notice of him.

The priest's voice dropped low in his throat. He addressed himself to John, 'Are you asking for any more proof than that?'

Before John could answer, the girl spoke, 'My grandfather will give him proof–he will show him his own power, and free him from you and your like. It is not God's will, as you preach, that he or anyone else should live in poverty and ignorance all his days. If they were made aware of their own power they would throw all this off.' She flung her arms wide and took a step towards the priest. 'You would stop them from thinking–for once they think, they question. And they mustn't question, must they? They must accept! It wouldn't do for them to realize there's no purgatory or heaven or hell but what they make themselves!'

Before John's eyes there rose the picture of Miss Llewellyn leaning back against the wind, saying, 'Take the heaven you are sure of.' Then his mind was brought back to this slip of a girl facing up to a man like Father O'Malley; not only facing up to him, but attacking him. What she was saying was quite mad, but she had courage.

The thought saddened him; it might be the courage of fanaticism, and she looked too sweet and girlish to be imbued with fanaticism.

The old man drew her back to his side, saying, 'Be serene, Christine. Remember, anger poisons.'

Father O'Malley's voice cast a deadly chill over the room as he said, 'The day is not far hence when you will rot in hell for your blasphemy!'

'The day is not far hence,' took up Peter Bracken, 'when your sect, if it does not throw off its dogmatism and learn toleration, will be fighting for its life; for there are seeds in the wombs of women, at this moment, that in thirty, forty or fifty years' time will shake the foundations of your preaching. The minds of people are moving. They are searching for the truth–they are reading. And what are they reading first?–the very books that are forbidden by your Church, for the first question the groping mind asks is: Why have these books been forbidden?'

Father O'Malley looked as if he was about to choke–black anger swamped his face. After a silence, tensed to breaking point, he addressed Mary Ellen, 'I leave you and your conscience to judge. And remember, I am warning you . . . disaster and damnation follow this man. If you wish to save your immortal soul and those of your family, throw him out as you would a snake!' His eyes burned into Mary Ellen's for a second, and then he was gone. And the banging of the front door shook the house.

It occurred to John that Father O'Malley had ignored him because he stood up to him; it was noticeable that the priest concentrated on his mother because she was afraid. He looked towards her. She was leaning on the table with one hand; the other was held under her breast tight against her heart. And she was shivering.

Dominic spoke for the first time: 'Don't take any notice of him; he thinks he's still in Ireland.' His words weren't spoken to his mother, but to the girl. But she did not return his glance, or answer him, for she was staring at Mary Ellen.

Into this tense atmosphere came Mick. He entered the kitchen, his head on one side and his hand over his ear. 'Ma, me ear's runnin' and it's ach . . .' He stopped short at the sight of Mr Bracken and glanced quickly from him to John.

No one moved for a second until Peter Bracken exclaimed in an exalted voice, 'Mrs O'Brien, I will show you! Your boy has earache, probably an abscess. I will cure it. Through the great healing power of God I will cure it.'

He made a step towards Mick, and in a moment the kitchen became quickened into life. Mary Ellen flung herself between them, intending to grab Mick to her, but Mick, thinking of last night and taking Peter's cure to mean much the same thing as when his mother boxed his ears, saying, 'I'll cure you!' sprang away from them both. Mary Ellen made a wild grab at the air, overbalanced and twisted herself to clutch at John's hands that were outstretched to her but missed them and fell on her side on to the mat.

Mary Ellen knew, almost as she fell, what had happened. The blinding pain, like a red-hot steel wire, starting in her womb and forcing itself up through her body and out of her head, blotted out even itself in its transit. When next she felt it she was lying on the bed–the pain was filling all her pores and forcing out sweat. She opened her eyes and looked up into John's face. She wanted to say to him, 'Don't worry, lad. Don't worry,' for his face was like death, but she could utter no word.

The hot wire was boring again, identifying itself from the other pains by an intensity that no previous labour had brought to her. It left no room even for fear when she realized that that Bracken man was near her; nor did she feel any element of surprise when she heard him saying, 'I'll go in and work at her head through the wall. Take her hand and don't let go.'

Mary Ellen felt her hand being taken between two soft palms, and she did as she was bidden when his voice came directly to her, as if through a thick fog, saying, 'Hold on to Christine, Mrs O'Brien, and the pain will go.'

As the pain forced her knees up and her head down into her chest, Mary Ellen gripped the girl's hand. And when she next regained consciousness she knew she was not on the bed but above it, lying on a sort of soft platform, and the girl was still by her side, while Hannah Kelly and Nurse Snell were working on somebody lying on the bed. And then the doctor came, not the shilling doctor, but Doctor Davidson from Jarrow, and she wondered vaguely who would pay him. He reached up and took her hand and tried to unloosen it from the girl's, but as he did so Mary Ellen felt herself dropping down into that contorted mass below her, and she clung on like grim death to the soft hand. She heard him say, 'You're Peter Bracken's grand-daughter, aren't you?' There followed a silence. Then his voice came again, 'Well, there are stranger things in heaven and earth than this world dreams of; and I won't despise your help, because I'm going to need it.'

She lay for years on the platform with queer sensations passing through her body, and the next voice she heard was that of Shane, muttering, 'Mary Ellen, lass, Mary Ellen.'

She knew he was crying, and she wondered at it. She thought of the time when he loved her and she loved him–it was all so long ago. What had happened since? Nothing. He still loved her, but she loved Katie and John. But they didn't love Shane–he had no one but her. What would happen to him when she died she didn't know–and it didn't seem to matter.

It was odd, but rather nice, lying here thinking untroubled thoughts. She hadn't to get up and see about the baking or washing or meals, or, what was more important, money. She had an ache somewhere, but she couldn't lay her finger on it. And she was conscious of smiling when the doctor reached up and, lifting her eyelid, exclaimed, 'Odd, very odd.'

The next voice that came to her was Father Bailey's. It was nice to have Father Bailey near; he brought a feeling of comfort. And as he made the sign of the cross and touched her lips, she felt a great happiness. She saw him standing at the foot of the platform and smiling, not at her, but at Mr

Bracken, who, she felt, was standing just behind her head. Father Bailey was saying, 'God's ways are many and mysterious. He has made these ways and only He can judge them.' She heaved a great sigh and fell into a kind of sleep, thinking, 'Yes, we are all one.' It was the answer Christine Bracken had given to Father Bailey.

The gas in the kitchen was turned low. It flickered up and down and spurted out of a little hole in the bottom of the mantle. In the dim light John knelt before the fire, taking out the ashes. He raked them slowly and quietly, and was glad of their warmth on his hands, for in spite of a good fire, he felt cold. It was the chill before the dawn, he thought. Was it only twelve hours since all this started? It seemed many lifetimes to him. And what it must be like for Christine, sitting in that one position by the bed, he could not imagine. He thought of her now as Christine–the night had joined them in a relationship that seemed to him to be stronger than any blood tie; he had wrapped a blanket about her and taken off her shoes, and put on her slippers. He had been next door for them, and had to find them himself, for the old man was sitting facing the wall and appeared to be asleep. He had taken her cup after cup of tea, and when, stiff with cramp, she could not hold the cup, he held it for her. Once she leant against him and he supported her with his arm. And an hour ago, he had tried to withdraw her hand gently from his mother's, but the result was the same as when others had attempted to do this–Mary Ellen's fingers became like a vice around those of Christine. His mother had been on the point of death, he knew, her life reduced to a mere flicker, yet whenever her hand was touched it held all the strength of vital life in its grip on Christine's. The doctor had said it was touch and go: 'I've done all I can,' he said. 'I'll be back first thing in the morning.' And looking hard at John, he asked, 'Do you believe in spiritual healing?'

John answered simply, 'I'm a Catholic.'

'So am I,' said the doctor. 'And I'm dead against it professionally and otherwise . . . yet . . .' He had stopped abruptly, buttoned his coat, and said, 'Good night. We'll know more in the morning.'

Father Bailey had left the house without saying anything, his face set and thoughtful.

Shane's reactions when he saw the girl sitting there were surprising to John. He had come back into the kitchen and stood looking down into the fire, his body strangely still. 'I don't care who keeps her alive–it can be the divil himself,' he said, 'as long as she doesn't leave me.'

He had turned and looked quietly at his son, and John realized that beyond the drinking and the fighting there still remained in his father a deep feeling for his mother. It surprised him and at the same time brought him closer to this man, whom at times he almost despised. A little while ago he had managed to persuade him to lie down–Dominic was already in bed, having retired there shortly after twelve. He had stood with the others round his mother when they thought she was breathing her last, but when she continued to breathe he said there was no point in the lot of them staying up, and anyway he'd have to be out early to see if he could get a start.

John knew that he, too, would have to be at the docks by six o'clock. There was a prop boat due in, and he might get set on–not that he liked prop boats, for there was no piece work–you received four shillings a day, and no overtime; but that would certainly be better than nothing, for with his mother bad, money would be needed now more than ever before.

Although he'd had no rest he did not feel tired; the training of working forty-eight hours at a stretch as a young lad when on tipping had hardened him. He thought nothing of working all day and all night to discharge an ore boat, and the men liked him in the gang. He could set the pace, and the pace meant everything when the quicker the discharging was done the sooner the men were paid. He looked at the clock . . . half past four. There were many things that should be done before he left the house; so he proceeded to tidy the kitchen, shaking the mats and sweeping the floor–his mother would want them to be dependent on neighbours as little as possible, kind as they might be.

He was setting the table for breakfast when Hannah Kelly came from the front room.

'I'll go over home a minute, lad,' she whispered, 'and get our Joe up. Then I'll be back.'

He thanked her, and asked, 'Do you think there's any change?'

'I don't know . . . perhaps there's a little–she seems to be breathing easier. Funny about that lass, isn't it?' She looked questioningly at John. 'Mary Ellen hanging on to her like that after saying she wanted no truck with them.'

John made no reply.

And after a moment she whispered again, 'She had me scared stiff, sitting so still. 'Tisn't natural. What d'ye make of it? And what are ye going to do if it goes on any longer?'

'I don't know,' he said.

Hannah shook her head: 'It's rum. Makes ye put yer thinking cap on, don't it?'

He nodded slowly, and she said, 'Aye well, there's queer things happen in the world. We'll know this time the morrer, likely.'

After Hannah had gone, he stood staring before him. What would happen to them all if his mother should die? She was the axis around which they revolved. Molly would soon be leaving school, but she would be less than useless to run this turbulent house. He looked down on her, lying in the corner of the couch. Her mouth was open, and even in sleep she looked what she was, feckless. Now if Katie were older . . . What! The thought shocked him. Katie work and slave after the lot of them! No. Let her have a better start than that, even though it be only in service. But his mother wouldn't die. Somehow they wouldn't let her die.

He classed Mr Bracken and Christine as 'they' when he thought of them in their strange and eerie capacity of healers; but as Mr Bracken and Christine, he thought of them as kindly folk, and in Christine's case, as bonnie and taking.

When he went quietly from the kitchen into the front room to replenish the fire, he saw them as he had seen them last–his mother, lying straight and still and curiously flat, with one arm outstretched to that of Christine, who was sitting close to the head of the bed; only this time there was a difference–inches separated Mary Ellen's hand from Christine's.

Christine smiled faintly. The smile seemed forced on to the chiselled whiteness of her face, her eyes looked vacant, like the hollowed sockets in a sculptured head.

John bent over her, whispering anxiously, 'Are you all right?'

She tried to broaden her smile, but the effort seemed too much, and she fell against him. He glanced at his mother. She was breathing evenly now, and a faint tinge of colour had crept into the greyness of her face.

Christine whispered, 'She's asleep . . . it's over.' She sighed, and her body pressed with gentle heaviness against him.

'Come into the kitchen,' he said.

'I can't yet. I've . . . I've got cramp. I'm stiff. In a little while.'

She sounded sleepy, and for a moment he thought she had fallen asleep.

Hannah Kelly came into the room again, and exclaimed softly, 'She's let go then.' She peered at Mary Ellen. 'She's better. Ye'd better get away to bed, lass,' she said kindly to Christine.

Christine, in an effort to rise, almost lost her balance, and John put his arm about her and supported her to the kitchen, followed by Hannah's quizzical glance and raised eyebrows. 'Aye, well,' she soliloquized, 'ye never can tell where blisters light. But my God, won't Mary Ellen go mad!'

John sat Christine on a chair by the fire, and stood helplessly watching her as she slowly started to cry. It was a gentle crying; the tears welled up from their source, spilling over the dark, thick fringe of lashes on to her cheeks, then down on to her clasped hands.

'You're all in,' John said. 'Come on, I'll take you in home.'

Like a child, she placed her hand in his, and he drew her to her feet.

'The cramp . . . it's still there'–she tottered as she stood–'my legs don't seem to belong to me.'

In the flickering light of the gas, she looked up at him and smiled through the tears. 'It's been a strange night, John.'

He nodded silently. He wanted to thank her for what, in the back of his mind, he felt that she and her father had done, but to say 'Thank you for saving my mother's life' would be to accept the strange and terrible power that was assuredly theirs, and some part of him was afraid. It seemed ridiculous that this slip of a lass could be anything but what she looked . . . a fetching, boyish-looking girl.

Christine sighed and said, 'Everything would have been perfect if the baby had lived. Will your mother be very upset?'

He couldn't answer for his mother . . . nor for himself, for he felt she would be shocked at his thankfulness that it was dead.

She swayed, and again he put his arm about her and led her to the door. Her legs gave way beneath her, and she clung to him saying, 'It's only temporary. In the morning I'll be all right, but now all my strength has gone.'

Stooping swiftly and saying, 'This is the best way then,' he lifted her up into his arms. She offered no resistance, but sank against him, her head on her shoulder. One of his hands was under her breast, and he saw the curve of it as her blouse and petticoat pouched, small, not much bigger than Katie's, and the sight of it brought no more excitement to his blood than the tiny mound of Katie's would have done. Some part of his mind wondered at this. His other hand was below her knees, and his face, as it bent above hers, was close enough for kissing. He could have dropped his mouth on to the lips and told himself it was in gratitude. And she too perhaps would have accepted his excuse. And it would have been a start. It would also have fixed Dominic. But he did nothing, not even press her close. Perhaps it was because he was worried about his mother, but he might have been carrying Katie, for his feelings were not aroused above tenderness. Vaguely, he was irritated by this. The night had brought them together in one way, a way that was deep and would be lasting, he knew, but it wasn't the way of a fellow getting off with a lass; it was a way that had missed his body and touched something beyond.

As he carried her into her own kitchen, she stirred and opened her eyes, and her hand came up and touched his cheek. And she whispered, 'You're so nice, John . . . so good.' And he knew that he would have started something had he kissed her, because she liked him in a way perhaps that hadn't gone past her body.

Chapter Five

The Comic

Katie moved the parcel on to her other hip. It was heavy; but not as heavy as the weight inside her; the weight was leaden. To go to the pawnshop with any parcel filled her with shame; to walk up the dock bank, under the knowledgeable stares of the men idling there against the railings caused her throat to move in and out; and to meet any of her schoolmates on the journey made her want to die; but when it was John's suit she was carrying every tragedy of the journey was intensified a thousandfold.

When her mother asked, 'Will you go down to "Bob's", hinny?' Katie had stared at her, speechless. She wanted to say, 'Our Molly should go, she's bigger,' but she knew from experience that Molly always got less on the clothes than she did, and generally too, she lost something, the ticket, or worse still, a sixpence. And because her mother looked so thin and white when she asked her she remained silent, and watched Mary Ellen go to the box under the bed and take John's suit out.

It seemed such a shame that it was John's, because he had started work only that morning. They all had, after being off weeks. But there was nothing in the house now to make them a meal, and although they would get subs, her mother was relying on these to pay the three weeks' back rent. Katie felt that once the rent was paid, her mother would look less white.

Going through the arches into Tyne Dock she met Mrs Flaherty.

'Oh, ye're not at school the day?' Peggy greeted her.

'No, I was sick.' Katie stared up into the half-washed face, criss-crossed with wrinkles, and her tone defied disbelief.

'Oh, that's a pity, it is. Ye shouldn't miss you iducation. Some day, when ye're old enough, I'll lend ye one o' me books; they'll iducate ye like nothing else will. When ye're old enough that is.' She snuffled and caught the drop from the end of her nose on the back of her hand.

'Thank you.' For as long as she could remember Katie had been promised one of Mrs Flaherty's books, and the promise meant nothing to her now. She said, 'Ta-ta, Mrs Flaherty,' and walked on, the parcel now pressed against her chest and resting on the top of her stomach.

Although she thought impatiently that Mrs Flaherty was always on about education, she wished her mother was a bit like her. She had almost given up talking to her mother about the examination and what Miss Llewellyn said, for her mother didn't believe Miss Llewellyn meant what she said–last time, she had stopped her talking, saying, 'Oh, hinny, you mustn't take so much notice of things; your teacher's only being nice. The examination she's on about is likely the one you have every year.' And when Katie had sat quietly crying, Mary Ellen said to John, 'Look, lad. I can't go down to the school and see what she keeps on about, I only have me shawl; will you go?'

'What! Me? Not on your life. Now that's a damn silly thing to ask me to do, isn't it! What could I say to the headmistress?'

'Well, will you go and see her teacher, then?'

John had just stared blankly at his mother, then picked up his cap and walked out of the house.

Katie thought the only one who understood was Christine. She liked Christine nearly as much as she liked Miss Llewellyn, but not quite. Life had taken on an added glow since Christine came into it; for Christine made her pinnies and dresses out of her own old ones. She gave her and Molly nice things to eat, too; and she had even given them money, real money, half a crown each. But only twice, for when they took their half-crowns into their mother the second week she made them take them back.

Katie could not understand her mother's attitude of not speaking to Christine and her grandfather. She allowed her and Molly to go next door, but Mr Bracken and Christine had never been into her house since that terrible day some months ago when their mother was taken bad. John and Dominic, too, went next door; and she often sat on John's knee while he and Mr Bracken talked. They talked about funny things, one of which stuck in her mind: Mr Bracken said you could have anything you wanted if you only used your thoughts properly. . . . There were so many things she wanted, but she wanted above all to be a teacher. Should she do what Mr Bracken told John, lie on her back with her arms outstretched and think of being a teacher until she felt herself floating away? Eeh no! she'd better not, for there were some people who said Mr Bracken was the devil. He wasn't; but anyway, she'd better not do it.

She always had a queer feeling when Dominic was next door, when she would wonder if he were trying to do what he was doing that night she went in unexpectedly. He had Christine pressed in the corner and was trying to kiss her. Her blouse was open, and the ribbon of her camisole was loose. Katie knew that Christine was frightened, for she held on to her until Dominic went out. Then she told her not to mention to John what had happened; and Katie only too readily promised.

At last she reached the dark well of the pawnshop, and listened, her eyes wide and sad, as Bob said, 'Only three-and-six, hinny. It's getting a bit threadbare.' He turned to a woman and asked, 'Will you put it in for her?' And the woman nodded, taking the penny Katie offered her. Katie wished she were fourteen, then if she had to come to the pawn she wouldn't have to pay somebody for putting the stuff in–a whole penny just for signing your name! It was outrageous, and she disliked the woman intensely for being so mean as to take the penny.

As she was leaving the shop with the money tightly grasped in her hand, Bob said, 'I've got something here that might interest one of your brothers. It'll fit nobody else round these parts. It's a top coat, and it's a bobby-dazzler. Ten shillings, it is. And I only wish I had what it cost when it was new. Tell one of them to have a look in.' Katie said she would.

She went on to the butcher's, and from there to buy a gas mantle. In Mr Powell's, she stood waiting while he hunted for the box which contained the turned down mantles. His search took him into the back shop, and Katie was left alone standing before an assortment of comics. They were arrayed on a sloping counter: *Rainbow*, *Tiger Tim's Weekly*, *Comic Cuts*, and others. Her eyes dwelt on them longingly. It was weeks and weeks since she was able to buy a comic. She would likely get a penny off John on Saturday. But Saturday was as far away as Christmas, and there stretched before her the rest of the afternoon and the long, long evening. And she daren't ask her mother for even a ha'penny out of the suit money. On the front of *Rainbow*, the Bruin boys were up to their games again: the tiger, the parrot, the elephant, and others, were playing one of their naughty pranks on Mrs Bruin. And inside the comic, Katie knew, would be the story of the little girl who was really a fairy and worked magic. Her eyes darted to the back shop. All she could see was Mr Powell's feet on the top of a pair of steps. Her hand went up and touched the *Rainbow*. It hesitated for a second, then with one swift movement, the *Rainbow* was inside her coat, and for the first time in her life she found herself wetting her knickers. The combined horror was too much for her. She ran out of the shop, down the dock bank to the arches. She did not stop to look inside her coat; her sin had already obliterated the joy of the comic. She was a thief! She had stolen! Mr Powell would miss the comic and put the pollis on her track; her mother would be taken to court and her face would become white again, and all at school would know . . . Miss Llewellyn would know!

Standing over the gutter, under the high, bleak arches, she vomited, and the comic slipped down from beneath her coat and became fouled with the sick.

There was a long row of boys and girls waiting to go into confession, for tomorrow was the first Friday in the mouth, on which day they all attended communion. They nudged each other and fidgeted whilst bending over in grotesque positions in supposed prayer. They whispered and passed sweets, and showed one another holy pictures; yet there was no noise at all, so practised were they. It was three week since Katie was last at confession, the longest period between her confessions she could remember. Although the chill autumn air was filling the church she felt hot and sick. She had been sick a number of times since the day she took John's suit to the pawn–she refused to think of it as the day she stole a comic. But now she had to think of the comic, for she was about to make her confession.

A teacher, not Miss Llewellyn, came and moved a row and a half of children down to the pews opposite Father O'Malley's box, which were singularly bare of penitents. This left Katie the next to go to Father Bailey. She was filled with a mixture of relief and fear, belief that she had escaped Father O'Malley's judgment, and fear that her turn was upon her.

A small, dark shadow emerged from one door of the confessional box, and Katie stumbled in. But for the faint gleam of a candle coming through the mesh from the priest's side the box was black dark inside.

'Please, Father, give me thy blessing for I have sinned,' she began. 'It is three weeks since my last confession.'

'Go on, my child.' Father Bailey's voice was like a soft balm falling on her.

'I have missed Mass once.'

'Through your own fault?'

'No, Father. It was me clothes; me ma wouldn't let me come.'

'Go on, my child.'

'I have spoken in church and I have missed me morning and night prayers.'

'How often?'

'Three times . . . no, four . . . perhaps a few more, Father.'

'Why?'

''Cos the lino's all cracked and it sticks in me knees when I kneel down.'

The priest made a noise in his throat and said, 'To strengthen your soul it is important that you say your prayers–prayers are the food of the soul like bread is the food of the body. . . . You understand, my child?'

'Yes, Father.'

'Then under no circumstances should you starve your soul.'

'No, Father.'

'Go on.'

But Katie couldn't go on. Her clasped hands, pressed against the elbow rest on a level with her face, were stuck together with sweat. The confessional box seemed weighed down with the smell of incense and mustiness.

'Is there anything more?' the priest asked.

'Yes, Father.'

'Well then, what is it?'

Silence followed his question. And after a moment he went on: 'Don't be afraid, my child; there is nothing so terrible that God won't forgive.'

'I stole.'

The priest's hand was taken away from his cheek and his face turned towards the mesh, and Katie looked up into two white bulbs. Then the hand was replaced again.

Katie shivered during the silence that followed; she felt her sin had been a shock even to the priest.

'What did you steal?'

'A *Rainbow*.'

'A what!' The hand was dropped again.

'A comic.'

The priest coughed. 'Now, my child, you know how it hurts our Blessed Lord when you do anything like that.'

'Yes, Father.'

'And will you do it again?'

'No, no. Never, Father.'

'No, I know you won't. And if you could find a way to pay the shopkeeper for the comic it would put everything right, wouldn't it?'

'Yes, Father.'

'Now, for your penance say one Our Father and ten Hail Marys, and tell Our Lord that never again will you hurt Him; and He will forgive you. And don't forget to kneel when you are saying your prayers, in spite of the lino; for remember the nails in the cross.'

The priest made the sign of the cross and said the absolution, whilst Katie murmured, 'Oh, my God, I am very sorry I have sinned against Thee, because Thou art so good and by the help of Thy Holy Grace I will never sin again.'

'Good night, my child, and God bless you,' said Father Bailey. 'And worry no more; He understands.'

In a holy daze, Katie walked out of the box, and in the same state she said her penance, kneeling in the corner of the dark church, straining her eyes up to the statue of the Virgin and the Child, knowing that her sin was wiped away. And on walking out of the church, there was John, standing under the lamp. It all seemed part of God's Grace. She ran to him and flung her arms about him, crying, 'Oh John! Oh John!' as if she had not seen him for years. Then she asked, 'Are you going to confession?'

'No,' John said; 'I was passing and I thought I'd wait for you.'

She knew this wasn't true; he never had to pass this way; he had come to meet her because she was crying when she left home. She seemed to have been crying for weeks. She knew that her mother and John were worried about her, for she couldn't tell them why she cried. But now she was free again–the dreadful weight was lifted from her.

John, looking down into her bright face, wondered what had wrought the change. He said teasingly, 'Has Father Bailey given you a pair of wings?'

'Eeh, our John!' She shook his arm as she walked by his side. 'But Father Bailey is nice, isn't he? He's so nice he makes me want to cry.'

'Well, in that case, I'll tell him to go for you the next time I see him, for you've done enough crying lately to last you a life-time.'

Katie did not speak for a time. And then she said softly, 'I won't be crying any more, John.'

'You won't? Well, that's something to know. Why have you been crying so much lately, anyway?'

There was a longer silence before she replied, 'I stole.'

Her statement came as a shock, stunning him for a while.

'You what, Katie?' he asked.

'I stole, and I was frightened. It was a comic from Mr Powell's. And now I've been to confession and Father Bailey says it's all right.'

'You stole a comic from Mr Powell's?' There was incredulity in John's voice. . . . Mick and Molly could thieve; Dominic and himself could lift things from the dock, although his own lifting was a fleabite compared with Dominic's–Dominic filled his trousers from the yorks up with grain, and sold it to anybody who kept hens; the only thing in that line he himself brought home was a few green bananas for the bairns, or an odd bit of fruit from burst boxes. Nevertheless, they all did it; but that Katie should lift anything seemed monstrous to him. It might only be a comic, but everything needed a beginning. 'Have you done it before?' he asked.

'No, only that once!'

'Why did you do it?' The question was ridiculous; as if he didn't know why she had done it!

'I hadn't had a comic for weeks, and I hadn't a ha'penny.'

'If you want a comic, ask me. Don't ever do that again, will you?' He stopped and looked down on her.

Katie couldn't see his face clearly, but she knew by his voice that he was vexed, more vexed than Father Bailey had been. 'Oh no, John, I'll never do it again . . . never.'

Yes, she could say that now, but there would be times, many times, when she would be without a ha'penny . . . and he too. What would happen then?

They walked on in silence, and he told himself it was only a kid's trick . . . Yes, it might be . . . any kid's, but not Katie's. It was this blasted, soul-shrivelling poverty, where a bairn was driven to steal because she hadn't a ha'penny! The thought persisted that because she had done it once she would do it again, and that by the time she left school and was ready for a place she'd be a dab hand at lifting. And then there'd be more scope. Nothing big perhaps; just a few groceries, an odd towel, or a hankie. . . . Oh, he knew what would happen. . . . Well, it mustn't; not to Katie, anyway. He must try and get more work, or different work, or something. He must see that never again would she be short of a ha'penny. But would that solve the problem?

He slowed his pace, and Katie, silent and apprehensive, glanced up at him. Suddenly he stopped again and said, 'What about this exam your teacher's on about? What have you got to do?

She peered up at him. 'Miss Llewellyn says that if I pass this examination I can do pupil training after I'm fourteen; and do another examination, and perhaps then I may be able to . . . to go to . . . college.' The last word was whispered, and John whispered back, 'A college?' He sighed, and they walked on again. It was fantastic . . . College! Yet why should it be? What did Peter Bracken say, not only say but lay down that it was a law? Anything to which you applied your thought you could bring into being. Peter had urged him again and again to put some of his methods to the test, but he had laughed at him, saying, 'No, Peter, I'm a Catholic; a poor one, I admit, but nevertheless that's my religion, and I'm trying nothing else.'

But Peter had said, 'This has nothing to do with religion, John; it's merely using your thought in a proper way.'

Well, here was a test. . . . Could he think Katie to a college? It sounded as daft as if he had said he would think her into being the Queen of England. Yet hadn't Peter given him proof of his power of concentrated thought? His mother was living proof. And she was aware of it too; that was why she never spoke of it, or to Peter; to her simple mind it was something too terrible for probing.

Peter said that once you set your mind and heart on something and concentrated on it day after day, things came to your aid in what seemed a mysterious way but which was simply your positive thought reaching out into the realm of all thought and making contact with its own kind.

John did not profess, even to himself, to understand half Peter's words, let alone their meaning, but this much he could, perhaps, believe . . . if you wanted a thing badly enough you could get it. But as Peter warned, beware of what you want, for sometimes that which you felt you wanted most could, in the end, wreck you.

Well, it would certainly be to Katie's good if she became a teacher, and he couldn't see that wrecking anyone. It was a wild and almost impossible dream, yet he would will it. But first he must know what he was up to. He would go and see Miss Llewellyn.

For the third time he stopped. Was he mad? Go and see that lass! She'd scare the yorks off him. Well, he wouldn't wear yorks. No, he wouldn't. To Katie's astonishment, he hurried on again, and now she had to run to keep pace with him.

Only Mary Ellen was in when they got home, and Katie stood listening to John with an astonishment equal to that of her mother's as he said, 'Look, ma, there's fifteen shillings'–he placed the money on the table–'I was saving it up towards a suit. I want you to pay the seven-and-six off that top coat and get me a new shirt . . . one with a collar.' He did not look at Mary Ellen when saying this, for never before had he asked for a shirt with a collar; it had always been a striped flannelette one and a new muffler. 'Get a good one,' he added, 'about five shillings. And get me a cap too, a grey one, darkish.'

'What's up, lad?' Mary Ellen asked quietly when he had finished.

'Nothing much.' He turned and smiled at Katie, and punched her playfully on the side of the head. 'I'm going to see her teacher about that examination, as you asked me, and I want to be decent.'

Chapter Six

The Visit

John stood sheepishly before Mary Ellen: 'Now if you tell me I look like the silver king I'll not set foot outside the door.'

Mary Ellen didn't proffer to tell him anything, she merely continued to stare at him. Who would have thought that a coat and a collar on his shirt would have made such a difference. He looked like a . . . well, like one of those adverts in the *Shields Daily Gazette* . . . no, better; there's never been a coat like this in Shields, she was sure. And anyway, the name inside the pocket said London. He was big enough, God knew, but the coat made him look even bigger. It was not shaped like those she was used to seeing, but hung full and was as thick as a blanket, with a check lining of fine flannel. A thrill of pride surged through her. Why, he could pass for a 'big pot'. His boots were shining as they had never done before, and the grey cap matched the dark, heather colour of the coat. She said, with a poor effort of offhandedness, 'You'll do. Mind, don't forget to take your cap off when you go in.'

'Now what do you take me for! I'm not a numbskull altogether.'

'No, lad, I know,' she said apologetically. 'Anyway, you'll likely not find her in . . . Saturday night and all. Why you couldn't go in the daylight, I don't know.'

'You know fine enough. Imagine me going down the street like this; the place would be out.'

Breaking the silence of her admiration, Katie burst out, 'They would have thought you were going to a wedding and shouted, "Chuck a ha'penny out."'

'Yes, they would that,' he laughed. 'Well, here I go. And if that Miss Llewellyn doesn't fall on me neck and say, "Oh, John, you look lovely," I'll skelp her face for her.'

He left them both laughing, Katie rather hysterically, her face buried in the couch.

Now he was outside in the dark street the jocular ease of manner he had assumed before his mother fell from him. He walked swiftly, passing people he knew but who failed to recognize him, and of whom he felt one or two turn as if puzzled and stare after him.

When he reached the dark stretch of road beyond the sawmill, he slackened his pace and, like a child, fingered the coat. He brought the lapel up to his nostril and sniffed. There was a faint aroma of tobacco mingled with another smell . . . not scent . . . he couldn't place it. He could only think it was a swell of a smell, anyway. But now he must forget about the coat and think of what he would say to Miss Llewellyn. God, what an ordeal! Would he be able to speak to her alone, or would her family be there? Had she a family? He supposed so. Anyway, as his mother said, being Saturday night she might be out. Likely with that Culbert fellow. But it was early, not six o'clock yet, so there was a chance he'd catch her. If he didn't he could try again on Monday, which would give him another chance to wear the coat. He chuckled to himself: 'I'm like a bit of a bairn, and as frightened.'

Katie had told him where the house lay on the outskirts of Simonside. She said he would know it, for it had a lawn in front and two gates, and that one of the gates had a wooden arch over it. He found it all too soon; it stood by itself, lying well back from the road. There was a light in an upstairs window, and the only light downstairs came through the stained glass of the front door. He stood at the gate looking towards the house until the sound of approaching footsteps, which had the ominous tread of a policeman, gave him the impetus to walk up the short drive.

His ring was answered by a maid, a little slip of a thing, all starch and black alpaca down to her feet. Very much like Katie would be if this didn't come off, he thought.

The maid spoke first, after having peered at him. 'Mr Llewellyn's not in.'

He almost laughed. They could titivate her up, but they couldn't titivate that accent; it was the broadest of Tyneside.

'Neither is Mrs Llewellyn,' she said, and was on the point of closing the door on him when he found his voice.

'It's Miss Llewellyn I want to see.' He smiled at her; he could be at home with her, anyway.

'Oh.' Her eyes grew wider, and she opened the door further. 'Well, you'd better come in. She's upstairs; she's just got back.'

John stepped past her into the hall, and she went to open a door to the right, then changed her mind, saying, 'Eeh no, you'd better wait in here.' She crossed the hall, passed the foot of the stairs and went down a short passage. And when he followed her she ushered him into a long, narrow room, at the far end of which a fire was burning.

She left him, only to return before he had time to look round. 'I forgot. What's your name?' she asked.

A great desire to laugh came over him. It could be Katie . . . no, Molly; Katie wouldn't have forgotten to ask the name.

'O'Brien.'

'O'Brien,' she repeated. Then, seeing the twinkle in his eye, her face refused to be uniformed like her body and she smiled broadly. 'I'm new, I've only been here a week.' She hunched her shoulders. 'I'm always putting people in the wrong rooms. This is Miss Mary's.'

She disappeared, and he stood, cap in hand, looking around him. Well, he was inside, in Miss Mary's room. So she was a Mary, like his mother. And she had a room to herself . . . not a bedroom either. He thought the Bracken's furniture wonderful. Then what could he say of this room?

As he gazed about him, the room took away the ease and self-possession the little maid had momentarily given him. It was a melody of colour. He had never imagined colour as part of a room–good, strong furniture, yes, but the colour never got beyond a shiny brown. Here there was russet and green, gold and white. The room was carpeted to the walls with green. Green curtains hung across the entire wall at the further end of the room, and a russet-covered chair and couch were standing cross-wise before the fire. Half of one long wall was taken up with a low bookcase, on top of which stood a number of china figures, gentlemen in ruffles, ladies in crinolines, their delicate colourings reflected in the dark surface of the wood, on which they endlessly danced or bowed. The yellow tone was supplied by early chrysanthemums, rearing with frosty elegance from a tall glass vase standing on a round table. . . . And then the white tone. He found his eyes drawn to this, and he walked a few steps towards it. It was a statuette of a woman, dead white and completely nude. The trailing hair covering part of one breast and falling across her stomach and over her womb only emphasized her nakedness. She was standing on an inlaid box by the side of the green curtains and reached just above the waist. She was about two feet tall, but she filled his entire vision, seeming to come alive before his very eyes. In the back of his mind, he knew that she was indecent and should not be in a good Catholic home, especially a schoolteacher's.

As he heard the quick, muffled footsteps descending the stairs, he almost sprang back away from her into the centre of the room again, and faced the door. Mary Llewellyn came in smiling, and as he looked at her he wondered at his nerve in daring to come and see this woman. Never before had he come into contact with anyone like her, and he was struck dumb. She seemed to move in a radiance. Did it emanate from the softness of her eyes or from the tenderness of her lips, or from the quick movements of her hands as she spoke? He did not know–he knew only that she was different.

'Hallo, Mr O'Brien.' Like her eyes, her voice was warm; and a slight catch of huskiness in it added to its charm. 'You wanted to see me? Come up to the fire and sit down.'

He followed her, his eyes fixed on the piled coils of her hair, and his inarticulateness was passed over in the process of sitting down.

He sat, half in the big chair, his cap in his hand, and she sat on the couch, across the hearth from him. She was wearing a blue dress with a dark red belt . . . she was like her room, full of warm, embracing colour.

'I suppose you've come to talk about Katie?' she smiled at him and waited.

'Yes.' The voice didn't sound like his own; it was as if he were shouting in a large, empty hall.

'I'm so glad you have, for I should like to know your plans for her. . . . Would you like her to become a teacher?'

'Yes.' Damn! Couldn't he say anything but yes! She would get the impression he was nothing but a numbskull.

'I'm glad of that. I know what to do now–I'll speak to the headmistress about her. Even if she only becomes an uncertified teacher, it would be something, wouldn't it?'

'Yes. Oh yes.' Was he a fool altogether? Yes, yes, yes. Why couldn't he be himself and say something, badly as he might express it?

There followed a silence, during which their eyes met and held. Hers were the first to drop away, and he felt she was embarrassed by his staring . . . perhaps annoyed. She leant forward and stirred the fire, and he suddenly began to talk–to straighten matters, as he put it to himself.

'I'm a poor envoy.' He wasn't sure if this was the right word, but he liked his placing of it; and he went on, 'There is so much I want to say about Katie, and so much to ask you. There's nothing more I want in the world than for her to become a teacher, but . . . Well, it's like this. You can guess how we are. . .' he substituted the word 'situated' for 'fixed'–'You can guess how we are situated. It's no good pretending, is it?' Without being aware of the transition, he was at his ease, talking frankly as he would have done to someone who knew all there was to know about him. 'There won't be any money to help her as far as I can see. If it's going to mean money, well, I'm afraid . . .' He lifted his shoulders expressively. 'If it was left to me and I could earn it I would, but I'm rarely on full time.' This was coming down to earth with a vengeance, he thought. So much for his coat.

Mary was leaning back against the couch now, and she too, as she listened to him, was thinking about his coat. Remembering how she had seen him before, she had expected to find him dressed in much the same way. The coat so altered his appearance that she hardly recognized him as the same person; he looked rather handsome. Well, not handsome. There was something too rugged about his face for it to be handsome. Attractive? Yes, he looked very attractive. His eyes, particularly, were nice, especially when he smiled. It was strange what a difference clothes could make, outwardly at any rate. Yet the first time she saw him, she remembered imagining how he might look if he could dress like Gilbert. It seemed odd now that she should have met him the day she refused Gilbert. . . . Suddenly she thought, I like him; he's nice–he's like Katie in a way.

She stood up hastily, saying, 'I haven't had any tea. Perhaps you'll have a cup with me, and then we can talk the whole thing out. Excuse me a moment.'

She gave him no time to refuse, but hurried away; and when she reached the door she turned, saying, 'Would you care to take off your coat?. . . you'll feel the benefit of it when you go out; it's nippy tonight.'

John stood up, staring down the empty room. This was a contingency for which he hadn't bargained. Against the coat, he knew his suit looked cheaper and shabbier than ever. . . . Well, she was no fool to be taken in by the coat–no doubt she had guessed he had come by it second-hand. He took it off and laid it with his cap over the chair. Then he stood on the hearth-rug looking down at his suit, and a determination was born in him: this was the last suit he'd ever get from a tally man. The coat had told him one thing: there were clothes that were made to fit a man. And he'd have them. How? He didn't know; but have them he would. If one rig-out had to last him a lifetime; he'd be dressed decent for once.

And she had asked him to stay and have a cup of tea . . . tea with Miss Llewellyn! It was fantastic.

He ran his finger round the inside of his collar; it felt tight against his neck. He glanced into the mirror over the mantel-shelf, and hardly recognized himself; the soft glow of the light seemed to make him look different. Or perhaps it was the collar. . . . And that was another thing . . . never again would he wear a muffler at the weekends, and perhaps not at nights either.

He had just sat down again when she came in with a tray; a silver one, with a teapot and jug on it. As he would have done to relieve his mother from carrying anything, he got up and took it from her. She smiled her thanks, and brought a little table, and set it between the chair and the settee, and he placed the tray on it.

The maid came in carrying another tray, which Mary took from her, saying. 'All right, Phyllis, I'll see to it.'

With a sense of unreality, John watched her pour out the tea. She had set a little table at his hand and told him to help himself. The bread and butter was so thin he could have put the plateful in his mouth at once. He watched Mary double her piece in two, and followed suit, refusing her offer of jam, for that would mean too much palaver.

And so, like one in a dream, he took tea with Miss Llewellyn, and listened with only half his mind while she talked of Katie. He was thinking of this room and of her and of the strangeness of the whole thing. . . . They were sitting here alone together, having tea, just as if . . .

He was startled back to the full import of what she was saying by hearing her repeat something he had said weeks ago: 'A day of high winds and far mastheads, and bonnie lassies.'

She laughed at his startled expression, and said, 'Now, when I find phrases like that in Katie's composition, although I know she's a clever child, I don't think she's that clever. Nor when she writes this: "The morning sky was massed with white clouds, like brakes ready for a day off."'

He felt the hot colour flooding up from his neck, and she asked, 'Have you tried writing these thoughts down and working them into something?'

'Writing them down?' he repeated. 'Me? Good Go . . . lord, no.'

'Why not?' she said. 'Burns did, and many others. I think you should. I was sorry when I had to make Katie scrap the composition in which she stated that ore on her tongue and sweat in her hair and bleeding nails meant gold on a Saturday and roaming round the market, hemmed in with the smell of tallow and the flapping of skirts.'

Now his face was scarlet, and he said, 'I'll have to be more careful of what I say. . . . You see, we go for walks—' He stopped.

'You should write them up, you know,' she put in; 'a lot of what Katie repeats has poetry in it. Why don't you try?'

He had been leaning back in the chair, quite at ease. He still leant back, but he was no longer at ease. His face drooped into a sadness, which conveyed itself to his voice, together with reproach and stark frankness as he said, 'I can't even speak properly.'

'Oh, please don't say that!'

It was Mary's turn to flush now. She stood up, and taking his cup, refilled it. 'You don't speak differently from anyone else. And that has nothing to do with putting your thoughts to paper.'

'I've been told there's such a thing as grammar.' There was a touch of bitter sarcasm in his voice.

'Yes, but that comes . . . you learn as you go.'

He made no reply, and she, too, became silent, furious with herself for being a tactless fool. He had been so at ease, with quite a charming naturalness, and she had to bring up such a suggestion as him starting to write, of all things! But on the other hand, she was perfectly sincere in all she said, for some of the things Katie repeated were surprising in their poetical content. But be careful of what you are about, she warned herself. Don't put into his head ideas that will make the life he has to lead more obnoxious to him. Remember, you are not talking to Gilbert.

She glanced at the clock . . . half-past six. She hoped Gilbert wouldn't put in one of his friendly visits; visits that were, she knew, manoeuvred by her mother.

John, noting her glance, said rather flatly, 'Well, I'll think over what you've said. I'd better be going now . . . Saturday night isn't a very convenient time to call.'

'No, no'–she put out her hand as if to press him back into his chair from the distance–'you haven't finished your tea yet, and I'm not going out again. And anyway,' she laughed in a renewed effort to put him at ease–'there are many things I want to ask you. Who, for instance, are Mr Bracken and Christine? Oh, Christine's wonderful!' She gave an imitation of Katie, closing her eyes and screwing up her face. 'You see, I get them every morning–while Katie is walking with me to school.'

John laughed with her. 'Our Katie's a chatterer. They are the people who live next door.'

'And Christine has a wonderful house, and cooks wonderful food, and has wonderful clothes. . . . Oh, she's wonderful!'

John's laugh rang out, free and unrestrained now–her imitation was so like Katie when describing anyone. 'I'm afraid Katie thinks a number of people are wonderful. Not that she isn't right,' he added hastily, realizing that sitting before him was, to Katie, the most wonderful of them all.

Mary, looking intently at him, wondered if he was in love with this Christine, about whom she heard so much. Katie talked of only two people, John and Christine; before, it was only John. . . . Our John said this, Our John said that . . . and the child had managed to convey a picture of someone quite out of the ordinary. Mary knew that the O'Briens were poor; not just clothes-poor, but of the poor who did not always eat well, which was different and more potent kind of poverty; but the child had made this John emerge as someone untouched by poverty, an independent being, living with yet not of them. Then lately, to this worship was added that of this Christine. . . . Christine and John, Christine and John.

How was it, Mary wondered, that some girls got men like this to love them, big kind men with a sense of humour as he had. At their first meeting, she'd thought he was to be pitied, but now she saw that she was wrong–he was intelligent and entertaining, the latter without making any effort to be so. He was certainly better company than Gilbert, even if he lacked Gilbert's taste in literature and art . . . or perhaps, because of it. Being a big man, like her father, was he attracted to small women, she wondered. This Christine, according to Katie's description was apparently small. So was her own mother, small and helpless. Helpless! The word brought a cloud over Mary's eyes, for she had come to recognize that beneath her helpless exterior her mother was pure granite; and to live in peace with anyone like her meant submerging oneself entirely. When she was young, her happy, loving nature did not question her mother's tyranny, and it was easy to accept 'Mother knows best'. How different her life would have been had she stood against her; for now her art study would have been finished. And who knows where it would have taken her–London–even Paris. Because her mother considered it wicked to draw bodies with no clothes on, she obediently put clothes on them. And again, when her mother said she would never make an artist . . . and anyway, artists weren't nice people . . . she subdued her natural talent becoming a schoolteacher, not through necessity, but because her father insisted she should have an occupation. But during these last few years had come a change, until now a state of undeclared war existed between her and her mother. The request to have a room of her own began it, and the refusal to be pushed into marriage with Gilbert Culbert, the son of her mother's old friend, widened the breach. And when, answering some inner urge, she bought the statue, and her mother demanded that it be removed from the house, the breach was further widened.

Lost in her thoughts, she did not notice that they were sitting in silence. How strange. She could never sit in silence with Gilbert. She lifted her gaze from her hands and found John looking at her, not intently, but rather reflectively. She smiled, and he blinked and roused himself.

'Are you interested in boats?' she asked. 'I mean the building of them.'

'Well, I know nothing about the building of them. I only know I get certain feelings when working in them. A feeling of friendliness for some and dislike for others. I suppose it has a lot to do with their cargo . . . and,' he laughed, 'the sweat in my hair.'

She laughed with him and asked, 'Would you like to see some models my father has made?'

'Yes, I would, very much.'

'Come into his workshop, then.'

She rose and went down the length of the room, and John followed her towards the green curtains. Before she drew them aside she gently moved the box and the statue. He watched her steady the statue with her hand, and it occurred to him as being strange that the statue no longer looked indecent but rather lovely . . . very like what she would be . . .

He was red in the face when she looked up at him, and she said hastily, almost apologetically, 'I came across it in an antique shop in Newcastle. It's an octoroon. I don't suppose you know any more than I did what an octoroon is; but, on looking it up, I found that she is the offspring of a quadroon and a white person, and a quadroon is one part negro and three parts white. Sounds very complicated, doesn't it?'

They were standing regarding each other now. Her hand was on the curtain and her face was unsmiling, and in her eyes he fancied he detected an appeal. For what exactly, he didn't know. But he said, 'I think it's very beautiful.' He, too, was unsmiling. And when she answered simply, 'Thank you,' it almost appeared as if the compliment had been meant for her. She turned swiftly and opened the french window, and stepped into the conservatory. He followed, going through a door close by and into the workroom.

It was in darkness, and she said, 'Just a moment. There are matches here, I'll light the gas.'

She gave an impatient exclamation as the box fell from her hand, and when, instinctively, they both stooped to retrieve it, causing them to collide and she to overbalance, his hands naturally were thrust out to steady her, and in the darkness he supported her . . . for one brief second his hands held her arms, and in that second the thing was done–the fuse that might have smouldered and died was fanned.

When the room was plunged into stark light from the double burner, John was still standing near the door. Mary did not speak for a moment, and when she asked, 'What do you think of them?' he moved slowly into the room and began to look round. There were dozens of models of small craft, set in stocks, on the shelves. In amazement, he asked, 'Your father made all these?'

'Yes. And most of them he's built full-size and sold. Do you recognize Mary, the tug?'

It was with genuine astonishment that he exclaimed, 'Your father's Llewellyn the boat builder then!'

'Yes. Didn't you know?'

He shook his head. He had never associated Llewellyn, the boatbuilder, with Miss Llewellyn the teacher. He knew Llewellyn by sight, as most of the dock men did. He had a little boat-building yard, tucked away on the side of the river. It still went under the name of Haggart's Yard, and it was known that Llewellyn worked in it as a lad by the side of his father. But that hadn't suited young Llewellyn; and he and his father built a boat on their own and sold it. It was said they built it in their backyard. That was a start, and eventually, when old Haggart died, and his own father too, Llewellyn bought the yard. He was known as a rising man. . . . And he was her father!

With this knowledge, she again assumed to him the unapproachableness of an hour ago. How had he the nerve to come here!

When she spoke to him, smiling over her shoulder and saying, 'Come and look at this little yacht, my father hopes to build her some day,' he went to her; but the ease had left him, and he held the model in his hand without making any comment. Her nearness made him uneasy. He suddenly wanted to get away from her and her politeness . . . she would act like this towards anyone, a begger on the road, even . . . she was made that way, courteous, easy of manner.

'What do you think of it? You have seen lots of boats, but have you see anything like her?'

She was looking up into his straight face, trying to draw him out again, when a voice from the doorway said, 'Hallo, Mary.'

They both started at the sound of the quiet, even tone.

'Oh! hallo, Gilbert,' she said, and after a pause, added, 'Come in a minute. . . . This is Mr O'Brien. Mr O'Brien, Mr Culbert.'

Neither of the men made the usual gesture to shake hands, but inclined their heads . . . John is an abrupt nod, and Culbert in a more leisurely movement. John knew that he was under Culbert's scrutiny, and after his first concentrated state, he did not look at the man but at Mary; for he was asking himself how anyone like her could take up with a fellow like Culbert, a weed of a man, narrow all the way up, right to the pointed head, over which his thin hair was meticulously brushed.

When Mary led the way back into her room John made straight for the chair over which his coat and cap lay, and she said nothing to delay his departure.

He nodded again to Culbert in farewell, and Mary escorted him to the front door. The feel of his coat about him did nothing to allay his renewed feeling of gaucheness.

'Well, thanks,' he said awkwardly. 'It's been kind of you to . . . to help me about Katie.'

They stood regarding one another, and she too seemed to have lost some of her ease of manner. 'I'll do all I can for Katie, I'm very fond of her. And she's a clever child. . . . Good night, Mr O'Brien.'

She held out her hand, and after the merest hesitation he took it. Firm and cool, it gripped his, conveying a sense of breathlessness and urgency. The feeling hung between them; even when their hands parted and he passed through the doorway it was there . . . a breathlessness.

He walked away down the path with her parting words acting like an opiate to his brain. 'If you feel there is anything you would like to know, at any time, please come and see me again.' It was odd, he thought, but she was the kind of person he could ask questions of.

But once out in the cold night air, the old brake of 'Steady your keel' thrust its reality upon him, and he said to himself, 'Well, that's that! It went off all right; Katie's set.'

As he reached the bottom of the Simonside bank, he deliberated whether to go into Shields and the market or walk slowly back home. If he did the latter it would mean thinking and going over every second of the past hour. He would go into Shields where there were lights and people. . . . But what about being seen in this coat? Well, what about it? It seemed that within the past hour he had lost and regained his self-confidence a number of times, but each time he regained it it was stronger, for now he didn't mind being seen in the coat; it was the portent of things to come . . . he would have things . . . his mother and Katie would have things. How, he didn't know; but they would.

His decision to seek company in the shape of the crowds did not immediately have the desired effect, and he found himself again thinking of Mary Llewellyn, but with a forced detachment. Fancy a lovely lass like her going to marry that . . . skinnymalink! Well, it was certainly no business of his. She had been very nice to him, more than nice; and she would help Katie; that was the only thing that mattered.

As he entered the first arch of Tyne dock a well-known figure, shambling towards him, brought him back with a bump to his own world. It was Nancy; and he could hear her snivelling when she was still some distance away.

'Hallo, Nancy. What's the matter?' he asked her.

She hesitated, shuffled off the pavement in uncertainty, then shuffled back when she recognized him. 'Eeh, John. Eeh, John.'

'What's the matter?' he asked again.

'It's our Annie. She left me in the market–she run away, and she had me tram fare. An' me ma said she had to look after me and put me on the tram for me place.'

'Have you walked all the way from the market?' he asked her gently.

'Yes. . . . It's our Annie. She run away, she did. An' me ma'll skelp me when I get in, she will, cos Mrs Fitzimmons said I had to be back to clean the shop out when they closed. An' me ma said our Annie had to put me on the tram.'

John put his hand in his pocket and gave her threepence. 'Now stop crying. You'll be back in plenty of time. There's your tram fare and a penny to buy some bullets. Stand over there'–he pointed back towards the bottom of Simonside Bank–'the Jarrow tram will be along in a minute.'

'Eeh! I can't get on the tram there, John. There's a bar there an' me ma says I've got to keep away from bars, cos the men come out.'

John could see the tram in the distance swaying towards them. He held out his hand to her: 'Come on, I'll put you on it.'

The tram jolted to a stop, and he helped her up, saying to the conductor, 'Put her off at the corner of Ferry Street, will you?'

As the conductor rang the bell, a figure leant forward from the end of the long wooden seat: 'Why, is that you. John?'

He recognized Mrs Bradley, and answered rather shortly, 'Yes, it's me.'

'Why lad, I hardly knew you. . . . Well I never.'

The tram rumbled away, and the last John saw was Nancy showing the coins in her hand to Mrs Bradley. The picture did not remain in his mind an instant, but he was to remember it, and, unimportant as it seemed, it was to assume such proportions that although it happened on this day of emancipation, when he had first worn a fine top coat and taken tea with Miss Llewellyn, its ugly significance was to blot them out.

Chapter Seven

Christmas Eve

Mary Ellen hummed softly . . . it was many, many Christmasses ago that she felt as happy as she did now. The morrow was Christmas Eve and she was really looking forward to it. She worked at the table in the middle of the kitchen, cutting out pastry for mince pies. Above her head hung a large, honeycombed paper ball, suspended from the paper chains criss-crossed under the ceiling. The kitchen was quiet and warm with an unusual air of cosiness about it. As she worked she planned for the morrow. She'd get up earlier than usual and blacklead the stove before lighting the fire; and then, after she'd got them all off to work, she'd get done and put everything shipshape; then she'd get the dinner ready, and have the afternoon clear . . . to go and get the coat.

Aye, it was a long time since she'd had a coat. A new shawl would have done her; but no, John had a bee in his bonnet, and she was to have a coat for Christmas. . . . What had come over him lately? He was the same to her, yet somehow he was altered. It wasn't only the new suit he had, although that made him look fine; no, it was in some other way he'd altered. Well, never mind, he was still her lad, and the best on God's earth. If only the other one was like him.

The thought of Dominic caused her to stop humming. Why hadn't he gone away, as he'd been hinting of doing for some weeks past? Then Christmas would have indeed been grand. She knew he had been inquiring after jobs in both the Liverpool and London Docks; anywhere, he had said, to get away from this hole.

When she came to think of it, Dominic too seemed changed. It was all that lass next door she supposed–he was set on her; but he didn't seem to be making much headway. Was John his stumbling block? This was another thing which puzzled her. John was always in next door, and often she heard his laugh joined with that of the girl's. But there it seemed to end. If he were courting her, he was doing it in a funny way; for he never took her out. Pray God he wouldn't either. No, no, that would be terrible if John really took up with her. Well, she wasn't going to think about it; she was going to enjoy this Christmas. She already had a piece of brisket and an aitchbone, and if John went down to the market last thing the morrow he might pick up a duck or something cheap. They sold them off for next to nothing rather than have them left on their hands. By, it'd be grand if he could get a duck! And on Christmas Day they'd have Christmas cake and the rice loaf she'd made. Nobody knew yet, but she was going to put icing on the cake.

By, they'd have a grand do.

A tap on the door broke in on her thoughts, and she called, 'Come in;' and Peggy Flaherty, after kicking her boots against the wall, stumbled into the kitchen.

'Oh God above, it's enough to freeze your liver! It's at it again, Mary Ellen–won't be able to stir hand or food outside the door shortly.'

'It hasn't started to snow again, surely?'

'It has so, Mary Ellen. As if it wasn't bad enough with everywhere frozen solid. God's truth, I've never seen anything like it! We'll have to be after watching the tap in the yard, Mary Ellen, or it'll be a dry Christmas in one way we'll be having. Oh, ye're lovely and warm in here, lass'–she wriggled her fat inside her many coats–'and the smell's good enough to eat. And did ye ever see such a picture of a kitchen, with all those bonny chains!'

'Sit down and warm yourself, and have a pie,' said Mary Ellen.

'I will an' all, for I'm chilled to the bone. I'm just back from Shields. Look'–she pulled three small packages from her bass bag–'some bits of things for the bairns' stockings.'

'Now, Peggy'–Mary Ellen compressed her lips–'that's madness, that is! You know you haven't got it to go and buy presents.'

'Why haven't I then? I haven't a bite of sup to buy for Christmas or Boxing Day, because out of the goodness of your heart ye've asked me down . . . so why haven't I? There they are'–she laid the packages on the mantelpiece–'we'll say no more about them. There's only one thing I regret, and that is I haven't got it to buy you all something. But business isn't what it used to be; divil the pennorth of advice I've given out this past three weeks. What's the matter with people, Mary Ellen? 'Tisn't as if there were no rows; God alive, they followed each other like flies down at the bottom end last week? If it wasn't for running me clubs I'd be hard set at times; but as long as I get my rent I'm all right. And God's good. There was last week-end I didn't know which way I was going to turn, when, coming up the yard, that blessed lad of yours slipped me sixpence. By, Mary Ellen, I think if ye lost everything in the world and ye'd only him left, ye'd get by. . . . Is he courting, Mary Ellen?'

'Courting?' Mary Ellen turned and with a blank face looked at Peggy. 'Not that I know of. Why do you ask?'

'Only I've seen him a number of times, three to be exact, and the last no later than this dinner-time, talking to the same lass. And a bonnier piece I've never seen. And mark ye, she wasn't from around these doors either. Today she had a fur coat on, and the tails hanging from the collar alone must have left a number of poor animals feeling cold around their backsides.'

'A fur coat?'

'The same. Tall she was, and strapping looking. And a voice like the gentry, for I heard her as I passed. And it's me that knows how the gentry talk–ye know that, Mary Ellen–for Mr Flaherty spent his life rubbing shoulders with them. And it's the same process, ye know: as ye can't touch pitch without becoming defiled, so ye can't mix among the gentry without picking up their lingo.'

Mary Ellen surveyed Peggy. 'You must have made a mistake.'

'Not a bit of it, Mary Ellen. John called out to me himself. "Hallo there, Peggy," he said, as true as I'm sitting here.'

Mary Ellen turned back to her baking board. . . . John talking to a lass with a fur coat on. Who could it be? And three times. He wasn't a one to stand talking to lasses at any time, only that one next door. She turned to Peggy again: 'It wasn't—' She nodded her head towards the fireplace.

'No. I may be short in the sight, but I'm not that bad. This was a big lump of a lass, in fact she was a woman: and twice the size of that scrag end next door, bless ye.'

Mary Ellen could question Peggy no more at the moment, for there was another knock on the door; it was Hannah Kelly.

She had a coat over her head, and she shook the soft snow off it before coming into the kitchen. 'What weather! The only ones enjoying it are the bairns. Hallo, Peggy. Is this where ye are? By! they smell good Mary Ellen.' Hannah nodded towards the pies.

'Help yourself, lass,' said Mary Ellen.

'Not now. Thanks all the same. I only came over to see you a minute . . . about something.'

Peggy, taking the covered hint with the abundance of her good nature, said, 'I'll off up, Mary Ellen, for I must make a start; I'm up to the eyes upstairs.'

'She never said a truer word,' said Hannah, when Peggy had gone. 'How she lives among that junk, God alone knows. I came over to tell ye about our Nancy, Mary Ellen; but I couldn't do it with her sitting there–she'd be offering me advice, and I'm not in the mood to take Peggy's advice the day.'

'Is anything wrong, Hannah?'

'It looks like it; I've had a letter from Mrs Fitzimmons about her. She says she's getting more queer every day, and she's getting that way she won't work; she just stands staring at her and says she can't. Ye know, Mary Ellen, that isn't like Nancy. As bad as she is she can do the rough work of half a dozen. Mrs Fitzimmons says I'll have to bring her home if it keeps on. . . . Oh, Mary Ellen, there'll be hell to pay again with our Joe if she's in the house all the time.'

'I'm sorry, lass. But perhaps you'll get her in some place else.'

'Not if she won't work. Ye don't mind me coming across and telling ye, Mary Ellen? Ye've got enough on your plate, I know, without my troubles stacked on top, but ye're the only one I seem to be able to talk to about her.'

'Why, lass, I only wish I could help you.'

Hannah sat down by the side of the fire and stared into the glowing coals for a moment. 'It's an awful thing, Mary Ellen, to know that a bairn ye've given birth to isn't all there.'

Mary placed her hand on Hannah's shoulder. 'We all have our loads, lass; if it isn't one thing it's another.'

Hannah gnawed at her lower lip. 'You and John are the only two who treat her like a human being. I know I don't. Sometimes I can't stand the sight of her. Oh, ye don't know, Mary Ellen, it's awful. But then, when I hear Joe going for her, I get a sort of feeling and want to protect her somehow.' She shook her head sadly. 'Well, the only thing I hope is she doesn't come home till after the new year. Joe's banking on a little bit of a do on New Year's Eve, but it'll be knocked completely on the head if she's home; he'll do nothing then; likely stay out most of the time.'

'She'll be all right,' Mary Ellen persisted, 'don't worry. Look, let's have a cup of tea.'

Mary Ellen bustled about making tea. In the face of the tragedy of having a partly imbecile daughter her load seemed very light. She had poverty and drink to put up with, but not that, thank God. Hers were all right up there.

The two women drank their tea and talked on . . . about Bella now. Hannah wasn't speaking to Bella, for whenever she did Bella made some excuse to come downstairs and ferret out her business. And Bella's constant presence in the house maddened Joe. Mary Ellen could well understand this, for she had no use for Bella Bradley, who was never happy unless someone else was in trouble . . .

As the snow thickened and the light vanished earlier than usual the kitchen was lit only by the glow of the fire–through necessity the gas was never lit until it was almost impossible to see, and Mary Ellen worked on, after Hannah had gone, more by feel than anything else. She began to sing softly to herself–her mother and grandmother had sung the song before her–the simple words expressing the tragedy of at least one phase of their love:

Love, it is teasing,
Love, it is pleasing,
Love is a pleasure when it is new;
But as it grows older and the days grow colder
It fades away like the morning dew.

Mary Ellen wasn't thinking of the words, or how they applied to her own life, but that she had much for which to be thankful: Shane had not been really drunk since she was bad that time, and his twitching had eased. There had been no row in the house for months either. Well, they said it was a long road that had no turning, and hers had turned.

On these pleasant thoughts the kitchen door was thrust open again. She turned towards it, but could not distinguish who was standing there. It could have been John, Shane or Dominic; but she was expecting none of them for another hour.

'Why can't you light the bloody gas!'

Mary Ellen groped for a piece of paper, which she lit in the fire and put to the mantle, then turned and looked at Dominic. She had seen his face portraying many moods, contorted with passion or anger, drawn tight with cunning; but his expression now was one she had never seen, his eyes were wide and hard, and to her mind, had the thick, dull shine of a beer bottle. He seemed to be spread in a new kind of anger, wide and high with it.

'I want me tea now. I'm going out!'

'Well, get in first, can't you! It isn't ready yet. Can't you get changed and have it with the others?'

'No, I can't! And anyway, you wouldn't expect God Almighty to sit down with me, would you?'

She stared at him. Had he gone off his head? She watched him fling his cap across the table on to the couch, pull off his coat and fling it after the cap. The coat, in its flight, whipped a number of pies on to the floor and sent a cloud of flour off the board.

'Here!' Mary Ellen cried, 'what's up with you?'

He did not answer, but grabbed the kettle from the hob and emptied it of hot water. He also emptied the pail of cold water, and proceeded to wash, the water splashing over the side of the dish and up the wall as he did so.

Mary Ellen cleaned up the mess from the floor; then picked up the kettle and pail and went cautiously down the backyard. The ashes on top of the ice were already covered with a layer of snow. The tap was running in a thin trickle and she stood on the fringe of ice and water, steadying herself against the wall as she filled the pail. . . . Always something to spoil things. What was it now?

She hunted around in her mind, but could find nothing. Whatever it was was connected with his work, for he was home early. And him saying, 'You wouldn't expect God Almighty to sit down with me.' Did he mean John? She couldn't fathom it.

When she returned to the kitchen, Dominic was in the bedroom, and she hurriedly cleared the table and set some bread and dripping and mince pies out.

When he eventually came to the table he stared down at the food. 'That's a fine meal for a man, isn't it!' His voice seemed to be torn from his throat.

'Well, you wouldn't wait. I'm going to fry.'

'You're going to fry!' he mimicked raspingly. 'Well, see that you do plenty of it; the big pot'll need it to fill his swelled head.'

Then his anger had to do with John. But how? What could have happened at work?

After having eaten all Mary Ellen had placed before him, Dominic left the house by the front way. As soon as the door banged behind him Mary Ellen went hastily into the room, and stood listening. Then, as she expected, came the muffled knock. He was next door.

She sang or hummed no more but, filled with the old dread, waited for John coming in–she had spoken too soon about her road turning. There was something afoot, and from the appearance of Dominic it was bad.

Katie and Molly rushed in, their hands blue and their noses red. 'Oh, Ma, is the tea ready?' 'And, Ma, our Katie's dirtied her knickers,' cried Molly.

'What!'

Both Katie and Molly burst out laughing at their mother's expression, Molly bringing her head down to Katie's, and the two of them pressing their faces together in their mirth.

'Not that way. She slipped on a slide and ended up in some broken ice and slush,' Molly giggled.

'Are you wet?' Mary Ellen asked Katie.

'No, Ma, it dried.'

'Tea won't be for some time yet,' said Mary Ellen. 'Here, take a bit of bread and get yourselves out again.'

Mary Ellen pushed a slice of bread at each of them. 'You can stay out for another half-hour or so. Hunt up Mick and bring him back with you.' It would be better, she thought, if she had the house to herself when John came in.

When at last she heard the clanking footsteps in the yard, she stood still facing the door. It might be Shane. The feet kicked against the wall, and the door opened. It was John, not with brows drawn and lips tight, but with an almost childish expression of pleasure on his face. He wasn't smiling–with an effort he was keeping his face straight–but the light in his eyes danced at her. She turned from him, puzzled. It couldn't be that lass with the fur coat. No, how could that affect Dominic?

'Is it still snowing?' she asked, as she bent over the pan on the fire.

John didn't answer, but came and stood by her. 'Anybody in?'

'No,' she said.

He took her by the shoulders and pulled her round to face him, so close that her head had to go back to look up at him. 'I'll give you three guesses.... What do you think's happened?'

'Why, lad, how should I know?'

'Go on.'

'You've been set on the Benisaf boat.'

John flung his head back and laughed out loud.

'Aye, lad, how should I know? Tell us.'

He stepped back, thrust his thumbs into the lapel of his coat, drew himself up to his fullest height with mock dignity, and said, in the deepest tones of his voice, 'Mrs O'Brien, behold . . . a gaffer!'

A gaffer . . . Mary Ellen could make no comment. Had he gone mad too? A gaffer. Her lad, and him only twenty-two. Why, there was something wrong somewhere. There was only one gaffer over the boats, and he must be a man steady in his years. The old gaffer had died a couple of days ago, she knew, but they couldn't have picked John. It was fantastic. Her face expressed her feelings, and John laughed and said, 'You don't believe it?'

'Well, lad . . .'

'Yes, I know it's hard to take in.' He was suddenly serious. 'I haven't taken it right in meself yet. I couldn't, for the life of me, believe they meant it.'

'Did the men pick you?'

'Yes, they voted for me to take old Reville's place.'

It was customary for the dock men who unloaded the boats to choose their own boss. They also paid him so much a head out of their wages. Most of the unloading was paid on tonnage, and the gaffer's job was to select men for the boat and at the end of discharging collect the money from the dock office, subtract his due and pay out the men. But this alone did not cover his duties, which often entailed taking off his coat and fighting it out with any man who thought he was not getting a square deal, and who said so forcibly. Another thing expected of the gaffer was to provide subs for men who were out of work and advances to those just being set on again.

This was in Mary Ellen's mind when she said, 'But lad, how can you do it? . . . The subs.'

'I've got over that. You know Mc'Cabe in the dock office. Well, when I went to tell him he seemed to know how I was fixed, and offered to lend me a few pounds to make a start . . . I'll be able to pay it back in a few weeks. And I won't forget him for it.'

'Lad, don't start on borrowed money. There's the twenty-five shillings for that coat. I don't need a coat; I've made . . .'

'Here . . . that's enough. You're getting that coat.'

'Were all the men for you?' She gazed up into his face; she was smiling now and her heart was racing within her breast. To think her lad had been picked for a gaffer. Oh, the road had turned all right.

'Not all. But the ones that mattered were.' He turned away and took off his coat. She knew he was referring to Dominic, and perhaps Shane.

'Does your da know?'

'Yes. He took it all right.'

She heaved a sigh of relief. Now perhaps Shane would get set on more often. No. She could quieten her hopes on that score–John would more likely be fair to the other extreme.

'Was none of the others after it?' she asked.

'Yes. But none of them were steady.'

Her eyes became misted. They had picked him, despite his years, because he was . . . steady. Her John a gaffer. And Katie set on the road to be a teacher. Oh, God was good.

The tears, gathering in her throat, threatened to choke her, and she turned away and put her apron to her face.

'Here! Here!' John pulled her round, and as his great arms pressed her gently to him a dam burst within her. No sorrow could have broken it; but this happiness was overwhelming, and she sobbed it out, leaning against him.

An hour later, when John saw Christine, he knew that she was already aware of what he had come to tell her; and after she exclaimed, 'Oh, John, what wonderful news! And at Christmas too,' he looked at her closely and asked, 'What's the matter? Aren't you well?'

'Yes. Yes, I'm all right,' she said hastily.

'No you're not, you're as white as a sheet. Has . . .?'

She turned away and picked up a half-dressed doll from the table. 'Dominic's just gone. He told me about you being made a gaffer,' she said.

'Yes, I bet he did; and he'll likely be the first one I'll have to take my coat off to. But that didn't make you look like this.'

Christine sat down by the fire with the doll on her knee, and proceeded to pull a frilled silk dress over its head.

'Look. If he's been up to any of his tricks . . .'

Christine cut him short with unusual curtness: 'He asked me to marry him.' She said it while looking John full in the face; the look was almost a challenge, and he experienced a feeling of guilt. Why, he couldn't fathom; but it was so strong that it swamped his indignation at Dominic's audacity.

'He wants me to go to Liverpool with him; then perhaps abroad.'

'Abroad?'

'Yes.'

'Are you going to marry him?'

'No.' She was still looking at him, the dress was only half over the doll's head. He blinked, and looked away from her down at his feet; and she sighed faintly and resumed the fitting of the dress.

John looked at her again. She was so sweet sitting there dressing the doll; why couldn't he go to her and put his arms about her and kiss her, just as often before he'd had the desire to kiss her? But he knew that, whereas for him it would merely be a kiss, to her it would be the absolute symbol of love. How he became possessed of this knowledge he didn't know, for, as he had asked himself on previous occasions, what did he know about lasses? If she were Jenny Carey or Lily McDonald he would perhaps have kissed her by now and let things take their course, but with Christine he couldn't, it wouldn't be fair. Was it even fair to come in so often? He supposed not, but he liked talking to her and Peter.

The strain that had fallen on them was relieved by David appearing. After glancing round, he asked, 'Has he gone then?'

'If you're staying in take your coat off, dear,' said Christine.

John knew to whom David was referring, he also guessed that Dominic had shooed David out.

'I'm getting a sculler for Christmas, John . . . a real one.'

'No.'

'Yes. Aren't I, Christine?'

The boy's large, dark eyes, glowing in his pale face, always aroused a tenderness in John. He was so thin, and almost girlish in his fragility.

John asked Christine, 'He doesn't mean a real one?'

'Yes. Grandfather has already bought it–it's at the quay corner. David's going to paint it himself and get it ready for the fine weather. Aren't you?'

The brother and sister smiled at each other. John realized that this was another of Peter's ways to eliminate yet another fear from his grandson. The child was highly strung and nervous, and had never quite got over the shock of seeing his parents killed in a collision between a tram and a cab when he was five years old. The episode at the gut no doubt added the fear that the boat was to erase. And the thought came to John, as it had often done lately, that Peter was a splendid man. How could anyone mock at him? By! he wished he'd been there when the crowd of hooligans burnt his hut down. They would have gone along with it.

He looked at the boy standing by Christine's side watching her put the bonnet on the doll. . . . They were like a little family of saints, tender with each other, kind to everyone, and forgiving beyond his power to understand. He sat for a while longer watching Christine finishing the doll. Then he said he must get indoors and give a hand, for there were still more decorations to be hung around the walls.

Christine smiled at him as he left: 'I'm glad about your job, John.'

'Thanks. I knew you'd be. . . . Tell Peter, will you?'

Christine nodded; and David cried suddenly, 'I'm going to stand at the corner, Christine, and wait for Grandfather.'

The boy chattered loudly as he and John walked down the yard, but outside, in the back lane, he pulled at John's arm and whispered, 'John, can I . . . I want to tell you something.'

'Yes, what is it, David?' John stooped to him.

'It's Dominic–Christine's frightened of him . . . she's always frightened of him. He made me go out and he said to Christine you wouldn't get her, but he would, some way. You won't let him, will you?'

John remained silent for a moment, looking at the blur that was the boy's white face, which stood out even against the newly fallen snow. It was straining up to him, appealing, pleading. 'Don't you worry, David. Christine will be all right; I'll see to that.'

'Will you, John? Will you?'

'Yes—' John patted David's hand, and the boy seemed satisfied and ran off in evident relief; and John turned thoughtfully into the backyard, to meet Katie coming out of the lavatory.

'Come in here a minute,' he said to her, drawing her into the washhouse and closing the door; 'I want you to do something for me.'

'Yes, John?'

He knew by her voice that her face was eager. 'Look; whenever you hear Dominic go in next door, you run in the other way, will you?'

'Yes, John. But if me ma . . .?'

'You can tell her you are going to return something of David's, a picture book or something.'

'Yes, John.'

'And no matter what he says, don't leave him alone with her. If he makes you and I'm in, come and tell me. You've got that now?'

'Yes, John.'

'Has he ever chased you out?'

Remembering Christine's warning, Katie merely answered, 'Sometimes.'

'Have you ever seen him . . .?' John stopped. 'Well, never mind. You know what to do, don't you?'

'Yes, John.'

Neither Katie nor Molly could remember a Christmas Eve like this one. They had faint memories of being excited at the prospect of hanging up their stockings, and a memory, not so faint, of disappointment at the meagreness of their contents when they opened them; but tonight was different. In the cupboard at the side of the fireplace were parcels, some that John brought in last night, some from Christine, and others. Katie and Molly would make running dives at the lower door of the cupboard, calling, 'I'm gonna open it, Ma! I am! I am!'

Apart from saying, 'You dare,' Mary Ellen took no notice of them. Her face wore a faint smile and her body seemed settled in contentment as her needles flew on the toe of a sock. They were the last few rows of a pair she was knitting for Shane. Why had she thought of knitting him socks for Christmas she didn't know–she could not remember ever giving him anything at Christmas, except the first Christmas they were married. She wouldn't of course, say that these were for a Christmas box; she would just put them out with his change of clean underclothes. Perhaps he would notice them, perhaps he wouldn't.

She glanced up as John came out of the bedroom, and she had to say to Katie, 'Leave John be, hinny, he's got to go out. . . . Stop clambering! you'll dirty his suit.'

'Give me a shuggy before you go. Come on, John, just one,' Katie coaxed.

'Well mind, just one . . . that's all.'

'You're worse than she is,' said Mary Ellen as John sat down and crossed his knees and stuck a foot out.

Katie clambered on to the foot, and he held her hands as he hoisted her up and down. And she giggled and shouted, 'But say it! You're not saying it!'

'Give over, Katie, John's got to go out! You'll be packed off to bed, mind. . . . Oh, what's the good! You're worse than she is,' Mary Ellen exclaimed, as John began to chant with each movement of his foot:

Father Christmas soon will come
Laden with all treasures.
I would like a boat to sail,
A rocky horse with a bushy tail,
A farthing or a spade and pail;
Katie wants a big, fat . . . dol-ly.

After the final heave, Katie fell off his foot, laughing, and John's eyes were drawn, for a moment to Molly. She was standing to one side, smiling, yet wistful. He suddenly realized he'd never had much time for Molly, and, scatterbrain as she was, she felt it. He saw it in her face now as she stood there. Impulsively, his hand went out and he pulled her to him, saying, 'Come on, you big soft lass;' and, laughing and giggling, she sat on his foot.

'Well I never. What next, I wonder!' Mary Ellen's tone was half laughing, half derisive.

Molly wasn't so easy to lift as Katie, and before John was half-way through the rhyme she had tumbled off on to the floor, where she lay, clasping Katie, helpless with laughter.

Mary Ellen, trying not to allow her gaze to linger on this son of hers, who was looking so grand, said, 'Get yourself away, lad, or else I'll not get them to sleep the night. And if you should see Mick, send him in.'

John put on his coat, saying, 'Well, expect me when you see me–I may have to follow the men to Newcastle to get the ducks. It's six you want, isn't it?'

He left the house with his mother joining in with the laughter of the children. The sound made him happy. There was something different about this Christmas. . . . Well, so there should be. A gaffer! He breathed deep of the icy air. But it wasn't that alone. There was a difference both inside and outside the house. Perhaps the difference lay in himself; life at last seemed to be opening.

He walked briskly to Tyne Dock, and stood waiting for the Shield's tram. The snow plough had been out, and the space opposite the dock gates had the appearance of land on which the grab had been at work; pale grey mounds lined the pavement, and the hurrying figures, passing in and out of the lamplight and the light from the bars, looked jet black against them. Some iron ore men, still in their working clothes, came out of a bar and hailed John: 'Why, man, you look as if you've had some money left you. Pinched our wages already? Or has the North-Eastern left you a prop boat?'

'Aye, they offered me one for Christmas, but I told them what to do with it: "A Benisaf or nothing" I said.'

There was loud laughter at this. 'I bet you did too! Well, a happy Christmas, and many of them,' they called as they moved away. 'And see we have full shifts for full bellies next year, mind.'

'Many of them,' John answered.

As he watched their unwieldy figures disappear into the darkness, he felt a thousand miles removed from them. They were good enough fellows in their way, with but one thought dominating them all . . . plenty of work, which meant plenty to eat and drink, or the reverse process. But somehow he didn't feel of them. It wasn't just since he had been made a gaffer, he had been feeling like this for some time past. Was it since he had got this coat? He didn't know; something had changed him . . .

The aisles of the open market were congested with buyers, and the shouts of the stall-holders were deafening. John saw that it would be hours yet before the stuff was sold at anywhere near his price. Ten or eleven would be the time to come back. So he walked down King Street, debating whether he should go to the second house at the Empire or the Tivoli. To whichever place he went, he couldn't go in the threepennies, not in this rig-out. It would mean the sixpennies, or even the ninepennies. That was one drawback of being dressed-up.

'Hallo, Mr O'Brien,' Mary Llewellyn stood in front of him, her arms laden with parcels.

'Good evening, Miss Llewellyn.'

They were blocking each other's path and that of the other pedestrians as, after the greeting, they stood mutely surveying each other, surprise showing in both their faces, as if this was the last place one would have expected to find the other.

'Did you ever see such a crowd?'

'No, I never have.'

John hadn't noticed the crush before, but now they seemed to be hemmed in on all sides.

'Are you doing your last-minute shopping?' she asked him.

'No . . . yes . . . Well'–his eyes twinkled–'I'm hanging around until they give the ducks away in the market.' And as he said it, he wondered why it cost him nothing in pride to admit such things to her.

They laughed, and one irritated shopper exclaimed, 'If you want to stand laughing your heads off clear off the flags and let people pass.'

They pulled long faces at each other, and Mary said, 'I suppose she's right.'

'Can I carry some of your parcels to the tram?' John asked.

'Well, I wasn't going home yet. But it would be a help if you'd relieve me of some of them for a time; I have a little more shopping to do.'

He took the boxes from her and stacked them under his arm. Then they turned towards the market again, John walking slightly ahead of her to make a way.

Laughing gaily, she left him outside while she went into a linen shop, and he stood gazing into the window, seeing nothing. He knew that this night was different. There was magic about; in the cold and the snow, in people's faces, and in meeting her. Strange, up till a few months ago, he had never set eyes on her. But since that night he had been to see her they had run into each other a number of times, mostly when he was coming from work; yet she didn't seem to mind his working clothes. The first time they met, it was she who stopped and talked, just as if he were all got up instead of being covered from head to foot with splatters of wet clay. He had been working on a boat from Sweden, and the ore was embedded in lumps of clay, which made the digging and picking heavy and dirty.

After these meetings, he never allowed himself to think, using his mother's formula . . . thinking got you nowhere. She was interested in Katie, and through Katie, kind to him. That was that. But this meeting, like everything else on this Christmas Eve was different. She had asked him to carry her parcels, and he was standing waiting for her as if he was her . . .

'I won't ask you to carry this one.' She was standing by his side, and he stared at her, not speaking; her face, under her fur-trimmed hat, shone at him like a star. For one brief second, the street and the hurrying crowds vanished, and she was alone in a vast emptiness, shining, and for him.

His face was unsmiling and his voice deep in his throat as he asked, 'Have you time . . . would you care to go to a variety show or the pantomime?'

He waited, tense and unthinking as her smile faded. The expression in her eyes changed a number of times in as many seconds, but not once did they portray annoyance or amusement.

'I should love to.' She turned away from him, and he fell into step by her side, thinking now, as he had never thought before: Had he gone mad? What of the Mr Culbert? It was Christmas Eve and perhaps she was expected at home for a party or something. What in the name of God had made him ask her! And what about money? He had five shillings of his own . . . would that do? . . . Yes. Somehow, he knew she wouldn't expect too much. But again, what in the name of God had made him do it! It was the last thing on earth he would have thought of doing. . . . Or was it? Hadn't he often wondered what it would be like to take someone of her stamp out? Yes, but just as one dreamt dreams, never for one moment expecting them to happen. The funny thing was she hadn't refused. She hadn't been merely polite, either; she seemed quite sincere when she said, 'I'd love to.' Well, now he must put his thinking cap on. They would have to go in the very best seats, and she'd have to have some bullets. Bullets! he repeated scornfully . . . chocolates. Get a little box. . . . A box! No need to go mad altogether. She wouldn't expect it anyway. He pushed his shoulders back. Expected or not, he'd get a box.

'Do you think there's time for me to make a telephone call?'

They were standing outside the Empire, and for a moment she drifted from him into the class that made telephone calls.

'Where do you have to go? The post office?' he asked.

'Yes; I won't be more than five minutes.'

'Of course. Come on.' He shouldered his way through the crowd. Class or no class, she was going out with him, this once anyway. And he'd do the thing properly; it would be something to remember.

In spite of her fur coat and rinking boots, Mary shivered as she waited in the telephone box. It had happened as she hoped it might. But where would it lead? . . . There was time enough to ask that later, she told herself. What she had to do now was to smooth things over with those at home.

She gave a gentle sigh when she heard her father's voice say, 'Yes. Who is it?'

'It's me, Mary.'

'Mary? Why, where are you? What's up? You should be home by now; we're nearly ready.'

'Look, dear. I won't be home . . . not until . . . quite late.'

'But where are you? You know you can't do that, Mary; we're going to Gilbert's! Look lass'–he cut her short as she was about to speak–it's Christmas, and we want things to go peaceable like. Where are you, anyway?'

'Shields Post Office.'

'What's made you change your mind?'

'I . . . Well, I met a friend.'

'But it isn't right. You know what a state this will put your mother in.'

'I never wanted to go. I've told her so all along. She shouldn't have accepted for me. . . . Look, Father, can't you see what Mother is trying to do?'

'Yes. I know, I know.'

'Well then why should you want me to go? And anyway, it isn't fair to Gilbert. She's giving him the idea that I can be coaxed round, and I can't.'

'Who's your friend?'

'Oh, you . . . you don't know him.'

'It's a man then?'

'Yes, it's a man.'

'Well, this is going to be a lovely evening for me.'

Mary laughed softly. 'It's yourself you're thinking about.'

'Well partly.' There was a chuckle. 'You'll be for it tomorrow, mind. And somehow I did think this was going to be a peaceful Christmas.'

'It's the loveliest Christmas I've ever known. Good-bye, dear.'

'Here! Mary . . . look, who's this fellow?'

'We may talk about him later.'

'Mary . . . you'll go to Midnight Mass? For God's sake don't miss that, or there'll be hell to pay.'

'We'll see. Good-bye. Wait. Do you want to know something?'

'What is it?'

'I like you, Mr Llewellyn.'

Laughing she hung up the phone, and almost ran to join John.

Mary Ellen yawned. She wished John was in, and then she'd go to bed. She leaned back and glanced up at the clock . . . ten-past eleven. Had he managed to get a duck?

She sat with her chair drawn up close to the fire, her feet on the fender, her skirt tucked up on to her lap, exposing her short legs to the dying ashes. The house was quiet, only Shane's and Dominic's snores alternating with each other's from the rooms. Behind her, the girls lay curled up under the thin brown blankets and a heap of coats; and, at each end of the mantelpiece hung their packed stockings, together with one for Mick.

As she yawned again, she heard the muffled pad of footsteps on the yard, and, pulling down her skirt, she got up to open the scullery door as John quietly lifted the latch of the back door.

Stupefied, Mary Ellen gazed at him; then, in a whispered exclamation, said, 'In the name of God! have you bought the market?'

John laughed softly as he lowered a great parcel on to the table, followed by a stone brown paper bag and a square box. 'You'll never guess what it is . . . it's a turkey! And this is a bag of fruit. And there's bullets in that box.' He spoke softly and rapidly.

'A turkey! But where'd you get the money, lad?' Mary Ellen looked closely at him. If she didn't know differently she'd have thought he'd had a drop–his eyes were shining, like coals. . . . Perhaps it was the frost.

'We . . . I waited till the last thing, and I got him for four bob.'

'But what's all this other?'

'Fruit.'

'A stone bag of it!' Mary Ellen looked amazed. 'Are they specked?'

'No, I should say not.'

John did not look at her. He had taken off his cap and was combing his hair. 'Miss Llewellyn sent them for the bairns.'

Mary Ellen stared silently at his profile. Miss Llewellyn.

John turned to her, putting on his cap again. 'I'm going to Midnight Mass at Jarrow. I'm getting the last tram up.'

Miss Llewellyn and Midnight Mass. Her lad going to Midnight Mass with Miss Llewellyn! It was funny, but she'd been thinking about Midnight Mass earlier on this evening, feeling the need to give thanks for all her good fortune at this Christmas time. It was years since she had been to Midnight Mass, and in spite of her tiredness, she'd thought: For two pins I'd go to Midnight Mass if John was in. She would have worn her new coat, although it wouldn't have mattered about going in her shawl; there'd be mostly shawls and mufflers there anyway. And she'd imagined herself kneeling as she used to do in the aisle, or even on the altar steps, wrapped about in the thick, incensed air, full of hushed rustle, so full would the church be. And for a brief hour she would really feel the Child was being born and be one with Mary in her travail.

But John was going to Midnight Mass, and he was going with Miss Llewellyn. She knew now the reason for the light in his eyes.

John tried not to show undue haste, but there was only a few minutes before the tram would pass the bottom of the street, and she would be on it. Already it was late, and perhaps they'd not get in the church. He did not want this to happen, for he had the desire to kneel at Mass with her, not only because it would mean being with her another hour or more, but because to go to Mass with a lass had a subtle meaning, which neither needed nor could be defined by words.

The four hours they had been together seemed to spread back down his lifetime. There seemed no moment when he had not watched the expressions dancing over her face like shadows in a garden, nor a moment when he had not been carrying her parcels or buying her chocolates, or when he was not sitting with her in the dark and laughing with her at a pantomime; or when was there a second in his life when she did not urge him to remain quiet while the stallholder, in desperation, brought his final and unmovable price of eight shillings a turkey down to four shillings! or when had he not watched her taking her choice of fruit, bananas, pomegranates, oranges, apples, pears, and nuts. And now they were going to Midnight Mass, and there would be no tram back. They would have to walk all the way from Dee Street, in the centre of Jarrow, to the heart of Simonside. It would be a long way for her, and difficult walking, for the pavements were sheets of knobbly grey ice; and it would be a long way to walk without touching each other. She might have to take his arm–he thought of it as 'link'–Miss Llewellyn and him linking!

A surge of feeling that demanded some form of expression swept through him, and, stooping, he kissed Mary Ellen swiftly on the side of the brow. Without a word, he was gone. And Mary Ellen stood fingering the place his lips had brushed. . . . Her lad had kissed her . . . for the first time since he was a tiny bairn. And because he was in love.

She had been worried lately, thinking he was struck on her next door, and had wondered where it would lead, for she doubted, if he took her, there'd be much happiness for him; not that she had anything really against the lass, only that terrifying religion of hers. God knew there was no happiness came out of a mixed marriage. With a Church of England one it would be bad enough, but with a Spiritualist! . . . And yet, as awful as that possibility seemed, he would have had a little show of happiness in a way, whereas now there was none for him that she could see. For what was the obstacle of religion compared with the obstacle of class? Had he gone mad? And that Llewellyn lass, too? Where did they think it would lead? Her da was a boatbuilder; and a docker, even a gaffer, would be so much midden muck to him. They had a fancy house, with even a lavatory inside, so Katie said, and kept a parlourmaid and a cook. Was the lass mad? There was no one better than her lad, no one in the wide world, but he was a docker and from the fifteen streets. And that lass must know nothing could come of it. . . . She was struck by his size and his ways, and she would shelve him when the novelty wore off. And what would it do to him? She thought of his eyes when he had come in, and slowly she sat down by the fire again and stared into its rose-grey embers.

Chapter Eight

New Year's Eve

It was a good thing New Year's Eve fell on a Saturday, John thought, for it meant one day less holiday. They would start work on Tuesday, the ones, anyway, who were sober enough. He wanted work, and more work. If he had his own way he'd carry on, night and day, for three parts of the week; he'd make them throw the stuff out of those holds as it had never been thrown out before. He wanted money. God, how he wanted money.

He sat before the fire, dressed in his working clothes, tense with thinking. Shane sat opposite him, sober and sullen; he'd been drunk only once during the holidays. This was a record. Was he turning over a new leaf? John wondered, or was it because he was forced to realize that the more he drank the more he twitched? But twitching or not, tonight he'd likely have a skinful. What would she say to this house and the lot of them? Would she take them as she took him? That was too much to ask. Whereas last Saturday night he thought he'd never known a moment in his life without her, now, across the vast space of time since he last saw her, he could not even recall her face clearly. Again and again he tried to visualize her; but always her face ran into a blur. Even when he attempted to recapture the wonder and the ecstatic feeling of achievement as, with her on his arm, he walked past the fifteen streets, huddled and sleeping under the star-carpeted sky, the feeling would slither away. It was strange, too, but he could not actually remember how he left her. What did they say to each other? Nothing much. They were quiet on the journey back; all the laughter and fun had been left in Shields market. As they walked up Simonside Bank, he had asked if she were tired, and she had replied that she'd never felt less tired. Yet she sounded sort of sleepy when she said it. . . . But there must have been more than that said. One thing he knew he hadn't said: 'Can I see you again?'

Why hadn't he, when it was foremost in his mind during those last few minutes with her? But foremost, too, had been the thought of money. He couldn't really ask her out unless he intended taking her somewhere. Well, he could have taken her out tonight.

All this morning he was hoping he would run into her as he came home from work. And when he didn't, he told himself it was the best thing that could have happened; there were many things he could do with those extra few shillings–his mother would know what to do with them. So perhaps it was all for the best–he moved impatiently in his chair. Perhaps . . . there was no perhaps about it. What was he aiming at, anyway? Was his brain softening, just because of that one night? If he were to see her again, what would it lead to? So intense was the urgency of the question that he almost spoke aloud. You are going stark, staring mad! Look around, and ask yourself what you and she can ever be to each other . . . even if she does like you. . . . He was on his feet, staring down into the fire; she likes me all right, I know it. She more than likes me . . . she feels the same as I do.

Mary Ellen could remain silent no longer; John's drawn, twisted face was wringing her heart. Shane was dozing now, and she whispered, 'What's up, lad?'

'Nothing. I'm going to have a wash.'

He went quickly into the scullery, and as he washed himself Mary Ellen gazed sadly at his back. She knew this would happen–she knew there'd be no happiness in it for him. She wanted to go to him and in some way comfort him; but her mind was lifted from him to Molly.

Molly's screeching voice came from the back lane, and Mary Ellen knew she was fighting again, for she was hurling rhymes at someone's head:

Annie Kelly's got a big fat belly,
And her belly wobbles like jelly.

My God! that lass nearly fourteen and yelling things out like that. Mary Ellen pushed past John and opened the back door.

'You, Molly! come in here!'

Molly was having her last word: 'You wouldn't do much for God if the divil was dead, Annie Kelly. You're mean, so you are. Poor Nancy!'

'Come in here!' Mary Ellen hauled Molly over the step. 'You can thank your lucky stars your da's dozing,' she whispered fiercely, 'or I'd bray you!'

'Well, I was only sticking up for Nancy,' Molly snivelled. 'She's been sent back from her place, Mrs Fitzimmons won't have her. And Annie wouldn't let her play with us; she punched her.'

'Sent back from her place,' Mary Ellen repeated to John. 'That means the do's off.'

'Damn good thing, too,' John answered shortly. 'They'll be yelling out for the money before the new year's in a week.'

'It'll likely be spent now, lad, in any case.'

The door opened again, and Katie rushed in breathless.

Mary Ellen hushed her: 'Be quiet, hinny! And close that door, the cold's enough to cut you in two.'

'Ma, can I go with Christine? And Molly too? There's a big stretch frozen hard, past Cleveland Place, and everybody's going there to slide . . . proper sliding. Christine's got proper sliding skates with knives on the bottom. And there's a man there with a fire selling roast taties. . . . Oh, Ma, can we go?'

'Go on, Ma, let's.' Molly joined her plea to Katie's.

'What about it cracking?' Mary Ellen asked John. 'Will it be deep?'

'It won't crack in this frost.'

He was drying himself, and asked Katie, 'How does Christine know there's skating? Has she been?' He hadn't seen Christine since Christmas Day, and then only to wish her a happy Christmas and to thank her rather sheepishly for the tie. He knew now why he hadn't kissed Christine, and the knowledge made him strangely embarrassed in her presence.

'Yes,' answered Katie. 'She was there yesterday, her and David. She says they're going to have a big fire on the bank the night to light the ice up.'

'How far past Cleveland Place is it?'

'It's in Roper's Field.'

'You'd better give it a miss,' said Mary Ellen; 'you'll slide the boots off your feet.'

'Not any sooner than with sliding in the streets,' said John.

'But it's them falling through I'm afraid of.'

'Don't worry,' he said; 'I'll take a walk up and have a look.'

He went into the bedroom and started to change hastily. Roper's Field . . . off the Simonside Road. There was just a chance she might be there.

In the kitchen of Cumberland Villa, the two maids were standing near the partly open door, straining their ears.

'Hear anything?' asked the cook.

'Not a word,' replied Phyllis. 'And the way the missis looked I thought she was going to explode. I bet you anything you like though she'd heard about that fellow.'

'I wouldn't believe a word of it,' said Cook. 'And I'd be careful what I was saying if I was you. Miss Mary walking out with one of the O'Briens! Huh! I'll believe that when I see it.'

'I tell you our Doris saw them in the market, and our Doris knows them both as well as I know you. She was standing behind them, and she said they were laughing and talking together like . . . well, like a couple who was walking out. . . . Sh! Listen.'

Phyllis's elbow stopped the cook's retort. 'There!' she hissed. 'Get an earful of that. Have you ever heard the missis go off like that before? What did I tell you?'

In the drawing-room, James Llewellyn was appealing to his wife: 'Look, Beatrice, leave this to me.' He spoke gently and soothingly; the jocular brusqueness, which was his usual defence against her, was gone from his tone.

'Too much has been left to you, and look at the result!' She turned from him, and again addressed her daughter, with quiet tenseness now, 'No wonder you wouldn't tell me who you were with on Christmas Eve! It is to your credit that you were ashamed.'

Mary stood with her elbow resting on the mantelpiece; her face was half turned from her mother, and she stared unseeing into the fire, her attitude belying the anger that was filling her body.

'You must have lost every spark of decency. You never, at any time, had a proper sense of what is correct. But this! Have you any idea how I felt when Florence Dudley told me they saw you in the Empire with a . . . docker?'

Beatrice Llewellyn spat out the last word, her thin nose and delicately chiselled mouth almost meeting over it. Her large pale blue eyes showed depths of purple, and her expression was weighed with actual hate as she looked at this girl whom she had come to think of as being by her but not of her. This last disgusting episode proved only too conclusively from which side she had inherited her qualities. 'Will Dudley says he comes from the fifteen streets and the family are notorious,' she ended.

Mary faced her mother, and her tone was infuriatingly quiet when she said, 'Of course they are. Anyone within a three-mile radius of the fifteen streets knows that. If you didn't shut out every unpleasantness from your life you would have heard it before. . . . One of the main things for which they are notorious is hunger. Dwell upon that the next time you're preparing for the Dudleys coming to dinner.'

Beatrice Llewellyn stood aghast–never before had Mary dared to address her so. 'They are poor because they drink and gamble. And you! You are a slut! You were out with that man until three o'clock in the morning. Do you think it won't be all round Jarrow and Shields by now?'

'I hope so.'

Mary's stillness seemed to lift the tension to breaking point. Her father cried, 'Here, lass! Here, that's enough!' and Beatrice Llewellyn perpetrated what was to her mind unforgivable . . . she screamed. 'You low creature!' The words seemed to emerge from the top of her head. 'You're utterly debased. I shall have Father O'Malley to you. Yes. Yes, I shall. . . . Leave me alone!'–she tore her arm from her husband's soothing hand, and flung like a small tornado out of the room.

During their twenty-six years of married life, James Llewellyn had never seen his wife lose control; this was the first show of sincere passion he had witnessed, and it left him, not only shaken, but worried. Usually she tried gentle tears and studied silences, alternated with the persistent reiteration of her point. But for Beatrice to lose her dignity meant this affair had indeed struck home.

'You've done it this time.' He came to the fireplace and knocked out his pipe against the bars. 'You know, lass, it was a bit of a shock.'

'To you too?' Mary asked sharply.

'Aye . . . yes. It's no good saying one thing and thinking another. But when Will Dudley got on about seeing you with one of the Big O'Briens I could have punched him in the face. Although he put it very nicely, I could tell it had afforded them a good topic of conversation all the week, and that was why Florence Dudley was so anxious for us to drop in this morning. When your mother came downstairs with her I thought she'd collapse. . . . How long has it been going on, lass?'

'It hasn't been going on, as you call it; that was the only time.'

'Oh . . . Well'–there was a measure of relief in her father's voice–'and are you . . . Well, is it finished?'

'I don't know.'

'You don't know! What do you mean, lass?'

'I mean that if it rests with me it won't be finished.' Mary turned towards him, nervously rubbing the palms of her hands together. 'I haven't seen him since, because he never asked me.'

James Llewellyn stared at his daughter. His lass, who was the best looking lass for miles, and who could have her pick, was in love. Even had she not practically put it unashamedly into words, he could see it in her eyes. She was in love with this dock worker, John O'Brien; and not in the light-hearted way that lassies fell in love, but in an earnest, stubborn, painful way, a way that would leave a mark on her, however things went. Well, he wasn't going to stand by and see her make a hash of her life, and say nothing. This was one time her mother was right. 'Now see here'–he planted his feet firmly apart and pointed his finger at her–'you know which side I've always been on, don't you? You know that life would have been much easier for me if I'd taken your mother's part all along.'

As his fingers wagged at her, Mary thought: he's nearly as big as John, and he has the same clumsy movements, a sort of endearing gaucheness. All the money in the world won't polish him. Anyway, he was once a dock worker himself, so why can't he understand about this?

'But I want you to understand, lass,' James Llewellyn went on, 'that I'm with your mother in this.'

'You'd rather see me married to Gilbert then?'

'I don't want you to marry anyone you don't fancy. . . . But yes'–he thrust out his head–'yes, I'd rather see you married to Gilbert than carrying on with this business. At least you wouldn't starve. . . . Oh, Mary'–his large leathery face crumpled–'stop while there's time. You don't know what you're running yourself into. Lass, I hate to say it, but I've seen those O'Briens rolling from one side of the arches to the other. I even remember the mother, years ago, a little body, standing outside the bars with the bairns clinging round her, trying to get a few shillings out her man before he blued the lot. I tell you, lass, they're noted.'

'He doesn't drink.'

'That's what he says.'

'He doesn't, Father.' There was a fierce ring in her voice. 'And he's not just a docker either; he's been made a gaffer.'

'What! Did he tell you that? How old is he?'

'Twenty-two.' Her head was thrust up in defiance, daring him to say, 'So he's younger than you.'

But what he said was, 'He's a damned liar! There's no fellow could be made a gaffer at twenty-two. Thirty-two would be more like it. He's stuffing you, lass. Can't you see?' He was angry for her.

'No, he's not. Anyway, it should be easy for you to find out.'

'Yes. Quite easy. But even so, if he is a gaffer, what's that?'

Mary did not reply but stood looking at him, her eyes wide and sad, for she too, was asking herself the same question. . . . He was worth something better than that.

To James Llewellyn, she looked at this moment pathetic, and he could never remember his joyous, laughter-loving daughter looking this way. Taking her by the hand, he said, 'Hinny'–using the endearing word that was banned in the house because of its commonness–'I only want your happiness. What do you think I've worked for all these years? To leave you comfortable. Look, my dear, tell me you'll drop this.'

The tears gathering in her eyes obscured her vision. Why, oh why, did they think money could buy off or replace a feeling that was made of intangible stuff? Money and love were on two different planes. . . . Yet were they so divided? Love needed money for its existence. Without it, more often than not it died, as the body, wherein it was housed, fought and struggled for life. Yet if the chance were given her, would she risk the survival of this love that seemed to be eating her away? Oh yes, yes. The tears spilled on to her face. 'I can't. If he asks me out again, I'll go.'

She watched her father leave the room and close the door after him with painful slowness . . .

Mary was sitting in her own room, crouched over the fire, when the dinner bell rang. She made no move to carry out its summons. Nor, as the time went on, did anyone come to inquire why. Never before had she felt so unhappy, and she couldn't see the unhappiness lifting; it stretched on and on into the future, for the only person capable of dispelling it was as class-conscious as her mother. She felt now that Christmas Eve had been merely a lapse of John's, and that during the quiet walk back from Jarrow he was already regretting it; he had left her with scarcely a word. Every dinner-time and teatime of this past week she had fought with herself not to stroll casually down through the arches, presumably on her way to Shields, in the hope of encountering him. But some hard core of pride said no . . . she wouldn't scheme to trap him into asking her out; if he wanted to see her he would find a way; and there was always the post.

What a New Year's Eve! She got up and wandered about the room. If only she could see him for a moment, run into him accidentally, as she had done last Saturday night. . . . But wouldn't it have been better had they not met at all–not last Saturday, but in the first instance. He attracted her that first night he sat in this room, and she had been unable to get him out of her mind since.

The memory of that meeting brought back the niggling envy of Christine. . . . Was that girl something to him? Was she the reason why he hadn't asked her to repeat the evening? She didn't know . . .

She went upstairs and put on her outdoor things, for she felt that were she to stay indoors any longer she would scream, as her mother had done this morning. Remembering her mother's voice and look, she realized that whether she pursued this business to its height or it merely fizzled out, the last supports of the barrier that had been erecting itself for years between them were hammered home today, and their combined life-times would not be long enough to break it down.

Standing on the bank at the edge of the field, John looked down in amazement on the scene. He had witnessed nothing like it before. The field, which dipped into a shallow valley, had every appearance of a lake, and there was scarcely a yard of its surface which had not its moving figure. Very few had skates; the main sport seemed to be concentrated on the long single and double slides. On the double slides, young men and girls crossed hands, skimming away with enviable balance towards the centre of the ice. Children had their slides nearer the edge, and were watched by the spectators, who outnumbered the skaters. Some of the young lads were already getting the bonfire going. The air was filled with laughter and shouting, the smell of burning wood, and the thick, comforting smell of roasting potatoes. The faces of the crowd seemed alight with a newborn joy.

The feeling of mass gaiety puzzled John. It was this whiteness; it had gone to their heads and caused a madness. The drabness of life was lost under the spell of its gleaming sparkle, and the people seemed to be deluded into thinking this clean, white world would remain–their house roofs were white, their window sills, their doorsteps. The docks and the ships, too, lay buried under the clean illusion–even on the top of the highest mast there was a virgin white cap of snow, fast and secure and promising to remain for ever. There would be no tomorrow, or the next day, when the gutters would be choked with brown slush, the roads become rivers, and the houses grey again, and they themselves grey and blue, feet wet, bodies shivering. It was cold now; but this was a dry cold, which quickened the blood, freed the perception and brought all the instincts to the surface, giving to each person an awareness of his existence, which demanded of the body that it be used, now, at this very time.

As he stood there John began to feel something of this mass joy. The whole scene, which seemed to have been dropped from another world, where only light laughter existed, bewildered him, and part of him realized that it was out of place in the realistic grimness of this area.

He watched Christine gliding gracefully in small circles near where Katie, Molly and David were sliding with other children. She looked little more than a child herself, a dark, elfin, slip of a child.

Christine caught sight of him, and waved and beckoned him on to the ice; but he shook his head and waved his hand in refusal. And after a while, she glided to where he stood on the bank.

'Isn't it wonderful! Come on . . . I'll pull you.'

'Not on your life,' he laughed.

He was relieved that there was no stiffness in her manner, for it must have been evident to her that he had avoided seeing her during this past week. She looked very fetching, standing below him with a red tam-o-shanter on the back of her head, and for a fleeting second he felt a regret that it was not she who was filling his mind and body at this moment, for then things would have been plain sailing.

'A big thing like you afraid of the ice!' she called up to him, teasingly.

'You'd be more afraid if you got me on there and I fell on you.'

'I'll risk it. Come on. Come on, John'–the pleasing was in her eyes and voice.

He shook his head: 'I've a number of other ways of making a fool of myself besides that.'

Christine saw that it was no use trying to coax him; nevertheless, she stood for a time gazing up at him. Then, without further words, she turned and skimmed away again.

John continued to watch her and the children, but between times his eyes would search the field. Although the light was fading he could still see the further bank, and he thought it would have to be very dark to prevent him from picking her out from the crowd. He noticed Katie leave the long line of sliders and walk quickly towards him.

'What's the matter?' he asked. 'Are you tired, or after a hot tatie?'

'Our Dominic's along there, John. He's watching Christine.'

John remained silent, and did not turn to the spot Katie indicated but looked to where Christine was still whirling unconcerned. 'Is he all right?' he asked; which meant, was he sober.

'Yes, he looks it . . . and . . . and he's got a collar and tie on too.' Katie's eyes fell to John's collar and tie, then to his new coat; and she added, with awe in her voice, 'He's got a new coat an' all, John.' Her eyes were round in amazement–the advent of any new clothes in the house was something to dwell upon, for in most cases their approach was awaited for weeks. As late as last night Dominic had no new clothes, yet here he was, all dressed up.

John's mouth moved into a twisted grin. Dominic wasn't to be outdone then. The buying of new clothes would be all to the good if it kept him off the drink; but John knew only too well that someone would have to whistle for the money for the coat. He glanced casually now in Dominic's direction. Yes, there he was, practically head and shoulders above the crowd, and even from this distance and the little John could see of him, the difference in his appearance was noticeable.

Momentarily John's attitude towards his brother softened, and he wondered if Dominic's feeling for Christine was anything like his own for Mary. But his wondering was definitely only momentary. . . . He would have gone about it in a different way if it was . . . and he still paid visits to 'Lady Pansy'. Moreover, his love for Christine, if it could be called such, had instilled her with nothing but fear.

He bent down to Katie: 'Don't forget what I told you about keeping with Christine.'

'No, John, I won't.'

'No matter what he says on the way home, don't you leave her, mind.'

'No, John.'

'Go on then, on your slide; I'll be here for some time yet.'

Groups of lads and lassies on the banks had started singing. 'Keep your feet still, Geordie, hinny' vied with 'Cushy Butterfield', and 'Bleydon Races' with 'Auld Lang Syne'. But now the careless made pleasure of the scene was dispelled for John, for Dominic was there. His presence acted like a pressure, forcing out the ease from his body and the quietness from his mind, and replacing it with antipathy, which was the only true bond between them.

As the daylight of the last day of the year faded, the twilight seemed to urge on the gaiety. The bonfire was well alight now, sending up showers of sparks through the grey dusk into the far reaching blue beyond. John found that after looking towards the fire and for a time the skaters on the ice appeared like dark, scribbled lines on a white canvas. He closed his eyes and pressed his eyeballs with his fingers. And when he opened them, there she was, standing not a yard from him.

When he was a child, his mother, if she had a piece of toffee for him, would say, 'Shut your eyes and open your mouth and see what God will send you.' He had shut his eyes, and look what God had sent him.

He took a slow step towards her–Dominic and all he stood for was gone, and the magic and madness of the scene was upon him fully now. No subterfuge need be used on a night like this; truth was easy, and desirable.

'I wondered if you would be here.'

At his words, her face, which had been set and strained, fell into a smile; not her usual, light-flashing smile, but one holding a tinge of sadness.

John did not detect the sadness . . . sadness and this girl were as apart as the earth and the sky. To his mind, she spelt radiance, to his body, magnetism; she was ecstasy and joy. But he had only plain words with which to speak: 'Have you ever seen anything to equal this around these parts?' He did not take his eyes from her face, but indicated the ice with a movement of his head.

'Never. It's like something you'd see in Switzerland.'

Her eyes, playing over his face, made him drunk with feeling; all the barriers between them were being swept away on a swift moving tide. The need was upon him to touch her, if only her hand.

'Have you been sliding?' he asked.

'I haven't any skates.'

'What about using our feet? It seems popular.'

'Here?' She pointed to the entwined throng below them.

'No. Let's go round to the other side; there are fewer people there, and if we fall there'll be less to laugh at us.'

Mary made an almost imperceptible motion with her head. The action was more pointed than words in its acquiescence.

They turned together. Then stopped. It was the red tam-o-shanter that brought itself to John's notice. Without it, Christine, at that moment, would have been merely another face–even Katie was just part of the crowd.

Christine and Katie stood hand in hand below them, silent and staring.

'Why! Hallo, Katie.'

'Hallo, Miss Llewellyn.' Katie's fat, rosy cheeks were very like the proverbial apples as she smiled.

'Are you having a lovely time?'

'Yes, Miss Llewellyn.'

'And did you have a nice Christmas?'

'Oh yes, Miss Llewellyn. Oh, lovely! And thank you, Miss Llewellyn, for the presents and all the lovely fruit.'

Mary's eyes were forced from Katie's to the girl in the red hat. The girl was staring at her; her eyes, dark and enormous, seemed to glow with a purple gleam. Even in the dusk, their light was penetrating, and Mary felt it stripping her. It was an odd sensation. It was almost as if the girl was looking into the very depths of her heart and finding there things of which even she herself was not aware.

When John said, 'This is Christine,' the girl, with a lightning movement, whirled Katie round and away, and in a moment they were lost in the moving figures and the dimness.

The situation had suddenly become awkward. Why had Christine dashed off like that? He knew fine well why! His neck became hot. Then a surge of relief swept over him . . . thank God he had never made up to her! He was free in that sense, anyway . . . free for Mary. Oh the daring, the audacity, the madness of it!

He turned towards her again, and this time the sadness in her face was clear to him. She too then had seen how Christine felt. He must make it clear to her that there was nothing in it.

'What about the slide?' he said.

Without answering, she turned from him, and they threaded their way among the crowd.

'Christine's a nice girl,' he began lamely.

'Yes, she looks it.'

They were forced to step apart to make way for a group of running children, and when they came together again, he continued, 'I don't think she'll ever grow up though. She's . . . well, she's just like Katie.'

She looked at him and smiled, a small, understanding smile. He smiled back at her, and they walked on in silence.

The far bank was almost deserted, the crowds having been drawn to the light of the bonfire and the man with the brazier and the roasting potatoes. The ice, too, was not so smooth here, for tufts of grass broke the surface.

'Shall we chance it?' He held out his hand, and she took it and stepped from the bank on to the ice. 'Single or double?'

'Single I think, for a start. . . . You go first, I haven't been on the ice for two years.'

'Two years! It must be at least eight since I was on a slide. . . . Well, here goes.' He ran and started to slide; wobbled, steadied himself, and wobbled again; then, with a suddenness that found every bone in his body, he sat down on the ice with a heavy plop.

With a sureness that spoke of past schooling, she reached him as he was getting to his feet. He was laughing, and said, 'Good job you weren't behind me.' And when he felt her hands gently dusting his shoulders he prolonged his own banging of his clothes to shake off the loose snow.

'Shall we try again?' he asked.

'If you like,' she said; but there was little enthusiasm in her voice.

'Do you want to slide?' He was facing her now, their breaths were mingling and their eyes holding. The words were a question that did not mean what it asked, and she answered with a candour that seemed to be of the very essence of the day.

'No.'

He reached out and took her hand, and they walked carefully towards the bank again.

'Would you . . . would you like to go for a walk? Or what about Shields?'

'Not Shields. Let's go for a walk.'

They walked down the narrow lane and on to the main road without speaking. Being a country road it was unlit, and in spite of the snow covering it, it appeared black after the glare of the fire-lit field. The darkness gave him courage, and he unclasped her hand and drew her arm through his, entwining his fingers through hers and holding them close to his coat. They walked on in step, and as he felt her hip moving against his he became conscious of the stillness between them, a stillness that seemed to be waiting only for the right moment to burst into sound . . . sound that would bewitch and delight him, because it would be her voice telling him what he wanted, above all things, to know. But as they walked on, it seemed to him as if the silence would never be broken.

When, of one mind, they turned down a side lane and stopped and faced each other, he told himself that never before had any man felt for a woman as he felt for her. But now the moment had come he seemed paralysed, and even the potency of his feeling could not lift him over the barrier to her. It was she who opened the way, with such words that flung barriers, prejudices and classes into oblivion: 'Oh, John, if you don't tell me I won't be able to bear it.'

There was a second of wonder filled time before his arms went about her, not gently, as he had imagined them so often doing, but savagely, crushing her into him until he could feel her racing heart pounding against him. He did not kiss her immediately. His lips travelled the whole surface of her face before they reached hers, but when they did, their bodies merged and rose, above the snow and ice, above their separate lives, away from this earth to some ethereal place where time is not. When, swaying together, their lips parted, it seemed to them both as if they had actually fallen into another era of time, so much did they know of each other.

'Mary.'

She did not answer but leaned upon him, moving her face against his.

'I love you.'

Her arms tightened about him.

'I'm mad . . . I shouldn't say that.'

'Oh beloved.'

Beloved . . . a woman had called him beloved . . . him! This beautiful woman, this girl, this . . .

'How is it you can care for a fellow like me? Mary! Oh, Mary!'

Her reply was smothered against him. And when he would have again begun deprecating himself her fingers covered his mouth. 'You're the finest person I know–there is no one to come up to you.'

She cut short his protest: 'John, let nothing ever separate us, will you?' Her voice was earnest. 'Nothing, nor no one. Promise. Never.'

The urgency in her voice stilled him–it was almost as if she was pleading with him. That she should be asking to let nothing separate them seemed fantastic.

Taking her hand gently from his lips he said, 'It's me should be putting that to you. What do you think will be said when this gets about? Will you be able to stand it?'

Her answer was the covering of his mouth by hers with such passion that all the longing, all the loneliness of his life, all that was drab and tawdry, vanished. Her love for him raised him to a new level of self-esteem.

'Oh, Mary, my love . . . my dear . . . do you know what you mean to me? Do you know what you stand for?' He was gentle now, holding her face between his large hands, peering at her, seeing each feature in his mind's eye: 'You're beautiful.'

'I couldn't be too beautiful for you.'

Her words were like notes of tender music, borne on the white wings of the snow. He shook his head slowly at the wonder of them. 'I don't know how you can love me . . . you, who have everything. I'm ignorant, and I'm ashamed of it. Mary'–his voice was shy–'will you teach me?'

'Oh, my dear, you don't need . . .'

He stopped her, 'Yes, I do need. And you know I do. I never want you to be ashamed of me.'

'John . . . John, don't.'

His humility brought the tears to her eyes, as he went on, 'And there's my folk. It isn't that I'm ashamed, only . . . well, I suppose you've heard of our family. There hasn't been much chance for any of us; my mother slaved all her days, and . . . and my father and brother . . .'

'Sh!' She leaned gently against him, stroking his cheek as a mother would soothe a child.

She murmured something, and he whispered in awe, 'What?'

And she repeated, 'It's a case of Ruth and Naomi.'

But still he did not understand, yet although the words held no meaning for him, her tone conveyed a deep humility, and he was filled with wonder.

Chapter Nine

Nancy

The home-made paper chains lay in a jumbled heap on one side of the table, the three bought ones lying neatly concertinaed by themselves together with the honeycomb ball. These would do for another year, Mary Ellen decided, if she could hide them somewhere. She had never before been so late in taking down the decorations; it was the 5th January, and she was just escaping bad luck by taking them down today, the morrow would be too late. But it had been nice to leave them up till the last minute, for they carried on the feeling of this wonderful Christmas and New Year. By!–she stopped in her work to look out of the kitchen window to the roofs beyond, where the last of the snow was sliding in a grey mass into the gutter–she had never known such a time. The stuff they'd had to eat! And Shane being sober, even on New Year's Eve; and no rows in the house. There was Dominic's surliness, of course, but she was used to that and had not allowed it to spoil things. And anyway, he was out most of the time . . . all night, once.

This business of John's troubled her at times; but what could she do, for he said nothing. He was going about looking like a cat with nine tails. She hoped to God something would happen to make it last. But how could it–him and Miss Llewellyn! Where would it end? . . . Well, she wouldn't worry–everything else was going fine; the coal house was full of coal and the bairns were rightly set up with clothes, the last, thanks to them next door–the thought of thanks took shape before she could stop it–well, anyway, they had been good, no matter what they were. She'd wished time and again she could go and thank them, but she was unable to bring herself to do so. The fear of them still held her, and she couldn't face them, so she had sent her thanks by the bairns and John. The fear had strengthened in an odd way too during these past weeks, for Mick's ear had stopped running for the first time in two years, and Shane . . . Why was it, after all these years, Shane had eased off the drink and his twitching had lessened? Did he find himself lying on a platform above the bed with Peter Bracken's hands moving over him? My God! She shuddered. It was the first time she had admitted to herself the influence of Peter Bracken on her the night the child was born. She put her hand inside her blouse and felt for her rosary, which she had taken to wearing round her neck of late.

Staring out of the window, she said her beads: Hail, Mary, full of grace, the Lord is with thee. Blessed art thou amongst women, and blessed is the fruit of thy womb, Jesus. . . . She had gone through two decades, when she saw the back yard door open and Hannah Kelly enter the yard.

Hastily, she fastened her blouse.

What did Hannah want so early in the morning? . . . There was something curious about her walk: she couldn't have had a drop already, surely. She watched Hannah fumble with the latch of the kitchen door, and when she came in and closed the door, and stood with her back to it, Mary Ellen exclaimed, 'Why, lass, you're bad! Come and sit down.'

Hannah shook her head and murmured, 'Oh, Mary Ellen!'

'What is it? Is it Joe?'

Hannah again shook her head. She tried to speak but the words refused to come, her mouth opening and shutting like that of a fish.

'What is it then? Nancy?'

Hannah's eyes drooped and her head fell on her chest.

'Tell me, lass. What is it?'

'Dear God, dear God,' Hannah said, and her voice sounded small and lost, and she looked like a bewildered child in spite of her long, bony frame. 'I may be wrong. Will you come over with me, Mary Ellen, and see? I came the back way, for Bella Bradley's on the lookout.'

'Is Nancy ill?' Mary Ellen asked, taking her shawl from the back of the door.

Hannah made no reply but went out, and Mary Ellen followed closely after her. . . .

Nancy was in bed, lying well down under the clothes, and Mary Ellen, as she entered the bedroom could see only her eyes. They held an odd look, a mixture of wariness and cunning, an expression not usual to their dullness.

'Hallo, Nancy,' said Mary Ellen.

But Nancy did not reply with her usual normal address; she just stared from one to the other.

Hannah, stripping the clothes from her, said, 'Lift up your nightie!'

With her eyes still darting from one to the other of the two women, Nancy complied. The nightdress was short and tight, and she had to drag it over her hips.

Mary Ellen gazed at Nancy's stomach. She knew now what Hannah suspected, and she exclaimed to herself, 'Oh, Jesus, don't let it be.' Nevertheless, to her eyes there was nothing really to justify Hannah's suspicions, and she looked across the bed to Hannah: 'Lass, what makes you think . . . ?' she said.

'She's past her time, and I've seen nothing; and I think that's what Mrs Fitzimmons twigged. And her being sick and not working.' She spoke as if Nancy wasn't there. 'Stand up!' she said harshly to her daughter.

Nancy lumbered out of the bed, still with her nightdress held above her stomach. And now Mary Ellen thought she could detect a small rise. But still she would not believe this thing possible; nobody in their right senses would dream of taking a lass like this.

'Look, lass'–she turned to Hannah–'it may only be wind. Or perhaps a growth,' she said hopefully.

Hannah, her eyes dead in her large, round face, turned away and walked into the kitchen.

'Put your clothes on, hinny,' Mary Ellen said to Nancy; and the girl immediately pulled her nightdress over her head and began to dress.

In the kitchen, Hannah was sitting dejectedly at the table, and Mary Ellen said, 'Get her to the doctor's lass. Take her now. It may not be what you think, and it'll set your mind at rest. . . . Anyway, it can't be that.'

Hannah, in dismay, turned and stared into distances beyond the kitchen walls: 'It's that all right. I'll take her, but I know.'

'Have you asked her anything?'

'Yes, I asked her if a man had touched her, and she wouldn't answer. And that's a funny thing in itself, for she always says right away, "No, ma, when men speak to me I run away." And then again, twice last week she disappeared. I had Annie out looking for her for three hours on New Year's night, and she found her round by St Bede's Church. She had come across the salt grass, but she wouldn't say where she'd been. . . . Oh, Christ . . . Christ Jesus!' Hannah burst out. 'What's going to happen? Joe will kill her. And if he finds out who it is there'll be murder done. Oh, Mary Ellen, what am I going to do?'

'Here, steady yourself, lass. Come on, get up and put your coat on and take her now.' She pulled Hannah to her feet. 'You'll catch him if you go now.'

While Hannah was putting on her coat, Mary Ellen went into the bedroom where Nancy was still laboriously dressing: 'Hurry up, hinny, your ma's waiting.'

Mary Ellen found she couldn't look at the girl. . . . If she were going to have a bairn and had kept quiet about the man, then there was some part in her that was sensible, Mary Ellen reasoned. Unless, of course, she was too afraid to say anything. But now that she came to look at her, the lass looked less afraid than she had ever done.

She bustled Nancy into the kitchen: 'There you are then, lass'–she was addressing herself to Hannah–'get yourself off. . . . And remember, whichever way it goes, don't worry. You can't help it; the blame can't be laid at your door, you've done your best.'

She watched them walking down the street, wide apart, like strangers, Nancy humped and shuffling, Hannah as stiff as a ramrod; and a sadness settled on Mary Ellen, the beginning of a long, long sadness.

John hurried out of the docks . . . Friday night and the first week of the new year over, and six boats discharging at the same time. He had just come from the weigh beam after paying off half the men. It was a strange sensation standing at the weigh beam with his pockets full of money and handing each man his due, and feeling that although he was young enough to be a son to three parts of the men they liked him, and trusted him to give them a square deal. As he left the last arch and passed the bottom of Simonside Bank he glanced through the darkness to the curving incline, and the thought that within the next hour he would be hurrying up there brought a leaping and tingling to his blood. The nights of the past week had been like glimpses of paradise–was there anyone in the world as beautiful and as sweet as her? Where was there a woman of her standing who would take him as he was? He had no notions about himself. Eight years in the docks had not filed him down, but roughened him. The only saving grace, he told himself, was that he was aware of it and would do his best to remedy it. He would have to if he were ever to feel worthy of her, even to the smallest degree. Moreover, another thing he would have to do was to find a better job. It was impossible for him to remain in the docks . . . even as a gaffer, for it would take more than a gaffer's wages to support her in the way to which she was used. Almost every night of the past week, after he had left her, his main thought had been that he must better himself; and he worked it out that there was no chance for him in the North, nor yet in England . . . America . . . the Mecca of the Tyneside Irish loomed before him like a lodestar. If she would have him he would go there. Perhaps she would go with him right away. . . . No; not for a moment would he consider that. When he had made enough money he would send for her. Not for one day of her life would she live differently because of him. . . . And then there was his mother and Katie. If he went to America he'd be able to send them money too. For look at the wages you earned out there! And it wasn't all moonshine. The Hogans from High Jarrow were doing fine, he'd heard; the father and four lads all in regular work, and sending for the rest of them this year. And there was that young

Stanley Tapp, who went out and had his lass follow him. So why shouldn't he, with his strength and fitness make a go of it! There was no job he couldn't tackle. Yes, that's what he'd do. But he'd have to wait a while before he put it to her; he couldn't ask her anything yet; it was too soon. Had he been loving her for only a week? It seemed now as though it had been going on for years. And each time they met the knowledge grew stronger that she loved him with an intensity that almost matched his own. This coloured his life, and lifted him to the heights whereon he saw himself wrestling a mighty living out of the world and giving her, not only the things that she was used to, but such things to which even she had not aspired.

He was whistling as he walked up the backyard, but stopped before he entered the house; his mother wouldn't have whistling in the house, it was unlucky. She was standing by the table, and before her, on the mat, stood his father and Dominic with their bait tins still in their hands. Shane's lower lip was thrust out, and he was saying, 'The swine should be crucified!'

'What's up?' asked John, loosening his muffler.

'It's Nancy,' said Mary Ellen, looking down at her feet. 'Nancy? What's wrong with her?' John took off his coat and rolled up his sleeves before reaching for the kettle from the hob.

'She's going to have a bairn.'

John's hands stayed in mid-air. 'She's going to what!' His brows met over the exclamation.

'It's true. Hannah's had her to the doctor. She's nearly out of her mind.'

Turning slowly, John looked from his father to Dominic, and back to his mother again. Nancy Kelly going to have a bairn! It was utterly incredible. He thought of her face as it really was without the veil of his pity covering it . . . the loose, repulsive mouth, the beady eyes, and the pushed-in nose. How could any man touch her, unless he too 'wasn't all there.'

Mary Ellen was saying, 'And the funny thing is, she's gone . . . odder'–she couldn't say 'brazen' to the men–'I can't keep her out of the house.'

Although Mary Ellen was filled with pity for Hannah and the girl, she had found the day trying beyond description, for when Nancy wasn't standing leaning against the stanchion of her own front door, staring across the street towards the house, she was knocking at either the back or the front door. Mary Ellen felt she could not say anything to Hannah as yet, for Hannah was distraught, not only with her daughter going to have a child, but at the change in her. It was as if now, with life moving within her, some part of Nancy had become activated into normality . . . a crude and shocking normality to the women, for she seemed proud of her achievement and was determined to show it to her world. Subconsciously through the years, she must have taken in, with perhaps a feeling of envy, the arrogance of the pregnant women standing at their doors, their arms folded across the bulks of moving life. And she may have laughed unknowingly at their jokes as they patted the tiny flutterings of their aprons, saying with raw wit the old, threadworn joke, 'Lie down, yer father's not workin'!'

Whatever had happened, she was now . . . brazened, and Mary Ellen's pity was turning to irritation.

Dominic sat down by the fire–he hadn't spoken–and Shane and John still stood regarding Mary Ellen.

'This'll send the little bantam clean off his head.' It was Shane who spoke, and he was referring to Joe.

As Mary Ellen was about to make some reply, the back door opened and Nancy sidled in.

'Look, Nancy!' Mary Ellen exclaimed sharply; 'get yourself away home.'

But Nancy, who never to Mary Ellen's knowledge had disobeyed a command in her life, simply ignored her. Instead, she came well into the kitchen and stood looking from one to the other of the men. They all stared at her, Dominic out of the corner of his eye. And when Nancy met his gaze, she flung herself round from him, showing him her back, like a child in the huff, and amidst silence, she walked towards John, and smiled her grotesque smile as she placed her hand on his sleeve.

'John.'

Tears almost came into John's eyes as he looked at her: God, but it was awful! Yet above his pity there arose a feeling of revulsion against her. Some subtle change in her was making itself felt–she was no longer the child.

She said again, 'John;' and he was about to say something to her when his head was jerked up by the sound of choking.

It was Dominic; he had risen from his chair, his body quivering with waves of shut-in laughter. Mary Ellen and Shane were staring at him. He lumbered past them and threw himself on to the couch, where he sat leaning back, facing them, his face working with glee.

Staring wide-eyed and questioningly at her son's contorted face, Mary Ellen was wondering what in the name of God had come over him.

Suddenly Dominic could control himself no longer, and his laughter filled the house. Bellow rolled on top of bellow. But as he rocked himself back and forth his eyes never left John's, and the implication was lost on none of them. He waved a helpless hand, encompassing Nancy and John. And John's voice rose above Dominic's laughter, almost deafening them, as he cried, 'You bloody swine!'

With one movement he flung Nancy aside and sprang for Dominic. At the same moment, Shane and Mary Ellen threw themselves on him. Dominic got up, his laughter gone now: 'Let him fight, the dirty bastard! Come on!' He tore off his coat and made for the back door.

John's rage sent Shane and Mary Ellen spinning away from him, and he was after Dominic; but as he crossed the step, Dominic's fist shot out and caught him full in the face: yet so little did it affect John in his rage, it could have been Katie's hand.

After the light of the kitchen, the backyard appeared black, and for a time they struck at each other blindly. But soon their fists met the other's body with quickening and sickening thuds.

'For God's sake, stop them!' Mary Ellen cried to Shane. She tried to push past him into the yard, but he barred her way, saying, 'Let them have it out.'

'No! No! He'll kill him. John'll kill him! For God's sake stop them!'

A small crowd was now gathering at the yard door, and the windows on the far side of the back lane were being thrown up–the cry had gone round, 'The O'Briens are at it.'

The one showing the least concern was Nancy; she stood against the kitchen table her arms folded on her stomach and a silly smile flicking her face.

The sight of her thus was too much for Mary Ellen. She darted back into the kitchen, and taking Nancy by the shoulders, pushed her through the front room and out into the street shouting, 'Go on! Go on, you young trollop, you! And don't darken these doors again!'

Back in the kitchen she tried once more to push past Shane, for blood was flowing freely now. It was running from John's mouth and from Dominic's eyebrow, and their shirts were wet with it.

Peggy Flaherty's voice came from the upstairs window, crying, 'Stop it! Stop it, you lads! Stop it, the pair of you. John, where's your sense gone? Do you want to break your mother's heart? Behave like a gentleman, can't you! Oh, if only Mr Flaherty was alive!'

Mary Ellen, through Shane's arm, could see the dark bulk of Peggy hanging half out of the window.

Peggy cried down to her: 'Mary Ellen, are you there? Will I throw some slops over them?'

Mary Ellen made no answer, for she was now staring at the lass from next door. Christine had come into the suffused light, paused for a moment near the battling figures, then walked right between them.

John's fist was travelling towards Dominic's body, and Mary Ellen closed her eyes tightly, for the girl's face, as she confronted John, was in line with it.

Only the sound of gasping breaths came to Mary Ellen. She opened her eyes slowly, and they were apart, with the girl standing untouched between them.

Christine lifted her hands and pushed John towards the kitchen door, where Mary Ellen pulled him over the threshold.

Then Christine turned to Dominic. He was leaning against the washhouse wall now, wiping his face with his shirt sleeve. He paused and looked at her, and said pointedly, 'This is one time I'm fighting in the right.'

'Fighting was never in the right.'

'No? Huh!'–he spat out some blood, then went on wiping his face–'not even when your wonderful John gives Nancy Kelly a bairn?'

There was a rustle among the crowd about the yard door. The whispers linked, forming a wave; then broke again, as one person after another darted away into the blackness. . . . John O'Brien had given Nancy Kelly a bairn!

When John at last arrived at their meeting place, Mary wasn't there, and his feelings became a mixture of sick disappointment and relief . . . and relief because of the uncertainty of her reaction when she saw his face. She would, he knew, be full of sympathy, but would she think that he was indeed one of the 'Fighting O'Briens', fighting for fighting's sake?–he'd be unable to explain why he had fought. So he walked towards her house, keeping on the far side of the road, and when he came opposite the gate he stood well back in the shadow of a hedge, and waited, wondering what construction she had put on his non-appearance.

The house was lit up, and occasionally a shadow darkened the blinds, but the shadow could have belonged to anyone.

How long he stood there he did not know, but a clock somewhere in the distance, struck the hour, and he guessed it was nine o'clock. And as he was making up his mind to move away, the front door opened, and she was there, silhouetted against the light. But not alone; a man was with her, and from his thinness, John knew him to be Culbert.

John's nerves tensed as he watched them standing talking, and his teeth grated when he saw Culbert's hand take hers. But she remained still and Culbert moved away, and the door was closed.

After standing for a while longer, John walked slowly away. He was cold, and his eye was paining, and the whole of his face was stiff and sore. Now the import of Dominic's wild laughter rose to the fore of his mind again; and with it came a paralysing sense of fear. Fear was the least of John's emotions–he could not remember ever having known real fear; he had been scared, but being scared had no connection with this weakening feeling of fear. What if it got around, what Dominic had suggested? God! he couldn't stand it. Anyway, people wouldn't believe it. Him take Nancy Kelly! . . . But wouldn't they? The lot around the fifteen streets would accuse Jesus Christ himself of it, if they were in the mood to do so. At times, it would appear they were utterly devoid of reason or sense, the rumours they believed and passed on.

As he neared the corner of Fadden Street, the huddled, darker blur standing out against the wall told him the men were there. It was usual for them to gather at the corner and crack, and it was their voices which generally proclaimed them. But tonight they were quiet. And as he passed them he knew a mounting of his fear, which almost reached the point of terror when he realized the rumour was already let loose.

A figure stepped from the group and walked for a few steps by his side, then stopped. John stopped too, and the two men peered at each other.

'I want a word with you,' said Joe Kelly.

John did not answer him, for the fear was drying his mouth. He waited, and Joe seemed to be waiting too.

Then Joe brought out thickly, 'What have you got to say?'

'What about?' John parried.

'Come off it, you know bloody fine!'

John made a desperate effort to bring reason and calmness to the fore: 'Look, Joe,' he appealed to the little man, whose face, even through the darkness, conveyed its trouble to him, 'do you, for a moment, think I would do such a thing? For God's sake, man, have some sense! Nancy's always made a set for me because I've been kind to her. . . . What do you think I am? I mean no offence, Joe, but I'm not that hard up for a woman.'

'Then why did you take her up the country?'

'Take her up the country? Me?'

'Aye, you! And give her money. . . . You might be big, John O'Brien, but

I'm going to kick the guts out of you!'

Before Joe could spring to carry out his intention, John's hands gripped his shoulders and pinned him against the wall, while he kept his body bent out of reach of Joe's legs.

'Listen here, Joe Kelly: if there's any guts to be kicked out, I can do a bit of it myself. But before we start that, let's get this straight. The whole thing's a pack of damned lies from beginning to end. You bring me the one that saw me up the country with Nancy; and let's get Nancy herself and ask her.'

'That's the ticket,' said a voice from the group of men; 'give him a fair crack o' the whip. I told you you were up the pole to believe it. Now, if it had been the other big sod . . .'

Another voice was added to that of the first: 'Aye, Joe. . . . Ask your lass, and get Bella Flabbygob to face him and tell him herself.'

Joe's writhing body was stilled. 'All right then,' he growled. 'If you've got the face, come and clear yourself.'

John, walking swiftly and tensely by Joe's side, said, 'I don't need to have any face, I've done nothing that I'm ashamed of.'

Thrusting open his back door, Joe cried to the startled Hannah, 'Get her up!'

After one bewildered glance towards John, Hannah went into the bedroom, and in a few minutes returned, pushing Nancy, half awake, before her.

Nancy had a coat about her shoulders, and her long thick legs stuck out, like mottled props, below her short nightgown. Her feet were bare and not very clean, and the whole picture of her was revolting to John. . . . That anyone should imagine he could touch a thing like this! The thought made him angry, and momentarily banished his fear. He confronted Nancy.

'Look, Nancy. Have I ever taken you up the country?'

Still only half awake, she blinked at him.

'Have I?' he persisted.

'No, John.'

John cast a quick glance at Joe.

'Now,' he went on, 'have I ever given you money?'

She blinked again. She was a child once more; her new-found self was lost in bewilderment and sleep. 'Yes,' she answered simply.

Joe scraped his feet on the floor as John said, 'Listen carefully now. When did I give you the money?'

She thought a while, then said, 'Up Simonside.'

They all stood silent. Simonside was the country. It was the place for lovers and courting. Hannah drew in her breath, and Joe bit out, 'Want to know any more?'

'Yes. How much did I give you?' John bent towards Nancy.

'Threepence.'

'And what did I give it to you for?'

'For being a good girl.'

Joe snorted and John turned on him. 'I know the night I gave it to her. I met her crying under the arches. Annie had left her in the market and she hadn't her tram fare. She was afraid to stand outside the bar, and I put her on the tram, and'–the face of Bella Bradley peering at him came back to John–'Bella Bradley was on that tram. It was her who put this into your head.'

'I've no use for that 'un,' Joe said, indicating Bella with a lift of his eyes towards the ceiling, 'but she said she saw you coming down the Simonside bank with her.'

'How the hell could she,' burst out John, 'if she was in the tram and it black dark!'

Joe had no answer to this. He turned from John to Nancy, his look indicating his detestation. Then he flung a question at her that made Hannah cry out and John wince.

Nancy stared back at her father, unmoved by the question itself. She was wide awake now, and she wriggled and flung her head to the side with a new defiance. As Joe, all restraint gone, went to hit her, she screamed and jumped aside like a grotesque animal.

Hannah caught her husband's arm, crying, 'Leave her be, man!'

Then Joe, Hannah and John were struck speechless, for Nancy, standing in the corner, her coat lying at her feet, her long neck thrust forward, was yelling at Joe: 'Leave me alone . . . see, you! You hit me if you dare, see! I'm gonna have a bairn, I am, an' be married. . . . Yes, I am. I'm gonna be married when the bairn's born I am.' She tugged her tight nightgown back and forward around her hips, then turned her face towards John: 'Aren't I, John?'

John stood gazing at her; he was dumb and sick. Had she remained the half imbecile child he could have dealt with her, but this new Nancy, full of craft and cunning, filled him with horror. When she came boldly towards him, her hand outstretched, he yelled at her, 'Take your hands off me!' and like someone possessed, he rushed from the house and started to run, with Joe's voice bellowing after him, 'You won't get off with it like that!'

Chapter Ten

Mary Llewellyn

Her home had always appeared a place of warmth and comfort to Mary, but not up to now had she looked upon it as one of the tentacles of her mother's possessiveness. Mary knew that, in her gentle way, her mother clung like a leech and sucked at one's individuality; and one of her sucking tentacles was the creating of comfort . . . good food, warmth, even the seductive fire in one's bedroom.

After Mary's victory of claiming a room to herself the creature comforts were diminished for a time; if she wanted a fire in this room she had to light it. Yet after a while, Beatrice Llewellyn saw that by pandering to her daughter's ridiculous idea of privacy, a new tentacle could be affixed. But since New Year's Eve, much to Mary's discomfort, this tentacle had been released. No fire had been lit in the sitting-room for a fortnight, let alone in the bedroom, and Mary's inquiry of Phyllis had been answered by, 'The mistress says there are fires in the drawing-room and dining-room, Miss Mary.'

For the first week of the new year it had not irked her, for her evenings were spent with John; and the fireless room was merely something that showed up her mother's pettiness. But for six days now she had seen John only once, and that under such circumstances, she would rather not have seen him at all. Added to this, the striking cold of her fireless rooms seemed to have brought her up against life with a vengeance.

Last night, after having gone fruitlessly to their meeting place, she wrote John a letter . . . a letter bare of pride. She had thrown pride over from the first night he failed to keep their appointment, for each dinner-time since, she had taken a roundabout way home, walking slowly through the arches, hoping against hope to meet him. Then today she saw him; but unfortunately only after she had met her mother and father almost at the dock gates. After her father's kindly greeting and her mother's fixed stare, they were walking on abreast, past the gates themselves, when John came out. His abrupt stopping brought them all to a halt; but before she even had time to speak, he was gone, across the road and into the Jarrow tram.

It was only by using all her control that she did not follow him. In a brief moment of meeting she could see something was wrong. He was in trouble, and he had been fighting. His eye was discoloured, and there was a scar across his lip. But it was the look in his eyes that shocked her. They were not the brown, kindly eyes of her John, they look haunted . . . even frightened.

It was disastrous that her mother should see him like this. Mary knew, by her mother's tilted chin and stiff profile, that she recognized him and was showing her disgust. And her father's repeated short coughs spoke, too, of his embarrassment.

Mary stood now in her bedroom, recalling the incident. There was another hour and a half before she would know if her letter had broken this estrangement for which she could find no cause. She pulled her fur coat tighter about her as she sat down by the window and looked out into the black garden. If he did not come tonight what would she do? Her life seemed barren and futile without him, and he had toppled her standards overboard. Up to a few months ago she was sure she knew what she wanted from life: culture, travel, and of course a lovely home. It was true she had never loved Gilbert Culbert, but it was his profession, she thought, had weighed her feelings against him; for she could not see herself going out to work when married, and thirty-seven shillings a week wasn't going to enable her to do the things she had planned, although she knew if she were to make this match there would be considerable help forthcoming from her mother. Yet, compared with John, Culbert was a man of means. But here she was, willing to forgo everything she valued for this man, who would hardly be able to feed her, as her father had so strongly pointed out, apart from supporting her in the smallest comfort.

She was helpless before the power of her feeling. No clear thinking would touch it. Nor did she want it to be touched, for she realized she had found something given to few, a love strong enough to defy convention. And not in the ordinary way; but to defy convention by living under its nose. For that's what it would mean if she, Mary Llewellyn, the boat-builder's daughter, married John O'Brien, the docker.

'Miss Mary!'

Mary started. 'Yes?'

'Your mother says she wants . . . she would like to see you in the drawing-room.'

'Very well.'

Mary turned from Phyllis, whose bright eyes were greedy for more scandal. Mary guessed her own doings were the high spot of conversation in the kitchen, and knew that, because she was associating with one whom they considered to be below their class, she was unworthy of their respect. It showed covertly in their manner, and she upbraided herself for being hurt by it. For this, she told herself as she went downstairs, was nothing to what she would have to put up with–she must get used to scorn, and the scorn of the poor was scorn indeed.

Her mother was sitting in her wing chair to one side of the large log fire, the heat of which met Mary as she entered the room. Beatrice Llewellyn looked smaller and younger and more fragile at this moment than ever before.

'You wanted me?' Mary halted in the centre of the room.

'Yes.' Beatrice Llewellyn paused, adjusted the lace cover on the arm of her chair, then went on, 'I would just like to ask you, Mary, to conform to the rules of this house if it is your intention to stay in it.'

Mary remained silent; it was like the ultimatum to a lodger.

'You know your meals are served in the dining-room! If you do not deign to have them there with us, then I'm afraid you'll have to eat out, for I'm not having them taken to your room.'

Anyone but Mary would have been deceived by her mother's tone into thinking that behind its evenness lay forbearance and toleration, but to Mary its studied calmness, in itself, was a danger signal.

'Is that all you wanted me for?' she asked.

'No, it is not all I wanted you for.' Beatrice Llewellyn lifted her eyes from the contemplation of the lace cover and looked straight at her daughter. 'You astound me, Mary. I cannot begin to understand you. . . .'

'No?' Mary raised her eyebrows slightly and waited.

'I can't think that one, even with your liberal tastes, can have sunk so low as to continue to associate with a man who is the father of an imbecile girl's child!'

The words glanced off the surface of Mary's mind. She was prepared to hear something against John, she hadn't thought her mother would speak otherwise, and at this moment she was feeling sick with cold and worry; so until, like a boomerang, their meaning rebounded back at her she just continued to return her mother's stare. There was a cause then for the six empty nights and his avoidance of her at dinner time . . . there was a reason; someone was going to have a baby by him.

What!–her mind jumped clear of its numbness–her John who was clean and loving and kind, whose love, so full of desire, was yet restrained, whose hands, even in their loving, were not the probing, groping hands of Gilbert . . . her John going to father a what!

She repeated aloud, 'What! What did you say?'

'You heard what I said.'

'And you expect me to believe you?'

'No'–her mother's voice took on a note of resignation–'No, all Tyneside could believe it, but not you. You are so obsessed by that . . . that man, that individual with the brutalized, battered face, whose licentiousness drives him to take a poor imbecile . . .'

'Be quiet! How dare you!'

'Don't speak to me like that, Mary!'

'I will! You sit there taking a man's character away . . . damning him . . . you, who know nothing . . .!'

'I take his character away! Can a man have any character who would touch that dreadful Kelly girl?'

'Kelly? You mean Nancy Kelly?'

'Yes, I mean Nancy Kelly.'

'You're mad! No man would . . . would go with that girl.'

'She's going to have a child, and you don't for a moment imagine it's an immaculate conception, do you?' Her mother was being unconsciously funny; if only the implications for John were not so terrible Mary would have laughed.

There was scorn in her mother's smile and maliciousness in her voice when she said, 'His exalted position of being a gaffer is in jeopardy too, I understand. For even certain dock men have standards of morals.'

The desire of her mother to hurt her was so palpably evident that Mary was stung to reply, 'Yes, for your sake, I should hope so, seeing that my father worked in the docks until he was twenty. You seem to forget that, don't you. I, in my way, am doing exactly what you did . . . taking up with a dock worker.'

Beatrice Llewellyn rose swiftly from her chair–she was no longer calm; Mary had touched a vulnerable spot, and she hated to be reminded that her prosperous husband had ever been other than what he was now. 'There's a coarseness in you, Mary, that disgusts me,' she said sibilantly. 'Your father was never a dock worker; he was apprenticed to a trade, as you well know.'

'What difference does it make?' Mary found she wanted to argue, to keep talking, so that she would not have to think.

But her mother ended the interview by leaving the room. She walked past Mary, her face tight and her blue eyes flashing with vexation, causing the air seemingly to vibrate with her displeasure. Mary did not move–she stood nervously tapping her lips with her fingers. . . . Nancy Kelly was going to have a child . . . that dreadful-looking girl who was no more than a child herself. And they were saying John was responsible. So that was why he looked as he did. And that, too, was why he had been fighting. How had he come to be accused of such a thing?

The old saying: There's no smoke without fire, came to her. But she refuted it with her mind and body; and she swung round and rushed upstairs. Yet the thought persisted; why had he been named?

Mary reached their meeting place half an hour before the appointed time. In the darkness of the lane she waited, each moment dragging itself out into seeming hours, filled with dread and anxiety. Twice she heard footsteps on the main road, but they didn't turn into the lane.

When at last she heard the heavy tread of feet coming towards her, she pressed back into the hedge, fearing lest it was not him. But as the dark bulk drew to a halt, she whispered softly, 'John.'

No answer came to her, and she moved slowly forward, and again she said, 'John.'

In the centre of the lane, he stood out against the starlit night, and she could feel the tense unhappiness holding him down. She reached out her hands and again spoke his name. This time he answered her. His arms went about her, and she was lifted into his embrace and held tightly against him in an unhappy silence. He did not kiss her, but bent his head and buried it against her neck; and his mental anguish engulfed her.

'What is it, my dear?' She purposely asked the question, for she felt he must tell her himself, and in the telling perhaps the strain would ease.

But he said nothing. And so they stood, wrapped close in an embrace that was full of questioning and stress. Then, as if his words had journeyed through many doors before finding a way out and were now tremulous in their release, he asked, 'Mary . . . would you marry me if I had enough money?'

The proposal was so unexpected–it was the last thing she had thought of hearing at this moment. She had imagined he would give some reason for their separation, if not speak of this dreadful other thing. For perhaps a second she remained still. Then she gently took his head between her hands and raised it. His face was indistinguishable in the darkness, but so well did she know each feature that his expression seemed at this moment to be outlined in light.

'Oh, my dear, I'd marry you now, just as you are.'

The question of Nancy Kelly flashed like a falling star across her mind, only to disappear into nothingness; its dreadful import could not possibly touch this man.

'No, no. Never that.' John's arms fell from her, but she held his face tightly, saying, 'Why not, my darling? Why not?'

'Because'–his head moved restlessly between her hands–'I'll never take you while I'm in the docks.'

'But, my dear . . .'

'It's no use.'

He gently released his face from her hands, and held them tightly: 'I couldn't do it. . . . Mary, I'm going away. Will you wait for me?'

'Where are you going?'

'America.'

'America! But John! Oh, my dear'–she pulled him towards her–'I can't let you go . . . not all that way, not without me. . . . John, take me with you. Let's start together'–she was pleading as if for her very life–'if we are together nothing matters.' She had her arms about him now, and he stood still within their circle, steeling himself against her offer, which for the moment had lifted him out of the terrifying depths of despair and revulsion to life that had almost overwhelmed him during these past few days, and which during that one brief moment had erased the picture of Nancy Kelly from his mind, so that he could no longer see her waiting for him at the corner of the street, or watching the house from her door or front window. His whole life had been coloured darkly by her. He would see her face reflected in the expression of the dock men's covert glances and in the too friendly overtures of a section of the men, who wanted him to know they didn't believe the rumour. The house that, during the holidays took on a semblance of happiness, was now a place of dread, and his mother seemed to have become bent under the load of it. Time and again he had found her watching Nancy from behind the curtains as she, in her turn, watched the house. . . . What would his mother do when he was gone?

He jerked his head as if to throw off this additional worry, and answered Mary, rejecting her offer, as he knew he must, but crying out internally at the necessity that drove him to it: 'No, it wouldn't work. I've got to go there and get a start, and make enough money to set up.'

The term set up and all that it implied lifted him back to a week ago, when there was no fear in his life, only the ecstatic feeling of loving her. He pulled her to him blindly and kissed her, and so was lost for a time, until she murmured, 'John . . . listen to me. Now don't get wild at what I'm going to say. But I've got a little money . . . only a little'–she felt his withdrawal and clung on to him–'Listen, darling, don't be foolish. It isn't much, for I've never bothered to save. It's what my grandfather left me. There's two hundred pounds. We could . . .'

'Mary . . . do you love me enough to wait a year, perhaps two?'

'It was as if she had never made her offer. She answered, 'Yes . . . for as long as you wish.'

'That's all right then.'

He kissed her again. Then said, 'I've been making inquiries; I'm going as soon as I can. I went up to see some people called Hogan in Jarrow last night. They've told me what to do.'

'Oh, John'–the huskiness of her voice was deepened by the catch of tears–'why. . .why all this rush?' And as she asked the question, Nancy Kelly came back into her mind. It was because of this he was going more than anything else. He was running away.

'John, what is it? What's worrying you? Tell me.'

He remained quiet, and she felt the stiffening of his body again. Then he put her thoughts into his own words: 'I'm running away. . . . I've been accused of something, and I can't face it. . . . Mary'–the muscles of his arms hardened against her soft flesh–'if you heard something bad about me would you believe it? I can't prove to you that I'm innocent, I can only tell you I am. . . . It's about . . . I'm . . .' He stopped and a shiver passed through his body. He could not bring himself to say, 'I'm accused of giving Nancy Kelly a bairn,' nor could he say, 'I'm as innocent as Christ himself, for I've never had a woman; nor will have until I have you, be it in two years or twenty.'

The cold dark bleakness of the night pressed down on them. They stood slightly apart, and Mary waited for him to go on and voice his misery. But he remained silent. The silence seemed to fill the lane and to widen the distance between them. At last she could bear it no longer, for now she was with him she knew without doubt that he was incapable of committing that of which he was accused, and she cried out, 'You would never do anything bad. Never! Oh, my dear, don't let this thing cause you to make hasty decisions. Don't let it drive you away. Stay and see it out.'

'You don't know what it is they are saying.'

'Yes, I do. I know all about it.'

The silence fell on them again, softly now, filled with reverence.

She knew all about it and she was here! He whispered, 'You know about Nancy Kelly?'

'Yes.'

The wonder of her love and faith coursed like a mountain stream through him, sweeping before it the fear and dread that had been intensified by the thought of her revulsion towards him should the rumour ever reach her. Her name burst from him on a broken laugh that could scarcely be identified from a sob.

She was in his arms, crushed tightly against him, and he was pouring words over her: 'Nothing matters now. I can face anything. I'll make money. We'll start a new life together. . . . Oh, Mary, my love, I'm as innocent of what they say as . . . as Katie is. I've always been sorry for the girl. I used to mind her when she was a bairn, and she would come to me when she was frightened. . . . She's changed; she's different now. But somehow, I think she's still frightened, and that's why she's made a dead set for me. And it's made them think. . . . But what does it matter now? Nothing matters, only you. We'll start life in a new land; and you'll teach me, as you were going to, and make a new man of me.'

She tightened her arms about him. . . . She teach him! What could she teach him but the superficialities, whereas he could teach her all there was to know of life.

Chapter Eleven

Ask and Ye Shall Receive

The February storm had raged for three days, during which hail, snow and rain was driven against the houses with such force as to almost penetrate the walls. It succeeded through many windows, and some of the people found it as dangerous to stay indoors as to go out and risk the flying slates and toppling chimney pots. But today the storm was lashing itself out. The streets were dry and the sun shone fitfully through the racing clouds.

It shone now on Nancy standing in her doorway. It showed her up vividly to Mary Ellen as she watched from behind her curtains. For the past three days Mary Ellen had seen Nancy only dimly, and appearing more grotesque than ever through the two rain-streaked windows. But now, there she was, as vivid as the picture that was seared on Mary Ellen's mind.

The girl, Mary Ellen knew, was possessed of a devil. This was the only way to account for her laying the blame of the bairn on John without actually saying so, and for her turning on Hannah and standing up to Joe. Mary Ellen knew that she, too, had become possessed of a devil. It entered into her the night Dominic and John fought, and when John stayed out all night, wandering the streets, after Joe Kelly had followed him into the house, demanding to know what he was going to do about supporting Nancy. The devil had frightened Mary Ellen, for he urged her to do Nancy a physical injury, and she prayed constantly to be relieved of all temptation. But from the night her lad told her he was going to America, she prayed no more, and the devil took full possession of her. She watched Nancy at every available moment, and there were times when she actually lifted the sneck of the front door with the intention of making a dash at the girl and tearing her limb from limb.

Nancy stood now scratching her head. She was doing it systematically, working over first one section then another; and Mary Ellen wondered for the countless time how anyone in their right senses could imagine her lad touching that thing. . . . But they not only imagined it, they voiced it. Since Bella Bradley had set the ball rolling, at least half the fifteen streets would swear to having seen John with Nancy Kelly in some questionable place.

She could have borne it all, Mary Ellen thought if only it wasn't driving her lad away. What would she do without him? The day he left the house, it would be as if she were laying him in his coffin, for she would never see him again. It was all right him saying he would send her money . . . he'd want all his money if he was going to marry that lass. And anyway, she didn't want money, she only wanted him. What would life be like when, cooking, washing and mending, she wasn't doing it for him?

She moved from the window and leaned against the wall, and pressed her nose tightly between finger and thumb, meanwhile taking great gulps of air–she mustn't start crying now, it was close on twelve o'clock, and John and Shane would be in soon, it being Saturday. Dominic was already in, sitting over the fire, picking his toes.

In spite of her efforts, tears started to flow. Unless Dominic got that job in Liverpool she'd be left with him and his beastly ways. John never sat over the fire, picking his toes . . . he washed his feet in the scullery. But not Dominic; he'd sit picking at the hard skin on the soles of his feet, or lifting the dirt from his toenails with his fingernails. There was nothing so ugly, Mary Ellen thought, as feet, and none so repulsive as Dominic's, big and broad and well-shaped as they were. She knew, with an overpowering certainty, that once John was gone and she was left to suffer Dominic, the devil would have his way. And there would be no door standing between her and Dominic, as there was between her and Nancy, acting as a deterrent to her uplifted hand. And the devil alone knew what she would have in her uplifted hand. Oh, if only her lad wasn't going to that America. Oh, God, if only something would happen to prevent him! She groaned and rocked her body. . . . Ask and Ye Shall Receive. Yes, but there were so many things she had asked of God, and had she ever received them? Perhaps she hadn't asked properly. Or she may not have wanted them as she wanted this one thing. If there was only somewhere she could be alone and kneel down, she'd pray to Him and ask Him. But the minutes alone were few and far between, especially at the week-end. . . . But she was alone now. She moved swiftly to the room door and closed it. Self-consciously she knelt down close by it so that she wouldn't be taken unawares if Dominic made to enter, and should anyone happen to glance in the window through the narrow aperture of the curtains it would look as if she were scrubbing.

Almighty God, she began, Almighty Lord of Heaven and earth, grant me this one prayer, and I swear unto You that never until the day I die will I miss Mass. Almighty and powerful God, grant me this plea. . . . She did not at once voice the plea, even mentally, but searched about in her mind for other words to denote power with which to adorn the name of God. But she could think only of Great and Almighty. She discarded the set prayers–she wanted something more powerful with which to contact Him. So she began again . . . Great and Almighty God, Ruler of our lives, You who can do all things, do this for me I beseech Thee . . . don't let my lad go to America. Make something happen to stop him. Only You can do this, Almighty God . . . only You.

Her joined hands were pressed tightly between her breasts, and her chin above them quivered with emotion. As she rose trembling from her knees, Katie's voice called from the scullery, 'Ma! Ma, I want you.'

Mary Ellen smoothed down her hair and rubbed her face over with a corner of her apron before going into the kitchen. She knew Katie must have seen Dominic and would not pass him, fearing lest his fingers were pushed beneath her nose.

Katie was standing in the scullery, trying to tidy her wind-blown hair before replacing her hat.

'What is it, hinny?' Mary Ellen asked heavily.

Katie whispered, 'Sh!' and pointed towards the kitchen. She pulled the door to, before going on in hushed tones, 'I just wanted to tell you I'm going to the slipway with Christine.'

'The slipway?' said Mary Ellen. And Katie again cautioned her. 'Sh! ma.'

'What are you going to do there?' asked Mary Ellen softly.

'The boat's there . . . Mr Bracken had it fetched from the quay corner this morning on a cart. It's all painted up. David did it all himself. Oh, it looks lovely, ma.'

'It's too windy, hinny, you'll get blown off the wall.'

'I won't go on the wall, ma. The boat won't be on the wall'–Katie chuckled at her mother's ignorance–'it'll be in the water!'

After a pause during which Mary Ellen adjusted Katie's hat, she asked, 'Who'll be there?'

'Only Christine and David.'

'Not Mr Bracken?'

'No.'

'Then you'd better not go, hinny. There should be no messing around with boats unless a man's knocking about.'

'But Christine knows all about boats . . . she can row! But anyway, ma, it's tied up, and Christine's not going out in it, she says it's too windy. She says, maybe the morrow if the wind goes down we'll have a sail . . . there's a sail in it too, ma!' She looked up at her mother with a mischievous smile. 'We'll take you out for a sail, ma . . . right to where the big ships are. And the boat'll rock, and you'll be sick.'

The picture of her mother being seasick tickled Katie, and she leaned against her, and put her arms round her mother's ample waist, and shook with laughter as she moved her from side to side, imitating the rocking of a boat.

'Stop it, hinny!' Mary Ellen felt far from laughter, but she smiled at this canny bairn of hers, and she had the desire to fondle her. She took off Katie's hat again and reached for the broken comb lying on the scullery window-sill, and began to comb the top of her plaits.

Katie made a protest, 'Ma, Christine's waiting!' But she still leaned against her mother, and the pressure of her arms tightened about her.

When Mary Ellen replaced the hat she patted Katie's cheek. Then, awkwardly, she stooped and kissed her. Katie's arms came up swiftly about her neck, and she returned the kiss with an ardour that seemed strange in one so young. Kissing was an uncommon ritual in the house, and Mary Ellen said, 'There, there. Now off you go.'

But although she told Katie to go, she still held on to her, buttoning her coat, lifting her plaits from off her shoulders, and yet again straightening her hat. When at last she closed the door after Katie, she stood for a time thinking of her, and the thoughts brought her a modicum of comfort . . . she'd always have Katie. For years and years yet she'd have Katie, and they'd cleave together even more so when John was gone. . . . That was another thing . . . Katie had to be told that John was going. What would her reactions be, for John was to her as a god?

A new fear entered into Mary Ellen. . . . Would it create an aim in Katie's life, and that aim to be to go to America to join John? She shook herself. This was going too far . . . this is what came of thinking. . . . Let God's will be done.

She steeled herself to go into the kitchen and to the oven where a hot-pot was cooking, for Dominic would still be on with his poking–she knew he prolonged it merely to tantalize her. But when she entered the kitchen he wasn't there; and further to her surprise, he came out of the bedroom, pulling on his old mackintosh. He had changed his trousers and was wearing his good boots. And he passed her without a word and went out, slamming the door after him.

Where was he off to in such a hurry? Surely he couldn't have heard what Katie said. If he did hear, he was off now to corner the lass at the slipway. It was quiet there, and nobody to stop him . . . only Katie. Well, Katie was as good as any.

Dominic's chase of Christine had aroused little interest in Mary Ellen of late. Under other circumstances the fact that Peter Bracken had forbidden him the house would perhaps have aroused in her a feeling of shame that a son of hers should have acted in a way to merit such treatment. At times, she did wonder at Dominic's persistence, and wondered too what it was about the lass that made him half demented for her. These past few weeks he had been drinking more than he had done since the Brackens came to live next door; not getting blind drunk, but just enough to arouse his temper and make him more detestable still. He was close on that stage now, having spent the best part of the morning in the bars.

Shane came in, and to her surprise spoke first.

'Lashing itself out,' he said gruffly.

It was some time before she answered, 'Yes, and about time too.' There was a change in Shane that bewildered her; he had almost dropped the drink, and he sat with her at nights instead of going to the corner. It began, she felt, when she was ill . . . or was it when John was made the gaffer? She knew that in his own way Shane was proud of that. And the change was more evident still since this trouble of John's. She felt dimly that he was trying to comfort her for what she was suffering on account of the lad, and dimly also, she felt a bigness in him for doing this, for it was John who had the affection that should have been his.

'Will you have it now or wait for John?' she asked, indicating the dinner.

'I'll wait.'

It was strange that she should ask him this and that he should comply. Not so long ago he would have bellowed, 'Who the hell's boss, him or me?'

When John came in she did not glance towards him, for she knew how he would look–his face would be straight and lean; the flesh had dropped from the bones these past weeks; the brown of his eyes would be darker, and in their depths would be a look she could not bear to see.

Mary Ellen's heart lifted towards Shane when, seated at the table, he said to John, 'We got her out in time all right, didn't we?' He was referring to the unloading, and her emotion almost choked Mary Ellen as she realized that her husband was trying to get on a friendly footing with his son; for never before could she remember him speaking in such a way, not only acknowledging John as an equal, but as his superior . . . it was how a man spoke to his gaffer; it was also how a father tried to convey his faith in his son.

John looked hard at Shane, then said quietly, 'You did that.'

They ate on in silence, and Mary Ellen went into the scullery to try to suppress the choking in her throat. As she stood, her hands pressed tightly against her neck, Molly's voice came screaming back from the back lane. 'Ma! Oh, ma! . . . Ma!'

What could she do with that lass? Would she never grow up?

'Ma! Ma!' Molly's voice came nearer.

Was she mad, screaming like that! By, she'd box her lugs for when she got her inside.

Molly's cries effectively suppressed Mary Ellen's emotion, and she pulled open the back door with an angry jerk . . . She'd give it to her; she'd swipe the hunger off her!

'Ma! Oh, ma!' Molly tore up the backyard and flung herself on her mother, ignoring the upraised hand: 'Ma! it's Katie . . . Katie and Christine.'

She stopped and gasped for breath as Mary Ellen gripped her shoulders.

'What's happened?' Mary Ellen asked with strange quietness; then called over her shoulder, 'John!'

As John reached the door Molly was gasping out, 'They're in the boat; they haven't any oars. . . . It's going round and round down the gut. It was our Dominic; he tried to get in the boat with Christine, and she pushed him back and Katie loosened the rope . . . I was behind the railings watching. Katie wouldn't let me go with her, but I sneaked down, and I saw our Dominic come. Oh, ma! and David's screaming in the slipway!'

John was running down the yard with Shane at his heels, calling, 'Make straight for the slacks; don't go down the slipway, it'll be in the main gut by now.'

Mary Ellen, with Molly at her side, followed them, whispering as she ran, 'What is this now? What has come upon us now?'

On the main road, passers-by stopped and gaped at the two great men in shirt sleeves tearing along as if the devil was after them, the old man behind the younger one, and the little woman and the lass behind the old man.

Someone called, 'What's up? Is it a fire?' But the running men took no heed, and one after another, the passers-by appealed to the woman and girl. And sometimes the girl answered, 'It's me sister . . . she's in a boat an' being carried down the gut.'

Children tacked themselves on to Mary Ellen and Molly, and men turned in their tracks to run back down the road towards the slacks.

When John came to the open space of the slacks his heart almost stopped. Without looking towards the gut he knew the boat was there, for the bank was lined with people. At this end of the slacks was the double tram line, where one tramcar had to wait for the others to pass. They were both standing empty, and their drivers were calling to people, 'We'll have to go'; but none of the passengers attempted to leave the bank.

As John ran on down the pavement towards the middle of the slacks where the gangway of timbers led from the bank to the edge of the mud, he had to push his way through the people pouring out from the streets known as the New Buildings that faced a part of the slacks. He thrust at them with his arms, knocking them aside and calling forth hot exclamations. Those standing on the gangway jumped clear of him, and he took the timbers four at a time. The noise from the bank died down and there was only the wind, on which was borne thin wails, and the squelch of the water between the timbers beneath his pounding feet. Automatically he paused at the cabin, which was mounted on a platform of lashed timbers in the centre of the great square, and grabbed up a long pole with a hook on its end that the timber man used for pulling the timbers together. Now the race was to reach the end of the timbers bordering the gut before the boat came abreast of him. He could see it was being held stationary at the moment; but by what he couldn't tell. If it was stuck on the other side of the gut on the great mud flat that extended to the river then it was almost a certainty that it would be sucked into this oozing morass.

Arrived at the end of the roped timbers, he had to take to the narrow planks that formed a precarious gangway to the gut. Here, he couldn't run, but had to pick his way over the green, slimy wood. The pole impeded him still further; and once he slipped and the water swirled about his thighs before he could pull himself up again. He had managed to retain his grip on the pole; and as he regained his footing a great 'Oh!' came from the bank. The sight of the boat speeding towards him lent wings of sureness to his feet, and within a matter of seconds reached the gut.

Clinging to the great post that was the last support of the foot timbers he shouted madly to the approaching boat, 'Grab the pole!' But the wind tore at his voice, carrying his words away from him and them.

The boat was now making swift circles; one second, he would see Katie's face over the gunwhale, her eyes staring in terror, the next he would be looking at the back of her head, her hat still on it. Christine was sitting in the middle of the boat, her arms still stretched taut, her hands gripping the sides in a pitifully vain endeavour to steady the tiny craft. She had seen John, for each time she fronted him her eyes held his for the second before they were torn away again.

It was not the wind that was driving the boat down the gut so much as the tide which was in full ebb; the locked waters between the floats of timbers were rushing madly back into the gut to meet the water draining from the mud flat beyond. Added to this, the suction of the cross channel, bordering the sawmill on the far side of the slacks, made the main gut a frothing boiling mass of water.

As the boat came abreast of him, John bellowed, to the very limit of his lungs, 'Catch the hook, Christine!'

Perhaps she heard him and was afraid to loosen her grip on the sides of the boat, or perhaps his voice became only part of the wind, for when he cast the crooked end of the pole towards the boat it fell close to it, and anyone on the alert could have grabbed it; but the fraction of time during which this could have happened was lost. The boat gave another mad turn and was away, past him. He saw Katie stand up. She seemed to stand perfectly straight and still, and he experienced the odd sensation that her face was floating to him . . . imagination! But it was not imagination when he heard her voice coming to him against the wind . . . 'John! Oh, John!'

The boat was now flung into the vortex of water where the channels of the gut crossed. It heaved and whirled. Then like a ball, held by some mighty hand, it became still, and John saw clearly two figures, their arms wound tightly about each other, crouched together; the wind was lifted, and the boat like a ball, was thrown up and over.

As John raised his arms to dive, two hands clawed at him and grabbed his belt. He half turned, screaming at the man behind him, but in wrenching himself free he overbalanced and toppled into the water. When his head broke the surface Peter Bracken grabbed his hair, and Peter's agonized voice screamed at him, 'It's no use! It's no use! They've gone. Don't make another.'

Two more hands stretched out and, gripping John's braces, hauled him on to the plank again, where he lay still with Peter Bracken bending over him. A great stillness was pressing down on him. It was the stillness of the dead of all time. In it there was no regret, no pondering, no desire, no recrimination, no feeling whatever; it was void, because it held no thought.

He looked towards the upturned boat; he watched Katie's hat, mounted on a crest of frothing bubbles, rise and fall, bobbing round and round the swirling boat, like the earth round the sun. Peter Bracken's tearing sobs came to him, and he did not wonder at them. Nor, when he turned towards him was he surprised to see a very old man. Time passed and the receding tide showed the shining mud about the planks on which they stood.

Men were walking cautiously along the planks now. First, Peter Bracken was helped back, and when the man said, 'Come, lad,' John allowed himself to be led back to the timbers, one going before him and one behind, steadying him as though he were a child.

The timbers were thick with men, soundless men. John walked alone now, and they made a path for him, they followed him to the bank, where the sobbing and wailing rose and fell like the waves of the wind.

Three people were standing apart at the foot of the bank, and when John stopped and looked at them, the stillness began to lift from him. The first impression to penetrate it was that his father had his tick back worse than ever. This was followed by the painful realization that his mother was a little old woman, and her not yet fifty, and that Molly would never be Katie. They looked at him, and the sobbing on the bank seemed hushed.

Then from the middle of a group of women, David's voice rose, crying, 'Christine! I want Christine!' and the stillness was lifted completely from John; and a name passed through his brain like a tearing flame . . . Dominic!

He threw up his head as if sniffing a scent, and his eyes swept the crowded bank from one end to the other. But from where he was standing below it, it was impossible to seek out anyone from the broken front line of the crowd.

A path was miraculously cleared for him when, turning suddenly from the agonized stare of his parents, he rushed up to the gangway. Across the main road was a rise of grassy ground bordering the New Buildings. He made straight for it. Now he was looking down on the congested road, and there in the far distance, on the very outskirts of the crowd he saw Dominic's head. It was hatless, and the fitful sunshine was turning the hair to gold. Whether Dominic had seen him John did not know, but as he tore along the comparatively clear ground Dominic's head disappeared; and when John reached the spot, Dominic was gone.

To a woman of the fifteen streets, John said only one word, 'Dominic?' and she pointed to the disused workmen's hall: 'He went round by the back of there, lad.'

When he reached the back of the hall John caught sight of Dominic . . . he was running across the middle of the field used by the chemical works as a dumping ground for their foul-smelling residue. The field was a mass of small mounds, and Dominic was leaping like a kangaroo over them.

As John raced over the field the distance between them lessened appreciably, and when he came out to the Cleveland Place road, there was Dominic, not twenty yards ahead, disappearing round the corner of the tram sheds.

They were both on the main road now, and the people struggling back to the fifteen streets called to John, 'Stop lad!' . . .' 'Give up, lad! . . .' 'What's done's done . . . think of your mother.' And when men's arms went out and tried to hold him he brushed them off like flies.

As they neared the fifteen streets Dominic was lost in the dense crowd awaiting news from those who had been down to the slacks. But John knew that Dominic would make for the stackyard at the top of the streets; here, in the maze of stacked timber he would hope to escape. He was right; he saw Dominic mount the wall and disappear.

John did not jump the wall, but stood on its top–his desire was teaching him cunning. He could not tell which way Dominic had taken, and once on the ground it would be like searching for a needle in a haystack; but up from here he could see Dominic's head as he moved between the stacks.

It was some minutes before John detected it, for Dominic's hair was in tone with the seasoning wood. Dominic had paused to glance behind, and John was off the wall, running swiftly and noiselessly, not in Dominic's direction but to the right of him. Dominic was making for the railway line at the end of the yard, and he'd get him there.

John reached the end of the stacks and waited, his eyes darting back and forth to the last three openings–it would be from one of these that Dominic would emerge. He came out of the middle one, running swiftly; and pulled up a few yards from John. His mouth was open and his jaw was moving from side to side. The brothers surveyed each other, John's eyes sending out streams of diabolical hate, while in Dominic's the hate was mixed with fear.

John did not say, 'You killed them . . . Katie and Christine, and now I'm going to kill you,' nor did Dominic say, 'It was an accident'; without any word they closed, and John, like a raving bull, smashed his fists into Dominic's face. From the start, Dominic was handicapped by his raincoat, but fear made him hit back desperately. It also made him aware that he could not stand up to the blows being levelled at him; so he used his knee. Bringing it up sharply, he rammed it into the lower part of John's stomach, and as John bent double Dominic ran back down the opening through which he had come, only to be brought to a stop by the cries of the men coming through the jumbled stacks. Assuming that the men were after him, he decided to carry out his first intention of taking to the railway. But when he turned once more there was John, at the opening of the stacks.

Blindly, Dominic rushed at him, using his fists and his feet; but it was as if John had set up a guard of flaying hammers, and soon all Dominic could do was to protect his face with his crossed forearms. He was pinned against a stack, and long after he ceased to fight John's fists pounded him, and he seemed to be kept on his feet only by the succession of lifting blows. At last, Dominic's knees gave way and he slid on to his side. John stood above him, gasping; then, using his foot, he pushed Dominic on to his back, and only then did he become aware of the crowd gathered about them.

Exclamations came from all sides. 'My God!' 'Leave him be, lad; he's had enough.' 'God Almighty, I think he's done for him!'

On hearing the last remark, John wiped the blood from his face with a sweep of his hand, and stared down at Dominic. . . . Was he dead? No, he mustn't be dead . . . Not this way, this easy way. He was going to die in the gut. He would drag him there, to the spot where they went down, where Katie's straw hat went round and round. The tide would be low, so he'd throw him down the steep incline of mud. He would be conscious and would claw at the mud as it slowly sucked him in. But–he looked up from Dominic and stared glassily at the faces of the men–they would stop him. Yes, if he attempted to do it now. Well, he would beat them; he would take this thing home. He moved Dominic again with his foot. . . . He wouldn't let him out of his sight, and in the night he'd get him to the gut. If he had to drag him every inch of the way he'd get him to the gut.

The exclamations came to him again, more shrill now, for the women had joined the men, after forcing open the stackyard gates.

'Oh, Jesus, have mercy on us! he's killed him. God Almighty, it'll be a hanging job!'

It'll be a hanging job! . . . The cry reached Mary Ellen, standing on the outskirts of the crowd, surrounded by a group of women, all with tear-stained faces, and all urging her, in one way or another, to return home. . . . 'You can do no good, Mary Ellen.'

'You must think of yourself and Shane.'

'Yes. Shane's lying back there bad, the shock's been too much for him. . . . Come on, lass.'

Mary Ellen stood quiet in the centre of them. She wasn't crying, there was no liquid left in her body to form tears. Her body was dry, it had been burnt up, and the flame was now going to her head. . . . If these women didn't get out of her way, she'd scream. She must get to her lad. He had killed

Dominic, so she must be with him. To her, this seemed to be the end of a long waiting–Katie was gone; Dominic was dead; and there was only John. . . . He had done what he said he would do–John always meant what he said. Now there was nothing else to wait for.

Mary Ellen knew that the agony within her was screaming to be set free. The agony was wide and deep, reaching into the bowels of the earth. In an odd way, she felt herself one with the earth . . . the dirt, the mire, and the richness. The scream of agony was tearing around in the dry emptiness of her body, and swiftly, in a spiral, it was mounting to her head. Once it was there, she would be set free, for when it escaped from her lips she would feel no more . . . at least, not with any feeling she would recognize; once she screamed, she would be changed for all time, for madness would possess her.

As her mind ran to meet the scream, she heard it. It seemed to lift her and the women from the ground. But it wasn't her scream; it was Nancy Kelly's. And it was mixed with laughter . . . the terrible laughter. The women covered their ears, but Mary Ellen stood listening. Then she thrust wildly at the bodies hemming her in, and forced her way through the men to the space where John stood, and Dominic lay with Nancy Kelly kneeling by him, pulling at his torn and blood-stained clothes and crying, 'Dominic! Dominic! Don't be dead! I've kept me mouth shut, Dominic . . . I did what you told me.' She pulled at him, trying to shake life into him again. 'Dominic, you must marry me when the bairn's born. . . . I've been a good girl, Dominic, I did what you told me.'

Nothing but her screeching voice could be heard; the crowd was as silent as the stacked piles of wood.

The blood pounded into John's head. Dominic, the father of the bairn! The swine! The god-damn, dirty swine! Reaching down, he grabbed Nancy and flung her to one side. Then he was on top of Dominic, crying out as he beat his fists into the inert, blood-covered face, 'You dirty swine! And you put the blame on . . .'

His words were lost as the men tore him aside. Fighting, they bore him to the ground, and so many held him that only his eyes were free to move.

As one of the men shouted to the others, 'look slippy there! Get him away can't yer!' John heaved in an effort to free himself. . . . If they got Dominic away they'd hide him. Why didn't he finish him off when he had the chance! He writhed and struggled until the uselessness of his efforts was borne upon him, and he suddenly became still. Well, wherever they took Dominic he'd find him! Oh, Katie! Katie!–he closed his eyes to shut out the men's faces as sorrow overwhelmed him.

When the men released him and he got to his feet, he saw his mother. She was picking at a button of her blouse, her eyes, dead in her white face, staring at him.

When he said, 'I'll find him,' she remained silent; then she turned and walked slowly away, and he followed her; and the crowd closed in behind, like a gigantic funeral procession.

Chapter Twelve

The Aftermath

There was no door in the fifteen streets that was closed to John; for three days he had walked in and out of the houses, into bedrooms, some tidy in their bareness, some a mass of jumbled old clothing and mattresses, and some indescribable in their squalor. He saw nothing of the conditions, he looked only for a concealed form; under beds, in cupboards, in rooms where the sick were lying, and where weary hands would reach out in a vain effort to give him comfort. He spoke to no one, and he trusted no one; he knew that in this time of trouble the people of the fifteen streets were united in one huge family to protect him, as they thought, from himself. So he did not search systematically, but after searching houses at the lower end, he would suddenly double back to the top or middle streets, and houses he had searched but a short time before would be gone over again. No harsh word met him; even if he stalked in on a family eating he would be greeted soothingly.

He had one assistant in his search: Peggy Flaherty. Her fat, wobbling body hugged by coats, she would accompany him at odd hours of the day, most of the time talking away at him: 'Never give up, John. We'll get him yet. By God! we will an' all. . . . He needn't run off with the idea he can escape you, can he lad? And he'll not get out of these buildings.'

Often, in his darting from one place to another, he would leave her behind; but she would be guided to the house where he was. And again she would tag along after him, nodding knowingly to the groups of people gathered in the street. Only at night did she leave him alone for any length of time, for then he paraded the main road.

John knew that Dominic would be in no fit condition for days and that it was practically impossible for him, up to now, to have made his escape by the stackyard, for since the breakthrough, the gates were doubly locked, and there remained only the wall as a means of an exit that way. So for two nights now he had watched from the main road. The night policeman, on his beat, would stop and talk to him, the darkness wiping away his officialdom: 'Is it worth it, lad? You know what will happen, don't you? You'll get time, if not the other. Anyway, how do you know he's not already gone? By what I hear, he's likely in hospital. If it hadn't been for your sister saying the little lass loosened the boat, we should have been on to him ourselves. And you can count yourself lucky, you know, one of us wasn't on the scene when you got at him. So don't look for trouble, lad, and get yourself home to bed.'

No words had penetrated John's mind since those spoken by the men when they were holding him; and it might have been that he did not hear this advice, for he made no reply. It was as though his mind, so packed with the weight of his sorrow and hate, could take in nothing more. During the first two days he did not actively think of Katie and Christine, nor yet of Mary, whom he felt to be part of his sorrow for all time, for she, in some strange way, was a partner in the guilt he was laying on himself. Because he had allowed the madness of his love to possess him, he ignored the danger in which Christine stood, and did nothing to protect her beyond ordering Katie to act as a buffer to Dominic's advances.

On this, the third day of the search, when the strain was telling on him, in the leaden weight of his limbs and his unsteady walk, and in his burning eyes that would close whenever he stood still for a moment, his mind, strangely enough, was beginning to sort itself out; thoughts were separating and presenting themselves, as it were, before him. He was standing leaning against the wall on the waste ground at the top of one of the streets, where he had paused for a moment during his search; and his hand moved over the three days' growth on his face. His body felt dirty, his inside empty, and his head light. But the thoughts came, one after another, isolated yet joined: I must stop sometime . . . if only they find them before they're carried out to sea; if I could see Katie once again it might not be so bad. Oh! Katie! Katie. . . . My father's done for, he'll not work again. Why am I not with my mother, she needs me? But she understands I've got to find him. She wants me to find him; she hates him as much as I do. . . . Why doesn't Peter Bracken look for him instead of yapping, 'Forgive us our trespasses'. Father O'Malley says Peter is the cause of all this, and if my mother and me had done as he commanded this would never have happened.

As if his thoughts had conjured up the priest, Father O'Malley, accompanied by Peggy Flaherty, appeared before him.

'Oh, there you are lad!' Peggy said. 'And here he is himself, father. . . . Away with you now!' she added to the children who were following them.

Father O'Malley confronted John: 'Come into the house,' he ordered, 'I want to talk to you.'

John blinked slowly and made no reply.

'Did you hear me?' demanded the priest.

And after a short silence, during which Father O'Malley waited, and the children sniffed, and a few women added themselves to the group at a respectful distance, the priest went on, 'This has got to stop! Who are you to take God's work into your hands? He will seek vengeance without your help. He has already shown you what He thinks of you going against His Holy Will–I cannot repeat too often, that had you kept that man Bracken from your house this state of affairs would never have come about.'

'It's hopeless,' Peggy Flaherty broke in. 'Time and again I've told him to give up his search. Oh! it's no use at all.' She proceeded to rattle on, in spite of the priest's gimlet eyes demanding her silence and John's blurred and bewildered stare as slowly the fact forced its way into his mind that she, and she alone, had urged him in his search.

There were murmers from the women: 'The priest's right. There's been no luck about the doors since that man Bracken came.'

'No! nor will there be!' Father O'Malley threw at them, effectually drowning the more considerate comment: 'Aye, but he's lost his lass too.'

'Come!' Father O'Malley commanded John.

John stood for a while longer . . . the priest and Peggy, and the women, were becoming blurred: he must rest and have something to eat if he intended going on. And so, in the eyes of the women and children, strength was added to the priest's power when John turned and obediently followed him. . . .

In contrast to John's ceaseless moving Mary Ellen sat almost immobile in the kitchen. At odd times she would go to the front room and attend to Shane; but she cooked nothing, nor cleaned, and, like John, she did not speak. And if at times she stared at Molly, her face did not show any surprise or wonderment at the change in this daughter of hers; for Molly was 'running the house'. She had screwed her plaits into a tight little bun at the back of her head and she wore her mother's holland apron, rolled up at the band. Overnight, Molly threw off her prolonged childhood; she was not now a girl, but a little woman. And she was spurred on by the praise of the neighbours: 'That's it hinny, you be your mother's right hand. You must take Katie's place now.' They talked as though Katie had been an elder sister.

Sometimes Molly would stand in the scullery and cry for Katie, while at the same time experiencing a feeling of relief that Katie was gone; for she would never have been needed had Katie still been here; and she was needed–they couldn't do without her. Why, she told herself, she was the only one in the house who hadn't lost her mind . . . except Mick; and he was no help, one way or the other. All he could do was to stand among awe-struck groups of lads, bragging that he knew where Dominic was hiding. . . . He didn't! She tucked her apron more firmly about her as she thought of that, of all the youngsters, she was the only one who really knew–Dominic was taken into a house at the top of the street when they carried him from the stackyard; but when John started to search they moved him. It was Peggy Flaherty's idea. They did it in the night and John hadn't found Dominic yet.

Thinking of John, Molly looked again at the screwed piece of paper in her palm. . . . After attending her father, the doctor had said, 'Look, my dear; take heed of what I'm going to say to you. Now do you think you can make your brother John some tea when he comes in and put these two tablets in without him seeing you? Be very careful of them; they are strong and will soon put him to sleep.'

She felt very proud it was she who was asked, for her mother was sitting there and he never asked her to do it. So there was a rising of excitement in Molly when she saw John and Father O'Malley coming up the backyard. She'd make the tea now, and offer a cup to the priest; and perhaps he would bless her and say she was a gift of God to her mother and them all at this time.

But the priest did not bless Molly, nor speak to Mary Ellen, but continued to talk to John, who was sitting with his elbows resting on the table and his hand covering his eyes.

Mary Ellen listened while she looked into the fire. Did he never tire? Would he never stop? Why did he persist that the Bracken man was accountable for all this, when it was she herself who had brought it about? Hadn't she prayed on her bended knees to God, and asked Him to make something happen to stop her lad from going to America? Well, He had made something happen . . . John would never go to America now. God was laughing out of the side of His mouth at her, she felt, and He was waiting for the climax between John and Dominic. The regret she felt in the stackyard when she knew that Dominic was not dead had soon changed to a dread that John would find him. By now, he must have been in every house in the place bar one, and if he were not half demented, that one would surely soon present itself to him. She cast her eyes towards the ceiling. . . . How much longer would Dominic remain there, hidden amongst the old furniture, the crocodile, and the poss tubs? She felt like his jailer, sitting outside the prison door, protecting him from a vengeance that haunted him. Had the hunter been anyone but John she would have let him in to do his work.

She turned to look at the priest drinking his cup of tea, and she wondered what she would do if he should propose that they kneel down and say the Rosary, for she was feeling hostile towards a God who had done this to her . . . using her own prayers to bring her to grief! Her eyes moved slowly to John–he was drinking his tea at one go. Soon he would be asleep, if Molly had done what the doctor told her. How long would he sleep? Long enough to get the other one away? And when would he go back to work?There would be only him to work now, for it was doubtful whether Shane would do a hand's turn again. . . . No. John would never now go to America.

She turned to the fire once more, and her old dominant self made an effort to oust the apathy. . . . Get up and see to Shane! it ordered. And that lass is wasting the food trying to cook it. You can't expect the neighbours to go on bringing stuff in. . . . But the apathy lay heavily on her and she allowed it to settle about her again as a protection.

The priest's voice was going on and on, and she was listening again. He was saying, 'You've been godless for years, and then you wonder why tribulation like this comes upon you. Can't you see, man, you can't defy God and get away with it; the ignoring of His Holy Mass Sunday after Sunday brings its tribulation. Make up your mind to turn over a new leaf. . . . Throw off all undesirable companions, and come to Mass.'

The priest's voice was falling to an almost sympathetic tone, it was quiet and even; and, as Mary Ellen listened, the wonder was born in her that he could be capable of such gentleness. As his voice became slower still, she turned to look at him. His eyes half closed, he was leaning across the table, for all the world like someone drunk, and he was emphasizing each laboured word with a wobbly shake of his finger.

Mary Ellen rose sharply to her feet, staring at the priest, her eyes wide and her mouth open. As Father O'Malley lifted his head and slowly comprehended her astonished look, he pulled himself upright. . . . What in the name of God had come upon him! This great, great tiredness. He shook his head in an endeavour to throw it off. Holy Mother of mothers, had he caught something? . . . But what could he have caught? Where had he been today? . . . The Flannagans . . . and the child with the suspected sleeping sickness. . . . In the name of God, it couldn't be! God wouldn't let his faithful servant suffer such a thing. But he had surely caught something–never before in his life had he felt so tired.

As Mary Ellen began to laugh, the priest rose slowly to his feet. These people! what were they? Ignorant hooligans, who could be driven to do the right thing only by fear. . . . Oh, God, don't let this thing fall upon me! he appealed. By the use of my strong will I will bring these people to You. . . . Only take this from me . . . that woman laughing! She was mad! . . . He must get home and to bed. He turned and staggered through the front room, with the terrified Molly behind him and Shane, half raised up in bed, following his erratic course in bewilderment and Mary Ellen's laughter becoming dimmer in his ears.

Mary Ellen had no power to stop the laughter; it swelled inside her, like the fire did a few days ago . . . or was it years? It shook every fibre of her body. She held one hand tightly against her stomach and a forearm across her wobbling breasts. John was standing over her, his glazed eyes blinking, and saying, 'Stop it, ma! Look; steady on.' He was holding her by the shoulders, and her wide-open mouth and grimacing face were doing more to bring back his mind to normality than all the reasoning in the world. It only wanted his mother to go mad to complete the whole thing. 'Look, be quiet!' His voice cracked hoarsely on the words.

'I . . . I can't, lad.' She moved her hands to her sides, where the pain of her laughter was tearing at her. 'The . . . the pills! she p-put them in the wrong . . . c-cup.'

John could not understand what her words were meant to imply. He shook her again: 'Ma! Ma! Stop it, I tell you!'

Shane's voice came weakly from the front room, calling, 'What is it? What is it out there? Why are you laughing? For God's sake!'

Slowly Mary Ellen's laughter subsided, and she gazed up into John's dirty, stubbly face, and for a second her own smoothed out into an expressionless mask before crumpling under the release of her tears; and her broken words, 'Oh, me bairn! me bonnie bairn!' cut through John, and completed his awakening.

He put his arms about her, holding her tightly, and her emotion rocked its way through him, and the burning of his eyes became unbearable. Like the rush of water when the main dock gates were opened to admit a ship, the tears came to him too. Silently flowing, they fell on Mary Ellen's brow; and their raining, more than her own, restored her, and set her once again in her rightful place as pivot of the house. And so, as always, they balanced each other.

Mary Ellen's body still shaking and her tears still falling, she drew away from John, and taking his arm, saying, 'Come, lad,' she led him to the bedroom. When he sat on the bedside she lifted up his feet, and as she loosened his boots he groaned and, turning his face into the pillow, sobbed, with the tearing, heart-rending sobs that only a man in sorrow can cry.

As Father Bailey hurried up Fadden Street he kept telling himself that this was not the time to be amused; tragedy had stalked this street, and was still doing so. But, nevertheless, only the darkness hid the twinkle in his eye and the quirk on his lips. The story the child Molly had brought to him was fantastic . . . giving Father O'Malley the tea with the drug in! And him staggering out into the street to be confronted by Peter Bracken, of all people. And then to be taken into Bracken's house! Oh, it was the limit of limits. In the wildest stretches of imagination, Father Bailey could not see his pastor allowing himself to be even touched by the hand of Peter Bracken, apart from being led into his house.

When Peter Bracken opened his door, Father Bailey said, 'You sent for me?'

'I did,' said Peter. 'Will you come in?'

Nothing more was said until they reached the kitchen, and even then not immediately; for the sight of Father O'Malley stretched out on the mat, with his head on a pillow and a blanket covering him, was almost too much for Father Bailey. Father O'Malley looked less prepossessing in sleep than he did awake. He looked, Father Bailey thought whimsically, as though he might be dictating to the sender of dreams as to their type and quality.

Father Bailey suppressed his mirth and left till later the relish this situation would provide, particularly for those times when his superior would be most overbearing. . . . Oh, the laughs he would get from this would last him a lifetime!

'How did it come about?' he asked Peter, without daring to raise his eyes from the floor in case this man, who was also in sorrow, should detect his mirth.

'I happened to be coming up the street,' replied Peter, 'and found him slumped against the wall near my door. Molly was with him and she told me what she had done. There was no one about at the time, but I knew that should anyone see him it would be said immediately that I'd put the evil eye on him.'

Without looking up, Father Bailey nodded.

'Or should he have been seen staggering about,' went on Peter, 'some would have said . . . well, that he was drunk. People only need to see a shadow to create the substance.'

Father Bailey slowly brought his gaze up to this man. . . . How many terrible substances had been created from shadows for him! And not a few by the priest at his feet. And yet he had endeavoured to save Father O'Malley from the stigma of drunkenness!

'You can get a cab and take him home,' Peter Bracken went on: 'Or you can leave him here till he wakes.'

Yes, he could get a cab, Father Bailey thought, and take him home. But then again, should he be seen being carried from the house, this man would be blamed for putting some 'fluence on him. . . . No; he would leave him here. And please God, he'd be here to see him wake . . . he wouldn't miss that for a bucketful of sovereigns.

'Would it be putting you out,' he asked, 'if he stayed?'

'Not at all,' said Peter Bracken quietly.

'And myself too?' added Father Bailey. ' I have some things to attend to, but I'll come back later if I may. . . . And I'd better look in on the doctor who issued those tablets.'

'There's something I'd better tell you,' said Peter. . . . 'It was important that John should have taken those tablets'–he nodded down at the sleeping priest–'for tonight it is arranged that . . . that'–he couldn't bring himself to speak Dominic's name–'the other one is to be got away.'

'You know where he is then?' said Father Bailey, with interest.

'Yes. But he can't remain there much longer. John will shortly regain his senses, and he will surely guess; for he's upstairs above him in the only house he hasn't searched.'

'Good God!'

'John is too good a man to suffer . . . for him. He must be got away!'

The priest nodded again, and asked, 'Where is he going?'

'I can't tell you that. I can only tell you he'll be put aboard a tramp steamer.'

'Will he be fit to work his passage?'

'Not for a time; but that has been arranged.'

Peter Bracken said no more, but Father Bailey knew that sick men weren't taken, even on tramp steamers, for nothing. And the man before him was the only one round these parts who could supply the money and arrange the whole thing. He shook his head. . . . Here, indeed, was a good Samaritan; and under such circumstances as to make the act heroic. He looked at Peter's shrunken figure and at the face, which during the last three days had drooped into deep lines of age, and he said: 'I think you're a very brave and forgiving man.'

The old man turned away, his lips trembling: 'I am not brave; it is that I can bear my sorrow easier than the others, for my child is near me. Death to them'–he nodded towards the wall–'even with their religion, is a severance that only death can join again. But to me there has been no parting, the main part of her is still with me.'

For the moment, the priest experienced a tinge of envy for this man's faith. . . . Here was faith as it should be. Would any Catholic think like this? No, he thought regretfully. Christ Himself was in the blessed sacrament of the altar for them, but their faith was so limited that it could not reach over the boundary to Him . . . so there were few miracles. They prayed to God to come to them, instead of boldly going to Him.

'Can I help in any way?' he asked. 'Is there anything I can do?'

Peter turned to the priest again: 'You can, if you will. John wouldn't suspect you. You could get more tablets and see that he takes them. If the men don't get the other . . . this done tonight, there may not be another chance for days. And then it may be too late.'

Father Bailey looked steadily at Peter Bracken: 'Why are you taking all this trouble over someone who has done you such a terrible injury?'

Peter's eyes closed, and his face set in lines of pain. He had lost the mainspring of his life and hopes, for Christine would have carried on his ideas. She had been brave; more so than him in some ways, for he was vulnerable to jibes–how many deaths had he died these past three days because of the attitude that had been taken towards Christine. It was as if his girl did not count . . . as if she too had not died the same death as the child, even the blame for the tragedy, in some subtle way, had been laid on her, while the perpetrator of it had even come in for a modicum of sympathy from a section of the people, and he himself was more hated and feared than before . . . and his heart was sore within him.

But he answered the priest calmly: 'Because I believe in the Great Plan of Life. I believe all that has happened had to happen. What I am doing I must do, for I feel also that it isn't in the Plan for John to commit a crime and suffer for it. There are other things for him, he has begun to think, and nothing can stop him evolving.'

As if expecting some deprecating remark, Peter's eyes held those of the priest for a moment before he went on: 'I believe he will eventually do something for the betterment of his people . . . I know he will, for Christine has told me; and she knows, for, you see, she loved him.'

Father Bailey's gaze was almost tender, as he looked at this old man, who, strangely enough, held views which were in exact keeping with some of his own; did he himself not always say that the path was all mapped out for each one of us from the day he was born, that the great Creator knew the shape of every pebble to be trodden by our feet. This man was a thinker, and was possessed of a spirit that wasn't un-Christ-like. He preached that he was part of Christ in his understanding and in his power, and although the doctrine he taught was divided by insurmountable barriers from his own, nevertheless the essence was very much the same. And he must talk to him; for whether he knew it or not, at this moment his need was great. Father Bailey knew that to extend to Peter Bracken the hand of friendship would be a herculean task; the main stumbling block would be, not so much the difference of their religions or opinions, but the priest now lying on the mat between them; and not him alone, but others of his breed, who with a little learning packing the narrow channels of their minds, set up theories bred of their own enlarged egos and used them under the stamp of the Church. . . . Well, this was one time he was going to make a stand. If this man and he could never see eye to eye, they would have gone far if each could respect the other's point of view. . . . A flash of enlightening candour through the priest's mind told him that the trying would be his work alone, for this man in his humility was advanced far beyond him.

He put out his hand and touched Peter Bracken's sleeve: 'I'll fix up that lad next door; then perhaps we can have a talk.'

After Father Bailey had gone, Peter, his eyes bright and head raised, stood by the side of the sleeping priest. He spoke as if to someone near: 'You were right, my dear; your going had a purpose. Never could this have come about otherwise. Will you ask all the guides of tolerance to help this man here? I, too, will work on him, that he may become more like him just gone.'

While Peter Bracken was sitting at the head of Father O'Malley the priest jerked violently–it was as if his spirit was up in arms at this outrage. From time to time his lips and cheeks would puff out and emit sounds like 'Pooh! poo-pooh!'

Peter did not smile–it needed Father Bailey to appreciate the humour of the situation.

The tin alarm clock on the mantelpiece showed twelve-thirty. Father Bailey sat looking at it, and from time to time he wondered whether it had stopped. But as he stared, the hand would give a slight movement, and once again he would tell himself that these were the longest three hours he had spent in his life . . . and the oddest. Was there ever such a situation! Here he was, sitting in this kitchen, after midnight, with this toil-worn woman opposite, so still she might be dead; and three cups on the table, the largest holding the white powder already mixed with the milk. And there on the hob was the teapot, stewing its inside out. They would likely all die from tannin poisoning if they were to drink the stuff. Well, pray God there would be no need. Less than half an hour now, and the men would be here and gone, and John could remain asleep or wake up just as he pleased, and no harm done. . . . And for himself, he would go next door, where at least there was a comfortable chair to recline in while waiting for the grand awakening, as he termed it, of his superior. . . . Was there ever such a situation! There next door was lying the man who was the sworn enemy of all spiritualists, and of Peter Bracken in particular and being tended gently by the man himself.

Father Bailey felt his eyes closing, and he was thinking sleepily that it was many years since he enjoyed a conversation like the one this evening . . . a very enlightened man that. Of course, God help him, he was entirely wrong in many of his opinions, but there were some which tied up amazingly with those of the Church. Peter Bracken's idea, for instance, that the spirits, termed guides, and through whom the healing was done, were the good people who had gone on, whom he and all Catholics termed saints. Now that was an interesting point. . . . He was awakened, startlingly, by a gasp from Mary Ellen.

They exchanged glances and looked towards the bedroom door; the bed was creaking heavily. There was a shuffling, a short silence, and John appeared at the open door.

It was only two days since Father Bailey last saw John, yet the change in him hurt the priest; he looked gaunt and twice his age.

But now was not the time, Father Bailey told himself, to waste on useless pity. Of all the times John could have chosen to wake up this was the worst; even if he drank the stuff this minute, as strong as it was, it was doubtful whether it would take effect before the arrival of the men.

John shook his head and ran his hand over his forehead. Then he looked dully but inquiringly at the priest.

And Father Bailey said promptly, 'Your father's not too good, John. Your mother called me in.'

John accepted this, and looked at his mother; then from her to the clock . . . twenty minutes to one! The pain of his existence flooded back to him . . . he had slept for hours! They would have got him away then. Well he had to sleep some time. But, oh God, why couldn't he have got him first, then this agony would have been appeased. Now it would go on for ever.

'Have this cup of tea, lad.' Mary Ellen was pouring the black tea into the cup with shaking hands.

John ran his hand round his face and shook his head: 'I'll have a wash first.'

'I could do with another, myself, Mrs O'Brien. Have a cup with me, John, it'll pull you together.'

The priest took the cup from Mary Ellen's hand and stirring it vigorously, passed it to John.

Without demur, John took it and drank a mouthful of the hot tea. He pursed his lips before replacing the cup on the table. Huh! the taste . . . his mouth was dry and thick!

Going to the hearth, he picked up the kettle. It was empty; and the occurrence was so unusual that he shook the kettle, then glanced at his mother. It seemed a symbol of the new life . . . nothing would ever be the same again.

Mary Ellen took the kettle from John's hand, whilst he went to the table and finished his tea. The priest sighed and sat down heavily, saying to John, 'Sit down, lad.'

Docilely, John sat down, as if his being knew nothing of hatred and the craving impulse to destroy.

Mary Ellen passed between him and the priest and placed the kettle on the fire. Then she too sat down, and the silence became heavy; until Father Bailey exclaimed, 'Well, Mrs O'Brien, I must soon be making my way home.' But he didn't move; and into the renewed silence came a soft padding. It bore no relation to footsteps. Mary Ellen and the priest exchanged quick glances, but John went on looking at the kettle, which had begun to hiss softly.

The padding which came from the wall at John's back now passed on to the ceiling. The priest turned his gaze from Mary Ellen and stared into the fire. . . . Well, if they made no more noise than that, it would be all right–the old stockings round their boots were quite effective. Another two or three minutes, and it would be over.

The minutes passed, and John stood up and lifted the kettle from the fire, forcing back into himself the urge to be going. What was he idling here for, anyway? In another few minutes he'd be asleep again. And there was still the chance he might find him; for how did they know how long he would sleep. They might have been afraid to risk getting him away. This time he would stay at the bottom end of the streets; it was ten to one he was there, for his cronies were in that quarter.

'That water isn't hot,' Mary Ellen broke in, getting to her feet–in the scullery he would be standing under the staircase, and the padding had started again.

'It'll do.'

As he made to pass her, he was brought to a halt by the sound of something falling on to the floor above. It could have been a chair or a box, or any piece of Peggy Flaherty's menage. Perhaps John would have let it pass as just that had he not looked at his mother and from her to the priest. The apprehension in their exchanging glances was like a revelation to him. . . . 'The bitch!' The words were forced out through his clenched teeth–at this moment he wasn't thinking of Dominic so much as Peggy Flaherty. It was as clear as daylight . . . her trailing round with him to throw him off the scent of that swine! What a bloody fool he was! He almost threw the kettle on to the hearth; but when he turned to dash out of the back door he found the priest barring his way.

'Get by!' he said grimly, towering over the tubby figure of Father Bailey.

'Listen, John. I'm not going to get by. . . . Now you listen to me!'–the priest stared up at John with as much aggressiveness as was in him to portray–'you can do nothing . . . you're as helpless as a new-born babe. Get that into that big head of yours. You've just swallowed an excellent sleeping draught, one that would put a horse to sleep. And that's where you'll be in a very few minutes.'

John stepped back and glared at his mother. Mary Ellen, her hands clasped, her eyes dumbly pleading, said nothing. He remembered her laughter, earlier on, and her jumbled words about Molly and the pills, and the queer turn of the priest. . . . Now Father Bailey sitting there waiting, with that tale about his father. Why, they'd all hoaxed him like a child! But he wasn't asleep yet. No, by God! not by a long chalk.

He swung up the bucket of water standing by the tin dish and bending, poured it over his head; then towelled himself vigorously. And before Mary Ellen and the priest were aware of his intention he was through the front room.

In the street, he ran as he had never run before, round the bottom corner and up the back lane. But when he reached the backyard he found only Mary Ellen and Peggy there. They were standing by the kitchen door, an epitome of the conspiracy against him and of its successful close.

In the moment of his pausing he was made aware of the effects of the drug, for he had the desire to push past them into the kitchen and to sit down. But the desire was swept away and he turned and ran again, for the main road now. However they tried to evade him, eventually they must make for the main road.

A cold drizzle was falling, and already his shirt was wet; but this would keep him awake. There was no one in sight, as far as he could see, and he stood in the shadow of the wall, scanning the openings to the streets. There was a lamp at each corner, but so far did the streets seem to stretch away into the darkness that he realized he must keep on the move if he hoped to discern any movement from the lower streets.

His lids felt heavy and drooped slowly over his eyes. He stretched them and swore grimly to himself. They had only to play a waiting game . . . they were in there somewhere still, he was sure. How much longer could he fight against this increasing drowsiness?

He had to lean against the wall. Gradually his anger died in him, and all he wanted to do was to lie down. . . . Blast them! He started to walk, briskly as he thought, but soon stopped again and leaned against a lamp post. His head was throbbing to the rhythm of approaching horse's hooves. Soon the black shape of a cab rocketed towards him, and ahead of it, on the pavement, he made out the scurrying figure of Father Bailey.

Panting, the priest came alongside John and laid a hand on his arm. He murmured something, but John did not hear what it was. He was looking at the cab, which was now abreast of him . . . and there was Dominic's face! His eyes were turned towards the window. They were sockets of darkness in a white blur. Time seemed to stand suspended, giving the brothers the opportunity to exchange their last looks of hatred. Then something sprang from John and leaped upon the sneering face of his brother. But whatever it was it had no effect . . . the cab rolled on, the bandaged face disappeared. And John, like a child, allowed himself to be led gently away by the priest; he was thinking dimly that all his life there would be a want in him . . . something uncompleted.

Chapter Thirteen

Renunciation

The under-manager of the sawmill watched John jump the wall; he was waiting for him on the pavement of the main road.

'You know, that's a punishable offence,' he said evenly.

John straightened his cap. 'I suppose so.'

'Well, I don't want to seem stiff'–the man was almost apologetic–'but it's got to stop. I shouldn't mind if it was just one doing it, but it only needs a start you know, and we'll have everybody living in Jarrow coming out this way, and I leave you to guess what'll happen to the timber. . . . It's got to stop, you see.'

John merely nodded before moving off; and the man, looking after him, thought 'poor devil'. It was right what they said, he had gone a bit queer. What other reason could there be for him not using the dock gates–for though the sawmill yard might be a short cut to Jarrow, it was difficult of access. Perhaps the lad thought he was still chasing his brother. Well, whatever he thought he was doing now, he'd have to find some other way of doing it but by this wall. . . .

John realized this as he strode homewards. But there was no other way to avoid meeting Mary; if he used the main gate sooner or later they would be bound to meet. For four weeks now he had come out by the wall; it cut off the arches and the length of road past the Simonside bank. It did not cut off the gut–no deviation could cut off the gut. At first, he was determined to avoid Mary only until he should feel strong enough to face her; but with each passing day he became weaker, and told himself that in the silence between them the madness would fade and he would not have to see her. Then her letters started to come. Every day for the past three weeks there had been a letter. They were all neatly stacked in his box under the bed . . . and all unopened. With the coming of the first one he knew he must not open it, for the words it held would break down his reserve.

In the long stretches of the night he would think of the letters and what they held, and it would seem as if their substance created Mary herself, bringing her into the room to him . . . at times, even into the bed. He would feel her there, even smell the faint perfume that was hers, and his arms would go out to her, and in pulling her to him he would come to himself and, getting up, would stand on the cold floor, staring out of the window into the black square of the backyard, or up at the piece of sky visible between the houses, and know that Mary and the magic world that she alone could make was not for him–this wherein he stood was his world, this his night view for all time . . . this was his far horizon; this was the limit to all his wild hopes; here in this house he would have to work out his salvation. Sometimes he would lean his head against the window frame and murmur, 'Katie, Katie,' as if asking her forgiveness. . . . If only he had never had the idea of making her a teacher! It was his fault, for she was a child and would have forgotten about it. Then he would never have got dressed up to go and see . . . her. And not seeing her, he would have come to love Christine; and the issue between him and Dominic would have been finished earlier, and his Katie and Christine would have been alive today. . . . Again, had the Brackens not come next door, and, like a disciple, he had not sat at Peter's feet, lapping up all his mad ideas about the power of thought, this would never have happened.

Well, he was finished with thinking . . . his mother was right–it got you nowhere. There would be no more wild imagining for him. The road he was on held no space for flights of fancy. He had been mad in a number of ways. Between her and Peter he had gone crazy for a time. She even made him believe that the quaint thoughts which came into his head were unpolished gems, holding poetic qualities . . . and Peter, that life held something gigantic for him, that one day he would lead men, not into battle, but out of it . . . out of the battle with squalor into brighter and better conditions. Peter even egged him to take on the job of being a delegate to the Labourers' and General Workers' Union. . . . God! how far above the earth he had walked; until that business of Nancy Kelly's! Even then he saw his Mecca in America. But now it was all over. He knew where his Mecca lay . . . in this house, in the fifteen streets and in the docks, working to feed his mother and father and Molly and that other growing Dominic.

Yet as he walked up the road, he knew that it wasn't all over; the hardest part for him was yet to come. He would have to see her and finish it. Far better make a clean cut than try to keep dodging her. Once it was done, he would feel better; he could not feel worse.

Saturdays were like the opening afresh of a wound; the week-ends altogether were a torture. And now another was upon him. Since jumping the sawmill wall, he knew how he must spend this one . . . he must read the letters! . . .

When he entered the kitchen, his eyes, in spite of himself, were forced to the mantelpiece. There was yet another letter against the clock. He thrust it into his pocket, then washed himself before sitting down to dinner. Shane was already at the table, and John, out of the pity growing in him for his father, answered his questions patiently. . . . Yes, the first boat of the year was in from Sweden with Lulea ore, and it seemed heavier than ever . . . yes, there was one due in on Monday from Bilbao.

'That'll mean piece work,' his father said . . . 'five shillings a shift.' He shook his head and looked down at his trembling hands. 'Perhaps if I made a start I would steady up . . . eh, lad?'

'Give yourself time,' said John, knowing that all the time in the world wouldn't put his father back in the docks.

'Yes. Another week then,' said Shane, with pitiable relief.

Silently, Mary Ellen moved between the oven and the table. Into the love she held for this son of hers was creeping a feeling of awe. The letters were creating it. That lass was writing to him every day, yet he was standing out against her. If ever a lad was in love, he was. But he was renouncing her . . . and for them. Where did he get his strength? She recognized him as a man with a man's needs, and her humility ignored the origin of his strength in herself. If only in some way he could have the lass. . . . But it was impossible, the house depended on him; they could only live by him.

Here was another Saturday. How she dreaded and hated Saturdays! She seemed to spend her weeks gathering strength to face the Saturdays. Yet life went on. Round the doors, it was back to normal. Already the incident was being referred to as something long past, in remarks, such as, 'That was a Saturday, wasn't it?' or, 'That day the two bairns went down.' The only ones outside the house who still felt the weight of that day were Peggy Flaherty and the Kellys . . . Peggy, because John, as she said, wouldn't look the side she was on. He wouldn't forgive her for duping him, and her fat was visibly disappearing through the worry of it. Her simple soul felt that until she was on speaking terms with John again nothing would be right. The Kellys were affected because now there could be no redress for Nancy. They would be saddled with her child and their scraping to live would become more difficult, while the possibility of yet another Nancy would be growing under their eyes. Mary Ellen, too, often thought of this. In a short while now, the child would be born, and she would be a grandmother. And always there would be Dominic across the street from her . . . from behind her curtains, she would look for the traits to show. She could see herself doing just that all down the years, for there was no possibility of her ever leaving the fifteen streets. Nor did she want to now; all desire for a change had long since left her, and she knew she must see life out to its close here. This did not worry her, but what did was that her lad would have to do the same. She hadn't wanted him to go to America, but that wasn't saying she wanted him to be stuck in the fifteen streets all his life. . . . Dear God, no. . . .

The meal was over, and while Molly cleared away Mary Ellen, taking Mick's shirt from the top of the pile of mending, cut off the tail and pinned it across the shoulders, before sitting down opposite Shane and beginning to sew.

John came from the bedroom, and looking hard at Molly, asked, 'Did someone call here a while ago? You know who I mean.'

Molly, after staring back at him for a second, hung her head and answered, 'Yes.'

'Why didn't you say?'

Molly turned her head a little and stared down to her mother's lap. . . . How could she say to him, 'You were all mad when she came?' She recalled going to the door on the Sunday afternoon and seeing Miss Llewellyn standing there. She had asked to see her mother or father, and Molly had said she couldn't, they were both bad. It felt nice, at the time, to deny something to her one-time teacher, a teacher who had never taken any notice of her; and when she was able to deny her John, saying that he was out and she didn't know where he was, she experienced a definite pleasure. There was no room in her to feel sorry for Miss Llewellyn, who looked pale and bad. She didn't want her here, anyway. She guessed that Miss Llewellyn had clicked with their John, and she was puzzled, yet made bold, by sensing the come-down it was for anyone so swanky to click with their John. And so, after Miss Llewellyn had gone, she forgot about her. And now here was John blaming her, and she didn't want him to be vexed, for the daily aim of her life was that he and her ma would come to like her as they had liked Katie.

When she gave him no reply, John went back to the bedroom. He picked up the letter he had been reading . . . 'Dearest, I felt I must come and see you. Judged by my own sorrow, yours and your people's must be unbearable. . . .' She had come here, to this house. Through the open door she must have glimpsed the conditions from the bareness of the front room, yet it had not put her off; nor the fifteen streets themselves. Nothing would put her off. She would go on believing that when he had accepted his sorrow he would come again to her.

He picked up another letter . . . 'Beloved, I understand. I will wait patiently. Each night I go to the lane, and I know that if you are not there there is always the following night, or the one after, or yet the one after that. . . .' He ground his fist into the palm of his hand, and getting up, began to pace the floor in his stockinged feet. . . . How much could a man endure! Of all the millions of women in the world, this one, who stood out above them, had to offer him a love such as this, a love men dreamed of, and died with it still but a dream. And it was his, it was being offered to him, John O'Brien, of 10 Fadden Street, of the fifteen streets. Yet he must renounce it, and do so now, this day. He must tell her in words that the mad dream was over. He must do it quickly and cleanly; the cut must be made without sentiment; there must be no tender good-byes, and no holding out hopes for the future. He knew what the future held for him . . . he was a gaffer, and he'd remain a gaffer; and there was not even the remotest chance of her even becoming a gaffer's wife.

John caught sight of Mary before she saw him. She wasn't in the lane but on the main road, walking slowly with her back towards him, and the setting sun cast an aura of white light about her as she moved. He paused and drew in to the side of the road. The sight of her back had taken all the strength and determination out of him–what hope had he then to stand firm when he faced her. It was easy to be brave in a room talking to oneself. There you asked the questions and fired the answers; there were no eyes to bore into your heart and no touch to set the blood racing. In the bedroom he had been brave enough to don his old style of dress; with a grim defiance he had knotted the muffler ends around his braces, put on his old trousers and heavy boots, and lastly his mackintosh and cap. This, he told himself, was getting back to what he really was, and it would make things easier for her; she would have less regret at what she imagined she was losing. But now he wasn't so sure. His decent clothes would at least have left him free of thinking of himself. Fingering his muffler he could only think of her reaction when she saw him like this–well, wasn't that what he wanted? He continued to watch her for some minutes, and his heart defying his head, cried out, 'Mary–oh! Mary!'

As if the voice of his longing had become audible, she turned, and John, knowing that the time had come, stepped into the centre of the path and walked slowly towards her.

Mary remained still, gazing over the distance towards him. She did not see his clothes, only his face. Even from a distance it sent out its lostness to her, and she murmured aloud, 'My dear! my dear!' and with a little cry she picked up her skirts and ran to him. John halted before she reached him, and the resistance needed to stop the automatic gesture of holding out his arms became a pain.

'Oh John!–my dear!' Her hands were on his chest.

He swallowed as if ridding himself of a piece of granite, and said, 'Hallo, Mary.'

'Hallo, my dear,' she smiled at him gently; 'how are you?'

'All right.' He could not take his eyes from her face. She was pale, but she was more beautiful than he had ever seen her, and the tenderness in her eyes caused him to groan inwardly.

'How is your mother?' she asked softly.

'All right.'

'And is your father better?'

'Yes.'

Her eyes fell from his to her hand. Her fingers were softly stroking his muffler. 'I've missed you, dear.'

It was unbearable. No flesh and blood could stand it. He moved brusquely away from her and began to walk; and in a second she was by his side with her hand in his arm. 'What is it, John?'

He did not reply, and she went on, 'Shall we go up the lane?'

He turned into the lane without speaking, his arm hanging straight and stiff under her touch. The action was boorish, but he knew that if he allowed himself one tender move he would be finished. They stopped by the field gate, where they had been wont to lean and watch the moon and make love. Beyond, the afterglow was tinting the field of young wheat with sweeping strokes of pastel colour. John did not lean against the gate but stood staring into the field.

'Talk about it, my dear. Katie would want it so. It will make you feel better.' Mary had withdrawn her hand from his arm, and now she stood by the side of him, waiting.

'No talking would make any difference to that,' he replied tersely; 'but there's something else I've got to talk about.'

She remained silent, and he went on, swiftly now, 'I am not going to America–that's finished. This business has put paid to my father. He'll never work again. And Molly and Mick are still at school. There's no money coming in, only mine.' He turned now and looked at her; the afterglow which was mellowing the world around had no softening effect upon his face. 'Nothing can come of it now–it's no good going on. You understand?'

'No,' she said, 'I don't.'

He moved his head impatiently: 'How can I? What will there be to live on?'

'We could wait . . . you asked me to wait while you were in America.'

'That was different. What could there be to wait for now?'

'Molly leaves school this summer, and your brother will soon be fourteen.'

'And what about my mother and father?'

'There are ways and means. You could always manage to keep them.'

'Out of what?' he almost shouted. It was as if he were fighting her now, and some part of him was shocked; but he went on, 'Where would we live, and on what?–just tell me that.'

She made no answer. And his head dropped, and he murmured, 'I'm sorry.'

'There's no need to be sorry.' She took a step nearer to him, but did not touch him. 'John, look at me.' She waited until he raised his head before going on: 'We love each other. There won't be anyone else for either of us–we know that–so don't let this happen. There is a way out, there must be–there is a way out of everything.'

Peter's words–'There is a way out of everything. Use your mind and it will give you the solution.' Peter's reasoning, added to the appeal of her voice and the entreaty of her eyes, broke the tension of his body for the moment, and he allowed his mind to clutch at a fleeting hope–could there be some way out? Could the madness be resurrected? Oh the joyful bewilderment of touching her again! Her face blurred before his eyes, and her voice became blended with the evensong of the birds.

'If you'll only listen to me, darling–I don't mind where I live or how I live, as long as I'm with you. We could be married and I'd go on working. John–I'll come to the fifteen streets. . . .'

The blur cleared. The mention of the fifteen streets held the power to betray dreams for what they were. No longer did he see the pleading in her eyes. He saw only her well-cut costume, the gold wrist-watch, the ring on her finger with the large amber stone in the centre, the patent leather of her narrow shoes, and the glimpse of grey stockings, which were of silk; and covering all, the perfume which emanated from her was in his nostrils, the perfume whose ingredients lay not in any bottle but in a sequence starting from a scented bath to fresh linen–and she said she would come to the fifteen streets! He laughed inwardly, harsh, bitter laughter, and said sharply, 'Be quiet! You don't know what you're talking about. Have you ever been inside a house in the fifteen streets?'

'No.'

'It's a pity you haven't.'

'There's no disgrace in being poor.'

'No? I used to think that at one time, but I don't any longer–it's a crying disgrace, but one that I can't alter. But I can do this–I can save you from yourself. You shall never come to the fifteen streets through me.'

'John, darling, listen.'

'I can't listen, I've got to go.' He stepped back from her out-stretched hand.

'John, please . . . Oh, don't go like this–John, I love you. . . . Don't you see, I can't go on without you?'

The stillness of the field settled on them. Outwardly they appeared lifeless things, fixed in their staring. Then, in spite of himself, he spoke her name, 'Mary.' And like a caress it touched her. But the caress was short-lived, for he went on, 'This has got to be–it's got to finish right now. It's no use going on–no–no!'–he silenced her quietly and with upraised hand. 'All the talking in the world won't make it any different. You'll forget–time will help.'

'It won't–I know that deep within my soul you'll remain with me for ever; I won't be able to forget you–John, oh, John–please! Please let us try to find a way out.' She held out her arms to him, and the humility in their appeal probed a fresh depth of pain in him. But he did not touch them, and Mary made a desperate final effort: 'Katie would have wanted it–she loved to think that we . . .'

'Don't! . . . Good-bye, Mary.' For a second longer he allowed his gaze to linger on her. A lark in the field beyond suddenly rose, singing, from the grass and soared into the dusk of the closing evening. When he saw the mist of tears blinding her eyes, he turned from her and went down the lane.

It was done!

Chapter Fourteen

Whither Thou Goest

Mary Ellen was puzzled by her own emotions. The sorrow of Katie's loss had not died or faded–it was as poignant as the hour when it happened–but she could bear it now with equanimity because of use. What puzzled her was that it seemed to have moved aside to make room for the sorrow she was feeling for John. Daily she watched him closing up–life seemed to be dying in him. He was becoming the kind of dock man he had never been, even before he had taken to wearing collars and ties. He had not yet taken to drink or lounging at the corners, but he never seemed to get out of his working clothes, and he never moved from the house once he came home from work. Nor did he sit in the kitchen, but spent hours in the bedroom–wrestling, Mary Ellen thought, with himself.

It was a fortnight since the letters ceased, and in some strange way their cessation had brought an added emptiness to her days. With their daily arrival, there remained the hope, however faint, that things would come right for her lad. Now hope was dead, and with it the part of him that had survived Katie's loss was dying too.

What was there to live for now? Mary Ellen asked herself, as she banged the poss-stick up and down in the tub, full of clothes. With no possibility of happiness for her lad and nothing she could do about it, her usual incentive to 'cope' was gone–if only an act of God would finish them all off and leave John free! But God never did things like that–nothing with any sense or reason in it. . . . There she was, going again. Her bouts of defiance against God brought her hours of fear and remorse in the night, yet mixed with her fear was a tinge of admiration at her day-time audacity at facing up to Him, and strange, too, was the contradictory feeling of late that she wanted to go to church–not to Mass, so escaping Father O'Malley's censure, but just to sit quietly in church, with no one there, and perhaps come to terms with God. She did not actually think of it like this–she had not advanced so far in her bravery to do so–but the feeling in her urged that should she go to church and sit quiet she would feel better. The feeling was strong in her now, and she stopped possing and whispered aloud, 'I'll go–I'll go now!' She rubbed her wet arm across her forehead and shook her head, and muttered, 'For God's sake, what's come over you? Have you gone completely up the pole? There's another two hours washing in front of you yet!' She stooped, and lifting the clothes from the tub, began running them into the mangle. There was a series of groans, squeaks and loud jolts, as garment followed garment.

The tub empty of clothes, she dragged it into the yard and poured the water down the sink, and she made no effort to move as the dirty foam swirled about her feet. Rolling the tub back into the washhouse again, she happened to glance up, and met Shane's eyes on her. He was standing at the kitchen window and his face bore the look of despair that covered them all. Although he had made no mention of it for weeks now, she knew that he, too, was continually crying out inside himself for Katie, and also that he was suffering because of the knowledge that through his dependence things were not right with John. She stood leaning over the empty tub for a moment, her eyes, gazing down at the water-worn wood. Then, as if she had found a command written there, she hurriedly left the washhouse.

In the kitchen, she dried her arms and combed the top of her hair. Shane watched her silently. Even when she put her coat on he did not question her. With her face turned from him, she said, 'I won't be long.' Then, as if compelled to expose her madness to him, she added, 'I'm going to the church.'

That any woman could leave her washing at two o'clock in the afternoon to go to church must prove, she thought, to a man like Shane that she was mad; but he made no comment on her extraordinary behaviour. Not until she was going through the front room did he speak.

'Mary Ellen.'

She turned: 'Yes?'

He was groping in his trouser pocket. 'Will you light me a candle?' He handed her a penny and their eyes met over it; and perhaps for the first time in their married lives they felt joined in thought and purpose.

As Mary Ellen opened the front door a pantechnicon passed and stopped at Peter Bracken's, and she saw Peter himself standing on his doorstep. For a space they looked at each other, and she knew that she should go to this man and say some word, for her son had been the means of killing his lass; yet through his lass she had lost Katie. With his very coming here, tragedy had entered her life. Peter's eyes were asking her to speak, but she found it impossible. It was strange that only once had this man and she exchanged words–that day in the kitchen, the day the bairn was born. Before she turned away she tried to send him some kindly message; but whether she succeeded or not she couldn't tell. She hurried away down the street, knowing that she had looked her last on Peter Bracken–he was leaving the fifteen streets and never again would they meet. Why had he come here in the first place? To relieve poverty and ignorance, he said. Oh, God, how happy she would have been in her poverty and ignorance had she still Katie. Yet she could feel no virile bitterness against him, which was strange. Instead, she felt they were sharing the same sorrow, and she wasn't troubled at her manner towards him, knowing intuitively that he understood. . . .

The day was dull and the sky low. Inside the church the light was as dim as if it were evening, and the air, as usual, was different from that outside–thick and heavy with the weight of stale incense. At the top of the centre aisle, Mary Ellen, her head bowed, made a deep genuflexion. She did not look towards the altar, where always and forever reposed Jesus in the Blessed Sacrament; somehow she wanted no 'truck' with Him; it was His Mother she needed. She went down the side aisle walking softly, as if trying to escape the notice of the Holy Ones standing in their niches with flowers at their feet.

There were no candles burning on the half-moon stand to the side of Our Lady, and she stood in shadow until Mary Ellen lit her candles, one for Shane, one for John and one for herself. Then The Virgin was illuminated, smiling down on Mary Ellen, half holding The Child out to her.

Mary Ellen knew she should kneel and say a prayer, and ask The Virgin about Katie and tell her about John, but she felt very tired and all she wanted to do was to sit. She sat in the end of the front pew, as near as she could get to The Virgin, and gazed at her, preparatory to speaking about her lad. But as she sat on, her feet resting on the long wooden kneeler and her hands joined in her lap, she found she couldn't think of John. It was as if he and his troubles had shrunk, her mind groping for them in vain. As the flame of the candles lengthened, the smile of The Virgin deepened, and it seemed to Mary Ellen that she moved and hitched the Infant higher up on to her arm as she herself used to do with Katie. The light of the candles grew brighter and brighter as she stared at them, and the church outside the ring of light became darker. A great peace swept over Mary Ellen. It started in her feet with a tingling warmth and coursed through her body, flooding her being with a happiness she could never remember experiencing before, or ever imagined possible. So great was her happiness that it left no room for fear when she saw The Virgin move and gently push someone towards her.

When Katie stood at the end of the pew and, smiling shyly, said, 'Oh, ma!' Mary Ellen felt no surprise. She leaned forward and gripped Katie's hands. 'Why, hinny, I thought you were–gone.' She wouldn't say 'dead'. And when Katie answered her, saying, 'It was only for a few minutes, ma. Things went black and then it was over,' Mary Ellen took it as a natural answer, and went on, 'You're not out there then, hinny?–not out in the sea?'

Katie's laugh tinkled through the church, and she glanced back at The Virgin, and The Virgin's smile broadened. 'We never went out there, did we, Christine?'

Katie turned her head and spoke into the shadows, and Mary Ellen asked, 'The lass, is she with you?'

'Why, of course! We're waiting together–it's nice waiting.'

'Waiting?' repeated Mary Ellen. 'For what, hinny?'

'For the time to come when we should have died, and then we'll go on–we went too soon, ma.'

'Yes, hinny, you did.'

Now death had been mentioned, a sweet contentment was added to Mary Ellen's happiness–she felt she was with death, and it was a pleasant thing, nay, not only pleasant, but strangely exciting. Her bairn was in it, and was happy. 'How long must you wait, hinny?'

'We don't know; but once it's over we'll start growing again–a different growing, getting ready to come back–won't we, Christine?'

Mary Ellen peered into the shadows but could see nothing, and Katie went on, 'Before we go, I'll come and see you again–and ma . . .'

'Yes, hinny?'

'Don't worry about John; he's going to be happy, so very happy.'

'How can you tell, hinny?'

'We know about those we love. Go home now, ma.'

Katie's lips rested on Mary Ellen's and the sweetness of them pressed down into her being . . . the sweetness like a gentle perfume was in her nostrils when she opened her eyes.

'Katie, hinny—' She put out her hand, gropingly. She could not see Katie, but something stronger than reason told her she was there. She whispered again, 'Katie, hinny,' then looked towards The Virgin. She was as she had first seen her, yet different, for her face seemed to hold the knowledge of all eternity.

Katie and Christine were all right . . . they were with her. It did not enter Mary Ellen's head to question how Christine–the spook's daughter–could be with The Virgin, who, above all others, was a Catholic first and the Mother of God after.

Smiling gently to herself, Mary Ellen left the church. Katie was happy, oh indeed she was happy–and everything was going to be all right for her lad. Katie had said so.

The ghoulish picture of Katie floating in deep water that had filled her mind for weeks was gone–Katie wasn't there–she knew where Katie was. . . .

Going homewards Mary Ellen walked with a lighter tread; there was an urgency in her to reach the house and tell Shane, although how she was going to tell Shane about Katie without him thinking her completely mad she didn't know. But Shane needed comfort, and if she could tell him in a sensible way that she had seen Katie she had no doubt that he would feel as she did now. She hurried up the backyard, ignoring the dead fire under the washhouse pot and the mounds of unfinished washing, and entered the kitchen. Shane was there, sitting in his armchair beside the fireplace, while opposite him sat the lass. Mary Ellen had never met Mary Llewellyn, but there was no need for anyone to tell her who this was.

Bright spots of red burned in the dull colour of Shane's cheeks: 'I told the lass to stay–you wouldn't be long.'

Mary rose to her feet and watched the little woman unpin her hat and hang her coat carefully behind the kitchen door. She had not spoken, and Mary began, 'I hope you don't mind, Mrs O'Brien . . . I wanted to talk to you.'

'Sit down, miss,' said Mary Ellen with strange gentleness, 'you're quite welcome. Can I offer you a cup of tea?'

'Please; I should like one.'

Mary Ellen pressed the kettle, which was standing on the hob, further into the fire. At the same time Shane rose, saying, 'I'll be lying down for a while.' He left the kitchen without glancing at Mary–it was as if she had been there always and was likely to remain. The room door closed behind Shane and the two women were left alone.

Mary Ellen, filled with a growing awe and wonder, silently placed the teapot to warm, and unhooked the cups from the back of the cupboard and put them on the table. Oh, Katie, Katie. Can this mean what you said about John's life? She dare not look at the lass in case she should disappear as Katie had done.

'How is John, Mrs O'Brien?'

Mary Ellen was forced to stop in her trotting to and fro and look at this woman, whom her lad loved. She said simply, 'He's not too grand, miss.'

Mary turned her gaze towards the fire, and after a moment asked, 'Do you agree with his decision?' Then before Mary Ellen could make a reply, she turned to her again and went on rapidly, 'Please believe me . . . I understand . . . I know that you have only him now to look after you, and I want him to do that always. But that is no reason why we should be separated–is it, Mrs O'Brien? We care for each other–very deeply, and there is a way out if only he would listen to reason.'

'You can't marry without money, lass.'

'Did you wait until you had money?'

Mary Ellen shook her head. 'This is different . . . you're different. He'd want money to give you a home.'

'I don't want that kind of a home, Mrs O'Brien'–Mary leaned forward and took hold of Mary Ellen's hands–'the solution is for me to come and live here. I must show him that I can do it. There are always empty houses going, and I could continue my work. Even if I didn't, I have a little money, enough to keep us a couple of years, living simply. . . . How much is the rent of these houses?'

'Four and tuppence.' Mary Ellen, her hands locked in the soft firmness of Mary's, was trying to measure the cost it had been to her lad to give up this lass, whose charm was already telling on her. . . . Aye, but it wouldn't work out. She would never be able to stick it here; it would strip her of everything but the capacity for regret. . . . Yet why should she stick here? Wouldn't John fight with every fibre of his being to take her out of this? That is, if she persisted in coming here and persuaded him to marry. . . . Peter Bracken's gone, the house next door is empty. . . . It was almost as if Katie was at her elbow–the voice in her head was Katie's. She remained still, listening to both Katie and the lass.

'Will you help me, Mrs O'Brien? I can assure you that you'll not suffer for it. Please, Mrs O'Brien, do help me. I want to come and live here, somewhere near. He will know nothing about it until it's done. I will show him that I can live here successfully . . . will you?'

'There's a house empty right next door, lass.' It was as if Katie had nudged her. 'It was the Brackens' you know . . . the lass . . .'

'Yes, yes, I know. . . . Oh, Mrs O'Brien, tell me what to do. Who do I see about it?' In her excitement Mary stood up, and Mary Ellen, her mind suddenly filled with doubt, turned away and mashed the tea. Would John want to live in a house where the lass Christine had lived? . . . She seemed to hear Katie's laugh tinkling again as it had done in the church. Now it was deriding her superstitions, and Mary Ellen set down the teapot, and turning back to Mary, said resolutely, 'I'll do anything to see my lad happy; although

I'd better tell you, lass, it'll be hard for you . . . at the very best it'll be hard going.'

'You doubt that I'll be able to stand it?'

'No, somehow I don't. If you care for him enough it'll keep the iron out of your soul.'

With a sigh that swept the tenseness from her body, Mary sat down again. As she took the cup of tea from Mary Ellen, they smiled at each other and a quietness settled on the kitchen as they sat drinking and thinking, their thoughts in different channels but flowing the one way.

The flat cart was at the door–a clean, respectable flat cart, but the sight of it and its import had prostrated Beatrice Llewellyn. She lay on her bed, faint with rage and self-pity. There was rage, too, in James Llewellyn's voice as he talked to Mary from the doorway of her room, moving from time to time to allow the removal man to pass. He only spoke in the man's absence, talking rapidly to get in all he had to say.

'You'll regret this to your dying day . . . do you hear me?'

'I hear you.' Mary, with her back to him, went on lifting books from the shelves and packing them into a tea chest.

'You don't know what you're doing–you can't! Why, woman, the scum of the earth live in the fifteen streets–he's not a man! No man who could lay any claim to the name would ask anyone like you to go there.'

'He hasn't asked me, he has refused even to see me.'

'And you have so little pride you are going to live there and push yourself on him?'

'Yes, I have so little pride I am going to do just that.'

The man came in and as he lifted the tea chest asked, 'Is this the lot, miss?'

'Yes . . . except the two trunks and the cases in the hall.'

James Llewellyn threw a murderous glance at the unfortunate man as he lumbered past him with the box. 'Have you got the place furnished?' he barked the question at her.

'No.'

'No? You mean to say you are going to live there with those few odds and ends?' He nodded towards the hall.

'I have bought a bed and a table . . . just the necessary things.' Mary kept her face turned from her father. She thought of the problem the buying of the bed had caused–whether to be modest and buy a single bed, or to be true to herself and buy what she hoped would be necessary. She had not asked Mary Ellen's advice about this. It was something she had to decide for herself. . . . And was she brave enough to face the comments of her future neighbours? for she did not delude herself into thinking it would escape their notice; and she could practically hear their comments on a single lass buying a new double bed. She knew already that the hardest thing to bear in the fifteen streets would be her lack of privacy.

She had ordered a double bed and by now it would have been delivered. She glanced for the last time round the room, her eyes avoiding her father's. He was standing, black and massive, filling the doorway. She did not mind her mother's censure, but his cut deep into her. She would have gone happily to the fifteen streets had he given her some kind word.

'You'll be the talk of the town–a laughing-stock!' He barred her way, and she waited, eyes cast down, until he would move aside.

'I'll not be the first, or the last.'

'Your mother's ill.'

'My mother isn't ill . . . she's merely angry, and you know it.' She lifted her eyes to his. His face was mottled with his emotions, and she could not bear to witness it any longer.

'I must go. . . .' She stepped towards the door, but her father did not move. He stood staring at her, his face working, fighting against the softening emotion that was breaking him down–his lass going to live in the fifteen streets! His Mary, who loved colour, and light and laughter, who was so close to him, closer than his wife, who could reason like him and laugh at the same things. She was going to live in one of those wrecks of houses, just to be near that big docker . . . God Almighty! it was unbelievable. . . . Yet he had given her credit for being able to reason like himself. Then could she be so far wrong? . . . Was there something worthwhile in the fellow? Worthwhile or not, she had no right to be doing this. She was mad.

'Mary, lass, don't go. . . . I'll try to fix something . . . a job or something, for him.' His face fell into pitying lines of entreaty.

She shook her head slowly and put out her hand to him, speaking with difficulty.

'It wouldn't work . . . he'd refuse. This is the only way, to take whatever he has to offer, however small, and make it do. . . . Perhaps later—'

'Oh, lass'–he pulled her into his arms–'oh, Mary, lass!'

They held each other for a moment, tight and hard. Then, thrusting her from him he went hurriedly down the passage, and Mary, trying to stem the flood of tears, listened in amazement to him barking down the drive at the carrier.

'Come in here, and give a hand with these things.' He came back, followed by the man, whom he bewildered with his torrent of orders.

'Get that china cabinet out, and that bookcase. And the couch and chair. Then up with this carpet.'

'Father–no, don't. Listen to me,' she protested, 'I don't want them . . . I must go as I am. It will only make it more difficult. He wouldn't want . . .' She stopped. Her father wasn't listening; he was in a frenzy of action. He passed her, carrying one end of the heavy bookcase, almost pushing the man off his feet, both with his confused orders and force, and she knew she must let him do this for her. However more difficult it would make the work ahead, she must accept these things.

When the room was at last bare, she walked down to the gate, her father at her side. In deep embarrassment they stood facing each other.

'Well, good luck, lass. I dare say I'll find my way to see you . . . what's the number?'

'Twelve Fadden Street.'

'You can always come back, you know.'

'Thanks, my dear.'

'Good-bye, lass.'

'Good-bye.' It was impossible to say more. Blindly she went down the road. The cart on ahead was a blur, and it remained so until she came within sight of the fifteen streets.

All afternoon they worked. They cut the carpet, and it covered the floor of the front room and bedroom. The kitchen boards were bare except for two rugs, which to Mary Ellen's mind were far too bright and grand for such a room. The things the lass had brought were lovely! She was glad the lass's father had made her take them, for now one of the main problems to the marriage, as she saw it, was removed . . . they were set up. But her happiness in this new turn of events was marred, and it was the statue that was responsible . . . that great, white, bare woman, as naked as the day she was born, and standing on a box where anyone at the front door would get an eyeful of her. The lass was respectable, she knew that, and apparently to her mind this naked woman meant nothing except what she was, a statue. But let them about the doors get a glimpse of it, and Mary Ellen knew the result as if it had already taken place. The women would dub the lass 'a loose piece', and from the start her life in the fifteen streets would be suspect. They would conjure up the men she'd had, and her lad would become an object of pity for having been caught, and never would the lass be able to pass the corners of the streets without hungry eyes and low laughter following her. If only she could explain to her . . . but it was a hard thing to explain. Mary Ellen knew she wasn't at her best with words, but actions now . . . yes. If she were to knock the thing flying accidentally . . . She stood looking at it. There wasn't much time left, for John was due any minute now. Molly was on the watch for him at the corner, and the lass was in the kitchen getting her first meal ready. Well, it was now or never. She lifted her hand and swiped the naked woman to the floor. As it crashed, she heard a gasp, and there, standing in the doorway, her face white and shocked, was Mary.

Across the debris they stared at each other. Mary Ellen, her face working, tried to explain. 'I had to do it, lass . . . they would think . . . the women would say . . . They wouldn't understand around these doors . . . I want you to have a good start.'

Mary gazed down on the fragments of her expression. The statue had been a symbol of truth to her; a figure indeed of her emancipation from cant and hypocrisy; a symbol of her growing freedom. But now it was gone. Never until this moment had she fully realized what coming to the fifteen streets would mean. She imagined at worst it meant living meagrely. Now she saw that was but a small part of it. To live happily, her life would not only have to be altered from the outside, but from within. Not only her actions, but her thoughts, must be restricted. This little woman had not broken the statue from malice, but from a desire to help her. Some deep knowledge of her own people had urged her to its destruction, and it might be only one of the many things which must be destroyed if she were to suffer this life. Could she suffer it?

'Lass, I didn't mean to hurt you.' Mary Ellen's face was pitiable, and her fingers, as always when she was in distress, picked nervously at the button of her blouse. Had she, with her mad action, destroyed what she wanted most? Happiness for her lad. The lass looked hurt and bewildered. She wanted her off to a good start, but she had achieved just the opposite. She bent her head in an effort to hide the raining tears . . . was nothing ever to go right?

When she felt the lass's arms go about her, she leant against her, faint with relief, and felt herself almost a child again as Mary patted her back, saying, 'There, there! It's all right. I understand. I should have had more sense than to bring it. Please don't cry! Just think'–she gave a little laugh–'if Father O'Malley had seen it!' They both began to shake, small, rippling tremors, which mounted into laughter; quiet, relaxing laughter such as Mary Ellen never thought to laugh again. Oh, the lass would get by. She knew what to laugh at.

They both stopped abruptly when a knock came on the front door, and Mary Ellen opened it to Molly.

'He's coming up the road, ma.'

'All right,' said Mary Ellen, 'you know what to do. Tell him I want him to come in the front way.'

Without looking again at Mary, she said, 'Well, lass, I'll get myself away in,' and she went through the kitchen and out of the back door.

In her own backyard she paused a moment. Within the next few minutes she would have lost her lad, for she had no doubt that once he stepped inside that door he would be gone from her and another woman would have him. She wanted his happiness didn't she? Yes, above all things she wanted his happiness. But with it she hadn't thought to feel this added sense of loneliness. Well, she'd have to turn her mind to the others. Shane, for instance, who needed her as never before. And Molly, who seemed to have been born when Katie died. And Mick, who'd need two steady hands on him to keep him from Dominic's path. Yes, she still had a lot to cope with. And her lad would be next door for some time yet–Rome wasn't built in a day.

Left alone, Mary felt unable to move. There were a dozen and one things she wanted to accomplish before seeing him; among them to change her apron and do her hair. But now she could only stand rooted. A few minutes ago she had asked herself if she could suffer this life. What a ridiculous question to ask, when her whole being told her she could suffer no life that did not hold him.

The heavy tread of his steps reached her, and she lifted her head to the sound. All the colour of life, all the essence of the music she had heard, all the beauty she had seen and felt with her soul's capacity, rose in her, and she moved towards the door. Not until she heard the sound of the knocker on his own door did she lift the latch.

It was some time before he turned his head towards her, and then he did it slowly as if afraid of what he would see. She held out her hand, and he moved towards her but did not touch her. It was she who took his arm and drew him over the threshold and closed the door behind them. Walking ahead of her into the room he looked about him, and his face was drained of its colour. He brought his gaze from the fragments of the broken statue lying by the fireside to her face, and he said grimly, 'No, Mary. You can't do it . . . that's how you'll end, like that–broken.'

'Some things are better broken.'

'I'll not let you do it.'

'You can't stop me, dear . . . it's done. Here I am, and here I stay until you have me . . . and after.'

His eyes travelled again round the room, and she smiled gently at him. 'Do you like it?' He made no reply, and she said, 'Come and see the kitchen.'

In the kitchen he stared at a table set in shining whiteness for two. The kettle, startlingly new, was singing on the hob. It caused something to break in him. He closed his eyes, striving to fight the weakness. 'You don't know what you're doing . . . you'll regret it . . . your father should—'

He could say no more. She was leaning against him, her arms about his neck. The oval of her face was lost in light. 'Hold me, John.'

His arms, telling his hunger, crushed her to him. The faint perfume of her body mingled with the acrid smell of iron ore, and in the ever increasing murmur of his endearments and the searching of his lips her words were lost:

> Whither thou goest, I will go: and where thou lodgest, I will lodge: thy people shall be my people, and thy God my God: Where thou diest, will I die, and there will I be buried: the Lord do so to me, and more also, if ought but death part thee and me.

A Grand Man

A Grand Man

Everything in this story is fictitious, except that which you yourself know to be true.

Chapter One

A Bit of Imagination

In the quiet corner of the school yard Mary Ann stood surrounded by a little band of open-mouthed, silent admirers. With waving movements of her thin arms she drew them closer about her, and when they were pressed near she warmed to her theme.

'And besides the great big house,' she said, her eyes moving from one to the other, like revolving saucers, 'we've got three servants and two cars and two horses . . . galloping ones.' She curved her arms into what she considered was the shape of the horses' legs, and she jerked them at a great speed to indicate the velocity of the steeds. 'And,' she finished in a voice weighed with awe, 'some day I'll show you them; and our house, and the car besides, some day when I have a party.'

The children stared at her in admiration. Then one after the other they put forth tentative offers that might act as a sprat to catch a mackerel.

'Would you like a stot of me ball, Mary Ann?'

'I'll lend you me thick skipping rope at the week-end, Mary Ann.'

'When I spent me penny on Saturda' I'll save you some, Mary Ann.'

Whether Mary Ann would have accepted any of these offers cannot be known, for at that moment an indignant figure came rushing round the corner of the school wall and startled them all by crying, 'Oh, you big liar, Mary Ann Shaughnessy! I've been listening behind the wall. You don't live in a big house, and you ain't got no servants or cars or horses. Oh, was there ever such a liar as you?'

The little crowd turned its eyes from the black-haired, vicious-faced accuser back to Mary Ann, and expectantly awaited developments.

Mary Ann felt no immediate anger against her enemy . . . Sarah Flannagan was always spoiling people's fun. And anyway, it wasn't lies she was telling, it was more in the nature of a story. Yes, that was it. This soothed her conscience, but she couldn't tell them that it was just a story. No, oh no. She felt a sudden spasm of pity for them; they had listened to her so intently–they were the best lot she had talked to for a long time. Looking back into the eyes of her audience, she realized that she owed them something, a show of defence at any rate. So she cocked her elfin face on one side and blinked her large brown eyes at Sarah Flanagan, and said quite calmly, 'You know nothing whatever about our house, or me da's car, Sarah

Flannagan; and I'll thank you to mind your own business.' She nodded at the children, and the nod said, 'There, that's settled her hash.'

The dark spoiler of dreams gasped, and for a moment was struck speechless; then sucking in her lips and making a sound that was a good imitation of frying bacon, she turned to the eager group, her head wagging as quickly as her tongue as she cried, 'Why! of all the whopping liars she's one. She lives right opposite us; and not in a house like ours either, but in Mulhattans' Hall. They've only got two wee rooms and a cupboard of a kitchen. And as for her da having a car . . . why! my! huh! He can't even keep down a job 'cause he's always on the booze.'

Knowing she had played her trump card, Sarah Flannagan's vituperation ceased, but her chin, thrust out towards the slight, quivering figure of Mary Ann, was defying her to get over that shattering piece of integrity.

Now the poised calm of Mary Ann had vanished, and her eyes were blazing with an anger that lent to her little frame the energy of lightning. She almost sprang on the indignant stickler for truth, stopped only, it would seem, by the jutting chin of her enemy. Her voice shaking with an emotion that could only be classed as uncontrollable rage, she shouted, 'You! you pig face! you wicked thing. I'll slap your face, so I will, if you dare say me da drinks. Oh . . . h!' She cast her eyes heavenwards. 'It's a wonder God doesn't strike you down dead. But you'll go to hell for your wickedness . . . Oh, yes you will.' She pointed an accusing finger, and had only to add 'I'll see to it' to give the stamp of absolute authority to this last statement.

Sarah Flannagan was not in the least intimidated by this threat to her future, but turned her fishy eyes on to the group that had widened and spread itself away from Mary Ann.

Mary Ann too looked at her late admirers, and beseechingly she entreated them, 'Don't believe a word she says. My da's a lovely man. He gets sick at times but he never drinks. And he tells the loveliest stories. Look, some day I'll take you . . . Home. . . .'

The words trailed away as Sarah Flannagan laughed: 'She thinks she's safe with you lot that comes from the Fifteen Streets; she doesn't tell them lies to anybody living round our way.'

The faces, whose attention Mary Ann had held so eagerly a few minutes ago, now looked at her in silence and condemnation, for to partake in the make-believe world of childhood is not to lie unless the word lie is actually uttered, but once it is then make-believe is wrong; it immediately becomes a sin–another weight to be carried on the head until the priest removes it in confession; lies were connected with penance and purgatory. Mary Ann Shaughnessy had been found out.

With one accord they backed away. Then turning together like pigeons in flight, they went hitching and skipping around the personification of truth as she walked triumphantly out of the school yard with a backward leer to where Mary Ann stood with trembling lips and the burning sting of tears in the backs of her eyes.

The blazing indignation had died out of her as quickly as it had arisen, and after waiting in order to give her tormentor a good start, she too walked out of the yard and made her way home. And to comfort herself, she decided that if she could cover the whole distance homewards without once stepping on a crack in the pavement any wish she might make would be bound to come true.

To this end she began a series of hops, jumps and long and short strides, of stepping into the gutter when confronted by a paving stone so cracked that it was impossible to hop, jump or stride over it. It was when confronted by such a stretch of pavement that she was knocked right into the middle of it by two boys rushing out of Stanley Street. Their wild stampede carried her before them and left her staring down at her feet lying bang across a crack.

Her face worked and her lips trembled, and she could have cried with vexation. She had so wanted a wish, just another wish to make doubly sure of the week-end. She couldn't have too many wishes to . . . keep the week-end right. And the week-end started tonight, because it was Friday night and her da got his pay packet the night. She stood uncertain for a moment, plucking at her lip. Then her face brightened and she hopped clean off the diseased pavement on to a whole but greasy slab. She knew what she would do; she'd go and have a talk with The Holy Family. If anybody could make sure of the week-end, they could.

This decision made, she hurried back along the main road, charitably forgetful of the times when the Holy Family had slipped up in their duty and the week-ends had been a failure.

As she neared the church, its external severity filled her with nothing but hope and its interior gaudiness lifted her heart and clothed her with peace.

Going up to the small side altar she knelt down below the life-size statues of the Virgin, with the Child in her arms, and St Joseph standing protectingly near. She gazed up at them for some moments in silence before beginning her routine. First she blessed herself; then she lifted the Sacred Heart Medal that was reposing on her chest at the end of a narrow brass chain, which she would have assured you was solid gold, and she laid this on the front of her coat so that it would not escape the notice of the influential ones. Then bringing to her face what she called her 'good look', she said, in a voice that was a mixture of Tyneside and Irish, 'Oh, Holy Family, I've come to ask you something; and I'll do anything you like for you if you'll grant my request.'

She waited, as if to let her offer sink in, before going on, 'I want you to keep me da from being sick at the week-end, 'cause he's a lovely da, as you know, and he doesn't mean to make me ma cry. He told her so last night himself when he thought I was asleep in bed. He told her it was sorry he was to the heart, and if only we could all get back into the country he'd give up the . . . I mean he wouldn't be sick any more; it's having to work in the shipyard and them factories that makes him want to be sick. And there's nothing but yards round here to work in. But mind,' she put in, hastily, 'I'm not blaming you for making so many yards; you've had to put them some place.' She nodded, expressing her sympathy at what must have been a dilemma to them.

Then she went on, 'But you see, me da doesn't like them; he likes the country. And he won't go into it to work without me ma and me and our Michael. And that's where the cottage comes in. You'll mind I asked you about it last week. If only you could see your way clear to getting us a cottage, just a little weeny one would do, I'd do anything for you, Jesus, Mary and Joseph. I'll even stop telling lies about the servants and the horses. I will, honest to God.'

She had a vague idea that something should happen at this point, a clapping of hands at least. She gazed up at the group of statuary in strained, expectant silence, and had to be content when the infant child looked up at his mother with a 'Well, what about it?' look on his face.

The Virgin must have taken the cue, for quite suddenly Mary Ann experienced a feeling of relief, and tears, which she was sure she had not started, ran down her cheeks, and she was powerless to stop them.

She blessed herself, and having risen, she genuflected deeply; then turned away and walked almost into the arms of Father Owen.

The old priest, with his bald head and long solemn face, hung over her for a moment and affected astonishment at seeing her. He made not the smallest reference to her tear-stained face, but he bent down and whispered, 'You've a great devotion to the Holy Family, I notice, Mary Ann.'

Blinking, smiling and sniffing, all in one movement, she whispered back confidentially, 'Yes, Father, 'cause it's nearly the same size as our family.'

'Oh, of course. Yes, yes,' he nodded at her. 'You're a good girl.' He patted her cheek, and the smile left her face and her head drooped, and she took small, quiet steps on her toes up the aisle, the priest walking as noiselessly by her side.

When she whispered something that he could not catch, he bent his long frame towards her, asking, 'What is it?' And she, still with eyes averted, whispered, 'I'm not a good girl, Father, I'm a howling liar.'

The priest's eyebrows moved slightly, and he said, 'Oh, indeed?'

And Mary Ann nodded to the heating grid over which she stepped carefully, and said, 'Yes.'

In silence they reached the end of the church and came to a halt where the holy water font was attached to a pillar. Mary Ann dipped in her fingers and once again blessed herself, and the priest, standing looking at her, sighed and exclaimed, 'Ah well. It's a good thing when we know what we are, but I think you're too hard on yourself. That's a bit too strong a name for you, Mary Ann.'

'It isn't, Father. Oh, it isn't,' she whispered emphatically.

She had called herself a howling liar, and the priest must take her word that that was what she was; he mustn't take things lightly like this. She stretched up to him and went on to explain, still in a whisper, 'You see, Father, I tell people we've got cars and horses and servants, and we haven't.'

'Oh, you do?' The priest's eyebrows moved again.

'Yes.'

'Dear, dear. Cars, horses and servants?'

'Yes.'

They stared at each other.

'Well, well; this is serious. They couldn't be just nice day-dreams you've been having?'

'No, oh no, Father.'

'Dear, dear me. Cars, horses and servants. What are we going to do about it?'

'I've talked to the Holy Family, Father.'

'You have?'

'Yes, Father. And I promised them I won't lie again. And I meant to promise them I won't get into any more rages either, but. . . .'

'Do you get into rages, Mary Ann?'

'I do, Father; when anybody says me da . . .' She hesitated and her eyes dropped once more, and she toyed with her hair ribbon which was hanging perilously on the end of one plait.

'Yes, Mary Ann,' prompted Father Owen. 'And what do they say?'

'Well'–she looked straight into the priest's eyes–'people say me da drinks; and you know yourself, Father, as he doesn't. You know he never touches a drop.'

The child and the priest regarded each other intently; and as Mary Ann watched the priest's nostrils quiver and his right eyebrow jerk spasmodically, very like the head of Mr Lavey, who lived on the ground floor of their house and who had the tick, she felt forced to press her point again.

'He might get sick now and then, but he doesn't drink. Does he, Father?'

The appeal in the great eyes, the strain visible in the thin wisp of a body, did not touch the priest as much as did the unseen but evident conflict of loyalties raging in the heart of this child who had the art of conjuring up and of living numbers of separate lives, each with the same focal point, her father . . . and him a drunken agitator, and not of the faith either! Which, in a way, was something to be thankful for. No, no–he chided himself for his thoughts–it could be the saving of him if he'd come in. . . .

'Does he, Father?' The whispered insistence made him pinch his quivering nose between his finger and thumb, and with a sliding glance at the cross hanging above the holy water font, he said, almost defiantly, 'Not a drop, Mary Ann. Not a drop. I know that.'

Mary Ann sighed, and she smiled, and her young mouth stretched wide in happiness as she said, 'I knew you would speak the truth, Father.'

Her pleasure, however, turned to immediate concern when she saw her dear, dear Father Owen almost choke. Something must have stuck in his throat, for he was going red in the face with coughing.

Still coughing, the priest led Mary Ann to the door, and patting her head, he nodded to her in farewell, for he was unable to speak.

In grave concern, Mary Ann watched him re-enter the church. Poor Father Owen; he had a bad cold. Eeh . . . the thought swept over her making her hot . . . what if he were to get the 'flu and die? Oh, but he wouldn't. God wouldn't let Father Owen die. She could not see the Creator being such a cold-blooded monster as to take away her confidant, friend, and what was more, her ally in defence of her father.

Suddenly she skipped off the church steps. Wouldn't that be one in the eye for Sarah Flannagan when she told her what Father Owen had said? 'Sarah Flannagan,' she would say to her, 'now shut your big gob and listen to this. Father Owen said . . . and mind he was standing near the holy water font and the cross above him when he said it, and not even you'll dare to say Father Owen tells lies. . . . Well, standing there, he said, "I've never known your da to touch a drop of drink, Mary Ann. And anybody that says it will go to Hell and be shrivelled up." So there!' By, that would be like a slap across her nasty big face.

For the moment she felt very happy. Father Owen was the bestest man in the world, next to her da. Eeh. Well, was her da better than the priest?

She spent most of the time that it took her to reach home in debating in which position of goodness she should place the two men who were a power in her life.

Chapter Two

Mulhattans' Hall

Mulhattans' Hall was a small tenement house jammed between two-storey houses consisting of two rooms upstairs and two down. In any other part of the country these would have been termed flats, but in Jarrow and the surrounding towns two rooms so placed was called a house, and if, as sometimes happened, the back-yard had been designed that each occupant had a slit of private concrete with a high wall cutting him off from his near neighbour, then that occupant had a right to feel that he was socially on the upgrade. It can therefore be guessed how far down the social scale were the five families living in Mulhattans' Hall, for here there was only one communal back-yard and from it water for all uses had to be carried.

The official name of Mulhattans' Hall was sixteen Burton Street. It had come by its title from a family of that name who had lived there some years before, and from occupying one 'house' the family, through marriage, had spread into the other four parts; and since they were all sons who had married the house had become a hive of Mulhattans, and far from a peaceful hive; and although the last of these Mulhattans had long since gone the name still remained.

Five families still occupied the Hall; the Shaughnessys on the attic floor, Miss Harper and the Quigleys on the first floor, and on the ground floor, on one side the McBrides, on the other the Laveys.

Tonight being Friday was bath night. Mary Ann didn't mind the bath, in fact she liked it, but she hated having to provide the means for it, for no matter how she talked to herself or what games she played she found that, even with their Michael on the other side of the handle, a bucket of water weighed a ton by the time she had reached the twenty-eighth step and the top landing. If possible she would have preferred to carry the bucket herself, for their Michael was the worst one on earth for playing games. What was more, tonight being Friday her grannie was sure to be visiting. That together with the bath was enough to try an angel with nothing on her mind; Mary Ann was no angel and she had a lot on her mind.

Once upon a time, she had hated to go into the house and find her grannie there, for as sure as life her grannie would want her to go and stay with her for the week-end, and to be in her grannie's company for just one hour seemed like a long nightmare, but now, although she still hated to find her there, all fear that she would make any such disagreeable request of her was past. If she thought her grannie was going to be so foolish as to ask her to go and stay with her, she had just to look at her with a certain look, which she kept now especially for her grannie, and that terrible old lady would dry up.

For years Mrs McMullen had put so many fears into Mary Ann's mind that it became difficult for the child to know which she was afraid of most . . . of hell, where she'd be made to sit on a red-hot gridiron all day without her knickers on, of being thrown clean out of the Catholic Church and plumb into the Salvation Army, or of being put away in a home so that she would never be able to see her ma or her da again till she would be an old woman of twenty. But now the old lady no longer instilled fear into Mary Ann with her prophecies; if possible, she kept out of her granddaughter's way, for Mary Ann had at last got her, if not exactly where she wanted her, at least under a certain control, and here she hoped to keep her. But Mary Ann knew she could only do this if she remained strong enough not to tell her da what had changed her grannie, for once she divulged the reason, her power, she knew, would vanish as quickly as a soap bubble, for he would roar for a month, and nothing she could think of would keep him from throwing his knowledge at his mother-in-law by way of a small repayment for what he had suffered at her hands during the past years.

Panting, Mary Ann reached the eighteenth stair and the landing before her own, and there, as usual, was Miss Harper, with her door open and sitting just where she could see who passed up and down.

'Hallo, there, Mary Ann,' Miss Harper called; 'your grannie's up.'

'Hallo, Miss Harper,' said Mary Ann. 'Is she?'

Unsmiling, she mounted her own flight of stairs. Miss Harper knew everybody's business, and she was the biggest borrower from here to John O'Groats.

She pushed open her own door, and there was her grannie, sitting like a lady in her astrakhan coat, and her hat, with the blue feather and veil on, cocked high upon her head.

'Hallo, Mary Ann,' said Mrs McMullen primly.

'Hallo, Grannie,' said Mary Ann.

'Have you just come from school?'

'Yes, Grannie.' What a silly daft question. Where would she have come from? Whitley Bay?

'Get your hands washed, and you can have your tea now,' said her mother.

'Aw . . . w,' Mary Ann protested, her face screwed up; 'can't I wait until me da comes?'

'Get your hands washed.'

When her mother spoke in that tone there was nothing to do but get your hands washed.

The ritual over, Mary Ann held up her hands for her mother's inspection; then sat down at the table. It was adorned with the best cloth, with the fancy work at the corners, and on a tray stood the three best cups, which if you held them up to the light you could see through, and the best tea-pot, which was of the same blue colour as the cups, but didn't match and had an odd lid.

In front of her grannie was a plate of boiled ham and a jar of pickled onions, and in the centre of the table was a plate of square, thin slices of bread which told all who beheld it that it was a 'cut loaf'.

Mary Ann watched her grannie eyeing the plate, and she said to herself, 'If she says a thing about it I'll say . . . "Milk Bottles!" I will, you'll see.' And she could almost hear her grannie thinking: Bought bread again, huh! Thought she didn't hold with it . . . nothing but brown, home-made wholemeal for her children. Must have their fancy vitamins. She hasn't a penny left to get the flour, that's it. And she got the loaf and ham on tick from Funnell's, I bet.

And Mary Ann also watched her mother avoid her grannie's eye and go to the fireplace. But she became so intent on again staring at her grannie that she did not notice her mother come back to the table; and she jumped when she said, 'Will you have jam or syrup?'

She eyed the small amount of jam in the dish, and knowing that Michael liked jam and hated syrup and thinking of last night and the names he had called their da, she said, 'Jam.'

'Jam what?' asked her mother.

'Please.'

'They hadn't to be told in my day,' said her grannie. Then almost choking on a mouthful of ham, she added hastily and in oiled tones to make up for her censure, 'Have you been picked for the procession, Mary Ann?'

Mary Ann attacked her jam and bread with vigour, but made no reply; and her mother said sharply, 'You heard your grannie talking to you?'

So Mary Ann, her eyes fixed on her plate, said, 'No, Grannie.' Oh, how she hated her grannie. She always asked about things that hurt you. For two pins she'd lean across the table and look her right in her old wrinkled eyes and say, 'Milk Bottles!' But once she had said it her hold would be gone, so she contented herself with just staring at her grannie in an irritating way and thinking back to that Sunday morning and the milk bottles.

She could see herself–it was very early and she had wakened with a cramp in her stomach. She was staying in Shields with her grannie, and as she usually did on such visits she was sleeping on the couch behind the kitchen door. It was the plums that were causing the cramp. Her grannie had made her eat them because she said they shouldn't be wasted. Yet they had been all soft and nasty. She'd got up and unbolted the back door and gone out to the lavatory. She had sat there for a long time, for the cramp kept on coming and going, and during the times her stomach was at peace she thought of home and her da and whether it had been a nice week-end. If it had he would be taking some tea to her ma in bed; and if she had been at home she'd have got some too, just as if she were grown up.

It was then she saw her grannie through the crack in the door. She watched her coming stealthily down the yard; then she disappeared from her sight as she went to the back door. Puzzled, she had listened, and she had heard her grannie open the back door and close it, and when she came within sight again she was carrying two pints of milk. She saw her stand within the shelter of the staircase wall, which also kept her out of the view of the upper window; and she watched her skilfully remove the milk-caps by inserting a needle under their edges, then pour the cream off both bottles into the screw-top jar, which she took from beneath her apron. This done, she filled one of the bottles to the brim out of the other, and after carefully replacing the cap, left the bottle inside the back door.

It was at this point that Mary Ann showed herself, and she watched her grannie hang on to the door for a moment and fight for breath as she exclaimed, 'Eeh! I saw what you did.'

She thought her grannie was going to have a fit; but before she could add anything further to her accusation she was grabbed by the collar of the coat she was wearing over her nightie and lifted clean off her feet and run up the yard as if the devil had her by the neck.

But if the terrifying Mrs McMullen had hoped to frighten Mary Ann she was mistaken. When at last Mary Ann was able to get a word in, with enraging calm and in her own words she reminded her grannie that it was only two weeks ago that Mrs Baker from upstairs, her that was deaf, had stood in the kitchen and complained of there being no cream on the milk, and she had blamed the milkman for swiping it and feeding his large, robust family with it.

There had followed a verbal barrage for power, which ended with Mary Ann putting on her clothes and saying she thought she'd go to mass in Jarrow this morning, and if her grannie would give her the threepence now for the bus instead of the night she'd be obliged.

Mrs McMullen had handed over the money, whilst her eyes had consigned her grandchild to the place from where through continued chastisement she had hoped to save her.

Mary Ann's last words as she left the house, which were apropos of nothing that had been said that morning, almost caused the final collapse of Mrs McMullen, for just a second before closing the door behind her Mary Ann said, 'Me da's a grand man.'

She had often wished since she had stayed just a little longer to have seen the effect of her words on her grannie, for even through the closed door she had heard the sound of her choking.

She looked now at the old woman guzzling the last of the ham. She hadn't been offered even the smallest piece. But what did it matter? She had more than ham on her grannie, and her grannie knew it. She could keep her ham and she hoped it stuck half-way down. She looked to where her mother was refilling her grannie's cup and wondered, and not for the first time, if her grannie was really her mother's mother. Her da likely wasn't joking when he had said her grannie had stolen her mother when she was a baby and she really never had been Lizzie McMullen at all but one of the first ladies of the land. Her da joked a lot at times, but still he was probably right about this, for what connection had her lovely mother with her grannie? None; none in the wide world. Her mother's hair was fair, like silver, and straight; not even a kink in it; while her grannie's was black and white and frizzed up like a nigger's. She got it that way by sticking it in thousands of papers. And her grannie's eyes were as round as aniseed balls but black, while her mother's were long and grey. And then again her grannie was little and stumpy and fat, and her mother was a grand height, and if she'd had nice clothes like Mrs Tullis, who kept the outdoor beershop at the corner, she'd have looked like a queen. No, like a princess; for in spite of her mother's great age of twenty-nine, she could be gay at times, like a young princess. No; her mother was no relation to her grannie. Would her mother have golloped all that ham herself? She wouldn't even eat any food if there wasn't much for her and their Michael. Her grannie was just what her da said she was, pig, guts, hog and artful!

'You can get down now.' Lizzie's voice brought Mary Ann's fixed gaze from her grandmother. 'Say your grace.'

Mary Ann said her grace. She knew why she had been ordered to leave the table, because she'd been staring at her grannie and her ma was afraid she'd say something.

Never slow to take advantage of a situation, she asked, 'Can I look at the album, Ma?'

Now the album was a treasure chest which, through an odd assortment of snaps, kept fresh the memories of the happy incidents that had taken place in the early years of Elizabeth Shaughnessy's married life, and as time went on she found it more and more necessary to refer to it to confirm that these memories were the stamp on her mind of incidents that had once actually taken place and were not just vague dreams.

Mary Ann could remember when she first saw the album. She was sitting between her ma and da and they were laughing and laughing as they turned the pages. She could remember the firelight shining on their faces, and they had both appeared so beautiful to her that instead of laughing with them she had cried. She could remember her da picking her up and carrying her upstairs to bed. Yes, she'd gone upstairs to bed, where Michael and her had a real bedroom. She couldn't remember very much about that house, only the real bedroom. There had been other houses; then rooms; and finally Mulhattans' Hall. In each place the furniture got less and less, until now none of it was familiar . . . only the album. The table and chairs might change, and even the beds, but the album . . . never. It was to her a land wherein she could wander and dream; but rare were the times she was allowed to wander alone. Only on such occasions as the present when her mother desired to keep her quiet was there a chance of getting the album to herself.

She saw that her mother was annoyed with her because she had asked for the album in front of her grannie, for it was a subject of controversy between them; Mrs McMullen considered that it belonged to her by right, having ignored the fact that her late husband had given it to his daughter on her sixteenth birthday.

'Wash your hands again,' said Lizzie; 'and be careful how you get it out of the trunk. And mind, don't disarrange the things. And stay in the room with it.'

Mary Ann did as she was bidden; and as she knelt on the floor to open the lid of the trunk that stood beside the little window which came down to the floor, she paused to wonder why the album should have been put into the trunk, for although it was usually placed out of her reach it was generally on show, for it was indeed a showpiece, being backed with fine leather and bound with brass hinges that spread across the back and front of it; it had once been owned by her mother's granda who came from Norway.

She lifted it tenderly out of the trunk, smoothed again into order the assortment of clothes, then went to the bed and, laying it there, she fell on her stomach across the bed, her heels playing a silent tattoo on her small buttocks. Sucking in her breath in anticipation of coming enjoyment, she lifted back the heavy cover and looked once more on Great-Granda Stenson. But his sidewhiskers had long ceased to be funny. She turned a number of thick pages, ignoring with an upward tilt of her nose the photographs they held; she knew them all; they were merely pictures of her grannie from the time she was a baby until she was married . . . and who'd want to look at them? But following the picture of her grandmother's wedding group the real pictures began.

Now she burrowed her knees into the bed. There was her ma with nothing on; and there was her ma on the sands with her spade and pail; and there she was again with her great long fair plaits and holding her school prize in her hand. There were many more snaps of her ma. Then they too abruptly stopped, and Mary Ann was confronted with two blank pages. They were like a curtain ending an act of a play, and although she was anxious to raise the curtain and continue the story, she did not hurry, but savoured what was to come. She knew there was not a lot more to follow, but it was the best, and, like the pork cracknel she sometimes had on a Sunday, she always conserved the nice things until the end.

Slowly now she turned the page, and there they were, her ma and da. She drew the air up through her nose as if inhaling a scent. Oh, didn't they look lovely? Anybody would know that her ma was a bride although she wasn't dressed in white but just in a costume. It was the . . . lovely look on her face that told you. And there was her da, dressed as a soldier. Oh, better than a soldier . . . an airman. And he wasn't just like any airman, for he had two stripes on his arm. He'd been a grand man in the Air Force, had her da. He had told her about the marshal, the one that sent the aeroplanes up. He had thought the world of her da, and he wouldn't think about lifting a finger unless first asking her da about it. . . . Oh my, yes; it was as her da said, the Air Force knew it the day he left.

Her ma, at one time, had laughed until she cried when her da was telling her about what a grand man he was in the Air Force. But not lately, not since they came to live here. In fact, when she came to think about it, her da never looked at the album at all now.

Suddenly her interest in the pictures waned; she found she didn't want to look at herself and their Michael in the various stages of undress. She looked up from the book and around the room. Its only articles of furniture were the bed, the trunk and a white-painted wardrobe. The floor had no covering except a clippie rug, but the boards were stained and polished and would have looked fine, she thought, had there not been so many wide gaps that let both draught and dust up through them.

Slowly she closed the book and wriggled back off the bed; and lifting the album, she returned it to the trunk. And not until she had closed the lid did she realize that it was the very first time she had put it away without being told . . . always her mother had to tell her again and again before she could be induced to close it. A pain not unlike a toothache came into her chest, and she stepped to the window and stood looking down into the street. Some of her friends were playing tiggie in the middle of the road, while others on the pavement opposite were endeavouring to walk on tin cans which they held tight to the soles of their shoes by pulling on string reins. The hurt feeling was pressing on her so heavily that it took away the wish that she might join them.

Her mind became a confused jumble of desires. They swirled around in her head and became tangled, as always, about the mainspring of her life; if only her ma and da laughed together like they used to; if only their Michael didn't make her wild by saying the things he did about her da; if only there were no week-ends in the week and men didn't get paid on a Friday; and if only her grannie could be wafted away to some far place; not hell; no, but some place from where she would find it impossible to come and visit her ma and talk in a quiet voice in the scullery, telling her what she should do about her da–her ma was always short with him after her grannie had been.

She leaned her head against the top of the attic window–it was just the right height for leaning against–and filled now with a pain that was almost of an adult quality, she stared unseeing through it.

Usually she was only too well aware that the Flannagans' window was straight below theirs on the opposite side of the street; but this evening with so much on her mind she gave no thought to it, until the curtains being jerked violently together attracted her attention. Then she straightened herself up, thinking, Eeh, I wasn't looking in. Eeh, I wasn't. She was about to withdraw when a too-well-known face suddenly appeared between the curtains and a tongue of remarkable length was thrust up at her. Before she could retaliate the owner of the tongue had withdrawn it, and the curtains were again closed.

For the moment, the weight of the family worry was lifted from her, and she compressed her lips and shook her head from side to side before muttering, 'Oh, Sarah Flannagan, you cheeky thing, you. Oh, you are! Just you wait.'

She could see by the bunched curtains that her enemy was still behind them, so keeping to one side of the attic window she waited, and it was no time at all before the curtains were jerked apart, and Mary Ann was ready at the instant. Not only did her tongue shoot out but it wagged itself violently for a second before returning limply to its residence.

Gasping with indignation, Mrs Flannagan threw up the window; but Mary Ann did not wait to hear what she had to say. With her fingers pressed to her lips she ran across the room, but before pulling open the door she composed herself to enter the kitchen so as not to give herself away. But she need not have troubled, for her mother and her grannie were in the scullery, as her grannie's voice proclaimed.

It came softly, but clearly audible, to her. 'You're a fool,' it said.

She stood, her ear cocked towards the scullery, and when her grannie's voice came again, her body began to tremble as if she was freezing with cold. 'Leave him. Get a court order; he'll have to pay. I'll take the bairns. And if you don't want to go back to office work there's plenty of clean factories to pick from now. If ever there's been a fool, it's you. If only you'd stuck to Bob Quinton you'd be living like a lady now. Look at the building business he's got up. And him never married. Oh, I wish the other one would fall into the Don on a dark night, I do, so help me God. And there's never a night goes by but I pray for it. God forgive me.'

There was a crash that brought the two women running into the kitchen, and for a moment they stood looking down at the blue cup and saucer lying in fragments on the hearth. Then they looked towards Mary Ann standing by the table, her face white and drained and her eyes stretched wide.

Mrs McMullen was the first to speak. Forgetting for the moment all caution, she reverted to her old manner. 'Well now, would you believe it? Anybody can see with half an eye that she threw it. Well, I ask you. And one of the good ones, an' all.'

'Shut up! Shut up! Shut up!' The words rose to a scream in Mary Ann's throat. The tears rained from her eyes, blinding her. As her mother's arms went about her she started to moan, and Lizzie, holding her tightly, cried, 'It's all right. It's all right. It doesn't matter about the cup or anything. We'll get another. Sh! . . . Sh! now.'

'A good smacked backside, that's what she wants.'

'Mother. Please.' Lizzie's voice checked the old woman. 'Go, will you; I'll be down on Sunday.'

Even the feather on Mrs McMullen's hat seemed to bristle. 'You're telling me to get out because of that 'un?'

'Yes. Yes. Don't you see? Just this once. Go on.'

Completely outraged, Mrs McMullen buttoned up her coat and marched to the door. But there she turned and said, 'Very well. But I'll expect you as usual on Sunday, mind. What's things coming to, anyway? Ordered out!' Her voice was cut off abruptly from them as the door banged.

For a moment Lizzie's eyes rested on the closed door; then lifting Mary

Ann up she set her on her knee and rocked her gently, saying nothing but looking away out of the window, over the roof tops, into a narrow stretch of clear sky, unpierced by even one tall chimney or crane or mast.

Was it wrong to wish to die? Was it wrong to wish from the bottom of her heart that she had never set eyes on Mike Shaughnessy? How much longer could she go on? . . . All her life, she supposed, until she was an old woman, inured to it all like Mrs Lavey down below . . . hope dead, love and respect burnt out. What more could she do? Only pray for something to happen. She shook her head. Pray? She was always praying, until now it had become only a form of talking to herself. Sometimes she thought her appeals never left her head–there was no force left in her to push them out. Her belief in the goodness of God was going, if not already gone. To believe in God's inevitable pattern for good you had to be made like Mary Ann and swear black was white, or be a saint. She was long past the Mary Ann stage, and she wasn't made of the stuff of saints. She wanted to lead a decent life and to have Mike the way he used to be. She wouldn't grow into a Mrs Lavey; she'd leave him.

She almost sprang to her feet, forgetting that she held the child.

The jerk caused Mary Ann to slip to the floor, and she stood dazed, and asked, 'Is he coming? Is it me da?'

'No,' said Lizzie, getting up: 'you slipped.'

'Ma.'

'Yes?'

'Me grannie . . .'

'Now'–Lizzie smoothed the tumbled hair back from Mary Ann's forehead–'forget what you heard your grannie say.'

'But she said . . .'

'It doesn't matter what she said. Everything's going to be all right.'

'Honest?'

Lizzie pressed her teeth into her lip and her head moved slightly. 'Honest,' she said.

Mary Ann sniffed and turned away. 'Will I start getting the water up?'

'No. Wait until Michael comes in,' said Lizzie.

'But he won't be in until six. Didn't he say that Mr Wilson wanted him for two hours the night?'

'Yes, I know. But it can wait until he comes in. You can go out and play for a little while.'

'I don't want to go.'

Lizzie looked down on her daughter, and she thought, Oh, let her want to go out to play. Don't let her start to reason and feel yet. But hadn't she always reasoned and felt, especially where he was concerned? If things came to a pitch, it would be her that would be the stumbling-block. If she were deprived of him she would die. 'Do you want the album again?'

'No.' Mary Ann shook her head. And as Lizzie stared at her the sound of footsteps on the stairs caused them both to turn and face the door, but almost instantly they recognized the steps weren't his.

There came a knock on the door, and when Lizzie opened it there stood

Mrs Flannagan dressed for the street; and besides wearing her best things she was using her best voice, the one that Mike Shaughnessy called her refeened twang.

'Mrs Shaughnessy, I must have a word with you. I'm sorry to trouble you as you've plenty on your plate, God knows, but I really must make a stand. It's getting that way that a body can't look out of her window.'

'What has she done now?' Lizzie Shaughnessy's voice was flat.

'Stuck her tongue out at me. A yard long it was. I was just pulling back me curtains before I went out. I was just off to the confraternity . . . I'll let the sun in, I thought, to warm up the room. It's a pity you don't get it across this way in the evening, it'd make all the difference. But there I was at the window, and she came and with real intent and purpose she leant forward and stuck her tongue out at me. I was so taken aback, Mrs Shaughnessy, I was really. It was uncalled for.'

'Did you?' Lizzie looked over her shoulder to where Mary Ann was standing behind her.

'Not at her, Ma. At Sarah. She had stuck her tongue out at me and dived behind the curtains; and I was waiting for her.'

'Now, now, now, Mary Ann.' Mrs Flannagan looked and sounded distinctly shocked. 'My Sarah was nowhere in the room, when I went to the window. You must not preevaritate.'

'I'm not,' said Mary Ann from behind her mother. 'She was. I saw her through the curtains.'

'Well! . . . That child!' To Mrs Flannagan's feelings was added indignation. 'It's one thing to weave tales as I know you do, but it's another thing to tell downright lies. I'll say no more, Mrs Shaughnessy. But I thought I'd come and tell you . . . one must make a stand. And I'm not a person to cause trouble, especially to those who are heavily burdened already.'

Mary Ann saw her mother's shoulders lift and heard her voice take on that note that made her different. 'You came to tell me about Mary Ann putting her tongue out. You have told me, Mrs Flannagan. I shall chastise Mary Ann. Is there anything more you want to say to me?'

There followed a short silence while the two women regarded each other. Then the older woman burst out, 'Don't come your hoity-toity with me, Mrs Shaughnessy; it won't wash. I pity you, I do, but I'll only stand so much.'

'Your pity is entirely wasted, Mrs Flannagan. . . .'

'It is that. It is that.' The deep rocketing voice came from the stairs, and Mary Ann sprang forward, only to be stopped by her mother's hip. She watched her father come into view, but he didn't look to where she was or at her mother, but straight at Mrs Flannagan.

'Good evening to you, Mrs Flannagan.' He doffed his black, grease-laden cap, and standing over the now wide-eyed Mrs Flannagan, he held it to his chest and moved it round between his hands in mock obsequiousness, and his voice took on a matching whine. 'Your pity's wasted on me wife, Mrs Flannagan. But now me, it's the very thing I'm needing. I'm needing pity so badly that you could bath me in it; you could hold me down in a bath full of it and I wouldn't drown. It has the same effect on me as beer, you know. Now, now, what's your hurry?' he obstructed her means of escape by standing at the head of the stairs. 'Don't go away, Mrs Flannagan, without sprinkling on me shamed head a few drops of your pity. It'd be about as effective as your holy water.'

'Mike!'

Mike took not the slightest notice of his wife's sharp demand, but advanced one step further towards the now retreating woman saying, 'Come now. Come now. You must make a stand. That's it, isn't it? That's your slogan . . . you must make a stand.'

'I'll call me husband, mind.'

Mike Shaughnessy's head went back and he bellowed forth a laugh. 'You've got a sense of humour, I'll grant you that.' Then of a sudden he dropped his posing and his voice lost its bantering tone, and he stood to one side, and, pointing to the stairs, said, 'Get down there, and don't come up here again unless you're asked, for if I find you at this door again I'll put me toe in your backside. That's if I'm sober. God knows what I'll do to you if I'm drunk.' He watched her scurrying down the stairs; then he turned to his own doorway, which was now empty, and entered the room.

Lizzie was at the table and did not look towards him, nor he to her, but he threw his cap to Mary Ann and she caught it deftly. Then she took his greasy mackintosh and dived into the inner pocket where his bait tin was, and opening it, discovered there one sausage. She smiled at him, and taking it out sniffed its smoky, stale flavour, then began to eat it hurriedly before her ma should remember it was Friday and stop her.

Mike divested himself of his coat, and, rolling up his sleeves, went towards the scullery, saying, 'What brought her here?'

Mary Ann and Lizzie exchanged glances. Then Mary Ann said, 'I put me tongue out at her; I thought she was Sarah behind the curtains.'

His head went up again, and he laughed 'Good for you.'

Mary Ann lifted the kettle from the hob and followed him into the scullery. She poured the water into a dish and stood waiting at his side with the towel while he washed himself. He did this with a lot of puffing and blowing, interspersed with remarks about Mrs Flannagan.

'You know the saying: "Put a beggar on horseback and he'll ride to Hell?" Well, it was started by just such another as her. Did you know that?'

'No, Da.'

'Well, it was. She means to rise, that 'un, or die in the attempt. It's a good job the poor are kept down.' He blew into the towel. Then peering over the top of it his brown eyes twinkled down at her. 'You remember the time she sent the note to your school saying Sarah had an illustrated throat?'

Mary Ann laughed up at him. She remembered it well. The note had been passed among the teachers and they had not been discreet about the cause of their laughter.

'And there was the time she asked in Funnell's for the liquidated milk. Do you mind that?'

Mary Ann nodded and chuckled, saying, 'If she couldn't have said evaporated she should have said unsweetened, shouldn't she?'

'She should that.' He buttoned up his shirt neck. 'Take my tip, Mary Ann. Anyone who tries to use long words in an aim to get above themselves, they're not much good. You can say all you want to say with your own kind of language.'

'But if you could get to the Grammar School you'd learn big words then properly, wouldn't you?'

'Yes . . . yes, you would then.'

'If Michael goes, he'll learn big words.'

Mike stopped in the act of rolling down his shirt sleeves and stared at her; but she did not flinch from the look in his eyes.

She might fight with Michael because he called this man names–Michael sometimes lay on the floor and beat his fists on the mat, grinding out from between his teeth such words as 'Big, rotten, drunken beast!' At such times she hated Michael and would think nothing of kicking out at him. Yet she knew why Michael said these things. He loved their mother and he was hurt when she was hurt, and he was ashamed of their da. He was going in for an exam for the Grammar School and he couldn't see himself holding a place there when his father's name was becoming a byword wherever drunks were mentioned–but her eyes were now telling Mike Shaughnessy that no matter how she fought with Michael she wanted him to go to the Grammar School, not so as she could brag about him, but because it would make her ma happy.

Suddenly Mike took her small face between his great hands and pressed it gently, and she pressed her hands over his before turning swiftly and running into the kitchen.

'Where's the kettle?' asked her mother.

'Oh!' She turned about again and collided with her father, and they both laughed.

Mike went to the table and looked significantly down on to the empty plates set there, and Lizzie, still not looking at him said, 'I didn't get anything ready.'

Mike gazed at his wife in silence for a moment before saying, 'You didn't believe me then?'

Lizzie moved towards the fire, and his eyes followed her.

'I swore to you.'

'You've sworn before.'

'But I thought it was a fresh start?'

Lizzie stood looking down into the fire, and he came and stood behind her, his red head topping her silver one. 'Liz'–his arms went about her–'help me; I am trying hard.'

She did not answer but made a choking sound, and he swung her round to him and held her pressed tightly against his chest.

Mary Ann stood at the door of the scullery, her eyes bright, watching them. It caused her no embarrassment to see her parents loving; rather, it filled her with bubbling joy. She listened now to her da's voice deep in his throat, and soft.

'Darlin', darlin'. I swear before God I'll make a go of it this time. Liz, Oh Liz. I should be hung for the things I've done to you.' His voice became lower. 'Never leave me, Liz. Promise you'll never leave me.'

No answer came from her mother, only the sound of her sobs. They were too much for Mary Ann and she turned into the scullery, and, leaning against the wall, began to cry. Oh it was going to be a lovely week-end. Oh her da was wonderful.

There was no connection between the man in there saying such words as darlin', beloved and precious, and the man who, just a week tonight, had rolled up the stairs at eleven o'clock singing at the top of his voice and proclaiming to all who would listen to him that at this time tomorrow he'd be a rich man, for hadn't he put three pounds on a sure winner, and the Sporting Pink would be red with his success.

There was no sound now from the kitchen, and after drying her eyes Mary Ann went in. Her mother was standing by the table opening her da's pay packet. She watched her shake out the contents. It was all happening as she had heard him saying last night it would.

Lizzie counted the notes, then moved the silver about with her finger. There was thirteen shillings, and she looked up at her husband and said, 'Will that do?'

He stared at it for a moment; then smiled with the corner of his mouth drawn in. 'Make it a quid. That'll do for me baccy an' all.'

She handed him the pound, and taking another four from the bundle of seven she stuck them in a jug on the mantlepiece, saying, 'That'll clear the rent.'

'Ah, Liz-a-beth. Must you do it all at once?'

His tone was joking, but Mary Ann knew that he didn't like what her ma had done.

'Look'–he caught hold of Lizzie's arm–'pay two weeks. You can clear it next week. You'll have more next week. I'm telling you, you will. What do you think? Look at me now'–he drew himself up a mock attitude–'and listen to what I am saying. Mike Shaughnessy is working the morrer–overtime till five.'

Lizzie and Mary Ann stared at him but said nothing, and he dived across the kitchen and, lifting a chair, brought it to Lizzie, saying, 'Hold on to that, for you'll need it.' He put her hands on the back of it, then stood away from her and proclaimed in an awful voice, 'Sunday an' all!'

Now Lizzie did show her surprise, and her expression gave him great delight; and Mary Ann stared up at her father her eyes like pools of gladness. He was going to do overtime; he was going to work on a Sunday; he must have forgotten clean about the things he called theories, for they usually stopped him doing overtime. He often had these theories when he was having a period of . . . sickness, and then he would talk a lot about them. She had come to understand that if all the men did overtime there soon wouldn't be enough work for them in the middle of the week, and they would be standing at the street corners again. She couldn't imagine the men standing at the street corners in the middle of the week, except Willie James, and he'd neither work nor want. Sometimes her da's theories took a different turn, as they had done last week-end when he talked all the time about the men stopping work on account of Harry Bancroft being sacked. He said Harry Bancroft had asked for it for he'd never done a decent day's work in his life; then he got bitter and said nobody had wanted to strike when he'd got the push, yet he did more work in a day than some of them did in a week, for he wasn't a gaffer watcher; and if every man pulled his weight there'd be no need for overtime. And he knew why he had got the sack. It was because he'd made his mouth go against the Union.

And now he was going to do overtime, and they'd have a lot of money next week and her ma would be happy and not listen to her grannie.

She ran to him, and throwing her arms round his leg clutched it to her. Mike laid his hand upon his daughter's head, and still looking at his wife, said, 'See? You see? I have me public.' Then hoisting Mary Ann into his arms, he kissed her and asked, 'Do you know what your da's going to do the morrer night?' And she, holding his beloved face gently between her hands as if it were something delicate and precious, said, 'Take us into Shields.'

He sniffed loudly. 'Shields! Newcastle it is the morrer night, and we're going to do a show; and in style.'

'Don't buoy her up.' Lizzie spoke quietly. 'I'm paying all the rent and you'll want your pound for baccy and for fares. And there's a bill to pay to Funnell's.'

'But I tell you I'll make a fiver over the week-end–you can pay it off next week.' He put Mary Ann down and moved towards his wife, saying, 'Ah Liz, be reasonable.'

But Lizzie moved away from him and went to the mantlepiece, and, taking the four pounds out of the jug, she turned to Mary Ann saying, 'Straighten your hair and put your hat and coat on.'

'What you going to do?' Mike's voice was stiff now.

'Send it to him.' Lizzie sat down at the table, and having written a note, put it with the money in an envelope, and when Mary Ann stood by her side, she said, 'Now you know where to go, don't you? Along Grange Road and turn to the right.'

'I know,' said Mary Ann. Her voice, too, was flat and had a touch of impatience in it. Oh, if only her ma hadn't got to do it. But she had; and there was her da looking at them, his face all hard again.

Her mother pinned the envelope inside the breast pocket of her school frock. 'Go on now, and don't speak to anyone; and keep to the main roads.'

As she moved towards the door no one spoke, and when she went out, closing the door after her, and stood on the landing, still no sound came from the room to her. An urgent, turbulent feeling filled her stomach. It had a voice of its own which cried loudly in her ears, 'Make them speak. Oh, make them speak. It'll soon be all right if they'll only speak.' She waited, her head bent towards the door; she couldn't go all the way down Western Road and Ormond Street across Dee Street to Grange Road to the rent man's house knowing they were not speaking.

'You're not taking any chances on me, are you?'

In spite of her relief, the tone of her father's voice hurt her; and her mother's added to the pain as she said, 'I've been taken in before; you wouldn't have rested until you'd had that rent.'

'My God! After all I said last night. All I was asking was that you paid two weeks and cleared it next. I wanted to give you a treat . . . take you away out of here for a while.'

'I'd rather get out of here permanently.'

'You shall, Liz–you shall, but I can't do it all at once.'

Her father's voice was so convincing; how could anyone not believe him. And it went on, 'Do you know it's Hell now–this minute my innards are burning for a drink.'

'Mike. Oh, Mike!'

There was a scrambling sound, and she knew her mother had flown to her da and that her arms were about him and that she was soothing and mothering him like she did Michael and herself when they were bad. Filled now with a sad happiness, she was about to turn from the door when a voice hissing between the banisters caused her to jump.

'You sneaking little pig. Just you wait–I'll tell me ma. Listening at the key-hole again.'

'Aw! you,' she hissed back at her brother. 'I wasn't listening.'

When Michael reached the landing he towered above her, his indignation making him seem even taller. In looks at least he took after his father; and he already looked more than his eleven years, whereas Mary Ann looked less than her eight; but in repartee and temper they were equally matched.

'I'd like to box your ears.'

'I know.' She pursed up her lips and wagged her head at him. 'But you'll have to grow a bit more, Michael Shaughnessy; and if you raise a hand to me I'll bite a lump out of you–see?' She edged round him and made her way down a number of stairs before turning and looking up into his angry countenance, and calling softly, 'Ginger! you're barmy.'

She did not stop to find out whether or not he was after her but took the stairs at a dangerous speed, almost taking Miss Harper's dustbin with her. But once she had gained the hall and found that she wasn't being pursued, her bearing suddenly changed and took on a graveness, as befitted anyone with a fortune pinned on her chest.

Chapter Three

Saturday

It was a funny Saturday, Mary Ann reflected, her da being at work in the afternoon; and it was pouring from the heavens and she couldn't go out; and it was cold, too. She was sitting on the fender near the oven where she was both warm and lapped around with the appetizing aroma of baking. The bread was out and arranged on the rack above her head, and inside the oven a bacon and egg pie was cooking. Her da liked bacon and egg pie. And her mother looked happier today and nearly young again–twice she had laughed at her when she'd had to push her along the fender to get to the oven.

Michael was sitting at the corner of the table writing on scraps of paper. He was doing sums. He hadn't passed the exam last year, and she wasn't a bit surprised, getting sums like he had to do. His teacher said he should have passed on his head. The teacher had come and talked to her ma and said Michael was worried and highly-strung and nervous. She was glad she wasn't going in for any exam. She didn't hate Michael today, she was sorry for him, yet last night she had stamped hard on his bare foot and pretended it was an accident. She had done that because he wouldn't answer their da nicely when he talked to him. Her da wasn't sick, even a little bit, because he had never been out, and he had asked Michael about the exam, and Michael had been surly and said, 'Oh, what's the use?' And he had gone out of the room and she had followed him and stamped on his bare toe. But today he too seemed happier, and he had been working at his sums all afternoon, except when he talked to their ma. Sometimes he talked quietly so that she wouldn't hear. She wasn't in the least annoyed at this because she liked to talk to her da in that way. Michael was talking quietly now, and she was pretending to read her comic while straining her ears to hear what he was saying. He was talking about clothes.

'I'd need a sweater and sports things; it wouldn't matter about a top coat, I never feel the cold.'

'Don't worry about anything.' His mother's voice was as low as his. 'You'll get all the things you need; you must keep all you earn from now on to help buy what's necessary.'

'Oh, no.'

'Yes.'

'Well, I will just this week.'

Why, Mary Ann wondered, should he want to keep his money just this week? And then with a start she remembered April the twenty-third was her mother's birthday, and today. . . . What was today? Yesterday at school had been the fifteenth; then this was the sixteenth. A week today! And she had nothing saved up. Well, only threepence. Still, she had to get her pay from her da yet. But that would only be sixpence at the most. She looked towards her mother's back. The skirt and jumper she was wearing both had a washed-out look. Oh, if only she had a lot of money and could go and buy her a dress. If she had a pound she'd buy her a lovely dress. There was a shop down Ormond Street that had lovely dresses. She had touched one once. There was a rack just inside the door and she had seen a woman pushing the dresses back and forward, and she had slipped in and stood behind the rack and fingered the dresses until the shop-woman had found her and chased her. Now, if she could buy her mother one of those dresses. If she could make a lot of money . . . oh, if only she knew the way to make some money. She was no good at knitting and selling things, or making kettle holders. Perhaps if she asked the Holy Family they'd show her the way. Yes, that was it. Bowing her head farther over her comic and pretending to read, she began supplicating conversation with the Holy Family.

'Are you in, Lizzie?' A voice broke in on her prayers, and exclaiming, 'Oh bust!' she raised her head.

It was Mrs McBride. Not that she disliked Mrs McBride, but she talked a lot and everything had been so nice, just the three of them; and now their Michael would go into the other room to do his work and it was cold in there.

'Come in, Mrs McBride.' Her mother never called Mrs McBride Fanny, like the other women in the house.

'Oh, these stairs, I don't know how you stand them.'

'Sit down. Get Mrs McBride a chair, Michael.'

Michael brought a chair forward and placed it near the fat old woman, then without a word he gathered up his papers from the table and went out of the room.

'Thanks, lad,' Fanny called after him. 'He still working at his books?' She looked up at Lizzie, and without waiting for any comment she went on, 'What I came up about was Lady Golightly. I've just heard this minute that she was over here last night and that Mike put a flea in her ear. Oh, I wish I'd been in; I'd have had a reception committee on the ground floor for her, fit for the Mechanics Institute. What was she after, Lizzie?'

'Oh'–Lizzie measured the jam into the tarts–'Mary Ann and Sarah had been having a squabble.'

'And what did Mike say to her?' Fanny asked, leaning across the table, eagerness expressed in each wrinkle of her sagging cheeks.

Lizzie laughed tolerantly and shook her head. 'I can't remember.'

Fanny sat back and with a sidelong glance looked up at Lizzie. She scratched herself under the breasts, then rubbed the end of her nose before asking 'Is it true what I'm hearing the day?'

With a touch of asperity Lizzie replied, 'Yes, it's true.'

'Well, well.' Fanny's face was beaming. 'He'll be workin' on a Sunday next.'

'He is.'

'Glory be to God! The things you live to see.' This indeed had the power to startle Mrs McBride and she shook her head. Then pointing a grimy finger at Lizzie, she cried, 'But you'll stand by me when I say I've always upheld Mike. Now, haven't I? Haven't I said time and again he's got one fault, and apart from that there's not a better fellow living?'

Mary Ann raised her eyes from the comic. Oh, she liked Mrs McBride. Oh, she did.

'And he's got eyes for no one but yourself–that's another thing in his favour–drunk or sober.'

'Sh!' Lizzie's voice came sharply.

'Oh, she's reading,' said Fanny, waving Mary Ann's presence away with her hand; and she went on, 'And I'm telling you, in a way you're lucky, for some of the flaming Janes round here would put up with his weakness just to have him around the house, for where will you see a better set-up man when he's sober? Or drunk, for that matter? I've known him for longer than anybody–I should know.'

'Sh! sh!'

Fanny sighed in exasperation. 'Why bother what they hear? You cannot keep them in glasshouses, they'll go their own road, some up, some down. Oh'–she leant back and began to laugh–'that reminds me. You'll never guess who our Phil's taken up with. Oh my, talk about reforming. What a week we've had! He's started courting a lass from Binns'–Binns' mind.' Her watery blue eyes narrowed. 'Stick that in your gullet and try to swallow. From no potty little draper's shop, but Binns' in King Street, in Shields!'

'Well, why shouldn't he? Phil's a nice lad.'

'Ay, he's nice enough; but we aren't.' Again she leaned back and laughed. 'Oh, my God!'–she slapped her thick thigh–'you should have heard him last night at our Peggy's young Joe. "You shouldn't say backside," he said, "you should say bottom." He had cornered him in the scullery. And there was me–I had to sit down on the fender or I'd have collapsed. Joe's backside was no longer a backside but a bottom, and all because of a lass from Binns'.'

Lizzie, trying hard not to laugh, said, 'I shouldn't tease him–he wants to get on and he likely wants the girl–you should help him.'

'Help him!' Fanny's voice rose in a crescendo. 'Me help our Phil? Why Lizzie, nobody can help our Phil. It's him that's out to reform the world. You know he's never been one of us, has Phil; you could never tell where you had him or what he was up to; not like our Jack. Now he's as clear as daylight, is Jack.' She sat back, quiet for a time, savouring the affinity between herself and her youngest son. Then suddenly leaning forward again, she said, 'Did you hear about Lady Jane Collins and the rent man?'

'Mary Ann!' Lizzie turned sharply. 'Go in and play with Michael.'

'But he's doing his homework, Ma.'

'Here,' Fanny beckoned Mary Ann to her, 'go down to our house, there's nobody in, and in the pantry behind the basin of dripping on the top shelf you'll find a bar of taffy. Take half of it. Go on now.'

'Can I?' Mary Ann looked at her mother, and Lizzie nodded. Mary Ann knew why she was being allowed to go in to Mrs McBride's. Her ma was afraid she'd hear something, like the time Mrs McBride had talked of how she had first seen her da as a little baby in the workhouse nursery. Mary Ann didn't want to recall this, although it didn't hurt now like it used to, not since her ma had made it into a story.

She did not immediately go down to Mrs McBride's but sat on the top stair thinking of and loving and pitying her da for not having had a ma and a da and for having been brought up in a Cottage Home.

She had first heard about this when Mrs McBride had laughed at her da for talking stronger Irish when he was sick. Mrs McBride had stood in their kitchen and said, 'Ah, Mike, it's real funny to hear you, and you never having set foot in the country. You talk it better than either me or me Colin ever did. God have mercy on him wherever He's put him.'

Mrs McBride had said a lot more, and her da had laughed, but it wasn't his nice laugh and her ma had pushed her outside and she had sat just here and cried. She had cried at intervals for a long time after that and then her ma had told her the story. And it went like this. Once upon a time an angel laid a baby in a basket outside Harton Institution gates. . . . No, no, she wouldn't think about it. She shuffled her bottom along the bare stair board to the wall. She'd begin where her da was a grand looking lad and worked on a farm, and her ma used to cycle past and watch him work the plough. . . . No, for that was a sad part too, for her grannie had found out and evacuated her ma miles and miles away. No; she'd begin where her ma was going along the platform on Hereford Station and she turned and looked towards the barrier, and there waving wildly was a man in R.A.F. uniform, and he was waving to her, and it was the boy with the red hair. She had walked back and through the barrier to his side, and when she stood near him he hadn't the sense to open his mouth.

Mary Ann sighed. That was the nice part of the story. It wasn't her ma, though, who told her how her grannie had tried to stop them getting married, it was her da, one day when he was–sick. Nor did her ma tell her that when her da came out of the Air Force he went to work on a farm near Kibblesworth, but that he wouldn't stay because he couldn't get a place where they could all live together; and he had come into the town and had worked for a time in Lord's yard before getting another job on a farm. But again he couldn't get a cottage, so once more he had come back to where they were then living in a house that had its own back-yard, and even a three foot wide piece of garden in front with an iron rail round it. Yet even in all this space he said he couldn't breathe–there was no air in his lungs. It was in that house she first remembered seeing him sick. Her ma never spoke of these things, but her grannie did.

Slowly now she went down stairs, past Miss Harper's open door, down the next flight and to the hall-way, and as there was no one in she did not trouble to knock on the McBride's door but pushed it open and walked across the room that was cluttered with furniture, all very much the worse for wear. But before reaching the scullery door she stopped and her head went to one side as it was wont to do when she was surprised or interested, and added to this her eyes now opened wide and her lips slowly parted, for her astonished gaze was resting on a couple locked tightly in each other's arms. Although their faces were so close together as to be one, she knew the man to be Jack McBride and the girl, Joyce Scallen.

Now she was not unused to seeing courting couples. When she came from confession on a Thursday night and it was dark she often bumped into them at the corner of the back lane, and their bemused swaying only evoked the term 'Sloppy doppies!' from her. But this couple was different. This girl was Joyce Scallen and she was a Protestant. Worse than a Protestant–her da was in the Salvation Army, and everybody knew that Protestants, especially Salvationists, were destined for Hell. This had always made Mary Ann feel sorry, at least for Joyce, for she was so nice, and up to now she had steadfastly refused to believe that every one of the Protestants would go to Hell, for this would include her da. Yet somewhere in her was the knowledge that once the Holy Family had had time to answer her special prayer on that subject and her da . . . turned, then there would be no further anxiety about the destination of the Protestant tribe, singly or collectively. But eeh! for Joyce Scallen to be kissing Jack McBride–and in the McBride's scullery an' all.

The joined figures parted and Joyce's voice came pleadingly, 'Oh Jack, let me go. You shouldn't have pulled me in; there'll be murder if I'm caught.'

'It's all right, she's upstairs; she won't be down for a while and you can hear her coming a mile off.'

'But I must go; me ma'll be in shortly and someone may come.'

'Will you see me the night?'

'I can't get out–there's a meeting.'

'Then tomorrow?'

'Oh–I don't know.'

'Look, we can't go on like this. Anyway, everybody knows about us but your folks and mine, and they're laughing, waiting for the balloon to go up.'

'Yes, and when it goes up think of me da. And just imagine how your ma'll go on.'

Yes, Mary Ann thought, Mr Scallen would create, but what would Mrs McBride do? Eeh! she couldn't make her mind imagine the scene that would ensue when Mrs McBride got to know.

At this point her quick ears heard a familiar voice–it was Don McBride talking to his wife as they came up the steps of the house. In a matter of seconds they'd be in the room and Jack and Joyce would be caught. Wildly, she looked about her as if she herself were trapped; then she decided there was only one thing for it. Swiftly, she dived into the scullery and her sudden appearance brought a scream from Joyce. But standing with her back to the door, she did a wild pantomime that could not have been misunderstood by the dimmest. Joyce needed no other warning. Like lightning she darted out of the back door, down the yard and into her own door opposite, while Jack stood looking down at Mary Ann, who was now beginning to enjoy herself and feeling completely in command of any wits that were left to the short thick-set young man.

'Taffy,' she whispered. 'Bunk me up to the top shelf.' The need for caution was gone but she wished to continue her part as long as possible.

As the voice of his brother came from the room, Jack hoisted Mary Ann up to the shelf and hissed as he did so, 'How long have you been here?'

On the ground once more and calmly breaking the bar of toffee in two Mary Ann said, 'Oh a long time–I'll go out this way.'

'Did you see—?'

She nodded, looking straight up at him.

She had reached the door when he thrust his hand into his pocket and brought forth a handful of silver. He raked amongst it and taking out half-a-crown pushed it into her hand, saying, 'You won't let on to me ma?'

Mary Ann looked down at this gift from Heaven and murmured, 'Thank you, oh thank you, Jack.'

She was half out of the door when she turned back and whispered, 'But I wouldn't have let on anyway, you know.'

Suddenly they smiled at each other and she darted away out of the yard, round the corner and up the front steps again, and not until she had reached the comparative privacy of her own landing did she open her closed fist to make sure her eyes had not deceived her. Half-a-crown! And just for doing that. She had only to help another seven courting couples and she'd have a pound! She looked up at the stained and peeling sloping ceiling of the staircase. . . . Oh Jesus, Mary and Joseph, thank you very much for showing me the way. . . . Now who would have believed they would have been as quick as that? She had only asked them a few minutes since. She shook her head at the tangible power of the Holy Family.

At half past five the table was set ready and Mary Ann, surveying it, thought that she had never seen a better. There was a knife and fork laid for her da, which meant he was going to have a dinner; then there was the bacon and egg pie, and besides that jam tarts and tea-cakes, and a big sly cake. She moved around the table examining it from all angles. Her mouth was watering and she was hungry, but she resisted the desire to ask for even a piece of bread because she wanted to eat a big tea; her da liked to see her eat well.

She looked at the clock. Only another five minutes and he'd be in. She looked at her mother. Lizzie was sitting by the fire patching, and occasionally she too would look up at the mantlepiece and glance at the clock. She hadn't spoken for a long time now.

Mary Ann went and sat on the fender near Michael. For once he wasn't writing, but just sitting gazing into the fire. The three of them were all tidied up as if it was an occasion. These last five minutes, she decided, were going to be the longest in the afternoon.

She nudged Michael and asked, 'Can I have a look at your Eagle?'

'I haven't got it,' he mumbled; 'I swapped Ned Potter.'

'Well, can I have a look at your swap then?' she asked.

'I didn't get a comic.'

'What did you get?'

'Oh–nothing.'

'You must have got something.'

He did not explain or argue further and Mary Ann's attention was drawn away from him, for the clock made a sound like hiccup as it always did when it passed the six. It was half past five. She looked towards the door, waiting and listening; her mother went on sewing, not lifting her head; and Michael continued to gaze into the fire.

The seconds ticked by, getting louder and slower in her ears, and just a small tremor of panic seized her when she found herself counting them. She had counted sixty eleven times when she rose from the fender. Their Michael was still staring into the fire and her ma was still sewing. She went and stood by the table, still counting. She counted sixty twice more, then she attempted to speak, but she got a frog in her throat and she croaked instead. It would have been funny at any other time, but not now.

When her throat was clear she asked, 'Can I go down to the front door, Ma?'

'No,' said Lizzie.

She stood staring at her mother, whose face seemed the same colour as her hair. Then she looked at the clock. It said a quarter to six. Well, he could have lost the bus–there were hundreds and hundreds of workmen waiting near the Mercantile for the buses. The feeling of panic swelled. Not on a Saturday though.

Then her mother spoke the words that sent the panic swirling through her body. Lizzie had risen from her chair and was folding up the mending, and she said, 'Come and get your tea.'

'No, no, not yet–oh, not yet.'

'There's no use waiting.' Her mother moved about the room as she spoke.

'Just a few minutes more–oh, Ma!'

'Now stop it!' Lizzie's voice was sharp as she turned on her, but it immediately softened as she said, 'It's no use.'

What was no use wasn't explained, and they looked at each other until Mary Ann's head sank, and, moving a step to the side, she slid on to her chair. Her mother then said, 'Michael.' But Michael's answer was to screw himself farther round until his face was hidden completely from them.

Lizzie passed a hand over her brow. She looked from the back of her son to the face of her daughter. If there were only Michael she knew what she would do–pack up this minute and go. And when he came rolling in at eleven o'clock, then perhaps he'd believe what she said. But there was her. She'd never get her away from the house no matter what ruse she used.

'Start your tea.'

'I don't want any.'

'Now do what you're told. Michael . . . come along.'

The boy did not move, and she went to him and, taking his arm, led him to the table.

With her eyes Mary Ann watched her mother mash the tea but with her ears she was trying to separate the sounds of the house and leave a wide space for the sound for which she was waiting. The clock said six, then five past, then ten past, and she still had her first piece of tea-cake on her plate. Michael across from her was eating slowly and stubbornly, and suddenly she had a deep concern for him as she had for her da. She thought, Oh don't let him cry, for if he cries he'll be wild at himself; and the blame would be her da's, and Michael would hate him more.

By half past six the panic feeling had given place to the awfulness, which was how she described to herself the anxiety, the fear and the love which combined to cause the feeling of utter sadness.

'Are you finished?'

'What?' Mary Ann blinked at her mother–she had been brought back from her listening. 'I mean–pardon?'

'Are you finished?'

'Yes.' They had all been finished a long time.

'Then say your Grace.'

'Bless us, O Lord, and these Thy gifts, which we have received through Thy bounty. Through Christ, our Lord, A—' She stopped. There were thundering footsteps on the stairs, not sick footsteps and yet not her da's usual steps. They sounded like someone bounding up the stairs two at a time.

All their eyes were on the door when it burst open, and Mike Shaughnessy came into the room, red of face and laughing . . . and sober.

'Da, oh Da.' She was hanging on to his arm, jumping up and down like a Jack-in-the-box, and he said, 'Here, here. Hold on. Stop it. Look, you'll have old Miss Harper's ceiling down.'

He looked from her to Lizzie. 'I'm sorry I'm late,' he said.

Lizzie stared at him, her face a mixture of relief and astonishment.

'You'll never guess what happened.' He moved towards her, and her head moved slightly.

'I got an accumulator up.'

'An accumulator?' Only her lips showed that she was repeating the word.

'I took a chance and backed Bird's Eye. It was a rank outsider in the two-thirty. I put ten shillings on. Yes I know, I know.' He quelled the protest in her eyes. 'But it came off. It was ten to one and the lot went on to Fancy Fair, and, God alive, that came up and then every penny was on Raindrop. It was the favourite and only two to one. If it had been anything of a price . . . Liz, don't cry. Aw, I knew what you'd be thinking, but I wanted to come home with the money, and I had to wait until the Anchor opened and Reg Brown paid out–I was afraid he might skedaddle with that lot–but I didn't even. . . .' He paused, and suddenly Liz sat down and dropped her face into her hands.

'Ma, don't.' Michael was on one side of her and Mary Ann on the other and Mike in front, and Michael repeated again, 'Oh Ma, don't.'

Mike said nothing, but drew her hands from her face and, taking a wad of notes from his pocket, he closed her fingers about them.

The tears dropping on their joined hands, she looked down on the notes.

'There's over thirty there. I've kept three, and no one's going to stop me from spending them.' He took hold of her chin, lifting her face up to him. 'We're all going to Newcastle.'

Lizzie could only blink and say, 'It's too late.'

'It's not too late.'

'You haven't had your tea.'

'All I want is a wash.'

'But—'

'Ma, Ma, come on.' Mary Ann pulled at her mother's arm, and even Michael added to her entreaty and said, 'Let's go, Ma.'

'Where's that water?' Mike swung round and Mary Ann dashed to the fire and lifted the kettle from the hob and had the water in a dish by the time her da had stripped himself to the waist. She watched him lather his hair, and when he gave a particular grunt she lifted an enamel jug of cold water, and as she poured it over his head, turning his thick hair into spirals of rust-coloured ringlets, her thoughts too flowed with it like benediction, bathing him with her admiration and love.

Chapter Four

The Blindness of Father Owen

Why was it, Mary Ann wondered, that happiness lasted for only short periods whereas unhappiness seemed to go on for ever? or was it, she pondered, that unhappiness was made of stronger stuff than happiness? It must be something like that, for she could recall vividly the numerous times she had been unhappy, yet when she tried to recall the happy times the memories were weak and elusive, like the vapour that floated over the river; she couldn't pin them down. Even that wonderful week-end when her da had won all that money and had taken them to Newcastle, that seemed now like something she had seen at the pictures, it wasn't real; yet it had happened only four weeks ago.

The week-end following it had promised to be the same, too, but her grannie had stepped in and spoilt it. Oh, how she hated her grannie. Why hadn't she said 'Milk bottles!' to stop her. But it would have been no use saying 'Milk bottles' or trying any other means of stopping her grannie that time. It had all happened on a Sunday. Her ma had taken her and Michael down to their grannie's in the afternoon because their da was at work, and Mr Quinton was there, and her grannie had a fancy tea all set out in the front room. And then Michael had made them all laugh, except, of course, her grannie, by saying for his Grace 'Oh Lord, make us able to eat all that's on the table.' She could remember being amazed at their Michael making anyone laugh; but since their da had been working overtime and hadn't been–sick, Michael had been different, even to their da. And all this had made their ma look really like a girl again, especially with the new dress and coat her da had bought her for her birthday. She herself hadn't been able to buy that frock she had set her heart on for her ma, although she had looked out for courting couples until she was tired. She had even got a clip on the ear off one girl who was having a row with her lad up a back lane off Ferry Street. It had been no use trying to explain she was only listening so as to be able to help.

But it didn't matter now, nothing seemed to matter any more since that Sunday night. She had become deader and deader inside since then. If she could feel mad, or scream or cry, it would be better than this feeling that made her want to die. She had actually been praying to the Holy Family for them to make her die this last week, and all through her grannie.

The scene, like all unhappy things, was held fast in her mind and she couldn't get rid of it. She had only to shut her eyes to see it all as plain as plain. They were having their tea and her ma was laughing at something funny Mr Quinton had said, when her da walked in. For a moment he had looked terrifying as he glared down on Mr Quinton, then he had laughed and said something to her grannie about when she was making plans she should always be prepared for set-backs. Mr Quinton had got up from the table and stared back at her da, but he hadn't spoken to him. Then he said good-bye to her grannie and her ma and he had called her ma Elizabeth, and when he had gone her da had said, 'And now E-liz-a-beth, with your mother's permission, we will go home. It seems a great pity I was finished early, I spoilt the party. And your mother must have gone to great pains to organize it.' Then he had suddenly dropped his quiet voice and, turning on her grannie, had cried, 'You old devil, you!'

After that she couldn't really remember what was said, except the feeling of terror her grannie's admission had brought to her, for her grannie had said she would go on planning until she had her daughter away from him. She could recall the terrifying stillness of the room and then her da saying, 'But what about a divorce? There's no divorce for a Catholic, is there? If your plan worked out you'd be making her live in sin, wouldn't you? You old hypocrite.'

On this her ma had got them all out of the house and they had come back to Jarrow, and no one spoke at all on the way until they got home; and then her da wouldn't believe that her ma didn't know Mr Quinton was going to be at her grannie's, and they fought in the bedroom, a different kind of fighting, talking low and quiet and bitterly. And at intervals during the following week they had talked like that. But still her da hadn't been sick until last Saturday, and even then he hadn't meant to be, for he had come in at half past five after doing overtime, and it was then her ma had told him she'd had the offer of a house, one of the newer ones, up Primrose Way. At first he had been pleased, and then he had begun to question her, and in a sudden burst of temper her ma had admitted it was through Mr Quinton's influence that the offer had been made. Her da had gone out then and got sick, not blind sick but just sick enough to talk and talk and talk; and twice during the week he had gone and got sick like that again; and last night as she held the towel for him he asked her quite suddenly 'Do you like Mr Quinton?' and she had lied promptly, saying, 'No, no, I hate him.' And as he dried himself he had said flatly, 'You can't lie to me–you like him because he's smart and has a fine big car and he never swears.'

'I don't.'

'And what's more, he doesn't get–sick–does he?'

She had fallen against him and clung to his leg and he had said something to himself that made her shiver. 'Life's hell,' he had said. He had loosened her hands from him and walked away. There seemed to be a deadness about him–he didn't bounce or rush or laugh any more–and the deadness was on her too, and she wished that she was really dead–dead as dead and in purgatory, and so taken up with going through it for her sins that she wouldn't have time to feel like this.

'If I have to speak to you again, Mary Ann Shaughnessy, you'll know about it. Are you going to confession?'

'Yes, oh yes, Miss Johnson.' Mary Ann dragged herself up out of her misery and from her desk.

'Then stop dreaming. . . . Now you'll all walk three abreast, and if there's any carry-on in the street like there was last Thursday you'll all be for it in the morning. Grace Smith, stop that pushing there. . . . All those going to Father Beaney at the front and those for Father Owen at the back here.'

Mary Ann joined the latter group. Not only did she not scramble for the front place but she took the inner side of the last three in the ranks which ensured her the unenviable position of being the last to go into confession, but that was what she wanted, for when she was last she could talk to her heart's content and the priest wouldn't hurry her on. Once she had told Father Owen all that was on her mind she knew that she would get some relief from this feeling. She had seen him a number of times during the past week but of course she couldn't tell him her trouble in any other place but the confessional box, for she didn't want him to know it was she who was troubled, or what she was troubled by, and in the confessional box he wouldn't know it was her, for as everybody knew God struck priests blind once they entered their part of the box so that they wouldn't know who was talking. They might peer through the grid but they couldn't see a styme. That's why you could tell them everything that was in your heart and not be afraid they'd split on you.

As the crocodile swung out of the school-yard it touched on a group of the bigger girls. They, too, were on their way to confession, but, because of their years, free and unhampered, and among them and near to Mary Ann's side of the ranks was Sarah Flannagan.

After mimicking the marching by striding along the gutter swinging her arms, Sarah addressed herself to Mary Ann's averted face and hissed, 'Convict!' whereupon Mary Ann, without turning her head but mouthing each syllable widely, said, 'Cas-i-bi-anca, flannel face!'

This retort had the effect of infuriating Sarah and with her fist she pushed Mary Ann in the back and knocked her flying into the girl in front, who, in turn, fell on to the girl in front of her. The result was four children lying on the pavement and Miss Johnson standing over them, saying, 'Who did this?'

There was a chorus of 'Mary Ann Shaughnessy, miss.'

'It wasn't!' Mary Ann denied emphatically. 'It was Sarah Flannagan.'

But since there was neither sight nor sound of Sarah Flannagan Miss

Johnson said, 'You come to me tomorrow morning,' which added bitterness to Mary Ann's collection of negative feelings and a new resentment against so-called justice.

In church she found it impossible to make her preparation for confession–she could only keep thinking that she wished she were dead. With one thing and another, she was fed-up and tired of it all. If only it was possible to die quickly–like that. She snapped her finger and thumb against her bent forehead. If something could happen and she could be struck dead. Laurie Carter had said her mother knew a man who had been struck dead because he swore at a priest. . . . She lifted her eyes over the back rest and looked across the church to where the Holy Family were enthroned in deep shadow. If she was struck dead she'd likely go straight to them. For the moment she had forgotten the required passage through purgatory. Suppose she swore at Father Owen. Eeh, what had put that into her head? Fancy thinking about swearing at Father Owen! But if it would make her die . . . No, not Father Owen. Well, which other priest did she know but Father Beaney? and she wouldn't have the courage to go up to Father Beaney and swear at him. She stared through the dimness towards the altar, and presently she thought, 'If I'm going to do it, Father Owen will be the best.' Suppose, as she was kneeling in the box, she did just a little swear at him. Perhaps that would do, and when he died he'd know she hadn't meant it. But what should she swear? Should she say damn? No, that wasn't quite big enough. Bloody? Eeh! no, that was too awful. She might be sent to Hell for ever for that.

The last penitent came stumbling out of the box, and rising from her knees, she sent up a quick prayer to the Holy Family in an appeal to be provided with the swear words necessary to cause her demise. She groped her way into the dark confessional and knelt down below the grid and began in her customary way, 'Pray Father give me thy blessing for I have sinned. It is a week since my last confession.'

'Yes. Go on.' The priest's voice seemed to come from a great distance and did not for the moment seem to be the soothing voice of Father Owen but of a priest who already knew all her sins and the blackness of her heart, so, quickly, she gathered her wits together and presented them to him, 'Please, Father, I have given way to the sin of hate.'

'Who do you hate?'

'Me grannie.'

'Why?'

'Well, she's always saying nasty things about me da and she wants me ma to leave him and she's got another man all ready for her. The other man's nice enough but he's not me da.'

There was a movement of the priest's feet, and he said, 'Your mother–what does she say about all this?'

'Nothing, Father–at least they fight a bit. She gets sick to the heart because he goes and gets a skinful. I mean he gets drunk.'

There, she had said the word. It was only in here in the fast secretness of this box with this blind priest that she could utter that word.

'When was he last drunk?'

'He had a few last night, Father.'

'Go on with your confession.'

'I've kicked our—' She stopped herself saying the word Michael, he might recognize her through that name; so she said, 'Me brother. And I've torn up the scraps of paper he writes on, and made him wild by calling him Ginger. And I've missed my morning prayers because I got up late, and I've looked over Cissy Tollard's shoulder into her exercise book.'

'Yes; go on.'

She was raking round in her mind for her other great sins when it came back to her that not a few minutes ago she had committed the worst sin of all by deciding to swear at him.

'Go on, my child.'

But she couldn't go on. And after waiting a while he said, 'Come on, my child, finish your confession.'

'I wanted . . .'

'Yes?' he encouraged.

'In the church, a minute back, I made up my mind to swear at you, Father.'

'You what?'

Two white bulbs came close to the grid and looked down on Mary Ann, but she looked fearlessly back into them knowing that the eyes were sightless. After a while they were withdrawn and the priest said, 'And why did you want to swear at me?'

''Cause I wanted to die.'

'Because you wanted to die?' There was utter bewilderment in his tone.

'Yes, I heard tell that if you swore at a priest you'd be struck down dead.'

Father Owen gave two short coughs, then he blew his nose before saying, 'And why, may I ask, do you want to die?'

'I told you, Father, it's about me da. I'm miserable and I never want me dinner and I don't care if I can go out to play or not. I even thought if I could find some poison I'd take it and when I was dead me da might be sorry and not get drunk again.'

'Poison?' The priest's voice was crisp now. 'Poison's no use, I've tried it.'

'You have, Father?' She was brought clean out of her own trouble with surprise and she stretched up to see better into the dimness beyond the grid.

'Yes, it only gives you the gripes in your inside and you're no better off.'

'Oh—' The thought of gripes in her inside turned her for ever from the thought of poison, but she went on, warming up to the situation, 'Last night I was so miserable, Father, and me ma wouldn't let me go out and look for me da and I thought if I could get out I'd a good mind to throw meself under the bus where it rounds the Ben Lomond in Ellison Street.'

'Under a bus? Oh, that's a worse idea altogether.'

'Is it, Father?'

'I'd say it is. What happens when you throw yourself under a bus? It chops off either your arms or your legs and you live on, and it's not a very pleasant state having no arms or legs, is it?'

'No, Father.'

'Well, forget about the bus, and pray to the. . . . Who do you usually pray to?'

'To the Holy Family, Father.'

'Oh, the Holy Family . . . well, you couldn't pray to a better Family, and you pray to them tonight and ask them for something nice to happen to you. What would you like to happen?'

'Oh, Father. For me da . . .'

'Oh'—he cut her short—'leave your da to God. Now isn't there something you want to happen to yourself?'

'Well, I wanted to get into the procession, Father.'

'And you're not in it?'

'No, Father, and all of them have been picked.'

'Yes. . . . Ah well, you go on praying to the Holy Family and you can be assured they'll make something nice happen to you.'

'They will, Father?'

'They will that. They never fail. Now for your penance say the first Joyful Mystery of the Rosary, and make your act of contrition.'

'O my God, I am very sorry I have sinned against Thee because Thou art so good, and by the help of Thy Holy Grace I will never sin again.'

'Good night and God bless you.'

'Good night, Father.'

Out of the confessional box, Mary Ann decided it would not be wise to stay in a now empty church to say her penance, for the priest, once out of the box and his sight back, would know it was her he had been talking to. And he'd remember about the drink and connect it with her da.

On the way home she wondered what nice thing the Holy Family would make happen to her; but this only played on the fringe of her thoughts, for deep in the permanency of her mind she knew there was only one thing that really mattered, one thing that would make her happy, and that was the happiness of her ma and da.

Friday was usually a nice day. It began by having your breakfast packed up and going off to Communion, then going straight to school and eating your breakfast in the hall, that's if you hadn't already eaten it on the road. Then there was Bible History, and one Friday in every four Father Owen or Father Beaney came and heard your Catechism. It was nice on the days Father Owen came, for he made you laugh. Then the class acted pages from history—today it was to be Flora Macdonald and Bonnie Prince Charlie. And in the afternoon there was the poetry lesson. She liked poetry and could remember long bits of it. When she was in Miss Harrington's class she used to get pennies for being the first to learn, but Miss Johnson didn't give you anything . . . only the stick if you didn't know it. But she never got the stick for not knowing her poetry. She knew long stretches of Hiawatha's childhood. It was easy stuff to learn because the man who wrote it kept repeating everything so as to make it easy to remember like:

'He was a marvellous story-teller,
He was a traveller and a talker,
He was a friend of old Nokomis,
Made a bow for Hiawatha;
From a branch of ash he made it,
From an oak-bough made the arrows,
Tipped with flint, and winged with feathers . . .'

Oh, she knew yards and yards of it.

'I have given you streams to fish in,
I have given you bear and bison,
I have given you roe and reindeer,
I have given you brant and beaver . . .'

Sometimes at night she put herself to sleep saying it.

Yes, she usually liked Fridays, at school anyway, but today the misery from last night still lay heavily upon her. She had arrived home from Confession to find her ma out, and she hadn't got back before her da came in, and they didn't speak. And he'd gone out after he'd had his tea and got a little sick; and in the night she had woken up on the camp bed where she slept under the sloping roof by the side of the scullery door and there, lying on the mat in front of the dead fire, was her da, with just a blanket over him. She felt so bad at the sight of him lying there in the cold that she began to cry. She had got up and the noise she caused brought her ma out of the room, and she made her get back into bed. And now here she was in school, with her breakfast still uneaten, and feeling more than ever that she wanted to die.

This morning was Catechism test and all the partitions of the school had been pushed back and Father Owen was up now on the platform talking. She wasn't paying much attention to him, for she was having her work cut out to keep her six inches of bottom space on the edge of the desk seat. All about her was a mass of heads and shoulders, except to the right of her where there was a little altar. It was St Anthony's altar, and he was standing on a pedestal in his brown habit with no shoes on, and his feet looked cold, she thought, and there were bits of dirt in between his toes. In a detached way she decided that when she was moved up into this class after the summer holidays she'd scrape out all that dirt. She didn't like dirt between her toes–her ma made her and Michael wash their feet every night before they went to bed. They were a rare family for washing, especially her da. The thought of her da brought back the thought of dying, and she looked once again at St Anthony. She had never laid much stock by him, yet she heard he was quite good at finding things for you if you lost them. She wondered, if she prayed to him now, how long he would take to bring about her wish. Anyway, it would pass the time away for there was nothing to see in front of her and nothing to hear but a mumbling of voices.

There had been quite a big stir at the beginning of proceedings because Betty Paul, who was to lead the procession dressed in a blue cloak and a crown like Our Lady, had gone and got the measles. Fancy anybody going and getting the measles when they were going to lead the May Procession and walk bang behind the statue of Our Lady hoisted on a platform and carried by four boys. She wouldn't have done a silly thing like that. But what did it matter, she wanted to die.

She looked up into the face of St Anthony and with first a little placation just to soothe him and make up for her neglect of him, she began, 'Dear St Anthony, I haven't prayed to you because I've been so busy, but I know full well how clever you are, and you could perform any miracle you like if you wanted to. Dear St Anthony, I'm very miserable, and you being in Heaven will know why. And please, St Anthony I want to die, oh, I want to die. I can't bear to think about me da. . . .'

'Mary Ann Shaughnessy–where is she?'

The priest's voice was lost to her, but a thump between the shoulders was an effective way of recalling her to it. A number of voices hissed at her 'Go on out.' 'Are you daft?' 'Don't you hear Father Owen calling you?' 'What's up with her?' The voices brought her to her feet and she looked towards the platform, and there was Father Owen laughing and beckoning to her with his hand.

'Come on, come on, Mary Ann,' he called. 'Were you asleep?'

As dazed as if she had been, she walked towards the platform wondering all the while what she had done to be called out. Surely it wasn't because of last night–she was going to report to Miss Johnson when her class assembled again. Her teacher was at the bottom of the steps, but said nothing to her, only pushed her up them, and not too gently either, and still in a daze, Mary Ann found herself in front of Father Owen and with a whole sea of faces around her, for on the platform was the headmistress and a lot of the teachers, and not one of them was looking pleasant.

What had she done to be brought up here? Only if you stole anything or broke somebody's windows were you yanked up on the platform and made an example of.

'Well, there it is. One person's bad luck is another's good.' Father Owen put his hand on Mary Ann's head and slowly screwed her around to face the school. 'As I've already said, nobody was more upset than myself when I knew that Betty had the measles and I had to find someone to take her place, so, as it is my privilege to pick from the school the leader of the procession, I have decided on Mary Ann Shaughnessy here. Granted Mary Ann is small'–he looked down on her–'but I've a notion that the Holy Mother herself was a slight body, and the gown may have to be shortened, but that can easily be done. I have chosen her because there is no black mark against her in school, and since she made her first confession fifteen months ago there has not been one week but she has attended Confession and Communion. Now let us give her a great big clap.'

He led the clapping by banging his long bony hands together. Mary Ann gazed up at him, then at the obedient clapping hands in front of her, then to the side where the teachers were clapping in such a way that would not have disturbed a sleeping baby, and she asked herself whether she was in bed having another of her dreams. But no, she wasn't, for her eyes were on a level with the bottom button of Father Owen's slack waistcoat and she could feel his fingers moving in her hair. She was just about to realize the wonderful enormity of the thing that was happening to her when out of the blue came the answer to her eager prayer of a moment ago. She felt it first starting in her legs as a shooting pain which screwed itself up through her chest and into her head. All the faces about her began to run into one. She made a great effort to steady herself and to keep her feet on the ground but it was no use, and when, without any warning, Father Owen's long thin figure began to swell before her eyes she knew, in an illuminating flash, what was happening–her earnest prayer to the Saint was being answered and she was about to die. The inadvisability of dealing with two firms for the one product was brought home to her–competition could evoke disastrous results. The efficacy of St Anthony's power was terrifying–he was as sharp as the Devil himself. She spun round to where his statue showed dimly in the distance, and there he stood laughing at her–she could hear him. She turned about to where the statue of Our Lady dominated the side wall above the platform and cried, 'Put it right with him, will you? I don't want to die now . . . well not just yet.'

But neither the Virgin nor the complete Holy Family had anything, it would appear, on St Anthony for quick service, for he strode from his pedestal shouting, 'It's nice to be able to play God,' and he picked her up in his arms and carried her off and rushed her straight through the air heavenwards.

The rush of the air made her gasp and his voice boomed in her ears as he shouted from the clouds down to the headmistress, 'I consider her need the greatest.'

Suddenly he dropped her and she gasped and gasped for breath as she fell. Having landed with a thump, she opened her eyes; then after one startled glance about her she lay back in contentment as she realized she was in the sanctuary of the Teachers' Room, lying on a couch, with the Headmistress on one side of her and Father Owen on the other.

'You're feeling better? That's it. Ah–that's it. You've been to Communion and haven't eaten your breakfast, I bet. Now, am I right?'

She made a slight movement with her head and he laughed and said, 'I knew it.'

'Father.'

'Yes?'

'It's true . . . about . . .?'

'You going to lead the procession?'

She nodded again.

'As true as life, but only if you drink a glass of hot milk and eat up a good breakfast.'

'I'm not going to die?'

'Die?' His long body seemed to fold up with laughter. 'I should say not. And you're going to wear that lovely blue gown.'

She gazed up at him. He didn't know it was her he had told last night to pray for something nice to happen, and she couldn't tell him for it would give the show away. But lifting her hands, she caught hold of his fingers and pressed them to her cheek. 'Oh, Father, Father,' she said.

Chapter Five

Mr Flannagan, the Coronation, and Mike Shaughnessy

Nowhere in Jarrow was the Coronation looked forward to and prepared for more than in Burton Street. For weeks there had been Committee Meetings. That the Committee grew in numbers and became divided in policy was to be expected, but that the divided parties should break up within themselves into smaller factions was to be regretted. Some were for teas in the street with games afterwards for the bairns, some, remembering rain-soaked street parties from the past, were all for the Baptists' Hall; but as Mrs McBride said, who'd want to get drunk in the Baptists' Hall? This called down censure from most of the factions. Who wanted to get drunk at all? Those who wanted that kind of a party had better take themselves down to the Fifteen Streets and not join in the festivities of a respectable neighbourhood. There was a nodding of heads and the murmuring of the name of Shaughnessy. Then there were those who suggested that every adult in the street should subscribe five shillings, the accumulated wealth to be used for sending three of them, these to be determined by a draw, up to London to see the actual procession. Before protests could rain down on this proposal it was haughtily thrust aside by Mrs Flannagan saying that if the Flannagans wanted to go to London they were quite able to provide their own train fare, thank you, and they had already refused the offer to accompany her sister and husband from Hartlepools who were going to her sister's husband's cousin and he had an excellent view already for them, from the window of the office where he worked, slap on the Coronation route.

At this, a combined murmur like the wash of the tide on a pebble beach came from all quarters, and it could have been translated into 'Oh ye-ah!'

Finally, after many meetings, a street party was decided upon, which as some of the Committee said, had been inevitable from the first. One stipulation was made: should it rain the bairns were to have their tea in the Baptists' Hall and Mr Gallon engaged to do his Punch and Judy Show. Of course there was one snag here, as those people who were not tired of arguing pointed out, they couldn't leave it until June 2nd to say if it was going to rain before engaging Mr Gallon–he'd have to be engaged wet or dry.

The day dawned and it does not need testifying that it was wet, but it took more than rain to damp the enthusiasm of the tenants of Burton Street and Mulhattans' Hall in particular. The children were wild with excitement, and the adults got rid of much of their suppressed emotion in trying to quell the exuberance of their young.

But put two hundred and twenty-six people in a hall that would be crowded with half that number and you will find all emotions subsidiary to the feeling of self-preservation. So at least thought Mike Shaughnessy.

He was sober and dressed in his best and standing in the corner of the hall. It would have been impossible to sit down had there been anything to sit on. The only advantage he had was his view–his head topped every other man's and woman's in the room–and he looked down on the rows of trestle tables lined with children and the rows of their admiring parents watching them eating as if they were accomplishing the feat for the first time in their lives.

Mike was not unaware that he was a subject of interest; that he was sober on such a day as this was a source of wonder to his neighbours. From different quarters he had seen covert glances and heard whispered words. At least he was a man who wasn't unknown. He smiled wryly to himself as his eyes roamed over the crowd, halting here and there to hold a gaze fixed on him in curiosity, and he wondered if anyone in this room would believe that ten years ago he hadn't known the taste of beer or whisky. Yes, there was one . . . she knew.

His eyes went to Lizzie. It was easy for him to find her, for he hadn't allowed her to move far from his sight all afternoon. She was like a queen among peasants, standing out far above them. My God, if ever there was a fool in this world he was one–to exchange her for a skinful of beer! He could only blame himself, not Quinton. He would lose her; then what would become of him? He'd be finished. Why did he do it? Why wasn't he as big and tough inside as he was out? Why did the smell of oil and tar and rope and the singey smell of hot rivets fill his stomach with the craving? Yet it was no use blaming the work and the sweat; he recalled the periods when he had sweated on the land. He had burned then for a drink, but a draught of spring water or a canful of milk had swilled it away. He was weak and he knew it.

It seemed like the twisting that Fate was apt to indulge in that he couldn't settle on a farm away from her and the youngsters, yet if she left him and he was adrift with nothing to hold him to this blasted town he would still be unable to return to the land. She mustn't leave him . . . ever. His heart began to beat rapidly, pumping as if at the end of a run, and he felt his pulse beat, as it had often seemed to do of late, in his eyes. Just the thought of losing her filled him with the terror of loneliness, that loneliness that he had known as a child and then as a boy, the loneliness that made him shun crowds and people, the loneliness that for its easing required only one heart to beat against. If she left him, the loneliness he had known before would be as nothing to what would come in the years ahead. But it needn't happen. It was up to him; he had only to go steady. She didn't mind him having a glass or two if he could stop at that. Yes, if he could. And then there was the other one tugging at the secret place in his heart. If anyone could keep a man straight it should be that child. His son, he knew, wouldn't care if he was gone the morrer, but Mary Ann. . . . He looked towards her and her eyes were waiting for him. She waved her hand and he waved back. The pride of him showed in her face, and he thought that she could be proud at any rate of her achievement in getting him here today. God knew she had worked hard enough at it, but he did not know for how much longer he could stand this crush and the warm, damp air of the room. The noise was a bedlam vying with that of the dry-dock, and he was feeling it pressing down on him. If only he could make his way towards that door and stand in the street a moment and get himself a mouthful of air. Judiciously he began to edge his way forward. He even got past the entrance to the hall kitchen where plates and trays were being handed overhead from hand to hand, but just beyond this and within a few steps of the door his progress was halted and he found himself wedged in another corner to make room for the hasty exit of a child who had eaten well but not wisely. She was being pushed through the crowd with the fiercesome admonition from her mother to 'Hold it.' The dire penalty of her refusing to comply with this order rose above the clamour. The situation amused Mike and he laughed, and so did the man at his side, and Mike turned his head towards him and said, 'Poor little beggar, she's between the devil and the deep sea.' The man looked back at him for a moment without speaking, then he laughed again, but not such a hearty laugh this time and said, 'Yes. Yes, you're right.'

'And,' commented Mike to himself, 'you're another poor little devil.' Anyone unfortunate enough to have to spend a lifetime with that upstart woman Flannagan had his sympathy. Mike chuckled inwardly. How often had he been threatened that he would suffer for his insolence at the hands of this little chap, and up to the present this was the nearest they had got to each other.

He said quite pleasantly, 'I'm trying to make for the door to get some air,' and Mr Flannagan replied with equal pleasantness, 'I'm heading that way meself.'

They nodded at each other, a strange, comradely nod that said, 'We may as well make it together then.'

'London's got nothing on this,' said Mike, when at last the double doors were reached.

'You're right there, Mr Shaughnessy.'

Oh, thought Mike, we're getting our title the day–Mr Shaughnessy it is. And to think we've seen each other every day for two years with never a 'Whatcher there!'

'Harry!' The astonished, strident voice brought Mr Flannagan swiftly round and he stood with his back to the door and faced his wife. 'Where you off to?'

Mr Flannagan did not answer for a moment, but his eyes flitted to Mike's back where he stood struggling with the long iron bar of the door. Then he said briefly, 'Outside.'

'Why?' asked Mrs Flannagan. 'What do you want to go outside for?'

Mr Flannagan's answer to this was drowned by Mike's laugh. Perhaps he was laughing at himself being unable to get the door open. With a quick jerk the bar went upwards and the double doors shot apart, and as he turned to close them his eyes met the malevolent glare of Mrs Flannagan, and he laughed in her face and closed the door on her words, 'Stay where you are till the air's clearer.'

Mike stood in the shelter of the porch for a moment and looked at the rain falling like a solid lead sheet across the opening, and Mrs Flannagan's voice, muffled now but still audible, came to him. He could not distinguish what she was saying but her tone told him that the poor little devil was getting it hot and heavy. As the door behind him opened again he turned his collar up and stepped out into the rain. He found it was not amusing to hear the little fellow being slated; rather, he was embarrassed. When a woman made a man look small it touched all men.

'Do you hear me?' Mrs Flannagan's voice followed him through the opened door. Then on a pitch of a scream it came down the empty street, crying, 'Harry!' and it told Mike that Mr Flannagan must be somewhere behind him. He did not turn round, but he thought with a glow of satisfaction, 'So he stood his ground . . . good for him.' And he slowed his pace until the little man came abreast. The odd thing was that Mr Flannagan made no effort to pass on, but suited his steps to Mike's, having to lengthen his stride to do so. This must have conveyed the worst to Mrs Flannagan, for her voice crying, 'Do you hear me, Harry Flannagan? Come back here this minute!' seemed to hit the two men in the neck. Anyway, it sent them forward at a quicker pace until they rounded the corner of the street. There Mr Flannagan, his face running with rain, looked up at Mike and asked quite solemnly, 'Would you mind me company, Mr Shaughnessy?' and Mike, successfully keeping his eyebrows stationary, replied in his politest tone, 'Not at all, Mr Flannagan, not at all.'

Mary Ann saw her da leave the hall, and for a moment the brightness of this wonderful day vanished, until she told herself that he had only gone out for a mouthful of air and he would be back in a minute. But he didn't come back in a minute.

The tea over, the children were bidden to sit where they were to see the Punch and Judy Show. Mary Ann tried to catch her mother's eye and ask her permission to attempt to leave the table, but Lizzie's eyes seemed to rest everywhere but on her daughter. Mary Ann did not care for Punch and Judy–the sight of poor Judy being beaten unmercifully with a stick always made her close her eyes–so at this point in the entertainment she followed the ruse of so many other children who were bored with sitting in one spot for so long, she put up her hand. It seemed to her that almost immediately her mother was behind her, and with a warning injunction for quiet, she lifted her off the form and carried her with some difficulty through the press, but not towards the backyard of the hall, but to the main door. Once outside, she put her down, saying, 'There are too many waiting, we'd better go home.' She did not say, 'You had better run home and then come back,' and Mary Ann knew that her ma wanted to go and see if her da was home.

It had stopped raining now and they hurried along hand in hand.

Mulhattans' Hall was quiet and had the air of a house that had been vacated in a hurry, especially in the hallway outside Mrs McBride's door, for there reposed a welter of oddments, the possessions undoubtedly of Mrs McBride's numerous grandchildren. Mary Ann ran ahead up the stairs and pushed open their door.

She did not call down to her mother that her da wasn't in, but her silence was telling enough for Lizzie, and when she entered the room she made no comment one way or the other but an anger rose in her against the man who was so weak and so selfish that he would not keep his promise to this child even for a day. The promise had not been given in words; but in a thousand and one ways Mary Ann had tried to impress on him the importance of Coronation Day and extract from him a laugh or the slow shaking of the head or a quick hoist in the air, and all these she took as signs that he would stay with them on that day and enter into the jollification.

Her own heart had softened towards him as it hadn't done for some time when she had seen him standing patiently with the crowd in the hall, for she knew how human contact in the mass could irritate him. But it had been too much for him. She had expected too much of him. Her anger made her silently vehement. He was weak, he was cowardly, he was rotten to the core. Let him hurt her, she could in a way stand up to it, but the look on the child's face when yet once again he had let her down was heart-rending. She turned to Mary Ann who was standing near the table picking at her fingers and said, 'I thought you wanted to leave the room?'

'I did.' Mary Ann turned and walked out and down the stairs, and Lizzie went into the scullery, and after staring down into the sink for some time she beat her fist three times in quick succession on the draining-board, and when the sound of Mary Ann's footsteps mounting the stairs again came to her she sighed heavily and went into the kitchen, and with an effort towards brightness she greeted her daughter, 'Well, shall we go back?'

'No, I don't want to.'

'Why?'

'Well, it will be nearly over.'

That was true. 'But,' said Lizzie, 'now that it's fair there'll be the races in the street and you've been practising for long enough.'

'I'm tired.'

'Now listen,' Lizzie spoke sharply. 'You're no more tired than I am,' which, if this had been strictly true, would have made Mary very weary indeed.

'I am,' persisted Mary Ann, sitting down.

'What about the prizes you were after? The big box of chocolates Mr Funnell's giving, and the doll to the best skipper?'

'I'm tired.'

Lizzie moved her head impatiently; then as a noise like a stampede of cattle came from the street she said, 'There they are, all back.'

'I don't want to go.'

'But we were going to see all the bonfires later on–what about that?'

Mary Ann looked straight at her mother and the look said, 'If he comes in roarin' will we leave him and go and see the bonfires?'

Lizzie turned and went to the fireplace, and with the raker pulled from the back of the grate a little more coal on to the low embers, then swinging round almost fiercely, she cried, 'Well, you'll go to bed mind, I'm not having you sitting there with a face like that.'

Even this threat could not bring Mary Ann out of her misery, and when she said, 'All right', Lizzie gave her one helpless look before walking into the bedroom.

She sat on the edge of the bed and rocked herself slowly, Oh, dear God, dear God. Was this to be her life? There was no likelihood at all that he would return before he was well soaked, and he would say, 'Well now, take you for a spoil-sport. Isn't it every creature that's drinking the Queen's health the night?' His voice would be thick with the Irish brogue, a tongue she had come to detest, for the deeper his cup the thicker it came. Once he had tried to explain to her the reason why he spoke broad Irish when he was drunk. You've got to belong somewhere, he had said; there are two things a man must have, a mate and a country. When you grow up knowing that you belong to nowhere or to no one and that no one belongs to you, that your very name was given to you by a committee, and one name being as good as another, they let you be called after the man who had picked you up from the gate, when a thing like that is the kind of thought you live with from the time you start thinking you begin to make up places and people that do belong to you. It was natural I should pick on Ireland with a name like Mike Shaughnessy, and for people it was as natural as breathing that I should pick on you the moment I saw you, with your golden hair and your promise of another world.

Oh, Mike, Mike. She leant her head on the bed-rail and her pity was resurrected. Why had life to be like this? Why wasn't she big enough to fill the loneliness that ate him up at times? He loved her, she was the only creature he wanted. He was capable of killing any man who would come between them, yet he could not kill or would not kill that which was a greater danger to their happiness than any man. Oh, Mike, Mike.

He had been gone three hours now. It would be another two or three before he would be back. She was weary and tired of thinking, tired of counting time, tired of worrying, tired of anxiety, tired of living. She raised her head and looked towards the window, for the noise and shouting from the street had suddenly increased. Was it only the echo of her worry or had she heard Mike's name called above the yelling and the shouting? She sat bolt upright, her ears strained. There it was again. Mike and Mr Shaughnessy. Mr Shaughnessy, the voice said.

Darting to the window she stopped and peered down into the street. The twilight had not yet deepened into darkness but the street lamps were lit and in the half-light she could not at first make out one figure from another; then her eyes were drawn over the crowd to a clearing, in the middle of which a man was dancing with his hands above his head. He was dancing a weird imitation of a Scotch reel, accompanied by the clapping and stamping of the crowd. But it was not Mike–it was Mr Flannagan. She dropped on to her knees and lowered her head to the bottom of the window to confirm that she was seeing aright. It couldn't really be Mr Flannagan, the solemn, miserable-looking little man, who rarely opened his mouth to anyone and was known never to have touched drink for years, not since he was converted to sobriety by the visiting mission. Without closer confirmation she knew that only if he had . . . 'had some' would he be dancing in the street. But Mike; they had been calling Mike. Where was he? Her eyes roamed wide over the crowd, peering through the distorted reflections of the lamps, only to come back to the cleared space. And then she saw him, and her amazement grew, for Mr Flannagan, who had stopped dancing, was pulling him by the arm in an effort to induce him to join the fray.

That Mike should need inducement to join in a bit of jollification was a sure guarantee that he was sober. She was completely mystified by it all; everything was topsy-turvy, Mike sober and Mr Flannagan drunk. Slowly she raised her eyes from the street to the window below on the far side of the road, and seeing the outline of Mrs Flannagan's face behind the curtain and being only human, she voicelessly said, 'Now how do you like it, Mrs Flannagan?' Then remembering the torture she herself had endured she added, 'But I wouldn't wish it on you, no matter what you're like.'

'Lizzie! Are you there, Lizzie?'

Lizzie turned from the window as Mrs McBride's voice came from the other room; and before she could reach the door it was thrust open, and Fanny, puffing and yelling, cried, 'Was there ever such a crowning to a day as that? Have you seen him?'

She carried Lizzie towards the window again with a sweep of her arm. 'Look at him!' She pointed into the street. Then looking across to Mrs Flannagan's window, she voiced the same sentiments as Lizzie had restrained. 'Ah, me fine madam. How d'you like it? This'll knock some of the stinking brag out of you. . . . Oh'–she turned to Lizzie, her broad beaming smile making her face resemble nothing so much as a dented and rather discoloured bag of tripe–'oh, if I've lived to see nothing else, this'–she indicated with a jerk of her thumb the again dancing figure of Mr Flannagan–'this would have been worth all me struggles. And if it doesn't keep the Duchess of Dam' All quiet for the rest of her life I'm a Hallelujah. Oh, isn't Mike the boy that gets his own back! If he had tried for a thousand years he couldn't have thought of anything better.'

'Mike?' Lizzie looked at the old woman. 'What's Mike got to do with it?'

'He did it. Took him along and got him bottled up. Didn't you see them leaving the hall together? Mary Prout said there was a do in the street with Lady Golightly.'

Lizzie's face hardened as she stared down on to the back of Mrs McBride's head. The things these people said. Mike had his faults, God knew, but petty vindictiveness was not one of them. Yet what about Mr Flannagan trying to get him to dance? If they hadn't been together would he have done that?

'The street's alive with it,' went on Fanny, again cocking her head up to Lizzie. 'Everybody knows the things she's said about Mike. Aw, who says the devil doesn't look after his own? Do you want to look down, hinny?' She put her hand out to where Mary Ann was standing now near her mother. 'Come and see your da. He's down there as sober as a judge, and it's Coronation Day an' all.'

'I wouldn't say that, Fanny.'

The three of them turned abruptly to where Mike was filling the doorway. His face was not clearly discernible in the dimness of the room, but his voice, the inflection of which could tell Lizzie whether he had been on beer, whisky, or both, told her now that he'd had a few beers, but that was all.

'Oh, there you are, Mike. How did you get away from him? You've got yourself a drinking pal from now on. But what in the name of God gave you the idea? If you'd spat clean in her eye you wouldn't have hit her harder.'

As Fanny threw her laughing remarks to him, Mary Ann darted across the room. She did not shout, 'Da! Oh, Da!' but just clung on to his arm, pressing her face against his sleeve in a passionate expression of relief.

Mike fondled her head and asked of Fanny, 'Who says it was my idea getting him drunk?'

'Who says! . . . Ah, what d'you take me for, Mike?' She pushed past him. 'Who says? Why everybody in the street, and they're all having a dam' good laugh, knowing the way she's held you up as a disgrace to the neighbourhood.'

'Has she now?'

'Has she now? Why are you playing so dumb all of a sudden? Has she now? Oh, you'll kill me with your fun one of these days. Well, here I am now going to see what happens when old Flannagan knocks on his door for admittance. I'll be seeing you, Lizzie. . . . Has she now?' She leered at Mike in farewell.

Lizzie made no comment, and not until the outer door had banged did Mike speak. 'I didn't get him full,' he said.

'Who did then? He's been with you, hasn't he?' Lizzie's voice conveyed neither displeasure nor amusement.

'Yes, he was along of me; I couldn't shake him off. It was at his suggestion we had a pint together . . . And then—' Suddenly Mike's voice broke, and his head went up and back, and his rocketing laugh filled the room. He took out his handkerchief and dabbed his eyes and said between gasps, 'Me. I had to put the brake on because of him. Can you see me putting the brake on because of Harry Flannagan? I kept saying, "No. I'll just have a gill. . . . No, no," I said, "I never touch whisky." And there he was with a double and a pint at his elbow. I tell you I had to get him out while he was still on his legs. If I'd waited any longer I'd have to've carried him back.' His laughter eased to a gentle shaking, and he looked at Lizzie and said, quietly, 'It's funny, don't you think, me having to keep steady to look after him? He wouldn't leave me; I couldn't shake him off.'

It was funny; the anxiety, the worry, the pain, and her recrimination of him were once again washed away with his elusive endearingness, the unfair endearingness that had the power to blot out all but the feelings of the moment. With one accord they moved swiftly to each other, and his laughter rolling out again, he caught her up and swung her about.

Mary Ann's laughter joined his, but it was a little too loud and a little too high to be natural, and it was too full of relief to stay as laughter. This was the first time since her da had won that money that she had seen him and her ma laughing together and with their arms about each other. It meant that everything was going to be all right, no matter what her grannie did or how nice Mr Quinton was.

Her laughter broke on a cry, and she fled from the room and through the kitchen into the scullery, and she leant her head on the sink and sobbed. But almost immediately she felt herself lifted up, and hiding her face, she buried it in her father's neck. And when Lizzie, stroking her head, said, 'Come, come, now we're going to see the bonfires,' her crying mounted, for it was the only way in which she could express her happiness at this moment.

Chapter Six

Sunday

The world was a beautiful place; there had never been any rain, or dullness, or darkness; there had never been any worry, fear or anxiety, for was not the sun shining brightly, and wasn't she walking in the country? In the country, mind, where the big trees grew, hand in hand with her da!

Not only was Mike solid and sober but he had on a new suit, and to crown his well-set-up appearance he was wearing on his head not the usual cap but a trilby. Mary Ann's gaze continually lifted from his face to the hat, and her heart was so swollen with pride that it was ready to burst from her body. Oh, he looked lovely in his new hat. Never, never in the world was there anybody who looked so wonderful as her da. Only one cloud touched him and the morning–Sarah Flannagan's eyes had not beheld the glory of him. Before they had left the house she had watched Sarah depart for Mass, and she had failed to induce her da to walk round by the church on their journey to the country in the hope that they would encounter Sarah coming out.

The thought of her enemy made Mary Ann once again put her hand tentatively towards the back of her head and feel the lump that even after a week had subsided very little. She touched it almost lovingly, for had she not received it in defence of her da?

On the morning following the events of Coronation Day Sarah had cornered her round the bottom of the back lane between the store shed of Tullis's outdoor beer shop and the Colyers' backyard wall. There in the narrow alley she had pinned her against the wall, and in language not strictly of school standard had accused Mike of making her da drunk and making her ma nearly throw a fit, and keeping them all up half the night, and, what was more, causing her da to lose the first shift in years because his head was so bad he couldn't raise it from the pillow.

Mary Ann had stoutly denied these accusations, saying that her da was solid and sober as everybody in the street knew, and he had never been inside a bar or smelt beer. As for Mr Flannagan, he was a disgrace. Hadn't she seen him with her very own eyes being dragged into the house by Mrs Flannagan? That was when her da was taking them all to see the bonfires. And hadn't Mr Flannagan made a show of himself by fighting Mrs Flannagan because he wanted to go along with her da?

That Sarah's rage only led her to bang Mary Ann's head repeatedly against the wall said something for her control. Whether she would have continued this restrained retaliation until she had accomplished Mary Ann's entire insensibility cannot be known, for Mary Ann's cries brought Mrs Colyer from her house, and Sarah reluctantly departed at a run.

The attitude of her parents concerning this attack was not quite clear to Mary Ann; even her da gave her little sympathy, and her ma did not show the slightest sign of going to Mrs Flannagan and telling her off. There was, she felt, injustice somewhere; but to explain it, even to herself, was beyond her. Only one thing was sure in her mind concerning the affair, she had got this great bump on her head and nearly died in defence of her da.

'That's the farm,' said Mike.

'Oh.'

Mary Ann looked over the yellow-green fields towards the flat-faced red-brick house and asked, 'Will the cottage be that size?'

'No. No, of course not,' said Mike. 'You know the size of cottages; they're like the little houses at the Quay Corner, two or three rooms at the most. But there's bound to be a good patch of garden.'

'And how'll I get to school?'

'You'll have to take the bus. But wait, I haven't got it yet.'

The altered tone of her father's voice made her lift her eye searchingly up to him. His smile had gone and there was a stiff straightness about his face that brought the shadow of anxiety back for a moment to dim the sun, and caused her to resort to praying rapidly that the job might be his.

There was no one in the farmyard except a sow with its stomach almost trailing the ground, and the sight of it brought Mary Ann from an anxious conversation with the Holy Family. She had never seen such a fat pig. She stared at it amazed, fascinated by the wobbling enormity of its flesh.

Mike left her to her wonderment and went towards a brick cowshed standing stark in its newness from amongst the time-worn, rather tumble-down buildings of the yard.

'Mr Campbell?' He spoke to a man who was unscrewing a nozzle from a pipe, and the man turned his head and said peremptorily, 'Yes, I'm Campbell. What is it?'

The tone slightly nonplussed Mike. But he went forward, and in a carefully guarded voice, said, 'I've come about the job; I was told you wanted a hand.'

'Oh, that.' Mr Campbell straightened his back, his eyes still directed towards the nozzle. 'You're too late, that's been filled nearly a week.'

The expression on Mike's face did not change, but he stood staring down at the bowed head of this under-sized little man and making a great effort to check a swift rush of temper. He hadn't got the job. That was bad, but by now he was, in a way, inured to disappointment; it was the offhandedness of the man that angered him. He was still intent on the pipe; it was as if he were alone, that nothing existed for him but the nozzle of the artificial milker.

Abruptly Mike turned and walked away, out of the cowshed, across the yard towards the road again, holding out his hand silently to Mary Ann as he went. His return was so quick and unexpected that she had to drag her thoughts back from the fascinating ugliness of the pig to take in exactly what this quick departure meant.

She moved towards him and put her hand in his. And so swift was his stride that she had to run to keep abreast of him. She could see he was flaming mad–she used his own expression to describe his temper–and she was sensible enough not to anger him further by asking senseless questions.

They had gone some way down the road when they were both halted by a shout. 'Hi! Hi, there!'

Mike turned slowly, paused a moment, then walked back towards the farmer. They stopped within a few yards of each other, and there was no prelude in the farmer's speech. 'Old Lord will be needing men; he's bought Coffin's farm. . . . You know Lord's place?'

Mike nodded.

'It was only sold yesterday. Coffin's taking his men with him. There'll be two empty cottages. . . . I suppose you want a cottage?'

'Yes.'

'Well, I would try there.' Then as if to explain his previous disinterest he added before turning away, 'I'm having trouble with the new machine. Not used to it yet.'

He had almost reached his farm-gate when Mike shouted, 'Thank you, sir.'

The man raised his hand in acknowledgment, and Mike and Mary Ann went on their way again.

'Are we going to Mr Lord's, Da?'

'No.'

'What for not?'

'Because it would be no use.'

'Why?'

'Oh.' Mike moved his head impatiently.

'If there's a cottage, Da?'

'You know who Mr Lord is, don't you?'

At the moment Mary Ann didn't know; she had to delve back in her mind. . . . Mr Lord? . . . Mr Lord? . . . 'Oh yes.' She smiled. 'He's the man with the big stone walls round his house, with the big trees inside. You can't see the house. It's up beyond the cemetery.'

Mike nodded.

'And he's got a wood farther along with barbed wire round and you can't get in.'

Mike nodded again.

But Mary Ann could see no reason why this should keep them from visiting Mr Lord. Her mind groped to understand all her da had left unsaid. Then suddenly she understood. Mr Lord was . . . the Lord. It was the nickname the men gave him in the yard, and her da had once worked in Lord's yard. And he had left when he was having a lot of talk about his theories. . . . Mr Lord and the Lord were the same person. Her spirits sank to a still lower ebb, and any hope of the cottage sank with them.

They boarded a bus that took them into Hebburn and then on to Jarrow, and when they alighted at the Ben Lomond, Mike said, 'You run off home, I won't be long.' And after one long look at him, Mary Ann turned silently away. The sun had gone, the day was dull, almost dark again.

She walked through the empty streets. The shops were shut and there was no one even sitting on a step, because it was Sunday. Everywhere looked bare and deserted and the atmosphere touched her low spirits and sent her off at a run to seek the security of the kitchen and the comfort of her mother. But her running ceased abruptly when she entered her street, for there she saw small groups gathered together on the pavement. There must, she surmised, have been a row. But not on a Sunday, surely. You could have rows up to quite late on a Saturday night, and they'd be quite in order, but it was shocking to have them on a Sunday. Smugly the thought came to her that it couldn't be her family, anyway. No, but it was in Mulhattans' Hall where the row was. She had evidence of this as she neared her home, and her surprise was almost stupefying as she mounted the stairs, for the shouting was coming right from the top of the house, and it was Mrs McBride who was doing it.

She passed Miss Harper's open door, and also the Quigleys', and when she reached her own landing Mrs McBride was shouting at her mother, 'Why didn't you tell me, you could have tipped me the wink?'

She stood in the doorway watching them. Mrs McBride was all dressed up in her Mass clothes, the tight black coat and the black felt hat she wore only on Sundays. Her mother was wearing the big apron she put round her when she was doing the dinner; she had the oven cloth in one hand and she kept pulling it through the other; but she didn't answer Mrs McBride; and Fanny cried 'The whole place has known except me, and never a thing would I have heard yet but for something Mary Prout said at the church door. She was talking to May Brice. "Join the army and see the world," she said, "and join the Salvation Army and see the other world. Wait till old Fan gets wind of it, Jack'll wonder which cuddy's kicked him." It wasn't long afore I had it out of her, and I nearly died when I heard. And let her take what she got, for I wouldn't believe a word of it. Yet there's no smoke without fire, and I came tearing home and tackled him, and he admitted it.'

She became silent for a moment, and her gaze turned inwards. She was seeing the astonishment on her son's face and feeling the tearing hurt of his words. 'Yes, it's Joyce Scallen. And I'm going to marry her. And just you try and stop me. And you make that rowdy tongue of yours go about it and I'll do it right away, I won't wait.'

But her tongue was her only weapon, the only weapon she knew of, and she had lashed it at him, and not only at him but at the whole family of Scallens.

Lizzie said gently, 'It might turn out all right. Just give them a chance.'

'A chance! A chance to do what, I ask you? Lead a hell of a life? What chance is there for happiness between a Hallelujah and a Catholic . . . because she won't turn? Do you know what her old father said to me? "It must be the will of God," he said. And he said that God was showing Jack the way and he'd be saved yet.'

'You see,' said Lizzie, 'Mr Scallen's taking it quietly. There'd be more chance with Jack if you could take it quietly an' all; you'd best Mr Scallen at his own game then.'

'So you think like me,' cried Fanny, 'he means something? Perhaps he's known about it all along, although the old swine said he hadn't.' She flung her short arms wide apart and lifted her eyes to the ceiling. 'Oh, what am I to do? Before you know it there'll be our Jack leading the band and knocking bloody hell out of the big drum, and I'll never be able to raise me head again on the whole Tyneside.'

Try as she might Lizzie could not suppress a smile, but her concern for the old woman was genuine, so much so that she addressed her by her Christian name as she said, 'Don't worry, Fanny, he'll not do anything silly; he's a sensible lad, is Jack; only be patient with him.'

'Patient!' Fanny spoke quietly now. She looked suddenly deflated. 'I've always been patient with him. Now if our Phil had done this I could have understood it. But not Jack. Not him.' Shaking her head, she moved towards the door, saying, 'This is what comes of missing Mass and neglecting his duties. It's two years since he was at them.' She paused near Mary Ann, and in a broken voice, said, 'There's worse things than drink, hinny. Remember that.' She patted her on the head, then went slowly down the stairs.

Mary Ann watched her. There was a lump the size of an egg in her throat–Mrs McBride was crying.

Her mother was standing by the table waiting for her to speak, but she couldn't for the moment, and Lizzie said, 'He didn't get it?'

She shook her head.

'Where is he?'

'At the Ben Lomond. He won't be long.'

Lizzie turned away and Mary Ann said, 'The farmer was nice. . . . He was sorry and he told me da about another job.'

'Where?' Lizzie turned about again.

'At Mr Lord's.'

'Lord's?'

'Yes. Beyond the cemetery.'

'The shipyard man?'

'Yes. Me da said it was no use going.'

'He was right.'

Mary Ann watched her mother go into the scullery. She too looked deflated. There was no comfort or security even here; and the whole world must be sad when Mrs McBride was crying.

Chapter Seven

The Last Straw

Although during the following week Mike was never paralytic, his inability to reach this stage being, he himself confessed, merely owing to the weakness of the beer, he was at times well set. Yet he had made no oration in the street, and hadn't sung until he reached the stairs. And although on this particular night he had to be alternately pulled and coaxed away from Miss Harper's fast-closed door, where he insisted on serenading her, not untunefully, with 'He was her man, but he did her wrong', this had been the only incident of the week.

But this incident, which had amused everyone in the house with the exception of Miss Harper and the Shaughnessys themselves, was the means of snapping the taut thread of Michael's strained nerves. He had sat for the examination, and during the waiting period prior to the results being made known, he was up in the clouds and down in the depths ten times a day . . . yes, he would be telling Lizzie, he felt he had answered most of the questions correctly; or no, he was sure he hadn't and had mugged everything.

It was earlier in the evening of Mike's serenading that Michael's pal had dashed in to say his parents had received a letter saying he had passed for the Grammar School. The last post of the day had been to Mulhattans' Hall and Michael had done his best to be pleased for his pal, but even his best was a poor effort, and Lizzie, keen disappointment filling her together with a heart torn with pity for her son, tried to reassure him that there was still tomorrow and that they wouldn't send all the notices out together. Michael had made no response to this except to shrug her hand off his shoulder and go into the other room and close the door after him.

It was eleven o'clock the same night, when Lizzie had to arouse Mary Ann from her bed to go down and coax Mike from Miss Harper's door, that Michael had begun to cry. His crying at first had been the broken sobs of a child, but when his father staggered into the room his sobs turned to angry gasps and when Mike, still singing, flopped into a chair he sat up and screamed at him: 'Shut up, you drunken pig you! I hate you, you rotten drunken pig!'

There followed a short surprised silence, which was suddenly broken by Michael crying again, 'Damn! damn! damn!' He thumped the bedclothes with his fist, and when Lizzie rushing to the bed tried to draw him to her he sprang up, thrusting her aside, and ran to where Mike, silent now, was surveying him. 'I wish you were dead, do you hear?' He pushed his face towards his father, who was now wearing a fuddled, surprised expression. 'They wouldn't let me pass because they knew about you . . . everybody knows about you. I wish you'd fall from the top of a mast and be smashed to bits.'

'Michael!' Lizzie dragged at him, but with the strength of his passion he again thrust her off, crying at her now, 'Why don't you go away and leave him? Why do you make us stay here? I won't stay; I'll go to me grannie's.'

With the aid of the chair Mike rose. He seemed much steadier than when he had sat down and his voice was only slightly fuddled when he said, 'Be quiet, do you hear?'

'I won't! I won't! I loathe you. I wish you were . . .'

'Quiet!' The shout vibrated from the walls, and in the silence that followed they all stood still, seeming to be stunned by the force of the order.

Mike was staring down into his son's face and his expression was frightening, but it seemed powerless wholly to intimidate Michael, who continued to glare up at him, and after a moment Mike turned from the loathing in the boy's eyes and, with only a slight sway in his walk, went towards the room.

Mary Ann watched her mother lead Michael to the bed. She watched her tenderly cover him up, then lie down on top of the bed beside him, and not until she began to shiver did she go to the corner where her bed was, and, climbing in, turn her face to the wall and thrust her fingers into her ears to shut out the sound of Michael's crying.

It was a long time later when her mother came and stood over her. She did not let her know she was awake, but kept her eyes closed. She heard her walk softly away and turn the light out, and when the darkness fell on her lids she opened her eyes and stared into the blackness. She felt her mother move across the room and into the bedroom. The door clicked softly. Then there was no sound. She could not even hear Michael's breathing. Poor Michael. Her thoughts were tender towards him. If only he had passed the exam, then he might not have minded about her da so much.

The words Michael had used to her father had not shocked her, for he had expressed them many times to her, and whereas she had always fought him when he upbraided Mike, tonight for the first time she felt in sympathy with him. But this did not mean she was less sorry for her father or that she condemned him, it only meant that within her small body was the capacity for understanding the agony of the personal disappointments of childhood.

For what seemed to her hours and hours she lay on her back staring into the darkness. Once a car passed down the street, and once Miss Harper had a fit of coughing and it sounded as if she was in the room. She was slowly falling into sleep when she was recalled to her wakefulness by the fog-horn wailing up the river, and she felt a little guilty that she should sleep when there was all this trouble in the house. Hastily she determined that she must keep awake. This was her last thought before sleep overtook her, but then it was a troubled sleep, for her dreams were on the surface and once or twice as was usual with her she told herself she was dreaming. Once she imagined she heard Michael get out of bed and go into the scullery, the door of which was near the foot of her bed, but it was all mixed up in her dreams.

She was not sure what woke her; perhaps it was the smell–she had been dreaming that she was being choked by the smell. She tried to sit up but found that her head was heavy and that she felt very sleepy. She also felt a little sick. Now why should she be feeling sick, for she had eaten no supper and she hadn't eaten any sweets for two days? It was a gassy smell, like when her mother turned the tap on and dropped the match and the gas came out of the oven and filled the scullery.

She was never to know exactly what drove her to rise against all her opposing inclinations and stagger to Michael's bed. It was empty, but she knew where he was . . . he was in the scullery. The scullery door was closed, and when she pushed it open the gas met her in a sickening wave. She could not see Michael but she knew he was there.

Staggering in her run, she burst into the bedroom and having groped her way to the bed pulled madly at her mother.

'What is it?' Lizzie was sitting up. 'My God!' Almost immediately she got the smell of the gas and was out of bed.

'Michael.'

'He's in the scullery.' Mary Ann's words were cut short by being knocked on her bottom in Lizzie's dive for the door.

'Wha's up? Wha's the row?' Mike's voice, thick with sleep, came from the bed, and Mary Ann, scrambling to him, shook him by his slack hanging arm, crying, 'It's Michael–he's in the scullery and the gas is on.'

Again she was almost knocked flat, and by the time she reached the door she heard her father's voice coming from the other side of the kitchen, saying, 'God in Heaven, what's he done?'

It was many hours later that Mary Ann recollected they were the only words she heard her da speak that night. It was her ma who did the talking. Fiercely she whispered, 'Open the window, and the scullery one, too, and let a draught through . . . and do it quietly.'

As Mike swiftly obeyed her command she said to Mary Ann, 'Get me the torch from the cupboard–mind the table.'

Mary Ann groped her way to the cupboard, groped for the torch, then groped her way back to where her mother was kneeling on the floor. Lizzie snatched the torch from her fingers and, switching it on, plunged its light on to Michael's face.

Mary Ann stared down at her brother. His face looked pink and smooth and swollen. He looked sound asleep, very sound asleep. She watched her mother grab him by the shoulders and shake him. She allowed her eyes to travel to her father's legs and up to where they disappeared beneath his shirt-tail, but she could not lift them to his face . . . until he bent his body over his son and his face came into the beam of the torch, and then she saw it was grey, an awful whitish grey, and that his eyes, although sunk deep into his head, had, at the same time, a popping look. His whole appearance looked wild and not a little fantastic. His strong wiry hair was standing up from his head in points and his shirt seemed too short and tight for his body.

Mary Ann moved swiftly back as he hauled Michael from the floor and carried him to the window. Her mother followed, directing the light towards the floor. Mary Ann looked to where her father, silhouetted against the darkness of the night and the blackness of the houses opposite, was shaking Michael, and when after a moment Michael's head lolled against his shoulder Lizzie turned to Mary Ann gasping, 'Get your things on, quick.' And she followed her to the bed saying, 'Run for the doctor, the nearest–that one off Ormond Road–Pimsel.' Her talking was in staccato whispers. 'Tell him . . . tell him that Michael . . . wait.' She stopped, and Mary Ann saw her turn to the window. 'No, don't go yet. Look, run down to Mrs McBride's. Go quietly without your shoes. Let yourself out the back door. She sleeps with the window open a bit. Try not to raise the house. Ask her to come. Go on now.' She pushed Mary Ann to the door, putting a coat about her petticoat and her thin bare arms as she went.

Mary Ann did not need to be told to hurry or to make no noise. She was used to the stairs in the dark, and when her swift light tread made them creak she took no notice for she knew they always creaked at night–it was the souls in purgatory being made to use them as a tread-mill that caused the creaking.

The cold of the yard struck up through her stockinged feet as she closed the back hall door softly after her and she knew a moment of fear at finding herself in the backyard made unfamiliar with the night. When she reached Mrs McBride's bedroom window she raised herself to the sill by digging her toes into the wall, and she called softly through the narrow opening, 'Mrs McBride.' On her third call she heard a rustling and she knew that she had woken the old woman, but not until she had repeated the call did she hear her speak.

'Holy Mother of God,' said Mrs McBride; and Mary Ann said, 'It's me, Mrs McBride . . . Mary Ann.'

There was a pause before Mrs McBride answered, 'Mary Ann Shaughnessy? In the name of God, what's up?'

'Sh!' said Mary Ann. 'Listen. Me ma sent me for you . . . our Michael's bad.'

'Bad?'

'Yes.'

Mrs McBride didn't seem to be unduly disturbed by this and Mary Ann had to say the dreaded words, 'He's put his head in the gas oven.'

It seemed to Mary Ann that almost in a single blinking of her eyelids Mrs McBride was at the back door. Dragging a coat over her dirty nightdress with one hand, she pulled Mary Ann into the scullery with the other and pushed her ahead into the room and across it; then quietly unbolting her door she drew Mary Ann into the hallway and preceded her up the stairs. She did all this, to Mary Ann's amazement, with the quietness and swiftness of a cat.

From the moment Mrs McBride entered the room she took command of the situation. She bent over Michael where he was now lying on the bed and put her hand inside his pyjama jacket for a moment, then turning to Mike, she said, 'Hoist him up and get him walking, he's not gone. . . . That's it.' She got on one side of him. 'Come on now, keep him going. Make up a good dose of hot salt water, Lizzie.' She turned her head in Lizzie's direction without pausing in her walk. 'He'll come to. That's it, keep him at it Mike, it's air he wants.'

In the light of the torch Mary Ann stood watching her da and Mrs McBride dragging Michael back and forward between the window and the bed, his feet trailing like dead things. It was a strange and weird trio, made more fantastic still by the torchlight. Suddenly Michael's body stiffened, his head came up and his chest swelled out and he retched and was sick over the floor.

'That's the ticket, get it up, lad. He won't need the salt-water now.' When they got him back to the bed again and Lizzie held a dish under his head, Mrs McBride exclaimed in much the same tone as another would use when viewing an objet d'art, 'Lovely . . . beautiful.'

Mary Ann moved a little closer. Michael was lying gasping now, his head moving heavily from side to side, and she could have thrown herself into Mrs McBride's arms when she heard her say, 'He'll be as right as rain; there's no need to worry.'

'Could I light the gas now?' asked Lizzie.

'Ay, of course, it'll all be gone by now. But I'd pull down the blinds,' said Fanny, 'or Nancy Cooper'll have her two bleary eyes glued to her window . . . she never sleeps.'

It was not until the gas was lit that Mary Ann saw her father clearly. He didn't seem like her da at all . . . his face seemed altered completely. It looked to her as if something had sucked all the blood from it, and his eyes looked–she could not allow herself even to think how his eyes looked, for fear was the last thing she would associate with her da.

It wasn't until Mike dragged his eyes from his son's face to gaze from one to the other of them in stupefied perplexity that he became conscious of his state of undress. He turned from the bed and went slowly into the room, and Lizzie, bending over the boy, called softly, 'Michael, Michael.' For answer he rolled his head and retched again, and Fanny, straightening her back with an effort, said, 'Ah, he'll do fine. There's nothing to worry about. You should have seen my Florrie the night she did it, when she found young Bob Lancaster had given her a bellyful. It was nearly touch and go that night and many's the time I've wondered since if it wouldn't have been better to let her go, for there she is now with seven round her, and to a no-good waster like Fred Boyle, and her young Bob gone off God knows where, and him the only one she gives a hoot for. Life's crazy, I've said it afore, but thank God even at the longest it's short. And it can't be short enough for me.' She sighed heavily, and Mary Ann knew she was thinking of Jack who was really going to marry Joyce Scallen. But what was that to worry about compared with what had nearly happened.

She shivered, and Mrs McBride turned to her, saying, 'What, are you cold, hinny? Why don't you jump into bed?' She bent over her, her breasts pressing out the front of her coat like great inflated balloons. And Mary Ann wanted to lay her head between them and put her arms about the not too clean neck and cry with relief, for had she not saved their Michael and was she not as anxious as her ma to keep the disgrace from the neighbours, for Mary Ann was fully aware of the disgrace that clung to a family should one of them stick their head in the gas oven. You were put in the papers then and everybody knew about you. That was why her mother had stopped her going for the doctor, for if the doctor had come it would have been all over the place and her da would have got all the blame. She glanced towards the bedroom door and Mrs McBride said, 'Don't worry, hinny, he'll be all right an' all, he's only getting into his things. Jump into bed with you now.'

Slowly she did as she was told and when Fanny's lips came down to hers she did not offer her cheek but returned the old woman's kiss. She watched her go and bend over Michael again, then walk towards the door pulling her coat about her. She saw her ma follow and she could hear them talking but not what they said. She saw Mrs McBride patting her mother, then she went out and her mother closed the door softly after her and returned to Michael.

It was some little time before her father came out of the room. He did not go to the bed but stood looking towards it to where Lizzie knelt stroking the boy's head. Michael was recovered sufficiently to cry again, but softly, and after a time, during which Lizzie gave no heed to Mike's presence, he went back into the room. Mary Ann watched her mother make a drink for Michael, she watched him refuse it and then be coaxed to drink it, then she saw Lizzie lie on top of the bed and put her arms about him, and she felt nothing but pity, until once again her father entered the kitchen. And when he stood silently looking at his wife and son the pity for Michael and sorrow for her mother combined into a fear, and the fear was formed around their allegiance and what it would mean to her da.

When once again her father returned to the room she saw her mother gently disengage herself from Michael and follow him. She had not turned out the light, so that meant she was coming back. Mary Ann sat swiftly up in bed and pressed her ears in the direction of the bedroom but the only sound she could hear was of a low murmur, and it was of her mother's voice. Her ears were so attuned to listening that she could distinguish what emotion was present in the murmuring of her parents' speech, but even without this facility she would have recognized disaster from the low, dead murmur of her mother's voice.

Knowing that she might be caught in the act did not prevent her from getting out of bed and moving swiftly towards the door. She had no need to bend down to the keyhole, for the door was ajar. She stood at the side nearest the opening, close to the wall, and listened to her mother. At first she could not disentangle the quick, low speech, but then she began to make out the words. They were dead words, yet alive with dread significance. They came to Mary Ann, bearing all the sorrow in the world. 'Don't think this silent, remorseful attitude of yours will touch me. You've tried everything in the past. You found talking yourself silly didn't work; well, you can save yourself this effort for it won't work either. If he had died I would have killed you, do you hear? Oh how I loathe you, you great weak hulk. . . . Well, it's finished, finally finished. I'm going.'

In the awful silence that followed, into which Mike threw no plea, Mary Ann stumbled back to bed; whatever more there was to be said could not surpass this. She lay watching the door. Her breathing seemed to have ceased, until suddenly, her lungs demanding air, she drew into her narrow chest deep gulps that almost choked her.

Lizzie came out of the room and stood for a moment, her hand pressed to her throat, before slowly moving towards the light and turning it down to a mere glimmer. After the springs of Michael's bed creaked, there was no more sound.

Mary Ann lay for a long time trying to discern objects through the glimmer, trying to shut out the thoughts that conjured up the future without her da, trying to stave off the dawn. Yet when its first light showed on the paper blind she realized she must have fallen asleep, for the gas was out and she hadn't seen her mother get up and turn it off. Soon she knew her da would come out of the room and get ready for work, and he would leave the house, and perhaps before he returned her mother would have taken them away to their grannie's. This might be the last time she would see him leave for work. The thought brought her from the bed. She must say something to him, tell him she would always love him and when she grew up she would look after him.

Gently she pushed the open door wider, and her eyes peered towards the bed. But he wasn't in it, he was sitting on the box to the side of the window. She could see the great dark huddled shape of him, and she was about to move softly forward when her step was checked by a sound coming from him. It was a familiar enough sound when connected with herself or Michael, or her mother, or anyone else in the world, but not with her da. It filled her body with a great, deep, unbearable pity. She stood listening to the sound until she could stand it no longer. It did not drive her to him to spread her comfort over him but back to her bed to lie huddled and sobbing herself. A god had fallen, not through his sins but through his weakness–for gods did not cry.

By the nine o'clock post the letter had arrived to say that Michael had passed for the Grammar School, but it did not make much difference; it had come too late.

Chapter Eight

Some Call it Auto-Suggestion (It's Their Ignorance, God Help Them)

As Father Owen listened to the child his heart grew heavy, not only with the weight of her sorrow but with the sorrow that seemed to be the heritage of all such as Mary Ann. Their very joy was tinged with sorrow, made so by their sensitiveness, a quality which should have been used merely to appreciate the finer things of life but which was deformed by constant worry. As he listened to her voice relating the happening of the last few days his mind rebelled against the sentence inflicted on childhood, a sentence inflicted by the parents themselves. Life at this stage should be a joyous thing; God made it so; away with all the twaddle that it was He who sent suffering.

Mary Ann was saying, 'He doesn't talk, Father . . . he says nothing, and he hasn't been full. He went out last night but he came back solid and sober.'

'When is your mother going.'

'Saturday, Father, I think.'

'And you're not going to your grandmother's?'

'No. She said only last night she'd got a furnished room round Hope Street and we go in on Saturday, and she's got the promise of a job, and Michael and me are to have our dinner at school.'

'And your da says nothing?'

'No, nothing; and he wouldn't let me pour the water over his head when he washed.'

'And does he seem upset at your mother going?'

Mary Ann did not answer the priest for the moment–upset could not describe the state her da was in, he seemed gone away somehow, dead. She was no consolation to him, and she knew, without knowing how she had come to the knowledge, that without her mother she had no power of her own to hold him. She herself could have done without even her mother as long as she had him, but in him it was her ma that infused the power to live. So she answered, 'When me ma goes I don't know what he'll do. I'm frightened, Father.'

'Now there's no need to be frightened. Just trust in God and everything will come out all right. For your penance, say one Our Father and one Hail Mary . . . make a good act of contrition.'

Slowly Mary Ann said the set piece–it was as if she were loath to leave the confessional and the comfort of the priest–she spread it out and was only induced to finish when Father Owen said, 'Now, good night, my girl, and trust in God.'

'Good night, Father.'

When she left the box the priest, after a murmured prayer, followed her. There would be no other children after Mary Ann. He was so used to her manoeuvres that he almost judged the time by her now. He saw her light a candle, then kneel with uplifted face to the altar of the Holy Family, and he turned to the church door and went through the porch and stood on a step, drawing in the fresh air as he looked up and down the street.

It was quiet now, the traffic of the day having eased. The shops on the other side were closed, their doors locked and barred, all except the door leading to the office of Mayland's, the solicitor. Likely, Father Owen surmised, there was a meeting going on up in the Board Room there. Ah, he shook his head at himself, he wished he had just the smell of the money that had changed hands in that room today. . . . But what was he thinking about? There would be no board meeting at this time of the evening. It was now six o'clock. Didn't his stomach tell him so? And what was more there were no cars about except one, and if he was not mistaken it was old Lord's. Likely it was him up there alone, settling the business of more land. What did he hope to do with it all? One thing was sure, he couldn't take it with him. Oh dear, dear; what men strove for. He shook his head again, this time at Mr Lord.

Peter Lord was an old man now, and what was in his life? Money and land. Yet God help him, he wasn't to blame entirely. Thirty years ago he had been a man splendid in his prime and if he had only managed his private affairs with the same sagacity as he did his business he would undoubtedly have had an exceptionally happy life, but like many another able man before him he had to go and pick on a feather-brained vain piece of a girl, and what a life she had led him. And she had given him nothing, not even a child; and then to leave him when she thought he was going broke. Oh, she had been a right bad piece that. And there he was alone in that barracks of a house where he lived like a hermit. Life was strange. Just imagine, if he had had someone to pour out love on him as did that child back in the church there on that hot-headed devil of a father of hers, it would have made all the difference in the world.

'Oh, there you are, Mary Ann.' He stood to one side and made room for her on the step beside him in the half-open doorway. 'Have you been to confession?'

He was well aware, perhaps not that he was blind in the confessional, but that he was to Mary Ann an entirely different being when once out of the box, and of being quite incapable of recognizing her as the same child who a few minutes before had poured her heart out to him.

'Yes, Father,' said Mary Ann, but there was no smile on her face tonight as she said it.

'That's a good girl . . . you'll be qualifying to lead the procession again next year, I can see that.'

'Yes, Father.' She managed a very faint smile. As he patted her head the sound of a car starting up made him turn his gaze up the street and as he watched it approach his hand became still on her head; then swiftly, without looking at her again, he gave her a little push backwards, saying, 'Stay there now.' And as Mary Ann stood within the shelter of the porch he stepped briskly to the kerb and hailed the driver of the car.

'Have you a minute?'

The car had not gathered any speed and Mr Lord brought it to a standstill, saying, 'Hallo–what are you after now?'

'Have you a minute?'

'Yes, and nothing else, and even that is valuable.'

The priest laughed and was in no way put out at the brusqueness of the tone. 'Oh yes, yes. Don't I know.' He bent his face down to the open window and cast his eyes sidelong at the erect forbidding figure sitting behind the wheel. 'Well it's only two minutes of your time I want, and I'll pay you when my ship comes in, or perhaps I'll just leave it to God and good neighbours.'

'What are you after now?'

'What makes you think I'm after anything?'

'If I know you it's something to do with money.'

'You're wrong then, this time at any rate. But if you've got any going . . .'

'Not a penny. Three hundred you had out of me last year.'

'Was it that much? Good gracious.'

'Was it that much!'

'Well, well, doesn't it mount up?'

Mr Lord surveyed the priest with a hard, forbidding look which did not intimidate Father Owen, who, putting his head and shoulders farther into the car, changed his tone and said, 'You can do me a favour if you would.'

There was no Yes or Nay or What is it? from Mr Lord, but in still silence he waited for the priest to go on.

'I heard you'd bought up Coffin's farm.'

Still silence surrounded Mr Lord.

'And I've heard,' said Father Owen, 'that Coffin took his hands with him, at least that's what I'm given to understand. They must have been fine workers; when a man gets good farm-hands these days he keeps them. Of course Coffin was good to the men. Didn't he have those two fine cottages built for them?'

Mr Lord closed his blue-veined eyelids for a second, then stared ahead through the windscreen and said, 'Come to the point, I want to get home.'

'All right–I want you to give a man I know a job–it may be the making of him. Have you stocked up? Have you got your men?'

'No.' Mr Lord turned his head slowly towards the priest. 'And I'm not stocking up with any of your riff-raff. I've had experience of your recommendations before and whoever you're wanting to palm off on me now would likely not be able to recognize one end of a cow from the other.'

'Ah, but you're wrong there–he's a right fine man with cows.'

Whether intentionally or otherwise Father Owen had adopted Mary Ann's voice and her words, and he had to laugh at himself for so doing. But his hilarity had an irritating effect on Mr Lord. He moved his hand on the wheel saying, 'You're wasting your time.'

'Look, just a minute.' Father Owen stretched out his hand and laid it gently on Mr Lord's arm. 'If you were to give this man a chance it would likely mean the saving of a family.'

'Why should that particular point be any concern of mine?'

The two old men stared at each other. Then Father Owen brought back the dim past when this man and he had been firm friends before the bitterness of life had erected the barrier between Peter Lord and all men, by saying, 'Peter, do this one thing for me.'

The use of his Christian name seemed to have little or no effect upon Mr Lord's feelings, for his countenance remained forbidding, but after a moment during which he seemed about to drive off despite the fact that Father Owen was half in and half out of the car, he asked, 'Who is it, and why are you so bent on getting him on a farm?'

Father Owen kept all eagerness from his voice as he said, 'Because it's his natural work–he's like a fish out of water in the yards.'

'But there's plenty of farm work going, they're crying out for farm hands.'

'Yes, but they're not issuing cottages to go with them; and you know yourself there are no set hours for a good farmhand, and the farms are so few and far between here that a man would have to stay on the job and travel home at odd times, and this fellow can't stick that. He's tried it. He wants his family with him. He's the kind of fellow who . . .' He did not finish this and add, 'who falls to pieces without his wife,' but said: 'Well, he'd pay you a good dividend in labour if you could settle him and his family in a cottage.'

'What's his name?'

'Shaughnessy.'

Mr Lord turned in his seat until he was square to the priest. 'Shaughnessy?' he asked heavily.

'Yes, that's him . . . a big red-headed chap.'

'Ha, ha!' It was supposed to be a laugh, but resulted in a dry splitting crack of a sound. 'You want me to take Mike Shaughnessy on? Why, if he was the last man on God's earth I wouldn't give him breathing space. Do you know what he did in my yard last year, or tried to do?'

The priest remained sadly silent.

'He would have had the men out–like that.' He snapped his fingers; and Father Owen said lamely, 'I hear he's a good worker.'

'A good worker!–he won't do a bat of overtime except with his tongue; besides which he's never sober. What do you take me for? Good-bye, Father.'

The farewell salutation was weighed with sarcasm and Father Owen withdrew himself from the car, which almost immediately shot forward and away.

As he turned towards the church again there was Mary Ann looking at him from the step, and he walked up to her, and they surveyed each other in silence.

How much had she heard? Her eyes were so full of strangled hope. He said, 'Mr Lord has a job and a cottage going for a farm-hand. I thought I might get it for your da.'

She did not reply but continued to gaze up at him.

'He's not feeling too well tonight–he's in a bit of a bad mood–or perhaps I just didn't put the case properly.' He smiled gently down at her. 'Now you, Mary Ann, would likely have put his case much better–I mean your da's.' His voice trailed off and he became uneasy under the fixed pain of her eyes. 'Well, we must never give up hope. Keep on praying, Mary Ann; it's amazing the miracles the Holy Family perform. Just you ask them for advice. They never fail you. Now I must be off to my tea. Good night, my child.'

He moved hastily into the church and her eyes followed him, but she did not speak, not even to answer his farewell, and after a moment she too moved away, walking slowly in the direction of home.

The kitchen was empty when she arrived, but she knew that both her parents were in, for her da's black cap was hanging on the back of the door and the table had not been cleared and her mother never went out without first clearing the table. She was removing her coat and hat when their voices came to her from the bedroom. They sounded normal, quiet voices and her hands became still and hope sprang afresh into her being and overwhelmed her for a moment, until, moving farther into the room, her father's voice, like the backwash of a mighty wave, sucked it away again.

'I'll allow you so much. . . . But don't take my word for it, have it done legally; you'll be safe then. . . . When are you going?'

'Saturday.'

'To your mother's?'

'No–a place in Hope Street.'

'Are you taking the bits?'

'No, it's furnished.'

'Well, you may as well sell them because I won't be staying here. Can I . . . see the bairns sometime?'

There was a pause before Lizzie answered, 'Yes.'

To Mary Ann the voices sounded even and untroubled; they sounded the same as when they were discussing something that had appeared in the *Shields Gazette*. They sounded like that but they weren't like that; they were final voices, voices that had ceased to shout or yell or fight, or even plead; they were voices from which emotion had been drained; and they frightened Mary Ann more than any other voices could have done. She fled into the scullery and, covering her face with her hands and pressing herself into the corner of the wall between the sink and the cupboard, she began to pray.

Chapter Nine

The Lord

The steps were very wide, the widest she had even seen attached to any house, and the house was the biggest she had ever seen. When she had pulled herself below the barbed wire and into the wood she had been scared at the size of the trees, at the thickness of the undergrowth and of the dim, weird light, but when she had emerged from the wood and seen across the meadow the house looking gaunt and weary with a sort of stripped look in the early morning sunshine she had been more than scared. It had taken her quite a time to cross the meadow and get through the fence. She hadn't seen a gate and she had walked through the pathless tangled garden, and here she was, standing on the top step, her hand hovering towards the great knobbly doorbell, and she was, in truth, scared out of her wits.

She knew she had had the dream in the night and that the Holy Family had told her to come and see the Lord himself, but they, as far as she could see, hadn't come with her, and never in all her life had she known fear such as this. She tried to recall the courage she had felt in the night when she had talked with the Virgin. She had actually gone right up to Heaven and seen the Virgin busy with her task of making babies, and the Holy Mother had stopped her work and took her on her knee and had listened to all that she had to say, and then she had told her what she must do. And St Joseph himself had set her to the gate. And then she had woken up full of courage. The courage had kept her awake until daylight. It had helped her to dress and get past her mother, who was asleep on a shake-down near the fireplace, and out of the door without awakening anyone.

She reached up a little farther and touched the bell, and of its own volition it seemed to come out of the wall for a surprising length, and the clatter it made would have raised the dead. She was still gasping with the shock of it when the door opened.

To say whose face showed the more surprise would be difficult. Mary Ann had expected to be confronted by . . . the Lord; instead, before her stood a thin old man in a baggy old suit. His head was long and pointed and without hair, and his shoulders stooped as if he were carrying a weight upon them, but it was his face that surprised Mary Ann. If she had not been overcome with fright and worry she would have laughed at it. His mouth hung open and his nose twitched like a rabbit's and sent the wrinkles across his cheeks with each twitch.

But of the two, she was the first to find her voice, and even if at first the words wobbled round her mouth reluctant to come out she made the effort and stammered, 'P . . . please I came to see the Lord.'

'What?' The old man's voice sounded cracked.

'The Lord–I've come to see – the Lord. I want to t-talk to him, if you please.'

.'How did you get in here?'

'Through the hedge–the gate was fastened.'

'Through the hedge?' The baggy suit appeared to swell with indignation. 'You got in through the hedge?'

'Yes, under the barbed wire.'

'Well, the quicker you get out the better it will be for you. Now away with you.'

He pointed a shaking finger over her head, but she did not move, and he said, 'Did you hear me?'

Slowly Mary Ann's mouth drew to a button which would have been a warning to anyone who knew her, and she answered with deceptive quietness, 'I'm not going till I see the Lord.'

'You're not what?' The bones seemed to rattle within the suit. 'We'll see about that.' His hand made as if to descend on her, and she rasped at him, 'You touch me and I'll bite a piece out of you.'

His hand remained threateningly over her, but it said much for her attitude that it didn't descend on her, but his voice rose to a shrill yet muffled cry as he exclaimed, 'Get out of this!'

'Not until I've seen the Lord.' As she spoke she placed herself in front of the stanchion, making it impossible for him to close the door.

'In the name of all . . . !' Her defence staggered him, and his pursed lips threw bubbles from his mouth. 'You would . . . defy me? Well, we'll see about that.'

'I'll scream, mind, if you touch me.' This threat seemed to intimidate him for a moment and he cast a backward glance over his shoulder; then whispered fiercely, 'You do if you dare.'

He made a grab at her but with a wriggle of her body she slipped past him and into the hall.

For a moment he stood looking at her as if she were something uncanny wafted into the morning from another world, and he asked, not without a trace of fear in his own voice, 'What are you after?'

'I want to see the Lord.'

'Who told you to come here?'

'The Holy Family.'

'The what—?'

'The Holy Family.'

Now understanding and a trace of compassion touched his face. The child was mad. But mad or no, he must get her out of this before the master came down, so he said softly, 'The Holy Family sent you?'

'Yes.' Mary Ann nodded emphatically.

'Ah, well, yes, now I quite believe that. And what did they send you for?'

'To speak to the Lord.'

'What about?'

'About me da.'

'And what about your da?'

'I'm going to tell the Lord.'

'Now come, come.' He advanced slowly towards her. 'You tell me and I'll tell the mast . . . the Lord. How about that–eh?' As the old man came on Mary Ann backed away from him until she was at the foot of the stairs. Here she stopped and said, 'I won't tell nobody, only the Lord.'

'Now look here'–the old man's patience was swept away by the defiance that embodied this minute child–'I'm having no more of it,' he declared. 'Do you hear? You get out of here this minute.'

'I'll scream mind . . . I will.' Mary Ann's warning cry had no effect this time and as his hand caught her none too gently by the shoulder she let out a high, shrill scream.

By now almost on the verge of hysteria himself, he was attempting to muffle her cries when a voice thundered over them. What it said neither of them knew but its mighty tone flung them apart and Mary Ann and the old man gazed up the staircase to where stood a figure with a pose of the avenging angel. Step by step the master of the house descended upon them, until he stood on the last step but one.

Had he, by one movement of his hand, now ordered them both to be shrivelled up in consuming flames it would not have been of the smallest surprise to Mary Ann. As he gazed down on her she actually stopped breathing, and when he thundered, 'What's this, may I ask?' she released her breath and opened her mouth still wider in an attempt to speak, but the old manservant forestalled her.

'I found her at the door, sir–she darted in.'

'What is she doing here?'

'She says she wants to see you.'

'Me?' Mr Lord brought his eyes from Mary Ann and laid them on his servant, as if to extract without further preamble the meaning of the outrage.

'That's all I could get out of her, sir. I don't think she is'–he made an effort to straighten his bent shoulders as he delivered his verdict–'compos mentis, sir. She says she was sent here by the Holy Family.'

Mr Lord looked once more at Mary Ann, and Mary Ann made haste to press home the advantage she imagined the servant had unwittingly opened for her.

'He's right,' she said, in a voice that was a mere reflection of her normal and anything but quiet tone, 'They did, last night. Go to the Lord, they said, and tell him what a grand man your da is, and everything will come all right.'

Mr Lord's bushy eyebrows gathered and hung over his cheek-bones like miniature palm trees.

At this point, collecting the shreds of her shattered courage, she half turned her back on the servant, and stretching to her fullest height, whispered confidentially in much the same tone as she used when addressing God, 'Lord, I want to talk to you.'

After staring down at her for a moment longer Mr Lord made an important movement and he shook himself as if throwing off some benumbing spell. 'Not this morning, no time.' He thrust her aside as he descended the last stair and grimly, in an aside, said to the old servant, 'Get rid of her.'

Mary Ann heard. The new world that seemed almost within her grasp was dissolving before her eyes. She was in the actual presence of the Lord whose power equalled God's and to whom all things were possible. This man could give her da a job; he could give them a cottage, and in a cottage in the country they would be fast closed round and safe-guarded from separation–if only her da could offer her ma a cottage in the country then she wouldn't leave him; she couldn't leave him if he'd give her a cottage in the country.

'Lord. Lord.' She dived at him and gripped his hand. 'If you only knew what a grand man me da is you'd give him the job.'

Mr Lord's veined hand hung slackly between the two small hands that clawed at it. 'What job?' he asked quietly.

'On the farm–he's a grand man with horses and things–he knows all about. . . .'

'Who sent you here?' Mr Lord released his hand slowly from hers.

'I told you Lord–The Holy Family.'

'Now, now'–the voice was grim–'none of that. Father Owen sent you, didn't he?'

'He did not . . . Father Owen? No.'

'Don't lie. You were the child that was standing at the church door last night, weren't you, while we were talking?'

'I was standing there, but he didn't send me, and I couldn't hear all you said–I heard some, and I knew you had a job going that would have just suited me da and I went home and prayed to the Holy Family. . . .'

'Father Owen told you to do that?'

'Yes . . . no . . . No, I always pray to them on me own.'

'The scheming old rascal!' Mary Ann heard the muttered words and her own troubles were forgotten for the moment as she came to the defence of her beloved priest.

'He's not a rascal; he's a fine man, as fine as me da, and don't you say a word against him. And anyway you'll burn in Hell for daring to call a priest a rascal. Maggie Simmond's Aunt Nellie spilled a big panful of boiling fat over herself and she died, and that was just after she'd had words with the priest, so there . . . look out.'

'Here, here, don't be cheeky. And come along. You've told enough lies and trash.'

The old servant once again bore down on Mary Ann, and this time she turned on him like a wild cat. 'I'm not telling lies, I'm telling the truth. After I had the dream I kept awake and I got up when the blind got a bit light on it and I come all this way to talk to the Lord about me da. And Father Owen's a lovely priest. D'you hear? And he put me in the May Procession, right at the head.' She seemed to be watching her voice as she sent it yelling up at the old bent figure. Then for a moment her face showed comical surprise as she heard it change. It began to wobble and crack, and her mouth began to quiver. She knew what was about to happen, and she fought against it with all her might, shouting even louder. 'There's a pair of you, so there is. You don't believe anything. You're like Sarah Flannagan, that's what you are. You wouldn't do much for God if the divil was dead.' And now, feeling that her case was hopeless and that her plea had failed, she turned on Mr Lord, crying in deep earnest, 'You can keep your job and your old horses, and the cottage; me da'll get a job on a farm. They'll jump at him, for he's a fine, steady man–he can work like a black. And me ma'll go back to him when he gets a job with a cottage. You'll see. So there.' She nodded her head up at him in short, sharp nods; then turning blindly to what she thought was the front door, she stumbled into the dining-room.

The manservant, about to haul her out, was checked by Mr Lord, who thrust his arm across the doorway, and after a moment of watching Mary Ann walking bewilderedly about the room, he said, 'Bring my breakfast.'

'But sir, she—'

'You heard what I said.'

One old man looked at the other. Then the servant who gave off his displeasure like the skunk does its smell, walked reluctantly away kitchenwards; and Mr Lord went into the room and sat down at the table.

He did not look at Mary Ann who was standing now before the great empty fireplace staring down on to the dusty hearth, her back turned purposely to him, but he moved the crockery which was set on a none too clean cloth on the corner of the long massive dining table first one way and then another. Then abruptly he commanded, 'Come here!'

Mary Ann did not at once turn towards him; she sniffed a number of times and moved her shoulders. Thus having expressed her independence, she turned slowly about and walked to the table, her eyes cast down.

'Your name is Shaughnessy, isn't it?'

'Yes.' It was a very small voice.

'Does your father know you've come here?'

'Oh no. He said it was no use coming.'

'So he did know you were coming?'

'No. No; he didn't. He said that the Sunday we went to the farm up Pelaw way. The job was gone there, but the farmer told him about you.'

'And he said it was no use coming?'

'Yes.'

'How right he was.'

'Well, he doesn't want your job. You can keep. . . .'

'All right, All right.' He hastily lifted his hand to check her swiftly rising voice.

'He's a grand man.'

'Yes. Yes.'

'He is. He is.' Twice her chin was jerked up at him.

'Very well. . . . Ah, there you are.' It was with evident relief that he hailed the servant entering the room with a tray. And when the man, placing a dish before him, lifted the cover, the audible sniff from Mary Ann caused him to look at her with a swift searching glance.

She had been unable to prevent the sniff and she bowed her head in shame.

She was hungry, but she'd rather starve to death than take even a bit of fried bread from the nasty old devil.

'Have you had any breakfast?'

'. . . No.' Her eyes, half raised, were just on a level with the big plate on which lay two pieces of fried bread, two rashers of bacon, an egg and two halves of a tomato.

'That'll do.' Mr Lord, making to attack his breakfast, gave the curt order. But on this occasion, the old man was apparently deaf.

'Ben.'

'Yes, sir.'

'You heard me.'

Ben walked slowly to the door and passed into the hall, where Mr Lord's voice, which nearly lifted Mary Ann from the ground, halted him.

'Ben!'

'Yes, sir?' Ben's disapproving body appeared in the doorway again.

'Close that door and don't come back till I ring.'

Ben closed the door, and his master, in much the same curt tone, said to Mary Ann, 'Sit down!'

Slowly she eased the big chair from under the table and wriggled herself on to its seat, only to find that even when she perched on its edge she was too far away from the table; so she got down again, pushed the chair further in and squeezed herself between it and the table and on to its seat again. But now, not a little to her consternation, she found she was much nearer . . . the Lord. She watched him place half a tomato on a slice of bacon which was already reposing on a piece of fried bread. This he had put on his side plate, and when he pushed it towards her she wanted to say in a very civil voice, 'No, thank you, I'm not hungry'; but what she did was to take the knife he handed her and cut the bread and bacon by holding it firmly with one hand, since there was no fork available, and despatching it without further quibble or hesitation.

'What do you drink? Tea or milk?

'Tea.'

'Then get a cup. You'll find one in there.' He pointed to a china cabinet, and she struggled off the chair again and went to the cabinet, and opening the doors took out a cup. It was thin and felt so light in her hand that for a moment she stood staring at it before returning to the table with it.

'Where do you live?'

'Mulhattans' Hall.'

'Where is that?'

'In Burton Street. Off Walter Street.'

'How old are you?'

'Gone eight.'

'Are you the only child?'

'No. There's our Michael. . . . He's going to the Grammar School; he passed an exam.'

'Indeed.'

'He's going to be a great scholar and earn a lot of money.' She offered this information in an ordinary conversational tone; but this soon changed when she heard him say, 'That's impossible, he can't do both.' The words were muttered more to himself, but immediately she took them up.

'He will! His teacher says he will. You don't believe anything.'

The cessation of hostilities was forgotten; the fact that she had just partaken of a miracle in the form of half his breakfast was neither appreciated nor understood.

'You're just the spit of Sarah Flannagan!' she finished.

'Who, may I ask, is Sarah Flannagan? Do you want a piece of bread and marmalade?'

'No. No, I don't . . . I mean, no, thank you. She's a girl lives opposite us. She goes to our school, and she's a big liar, and she never believes anything.'

'And I'm like her?' He helped himself to marmalade, while Mary Ann paused to reconsider her verdict, blinking at him the while.

'Well, you don't believe anything, do you? You don't believe about me da, and that's like her. It's a wonder she's not struck down dead the things she's said about me da.'

'What kind of things?'

'Well.' Mary Ann paused as if there was need to recollect. 'Well, she said me da drinks. Now would you believe that?' She leant a little towards him; and he leaned back in his chair and surveyed her.

'And you say she's lying?'

'Yes. She's a bigger liar than Tom Pepper.'

'You did say your name was Shaughnessy, didn't you?'

'Yes.' Mary Ann was quite emphatic about this.

'And your father is called . . . Mike. Is that right?'

'Yes.'

'And he's a big man, with red hair?' He waved his hand round his own white head as he spoke.

'Yes, that's him. Do you know me da?'

He ignored her question and said, 'And you say he doesn't drink?'

She stared at him, unblinking. Then she said quietly, 'Yes.'

As his head moved down towards her, her body began to stiffen but she continued to look him defiantly in the eye.

'Do you mean to sit there and tell me that your father doesn't drink at all?'

She moved her bottom quickly back and forward on the seat until the leather began to squeak. Then she brought out, 'I do. And,' she continued, slipping off the seat, 'I don't want any more of your tea or your breakfast, for you're as like as two pins with her. You can ask Father Owen about me da. He'll tell you what a right man he is.' She bounced her head once at him with finality. Then turning on her heel she marched towards the door.

'Where are you going now?'

'I'm going home.' She threw over her shoulder.

'Come here.'

Mary Ann found that she was forced to turn at the command, and when once again she was standing by the side of the chair she had just left, he said again, 'You say your father doesn't drink?'

'I've told you.'

'You're a Catholic, aren't you?'

'Yes.'

'And still you say your father doesn't drink? Be careful now.'

Mary Ann stared at him, and her answer did not come immediately. But when it did it was still quite firm. 'I do.'

'Would you swear on it?' Now he seemed to be towering over her, and there was an odd look on his lined face. It had shed its stiff, hard mask and had taken on an expression that could only be called excitement; it sat strangely upon him, and he looked like a man who was watching a race.

Mary Ann's eyes widened, stretching across her face until they seemed almost to encompass it. It was one thing to fight the whole world for something that you wanted to believe, but to be made to swear on it . . . that was another thing entirely; and to be reminded that she was a Catholic into the bargain made things a thousand times worse. The Holy Family, with hurt expressions, were on one side of her, purgatory, hell and damnation gaped widely on the other; but in front of her, blotting out them all, even the face of this terrifying old man, stood her da, looking as she saw him last night before she went to bed, a drawn, changed, different da. Her lips began to tremble and her nose to twitch, but her eyes met Mr Lord's without flinching. 'I would swear on it,' she said.

There was a taut silence in the room; then it was split by a laugh, the strangest laugh that Mary Ann had ever heard. She watched Mr Lord lean back in his chair, and his thin body seemed to crack each time a staccato sound escaped his lips. The sounds mounted, and when he pressed his hands to his side Mary Ann's concern for him brought her to his knee.

'Have you got a stitch?'

Her attitude and concern only aggravated the stitch, for his laughter mounted. Neither of them noticed Ben come into the room and it was not until he spoke, asking in an awed voice, 'Are you all right, sir?' that Mr Lord, with a noticeable effort, took hold of himself. His laughter weakened and became spasmodic, but Ben's concern grew when his master, looking at him with streaming eyes, said, 'The greatest of these is loyalty.'

The old man looked at Mary Ann and there was fear in his eyes, and when he turned to his master once again Mr Lord waved him away. 'Go on–go on,' he said; but as the old servant went again reluctantly out of the room his master's eyes followed him.

Mr Lord had never considered before that he had been the recipient of loyalty for over forty years. He had taken Ben for granted. He had growled at and abused him, first because no other servant would live with him, then because of the state of the house, then just because it had become a habit. He had sacked him countless times; he had even stopped his money to make him go, but it had made no difference. For years he had seen Ben as an old nuisance who hung on because he wouldn't be able to get a job anywhere else. Ben was twenty-eight when he first came to work for him, and he knew everything there was to know about him. He had witnessed the madness of his marriage; he had seen its end; and as isolation had become his defence he had clung closer to him. Yet, it was strange, he had never before this morning looked upon Ben's service as loyalty. It had taken this child, who could lie with the innocence of an angel and the purpose of a priest, to show him just how much of the same loyalty had he himself been receiving all these years.

Mr Lord wiped his eyes. But why should he have laughed? It was many a long year since his body had shaken with such laughter as this child had inspired. He looked at her through his swimming eyes. Her face was like a film flickering the thoughts of her mind across its surface; she imagined that she had only to stick to her guns and he would see her father as she saw him. If he hadn't known Mike Shaughnessy he would have, without doubt, believed every word she said. She did not look a bit like Red Mike, yet there was something of him there. Perhaps it was her tenacity–given an idea she would hang on to it until she died–that was him. If only he had the right ideas. But apparently, to him, they were right for he was willing to lose his job for them–yes, and to cause strikes through them. No, he must be fair to the man–he would have caused no strike in his yard; he was too much of an individualist; he could sway neither side completely for he pointed too blatantly to the rottenness of both. It was because his own conscience had been pricked by the man that he was so mad at him. Yet it was strange that all this big red-headed hulk wanted was to work on the land and have his family near him.

'Are you all right now?'

He nodded to her. 'Yes, yes, I'm all right.'

'I get like that when I go to the pictures and I see a comic, the stitch gets me in the side and I want to cry when I'm laughing . . . it's awful. Will I pour you out another cup of tea?'

'Yes–can you?'

'Oh yes, I often do the tea at home. There.' She pushed a cup towards him, and he lifted it and drank while he continued to look down at her.

'What are you going to do when you go back home this morning?' he asked.

Her eyes dropped from his, and she replied dully, 'Nothing.'

He handed the cup back to her and with the side of his finger he smoothed down his white moustache; then hesitantly, almost as if he wanted to find favour with her, he said, 'Will you have time then to take a little ride with me to . . . to the farm?'

They looked at each other. The significance of the request took on a tangible form; it shone between them, blinding Mary Ann with its promise; it formed a fairy-like castle on a high mountain; and she was choked with its wonder. She could bear no more. She flung herself at his feet, her arms about his legs, and when he, making strange tut-tutting sounds, attempted to quieten her noisy sobs, her crying only increased. With gruff tenderness he coaxed her up, and when she leant against him it seemed the natural sequence that he should then lift her on to his knee.

He had in his time been kissed both passionately and falsely by women, but never had he been kissed by a child, never had he felt that ecstatic grip of thin arms about his neck. In this moment he would willingly have changed places with Mike Shaughnessy.

Chapter Ten

The Truth, and Nothing But . . .

It had been a grand morning, a lovely morning. Mary Ann wanted it to go on for ever, but there was her ma and her da and the letter. Lovingly she touched the pocket in which the letter reposed and edging herself further towards the front of the car seat, she smiled up at Mr Lord. 'Will you take me round by our school?'

'Where's that?'

'Not far from the church, you know. Round Dee Street.'

'Oh.'

'Do you think we might be able to have a dog and a cat?'

'I don't see why not.'

'Have you a dog?'

'No.'

'You should have, in a big house like that, because it would scare burglars.'

'Yes . . . yes, you're quite right.'

'Haven't you anyone to tidy up for you besides him?'

A spasm passed over Mr Lord's face, moving the wrinkled skin like small lapping waves on a ridge of sand, but the answered quite seriously, 'No, only him.'

Mary Ann shook her head. 'Me ma's the right one for tidying up.'

'Is she?'

'Yes. Our house is like a new pin. Look . . . there's our school. You see that second window along the top? That's our class.'

Mr Lord bent his head and looked up at the window, saying. 'Yes. Ah yes, I see.' Then he added, 'Can I put you down here? Can you find your way home?'

'Yes. Why yes,' she laughed up at him.

He was funny. Find her way home indeed . . . she could find her way all over Jarrow by herself.

It was at this point when Mr Lord was about to apply his brakes that Mary Ann, peering through the windscreen, saw in the distance a group of children, five in number, and all well known to her. One head in particular was so familiar that she almost choked with excitement and actually nudged him. 'Look . . . along there. See those girls? Can I get off there? Will you ride me along there?'

Mary Ann, thinking she detected a slight hesitancy in Mr Lord's manner, added urgently, 'The long one, that's Sarah Flannagan.'

'Oh-h.'

The car moved on again, and Mary Ann, her eyes starting from her head with the force of her feelings volunteered the information, 'She's the one as I told you of. When I've been telling girls about our car and horses she's always spoilt it . . . she never believes it.'

'Dear, dear, doesn't she?' said Mr Lord.

'No. But I was only making on, you know. But still, she should have believed it, shouldn't she?'

'Of course. Of course.'

'Well, now she'll see. She'll get the shock of her life. It wouldn't be any use me telling her on Monday that I'd been for a ride with you in a car. She'd say I was loppy and wanted me head looking.'

'She would indeed.' Mr Lord brought the car to a slow stop just where the group of girls stood on the pavement, and leaning across Mary Ann he opened the door. With a grateful sidelong smile at him she edged herself off the seat, gave a little jump and landed on the pavement, face to face with Sarah Flannagan.

That Sarah was surprised is an understatement. She goggled, her mouth as it fell open looking out of all proportion to her face. Mary Ann gazed up at her, long and steadily, before allowing her shining eyes to flicker over the rest of the group, two of whom had been listeners to the . . . big house, cars and horses tale, which Sarah Flannagan had shattered that particular night in the school-yard. Now Mary Ann, addressing herself solely and pointedly to Sarah, said, 'I've been for a ride and I've had me breakfast in a great big house. Like a palace it is. And we're going to move into a fine grand cottage with a great lump of garden, and me da's going to be somebody and me ma'll have nice clothes.'

To give Sarah her due she did try to speak. Her lips formed the usual phrase, but soundlessly, and they only got as far as 'Oh you great big . . .' for her eyes lifted to the old man in the car. She knew who he was, everybody in Jarrow knew who he was, and Mary Ann Shaughnessy had just stepped out of his car.

Mr Lord watched the little play, and groping back and clutching at a faint spark of devilment from his youth, suddenly brought all eyes towards himself, including Mary Ann's, when he said with slow pomp and using her name for the first time, 'Where did you say you wanted to go for a ride tomorrow, Mary Ann?'

A message that could only be read by Mary Ann came from his eyes, and she answered it with one that was touched with love. She moved towards the car window, 'Oh, Whitley Bay.'

'Whitley Bay it is then. And what time will I come?'

'Come for me, in the car?'

The proposal was filled with such phantasy that even she didn't for the moment believe it was true.

'Of course.' Mr Lord's voice had a touch of the old asperity about it, and this itself conveyed to all present the serious and truthful intent of his purpose.

'Oh.' On a surge of rising joy came an inspiration to Mary Ann, and after casting a glance about her at the amazed faces she swallowed hard and said, 'Would you call for me then after Mass, the ten o'clock, at the church door?'

The meeting place obviously was a surprise to Mr Lord, and his brows contracted for a moment as he repeated, 'The church door?'

'Yes.'

It was evident that the church door did not meet with Mr Lord's approval. The sound that came from him was akin to a groan, and Mary Ann, looking apprehensively, said in a small voice, 'Well, can you?'

He moved back in his seat pulling the car door closed as he did so. His expression looked to Mary Ann very like the one he was wearing before he'd had his breakfast.

'Good-bye,' she said softly.

'Good-bye,' said Mr Lord.

Suddenly she knew she couldn't let him go like this. Reaching up, she peered over the lowered glass of the window and whispered, 'Are you vexed?'

For a moment he looked at her; then his eyes crinkled into a smile and his hand came out to her cheek, 'I'll be there.'

Until the car had passed from sight around the corner of the street Mary Ann did not move, and when she did it was to walk away with her chin in the air and without even a glance at or word to Sarah Flannagan and the girls. The ground was still shaking under her feet; she fully realized it had been touch and go about the church door; also that its accomplishment was a glory that wouldn't come her way twice. Tomorrow morning when all the school was coming out of church there would be the car to meet her. Sarah Flannagan and all the lot of them, even the teachers would see her. The emotion was partly agony.

She had reached the corner of the street before she realized that not a solitary jeer had followed her, not even the usual gibe of 'Mary Ann, frying pan!' She turned round, and there they were where she had left them, standing like dummies. Unable to resist a parting shot she turned her back, lifted up her short skirt, and thrust her bottom out at them.

The voice of Fanny McBride rang up the staircase with the force of a sergeant-major on the barrack-square. She was holding on to the bottom banister with both hands as she cried once again, 'Mike! Mike! You, Lizzie–she's here, walking down the street as large as life.'

She had scarcely finished before Mike was descending the last flight of stairs towards her.

'Look for yourself.' She followed him to the door and called out over her shoulder, 'What did I tell you, Liz? I knew she would turn up. She's not the kind to go and tip herself in the river . . . not Mary Ann.'

Mary Ann walked up the steps towards her parents. Her eyes darted from one to the other. She spared no glance for Mrs McBride or Miss Harper, or the Laveys who were now crowding the hallway, but the suppressed excitement about her made itself felt, and she asked in an airy tone, 'What's the matter, Ma?'

'Listen to her. What's the matter, Ma?' Fanny's laugh vibrated round the hall. 'Only half the town looking for you, polismen an' all.'

Mike and Lizzie both stood staring down on her as if they were finding it hard to believe the evidence of their eyes, and it was Mike who eventually spoke. 'Where've you been?' he asked.

Mary Ann did not at first reply, but looked up at her father. His voice was harsh and his face was harsh and he wasn't like her da at all. His face looked even worse than it had done last night, and his manner had the power to crush her gaiety and she replied meekly, 'In the country.'

'In the country . . . well, I'll be damned!' Fanny slapped her thigh, and Lizzie, saying nothing, reached out and taking Mary Ann's hand led her through the little press and up the stairs.

Once in the room and the door closed, Lizzie suddenly sat down. It was as if her legs had been whipped from under her. She put her hand for a moment to her brow and covered her eyes, then softly she asked, 'Where've you been? I want the truth, mind.'

'In the country, Ma.'

'Why did you go out like that . . . so early?'

Mary Ann looked from her mother to where Mike was standing glaring down at her, and she found she couldn't say. There wasn't very much time left, so she substituted, 'I wanted to get back soon but we went for a ride in the car.'

The room became so still that Mary Ann scraped her foot on the lino in order to make some familiar sound.

'Whose car? Who have you been with? Now no lies.' The tone of her father's voice wiped the remaining joy from the morning. It was if she had done something wrong . . . and him saying 'no lies'. As if she told lies for herself–she told lies only to make things come right for him. Her lips trembled and her head drooped and she muttered 'Mr Lord's.'

'Mr Whose?'

'Lord's . . . him who has the farm.'

Slowly Mike came to her. 'You went to Mr Lord's? What for?'

'To tell him . . . to tell him . . .' Now she was sniffling and Lizzie said, 'Sh! There now. Just tell us what happened and you won't get wrong.'

'I went to tell him what a . . . a grand man you were with . . . with horses and cows and things.'

For a brief moment Mike's eyes held Lizzie's; then he turned slowly towards the fire, and Lizzie, gathering the child to her said, 'Tell me what happened. How did you get into Mr Lord's place?'

'I got through the barbed wire, and the old man let me in, and Mr Lord give me half his breakfast. Then we went to see the cottage.' She lifted her head from her mother's breast and still sniffing continued, 'Oh it's a lovely cottage, Ma; he's given us the best one.'

As Mike swung round exclaiming, 'What did you say?' Lizzie pressed Mary Ann away from her, and holding her at arm's length demanded, 'What are you talking about, child?'

'The cottage that goes with the farm, Ma. He gave me a letter–here—' she pulled the letter from her pocket, and turning, handed it to Mike who took it and opened it without taking his eyes from her. When he did begin to read both Lizzie and Mary Ann watched him. Then he slowly lifted his head and silently contemplated Mary Ann. His head shaking with a slight bewildered movement, he handed the letter to Lizzie and went into the room, walking, Mary Ann thought to herself, as if he'd already had a few.

After a moment Lizzie's hands dropped into her lap and she too stared at Mary Ann in a bewildered fashion; then without any warning she began to cry, not a quiet easy crying, but a crying that was tinged with laughter and touched on hysteria. It brought Mike back to the kitchen and after only a moment's hesitation, during which his face worked convulsively, he went to her and gathered her into his arms and smothered her wild cries against his breast.

Mary Ann stood apart, watching. The emotions that were coursing through her were too tangled and complex for her to experience any one of them consciously; she could not put a name to the feeling of deflation their combined force created; she could not even think that her da holding her ma in his arms again portended nothing but good. One thing only was evident to her, everything had turned out quite differently from what she had imagined. Her news hadn't been greeted with open arms; she hadn't been hugged and kissed and told what a clever girl she was; instead, she had been accused of lying. Why, when she came to think of it, the only one who believed her was the Lord himself. He thought she was a clever girl; he had told her so when he put the letter into her hand. And because he realized she was a clever girl she had given him her entire confidence–she had related graphically just how Sarah Flannagan had banged her head against the wall because of what happened on Coronation Day, and he had laughed and laughed. She had even told him about how she went in the black dark for Mrs McBride the night their Michael put his head in the gas oven. The more she told him the more he laughed and she knew he believed everything she said.

She had decided much earlier in the morning that she liked Mr Lord. She had even decided to take him under her wing, for all he needed was a good laugh and his house tidying up and he'd be all right.

She watched her da lead her ma into the bedroom, and when the door closed on them she felt indeed alone. She stood irresolute for a moment; then with a flop she sat on a chair and was preparing herself to feel very misused when the outer door burst open and Michael appeared. He gave no welcome cry at the sight of her but in his brotherly fashion advanced towards her demanding, 'Where do you think you've been?'

She did not answer but looked up at him with a sidelong glance fully calculated to aggravate his already harassed feelings.

'Where's me Ma and Da? The motor cops are looking for you.' He looked around the room. 'Where's me Ma?'

Still Mary Ann said no word, and her air of superiority, which at any time had the power to annoy him, infuriated him now. Without further words he stretched both hands out to grab her, but like lightning she slipped beneath them and, still without speaking, she aimed one well-cobbled toecap at his shin.

On his cry of real pain the morning suddenly balanced itself again and her depression lifted. Life was normal, the world was full of magic, she was cleverer than their Michael even if he was going to the Grammar School; they had a cottage in the country, her ma and her da weren't going to leave each other . . . and there was Mr Lord. And tomorrow morning he'd be at the church waiting for her for all the world to see.

Michael, hopping on one leg, cried, 'For two pins I'd . . .' and she answered pertly, 'Oh, would you? Well wait a minute and I'll get them for you.'

'Mary Ann.' On her name being called softly from the bedroom door, she swung round and there stood her da. They looked at each other for a moment before he held out his arms to her and almost in one leap she was in them, hugging and being hugged with such intensity that even Sunday morning became blotted out.

Now came the Elevation of the Host. Mary Ann knelt with bowed head and beat her narrow chest with clenched first as each tinkle of the bell came from the altar and she murmured with every thump, 'Lord be merciful to me, a sinner; Lord be merciful to me, a sinner.' She drew a deep breath as she raised her head after the last tinkle. Ah, that was over. There wasn't much more now. Soon John Finlay would carry the big book from one side of the altar to the other and then Father Owen would say 'Our Father' and 'Hail Mary' and a little bit more, and then. . . . The excitement began to tear round inside her again, almost making her feel sick. Eeh, she mustn't be sick. She had been sick last night, but she hadn't minded for both her ma and her da had held her head, and it wasn't because she had eaten any sweets or anything or had had anything fancy for her tea. She had felt the sickness coming on in the afternoon while she waited for her da to come back. He had gone out all dressed up to see Mr Lord and he hadn't returned till nearly seven o'clock, but for once her ma hadn't looked worried. She had looked quiet and calm–she had looked like that since she had unpacked their clothes–and her da had looked quiet too. She remembered at dinner time they had all sat round a makeshift meal, and Mrs McBridge had come up and had cried, 'Lord, ye're as quiet as a bunch of survivors from a wreck,' and her da had said in an odd way, 'Just as quiet, Fanny.' And when he came back from Mr Lord's he was still quiet and he wasn't quite himself, but he wasn't sick or anything. Oh no, for she knew he hadn't touched a drop. But he seemed as if he must have her near him; and after she was sick he had even washed her himself and put her to bed. Oh, it had been a grand week-end, a lovely week-end. And it wasn't over. Oh no, not by a long time–there was all today.

Oh, if Father Owen would only put a move on . . . Eeh, what was she saying? After all the Holy Family had done for her, and . . . She tut-tutted to herself. Would you believe it, she had never even thanked them properly. She turned her face to the side altar and found to her surprise that as she had nothing at the moment to ask of them she was a little at a loss for words. Hesitatingly she began, 'Dear Blessed Holy Family, thank you for all you have done for me, for getting me da a job and for the cottage.' It all sounded so inadequate, sort of mean. She felt that something was expected of her, some present of some sort. Well, she'd light a candle the morrer–she just couldn't spare the time this morning. The mean feeling persisted and she thought, 'I know what . . . I know what'll please them more than anything.' She unlaced her fingers and put her hands finger-tip to finger-tip as she usually did when dealing with matters of import. 'Dear Holy Family. I promise you faithfully, so help me, that I'll never tell another lie. May I be struck down dead if I do.' There, she felt better, and the Holy Family looked very pleased, but it still felt funny not having anything to ask them to do. She was about to turn her attention back to the main altar where John Finlay was now moving the book when she suddenly thought of her grannie. Now there was something they could do to get on with. Solemnly and fluently now she beseeched them, 'Dear Holy Family, could you do something about me grannie to stop her from coming out to our cottage? Could you give her a bad leg or something? You needn't kill her off, just stop her. In the name of the Father, Son, Holy Ghost, Amen.'

She got that in just in time to give the responses with the rest of the children to the priest saying the first half of the 'Our Father.' On the third 'Hail Mary' her responses were loud and clear and very definite, as if she herself had some proprietary right in their saying . . . 'Holy Mary–Mother of God–pray for us sinners–now and at the hour of our death–Ah-men.'

Ah . . . there, it was over. Father Owen had not disappeared through the vestry door before she was on her feet.

'Sit down and wait until the class is out.' A hand on her shoulder and the hissed command from Miss Johnson brought her bottom abruptly into contact with the hard seat.

Oh, Miss Johnson! She had eyes like a gimlet. Oh dear! Bust! Now as like as not she'd keep her back till the very last.

Which was exactly what Miss Johnson did. Row after row of children swarmed methodically into the aisle. With noisy caution they kicked against the wooden kneelers, gasped audibly as they genuflected towards the altar, and invariably scraped their feet on the heating grids.

Mary Ann kept her eyes riveted on Miss Johnson's back, but Miss Johnson seemed to have entirely forgotten Mary Ann's presence. She was standing six rows away and apparently in another world.

Oh the beast . . . oh she was awful. Mary Ann wriggled on her seat as if she were already on that gridiron so often prophesied by her grannie. Everybody would be gone home. Perhaps even Mr Lord would think she'd gone, and he'd go away. There was no fear strong enough to keep her in her seat; she rose to her feet and, moving quietly into the aisle, genuflected and bowed her head to the altar, only to lift it to Miss Johnson's legs which she surmised had been whipped in front of her by lightning, or the devil.

'I thought I told you to wait until the church emptied?'

You don't argue with a teacher or Mary Ann would have said, 'You said wait until the class had gone, which is quite a different thing from waiting until the church was empty.'

Perhaps the swish of Father Owen's gown had some influence on Miss Johnson's censure, for she murmured softly, 'Go on now; but come to me in the morning.'

Without a word Mary Ann turned away, and it was only with the greatest restraint that she stopped herself from running up the aisle–or was it the fact that she was 'twixt the devil and the deep sea, with Miss Johnson behind her and Father Owen in front?

Father Owen paused before going out into the porch and patted the heads of self-conscious philanthropists as she or he made a great show of putting a penny into the poor box or lighting a candle to their favourite saint. Mary Ann did neither, but she was going past him, actually without looking at him and on the verge of a run now, when his hand descended on her head.

'What have you been up to?' he whispered.

'Nothing, Father.'

'You were kept in.'

'Yes, Father, 'cause I wanted to get out quick.'

A twinkle in his eye softened the harshness of his words. 'Out quick? away from God as quickly as you can?'

'No, Father. But you see, it's a special morning.'

Oh dear, dear. Wouldn't he take his hand off her head? She glanced with evident longing towards the door. 'What's extra special about it?'

'Mr Lord–he's come to take me for a ride . . . I was going to come and tell you last night but I was sick and vomited all over the place.'

'Mr Lord?' The pressure on her head became heavier and her hat was hurting her ears. The priest bent nearer to her. 'What were you saying about Mr Lord?'

'He's given me da a job and a fine cottage. I prayed to the Holy Family and they told me to go and have a talk with him, just like you said yourself, Father. Oh Father, can I go now?'

He took his hand from her head but said, 'Wait a minute. When did you talk to him?'

'Yesterday morning, Father. I got up early and crawled through the barbed wire and knocked on his door.'

Father Owen straightened up. He could not step back for he was already against the wall, but he drew his chin in and half closed his eyes as if to focus her better, then he began to chuckle.

Mary Ann could not go without his word, but she moved from one foot to the other just to show him the extent of her need to hurry. But he only continued to chuckle. 'Where is he going to meet you?'

'Outside, Father, just outside—' she pointed to the door and moved a step towards it, trying to draw him with her.

'Did you ask him to meet you outside here?'

'Yes, Father.'

He continued to stare at her, but he remained where he was. He knew exactly why she had requested the car to be brought to the church just after Mass but he could not for the life of him imagine what form her persuasion had taken to make Peter Lord agree to bringing it. His head wagged. 'Well, well.' And he had given Mike the job. Again 'Well, well.' And all through this little mite's tongue. . . . Nothing she would do or say would ever surprise him.

But here Father Owen was wrong.

'Will you come and see, Father, or else he'll be away?'

'No. No, Mary Ann . . . you run along.'

This was her hour. He knew his presence out on the street would only deflect some of the children's attention from her and he guessed he'd be the last person Peter Lord would wish to see this morning. No, he'd stay where he was.

'I'll come and tell you all about it the morrer. Good-bye, Father.'

She was gone; and after waiting a few seconds Father Owen's good intentions were also gone. Cautiously he went into the porch and towards the main doorway.

The crowd that awaited Mary Ann was somewhat disappointing. There weren't more than twenty-five altogether. . . . It was that beastly Miss Johnson's fault. They had all gone home; and the car wasn't right opposite the church door either, but some way along the street.

However, the number of the crowd did not matter so much, it was the quality of it that counted. And the quality to her was of the best, for it consisted of most of her class and, pleasure upon pleasure, Sarah Flannagan.

The car was facing her and as she ran towards it holding on to her hat with one hand she waved to the grim face behind the wheel with the other, and it was no imagination on her part that the face relaxed into a smile and a hand was raised in response to her salute.

'Get by!' Mary Ann directed this command to Sarah Flannagan who was standing on the pavement well to the side of the car door. In fact, all the children had kept a respectful distance from the car. Sarah was no more in Mary Ann's way than were two or three of the other children, and she did not, as some of the others did, shuffle a few steps to the side, but she stood her ground. 'Get by yersel,' she said.

Mary Ann got by. She walked round her enemy with her lips and her nose pursed and eye to eye with her, for Sarah slowly pivoted in the same direction.

As Mary Ann reached the car door it opened, but she gave no word of greeting to Mr Lord, only smiled warmly at him before ducking beneath his outstretched arm to sit herself with dignity on the edge of the seat. The door banged and there was a soft purr, then from the open window she faced the little crowd of children, now gathered closer about the car; but her eyes rested only on one, and to Sarah she addressed herself.

'Now you see who's a liar, Sarah Flannagan. You wouldn't believe about our house and the cars and the horses, would you? Well, we're going into our new house the morrer, and there's four horses, and me da's got a right fine job, better than your da will ever have, 'cause he's a drunken no-good and'–her voice rose to a shrill pipe and all her dignity vanished–'if you dare to call me a liar again you won't half catch it, because this . . .' she cried finally, sticking her head out of the window now and jerking her thumb over her shoulder, 'is me Granda!'

There was a shocked silence in Heaven, while down in the church porch Father Owen bent his head and covered his face with one hand.

'There you go–I tell you it did happen. Ooh! you'll believe nothing–it's like Sarah Flannagan you are.'

Feathers in the Fire

Feathers in the Fire

He born tethered to a byre
And he born upon silk,
Both suck the sap of milk;
Life above or below the sod
Viewed coldly by the Gods
Is but a feather in the fire.

BOOK ONE

1881

Chapter One

'I tell you I know nothing about it. God in heaven! I've said it four times already, I didn't give it her.' Davie Armstrong turned on his father, crying, 'An' don't say again it couldn't get there on its own; bloody well I know it, it couldn't get there on its own.'

'All right, all right, lad.' It was his grandfather speaking, and he came towards him and petted his arm and, his voice soothing, said, 'I believe you. We all believe you, lad.' He glanced fiercely at his daughter and his son-in-law; then looking at his grandson again, whom he loved better than he'd ever loved his one and only offspring, he added quietly, 'But you know, you'll be given the blaze for you were courtin' her.'

'Courtin'!' Davie glared at his grandfather now. 'I might have been knockin' on but we weren't courtin'; except for a dance in the barn and taking her to the fair and a nudge on the quiet, that's all it's been. I tell you she ran off from me when we were at the fair, an' I didn't see hilt or hair of her till I got back here, eight o'clock. It must have happened then; but I wasn't at t'other end of it, honest to God.' He now looked at his mother who was standing at the far side of the trestle table that was set for a meal. She had her hands on the lid of a black cooking pot set on a square of wood; her fingers were beating an unconscious tattoo on the handle, while her eyes, unblinking, were riveted on her son; and now she said, 'Come and sit up and have your meal, time is passin'.'

'I want no meal.'

Her hand lifted the lid and she banged it down on the table and, her voice harsh now, she said, 'You'll eat, we'll all eat. We've got to work, so we'll eat.' And at this she began ladling out thick mutton broth onto four plates. When they were filled, she cut large shives of crusty bread and stuck one in the middle of each plate, which she then placed at each side of the table.

Ned Armstrong sat down, and old Sep sat down, but Davie still stood. He had his back pressed to the dresser, his square chin was thrust out and stiff with the tightness of his jaw bones. His mother said to him quietly, 'You know I won't sit till you're set, so how long do you intend to keep me standin'?'

His head drooped to his chest, his lips pushed against each other as he sucked them inwards; then thrusting his body from its support, he came to the table and sat down, but not before banging the high railback wooden chair hard on the stone floor.

Winnie Armstrong now sat down and picked up a spoon, and they all began to eat. Only the munching and the slopping of the stew filled the silence until old Sep, putting his spoon down on the bare table and placing his hands one on each side of his plate, leaned across towards his son and said, 'You know summet, I smell a rat.'

'How?' asked Ned, gulping on a mouthful of food, his spoon held in mid air.

'Geary, that's how, Geary.' The old man's voice was low and he jerked his head back and slanted his gaze in the direction of the fireplace and the wall to the side of it, the wall that divided their cottage from the Gearys'. Then casting a glance, first at his daughter Winnie, and then at his grandson, he brought his attention back to Ned and said softly, 'He finds their Molly has fallen an' what does he do? He goes to the master and demands that she be chastised . . . flayed! There's no woman been flayed on this farm since I was a lad sixty-odd years gone, and then it was the master's grandfather what did it, and then he had to be roaring drunk afore he could tackle it. You mind, I've told you 'bout Nellie Cassidy pinching the gold retriever watch, and he gave her the option of goin' along the line or standin' a flaying. She took the flaying. But Geary there—' he again jerked his head back, 'who's got no feelin' for either God, man, or beast, but he doesn't lift a hand to her.' He now turned and looked at Davie and said, 'Lad, just think; imagine that house and Molly comin' in and sayin' she's fallen; what do you think he'd do?'

Davie looked at his grandfather, then answered slowly, 'Knock hell out of her.'

'Aye, you've said it, lad, knock hell out of her and take joy in doin' it. But he doesn't knock hell out of her, he goes to the master and asks him to do it for him. I tell you, I smell a rat.'

The three men looked at each other; then they turned their gaze on Winnie and she stared back at them for a moment before saying, 'Well, you've added up two and one, not two and two, you haven't reached four yet, so what do you make of it?'

Her eyes came to rest on her son, and Davie answered her, 'I don't know, but I mean to find out.'

'Do,' she nodded her grey head slowly at him, 'but go about things quietly. Remember, to all intents and purposes, it's you who are named; never was it so silently done, but never so clearly.'

As she rose from the table she said to no one in particular, 'Now I must be goin'. Flood, storm, or tempest, the master will want to eat. But how I'm goin' to put up with that one flitting about me in the kitchen I just don't know. I've always said she was a flighty-cum-jaunting-Sunday. I told you,' she nodded down towards her husband, 'didn't I, I told you I caught her dancin' in the sitting room to the musical box when the mistress was out. Dancin', mind, in the mistress's sitting room.'

'Aw, Ma.' Davie's chair scraped back over the stone floor as he got to his feet and, confronting his mother across the table, he said, 'Let's get things straight. There's no harm in a bit of dancing.'

'I'm not sayin' there is, but there's a time and a place for everything. And it's how you dance. There she was with her skirt held right above her knees like any quay trollop.'

'Quay trollop!' Sep looked up at his daughter and, his good humour returning, he slapped out at her thigh with his hand as he repeated, 'Quay trollop? You wouldn't know a quay trollop, me girl, if you saw one.'

'Wouldn't I, Pa?'

'No, you wouldn't; so go on and get about your business.'

'I'm goin'.' She nodded her head sharply at him. 'And you get about your business and see that you wash them plates up properly and don't leave them stuck thick with grease.' And on this she went out to her work.

The three men, left alone, said no word to each other, but Ned got up and, going to the mantlepiece, took from a rack two clay pipes and, picking out a long twist of brown baccy from a jar standing near, he cut two pieces off the end, then handed one of them, together with a pipe, to his father-in-law. When he sat down again, each worked the knot of tobacco loose by grinding it with the stub of his left hand into the palm of his right hand. When the tobacco was sufficiently shredded, almost simultaneously they filled their pipes and Ned lit them from the same spill.

While this was going on Davie had been standing looking out of the small window and along the mud-dried road that curved in front of the house to end abruptly, cut off by a railing that circled a dark mass of trees.

The Armstrongs' cottage was the end one of the three labourers' cottages, farthest from the farmhouse, which was a hundred yards away. They had been built ninety years ago when the new additions had been made to the farm. There were no gardens at the front, but at the back of each was a piece of land as wide as the cottage, which was sixteen feet. It ran in a narrow strip for about seventy feet, downhill to the brook that supplied water for all purposes. The ashes from their fires formed dry middens, the contents of which, together with that from the house, was collected once a week by a farmcart and dumped in the old workings of a lead mine half a mile away.

Davie had been born in this cottage, and up till this very day he had considered himself lucky to have been brought up on this particular farm, for the master, although strict in all ways, and narrow and churchy in his views, was a go-ahead progressive employer, as his efforts at modern sanitation proved–no stinking cesspools and middens near the house for him. He had once overheard him say that the excrement from animals was sweet compared to that of humans, and it was the badness in humans that made it as it was. Moreover, the master had not allowed him to start work until he was six. No child on the farm started work until he was six, even at scarecrowing. And then, since the master took over twenty years ago, every child on the farm attended Sunday School, and this was long afore school going was made compulsory. He had been very strict about them all going to Sunday School, and so they all learned their letters, those who could take them in. He himself had taken them in, sucked them in–he had lapped it all up. He still did; the older he got, he knew the more there was to learn. He was proud of what knowledge he had; he could count, he could add and subtract, and he could write a letter. However, he had never yet written a real letter to anyone, for there was nobody to write to. But if it ever came to pass that he had to write a letter, he would be capable of doing it. And he could read, oh aye, he could read.

He had got this far in book learning because he was interested. He wanted to learn something else besides milking cows and the other work on a farm, and Parson Hedley was out to learn anybody who wanted to learn. Not so Parson Wainwright; oh no, old-nose-in-the-air Wainwright only gave you his blessing when he knew how much money you were likely to leave to the church, or, to put it plainly, to him.

Parson Hedley had said only last week, 'I'm going to loan you a book by Mr Dickens, Davie. It is called *Great Expectations*. And you know, Davie,' he had added, 'that is a very good title, *Great Expectations*. It's based on hope, and hope is a mighty fine thing to carry you through. And by the way,' he had ended, 'bring Molly to the readings. She hasn't been for a long time and she was getting along fine.'

Bring Molly to the readings! She hasn't been for a long time. No, Molly had been otherwise occupied. Blast her. But with who? Who? His Granda was right about smelling a rat. There was a big stink here somewhere. Nothing escaped his Granda.

He turned slowly and looked at him. He was puffing quietly at his pipe, his eyes were closed, his shoulders stooped; he looked old, worn out, yet Davie knew he was much more alert mentally, even at his age, than his son-in-law.

He cared deeply for his grandfather and he always felt a pang of anxiety when he saw him sitting like this, his body sagging, his lids drooping, for then that vital spark of life which showed in his eyes was hidden. He said flatly, 'I'm off,' and at this his grandfather opened his eyes, his father lifted his head, and they both said, 'Aye,' and he went out of the front door onto the road.

He passed the Geary house, which was strangely quiet today. It wasn't very often he passed this door without hearing Casey Geary bawling at one or the other. If it wasn't her husband, it was the two lads, or Molly. It was worse before the three younger lasses went into service. The hardest worked part about Mrs Geary, he considered, was her mouth.

He passed the next house, which was always quiet, having only Will Curran in it. But even when Mrs Curran had been alive, and their grown-up son and daughter in the house, it had always been quiet; Will Curran was a domineering man who would be obeyed. He wanted to be a master did Will

Curran, and he practised it hard under his own roof. His son had run off to sea and his daughter had done a moonlight flit with a fellow from across the valley.

He went on down the road and into the farmyard.

Everything here looked neat and spruce, especially since the mud was baked hard. There had been no rain to speak of for weeks, but it wouldn't be long before they had it, for the clouds were breaking up. He passed the house lying back to the left of him, then turned at right angles into the long yard that lay between the byres and barn at one side and the stables and store sheds at the other. He stepped over the channel of water which ran down the middle of the yard. Fed by inlets from the byres, it took the main part of the slush and muck.

When he entered the byres Fred Geary was already at work, which was unusual so early in the afternoon session. The man turned his small thin body and looked towards him but didn't speak, and Davie hesitated just within the doorway, wondering what he should do. His first impulse was to go up to him and say, 'Look here; you can think what you like but I know nawt about it.' But he thought better of it; what had to be said he would let come from him first.

But when fifteen minutes passed and Geary said no word to him, good, bad, or indifferent, he covertly watched him as he clumped back and forth to the dairy. He still had the explosive look on his face that had been noticeable when they were all called into the barn to witness the chastisement.

The chastisement. He couldn't get over it. When the bell had rung, he had dashed from the beet field thinking there was a fire, for the bell was only rung to gather them together for the march to church on a Sunday or in case of fire or flood; it was also rung merrily for a birth, slowly for a death. But this morning his Granda had been pulling it at the rate he did on Sundays, and so he had cried at him, 'What's up?' His Granda had merely pointed along to the barn.

When he had reached the barn it was to see the master and Molly standing up on the weighing platform, and below them the five Gearys, Will Curran, his own mother and father, and the mistress and Miss Jane. The master had looked down on Miss Jane and ordered, 'Go to the house and stay there,' and the girl had hesitated a moment before doing as he bade her. Then the master had said, 'There is trouble among us. Fred,' he had nodded towards Geary, 'Fred has come to me with bad news concerning his daugh . . . Molly here.' He had hesitated over his words, which was unusual for the master, but it was plain he had no stomach for what he was about to do. Then he continued, 'He tells me she's in trouble and will not name the man, and because of her stubbornness he has asked me to chastise her. I have no heart for this, but he demands it be done as was usual. . . .' It was at this point that his Granda had cried out, 'But them days are past, Master!' And the master had replied, 'I have already pointed this out to Fred.' 'Then why do it, Master?' his Granda had dared to question, and the master's reply was, 'If I don't, he will take her in hand himself, and I think in this case I am the lesser of two evils.'

At this he had asked Molly again to name the man, but all she had done was to shake her head. And then he had told her to grab hold of the stanchion post and he had laid his horsewhip across her back. She had on a cotton blouse and although his hand was not heavy, she jerked at each of the five lashes, especially the last, for the tail-end of the thong caught her on the bare neck.

When it was over Molly had walked away with her head down, she had not cried. He had stared after her helplessly. The whole thing had come upon him so suddenly he couldn't believe it had happened. Everybody seemed stunned, all except Geary, who showed no satisfaction in the outdated punishment he had demanded.

He had wondered at the time why Geary's big-mouthed, slovenly wife hadn't done something to prevent the whole business; but no, she had just stood there and watched her seventeen-year-old daughter being made a public spectacle.

When he came to look at the affair from a distance he couldn't make it out, because Casey Geary was the one to spew mouthfuls of abuse on anybody who laid a finger on a member of her family, even when they were all bairns together and in a straight farmyard fight. As his Granda had said, there was a smelly rat here somewhere. But where?

When he had finished his work in the byres, he went out and across the yard to the harness room. There, young Mickey Geary was sitting on a high bench with his back towards the wood-panelled walls, and he was almost entirely obliterated by a saddle arched across his knees. His face was bright and cheery. What he had witnessed happening to his sister this morning had apparently left no impression on him, for he said airily, 'Want me to come now, Davie?'

'You finished that?'

'All but.'

'You've been some time; you started it first thing.'

'Aye, but I've cleaned it bonny.'

Davie lifted the saddle away from the boy and examined it, then nodded and said, 'It'll do.'

'We goin' for the cows?'

'Aye.'

The child slipped agilely from the bench onto the floor, where his diminutive height and thinness questioned his eight years. But for all his smallness he was a bright little fellow and a favourite with Davie, or had been up till today. Now he hated the whole job lot of Gearys.

As Mickey trotted beside him he chatted. 'You goin' to make up some polish the night, we're nearly out, Davie?'

'We'll see.'

'Can I help you? Can I stir the wax, you said I could last time?'

'We'll see.'

'When is Primrose gona calf?'

'Soon.'

They went out of the farmyard into the road, through a gap in a dry-stone wall opposite, across a field and over a stile towards the steep hill they called The Ridge. The grass was slippery and Mickey measured his length once or twice, but Davie didn't stop until the small voice suddenly said, 'Ee bugger! I'm not 'alf hungry, me bloody belly thinks me throat's cut.'

Another time this would have brought a smothered laugh from Davie and he would have cuffed the boy's ear while admonishing him, but now he just admonished him sternly, saying, 'Let the master hear you an' that language an' he'll sort you out.' Then staring down into the small round face, he asked, 'Didn't you have no dinner?'

'No. Me ma never made none, she's in a hell of a sweat. Everybody is. You gona marry our Molly?'

Davie's face stretched; his whole body stretched, and before he could say anything, the boy backed away a step, saying, 'Well I only axed, 'cos our Johnnie said you had a shy on her.'

'Well, you can tell Johnnie to keep his mouth shut,' he bellowed at the lad, then turned away and closed his eyes for a moment before tramping sharply on again.

On the top of the ridge he waited for the boy to catch up. From where he stood he could see a great expanse of land beyond the boundary of the farm. To the right of him were hills, young mountains some of them; showing green and brown, with here and there great black patches, telling scars of dead lead mines. To the left the land rolled into moorland flatness on its way to Haltwhistle and the South Tyne. In front of him, eight miles as the crow flew, twelve miles by the twisting road, lay Allendale in its nest of moors.

Even in the winter he always paused at this spot to breathe in the air; it seemed purer from up here. Today, a late hot summer day, it was thin and clean and scoured his ribs as he drew it inwards. It was almost as good, he considered, as the air you breathed from the top of Shale Tor.

Mickey, crawling to his side on all fours, straightened himself and gasped, 'Whew! I'm out of puff. It's all slack. When the rain comes, I bet it'll be claggy,' and Davie, now looking down at him, half smiled and cuffed his ear gently, and the boy laughed and ran ahead of him down the slope and into the field where the cattle were grazing.

They did not bring the cattle back the way they had come, but by a narrow track that skirted the hill and finally led across the twenty-acre field and into the farm by the back road.

But before they came to the field, they had to pass along a road so narrow that the cattle walked in single file. Lowing and ambling at their own pace, their bags, almost touching the ground, swung rhythmically from side to side.

More out of habit than in any effort at persuasion, Davie ambled behind the last stragglers, crying, 'Git up! Git up there! Move, Daisy! You, Belle, move! Move, I say!' and when he stopped issuing his fruitless commands, Mickey took them up, 'Hie-up there! Hie-up there, Daisy! Hie-up you, Belle! Get along, Vicky, along you get.'

As Mickey's piping went on, Davie happened to glance to his right beyond a low scrub hedge where the land fell away over what was termed the shale field. It was a large strip of land, almost on the north boundary of the farm, and in most parts useless because of the outcrops of rock and shale shelves protruding from the ground. Grass did grow in the far corner of the field; contrarily a couple of acres gave luscious grass; perhaps it had something to do with its proximity to the old malt house.

The malt house was in ruins; it had been a ruin when Davie's grandfather was a boy. One section alone remained. This had been the habitation, but now the ground floor was used as a shelter for the horses in rough weather, and the mares and their foals were brought out here to grass. Halfway across the ground floor an open stairway led to a gallery, which had once, in turn, led to rooms which adjoined the malt house. But now all that remained of these was a wall of doors; the gallery itself was given over to storage of hay and bags of oats.

What had drawn his attention to the malt house was the figure running in that direction; although some distance away, he recognized the slight form of Miss Jane. She was holding her skirt in both hands, and her legs were leaping over the ground; from this distance she put him in mind of a two-legged deer. He thought she was going to the mare and foal, the foal being at the pretty, enticing stage of four weeks, but when he saw her pass them and make for the malt house, he stopped. Mickey stopped, too, and, his small face screwing up, he exclaimed, 'Yon's Miss Jane, an' she's fallin'.'

When seconds passed and the form on the ground made no move to get up, Davie said quickly to the boy, 'Take them on, I'll go down and see what's wrong with her.'

He now hurried back down the narrow path to where the hedge was thinnest and, having pushed his way through, he ran quickly across the field; but before he had covered half the distance he saw his young mistress get to her feet and start running again, not so quickly now and slightly erratic. She made for the malt house.

When he reached the front of the house, which was paved with large flags of natural stone and was on the side facing away from the field, he paused for a moment before walking quietly to the doorless gap. The stanchion was rubbed smooth in one part by the horses' hides; the floor inside was of stone, too, but the flags were smaller and covered with horses' droppings. The atmosphere was hot and dim and the odour pungent.

He looked about him, then upwards to the railless gallery as the sound of stifled sobbing came from the bay. Slowly and quietly he ascended the open stairs to the floor above.

'Miss Jane!'

There was no answer.

'Miss Jane! Are you hurt? It's me, Davie. Are you hurt?'

He walked quietly and slowly towards the bay. She was lying deep in it, and after a moment she turned on her side and looked up at him. Her face was awash with tears, her mouth was wide, and her tongue jerked on each sob.

'What is it? Have you hurt yourself?' He dropped onto his hunkers beside her, and she closed her eyes and shook her head.

'You fell, I saw you fall; I was takin' the cattle in. Are you all right, Miss Jane?'

She nodded her head while she gulped.

'You're sure you're not hurt?'

'No. No, Davie.' Her voice was a cracked whisper. Then she looked at her knees that were exposed by her rumpled skirt. One grey stocking was torn and showed scraped flesh oozing specks of blood, and as she eased the stocking off the skin she muttered, 'I'm not crying because I fell, but because Father . . . Father whipped Molly. He whipped her, Davie, you saw. . . .'

He blinked his eyes and looked down and away from her, then said, 'The master told you to go to the house. Anyway, it's done, over, so forget about it.'

'I can't, Davie. I keep thinking, and just can't believe that Father. . . .'

When she began to cry again, he said briskly, 'Now, now. Come on, dry your eyes and come away home. The mistress will be wondering, it's on your dinner-time.'

'No.' She shook her head. 'Father's gone into Hexham; he . . . he didn't want any dinner, nor . . . nor did Mother.'

'Well, that doesn't mean because they don't eat you've got to starve. Come on now, Miss Jane, up with you!'

He was about to rise from his hunkers, and he had his hand extended towards her, when there came to them the unmistakable sound of horse's hooves on the stone paving. The sound in itself should not have caused any surprise, for was there not a mare and her foal in the field? But this sound was of a single animal, and it had a rider. When the order came for it to stop, he recognized the voice. And he wasn't alone in his recognition; Jane was staring towards the glassless window at the end of the gallery. Then she quickly turned her head towards Davie, and he was on the point of saying, 'It's the master,' when a question flashed through his brain: Why should the master, who was supposed to be in Hexham, which was in the opposite direction from this, be coming into the malt house?

He put his hand out and pressed Jane back into the bay with a warning to be quiet, and by moving his head just the slightest he could see, around the mound of hay and between the sacks, the figure of his master framed in the doorless aperture. He was standing with his back towards the room looking out.

The master was waiting for somebody but he was wearing his town coat, three-quarter length, slightly flared; it had a velvet collar and was cut to his figure. His brown leather gaiters were shining like burnished copper, thanks to the elbow grease of young Mickey Geary. As the riding crop hit the leather the crack startled not only Miss Jane but also himself, and for a moment he almost lost his balance.

When a new sound broke the silence he put his fingers to his lips and warned his young mistress to silence. The sound was of light running steps. The steps turned the corner; then a small plump figure came flying straight into the arms of the waiting man.

The grim tautness of his body was broken by the smothered gasp from his side; the young mistress had moved. She was seeing what he was seeing; her mouth was dropping into a wide gape, and he knew within a second there would issue from it a cry, and then all hell would be let loose, for if he went down there, God alone knew what he would do to either of them. But what was equally important, if they looked up and saw him here in the straw with the young mistress, their mucky minds would be capable of putting two and two together. The young mistress was but twelve, but that wouldn't matter when people were looking for ways to defend themselves.

His hand gripped her jaw tightly and, staring down into her eyes, he moved his head twice. Then the voice from below brought his head round, for his master was speaking and using words of passion that a man should use only in the darkness of the night, and he finished them with, 'Oh! Molly, Molly my love, forgive me. How could I! How could I! To beat your flesh like that! Oh! my sweetie, my sweetie.'

'Aw, don't you worry, Master, don't you worry your head. Each stroke was like a kiss 'cos it came from you.'

The girl's voice was as impassioned as the man's, and Davie now tried to press Jane back into the bay so that her eyes should not witness her father's actions, for the master had pulled down Molly Geary's blouse and was moving his lips over her flesh like a man demented. He closed his eyes against the red flick of the tongue as it washed the weals and to the girl's flung-back head, her face filled with unholy ecstasy.

When he next looked at them the master was holding her tight, his hands were on her buttocks pressing her into him, while he talked rapidly: 'Your father, he came last night. He didn't come out in the open, he's too sly for that. "I've asked her to name the man," he said, "and she won't." Do you realize, Molly, he's known all along.'

'Aye, Master, I do now. But I didn't till this mornin' when I vomited and he came out with it, not naming you, but hinting at it. It's money he's after, an' a house . . . new built, separate.'

'He'll get both if he's sensible, give him to understand that. I won't be blackmailed, but I'll do anything, you know I will. . . .'

There were more words, too low now for Davie to hear, but they caused Molly Geary to bury her face in her master's chest, then suddenly to fling her arms around his neck and cover his mouth with her own while her body moved on his like that of any whore on market day.

His own body was writhing with rage, and again he was only checked from jumping up and diving down the stairs by a movement from the wide-eyed, staring girl at his side. She had her own hand tightly across her mouth now, but she was no longer crying. He had always thought she had a fine pair of eyes, Miss Jane, the best feature in her face, and they would likely stand her in good stead later on if she grew up as plain as she was now. The look in her eyes had been like a picture mirroring the simplicity of her nature; now the look was gone, never, he guessed, to return. It was a known fact among them all that she worshipped the master. It was also a known fact that she was a disappointment to him, for he had wanted a son. But he was never harsh with her, although not tender either, and up till now his unspoken wish had been her law. As he looked down into her face he likened the look in her eyes to that of a young fledgling being rent by a hawk.

And the master was a hawk, a buzzard, a vulture. God Almighty! And to think how he had always looked up to and respected him. His train of thought was punctured by his master's voice coming to him clearly now, saying, 'You'll have to come out in the open and name a man, for you must marry; the child must have a name. Whom do you choose?'

'Davie, Master.'

'Yes, I thought so.'

'Aw Master, Master, no need to look like that, none, for no matter whose name I take there'll only ever be you; always remember that, there'll only ever be you, Master.'

They were joined again, and the silence that settled on the ruined house was stupefying; the place was filled with heavy air like that which comes before a great storm. And the storm might have broken at this point had not young Jane's hand come on his; and now there was a share of the horror and hurt in her eyes for him. They both turned their heads and gazed down on the locked couple below as the master said, 'I'll tell him tonight.'

'What if he won't, Master?' This was the first note of uncertainty she had expressed.

'He'll do as he's bid, leave it to me. Go now, I should be in Hexham, and I'm late, I must hurry. But,' his voice changed and, his tone like that of a young ardent lover, he ended, 'how will I ever do without you, how will I manage, what will I do when you are at the beck and call of a husband?'

'Aw, don't worry your head, Master; leave it to me, I'll fix that.' Her reassurance could have come from a mature woman, not a girl of seventeen.

They embraced once more, then she went out, backing from him, buttoning her blouse as she did so.

Two minutes later, her master followed her.

When the sound of the horse's hooves going over the flagstones faded away, he got to his feet. His whole body was trembling, his legs felt weak. He had never experienced such a feeling in him before. He wanted to hit out. But at what? He had a desire to kill that bitch . . . and the master an' all. They were a conniving pair of devils. Be told off to marry her, would he? By God! Not as long as he had breath and legs.

'Davie!'

Although he had been looking at the young girl, he hadn't been conscious of her. Now, seeing her stricken face, he swallowed to clear the dryness from his throat and muttered thickly, 'Don't worry, Miss, don't worry.'

'But Father, and . . . and—' When she shook her head desperately and bowed it, he put his hand out and, taking her arm, drew her upwards, saying, 'Get away back to the house; the mistress will be missin' you.'

'Oh, Davie!'

Now she was holding her face with both hands and her mouth was pressed into a soft shapeless gap as she whimpered, 'Mother! If Mother gets to know, oh! Davie . . . what must I do?'

'You know what to do, don't tell her, tell nobody.'

'Nobody?'

'No, nobody; least of all the mistress, for you know she's in a condition.'

Jane stared up at the young man whom she could remember since she first remembered anything. He was as familiar to her as were her parents, perhaps more familiar than her father because he had always been kind to her, jolly. He used to make her laugh. He had said that her mother was in a condition as if he were telling her something. She knew all about such conditions; conception and birth were natural to her, she had watched them both. It was something that God made happen to animals, but she hadn't, up to a few minutes ago, associated it with people. Even her mother's rising stomach hadn't caused her to liken 'the condition' to Betsy, Rene, Flo, and Jessie, who were all in calf. It was a different condition, a condition as yet not probed. She had not begun her periods, and she had no companion of her own age with whom to discuss the secrets of the body. Her mother did not talk of such things or encourage her to probe. It was sufficient that her mother loved her, and she gave her great affection in return because she knew that the love her mother had for her was the same as that she herself had for her father. And not to get a love returned was a very painful thing, so she was always extra affectionate to her mother, no matter how she felt.

But now she was probing and had opened a deep well in her mind. She saw pictured in it the thing that happened between her mother and father, the private thing. But she also saw the same thing happening between her father and Molly.

She knew Molly as well as she knew Davie. Molly had been a kind of elder sister to her. Although there was only five years between them, Molly had taken care of her when she was small, and had often washed and dressed her. But when she was seven years old her mother decreed that she should do these things for herself. She had also pointed out at that time, too, the difference in their stations. So Molly had been relegated to helping in the kitchen and doing the housework. And now Molly and her father. . . . She turned and threw herself face downwards onto the hay again. But almost immediately Davie's voice roused her, crying sharply, 'Come on! Come on now, none of that. An' I've got to be on me way. It's milkin' time, and they'll be crying out for me. Come on now, get up.'

He pulled her none too gently to her feet and pressed her forward across the balcony and down the stairs, and when they were once more in the open he said, 'Go on over there and wash your face in the brook, then make your way home an' leave things as they are, they'll work out. Do you hear me?'

When she didn't speak he bent down to her and said gently, 'Miss Jane, did you hear what I said?'

She lifted her face to him but still she didn't speak; then turning, she walked from him over the grass and towards the brook. And he went up towards the track again, but he didn't run, nor even hurry; he was too stunned to do either. He felt like a dolt. Molly had made a monkey out of him. He had denied courting her for he hadn't been over fresh in his advances; she was saucy and so he had kept her guessing. But inside he had courted her; he had even seen them married and got as far as wondering if the master would build them a new cottage. The master! He spat vehemently onto the grass.

'I was right then.'

'Aye, you were right, Granda.'

'My God! I still can't believe it. But then, you know your ma's always said she was a scut. Your ma's never far out when she's judgin' people. Your ma's told us on the quiet that she was at it when she was little more than a bairn, not thirteen. She caught her on with young John Curran and she scattered the pair of them. It's a wonder to me she's not had your trousers down long afore now, lad.'

'Aw, Granda, what do you take me for?'

'A man, lad; that's all, just a man. But you're probably late in startin'. It's them books. I was sayin' to Ned only this dinner gone it's them books, an' Parson Hedley. But then the master's a read man an' all, but it hasn't stopped him. No begod! It hasn't stopped him. But then it's his time of life; turned forty, something happens to you, lad.' He nodded at his grandson and his eyes stretched in owl-like wisdom. 'You have the urge to plough another field. At least that's how the ordinary man feels. But then the master, I didn't take him for no ordinary man. I've followed him to church Sunday year after year, sunshine and shadow, sleet and snow, not because I wanted to hear old Wainwright but because I was following the pattern of a good man, a man o' God. Aye, I always thought him an upright man o' God.'

'Upright man of God!' Davie was walking the kitchen floor: six strides from the door to the settle, around the table, four strides back to the door; here his fingers lifted the latch, then dropped it again, click-click, click-click. After he had repeated the pattern four times he turned fiercely and cried at his grandfather, 'Man of God! And coolly planning to shove the blame on me, the both of them. If you could have heard them. How in the name of heaven I didn't show meself, I'll never know.'

'It's a wonder they didn't spot you,' said Sep, ''cos by the sound of it that was their nest. An' very comfortable. An' who of us goes down there, except young Johnnie or Mickey to see to a mother and foal, and the cart once a week with the fodder. Stop prancing, lad,' he said now; 'go on back to your work. Say nawt to nobody; we'll talk this over when your ma and da come in. He won't be back from Hexham afore seven and that'll give us time to think.'

By seven o'clock they had thought a great deal, but it hadn't got them very far, and the four of them were sitting in the kitchen now waiting for the summons to the house. For countless times in the last half-hour Winnie had exclaimed, 'I cannot believe it, the master, and him a God-fearing man.' And now it was not Davie but her father who turned on her harshly, crying, 'Aw, have sense, girl, have sense. God fearin'? Even God is no longer afeared when the body cries its needs.'

'Oh Da! Stop talkin' such.'

'I'll stop talkin' such when the Almighty decides to change the pattern.'

Ned now spoke. He looked at his son from where he was sitting in the corner of the settle, his arms folded across his chest, and he said in a conciliatory tone, 'I would let him have his say, Davie, and whatever you answer, I mean when you tell him you're not for havin' it, do it quietly, because we don't want no trouble. What I mean is. . . .'

'What you mean is—' Davie's voice was barking, but it was brought tones lower by wild gestures from his mother with her arms flung out towards the wall, indicating that it had ears, the ears of the Gearys. 'What you mean is that he could give us all the push, bonded or not bonded. Well, here's one that needs no push, Da, 'cos I'm goin'.' He got on his feet now, staring back into the three pairs of eyes riveted on him, and his mouth worked for a moment before he added, 'The world's wide, there's things out there I've never even dreamed of, so . . . so I'm goin'.'

'Aw, no. No.' Winnie came towards him, her two hands joined together as if in supplicating prayer. 'No, boy, no, don't go as far as that. Think, now think.' She tried to press him into a seat, but he pushed her away, then looked at her, half in apology, and, his voice toned down, he said, 'It'll be all right; he can't do anything to you if I go. He wouldn't it would be cuttin' off his nose to spite his face. Where would he get another like you, cooking, cleaning, dairy, the lot? You do the work of two and a half women.'

Winnie now bowed her head to the side, and it was as if she were, by her gesture, indicating her husband and his rheumsticky twisted hands. Rheumatism had struck him early, whereas her father had reached the middle fifties before his joints had knotted. But Ned wasn't of the stamina of her father; he suffered greatly from his aches, and had done for the past ten years. And now at forty-three, the winters presented a nightmare; wet sacks over his head and shoulders, and feet often so swollen and painful that his boots had to be eased off them–it had taken an early toll.

Four generations of the Armstrongs had worked on Cock Shield Farm. It was their home, their place, and now Davie was rocking the very foundations of their livelihood because, like herself, he did much more than his share, and between them they made up for any slackness on Ned's part and the fact that her father had to be cared for. True, the old 'un still did odd helpful jobs here and there about the place, in the summer that is, but in the winter he didn't earn the one and sixpence pension the master gave him. But the master made no complaint because most of the work he used to do Davie had taken on. Besides his own work as second cowman, Davie acted as coachman when the master and mistress went in style to their twice-yearly visits to The Manor, he took a turn on the plough, and he saw to the hunters; there wasn't a job on the place he didn't turn his hand to. He had done a fourteen-hour day for years and rarely grumbled, because he was young and strong and willing; but he was also stubborn, hot tempered, and had ideas in his head beyond those of his station, and all through Parson Hedley and his books.

Davie knew they were all looking at him, their thoughts hard on him, but he continued to stare out of the window until Johnnie, Fred Geary's eldest son, aged ten, came running down the road.

As he knocked on the door the boy called, 'Davie! Davie!'

Slowly Davie moved a few paces towards the door, lifted the latch, and looked down at the boy.

'Master's back, Davie, and askin' for you. He says come to the office.'

When Davie didn't answer him, the boy repeated. 'He's askin' for you now, the master.'

'All right, all right.' His voice was tight and thick, 'I'll be along.'

They nodded at each other; then Davie turned and looked at his people, all standing now.

His mother said tentatively, 'I'd put a clean smock on.'

At this he tore off his soiled smock, threw it on the floor, then swung round from them and went out, banging the door behind him.

As he walked down the dusty road in the direction of the farmyard, his angry gaze lifted towards the house. He had always liked the farmhouse, the shape of it, the mellowness of it; it was the best of its kind for fifty miles in any direction you went. The old part of it dated back to 1699 and had three stories. The lower floor was now the dining room; it was a very large room. Above it the same space was divided into a bedroom and two small rooms, one used as the master's dressing room and one as a night water closet. Above these there had been two attics, but the dividing wall had been pulled down to form a large storeroom for all the odds and ends of the house.

The new part of the farmhouse, which was built in 1794, had only two stories, and the bedrooms were on a lower level than that of the old part. Four steps led down from the old house into the new, and onto a fine big landing, as big as a room, with six bedrooms going off it. The house had been built for a family, and at one time these rooms had held seven sons and three daughters. This was because they had been lucky enough to be born and reared between the bad plagues. On the ground floor there was a fine sitting room, and at the end of a passage leading from the hall, a room that had once been the breakfast room (the house had been styled on those of its betters) but now was the master's office. The end of the passage gave access to the kitchen, and this room, like the old dining room at the opposite end, was stoneflagged, and held everything that a kitchen should hold, from a pepper mill to a row of twelve graded pewter pots hanging above the long mantelshelf, seeming to form a bridge between the great copper pans that gleamed, also in rotation of size, where they hung on wooden pegs down each side of the fireplace.

If Davie had ever had a wild dream, it hadn't up till now been of sailing the seas and discovering new lands, as did the people he had read about, but of owning a house such as this, with a kitchen where he could enter without scraping his feet, taking off his cap, or touching his forelock.

He now scraped the dust off his feet on the scraper and then on the roped mat outside the kitchen door.

He paused inside the door and there, at the long wooden trough sink, stood Molly Geary washing dishes. She turned her head quickly towards him, her hazel eyes narrowed, a faint smile on her face. 'Hello, Davie,' she said softly.

He glared at her, then walking slowly to the edge of the sink he bent his shoulders slightly forward and said in a low voice. 'You go to hell's flames, Molly Geary, and as far beyond; and you can take that,' he stabbed his finger down at her stomach, 'along with you.'

Her eyes stretched wide, her mouth fell open, and she turned her head quickly and looked towards the far door that led into the passage, as if she would run to it; but Davie was walking towards it. Before he went through he turned and looked at her again and, his voice still low and his words spaced, he said, 'The master wants me,' and he laid strong emphasis on each word.

Her face showed him that she was in no doubt as to how much he knew of the truth of the situation. He went into the passage and towards the office door, and there he had to force himself to knock.

'Come in.'

Slowly he opened the door and entered the room, then stood with the door in his hand, looking at the man seated behind the desk.

Angus McBain glanced upwards as he pushed a ledger to one side and rearranged some papers on the desk; then he said, 'Come in and close the door, Davie.'

Davie did as he was bidden, and slowly walked up the narrow room until he was standing in front of the desk, looking down into the face of his master. The face looked all thin–nose, lips, eyebrows–yet the hair on his head was black and thick. It lay like a silk sheath and was as yet untouched with grey. Until this moment Davie hadn't realized how thin the master was in all ways. His body was tall and thin, his face was long and thin, even the grey of his eyes was a thin colour; and his voice was thin–clear, sharp, and thin.

'Do you know why I've sent for you, Davie?'

Should he say 'Yes, Master,' or 'No, Master.' He stared down into the flickering half-veiled gaze. The drooping lids suggested that they could close at any moment, and he said, 'I've got a good idea,' he paused a second before he added, 'Master.'

Angus McBain brought his attention once again to the papers on the desk and his Adam's apple made a rapid movement in his neck, stretching the skin in its passage. 'You have been courting Molly for some time. . . .'

'I've never courted Molly, Master.'

Again they were looking at each other, and now McBain's eyes were wide and his voice stiff as he said, 'I have seen you myself walking the fields.'

'You can walk the fields, Master, without courtin'.'

Again there was a pause before McBain said, and thickly now, 'The girl is with child and she won't name the man.'

'Won't she, Master?'

McBain made no reply to this. At another time the young fellow's tone would have brought his tongue lashing at him, for he allowed no servant, man or woman, young or old, to approach him as an equal. His forebears had always run the farm as gentlemen farmers, not like the ordinary trish-trash who worked neighbouring farms and allowed their people to pig in with them at a central table in the kitchen. Those he employed knew their place and gave him his. He was a good master to them and acted as their counsellor. He demanded respect and subservience as his right.

But there was neither respect nor subservience in young Armstrong's manner. Of course, he was peaked at discovering Molly had fallen and he'd had no hand in it; it was natural he supposed, and, therefore, he must make allowances. Well, the thing to do was to get it over and quickly. He picked up a sheet of paper from the table, scrutinized it for a moment, then laying it down but his eyes still on it, he said, 'You will marry Molly.'

'. . . I'll not, you know . . . Master.' Again there was the pause before 'Master.'

'What!' The thin face was thrust upwards now. 'Did I hear you aright?'

'Aye, you heard me aright.'

'You would defy my order, and leave her with an unnamed child?'

'Aye, both, Master.'

McBain's eyes were wide now. There was more in the young fellow's attitude than frustrated virility; he felt a sense of uneasiness. Had Geary, because he had been thwarted in his attempt at blackmail, hinted something to the fellow? Surely the man would have had more sense. Had he not a family to support? And did he not realize that the roads were crawling with farm workers begging for work? Nine shillings a week he was paying Geary, and three shillings between his sons; that was a tidy sum, not counting the two shillings a week from Molly. Then there was his cottage, milk, potatoes, and two cords of wood a year. Surely the man wouldn't jeopardize all that? No, for he was a cunning individual, was Geary. What he wanted for his knowledge was a raise in pay, a house, more perquisites. He would not jeopardize that. But why then young Davie's attitude?

The muscles of his face tightened as he looked into the brown eyes, almost black now with what he recognized as suppressed rage. He leaned back in his chair and surveyed the young fellow as from a distance, and it was as the master of destinies that he slowly spoke. 'If you disobey my wishes you know what it could mean?' He held up a finger as Davie was about to speak, and continued, 'Now think, think hard. I'm not a man to use empty threats. Those who do me service are repaid, well and truly repaid, as you and your family know. You have a good job: ask yourself, where in this county would you get seven shillings a week? What is more, there is a great deal of money going into your house from my pocket.'

'Aye, and you're gettin' a great deal of work for it, Master. Me ma and me both do two people's jobs each; me Granda did the same for years till he was worn out.' He did not mention his father.

McBain was sitting upright now, stiff as a ramrod. His voice had a steel thread to it as he said, 'You are forgetting yourself entirely. Be careful, Armstrong, be careful.'

'No, Master, I'm not forgettin' meself. You sent for me, didn't you, to tell me I had to marry Molly? Well, I'm tellin' you I'm not goin' to, 'tis a free country.'

'You are a bonded man.'

'Bonded, or no bonded, I've only got a few months to go. I could leave at the end of the year and you could do nothing about it.'

McBain slowly drew himself up from the chair, stretching himself until he appeared to stand head and shoulders above Davie, although in fact with his six feet he could give him only two inches, and his words had an ominous ring. 'Yes. Yes,' he said, 'you could leave at the end of the year and I could do nothing about it. But I could do something about the cottage and your father. Don't you want time to think, boy?'

'All I can think, Master, is you'll go a long way afore you'll get anybody to work for you like me ma does, an' me da an' all; they both do a twelve-hour day, more, never no less. And you won't find me da droppin' asleep on the job either. An' me, my hours never end, you see to that. An' you've no need to tell me the roads are crawling with families looking for situations; I know it, but what I also know is that Farmer Hetherington from over Hunstenworth would jump at me ma like a shot. His wife's been on her back for years an' he can't get anybody right for the house; he's asked me ma twice . . . that's news for you, Master. . . .'

'Stop! Stop your insolence this minute!' As McBain came round the desk Davie did not retreat, and when his master stood within an arm's length of him he faced him unblinking. It was strange for him to realize that he had no fear of this man now, even in his wrath, for he had always stood slightly in awe of him, not only as a master, but as a man. Because he appeared away above the ordinary mortal, his example was something to follow. But for three years now he had questioned the church going and psalm singing; strangely, it had been the books Parson Hedley himself had recommended that had brought the vague questioning doubts to the forefront of his mind; without his reading he doubted if he would ever have troubled to think about it.

God was in his heaven,
The cattle were in the field,
Men ploughed and sowed
And lived off the yield.

That was the pattern he could, like his folks, have lived and died by. Yet his reasoning told him, even in this moment of stress, that it was this man, this enraged master towering before him, who had allowed him to go to Parson Hedley's Sunday School. However, he questioned the man's progressiveness in the face of the prevailing parsimoniousness of thought and asked himself, would he have been allowed such a privilege if the master hadn't been a friend of old Parson Wainwright, and Parson Wainwright hadn't been full cousin to Lord Powlett, and Lord Powlett's niece hadn't married Sir Alfred Tuppin, who lived in The Manor. The master had a taste for high company; it was known around the county he didn't live like any ordinary farmer. So the sending of him and the rest of the young 'uns on the farm to Sunday School he saw now as a means of impressing Sir Alfred and the rest of the gentry with his progressiveness.

He had a mental picture of his master reading the Lesson; that was when his awe of him had first begun, for he did not seem like a farmer, or his master, but a man full of God. A man full of God! The words ran through his mind like an audible sneer. In this moment he had the desire to spit them into the face before him.

The master was speaking. His voice low and very thin now, he was saying, 'You have your choice, you'll marry Molly or you'll go.'

'You've had me answer, Master, and I'll add something to it.' His own voice was low and thick. 'I'd rather be crucified than give me name to her an'—' there was a long pause before he ended, 'your fly-blow.'

He watched the colour drain away from the thin face, leaving the skin grey and muddy looking, except for two white spots on the cheeks where the bones showed through. He could not continue to look at the fall of a god, as it were, so he moved to one side, then went towards the door, only to be checked by McBain saying, 'Wait!'

Again they were looking at each other, but Davie saw that the master had recovered quickly, and the tone of his voice bore this out as he said, 'I could horsewhip you, or take you to the Justice for defiling my . . . my character. Do you know what you have said, accused me of?'

'Aye, Master.'

'Well, it's a lie, bred of your jealousy. That is final, you'll go, and if you spread this lie around I'll have you transpor. . . .' He had been about to say 'transported,' but realized he was more than sixteen years too late for that; but Davie took it up.

'And Miss Jane along of me, Master?' he said.

There was a short silence before McBain muttered, 'What!'

'I said Miss Jane along of me, Master?' His voice was quiet. 'She was in the malt house s'afternoon, as I was meself. I was bringing the cows in and I saw her fall. She was running towards the malt house. When I got to her she was up in the straw, you know,' he inclined his head forward, 'the straw that's in the gallery. She had cut her knee and was cryin'. She wasn't crying 'cos of her hurt, not that kind of hurt anyway, she was crying for. . . . Now who do you think she was crying for, Master? She was crying for Molly, 'cos you had flayed her. And then she sees you, Master; we both see you comin' in and waiting. I don't need to tell you any more, do I? It isn't me you've got to worry about, Master. Not me, it's Miss Jane.'

He walked from his master's presence without being given leave, and he didn't bang the door.

Angus McBain put his hand behind him and gripped the edge of the desk, then took a step back and rested his buttocks against it. God above! What was this? His mind leapt back to what he had said to Molly in the malt house . . . and what he had done to her, kissing her flesh, fondling her. Ah, dear Lord!

It was characteristic of him that he wasn't concerned so much over the impression his infidelity might have made on his daughter as by the fact that a member of his immediate family should be aware of his intrigue. That his employees should have knowledge of what was going on was, after all, of no great import; they would never dare voice, or even hint of any such thing to their mistress. They could, and would, talk among themselves, but what did that matter? He had after all only done what was commonplace all over the countryside, taken his pleasure with a serving maid. This might even add to the respect granted him in some quarters, and arouse it in others where it had been lacking; their knowledge of his peccadillo would have made him appear much more a man of the world. What was shaking him now with fear and foreboding was the possibility that through his daughter the facts might come to his wife's ears. But again his particular worry did not concern the effect it might have on her, but on what she was carrying. She had carried for nearly seven months, the first time since Jane was born, and he had willed it be a son, willed, and willed, and willed it to be a son, until, deep within him, there was the sure knowledge it would to be a son. A few more weeks and he would have a son. Molly might have a son, but he could never claim it.

Molly! Even the name coming into his mind made him feel weak. He had never had a desire for anyone like he had for her. Ignorant, untutored, it did not matter, her body was a delight to him. He liked young things, soft, rounded things. His first wife had been like Molly, all flesh. She had died and taken their first child with her, and that had been a son. Why then, with his inclination running to tender soft young things, had he picked on Delia to bear his children? Delia had been twenty and thin; pretty, yes, but thin, almost as thin as himself. She was still thin; she had got thinner with every miscarriage. Seven of his children she had dropped; he had grown weary of trying to bring permanent life out of her bony frame. Now for the first time in thirteen years she was holding his seed, and nothing must cause her to drop it before it was due. Where was Jane? He must find her, explain to her; she was twelve years old, old enough to understand.

He seemed to be catapulted from the desk, out through the door along the passage and into the kitchen, only to find it empty. He went into the passage again, then on into the drawing room, calling 'Delia! Delia!' When his wife didn't answer, he went into the hallway and out through the front of the house. The garden was deserted. Delia, he saw, had been on the lounge chair, for her work bag was lying on the grass. He went through the house again and out into the side yard, and there called to young Mickey Geary, 'Have you seen your mistress, boy?'

'Aye, Master. Her and Molly are lookin' for Miss Jane; she didn't come home to no supper.'

He bit tight down on his lip before asking, 'Which way did they go?'

'I don't know, Master; they just went round 'n' round the place callin'.'

Swiftly he made his way out of the yard and into the road. Then he crossed the fields almost at a run, leaned over a low stone wall, and made for Shale Tor. He slipped as he scrambled up the steep path and when he reached the top, he was gasping.

The evening sun was in his eyes and he put his hand to his brow and peered around him. Then he saw them, two small figures a good distance apart, his wife on the cow track above the malt house field, and farther away the unmistakable figure of Molly running down towards the brook; he could not see his daughter. He left the top of the hill and took the curving path at a run, which he kept up across the fields. He could not remember running like this since he was a boy of fourteen.

Delia McBain had been looking for her daughter for the past hour and a half. She had started the search quietly. Rising from her outdoor couch, she had gone into the kitchen, where she had asked Molly if she had seen Miss Jane. Molly had answered, 'No, Missis, not since dinner-time.'

As Delia had gazed at Molly she had for a moment forgotten that she was looking for her daughter, and had, in spite of this girl's sinning, felt overcome with compassion for her. She herself had been quite unaware of the reason for ringing the bell: the sound of it had brought her swiftly from the dining room, and she had asked Angus as he was crossing the hall, 'What is the matter? What has happened? Why have you ordered the bell to be rung?' and he had spoken to her over his shoulder as he went out, saying, 'Come to the barn and you'll find out.'

And having found out, she then understood her husband's reticence in speaking to her of the matter, for she knew him, in spite of her private knowledge of a certain facet of his character, to be a very moral man. But when she had seen him lift the whip to Molly, something within her had become outraged. Those undercurrents in her apparently placid nature, which were known to no one but herself, swept up through her in a torrent and almost escaped her lips in protest. She reminded herself only just in time that any protest of hers would appear as if she were censuring her husband, and would present a bad example to his people. She always thought of the workers as his people, not her people, but Angus's people; she was no Queen to his King, and she had always been aware of her inferiority with regards to him, for Angus had a great mind, a cultured mind.

She herself came from a well-connected family. Her grandfather having once been a shipbuilder (that was before they brought the iron ships in), if her father had not squandered his inheritance, she would, no doubt, have never been allowed to marry a farmer, even such a one as Angus McBain. But penniless and living on the bounty of a cousin, and having reached the age of twenty and no one having as yet asked to marry her, the widower, the young, lean, stern-faced widower had appeared to both her and her cousin's family like the answer to many prayers.

She had not loved Angus when she first married him, but in a very short time she had been consumed by her feelings for him, and it wasn't until the fifth year of their marriage that there began the long, slow, dying of her love. He blamed her for the loss of each child. The third month of pregnancy was agony to her; as the blood flowed from her, carrying away yet another of his frenzied efforts to make her body bear his son, she died afresh.

As the years wore on and she sat in church Sunday after Sunday and heard him read the Lesson with as much or more feeling than either Parson Hedley or Wainwright put into their readings, she began to contrast him with the man of the night, the man who tore at her body like a hungry lion at a doe. Yet she knew she must suffer this, as it was the lot of all women; men's appetites must be satisfied. But the daring, probing part of her mind questioned God's handiwork in combining in her husband His adherent and the wild beast of the night.

So her love died. But not her respect for his superior knowledge. He was well read. His office walls showed lines of books like you might find in a library, and Sir Alfred Tuppin always referred to the office as the library, and never failed to admire her husband's taste in literature when he called, as he did sometimes after a meet. And what was more, both parsons respected his knowledge.

She found pleasure of an evening when Parson Hedley came to supper, and after the meal she sat with her handwork and listened to her husband and the minister discoursing on all subjects, lately about Disraeli, Parliament, and the Queen. From their conversation she had visualized the Red Sea and the Mediterranean joined by a great canal. She had listened attentively to the discussion on a man called The Khedive. He was the ruler of Egypt, and he had sold his shares in a canal called the Suez Canal to Mr Disraeli, or at least Mr Disraeli had bought them for the Queen and the Empire. Of course neither her husband nor Parson Hedley agreed with all Mr Disraeli had done; they criticized him a great deal and were pleased when his Parliament fell. But they didn't seem much happier with Mr Gladstone, who was now Prime Minister. Undoubtedly he was a moral man, a righteous man, but he was, they said, swaying the people, the working men, and not, they both agreed, in the right direction.

They were very enlightening and enlivening evenings when the parson came to supper. When they had supper alone her husband never talked to her except upon household matters, or visits that had to be made. And if such a visit were to be special and to occur some little time in the future, he would advise her to plan for it and would give her the money to buy the material for a new gown.

For this purpose she loved the trips into Hexham, and twice over the years she had been as far as Newcastle. The shops in Newcastle had beautiful material, such an assortment; foreign silks straight from the boats, beautiful velvets of the gentlest hues. Her husband was generous when he wanted her to appear well dressed, and of late he had been more generous. When she was safely past her three months pregnancy, he had given her twenty pounds and ordered Davie to drive her into Hexham, there to choose a material for a gown that she could wear during her last month. This she looked upon as a tender extravagance, as it would have to be taken to pieces later and remodelled.

She had never known such contentment as that which had filled her these past three months; all fear had dropped from her. She knew she would carry this child, and it was all due, she knew, to Mother Reckett. Why hadn't she gone to the old woman years ago? She knew why; it was foolish to ask herself this question. When, after her second miscarriage, she had said to Angus, 'There is an old woman called Mrs Reckett who I understand makes up potions . . . ,' he had silenced her before she had got any further. Mother Reckett was a heathen, a woman with the evil eye. He wasn't a superstitious man, he told her, but he knew that Mother Reckett possessed powers of evil;

some people gave her credit for the power to cure animals, but she also had been given credit for bringing blight and disease to the land of many a man who had crossed her.

So for years she had resisted the temptation of consulting Mother Reckett, until desperation and a word from Mrs Swinterton, when taking tea with her at her house outside Haltwhistle, had supplied the courage. Mrs Swinterton was an old lady herself and had been a friend of the McBain family for years. She had expressed sorrow for her many miscarriages and suggested that, unknown to her husband, she seek help from Mother Reckett; and Mother Reckett had worked the miracle.

It was now eighteen months since she had taken her first bottle of medicine. It had been as clear as water and as bitter as gall, and she had drunk it as if it were nectar. Three doses a week she had taken for twelve months, and then the miracle had happened. For four years prior to this she hadn't even conceived. At times she had longed to conceive even though it would mean carrying the child for only three months, for following a miscarriage Angus always let her body rest for some weeks.

Once she had conceived again, Mother Reckett had changed the medicine to a thick substance that had a sweet acrid taste and which had to be taken by the teaspoonful three times a day. And so periodically she went for a walk over the moor. Angus was used to her taking long solitary walks, when she might be absent for three hours at a time, and so he had not questioned her journeyings. From her last visit to Mother Reckett's cottage on the outskirts of Harper Town she had brought back enough medicine to last her until her time was up because her body was already heavy, and she was tiring very easily.

But here now was Molly, and she, too, was carrying a child, even if it was the product of sin, and this morning she had been whipped. She had the desire to go to her and comfort her. But Molly was apparently still suffering from the injustice of her treatment for she turned her head from her.

When she asked, 'Have you seen Miss Jane?' Molly, still with her head down, muttered, 'No, Mistress, not since dinner-time, when she wouldn't have nothin' to eat.'

'Oh, but she was here well after that. It's now close on seven. I'm worried; she seemed upset.' She did not go on and say, 'The fact of your being whipped upset her; she did not do as her father bade her but witnessed the scene through the back of the barn,' but added, 'We'd better look for her. We'll take the cow path to the burn, she may be there. You can run down; she is often at the burn because the foal is near.'

Molly dried her hands, then turned from the sink and said, 'Master's back, Missis.'

'Oh, I didn't hear him. Is he in his office?'

'Yes, Mistress, but Davie's with him.'

'Oh!' Delia looked at the girl and thought she understood. It would be Davie. Of course it would. She had seen them together. But she was very disappointed in Davie; if he had come forward, he could have saved this poor creature from being flayed; she had thought better of Winnie's son. She liked Winnie, she considered her a fine woman, in her place of course, and she had at times envied her her son, for she considered Davie an intelligent boy, worth perhaps something more than the position of second cowman. But she was sure that her husband recognized this and would bear it in mind for his future. She had said as much to Winnie. But now the boy had come out of this situation without any honour; he would get a severe rating from Angus, that was sure, and serve him right, but once they were settled, Angus, fair man that he was, would no doubt see to building them a cottage of their own. Some time ago he had talked of renovating the old malt house. The foundations and part of the structure were still good; it was a picturesque place and a shame that it should be given over to the occasional stabling of a mare and foal. He had seemed very keen on the idea. That was some time ago; he had not mentioned it for months past. But now it would likely come to his mind again. It would make a most superior dwelling, fit for a bailiff, or in his case, foreman. And why not? If Davie behaved well from now on he could in time rise to that position, for Angus had talked more than once of engaging an intelligent man to act as a kind of manager, so that he himself could have more time to devote to other things, which, she had thought indulgently, included hunting and fishing. Last year he had been invited by Sir Alfred Tuppin to his Scottish estate to indulge in the latter sport when the salmon season was on. It was at that time he had talked about employing a capable manager.

But now she was sure everything would work out both for Molly and Davie and the household, for Molly, being trained under Winnie, would take over when Winnie was too old to carry on; and outside, Davie, she was sure, in spite of his lapse, would run the farm in the interests of his master.

They went out, not together, Molly walking a foot or so behind her mistress, as was right, and Delia spoke to her over her shoulder. 'I'm seriously thinking of sending Miss Jane to Madam Lovell's private school in Hexham.'

'Oh, aye, Mistress.' There was little interest in Molly's response.

'She is too old for the day school now, and it is not advanced enough in its teaching. The master agrees that she should attend Madam Lovell's.'

Again Molly said, 'Oh, aye, Mistress.'

'She will learn French and music, although she is quite good at the pianoforte now.' She paused, then ended, 'I thought I might like her at home to help with the . . . the baby, but the master is arranging to have a nurse. She will attend me as long as is necessary.'

When Molly did not answer, she turned her head slightly and looked at the girl. Her face was sweating; there were beads of perspiration running from her hairline and down over her plump cheeks. She wanted to reassure her and say, 'Don't worry, everything is all right, the master will see that you're cared for.' Instead, she said, 'Run on ahead, Molly. Go down to the brook and see if she's there; I'll have to take my time. But you be careful, too.' She smiled at the girl, but it brought no response, for when she passed her she hung her head, and she noted that she kept it down as she ran along the lane. She watched her sit atop the dry-stone wall that hemmed in the burn bank and kept the cattle from straying; she saw her swing her legs over one after the other; then she was lost from view.

She herself was very hot and feeling weary. Her step slowed. She hoped that Molly found Jane down there and also that she had got over her distress. She was a highly sensitive child, very young in some ways for her years, yet in others she was old beyond her years. She had a great fund of natural sympathy and affection, but she had one shortcoming in that she was given to wild fits of temper. This trait, she was sure, her daughter did not inherit from herself, for no matter what her own feelings, she was always able to conceal them. And she certainly did not inherit it from her father; Angus might get angry, but it was a controlled anger.

Sometimes she thought that the free life her daughter led might tend to make her become wilful; it was with the thought of erasing any possibility of this that she had suggested Madam Lovell's school to her husband. In making this suggestion, she had made a personal sacrifice, because up to now Jane was the only proof she had to show that she was capable of bearing a child. So, therefore, she loved her very much. And the child had always given her affection and comfort, but never, she knew, love. That she had kept for her father.

She started as she heard Jane's voice, high and shrill now, coming from the direction of the burn. It was as if she were crying, and in distress. She hurried along the lane to the spot where Molly had crossed the wall, but to make her descent, she herself had to go much farther along the winding path to where a gap gave way to natural slate steps down to the burn itself; and all the while she hurried, she could hear her daughter's voice.

When she reached the gap she looked down the slope, and the sight that met her eyes astounded her. Jane was actually fighting Molly, striking out at her with both hands and feet. She had never witnessed anything like it. Molly was protesting, but not loudly, just warding off the blows, saying, 'Aw, Miss, give over, give over. For God's sake, Miss. Aw, for God's sake, Miss, be quiet, it'll cause trouble. Aw, Miss, Miss, come on away, come on up home.'

'Don't touch me, don't dare touch me. You're filthy, filthy. Molly Geary, you're filthy.'

Delia was about to call out and command her daughter to stop making such an unladylike spectacle of herself and demand to know the reason for the scene, when Jane's next words gave it to her without further questioning. 'I hate you, Molly Geary. You and father . . . I saw you both. I saw you in the malt house. You were horrible, and you let him whip you while all the time you knew it was him. You are horrible, horrible!'

Delia stood transfixed, looking down on them. Her daughter was still gabbling and Molly was still pushing off her hands and feet.

Like someone sleepwalking now, she slowly descended the shallow steps where they turned in a half moon towards the burn. Jane was now spluttering, 'Planning with Father to make Davie marry you, pretending it was him. You are horrible, dirty. I hate you, Molly Geary.'

'Jane!' Delia had not spoken loudly. She was amazed herself at the quiet tone that issued from her lips, for inside her head her thoughts were whirling and screaming.

They both turned towards her now, Jane staring up at her, her face dirty, tear-stained, and, at this moment, ugly; but Molly, after one glance at her mistress, drooped her head onto her chest and stood limp, her arms hanging downwards away from her body as if she no longer had any control over them.

'What is this?' Delia was addressing her, and when the girl did not lift her head, she cried at her, her voice expressing her emotions now, 'Answer me, girl! What is this I hear?'

When Molly raised her head, startled as much by this new aspect of the mistress as by the fact that she was advancing on her, she could only stammer, 'Oh, Mistress, Mistress.'

Delia stopped within an arm's length of the girl and now demanded, 'Tell me that my daughter is deranged and not speaking the truth.'

Molly now swung her head from side to side, gulped in her throat, opened her soft wet mouth wide, closed it again; then her head seemed to be jerked off her body by a blow first to one side of her face and then to the other. As she cowered down a voice thundered over them, crying. 'Delia!' and Delia turned and looked up the steps to where her husband was standing in the gap.

McBain had taken in the situation; he was too late. Well, what was done was done, and couldn't be undone; what he must do now was to calm her down. She mustn't get excited, not at this stage.

He came rapidly down the steps. He looked neither at his wife, nor yet at his daughter, but addressed Molly, whose eyes were on him, her manner now showing her confidence in his protection–the master, her love, whom she knew she could twist round her little finger. He would show the mistress and the young one an' all what was what.

Her confidence was wiped away and her mouth brought again into its soft gape by the master addressing her as if someone of no account. 'Get back to the house, girl, and get on with your work.'

She paused a moment before obeying him. Even before that night when the master had come into the kitchen late on and found her with her skirts above her knees dozing in front of the fire, and she had waked to find his hand on her groin, even before that, he had never spoken to her uncivilly. It had always been, 'Molly girl, do this. Molly girl, do that.' But now he had spoken to her in the voice he used to gypsies and tramps on the road who came abeggin' and wanted food without offering to work for it.

As she sidled past him she cast a quick glance up at him, but his face was stern; she didn't recognize the man who only a few hours earlier had held her tightly and kissed her wounds. She scurried up the steps and when she reached the road, she burst out crying.

Now McBain looked at his daughter and he said, 'And you, Miss, get back to the house and to your room, I will talk with you later.'

Jane stared at her father, amazed that he was putting her in the wrong. It was as if she had committed the crime against her mother, and against himself, for in destroying his image he had destroyed the beauty of life for her. The rage that she had nurtured against Molly all afternoon, then had released on her, was now over like something that had never been. She felt weak and spent, and she did not seem to have the strength even to cry anymore. She wished she could die like the foal last week, just lay her head sideways on the straw and die, or be frozen stiff in the snow like the young lambs. Or, at this moment, she would even thank someone to stick a knife in her neck as they did with the pigs. She had not known how the pigs were killed, and when her curiosity had been satisfied, she was sick for days and wouldn't touch bacon for a long time.

She didn't want to live, and if it wasn't for her mother, she wouldn't live. But her mother was going to need her. As if she were being given a glimpse into the future, she knew she was the only one on whom her mother would be able to rely; she also knew that now all talk about her going to Madam Lovell's school in Hexham would cease. She would never go to that establishment and learn French and music and dancing.

A similar train of thought was passing through Delia's mind. The knowledge that had come to her in the last few minutes would alter life for all time. It wasn't just the fact that the man before her had had his way with a kitchen slut; she was no fool, there was hardly a household of any standing for miles around where the masters did not demand their pleasures from their female employees, and not only from girls not yet wedded; a working man's wife had to have a strong personality and be virtuous indeed if at least one of her many children did not show a marked resemblance to the man who employed her husband. And the husband might black his wife's eyes because he couldn't dole out that very medicine to the man on whom he relied for his bread.

No, it wasn't entirely the fact that her husband had been sporting with that skit of a girl while she herself was carrying his child. What was filling her with rage was that this man, who was looked up to, whom she herself had been forced to respect even while she had stopped loving him, was nothing but a hypocrite, a sanctimonious hypocrite, daring to stand in the pulpit Sunday after Sunday and read the Lesson, and sit smugly in their pew listening to old Parson Wainwright singing his praises after yet another donation towards the upkeep of the church: 'Our good Brother McBain has yet again come to our rescue.' She could hear the thick fuddled voice of the minister who more often than not was still carrying the previous night's load of port when he ascended the pulpit. And then Sir Alfred Tuppin, she could hear his thick guttural voice saying, 'Your husband, Mrs McBain, is an upright man. There are so few left in this England of ours today. Good stock, good stock, the McBains.' Such praise had even silenced her cynical self which at times would rise up and present her with a picture of McBain in the night. And she would recall the advice her cousin had given her before she married: 'There are two men in every husband,' she had said, 'a night man, and a day man. See that you satisfy the night man, and you will be both master and mistress of the day man.' Yet even as she offered this sop to herself from time to time she knew it to be trite and untrue, except in very rare cases. There was no opportunity given a woman to satisfy a man; the animals and the birds were more courteous to each other, more patient than a husband.

But still she could have forgiven all that, as she had always done, accepting it as part of a woman's existence. But not his play acting, his lapping up of homage as due payment for his integrity, the head held high, the clear eyes, the tones of the sage–in all appearing like a reflection of God, as it were.

'Take your hands off me!'

'Now, Delia, you must listen to me. I, I want you to listen to me.'

'You may want, Mr McBain, you may want.'

'Delia!'

'That, Mr McBain, is your "Thou shalt not" tone. Well, I may tell you that for some time now it has ceased to fill me with awe. Yet I have respected you . . . but never no more.' They were glaring at each other when she asked grimly, 'Will you go to church on Sunday, Mr McBain, and read the Lesson? Will you?' The last words were high and piercing, and he answered coolly, 'Delia, I command you, be quiet, keep calm for your own good. You must not get excited; you must think of the child.'

'Which child? Whose child? Mine, or hers?'

'Don't talk stupidly, Delia.' He again extended his hand towards her, saying briskly, 'Come.' But she stepped back from him, and she said again, 'I ask you, will you go to church on Sunday and read the Lesson?'

His patience was running short now and he answered grimly, 'Very likely, I see no reason why I shouldn't.'

'Do, do that, Mr McBain, go to church and read the Lesson. And do you know what I shall do? I shall scream the truth to the rafters. Enter that church again and I shall scream the truth to the rafters. I could forgive you for sporting with a low scut if you had ever accepted that you were an ordinary man, but you sported with her while playing God. In two months' time they are unveiling the stained glass window. Do you remember why you donated the window to the Church? In your own words you told Parson Wainwright it was because God had allowed your wife to carry your child. The window is to be unveiled the day your child, your *son* is born; it wasn't to be another daughter, no, no, you had told the Almighty it had to be a son and. . . .'

'Quiet, woman. How dare you!'

McBain's thin pale face was almost purple with rage now, but it was having no effect on his wife, for, looking at him, her eyes full of disdain, she said, 'I dare, Mr McBain, at last, after thirteen years, I dare.' And with this she passed him and walked with firm but heavy tread up the steps and onto the road.

McBain watched her, but he did not follow her; he stood now with closed eyes, his fists clenched tightly by his sides. There was running over his entire body a cold sweat. No one in his life before had dared talk to him as his wife had done. No one, except himself, had seen the man beneath the skin; but now his wife had seen him. She had called him a hypocrite, and he supposed she was right, he was a hypocrite, not only since he had begun to ease himself on Molly, but in the man he presented to outsiders, for this man had no connection with the one his wife was acquainted with in their personal life. He had used her roughly for years. But then that was his nature; it was ravenous for something he couldn't attain. He would have respected her more if she had turned on him and refused to put up with his madness; but she had never protested, and so he had used her. Yet all the while, underneath her apparent calmness, she had known him, known him for what he was, for what he knew himself to be, a man with an insatiable appetite that was like a disease. A two-faced man, a hypocrite.

He rubbed his hand hard around his face. What was he to do? If he stopped attending church, what excuse would he give? Illness? No. Dissent? No. He was a firm Protestant. The thought came to him that perhaps by Sunday he would have reasoned with her. He turned it aside. He had not been mistaken in his early suspicions of a self in her that he had no access to. He'd had glimpses of it when they first married, but he had soon subjected her to his wishes and, consequently, he had imagined, stifled all life out of the wayward self. But now he knew that that self had remained very much alive. There were two women in his wife, just as there were two men in himself.

But dominant self or no dominant self, she must not be allowed to get the upper hand. At the same time, he must tread very warily, even gently, with her until the child was born; once that was accomplished she could show to him whatever self she liked and he would deal with it.

He turned now and followed her, hurrying to catch up with her, so that they could enter the farm together. He must put a bold front on things, keep appearances normal, because he knew that the whole incident would blow over.

Chapter Two

McBain was more disturbed than he would admit to himself. The blowing over of the affair was going to take a stronger wind than he had anticipated. Something quite unprecedented had happened last night: Delia had refused him his bed. She had dared to refuse him his bed.

Sitting straight up against the pillows, a hand pressed tightly down on the bedclothes at each side of her, she had stared at him as she said, 'No more, Mr McBain. If you insist on getting in I shall get out and take up my room across the landing. And I promise you I shan't do it quietly. But you can save your face by going into another room; you might even convince people it is out of consideration for my condition. At least you can order them to accept such an explanation; what they might think privately is a different matter altogether.'

McBain was a passionate man but not a violent one. In that moment, however, he had the urge to knock her flying out of the bed and, more so, to use the whip on her, for he considered that she had earned it much more than ever young Molly had done, even if he hadn't been the man responsible. Yet while his desires raged in him, he had stood dumb before her, knowing she had him in a cleft stick; excite her, upset her, and the child could be brought ahead of its time. Like a cow in calf being chased by an unruly dog, she would drop what was in her without its being fully fledged.

Only his deep-seated craving for a son, a legitimate son, gave him the strength to turn from her without uttering a word.

By morning he had decided that if she could see Molly married and apparently out of reach of his hands, this would calm her. There was only one eligible man on the farm and that was Will Curran. He was forty-two years old, the same age as himself, and he was certainly not the man he would have chosen for Molly. But what other course was open to him? He had no doubt but that Curran would be willing; he was a widower these past five years. About Molly's reactions to the man he gave no thought. She would do as he bade her.

He rose, as he always did, at seven o'clock in the morning and followed the same pattern as always. Leaving the bedroom, he went into the closet room. One side of the room was taken up with a long wooden seat with three holes in it; underneath stood three pails, and high up on the wall behind each hole, suspended from a hook, was a lavender bag. Flanking the wall opposite the row of pails was a long narrow table, and on it, placed upside down in a neat row and ranging in size from an extra large one to a very small one, were ten spare chamber pots.

The first part of his ablutions over, he went into the dressing room. Here the whole length of a wall was taken up with a huge wardrobe, of which the frame was shining rosewood encasing three huge mirrors. Underneath the window at the end of the room stood a table, and on this there were two wash basins, with jugs inside. Over one was draped a white towel, through which a thin film of steam was permeating. A couch, a chair, and a bow-front chest-of-drawers were the only other articles of furniture in the room. It took him fifteen minutes precisely to wash and shave and dress. His working clothes were simple, consisting of cord knee breeches and a short homespun coat over a fresh white cotton shirt. His feet were encased in black boots freshly dubbined, his legs in black gaiters equally so.

He did not even glance at the communicating door leading into his bedroom as he passed it, but went out and across the landing and down the steep oak stairs.

When he entered the kitchen, Winnie was there alone. She did not look up from where she was cutting thick gammon rashers from a ham, but she said, as always, 'Mornin', Master,' and he replied, 'Good morning, Winnie.'

She now went to the stove and took from the hob a china teapot that was standing next to a homely brown one. She went to the end of the table where stood a tray holding a cup and saucer and a sugar basin, and having poured out a cup of tea that looked jet black, she spooned four heaped teaspoonfuls of sugar into it; then she handed the cup and saucer to her master.

Now, the master should have walked to the kitchen door, to stand looking out onto the farmyard, taking in in one sharp covering glance that everything was as it should be. Even in winter the procedure never altered. Sometimes she wished she could shout at him, as she would have to one of her own, 'For God's sake close that door, me legs are froze.' But this morning the master surprised her by walking towards the door through which he had entered only a few minutes previously, saying as he did so, 'Get Will Curran to me. If he has already gone to the fields, send a boy for him. I'll be in my office.'

Winnie did not say, 'Yes, Master,' until the door had almost closed on him.

Will Curran, on the point of leading the horses out of the yard and to the plough, was given the message by young Mickey. 'Me?' he said. 'Just gone seven in the mornin', Master wants me in the office?'

'That's what Winnie says,' said young Mickey.

'You're not havin' me on, boy, as hope?'

'No, Will, no. Winnie . . . look, there she is.' The boy pointed, and Will Curran looked towards the kitchen door where Winnie was waving him forward.

Three minutes later, chaffing his hands together as if to rid them of dirt, then wiping them down the back of his breeches, he knocked on the office door and was bidden to enter.

McBain looked at his ploughman and he didn't like what he saw; he had never liked the man. Perhaps it was his appearance that put him off, red hair, red nose, nearly always with a permanent drop on the end. He was an ignorant man–dull-witted in one way, yet sharp and sly in another.

His voice curt, the words clipped, he said, 'I won't beat about the bush, Curran. Are you agreeable to take a wife again?'

'A wife! Me, Master? What wife?'

'Molly.'

He watched three drops in rapid succession leave the end of Curran's nose, two being caught by the man's chin, and one falling to the floor. It was odd, but a thing like this could make him feel sick; there were niceties in him that years of dealing with animal nature had not erased.

Curran was now rubbing the palms of his hands together in a circular movement, but his voice had a touch of genuine amazement as he said, 'Molly! Why, she'd have no truck with me, Master; I'm a couple of years older than her dad.'

Ignoring this, McBain said, 'She wants a father for her child; no man has come forward. She will do as she is bid, if you are willing.'

Will Curran's head wobbled on his shoulders. A smile, sly, yet filled with amazement, spread over his face. 'I'm willin', Master. I'm as willin' as a tethered bull.'

'Very well. Get back about your work; I'll see you later.'

'Thanks, Master. Thank you, Master, thank you right kindly.' Will Curran was backing towards the door, touching his forelock, when McBain said to him, 'Tell Winnie to send Molly in to me.'

'Aye, Master. Aye, as will, Master.'

McBain sat back in his chair, drooped his head onto his chest, and waited. The term 'lamb to the slaughter' came to his mind. But Molly was no lamb; she hadn't even been a virgin when he took her for the first time, and she wasn't sixteen then. Whoever had taken her virginity she hadn't said, not even hinted at it; but one thing seemed certain, it hadn't been young Davie. The name coming into his mind made him think he was going to find it hard to replace young Davie; but still, there was never a good but that there was a better. Even so, he didn't like new faces about the place, and he'd always had a personal liking for the boy. But not for the man he had suddenly sprung into; it was no boy that had faced him across this desk yesterday. Still, it was a pity he had to go. But go he must; he could not allow himself to be thwarted by one of his work people.

When the tap came on the door he answered softly. 'Come in,' and Molly entered.

After closing the door behind her, she rested her buttocks against it for a moment, then came slowly forward. She had her eyes tight on his face, and she hesitated at the side of the desk wondering whether to go round to him or to stand with the desk between them as a servant should. Something in his face made her take the latter course and she took two further steps, then stopped and stared at him. What she saw disquietened her.

He wasn't the master of the malt house. He wasn't the man who tumbled her in the straw. There was no vestige now of the man who had to slip back from the fair to the malt house, nor of the man who had arranged there should be no one on the farm but old Sep Rummery, having taken the mistress and the young miss to Allendale visiting, and leaving them there while he supposedly went into Hexham on business. The business he had done was to take every stitch off her until she was as bare as the day she was born, and although she had experienced his lovemaking before and been surprised by it, there were things had happened in that one hour that she was sure had never happened to anybody else on God's earth. And she had protested against not one of them, but joyed with him; oh aye, she had joyed with him, and would be willing to die for just one such hour again.

She said softly, 'You sent for me, Master?'

'Yes, Molly.' He did not even put his hand out towards her. 'I have something to tell you.'

She watched his thin lips wetting each other; then her eyes sprang wide at his next words.

'I've arranged you should marry Curran. He is willing.'

She pushed her head back onto her shoulders and her mouth widened; then she swallowed deeply before gabbling, 'No! No! Master, not Will Curran. I couldn't, not him; him with his runny—' she had almost said *snotty*, 'him with his runny nose. And he's old, old . . . aw, Master, not him. Not Will Curran.'

He looked at her for a moment in pity while at the same time feeling gratified that she did not consider himself to be old. 'The child must have a name, Molly,' he said quietly.

'But Master!' She was now leaning across the desk, her face only a foot from his. 'I don't mind, I don't mind having the bairn and him claimin' no name, I don't, I don't.' She moved her head slowly now and, her face full of pleading, she gazed at him. And he could have been softened by the look of her if it weren't for the fact that if she were to roam loose about the place she would be a thorn in Delia's flesh, an agitation; and he could not risk that agitation. He said firmly, 'You must be married, Molly. I want to hear no more.' He rose to his feet.

'Master!' She rushed round the desk now and caught at his hand. 'I'll plead with Davie, I'll beg him to take me. I can make him do it; just give me time.'

'Your time will be wasted; he was up in the gallery of the malt house when we met yesterday.'

She put her hand tightly over the lower part of her face, and he nodded slowly at her. 'He had seen Miss Jane in distress and had gone to fetch her.'

Slowly she took her hand from her mouth and her head drooped, and like this she whispered, 'Will I be able to see you again, Master, if . . . if I marry Will Curran?'

Tenderly now, he put his hand under her chin and raised her face upwards and, his voice as low as hers, he answered, 'You'll see me again, Molly, when the time is ripe, never fear. Go now and do as you're bid and I'll always see that you are well looked after.'

She stared up into his eyes. She had been loved by this man, and she had known pride because of it, and power an' all, aye, power. She had defied her da because of the secret power her master's patronage had given her. But now she no longer felt she possessed any power. In spite of the master's promise, he was different. She couldn't understand it. Why? She had imagined she had him in the hollow of her hand. Her head on her chest, she walked out of the room.

McBain turned to his desk and, seating himself, he placed his hands palm downwards on the ordered pile of papers in front of him and stared ahead for a moment. This part of the business might not turn out so bad after all. If she had married young Davie, there would not have been much hope of their continued intimacy, no matter how much she manoeuvred, for Davie was no fool. But with Curran, she could handle Curran, and things would go on as before, for now that he had been deprived of his wife's bed until the child should be born and for some time afterwards, he must find release in whatever quarter was available. And he knew of none sweeter than Molly; neither of his wives had satisfied him as she had.

Until eleven o'clock in the morning he saw to the business of the farm, visiting the dairy, the byres, inspecting the animals; his eyes ranged knowledgeably around the harness room and the coach house where Davie was getting the gig ready. He passed him without a word. But when, in the grain store, he gave a good morning to old Sep, who was setting the terrier onto a rat's nest, and received no verbal reply, only a curt motion of the head, he walked briskly out and across the yard and into the fields. He was annoyed. There had been disdain in the old man's look, and the movement of his head had been no answer to his morning greeting, rather it had been one of censure.

He walked to the top of Shale Tor from where he could see his sheep, well outside the precincts of the farm, away up on the distant hills. And nearer, his herd of eighty cows were grazing in the morning meadows. They were the best herd he had reared and he was proud of them. He was going into Hexham this morning to meet Parson Wainwright and the Hospital Board with a view to passing on to the hospital any milk which was surplus to that which he sold to the town. He was a member of the Hospital Board, and also of the Board of Guardians. Parson Hedley had proposed that he should allocate the milk to the Workhouse, but he was not for this at all—not good, full cream milk. He had already made an allowance of skimmed milk to that establishment, and he did not believe in pampering the poor and feckless; Parson Wainwright seconded him strongly in this.

By eleven o'clock he had returned to the farm and was ready for his journey to town. Going into the kitchen, he said to Winnie, 'Where is the mistress?'

'In the sewin' room, Master, along o' Miss Jane. The seamstress has come from Allendale.'

He noticed that Winnie had not stopped her work when he spoke to her, nor had she looked at him once today. He felt angry that she dare show her displeasure at the turn of events. Who were they, these Armstrongs? What were they? Chattels, depending entirely on him for their livelihood. They lived well, he was a good master to them; his private life was no concern of theirs and should have brought no response from them. He said curtly, 'Tell your mistress I shall be back in time for dinner,' and on this he went out.

Winnie looked towards the door that had banged closed, and she muttered under her breath, 'Aye, I'll tell her, but not that she'll care much what time you'll be back, not from the looks of her this mornin'.'

In this moment she loathed the master. She had always looked upon him as a good master, not too easy to get on with, but fair and honest in his dealings. But now that she knew him for what he was, she realized that she had never liked him, and she hated him now for being the cause of her losing her son. And she was going to lose Davie, for he was bent on leaving. Any day now he would just walk out and tramp to Newcastle, that was what he was going to do, and there find a ship, a ship that would take him round the world so that he could see places. That's what he said. He was glad, he said, things had happened as they had done, or otherwise he would have been stuck here for life and never known what he was missing.

She stopped kneading the dough in the big brown earthenware dish and looked down at her hands half lost in the elastic mounds of paste. Her life would be empty without her lad. She had never imagined them parted. He would marry, of course, oh aye, and have children, but she had imagined her life would start over again with his children. And now she was to be left with her father and her husband; her father, galloping rapidly towards the grave, and her husband a creaking door that might go on forever, yet so eaten up with rheumatics that he had forgotten, even now, how to live. The prospect of life ahead was dull and empty because the days would pass and the weeks would pass, aye, and the years would pass, and she might never see her lad again.

McBain returned at quarter to three in the afternoon. He was wet to the skin, for the weather, which had been unusually fine for the past two weeks, had suddenly changed, and he had driven through heavy rain. He was highly irritated and not a little troubled. The meeting with the Hospital Governors should have been pleasant. Usually, the manner of individual members towards him conveying their respect, which he had come to look upon as his right, pleased him; but there had been something lacking in their attitude today. One, a farmer from as far away as Haydon Bridge, had slyly prodded him with the words, 'Hear you had to do a little chastisin' of a female yesterday gone.'

He had stared at the man fixedly for a moment; he was a person for whom he had no feeling, a type of farmer who smelt strongly of the byres even in his best clothes. He had answered him, 'News travels fast,' and the man had come back with, 'As fast as the crow flies.'

The crow would have had to fly all of fifteen miles to get to this man's farm, and he gauged that if he knew about the incident, so then did the others present.

During the remainder of his short stay in the Assembly Rooms he had searched one face after another, looking for some reaction to the news that he had flayed a maidservant, for, to a man, he would have expected them to say, 'Those days are gone, the time is past when you can flay a servant.' All except one, that is. Old Parson Hetherington, the parson, was for subjugation of the flesh.

When he entered the yard no one ran to take the horse's head, and he glared about him before he got down from the trap. Where was everyone, skulking away because of the wet?

It was his practice whenever embarking on or returning from a journey, however short, always to leave and enter the house by the front way, but as he crossed the yard he saw Winnie coming from the direction of the kitchen door. She had a ripped sugar bag over her head, the corner not standing straight up but weighed down with water, and the expression on her face and her wet condition brought from him, 'What is it? What's the matter?'

'The mistress, Master, she left the house shortly after you was gone; to take a walk, she said, but now it's past four o'clock an' has been stormin' hard this two hours or more.'

'Where did she go?' As he spoke, he glanced around as if about to dart off, and she said, 'It's no knowin', Master; I've sent them out in all directions. I was anxious afore it started to rain an' sent Mickey lookin'. And Miss Jane was along the road waiting for her long afore that. But there wasn't a sight of her, and so I took the liberty of tellin' my Davie to take Prince and ride over towards Harper Town.'

'Harper Town? She would never get as far as Harper Town.'

'The mistress is a good walker, Master, and she had a hankerin' after that part, to look at the Castle over Featherstone, an' the river. On the other hand, she might have skirted it and gone straight over to Plenmeller Common.'

'Don't be a fool, woman.' He turned on her angrily now. The very thought of Delia walking as far as Plenmeller Common, let alone being on it in a storm such as this, filled him with anxiety, for the mist coming down unheralded, as it was apt to do in these parts, could in a matter of seconds turn a warm atmosphere into an icy blast and blind one to direction; unless you knew the ground with the knowledge of a shepherd, you could wander for hours.

'You have no idea of the direction she took?'

'None, Master.' Winnie's tone was stiff.

'Well, then,' he cried at her, his voice still angry as if she alone were responsible for the situation, 'she could have gone over there . . . over there . . . or over there!' He pointed rapidly in three different directions. 'To Whitfield Moor, or Slaggyford, or she could even have reached Glen Dhu and gone over the waterfall, or to Nine Banks and taken up residence in the Peel.'

Winnie stared at him. He was being sarky, but that showed he was very troubled, and right he had to be troubled an' all.

He was stalking away from her when he turned and shouted, 'Why had you to give him Prince?' and, forgetting for a moment that she was talking to her betters, she bawled back at the top of her voice as she would have at one of her own men, ''Cos he was the fastest thing on the place, if you want to know.'

Her manner checked him for a moment, but only for a moment; there would be time to deal with her later.

There was no one in the stables and no one in the harness room. He grabbed up a saddle and hurried with it to the stable, passing the gig and the patient standing horse. He could have gone searching in that, but only on the main roads, and then they, too, would soon be quagmires. Anyway, of one thing he was sure, wherever Delia had gone, it wouldn't be for a walk along the main roads. She had done this to spite him. If anything happened to his child, if this brought her on before her time he would. . . . He paused, checking the thought that he would kill her with his own hands.

As he galloped out of the gate little Mickey Geary came plodding along the road towards him, and he pulled the horse up and shouted down at him, 'Well!'

'No sign of mistress, Master. Bin up on Peel and as far away as the start of Whitfield.'

He urged the horse on into a gallop and in the direction of Beltingham; this way he could take in Plenmeller Common from the east side.

The rain increased, and when a distant roll of thunder came to his ears he gritted his teeth. God help her if she succeeded in thwarting him.

Two hours later, soaked to the skin, outwardly cold yet burning inside with a mixture of righteous indignation and fear, he entered the farmyard to hear sounds coming from the cow byres. The animals were in and had been milked. He barked at a figure crossing the yard half hidden by a sack. 'Here! Take him,' and Fred Geary turned and came towards him.

Dismounting stiffly he said to the man, 'Your mistress, has she returned?'

'Aye, she's returned, Master.' Geary's tone gave him no information, it was just a statement.

He drew in a deep breath and hurried from him and into the house. Winnie was coming down the stairs. She paused halfway, then came on towards him.

'How is she? Where has she been? How long has she been in?'

She answered the three questions in their order. 'She's in some distress, Master. She lost her way on the Common in the rain. She's been back this half hour.' Then she added, 'Miss Jane found her.' She prevented herself from going further and saying, 'The child was in as bad a state as her mother,' for she knew he wasn't concerned with his daughter's welfare, not yet for that matter with his wife's: his main thought centred round what she was carrying. He was a single-minded man was the master, always had been, except for diversions now and again. Since yesterday she had called to mind a diversion he'd had some years ago. That had been with a girl hardly out of childhood an' all. A strange man was the master. She went on into the kitchen, he up the stairs, and without ceremony he entered the bedroom.

Delia was undressed and in bed. Her face was pale, and her breathing was deep and inclined to gasping. He stood over her and stared at her, but she did not return his look. Her eyes were hooded, their gaze directed over the mound of her stomach towards her feet.

'What madness have you been up to?'

She remained silent while she imagined, as she had often before, that there was no measurement she knew of which could take the depth of his voice when he was angry or even merely displeased. The tone was so thin it flattened the words until they had no substance, yet it held and maintained some element that pierced like the point of a knife.

'You did this on purpose, didn't you? In retaliation.' He waited for some response before going on, 'All right, retaliate against me, but save it until the child is born. You can spend the coming weeks working out ways and means to make me suffer for my lapse, but I warn you. . . .' Now his body was bent over hers, drips of water from the front of his hair actually dropping onto the breast of her nightgown, 'If you purposely harm that child, if you have harmed it by your escapade today, you will live to regret it. You know me, Delia. When I speak, as now, I don't make idle threats.' Slowly he straightened his body, and again he waited, but still she made no response.

Not until he had left the room did she raise her eyes. Then she looked towards the door, and when she heard him shouting from the top of the stairs: 'Winnie! See that I have hot water for bathing in the closet room immediately,' she knew how far she had tested him, for he never shouted his orders around the house. Always on his guard, always giving the good example, his tone might be icy, but he kept it controlled. Now, like any ordinary common farmer, he was bawling at his servants.

She lay staring up at the ceiling. She felt exhausted, slightly ill. She'd had no intention of hurting the child. What had happened today had come about purely by accident. She was on the Common and about to turn for home when the storm had overtaken her. At one period she had become frightened, at another resigned, and had thought, If I lie down and this rain continues all night, I could be well on the way to death in the morning, and it with me. But she had not lain down, she had tried to find her way home. She had not known that she was only a short distance from the road until she heard Jane's voice crying, 'Mother! Mother! Are you there, Mother?' But for her daughter's timely coming, she might have had to lie down through sheer exhaustion. That being the case he would have said it was deliberate, as he did not. But what matter? What matter anything? She was very tired and no longer cold, her body was burning, her heart was burning, scalded.

Chapter Three

'Don't talk of the morrow, lad.' Winnie, her shoulders stooped with weariness, gazed sadly at her son. 'Wait until I have time to get me breath an' talk to you, quiet like, and know what you're going to do. As it is, I'm run off me legs over there and I'm droppin' for want of sleep. He says I've got to sit by her the night again. I wonder what he thinks I am, a machine that doesn't need rest? So, lad,' she put out her hand and touched Davie's shoulder, 'let it rest for a day or two. He hasn't actually told you to go, now has he? If you're determined to go, well, you can pick your own time, but wait until the mistress is on her feet again.'

'But when will that be, Ma?'

'Soon as the fever goes down, a couple of days at the most I should say.'

'Is she goin' to lose it?' Sep leaned forward in his chair. 'A fever such as this could bring it on.'

Winnie bit on her lip and turned her head to the side as she said, 'I hope to God she doesn't, there'll be hell to pay, he'll go mad. Yet I could bet ten to one she's havin' her pains, though she doesn't say.'

'How could she keep quiet, havin' pains?' Ned cast a disdainful glance at his wife.

'She could.' Her voice was harsh. 'She's got an inner stubbornness. It doesn't show, but it's there. I've 'tected it more than once. Still I hope to God I'm wrong; she's had enough to put up with in her life without this final blow. An' if he were to lose his son. . . .'

'Son be damned!' Davie's voice cut her short. 'How does he know what it'll be, has he had a word on the side with God Almighty? I bet he thinks he has, the psalm-singing holy lecher.'

'That's enough!' His father's voice cut him short, but he turned on him, crying, 'It isn't enough, Da. An' don't try to shut me up here; if I can't speak me mind in me own home, then I'd better clag me mouth up altogether, for I can't open it outside.' He paused and looked from one to the other, then ended, 'By God! Things want changin' in this country; they've got us all so bloody nooled, we're no better than the slaves, it wants a Wilberforce here. Charity begins at home. An' they're pattin' themselves on the back for freeing the Boers from the Zulus, when it's us that wants freeing. As do the Irish; no wonder there's risin's there. If they can free the bloody Boers, why can't they let the Irish rule their own country and not have them floodin' us an' takin' the bread out of our mouths. They hate Parnell; I say good luck to him.'

Mother, father, and grandfather gaped at him. They had never heard of Parnell, nor yet of Wilberforce; no one of them could read. The bedroom in the roof held a conglomeration of old newspapers and three books, all passed on to him by Parson Hedley. He never discussed what he read, but, in this moment, his garbled smattering of world events made him appear as a being apart, a creature of another species, older than themselves, very learned.

Winnie felt a warm pride flood her, a pride that brought a smarting of tears to the back of her eyes. This lad of hers would go places, he would become something; with a mind as knowledgeable and inquisitive as his, nothing could stop him once he got away. No matter what her private feelings were, she knew it was a good thing for him that he was leaving the farm.

To stop her tears from falling she applied herself to everyday necessities by saying, 'That's as it may be, but there's a meal to see to and I cannot get it; you'll have to fend for yourselves 'cos I'm away across again.' She went hastily towards the door, but there she turned and looked at Davie, and as their gazes linked and held she knew he would do as she had asked and not go yet awhile.

As she went out of the front door of the cottage Ned rose from his seat and went out the back way, down to the midden. He was distressed at the thought of his son going, but could not show it. But not so old Sep. The old man, looking at his grandson, said slowly, 'You're fixed in your mind then, lad?'

'Aye, Granda.'

'Well, I'm not blamin' you, no fraction of me is blamin' you, but I'll tell you one thing. Things'll never be the same when you're gone. If you take to the sea, how long do you reckon you'll be away?'

'Hard to tell, Granda. It could be a year, two maybe, or three.'

'Aye, that is what I was fearin'.' He nodded. 'Well, I only hope I'll be here when you come back. Now,' he raised his hand, 'I'm not latherin' you with soft soap; I'll go when me time comes an' not afore. But I can tell you this much, if I was your age and livin' in this changing day–although I can neither read nor write I can tell the signs, you've only got to be half an hour in the town to see them–aye, things are changin' and changin' fast, an' as I said, if I was in your shoes, lad, I'd be off the morrow and matchin' up to the times, for after all what is life but a feather in the fire. We're all feathers in the fire; time passes on us like a flick of flame. One minute we're there, the next we're gone, forgotten, as if we'd never been.'

'I wouldn't say that, Granda.'

'It's true, it's true, lad, and remember it. Kings and great men are forgotten, so why should the likes of us be remembered.'

'I'll never forget you, Granda, never fear.' Davie walked towards the old man and, bending, put his hand on his shoulder. It was an unusual gesture of affection, perhaps the first open expression of their love for each other since he had been a small boy. 'You're a wise man, Granda. I have always known you to be a wise man, and you'll not be forgotten, at least not by me. Anyway—' he punched the old man playfully in the chest, 'what you talkin' about? You'll likely be smokin' that stinking old pipe of yours when I'm pushin' the daisies up, or more likely chasing the mermaids at the bottom of the sea.'

Although old Sep laughed now, he said, 'Don't talk like that, lad. If you pray for anything, pray that you die on dry land and be settled to rest firmly in the ground.'

At this point the back door opened and Ned entered. Looking from one to the other he asked sharply, 'Does nobody want to eat?' and at this they all three set about getting the evening meal, which was, as usual on Friday, as on Thursday, Wednesday, and Tuesday, mutton broth.

For the second night running Winnie sat by the mistress's side, and tonight there was more need for her presence. Although the mistress wouldn't admit it, Winnie was positive she was having pains; if not, then she must be suffering some sort of cramping seizure.

The truth was that Delia was having pains. Though her temperature was high and at times her head swam and was full of strange thoughts, she nevertheless knew she must not admit to the pains. She told herself to lie still, perfectly still, and everything inside her would settle. Anyway they were not true pains; the intervals between them, she considered, were too long to be true pains, and she mustn't have true pains. When she thought of true pains, she saw McBain's face hanging over her. She heard his voice again, saying, 'If you purposely harm that child, if you have harmed it by your escapade today, you will live to regret it. You know me, Delia. When I speak as now, I don't make idle threats.'

She was aware that he visited her frequently, but she never looked at him. Although her hidden strength had come to the surface and she dared now to defy him, there still remained in her a fear of him. The fear had been with her too long, and was too well founded on her private knowledge of him for her to erase it now, and she dreaded the consequences if she failed to carry his child to its time.

It was towards eleven o'clock at night that a pain attacked her which told her that the child was coming and nothing she could do would prevent it. She had been waked from a nightmarish dream by a grinding in her loins; it was a well remembered experience and couldn't be disregarded. As it forced the truth on her, she gripped handfuls of the bed tick in an effort to stifle her moans and still her fear. Winnie was sitting by the bedside, her head drooped in sleep, and when she put out her hand towards her, Winnie didn't move. The pain subsided, and she gave herself the ease of gasping.

She leaned on her side and stared towards the fire. It was bright and had recently been tended. The lamp, too, was burning steadily. Should she waken Winnie? No, no, what was she thinking about? She'd run straight to her master. Anyway, she was tired, worn out. Let her sleep. She lay back and looked at her servant, and wished from the bottom of her heart that she could change places with her. She was the centre of a close family, the pivot around which father, husband, and son revolved. She envied her her life.

Winnie opened her eyes and blinked; then bending forward, said quickly, 'You all right, Mistress?'

'Yes, Winnie.'

Winnie put out her hand and touched the deep brow. 'Ah, that's better, you're cooler.'

'Am I, Winnie?'

'Yes, Mistress.'

'Winnie.'

'Yes, Mistress.'

'Hold my hand.'

Slowly Winnie put out her square, broken-nailed hand and clasped the slender white one held towards her, and after a moment she asked softly, 'Are you sure you're all right, Mistress?'

Delia didn't answer, she just nodded, and at this point Winnie, who was never given to tears, had for the second time in two days a strong inclination to cry.

At seven o'clock the next morning when she handed McBain his tea in the kitchen, she answered his question. 'She's better in that the fever's gone down.'

As he took the cup from her he said shortly, 'Well, is there anything else?'

'I can't say, Master, only that she seems tired.'

'Rest will cure that. There's . . . there's no sign of the child coming?'

'She doesn't say, Master.'

'Say or not,' his voice had risen, 'you'd be able to tell.'

And now, also for the second time in two days, her voice rose to answer him. 'How can I tell when she gives no sign? I am no doctor.'

He gritted his teeth while he stared at her; then forcing himself to calmness, he added, 'Well, you don't think the fever has had any effect?'

She turned her head to the side and shook it as she answered, 'Not that I can say at the moment, Master. Yet the mistress is not herself.'

He turned away and walked to the door. He was well aware that she was not herself, but her emotional condition didn't trouble him; as long as she held on to what was in her and gave it a chance of life, that's all that he was concerned about at the moment.

So much did this matter take up his mind that Molly, coming out of the far door of the dairy, caused no ripple to pass through him. She was carrying two large pails of skim and dropped them with a clatter on a small platform ready for Johnnie to pick up and take to the pigs, and when she hitched up her full breasts with the cushions of her thumbs, there was no tightening of his loins, no deep drawing in of breath.

He finished his tea and turned from the door and, coming back into the kitchen, said, 'You think she necessitates the doctor?'

Again Winnie turned her head to the side and shook it before saying, 'That's up to you, Master. That's up to you.'

Yes, that was up to him, but the last person he wanted to talk with Delia at this moment was old Cargill. He was a fusspot, a gossiping, probing fusspot. By now, like all those in Hexham, he would have heard of the flaying, and were he to call, he would, with a question here, a nudge there, as he sauntered around the farm, come to the truth quicker than any judge, after which he himself would be in for a long rigmaroling admonition. No, he didn't want Cargill here just to attend her in a fever. But if he thought there was the slightest suspicion that the child was affected, then he would gallop into the town himself and fetch him.

He glanced at Winnie again. She'd know. She was a knowledgeable woman, a sensible woman, and she had an affection for her mistress, so therefore her perception would be keener.

Winnie brought his attention to her again as she said, 'Who's to stay when you're all at church, Master? I think it should be somebody who could use his legs, just in case; me da's not much use in that way.'

He was walking towards the door again as he said briefly, 'I'll be here.'

Although Delia in her present state could not carry out her threat of denouncing him in church, he thought that her indisposition would not only supply an excuse for his absence today, but also for the coming Sundays ahead until the child was born. After that he would meet events as they came. One thing he was certain of, once the boy was born, he'd put her in her place again.

The pain that now rent her body seemed to split it in two. It had attacked her quite suddenly, waking her from a half-dazed sleep. To save herself from crying out against it, she bit tight down on the side of her hand, and when it had passed she lay gasping.

The sound of her heavy breathing should have brought Molly from the dressing room, but it didn't. When the sweat had cleared from her eyes she looked towards the open door where, reflected through the mirror of the wardrobe in the light of the lamp, she could see the girl, her head lolling to the side as she slept in an upright chair.

She had said to Winnie, who was very tired, 'Go and rest, I'll be all right,' but Winnie wouldn't listen until McBain had commanded, 'Go to bed, woman, the girl will take your place.' Then she herself had been forced to protest and had cried at him, 'I do not need a watchdog. Anyway, Jane can sit with me.'

To this he had replied calmly, 'Jane has been on her feet all day, she is worn out. Anyway, you need a night-attendant, a nurse, and tomorrow morning I'm sending into Hexham for one, and the doctor, too. You have been too long in this state for your health.'

She had lifted her hand and dismissed Winnie from the room. Then looking at him fully for the first time in days, she had muttered from deep in her throat, 'I will not have the girl in this room. Nor will I have her in the house once I am about.' And he had turned his back on her as he gave her his reply, 'She will sit in the dressing room within call. As for your whims, we will deal with them when the time comes.'

Winnie had come up before going home at nine o'clock and had said soothingly, 'I will just take a few hours, Mistress. In the meantime, if you should feel you want me, call to her and she will come and fetch me.'

She had almost put her hand out and said, 'Sleep here, Winnie,' but had she done so, it would have shown her alarm, and so she had allowed them to install the girl in the dressing room, and for well into the night she had lain and watched her. Twice she had disappeared from view and gone into the closet room. At this, she had wanted to shout, 'Come away from that room, girl. How dare you! Go out to your midden, that is your place, the midden.'

Yet as she berated the girl in her mind, she knew the situation wasn't of her making; although she had become a party to it she would never, in the first place, have dared to approach McBain.

As another pain seized her she wondered why she was trying to hide the fact that the child was about to be born. What would it avail her now? She brought up her knees to her chest and groaned; then she cried aloud as the whole of her inside slipped into a flaming hell of pain, and now with her eyes screwed up tight, she groaned, 'Girl! Girl!'

When the spasm eased for a second and she opened her eyes, there was no one by her side. She could not see the girl through the mirror now because her vision was blurred with sweat. Again her body was shot into pain, so excruciating this time that she lost consciousness. When she came to herself she was lying on her back, her legs wide apart, and the child's head had thrust itself into life. When the shoulders followed, she screamed a thin, high piercing scream, and to her own voice was joined another, and she knew the girl was with her. She heard her yelling, 'Master! Master!' There followed another pain . . . and then another . . . and then great ease.

Her eyes were closed, everything was quiet. She felt that she herself had stopped breathing. In the peace she lifted her lids and saw McBain standing halfway down the bed. He had on his long nightshirt and he was staring downwards, as was the girl standing by his side. Slowly she allowed her limbs to relax, and now she lifted her head slightly and looked down along her deflated body, and there, lying between her legs on the blood-stained sheet and still attached to her, was her child–or part of her child. There was something wrong with it, something missing. She looked upwards to her husband's face, and God in His wrath could never have looked like this. She took refuge against it in unconsciousness.

The turmoil in McBain's brain was something beyond even his own understanding, for the feelings of revulsion, anger, and disappointment were so deep, so desolate, that they combined to a torture, and when he looked back he knew that for a space of time his brain had been turned, and that, like any madman, he might have committed a crime, except that Molly had torn his hands from his wife's neck, then had dragged him into the dressing room, pleading with him while she repeated just one word, 'Master! Master!'

Not until she had managed to thrust him down into the chair, saying, 'Stay, stay, Master, for God's sake, while I get Winnie,' did a little of his sanity return, and he checked her with his hand gripping her arm. Then he wiped the sweat from his face while he gulped air into his lungs, and he continued to hold her until he had the power to speak, when he said, 'Take . . . take it out and bury it.'

'Master!'

'Do as I bid you.'

'B . . . but, Master.'

'Go on, do what I say. And quickly.'

She backed from him and slowly went into the bedroom, and as if approaching a lion's cage, she went towards the bed. And there she separated the mother and child. The cutting of the umbilical cord was not new to her; she had helped her mother on several occasions. And she knew what to do with a newborn child; if it didn't yell straight away, you took it by the legs and held it upside down.

Frantically she looked about her for something to put round the child. Her eyes alighting on the mistress's cashmere shawl, she grabbed it and put it over the infant, then rolled it onto its face, so that she could lift it up without touching it. As she straightened her back it gave a thin cry, and at this her eyes and mouth sprang wide and her terrified glance went towards the dressing room door, then returned to the wrinkled face peeping out from the folds of the shawl, and she muttered, 'Oh, God Almighty!' Placing the child on the day couch at the foot of the bed, she ran into the dressing room and, standing before McBain, she spluttered, 'I, I can't. I c . . . can't, Master, 'tis alive, breathin'.'

McBain had been sitting with his head deep on his chest, almost as if he were asleep; and now his whole body jerked upwards and he grasped her again, by both arms this time, and slowly he said, 'Listen to me, girl. It's for the best. You have seen it; imagine if it were allowed to live. Each time I looked on it I would see it as God's hand on me in retribution . . . you understand?' He stared into her red sweating face. He knew she was a simple girl and here he was, asking her to understand something he was only dimly comprehending himself. It was all bound up with the saying that God is not mocked. Delia had been right, but he felt the retribution wasn't because he had lusted with this young girl so much as that he had done it while praising God. Jesus Christ's one abhorrence was a hypocrite, and the thing in there was God's answer to hypocrisy. And in this moment he hated God for it.

'No, Master, no.' She was whimpering like a hurt animal.

'Molly, you love me?'

'Aye, Master.'

'Then do as I bid you. Look.' He got to his feet, still holding her. 'Take it to the copse and drop it into the pool, the bog part.'

Her head was back on her shoulders wagging in desperation, 'But what'll you say, Master, what'll you tell them? Dead or alive, Winnie and Miss Jane, they'll expect to see it.'

He shook her impatiently now, then whispered, 'It came away in bits. Tell them that, it came away in bits and you put it in the muck cart. When you come back, you can take the after-birth and dump it there. Go now, go on.'

He thrust her towards the bedroom door, and like someone drunk, she staggered into the room again. Stopping for a moment she looked over the foot of the bed at the inert, distorted, unsightly figure of her mistress; then she grabbed the small bundle in the shawl and crept out of the room.

When she reached the bottom of the stairs and heard a door above her open with a squeak, she knew that Miss Jane had waked up, and at this she took to her heels and flew through the kitchen, out into the yard, and along the road towards the copse.

Davie sat on the side of his bed looking out of the low attic window. The rain had stopped, and the moon was shining and seemed to be wafted from one scud of clouds to another by the high wind that was blowing. There were only the clouds and the noise in the chimney breast behind him to indicate the strength of the wind; as far as he could see, the land was treeless, and fell, to rise again sharply to the hills beyond. His vision did not take in the copse that lay to the right of him, for his head was resting against the wooden shutter that barred the window from the inside and kept out the weather in the winter.

This was to be the last night he would sleep in this room for a long time to come. He didn't know how long, years perhaps, or never again. He felt sad, depressed. Yet at the same time he was experiencing an odd kind of elation, for whatever lay before him would be strange and exciting. He gave no thought to a hungry belly, or hardship; he was young and strong, and, as he told himself, he had his wits about him; what was more, he had advantage over the majority of his kind, for he could read and write and, if it was required of him, talk with the best of them, at least so he told himself. But nevertheless, he was sad, deeply sad. He was going to miss his mother, and he would even miss his father; but most of all, aye most of all, he'd miss his Granda.

It was odd, he thought, but if the events of yesterday had not taken place, he might in the end, in fact he knew he would, have married Molly Geary and remained for the rest of his life on this farm, in this hollow in the hills, and might never have got even as far as Alnwick. He had promised himself for the last two or three years that one day he would go to Alnwick and see the castle, the stronghold of the Percys. Parson Hedley had told him quite a bit about the Percys—great fighting men, the Percys, men it was an honour to serve. He wished now he could go back down the centuries and ride by young Hotspur's side, even if he was but a lad of twelve, and with him retake Berwick and kill every damn Scot in it, his master included. For it was McBain's boast that his forebears went back to the fourteenth century. He had a sword hanging in the hall that he was forever pointing out was used at Duns when the Scots routed the English, but he never said nought about the defeat of 50,000 of the hairy-legged galoots being beaten by half their number at Neville's Cross. Why, when he came to think of it, what was McBain, compared with men like the Percys? Midden muck, that's all, midden muck.

Two days ago he wouldn't have thought of the comparison, but now it seemed apt, not because he had found out about the master whoring, nor that he had hidden his escapades under a cloak of piety. No, his animosity was derived from the personal insult McBain had directed towards his manhood. He had wanted Davie to marry Molly, to cover up for his own fly-blow. Like hell he would. If he was to father a child, he would know the beginnings of it as well as the end. Oh aye. By, she was a rampant cow, that Molly. You found them here and there among the stock; not for them, waiting their turn. Right at the front they were, almost putting the bull to shame.

As if his thoughts had conjured up their substance into form, he saw her. She came running into a patch of moonlight opposite Curran's back gate. She was on the grass bank raised above the lane and was carrying something in her arms. He bent forward, his face close to a small pane. What was she up to at this time of night, or mornin' as it was? Where could she be making for, running along the bank? It was a dead end, the railing shut off the copse.

A cloud distorted her shape for a moment. The wind was lifting her skirt into a half circle behind her legs, and she looked as if she were flying.

He stood up but still stooped and moved his head to the other side of the window. He saw that she had reached the railings, and he watched her drop the bundle onto the ground, and climb over, and then she was gone into the low shrub, all except her hands that came out and pulled the bundle under the bottom rail.

He stepped three paces back from the window to where the ceiling allowed him to stand straight and he looked from one corner of the little room to the other as if he would find the answer to his thoughts. What was she taking into the copse at this time of night? It was dangerous in there in the daytime; there was bog all round the water hole. Whatever she had with her was meant for the water hole. But what?

He did not wait any longer for an answer but pulled open the door and ran down the stairs; and as he rushed out of the back door, he heard his mother's voice crying, 'Is that you, Davie, you awake?' Within seconds he had reached the railing and was over it and into the copse. He paused for a moment and listened; but the wind covered all sound but its own thrashing. There were two narrow paths not more than twenty feet apart, and both leading to the water hole. They had been made many years ago before the springs had started to divert and make the place a danger to man and cattle.

Before he reached the end of the path he had taken, he saw her. She was standing on the edge of the bog looking down at the thing she was holding in her hands. The moon was full on her and she was rigid, but she was evidently going to throw whatever she was carrying into the pool, and once in there, it would be lost forever–it was said to be bottomless. He had never tried to prove this; even his adventurous boyish spirit hadn't been brave enough to test the depth of this awesome place, not after he had seen the cow sink like a stone in the mud at the edge.

'What you up to?' He thought for a moment she was going to fall backwards into the bog and he rushed forward and gripped her arms that were in turn gripping the bundle to her.

'What you up to? What's this?' He had to hold onto her to keep her steady, for her whole body was now shaking like a cart going over a rutted road. He took one hand from her arm and touched the top of the bundle; then he pulled the blanket back and gazed downwards.

'Aw, my God! You! You! You wicked hussy, you!'

'No, no, Davie, no, no, I would-n't, I could-n't have.'

'What did you come in here for then?'

'The master. But . . . but I couldn't.'

'You would if I hadn't stopped you, an' it breathing an' all.'

He pulled the shawl farther away from the face; then he said in a deep tone that might have been used by Pastor Wainwright, 'If there's a hell, you'll go to it for this.'

'Davie! Davie.' She was crying now and loudly. 'I wouldn't, I wouldn't.'

'Shut up! an' get back.' He gripped her by the shoulders and pushed her forward, and she tried to turn to him as she spluttered, 'You don't know, you don't know, Davie.'

'Go on, out of it.' He thrust her along the path until they reached the railings, and there he let go of her. She pushed the bundle under the bottom rail, and when she tried to climb over, she almost fell onto the other side. She did not stoop immediately and pick up the bundle, but stood leaning against the rails gasping as she looked up at him. The tears were raining from her eyes, her mouth was wide; she tried to speak, but the words were choked in her throat.

He bent down to her.

'Get!' He pointed, and at this he stooped and picked up the child again. And once more he was pushing her forward and toward the figure that was now standing in the road outside the front door.

Winnie, a coat over her calico nightgown, came towards them, saying under her breath, 'What in the name of God is it! What's happened?'

'Get inside.'

Her eyes flashed from him to Molly; then she hurried back into the cottage and he followed her, still thrusting Molly before him.

Although there was a candle burning on the kitchen table, the light in the cottage was dim compared with that outside. Davie peered towards the stairs, where his father was descending with his Granda behind him. His Granda was saying, 'What's up? What's up, lad?'

For answer he turned to Molly, saying, 'You tell them.'

Molly now dropped the bundle on the table and leaned over it, shoulders shaking, her sobbing uncontrolled, and Winnie, going to her, said, 'What is it, girl, what is it?'

But all Molly could say was, 'I wouldn't have, I couldn't, I couldn't.'

Winnie put her hand out tentatively towards the bundle, asking now, 'What have you in there?' and before Molly could answer, David cried, 'Go on, tell her. Tell her what you've got in there, an' what you were aiming to do with it.'

They were all surprised at Molly's next reaction for, turning from the table and gulping on each word, she bawled at him, 'You! You! God you are, aren't you? God. Well I wouldn't have, no matter what you think, I wouldn't have. I couldn't, I was just wonderin' what to do. Even though the master bade me.'

Taken aback for a moment Davie remained silent, as they all were, and then he said, 'He told you to drown a bairn? The missus's bairn . . . couldn't be anybody else's.'

'Aye, aye, he did. An' 'cos why, cleversides. Look, look.' She now swung round to the table and tore the blanket first one way and then the other from the tiny form.

They all stared down at the little creature. It had a head and two arms and a body, but no legs. There were two fleshy protrusions where the legs should have been and from these hung two pieces of distorted flesh, what might have been termed, with a stretch of imagination, a pair of feet.

'God save us this night.' It was a faint whisper from Winnie, but it was echoed in the eyes of the three men.

There followed a long silence, which wasn't broken until Winnie went to a table in a corner of the room on which stood a bucket and a bowl, and took from its drawer a square of rough linen. Having dipped it into the bucket of water, she came back to the table and gently wiped the slime from around the child's eyes; then she passed the cloth over its face, and as she did so, it cried out loud for the first time in its life.

It was Ned who spoke first. Quietly he said, 'I can understand why he wanted to get rid of it, it's natural.'

'Natural! God! Da! You say it's natural, a child livin' and breathin'. And then he hadn't the guts to do his dirty work himself. Natural!'

'It hasn't happened to you, lad. You're born but you're not buried yet.' His father's voice was harsh, and Davie cried back at him, 'Well, if it did happen to me, I'd put up with the consequences. Anyroad, I'd do me own murderin'.'

Sep put in quietly now, 'There's bairns been born without legs afore the day and lived to be old men, good old men at that. You remember the Millburns over near Newbiggin? Well, they had a lad who hadn't a leg to stand on so to speak, and he was a potter, one of the finest in the county, and died worth a bit. An' he married at that.'

'Aye, well, when you're on remembering,' Ned nodded his head vigorously at his father-in-law now, 'also reckon on Harry Watts's daughter, one stump of an arm and no legs and her head the size of two. And then not five years since there was a child they tell us born over near Beltingham, not an arm to him, everything got to be done for him. There's somethin' to be said after all for makin' a quick end to such.'

As Davie turned away from the table, Winnie said, 'What's to be done?'

'He'll have to be taken back, lass,' her father answered, and at this Molly cried, 'No, no, Eeh! No. The master wouldn't have it, he wants a son, a real son.'

'Then you'll have to give him one, won't you.' There was a deep bitterness in Davie's voice, and Molly again faced him, but all she could say this time was, 'You! You!'

'Look, lass.' Sep touched her arm gently. 'He's got a son, a bit short in the limbs perhaps, but you never know. God works in strange ways, and he might turn out to be a comfort to him.'

Molly's head swung from side to side as she muttered, 'I can't, I can't take him back.'

'All right, lass, I'll take him.'

The girl looked up into Winnie's face and whimpered, 'He won't have him, Winnie, he won't.'

'We'll see about that. Come on, Ma.' They all looked at Davie now. He was standing with the open door in his hand and when his father said, 'You stay out of this, it's none of your business,' he jerked his head towards him. 'No, none of my business. I've saved its life, haven't I? Another minute and it would have been at the bottom of the quarry. She can say what she likes but that's what would have happened to it, so I take it, it is me business. Anyway, in a few hours I'll be left this place an' I want to do him one last service. Come on, Ma.'

Winnie heaved a deep sigh, lifted the child from the table and followed her son out, and Molly, after glancing from Ned to Sep in a desperate fashion, went after them.

No one spoke until they were crossing the farmyard; then Winnie turned and whispered to Molly, 'The mistress, how did she take it?' And Molly muttered through her crying, 'Bad, she passed away in a faint.'

'Why didn't you come for me earlier?' They were nearing the kitchen door now and Molly, hanging back, said, 'I didn't know, I dozed; an' then I heard her cry out, an' there it was on the bed.' She stood still before she added, 'I'm not comin' in, I'm . . . I'm afeared.'

'Don't be silly, girl!' Winnie's voice was low and harsh. 'Somebody's got to see to the child, 'cos I'll have to attend the mistress. Here, take him.'

Backing from Winnie, Molly shook her head and muttered, 'I daresn't, I daresn't, Winnie, I daresn't.'

'Give him here.' Davie's voice was quiet, even calm sounding, so much so that his mother looked at him in enquiry; then after a moment's hesitation, she handed him the child, saying, 'He'll have to be kept on the side for a time, away from both of them.'

'You mean you're not goin' to tell him it's back?'

His tone was as it had been before, and she answered with equal sharpness, 'Of course he'll have to be told; but let him get his breath. Molly—' she turned to where Molly had been standing, but Molly was no longer there. There was no sight of her in the yard, and again Winnie heaved a deep sigh, then said, 'Keep it warm; I'll rouse Miss Jane.'

The sound of a loud wail coming from up above startled them both. When it rose to a scream, Winnie rushed out of the room. After a moment Davie went towards the fire, pulling a cracket after him. Seated on it, he looked down at the baby on his lap. The face was wrinkled, the eyes in the lowered light from the oil lamp looked dark, black; the hair on the head was fair. He had never considered babies to be as attractive as young calves, at least not until they started to gurgle and move about a bit, but there was something about this one's face that kept his eyes riveted on it. Somehow it didn't look like a baby's face at all; not that it was marred, it wasn't. He supposed many would consider it bonny for a newborn babe, but there was a look of age about it that wasn't suggested by the wrinkles.

He started again as he heard another high scream from the room above. The missis was taking it badly. There came the sound of a door banging loudly, and then the screaming died away.

He never heard McBain enter the room; the door from the passage was open. McBain was wearing slippers, but he had no sooner stepped over the threshold than Davie became aware of his presence, and he turned slowly and looked at him. But his master did not return his glance, for his gaze was concentrated on the bundle Davie was holding on his knee.

As McBain came towards the middle of the room, Davie rose from the cracket and went towards the table, and there they stood, one on each side.

McBain's face was ashen. He no longer looked at the child, but straight into Davie's eyes, and if it had been possible to strike him dead at this moment, he would have done so; if their had been a weapon in his hand he would have used it; the rage in him was molten steel, white hot, fusing all his emotions into a bar of hate.

'You mustn't blame Molly, Master.' Davie's voice was low and cool sounding. 'She did her best to carry out your instructions, I just managed to stop her in time.'

'Get out! Get out of my sight, off my land.' McBain's voice was choked with his passion, and Davie, dropping his quiet pose now, cried back at him, 'Aye, I'll get out of your sight an' off your land. I'll leave at dawn and not afore, because I don't want to wake up Parson Wainwright and Parson Hedley afore the sun is up, because I'm going to give them a message. I'm going to tell them that your son's been born and you want either one of them to come over and christen him proper like, because you don't know what might happen to him. I'll make it me business to tell them both, 'cos if I was only givin' me message to old Wainwright, it's my belief it wouldn't take much for him to finish off what Molly started so'll you'll keep his hand greased. But not Parson Hedley, no. So I'll see that they both know that your son has been born. I'll tell them he's without legs, but, as me Granda says, he's likely been given something else to make up for them. They say God's ways are strange.'

A gasp from the doorway brought his lightning glance to Jane. She was standing with one hand on the side of her face. How long she had been there he didn't know, but he dared to call to her and say, 'Come here, Miss Jane, and take your brother, he needs care.'

There was a wooden mallet lying at the end of the table–Winnie used it for tenderizing the meat–and when like a flash McBain's hand went out to it and gripped the handle, Jane sprang towards him, crying, 'Father! Father!'

It was not her puny strength that stopped him but the fact of her presence, and as she hung onto his arm she cried at Davie, 'Go on, get out! Get away, go on!' and he went.

Slowly he walked out of the kitchen and across the farmyard and up the road into the cottage. He had burned his boats.

In the kitchen his father and Granda were sitting by the rekindled fire. 'What happened?' asked Ned anxiously, and he told them, ending, 'He would have brained me, yet if I had lifted me hand he would have had me jailed. There's somethin' wrong with the laws of this land when a working man's life is held so cheaply.'

Ned looked at him, then said quietly, 'I'm sorry to say it, lad, but if he had hit you, you'd only have got what you asked for. You tried him too far; a man, good or bad, can only stand so much.'

'Whose side are you on, Da?' Davie's tone was hurt and harsh.

'I'm on nobody's side. Only this I'll say, an' I don't want to, and at this time. You'll be gone in a matter of hours, an' we're left here, an' he's still our master. You're young, lad, and have your furrows to sow, but you should gave a thought to others.' And on this he rose and went heavily up the stairs.

Davie stood looking hangdog for a moment. Some part of him knew his father was right, yet his youth protested against the injustice as he saw it, and he turned to his grandfather and said, 'Well, what d'you think of that? Nice partin' gift. There's something I'm gona tell you, Granda. I'm never going to let any man master me like they have him. As I said, an' I'll say again, lives are held too cheap, not worth a farthin' candle, they're not.'

'All life is cheap and brief, lad,' said Sep sadly. 'After all, we are nawt but feathers in the fire; we're blown into life, then we're nipped out, king and commoner, all the same. But what I say is, God help the little feather that was born the night, for his comin' will bring changes. Aye, it will that. This farm, this happy farm, for it's been that, say what you will, will never be the same again, nor nobody in it.'

BOOK TWO

1884

Chapter One

It was a week since the snow had disappeared, but it was still only March, and there would likely be more flurries, if not a deep fall, before spring really settled on the hills. The bright hard sunshine was giving the impression that it had already come to stay and was agitating the restlessness in all life. It was working strongly in Jane, now bordering on sixteen years of age, but she didn't recognize it except as a desire to get out and walk; walk the hills, the moors, walk towards Allendale and climb the crags or lie on a high fell and watch the water racing down in froth-tipped leaps over stubborn stones to the river.

It seemed a simple desire, one so easy of fulfilment, for she was surrounded by the means of bringing her wish to life. But nearer at hand, within two arm's lengths of her, was the reason why she could not just walk out and over the hills. Amos McBain, three years and six months old, was seated in a chair, the seat of which was nine inches from the ground. The boy's body was sturdy. The arms were rounded and filled the sleeves of his dress. His face had a squarish look; the mouth was wide, the nose thin, but it was the eyes that caught the attention. They were almond-shaped and gave him a curious appearance. His hair, very fair, clustered in unruly curls about his head. Altogether it wasn't a face, you could say, that typified those bred in the northern dales. The colouring and shape of the head might have suggested Scandinavian blood, but the eyes, dominating the whole of the face, brought one firmly to the conviction that somewhere along the lines of either the McBains or the Lawsons there had been oriental blood. This conviction would have been entirely misleading, for both families had been firmly entrenched in the north of Britain, the McBains going no farther north than Edinburgh, and the Lawsons south to Yorkshire.

The overall impression given out by the seated child was one of a strange fascination; that was until, thrusting himself forward, he attempted to walk; then embarrassment and a slight revulsion, which could not overwhelm pity, would have been the first reaction of any visitor. But then this contingency never occurred, for there were no strange visitors to the attic in the old part of the house. The only people who had ever entered the room, and who made up Amos McBain's world, were Winnie, Molly, Parson Hedley, and Jane.

But Winnie and Molly, and even the parson, were as visitors in his life; only Jane was permanent in his narrow world, the world that was like an eggshell about him and out of which he was now aiming to break through and be born.

'I want to, Jan,' he said; 'I want to.'

'Not today, dear; some . . . some other time.'

'When? When, Jan?'

Jane turned from making the low bed set at right angles to the fireplace and looked at him where he was sitting beside the window, gazing down onto the farmyard. In her look was love and pity and concern, deep concern. She knew that the child could not be kept up here forever, no matter what her father said. He would one day soon be able to fight his way out, and what then? He was extraordinarily strong already for his age, his arms could thrust her off; she was amazed at his strength, as she was by his mind. She herself could not remember being able to read before she was five, and she had been nearly seven before she could recite her ten times tables. She didn't know at what age she had begun to write, but it was certainly not at three and a half years old; and yesterday Amos had written his name. True, the letters were unwieldy and only discernible to herself, but nevertheless he had written *Amos*, and he could go through the alphabet in the primer.

It astonished her how quickly he grasped things. He could remember small details of a story she had told him weeks previously. Should the telling of a story divert from its original theme, he would quickly call her attention to it. This brightness confused her, and she had to be on the alert against it.

When she looked into the future, she became apprehensive. What lay before him? She had put this question to Parson Hedley and he had, in his own inimitably kind way, reassured her, saying, 'Don't worry, his head will carry him through. God has strange ways of dealing out compensation. He will, if I'm not mistaken, have a thirst for knowledge which may lead him to make his mark in the world.'

Jane wondered what she would have done over the past three and a half years if it hadn't been for Parson Hedley. He was thirty years old, but he laughed and acted like someone of her own age, and he always succeeded in brightening the dullest day for her. Moreover, he was kind to everyone, even to her father after he had found out what he had tried to do to the child.

On the morning of that dreadful day when he had come to christen the child–because Davie Armstrong had kept his word and on his way to the sea had called at the Vicarage–Molly had had hysterics in the kitchen. She had gone onto her knees before him and begged him to ask God to forgive her, and into his astonished ears she had poured her confession–her intrigue with the master, her being the cause of the mistress's coming on before her time, and then in her spluttering and crying, she had brought out the fact that she had been ordered to drown the child. But she had insisted that she wouldn't have done it, no matter what Davie Armstrong said.

He had lifted her up and held her and given her no word of censure, but Jane knew that if Parson Wainwright had been the one to listen to her confession, he would have damned her to hell's flames and branded her over the countryside, more so than she was already.

And knowing all this, Parson Hedley never failed to visit her father at least once a week; even her father's changed ways did not deter him, not even when he cursed God, as he sometimes did now because he had become a slave to drink, strong drink. Scarcely a night went by when he didn't indulge himself; although in the daytime he still carried out his duties as a farmer, he was no longer the master he had been. Where once he had inspired awe through respect, he now inspired hate from some quarters, and disdain and condescending pity from others.

It was the disdain, Jane guessed, that disturbed him most, for the disdain came from the townspeople. True, they said, he had been dealt a blow by his wife bearing him a bit of a monstrosity, but why hadn't he taken it like a man? And there were the rumours concerning him: some said he was for cutting the child up and throwing him into the cesspool; others said that, not having the guts to kill the child himself, he had sent out the young trollop, who was really the cause of all the trouble, and told her to bury it alive. Well, whatever the rights or wrongs of it were, it was well known that he had banished the child to a fortress at the top of the house and had never looked upon it from the morning it was born. Nor, it was said, and this in stern condemnation, had he spoken a word to his wife, and she was almost as great a prisoner as the thing she had given birth to, for she was confined to her bed most of the time.

The townsfolk of Hexham still saw him once a week, but he no longer graced the boardrooms of either the Workhouse Guardians or the Hospital Governors, nor yet was he seen at the Agricultural Show at Stanhope, nor at that of Allendale. Either Fred Geary or Will Curran took the cattle to the shows, but they brought back no prizes, not even a third.

In the gossip in the markets and at the fairs they said Cock Shield Farm was finished; some said, God is not mocked; others said, the sins of the fathers are surely visited on the children; but it was only the women who said pointedly that all this tragedy was the result of his carrying on with the scut under his wife's nose. The men did not voice this opinion, for few had room to speak.

Jane was fully aware that her father and mother were not the only people whose lives were changed with the coming of the child. She knew she had been prematurely thrust into womanhood the morning she had stood in the doorway and watched her father and Davie Armstrong facing each other across the kitchen table, the bundle between them. It was when she had picked up the child that she had ceased to love her father, and her heart and emotions had become centred on the legless infant. Strangely, too, about this time, her brief hate of Molly disappeared. When the child was but four days old and already ensconced in the attic room that was to become its world for years ahead, she had found Molly bending over it, the tears raining down her face. The girl had looked at her and, heartbrokenly, said, 'Will you believe me, Miss, I would never have done it, an' that's the truth. I'm wicked, very wicked, I know I am, but I hope God strikes me down dead this minute if I'm tellin' a lie; I wouldn't have done it. I was for turning and coming back when Davie collared me. But you couldn't make him believe that, 'cos he loathes me hide; he'd have me strung up if he had his way. I'm sorry, Miss, I'm sorry for all I've done to the mistress; I'd never, never in me life do such a thing again, never, never. An' I'm not gonna marry Will Curran, Miss, I'm not, I'm not. What's in me—' she had touched her stomach gently, 'I'll care for on me own, and work for it, but I'll not marry Will Curran, not if the master was to beat me black and blue, I'll not.'

Jane had been surprised, too, at her own reactions, for she had gone to Molly and put her arms around her, and like two young girls, they had clung together and both cried.

Afterwards when she thought about the incident, she knew she shouldn't have embraced Molly, for by doing so she was condoning her sin, the grave sin Molly had committed with her father. Yet, nevertheless, something in her was glad that she had forgiven Molly.

In those terrible early days, she had only known that she must look after the child and that for the rest of her life he'd be her care, her responsibility. Winnie could see to her mother, but she must see to the child, for no one wanted him or would ever want him. But as the years went on she'd had to reconsider this last statement, because there was something appealing about the child; it wasn't his handicap, it was something in his face and nature, the way he had of looking at you–except, that is, when he was in a rage, and then she had to admit he became fiendish. His spasms were not just bouts of childish temper, but extraordinary rages, when she could not control him, when he twisted his body like an eel in her arms and flayed at her with his hands until she was bruised.

It was with the dread of such a rage now coming upon him that she went to him and, coiling herself on the floor in front of his chair, took his hand and said, 'Only be patient, Amos. Soon, soon you'll be able to go out; I promise you.'

He stared back into her eyes before asking flatly, 'When soon?'

Her lids fluttered, her head moved in small jerks.

'I want to see that little girl.' He pointed to the far corner of the yard where Molly's daughter, Biddy, was running towards the road. 'I want to see her.'

'You will soon, darling.' She went to pat his hand, but he pulled it away from her.

'Always you say "soon". I want to go now. If you don't take me, I'll ask Molly. Molly is her mother.' He looked down into the yard again, then asked slowly, 'Why has she got legs?'

She had been waiting for this question. She had wondered why it hadn't come before, and now she was dumb. There was no strength in her hands to stop him when he pulled up his dress, then his calico petticoat and his two flannel ones, and exposed to her gaze and his own two firm stumps of about six inches in length, from which protruded a pair of distorted feet.

'Everyone there has legs.' He nodded his head towards the window now. 'Why have I not legs?'

She kept her tears from brimming over, but they were in her voice as she said, 'Well, you see, darling, you . . . you had an accident.'

'An ac . . . cid . . . ent? Did a giant chop them off, like in the story with the bad man's head?'

'No, no, Amos. The accident was to your mama.'

'My mama?' He stared at her. 'Why does my mama not come and see me?'

'I've told you, I've told you several times, she is sick in bed.'

'You could take me to see her.'

'She's . . . she's too sick to see anyone at present.'

'My papa is not sick. There's my papa. Isn't that my papa?'

Jane looked down into the yard. Her father was going towards the stables. Being Tuesday, he'd be riding into Hexham; he'd be gone for at least four hours.

The idea coming into her mind was interrupted by the child saying again, 'You said that was my papa?'

'Yes, dear, that is your papa.'

'Then why doesn't he come up to see me?'

'He is very busy, there is a lot to do on the farm.'

'Parson Hedley comes to see me.'

'Yes, dear, but Parson Hedley hasn't a big farm to run.'

'I like Parson Hedley.'

'So do I.'

They stared at each other for a moment, then with one of his impetuous gestures that brought joy to her heart he brought himself forward and flung his arms around her neck, and with a heave of his body landed on her knee. But the way she was sitting forced her to lose her balance and they rolled over together on the floor, and she laughed now with him as if she herself, too, were a child.

Winnie, coming into the room at this moment, stopped and exclaimed, 'Well! Did you ever! What are you two up to?'

Still laughing, Jane got to her feet, and the child, with an expert twist of his body, turned onto his hands and, using the stumps as another child would its knees, went towards Winnie at a remarkable speed, then, dragging at her skirts, he pulled himself upwards and, standing on his stumps, dropped his head back on his shoulders and said, 'Jan, she says I am going down soon, I am going down into the yard to the people, I am, I am.'

As she patted the boy's head Winnie looked at Jane, and Jane made a slight movement with her shoulders.

The boy now shook Winnie's skirt vigorously and cried loudly, 'I said I am going down.'

'I heard you, I heard you, Master Amos.' She tapped his cheek, then said, 'Now leave go of me, leave go of me afore I slap your backside.' She bent down and playfully tapped him on the buttocks, and at this he let go of her, dropped onto all fours and, in a crab-like fashion, his middle body swaying, he scurried to the window.

Winnie now went to the other side of the bed where Jane was spreading the quilt and once more they exchanged glances, and Winnie murmured under her breath, 'It's got to come, Miss Jane. One of these days he'll be out of that door afore either of us can stop him, and like a dog off a leash he'll be down the stairs. You should speak to the master.'

'I . . . I can't, Winnie, not again. You know what happened when I broached the subject before; he didn't open his mouth to me for weeks.'

'Well, you can see for yourself, Miss, somethin' 'll happen sooner or later, an' then the master 'll have to face up to it. It isn't as if,' she jerked her head backwards, 'he's an idiot. Never in me life have I seen one so bright. If the master would only bring himself to look at the child, or even the mistress, for that matter. But then, I think there's less likelihood in that quarter than in t'other. Aw, it's a nice kettle of fish. Look,' she came round to Jane's side, her voice a whisper now, 'The master's gone into town, left as I was comin' up. Why don't you take him down now? There'll be no chance of him seeing anybody that matters. The mistress hasn't been out of her room for three months. An' there's another thing,' she now stabbed her finger into Jane's shoulder, 'you're gettin' as pale and peaked lookin' as a lady in decline. You've got to get yourself out, an' you've got to take the chance as it comes. Look, why not take him down this minute an' I'll get one of the lads to carry him up to the Ridge. By! That will open his eyes, for the child to see the world for the first time from the top of the Tor. An' think of the good it'll do yourself. Now, what about it?'

'Oh, Winnie, do you think I dare?'

'If you never dare now, Miss, you'll never dare at all. It's a bonny day. The wind's fresh, spring's in the offing, and that child has got to get out of this room sometime, or other else he'll break out. Come on, come on, it's now or never.'

There was a flutter in Jane's heart as she ran to the cupboard and took out a shawl. The child had no outdoor clothes, there seeming to be no necessity to buy any. When she went towards him holding the shawl out before her, he seemed to anticipate the excitement in the air for leaving the support of his low table, his body seemed to fold up like a concertina before he sprang it upwards and into her arms.

'There now, there now, don't get excited.'

'I'm goin' down, Winnie! I'm goin' down!'

'Darling. Listen!' Jane shook him, bringing his attention to her. 'Listen. You must be quiet until we get out of doors, understand? Your mama is not well. Don't talk until you're in the open. Now do you understand?'

His face now soft, his mouth closed, he nodded at her, and to show her that he was falling in with her wishes, he pressed his lips tightly together. But when the door was opened and closed behind them and he did not hear the sound of the key turning in the lock, he looked down into her face; then as they went along the passage, his mouth fell into a childish gape, and on descending the stairs his head turned from one side to the other in wonder.

'Go down the back way, Miss Jane,' Winnie whispered from behind her.

Jane didn't answer but nodded her head once, and when they came onto the floor below, she turned sharply to the left and went down the four steps onto the next landing, past the doors of her father's bedroom and of the room that had once been her own and still was, although she slept with the child in the attic. Then passing the head of the main stairway, they turned left again, and went through a door and down the backstairs that dropped into a passageway. This in turn gave onto the side yard.

The yard was paved for only half its length, the rest being covered with turf which continued round to the back of the house, inlaid here and there with flower beds. The paved half terminated at the corner of the house and was shut off from the main yard by a thick wall, part of which had a dubious claim to Roman structure. The archway leading into the farmyard proper, although deep and ruggedly built, was of modern design.

It was as Jane entered the arch from the side of the house that her father also entered it from the main yard.

Which of the two was the more affected was hard to tell. Jane thought for a moment that she would drop the child, so weak did her fear make her.

The boy could have put his hands out and touched his father, but the touch would have scorched him, for McBain was full of a body-burning rage. His livid glance touched on the child for but a second or two, and its pale flat face and almond-shaped eyes hooded by the shawl only emphasized the impression of the monstrosity he always carried in his mind.

'Take . . . it . . . back.' The words were sieved through his teeth, which were clenched, the lips straining away from them.

'No . . . No, Father, I can't. He must . . . he must have air.'

'Take it back.'

She stepped away from him while shaking her head as she defied him, saying, 'I can't. He's a human being, I can't.'

'You are my papa.'

If a pig had walked on its hind legs and spoken these words, McBain could not have been more surprised, they were so clear, so firm, so normal sounding. The thing had said, 'You are my papa.' The shawl had dropped from around its head, and he saw the mass of fair curls. But they could have been a crop of horns he was looking at. No male McBain had ever been fair, all had been raven black; the fairness he was looking upon was no ordinary fairness, it was a weird, strange, silvery fairness. Yet the voice was ordinary, normal. But no, there was even something weird about that, too, for it wasn't the voice of a child. The thing did not look like a child, and it showed no fear of him.

When it said in the same clear ringing tones, 'Are you going to ride your horse?' he brought his shoulders up round his chin as if to protect himself against some hideous attack and, turning about, almost ran from them and disappeared into the main yard.

Jane now leaned against the wall, the child clutched to her. Then she turned her head slowly and looked to where Winnie was standing some little distance away, and Winnie, as if coming out of a trance, now darted towards her. 'Give him here. It's all right, it's all right, give him here.'

The weight of the child taken from her, Jane felt the strength returning to her body; but the sweat was running down her face and, looking at Winnie, she whispered, 'What now, what shall I do now?'

'Take him to the Ridge as you intended. It's well it happened, it's over, you've won.'

'I have?' She was like a young dazed child herself, asking the question.

'Aye, lass. Or at least he has. He's proved that he's no oddity, not up top anyway. "You are my papa," he said. Didn't you lad?' She hugged the boy to her. 'Come on, come on back into the kitchen and I'll make a cup of tea. There's no need to hurry anymore; that over, you'll go out into the open whenever you like from now on an' take him with you.'

'Oh, Winnie! Winnie!'

'There you are, Miss, there you are.' She put one hand around Jane's shoulder and as she led her back towards the door, she said, 'Don't fresh yourself, Lass, don't fresh yourself. You did splendidly. By! You did that. Things should go plain sailin' after this.'

Chapter Two

Jane was to remember Amos's fifth birthday and look back on it as a day of happenings, happenings that were the beginning of events which would shape her life . . . and Amos's.

The first happening took place at nine o'clock in the morning. She had risen before six and, leaving the boy sleeping peacefully, she had gone out, locking the door as usual, which was more necessary now than ever. Then she had gone downstairs and prepared their breakfasts. But before bringing them up, she returned to her room on the first floor and gathered together his birthday presents, one of which was a coat that would serve him in the winter. She had sent into Hexham for the material and had had the seamstress make it up to her design, with a cap to match. Both were of a soft brown colour which, she knew, would suit the boy's fairness. Also, there was an engine that ran on wheels and had what appeared to be smoke coming from its funnel when a string was pulled. She herself thought this very ingenious, as the smoke was supplied by flour, or any other powder you had a mind to put in the box beneath the funnel. She had been told that the engine was an exact replica of the one that ran between Newcastle and Hexham. Also, she had a bag of coloured marbles for him, as he loved to play marbles.

But, this birthday, there was a very special present for him, and not from herself, but from old Sep. Sep had made a pair of crutches which, he had told her, would serve the boy as good as legs, with a little practice. The arm supports were padded with blue velvet. She had supplied the material and

Winnie had done the padding. She was as excited about the crutches as if she were going to use them herself.

It was half an hour later when she woke him up. She had sat on the floor gazing at him for some time before doing so. She often sat watching him while he slept, but this morning she looked longer and deeper; today he was five years old. In years he was still a child, yet in some strange way he had leapt beyond childhood; in fact, on looking back, she could hardly remember his being a baby; he seemed to have been born with age on him. His head seemed full of all kinds of things that shouldn't occur to a child. At times she became afraid for him. Being so forward now, what would he be like when he was, say, ten years old? Would his brightness emphasize his handicap? Would he be hurt by it more because he possessed an awareness more keen than others? Suffer more? Still, that was all in the future. There was today, and this was his birthday.

'Amos.' She shook him gently. 'Amos, wake up. Look what I've got for you.'

Slowly he opened his eyes and stared at her. His face was soft and warm and beautiful.

'Happy birthday, Amos.' She bent and kissed him, and immediately his arms were around her neck and he was kissing her in return and crying, 'I am five. I am five. Have you my presents?'

'Yes, here they are.'

He tore the paper from the first parcel she handed to him and revealed the coat and cap, and within seconds he had them both on, tugging the arms over the sleeves of his nightshirt. When he put on the cap, Jane laughed out loud, and running to the dressing table near her bed, she brought back a hand mirror. When she held it before him, he glanced at her, his mouth wide, and said, 'I am pretty,' then lay back on the bed and laughed.

Next she gave him the marbles, and he juggled with them expertly, for they had played chucks together for years.

When, next, she lifted the unwieldy parcel onto the bed, he paused before opening it, and asked, 'What is it?'

'Look and see.'

When he saw the crutches, he sat straight staring at them. His whole manner was changed, all the gaiety gone. This often happened when his deformity was brought to the fore.

Last year Ned and Sep had contrived between them a go-cart for him, so constructed that, sitting in it, he could guide himself wherever he wished, except up steps. They had gone to a lot of trouble with the cart, especially with regards the wheels, concerning which they had consulted the wheelwright over near Ninebanks. He was an old man, as old as Sep, and finished with his trade, but he had been kind enough to construct four broad-rimmed wooden wheels, each with a fancy hub. Yet when they had presented the boy with the cart, his face had flushed to a deep red, scarlet in fact, which was usually the prelude to a burst of temper; but she had been swift to lift him into it and put his hands on the front wheels and propel him forward. As he felt the movement, the hot colour in his face had subsided and the light had come back into his eyes, and as if he had been used to propelling it every day of his life, he whirled it round the yard, scattering the hens and ducks, causing the dogs to bark and the bull to roar and making everyone laugh.

This had happened on a Tuesday. Of course, they had picked the day to present him with it when the master was in the town.

And now the crutches were having the same effect on him. The laughter had died from his face, his mouth was tight, his colour was rising, and there was that look in his eyes that even now brought a thin thread of fear into her. As with the cart, so now she again acted quickly. Lifting him out of the bed, she swiftly tucked a crutch under each arm. Their sizes were exact; they touched the floor at the same level as his distorted feet.

'Like this,' she said excitedly. 'Your feet on the ground, so, then put your weight on your oxters, like this . . . That's it. That's it.' When he almost overbalanced, she put her hand gently at his back; the next minute he was away from her. Wobbling, the crutches sprawling out away from him, he went up and down the long room. Twice he fell, but pushed her hands off when she went to help him up. Soon he had the feel of them and swung into a rhythm.

She stood and watched him, her hands held tightly together under her chin, and when at last he stopped in front of her, his shoulders hunched, each hand gripping the middle bar of the crutch, she dropped onto her hunkers and took his face between her hands and shook his head from side to side. And as the tears flowed from her eyes, she whispered, 'You can walk. You can walk now.'

'I can walk.'

They looked at each other. Then, his voice holding a tone like that of an adult, a man, he said, 'I won't have to wait for anyone anymore, I can walk on my own. I won't have to wait for anyone. . . .'

She rubbed the tears from each side of her cheeks and on a breaking laugh said, 'I hope you'll always wait for me, Amos.'

As the brightness slowly seeped from his face, so it did from her own, and again in a voice like that of a man he said, 'Oh yes; I'll always wait for you, Jan.' Then he brought his head forward until it touched her arm, and she held him, and her tears flowed fast.

For the next few hours he became totally engrossed with the crutches; the distance he covered in the room must have amounted to miles. She felt dizzy with him going round and round. She had to make him stop in order to tell Winnie to thank her husband and father for their wonderful gift.

Winnie, staring at the boy careening round the room, said, 'Why didn't we think of it afore, Miss, I mean giving him crutches? He could have been on them since he was three. They should have got the crutches instead of the cart in the first place. Didn't you ever think of them, Miss?'

Jane nodded her head as she said, 'Yes, but . . . but for the future; somehow I couldn't see him balancing.'

'Why not?' said Winnie. 'He balances on his stumps.'

Jane nipped slightly on her lower lip. It always did something to her to hear his short appendages referred to as stumps.

As they stood watching him, Winnie voiced a fear that was already growing in Jane's mind. 'The job now,' she said, 'will be to keep him put. You knew where you had him afore, but now he'll be as free as the rest; and you can't go on forever locking the door.'

'No, don't lock the door again.' They both started. The boy had stopped and was staring at them. His face was straight; it was wearing the set look of determination they both recognized. They were amazed that he should have heard their low-pitched conversation. It came to them in different ways that he must have heard all that they had ever said in that room, be their voices ever so low.

Jane moved slowly towards him and, dropping onto her hunkers again, she said, 'I must lock the door, darling.'

'No.'

'Yes, yes, I must. You see, your mama is not at all well.' It was strange, but she herself had never called her mother 'mama' or her father 'papa', but in placating the child when answering his first questions about his parents, which incidentally came after she had explained that Molly was the mother of the little girl he often saw down in the yard, she had used the terms mama and papa. They seemed softer, warmer somehow, making up for the lack of the physical presence of what they represented.

'If I saw my mama I would be good, I would not make a noise.'

She glanced back at Winnie, and Winnie said softly, 'Your moth . . . your mama has to be kept very quiet, and can't have visitors. That's what the doctor says.'

'Does no one see my mama?'

'Only the doctor and . . . and Parson Hedley.' Winnie nodded down at him, and he stared back at her for a moment, then turned from them both and began once more circling the long room on the crutches.

Winnie turned towards the door, saying, 'Well, I'd better be gettin' a move on, Miss, but I'll just slip across the way first and see if my lot have eaten, and tell them about . . .' she nodded towards the boy, 'and that they are fine, just fine.'

'Thank you, Winnie.' Jane went to the door with her. 'Tell Sep and Ned I'm so grateful, and we'll be over later. He'll,' she jerked her head backwards, 'he'll thank them himself.'

'They'd like that.'

When the door had closed on Winnie, Amos came towards Jane, walking slowly now, the crutches making a clip-clop clip-clopping sound, and he said, 'I want to go down and show Biddy.'

'As soon as I've tidied up and you're washed. You must be washed and dressed, for you can't go out like that, can you? You can wear your blue velvet dress today.'

The boy looked down towards his feet, at the hornlike big toe sticking out from beneath his nightshirt, and he said, 'When can I wear trousers?'

'Oh!' She was nonplussed. 'Later. Later, you can wear trousers.'

'When?'

'Well, when I get them made for you.'

'Soon?'

'Yes, soon.'

'I should wear trousers, I am a boy. I'm not like Biddy; Biddy has to sit on the ground to pee.'

'Oh, my God!' She actually muttered the words aloud. Not only were his observations distressing to her, but more so was the fact that he had a very keen interest in Biddy. One day he would have to be told of their relationship, for his attraction to their half-sister–because that was what Molly's daughter was–was troubling her even at this stage. It would have solved the problem if Molly had left the farm years ago. But where could she have gone except into the workhouse, because employers didn't take on young mothers with suckling babies, a suckling baby deprived a mother of some of her strength.

It was half an hour later that she went out of the door and turned the key in the lock and was immediately startled by a loud hammering on the door from the inside and the child screaming, 'No! No! Jan. Don't lock it. No! No! Don't lock me in. I can walk, Jan. I can walk.'

When she quickly unlocked the door and thrust it open, she pushed him onto his back, and he lay there looking up at her with a crutch in one hand.

'Oh Amos, Amos.' She brought him upright. 'Oh, I'm sorry, are you hurt? But I've got to lock the door, I must.'

'No!' He shook his head slowly. 'No, Jan, not anymore. Please, please, Jan, I'll be good. But if you lock it, I'll scream, I will, and better, yes, with the crutch, I will all the time.'

She lowered her head onto her hand and closed her eyes; and after a moment she looked at him and said softly, 'Well now, listen. If . . . if I don't lock the door, will you promise not to leave the room until I come back?'

He stared into her eyes for a moment then drooped his head, and she passed her hand over his curls and murmured, 'That's a good boy. Now I won't be more than five minutes. Play with your toys, and when I come back, we'll go out. We'll go and see Sep and Ned and you'll thank them for their present, eh?'

He nodded his head but did not look at her, and so she backed from him, then turned slowly and went out and closed the door. On the landing she stood looking at it, at the lock, and only resisted the temptation to turn it by hurrying away and running down the stairs.

At the bottom of the stairs she paused and glanced across the landing towards her mother's door. It was time for her morning visit but she must go to her own room first, there to attend to her personal needs which she had never been able to perform in front of the child.

Delia heard her daughter come down the stairs, and she heard her hesitate before going to the lower landing and to her room. There was no movement that her daughter or the child made that she did not hear. Sometimes she might only be dimly aware of the activities in the room above her, especially after she had taken the strong medicine that Doctor Cargill prescribed from time to time, yet some part of her mind was always conscious of the activity in the attic room. She knew when they went to bed, and when they awoke in the morning. She heard the child cry, and scream, and laugh, and at times she heard her daughter laugh with him. This, strangely, hurt her most of all.

In the past eighteen months she had been only twice out of the room. Prior to that, except during the first six months after the child's birth, when she was prostrate and often not in her right mind, she had periodically made an effort to get back into life. It might be once in two months, or three. She would dress and go downstairs into the sitting room, but she never went outside; her legs didn't seem strong enough to come in contact with the hard earth, nor her face the sharp air. But for the past nine months she had not even moved out of the bed.

No one spoke to her of the child, and his name was never mentioned. But then she saw so few people. Only four in fact: Winnie, the doctor, Parson Hedley, and, of course, Jane.

She wondered time and again why she was not dead. She had no strength in her body, and seemingly very little left in her mind; what she had, she used in the wish to die. She knew she was dying, but the process was slow, a fading away.

From early this morning she had listened to the strange sounds above her. They were not the usual sounds and they had gone on for hours, a hard clip-clop, clip-clopping all over the ceiling.

Years ago she had wanted to leave this room, fly from it and never see it again, but were she to move to the other landing, she'd be near her husband, and that situation would be more unbearable than this. Never one word had they exchanged from the night he had stood over her and cursed her for bringing a monstrosity into the world. When she had come to herself, the thing she had given birth to was gone; but he was there, and there had been murder in his eyes, and he had said things to her that could never be forgotten.

Sometimes she had seen him from her window, striding about the farm. Only twice had she encountered him face to face. Even then they had not looked at each other; she had passed on into the sitting room and he across the hall, as if both were blind ghosts. Yet even if he didn't look at her, or speak to her, from time to time she heard his voice; although his office was not below her room, the one below being the dining room, its chimney flue connected with the same main flue as her bedroom's, and through this funnel she heard his distant gruntings when he was in drink.

The fact that he had taken to drink was, even in her dim and half aware state, surprising. Only when there were visitors at dinner had he indulged in wine, and then in moderation; he would pour it out generously for Parson Hedley or Parson Wainwright, oh very generously for Parson Wainwright, but he himself drank very little. But now, not infrequently of an evening, and more towards midnight when the house had settled, she would hear his mutterings, and although unintelligible, she gauged the ferocity of his mood by the inflection of his voice as it was sucked up the funnels of the chimneys.

Beneath the laudanum-dulled layers of her mind there was an activity, a threshing process that winnowed all the sounds in the house and brought the residue near enough to the opiate to bring her some awareness.

The stamping on the floor above had stopped, just before Jane had come down the stairs; but now it had started again, only the rhythm was different. There was a longer time between each clip-clop, and each thud seemed to be lighter, such as the difference between walking and tiptoeing. The sound turned into a tap-tap. She followed it. It was no longer above her head, but on the stairs. The child was coming down the stairs. But how?

She knew when he had reached the bottom. She made an effort and pulled herself up further onto her pillows. She could see over the rail of the bed now, and to the door opposite. The sound had returned to what it was when above her head, a clip-clop, clip-clop, clip-clopping sound.

She felt she was drawing her last breath as she watched the door handle slowly turn, and with a sharp thrust the door was pushed back wide, and there came into the room, and towards the bed, her son. The nearer he came towards her, the less she saw of him, until he moved to the side of the bed and two movements of his crutches brought him within a yard of her pillow.

She was unable to breathe, the constriction in her throat was choking her. She stared at the curly head, into the face with the almond-shaped eyes.

'Are you my mama?'

The voice was as surprising as the rest of him. It brought her face stretching and her breath fighting for escape from her throat.

'Can't you talk?'

No, she couldn't talk, she could not utter one word to this son of hers.

'Are you sick?'

She wanted to make a motion with her hand, but it refused to obey her. What was more, she wanted to do something else. Every fibre in her wasted body urged her to lift up her arms and stretch them outwards and grasp this child, this child who spoke so clearly, who looked so bright and intelligent. It might have only half a body, but he was a child, not a monstrosity. What had she done lying here for five years listening, while up above was this child, her child, someone who could have brought her comfort? An agony filled her body as she realized she had rejected comfort, and that was what she needed most, comfort.

She lifted her hand and slowly moved it towards him, and as slowly, he moved back from it, and what he said to her was, 'I don't like you.' On this, he swung his body round and stumped out of the room. But he had no sooner passed out of the door when he was grabbed and lifted bodily upwards, and when the crutches fell to the ground, these, too, were lifted, and Molly's voice hissed in his ear, 'Oh, you bad lad, you, you bad lad!'

'I'm not. I'm not.'

'Ssh! Be quiet! Wait till Miss Jane finds out.'

'Put me down, I can walk.' He was beating at her with his fists, and she hissed at him, 'Give over, Master Amos, 'cos I'm not puttin' you down; you're goin' back upstairs.'

She had to make a detour round the main landing to reach the backstairs again because she couldn't pass the mistress's open door. She knew the mistress couldn't stand the sight of her; she was a thorn in her flesh.

As she turned onto the main landing the boy struggled so much that she was forced to put him to the ground, and as she did so, she exclaimed under her breath, 'Oh, you are an imp, you are that! Here.' She pushed the crutches at him. 'No, not that way, back up the stairs.'

'I won't! I won't!'

Neither of them was aware of the door opening until McBain's shadow fell over them, and then they both looked up. Molly's was just a fleeting glance before her eyes dropped away from the master's face; but not so the child's. His face now red with anger and indignation at Molly's rough handling, he glared up at the man, the man who passed him at a distance without turning his head in his direction, the man who was his papa but who would not speak to him. His next words linked up with those he had said in the bedroom, as if he were just finishing a sentence. 'And I hate you, too, I do,' he said.

In no way intimidated by the rage-filled countenance high above him, he continued to stare up into McBain's face for some seconds before he turned his back on him and stumped away. He did not go upstairs towards the prison that had been his since birth, with rare escapes to the yard below, mostly on a Tuesday, but down the main staircase, stumbling once and nearly going headlong to the bottom, through the hall and across the farmyard, passing gaping faces, in the direction of the Armstrongs' cottage.

One thing had been made certain to Jane, the child could no longer be kept a prisoner in the attic; and this fact had got through to every occupant on the farm, including its master.

After the encounter on the landing, McBain went back into his room, and there he paced the floor trying to face the fact that this half-being could no longer be concealed.

He still looked upon the child as a monstrosity; even the fact that it might be intelligent did not veer his thoughts from the ignominy of having produced such an object. He thought of the child as 'it'. He spoke of it, when he spoke of it at all, by that term. To him the boy was an object, a threefold curse, emphasizing first his lack of judgment in taking a wife such as Delia; second, forcing the question that his own genes might be at fault; thirdly, and most important of all, he looked upon the boy as an act of God, a punishment to expiate his lust, the lust that had eaten him up for years, and that could only be satisfied by the very young. And now this same lust had turned sour on him; Molly, who had excited him as no other had, at least at the time he was most in need of her, had repulsed him, not once, but twice, and yet a third time. He was a proud man, he would not beg, so on a Tuesday he went into Hexham, and sometimes as far away as Newcastle, and when his business was done, he paid for the release of his passions. But it was never the same as before.

Nothing was the same as before. He did not command the respect as he had, at one time, in the town. He sometimes wondered whether, if he had accepted his tribulation, taking it into the open, and drawing pity to himself for it, life would have been better, easier.

At one time, on his own land, he had been looked up to as a god. He had felt as a god. Now he was a fallen angel. And the only succour he received was from the brain-dulling effect of whisky.

Concerning the present situation, he asked himself what was to be done. He could not have 'it' running about the place where he would encounter it at any time of the day. He could send it away, put it in a home, or a school; there were places for such as he. But, there was a question here. Were he to do that, what would be the effect on Jane? He could not risk alienating her. Jane, the child, had loved him at one time; he doubted if Jane, the young woman, still loved him. But, strangely, he loved her. She was the only thing left in his life that he could love, and he knew that whatever he did to the child in an adverse way would affect their relationship. They might not have much to say to each other now, but she was the only human being in the house to whom he could talk. What was more, her understanding was deep. She could accept his ignoring of the child, but he knew that she would never forgive him were he to dispose of his son in some institution.

There seemed nothing for it but that he must face this situation as best he could. But one thing he would never allow–he would not allow 'it' to eat at his table, ever.

As if this decision had in some way made his position bearable, he straightened his shoulders, stretched his neck with a chin-wagging movement up out of his loose cravat, then marched from the room.

When Molly informed Jane of what had happened, she ran and almost dragged Amos from old Sep and back to the house, and all the way he had protested as he had never done before; not crying like a child of five might do, but arguing and questioning with a reasoning that startled her. Why must he stay up in his room if he could walk? Why wasn't he allowed to go round the farm? Had his papa said he must not go round the farm? Was it because he had no legs?

It was after the three o'clock dinner that Molly, coming upstairs to clear the dishes, said in an aside. 'It's done this, the ice is broken, so why don't you let him go out on his own? Or better still, the day being fine, take him up on the Tor; by! that would be an eye-opener for him.'

Jane looked at Molly, and as if Molly read her thoughts, she said, 'I can look out the landin' window and see whether he's about . . . the Master. An' you can slip out the back way. 'Bout time you did get out an' about, 'cos you're gettin' more peaked lookin' every day.'

Yes, she knew she was peaked looking. White, thin, and shapeless, that's how she saw herself, whereas Molly, who worked fourteen hours a day and saw to her child as well, remained plump and rosy-faced and bonny.

Molly was a woman of nearly twenty-two. She was almost, Jane considered, past marrying age, yet she seemed to grow prettier every year. But she was no longer flighty; her manner in fact was inclined to staidness, much more so than her own; but this, Jane considered, befitted her years. She wondered sometimes about Molly, she wondered why she didn't marry. Was she still attached to her father? She doubted this. Perhaps she was waiting for Davie Armstrong to come back. But she doubted very much whether Davie Armstrong would ever come back, for there had been only two letters from him in five years, one from London, and one all the way from Barcelona, and this second one had come some eighteen months ago. She had read them both to Winnie, and Winnie had told the men what they contained. They were quite interesting letters, but the spelling wasn't good and the writing left a lot to be desired. No, she thought that Molly would have a long wait if she waited for Davie Armstrong to come back.

Again and again Jane had asked herself over the years how it was she had turned completely about face in her attitude towards Molly, because at first she had held Molly responsible for the ill fate that had come upon her mother. But on reflection, she owned up to the fact that her mother would have given birth to Amos as he was, even if she had carried him for the full time.

Perhaps, she thought, she liked Molly because she was the only person near her own age on the farm, or for miles around for that matter; no one visited them now except the parsons and the doctor, and they, in turn, visited no one. Sometimes she was filled with envy when, on her rare walks to the top of the Tor, she saw in the distance, the Reed girls cutting across the bottom field with the hunt. You could always tell the Reed girls. The three of them had red hair and they dressed flamboyantly. Their names were bandied about quite a lot. Even the youngest, Agnes, who was just on sixteen and almost two years younger then herself, was allowed to go to balls. She understood that the sisters were the belles of every ball they went to, and it was said that men came to fisticuffs over them. There was no possibility of men coming to fisticuffs over herself. Well, it didn't matter, as long as she had Amos to look after and he was happy; that was all she cared about.

Although she no longer went to church, she felt that God had given her an allotted task in life: He had put Amos into her care. But Amos, more often than not, disclaimed any connection with his heavenly Father, and did not live up to his name at all, the name that Parson Hedley had given him on the first day of his life. As no one had been forthcoming with a name, Parson Hedley had said, 'Well, we'll call him Amos, for Amos was a farmer who eventually did great deeds and was good in God's sight, as this child will be.' And she knew he would be, for Parson Hedley was always right.

She said to Molly, 'I'll do that, it's a lovely day.'

'There's heather in plenty on the Tor, you could gather some on your way back. He's never gathered flowers; he'd like that.'

'Oh, yes. Yes, I'm sure he would.'

They both turned and looked at the boy. He was staring at them. He had heard all their conversation and he said bluntly, 'Shall we go now?' and Jane and Molly looked at each other and suppressed their laughter with tight pressed lips, and Jane said, 'Yes, we'll go now.'

The sky was endless, seemingly without horizons. The bracken on the right of the Tor was shoulder high, some already tinged yellow, forerunner of the reds and purple that would turn the fells and hills into a warm flame. At the foot of the Tor were clusters of bilberry bushes, their fruit standing out like black and purple stains, and she pointed this out to the boy. But he didn't seem interested, for his gaze was directed to the top of the Tor.

The easiest way up was through the bracken, but the child would be enveloped in it, the fronds would impede him, and they could easily cut, so she led the way along the narrow road that skirted the foot of the Tor on the north side, where it was mostly shale, giving place to rough rock. Starting from the road was a path, cut diagonally, and slowly mounting its way to the summit, and she took this. Picking Amos up in her arms with the order for him to hang onto his crutches and not get excited for fear he overbalanced them both, she began the ascent. The end of the path was out of sight on the east side of the Tor and away from the road, and when she finally reached it, she dropped the boy to the ground, then sat down on a rock and, panting and laughing, said, 'Well, here we are.'

The child was standing supporting himself on his crutches. She stared at his face; it was wearing the strangest expression. He was looking towards Whitfield Moor and the hills beyond. She watched him look from one side to the other, taking in the great range of space; then his head went slowly back on his shoulders and he gazed up into the sky.

'Isn't it beautiful?' She put out her arm and encircled his waist, and he turned and looked at her and smiled. And he was beautiful too. This face often made her sad, but not today; it was as if she also, like him, were seeing the world outside the farm for the first time. She gripped him to her and he dropped his crutches, and as she had been wont to do since she was a small child, until she was twelve years old, she rolled on the grass, but now with him pressed tightly to her. When she stopped they lay, their faces close together, laughing; then like an eel he was away from her, scrambling over the grass on all fours, his body, from his waist to his hips, wobbling from side to side. When he reached his crutches he began to run wildly here and there like someone demented, and she chased him, laughing as she called, 'Amos! Amos! Stop! Keep away from the edge! Be careful. Be careful.' Every time her hands went to grasp him, he ducked or slithered from her hold.

The agility on his new-found legs amazed her; it was as if he had used the crutches from birth. It seemed that Parson Hedley was right, he was going to be very adaptable. Parson Hedley said he was the brightest child he had ever come across. For a moment a cloud passed over the bright day as she thought, if only her father could see him as Parson Hedley saw him; or for that matter, if her mother had viewed him as a human being; if only one of them had taken him to their hearts. Anyway, he had her, he would always have her.

She lifted up her skirts and raced towards him, for now he was some distance away and nearing the edge of the Tor where it dropped almost sheer to the road below. This part was strewn with loose rocks and boulders and, as he went twisting in and out of them, she had a job to outmanoeuvre him. When at last she caught him, she sat down with her back to a boulder and laughed as she rocked him. Then quite suddenly, as he was apt to do, he asked a most disconcerting question, 'Why haven't I got legs like you, Jan?' He sat back from her straight up on his buttocks, then with a swift movement he lifted her skirt and petticoats back up to her knees.

'Amos!' Her voice held a sharp note. 'You mustn't do that.'

'Why?'

'Well, just because.'

'But why have you got legs and I haven't?'

'You . . . you had an accident.'

'When?'

'Oh.' She closed her eyes and swallowed. 'It was before you were born.'

'What . . . what kind? Did I fall?'

'No.'

'Well, what kind of an accident?'

'You . . . you mustn't ask such questions.'

'Why?'

She couldn't say to him 'because she didn't know the answers', for he expected her to know all the answers. She was saved from further embarrassment by the sound of a pony trap below them. It was coming around the bend of the road. Jumping to her feet and pulling the boy with her, she raised her hand and shouted, 'Parson Hedley! Parson Hedley!'

The man in the trap stopped and looked about him, then lifted his head. She waved down to him again, and at this he waved back, then he lowered his hand and stared at the small figure by her side, and she knew that he was very surprised at what he was seeing. She put her hand to her mouth and shouted, 'We'll come down,' and at this he called back, 'No, stay there, I'll come up; just let me fasten Toby.'

She watched him drive the trap to where the ground levelled off sufficiently for him to take it off the road and where there was grass for the pony to nibble; then she followed his movements as he made his way up the winding narrow path, and when he was below them, she laughed down at him. Then with Amos stumping by her side, she ran back towards where the path came out on the summit. They reached the spot simultaneously and their greetings were high and pleasurable as if they hadn't met for some long time, instead of twenty-four hours previously.

The parson was a man of medium build. He had flat rather blunt features, none of which had any claim to good looks, except perhaps his eyes; even these were nondescript in colour, being of a flecked grey. But it was the eyes that gave interest to the face; perhaps it was the kindliness and understanding in their depths, and a certain sharp keenness in their glance, which rarely held censure, that made them attractive.

He gazed down at the boy who had become a deep interest in his life, as also had his sister, but whereas he could express his feelings on the former, he had to hide them on the latter. For all her capabilities, he still considered Jane a child, and even if she hadn't been, there remained circumstances which prevented him from presenting himself as anything but a friend, pastor, and tutor. But with the child it was different, and now he exclaimed loudly, 'Well! Well! A day of miracles. What is this?' He stood back and surveyed the boy standing erect, shoulders hunched, on the small crutches; and when Amos, in his forthright manner, stated, 'I've got legs,' he had to pause before answering, 'Indeed, indeed you have, Amos. Now why didn't we think of this before, eh Jane?'

Jane smiled widely at him. 'That's the very thought that came to me a short while ago, Parson. Perhaps it's because I thought he couldn't manage them. . . .'

'I can manage them, look, look,' Amos interrupted while he demonstrated, going round in small circles, and she laughed as she caught him, crying, 'We can see. Yes, darling, we can see. But you'll make yourself dizzy. Come along, sit down.'

When they were seated on the grass, Arnold Hedley gazed before him for a moment in silence, then said, 'It's years since I was up here; I'd forgotten how magnificent was the view.' Then glancing at the boy who was sitting to the side of Jane, he said low, under his breath, 'It was good for him to see the world for the first time from this spot. It was like you to think of bringing him up.'

'It wasn't my idea, Parson, it was Molly who suggested it.'

He looked into her face. She was so honest, she would not even take a little credit to herself when it rightly belonged to someone else. Her face to him was beautiful, for it held the beauty of honesty, the beauty of an unselfish nature and a kindly heart. True, she was given to bouts of temper, but then she was but human. And she was young, so young, too young to have the responsibility of mothering this boy and running that disemboweled tortured household. He was often amazed at the gaiety she managed to maintain. But then her charge, although terribly handicapped, was a lively, intelligent little fellow, too intelligent, he considered at times, for his age. But he supposed God in His wisdom had given him the gift of memory and keen perception to make up for his lack.

He was bending forward towards Jane to make a further comment when he was pushed aside by Amos's roughly forcing himself between them from behind. The force levelled by the child's arm into his ribs was of a strength one would associate with a boy of ten or twelve. He held back his head and surveyed the child as Jane admonished him, saying, 'That's naughty, Amos. You mustn't push like that. That's very naughty.'

Amos was now sitting upright between them. There was a slight smile on his face, and with a lightning movement he turned to the parson, raised his hand, and viciously nipped the lobe of his ear.

When Arnold Hedley actually cried out with equal amounts of surprise and pain, Jane, snatching the boy's hands, slapped them hard as she cried, 'That's very wicked, Amos, very wicked. How dare you!'

Amos stared wide-eyed up at her, and, his smile sliding into a grin now, he said, 'He pulls my ear.'

She exchanged a glance over his head with Arnold; then she swallowed and said, 'Parson does it playfully, he never hurts you. There is a difference between pulling and nipping. If you ever do that again, you'll get a sound smacking, a real smacking.'

The smile slid from the boy's face, his eyes clouded, and his lips fell firmly one on the other. In another child of similar years this might have been a prelude to tears, but he showed no signs of crying; instead he threw himself forward onto his hands and knees, crawled swiftly to where his crutches were, stood up on them and, looking from one to the other, said firmly, 'I'm going down to the farmyard.'

'You will wait a moment.' Jane put out her hand to stop him, but he was gone, and when she rose and ran after him, Arnold Hedley got to his feet. His ear was still stinging; the boy's nails had almost pierced the skin. He felt the lobe gently as he looked to where Jane was struggling to hold the child from going towards the path, and now he went swiftly to them saying, 'Let's go down; I've got a lot of calls to make before evening. Here, you take the crutches and I'll carry him.'

When he stooped and lifted the boy up, Amos smiled into his face, and he smiled back at him; and he said as Molly often did, 'You're an imp, young fellow, you're an imp.'

'Can I ride in your trap?'

'Yes, of course you may.'

'I'm going to have a trap and a horse.'

Arnold turned and glanced enquiringly at Jane. When she shook her head, the motion did not go unnoticed by the boy, for he twisted round and cried at her, 'I am! I am, Jan. I'm going to have a horse and trap. And I'm going into the town, I'm going to race papa into the town.'

Neither of them gave any answer to this. In single file they made their way down the sloping path of the Tor, and along the road to the pony and trap. There was a quietness on them now, a restraint, and Jane was acutely aware of it; she was to remember this day for as long as she lived, the day when Amos had nipped Arnold's ear.

Chapter Three

The sun was going down as Davie Armstrong came up the south side of the Tor, walked over the top, and stood on the summit, almost in the same place where Jane and Parson Hedley had sat a few hours earlier. A feeling, long starved of expression, rose from the depths of him and escaped on a long, long breath. He sighed before muttering aloud, 'The bonny hills. Aye, the bonny hills.' There was a softness in his tone and a moisture in his eyes as if he were being reunited with a loved one.

He hitched the canvas bag further onto his shoulder as he looked to the left of him where he could see the smoke rising straight up from the farmhouse chimneys and, a short distance away, three straight spirals in a row from the cottage chimneys. His gaze moved over the fields into the far distance to the ridge on which he used to pause for a moment before going down to the meadows to collect the cows. It was a fine view from the ridge, but up here was finer, wider, grander. In his remembering, it had been from this point he had viewed his land, and when he compared it with the places he had seen over the last five years, he had always found them wanting.

He had landed in Newcastle last night, and for the past week he had been telling himself that that was as far as he was going to go into Northumberland. Although he was longing to see his folks he knew that, once back, the sickness would start up in him again, the sickness for the hills, for the wide sky, wider it seemed than any he had viewed on the oceans that he had crossed. There, you couldn't tell which was sky and which was water, but here the sky was an endless canopy of clear light. And up here you knew it went on forever and ever.

'Aw well, enough of this.' He spoke aloud, then stepped over the edge of the Tor onto the winding path and went down onto the narrow road, along it and onto the main road, and slowly, with steady step and a slight swaying to his carriage, he came back to the farm.

Mickey Geary was the first to see him. Mickey was coming along the road with a dog by his side. The dog barked and ran from him and towards the oncoming stranger, and as it stood yapping the boy stopped and, his jaw dropping and his face spreading into a wide grin, he exclaimed. 'Why! Why, it's you, Davie. Eeh! You've come back. Why, man? Eeh! We never thought to see you again.'

Davie came up to the small boy, for Mickey at thirteen was still undersized, but his face as always was round and bright. He put his hand on the boy's head and ruffled his hair, saying kindly, 'By lad! Mickey, how you've grown. I wouldn't have known you,' although he was thinking that the boy had hardly changed in five years. 'Well, well! An' how is everybody?'

'Oh, you know.' Mickey jerked his head. 'Things 've changed a lot since you left, Davie. Eeh! Your ma 'll be over the moon.'

'Granda all right?' He asked this question tentatively; it had been a fear in him for a long time that he wouldn't see his Granda again.

'Aye, oh aye, like a linty. Me ma says he'll never die, they'll have to take him to the slaughterhouse.'

Davie laughed and jerked his head, then said, 'Well, I'll be seeing you again, Mickey. So long for the minute.'

As he walked away the boy called, 'You home for good, Davie?'

'No, no, lad, no farm life for me, not after being on the briny.' He saluted from the peak of his cap, and the boy stood watching him in admiration as he stepped off the main road, crossed over the wide grass verge and onto the narrow path fronting the cottages.

Just before he opened the door he dropped his bag from his shoulder and took off his cap; then thrusting the door back with a flourish, but still holding the knob, he bent forward, his hat held like a quoit in his hand, ready to throw, as he cried, 'Do I have to chuck it in to test me welcome?'

'Oh my God!' Winnie muttered the words, but she didn't immediately rise from her chair or put down the pair of moleskin trousers she was patching, nor did Ned take the tacks from his mouth or lift the last from his knee on which was a boot he had been soling. It was Sep who first rose to his feet. The clay pipe had dropped from his hand onto the mat, and he made no effort to retrieve it, but came slowly across the room. Yet before he had reached Davie, both Ned and Winnie were by his side. Then on a gabble of high exclamations, they all stood entwined, and it was Winnie who held onto him to the last. The tears raining down her face, she kept saying, 'Oh lad! Oh lad! What a shock,' until he pressed her from him and, holding her at arm's length, cried, 'Well, if that's the way it's gona be, I'd better make me stay short, eh?'

'Sit down, sit down, and let's look at you.'

'You'll get a better view standing up.' He posed before her, spreading his arms wide and turning round. And she laughed, they all laughed; and then, still looking at him, still crying, she said, 'Eeh! I'd better put the kettle on. Are you hungry, lad, have you had anything to eat? Why didn't you let's know you were comin'? Where've you been? I mean where've you come from?'

'Hold your hand, woman.' Ned pushed her in the shoulder. 'Give him time to get his breath; it'll take him a week to answer that lot. Come and sit down, lad. Come and sit down.' His voice was soft and breaking and he stood aside and watched his son take his own seat by the fire.

Davie looked at his father, and Ned said quietly, 'It's good to see you, lad.'

'You, too, Da.' He felt a warmth towards his father that was new. He had expected to find him much older looking, more crippled with the rheumatics, but it was as if he had left him only yesterday; and his grandfather, five years added to his sixty-seven had done little to alter him outwardly, except to bleach his hair to a silvery white and turn the stubble round his face to a dirty grey. It was his mother who was altered. Her hair had been touched with grey, but now it was all grey, not a brown streak to be seen; and her face was thinner, she was thinner all over. He leaned forward and caught her hand as she stood with her back to the table gazing at him, and she came to his side and with a quick movement pressed his head against her breast before pushing it from her again and turning away to busy herself with making the tea.

'I can't believe it, lad.' Sep was shaking his head now. 'Out of the blue, just like that. When did you get in?'

'Last night, Granda.'

'Where've you been?'

'Where haven't I been!' He pulled his brows down and moved his head slowly.

'Well, wherever you've been, it's broadened you.' His father's eyes were looking over him, from his brown hair that seemed lighter now, over his tanned features, over his shoulders filling his melton-cloth coat, down to his stout boots, and he ended, 'You've put on some weight I'd say.'

'Aye, Da; but mind,' he pointed, 'it isn't from the good grub they feed us, by! no.'

'Bad?' Sep poked his head forward, and Davie nodded at him. 'Rotten would be a better word, Granda; terrible on some boats. You mightn't believe it,' again he was pointing his finger, 'there was many a day during the first year I was away I envied the pigs their swill. By lad! When I think what I used to give those pigs, and what we got on that boat.'

'You've been on more than one boat?' Winnie turned from the table, and he looked towards her and said, 'Aye, Ma. This one now is me second; I've been with her nearly four years. It's a good ship, that is if you can say any of them are good.'

She turned her attention fully on him now and stared at him in silence for a moment before saying softly, 'You don't like it, I mean the sea?'

'Well, Ma—' He leaned back in his chair, stretched his legs out, then flung his arms wide and said, 'That's a question that's going to take me three full days to answer, for sometimes I do, an' sometimes I don't. When I'm on it I hate it, when I'm off it and on dry land I'm longing for it. Tell you truthfully, I don't know me own mind. Yet there's one thing I do know.' He nodded first at his father, then at his grandfather, before he continued, 'It's a damn sight better than working on the land, I mean the prospects. Don't you notice anything about me?' Now he was grinning at them, sweeping them with a merry glance; and they looked him over again and shook their heads while they laughed back at him, and he said, 'Oh well, a prophet in his own country. That's what I'm always saying.' The phrase was not applicable to the situation, but it sounded fine, and learned. And one thing that he was always quoting was true, 'You're not looking on any ordinary donkey room pony, you know.'

'No!' Old Sep's mouth was wide, his face one great beam.

'No, Granda, no; you see before you a second mate.'' He now sat up and preened himself, and his chest swelled naturally when they murmured, 'Second mate on a ship!'

'Well, the *Arcadia* is not a fish barrel, although mind, I have to confess she's had to stoop low sometimes when she's been short of a cargo out there and fill her hold with whale carcasses.'

'How in the name of God did you come into that, lad?' His grandfather's face was screwed up with an enquiry. 'I thought you had to sit for your ticket for that kind of thing.'

'Well, he can read and write, can't he? He could have sat for his ticket . . . did you?' Winnie was looking at him.

'Not exactly, Ma, not in the ordinary way. You see when you're out there plying between one port an' another, scrounging cargoes, you're likely to get half eaten up by the thousand and one different kinds of flies that they breed, and some folks' blood objects to them. Like those beggars polished off two second mates within nine months. So nobody seemed to want the job, 'cos there was the idea that them flies made a bee line, so to speak, for second mates, though how they picked them out beats me, not being able to read. Well, as I said to the captain, there's one born every minute, so I'll take the job, thank you very much. An' that's how it came about.'

At this there was a gale of laughter, and Winnie wiped the mixed tears from her face as she handed him a mug of tea. Then after he had drunk more than half of it at one gulp, he said in a more serious tone, 'That was how it happened in a way. But as me ma said, it was because I could read an' write, and I wasn't slow to pick up things.' He smiled quietly now and looked from his father to his grandfather and added kindly, 'You must have given me something atween you; or did I get it from me ma?' He was laughing again and he reached out his hand and slapped Winnie's buttocks, and she turned round quickly, her face a bright red as she exclaimed, 'Well, I never! You're never done that in your life afore. By! It would seem you have learned more than sailing a ship since you've been away.'

He grinned at her now as he said, 'Could be, Ma, could be.' And they laughed again.

They laughed while the meal was being prepared. They laughed during the eating of it. They laughed until Winnie, rising from the table, said, 'Eeh! I've forgotten all about it, I should be over the road; the missus will think I've forgotten her.'

'Nine o'clock!' Davie looked up at her. 'You go over there at nine o'clock at night?'

'I've got to settle her for the night.'

'Why?'

'Oh, it's a long story. She's hardly been out of bed since . . . well, you know, since that night.'

He looked from one to the other. He hadn't asked about the concerns of the house, about the master, or the legless baby, yet it wasn't because they hadn't been in his mind; he had thought he'd let the topic come naturally. But nobody had mentioned the house until this minute, perhaps because up till now he had been having all the say. He looked at his mother now and said, 'Well, don't be long then'; and she smiled back at him as she answered mischievously, 'I won't. I'll be back in time to put you to bed.'

'Go on with you.' As he slapped her buttocks again, his mind leaped back to the days when, as a small child, well under five, he had refused to go to bed unless she was there, and she would say to him, 'Now sit still an' don't wander, an' I'll be back afore you know it and put you to bed.'

When beat she had gone and they were sitting before the fire, he asked a question. 'How are things round about?' he said, and they told him, Sep doing most of the talking, while Ned added points that sounded pessimistic, even beyond his checkered outlook on life, such as when, speaking enthusiastically about Amos, Sep said, 'Eeh! He's a marler. You've no idea. And as bright as a button. You should hear him talk, talk about a sea lawyer. Just you wait till you hear him. And you should see him on his new legs. Ned here made him a pair of crutches; you'd think he'd been on them since he was born an' he just got them the day. Aw, he's going to be a bright spark, that 'un.' It was at this point that Ned put in, 'Aye, but he's got a cruel streak in him, I think.'

'What d'you mean, cruel streak? He's no less of a lad 'cos he hasn't got any pins. You mean 'cos of what happened with Biddy the day?'

'Aye,' said Ned. 'But that isn't the first time that he's swiped her, nor taken her glass alleys.'

'Aw, that bairn's playin'; Miss Jane always brings them back.' Sep now turned to Davie, explaining, 'He plays marbles with Biddy. You want to see them both at it; she's nearly as good as him, but he always manages to win her best blood alley. He's even beat Mickey at it. Oh, he's a great one with the plonkers.'

'Who's Biddy?'

Sep was about to speak, but his breath caught in his throat, and he coughed, then, rubbing the tip of his nose with his first finger, he mumbled, 'Molly's bairn.'

There was a short silence while the three of them looked at each other, and then Davie, his eyebrows rising, his lips pursed, repeated, 'Molly's bairn?'

'She's a nice child,' it was Ned speaking.

'No doubt.'

So the master's son and Molly's child played marbles together. Well, well.

'What's past is past,' said Sep quietly. 'Molly's turned out a hard workin' lass, an' sensible at that. It's five years, you know, lad, since you left, an' she's worked every day of that time, from mornin' till night she has, an' she's bringing the child up decent. Dresses it well and spends most of her wages on it; that's after she pays that old skinflint Casey for minding it.'

'She didn't marry . . . she didn't marry Curran then?'

'No, no; she refused flatly. She did that.'

'What! After her lord and master giving her her orders?'

'Aw now, now,' Sep wagged his head, 'that's all over. As I said, five years is a long time, and she was little more than a bairn herself.'

'By! lad—' Davie grinned sardonically now, looked first at his grandfather, then at his father, then back to his grandfather again before he said, 'We've changed our tune, haven't we?'

'Speak as you find.' Ned's voice was quiet. 'Whatever harm she did she's payin' for it in the only way she knows how. She's devoted to Miss Jane an' works like a horse to ease her plight.'

'What plight? What's happened to Miss Jane?'

'Nothing's happened to her except that she's had to give every hour of her time, not only wakin' but sleepin', to the child. She's brought him up, and for the first three years of his life, she lived in the attic with him an' hardly left it.'

Davie slowly moved his body forward and repeated, 'The first three years she lived in the attic with him? Why in the attic?'

Now Ned and Sep exchanged fleeting glances, and it was Ned who in his brief terse way gave a rough description of the circumstances under which the child had been brought up; and when he had finished, Davie sat straight in his chair and stared at his father. Then he said softly, 'And you mean to say that neither of them, him nor her, ever speak to the child? You mean that all these years they've kept it up?'

'Well,' Ned reached out his hand and knocked the doddle from his pipe against the hob, 'the mistress, she's been more or less bedridden. It's said she could slip away any time. Winnie believes that some mornin' she'll go in an' find her gone. As for the master's attitude, well, you know as much about the cause of that as any of us. He's a changed man an' I never thought I'd be able to say I pity him, but I do! In his eyes, he has neither wife nor child while havin' both.'

'Aren't there any young heifers left round about?'

Ned lowered his head at this and remained silent, leaving it to Sep to say quietly, 'As your da says, lad, the master's a changed man. He's got nawt left, not even God. Parson Hedley comes twice a week to tutor the boy, and has a word with him. But it's got no effect, the only one that he has any use for is Miss Jane. The whole household seems to hang on the lass an' I wonder meself how long her thin shoulders 'll be able to bear it. But now that the young master can get out and about, things should be better for her.'

'What'll happen if she wants to get married, what'll they do then?'

'Oh! Married?' said Sep. 'I can't see Miss Jane marryin', her whole life's taken up with the child. You'd really think it was hers. An' he won't let her out of his sight. She's mother, father, nurse, the lot to him. No, I can't ever see Miss Jane marryin'.'

'Well, well.' Davie again pursed his lips. 'What a prospect for a young lass. What does she look like?'

'Oh,' Sep put his head on one side as he smiled, 'still plain, some would say, an' no figure to speak of, but she's got somethin'. Hard to tell, hard to put a finger on, but she's good for a crack, she'll listen to you, she seems to want to listen to folks. If she hadn't been handicapped with the child, I think she might've blossomed into somethin' fine. What I mean is, if she'd been able to mix with them of her own age, 'cos she's got a sort of gaiety about her. It's quiet, under the skin like, but she's not without spirit. Oh no, she can take a firm hand with Master Amos. Sometimes when I've looked at her, I've thought she's just missed being bonny; but there, she's a sensible young woman.'

Davie got to his feet and placed his pipe on the mantelpiece; then punching his grandfather gently on the side of the head, he said, 'God save me from sensible young women, Granda.'

As he went slowly towards the door, Sep asked quietly, 'What kind of women have you seen, lad?' There was more to the question than the actual words conveyed, and he turned and laughed at them over his shoulder as he said, 'I've three days afore I go back, I'll give one of them up entirely to tellin' you all about that, an' likely at the end you'll get the parson to me, aye. By the way, how are they? Has old Wainwright kicked the bucket yet?'

'No, lad.' Sep laughed. 'But Peter Skillet was past here t'other day an' he said the old codger can hardly stand on his pins. He said, when he was takin' Alice Knowles's burial service, he wanted to say "Go careful, parson, else you'll be lyin' on top of her, then it'll be a toss-up whether to cover you up or pull you out."'

Davie chuckled, then asked, 'An' Parson Hedley?'

'Oh, he's all right. Good man, Parson Hedley. But I'll tell you something. You remember Clarke, Sam Clarke?'

'Sam Clarke, the verger? Of course.'

'Aye, cast-thy-bread-upon-the-water-Clarke, an' the size of the bread he'd cast wouldn't choke a sparrow. Well, an uncle in Australia died an' left him a fortune.'

'Go on.'

'He did, it's a fact. Ten thousand pounds they say.'

'Whew!' As Davie shook his head his father put in quietly, 'He cast his bread an' got a bakehouse back, full o' dough.'

Davie had never heard his father crack a joke in his life, and this was a real good one. He lay against the door, his head back, his mouth wide, and bellowed, and they joined him.

It was good to be back.

After he had wiped his eyes he said to his father, 'Don't think I've heard better, Da, since I've been away,' which compliment brought a slight flush to Ned's face.

He now opened the door and stood looking out onto the roadway. The twilight was deepening rapidly, and a missel thrush, making a late journey up the road towards the copse, shrilled petulantly as it passed him. There came the sound of a single moo from the direction of the farm, and somewhere in the near hills a fox barked.

For five years he had dreamed of these sights and sounds, and now they were his again, but for only three days. If things had been different and he had left this place in ordinary circumstances, he would have gone this very minute to the master and said, 'Have you a place for me, it doesn't matter what?'

The feeling in him to remain was like a pain. He longed to rest in the folds of the fells and to be invigorated in turn by climbing the hills; he wanted to struggle against the keen winds and breathe in the same air that he had taken with his first breath, to come back, in fact, to where he belonged. But this he knew was an utter impossibility, so he would make the best of the time he had. He would put a face on things; he would preen himself in his new position, which wasn't so bad after all was said and done for a raw farm lad to have achieved.

As he stood he saw a figure coming out of the farmyard gateway and into the road. He did not recognize it until it reached the bend of Will Curran's cottage, and then it slowed and he saw the mass of auburn hair topping the woman now, not the girl. He watched her walk slowly towards her own door. Her eyes were on him, and his on her, but neither of them smiled at the other, and neither of them spoke. But she paused a moment before she disappeared from his sight, and in that moment he thought he saw what his grandfather meant by the change in her. But ah! he told himself, she'd still be the same Molly underneath, as he was still the same Davie. Leopards didn't change their spots, and human beings didn't change their natures, only their coverings.

He walked out of the door, crossed the road and jumped up onto the high grass verge, and so on to the fells, with the wish strong in him now that he had resisted the urge to come back. It had been a mistake, and one he would likely pay for in the months ahead.

Chapter Four

'You must keep it out of my way, Jane.'

'But, Father, that is impossible. And . . . and he isn't an *it*, Father, he's a child. And . . . and don't you realize, won't you realize, he's a very intelligent child. Parson Hed. . . .'

'Jane!' He turned from her, his hand on his brow, his eyes closed. 'I'm not going to go through this again. Do you want to make me angry, really angry?' He swung around and faced her. There were two high spots of colour on his thin cheekbones and his grey eyes held a light that glowed under their dullness, like the setting sun reflecting on ice on a dirty pond, and he growled at her under his breath, 'If you persist in letting him get under my feet,' the anomaly didn't apparently strike him, 'I will have him sent away; yes, yes, I warn you. . . .'

Jane stared up into the distressed face. She understood his attitude, and she was full of pity for him, but nevertheless, his words had made her turn pale, and as she often did when afraid, she now showed courage, for she said, 'Father, if you were to do that I would leave with him. I would take up a position of some sort as near to him as possible, and not even mother's predicament would keep me here, nor the fact that I'm still under your jurisdiction. Only by force, Father, would you keep me if you sent him away.'

She did not know what reaction her words would evoke, but she did not expect him to sit down suddenly in his chair and drop his head into his hands.

His acceptance of defeat brought tears to her eyes, and she went swiftly to him and put her hand gently on his shoulder, saying softly, 'I, I will do my best to curb him, I promise you. But . . . but if only you could bear to tolerate him, just speak a word to him now and again, you would, I am sure, get to. . . .'

He raised his head and looked into her face and said quietly, 'Too late, Jane, five years too late. I grant you he's intelligent, intelligent enough to know that I have rejected him, and still reject him, for I cannot do otherwise, so put out of your mind any idea of reconciliation.'

Her heart was sore for him. Slowly she bent her head and kissed his cheek. It was the first time she had done this since she was a small child; and she was saddened further when the close proximity to him brought to her the strong smell of whisky. It was but eleven o'clock in the morning and he had begun already. She had thought he kept his drinking solely for the late hours.

She went out and up the stairs to her room. It wasn't often she could sit alone, but now she gave herself a few minutes' respite. Amos was in good hands at the moment; Winnie had taken him across to the cottage to see Davie. Davie had come home. She had never seen Winnie so happy for years. She must go across and give him a welcome, but for the moment she would just sit here; she felt tired, weary, not only in her mind but in her body. She'd already had a tussle with Amos before eight o'clock this morning.

She had overslept and had waked to see him going through the door dressed for outside. When she tried to prevent him from going down the stairs, he had fought her like a young wild animal. But though she had managed to keep him quiet until she was dressed, once outside he had raced about the yard like a dog off his chain.

When he would not return upstairs to have his meal but wanted it in the kitchen, it was then she made the mistake of saying, 'We don't eat in the kitchen, we eat in the dining room.'

Oh! Then he would have his meal in the dining room.

There had been more explaining, more argument. His powers of reasoning were, in a way, beginning to frighten her. He could detect subterfuge better than an adult; moreover she had known long before yesterday, when he had nipped Parson Hedley's ear, that he could be loving one moment and vicious the next. The latter trait she put down to frustration, for, with his temperament, restriction must be a form of torment.

Sadly, wistfully, she thought again that if only her father would countenance the child's presence in the house, life would be so much simpler, in fact it would be wonderful. It did not matter so much her mother ignoring his presence, for they need never meet.

The thought of her mother reminded her that she had been without Winnie for the past half hour, so she must go and visit her. She rose slowly and went out across the wide landing to her mother's door and knocked, as always, before she entered the room. To her great surprise she found that Delia was out of bed, actually sitting in a chair by the window, and she ran to her, crying, 'Oh! Mother. You feel so much better?'

'Yes, dear. I, I thought that . . . that before the winter comes I may get downstairs and go out in the fresh air.'

Jane stared down into the faded blue eyes, the thin worn face, and she said softly, 'That would be wonderful, wonderful. Shall I help you to dress now?'

'No, dear, not today, I will just sit here. I . . . I can see the gate from here. I saw Winnie; she . . . she had the child with her.' Delia turned and looked at her daughter and, putting out her hand, that was like a bony claw now, she clutched Jane's and with a break in her voice said, 'I . . . I have made a grave error in . . . in shutting him out. It was wrong of me, very wrong. I . . . I must try to make amends.'

'Oh! Mother, Mother.' The tears slid slowly down Jane's face; she gathered the two hands to her, and holding them tightly against her breast, she said, 'Oh, that's wonderful, wonderful. He's so bright and clever, he could grow up to be anything he chose. Parson Hedley says that he has great hopes for him.' And now she bent forward and kissed her mother on the cheek, and she had not done this, either, for many years.

For a moment Delia stroked her hair, then, her attention drawn to the window, she looked out and towards a small figure toddling across the yard below, and she said quite calmly, 'Molly's child is quite pretty, don't you think?'

Jane gave no answer to this—she was too overcome at the turn of events; she just watched Biddy toddling in the direction of the cow shed. Before she reached it, however, her father emerged. The child looked up at him, but he paid no attention to her; he ignored her as he would have done Amos.

Jane looked at her mother. She was staring down into the yard following her husband's progress. Her gaze still on him, she said quickly, 'He's getting old.'

There was such a deep note of satisfaction in the remark that again hope and joy were dimmed in Jane; whatever reconciliation would take place between her mother and the child, there could never be any hope of such happening between her parents. Beneath her mother's fragile exterior she sensed an ever growing hatred of her husband. She turned away and went out without saying anything further.

Down in the kitchen, Molly was busy cooking the dinner. Besides the housework and the dairy, she now did most of the cooking. But the long hours and hard work seemed to have little effect on her–she was strong and straight-backed. She turned from the table where she was dressing a bird, saying, 'Eeh! Miss Jane, I think you're goin' to find these partridges as tough as your boots. This lot must've dodged the gun for the last ten years, an' they'll be stringy. Still, there's some saddle o' mutton left, an' I've made a plum puddin', you can fill up with that.'

She drew the inside out of the bird as she said, 'You could do with a bit of fish, we've never had any for over a week. Our Johnny's goin' eeling the night. Now if he gets any I'll collar one and that will be a bit of a change for the morrow, start the first course off. . . .'

'Yes, that will be nice, Molly.' For a moment she stood watching her larding the birds, then she said, 'I've often wanted to cook. Perhaps now Master Amos can get about on his own I'll have more time; you'll have to show me.'

'No, not me, Miss, you'll have to get Winnie to do that. Winnie's a grand cook; given the time, she can turn out anythin'.'

'Yes, given the time,' she repeated sadly; then on a brighter note she asked, 'By the way, you know that Davie's back?'

Molly did not look up from what she was doing, and she did not speak immediately, and when she did her tone was noncommittal. 'Yes, Miss,' she said, 'Yes, I know he's back.'

Jane went out thinking that perhaps she shouldn't have mentioned the fact that Davie Armstrong had returned. Yet why not, it wasn't a thing you could hide. It was a pity though he had gone away in the first place, for in spite of everything, he and Molly would likely have been married by now.

Again she commented to herself how strange it was that her feelings towards Molly were utterly devoid of animosity; she would like very much to see her happy with a man who could be a father to Biddy, a real father.

It was rarely she thought of the relationship between Molly's child and herself, and when she did, she could not take in the fact that they were half-sisters.

She walked out of the gate and down the road towards the Armstrongs' cottage, and long before she reached it, she heard Amos's high squeals of glee.

The cottage door was open and she stood unobserved for a few minutes watching the blue-clad sailor, whom she hardly recognized, holding Amos up with one hand towards the beam that spanned the width of the stairs about a foot below the ceiling. There was a similar beam at the head of the stairs in the farmhouse; each acted as a span between the stout oak pillars to which the balustrade was attached. A fox's skin was nailed across the beam in the house. She stood breathless now as she saw Amos swinging from the beam without any support.

Davie Armstrong had withdrawn his hand and with his head back he was laughing up at the child, crying, 'Go on, move along it, hand over hand like I showed you.' And Amos followed his instructions. Six times he moved one hand in front of the other and swung himself along the beam. Then she put her hands swiftly to her mouth when, pulling himself upwards with the strength of his arms alone, he squeezed between the beam and the ceiling and, his head hanging over the side, he laughed down at them, until Winnie said, 'Come on, come on, that's enough.'

'No, no, I'm not coming down.'

'Time's up, lower away.' She watched Davie Armstrong put up his hands towards the boy, but Amos just laughed at him and defied him.

She was about to enter the room when Davie ran up the stairs, then turned and stepped onto the banister. One hand outstretched, supporting himself against the staircase wall, he leaned forward and gripped the back of Amos's coat and with a swift tug he pulled him from the beam and held him dangling in mid-air; then jumping down onto the stairs, he hoisted him onto his shoulder. When he came to the foot of the stairs, he stopped as he saw Jane standing in the doorway.

Amos also catching sight of her shouted, 'Jane! Jane! Look. See what I can do. Push me up again.' He bent forward and looked down into Davie's face, and Davie said, 'Enough is enough, young man,' and lowered him to the floor.

'Hello, Davie. I'm glad to see you back home.'

He took her outstretched hand and shook it twice before he said, 'Thank you, Miss Jane; I'm glad to be back. I'm only sorry me stay will be short.'

They looked at each other smiling, and she thought, he's changed so–bigger, broader, and very self-assured. The second cowman was gone, there was no remnant left of the young man who had comforted her in the straw of the malt house, then put his hand over her mouth to stop her crying aloud at what she was seeing and hearing; nor yet of the young man white with anger who, in the dead of the night, had put Amos into her care. She noted that he wasn't dressed like the common seamen. She knew how these dressed, she had picture books of them, and Winnie had already told her of his promotion, and more to follow. First mate he'd be soon, she had said, and then, who knew, captain. And she didn't doubt that Winnie was right. Davie Armstrong had grown into a man, a determined-looking man.

'How are you, Miss Jane?'

'Very well, thank you, Davie.'

He considered she had a nice voice, not la-de-da or anything like that, and it had a lilt to it. He remembered that she had always spoken nicely, due to Parson Hedley's coaching, no doubt; and her face–his Granda had said she was plain, well, he wouldn't have said that, not really, not when she smiled; she had a right bonny pair of eyes on her. She was on the thin side, but then she was young, and would fill out. She hadn't changed all that much; he could like Miss Jane, the young lady, as much as he had liked Miss Jane, the young girl.

'You've got a handful here.' He nodded down at the boy, who was now standing between them looking up first at one and then the other.

'Yes, I'm afraid so, Davie.'

'He's a bright spark.'

'He's a naughty boy at times.' She looked down in mock sternness on the boy where he was now supporting himself by gripping Davie's thigh, and Amos, his head back, gazing up at Davie, said, 'Will you stay here? I want you to stay here.'

'Well, now.' Davie nodded at Jane. 'Tell me, is that an order or merely a request from the captain? Oh, I'm forgettin', captains never make requests, they just give orders. But I'm afraid, Captain,' he saluted the boy now, 'I'll have to disobey your command. It's mutiny I know, farmhouse mutiny on the high fells, but it's off to sea I'm going the day after the morrow.'

Sep laughed, and Winnie laughed, and Jane laughed, but the boy didn't; what he said was, 'You are laughing at me.'

Davie looked down at the boy, who was a small child one minute, allowing himself to be hoisted up to the ceiling, but the next, refusing to be treated as such. He was disconcerting. That word fitted here, he thought. It was his captain's nickname: Disconcertin' Surtees, they called him, for the only response that disaster, from minor to mortal, provoked in him was the term, 'It's bloody disconcerting.' And so was this youngster's attitude. He was an old child, and it was odd when he came to think about it, but whatever he turned out to be, he, in a way, would be responsible for it. In himself he was still convinced that had he not appeared on the scene, Molly would have done the job she had been ordered to do.

'Come along now, Amos; you mustn't be a nuisance.' Jane caught hold of the boy's hand but he thrust her aside and clung onto Davie's leg as he looked up and pleaded, 'Will you play with me?'

Davie stared down into the long narrow eyes and, assuming a stance, he said, 'Well now, let's see; when does this watch finish?' He looked around at his mother, 'Twelve o'clock dinner, is it?' And when, laughing, she nodded at him, he returned his gaze towards the boy, demanding, 'What time do you have your dinner?'

'Three o'clock.'

'Then at two o'clock meet me at the burn and we'll have a swim. What about it?' The last words were addressed to Jane; and now she blinked and stammered slightly as she said, 'He . . . he has never been in the water.'

'Well then, it's about time he made a start. All right, young master,' he pointed his finger down at him, 'two o'clock sharp. Not a minute afore, nor a minute after. Meet me on the cow path.'

The boy stared at him for a moment longer, his face alight; then swiftly he took his arms from about Davie's legs, scrambled on all fours to where his crutches were leaning against a chair, tucked them one under each arm, and was out of the door, all within a matter of seconds, and his voice came to them as he cried loudly, 'Biddy! Biddy! I'm going to the burn. I'm going with the sailor to the burn.'

'Oh, dear me.' Jane was turning hastily to the door when Winnie put her hand on her arm, saying, 'He'll be all right, Miss Jane; just let him go his own road. It's got to be like that, he's doin' no harm. Remember he's a lad an' he's got to run his energy off.'

'But . . . but I promised Fa. . . .' She stopped, aware that Davie Armstrong's eyes were on her, and aware too that there was still one thing left of the second cowman, his hate of her father, and her father's hate of him. She ended haltingly, 'You won't let him stay in too long, he may catch cold not being used to it?'

'He won't catch cold; there's no chill on the water, I was in this mornin'.'

'Oh!' She stared at him, until a flush came to her face, then she turned quickly away and went out of the door. Slowly he followed her and watched her walking to where the boy was standing, leaning on his crutches looking down on a little girl who was sitting on the grass verge cuddling a wooden doll, and he thought, It's a damn shame.

He carried the boy piggy-back down from the cow path to the burn. It was a strange feeling because there were no legs around which to entwine his arms. He carried the crutches under his arm and he did not hold onto the boy's hands clamped round his neck, for he was clinging like a monkey and his arms seemed as strong as any man's.

He did not stop at the bottom of the steps but walked along the bank until he came to the shelf of rock from which he had dived since he was a small boy. He couldn't remember having learned to swim, only that he had once fallen in and that after that it was easy. The water above the shelf of rock ran two feet deep, but he had never yet touched the bottom beyond the shelf, although he had tried many times.

He sat down on the grassy bank and let the boy slide from his back. 'There, get them all off.' When the boy hesitated, he cried at him, 'Come on then, off with your gansey first.' He laughed as he watched the boy struggling with the tight neck of the jersey, and he helped to ease it over his head, saying, 'Don't start by chokin' yourself.'

In a matter of minutes they were both naked.

'Come on.' Davie held out his hand, but the boy didn't rise from the grass; he was staring up at the firm, thick-set bare body. His eyes moved up and down it two or three times, and then he turned his gaze onto his stumps with protrusions, which should have been feet, and his face crumpled as if he were about to cry. Whether or not he would have cried he didn't know, for the next minute he was jerked from the ground and Davie was saying, 'No, not on all fours, stand up straight, you can walk on them. Use them like feet; come on, let's see you. Hang onto my hand. That's it, come on. Toss your body from side to side like this,' he demonstrated, 'an' you'll get it. Come on now, have a shot . . . Aye, aye, that's it.'

When they reached the water's edge he said, 'There now, you keep that up and you won't need those crutches half the time; and your muscles will harden and be as good as any feet.'

Amos looked up steadily into his face and Davie nodded down at him, saying, 'I'm tellin' you, it's true. Try standin' straight, try walkin' straight. Keep off your benders; that's no way to get about, on all fours it isn't. Come on now.'

When the water rose above his stumps and touched his loins Amos shuddered, then gurgled, then laughed aloud, and when it reached his chest, he closed his eyes for a moment as if experiencing ecstasy.

'There now, let yourself go, I've got a hold of you. Just let yourself go, you'll float on the water. Move your arms . . . Aw no, not like that, not up and down like the dogs. Look, stand there a minute and watch me.' He now lowered himself from the shelf of rock into the deep water and swam back and forth for a short way, calling as he did so, 'Like this, see. Like this. Use your arms and your shoulders.'

When he got back onto the shelf he laughed out loud when the boy fell fearlessly onto his face in the shallow water and began to imitate him.

'That's it, that's it. Well, I never! You're like a duck.'

Amos righted himself and stood up, and still with the ecstatic look on his face, he began to move his hands over his naked body as if he were feeling contact with it for the first time. Then of a sudden he seemed to go mad. He jumped and waved his arms about and shouted. He did not shout words, just sounds, but the sounds indicated glee, pure unadulterated glee. When, the water supporting him, he began to prance like a mythological horse, Davie cautioned, 'Steady on, steady on'; but Amos had found that by jumping up he went further down into the water and hit the rock bottom, which sent him up again.

It happened so quickly that Davie didn't realize that it had taken place until he saw the body sinking into the depths; and then he dived. Head first he went through the water that appeared like a silver curtain. His mouth was closed tight but he knew that he was bawling out inside, 'God Almighty! God Almighty!' For a moment he couldn't see the child; then there he was. His hand darting out, he grabbed him by the hair and in the filtered sunlight he saw the boy's face and it had not a vestige of fear on it. So calm was the countenance that for a moment his mind cried at him, 'God! He's dead. He's dead.'

When he broke the surface again, he held the boy up under the armpits and he pushed him onto the ledge and scrambled after him. Then stooping quickly, he carried him up out of the water and onto the bank, and there, putting him onto his face, he began to pump him. When, after a few minutes, he realized he was breathing, he turned him round and onto his back, and the boy gazed up at him, his eyes wide. Then swiftly the child thrust his arms around his neck and pulling himself up to him, pressed himself close while a deep gurgle came from his throat before he exploded on a high piercing note, 'I can swim! I can swim!'

'Swim!' Davie gazed into the face so close to him. His own body was trembling; he'd never had a shock like that in years. It would be odd that, having once saved his life, he had now to go and drown him. By! He was a little marler; he was going to be a handful all right. He didn't envy Miss Jane, or anybody else who had to look after him. By God! He had got a shock. What he could do with was a drink; he was shaking like a leaf. 'Come on,' he said, loosening the arms from around his neck. 'It's time to dry off and get into your togs; enough for once.'

'No! No!' Amos now threw himself on the grass and began to gambol about on all fours; then lying down, he rubbed his body backwards and forwards like a dog rolling in excrement, and with much the same delight on his face.

'Here, come on, stop your antrimartins and get into your togs.'

As he went to pull the boy upright, he let out a high cry of pain, for with a lightning movement Amos had plucked a long black hair from his groin. 'God Almighty! You young devil you. Now why had you to go and do that, eh? For two pins I'd lather you.'

They stared at each other now intently, so intently that they did not see the small figure, until Davie, catching sight of Biddy out of the corner of his eye, again exclaimed, 'God Almighty!' He dropped onto his face and reached out for his shirt and pulled it roughly around him. Knotting the sleeves at the back, he now looked at the little girl who was surveying them both; but before he had time to give her any greeting, Amos had risen onto his stumps and was shouting at her. 'Go away you! Go away. He's my sailor.'

'I don't want your sailor; I was just lookin'.'

'You mustn't look. Go on, go away.'

'I'll not.'

The blow from Amos's flat hand knocked the child onto her back; the next second he himself was swung round and knew what it was like to be really struck for the first time in his life. The blow across his ear was not forceful but it was hard enough to knock him, too, onto his seat and make him gasp, as much in surprise as in pain.

Biddy was crying now and Davie, attempting to maintain the shirt in its precarious position, lifted her to her feet with one hand, saying soothingly, 'There now, there now, you're all right. Go on away with you to your ma. Go on now.' He turned her about and tapped her bottom gently; then he returned to the boy and said sharply, 'Let that be a lesson to you. By the looks of you, you've had too much your own way, young man. Get into your clothes, and sharp.'

'Jane helps me.' The voice was sulky now.

'Well, Jane's not here to help you now, and you're big enough to dress yourself. If you're big enough to belt little girls, you're big enough to get into your togs, so the quicker you start, the quicker you'll finish.'

Davie got dressed and waited patiently for the boy to get into his clothes. He knew as he slyly watched him that he was purposely lengthening the process. By! He was a strange youngster. Loving you one minute, not like a lad might but like a little lass would do, then pulling the hairs out of you wholesale the next. His Granda had been right, there was a vicious streak in him, and if it wasn't curbed, somebody was going to suffer, and by what he was learning of this young gentleman, it wouldn't be himself.

'I'm going to tell Jane that you slapped me.'

Davie jerked his head round and looked sternly into the face looking up into his, and he said, 'Do that. You do that, and you can tell her that I'll do it again if I catch you at the same trick. Come on, up with you, get onto your crutches.'

'Aren't you going to carry me?'

'No. You're a big fella, at least to yourself, so you walk up those steps. Get goin'.'

And casting speculative glances at the sailor, Amos got going.

It wasn't until Jane was putting him to bed that night that he said to her, 'The sailor struck me.'

'What! You mean Davie?'

'Yes, Davie, the sailor. He boxed my ears like Mr Geary does the boys!'

'He never did!'

'He did.'

'But . . . but why?'

He blinked at her, then grinned, saying, 'I slapped Biddy, I knocked her down. She wouldn't go away when we were bathing. I told her he was my sailor and she had to go away and she wouldn't, so I slapped her; and he slapped me. But I still like him, he's still my sailor.'

Jane ignored this last, she felt highly indignant. How dare Davie Armstrong slap the child, even if he had first of all slapped Biddy; children often slapped each other. She would have a word with him about it, indeed she would. He would have no right to do such a thing even if the boy had been an ordinary boy. Had he no feelings for his handicap? She was surprised at Davie Armstrong, especially as the child had taken to him and had openly shown affection for him.

She couldn't really believe it; perhaps the child was romancing. Anyway, she would find out tomorrow, she would ask him outright. And if Amos had been speaking the truth, well then. . . . She paused in her thinking. How did one chastise a man like Davie Armstrong had turned out to be? He had been a headstrong youth before he had left the farm, even Winnie admitted that, but now he was a man who sailed the seas and he had gained a certain position. Whether this had given him his authoritative attitude she didn't know; what she was aware of was that he wasn't a person one could chastise. Still, if he had struck the child it was her duty to do something; after all he was but a labouring man. Oh really! Some part of her flounced at her priggishness, but she defended herself by muttering aloud, 'Well, you just can't let a thing like that happen and do nothing about it.'

Before she went to sleep she definitely decided to have a private word with Davie Armstrong in the morning. But before nine o'clock the following morning she was standing in the dining room defending him.

'Why,' said McBain angrily, 'did you not tell me that Armstrong was back?'

'It . . . it never crossed my mind, Father.'

'It never crossed your mind!' He brought his closed fist down on the dining room table. 'You are no child, so don't act like one. You're bound to know that the very sight of that man will make me want to use a gun on him.'

What she did know at this moment was that five years ago the enraged man before her would not have thought of using such an expression, no matter what his feelings were. She had always been aware that he had despised the more ordinary farmers roundabout, but now his own manner of living and speaking wasn't much removed from theirs, and this unfortunately was reflected in the farm.

There was no real outward sign that the standard of the farm had depreciated, but she was aware that it had. The hand that had once held the reins of the business had been a sober hand, sober, strict, and knowledgeable, and this made for good husbandry, but now his knowledge wasn't used because he woke each morning to a mind fuddled from the excess of the night before.

The name of Davie Armstrong had never been mentioned from that awful night they had faced each other across the newborn child in the kitchen, but instinctively now she realized that Winnie's son had been growing like a canker in her father's breast, because but for Davie's interference, Molly, he felt, would have carried out his orders and there would not have been gamboling round the place a child he looked upon as a monstrosity.

She said quietly, 'You cannot stop him visiting his parents.'

'Can't I? I can turn the whole damn lot of them out.'

The muscles of her face tightened, her mouth set against the unreasonable injustice of this threat; and now, her voice rising, she dared to say, 'You'd be hard put to it to find anyone like Winnie; you don't appreciate what she does. Have you ever thought what it's like looking after mother seven days a week?'

'Be quiet, girl!' His face had a bleached look, even the mottled pattern of blood veins on his cheekbones had paled.

She remained quiet for a moment while they stared at each other and then in a controlled but stiff voice, she said, 'He'll be gone tomorrow and if you're wise, Father, you'll say nothing against him to Winnie, for things are not so bad over the countryside that she wouldn't be snapped up; there's still Farmer Hetherington and his wife is still alive. And I must remind you,

Father, that I cannot take on anymore, my hands are full from morning till night, I'm. . . .'

Her words faded away as she watched his head droop heavily forward and his shoulders hunch as he lowered himself down into the chair, and with his fists pressed together on the desk, he brought out in a voice like a groan, 'Don't . . . don't keep on, Jane.'

When, after a moment, he raised his head and looked at her she was so swamped with pity she wanted to put her arms about him and press his head to her, for she had never seen such need for comfort in any human being; his need she felt was greater than her mother's, or the child's . . . or her own. What was her need? She refused to go into it now; this was something that one wrestled with when unable to sleep. And anyway, it was only a part of life, for as the Bible said, the body was not one member but many. The Bible also said, 'Though I speak with the tongues of men and angels, and have not charity, I am become as sounding brass, or as a tinkling cymbal.' The thought urged her to carry out her desire and comfort her father, but as she made towards him he turned his head from her as if in shame, then rose from the table and went out of the room. The moment was lost, never to return, and she knew this and was saddened to the depths of her.

When she went to collect Amos from the kitchen, where she had left him, Molly turned from the stove and said, 'It's no use, Miss; might as well try to tether a streak of lightnin'. He scooted out of the door afore I could stop him.

'Hold him, Miss? I tell you I'd just as soon try to hold onto the bull. But don't worry–' she gave a thin smile–'He'll come to no harm, he's gone down to the Armstrongs'.'

'Dear dear! He'll make a nuisance of himself.'

'I don't think so, Miss.' Molly lifted the black stock pot from the stove and brought it to the table.

Jane noticed that Molly had made no further reference to the visitor in the Armstrong household, so she herself did not bring his name up. Under the circumstances it would, she felt, have been indelicate.

Molly now said, 'Would you like a blueberry pie made, Miss? The bushes at the back are laden.'

'Yes, that would be nice. Could I gather them for you when I get the child?'

'No, no, Miss; you'll get all messed up and you've got your new print on. I like that one.' She nodded at the mauve print dress that Jane was wearing which had a thin gold stripe running through the material; the skirt was full and the bodice fitted her narrow waist. 'It suits you; mauvy tones suit you.'

Jane flushed slightly as she passed her fingers over the front of the skirt; she was feeling a deep embarrassment, as if she were being paid a compliment by a man, for it was the first time anyone had ever remarked about her clothes, or her appearance. She thought again that Molly, in spite of everything, was a kind creature.

Molly watched her young mistress go hurriedly from the kitchen, then she went to the window and watched her progress across the yard. She was running like a young girl should. She watched her pick up her skirts away from the slime as she jumped the drain down the centre of the yard, and aloud she muttered three words, 'God help her.' She was as sorry for Miss Jane at times as she was for herself. In a way they were both in the same boat. Miss Jane had as much prospect of getting married as a bitch in a brothel; and then there was herself; she'd had two offers in the past year, not counting Will Curran, who watched her like a chained dog. Both the offers would have given her a better life than she had here, so why hadn't she taken them, why? In the past she had refused to answer this question; now as she returned to the table she cried at herself, 'Stop damn well askin' the road you know.'

He was along there, a few hundred yards from her, Lord Davie Armstrong . . . God Almighty Armstrong, and he had never opened his mouth to her. She thought she would have dropped down dead when she saw him through the dusk two nights ago, and she had tossed and turned half the night as she lay with the child by her side, knowing that there were only two layers of brick atween them.

The dawn had come before she closed her eyes, for she had faced up to the fact that she had been a bloody young fool. Yet she wasn't going to take all the blame, she wasn't going to pour more guilt on herself than she had already done; she had enough to carry; she looked back on the episode with the master as a sort of summer lunacy. Her Grannie Talbot used to tell her about such happenings when she was a girl, things that happened after the Harvest Supper; things that had made her put her hand across her mouth and giggle and say 'Eeh! Grannie, you're spinnin' 'em.' Now she knew her grannie hadn't been spinning them; the master had ravished her and, let her face it, she had enjoyed it. When John Curran had first taken her, there had been no joy in that. She hadn't wanted it, but he had forced her and she had been frightened. But John Curran was a babe in arms, in fact an unborn child compared to the master, and yet what had taken place between them had not frightened her. Looking back on it though, over the distance, the mere thought of it now sickened her; it was as if she had been mesmerized and changed into another being.

If she had at that time taken any of Mother Reckett's medicine she would have blamed it on that, for Mother Reckett's doses had been known to do funny things to people; she had known that the mistress had visited Mother Reckett, for she had found the hiding place where she put the bottles. She had never let on to anyone about that, not even to Winnie, and certainly not her ma, though her ma knew all about Mother Reckett. The old woman had got rid of three of them for her ma, although each time it had made her feel bad, and she had never been right since the last do, tired all the time. Anyway she couldn't blame Mother Reckett for what had happened between herself and the master, she only knew that her whole attitude towards him changed when she had stood on the side of the bog with the child in her arms. She had known then that the master was the kind of man who would sell God to the devil if it suited him; and it was strange that what rankled in her mind most was that she had allowed herself to be flayed by him. She did not think of it as a piece of utter hypocrisy, she just thought that no real decent man would have put her up to it, then done it himself. But the bitterest pill of all was the knowledge that through her madness she had thrown away the chance of getting a decent man. And not only that; she had a feeling for Davie Armstrong, not the same kind of feeling she'd had for the master, it was different, deeper, going right back to the days when she first began to follow him into the fields when he was crow scaring. He had never pushed her off when she pestered him, and as she grew up she had thought of him as her property. She was fourteen when she had slapped their Lena's face for saying that she, too, liked him. She had wanted to tell him about John Curran, but she didn't dare, for she felt he would have bashed his face in for him, and she knew it was very important that everybody should get along with everybody on the farm.

But from the night the master had gripped her thigh, she seemed to have lost her senses, gone stark staring mad. Strange, she had thought no less of Davie, but the master's passion and attention had drugged her almost to death. It was as if she had chewed foxgloves and raw poppies.

The whole thing now appeared to her like a bad dream, something that could not have happened in reality. But she had only to look at the master, watch his thin legs in the cords and polished gaiters hanging each side of a horse; it was at such times that she knew it wasn't a nightmare, for she had seen those legs, hairy and bare, prancing and dancing like a dervish.

What madness got into people! She couldn't understand it. She couldn't understand why, when Davie Armstrong wouldn't look the side she was on, when his contempt for her was deep in his eyes, that the feeling inside her for him should grow, and keep her lying alone when her body ached for lack of use.

She picked up her basket and went out of the kitchen by a side door, through the arch into the paved court, and through a gate into a lane that led to a copse where grew the low blueberry bushes.

There was a tangle of undergrowth behind the bushes and she hadn't put her hand out half-a-dozen times to pluck the berries when Davie walked round from behind the bushes.

Although he had been in her mind up to that very minute, nevertheless the sight of him made her start. Determined not to speak first she went on picking until he said, 'Why hello, Molly Geary.' It could have been that they had just met after a long time, except that his tone was weighed with mockery, 'Fancy running across you. I would have thought you would have been up and gone to the big city years ago.' And then she turned on him saying, 'Think you're funny, don't you?'

'Me funny? I never thought I was funny in me life . . . me funny?'

'You're born but you're not buried yet.'

'Tut! Tut!' He made a clicking sound with his tongue. 'Where've I heard that afore. Aye, me da; it's a favourite sayin' of his. And it's a daft saying when you come to analyse it. Of course we're born, and some of us get the chance to live. . . .' He paused and their gaze held before he finished, 'Long enough to know that they'll be buried some day.'

'You still don't believe me, do you?' Her voice was quiet now, full of pain.

'You'll go down to your grave not believin' me; nothing will ever make you think other than I meant to do it, isn't that true?'

'Aye, that's true.'

'Well—' she gulped in her throat. Then her voice rose. 'You're wrong then, you're blasted well wrong. You think as you do 'cos you wanted to think the worst of me. It gave you something else to pin on me . . . t'other wasn't enough.'

It was a few moments before he said, 'T'other was enough, but you went a long way with the bairn afore you changed your mind, didn't you?'

'Aye, I did; right to the very brink. But I did change it. I'd changed it afore you came on the scene and played God. You're good at playin' at God, aren't you?'

'Sailor! Sailor!'

They both turned sharply and looked down the road, where Amos was hobbling towards them on his crutches, followed by Biddy. Both children were panting when they came up to them and Amos cried, 'I've been looking all over for you. Do you know I've been looking all over for you? Where have you been?'

'Up to London to see the Queen.'

Amos didn't follow this, but Biddy did. On a high clear laugh she looked up at Davie and chanted, 'Pussy cat, pussy cat, what did you there?' And laughing, Davie finished with her, 'I-chased-a-big-mouse-from-under-her-chair.'

'Good, good!' As Davie looked kindly down on the child, the while ignoring its mother, Amos put in sulkily, 'I don't like that.'

'You don't?' Davie turned to him. 'Then you don't know a good rhyme.'

'I know 'nother one, Mister.' Biddy was smiling up at him, and without more ado she repeated:

What's your name?
Mary Jane.
Where do you live?
Up the lane.
What do you keep?
A little shop.
What do you sell?
Gingerpop.

Amos was supporting himself now on one crutch, the other lifted breast high, the point end thrust towards Biddy, when Davie cried, 'A-ah! You do, young fellow, you do. Remember yesterday?'

Their eyes held, the boy's and the man's; the crutch was lowered and tucked under his arm, and then he said, 'She shouldn't say lines to you.'

'And why not, boy?'

'Because I don't want her to.'

'Oh! Well, let me tell you somethin', young man.' Davie went down on his hunkers before them both. 'What you want, and what you're going to get out of life, are two different things, and the quicker you learn this the better. Now off you both go onto the green there and play.'

'I want you to come.'

'I'll come in a minute; go on with you.' He gave the boy a push that almost unbalanced him, then stood watching as he hobbled off, sulking, following Biddy this time. When he turned towards Molly she was staring at him, and he returned her glance for a full minute before saying, 'There's not much resemblance atween them, is there? None at all I should say. But it should show somewhere, don't you think?'

Her lips were quivering, and the muscles of her face worked before she said from deep in her throat, 'You're a cruel bugger, Davie Armstrong! That's what you are, a cruel bugger.'

Jane did not have her private word with Davie until about an hour before his departure the following day. Her determination to reprimand him with regards to his treatment of Amos had faded, but even if it hadn't, she doubted if she would have been able to carry it through.

Thinking of what to say to Davie Armstrong when out of his presence was a simple matter, to say it in his presence was a different matter altogether. Although his manner was pleasant, even jocular, he had an air of authority about him which she had noticed from the beginning. Nevertheless, they talked of Amos, and in the boy's presence.

Davie stood at one side of the hearth in his mother's kitchen with Amos clinging to his leg while Jane stood at the other side. She watched him put his hand on the boy's head and ruffle his curls, curls that had taken her quite some time to comb into place; and he looked down on the child while he addressed himself to her, saying, 'He wants a firm hand; as I said yesterday the bit wants tightenin'.' And when he added with a glance at her, 'Though it's none of my business, Miss Jane,' she prevented herself from answering, 'You're right, it isn't.'

She remained silent looking into his face, while she thought, I'm glad he's going away, he'd be a disturbing influence here. And then he brought the colour flooding to her face with his next words, 'I went over to the vicarage last night,' he said. 'I had a long talk with Parson Hedley. Fine man, Parson Hedley. An' he thinks highly of you, Miss. Talked at length about you, he did. Lonely life for a man stuck in that big barrack along o' that old hypocrite. Real old face-both-ways is Parson Wainwright. I said to Parson Hedley he should get himself married 'cos he looked more lonely than a sailor in a dead calm. You should be thinking along those lines yourself, Miss Jane. Coming up eighteen, aren't you?'

The heat rushed down her body to her very feet. He was talking to her as if she were a child, or a girl of the farm. She managed to say with some dignity, 'Really!' And then her colour went a tone deeper when he burst out laughing. 'Aw now, Miss Jane; don't come the fine lady, you're too nice for that. An' I meant no impitence, I was just thinkin' about your future, 'cos somehow I don't think you'll bother much about it yourself. You won't get much chance will you, not with this?' He again ruffled Amos's curls while the child stared up at him, his mouth slightly apart as if he were sucking in every word.

Her lips tight, her expression prim, like that of a maiden lady of twenty-seven, not a girl of seventeen, she lowered her eyes from his, then held out her hand towards Amos, saying, 'Come along.' But Amos answered her quickly with, 'No! Not yet. I'm going to see old Sep; he's in bed bad.'

Jane turned her head to the side with impatience, not only at his disobeying her, but at the term 'he's in bed bad.' She'd have this to contend with, too. The more the child went about the farm, the more of the jargon, the bad grammar, was he likely to pick up. She covered her annoyance by asking, 'Is old Sep really ill?'

'No.' Davie's left eyelid drooped. 'But he thinks that if he puts on his rheumatics it'll keep me here another day or so. He won't believe that cargoes, like time and tide, wait for no man. To hear him talkin' you'd think I was second-in-command to "Tug" Wilson.'

When he saw her eyebrows rise slightly he laughed and said, 'That's what they call Sir Arthur Wilson. He's Admiral of the Fleet, you know.'

'Oh! Oh yes, of course.' She hadn't known who "Tug" or Sir Arthur Wilson was and he knew it, so he sprouted his surface knowledge, gained mostly from the deriding of the navy in the forecastle of the merchant ships, saying, 'He took over after Captain John Fisher, you know, Lord Fisher. He got the title for knocking hell . . . for bombarding Alexandria. You, know, about three years back.'

'Oh yes, yes.'

'He commanded the *Inflexible* . . . No! No! I'm tellin' a lie. Not altogether though, 'cos the *Inflexible* was among the lot. . . .'

'I want to see Sep. Carry me to see Sep.'

'Aw well, come on then; there'll be no peace till you get your way.' He hoisted the boy up into his arms. 'Young devil you are . . . Isn't he?' He addressed the question to Jane as he passed her, and his left eyelid flickered again.

She watched him mounting the stairs, talking all the while to the boy who had his arms clasped tightly around his neck. He had winked at her twice within the last few minutes. Davie Armstrong had winked at her. She did not have to remind herself that this Davie Armstrong was not the Davie Armstrong that she remembered. Really! She was glad he was leaving, otherwise the situation would become most embarrassing. He didn't seem to realize that she was Miss Jane, in charge of the household, which she ran very efficiently. And what was more important, she was in charge of the child. She realized that her position with regards to Amos would become untenable were he to remain here, for he treated her as little more than a girl, a very young girl at best. Yet he had suggested that she was old enough to marry, and had even put a name to the man, Parson Hedley. Really! He was outrageous. Parson Hedley was almost thirty years old.

Davie stood on the top of the Tor on the same spot on which he had stood three days before.

The sailor's bag rested against his leg. It was much lighter than it had been on his arrival, but it had in it something more valuable than baccy, whisky, and trinkets, for it held three large crusty loaves of bread, the like of which he wouldn't taste again not for many a year.

There was in him a new sadness; he knew that he was unlikely to see his grandfather again. Moreover, over the past three days the sea had fallen away from him and the soil had seeped back into his being. But he was already empty with the loss of it, even while it weighed him down; these hills, these mountains, the fells and the valleys, how could a man tear his roots from them? They said the mandrake cried when it was pulled from the earth; he was crying at this minute, his body was sweating his tears, only his eyes were dry.

He looked towards the farm for the last time and when he saw the dim outline of a figure come out of the gate and walk along the road towards the cottages, he thought, but for her I'd be down there still. A cruel bugger, she had called him, and she had been on the point of crying as she said it. He was glad he could hurt her. He stooped down and swung the bag onto his shoulder and, turning abruptly, he walked over the Tor to where it sloped into a bracken-covered hillside, and he went through this until he dropped onto the fells and then onto the main road.

He had been walking on the road for only a matter of fifteen minutes when he heard the familiar sound of a trotting horse. It was approaching round the bend from which he had just come. He walked onto the grass verge, turning every now and again to watch its approach. It could be a carter or some friendly soul who would give him a lift into Hexham, from where he would take the train to Newcastle.

When the trap came into view and he recognized its driver he turned abruptly and walked smartly forward, his gaze directed ahead. The trotting came nearer, and it was just behind him when McBain's voice cried, 'Get up there!' There was the crack of a whip, then the trap was abreast of him. When the whip cracked for the second time and the tip of it came over his kit bag, whipped his hat off his head, and struck its thong against his left temple, he staggered and almost fell into the ditch. Recovering his balance, he threw down his kit bag and, running into the middle of the road, he bawled, 'You bloody cowardly swine, you! That's all you are, a bloody cowardly swine!'

He stood staring after the racing trap; then he put his hand up to his face and looked at his fingers. There was no blood on them, but he could feel the swelling rising from his cheekbone to his temple. He picked up his cap and thrust it on his head and hoisted his bag once more onto his shoulder.

He walked slowly, hesitantly now, along the road, for he had the desire to go back and set the whole farm on fire, do something to get even with that smarmy hypocrite.

He had congratulated himself that he had kept out of the man's way during the past three days, and then this to happen at the last minute. Well, it was five years since he had been here, it had better be ten before he came back again. It would take that long for his temper to cool. But five, ten, or fifteenone day he'd get even with that swine, by God he would.

BOOK THREE

1896

Chapter One

Up till a few years ago Cock Shield Farm had been pointed out as an example of how a farm should be run. The example extended back to McBain's great-grandfather and the pattern appeared so set it seemed impossible of alteration either for the better or the worse. But for some time now McBain's neighbours, both immediate and those not so, had taken great satisfaction in watching the example disintegrate.

McBain, it was said, was rarely sober now. He was no longer in command of his own business. There was slackness on the farm, and it was not only hearsay, you had just to pass the gate and there you saw evidence of it; more evidence still in the cattle he sent into market; and his milk yield had gone down, so much so that he had stopped the supply of milk to the hospitals.

Not that some of the more kindly neighbours didn't pity him, for his son, 'McBain's bit' as he was cruelly nicknamed, was a handful. He might be without legs, but he caused more uproar than a human centipede. Not quite sixteen yet and throwing his weight about like any man, but then he had looked like a man for years. To see him sitting in the trap you'd swear you were looking at a man in his twenties. And his trap was something, too, made up from an old one and mostly by himself they said, with a set of portable steps at the back up which he could hop. A seat for himself on one side was higher than a low one for the passengers at the other, so that generally his head would be above theirs, except when he drove young Biddy Geary into Hexham, and she topped him.

That was a nice state of affairs, the people of Hexham said, when at the age of fourteen he had first driven her into the town.

It was noted that from the time the boy drove into Hexham, McBain ceased to attend the market. Fred Geary went in his place, and everyone knew that Geary was as bottle conscious as his master. And it was Geary who, when well oiled, gave the avid listeners details of the happenings at Cock Shield. He never tired of repeating the fact that father and son had uttered not one word to each other, except, that is, but once, when the youngster had hobbled into the dining room and seated himself at the table. He was ten years old at the time and McBain had cried at him, 'Out! Out!' and when the boy hadn't moved, he had picked up a carving knife. What might have happened if Miss Jane had not thrown herself between them was anybody's guess, so Fred Geary said. But mind, Geary always added, not that he would want Master Amos sitting across the board from himself, for did you ever see such eyes as he had in his head, long and narrow, but so sharp looking they could pick winkles. And that fair hair of his that grew thicker than wool on a sheep's back, it made his head look twice its size. Even then it didn't do anything to diminish his shoulders. Did you ever see such shoulders and arms on an ordinary man? Mind, he would say this, given a pair of legs he'd have been a remarkable specimen, six foot at least when fully grown he guessed, and as broad as a bull with it. But having no legs didn't stop him prankin'. The things that lad got up to, even from he was a mite, was something nobody'd believe. Teased the life out of the lads he did, and the cattle an' all. He wasn't seven when he lashed one of the cats' tails to Rover's, then hung a kitten around his neck. Old Rover was as quiet as a lamb, but that day, God, he nearly tore the place apart, they thought they'd have to put him down after.

Bossy, he was an' all. Everything had to be his. He sort of claimed people; Miss Jane, well, she hadn't a life of her own. As far as he could see she'd never marry Parson Hedley although there'd been an understanding 'twixt them for years. She had her hands right full had Miss Jane. He was dead sorry for her. What with bringing that young 'un up and then the master, and the mistress. Never put a foot out of bed had the mistress from the day the young rip bashed her across the ankles with his crutch, and that was some years ago. It was the very day after Davey Armstrong had gone back to sea. He remembered it as if it was yesterday.

It was in the late autumn of '94 that something disastrous happened at Cock Shield, but Fred Geary was unable to relate it. Typhoid struck the farm, and not only the farm but most of the county. The epidemic brought forth indignation as well as horror, indignation because it was thought that typhoid had been overcome. Hadn't all the corporations been ordered to see to their drainage, to pull down slums where congestion led to filth, and filth to disease? Parts of Shields, Jarrow, and Newcastle had been breeding spots, but much had been done to eliminate them. Hexham had done her part, too. The huge rubbish dumps lying on the banks of Skinner's Burn had disappeared, and everything had been done that was possible to eradicate the fever, so how had it reached this part?

It had reached the farm through a carrier, a man named Peter Hanratty. He had brought Jane some packages from Newcastle that she had ordered by letter, and for Winnie he had brought two pieces of leather for soling and heeling the boots. There was a stall from where he picked up pieces cheap, so cheap that he could afford to add coppers to their price and still leave the leather at half the price Winnie would have paid for it in the shop.

Strangely Winnie didn't get the fever, nor yet did Jane. The first one to go down with it was Delia. She died within four days. Ned was next, he went quickly like the snuff of a candle. The following week Fred and Cassy Geary died within a few hours of each other. One by one the other occupants of the farm waited for death.

With the exception of the doctor and Parson Hedley, no one came to the farm and no one left it, they weren't allowed to.

And no outsiders came to the funeral of any of the four who died. The farm itself seemed near its final end. Even the cattle made sounds like echoes of the death throes.

Yet when the epidemic finally passed and they could throw off the fear of catching the fever, each individual acted as if he had been given a new lease of life. First, Johnnie Geary went to the master and told him he wanted to be married, and could he have the malt house, he'd do up the big room and make it habitable.

McBain's prompt answer to this was, No, he couldn't have the malt house. He had other uses for the malt house. If he wished to marry, he could bring his wife to the cottage that he shared with his sister. It was big enough; hadn't his mother and father reared seven in it?

Johnnie Geary had to be content with this.

Mickey, too, went to the master. But he posed a very odd question. Who was his master? he asked. Who had he to take orders from, himself, or Master Amos? Mickey pointed out that he just wanted to know where he stood.

McBain's answer to this was to say grimly, 'Where you're always stood. You know that without asking.'

It was after Mickey's visit to him that McBain, too, seemed to change. He reverted back to a shadow of his former self. It was noticed that there was no smell of liquor from him in the morning now; he moved briskly around and he gave orders so that all could hear. Moreover he brought in two day labourers to help out the three men who were left. Two further surprising things. First, he began riding again, and then, six months after Delia died and, for no apparent reason, he engaged builders to renovate the malt house.

The first indication Jane had of her father's intention with regards to the malt house was when she was walking along the cow path. Looking down over the scree-studded field, she saw men at work on the roof and others unloading a wagon full of bricks. She did not go down to investigate but returned quickly to the house in search of her father.

McBain was not to be found on the farm. She asked here and there, everyone in fact except Amos–she never mentioned her father to Amos. It was Will Curran who at last informed her that the master had gone down to the bottom pasture to see what the animals might be picking up, as three cows had dropped their calves during the past month.

She did not give way to her feelings and run down to the lower cow pasture; she was wearing her twenty-seventh birthday and her running and scampering days were over, but she hurried almost on the point of a run.

The ten years that had passed had not altered Jane very much. She was a little taller, a little less thin, but she was still neither pretty nor yet plain. Often, in a matron of twenty-seven, you could add the word comely, but not to Jane, there was nothing comely about her. If she had ever thought of dressing up like a boy, she could have passed for one. She would have been shocked at the suggestion, for within herself she was utterly feminine, and being so her emotions tended to guide her tastes. She liked a good story with a love interest in it. She was a devotee of the Brontë sisters; on the other hand; she didn't care much for Mr Dickens, whose writings smacked too much of caricature, and caricature, she thought, was cruel; and all the pictures in Mr Dickens's books tended to show queer creatures. In music her taste was towards Strauss and did not go beyond Mozart. She thought that it was because her tastes were so plebeian that nothing satisfied her. In spite of being betrothed to Arnold she felt lost. Amos no longer needed her, even when he persisted that she keep him company. It was only her father, and of course Arnold, to whom she could act as a staff. Yet Arnold, as dear as he was, had for twenty-five of his forty years taken care of himself. His only need of her, she felt, was as a loving companion. Well, what more did she want at her age?

She lifted the top bar of the gate from the hook attached to the low stone wall, closed it after her, then went across the field to where she saw her father standing breaking up a tuft of grass with his foot.

'Father.'

He turned, showing slight surprise. He hadn't heard her coming. 'What is it?'

'I've . . . I've just passed the malt house. There are men there, workmen.' She watched his eyes flicker to the side. It was an evasive action; she knew it of old when he was reluctant to discuss the matter in hand. 'What are they doing, Father?'

'Well, what do you imagine builders do when they go into an old house? They restore it. I'm having it restored.'

'The malt house?'

'You've just said you've seen them there. Yes, the malt house.'

'Have you changed your mind? Is it for Johnnie?'

His eyes flickered away again, and his lips went into a hard line; then he brought his head sharply upwards and looked at her, saying, 'No, it is not for Johnnie, it . . . it is for you . . . and . . .'

'Me! Father?'

He did not immediately answer her startled exclamation but dusted a straw from his breeches before saying, 'It will be your home when I remarry.'

She thought she was going to sink into the ground; she actually recoiled as if from a blow. It was her expression that brought his head up and his body straight as he said rapidly, 'I am not an old man, I am but fifty-six, I have lived an isolated life long enough. Anyway, this should be good news for you, for when I take a wife you will be free to marry. I have been a hindrance;

you might never have married, with me at this end and old Wainwright at the other.'

Her body slumped slightly; the shock was leaving her, being replaced by a certain tenderness. He wasn't remarrying out of purely selfish motives, he had been thinking of her. It was true what he said. With him holding her here and Parson Wainwright refusing to allow a married woman to share his home, they had been handicapped, for Arnold's stipend wasn't sufficient to provide for himself and a wife. And this state of affairs might have gone on until they were too old to care, but her father had thought of this. She blinked her eyes and said softly, 'I . . . I understand, but . . . but what about Amos?' The eyes flickered away again. 'He'll go with you of course; that will be one of the crosses you'll have to bear in your married life.'

She would have liked to say, 'Oh, Amos won't be any cross, Father,' yet she knew that he would be, for he was of a jealous nature. He did not even like to see Arnold touch her hand. They had to be very circumspect in his presence. But that didn't matter; that contingency would be met in the future. As Arnold would quote, 'Sufficient unto the day is the evil thereof.' She gazed at her father tenderly now. Perhaps things were taking a turn for the better at last. Perhaps the woman he was marrying–although at the moment she couldn't think of anyone he might have chosen–perhaps she was motherly and she would grow to love her.

Then it was as if a mighty hand passed over her, sweeping her generous thoughts away into the wide sky and filling her body with anger and resentment, for her father was saying, 'I want you to prepare a dinner for a week come Wednesday. I will be bringing the Reeds over. They are aware of my intentions; I will be settling the matter with them at the weekend. I am in little doubt but that Agnes is willing.'

AGNES REED! The name came spiralling upwards and seemed to dive out of the top of her head like a startled lark, the echo of the name filled the sky. 'You can't mean AGNES REED, Father!'

His colour changed, the nose that had at one time been thin, but was now bulbous, turned purple, and the tinge spread up over his eyes and brow into the bald dome at the front of his head until it became lost in the black and grey streaked hair sprouting above his ears.

'She's younger than me!' she was yelling at him. 'You can't. You can't, Father, not Agnes Reed. She's flighty, common, the talk of the countryside, she's . . .'

'Be quiet! I command you, hold your tongue. She's a fine young woman of proper . . .' he had almost said 'proportions', but quickly altered it to 'principles'. 'Because a young woman rides a horse as good as a man, why should she be slandered?'

Her indignation was burning her up. As she glared at him she saw him as he really was, as he had always been, a man who favoured young girls. She had a picture of him as he held Molly to him; she saw his lips like wet slugs sucking her breasts. And Molly hadn't been the first. No, her mother in her delirium had mentioned the name, that of another girl, a very young girl, who was now a married woman but also had always looked at her strangely when they met in Hexham. And his jaunts into Newcastle on a Tuesday, what did he do there? He had no business in Newcastle. Oh, she knew what he did there.

But Agnes Reed; that silly addleheaded girl. She hadn't met her more than half-a-dozen times, but once would have been enough to know the type she was. And now she was to be turned out of her home, the home that she loved, that she had helped to tend and care for over the years, the home where she had thought she and Arnold would be spending the rest of their lives, when they married. It was no use her reason telling her that even if her father had chosen an older woman, she would still have been turned out of the house; for she knew the house would not have been closed to her, as it would be if Agnes Reed became its mistress. She shouted at him now, 'You can't do this, Father, you can't! It's indecent. Arnold won't marry you. He wouldn't, he couldn't coutenance it.'

'Arnold shan't be asked to countenance it; I shall be married in Hexham.'

They stood glaring at each other now. The wind had loosened her hair and a strand had fallen over her eyes. She pushed it to one side and with it the first tears, but so full was she of anger that they ran slow. But not so her legs when she turned from him and, picking up her skirts, raced through the fields.

When she entered the farmyard she looked like someone demented. Amos was coming out of the stables and he called to her, 'What's the matter, Jane? Jane! Stop a minute. What is it?' But she took no heed. Nor of Molly in the kitchen who came from the sink, saying, 'Good God, Miss, what's happened to you?' She ran past her and up the stairs and to her room, and there she stood gasping for a minute before throwing herself onto the bed.

It was only seconds later when Molly entered the room and, putting her hands on her shoulders, said gently, 'Tell us, Miss, what is it? What's upset you?'

'Nothing, nothing.' She shook her head from side to side.

'Aw, Miss; now come on, you don't get in a state like this, not you for nothin' you don't.'

'What is it?' Amos came hobbling into the room and, thrusting Molly aside, he dropped his crutches onto the floor and hoisted himself onto the side of the bed and, pulling Jane round to him, gazed tenderly down into her tear-swamped face, saying, 'Tell me, tell me what's happened. Someone done something?'

She gulped in her throat, then drew her fingers across her eyes, groped for a handkerchief, wiped it round her face, and, looking at him, gulped quietly, 'Father . . . Father's going to marry again.'

The expression on Amos's face remained as it had been a moment before, full of concern, kindly; then as the seconds passed, it slowly took on a look of utter blankness.

'He . . . he is having the malt house reno . . . renovated for us?' She glanced from him to Molly, who was standing near the door now. Somehow she felt it was right that Molly should hear the news first-hand. 'But . . . but Amos–' she moved her head from shoulder to shoulder'I wouldn't mind him . . . I wouldn't mind him remarrying, but . . . but it's who he's going to marry.'

'Who is he going to marry?' Amos's enquiry was quiet.

'Agnes Reed.'

'Reed? Agnes Reed, the twin girl?'

She nodded her head. 'She's two years younger than me, it's indecent. And, and Amos, it's not fair . . .' the tears were still raining from her eyes as she gazed into his face, 'is it? Is it?'

He did not answer her, nor did his expression give her any indication of what he was thinking, or if he was thinking at all. But he was thinking; his mind was galloping ahead into the future.

Sitting taut, his body straight, he could have been taken for a tall, hefty young man sitting on the side of a bed with his feet on the ground, so much so that he knew exactly what to expect from life, but also what he meant to demand from it by way of compensation. Going by age, his father was not really an old man, but in the jargon of the farmyard, which he used more often than the stilted form of speech taught him by the parson, he considered his father was not long for the top–frustration and drink had played havoc with him over the years. And it was not a thought brought up from his deep subconscious when he wished his father dead, but an ever present desire in the forefront of his mind.

The hate for his father had increased with the years. He had hated him before he learned, through eavesdropping on Will Curran talking to Johnnie Geary in the harness room, about his father giving orders to drown him, and how Molly Geary was said to have hesitated, and the question still remaining open whether she would have or not if Davie Armstrong hadn't appeared on the scene. He had heard vague reference to the episode of his father whipping Molly Geary because she had fallen, and he knew that his mother had taken to her bed, not only because of his birth, but because his father had had a woman on the side. He hadn't as yet learnt the name of the woman, but it wasn't of any interest to him anyway. He was also aware that there was sniggering in certain quarters with regards to his friendship with Biddy, but he put this down to her being Molly's fly-blow and himself McBain's son, which in one way was correct.

He gathered a great deal of information through his quiet approach. There were rubber cups on the ends of his crutches, and he wore handmade, soft leather shoes on the appendages referred to as his feet; he came upon people so suddenly that he startled them. He had discovered this trick early in life and had always used it to advantage, sometimes to scare an unsuspecting worker almost out of his wits, or to creep up on a conversation.

He had worked out for some time past what he was going to do with the farm when it became his. He would sell all the lower land lying towards the river. Sir Alfred had been after it for years, not only in order to extend his own land but with idea of building a house for his son, for from the rye field, there was one of the finest views in the county. The Manor had nothing to compare with it; all the manor lands lay too low; whereas this particular part of the farm took in the source of the burn; it sprang from high up in a rock wall as out of a gorgon's mouth; it was a silver spray in the summer and a roaring cascade in the winter. But who saw it unless they made the rough journey to it. No, that part could easily be done without, and it would bring in a pretty penny. He could enclose the farm, bringing it down to workable size so that they needn't employ outside labour. What had to be done would be done by Will Curran and the two Gearys. What the farm wanted was reorganization; less land would need less scattered labour on walls and ditches and hedges. And he'd get rid of the hunters; they ate money, hunters. Look at what was spent on them and look at what was doled out to himself. On the first of every month Jane gave him a pound, the allowance his father made him–a pound! He wanted to spit at the thought. At one time it had been only five shillings, and he had been forced to supplement it with his winnings from marbles and chucks. Even as a child he could beat the men at their own game. A ha'penny a game he would play. They had thought it funny at first, until, losing as much as three-pence a week, they called a halt to his monetary gains.

Lately he'd had a craving for money. He had designed a new trap, a spanking affair, something different from the makeshift he used now. It was to have a portable hood and a soft leather seat shaped like a tub armchair from which he could drive. He imagined himself galloping into Hexham or even as far as Newcastle in the rig. In it he would feel the eyes on him, women's eyes, in fascinated admiration. God, what he would have done to them if he'd had legs! But he wanted to rivet their attention onto what he had become without legs, a smart dashing figure in a spanking rig.

With money he'd have a tailor who'd make clothes to suit his bulk. And trousers. He had even designed a pair of false legs made of light wood, strapped to his waist by leather. And the picture in his mind was of him walking up the aisle of the church with Biddy on his arm.

Apart from her being the only one who was likely to have him, he loved her, craved for her. He hadn't seen her bare body since she was ten. She'd got shy and proper after that, but every time he looked at her he stripped the clothes off her. It made not an atom of difference that she was old Geary's granddaughter and that she didn't know who her father was. What the hell did that matter?

And the idea of marrying Biddy had an added attraction, for it would cause a stink roundabout. One thing he was sorry for, his father wouldn't be here to see it because all this could not happen until he died.

Now Jane was saying he was going to marry again, and to Agnes Reed, which would mean he would start a family, for the woman was a frustrated breeder by all accounts. Good-bye to the farm; good-bye to dreams; good-bye to compensation; where would he end his days? Up in the attic? The bogey man to the litter that would fill the house. As if he had asked the question aloud, Jane said, 'He's . . . he's having the malt house renovated for us.'

'The malt house?' He gaped at her, then brought his head down towards her and repeated, 'The malt house?' She nodded silently. 'Well, well, that is kind of him. It's quite a way to the malt house from the farm, we'll be nicely tucked out of his sight.' He now put his hand onto her shoulder and, gripping it, said, 'Don't worry; he hasn't done it yet. He could have a stroke.'

For a moment, she looked horrified; then hastily wiping her face she muttered, 'Oh, Amos, don't say things like that.'

'I was just hoping.'

'Oh, Amos!'

He brought his joined hands together and pressed them down into the coverlet between the stumps of his legs. Then he turned his head and looked at Molly, who was still standing by the door, and as if he too considered her one of the family he asked, 'And what do you make of it?'

'I'm not all that surprised,' Molly answered, then turned and walked out, down the stairs and through the kitchen and into the dairy, where Winnie was scouring milk pans, and without any lead up she said, 'He's gona marry again.'

Winnie turned her head, her face wrinkled in perplexity, then she repeated, 'He?'

'Aye, the master.'

'No!'

'Aye, it's true. An' who do you think it is? That Miss Reed, the horsey one, the one that got her name up two or three years back and went away for a long holiday abroad they said, you remember?'

'No, never! She's younger than Miss Jane.'

Molly now folded her arms and patted her bare flesh as she said, 'Well, here's one who won't stay and welcome the bride.'

'Where will you go, lass?'

'I don't rightly know as yet, Winnie, but I think it's time I was making a move, for more reasons than one, don't you?'

They looked at each other in silence now. The reason was speaking from both their eyes, and Winnie, turning to her work again, said, 'Well, perhaps you're right, lass; in fact, I know you are. Pity you didn't tell her years ago.'

'Aye, it is. But then there are some things that are hard to get out.'

Chapter Two

The dawn was breaking when Amos slipped out of the house the following morning. Molly was not yet in the kitchen, or Biddy in the dairy. Their time for arriving was half-past five, half an hour earlier than in the winter, but winter and summer now Winnie did not begin work until half-past six, it was a concession to her age.

There was a ground mist over the land and his head just came above it; as he bobbed along on his crutches, he appeared to be swimming in it. He was careful when going along the Tor path, for there was a drop on the off side, not over steep but enough to keep you rolling until you reached the valley bottom should you step off the road at certain points.

He left the ground mist behind when he took the Tor path, and when he reached the top the sky had a warm glow to it, although as yet he couldn't see the sun.

It wasn't the first time he had been on the Tor at dawn; since his first visit the Tor had held a fascination for him. But when up here he liked to be alone, even Jane's company irked him. He seldom dreamt when in bed, but he always dreamt up here. The Tor soothed him, brought him peace, and gave him a sense of power. He knew it had a power all its own. And this seemed proved to him one day when, the rain pouring down on the hills around, the sun still shone onto the top of the Tor and it remained dry. And there were days when it matched his black moods, when the rest of the surrounding country was bathed in light, but dark clouds remained stationary, shadowing the Tor rocks, tinting their hue to the despair of his mind.

He knew the history of the hills: the mud-rocks, beaten by time into slate; these would take grass and wear it like a cloak, whereas the slates born of volcanic lava were as cold and hard to the buttocks as steel. But his tor, like a human being, was a mixture. The north side above the path was made up in part of loose scree, yellow or grey or black according to the light; put a wrong foot on it and away you went tumbling down into the road. But on the top, like a soft mantle studded here and there with rock gems, were great stretches of turf, moss, and lichen, which sloped down southwest to a wooded area.

But he wasn't interested this morning in the softer aspects of the Tor. What took his attention was a cluster of boulders, eight in all, situated about twelve feet from where the land dropped at its steepest to the road below. As a child he had played in and out of these boulders, chasing Jane and being chased by her. There was one he could rock back and forward. When he was seven years he stood as high as it, now he could support himself by leaning his arm on it, and he often did while rocking it gently.

There had, in the past three years, been two rock falls from the Tor, both occurring after prolonged periods of rain. The last fall had blocked the road to a height of ten feet, and some of the fall had spilled down into the valley below. A good job, everyone said, it had happened during the night, for someone might have been coming round the bend, and then it would have been a bad outlook for them.

He walked on his crutches to within two feet of the edge of the rock and above the point at which the road below began its curve around the base of the Tor. The rock, shale here, was slack in parts. There was a deep split, a two-inch crevasse, not more than a foot from the edge. A few boulders placed on the outer part could bring it down, but perhaps at the wrong time. They would have to be placed just this side of the crevasse. But how to get them this far.

He went back to the boulders and rocked his favourite stone, but try as he might he couldn't budge it. Yet when he tried the same manoeuvre on the one to the side, he was greatly surprised when he found he could move it with comparative ease.

Within a short space of time he had moved four boulders to within four feet of the edge of the rock, and then he sat back and surveyed his handiwork. If the combined weight of them didn't cause a slide, one of them alone, toppled at the right moment, could sent a pony and trap, or a horse and rider, skitting down into the valley below.

Now on all fours, he scrambled to the very edge and peered over, and as he stared down he had a vivid picture of his father looking up at him in that split second before the boulder hit him, and he anticipated the feeling the picture would give him when it took on reality.

The feeling that he had for his father, which was bred of hate, would at times take on a raging feeling of lust for revenge. Apparently small things could awaken this feeling, such as the sight of Winnie carrying in the cover dishes to the dining room, or his father throwing a leg over a horse.

He had known before he left Jane last night what he intended to do; the only question now was when–it was all a matter of time. There was only one snag that he could see. His father didn't always take the Tor road; but if he was going to the Reeds he'd surely come this way, for it was the nearest road to the village, and the Reeds lived beyond the village.

He shambled back, picked up his crutches, and stood looking at the boulders. If Jane should come up here before he could carry out his intentions, then he would suggest that it was the work of some village lads, up to their pranks. It was well known that they came poaching. But he wasn't worried about Jane, he could always convince Jane of anything he wished.

It was Thursday night; his father had been out twice and had not used the Tor road, neither going nor coming. He had waited through the long twilight last night, even until it was dark. Jane had questioned him as to where he had been, and he had snapped at her, 'Let go of my halter,' and had felt little contrition when he saw the tears coming into her eyes.

His father had returned at nine o'clock this evening from wherever he had been, and was now in the sitting room drinking, and he would be there until midnight. Or perhaps not. He recollected that over the past few nights he had come upstairs to bed a little earlier; perhaps, he thought, he didn't need so much drink now he had comfort in anticipating the pleasures of a young wife. What a pity he didn't get drunk enough to fall downstairs and break his neck.

The thought brought his body slowly upright where he sat in the leather chair before the low toilet table that held a standing mirror. In the candlelight he looked at his reflection. His eyes were slowly widening, his lower jaw drooping. He leant forward and stared at his face. It was a habit with him. He had spent a great deal of time over the years looking at his face. He knew it was an extraordinary face, very uncommon, beautiful in a way. His mouth was full-lipped and looked tender, his nose was straight, his cheekbones flat, and his eyes, his eyes were really extraordinary. He knew he resembled neither of his parents, nor yet any of his forebears. Jane had introduced him to the two albums of forebears when he was very young. 'That is your grandmother McBain; and that is your grandfather McBain. That is your great-grandfather McBain and that is your great-grandmother

McBain. And that is your grandmother Lawson and that is your grandfather Lawson.' On and on. She had always stressed his claim to his forebears to make up to him for the lack of parents, who had been as dead to him from the day he was born.

He had, over the years, worked out for himself the comforting thought that perhaps he was a changeling, a being from some other existence, another world where no one had legs, just short appendages thrusting out from the hips. The feeling of being different from those around him was emphasized when he was visited by strange and weird ideas, ideas more fearsome than those in the stories of Mr Edgar Allan Poe, ideas that would have horrified Parson Hedley had he voiced them, for Mr Poe had never thought up ideas so macabre as the ones his mind prescribed for his father.

And now his thinking had offered him a solution, not a very original one, he admitted, but it could, like the landslide from the Tor, be set down as an accident. He wondered why he hadn't thought of it in the first place.

He slid down from the chair and, going to the door, opened it slightly and listened. He did not expect to hear any sounds. Jane had gone to bed early with a toothache; Winnie had given her some herb tea and a dose of laudanum, she would be fast alseep by now.

He turned and peered through the candlelight at the clock on the mantelpiece. It said ten to eleven. Swiftly now he sat down and pulled off his soft leather shapeless boots. He was about to take off his coat when he changed his mind, thinking, no, he might have to lie there for some time and it would act as a pad against the wood.

As silently as a cat, and not unlike some huge animal, he went along the passage and down the stairs, across the landing and down the other four steps onto the main landing. When he reached Jane's door he stood for a moment and listened; then he went on to the top of the stairhead.

There was a table to the left hand side, on which stood a lamp. Its wick, only half turned up, gave a dim glow to the head of the stairs. He turned it down lower still. At the right hand side, against the open balustrade that gave to part of the landing the effect of a miniature gallery, stood a heavy wooden monk's chair. Gently, he eased it a foot further until the stout back was within a few inches from the square upright post that ran from the ground floor up past the head of the stairs to the ceiling above and acted as a support for the lintel beam placed about two feet from the ceiling.

Pulling himself onto the chair, he stood peering up at the lintel. It was a replica or, more correctly, the mother and father, of the one in Winnie's cottage. Since the sailor had first introduced him to it, it had become a practice that whenever he was in the cottage, one or the other of them would lift him up and he would swing from the beam. Often, as he had on that first day, refusing to come down, he would lie, his head hanging over the side, laughing at them. But he had stopped swinging from the beam when he was nine or ten because he had become too heavy for them to lift.

This beam was more than twice the width of the one in Winnie's cottage and he had no doubt that once up, he would rest comfortably on it. But it was the getting up; he had only his arms to rely on.

The back of the monk's chair was about six inches higher than the top of the balustrade. It was made of black bog oak and the top horizontal rail was flat, but he knew that even if this supported him there would be more than four feet to go before he could reach the beam. He himself stood exactly four feet from the end of his stumps to the top of his head. His arms extended, measuring from the top of his head to his wrist, would give him another foot or so. But the point was he wouldn't be able to extend his arms, his arms would have to act as legs and grip the post while supporting his weight, and his body would then be as a concertina. He could grip tight with his stumps if he could get the object between them, but this post was too wide for that. Once he left the support of the chair he'd have a perilous foot to traverse; he could hang and swing from a bough like a monkey, and slide down a tree, but he had never attempted to climb up one, fearing that the feat would end in defeat, and he couldn't countenance defeat.

He heard a movement somewhere in the distance below him, and it acted like a starting pistol. He flung his arms upwards and to the side, and as he gripped the post, his body swung into mid-air. When he felt himself beginning to slide he spread his stumps as wide as it was possible for them to go, and when each one pressed tight against a corner of the wood the pressure was like a hot iron searing his flesh, but it checked his descent. Drawing in a deep gulp of air he moved his arms upwards once, twice; and then he thrust out a hand and clutched the top of the lintel. He had made it, he was safe. Letting go the other hand, he encircled the beam with his arms, then slowly drew himself up, onto the top of it, and there he lay breathing heavily, one cheek pressed tight against the wood.

After a moment he moved cautiously, easing his body into a more comfortable position for the wait, however long it be.

It was longer than he anticipated, long enough to make him realize that he wouldn't be able to swing forward from this beam, for it was too wide for him to grip with a single hand; he'd have to join his hands over the top of it if he wanted to put force into his body. He also realized that his movements must be swift; he must not expose himself until his father reached at least the fourth step from the top. Then he would swing sideways and catch him on the third or the second step.

By the time the clock in the hall struck half-past eleven his body was becoming cramped, and he knew that he could not lie like this much longer, nor could he ease his position on the beam, for his previous movements had brought him into contact with nails. The lintel, he had discovered, was a fake as to its width. Below, it appeared like one massive piece of wood, but he had found it was made up of two beams nailed and belted together in parts. Moreover it was thick with dust; twice he had to pinch his nose to stop himself from sneezing.

As the clock struck a quarter to twelve he heard a door open, then close, and footsteps coming across the hall. He did not see his father until he was actually mounting the stairs, for McBain had stopped to turn out the lamp in the hall. His body stiffened; he raised it slightly upwards and watched the oncoming figure.

McBain had his head down, looking at each stair as if deep in thought. His step was steady, for his drinking had been moderate. He left the sixth step and it was on the fifth that something caused him to raise his head and look up, and the cry escaped him when he lifted his foot and put it on the fourth stair. But it was throttled in his throat as the stumps of his son's legs caught him under the chin and lifted him into the air and sent him tumbling to the foot of the stairs.

Jane was awakened by a scream and someone shouting. Or had she been dreaming? She'd had a nightmare. The pain from her toothache was gone, but her head was very fuzzy. What was it? She lifted her legs slowly out of the bed and sat on the side of it. She was sure she'd heard someone call out. Had something happened to Amos? But what could happen to Amos?

She stumbled across the room, not bothering to put on her dressing gown, and opened the door and looked out onto the landing. The light was still burning, but it was dim and she couldn't see very far. She glanced towards the stairs that led from the landing to the next floor; then she turned her head slowly and looked towards the head of the main staircase. Could it have been her father calling?

At the top of the stairhead she stood peering down. Then she was crying aloud as she raced down the stairs. 'Oh Father! Father!' She had her joined hands tight against her mouth as she stared down at the contorted figure at the foot.

McBain was lying half on his side, half on his back. One leg was twisted underneath him, the other was across the bottom stair. His arms looked at strange angles; his face was deadly white, his eyes were closed. There was no sign of blood on him. She cupped his head in her hands as she moaned, 'Oh dear! Oh dear!' She looked wildly about her into the dark hall. Then laying his head back, she raced up the stairs again, across the landing, calling all the while, 'Amos! Amos!' She burst open his door. 'Amos! Amos!'

There was no light. She groped her way to the bed and shook him. 'Amos, wake up! Amos!'

He grunted, saying, 'Wh-at is it? What's the matter?'

'Father . . . Father, he's fallen downstairs. Get up, get up and go for Winnie. Go for the boys. Quick! Quick!'

'How . . . how did he. . . ?'

'I don't know, I don't know, only get up.'

'Is . . . is he dead?'

'I don't know, I think so. Amos! Amos! Please, don't ask questions, just get up and go for Winnie and get the boys, he'll have to be moved. Hurry, he's all twisted up. Come on.'

She went out of the room, and he allowed a short time to elapse, time enough for her to imagine he was getting into his clothes, before he went out and down the stairs. Without an upward glance he passed under the beam, and when he reached the foot of the stairs, he rested on his crutches and looked at the figure lying there and felt not the smallest spark of contrition.

Before he stepped over his father he asked again of her, 'Is he dead?' and she answered, 'His heart is still beating, but faintly. Amos, please, will you hurry!'

He hobbled away on his crutches, and as he was going out of the door, she shouted at him, 'Please, Amos.'

He did not hurry as he crossed the yard, nor as he went up the road to the cottage. He decided to go to Winnie's first and was surprised when he passed the window to see a light through the shutter, and as he knocked on the door his surprise mounted at the sound of voices and laughter coming from within.

The door was opened by old Sep who gaped at him, asking, 'What's it, Master Amos, what's it?'

'Father, he's hurt, he fell down the stairs. Jane says to call the boys.' He looked beyond Sep and into the room. In the reflection of the lamplight and bright firelight he saw Winnie standing by the chair in which the sailor was seated.

He would have recognized the sailor by his clothes, if not by his face. It was more than ten years since he had seen him, but the memory of him had always remained fresh in his mind; twice the sailor had given him life, and through water: first, saving him from Molly and the pool, and then rescuing him from the burn. He lifted his crutches over the threshold and stared towards the man who was staring at him, and he said, 'You've come home again then?'

'Yes, I've come home again.' The voice was deep, thick, and rich, and it was as if he had heard it only yesterday.

Winnie interrupted now, saying, 'The master's hurt, badly?' She did not wait for an answer but grabbed up her shawl, adding, 'Oh my God! This is awful. Come on, come on.'

'I'll come along with you.'

Winnie turned on her father crying, 'You'll do no such thing, you'll stay put.'

'Jane said to call the boys,' Amos said again. His voice was flat and unemotional and she answered, 'Aye, yes, that's who we must get, the boys. Come on then.' She put her hand on his back and went to turn him around, but he shrugged away from her and, looking towards the sailor again, said, 'How long are you going to stay?'

'I don't rightly know, a week, perhaps two.'

'I'll be seeing you then?'

'You'll be seeing me.'

When he stepped outside, Winnie was hammering on the Gearys' door, shouting, 'You there, Johnnie, Mickey, you there! Get up! Do you hear?'

When the upper window was opened it was Molly who put her head out, asking, 'What is it?'

'Get them up; something's happened the master.'

Amos stood peering up through the darkness waiting for some word from Molly, but she didn't speak and it was almost a minute before she moved.

Winnie was now rapping on Will Curran's door, but Will was already up, the commotion having roused him; hanging out of the window, he cried,

'Fire? Is it a fire?'

'No, Will. The master's fallen downstairs. You may be needed, you'd better come along.' At this she hurried away and Amos followed behind, but slowly, taking his time.

At the entrance to the farm gate he stopped. There was the sound of activity coming from the cottages, doors slamming, voices calling, feet running. He looked towards the house across the yard. There was a light gleaming now from the fanlight above the front door. He brought his gaze in the direction of the byres and the stables from which were coming faint comforting rustlings.

For years he had hungered for possession of the farm and all it would mean to him, and the feeling in him now was like one of glorious surprise, as if he had waked up and found that he had legs.

He moved on as the running footsteps of the men came nearer, his men. A rush of pleasure and power mounted in him until he reached the hall and there saw his father still lying on the floor, but straight now, Winnie on one side, Jane on the other. His eyes were open and he was staring at Jane while he tried to speak, but although his mouth opened and his lips formed words, they made no sound. The feeling of power seeped from him and he felt sick.

During the next few minutes he stood to one side and watched Johnnie, Mickey, and Will Curran lift his father and carry him up the stairs while Jane admonished them: 'Be careful. Don't . . . don't hurt him. Be careful, he'll be in pain.'

Some short time later he was sitting in the kitchen. When Molly rushed in and, whipping up a kettle from the hob, was on the point of going out again, he said, 'Is . . . is he dead?'

She turned on him. 'No, no, he's not dead. It looks to me he's had a stroke, an' he could weather that.'

She went out of the kitchen, and he was left alone, and for the first time in his life he experienced fear. If he could have picked a death for his father, it would have been slow and very painful, but not under the present circumstances; for if he were to speak now, anything could happen. They could put him away. He wanted to vomit.

He knew it would be no use pleading that his father had treated him like an animal for years, even less than an animal, for animals now and again were given pats and kind words, whereas all he had received from the man who had fathered him were looks of abhorrence and disgust.

What must he do now? He'd have to think. He took up his crutches and went towards the drawing room, the room in which he'd never been allowed to sit. But at the door he paused, then walked farther on and opened the dining room door. It was dark inside. He could see nothing but he knew where everything was; every stick of furniture in the room where he had never been allowed to eat was engraved on his mind, and such was his mind that, even in the state it was now, full of fear, he hobbled into the room, groped for the armchair at the head of the table, and hoisted himself into it, as if he were already master.

Chapter Three

'He keeps trying to say something all the time, Winnie, a word. Look, his lips come together, like this.' Jane imitated the movement of McBain's mouth. Then looking down at him again, she said, 'W . . . w . . . w . . . wound? Work? Worry? No?' She shook her head as she gazed into the eyes that were staring up into hers, their colour paler than ever now, yet their expression keen, even piercing. 'Will . . . Will Curran?' She glanced quickly at Winnie. Her father's eyelid had flickered, then stopped. She said softly, 'Will Curran?'

The lids closed and remained closed.

It was Winnie who said on a high note of excitement, 'Will . . . you know, his will. That's what it is. Master–' she was bending over him–'your will?'

Now the eyelids blinked slowly and definitely, and Winnie raised her head and looked at Jane and stated excitedly, 'That's it, his will!'

Jane's voice, too, was excited. 'You want your will, Father? Don't worry, I'll get it, I'll find it.'

Hurrying out, she ran down the stairs, across the hall, and burst into the office, then stopped dead within the doorway at the sight of Amos sitting in her father's chair behind the desk.

'What are you doing?' There was an abruptness in her manner.

'What does it look like?' he answered coolly. 'I'm looking through the bills and things, somebody's got to keep things going. Or,' he pushed his shoulders back, 'do you think it would be better if I went upstairs and locked myself in the attic?'

'Don't be silly, Amos. And at a time like this. But you know that's Father's desk and—'

'And,' he mimicked her, 'I was never allowed in here. You don't have to remind me. And I'm going to ask you something. Do you think he'll ever use this desk and chair again? He's totally paralysed, and no matter what kind of a monstrosity he considered me, I'm his son, and I'll take over when he's gone.'

'Amos, you talk as if he were already dead, it's dreadful.'

'Jane. Jane.' He screwed himself backwards into the chair, then bent his body forward over the desk. 'It's dreadful, you say. Because I'm honest, you say it's dreadful. You don't say that his treatment of me over all these years was dreadful, inhuman. That's the word, inhuman. And you know something? He's made me almost inhuman, because if they got him out of that bed now and hung him on a cross, it would not arouse one spark of pity in me. And that is dreadful, don't you think, Jane? That is really dreadful. Don't you realize that if it hadn't been for you, I might have been a real "thing"–a real *it* left crawling around that attic. He would have had the windows blocked up; he would have made me into an imbecile. . . .'

'Amos! Amos!' She was covering her face. 'He wouldn't, he would never have done such a thing. He's not like that at all. He's . . .' She stopped, then sank on to a chair, her face still covered, for even as she defended her father, denying all Amos said he was capable of, there was some part of her that recognized that what her brother said might have taken place if she herself hadn't been at hand was true. Human beings were capable of the most hideous things. It has been a hard lesson to learn, but she had learned it. She shook her head wearily, then her gaze focused intently on Amos. Somebody's got to keep things going, he had said. It came to her with an unpleasant shock that he was already running things in his mind; the farm was already his. She felt a shudder of apprehension. Strangely, she did not want Amos to be in control of the farm. True, he was his father's son and sons inherited without question, but her father would not have wanted Amos to have the farm. No, never.

The will. She must find the will. She rose and went towards the desk, saying. 'Have you come across the will?'

'The will?' He shook his head.

'Well, it must be here somewhere.'

She began to search, and he, too. They pulled out drawers, they looked through papers, until, stopping abruptly, she said, 'What am I thinking about? It'll be in the wall safe.'

She went over to the fireplace and, lifting down the picture from the wall above the mantelshelf, she exposed a door. It was an old-fashioned wall safe, having a keyhole to the side. She went back to the desk and, picking up a bunch of keys, said, 'It's one of these.' After trying a number of keys she found the right one and when the door was opened she took out a bundle of papers, some yellow with age, their seared edges curling. When she placed them on the table Amos grabbed half of them towards him and began looking swiftly through them. After a time he said, 'These are all deeds, old deeds, of the house and land.'

'Most of these, too.' She spread her fingers over the papers and bank receipts, then looked about her. 'It must be somewhere.'

Amos remained seated and quiet. He watched her going round the room, searching the cupboards and drawers. She hadn't as yet come to the old-fashioned desk standing in the corner to the right of the window. The desk was a warm brown veneer; it had a four-inch flat top from which dropped a curved lid hinged in the middle which folded back. The writing flap pulled out in slots, and the inner panel could be raised up at an angle for ease of working. There were three doors down one side of the desk and cupboard space at the other. He knew all about this type of desk, he was interested in furniture, at least in wood, and it was through this interest that he had read books on period furniture. There was nearly always in such pieces a secret drawer. He wondered if Jane knew about it. He watched her lifting up the lid, pulling out the writing flap, and opening the little drawers above it. When she spoke to herself, saying, 'It couldn't be in here at any rate, it would be too large,' he made no comment. He watched her pull out the drawers at the side of the desk, and again he made no comment when she said, 'These are full of old bills dating back . . .' she paused as she scrutinized the sheaf of papers in her hand, then ended, 'Dear, dear–a seed bill from 1822.'

Her examination of the cupboards at the other side revealed only further bundles of bills, and when she straightened her back and asked, 'Where can it be?' he answered, 'If you don't know, how should I?'

She stood biting her lip for a moment, then said, 'I'd better get back; he may be able to give me some indication.'

He watched her go out of the room. Then slipping down from the chair and moving on all fours to the desk, he pulled himself up. Having raised the lid, he drew out one of the small drawers above the writing flap and gently moved his fingers along the roof of the drawer and, as he expected, came upon a knob, and when he pressed this gently, the whole top of the desk rose slowly and exposed a long narrow shelf with a similar drawer beneath. On the shelf lay what Jane was looking for. Without examining it, he thrust it inside his coat. Then reaching out he pressed the top of the desk down into place again, closed the flap, crawled back to his crutches, and went out and up the stairs to his room.

The door closed, and having no fear of interruption, he sat down near the window and unfolded the long piece of parchment, to find it held a similar piece inside. He held them up and looked from one to the other; then he read the outer one first. It began in legal terms:

'I, Angus Forrester McBain, of Cock Shields Farm in the County of Northumberland, revoke all wills and testamentary dispositions heretofore made by me and declare this to be my last will.

I appoint my wife, Delia Florence McBain, to be the sole executor of this my will, but if she shall predecease me, or die without having proved this my will, I appoint my daughter Jane Mary Alexandria McBain, to be the sole executor.

Should my daughter have predeceased me, I appoint my only brother, James Francis McBain of 8 The Knole, Birkside, Edinburgh, to be the sole executor. In the case that he has predeceased me, my estate to be divided among his children.

I state here that I hope the above contingency does not arise as I have not seen or associated with my brother or any member of his family for twenty years.'

There was more, but Amos stopped here. This had been written before he was born; it was meaningless. He looked at the other parchment. It was dated *10th day of September 1889* and was not in the beautiful script of the other paper, but was written in a thin spidery handwriting; nor was the wording so official as in the other, although there was a legal turn to the phrasing of one paragraph which stated:

'I, Angus Forrester McBain, hereby revoke all my former wills and declare this to be my wish and last will. I leave my estate and all it entails completely to my daughter Jane Mary Alexandria McBain. I do this unconditionally. Signed Angus Forrester McBain and witnessed by . . .'

Underneath was the almost unintelligible signature of The Reverend John William Wainwright and underneath that, the signature of The Reverend Arnold Hedley.

He held both parchments out before him. His jaws were tightly clenched. No word of him, not even a reference that Jane should provide for him. This last will was written when he was nine years old, the day following his birthday, the very day his father had turned him out of the dining room. Would anyone believe that a man could disown his own in such a way, even if his own had grown to be an idiot?

If there had been a spark of remorse in him for anything that he had done, it would have fled at this moment; this deed vindicated his action. His gaze dropped to the papers again. The last one had not been drawn up by a solicitor, but it would be held valid: the signatures of two such witnesses would be enough for that. And where would it leave him? At the mercy of Jane's generosity. Oh, she would be generous, she would look after him until he died.

He slipped from the chair and stood upright on his stumps. From now on there was no one going to dictate to him, not even Jane. He would rule, he would be master of this house or die in the attempt. It was either he or his father.

This last will taken care of, there remained only the other one, the legal one, which left everything to his mother; and his mother was dead, and he was his mother's son. Nobody could get over that, could they? And should the parsons remember that they signed a will in 1889, what could they do if it couldn't be found?

He went swiftly to the table near his bed and, taking up a box of matches, he lit a candle, and when it was well alight he held over it the piece of paper that would have robbed him of the recompense he considered his due. When it was burnt two-thirds through, he moved on his stumps in a body-twisting motion and dropped the paper into the empty grate and watched it curl into black ash. Then he picked up the other will and, putting it into his pocket, he went to find Jane to tell her that she needn't worry anymore, he had found what she was looking for.

Chapter Four

'What is it?' Winnie looked at Molly as she came slowly into the kitchen. 'Is he worse?'

'Aye, I should think so. He's agitated, got somethin' on his mind.'

'Well, that's natural,' said Winnie. 'It's likely that Miss Reed. Did Miss

Jane tell him she'd called?'

'Not when I was in she didn't.'

'I'll take this broth up.' Winnie went to pick up a tray from the table, adding, 'Then I'll slip along the road for half an hour and get them something. Davie says he can manage, an' I dare say he could, with a galley concoction.'

'Well, leave it down, I'll see to it. I've got to go up again anyway.'

'You sure, lass?'

'Yes, yes. Get yourself away. An' you needn't rush, 'cos the dinner here's all ready. Not that anybody'll eat it.'

'I know one will.' Winnie's voice was low, and when Molly didn't answer but stood gazing down at the steam rising from the broth, she went on, 'I know he hasn't been treated fair but he's struttin' around like a stumped peacock, as if he was already master. . . .' Winnie stopped and, looking closely at Molly now, asked under her breath, 'What is it, lass?' But as soon as she had put the question she thought it was a stupid thing to say, for there were three things at least that could bring Molly low at the present moment. There was the master near death, and if there had been nothing between them for years, there had been at one time, and the evidence of it was in the dairy at this minute. Then there was the face of her Davie coming back. Fifteen years was a long time, time enough to forget a man and marry, but she hadn't married. Then there was a third thing that was always worrying her, Master Amos and his constant chasing of Biddy, and his acting at times like a normal man who owned her. Yes, she had a lot on her plate had Molly, and she was sorry for her. She had grown to like her over the years, and that was odd, because at one time she had thought her fast and brash, but at that time she had been fearful of her hooking Davie, and she had wanted someone better for her lad. She still did, but there was no fear of Davie falling again. Davie the man was a different kettle of fish from Davie the youth, or even the young sailor who had turned up five years ago in much the same way as he had come in the other night.

She watched Molly pick up the tray as she said, 'Oh, I'm like the lot of us, just tired,' and smiled weakly as she added, 'Go on an' get them something, an' as I said, don't hurry back, Biddy'll help me here. There'll only be one for the dining room; Miss Jane will have hers upstairs.'

'Thanks, lass.' They nodded at each other, then Molly went out with the tray and as she crossed the hall she looked towards the dining room and she repeated to herself, 'Only one for the dinin' room.' That maimed skit would be lording it in the master's chair when he should be in. . . . She gulped and gripped the tray tighter. She'd have to tell somebody and the only one she could talk to was Winnie. But then Winnie might let on to Miss Jane, Winnie wasn't all that cautious. And what would happen then? Miss Jane had had nothing out of life but worry and frustration. Courting the parson for years, a walk across the fields on a Sunday or up to the Tor. There hadn't even been the comfort of a roll in the hay. No, Miss Jane mustn't know; but she must tell somebody about that devil or bust.

She had always known he was bad; she had tried to make Biddy see he was bad, but Biddy was sorry for him. Biddy said she understood him. And well she might.

When the master died, he would take over completely; then God help them all. God help Biddy. Eeh! She'd have to talk to somebody. Parson Hedley? No. No, he was too near to Miss Jane. If he were to expose Master Amos as a murderer, then how would Miss Jane take it?

When she entered the room Jane turned from the bed and, coming towards her, whispered, 'He's so exhausted. He seems to be sleeping, I wouldn't give it to him yet. And while you're here, Molly, I'll slip to my room, I must change my clothes.'

'Do that, Miss. And don't worry, I'll call you if there's any change. Have a wash and it'll freshen you up.'

Jane nodded at her, then went towards the bed again and looked down at the still grey face for a moment before turning away and saying under her breath, 'I'll leave the door open so you can call if you want me. I'll leave mine open, too.'

'Do that, Miss. Yes, do that.' Molly nodded at her, then took her place in the chair at the head of the bed.

As she sat staring at the still form lying there, she did not see the man who had once showed her ways of loving that had been as enchanting as witchcraft . . . at the time. Reality had faded with the years until now she imagined she had dreamed most of what they had experienced together. Even at night when her body ached for comfort and love, her mind bypassed that early episode as if, like leprosy, it would contaminate her present existence; yet the thought was ever present in her mind that her life would have been different if his hand on her thigh hadn't awakened her from sleep on that night.

When his eyes opened and looked at her, she bent quickly forward and said, 'Would you like a drop of broth, Master?' She watched his nostrils dilating, his breath coming in short laboured gasps, and when she saw his tongue come out and pass over his lips, she took a square of lint that was floating in a bowl of water on the side table and gently drew it around his mouth. She asked again, 'Would you like a drop of soup, Master?' and when his eyelids closed once, she knew he did not want any. As she watched his tongue move over his lips again she said, 'A drink of water?'

His eyes remained open, and she nodded at him and smiled. 'I'll get you a nice cold one, there's a jug fresh from the well. I won't be a minute.' She nodded at him and hurried round the bed and into the dressing room.

The glass was full in her hand when she heard the stifled cry. It was like the death rattle of a calf, a strangled whining sound. It froze her for a moment, and she almost dropped the jug from her hand and the glass with it. The water spilled from the glass as she ran towards the door. Just within it, she stopped. The master had moved. His head was up and he was choking, and there, standing between the door and the bed, was Master Amos.

'Get out, you! Get out, you!' She was bawling at him at the top of her voice. But he didn't move. His eyes flickered towards her, then returned towards the bed and to his father.

Thrusting the glass onto the mantlepiece, she rushed at him, hissing, 'Get yourself away! Get out of here!'

'Take your hands off me!'

She took her hands off him and stepped back. Her eyes darted from the door to the bed. Then she ran first to the door and yelled 'Miss Jane! Miss Jane!' Before rushing back to the bed. She slipped her arm under McBain's shoulders and tried to hold his heaving body, and she cried again at the hunched figure standing immobile on his crutches, his stare fixed as if he, too, had suffered paralysis. 'Get out! Do you hear? Get out! You're determined to finish him, aren't you?'

'Amos! Amos!' Jane came rushing into the room. 'Oh Amos, how could you! Go away. Please, go away.'

But he did not obey her immediately, not until she had rushed to the bed and had taken her father from Molly's arms and the bobbing head had fallen to the side and become still. Then he turned and hobbled out, and Jane slowly laid McBain back on the bed.

Standing side by side, Jane looked down on her father and Molly on her one-time lover, and they bowed their heads and slowly they began to cry.

Chapter Five

'No, Ma. Now don't keep on asking me, for I'm no hypocrite. I stopped followin' him years ago, so I'm not going to start again on his last ride; nor am I going to say I'm sorry he's gone.'

Winnie closed her eyes tightly and shook her head as she said, 'Oh, don't be like that, Davie, it upsets me. Bad enough with that one across there. Dear God, there's going to be changes on this farm, if I know anything. Fancy,' she now looked at old Sep where he sat in his chair by the side of the fire, 'have you ever heard of such a thing, not goin' to have plumed horses and wantin' to cut the carriages down to two! Miss Jane had to have a stand-up fight with him, Eeh! That lass is upset. There's something funny somewhere; the master would have never left things so that that young devil could take over. If he cared for anybody it was for Miss Jane. And then,' she turned to Davie now, 'Parson Hedley remembers signing a will just a few years back, and he told Master Amos straight. I never heard him talk like that afore. He's quiet like, you know he is, but not this time, oh no, he was fighting for Miss Jane's rights. When the house was clear yesterday she turned the office inside out. She's upset, she is that.'

'But there'd be a copy wouldn't there, there's always copies of wills? They've got a solicitor.'

'Aye, of course, an' as far I can make out he's got a copy of the old one, but not of the one Parson Hedley's on about.'

'Winnie, I'd like to go.' They both turned and looked to where Sep had risen from his chair, and Winnie cried at him, 'Now, Da, don't be silly.'

'Silly be damned, woman! I said I'd like to go an' I'm goin'. You get me suit out. It'll likely hang like a sack on me, but what matter!' Old Sep now looked at Davie and said firmly, 'Speak as you find, lad. He was always decent to me an' he give me me one an' six a week when he had no need.'

'Speak as you find, Granda.' Davie nodded back at him, smiling quietly. 'Always speak as you find. You go if you want to.'

'My God! What a pair.' Winnie went towards the door, shaking her head. 'The one who could go won't, and the one who shouldn't go out the door will.'

When she had gone they both looked at each other and laughed quietly; then Davie said, 'I'm goin' to stretch me legs, Granda.'

'Aye, lad,' said Sep, sitting down again. Then he asked quietly, 'Getting restless?'

'Restless? No, Granda. I could do with a lot of this.'

'Then why go back, lad?'

'Well,' Davie pursed his lips, 'what else is there for me? And who knows,' he grinned now, 'the first mate might drop down dead and I'll get his place. That's the worst of likin' your captain an' mate and staying with a boat too long, you get into a rut, or I should say trough, shouldn't I?'

'If you sign on again how many years will it be this time?'

'God knows, Granda, God knows. Still, don't worry, old 'un, I've found that God doesn't want me to die by drownin'; He's tested me twice, as I've told you.'

'The third time might be catchy time, lad.'

'That's what they say, Granda, third time catchy time. But I'll have to chance that, won't I? Now don't you worry, just think of how you're going to stop slipping through your good suit.' Again they both laughed; and now Davie took his hat from a nail by the door, pulled it firmly onto his head, and went out.

He paused in the road, taking in deep gulps of air, and after looking first to the right and then to the left of him, he decided to take a walk towards the burn and to follow it down to the river.

He went along the road and past the farm gate, and saw coming around the corner of the barn, which backed onto the road, young Biddy. She was a bonny piece, fresh looking, well made, with no resemblance to Molly at her age, for the features were thin, like him that was responsible for her. But there was a soft delicateness in the thinness. He had seen her before in the distance but hadn't as yet spoken to her. He stopped in front of her and said, 'Why, hello there! You're Biddy.'

'Hello,' she said. 'An' I know who you are, I can even remember you.'

'You can? It's almost ten years.'

'I know, but I can, faintly, sort of. You were down by the river an' you were swimmin' with Amos.'

He was quick to note that she didn't say Master Amos. 'Well! Well!' He shook his head at her. 'You have a long memory. I remember that day an' all. That young devil nearly drowned himself.'

She smiled as she said. 'He's always been grateful to you, learning him to swim. He's like a fish in the water now.'

He noted also the word now. She must watch him swimming. He asked her, 'Do you like farm work?'

Her shoulders moved up in a shrug before she replied, 'Sometimes; yes and no. I'm taken more with the house than the dairy.'

'You still go to school?'

'No.' She flapped her hand at him now in a familiar way, then laughed. 'I'm fifteen, goin' on sixteen. But I still read. I like readin', when I get the chance.'

'What kind of reading?'

'Oh, all kinds, that Amos lends me. Some of the books are . . .'

'Biddy! You, Biddy!' They both turned and looked towards Molly, where she was standing by the farm gate. Then the girl looked at him and said, 'Seein' you.' And he nodded at her and answered, 'Aye, seein' you.'

He did not turn away immediately but stared along the road towards the woman standing in the sunlight, and he wanted to laugh loudly and shout at her, 'What you afraid of, like mother like daughter?' but he turned away wondering why it was that every time he set eyes on her he wanted to flay her with words, stir up the dead past; for it had all happened so long ago, fifteen years ago. She was what now? Thirty-two. Why had she not married? Perhaps she had no need to; she could get what she wanted on the side. And she would want it, after the practice she'd had in her early days. By! She had been a young cow if ever there was one. 'Now, now!' he chided himself, and grinned as he came back with, 'Don't insult the animals.'

Ten minutes later he was on the point of dropping down the steep path towards the burn when he heard her voice calling his name. It startled him, he thought he was imagining things. He turned fully round, and there she was running along the path that led from the back of the house to the garden. About two yards from him she stopped. She was panting and her full breasts were lifting the front of her print dress up and down.

'Well! Well!' He gave a short laugh, but his face was straight as he waited for her to say, 'Don't you talk to my Biddy.' It would be just like her to think he would try to get his own back through the young lass. What was nineteen years anyway? Captain Surtees had married a lass twenty years younger than himself; it was done all the time.

'Can I talk to you?'

He was slightly taken aback. He raised his eyebrows and jerked his head to one side. What was this? Her voice was quiet, soft, it even had a tremor in it. 'Talk to me?' he said. 'What do you want to talk to me about?'

'The young master.' She gulped, cleared her throat, then went on rapidly, 'I've got to tell somebody an' I can't tell anybody back there in case they tell Miss Jane.'

As he stood looking at her with narrowing gaze she stared back at him, deep into his eyes, and the secret part of her whimpered, 'Oh God, I was a fool.' Then she brought out in a rush, 'He . . . the young one, he killed the master.'

'What!' His whole face was screwed up now.

'It's a fact.' She moved a short step nearer to him. 'You know the beam at the top of the stairs, like in our houses? Winnie said Ned used to lift him up onto it, and he used to swing from it. Well, he swung from the one at the top of the stairs an' . . . an' on purpose. I . . . I found the chair had been moved, the monk's chair. It's heavy and I always put it back in the same place, but there it was against the post. It was that that made me look up, an' I saw the piece of rag hanging from the beam. We only go up there when it's spring-cleanin', it's always dusty; so I got the step ladder, an' found that most of the dust had been wiped off. I mean on top of the beam. An' there was this piece of cloth caught on a nail. Then I went to his wardrobe and there was his coat. It was from the inside of the facing.'

'But . . . but you can't believe that, that he. . . . ' He shook his head.

'I do. I know he did it. Mind, I won't say he hasn't had cause; the master's never looked the side he was on, an' he's never had a penny in his pocket, only what Miss Jane gave him. If it hadn't been for her, God knows what might have happened to him earlier on, he mayn't have lived. . . .' She now bowed her head and, her tone changing into thin bitterness, she said, 'That was the wrong thing to say, but. . . .' Once more she was looking at him. 'I swear to you again I would never have done it. I was beside meself. He made me take it, but I'd never have done it.' She was shaking her head widely now.

She had stopped speaking, but he didn't break the silence for some time, and then he asked, 'Why did you tell me, what can I do?'

She put her hand to her cheek and pressed it tightly, while looking to the side. 'I don't know. But I just had to tell somebody, it seemed too big to carry meself. The right thing to do would be to tell Miss Jane, but . . . but I don't want to be the one to bring trouble on her. She's been good to me, more than good, and she has no life, no more than . . .' she stopped herself from adding, 'me'. She brought her pained defiant gaze onto him again, and after a moment she said, 'There's one thing I know, he's dangerous. He's but a lad, just on sixteen, but he's sixty in his head an' his ideas. And he's got a cruel streak in him, vindictive. I don't think Miss Jane can see it. She's always making excuses for him, and that's natural enough, 'cos she's been mother, father, and sister to him, everything. She lived in that room with him night and day until he was ten. How she stood it, God knows.'

He made no comment, and she went on, more slowly now, as if she were repeating old news, 'She should have married the parson years ago, but the master wouldn't have him here. And old Wainwright wouldn't have them there. And then the master going to marry that Miss Reed nearly finished her. That's what made the other one do it, I'm sure of it.' She nodded her head at him. 'It would have put his nose out. And he always wanted to boss. He's a weird creature, frightenin'. . . .' She looked up at him for a moment without speaking, then asked, 'What am I to do?'

He rubbed his ear with his hand, then brought it over his stubbly chin and to the other side of his face before he said, 'I can't see what you can do except keep quiet if you don't want to hurt Miss Jane and cause a stir for miles. Not that, from what you say and what me ma's told me, there won't be a lot of sympathy with the lad. And you can understand him being a bit weird, handicapped as he is.'

'He doesn't see it as a handicap.' There was bitterness in her tone now. 'He can do most things, too many for that matter.'

He looked at her enquiringly, but she took the subject no further. Instead she said, 'Well, I'd better be gettin' back. But I had to talk to somebody. You don't mind?'

'No, I don't mind.' His voice was noncommital and she half smiled at him, until he said, 'Though I don't know who it's going to aid, you telling me, 'cos I'll be on me way shortly.'

She stared at him for a moment longer before turning away and walking quickly up the path. He continued down towards the burn and stopped opposite the spot where he had taken Amos in and taught him to swim, and by way of thanks had had the hairs pulled from his groin.

She had said the boy was dangerous. Yes, he could say he would be if he was thwarted and didn't get what he wanted.

He had a sudden desire to be away from this place, yet all the while knowing that this was where his heart lay. He would go into Newcastle tomorrow and see how they were getting on with her bottom; a fortnight or three weeks, at least, they had said. Still, it could be sooner if the captain had got round them. Let's hope he had.

The following morning early he went by the carrier cart into Hexham, and from there took the train into Newcastle. Here, he mounted a horse bus that eventually brought him into Jarrow and the dry dock.

The *Arcadia*, out of the water, looked enormous, but she appeared old and battered. She did not arouse love in him as she did in the captain, perhaps because his quarters on board had never been as comfortable as the captain's, nor the first mate's, for that matter; his had just been a couple of short steps above the deck hands'.

On enquiry he was told the work would take another ten days to a fortnight, for it had been discovered that one of the boilers would have to be renewed. He saw no one he knew belonging to the ship. The captain, they said, had been over yesterday from Hull, where he lived. The first mate lived nearby in Shields, but he was spending most of his time in Edinburgh, where his parents were.

He left Jarrow and returned to Newcastle. The city did not attract him. It was like any other city, and made him feel like a fish out of water. As he wandered about the streets, glancing in the shops, he knew he was wasting his time. He had a longing to get away from it, away beyond Hexham and into the hills.

He went through the Cloth Market and the Bigg Market towards Grainger Street, deciding that on his way to the station he'd drop into a pub and have a drink. Unlike most sailors, he could take drink or leave it, but he felt in need of one today.

It was as he turned the corner into Grainger Street that he bumped into her. He went to side-step, saying, 'Pardon, Ma'am,' when he exclaimed on a high note, 'Oh w . . . why! Miss Jane!'

'Well!' Jane shook her head. 'Of all the places to meet.'

'It's right what they say after all; it's a small world.'

'Yes, yes.' She laughed gently. 'As you say, it's a small world. I . . . I was just making my way back to the train.'

'Well, so was I, Miss.'

'Oh!' She remained still, her face slightly flushed. She felt embarrassed. If she had met Johnnie or Mickey or Will Curran, or anyone else from the farm, she would have walked with him down to the train and thought nothing of it, but this man, this sailor, was not of the farm, not anymore, and his dress denied all connection with the country; he was very well set up, quite spruce; he had grown into a fine man had Winnie's Davie, but she found him a little disconcerting. She had spoken to him twice since his return and each time she had been made uneasy by his presence. It was as if he forced himself on her notice. But that wasn't true, because his manner was most correct.

'Will I take those for you?' He was lifting the packages from her arms, and she said, 'Oh. Oh, thank you Davie.' It did not feel natural to call him Davie, it was as if she were taking a liberty. But what else could she call him? Not Mr Armstrong.

When, her four parcels held in one arm, he took her elbow and, turning sidewards shouldered his way through the crowd so that she could remain on the pavement and not be pushed into the muddy road, she thought he had quite good manners. She had understood that most sailors were gauche and cumbersome owing to their being deprived of society for such long intervals, but then country people too were considered gauche.

His courtesy surprised her further when, as they approached the station, he asked her would she care for some refreshment. She thanked him kindly and told him that she had just eaten, which was not true. She could have done with a cup of tea–in fact, she had intended to go and have a light meal before catching the train. She didn't know why she hadn't made this clear to him.

They were fortunate in having to wait only ten minutes for the train and as they stood on the platform, he said to her, 'I don't know whether we'll be able to travel together, Miss Jane. I've only a third-class ticket.'

'We'll be able to travel together.' She nodded slowly. 'I have a third-class ticket, too.' They smiled at each other, then laughed gently.

As he looked at her he thought, her skin's as white as milk, black suits her. Funny how she's escaped being beautiful. She could have been, at that; she's just missed it somehow. Now if her expression were different, more happy like. There's something missing. How old is she? Twenty-six? No, twenty-seven. She looks older, thirty, if a day. She carries herself well; she's straight, a bit too straight perhaps. Pity she hadn't a bit of what Molly has up top. Well, not quite up top–he smiled inwardly–say, just above amidships.

'Are you looking forward to returning to sea?'

'Well, yes and no. All the time I've been away I've dreamed of the farm and the country around, you know, and now when I'm back I feel at a loose end. I suppose it's not having anything to do. If I were working, it would be different.'

'You wouldn't like to return to the land?'

'Ah, that's a difficult one, for what is there for a man in my position on the land these days?'

'Yes, things are difficult.'

The train came in and they took their seats, sitting side by side, and the silence that now fell between them caused little embarrassment because of the other occupants in the carriage and the rattling of the train itself.

It wasn't until they reached Hexham and were making their way to the stables to collect the horse and trap that they began talking again. Their conversation now took the form of question and answer, and strangely it was Jane who asked the questions: What did his work entail? What did he do in his spare time? Did he still read? To this last he answered with some pride, 'Oh yes, Miss Jane, everything I can get me hands on. I stocked up well afore I became second mate, the fo'csle was like a schoolroom.' He laughed. 'You wouldn't believe, Miss, what it means to a man when he can write his own name; gives him a sort of dignity. In some boats there's not much difference atween the rats in the holds and the humans below decks, because they're not treated any better than you would treat vermin; an' there was many such in our boat. But you know, Miss, once those fellows could spell *cat*, *dog*, *rat*, and *fat*, an' write their name, why, it was like a miracle, what it did for them. But mind, I'm not saying it acted in all cases, for some of them had nothing in their noddles, and a belaying-pin wouldn't have knocked it in.'

'How wonderful!' she said. 'What a thoughtful thing to do, to teach men their letters.' And she did think so. Although his grammar left a lot to be desired, she recognized in him an intelligence above the average, and the fact that he wished to impart his little learning to others gave him a prestige in her eyes.

At the stables she said, 'Will you take the reins, Davie?' and he answered, 'I'd like nothin' better, Miss.' And so in the growing twilight they drove home together, and laughed and chatted all the way.

Later, they both remarked to themselves in private that it was strange, but they had not spoken of her father, or of Amos, or of Parson Hedley.

It was the following morning that Amos made his way to the cottage to see Davie. He'd had no real conversation with him since he had returned, but this was not to say that he hadn't thought about him; Davie had been in his mind constantly.

The feeling that he'd had as a child for the sailor still remained. He liked him. In his company, he felt a man, a whole man; they were men together. He would like him for a friend. Yes, and the balance of possession would weigh heavily towards himself, for the relationship would give him both a friend and a servant, a double advantage.

He knew Winnie was about her duties in the house, and he hoped old Sep was still abed. And this he found when he knocked on the door and it was opened by Davie, who stood aside to let him hobble into the empty kitchen.

Going straight towards a chair he hoisted himself expertly onto it, laid his crutches to the side, then, a hand on each arm of the chair, he leant back and said, 'Now then.'

Davie stood at the end of the mantelpiece and looked at the massive upper body of the boy, his width exaggerated still further by the grotesquely short stumps and feet. He had spoken to him as a master might speak to his man: "Now then, let's get on with it.' He reached out and took his clay pipe from the rack above the mantelshelf, bent down and knocked the dead doddle out against the bars, then peered down into the empty bowl before opening a penknife and scraping it.

'Eeh! Oh! That puts my teeth on edge; why don't you smoke a wooden one?'

'This does me.'

Amos looked at him through narrowed lids. He sensed a lack of friendliness in his tone, definitely a lack of deference. Still, he wasn't his master . . . yet. 'Winnie tells me you went to see your ship yesterday.'

'Yes, I did that.'

'How did you find her?'

'Oh,' Davie allowed himself to grin, 'with her backside bare, she wasn't a nice sight.'

Amos's high fresh laugh brought Davie's eyes tight on him, and in this moment he was doubting Molly's tale; the laughing face looked good, incapable of such destruction as killing, and the victim his own father, be he what he may. Yet put himself in the lad's place, ignored for years, treated like an animal, what would he have done. Very likely have tried to have a go at the old man long before this. You couldn't judge such things, a man could stand only so much. And what was more, this was no lad, no boy; although his years were few, he was a man. Funny, his mother had said the same thing last night when they were talking. 'He was born a man,' she said, 'in his mind, that is.'

'Are you anxious to get back to sea?'

Davie was shredding a plug of black baccy in the palm of his hand, and he contemplated it before answering, 'Yes and no.'

'What do you mean by that?'

'Just yes and no. It's my job, but I'd be happier if my ship could sail around these hills.'

Again Amos laughed; then, his face settling into its sombre pattern, he watched Davie filling his pipe. He watched him light it with a spill before he said, 'You needn't go back, you could stay here and work for me.'

Slowly Davie turned his head to the side and looked at the figure sitting in the chair, the big head held up, the neck stretching away from the shoulders, the back straight. For a moment he was reminded of a figurehead such as one or two of the old ships still carried. He had not said, 'You can come back and I'll find you a job on the farm,' but, 'you can work for me.' It was as his mother said: he was playing the master all right. He now threw his own head back and laughed, a deep short laugh, and, as if he were dealing with a child and a joke, he said, 'Oh yes, work for you. And what would you offer me?'

'Fifteen shillings a week.'

He took the pipe from his mouth, puffed out a thin stream of smoke, then raised his eyebrows, pursed his lips and repeated, 'Fifteen shillings a week.'

He would pay fifteen shillings, well! well! And in these days, when a farm labourer who received ten shillings together with his cottage and perks would consider himself damn lucky. He was only picking up twelve shillings himself and sometimes the food turned his stomach, biscuits that walked towards you drawn by weevils, and meat that heralded its approach with a whiff that would knock you down. Fifteen shillings, well! well! His mouth moved into a twisted smile as he said, "And what would you be expecting of me for fifteen shillings, because, you must remember, I haven't been on a farm for this many a long year, I've almost forgotten where the milk comes from. A fellow I once knew thought it came by pumping the beast's tail, and I'm not much better. Fifteen shillings. You'd want something for your fifteen shillings, now wouldn't you? And would you mind telling me what it is?'

'A gaffer, manager, someone to see to the others; there's a lot of time wasters about. Mickey's all right, but Johnnie's a dodger, and Will wants stirring.'

'And I would have to stir?'

'You would have to stir.'

'Well!' He let out a long breath, then drew on his pipe again before saying, 'You won't remember it, but there was a time when it took nine men going at it hard to run this place. Well, perhaps I shouldn't say they were all men because the two Gearys were young, but they worked hard, as did Curran's two. They were doing a man's work at ten, and now with only three left to do the work, you want me to hustle them.'

'The place isn't run as it was years ago, and you already know that, if you've walked round; here's walls down, gates hanging off. Anyway, I intend to cut the land.'

'Cut the land?' Davie's face was screwed up in enquiry.

'Yes. Sir Alfred's been after that bottom stretch for years. It's not productive, only pretty, and we can do without that.'

'That'll mean letting the burn and the malt house go.' There was indignation in Davie's voice but Amos did not seem to notice it, for he went on. 'The burn will go, yes, but I'm keeping the malt house; that'll be for Jane and the parson when I marry.'

Davie felt the muscles of his face sagging. He just stopped his jaw from drooping and from repeating the word marry.

When this young fellow here talked you could forget he hadn't legs, there was a virility in his voice, certainly a virility in his torso. The way he had of sitting straight, without movement, gave the impression of power. But when he spoke of marriage as if it were a certainty, you remembered he hadn't legs. Still, his shoulders made a slight movement, what of it; he had the necessary to make a marriage work, in one direction that was. But who would take him on? Which lass would be willing to go to bed with that? Oh, again there was a movement of his shoulders as he answered himself, some would. When they got past twenty, there were those who'd hook up with a blind beggar, so desperate they became. There were others, who he thought were in the majority, who'd become sick at the thought, that is unless they cared for him. That was the word, cared. Not so much loving, but caring. There was a big difference here. He had learned that from watching his mother and father. He doubted if his mother had ever loved his father; but she had cared for him, and they'd been happy together. Yes, if the lad found somebody who cared, somebody of the type of Miss Jane who was all heart and sacrifice, he would marry. But there were few Miss Janes about.

'Well, what do you say?'

'Aw, you're not serious?'

'Serious? Of course I'm serious.'

Davie stiffened at the tone, and his own matched it now when he replied, 'It's a thing that'll need considerin', a lot of thinkin' about. I could say no right away, for I don't know whether I'd like working for you anymore than I did your father. . . .'

His words were cut off by Amos letting out a high laugh, and he looked at him in surprise, for the master was gone and the boy was back as he said, 'You know that's what I like about you, Davie; you're different, you're not afraid to say what you think. I remember, all those years back, you clouted me, didn't you? Any other one on the farm wouldn't have dared, but you did.' He reached for his crutches and slid from the chair, and looking up at Davie, he said, 'Think hard on it, I'd be obliged if you'd stay.' He paused, then ended, 'I need you, someone like you, to balance things. And remember, it would make your mother happy.'

Davie made no answer to this, but watched him going towards the door. He hadn't rushed to open it for him but had left him to manoeuvre it himself. Not until he had gone through the door and was some way down the road did he go towards it and close it. Then he returned to the fireplace and, bending down, leant his forearms on the mantelshelf and laid his brow on his hands and looked down at the fire.

A short while later, when he went upstairs, old Sep said, 'Did I hear the young master down below?'

'Aye, Granda, you heard him.'

'What's he after?'

'He's offered me a job, manager of the farm, sort of.'

'What!' Sep pulled himself up in the bed with startling agility, seeing that he could hardly move with rheumatics. 'Name of God! He didn't!'

'He did. Fifteen bob a week.'

'Name of God!' The exclamation was higher this time. "Fifteen bob a week! Aw, lad. Well, I always knew you'd make it one day.'

'Now, Granda, now, now. You lay yourself down; this needs thinking about.'

The old man, now gripping his hand, looked up at him and whispered, 'Stay, Davie, stay.'

'We'll see, we'll see. As I said, it needs thinking about.'

But as he went down the stairs, he knew he had already thought about it. He was manager of the farm.

Chapter Six

Jane stood before the desk in the office and looked down on Amos. Her face was tight and there was anger in her voice as she said, 'Please don't send for me as if I were a servant, Amos. And if you wish to talk to me, I prefer that you do not sit in Father's chair and behind his desk.'

He stared at her, his face equally tight and his voice grim as he said, 'And you forget that times have changed, Jane. This is no longer Father's chair and desk, it is mine.'

Their glances held for a moment; then he quickly tossed his head from side to side and, his voice and manner changing completely, said, 'Aw, Jane don't let's quarrel. Look, I'm sorry. I just asked Winnie to tell you I'd like a word with you.' He leant across the desk and put his hand out and caught at hers, saying softly, 'Please, come on, sit down.'

She remained straight and stiff for a moment longer; then slowly she turned about and pulled a chair forward and, seating herself, looked at him, once her beloved child, her charge.

For sixteen years she had spent her energies and her love on him, and although her life had been hard, tiresome, and dull at times, it had been without fear. But since her father died, she had been full of fear; of what, she didn't rightly know, for she wouldn't admit to herself that it was fear of him.

In two short weeks the whole atmosphere of the place had changed. Everyone was on edge. The only good thing he had done was to persuade Davie Armstrong to become a working manager. Yet this hadn't found favour with the others. Will Curran was openly opposed to it, as also was Johnnie. Mickey was the only one who welcomed the innovation, at least among the men. Winnie, she knew, was over the moon. And Molly–one couldn't tell what Molly was thinking. But Molly wasn't acting like herself these days either, so perhaps she, too, was disturbed by the new arrangement.

Arnold thought it was a very sensible move on the part of Amos, but then he had always been very fond of Davie, although he had pointed out that a sixteen-year gap was a long time to be away from farm work, for things on the land had changed a lot. Davie's job wouldn't be easy if he wanted the place to pay its way.

This was another thing; she had discovered that the farm, far from paying its way, had been losing money; there was a heavy mortgage on the house. She had found out a great number of things when she went to Newcastle to see the solicitor. She had gone to him purposely because she couldn't believe that her father had made no provision for her.

Knowing the strength of her father's feelings concerning his son, she was convinced that Amos had no right to be sitting in that chair; it was she who should be in charge of the farm. She was sure that her father would not have been so negligent as to omit leaving a document that would ensure that Amos would not inherit. In fact the thought was adamant in her mind that he would have ignored Amos's requirements, as he had always done, and left his future in her hands.

The solicitor had been of the same mind, but as he said, if there were a later will, they must stand by the present one until such time as it might be found. He suggested that she search the house, particularly the office. This she had done over and over again, but with no success.

Amos startled her by saying, 'I've ordered them to finish the malt house.'

'The malt house! But why? It won't be necessary.'

He leant over the desk and although she was out of his reach, he extended his hands towards her, laying them palms down on the papers. 'You want to get married, don't you? You've waited long enough.'

'Yes.' Her chin was slightly to the side. 'Yes, I've waited long enough. But, oh,' she smiled now, 'I see.' She nodded towards him. 'You don't want to live with us, you want a place of your own. I can understand, and it's thoughtful. . . .'

'No, no,' he was shaking his head vigorously, 'you've got it wrong. Turn it round. It's for you . . . and Arnold.'

'You mean . . . ?' She got to her feet. 'You mean I'm . . . , we're to go to the malt house?'

'Well,' he pulled his arms sharply back across the desk, 'I'm going to marry some day, and before long I hope, and two mistresses under the one roof wouldn't work.'

'You're going to . . . ?' She stopped. She had never thought about him marrying, not even that the idea would ever enter his head. Who would . . . ?

'Don't look like that!' He was bawling at her now. 'My God! Underneath you're like the rest of them. I'm not a man, am I? Just a thing!'

For the moment the malt house was forgotten as she tried to reassure him, saying, 'Don't be silly, Amos. And that's most unfair, you know it is. It's only that you're so young and . . .'

'And I'm odd. Who would want to take me on? That's what you're thinking, isn't it? That's what they all think. Well, I won't have far to go to find someone willing. I might as well tell you now, I'm going to marry Biddy.'

She felt the blood draining from her face, from her arms; she had the sensation that there was a tap in the soles of her feet letting it flow away. She felt for the moment that she was going to faint. She knew that Arnold had been right when he had advised her to tell the boy when he was no more than eight years old. He had again brought the subject up when Amos was ten, and then twelve, but she couldn't risk embittering him further against his father and taking from him the only young companionship he had. Anyway, she had foreseen the problem solved by Molly sending Biddy away into service, when she became twelve, with either Lena or Katie. Both of them had married, but had remained in service. From time to time Molly had spoken of Lena, saying she could get Biddy into her household, but nothing had come of it. Molly, she knew, was loath to part with her daughter, for she was the only thing she had.

He was yelling at her again. 'Oh, for Christ's sake! Don't come over all class conscious. Anyway, who cares? We're in the backwoods here, and we might as well be on an island for all the visitors we get. And that's how I want it, I want it to be an island, I'm going to turn it into an island. I've written to old Tuppin about the bottom land. I'm having the walls and fences done, gates put up. I'll make it an island where we can. . . .'

'Quiet! Do you hear, be quiet!'

'Jane!' His voice was deep in his throat and, without looking behind him, he groped for his crutches and, drawing them forward, tucked them under his arms and came round the desk, to stand in front of her. And with his head just slightly back, he looked at her and said slowly, 'Gone are the days when you could tell me to be quiet.'

She moved one step back from him; then two. When she bumped into the chair she turned round and pushed it out of her way, then took another step in the direction of the door.

He stood watching her for a moment before he demanded, 'What's the matter with you? Why are you looking like that? You've always liked Biddy, and she's tractable and not ignorant; she can read and write as well as the next.'

'A . . . mos!' His name was strangled in her throat. She gulped spittle into her dry mouth, then breathed deeply three times before she said, 'You cannot have Biddy, ever . . . ever; it's . . . it's impossible.'

'I cannot have Biddy? What do you mean?'

'I . . . I should have told you before now, years ago, but I thought it . . . it would make you dislike Father more. And I didn't think you would . . . I never thought about marriage. It's impossible. Biddy . . . Biddy is your . . . our half-sister.'

For a full minute he did not seem to comprehend the meaning of her statement. His face screwed up, the almond eyes became long narrow slits, his whole body was still; then in a lightning movement he came to life and she sprang back towards the door and screamed, 'Don't! Don't, Amos. Don't!' as a crutch came spinning through the air like a boomerang at her. It struck her shoulder and she cried out again and ran into the hall.

Molly, coming from the dining room, enquired urgently but quietly, 'What is it? What is it, Miss?' and Jane rushed towards her and clung to her for a moment; then grabbing her hand, almost dragged her up the stairs and into the bedroom.

'In the name of God, Miss Jane, what is it? What's he done?'

Again Jane was clinging to her, 'I . . . I had to tell him about Biddy; he . . . he said he was going to marry her.'

'God Almighty!' Molly's response to this was so quiet that it had a calming effect on Jane, and she dropped onto the side of the bed and joined her hands tightly on her knees and asked, 'What are we going to do?'

Molly didn't answer her directly but said, 'I've . . . I've been half expecting it, Miss. It made me write to our Katie and Lena some weeks back. The place has been filled in Lena's, but they're looking for a stillroom maid in Katie's. But . . . but I didn't want to let her go that far; it's right down in the south of the country, back of beyond, near a place called Teignmouth. Beautiful, Lena says, but lonely. Worse than this. I . . . I didn't want to send her to the back of beyond 'cos she's young. Yet she was for going when I mentioned it. I wish to God I'd let her now.

'Don't shake so, Miss Jane.' She came slowly to the bed and, sitting down on the edge of it, she put her arm around her and held her close, and Jane said, 'Oh, Molly, Molly, what have things come to?' and Molly turning her gaze to the wall said flatly, 'Parson Hedley would say it's the sins of the fathers and of the mothers.'

'Oh, I wasn't meaning that, Molly.'

'I know, Miss, I know, but I can't help thinking that it's right; I carry a weight about with me all the time.'

'Oh, Molly!' Jane leant her head against her and in this moment they could have been the half-sisters.

After a time Molly rose to her feet, saying, 'You stay here quiet for a while, Miss Jane, till things settle down. But we'll have to put our thinkin' caps on, 'cos something must be done.'

On her way to the door she glanced out of the window, then stopped and exclaimed on a high note, 'Oh, my God! There he goes into the dairy.' And with that she turned and ran from the room and down the stairs and out of the house.

As if Amos knew that Molly would come, he had immediately dropped the bar over the door when he entered the dairy from the yard, and now he stood with his back to it and looked towards Biddy, where she had turned from the marble slab on which she had been patting up butter and stared at him. It was she who spoke first. 'What is it?' she asked. 'What's the matter? What you barrin' the door for?'

He did not answer her, only continued to stare, and she turned from him and picked up a cloth and wiped her hands before looking at him again and repeating, 'What's the matter? You bad or somethin'?'

His face was colourless but running with sweat, as were his hands gripping the bars of the crutches. He leant back against the door as he asked, 'Do you like me?'

'Like you?' She twisted her face at him. 'What's up with you?' The question was high.

'I said, do you like me?'

'Well,' she wagged her head, 'I suppose so, Aye, yes, I like you.' She looked him up and down. She never thought about him having no legs; she was so used to him that way, and so she had never been sorry for him because of his disability.

'Would you marry me?'

'Wh-at! What did you say . . . marry you?' Her dark brows had moved into points. Then she gave a little laugh as she said, 'Don't talk daft.'

'Biddy!' He bawled her name as she went to turn from him, and at the same time it was shouted from beyond the door. 'Biddy! Biddy! Open this door. Do you hear me?'

Biddy stared at the door above his head, then down at him. 'That's me ma,' she said, 'Open the door.'

'Answer me first, will you marry me?'

As the glinting light of his eyes held her gaze, she almost said, 'Marry you, are you mad? Who would marry you?' but she had some of her mother in her and so her answer was, 'Now look, don't act so daft; I'm not marryin' anybody, nobody.'

'Biddy! D'you hear me? Open this door. Push him out of the way an' open this door.'

'You'd better get by,' she said quietly, 'else I'll have to push you.' If she pushed him, he'd unbalance, and she was quite capable of pushing him. During the years he had sparred with her, she had learned to defend herself the hard way, although he had always got the better of her once they were on the ground together. And so he made no effort to stop her when she moved close to him to swing the bar back into its socket.

When the door burst open it almost knocked them onto their backs. Standing in the opening, red in the face and enraged, Molly looked from one to the other before addressing her daughter. 'What's he done? What's he said?' she demanded.

'Nothin', Ma, nothin'. What you yellin' for?'

'Nothin' you say? Why did he bar the door then?' She turned her glance swiftly to Amos, who was glaring at her with a look of deep hatred on his face, and it came over in his voice as he said slowly, 'I asked her to marry me. . . .'

'You dirty. . . .'

'Don't say it. Don't say it, Molly.' As his head went down, his eyes moved upwards under his lids, giving him a demoniacal look.

'I will say it.' She now turned to Biddy. 'You get out. Get out of here, and go up home.'

'What? Why?'

'Do as I bid you, girl. Go on up home.'

Biddy went slowly out, and Molly banging the door closed again, leant against it as she growled, 'Knowin' what you know, you asked her that?'

'Yes, I asked her that. And it makes no difference.'

'You mean you would . . . ?' Her lips moved away from her teeth and he finished for her, 'Yes, yes, I would. And she would an' all if you left her alone.'

'Never! Never! In this world. An' when I tell her, that'll be the finish.'

He moved slowly towards her and stopped only a few feet from her before he said thickly, 'If you make it the finish, it'll be the finish of you, too; I'll send you packing quicker than a rocket.'

'You will, will you?' Her head was jerking in small movements. 'That's what you think.'

His expression showed he was surprised by her defiant attitude. But he spat at her, 'And you won't get a reference other than I'd give to a whore.'

Her lips became tight, her rounded chin knobbled. It was some moment before she spoke and then she said, 'I'm no whore, never was. Compared to you, your father was a gentleman. An' that's what you'll never be, not even half a one.' She flicked her eyes down towards his lower limbs. But in spite of her brave front, she became fearful for a moment by the look on his face. Even so she went on, 'I'll leave this farm when I feel so inclined an' not afore, and you can't do a damned thing about it, Mas . . . ter Amos.' She watched his lids blinking, his brow moving to a furrow of thought. 'That's set you thinkin', hasn't it? An' I'll tell you somethin' more. I've got in me power to put you along the line any minute I choose. You killed your father; you swung from that beam an' you killed him. An' I've got the evidence of it. Not only have I got the torn piece from your coat, but I've got the coat an' all. You made the mistake of givin' it to our Johnnie when you were rigging yourself out with new finery. No, don't, I'm warning you,' her arm went straight out, her finger pointing at him, 'don't think you'll wallop me with that crutch an' get off with it; I'm not Miss Jane, I've got no niceties about me. You lay a finger on me, whether it's by hand or wooden leg, an' by God! you'll live to regret it.'

They glared at each other for a moment longer. Then she turned to open the door. Her hand on the bar, she cast her glance back at him and said softly, 'An' don't try and concoct a way of gettin' rid of me, 'cos if anything happens to me you'll be for it surely, 'cos I'm not the only one who knows, I've seen to that. You see I know you, Master Amos; I've known you for a long time. Long afore others twigged what was in you, I knew you.'

She held his gaze before turning away. Her legs were trembling under her long skirt and the sweat was running from her oxters. She made herself walk steady because she knew he was watching her.

A few minutes later in the kitchen of her cottage she stood looking at Biddy, who was crying loudly while she muttered, 'You should have told me, Ma, you should have told me.'

'Aye, I know I should. It's my fault, but . . . but I thought you'd be gone years ago to your Auntie Lena or Katie's.'

'You, you can't blame him for carryin' on, you can't, 'cos he must have got a shock an' all, he must, Ma.'

'Of course he got a shock, I'm not denyin' it, but in spite of gettin' a shock he went an' put that to you. Marry him, he said. If he had been an ordinary being it would have been bad enough, not right, against God like, but him as he is, offerin' you a double handicap. Now stop cryin', do. Dry your eyes. Come on, dry your eyes.'

'I feel all of a dither, Ma.'

'Aye, lass, I understand. You're bound to. Look, I'll make a sup tea an' then I'll have to get back. But you stay here. Mind, I'm tellin' you, you stay put until I get things arranged.'

As Molly went to the hob and lifted the kettle Biddy said quietly, 'I can't take it in, the master being me da . . . father. He never looked at me, or spoke to me, no more than he did to Amos.' There was a pause before she ended. "Funny him being me father. I'm not just nobody then. I used to wonder. But I'm just not nobody, am I?'

Molly set the kettle into the heart of the fire, then she turned and looked at her daughter. It was odd that she should lay stock on who she came from. Yet not so odd when you came to think of it; she must have wondered many a time.

And Biddy confirmed this now by saying, 'You know, Ma, I used to think it was,' she thumbed towards the wall, 'Mr Armstrong . . . Davie. I used to think he was me da, an' that's why he went away.'

Molly turned again to the fire, saying grimly, 'Well, you thought wrong then, didn't you?'

'But Ma, why . . . why haven't we heard afore, either him, I mean Amos, or me? It's a wonder nobody let it out, isn't it? Me Uncle Johnnie or Mickey, or Will Curran, or them at the Sunday School. It's a wonder they didn't pelt me with it, 'cos I was called a bastard more than once.'

As Molly measured the tea into the earthenware pot she said quietly, 'In Sunday School they were from well around, the places are spread out, they wouldn't know. An' anyway, they were just bairns like yourself.'

'Jim Doolin, or Frank Pearce, they're not bairns. Jim Doolin is after me proper; he waits for me market day.'

'Well, it's not likely that they would say anything even if they knew, is it? An' if they knew the master had been your da, it might have been a feather in your cap.'

'I don't know.' Biddy considered. 'Men are funny about such things. I know Frank Pearce's mam and dad wouldn't have liked it, they're stiff chapel.'

'Well, you won't have to worry about what any of them think; you'll meet a different class with your Aunt Katie. Down there there's butler, an' footmen, an' proper coachmen, an' everything down there she says.' She leant forward and touched her daughter's cheek. 'You're a bonny lass, you'll likely make a good match.'

'I'll miss you, Ma.'

'And I'll miss you, lass.'

They put their arms around each other and remained quiet for a time until Molly said, as if she had been reconsidering the matter, 'It's no good, you've got to get out of here an' as quick as possible.' She moved briskly away now, saying, 'I'm goin' across to see Miss Jane. She's in a state an' all, poor soul. My! If anybody's had the rotten end of the stick, she has. Make yourself some tea, an' no more cryin'. You've got a life afore you, an' it would be wonderful.' She smiled weakly; they both smiled weakly; then she went hurriedly out.

On entering the house she immediately heard the shouting coming from upstairs, and going swiftly through the kitchen, she found Winnie standing at the foot of the stairs. There were high spots of scarlet colour on her cheeks, the rest of her face was white. 'He's like a devil,' she whispered. 'He went for Miss Jane like a madman. Look.' She pointed to the corner where a vase lay broken on the floor. 'He swiped that off with his crutch. I thought he was going to hit her, I did. Where's Biddy?'

'Over in the house. I've got to get her away to Katie's as quick as possible.'

'Aye, the sooner the better. But how will she go? It's the other end of the country, and she's never been farther than Hexham in her life.'

'I'll take her meself.'

'Right away, down there?'

'Aye, right away down there.'

'You'll come back?'

'Oh aye, Winnie; I'll come back.'

They both looked at each other; and they both knew why she would come back.

Molly asked quickly now, 'What's time's Davie goin' in for the stores?' and Winnie answered, 'Around twelve, I should say.'

'He would take us into the train, wouldn't he? He could pick us up along the road on the quiet.'

'Aye. Aye, he could do that.'

'I'll go an' ask him.'

They both hurried away as a door banged overhead, and in the kitchen Molly asked, 'Will you look after the lads for me the time I'm gone, Winnie?'

'That's the least of your worries, lass,' Winnie answered. 'Go on now, and arrange it with Davie.'

She found Davie in the grain store where the rats had been playing havoc, and without any preamble she said, 'You goin' into Hexham the day?' and he nodded as he replied, 'Aye, I'm going into Hexham the day.'

'Around twelve your mother says.'

'Yes, that's right, around twelve.' It was an aggravating habit of his to repeat everything she said.

'Will . . . will you give us a lift, Biddy an' me? I'm taking her away.' Now she had his attention.

'Why? What's happened?'

She looked down for a moment; then moved one lip over the other. 'He . . . he wants to marry her.'

'No! You mean?'

She still had her head down as she nodded. 'He's playin' hell, goin' mad. Even when he knew how they stood to each other, he still went and asked her. I'm . . . I'm takin' her down to our Katie's. It's a long way an' I can't let her go on her own.'

'No, no, of course not. Where will I pick you up?'

'Round the bend of the Tor.'

'Good enough. How . . . how are you off for money?' His voice was gruff.

'Oh, I can manage, I've got a bit put by.'

'Enough to take you there and back? You're coming back?'

She looked up at him, a gleam of hope in her eyes. 'Yes, I'm coming back.'

'What if he won't let you?'

She nodded her head now as she said, 'Oh, he'll let me all right; he can't do anythin' else; I told him what I know about . . . about what he did.'

'You told him that?' He asked the question in a thin whisper.

'Aye, I had to. He was giving me the shove an' . . . an' this is me home, it's the only place I've got. An' what's more I like working along of Miss Jane.' As she lowered her gaze again, he asked quietly, 'Do you think it's wise to come back? You could get a job anywhere.'

'I know that, but as I said, this is me home, I was born and bred here.'

'Aren't you afraid of what he might try an' do to you?'

'I put a stop to that an' all; I told him I'm not the only one who knows.'

He stared hard at her before he asked, 'Did you tell him it was me?'

'Oh no, no, of course not; he might try to do us both in. I wouldn't put it past him.'

'He might at that.'

She heaved a sigh, then said dully, 'Don't let on about where she's going, will you? I mean not to Will Curran, 'cos he'd sell his soul for a penny bun. I'll have to tell the lads, but he won't get it out of them.'

'Don't worry,' he said; 'he certainly won't get it out of me. Be along there around twelve.'

'Ta,' she said, then she went out; and he picked up a handful of grain and ran it through his fingers. There was going to be trouble when he found Biddy gone, for she must have been his one solid hope of fulfilling himself as a man. He remembered the lad used to act as if he owned her when they were small children together. That feeling must have increased rapidly with the years. In this moment he experienced a strong sense of pity for the boy; but the very pity created a stronger sense of foreboding.

Of a sudden he had a longing to be back at sea.

Chapter Seven

'Where's she gone? Where's she gone I'm asking you, woman?'

'Take your hands off!' Jane slapped out at him. 'Take your hands off me. I tell you I don't know. Amos, stop it!' When she fell back onto the foot of the stairs, she let out a high cry as her elbow struck the wood and the pain of it for a moment blotted everything from sight; but she was conscious of steps running from the kitchen and Winnie shouting, 'Give over! Master Amos, for God's sake, give over!'

But she wasn't aware of Davie's presence until Amos was lifted bodily from her; then she saw Amos scrambling on all fours towards the wall where he grabbed at one of his crutches and hurled it at Davie's legs. She closed her eyes tightly when the other crutch went hurtling after the first one. And then Davie's voice, seeming to shudder the roof, yelled, 'Don't you come any of that with me, Mister, for you've picked the wrong one!'

'Come away. Come away out of it.' Winnie was pulling her to her feet, and she groaned with the pain in her elbow. She glanced fearfully to where Amos and Davie were confronting each other, both strangely of a like breadth, the only difference being in height; yet Amos's lack of legs did not seem to handicap him, for of the two at this moment, he looked the more ferocious.

She was passing through the door when she heard Amos speak and she went to turn back, but Winnie pulled her on into the kitchen and banged the door behind them.

What Amos had said was, 'You'll find it better, Armstrong, if you mind your own business.'

'I take it as my business to stop you beltin' into your sister. What's up with you anyway? What's come over you?'

'You're not stupid, so why do you ask? You know what's come over me. And you know where she's gone, don't you? You know where that bitch has taken her. They didn't walk to Hexham, you must have given her a lift on the cart.'

'That's right, I gave them a lift on the cart. But I don't know where they've gone. An' if I did, I wouldn't tell you.'

He lied so convincingly that Amos believed him, and like the draining of a barrel the anger and the rage slowly seeped out of him, and he was left with a great sense of frustration and the futility of going on; for the moment the farm and his new power were as nothing to him.

Slowly he turned away, and as Davie had taught him to do years ago, he shambled towards the stairs by throwing his body from side to side. When he reached them he sat down on the bottom stair and, gripping the oak post, he laid his head against it, and there welled up in him the torrent of emotion that had been dammed for years; for the first time in his life he began to cry–great, tearing, shoulder-shuddering sobs. But when Davie's hand came gently onto his shoulder, he turned fiercely on him. Water spurting from his eyes and nose and spluttering from his mouth in bubbles, he gasped, 'Somebody will pay for this, they will! They will. They will! God Almighty! They will. I'll see they will.'

And they did.

BOOK FOUR

1898

Chapter One

'Now, my dearest Jane, don't worry. Nothing can happen. A week from today we will be together forever, forever and ever; living or dead, we'll be together.'

Arnold Hedley held her thin hands tightly to his breast; his nondescript features glowed with love and happiness. He had waited so long for his superior to die and for Jane to throw off the chains that bound her to Amos, but now everything at last had come about, everything was arranged. Seven days hence she would leave the farm for good and all, and come here to the Vicarage to make it a home. And he so wanted a home, for he had never known one. His parents had died young, and he had been brought up in the care of an uncle who had rid himself of him as soon as possible by sending him to boarding school. From there he had gone into the seminary, and from the seminary he had come to this house, a house that had been dominated by John William Wainwright, a man whom he knew in his inner heart was not really of God, but a selfish, vain, self-seeking man. But he must not think harshly of him anymore, for Wainwright was where God willed him to be these past three months. And the Bishop had confirmed him in the living and so made his way clear at last to make Jane his wife.

Yet although he had said to her that nothing could go wrong, there was an uneasiness in him and he knew he wouldn't feel that all was right until Jane was safely installed in this house and away from the farm, or rather, Amos. Never had he been so mistaken in judging human nature as he had in that boy. Through all his early days he had prophesied great things for him. With such an active mind he could have become a writer, a profession he could have followed without exposure to the public. But what had he done? He had used his powers to become a gambler. As a child he had been adroit with the game of marbles. He himself had been amused by his prowess in this direction. Now he was horrified at where the simple game had led him. The farm faced utter disaster if some check were not put on his activities. But who could check such a one as Amos had become? And there was not only the gambling, there was the scandal of his trips into Hexham, trips that kept him there two and three nights at a time. His jaunts on this business at times took him as far away as Newcastle. He could be away for as long as four days to a week. Only one good thing resulted from his absences: the inhabitants of the farm during such times knew a little peace.

Arnold recalled the time when he first came to this parish. There had been eighteen souls all told at Cock Shield; now there were but seven. In the last twelve months two more had gone from the place: Johnnie Geary had married and taken his young wife with him to another farm; and Winnie, that hard-working faithful servant, had gone to her long rest but two months ago. It was strange that old Sep should have outlived his daughter and her husband, and also weathered the epidemic that took four of them in a week. He supposed there was a purpose in it, God's ways were strange. He was thankful that the Lord in His wisdom had seen fit to bring Davie Armstrong back, for without him he dreaded to think what might have come to the place. He had not been wrong in his summing up of Davie. A fine man was Davie in spite of his lack of faith, hot-headedness, and sharpness of tongue at times. He was very fond of Davie, as was Jane.

He led her now across the brown-painted dismal hall and into the brown, darkly furnished, equally dismal sitting room, and, pressing her into a chair, he said, 'Now sit there quietly, my dear, and I'll go and tell Mrs Spense you've come, and she will make you a hot cup of tea.'

'Yes, Arnold, that would be nice,' Jane said dutifully, knowing at the same time that Mrs Spense was well aware that she had arrived and that if she made her a cup of tea, it would be with reluctance. Mrs Spense was not looking forward to having a mistress in the house.

She looked slowly around the room. How would she ever be able to think of this place as home? Could she even succeed in making it homelike? Could she ever be able to erase Parson Wainwright's presence from that great leather chair, the indentations which even now gave the impression that he was sittin in it; he who smiled at her while he fought her off with unctuous charm? She looked at the heavy black sideboard taking up almost one wall of the room; the high glass cabinet of stuffed birds dominating another wall; the curtains of an indefinable colour hanging limply at each side of the narrow, deep stone window which she guessed had never been washed for fear of disintegration.

If she'd had some money of her own and had been able to strip the whole place and refurnish it, she would have been happy, for at least it would have given her an interest in her future; but she had no money. She had come to Arnold with only her clothes, her books, and a little jewellery to which, under the present state of affairs, she had no right. She had handled no money for almost two years now, since Amos had taken over, he had seen to all the bills. Amos had treated her shamefully, and she didn't deserve it. No, she didn't deserve it from him, for she had given him her life.

He had blamed her for helping to spirit Biddy away. For months after that dreadful night when he had smashed nearly all the furniture in the sitting room, he had refused to speak to her, treating her much in the same way as her father had treated him. Their normal relationship had never really been restored until three months ago when Parson Wainwright had died and she had told Amos that she was going to marry Arnold and make her home in the Vicarage. She had been surprised at his first reaction to her news, for he had appeared again like the young Amos who had demanded her whole attention. 'No, you can't,' he had said. 'Oh Jane, you can't. You wouldn't leave me here on my own.' But she had replied that he had little need of her now.

'That isn't true,' he had said, 'I do need you, I need you all the time. You're the only thing I have left. No matter what I do or how I act, you know you're the only thing I have to call my own.'

Although this had touched her, she had remained quietly adamant. She was going to marry Arnold, she said; it was settled, finally settled. She could have added that she must marry Arnold for more reasons than one.

Shortly after this Amos had compromised. 'All right then,' he had said, 'all right, but come and live here. I can't be left alone, Jane, I can't.' But even against this entreaty she had remained firm, saying she was sorry but the place of a parson's wife was in the Vicarage.

The place of a parson's wife was in the Vicarage. She now looked into the black iron grate where a low, dull fire was burning. She hated this house, she had always hated, but it was her only refuge: this, and Arnold. Dear Arnold. So kind, so thoughtful. And so loving; she wasn't worthy of him. If he could see into her heart he would be astounded, for he would find nothing there but a thirty-year-old shrivelled case. How long ago was it since she had given the core of herself away? She didn't know, for at the time she hadn't realized she had parted with it. It was only during these past two years that the knowledge had come to her, the shocking knowledge that she loved a man who, even in her reduced circumstances, was beneath her. Davie might be managing the farm, what was left of it, but he was still remembered as McBain's cowman.

Arnold came hurrying back into the room. He was smiling. He closed the door behind him, a precise action, then came towards her, his hand extended.

'There you are, that's settled. The kettle is on, and in ten minutes we'll have a cup of tea.' It was as if he had achieved some extraordinary feat of diplomacy.

When he drew his chair up to hers she put her hand on his and said, 'There was no need to trouble Mrs Spense, Arnold. It's not long since I had dinner.'

'You've walked all this way and I'm not going to allow you to walk all the way back without some refreshment.' He now leaned nearer to her and, his voice dropping, he said, 'I have a nice surprise for you. I have acquired the third book in the trilogy by the Reverend Ingraham, *The Prince of the House of David*, and two of Mrs Henry Wood's books. Ah-ha!' He wagged his finger at her. 'I am not going to tell you the titles of those, I am keeping them as part of our recreation. I have it all planned out. One evening you shall read to me, the next I to you; when we're . . .' Only just in time he checked himself from making use of the embarrassing term in bed, and substituted, resting.

Jane looked at him with a deep, tolerant warmth in her eyes. She had a vivid picture in her mind of them both sitting up in bed, one reading, the other listening, and although the picture didn't bring her any joy, she appreciated the gesture he had made in buying the latter two books, for his taste did not incline towards Mrs Henry Wood, but to much deeper subjects, slightly controversial subjects such as science. He talked a great deal about Mr Huxley and admired him, yet he could not countenance his attitude to religion. Mr Huxley, she understood, had brought into being a new word with regards to irreligious people: he called them agnostics.

Arnold was now moving his fingers gently around her wrist. Back and forward, back and forward they went, as if forming a bracelet. She couldn't stand it. She had never been able to stand this affectionate gesture of his. She wanted to jump to her feet, but she forced herself to rise slowly, saying, 'I must be getting back, I have so much to do.'

'But, but what about the tea?'

'Oh, thank Mrs Spense and apologize for my going.'

'Yes, yes, my dear.' His voice was hesitant. Then he added, 'I feel guilty at not being able to accompany you, but I have the meeting with. . . .'

'Arnold, Arnold,' she chided him gently, 'I have often walked those two miles on my own. Don't be silly.'

'You might have, my dear, but I still want to accompany you. And let us say, in place of guilt, I feel a sense of loss in being denied your company.'

They stood under the porch of the Vicarage and looked at each other; then he bent forward and kissed her gently, as a father might, and she went from him down the grass-grown gravel drive to the gate and out into the road, telling herself all the while not to be silly, she mustn't be foolish, she must not cry.

She was deeply fond of Arnold, he was the best man in the world, and she reminded herself that she was near thirty and this would be her last chance of marriage. She wanted marriage, for she wanted a child. Oh yes, once she had a child everything would fall into place; her body would no longer torment her once she had a child.

She had entered the farmland and was within five minutes' walk of the house when she saw Davie. He was at some distance, but she knew it was he and that he was attending an animal. She cut across the fields in his direction, and before she came up to him he heard her approach and turned towards her, but it was she who spoke first. 'Is anything wrong?' she asked.

'Flo here, Miss Jane. If I'm not mistaken, she's going to drop her calf an' all. If that happens it'll be the fourth in three weeks. Something should be done.' He stared at her, and she turned her eyes from his and looked sideways down onto the grass.

'I've told him it's the lack of something. It's understandable one dropping now and again, but this'll be the seventh this year. He should get advice. An' you can, you know, Miss, they're looking into these things now. There's a place where you can send. I've got the name and. . . .'

He stopped talking when she looked up at him and said quietly, 'You've tried it, Davie, and I've tried it; we know it's no use.' She turned away, and he turned with her, saying abruptly, 'It's a thankless job. I'm telling you, Miss Jane, if it wasn't for me Granda, I'd be gone the morrow.'

'No, no! Davie.' She had stopped abruptly, and again they were looking at each other. 'If you desert him, well . . . well, the place—' she shook her head, then slowly looked about her and, as if to herself, she finished, 'Twenty years ago it was the most thriving farm in these parts; no other could touch it.'

They were walking on again when Davie said quietly, 'I hear he's for selling the land beyond the Tor.'

'That's what he says, Davie.'

It was noticeable that neither of them referred to Amos as Master, or Master Amos–he was *he*, as he had at one time been *it*.

'I was worrying about losing Mickey, but if this goes on it won't matter; it'll soon be a one-man plot. All that'll remain will be a small holding left us by the grace of Sir Alfred. God Almighty! It's terrible when you think of it. Aw, I'm sorry, Miss.'

'It's all right, Davie. I say it too. God Almighty! It's terrible when you think of it.' She did not ask herself what Arnold would have said to her using such an expression, but she added, 'I didn't know Mickey was thinking of going.' And he answered, 'Well, you can't blame him.' He didn't look towards her as he added, 'There's one good thing, you'll be finished with it all next week.'

Slowly they turned their heads towards each other, but they kept walking. 'The weight of it will still be on me wherever I go, Davie, and I feel as if I am deserting and leaving a sinking ship.'

'Don't feel like that.' His voice was quiet and deep. 'If anybody in this world deserves a little peace, it's you . . . Miss.'

She kept her head down as she said, 'Thank you, Davie.'

They walked in silence into the farmyard; then she went towards the kitchen where Molly was standing at the door, and he went towards the cow byres. But he passed them and let himself into the harness room.

When he had closed the door behind him he stood looking about him from one article to another, from the table that held spoke, and waterbrushes, bit and dandy-brushes, and leathers all jumbled together. He had ceased ordering Mickey to arrange everything neatly; there was no time for it. There was only time for keeping his gig spanking, for His Lordship. With the exception of one, the saddles on the walls had all gone dry, for the boiler was rarely put on now and the room was cold.

He moved slowly to the wooden block near the bench and sat down and dropped his head into his hands for a moment. Supporting it with his thumbs, his fingers moved across his brow, and not for the first time he muttered aloud, 'I must have been up the pole, bloody well up the pole to take this on.' If he had gone when he should have, he'd be free now on the seas, not working for a young snot whose head he wanted to bash every time he looked at him. Not that he wasn't civil to him, himself; oh, butter wouldn't melt in his mouth at times; but ask him to lay out a penny on the cattle or the place and what did you get? Just that blank, closed look that you couldn't get through.

He had spoken only half the truth the day he'd found Biddy gone, when he had cried and said he'd make somebody pay for it; he'd made everybody pay for it. But her, most of all.

His fingers now stopped moving on his brow and pressed tightly against his temple bones. She didn't want to go through with it, he was sure of it. Well, say she didn't, where did that leave him? Aw, why in the name of God hadn't he gone when the going was good? Why? Because he had gone barmy. You couldn't want two women at once, or could you? What was he on about? He didn't want two women; never in his life would he take Molly Geary, although she was hanging like a ripe plum just waiting to fall into his hand. Throwing herself at him she was. Never by a word, no, no, but he could tell, he could read the hungry look in her eyes. Well, she could throw herself from now until she was toothless and she would still bounce off him. But the other, Jane–he did not add the prefix of Miss in his mind–how did she affect him? He was puzzled with regards to his feelings towards her. All he knew was that they had grown out of pity. He had been sorry for Miss Jane, used by her people since she was a child, and now left with only one refuge: to marry the parson. He had nothing against Parson Hedley, oh no; if he respected anybody, it was the parson. But not as a husband for her, a man to love her. No, he couldn't see the parson filling those roles. And Jane needed both, for she was warm and loving. But she was lost. For months past now every time he had looked at her he had wanted to take her into his arms. Just to comfort her, nothing more, just to comfort her. At least, it had been nothing more at the beginning.

It was, he told himself, a hell of a situation, for these were the nights when, lying in his bed, he was as conscious of that one beyond the wall as if she was tucked in to his side. At times he felt she was willing herself into his bed. There had been one night not long ago when he'd had the urge to get up and hammer on the wall and yell, 'Stop it! Stop it! You're wasting your time. Once bitten, twice shy.' He fought with her ceaselessly during the night, yet in the daytime he was civil to her. He called her by her name, and spoke the time of day, and at times talked of this and that. He also thanked her frequently for what she did for the old 'un; but then in this case, there was likely more method in her madness than generosity. Aw, no! He had to give her her due there, she was kind. By nature she was kind, and it was in her favour, too, that she'd always been kind and loyal to Jane. But she'd been kind to Jane's father an' all, hadn't she?

He rose abruptly from the log and went outside. He had better see what Will Curran was up to. If he hadn't been an old man he'd have sent him packin', lazy beggar that he was.

'Jane.' Amos stretched his hand along the dining room table towards her. The gesture and his voice both held supplication, and his large, fair face was soft with it.

It was a long time since she had seen him like this, but she remained untouched by it. Sitting straight in her chair, she looked at him as he said, 'I'm speaking for your own good as well as mine. Oh, I know I'm pleading for myself, but . . . but on the other hand, I know your heart isn't in this. Look, it's not too late to call it off. And I promise you, I swear on it, Jane, I'll take a pull at myself. I won't sell the bottom land, I'll get another hand in. I'll see to things myself, I'll take over. . . .'

'You couldn't do better than Davie does.'

He drew his hand a few inches backwards and stared at her before he said, 'No, I know I couldn't. I'm not saying I could. I'll always need Davie. But . . . but there's things I could do to. . . . Oh! Oh!' He now waved his hand in front of his face. 'I know I should have done them before, but Jan—' he used his old pet name for her, 'don't marry old Hedley, don't leave me, please.' On the last words his voice had dropped to a thin whisper.

Two years ago, even a year ago, if he had made such a plea she would have flown down the table and put her arms about him and held his head to her and said, 'As long as you need me, Amos, I'll never leave you.' But she knew now, and with a deep certainty, that were she to comply with his selfish demand, he would, in a very short while, forget his promise to reform and argue and defend his rights. Oh, she knew Amos. To her cost, she knew Amos. Never had she imagined that there would come a time when she would look at him coolly and see him as he really was, a bitter, totally selfish man; for, at eighteen years, he was a man in looks and mind, and in one other particular as well, which was certainly not affected by his handicap.

As she walked from the table, she said, 'I am marrying Arnold next week, Amos, and nothing you can say will change my mind. It's too late.' She was, she imagined, passing beyond arm's length of him when, with the agility that always surprised her, he leaned sideways, stretched out one arm while hanging on to the table with the other hand and, grabbing hold of her skirt, tugged her fiercely towards him.

As her hip hit the table she cried out, 'Amos! Stop it! Have you gone mad?'

'No, I haven't gone. I am. Remember? You have told me on several occasions over the past two years that I am mad; everything I do comes under the heading of madness to you. Now, before I show you how really mad I can get, I ask you again not to leave me.' There was no plea in his voice now, and although he had said, 'I ask you,' it was more in the nature of a command.

'Let go of my skirt.'

'I will when I'm ready. You're going to listen to me. What do you expect to get out of a marriage with old Hedley? And don't tell me he's only forty. I know his age. But add twenty years onto that and you've got the real man. Why, you'd get more out of Will Curran than you would out of him. He's never seen a bare backside in his life, not even a child's. Do you think he'd want to look at yours . . . ?'

The force of her blow sent his head bumping against the back of the chair. If she had attacked him like a dog and bitten him, he couldn't have been more surprised by her reaction. She stood back from him. Her face was not flushed with indignation but drained like a piece of bleached calico. The pumping of her heart was heaving her small breasts and pulsing in her neck. Her words, when she spoke, spouted out in jerks as if each one had to surmount an obstacle. 'F . . . Father was right. He . . . he was right all along with regards to you. I've . . . I've heard said you were a devil, and . . . and you are, a . . . a wicked-minded devil.'

She ran out of the room while he remained seated at the table, his hands spread out before him as if taking his weight. Her attack had surprised him in more ways than one. What had he said to make her so mad? That old Hedley wouldn't want to see her backside? He had said worse things than that in her presence. He had never seen her so wild, not even on the day he aimed at smashing up the whole house and she had literally fought with him, braving flying vases and bric-à-brac. Did she care for old Hedley all that much? No, she couldn't; she was just keeping to an agreement made years ago.

He lifted one hand now and felt his cheek. She had struck him, and no light blow, but he wouldn't hold that against her. It was a wonder she hadn't done it years ago; he knew he had tried her patience beyond endurance at times. But didn't she understand that you always tried the patience of those you loved? Didn't she understand that he loved her, that in spite of everything he had done to her, he loved her? Anyway, she was all he'd had to love since they took Biddy away. And now Biddy was going to be married. Her mother had made a point of telling Will Curran within his own hearing. By God! He'd like to slit that one's throat. If there was anyone on this earth he hated, it was Molly Geary, and he would have given her short shrift before now if it weren't for the fact that she had him nobbled. It was true he had only her word for it, but he had to take it just in case. And now it looked as if he were going to be left with her. She would order things pretty much her own way once Jane was gone.

There were so many reasons why Jane shouldn't go, so many. What would it be like at night in the winter when the snow was on the ground for weeks on end and he couldn't get into the town to ease his body's needs? He had been like a caged lion last winter, but a lion with a gentle keeper, a keeper he knew he could devour, metaphorically speaking, any time he chose. Now his keeper was leaving him, and there was the winter ahead.

But there wasn't only the winter to worry about, there were the nights in the near future when, because his bank balance was almost nil, he would be unable to enjoy the one thing that gave him real pleasure.

Over the past eighteen months he had become a respected patron in Rafferty's Rooms; a seat was kept especially for him. There, he was a man among men. There, no one treated him as a youth, and he knew that some of them were afraid of him. For the first six months his luck had been just average, then there was a time when everything he touched came up for him. During this period he had never gone to the tables more than twice in the same coat and waistcoat; what was more, Rafferty's niece had been very attentive to him. She was a bit long in the tooth, but after all, he had to face it, his choice outside the brothels was limited.

But it was those long winter nights ahead of him that were really worrying him, when, with Jane gone, he'd be deprived both mentally and physically. There would be no one to talk with. He no longer found even slight amusement talking to those about the farm. What had he in common with Will Curran, Mickey, or even Davie Armstrong for that matter? It was strange about Davie. He would have been more than willing to listen to his yarns of the sea if they had been forthcoming, but the man was reticent. There was an aloofness about him that did not fit his position. True, he would discuss any point concerning the farm, but beyond that it was as if he had drawn a line. At one time he had wondered if it was he who was Molly's confidant, but had discarded the suggestion, going on what Will Curran had said–that she was as much cow splatter to Davie–and he treated her as such, stepping out of her way whenever possible.

But in spite of Davie's manner, which irritated him at times because of its entire lack of subservience, he still retained for him the feeling the man had engendered years ago. He liked the sailor. In fact, when he came to consider it, he liked the sailor better than anyone else he knew, except, of course, Jane.

Jane . . . Jane. He touched his cheek again. Next week, and for the rest of her life, she'd be in the Vicarage with old Hedley. Apart from everything else, it wasn't right; she might be thirty and past the marrying age, but in a strange way she still remained a girl, a very young girl. It didn't seem right that she should be broken in by old Hedley.

He sat quite still for almost fifteen minutes; his face had taken on a look of deep concentration. When at last he slid off the chair and got onto his crutches, he hobbled slowly from the room, went out through the front door, across the farmyard, and over the fell towards Shale Tor.

Chapter Two

'Is that you, Davie lad?'

'Aye, Granda, I'll be up in a minute.' Davie took the brown teapot to the hob and mashed the tea from the black spurting kettle. Then, putting out his hand, he went to pull a chair up to the fire to sit for a few minutes while the tea brewed, to give himself a breathing space before going upstairs to talk and listen to the old 'un. But his plan was halted by old Sep's voice, high now, calling, 'Davie! Davie! Come up a minute. Here, quick!'

Thinking there was something wrong, he bounded up the stairs and burst into the small low-ceilinged bedroom to see his grandfather leaning towards the window, peering out into the deepening twilight.

'Come here a tick.'

'What's up with you, old 'un?'

'Nawt, nawt. Just get on your hunkers and follow me finger.'

Leaning over the bed, Davie looked in the direction in which the horny finger was pointing, and after screwing up his eyes he studied the far landscape for a moment. 'What you hoping to see?' he asked. 'There's nothin' out there.'

'Hold your horses, an' keep your eyes on this side of the Tor, above the road. Now, what do you see?'

Again Davie paused, then said, 'It could be a sheep going up the path. No, too big for that. Well, a wild pony strayed in.'

'It's no sheep an' no wild pony.' The old man's voice was low. 'Four nights running he's gone up there and around, on dark. Yon's Master Amos.'

'Master Amos! Don't be silly, old 'un; you can't make out what that is from this distance, man or beast, not in this light you can't.'

'Can't I, lad? Well, there's one thing I've kept, an' that's me keen sight, together with me mind; I'm neither blind nor in me dotage. No matter what's gone wrong with me limbs, those two faculties are much as they always were, an' that thing you see movin' over yonder is Master Amos. I tell you he's skitted across those fields like a divil in a gale of wind these past few nights, an' always on dark. Now why, I ask you, why?'

'Perhaps he's got some piece from the village he meets up there. Some of them's not particular.'

Sep shook his head. 'Why should he go there for his sport when he can get it in Rafferty's backroom? Anyway, it would be a bit uncomfortable. Blow the hairs off your chin up there. No, you know what, lad? I smell a rat.'

Davie turned his head and looked at the old man, and like an echo rising from the past the words conjured up the scene in the kitchen all those years ago when his Granda had said, 'I smell a rat,' and the rat had turned out to be the master. His Granda was good at smelling rats, although he couldn't unearth them. And now he smelt a rat with regard to Master Amos.

What was that legless giant doing up on the Tor at this hour? Tomorrow morning, first thing, he'd make it his business to take a walk up there. It was some long time since he had been up there himself, for with one thing and another he had more than his hands full down here, but tomorrow morning as soon as it was light he'd take a dander to Shale Tor, and maybe he'd unearth the rat.

At about the time Sep had called down to Davie, Jane was helping Arnold to pack the last of her possessions into the old Vicarage trap. And it was an old trap. It was old when Arnold had first taken up his position at the Vicarage, and since then its shafts had only known two ponies. The present one, Betty by name, was eighteen years old. She was sweet natured and patient, as a pony that pulled a parson should be. She had never taken fright or bolted; she was known far and wide and was loved by old and young alike, and her middle was inclined to thickness because of the fruit and tidbits she received.

Jane went to the pony now and patted her head while Arnold lit the side lamps, remarking as he did so, 'The glass has cracked in both panels of this one. You wouldn't think a candle could generate so much heat, would you?'

'No, Arnold, no, you wouldn't.'

They stood together now at the back of the trap. She could just see his face. His eyes were so kindly, so full of tenderness and concern. She told herself yet again that she was very fond of Arnold, very fond; yet when he put his arms out and drew her gently into them, she stiffened. It was only the slightest movement of resistance, but he felt it and said reassuringly, 'It's all right, my dear, there is no one about.' He turned his head to look one way, then the other. 'All are going to their nest, animals, men, and women alike. God made the night for rest and for. . . .' The word that jumped into her own mind was love, but when, after a slight pause, he added 'peace', she wondered if in the future his stilted phraseology, his pedantic way of speaking, might not get on her nerves. He had taught her to speak correctly, and he had corrected her diction from when she was small; later, he had tried to guide her thinking, but in the latter he had never succeeded, for her thoughts had always run wild.

When his lips touched hers they created no responsive feeling; his fingers caressing her wrists twanged the strings of passion in her more than his lips did; but he was Arnold, dear, dear Arnold, and the day after tomorrow she would be his wife.

Her books and two cases of clothes were all the personal possessions she was taking with her, although Amos had been surprisingly generous at the last. He was giving her the china cabinet from the drawing room and at least a third of the cutlery, besides the small silver tea service that had never been used, and also the furniture from her bedroom; all these would go to the Vicarage tomorrow on the farm cart.

Over the past few days Amos's manner towards her had been exemplary; she had never known him to be kinder or more considerate. He was, she knew, trying to make up to her for the scene in the dining room. As he had said last night, he had only one sister and he wanted her to go on loving him, no matter where she was. She had been very touched, and she told herself again that if only he had been like this over the past two years, she could not have borne to leave him.

'Good-night, my dear, dear Jane. Only one more parting and then we'll be together, always together.' He now took her face tenderly between his hands, adding, 'Don't be afraid, my dear, of anything. Your peace of mind will be my whole concern; you will know nothing but tenderness and consideration at my hands.'

'Oh Arnold! Arnold!' She was near to tears, and impulsively she clung to him, almost fiercely, until he laughed shakily and said, 'There now, there now, I must be away. Even Betty is getting impatient.' His lips touched hers gently, and then he got up into the trap, and immediately Betty moved off.

She followed the trap until it passed through the farm gates into the road and there she called, 'Good-bye, Arnold. Good-bye.' And he answered her, 'Good-bye, my dear, Good-bye.' Then she stood watching the jogging lights disappear into the distance.

It was dawn the next morning when the trap and pony and parson were found at the bottom of the valley. The parson was lying beneath the pony; the trap had disintegrated into matchwood underneath the boulders that had come down in the landslide from Shale Tor.

Chapter Three

'She's like someone demented.' Molly stared down at Davie. 'She's bent on getting up, but the doctor said she had to stay put for at least another week or so. An' she hardly opens her mouth, except to say "Yes, Molly. No, Molly. Thanks, Molly." She lies there, starin' ahead, for all the world as if she was seeing something that wasn't there. You know what I mean?'

Davie nodded, then absent-mindedly pushed away from him the head of the cow he was milking.

'And you know somethin' else? She's never opened her mouth to him, not once, leastways not when I've been there.'

Davie turned his head sharply towards her now as he asked, 'Has she said anything, I mean why she's not speakin' to him?'

'No, not a word. But I can say this, he's been different since the parson went. Give him his due, he's done everything in his power. . . .'

'Aye, he's done everything in his power.'

'What did you say? What did you say, Davie?'

'I was just thinkin'.'

Molly continued to look at him for almost a full minute before she said quietly, 'Biddy's bein' married the day.'

Again his head jerked towards her. 'She is? Well, well. Now why didn't you go down? Why didn't you?'

'I was, I was for it, but I ask you, could I leave Miss Jane like this? She hasn't a soul to turn to, and not even the old crabs who used to swarm round the parson come visitin' her. But that's 'cos of him. They're feared of him. I've never seen anybody so lost lookin' as her, so I couldn't go off.'

Davie stared into her round, hazel eyes. She had a heart for people's troubles. As he had said afore, he'd give her credit for that. But it wasn't right, she should have been at her lass's wedding. She should have had that much out of life. He checked his softened thinking with regards to her; he no longer held any animosity towards her, yet he was still determined within himself that she wasn't getting any further than his outer skin. And so he said, 'I think the best thing would be if she did get up. Lying there, she'll just brood. The days are cuttin' in; she should get out in the air while the weather's fit. I would let her get up if I was you.'

'Aye, perhaps you're right.' She gazed at him as she nodded; then she turned slowly away.

Again he pushed at the cow's nuzzling head. Then rising, he unloosened the chain that held her to the milking stall and slapped her rump as she backed out and followed the rest of the small herd into the fields. He then carried the last pail of milk into the dairy where Mickey, pausing in the business of filling a churn from surrounding buckets, remarked flatly, 'Don't know how much you've got there, Davie, but this's down again; soon won't be worth the cartage into town.'

Davie was on the point of retorting sharply, 'Well, that's not your worry,' when he checked himself. Mickey was a good lad, and in a way he was concerned for the place, for he had been bred on it. It was his home, and he had known no other, but the lass he was courting had no mind to start life here. Moreover, she was scared to death of Master Amos, so in a short time he'd likely follow Johnnie and start his married life elsewhere. What he said was. 'It's a problem I wish I could see the end of.'

Mickey asked now, 'Do you think there's any truth in this business of him sellin' the bottom fields?'

'I should say there's no smoke without fire, lad.'

'But how's he goin' to go on for hay and winter food? He's not daft, he knows that if you can't grow it you've got to buy it.'

'You don't need winter feed if you haven't got any cattle.'

'You mean . . . you mean he'd do away with the lot? But, how would he live?'

'Sheep and pigs, he says. Sheep on the hills and just enough tatties, an' a cow or two for his own use. That's how he sees things.'

'God! The place'll be no better than a shanty plot.'

'You've said it, lad; no better than a shanty plot.'

'Eeh! It's a wonder the master doesn't turn in his grave.'

'It's my guess he's turned so often of late he's so dizzy he's havin' to hang onto the handles.'

Mickey's burst of laughter brought a slow chuckle from Davie, then he was laughing as loud as the young fellow.

'Eeh! That was funny, Davie.' Mickey wiped his eyes. 'It does you good to laugh.'

'Aye, Mickey, it does you good to laugh.' He turned away thinking, 'tis strange how a man changes, for who would have thought I'd crack a joke over McBain.

A few minutes later when crossing the yard he stopped as he saw Molly come running from the house. 'What is it?' he asked.

'She's up an' gone, she's gone out. She's not in the house anywhere.'

'Well, don't frash yourself. She's done what we said she should do; she's gone for a walk, taken the air.'

'No, no.' She shook her head. 'I don't think she's put any clothes on, and she doesn't seem right in her mind. There's no knowin' what she might do.'

'No clothes on!' He screwed up his face, then said quickly, 'I'll go up on the ridge and look over the land from there, you go down by the burn.'

'But if she's not there. . . .'

'Well, go and see, woman. How do you know she won't be there until you go and see?' His voice was harsh, and he saw her bridle for a moment before she turned sharply away.

He ran swiftly into the road now, across the fields, over the stone walls and up onto the ridge. The sky was high, the light was clear. It was silvery white light through which you could see for miles. He picked out the various paths and roads, and saw on one what could be the trap returning from Hexham, bearing the Lord of The Manor back to what remained of Cock Shield farm. His thoughts were always tinged with sarcasm when they dwelt on Amos. Finally, he looked up towards the Tor, because that was the last place, he imagined, she would make for. But there, on the winding path, moving around the face, was a figure. It could have been anyone from this distance, man, woman or child, but immediately he knew it was she.

He leapt down the slope, the impetus acting like springs to his feet, then raced across the fields, swung himself over three low stone walls, then dropped into the valley just to the right of the spot from where he had helped to lift the body of the parson in the early morning of the day before he was to be married.

He was gasping hard when he reached the Tor road. Then he was running up the winding path, and when he reached the summit he stopped, both from lack of breath and surprise, for there she was in her night attire standing in front of the rocking stone, her finger pointing down to it, as if she were accusing it personally.

He drew in a number of short breaths before he moved slowly towards her. He reached to within three yards of her and she didn't turn or move from her position. Very softly he said, 'Miss Jane!' Then again, more firmly now, 'Miss Jane!'

Her finger wavered, her eyes blinked. Slowly she turned her head and looked at him. Then like a child whimpering after receiving a fright, 'Davie . . . Oh, Davie.'

'It's all right, Miss Jane.' He moved another step towards her. Her arm had dropped to her side now. Her body looked limp, slumped. She didn't seem aware that she was still in her night attire. Her nightdress was made of lawn with a small frilled collar; the sleeves came down to the wrists and ended in frills; the hem fell below her ankles and showed a faded pair of blue velvet slippers, dust covered now, as was the hem of the nightdress. He said gently, 'It's all right, Miss Jane, it's all right. There's nothing to worry about.'

'Oh yes, Davie, yes, there is something–something to worry about.' She was speaking like a child now, her words resting on her tongue before she delivered them. 'The stone, Davie.' She turned now and pointed again to the stone. 'He could never move this . . . not this one.'

God Almighty! She knew. That's what it was, she knew. It had turned her brain because she knew. His Granda was right, with his smelling of rats. What was to be done?

'Davie.'

'Yes, Ja . . . Miss Jane.'

'Look.' She held out her hand and caught his, and now she led him across the top of the Tor to the raw jagged edge left by the fall. He had to check her from going too near. Her finger was again pointing stiffly, but downwards towards their feet now, as she said, 'He had them all lined up here. The boys from the village, he said the boys from the village had moved them, but I knew a long time ago he had done it himself, Davie.' Her voice was breaking now and her face, like a child's, was crumpling into tears. 'Da-vie, he killed Arnold. Amos ki-lled Arnold. I . . . I heard Betty scream. A horse screams when it's frightened, Davie. It screams louder than anything in the world, a horse does. Davie, Davie, he killed Arnold. He said he wouldn't let me leave him, that he was lonely. He wouldn't let me go, so he killed Arnold.'

The tears were falling over her lower lids now, big, slow drops. They seemed to be falling into his own throat, swelling it. She still had hold of his hand. He put out his other and took her arm and drew her gently back from the edge. Now she was gulping her words out while she blinked up into his face. 'He . . . he was drinking when I went into the dining room that night. He didn't expect me. Davie, he didn't expect to see me. He . . . he started, and, and he was drinking. Amos doesn't drink. He gambles, but he doesn't drink. Whisky, a big glass of whisky. Gulping . . . gulping it.'

'There, now. There, now. Don't distress yourself.'

'Davie, I'm lost and I've nowhere to go. I can't . . . I can't get away from him, and I cannot tell the police because . . . because I still love him, Davie. He's my brother and I'm all he has, but . . . but I hate him, Davie. I love him, and I hate him.' Her voice had risen; her face was contorted; the tears were choking her, her sobs turning into wails. When she fell against him he put his arms about her and stroked her hair while he murmured, 'There, there. There, now, cry it out. That's it, cry it out.' And all the while he was aware of her body near his, Miss Jane's body near his. No, not Miss Jane's body, Jane's body.

His face was resting in her hair and her wailing was subsiding when Molly's head and shoulders appeared over the edge of the Tor. He stared down at her but didn't move. She looked up at him and for a time she didn't move either.

When she came up to them his head was straight but he still had his arms around Jane, and he said, 'She's cried it out, she'll be better now. Let's get her down.'

Between them they led her down the Tor and back into the house. Then Molly took her upstairs and put her to bed, and almost immediately Jane went to sleep.

Later, when Molly entered the kitchen, she was surprised to see Davie waiting for her. He said, 'She knows that he killed the parson.'

'Who? You don't mean that he . . . that he did that an' all?' There was horror in her face and voice.

'Aye, this is the second notch on his stick.'

'Oh, dear God!'

'If I had gone up that night when me Granda told me, I could have prevented it.'

'You've known then?'

'Aye, sort of. The old 'un had spotted him going up the Tor a number of times when it was late. He must have been waiting for the parson going home. Still,' he turned slowly about, 'he would have got him some other way, he wouldn't have let it be. He's a devil, a devil from deep hell, that one.'

'What are you gona do about it?'

'What can I do? There's no proof; no one saw him do it, no more than they saw him kick his father downstairs.'

'I've still got the coat to prove that.'

'It's only your word against his, and who's going to believe that a legless man could climb that staircase post? It would take me all me time to reach that beam. No, you would come worse off out of that, I'm afraid, as I would if I went to the police about this, because I doubt if Miss Jane would speak against him.' He moved towards the door and, his voice thick, he muttered, 'There's only one thing I wish now, that I were away to hell out of this.'

She stood looking towards the closed door. She, too, wished he were away to hell out of this; but she knew that she was the only one who did wish it, because he himself didn't. Nor did Miss Jane.

There had been something niggling at her mind for a long time now, for two years in fact, ever since he came back onto the farm, and this was it. It had come to light when she saw them standing together up there.

Miss Jane might have been out of her wits, but he wasn't. His face had been buried in her hair like that of a lover.

She couldn't stand this, not this. She couldn't bear any more, she was tired, weary. She began to cry, slow tears which rolled down her cheeks unheeded until, sitting down at the kitchen table, she dropped her head onto her folded arms and gave way to the pain inside her. As her tears, like a rising river, gushed down her face, she cried out against her life and fate. She didn't deserve to be treated like this, she didn't, she didn't. She had paid for what she had done. People changed; she had just been a lass, he should understand that. Was he doing it to spite her? No, no, she didn't think that; it was one of those things that just happened. But it had happened between the two people she liked best in the world, loved best in the world. God, she wouldn't be able to witness it, she couldn't, she'd have to get away. Fred Bateman would have her. He had been knocking on for her since his wife died. He had five bairns and there was still time to have some of her own. God in heaven, what a prospect! But it was either that of stay here and watch them grow closer.

Slowly she raised her head and blinked rapidly as she stared at the fireplace framed in its gleaming copper pans and brass, and she said to herself, 'But . . . but they haven't started yet, the parson's been buried but a week. Don't meet trouble halfway, wait till they start, wait till it's in the open. And then there'll be nothing you or anybody else can do about it.'

On this last thought she suddenly exclaimed aloud, 'Oh my God!' There was one who'd do something about it if she knew anything. They said everything went in threes. Well, Davie Armstrong was no fool, so if anything would deter him from letting his ideas run wild with regards to Miss Jane, the knowledge that he could be Master Amos's third choice should do it. She was a fool, but she'd sit tight and wait.

Chapter Four

It was almost a year to the day before it came into the open. Molly had watched it gradually grow. She had watched them both fighting it, and in the process she had become sorry for them, and many a time she had wished to God they would get it over with and put her out of her misery.

Davie, too, wished it would come to a head, while at the same time fearing to speak. Not just because any alliance between the daughter of Angus McBain and himself would be derided from all quarters; for he was well aware that the Manor would, for a convenient time, forget that Cock Shield was not the place it once had been and that Jane was no longer the daughter of a gentleman farmer, they would consider only that, in stooping to him, she had broken a social code. The main deterrent was the fear of what Amos would do. What would be the outcome if he were to go to him and say, 'I want to marry your sister and, what is more to the point, she wants to marry me'? Hadn't he already accounted for two people who had stood in his way? He could understand him doing for his father, but not the man who had been kind to him from birth, who had tutored him and been his friend, his only friend, other than Jane; if he could kill the parson in cold blood, what value would the madman put on himself?

What Jane's thoughts were concerning Amos's reaction on this particular subject, he did not know; but he was sure of one thing, he had only to speak and she would be his.

Besides everything else, his days were heavy with work and worry concerning the farm; also that his grandfather was slowly letting go of his vital grip on life. For the past few nights he had sat by the old man's bedside, and each time that sleep had overcome him, he had awakened to the thought, he's gone. But no, there he lay, looking into the candlelight, his breathing scarcely audible. Yet sometimes the old man would speak in a strong clear voice as if twenty years had slipped from him. 'Are you there, lad?'

'Aye, Granda.'

'Now, why can't you get yourself away to bed? You've got work facin' you in the mornin'.'

'I'm all right, Granda.'

'All right be damned! Look, lad, when my time's near I'll know, an' I'll tell you. An' don't worry your head. Now I'm tellin' you, don't worry your head, 'cos we've all got to go. Feathers in the fire; that's all we are, lad, feathers in the fire.'

Feathers in the fire! Aye, that's all they were, feathers in the fire. Life slipped by. It was galloping by him, and what was he doing with it? What had he done with it? Nothing. He should have a wife and a family now, be a settled man, and here he was, neither flesh, fish, nor fowl.

Last night he'd had a full night's rest, for the old man seemed so much better. It was as if he'd had a new lease on life. And now today for his dinner, he had drunk every drop of broth Molly had brought up.

Davie took the basin from his hand, saying, 'Well, you made a clean sweep of that, old 'un?'

'Aye; never tasted better, lad. She's a good cook, is Molly.'

'Aye, she's a good cook, Granda.'

'And a good lass an' all.' The old man's pale blue eyes looked up at Davie, and he repeated, 'She's a good lass an' all, Davie.'

He was on his way to the door as he said, 'Yes, she's a good lass, Granda.' Then turning about he added, 'Now don't forget I'll be gone for a few hours; there's hardly a mouthful of hay for the animals. But whether Morton'll give us any more tick remains to be seen.'

'You say he's been gone since yesterday, lad?'

'Aye, Granda, our lord an' master has gone on his monthly spree. He must have got the money for the land some time last week. Well, it's to be hoped he cleared up Morton and Rymill; if not, it won't be only the horses that'll go without their feed.'

'He's a bad 'un, that one, a real bad 'un. Lookin' back on things, it's a pity Molly didn't do what she set out to do in the first place, that's what I say.'

'I'm with you there, old 'un.' And strangely, he was; the time was long past when he had stopped condemning Molly for attempting to drown the child, and now he blamed himself for having interfered. That's what you got for doing the right thing. Playing God, as Molly had said.

'God help Miss Jane, that's all I say.'

Davie could have added, 'And I'm with you there an' all,' but instead he said, 'Now mind, behave yourself. I'll be back as quick as I can; Molly will keep lookin' in. Ta-rah.'

'Ta-rah, lad. Don't hurry yourself. Take it easy for once.'

He went across the narrow square of landing and into his room, and there he changed into his town clothes, which were the trousers of his seafaring days and a worsted coat of a lighter shade. He put on a clean blue striped shirt and a neckerchief; then he picked up his hard bowler and went downstairs.

He had already harnessed the horse to the wagon, and when he reached the yard he was surprised to see Jane standing beside it. She, too, was dressed for town, and she said to him, 'Will you drive me in, Davie? I have business in Hexham.'

'On the wagon, Miss?'

'Yes, Davie, I . . . I don't mind the wagon.'

'But look—' he jerked his head up towards the sky, 'there's a storm brewin'. We might be caught in it, and there's no shelter unless you get under the tarpaulin.'

'I'll risk that, Davie. But . . . but I must get into town.'

'Very well, Miss.'

As he held out his hand and helped her up onto the high, wooden seat, Molly came to the kitchen door, and he was aware of her eyes tight on him as he walked around the horse's head to the other side of the wagon and pulled himself up. Before giving a command to the horse he paused and, looking across the yard at her, he asked quietly, 'Will you give an eye to him?' For answer, she inclined her head but didn't speak. 'Gee-up! there,' he said. 'Gee-up!' And the cart rumbled out of the yard.

They had gone some distance in silence when Jane said, 'You don't mind taking me in, Davie?'

'Mind?' He turned his head quickly towards her. 'Why should I mind?' He could have said, 'That's a daft question, Jane; I'm in no position to mind, now am I?'

She dropped her gaze from his and looked down at her hands, then said softly, 'I'm . . . I'm going to the jeweller's, I'm going to sell some trinkets.'

There was a pause before he asked, 'Didn't he give you anything out of the sale?'

'No.'

'It's a bloody shame. Excuse me, Miss.'

'It's all right, Davie. I . . . I can endorse what you say; I, too, feel like saying, it's a . . . bloody shame.'

They glanced at each other. It was a moment when they should have smiled, laughed. She had sworn. Once she had repeated after him, 'God Almighty!' and that had tickled him, but now she had sworn, even if politely, but they didn't smile.

They were looking ahead again when she said, 'I don't know whether they're saleable or not, but Mr Pearson is a very fair man. He would not cheat me. There isn't much: two signet rings, a gold lever watch and chain, and a gold and ivory cameo of my grandmother. They all belonged to my grandfather, and I came across them in a separate drawer. If . . . if he had seen them first, I wouldn't have them now, for he claimed all that he could lay his hands on at the time. But . . . but I felt justified in keeping these.'

'You were that. Aw,' he moved his head slowly, 'words fail me. They do.'

There followed another silence before he asked quietly, 'Where's it all going to end?'

'I wish I knew, Davie.'

'You can't go on like this forever, you know.'

She made no answer, but after a while she asked, 'Do you think you'll get the hay?'

'If he's paid something off to Morton, I will. If not, I can see me coming back the way I'm goin'.'

They had jogged on for almost a mile before he spoke again, and then he remarked, lightly, 'Well, it looks as if we might miss the storm.'

'Yes, yes, it does.' She turned her eyes towards the sky, and now, her voice little more than a whisper and as if talking to herself, she said, 'I used to think there was no place in the world like this. I know I haven't travelled, but I have read a lot about other places and I always found them wanting in comparison. Now I want to run from it, lose myself in a town, or a city, where everything is flat. I never want to see a hill again.'

He passed no comment, but his hands gripped the reins tightly and the horse shook its head, impatient at the pull on its bit. It knew its pace along this stretch of the road and it was going to go no faster or no slower than was usual.

After a moment she said, 'You have seen most of the world, Davie, how do you compare it with this?'

'Oh, well, like you, I found every place wantin', but like you, I've changed. Yet you can't blame the place, can you? It's people who want to make you stay or go, after all's said an' done.'

'When old Sep dies, there'll be nothing to keep you?' Her face was turned towards him, and he didn't look at her for as long as it took the horse to do twenty paces. Then, his eyes slowly turning to meet hers, he said quietly, 'That depends.'

'On what, Davie?'

He saw that her lips were trembling and that her hands were locked tightly over her beaded handbag.

If he said, 'You,' he could be signing his death warrant. Yet that didn't really worry him; forewarned was forearmed. He could let that young maniac know that he was aware of his two exploits and had taken his knowledge a step further than Molly had. He could tell him that he had sent a letter to a solicitor in Newcastle which was to be opened if anything happened to him. He had read about that trick in a book when he was at sea, but he could apply it here all right, and it would put a stop to his gallop. So what was he hanging back for?

The answer he gave her was, 'Oh, a number of things,' and when he saw her turn her head slowly away, he wanted to draw the horse up and pull her into his arms and say, 'Jane, Jane, let's stop playing games, let's go ahead with what we both want, and be damned to it.'

They spoke no more until they reached Hexham, and as he helped her down from the cart, it began to rain.

'How long are you likely to be?' she asked.

'Half an hour, if I get the hay; if I don't, well then, just the time it'll take me to get to Morton's and back.'

She looked along the street now and said, 'The tea rooms–I'll go and have a cup of tea after I have finished the business at the jeweller's. I will see you from the window. But in any case, I'll be here in this street.'

'Good enough.' He nodded at her, then added, 'Don't let him beat you down.'

'I won't.'

He watched her walk up the street towards the jeweller's shop. From behind she looked like a young girl, and she walked like one, quick and sprightly. But that was from the back. From the front she looked like a lost woman, a lost and lonely woman, a woman who had missed life. Even Molly didn't carry the look on her face that she did. But then, Molly hadn't missed life, had she? She'd had it to the full: 'No matter whose name I take, Master, there'll only ever be you. Always remember that, there'll only ever be you.' He had lived with those words for years. But lately he had scarcely recalled them, and so he didn't know why he was doing it now. Oh yes, he did; it was a sort of comparison. The figure going along there hadn't been handled by any man; she was as a man expected a woman to be when he took her to his wife, whereas Mistress Molly had given her virginity away, first in a hay rick, then, while still a very young lass, had let an old man take her, slaver over her. Aw! To the devil! He should be worryin' about the hay; it was the animals' needs he must think about at the present moment; his own must wait.

To his surprise, Mr Morton met his order without comment; which meant that Amos had settled the bill, or at least had paid something off it.

Within a few minutes of his drawing the cart up outside the tea shop, Jane made her appearance at the door, and, without speaking, he helped her up into the seat. As they drove off it began to rain, and before they had left the town, they were sitting under a downpour.

Urging the horse into a trot, he said, 'I think we're in for it. Look over there.'

She turned her head and peered through the rain over the gooseberry fields and orchards and remarked briefly, 'Yes, it's black.' Then looking ahead again, she added, 'It doesn't matter.'

'You could sit under the cover at the back, that would save you some.'

'No, no, Davie; don't worry, I'll be all right. It won't be the first time I've been wet through.' She gave a little laugh. 'But this is going to be a bad 'un by the looks of it.'

By the time they came to the crossroads and were still four miles from home, the lightning was flashing and the thunder was rolling like an army of drums above their heads, and he shouted to her, 'I'll take the main road; it'll be longer but it won't be so bogged.'

She didn't answer for she had scarcely heard him. She had her head down and her shoulders hunched against the onslaught of the wind and rain.

When a terrific clap of thunder burst above them the horse stopped, tossed its head, then attempted to rear, and it took Davie all his time to hold it. Pushing the reins into her hand and shouting, 'Hold hard!' he jumped from the cart and went to the horse's head and led him farther up the road to where a gap in the stone wall opened into a field. Tying the reins firmly to an iron spoke that had once supported a gate, he then reached up and almost pulled her down from the seat, and ran with her to the back of the cart. There he pushed her unceremoniously underneath the tarpaulin cover and in between the bales of hay; then he drew himself up and in beside her.

It was black dark under the cover. Their heads were touching it and the rain was beating on it and into their brains like so many hammers; they were half sitting, half reclining, and close together. There was no lead up to the beginning. He put his arms about her and held her quietly for a moment to gauge her reaction, and when her face fell to the side of his and her lips moved over his ear he pressed her thin body into him. His hand made no fumbling movement as it went among her wet clothes, and she did not utter a word; no words at all passed between them. When she moaned it was more like the muffled lilt of a song. . . .

Half an hour later he lifted her down from under the cover, and she stepped into another world. The storm had passed, the last rays of the setting sun were jewelling the whole world, her whole world; as far as she could see, everything was sparkling. She brought her gaze to his face and she muttered on a cracked note, 'Oh! Davie . . . Davie.'

'Jane!' His arms went round her again, but gently now.

'Are you all right? You . . . you won't regret it?'

'I'm all right, Davie. And no, never. Whatever happens, never, never will I regret it.' There was no break in her voice now, her words were clear and strong, and she added, 'It's been a long time.'

'Too long. Aye, too long. Ten years too long.'

Her face widened into a smile, and she asked now, 'Did you care for me then?'

He blinked, trying to recall how he felt ten years ago, and he threaded his imagination with kindness as he said, 'I must have; anyway, I knew you should be married. And . . . and now I think the same, but what about it, how do we stand?'

'Oh! Davie, I'd marry you tomorrow, or now, now.'

'How's he going to take that?' He stared down into her face. 'We've got to be prepared for him trying to get rid of me.'

'Oh, no! He wouldn't.' Her voice was filled with horror. 'Not that; he'd never go that far. Besides, he . . . he likes you.'

'He liked the parson at one time. If he only killed where he hated, like he did with your fath— . . .' He stopped. She was leaning back from him, still within his hold, but with her mouth dropping open. 'No . . . O!' She brought the word out slowly.

'Yes. Swinging from the beam at the top of the stairs.'

'Oh, dear Lord!' She put her hand over her mouth. He said softly, 'I'm sorry. I'd have to let it come out now. I'm a fool; it's spoilt it.'

'No, no.' She forced her attention back to him. 'No, no, Davie; nothing could spoil this. It was just the shock. And yet . . . yet, you know it wasn't such a shock as it should have been; I feel I must have known all the time. All the things he did, then the way he went on, and the will. He looked for the will.' She shook her head. 'Davie—' she was clinging to him now, 'we could go away, we could work together. I got thirty-five pounds for the things. I . . . I think it was a fair price. We could go any time. . . .' She stopped, the words hanging on her lips, then she muttered, 'I forgot . . . I forgot . . . old Sep. But . . . but Davie, as soon as you are free, we will go?' It was a question.

'We'll go. That is a promise. As soon as Granda goes, we'll go.'

'We mustn't tell anyone about . . . about us.' Her face was flushed and her eyes held a shyness. 'We must act as if nothing has happened; we must not even let Molly know.'

When his look altered just the slightest and a shadow seemed to pass over his face, she said quietly, 'Molly, . . . will this hurt her?' And he answered on a high note, 'Hurt Molly? No, no; why should it hurt Molly?'

She had not questioned his feelings with regards to Molly. It was herself he loved. Had he not proved it? So he could not think anything of Molly.

'Come along, we must get back.'

She did not move immediately, but stared at him for a moment. Then, with an impetuous gesture that she might have used when she was seventeen, she flung her arms around his neck and, gazing up into his face, whispered, 'Oh, I love you, Davie. I love you, I love you. I've always loved you. I cannot remember the time when I didn't love you. Oh, darling, my darling.' When her mouth came on his he did not answer it for a moment; his whole body was still under a sense of wonder–the wonder of her voice, her words and what they were telling him. This would be a different kind of love altogether from that which he would have experienced if he had taken up with anyone of his own standing, such as Molly Geary or her like. This was going to be not only a love of the body and its wants, but of the other emotions, of words and tenderness. He was going to learn a lot from this love.

'Aw, Jane! Jane!' He held her from him and looked his wonder into her face. Then drawing her to him he kissed her, a gentle lingering kiss.

Chapter Five

Jane stood in front of the window peering out into the dark night. She was standing in blackness, for she had quenched the light in her bedroom. She turned about and focused her gaze on the door, then groped her way towards it and stood listening. There was a strong wind blowing, and although it could not penetrate the thick walls, it rattled the windows and created strange echoing sounds around the chimneys. In her mind she separated these noises from those usually heard in the house, and the house appeared silent.

He had been up in his room for more than half an hour now, but she must wait a little longer to make sure he was asleep. He had taken to drinking of late, not whisky like her father, nor yet wine, but beer, strong, thick stout. Stout was supposed to induce sleep, and she was hoping that he had drunk enough of it to send him off quickly tonight. She would soon tell once she was outside his door, for he snored in his sleep. He always had; it was, she thought, because of his short neck and deep chest.

Earlier in the evening she had felt like boldly saying, 'I am popping over to see old Sep; it may be for the last time.' But then, she had used that excuse before, and old Sep hadn't died; she had never known anyone take so long in dying.

It was six weeks since the day Davie had driven her into Hexham–six weeks since she had been reborn, into joy, into ecstasy. But only once had they managed to be together since that night. She was being very careful, most circumspect, but it was so hard at times to control her feelings when she saw Davie. She had never paid so many daily visits to the cow byres as she had done these past few weeks, for she felt impelled to see him often; at times she was driven to leave what she was doing and go into the yard on some pretext, just to watch him at a distance. Sometimes she thought Molly had guessed her secret, for she would look at her with a strange look–she could not put a name to her expression.

She turned her back to the door and leaned against it, and, clasping her joined hands to her mouth, she bit on the knuckles of her thumbs to prevent herself from hoping that old Sep would die tonight. Within a week of his going they could be away. The Gladstone bag was already packed in the bottom of the wardrobe; she required so little. The most important thing was money, and the thirty-five pounds was safely hidden in the bottom of the bag.

It was strange, she considered, that Davie should have more money saved than she–she, who was the daughter of Angus McBain, at one time the richest farmer for miles around. If her father were to come back, he would die a thousand deaths to see what had happened to his farm. Although, towards the end of his days, he himself had let it go somewhat, the place was now little more than a glorified smallholding with land hardly able to sustain a dozen cows, and that land so poor and deficient in the vital minerals that they had lost two cows during the last three weeks. Both had died with the shivers. The shivers had always been a warning that animals needed a change of pasture, but now there was nowhere for them to change to.

She turned and opened the door slightly and, putting her head on one side, listened. She thought she heard a movement from along the corridor. She knew that once he had the slightest suspicion of what was afoot, he'd be quite capable of playing with her like a cat with a mouse. One thing she was certain of now, her brother was deformed not only in his body, but also in mind, and that if she had to spend the winter with him, the spring would not find her sane. Last night he had looked at her across the dining table and with the smile on his face that wasn't a smile, he had said, 'It's going to be a long winter, Sister.' He had never before called her sister. 'Soon there'll only be the two of us, now Mickey's gone, old Sep dying, and old Curran on his last legs. That only leaves Davie and Molly, and they'll likely go off together. I shouldn't be a bit surprised. What do you say?'

She hadn't been able to say anything; she had simply stared at him through the lamplight like a rabbit would at a stoat, until he added, 'Mind, I don't envy him that piece. But then, there's been nobody else about to ease him, has there, and a man has his needs.' Then she thought she'd be sick.

She had risen from the table, saying, 'If you have no other topic of conversation, I'll bid you good-night.'

When she went to pass him he had put out his hand and held her, as he had done once before, and had said softly, 'You're an old maid, Jan; you'll go down to the grave an old maid. But I don't mind, I like you this way. As I said there'll soon be nobody else here but us, just we two, as it was in the beginning up in the attic. Yes, as it was in the beginning, is now, really, and ever shall be.'

Having wrenched herself from his hold, she had to prevent herself from flying out of the house, yelling, 'Davie! Davie!' She was filled with panic at the thought that perhaps he knew and was playing with her. But then, in the quietness of her room, she reasoned that it was impossible for him to know anything The second time that Davie and she had met privately had been on a black night, down by the burn, and at a time when Amos was away from home on one of his jaunts. So, she reasoned he could not know anything about them, and that it was just the fear of what he might do to Davie were he to find out that was making her suspicious.

She tiptoed along the corridor, paused opposite his door, and when the rhythmic sound of his snoring came to her, she went on and down the stairs and out of the house.

Amos heard her go. He rose from the bed fully clothed, donned a dark coat, pulled a dark cap onto his head, then onto the end of each crutch he tugged a lambswool stocking. When he went from the room his movements were not audible, not even to himself.

The play, he thought, was nearing its end. Jane was a fool. She had always been a fool, a soft-hearted fool, but he had given her the credit for more intelligence than she possessed.

If he hadn't ridden the main road on his way from Newcastle in the storm that day and seen his horse and wagon in the field and glimpsed the contortions under the tarpaulin, he would still have known there was something between them, for her every action when she returned to the farm had betrayed her. He hadn't known how much he loved her until he had watched her get down from the cart, her face aglow. It was then that his own body had been rent in two with a torment that was fresh to him.

The love that he'd had for Biddy had been that of a boy for a girl; yet if it had been fulfilled, it might have satisfied him, half-sister or no half-sister; but the love he now felt for his sister dimmed the feeling for Biddy, as a star would an oil lamp.

He had debated for some time what to do about Davie. The fact that he was the only man he had ever really liked had checked the suggestion of putting a quick finish to him–checked it, not actually dismissed it. In some strange way Davie represented life to him. He remembered that he had first realized he was alive that day he jumped into the deep water in the burn, and it was ten to one he would have drowned if the sailor hadn't come down and got him. Moreover, hadn't he given him life in the first place? So he felt a certain reluctance about taking his life. He would be satisfied, he told himself, if he could put him somewhere where he would no longer be able to interfere.

He went noiselessly out into the yard, then in the direction of the cottages.

Molly was in the kitchen brewing some tea; her movements were slow, as if she were carrying a weight on her body, and in her way she was, for her heart was like lead.

She knew things were fast drawing to a head. Old Sep upstairs there; he'd surely go this time, then they'd leave, too. And what was left for her? What was she to do? Stay here and look after him? No! No, begod! Far better Fred Bateman and his brood than be here alone with that maniac, for who knew but he'd try and do her in next. She was no weakling, but she'd have a job to fight off arms like his. He was a dirty fighter. She had seen him, supposedly in fun, in the yard there. He went for the legs and whipped them off the ground, then held on with a grip that was like no other man's!

She pulled a chair round to face the fire; she'd sit down a few minutes, for she was tired to death. What was more, they could do without her going up there, oh, aye, they could do without anybody's going up there. For a moment bitterness like acid ran over her feelings for both of them, and she bowed her head and shook it slowly. Then it was brought sharply up and a startled exclamation came from her as she looked towards the back door and saw the muffled form of Will Curran standing there.

'In the name of God! What's up with you, sneakin' in. . . .'

'Ssh! Ssh!' He held up a warning hand, then closing the door softly behind him, he came towards her saying, 'Are those curtains closed?'

'Curtains?' She turned her head sharply. 'Aye; what's up with you? You nearly scared the wits out of me.'

'The wits are nearly scared out of meself, never mind you.' He thrust his head towards her, muttering thickly, 'If he finds me here, he'll do for me, he's capable of it.'

'Who?'

'Who do you think? Look, I've left the trap tethered near the turnpike an' I had to practically crawl back in case he spotted me. I'm on me way into Hexham for the police.'

'For the what!'

'That's what I said, for the police. They're to come round at first light, he said, and 'vestigate; he's lost some things.'

'Name of God!'

'Aye, name of God. I said more than that when he got me out of me bed, me at my age. I told him I wasn't goin' at first, an' he put the screws on me. Near me time, he said, I wanted to finish me days in the cottage, didn't I? This night might be cold, but the workhouse would be colder. That's what he said.'

'But who does he want the police for?'

'Need you ask? There's only one he wants out of the way now, Davie. He's spotted what's been goin' on and found a way to put a stop to it. He's a cunnin' devil if ever there was one, by God! He is that. An' wicked. Aye.'

'How do you know what's going on?' She stared at him with her mouth slightly agape.

'I'm not blind.'

'What you going to do?'

'What can I do? I'll have to go, only I thought I'd put him wise, an' if he's got any sense, he'll be out of it afore the mornin'.'

Molly stared at the man standing before her, and realized that Will Curran was an old man. She had never liked him, and the thought of taking him for a husband had made her sick, yet in this moment she wanted to put out her hand and shake his; more so when he next said, 'I've got no love for Davie Armstrong, for he stepped in to the place that should rightly have been mine; comes back after fifteen years and just walks into it. It wasn't fair. But then, there's nawt fair in this life.' He stared at her. 'The luckiest one among us I guess is the old' un upstairs; he's gettin' out of it.'

She said nothing–words were hard to come by in a situation like this–but it was odd, she thought, that everyone had to suffer, even the ones you had no time for, ones you thought were too thick-skinned and dim-witted to feel. They too passed along a similar road to yourself, tripping over disappointments and heartbreaks all the way.

She stood staring at the door through which he had sidled out into the dark. Then she turned about, and rushed out of the room and up the stairs, remembering to tiptoe into the bedroom only at the last minute.

Old Sep was lying as he had been for the last twelve hours; he was in a coma, and this time he wouldn't wake. She looked at Davie and Jane within a joined handclasp from each other; she had no doubt but that their fingers had been linked a moment before. Beckoning them to come out onto the landing, she looked from one to the other in the dim light before she gabbled, 'Now listen, listen. He's on the warpath, he means business. Will Curran's just sneaked in by the back door to tell me he's on his way to Hexham for the police. They'll be here by first light. It's . . . it's you he's after.' She pointed her finger at Davie. 'The message he's got to give is that they must come and 'vestigate 'cos there's things missin'. He's . . . he's likely planted something in here.' She made a circular movement with her hand now. 'He's come in to see the old 'un when we've all been at work; he could easily have done it, planted somethin'.'

Neither of them had spoken while she was talking, but now Jane, turning and grasping Davie's hand, cried softly, 'Oh! Davie, Davie, I knew something like this would happen. You must get away; else he'll . . . he'll have you imprisoned.' She stopped, and they both looked at Molly as she said, 'You'll both have to get yourselves away.' Her eyes came to rest on Davie's for a moment, and he gazed back at her. He was about to speak but changed his mind and, swinging around, he beat one fist into the palm of his other hand, saying, 'Who would believe it? I ask you, who would believe it?' Then he looked through the open door and to the bed and the heaving chest of his grandfather, and after a moment he said flatly, 'I'm not goin' till he goes, no matter what.'

'Don't be a blood . . . don't be a fool; the old 'un's already gone, he'll never wake again.'

'She's right. Molly's right, Davie, Molly's right; it's only a formality now. Please, please.' She had hold of his hands again. I'll stay until old Sep goes, and . . . and then I'll join you.'

He did not answer her for a minute. Then, his face screwing up, he said, 'God damn! If he's planted something in the house, then the thing to do is to find it. Look—' he touched Jane's arm, 'you sit by the bed, and Molly and me here, we'll scour the place. It shouldn't take all that long; if there's anything to find we'll find it. We'll start downstairs. You take the scullery, Molly, I'll take the kitchen, an' we'll work our way up. And if there's any change . . .' he motioned his head towards the bed, 'give us a shout.'

Half an hour later the three of them were again standing on the landing looking at each other. They had scoured every crevice and cranny of the cottage. Davie had even turned out his old sailor bag, and remembering Amos's agility concerning beams, he had looked on the beam at the top of the stairs, but with no success.

'We don't even know what we're looking for,' he said thickly now.

'It'll . . . it'll be some form of jewellery,' Jane said. 'Not money, you cannot identify money.'

'Perhaps he stuck it in the cowshed somewhere,' said Molly. 'But then that would involve Will, wouldn't it?' She shook her head. 'No, whatever it is, it's in here. I feel it's in here.' She looked around for a moment; then fixing her gaze tight on Davie, she said, 'He'll have you, he means it. He must have been workin' up to this for some time, he doesn't do things by halves. Remember the other two. Look, I'll tell you what. As soon as it's light, have your things ready and go down to the malt house. If he thinks you've gone, he'll imagine you're far afield; he won't think you'd stick around here.'

Davie stared into Molly's face for a moment, but without seeing her. Then he said slowly, as if having weighed everything up, 'I can't go while there's breath in him.'

'Do you think he would be happy knowing you were in prison?'

He turned and looked at Jane. Her face was white, her eyes large, and filled with love and pain. 'Go to the malt house as Molly suggests, and . . . and I'll stay here with Sep until the end. Then I'll join you.'

Molly's tone was weary as she put in now, 'He's got you both taped. He's got us all taped. It'll be better, Miss Jane, if you go back to the house an' pretend to go to your bed. And you, Davie, do as we said, go down to the malt house. An' if when the police comes, the idea that you might be down there enters into that maniac's head an' they make for there, I'll ring the bell good and hard. What do you say?'

There was silence among them for a moment, then Davie, nodding, said, 'You make sense, Molly; you've got to play him at his own game.' He turned to Jane. 'Go now, as Molly says, and try an' rest if you can, because there's a long day afore us, and God knows what's in it.' He did not touch her, nor she him, but they looked at each other deeply before he turned and went into the bedroom; then she went down the stairs and Molly followed her.

Chapter Six

Jane awoke from what appeared a nightmare. She was aching all over, particularly the back of her head and the bottom of her spine. She was lying on the bed in a dim light, candlelight, and there was a face above her and a voice was saying, 'Drink this.'

Where was she, and what had happened? The last she remembered was groping her way along the passage and entering her bedroom. This . . . this wasn't her bedroom, this was . . .

'Come along, drink this.'

She took a mouthful of the liquid, then gulped, as her taste registered laudanum. It was the medicine her mother used to take to soothe her nerves and put her to sleep. As she spluttered, she knocked the glass flying. Then, her eyes wide, she went to pull herself up, but the hand on her chest prevented her, and Amos's voice said, 'It's no use, so you might as well give in gracefully. You're here and you're staying here, for the time being at any rate, until you learn to behave yourself. I'm surprised at you, Jane, letting yourself down to the level of a farm labourer.'

'Let me up!'

'You're not getting up. I'll give you a choice, you either drink more of this—' he moved his head towards the bottle standing on the side table, 'or I'll tie you up and gag you. You have your choice.'

'Amos! Amos!' She began to plead now. 'Please, I beg of you, don't do this, let me go. I'll go eventually; you can't keep me.'

'Can't I? You'd be surprised what I can do.'

'No! No!' Now there was no pleading in her voice and she barked at him, 'I'd never be surprised at what you can do after . . . after murdering Arnold.'

'Oh!' He raised his eyebrows. 'So you've known about that?'

'Yes, I've known about that.'

'And you didn't give me away. . . . Why didn't you give me away?' He waited for her answer, and when none came, he said, 'I'll tell you why, because you loved me. And I'll tell you something else, I love you, and that's why I can't let you go. You understand what I'm saying, Jane? I love you.'

She felt her body shrinking back into the bed in terror now. She had no need to look for a definition of his word love, she was well aware that the prefixes of motherly or sisterly wouldn't fit the love he was speaking of. The horror of the situation lent strength to her arms, and now she was struggling with him like someone demented, while she screamed, 'Davie! Davie! Molly! Davie! Davie!'

They were on the floor rolling together as they had done years ago on top of the Tor, and all the while his arms held her as if in a vice, and from time to time his body lay on hers. She had only one advantage over him, her knees, and she used them when she could. One vicious jab into his loins caused him to yell and release his hold on her for a moment, and, her hands groping wildly at the wall, she dragged herself to her feet and found she was near the window. She had just managed to open it when he was on her again; and now she screamed at the top of her lungs.

They both heard it together, it came like a thin high voice on the wind. It brought Molly from a light doze by the fire and Davie to his feet in the bedroom; then they were both at the bottom of the stairs looking at each other.

'It was a scream; it sounded like a scream.'

Before Molly had finished speaking, Davie was running out of the house and she after him.

When they burst into the kitchen and paused for a moment, the sound of the struggle came to them from above as some article of furniture overturned and crashed to the floor.

Davie took the stairs two at a time, but when he reached the first landing he stood looking upwards, unable to see the stairs that led to the attics. It was odd that he should have lived close to this house for the first nineteen years of his life and never got beyond the ground floor.

'Along here! Along here!' Molly was now running past him around the dark corner of the landing and up the four steps onto the old landing. But here he passed her and made for the dim narrow stairs that led to the attic.

When he thrust open the door he saw nothing for a moment, then at the sound of panting coming from the far side of the bed he rushed across the room, and there she was, spreadeagled on the floor, with Amos on top of her, his arms pinning her down.

He uttered no sound, but his hands flashed out and, gripping the back of Amos's collar, he hauled him upwards and flung him against the fireplace.

When he went to lift Jane from the floor, Molly was already by her side, and between them they guided her to the door.

He had his back to the room as he said thickly, 'Get her downstairs,' and it was as he turned to see what the maniac was up to that the end of the poker hit his shinbone, and he cried out aloud as he leaped into the air.

Bending now and holding his leg tight against the excruciating pain, he looked to where Amos was grabbing up a pair of tongs from inside the fender. With a lopsided leap he flung himself on him, and again Amos was rolling on the floor, but with a difference this time, for now he was like a mad bull and with a mad bull's strength, and it wasn't until he sank his teeth into Davie's wrist and blood spurted that Davie became a match for him. Filled with rage, he fought as he had seen men fight on board ship, like savage animals; yet it took him all his time to free himself from Amos's hold, for his arms seemed to be everywhere. They were like the tentacles of an octopus; you released yourself from one, and another caught you. Only when he used his knee as Jane had done did Amos go flying from him and straight through the open door onto the landing.

He lay still now, and Davie stood gasping while he watched him. The blood was pouring from his wrist, and he gripped it in an effort to stop the flow; his leg was paining damnably; his body felt as bruised as if he had been tossed about in a bilge in a storm.

Slowly he moved towards the still figure and stood looking down on it for a second; and it could only have been a second before, once again, he found himself on his back. Amos, having swept his legs from under him, was in the act of jumping on him, when Davie's hands came instinctively upwards and with a mighty effort he hurled the stunted body backwards over his head. Then he lay still, his arms outspread, listening to the repeated thumps and guttural cries.

In the silence that followed he slowly turned himself onto his hands and knees and peered down the dark stairway to the darker form lying at the bottom, then, helping himself to his feet by pulling on the balustrade post, he descended the stairs.

At the bottom he stood looking at the humped body, but this time did not stoop towards it. Not until he satisfied himself that there could be no more tricks did he bend over him; then his hand slowly dropped onto the high chest and he held it there for a second, just long enough to feel the faint heartbeat and to experience a strong emotion of fear and disappointment mixed.

He wasn't dead. Like his father, he could linger on for months; and what then?

He wasn't conscious of having knelt on the floor, only of the hesitation in his mind whether to put his thumb on the gullet or his hand tight across the mouth.

'Are you all right?'

When Molly's hand came on his shoulder he froze.

'Is he dead?'

'N . . . not quite.'

'Pray God he soon will be.'

'I second that.' He stumbled to his feet.

'You're, you're bleedin'. Look at your wrist.'

'I'm all right; it'll clot. How is she?'

'In an awful state; can't stop cryin'. She's in hysterics I think, on about him. Aw, if ever there was a swine on this earth, he's one.' She prodded the inert body with the toe of her boot, then said, 'I think you'd better come down. But . . . but what are we going to do with him?'

He hesitated, then said, 'Give me a hand with him; we'll put him in his bed and let the devil take care of the rest.'

When, after a struggle, for the stumped body was a dead weight, they had laid him on the bed, Molly asked, 'Hadn't you better lock the door in case he comes round?'

'I don't think it'll be necessary, but we'll do it nevertheless. If he does come round, he won't do any hoppin' for some days, I should imagine.'

As they went out and locked the door, Jane's cries came to them, and he ran down the stairs and into the drawing room and taking her shivering body into his arms, he muttered, 'It's all right, it's all over. Quiet now, quiet. Don't cry like that.'

'Da . . . vie! Davie!'

'Yes, dear. Now, it's all right, don't worry.'

'He . . . 'll k . . . kill me. He'll kill me.'

'He'll kill nobody else.'

Gasping, her face contorted, the water running from her eyes, nose and mouth, she spluttered, 'Dead! . . . Is he dead?'

Regretfully he shook his head and answered slowly, 'Not quite.' He now turned to Molly. 'Make some strong tea, will you?' he said, and when she replied, 'The kettle's on,' she also added, 'Shouldn't one of us be along the road?'

'Aye, yes.' He nodded at her. 'I'll slip along.'

But when he went to move away, Jane clung to him and he said soothingly, 'There now, there now, I won't be a tick. I promise you. It's all right, he's locked in. Even if he could move, he can't get out.'

When she continued to cling to him, he looked at Molly with a shamefaced look, and Molly, bustling, took her from his arms, saying tersely, 'Come on now, pull yourself together. It's all over, or soon will be.'

Hurrying out of the room and the house, he ran up the lane to the cottage. But as soon as he entered the room, he knew that he was too late, his Granda had gone.

He stood looking down on the old man's face. The eyes which had been closed for days, were now open. The mouth, too, was open, as if he were about to speak, to say something pleasant, for his whole face looked at peace. At the very last moment he must have wanted to look on his own, and his own wasn't there.

A great bitterness flooded him and he had the desire to go back to the house and finish off that maniac with his own hands. He regretted not having done so when the urge was on him.

He went to cover the still head with the sheet, but halfway in the act he stopped, and slowly he knelt down. He was no praying man; he had never been on his knees in prayer, nor had he uttered a prayer since McBain had disillusioned him. He didn't pray now, but he took the bony blue-veined hand in his as he whispered aloud, 'Good-bye, Granda. If there's a God an' He's just, you'll have a happy passage.' His bottom lip trembled and he pressed his teeth into it, but this did not stop the tears from raining down his face.

On his return to the farm he walked slowly. When he entered the sitting room, Jane was lying back on the couch. She was quiet. She looked towards him, as did Molly, and it was Molly who spoke. 'He's gone then?' she said; and to this he nodded.

'Did he wake at all, come around?'

'I don't know; he had gone before I got back.'

'Oh! Davie.' Jane was sitting up and holding her hand out towards him, and as he went to her they were all brought into a fixed stillness by a sound coming from the kitchen. Molly, her eyes flashing from one to the other, whispered, 'It can't be, we locked the door.'

'Stay there.' Lifting his feet and treading as softly as he could, he went from the room. Warily he glanced round the hall and up the stairs, then made his way to the kitchen, and when he burst open the door he drew in a long slow breath at the sight of Will Curran leaning against the table.

'What's up?'

Holding his hip and limping towards a chair, Will said, 'Bloody horse took fright at a rabbit or hare or summit goin' across the road, and side-stepped into a ditch.'

'Whereabouts?'

'Beyond turnpike.'

'Is he hurt?'

'No, just frightened. I managed to get him out of the shafts. I tried to get him to pull the trap out but the wheel had buckled. It's a good job he was on his feet lest I'd never have got him out.'

'You brought him back?'

'Aye, but he wouldn't let me get on him, I had to walk him. He's skittish as a new foal. Bloody rabbits!'

'You didn't get to Hexham then.' It was a statement, not a question.

'Hexham? How could I?'

'That's all right, Will, that's all right.' Davie sighed within himself. That was one bit of trouble waived anyway. 'Help yourself to some tea,' he said, 'and I'll try to get you a drop of something.'

As he went towards the door Will Curran asked, 'What's up anyway? I came 'cos I saw all the lamps on. What's happened that you're in here this time a night?'

Davie paused for a moment before he said, 'He had a go at Miss Jane, almost did for her. He fell down the attic stairs.'

'He's hurt?'

'Aye, I should say so.'

'Bad?'

'I hope so, Will. For everybody's sake, I hope so.' Then he added, 'Thanks for tipping Molly off. It was good of you, knowin' how you feel about things. Oh—' he turned his head away and waved his hand in the air, 'I know, Will, I know. I would have felt the same in your place, worse in fact. But hang on, for things might take a turn for the better from now on. When Miss Jane runs the place, she'll see you're all right.'

'Aye, Davie, aye.' Will Curran's tone had changed, the look on his face had changed, and when Davie said, 'Soon as you drink your tea, get to bed, 'cos you'll have to go for the doctor when it's light,' Will again said, 'Aye, Davie, aye,' as if he were speaking to a friend, although he had never before shown anything in his manner towards Davie but envy and obstinacy.

When he entered the sitting room again, he said immediately, 'There's one trouble we haven't got to face–the police won't be here in the morning'. The trap went into the ditch, and Will's come back with the pony.'

Jane closed her eyes and put both hands over her mouth and spoke through her fingers as she said, 'Thank God! Oh, thank God!'

'Were they hurt, the horse or him?'

He looked at Molly and shook his head, saying, 'Will's limping a bit, that's all. He's for bed, and—' he turned his head towards Jane, 'that's where you're going.' When she began to protest he said, 'Now no more words, not tonight. Just go to bed, and me and Molly will see to things.'

Molly was standing apart now. It was right, she thought, that Miss Jane should go to bed, she had gone through something the night. But she herself was tired to death. She'd never had a full night's rest for weeks now. She could sleep standing on her feet, but he had no feeling for her. 'Me and Molly will see to things,' he had said. He hadn't a kindly thought in his whole body towards her. Oh, he was civil enough now, but that was all. She'd had hope while he slated and scorned her, but not since he had spoken civil to her; from then she had known that he had closed the door on any feeling he might have had for her. And he'd had feeling for her; oh aye, a man doesn't get angry and shower his scorn on a woman he doesn't care for. But now he was civil spoken.

When Jane, looking at her, said, 'But Molly's worn out, too. You should go to bed, Molly,' he put in quickly, 'Don't you worry about Molly, she's as strong as a horse.' Molly felt that she was about to make a fool of herself and burst into tears.

That's how he would look on her for the rest of her life, 'as strong as a horse,' a beast of burden. Could she stand it? Was she up to it? No, no, she wasn't.

The doctor came out of the bedroom, and Molly followed him. They walked to the top of the stairhead before he spoke. Then, his voice low, he said, 'You tell me he attacked his sister?'

'Aye, he did, Sir.'

'I'm very surprised at that, I always understood that they were close. She was more like a mother to him than a sister. It is very surprising. Was there any reason for it?'

'She told him she was going to leave, Sir. Things hadn't been going too well here, you might have heard?'

'Oh yes. Yes, you hear all kinds of rumours, and there's no getting away from the fact that the place has changed drastically since your master died. But to attack her. How did he do it?'

'It was in the dark, Sir. He knocked her out, then must have dragged her up to the attic.'

The doctor's face was showing his disbelief as she put in quickly, 'Oh, he could, Sir. He used to sit on his backside . . . well, I mean he used to sit on the stairs and hoist himself up backwards, and pull things up that way. It was amazing the things he took upstairs. He was only about five when he dragged his four-wheeled cart up there, and now he's as strong as a bull. Leastways, he was.'

'Yes, leastways, he was.' He wagged his head; then said, 'Miss Jane . . . where is she?'

'In the sitting room, Sir, she's got her feet up. She's still not herself.'

She led the way down the stairs and opened the sitting room door for him, and he entered saying, 'Well! Well! Jane. Well! Well!' When he took the seat by the side of the couch he looked down and added, 'This is distressing news, distressing.'

Jane said nothing. She was in a high state of nerves. She was feeling much worse than she had done in the middle of the night; moreover, she was anxious to know his report on Amos, and when he said, 'I'm afraid your brother is in a very bad way, Jane,' she still made no comment, simply stared at him wide-eyed, waiting.

'Besides concussion and a dislocated shoulder he has, I'm afraid, seriously injured the bottom of his spine. I suspect it may have affected him internally, for he is—' he hesitated on the word, 'incontinent at the present moment. This is a bad sign. It may be that he is paralysed from the waist; I cannot make a final examination until he's fully conscious. I will come back tomorrow and look at him again.'

'He is going to live?' She made the statement slowly, her eyes in a fixed stare.

'That, too, I cannot say with any certainty at this stage. Now, about you. How do you feel?'

'Not very well, Doctor.'

'No, you don't look well. Now what you must do is to rest for a few days. I understand from Molly that you've had something of a shock. If you can send into the town today, I will make up a sedative for you. If not, I will bring it tomorrow.'

'Thank you.'

'Now just rest; you need rest.' He got to his feet. 'Well, I must be on my way, but remember, Jane, you must rest.'

'Yes, Doctor.'

He stooped and patted her head as if she were a child; then straightening his creaking back, he bade her good-bye, and she answered, 'Good-day, Doctor.'

A few minutes later Molly came back into the room saying, 'Well, that part's over.'

'He didn't question about his falling?'

'No, I just told him what we said I should.'

'What will happen when he regains consciousness? He might tell the doctor it was Davie.'

'You leave that to Davie; let's meet the trouble as it comes.'

'If . . . if he lives, he'll need nursing, Molly.'

'Aye, aye, he will.' Molly was replenishing the fire now, and she had her back to Jane as she spoke.

'It isn't fair to ask you to do it.'

Molly thrust the poker through the lower bars and raked vigorously. It was on the point of her tongue to retort, 'There's nothing fair in this world, Miss,' but she checked it and made herself say, 'Don't worry your head about that.' Dusting one hand against the other and picking up the empty scuttle, she said, 'Lie quiet,' and went out.

She did not go straight through the kitchen and into the yard to fill the scuttle, but put it down by the side of the wide hearth and stood looking at the black pot on the fire, which held a meat pudding she had made an hour ago.

During the past few hours she had laid out old Sep, she had stripped the clothes from that one upstairs, cleaned the filth from him, and changed his bed. She had cooked the breakfast, prepared the dinner, and tried to get Miss Jane to eat something, but instead had had to hold her head while she vomited. It was this last that hurt her most, for this wasn't the first time that Miss Jane had vomited in the morning. She wondered if she knew what was wrong with her. She wouldn't be surprised if she didn't. She was guileless. Living on a farm where conceiving and birth were as common as God bless you, she had somehow never been part of it.

She reached up and laid her forearms crossways on the mantelshelf and rested her head on them. It was a favourite position of hers when she wanted to think. But now she was past thinking, she was tired. Her body was crying out for sleep, and her heart was crying out for something she would never have in this world.

She let out a high squawk as the hand came on her shoulder, and Davie had to steady her or she would have fallen into the fire.

'You . . . you were half asleep, didn't you hear me come in?' He still had hold of her and she gazed at him through her blinking lids while he looked down at her. They stood like this for a full minute, and some quality in the look in his eyes which she had never seen there before made her weak, so much so that she put her hand back and grabbed at the chair. When she sat on it he still kept his hand on her shoulder. 'You're all in,' he said. 'It's too much to expect. You're been on your feet for weeks now, what with the old 'un an' one thing and another, and I'm . . . I'm not ungrateful, Molly, I'm not.'

Again they were staring at each other, when he said, 'Jane's just told me what the doctor had to say, but as long as he lives I'll help you tend him, you can't do it alone. One thing we mustn't do, and that's let her go near him. Not that she will want to, she's scared to death of him now. She won't say exactly what happened, but I've got me own opinion on that, an' it makes me sick.'

Her head came forward; she pulled herself away from the chair and his hand; then going towards the side of the fireplace she picked up the empty scuttle and made for the door. The latch in her hand, she turned and looked at him and said quietly, 'Talkin' about being sick, did she tell you she's been sick in the mornings? It might only be a nervous stomach, but then it mightn't. But you should know.'

BOOK FIVE

1899

Chapter One

Davie stood to the side of the bed, not too near it; he did not want to grapple with the one good hand Amos had left. But he let his glance rest on it for a moment. The fingers were plucking the bed cover. The left shoulder was mending but the rest of him would never mend, so the doctor said. He was now paralysed from the waist. It was a terrible predicament for any human being to be in, yet he couldn't pity him. He was but a lad of nineteen, broken in what body he had and twisted in mind. Forgetting all his past deeds, even the one against himself, and that had been mean, for to plant six pieces of jewellery under the mattress of a dying man took some beating; even so, his present condition should call on his compassion, but it didn't, for he was still wary of him, still suspicious of him and the power of his mind. The power showed in his face when his eyes fixed you with that dense stare; you had to use your will not to drop your gaze away from them, not to allow the jerking in your stomach to pass like a tremor through you.

He watched the strong white teeth come slowly apart, and then Amos was asking slowly, 'Do you sleep in the house?'

'Yes, I sleep in the house, and have done for the past month.'

'You have no right, you will go back to your cottage.'

There was a short silence while they stared at each other. Then Davie, his tone in levelness matching that of Amos's, said, 'I have no intention of returnin' to the cottage, now or at any other time. For the rest of me life I am stayin' in this house; I am marrying Jane the morrow.'

The hand stopped plucking the eiderdown and formed itself into a fist. 'You can't. You won't. You daren't. Do you hear me? You daren't.' He raised the upper part of his body from the bed by lifting one shoulder and resting on his elbow, and his head craned forward as he yelled, 'You can't do this, do you hear? You won't, and I can stop you. When Cargill comes, I'll tell him how I got this. It was you, you threw me down the stairs.'

'Do that. You do that—' Davie nodded at him, 'and I'll tell him and . . . and the Judges an' all that I came in answer to your sister's screams when you were trying to rape her.'

'That's a lie.'

'Well, say it's a lie, say you intended that for future use, there's still the little matter of Parson Hedley conveniently put out of the way the night before he was going to marry your sister, and Jane would explain how you did it. Then there's the other matter of your father's end. Molly would have a lot to say about that. Anything you could say against me wouldn't help your case at all. Nor would the predicament that you're in now. There are prison hospitals where men end their days, an' I would see you taken there without blinking an eyelid, so . . . think on it. You're got a choice, you can rest comfortable here until you die, or you can pay for what you've done. It's up to you.'

In one movement Amos fell back on his pillow while his hand went out and gripped the heavy glass water jug from the side table, and as quickly Davie's voice came barking at him, 'You do! Just you do and I'll punch your lugs for you until your face is twice the size it is now.'

They glared at each other for a long moment. Then Davie turned and made for the door, but stopped before he reached it and, glancing over his shoulder, said, 'One more thing. You be civil to Molly or I'll see you lie in your muck. And that's no idle threat.' And on this he went out. But once on the landing the stiffness went out of his shoulders and as he walked down the four steps onto the lower landing and to the room that was now his, his whole body slumped.

Seating himself in the high-backed chair near the window, he let out a long slow breath; then half-aloud he said, 'He can't do anything. Anyway what could he do? He won't tell the doctor, so what can he do?'

No answer came to his mind, nor yet no reassurance that nothing could happen before tomorrow when Jane would be his wife and together they would sleep in that bed.

His head actually nodded towards the bed, the bed in which McBain had slept; the bed which had refused him rest of any kind the first night he had been in this room. He had thought at one time that McBain himself was in the mattress prodding him into wakefulness, trying to kick him out. In the end he had got up and dozed in this chair by the window.

He looked out of the window now down onto the paved court and the arch that led into the main yard, then over the garden towards where, in the far distance, was the cow path above the malt house. Tomorrow, by law through his wife, he should be master of all this, this house that had been like a star to him in his youth, and, like a star, just as unreachable. But as it was he'd be playing at master, for the owner was still alive, the mind alert in a mangled body, and, as things stood, he'd be quite capable of willing everything away from Jane, even though it was mortgaged up to the hilt and beyond.

At this point there came to him a clear understanding of the desire that had driven Amos to get rid of those who stood in his path. He rose abruptly from the chair and went downstairs.

Chapter Two

The morning was bright; there was a tang about that promised winter; the trees in the copse were tinged with brown, some leaves having already fallen; the sky was high and cloudless, and the air caught at the throat like a sharp wine.

Jane stood in the hall, with Molly beside her. They were both pale. Molly was wearing a clean holland apron, the side of which she crumpled in her hand one minute and smoothed down the next. After a while she said, 'You look bonny.' She did not add 'Miss Jane.'

'Thank you, Molly; but . . . but I don't feel bonny.'

'Well, you are. Blue's your colour and corduroy always looks cozy. Mrs Bennet made a good job of that although her hands are not what they used to be.'

'Yes, I think she made it very well.'

Now Jane smoothed down the front of her three-quarter length corduroy coat with its matching skirt and, her head lowered, she said, 'I'd feel much happier if I thought I wasn't going to lose you.'

'We can't have everything in this life.'

Jane's head was brought up sharply by the tone and she stared at Molly whose face was now suffused by a deep blush. 'What I mean is, Miss Jane, you'll be married an' you'll have Davie, and Will has promised to look after him.' She jerked her head upward. 'He said he won't mind doing that, 'specially with winter comin' on, it'll keep him out of the weather. Will knows when he's on a good thing, an' Davie will get another man. We've been into it, haven't we?'

'Yes, Molly, we've been into it. When are you going to see Mr Bateman?'

'Oh well; this afternoon, maybe, I'll take a walk over.'

'You can't walk all that way; Davie'll take you in the trap.'

'He'll do no such thing.'

There was the tone again that brought them looking at each other in silence. Then Jane said apologetically, 'Well, I only thought, it being on six miles . . .'

'Aw, what's six miles?' Molly was looking down at her hands twisting her apron once more. 'Do me good to stretch me legs. I'll have to stretch them longer than that to keep running after that squad.' She gave a nervous laugh; then they both turned and looked at the stairs, which Davie was descending, a new-looking Davie, a slightly awkward-looking Davie.

And he felt awkward in his new clothes; he had never worn such a light colour before, nor yet such tight trousers. The suit was made of tweed and the clothier in Newcastle had promised him it would last a lifetime. That, he had remarked to himself, remained to be seen; a little more weight and he wouldn't be able to get into it.

As he looked down at Jane waiting for him at the bottom of the stairs he felt he should apologize, for things were in their wrong order; it was the man who should be waiting for the woman. But he had been up since first light this morning seeing to the cattle; afterwards he had taken a bath in the closet room. He had humped the hot water up from the kitchen and for the first time in his life he had been immersed all over at one go with warm water. He had stayed too long in it and then had to scurry.

'Well then, we're ready for the off?' He screwed his chin upwards out of his shirt collar–he wasn't used to anything so tight round his neck–then he pulled his white shirt cuffs well below his grey coat sleeves, and Jane, looking at him with love-filled eyes, replied, 'Yes, Davie, we're ready for off.'

Molly said nothing.

They walked out of the hall, Jane going first, he following, and Molly coming up in the rear. They went on to the drive where the trap stood, Amos's trap, the seats altered, the low steps taken off the back. It was a gig to be proud of.

As he went to hand Jane up into the trap she turned impulsively to Molly, and, catching her hands, said, 'I wish you were coming, Molly. I do. Oh, I do.'

Molly seemed to find difficulty in answering; then she said, 'I'm where I'm needed most, Miss; Mickey and his wife can both write and that's all that's needed, just to sign their names.'

Jane shook her head slowly before turning quickly and getting into the trap.

Davie, his foot on the step, paused and looked at Molly, and she at him. For one long moment they looked at each other and the years fell away and they were walking through the fields again, both chewing rose hips, and when their shoulders touched they bounced from each other like rubber balls and laughed.

Now he bounced up into the trap, and it rocked like a boat.

'Gee-up there! Gee-up there!'

The pony trotted smartly out of the yard and when, going through the gate, Jane turned to wave to Molly, she saw that the yard was empty.

In the kitchen Molly stood with her back to the stout oak door. She had her thrumb thrust deep into her mouth and was biting on it so hard that she could scarcely endure the pain. But it was either that or giving way, and that must wait, she didn't want to face them at their breakfast with red eyes. She wouldn't give him that satisfaction, and she wouldn't upset Miss Jane, or Mrs Armstrong, as she'd be in an hour's time. What she must do, she told herself, was to go and clean that one up, and that would keep her occupied and her mind off herself; her mind couldn't wander when she was seeing to him.

As she opened the bedroom door he raised himself on his elbow and cried at her, 'You've taken your time. Didn't you hear me shout?'

'Aye, I heard you, but I've been busy.'

'Busy! I'm your first concern to be busy about.'

'Now you watch it!' She nodded her head at him as she stripped off the top cover. 'Keep that up and I'll leave you lying in it.'

He sank back into the bed and lay gasping for a moment; then closing his eyes, he asked her in an entirely different tone, 'Have you any idea how I feel lying here?'

She glanced sharply at him, then said nonchalantly, 'No; how could I, not being you?'

'That's the point, not being me, you couldn't understand what it's like. Molly—' he put out his hand towards her, 'I . . . I want to see Jane. He won't listen to me.' It was odd that Davie had now become *he*. 'I promised him I wouldn't upset her. I . . . I just want to see her, just to have a word. Look, Molly, I'm sorry if I've gone for you, I am, I really am.' He gazed at her, his slant eyes soft. 'Ask him, will you? Just for a minute. She needn't come near me, just so's . . . so's I can see her. I'll go mad, more mad than I am now. Yes, I will. I'll go stark raving mad lying here seeing only you and him. I loathe him, do you know that Molly? I loathe and hate him, and I used to like him, almost love him. But now I hate him even more than I did my father. God! How I hate him.'

She stopped stripping the bed and stared at him, and for a second she felt so sorry for him she almost put her arms around him. He looked like a very young lad on the verge of tears. After all, as he said, it was terrible lying here, helpless, seeing only her and Davie and the doctor. He was at their mercy, so to speak, and it must go against the grain with a character like him who wanted to dominate everyone, who did dominate everyone, crippled as he was.

'I've got to see her, Molly, I must. We understand each other, she and I. I've got to explain to her why he wants to marry her. It's just to get this place. He doesn't love her. She's plain, she's got nothing about her to attract a man like him; his kind don't go in for character, and that's all Jane's got, character, a sweet, sweet character.' He shook his head. And now, again pulling himself up on his elbow, he appealed to her, 'Look, ask yourself what harm can I do from here. The only thing I've got is my mind, such as it is, and I don't know how long I'll have that. Tell her I promise I won't raise my voice or say a word out of place, if she'll just come in for a moment . . . Where is he?'

'He's gone out.'

'Well go on, Molly, ask her now, please.'

'I can't.'

'Why? Why can't you? Are you aiming to get your own back? I know you never liked me, and that's my fault, but you have the better of me now, so I beg of you do this for me, just this once. Please, Molly.'

'I would if I could an' I mean that, but . . . but you see, she's gone with him, they're on their way to the church now, they're to be married at nine.'

He made no sound for a full minute; then swinging his head from side to side he cried, 'No! No! NO! No! . . . No! No!' As his voice got louder she shouted at him, 'Now stop that, stop workin' yourself up. They had to be married, they just had to. If you'd been up it would have made no difference, they would have been married.'

'Never! Never!'

'You can say that—' she was yelling back at him, 'but I tell you she would have married him, unless she wanted to be like me and my Biddy . . . she's been carrying his bairn for two months.' The bitterness in her voice brought her to stillness and there fell about them a silence in which they both seemed embalmed for a moment; the only live thing in the room was the smell of excrement emanating from the bed and his exposed stunted limbs.

When he slowly brought his fist up to his wide mouth and rammed his knuckles between his teeth, she thought how she herself, a short time earlier, had tried to stem her own agony, and she went to him and put her hand on his head. But he moved away from her touch, not abruptly or harshly; he just turned his head round and buried what he could of it in the pillow.

There was a great swelling of pride in Davie as he sat at the head of the table. He had eaten at this table for some weeks now but he had never sat in this chair; at Jane's insistence, he had taken the seat at the top of the table.

To all intents and purposes he was master of Cock Shield, what was left of it, fifty acres at the most. Still, it was up to him now. And he intended to start the way he meant to go on, as if Amos were already dead and buried. The doctor had given him six months, perhaps less; it all depended. But Amos dead or alive, he would work as if the place were his. It would likely take him the rest of his life to clear the debts on it, but he would do it.

He looked at Jane. Her face had picked up the white light of the morning. He had always thought she had just missed being beautiful, but when she had turned to him on the altar steps, she seemed to have caught up with the beauty that had long evaded her. From now on, given the chance, she would blossom; her body would grow plump, her breasts would fill and remain full, and she'd be a woman, not an old maid of thirty. He put out his hand to her and asked softly, 'How do you feel?'

'Oh, Davie! I can't tell you, I haven't words to explain. Wonderful, fulfilled, marvellous, yet . . . yet still a little fearful.'

'Now, now.' He raised his finger to her. 'Remember what we said, it's our life and we're going to live it; the past is past. There's just you and me.'

'That's . . . that's what I'm fearful of, it seems too good to be true . . . Davie.'

'Yes, me dear.'

'I love you. I love you so much. I—' she smiled faintly, 'I feel indecent at times because I love you so much.'

She had the pleasure of seeing him put his head back and laugh. Then bringing his face down close to hers, he said softly, 'Go on being indecent; I like you being indecent.'

'Oh, Davie! Oh, Davie!' She lowered her eyes at him, then softly they laughed together.

A moment later she looked down the table and said, 'Molly has done everything so nicely. Why didn't she stay until we got back?'

He took a mouthful of cold pork and chewed on it before answering, 'Well now, she did tell you that she was going over to Bateman's, didn't she?'

'Yes, but I thought not until around noon.'

'It's a good stretch.'

'Well, I told her you would take her but she said she wanted to walk. And . . . and what's more, Davie, I don't fancy the sound of this Mr Bateman and his house full of children. She's had a hard enough life here.'

'She doesn't mind youngsters, she was brought up among a crowd.' He continued eating, then breaking off a crust of new bread, he covered it with butter before he ended, 'She's like everyone else, she wants to marry and have a place of her own. It's understandable.'

'Yes, yes, of course.' She smiled at him, then said thoughfully, 'But . . . but she's had lots of chances over the years. You know, Davie—' her voice dropped, 'I used to envy her. She had a way with her and men seemed to gravitate towards her. Look . . . look at my father. . . .'

He took a long mouthful of tea before he answered, 'That was in her young days, she's getting a bit long in the tooth now. I haven't seen anybody scampering around her. And what is she? Going on thirty-six. You're showing wear at thirty-six.'

'Oh! Davie, Molly showing wear! Don't be silly, she's bonny. She'll always be bonny; women like her don't seem to age. Anyway, age or not, I'm going to miss her . . . Davie.'

'Aye, I mean yes?' He poked his face playfully towards her, and she tapped his cheek with her finger, then shook her head at him before leaning forward and proffering him her lips. After he had kissed her, he asked, 'What were you going to say?'

She was looking into his eyes as she answered, 'Oh just that at one time I . . . I was jealous of Molly. I thought when you came back you might . . . well you might pick up where you left off years ago, because what happened wasn't really her fault. . . .'

He rose abruptly to his feet and half turned from her as he said, 'Now, now, none of that. What put that into your head? That was over and done with afore we finished Sunday School. And I told you, didn't I, the past is past, all of it. So no more goin' back. Well now.' He tapped each lapel of his grey suit as he ended, 'These togs must go in the drawer with the moth bags, and the Lord knows when they'll come out again.'

'They will not go into the drawer with any moth bags, you're to wear them when you go into the town.' Her voice was prim, and laughingly he answered in the same vein, 'Yes, Ma'am. Yes, Ma'am.'

'Oh! Davie.' She came round the table, running like a girl, and into his arms. 'I'm so happy. I'm, I'm almost perfectly happy. Almost.' As she cast her eyes towards the ceiling her face clouded and he said sharply, 'You are perfectly happy; don't let your mind dwell on that part of the house. As far as you're concerned, it doesn't exist. Remember what Doctor Cargill said, you're not to go near him. Your system, your nervous system, won't stand up to much more. He said that, now didn't he? So leave him to me and Will, we'll manage him atween us. And promise me, now promise me that on no account do you go up those stairs onto that landing.'

She stared into his eyes for a moment before she said, '. . . I promise you, Davie.'

'That's a good girl.' And when his lips touched hers again, she felt like a girl. For the first time since she was twelve years old she felt like a girl.

Davie worked for the rest of the day, and he planned as he worked. He'd split the herd and try a few of them down on that patch near the malt house. The grass was lush there, and from the returns he got from the milk, now that Master Amos couldn't get his hands on it, he would put a little aside and so be able to engage some casual labour. Perhaps only for a day or two at a time, but that would be a help, and such hands generally worked like slaves in the hope of being kept on. And should he come across an exceptional one, he'd make him an offer, his food and a cottage and a small regular wage until things looked up. A decent man would take a chance.

At three o'clock in the afternoon he had gone in to a dinner cooked by Jane. It wasn't up to the standard of Molly's cooking, but he praised it. By five o'clock it was raining heavily and Molly hadn't returned.

'She'll be wet to the skin,' Jane said, when she came yet again to the cow byres to have a word with him.

'Not her: she won't be making the journey back this night, that's certain. The top an' bottom of it is, once he got her there, he wouldn't let her go, so stop worrying on her account; Molly can take care of herself, never fear.'

It was around eight o'clock and the rain had fallen to a steady drizzle as he made the last round of the day. He went from the cow shed to the stables, where he spoke to the horses and the pony; he went round the hen crees and the piggeries; he passed the open barn where the dogs were, but knowing his step they made no movement, only blinked in the lantern light; then he walked by the side of the big barn and into the road and towards the main gate. And it was then he saw her, in the swinging gleam of the lantern, shambling slowly, like a drunken woman, towards him.

'That you, Molly?'

She didn't speak, and he came close to her and held the lantern above his head. And not even then did she say anything; her face, running with rain, was crumpled as if she were crying.

'What's happened you?' he asked. 'You're wringing to the skin.' He touched her shoulder and it was this that seemed to loosen her tongue, for now she began to gabble in such a way that it was difficult to distinguish whether she was talking through laughter or tears. 'So much for the bolt hole; I thought I just had to walk in. And that's what I did, just walked in, large as life, an' there she was settled, a trollop if ever I saw one, a dirty, lazy, fat trollop, the end part of a trollop at that, for her best days were over. She'd lost most of what she'd had except her tongue.' She gulped now and her head wagged again before she ended, 'He didn't open his mouth, just stood there like a pie-can, an' 'twas only a month gone since he begged me to take him an' his brood on, just a month.'

'Come on inside,' he said gently, 'an' get your things off. You'll get your death, it's turned bitter. And there's one who'll be glad to see you; she's been worried about you.'

She became still now as she peered at him through the lantern and the rain. Then, her voice low and her words slow, she said, 'Aye, she'll be glad, but not you. You wanted me out of the way, didn't you? Well let me tell you somethin'. I wanted to get out of your way an' all, so there was a pair of us wantin' the same thing. But now you're stuck with me until I find a place. When I'm prickin' your skin like a holly leaf, just remember you're doin' the same to me. But it won't be for long; a day or two, I'll get something. Aye, I will; I can work anywhere.'

'Don't be silly, woman, don't be daft.' His voice was harsh. 'You have no effect on me, good, bad, or indifferent, so you can stay as long as it pleases you. It's up to you.'

Her face seemed to swing with the movement of the lantern. He saw her mouth open wide and her eyes close before she flung herself round and leant against the gate post; her head buried in her hands, she cried uncontrollably like a child would who had fallen down and grazed its knees, and he stood gazing at her helplessly while he warned himself not to touch her.

Chapter Three

'Davie, please, please let me see him. It's like my father all over again, keeping him tied to the attic.'

'Jane—' he put his hand over his eyes, 'you know what Doctor Cargill said, an' just a day or two gone. "It would be advisable," he said, "if you didn't disturb yourself in any way." Those were his very words, weren't they?'

'But my nerves are all right now, I've never felt better in my life. And he keeps going for Molly, shouting at her. I'd have to be deaf not to hear him. I . . . I won't go any further than the foot of the bed. And Davie . . . Davie—' she took his hands in hers, 'it isn't that I really want to see him, but morally I think I should. I've . . . I've forgiven him. And he needs forgiveness, he's dying.'

'Is he? I'm beginnin' to have me doubts about that. Six months now he's been lying there. Doctor said that was his limit, but he shows no weakness to me. In fact he can use those arms of his as well as ever he could. And—' he paused and brought his head down to hers and, his voice low, he ended, 'that's what I'm afraid of, those arms of his, tentacles; let them get hold of you and you'd swear he was an octopus.'

'But I promise you I won't go any further. . . .'

'No, Jane. Not now, not at this time. When the child is born and if he's still here then you can go in to him, but as you are now, the very sight of you like this,' he tapped his first finger against the dome of her stomach, 'this would drive him mad. I know him, I know him better than you. I told you a while back that he's lying there concocting mischief, I can see it in his eyes. And another thing you'd better know, Molly's got the idea that he can move more than he lets on; in fact she's sure of it 'cos she watched him through the keyhole and saw him bumping himself up in the bed by his arms. The next thing we'll know he'll be pulling himself out of the bed.'

'He couldn't, Davie, he couldn't do that, it's too high. Anyway, once he was out he'd never be able to get back.'

'Jane—' he cupped her face between his hands and gazed at her for a moment before saying, 'It's only six weeks. . . .'

'Nearly seven.'

'Well, nearly seven. You've stood out all this long time, keep it up a little longer, just for me, and . . . and I'll promise you one thing, if I suspect at all that he's near his end, you'll see him. Now I give you me word on that, so will you give me your word again, you won't go in to him on your own?'

She stared into his face, into his beloved face, into the face that had given her rebirth; for if ever a woman had been reborn, she had. If it weren't for the thought of Amos constantly niggling at her mind, she'd be so happy it would be unbearable. Her love for him was almost like a pain in itself. And it was true what she had said, she'd never felt so well in her life. And this in spite of carrying a child and working as hard as any hired maid. She had completely taken over the dairy; she made butter and cheese as good as Molly now; she helped to milk the cows, feed the pigs and chickens, and groom the horses. During her thirty-one years on the farm she had never spent so much time outside the house. Her mother would have thought it beneath her to lift her hand to an outside chore, and the kind of farmer her father had been, he had not expected it of her, so she had not thought it odd when she herself had not been trained in the ways of butter and cheese making and the like. There had always been Molly, and Winnie, and, before they had gone out into service, the Geary girls. But now she was rarely in the house during the day. And this was fortunate, for outside she did not dwell so much on Amos and his plight. She felt that Davie had arranged things so, giving her tasks that would keep her away from the house.

'Very well.' Her voice was soft, and her arms went up and round his neck as she said, 'I can't say no to you in any way, my dearest.'

When he had kissed her firm and squarely on the mouth he pushed her from him, saying on a laugh, 'What would they say if anyone saw us, husband and wife kissing at ten o'clock in the mornin' in the barn? They can't be married, they'd say. That's what they'd say, they can't be married.'

'Oh Davie, go on with you!'

'Aye, an' I'd better go. You see that sky.' He pointed out through the open door. 'That's been coming up from the northwest since late yesterday; I know that sign, we're in for a bad 'un. I'd better get Will to help me tie down the ricks.'

'I'll help you.'

'You'll do nothing of the sort. Go back to the dairy, woman, about your business.' When he slapped her buttocks she put both hands on the place and hurried away, glancing at him over her shoulder, her eyes alight as if he had just bestowed a gift on her.

As he went out of the main gate and across the road into the open meadow where the two ricks were, he was still shaking his head and half smiling. She was like a young lass. He had never seen a change like it in his life; she seemed to have gone back to what she was all those years ago before that day in the malt house. And that's how he wanted to keep her. And he would keep her like that, as long as she didn't see that maniac.

The storm broke at noon. It followed a dark, dead calmness in which nothing moved. The bare branches of the trees in the copse looked as if they were painted on the low sky. The washing that Molly was grabbing in from the lines was hanging limp. The animals too were affected by the stillness, for they made no sound. There was no grunting or cackling or mooing; they, together with all life on the land for miles around, seemed to have become paralysed with the stillness. Even Molly's bustling movements were checked once she got inside the kitchen, for having dropped the wash basket onto the floor, she went and stood near the window and peered out into the yard, across which she could now scarcely see.

The first drops of rain were spaced and the size of hailstones; then with the suddenness of lightning the sky unburdened itself and the water fell in sheets which blotted everything from sight.

She stepped back from the window, saying aloud, 'God in Heaven! We're in for it the day. Eeh! I can't see a stime; I'd better light the lamp.'

She lit not only the lamp in the kitchen but also those in the hall and the dining room; then she went upstairs and lit the one that stood on top of the landing; and finally, the lamp in *his* room.

When she brought it from the central table to the bedside table so that he could see to read, she had to raise her voice to make herself heard above the din on the roof. 'We're in for it! . . . I said, we're in for it!'

And the answer he gave to this remark was, 'Did you do as I asked you?'

'Now don't start that again, not at this time. We'll have enough to think about it strikes me afore this one's over.'

'Did you do what I asked you?' He was shouting now, and she shouted back, 'No, I didn't, 'cos I've told you a hundred times afore, it's no use.'

She watched him drop back against the head of the bed in that desperate fashion that hurt her, and when he spoke again she said, 'What did you say?'

'It's inhuman.'

She stepped back and stared at him. Aye, she supposed it was inhumam. She had never thought Miss Jane would stand out this long; but she was like a child in Davie's hands. His word was law to her. She herself used to say that he played at God, and Miss Jane had, in a way, turned him into one. But the plight of this one here hurt her sorely at times. She never thought there'd come the day when she'd feel heart-sorry for him, but, dear God, you'd have to be made of stone not to be melted by his predicament.

At times she felt fearful over his constant demands to see Miss Jane, for then he worked himself up into a frenzy. She had thought, and more than once, it wouldn't have done Miss Jane any harm just to stand at the door and have a word with him from there. He wasn't long for the top, the doctor said, so what harm could he do? As long as he stayed put in bed, that was.

'Now mind you don't knock the lamp over.' She was shouting again. 'There's your books an' your drink, you've got everythin' to your hand. I'll bring your dinner shortly.' She nodded at him, then went out.

After staring towards the door for a long moment, he turned his head slowly and looked at the lamp.

By seven o'clock the storm had in no way abated, in fact it's fury seemed to be getting worse every moment. An hour ago it had lifted the roof completely off the hen cree and the birds had been tossed about the field like bits of straw. It had taken Davie, Molly, and Will Curran all their time to marshal them into the main yard and to the barn; and then their efforts had resulted in only half the birds being brought to safety.

The tall tree at the end of the copse had been torn up by the roots, and its top branches had just missed the last cottage by a few feet.

The yard itself was strewn with slates from the house, and Davie had continually yelled at Jane to keep indoors in case she should be struck by one.

Right up till the hens had scattered she had worked by his side; now she was sitting near the kitchen table panting and spent. She ached in every limb; her head was bursting with sound; she was so weary that she told herself she wanted to die, then contradicted the statement hurriedly as if her wish would be granted. No, she didn't want to die–ever. She put her hand on the side of her stomach, just below her ribs. The child was kicking furiously, annoyed, as it were, by so much activity. She looked down tenderly at the bulge and thought with an inward pride that when her time came she'd be so big she wouldn't be fit to be seen. Last night Davie had moved his hands over her stomach as he said, 'You're carrying so high, there's room for two underneath,' and at this they had smothered their laughter against each other. Oh, life would be wonderful, if only. . . .

She rose heavily to her feet. She must see to the broth; they were all frozen.

As she neared the fireplace a blast of smoke came down the wide chimney and almost choked her, and she turned, coughing, and leant against the table. Through the window she heard a distant sound of grating; then a crash outside the back door which told of more slates coming off the roof.

For twenty-five years back she could recall storms, terrible storms when the river flooded, and the burn from its source became a great waterfall. During one such storm two ponies in the malt house had only been saved because they had been washed onto the stairs and so had managed to climb to the gallery. Then there was that weird and strange storm when there was no rain and the lightning struck the ricks and set them on fire. But these storms seemed to have come and gone within a limited time, gradually mounting, then easing away. This one had been raging at the same pitch since noon, and showed no signs of abating.

The door burst open and the wind rattled the crockery hanging on the dresser, bringing from it a sound like that of cracked bells. Molly stumbled in, followed by Will Curran and Davie, and it took Davie all his might to force the door closed.

'God in Heaven! Did you ever know anything like it?' Molly tore the hood from her head, then pulled off her sodden coat, adding, 'I'm wringin' to the skin.'

'Did you change?' Davie was not addressing Molly, but Jane, and she answered, 'My cape had taken most of it, I changed my shoes.'

'You should've changed altogether, you can't help but be wet through.' He felt her shoulders, which were dry, and she smiled at him and said, 'There! Satisfied?' then added, 'It's you who needs to change. And you, too, Will.' She turned her face kindly towards Will Curran, and he replied, 'Wet doesn't worry me, Miss Jane. So used to it I take scant notice, 'climatized, sort of.' He smiled at her, and she smiled back at him. He wasn't such a bad sort after all, Will. She had never liked him because of his appearance and his perpetual drip, but of late she had found him kind and willing. There was good in everyone if you only looked. The thought brought a sadness to her and she turned sharply from him, saying, 'We must all have something to eat, the broth is ready.'

As she went to the fireplace to lift the pot, Davie came to her side, saying sharply, 'Now leave that alone. Haven't I told you? God in Heaven! You're like a child. I have to keep on at you.'

He was reprimanding her before the servants, but they took no notice, and she smiled as if he had paid her a compliment. And he had, for he was showing concern for his wife, and like any wife she replied, 'Oh, don't be silly, I've lifted heavier than that.'

Five minutes later they were all sitting round the same table eating, and no one of them but thought that times had changed, but for the better.

Towards nine o'clock the rain stopped, but the wind seemed to gain in momentum. At half-past nine Davie and Will Curran made one more round of the place. Then Will went to his cottage.

It was close on ten o'clock when Molly went to hers. She had left Amos right for the night. She had seen Jane to bed, and she had stood for a moment in the kitchen alone with Davie and remarked, 'There'll be some clearin' up to do the morrow,' and he had replied, 'You've said it there, but no matter what we've got to do, I think we'll be lucky compared to those down the valley near the river. Bet your life there's been some cattle lost there the day. I shouldn't wonder if some of the bridges aren't down. A force like this pushing at water will test the stoutest pillars. I don't think I've seen a worse, even at sea . . . Look, will I walk along with you?'

'Walk along with me?' She cast a glance at him over her shoulder. 'No! No! I've kept me feet so far, so I'll trust to them to get me there. It's me feet that's keepin' me down, they've always kept me down.'

He had never known her to joke with him, although he'd heard her joke with others, and he laughed now and said, 'Aye, some of us would be right upstarts if it wasn't for our feet.'

She stared at him for a moment longer. He could have been speaking against himself, but he wasn't, for since he had taken on the mastership of the farm he hadn't played the big boss or cracked the whip, all he had done was to work harder, if that was possible. His efforts were paying off at that, for things were better than they had been for years; the place was beginning to look like it used to. Of course, it would never be as it was; there wasn't the land, or the cattle, or the people to run both, but nevertheless a change had come over the farm in the last few months. She fancied at times he forgot, like they all did, that the real master of the place was still upstairs.

'Have a good night,' he said.

'A good night!' She raised her eyebrows. 'I can't see anybody havin' a good night in this!'

'Well, here's one that's going to.' He nodded at her. 'Let me head get on the pillow and I won't have any say in it.' He smiled at her, but she didn't smile back. She knew what would happen when he got his head on the pillow; she had gone over it every night for months past. She couldn't break herself of the habit. She no sooner got into bed than the picture of them rose before her. At first she had thought it wasn't right. Apart from everything else it wasn't right, him havin' Miss Jane; until she remembered herself and the master. And she didn't like remembering that now. Anyway, this was different, she supposed, because they were married. He had put a ring on her finger; the ring made everything right.

Marriage was a funny thing, when you came to think about it. The parson said a few words, the man put a ring on your finger, and you could run round bare-arsed between sunset and dawn and it was all right, because it was done in the eyes of God. Odd, how much stock God laid on a ring. He classed the same thing bad without a ring, but good with it. She'd never laid much stock on God herself, and she laid less as time went on. She wished now she'd had some book learning, it might have cleared things up for her.

When he held the door open for her she went out into the tearing wind, her head down against it . . .

But it was as Davie had said, he'd hardly put his head on the pillow before he was asleep. And Jane, too. She had kept awake until he had come to bed, but after he had taken her in his arms and kissed her, her lids closed and she was away.

She didn't know what time it was later when she awoke and realized that he was no longer by her side but moving about the room. She pulled herself up in agitation, saying, 'Davie! Davie! What is it? Surely it isn't time yet; I don't feel I've been asleep . . .'

'It's all right, it's all right. Lie down. Wait till I light the lamp.'

'What time is it?'

'I don't know yet, but it's early on I think. Listen to that.'

She listened, but for a moment could only hear the howling of the wind. Then, as if from a far place, there came to her ears in between the gusts a high thin neighing, the unmistakable cry of a frightened horse. 'It sounds like Benny,' she said.

'Aye, it's him all right. And I put him in a stall by himself in case he started his antrimartins. He's likely kicking hell out of his box, and he'll set the others on.'

The lamp lit, he peered at his watch. 'Quarter past twelve,' he said. 'Oh Lord! I hoped it might be near morning. Now you stay put and go to sleep, there's nothing you can do, not tonight anyway. There'll be more than enough for you tomorrow.'

'Be careful, Davie.'

As he went towards the door there came the sound of a crash from somewhere in the house, and he stopped for a moment. Then wrenching the door open, he ran onto the landing, and there at the end where the steps led up to the old part of the house a window had blown open. When he reached it, she was behind him, and as he forced it closed he shouted at her. 'Now look! It's all right. Get back into bed.'

'The glass is broken, mind your hands!' She was shouting back at him.

'Well, we can do nothing about it now, we'll see to it tomorrow. Now get back into bed, I won't be long.' He pushed her across the landing and into the bedroom, then closed the door on her. And at the head of the stairs he paused a moment and turned up the lamp that had been glimmering low, then ran down the stairs and out into the night.

Amos, resting on his elbows, strained his ears to distinguish the sounds not caused by the wind, and he knew when Davie had reached the bottom of the stairs.

Patience was a virtue. Old Hedley used to quote that ceaselessly to him. 'Patience is a virtue, my boy.' He had been patient for months, knowing that sometime, somehow, a solution would present itself to him. If she had relented and come and had a word with him, perhaps he might have seen things differently. Yet no; he knew that he would never have looked upon this situation differently. The only solution to the situation was to give it an end, a final end.

They had been waiting for his end, and not patiently. His clinging to life was disturbing them. He could see it in Armstrong's face; he even detected it behind Molly's sympathetic attitude towards him. Well, now they would get their wish, he'd bring it to a head. But he'd want company on the journey, he wasn't going alone. No, by Christ! He wasn't going alone. 'Go back to bed!' he had cried at her. 'Go back to bed!'

There was a great rattling above his head and he looked upwards. The slates were rolling off the attic roof. The wind would be rushing in, the cleansing wind; the wind from the hills would be sweeping his prison. Although he had lain here for months past in the room in which he had been born, his mind had been back in the attic reliving the experience of his childhood again. But soon the attic would be cleansed of thoughts and memories and he would be free.

Putting out his arm, he leant over the side of the bed and when his fingers touched the floor he heaved with his shoulders and his useless body slid with a heavy plomp onto the carpet. He rested a moment, for he discovered he was weaker than he thought; then raising himself on his elbow, he stretched out one hand and gently tipped towards the bed the side table on which the lamp was standing. It was a second before the flames burst upwards, and then the feather mattress and the pillows crackled into a furious blaze.

He didn't stop to see the progress, but, clutching at the carpet, he drew himself hand over hand towards the door, and it was a simple thing to reach up and turn the knob. Once out on the landing, he pulled himself towards the short flight of stairs. Here he found difficulty in descending for he had to try and prevent his useless stunted limbs from slewing sidewards and bring him rolling to the main landing.

There was a wind blowing along the landing from the broken window, and it covered the sounds of his gasping breath. Instinct led him, not to the room that had previously been Jane's, but to the one that his father had occupied; and he knew his instinct had led him aright when he saw the thin stream of light coming from under the door. Softly now he reached up and turned the handle, and softly he pressed the door open. If the movement of the door made any sound, it too was obliterated by the noise of the storm. He looked upwards towards the bed. It appeared a long way from the door. He could not see whether she was asleep or awake because of the draperies; in any case, she was apparently not aware that the door had opened.

Slowly he drew himself over the carpet to the side of the bed, where stood the table with the lamp on it; and then he saw her. She was lying well up on her pillows as if she were patiently waiting. His two hands gently clutched the side of the bed and with an effort he pulled himself upwards until his head came just above the mattress, and there he held himself still while he looked at her.

He had no intention of speaking before he had done what had to be done, but his concentrated gaze must have penetrated her light dozing, for her eyes sprang wide as if she had received a shock or heard a loud noise. And then she was gaping at him. Every muscle of her face stretching, she tried to speak, but only her lips moved. When a strangled gasp came from her throat, her hands went instinctively to it as if to stop herself choking.

'Hello, Jan.'

Her terror increased.

'It's a long time since we've seen each other. You've changed, Jan.' His gaze moved down to her hands which were now gripping the bedclothes above her stomach, then back to her face again, and he asked, 'Why wouldn't you come and see me? Was it because you were afraid of him? You were always afraid of someone or something, weren't you, Jan?'

As he waited for her speak, his hands began to lose their grip on the mattress, which he took as a sign that his strength was going. He knew he must get her into his arms before he overturned the lamp. Once there, he'd have sufficient strength to hold her until the end.

It was the combination of the look on his face, his clutching hands, and a sudden awareness of a smell of burning permeating from the landing, that triggered off the scream that had been whirling upwards through her since she opened her eyes and saw his head like a disembodied thing sticking to the mattress. It spiralled out of her as she sprang to the other side of the bed in a frantic effort to get out. At the same moment he tipped the lamp, as he had done the other, but more sharply, onto the bed. And then he was scrambling round the foot towards where she had just risen from her knees. Within a split second she was on the floor again, her body hitting it with a sickening thud as he brought her down by clutching her legs, and although she fought him, it was in a dazed way, without much effort.

It was as Davie battered on Will Curran's door, shouting, 'Will! Open up, I want a hand. The stable roof's caved in, they're pinned, two of them. Will! Do you hear me? Will!' It was at this point that he turned his head in the direction of the house. The wind was blowing full on him and it brought to him a strong smell of burning.

He lifted the lantern high and swung it, but could see nothing, the house was too far away. 'Will! Will!' he bawled now. 'Come on, man! Come on!' But he was back down the road as he shouted.

When he reached the yard he saw the flames leaping red through the bedroom window to the side of the house, Amos's room, and he thought he was imagining things when, looking along the front towards the window of his own room, there was a reflection of the flames. He raced to the front door, through the hall and up the stairs, and although when he pushed the door wide, he couldn't credit what he was seeing, he knew that he had feared and expected something like this for months past.

'Jane! Jane!' He screamed her name as his arms wafted wildly at the smoke. The whole bed was alight, not only the mattress and the draperies, but also the posts which, being old and brittle dry, were burning like oiled paper.

'Dav-ie! Dav-ie!' It was more like a moan than his name but be rushed to the far side of the bed, and there through the smoke and flames he saw them. They were lying locked together near the wall.

Falling onto his hands and knees he tore at them both in an effort to separate them, but Amos's fists lashed out at his while with his other arm he clung on to Jane.

He was choking with the smoke, they were all choking with the smoke, and he knew for a certainty that they would all die joined together here in the next few minutes. When his groping hand found Amos's windpipe he pressed hard, relaxing his hold only when he felt the body sagging. But when he grasped Jane's shoulders, intending to drag her from the room, he was again brought to the floor by Amos's last effort.

As he measured his length almost on top of Jane, a madness seized him, and, coughing and spluttering, he hurtled himself upwards, then kicked out at the demoniacal face lit now not only by the flames from the bed, but also from Amos's nightshirt.

As the body fell backwards he swung round and, again grabbing Jane, he dragged her limp body out of the door and well onto the landing, and there, coughing as if his lungs would burst, he beat at the bottom of her burning nightdress with his hands.

'Oh my God!' He wasn't aware of Molly's presence until she shouted, 'Is she all right? Is she all right? The whole place is afire . . . both ends. Oh my

God! My God! Come on, get out of it.' She, too, began to cough and choke now with the smoke.

Unable to speak, he gesticulated wildly towards Jane's legs, and between them they carried her down the stairs. As they were crossing the hall, Will Curran burst in from the kitchen, but stopped at the corner of the passage for a moment and gaped at them before crying, 'The old part, Davie, the old part's alight. It's alight!'

Davie made no answer to this; instead, still coughing, he said between gasps, 'Give's a hand . . . with her, to . . . to the cottage.'

As Will Curran took Jane's legs, he shouted, 'She'd be better on the trundler?' and at this, Molly ran along the front of the house and into the yard and, picking up the shafts of the wooden-wheeled handcart, she dashed with it back to the house and held it while they laid Jane on it.

As Davie began to push the cart away, Will called to him, 'What's to be done?' and Davie shouted back, 'See to the horses first. There's one pinned under a beam. The roof's caved in. Give him a hand, Molly.'

'What about this?' she screamed and waved her hand back at the house as she ran by his side. 'We should get some of the things out; it'll be like a bonfire in no time,' and he yelled back at her, 'See to the animals first, then do what you can. I'll be back as soon as she comes round . . . If she comes round.' The last he added to himself as he ran the cart towards the gate. Before he went through it, Molly was by his side again, shouting, 'Go into my place, your beds will be damp, sodden.'

He nodded, then guided the barrow through the gate and onto the road, and then he began to run.

Perhaps it was the jogging of the cart or the pain of the burn on her leg that brought Jane back to consciousness, for she put out her hand and groped at the air.

When he faintly discerned her moving hand, he stopped the cart and, peering down at her through the darkness, he said, 'It's all right, it's all right. Don't worry, you're all right. Just lie still until we get to the cottage.'

When he reached Molly's door, he pushed it wide; then returning to the cart, he put his arms under Jane and carried her bodily inside.

It was strange but he had never been in this cottage since he was a young lad; he had no memory of what it was like, except that it was muddled and not over clean; not like his own home, which was spanking.

There was no light, but a dull flow from the fire showed up a wooden settle with a high back standing at right angles to the fireplace, and on this he laid her, saying softly as he did so, 'Are you all right, Jane? Are you all right?'

'Yes, Davie, I'm all right.'

'Are you burnt? Let me look.'

'No, no.' She put her hand on her knee. 'I'm all right. It's . . . it's only shock. Go back; please go back and . . . and try to put it out.'

'I couldn't, I couldn't put that out, Jane; it's at both ends.'

'Try . . . try to save something from the bottom floor, the small pieces, the silver. Go one, Davie, please, please try to save something, otherwise—' she stopped and shook her head.

'You'll be all right then?'

'Yes, I'll be all right. I'll . . . I'll lie quiet.'

'Promise?'

'I promise.'

He looked around the room. There were two of Molly's coats hanging on the back of the door. These he brought and put over her; then touched her tousled hair for a moment before hurrying out.

Once on the road, he raced along it. The whole place was illuminated now with the flames. The glass in the window of the side room had burst, and the crackling of the fire and the raging of the wind appeared to him like hell gone mad. Smoke was pouring out of the front door in billowing waves and the deep red glow from his bedroom window showed the furnace within. If there had been any thought in his mind of going up there and trying to drag that one free, now that his rage had subsided somewhat, he dismissed it; but perhaps there was still time to save the furniture from the bottom floors.

He dashed along the yard and towards the stables, and there saw Molly and Will struggling to lift the beams that were shutting in the two terrified horses. He noted instantly and with relief that the animals, although very frightened, were both unharmed. Stooping down and getting in between Molly and Will, he put his shoulder to the beam; but immediately it began to move, he saw the danger. The end of it was supporting another beam which was balancing precariously within a few feet of yet another one, and were that to slip it would break the animals' backs.

'Hold your hand! Hold your hand a minute!' He took his support from the beam, crying, 'Keep her steady till I get that down.' He pointed upwards; then climbing on to the partition between the boxes, he leant against the wall for support and, putting up both arms, he took the weight of the beam and slowly eased it sideways and down towards the floor. He did the same with the second beam. When he jumped to the ground again, he put his shoulder to the main beam and between them they eased it from where it was jammed across the front of the box.

The animals freed, they now had their work cut out to hang onto them, and when they led them into the yard, the smell of the fire so increased their fear that it was almost impossible to hold them.

Once they were in the field, Davie yelled, 'They'll be all right, let them go.' Then shouting, 'Come on!' he turned and raced back to the yard. But at the entrance he stopped. Whatever hope he'd had of saving anything was gone. Although the flames hadn't reached the bottom floor, the smoke was finding every outlet.

When Will Curran said, 'We'd never be able to get in there, we'd choke to death,' he made no response.

'Perhaps the kitchen, pans and things.' Molly looked at him and he at her. His eyes were red-rimmed and running water, his face looked grey like that of an old man. Like someone coming out of a dream he repeated, 'Pans and things.' Then on a high note he cried, 'My God! Where's me wits. The money, all there is! It's in the office desk.'

'Well, it'll have to stay there 'cos you'll never get beyond the passage.'

'I've got to take that chance, it's all we've got.' He was running towards the house, she hanging on to him, crying, 'Don't be mad, Davie! Davie! Oh my God! Don't do it.' She had one arm around his neck, and he paused, but just for a second, and looked at her; then he thrust her aside, saying, 'Don't be so damned stupid, woman.'

The kitchen, being separated from the hall by a passage, was not yet impenetrable, but when he opened the door into the passage the smoke came billowing into the kitchen. Molly put her hands over her mouth, then closed the door and stood with her back to it.

Minutes passed, then she saw Will Curran through the smoke. He was shouting, 'The wind's changed. A spark could catch the byres. We'd better start pumping . . . where's he? He's not gone in there! There's no chance Master Amos's still alive. Anyway, I'd let the young devil go—better that way.'

Molly turned from him now and with a frantic movement pulled open the door and, her head down, she ran into the passage.

It was the bottom of the stairs that she felt him. He was crawling on his hands and knees, and after the shock of her touch, he pulled her down with him and almost dragged her back along the passage. When they got into the kitchen he stumbled to his feet, still holding her, and coughing and choking they rolled like two drunks out into the yard. And there he thrust her from him, saying between gasps, 'Bloody-silly-thing to do. More-bother-than you're worth. Could . . . could have missed you. What then?'

She was standing up now drawing great draughts of air down into her breast, and after a moment she shouted back at him, ''Twas a bloody silly thing for you to do, wasn't it? Clever bugger, as always, you are. Always playing God Almighty. Always have, always will.'

He passed his hands over his streaming eyes, then peered at her, and suddenly his body seeming to go limp, his head bowed and he muttered, 'I'm sorry. I'm sorry.'

She did not speak for a moment, and when she did her voice too was quiet. 'Did you get it?' she asked.

He nodded once and tapped his pocket, then said, 'Where's Will?'

'Pumping. The wind's changed. Look.' She pointed. 'It could take the dairy an' the cow sheds.'

'My God! My God!' He was running again, and she by his side. And it was there she stayed until well on into the night, carrying bucket after bucket after bucket of water while their world grew into a great red waving mass of flame.

Towards dawn the house roof fell in and they stood, bodies slumped and weary, looking at it, and Molly said quietly, 'Well, that's put the lid on his coffin.'

Chapter Four

The house smouldered for a week until there was nothing left but the blackened window-gaping stone walls and pieces of charred wood.

The Justice of the Peace together with an official of the Police Force came from Hexham. A man had been burned to death, how had it happened? A lamp had been blown over in the storm and the wind had caught it–they had all agreed that this was how it should be told. Will Curran knew no other but that it was so.

A gentleman, sombrely dressed in a high stiff collar and a three-quarter length coat, came from the bank in Newcastle. He had a clerk with him, and they arrived in a hansom cab. The gentleman talked to Jane of the mortgage and reparation through insurance, reparation to the bank, but not to her. It appeared that her brother had been warned several times that if he did not meet his commitments on the mortgage, the bank would be forced to foreclose. Had she been aware of this matter?

No, she had not been aware of this matter. Nor had she found any letters from the bank concerning it.

He said he was very sorry and he would do the best he could for her. He hoped when the matter was settled there would be no need for them to restrain on the cattle and land.

The third dignitary who visited them was Sir Alfred Tuppin's younger son, and he began by asking Molly if he could see Miss McBain. He was standing at the cottage door, and it was Davie who answered him. Coming from the scullery, he crossed the room quickly, saying, 'There's no Miss McBain here; if you wish to see Mrs Armstrong, you can come in.'

The young man had stared insolently at Davie for a moment before looking beyond him and Molly to where Jane sat on the settle near the fire. And he had gone towards her, saying, 'My father wishes to know if you're in need of anything.'

When she replied, it was like an actress on the stage saying her lines.

'Thank your father for me. Tell him I'm obliged to him, but I have everything I need.'

He had become nonplussed for a moment; then with slight smile he had bowed slightly towards her, saying, 'I shall give him your message. He'll be glad to know that you're well provided for. Good-day to you.'

Jane did not answer him, but when he walked out she bowed her head and bit tightly on her lip. Davie had gone over to the fire, and with his jaws clenched he had stood gazing into it. Molly, after looking from one to the other, went into the scullery and left them alone.

The days that followed were days of grinding labour from morning till night, at least of Davie and Molly. Jane could do very little. Apart from her time drawing near, she had a burn on her leg which refused to heal and caused her intense pain at times, and she was forced to rest more than she would have done under ordinary circumstances.

Although Will Curran did his best, and with a good heart, ten hours' work was as much as he could achieve, and then, during the second half of the day, he slowed up considerably.

Davie sawed up the tree that had fallen near the cottage and kept the fire going day and night to air his old home. Molly scrubbed it down from top to bottom and washed the bedding, and for the last two weeks they had been installed there.

Davie was back where he had started.

The first night he lay with Jane by his side in the bed that his parents had shared for years, in the bed in which he himself had been conceived and born, he had thought: everything goes full circle. He had worked like two men all his life, and what had he to show for it? Well, he had Jane and the child that was coming, and he had a piece of land and a few cattle. But hold your hand! Don't count your chickens, he had warned himself; these last weren't sure. He was waiting to hear about them; he wouldn't be surprised if the next thing they would say would be that they were going to take the land. He'd be surprised at nothing anymore.

Three weeks before her time, Jane started her pains. She had felt ill for days, but she put that down to her leg. There was a hole in it now. When the bandages were taken off, the matter poured out. Doctor Cargill said she must keep it well covered up, but it was so painful she could hardly bare the linen strips near the flesh. Molly had put goose grease on to prevent the cloth sticking, but that hadn't helped.

She was woken from her sleep by a searing pain circling her middle. When she clutched at Davie he roused himself, saying, 'What is it? What is it?'

'I've got a pain.'

'Pain? But . . . but it's not due . . .'

'I know, I know, but . . . but it's a definite pain.'

'I'll . . . I'll get Molly.'

'No, no, it may be nothing, it might go away. Perhaps it's just a cramp . . . flatulence.' She never said wind.

The pain hadn't gone away by dawn, but increased, and he went into his old bedroom and knocked sharply on the wall, and a few minutes later Molly came running in, fastening on her clothes as she did so. Her teeth were chattering with the cold as she asked, 'Wha-at is it? What's up?'

He was standing at the top of the narrow stairs as he said softly, 'She's started her pains.'

'But it's not . . .'

'I know, I know. But it's them all right.'

'Not a fluke?'

'No, I should say not. I'm going to ride in for the doctor.'

'But she might be hours, a day or so.'

'I doubt that; not the way they're comin'. And he promised her he'd be here at the time, with her leg the way it is and the state she's in with one thing and another.'

As she passed him, she said, 'He won't thank you for goin' at this hour.'

'I can't help that. Anyway, it'll be on light when I get there.'

She passed him and went into the room and bent over Jane, and they stared at each other, both wide-eyed.

'You think it's them?'

'Yes, Molly.'

'Now don't you worry, everything will be all right. Davie's goin' for the doctor. He's good is Doctor Cargill with bairns. Not that I can't bring it meself, I've had nearly as much experience as him.' She smiled, but received no answering smile from Jane.

'I'm worried, Molly.'

'What've you got to be worried about? First 'un's always come days afore or days after. Me ma always said our Lena was so long in coming she thought she was goin' to go the full eighteen months an' have twins.' Her smile was wide now and she laughed. And Jane laughed with her, a short weary laugh. But the next minute she was hanging onto Molly while she gritted her teeth and the sweat ran down her face.

When it was over Molly drew in a deep breath and said, 'You made no mistake, it's them all right, short and sharp. Lie still now, I won't be a minute.'

When she reached the kitchen, Davie was brewing tea and she said abruptly, 'You'd better leave that and get a move on if you want him to be here when it comes.'

'Eh!' He dropped the teapot on the table. 'As near as that you think?'

'Nearer, I wouldn't take the trap, I'd just ride Benny, he's fresh, you could be there in less than an hour.'

Before she finished speaking he had grabbed up his coat from the door; but as he went to go out he looked towards the stairs. But he said abruptly, 'There's no time for that,' and he turned and faced her for a moment, his face red and angry looking. Then he went out; but the next minute she was calling to him as she ran after him, 'Look here, put these gloves on, the reins will sear your hands. They're bad enough as it is.'

He grabbed the gloves from her without thanks, and she stood for a second in the dark listening to his feet pounding the road as he ran towards the stables.

An hour and a half later the child was born and Molly delivered it and cried joyfully as she saw the perfectly shaped feet slip out of the womb. 'God in Heaven! I've never seen anything so quick in me life. Well! Well! Would you believe it. Aw, lass, lass.'

'Molly.' Jane's voice was a faint whisper.

'Aye, lass. Aye, Miss Jane.'

'Is . . . is it all right?'

'All right? Why, it's perfect. A little lass and it's perfect. Hair on its head an' all. Now lie still, lie still, don't move, I've got me work cut out. An' listen 'er, just listen 'er. She's lettin' you know she's here.'

She severed the cord and knotted it before wrapping the child in a warm sheet; then she attended to Jane, saying, 'Lie still, lie still, the afterbirth will be comin' away any time now. There, let's wipe your face. By! You look bonny. Aye you do, white, but bonny.'

'Oh, Molly! Molly!' Slow tears ran down Jane's face. 'Oh, Molly! Molly!'

'There now! There now! Don't start me on, else I'll flood us out.'

'Molly.'

'Aye, Miss Jane.'

'I . . . I don't know what I would have done without you, ever. Thank you, Molly.'

Tears gushing from her eyes, Molly turned away abruptly, saying, 'I told you, didn't I? I told you, an' as soon as he comes in the house he'll go for me. Bubbling your eyes out, he'll say, and upsettin' her. That's what he'll say, he always blames me. Aw!' Her tone changed as she bent over the white bundle. 'Aw! But she's lovely.' She lifted it up and carried it to the bed, saying between sniffs, 'Look. Look at her. Now just take her in your arms a minute, just a minute, 'cos I've got to get her cleaned up, she's in a mess.'

It was at this point that the door opened and Davie came in, and he stood stock still for a moment looking in amazement towards the two women and the child. Then he moved swiftly to the bed, and Molly stepped aside and went out of the room.

Slowly now he dropped onto his knees and stared at the little wrinkled face peering out from the white sheet. Then looking at her, he murmured, 'Jane . . . Jane,' and he kissed her gently and stroked her face while she gazed up at him, unable to speak. Slowly now he undid the wrapping round the child and looked down on its perfect limbs.

'A girl,' he said softly.

'You don't mind?'

'Mind? I wouldn't mind if it was a heifer.'

'Oh! Davie.' Her face crumpled into a broken smile. 'Don't. You're as bad as Molly. I . . . I don't want to laugh, I feel so tired.'

'Aw, my dear.' As he took the child and laid it on the bottom of the bed there was a bustle outside the door as Molly announced her entry, and she came in saying, 'I'd better have it afore it needs a pick and shovel to get it clean.'

He looked at her as she picked up the baby and bustled out again. He wanted to say, 'Thanks, Molly, thanks.' And he would later. He knelt again by the side of the bed and stroked the wet hair back from Jane's forehead. 'Go to sleep,' he said. 'Go to sleep, my dear, my very dear.'

'Yes, Davie, I'll go to sleep, I'm very tired, so tired. But the afterbirth hasn't come yet.'

'Don't worry about that, it'll come in its own good time, and Doctor Cargill will be here shortly. By! He'll get a gliff, just like I did.'

He watched her eyes close and her breathing get deeper. Then slowly she half opened her lids again and said in a thin, thin whisper, as if her thoughts were escaping in spite of herself, 'You have never said you loved me, Davie, do you know that, not once. You have never said you love me.'

The muscles of his face dropped as he stared down at her. Had he never said he loved her? But hadn't he proved it in a hundred and one ways? Yet had he never said he loved her. No, he hadn't, he hadn't said it in so many words. Oh Jane! Jane! He went to put his lips on hers, but realized she was fast asleep, and slowly he rose from his knees and stood looking at her.

He wasn't given to soft words, but he must try to put this thing into words to please her, for she herself put it into words every day. Women were queer cattle; all of them were queer cattle.

The afterbirth didn't come away. When Doctor Cargill arrived at nine o'clock that morning, it showed no sign of coming. Two hours later when he left, it still hadn't come, and Davie returned to Hexham with him to collect some medicine that would help it on its way.

By evening Jane was in a high fever and Davie sat by her side wiping her brow with a cold cloth.

At six o'clock Will Curran took the trap into Hexham, and at halfpast eight Doctor Cargill was again in the house, and everything was bustle. Sprinkling chloroform on a pad of cotton wool he held it above her face for a moment as he said, 'Just breath deeply and when you wake up everything will be all right.'

But when she woke up everything wasn't all right, for she was bleeding heavily. She held tightly onto Davie's hands while she retched against the sickly smell of the chloroform, and Molly, under the direction of the doctor, wrung out cold clothes from a bucket of well water and placed them on her stomach in an effort to stop the flow of blood.

Just before midnight, before losing consciousness, she whispered, 'Davie! Davie!' and, his face close to hers, he said, 'Yes, my dear; yes, my dear.' And her last words to him were, 'Name her Delia. My mother would have liked that. . . .'

She died as the dawn was breaking, and he could not believe it, he would not believe it. He held her to him and rocked her and moaned, 'No! No! Jane. No! No!' and the doctor, worn out with his efforts, and Molly, near to collapse, left them alone.

After a time he laid her back on the bed. Her face was white and smooth and beautiful; the beauty that had always just evaded her, except on her wedding day, had been permanently released by death.

Feathers in the fire. That's what his Granda had said they all were, nothing but feathers in the fire. But why did the burning of a feather leave so much pain in the beholder?

Chapter Five

The summer had gone. It was October again and the winter loomed ahead. The child was six months old. It was a fat, bouncing, gurgling baby; strangely it had not suffered a day's illness since its premature birth. It laughed a great deal, and only cried when it was hungry; and when it was hungry, it wouldn't be put off with a dumb-tit.

Molly cared for the child. She washed, dressed, and fed it, carried it in a wash basket and laid it in the yard outside the dairy whenever it was fine; when it wasn't, she left it in the dairy. She never left it alone in either of the cottages, for fires were burning there night and day, and now she had a horror of fire.

She missed Jane as she would have a dearly beloved sister, yet at the same time she felt relieved at her going, but suffered for this failing with self-recrimination.

She had given him three months to get over the worst of his grief, but when three months had past, during which it had been difficult to get a word out of him, and he still showed no interest in her, and at times appeared barely civil, she experienced a new despair, a final despair. For if working alongside him from morning till night like a galley slave, if tending his child as if it were her own, and it could have been, judged on the feelings she bore towards it, if cooking for him and keeping his house clean could not draw from him a kind word, let alone a glance from his eyes that told her she was still a woman, then nothing could.

Her past, she felt, was as alive for him today as when it had happened all those years ago, a long lifetime ago. He had been a stubborn, blockheaded youth then, and was now grown into a hard, unforgiving man.

She had made allowances when, following the fire and Jane's death, she would watch him at odd times, mostly in the late evening, looking at the great shell of the house. She had only realized of late that Davie Armstrong had been an ambitious man, and the knowledge had created the thought that this could have been the reason why he had married Miss Jane; but she had dismissed it. She wouldn't give him the bad credit for being so mean. But nevertheless he'd had a feeling for the house and the land more than was usual in a worker.

Then to cap all, today she'd had a shock, and it had released a frightening prospect. They'd had a visitor. Into the yard, around three o'clock, had ridden Miss Agnes Reed. She had said she was thirsty and could she have a glass of milk, and while she drank it, she had sat looking at the blackened house; then she had said, 'Mr Armstrong . . . is he about?'

'In the fields.' Her answer had been short and sharp. She had watched her ride down the road and through the gap in the stone wall.

The Reed girl had never shown her face at the farm after the master had died. What was she after now? Need she ask? She knew what she was after. She had a name, that one, a clothes prop with trousers on would do her, as long as it acted like a man. But Davie was no prop with trousers on, he was well set up, attractive, handsome; although his face was grim, he was still a handsome man, and what was more, he had sense. But did any man have sense when a woman threw herself at him, and from the height of Agnes Reed's station? It was enough to turn any man's head.

Fifteen minutes later when she returned to the gate and saw him walking up the field by the side of the horse and rider, all she could say to herself was, 'My God!'

Davie, too, said the same words, but to himself as he looked up into the smiling face of Miss Reed. But he added 'What they'll stoop to!' And that Miss Reed was stooping, he had no doubt. It wasn't the first time he had seen her since Jane had died; he had encountered her a number of times in Hexham, and although she hadn't acknowledged him with a movement of her head, her eyes had remained fixed on him much longer than was seeming in a woman of her standing. But what standing? From what he could gather, she was nothing but an upper class unregistered whore.

'It seems strange,' she was saying as she looked down into his eyes, 'but if things had taken their course, I would have been the mistress of that dead pile. However, the course took a turn, and now you are master of it.'

'That's so.' He jerked his head, his face unsmiling.

'What do you intend to do with it? It's an eyesore as it stands.'

'Yes, you could say it's an eyesore, but . . . but I have me plans for it.'

'Really! I'm pleased to hear that. You must tell me of them some time.'

He made no answer to this, just stared back into her pale grey eyes, eyes that strangely reminded him of McBain's. They had reached the gap in the wall, and he stood aside and said, 'Good-day to you,' and after a pause she said, 'And good-day to you, Mr Armstrong.' Then digging her heels sharply into the horse's flanks she cantered off, while he stood looking not after her, but down onto the top of the wall. The end sandstone brick had been worn smooth with the hands that had grasped it over the years as they went in and out of the field, and now he grasped it tight as he thought, slut! And the nerve of her, thinking he would jump onto her hook. Clients must be getting scarce in her quarter.

He was filled with a sudden wave of indignation as if he had just suffered an insult. He watched his fingers moving backwards and forwards rubbing the stone, and there returned to him her words, 'If things had taken their course, I would have been mistress of that dead pile. However, the course took a turn and now you are master of it. What do you intend to do with it?'

What did he intend to do with it? He had thought once or twice lately that he would gradually knock it down and with the stone build a wall on the north boundary that would show old Tuppin he wasn't coming any farther.

When it had become known that the land, and what was left on it, was legally his, Sir Alfred's solicitor had written him a letter offering to buy the place and had stated a sum he wouldn't have taken for the cow sheds. In his best writing, and his best manner, he had written back and said he had no intention of selling the farm now or at any time in the future. He had heard nothing since.

He was well aware that everybody was giving him the cold shoulder; he was out of favour in both camps, that of his own kind and that of those in power. He had been condemned by the former because he had gone to Jane's funeral in his wedding suit; true, he had a black band on his arm, but who had ever heard of a man going to his wife's funeral in a light grey suit? Jane had loved him in that suit, she had been proud of him when he wore it. And he hadn't cared a damn what anyone thought.

And he had worn it again when he had been summoned to the bank in Newcastle, and there he had met the manager's condescension with arrogance, and had the last word in the interview, saying, 'I am not thanking you for letting me keep what I consider me own through me wife.'

No. No one had come to his aid, for he was, on all sides, considered an upstart, and they had left him alone. Except for the visitor today. He turned now and looked along the road; then gave a short mirthless laugh before walking briskly back to the farm.

Crossing the yard, he approached the house. He had never been in it from the day they had unearthed from among the charred beams what remained of Amos. Now he went through what had been the front door and, his feet crunching into the burnt wood, he stood where the stairs had been and looked upwards and into the high clear blue sky.

He remained standing in the hall for almost ten minutes, ten minutes idling, doing nothing, but thinking.

When he came out Molly was passing down the middle of the yard with the basket on her hip, the child in it, and he called to her, 'Molly!' When she didn't stop, just turned her head towards him, saying, 'I'm goin' to make the meal,' he looked after her, puzzled for a moment. She seemed upset about something.

He hurried after her, shouting, 'Molly! Here, wait a moment.' When he caught up with her, she said, 'What is it? What do you want?'

'What do you mean, what do I want?' He stared into her face. She was in a temper. She had shown him nothing but kindness and consideration for months past; he felt he would have gone mad without her; but now she was fuming. 'Is something wrong?' he asked.

'Now what could be wrong? I ask you, what could be wrong?'

'All right.' He nodded at her. 'As you say, what could be wrong? You'll tell me in your own time, I suppose, but . . . but listen, I've got an idea.' He pointed towards the house. 'I'm going to rebuild it.'

'What!' She jerked the basket on her hip and the child gurgled.

'Aye, I was for pullin' it down, but I'm goin' to rebuild it. Not the old part, that'll go. It's had its day anyway. Look, give her to me. Here.' He grabbed the basket from her. 'Come on, I'll show you.'

She did not now walk by his side but remained a couple of paces behind him. In front of the house he placed the basket on the ground, then pointed to the front door, saying, 'I'm going to clear it all out. That's the first thing, clear it all out. Then brush the stone. The stone's all right except for a crack here and there, and that's easily remedied. Then I'll lay the floors, an' fix in the beams.'

Her voice came at him, derisive, saying, 'It'll take a lifetime. An' where are you goin' to get the wood, beams an' all that?'

He turned to her. 'Five years. I could have it up in five years. As for the wood, I'll buy a bit at a time for the floors. The beams, why–' he pointed out towards the road, 'there's all those trees in the copse. That's the first thing I'll do after clearing it out, get them down so they can be seasoned. I'm going to build, Molly.' His shoulders were bent, his head thrust towards her. 'The old house meant something to me, but it'll be nothing to the one I'll build. That'll be mine. Are you with me? Will you help me?'

She stared at him while the muscles of her face sagged, 'Help you?' she said.

'Aye, help me.'

'Well,' her shoulders jerked, 'you pay me, don't you, so I don't suppose it matters which way I earn me money?'

He stared hard at her for a moment. Then his gaze dropped away from hers, and he stooped and picked up the basket and, holding it out to her, said, 'I'll manage, I want no forced labour.'

Her mouth was tight as she turned away.

It was pitch dark and he hadn't come in. She looked at the child sleeping peacefully in the basket by the side of the fire. Will Curran had been finished this past hour.

The usual procedure that ended her day was that she cooked the meal in her own oven and between times washed the child and got her ready for the night; then when she heard Davie come in, she gave him time to get his wash before taking both the meal and the child next door.

They had eaten together for months past now, but they were cheerless meals. Sometimes he didn't open his mouth. When he did it was on some aspect of the work. He always took the child upstairs with him at night.

When another half hour passed and there was still no sound of him, she pulled the basket well away from the fire; then, putting a coat around her, she ran out and down the road and into the farmyard.

The gleam of the lantern showed him bringing an armful of charred wood into the yard and placing it on the barrow. She called to him from the distance, 'Are you going to stay out all night?'

'Just comin',' he answered back.

'The meal's spoilin'.'

She was walking towards him as she spoke, and when she was near enough to see him she exclaimed, 'My God! You're a sight. You'd think you'd been down the pit.'

'Aye.' He knocked one hand against the other. 'I'll have to go to the burn to get this off.'

'What! The night? It's freezin'.'

'Well, I can't go inside like this, can I?'

She stared at him for a moment, then said, 'Another ten minutes; then come on home an' I'll have some water hot an' you can have a wash down in the scullery.'

'Oh, ta. Thanks.' He nodded at her, and she saw his blackened face move into a smile. It was the first time she had seen him smile since the child was born.

She turned away and hurried out of the yard and up the road. In the cottage she ground a kettle full of water on the fire, then went next door and put a full kettle on his fire. Taking a zinc bath from the nail on the outside wall, she placed it just inside the scullery door, and scooped rain water into it from a barrel in the yard. Following this she took the kettle from her own cottage and stood it on the hob against the other one; then she went back and waited.

It was almost three-quarters of an hour later when he knocked on the wall, and at this she lifted the basket and took the sleeping child in to him, then returned and took the meat pie from the oven.

When she set the pie on the table he was standing with his back to the fire, and he looked down on it and said, 'By! I'm ready for that. That wash was a god-send, I feel I could start all over again, night shift. I'm going to get up an hour earlier in the mornings an' do two hours extra every night. That's the least I'll do because in the winter there won't be so much goin' outside, and there'll be time enough to spare. I'd like to bet if I stick at it, I'll have the kitchen and hall roofed by spring. What do you say to that?'

She had just put three-quarters of the pie onto his plate, and she only prevented herself from banging it on the table and saying, 'What do I say? I'd say you've found your tongue all of a sudden. Strange what a visitor will do for you.' But what she said was, 'It'll take you, to be going.'

'I'll go all right.' He pulled a chair up to the table and sat down. 'And right from rock bottom, starting practically from scratch. An' what I make from now on will be me own. After all, fifty acres is fifty acres. There's many a man made a small fortune on less. This is good.' He chewed a mouthful of pie, swallowed, and then looked at her.

She had her eyes cast down; she was eating slowly, quietly.

The urge came into him, as it had done over the past few weeks, to put out his hand and touch her. It wouldn't have been disrespect to Jane; Jane would have understood. As for anybody else's opinion, he didn't care a damn. Anyway, who was around here? Only Will, so what was stopping him? The old picture of her wantonness? No, no; that had faded into the past, years ago. No, he knew what was stopping him; and until he faced up to it and admitted it to himself, he would never be able to make a move towards her.

For years he had denied that she meant anything to him. Inside himself he had scorned her, yet all the while he had known he was hiding something, feeling that if he let it see the light, he'd be less of a man, for men, real men, didn't love trollops; they used them for their needs, but they didn't love them.

For years he had thought of her as a trollop, but today, when that real trollop had come on the scene, she had, in some strange way, wiped Molly's slate clean; she had certainly made him face the truth that had been buried for so long, and part of that truth was that he had even used Jane to help smother the undying feeling. Yet he had cared for Jane. Oh yes, yes, he had cared for Jane. But had he loved her? For long after she died, the words that were almost her last had burnt him. 'You never said you loved me, Davie.' If only by way of thanks for all she had done for him, all she had given him, he should have made the effort and said those words to her without being prompted. But he never had.

'You're not eating,' he said.

'I'm not very hungry.'

'You're tired,' he said.

'Aye.' She looked at him. 'I think that's it, I'm tired.'

'I've worked you too hard; I haven't been thinking.'

She lifted her head and looked at him. The kindness, the consideration, even the tenderness in his tone was too much. For twenty years she had longed for it. She had not supplemented the want of his tenderness with another man, or men; yet it wasn't for want of the chance. Over the years she had scourged her body into submission; from where had come the strength she couldn't tell, for she knew herself to be of a loving nature, wanting to give everything, aye everything. During his long absence at sea she had asked herself what she was waiting for, was she barmy, for even when he came back he wouldn't look the side she was on. But she reckoned that it would be just her luck that if she committed some indiscretion he would turn up, and then her chance with him would be gone forever. She had seen him looking at her with those eyes of his, and they would say, 'You trollop.'

She tried to quell the flood of emotion that was rising in her. She looked into his eyes through a haze of tears, and with the contradictoriness of human nature proving itself to her, she cried inwardly, 'It's come too late, too late. I can't stand no more, I'm finished.' On top of this thought tumbled another that brought her fighting instincts to the fore again. Was he just soft-soaping her because he had his eyes on the rider this afternoon, and knowing that that piece wouldn't want to soil her hands, he would still want someone to do the donkey work?

He was saying to her, 'I don't expect you to help with the house, I'll see to that meself. And you were saying that Mickey would like to come back when I get on me feet. Well, I see no reason. . . .'

The storm broke. Twenty years of agony of both body and mind erupted; the pain of all the nights she had lain in her bed with her hands on the wall that divided them. Even during these past months she had lain like that. If there was no wind and the night was still she could hear the creaking of his bed springs, and their movement mangled her heart.

She had reckoned on a certain time for him to recover completely from Jane's loss, six months, but a year perhaps would be more decent; she didn't mind as long as he gave her a sign. She had waited so long, what were a few more months? But then today the arrival of the horse and rider and the knowledge that he could, and would, take a wife was more than she could endure.

'What is it? What is it? Don't cry like that.' He was standing over her, his hands on her shoulder. He recognized that she had reached the end of her tether; something had happened today that had been too much. He looked back to the only difference in this day from any other, the visit from that Reed trollop . . . that was it. She must have thought. . . . God! She couldn't have thought him capable of doing that to her? He had been a bit of swine to her over the years; more than a bit at that. He had made her pay a whole lifetime for something that could happen to any lass, that did happen to half the young lasses in her position; human nature being what it was, how could they resist the advances of the master who had power over their very livelihood, their right to eat?

There might have been an excuse for his retaliation in the early days; he was hot-headed, hurt, and the power of his own manhood had received an assault. But there had been no excuse when he had come back. Well, perhaps still a bit, on his first visit, but not when he had taken up the job on the farm, for he had seen then that she was different. She had changed; and yet she hadn't, she was still the Molly he had known, the girl who had bothered him. Yet not even the fact that she had been respected by all those who had been against her, his own family in particular, had carried any weight with him. And why? Because deep inside him he had known that she held him in the hollow of her hand, and even as a grown man he wasn't big enough to admit to it.

His hands went under her oxters and he lifted her from the table and turned her towards him. Her head was hanging, her whole body was shaking with her emotion.

'Molly!'

She took no heed. She was consumed with an anguish that had to flow out of her.

'Molly! Look at me. Give over.' He became concerned and shook her by the shoulders, saying sternly now, 'Come on, come on. Enough is enough.' He had never seen anyone give way like this; even Jane's crying on that night Amos had first gone for her had been nothing like this; and Jane with her finer calibre was the more likely to give way to hysteria. At this point he bludgeoned himself mentally for this thick-skulled thinking. This woman here had suffered through him as Jane had never done through Amos, for he had deprived her of bodily satisfaction for years while mentally attacking her. He knew in this moment that he wouldn't live long enough to make it up to her.

When he drew her into his arms, her emotions shook his body; and now he made no effort to check it, but stroked her hair.

The fire crackled and fell in with a plomp. The lamp flickered, the child stirred in its sleep, and still they stood in the middle of the kitchen until, her sobbing easing, she lay against him spent.

Still he stood quiet, uttering no word.

When at last she raised her head from his breast and looked at him, he pressed her slightly from him and, stooping and taking the bottom of her apron, a clean one, which from habit she donned before serving the meal, he passed it gently round her face; then turning her about, he pressed her into a chair, saying thickly. 'Stay put.' Then swiftly he lifted up the basket and the child and took them upstairs. He was down within a minute and, standing before her, he held out his hand to her and, looking into her eyes, he said, 'Come on, Molly love; it's been a long time.'

Through still streaming eyes she gazed up at him; then slowly she placed her hand in his, and as he led her to the stairs he put out his other hand and shot the bolt home. It stuck at first for it was many a day since it had been used.

They had to go up the stairs in single file but he still held onto her hand, and each step took her from her mundane, work-weary, bodyscourged life, right back to the beginning when Davie Armstrong had filled her sky from one end of the moors to the other. Yet there was no ecstatic feeling swamping her. She was numb, twenty years numb. The thawing would take time. Life was funny, crazy.

'Come on, Molly love; it's been a long time.'

The Blind Miller

The Blind Miller

To
Theresa and Colin

Though the mills of God grind slowly, yet
  they grind exceeding small;
Though with patience he stands waiting, with
  exactness grinds he all.

HENRY WADSWORTH LONGFELLOW

BOOK ONE

Chapter One

'I should have known.'

'Why should you?'

'Me mother should have told me.'

'How did she know that they were going to give you fruit with your tea? And, anyway, you said you used the fork all right.'

'I felt clumsy. It was awful . . . awful.'

'What's up with you, our Sarah, worrying about using a fork to fruit? Lord, if I was in your shoes I'd be thinking about what they thought about me . . . along that line.'

'Well, I am . . . that's what I'm doing. What'll she think about me using a fork as if it was a pick shovel?'

'Look, forget about the fork and tell us what it was like, the house and everything.'

'Oh, it was lovely, lovely. You've no idea, Phyllis.

The two sisters sat on the edge of the bed, their thighs brought together by the sagging mattress. They looked at each other, one bursting to unload her experiences over the hump of humiliation brought about by a new venture in table manners at a Sunday high-tea, the other waiting to be warmed in the glory that had befallen her elder sister.

'There was a beautiful linen cloth on the table; everything was to match, china and all that, and tea-knives besides the knives and forks. I knew what they were for all right.' She pulled a face; then her features flowed into a quick smile that illuminated her surroundings like a light through a dirty window. 'And they've got a proper dining-room, they don't eat in the kitchen.'

'That's because it's a corner house, it's double like.'

Sarah nodded quickly. 'And there's a carpet in the front room, and there's a whole suite; and a piano, and a cabinet–glass-fronted you know, with best china in it. Oh, Phyllis, it was lovely.'

'Did you get upstairs?'

'Yes, she took me up to take me things off.'

'All of them?' Phyllis pushed Sarah in the shoulder and they swayed from each other before the bed brought them close together again.

'Don't be nasty, our Phyllis.' Sarah's eyes were blinking; her face was straining not to laugh now. 'That's what they do. An' you know something . . . they've got a flush lav.'

'No!'

'Yes, truly.'

'Coo! Did it wet your things?'

'Don't be silly.'

'I'm not; I sat on one once and pulled the chain. Ooh, lor! I was wringing.'

'You are a fool you know, our Phyllis; you don't pull it till you get up.'

'I know now. But go on. Did they leave you in the front room to do your courtin'?'

Now it was Sarah's arm that shot out, and so quick was the thrust that it knocked Phyllis from the edge of the bed on to the floor. Within a minute they were back into position again, holding each other as they rocked silently together.

When they were sitting upright once more, their faces wet with their controlled convulsions, Phyllis said, 'I wouldn't have been surprised if they did, you know. Coo! He's not slow on the uptake, is he? You've only been going with him for three weeks and he asks you home. There's May Connor, she's been going with Harry Willis for six months and never darkened his mother's door, and they're supposed to be goin' strong.'

'That's different. . . . I don't suppose Harry's particular for May to see inside the house.'

Phyllis wriggled her buttocks on the bed, which brought her feet from the floor, and she lifted them upwards and looked at them as she said, 'They're talkin' about you next door. Old Ma Ratcliffe had her head over the wall the minute you went round the bottom corner. She said to me mother: "Sarah's looking bonnie the day".' Phyllis nudged Sarah with her elbow and stuck her tongue well out. 'That was a sure lead-up to the old snake sticking her fangs in. Will I tell you what she said?'

The eyes of the two girls were now slanted towards each other. 'I'll likely have heard it all afore,' said Sarah.

'You haven't, not this bit . . . we're all one family now.' Phyllis drew her upper lip to a point, showing her large white teeth, and, thrusting her chin out, brought her face into a good imitation of that of their neighbour as she said, '"Well, Annie, you know nothing can ever come of that, we being at the bottom end." We, you note . . . we're all one big family now . . . no looking down her nose the day. "Stink-pots like the Hetheringtons couldn't be expected to walk this way with wedding rings." That's what she said.'

'Who's talkin' of wedding rings?' Sarah's voice sounded hoarse and threatening.

'Well, I'm only tellin' you what she said. And she didn't forget to rub it in an' all about them being chapel. And then she fired her last gun afore saying she had to get the tea ready. "You'll be having the priest sitting on the doorstep from now on," she said.'

'Damn her!' Sarah got to her feet and walked the two steps to the window, and Phyllis, looking at her straight back, said, 'Eeh! our Sarah, fancy you sayin' that; I thought you had said you'd promised Our Lady never to use a swear word in your life.'

Sarah did not turn her head but stared through the lace curtain to the row of chimneys opposite. Her whole being was flooded with an anger that was not just the outcome of the moment, but stemmed from years of puzzled thinking, of probing and groping blindly to know the reason why. She had been protesting constantly for ten years now from a particular day when she had seen, as if in a revelation, the whole of her life being spent in the lower end of the Fifteen Streets. She'd had a bad cold and her mother had given her nearly half a bottle of cough mixture. It had knocked her silly, and she'd seen funny things, most of which she had forgotten. But she hadn't forgotten the mud picture, as she now thought of it. In the picture she not only saw her mother and Phyllis and her new step-father, wallowing, choking, in a sea of mud, mud like that which filled the huge timber pond at Jarrow Slacks, a mile down the road, but all the people of the Fifteen Streets, all of them, were choking in the mud; there wasn't one of them who wasn't up to the neck in it. And she knew that they all knew there was no hope of getting out. Yet they still struggled. Some upheld others, but some, like Mrs Ratcliffe next door, put their hand on the heads of those nearest them and pushed them under.

'I hate that woman.' She was glaring down at Phyllis now. 'She's never so happy as when he's goin' for us. But I'll show her. I'll get out of here, you'll see.' She bounced her head at her sister, and Phyllis nodded back, saying under her breath, 'An' the day you go I'll be on your heels.'

Again they were seated close, and Sarah's voice, stripped now of all anger, asked softly, 'But what about me mother?'

Phyllis, sitting straight on the iron frame, eased her hip to one side before she said, 'She wants us to go, an' as soon as possible. There'll be no peace until we get out.'

'She told you that?'

'No, no, of course she didn't, but she could manage him if we were out of the way.' Phyllis sighed now, and, tossing her head back and her long fair hair from her shoulders, she supported herself with her hands, gripping the iron frame of the mesh base as she looked up to the ceiling, and said dreamingly, 'I wish I had a bust like yours.'

This remark brought from Sarah a quick downward jerk of the head. The movement showed impatience and an effort to crush down laughter. She got up from the bed, and with her back against the narrow window-sill she looked down on Phyllis, and once again tried to understand this mercurial sister, who could change not only a conversation but her manner so quickly as to leave you bewildered. She said, 'You can have it, and welcome.'

'That's what they go for, a bust.'

'Don't be nasty, our Phyllis, I've told you.' In embarrassment Sarah gathered the frayed end of the lace curtain in her hand and laid it in a bunch on the sill.

'I'm not. I tell you I've watched you going past the bottom corner. An' I've seen the men. Some of them look at your legs sometimes, an' others at your face, but their eyes nearly always finish up on your bust.'

'Our Phyllis!' Sarah was now kneeling on the bed with one knee, pinning her sister down by the shoulders with her hands as she hissed, 'Stop it! Stop such talk! And you only seventeen. You're as bad as the women up the street standing round their doors.'

The bed began to shake and once more they were enfolded together, their arms tight round each other, rocking from side to side, the springs making a zing-zing sound as they moved, until Sarah choked, 'Stop it! You'll have me mother up.'

'I can't help me bust.' They were lying quiet now, their faces wet with their laughing.

'Don't try, you've got something there.'

Again their arms were round each other; again the springs were zing-zinging.

'Do you know you'll have to go to Confession?'

'What for?'

'Well, talking about such things.'

'Oh, our Sarah! You know you are a bairn in some ways. Do you mean to tell me you'd tell Father Bailey about your bust?'

Sarah pulled herself off the bed; a battle was now going on inside her. This too was an old battle. She wanted to laugh loudly at Phyllis's suggestion, but she knew that it was no laughing matter, for if she had been guilty of bringing up the conversation about her bust she would definitely have had to confess to bad thoughts.

As she stood up there came from below the sound of a door banging, and the sound brought Phyllis from the bed too.

'Better get in.' They were whispering.

Quickly they began to undress, standing where they were in the two-foot space between the wall and the iron bed. As they bent down to pick up their clothes their buttocks bumped and this brought a suppressed giggle from Phyllis, but Sarah, swiftly hanging her things on a hook behind the door, motioned her to silence. Then almost simultaneously they knelt down side by side and, crossing themselves, said their prayers.

Sarah, holding the spring taut with gripped pressure from her hands, waited for Phyllis to crawl cautiously to the far side of the bed, and not until her sister was settled did she take her hands away. Then, sitting on the edge of the bed, she slowly allowed her large frame to sink towards her sister; and when they were close once again Phyllis whispered, 'He'll be disappointed that we're in; he'll have to find something else to yell about.'

Sarah nodded, then whispered. 'Goodnight.'

'Goodnight,' said Phyllis.

They both turned slowly on to their back and lay looking up at the flaking ceiling, fading now in the light of a summer evening.

It was ten o'clock on this Sunday evening. It was warm and nice outside; couples would be strolling up in the country still, yet here they were packed off to bed as if they were still bairns. Well, Sarah supposed Phyllis wasn't much more being just seventeen. But she herself was nineteen, nearly twenty. It couldn't go on; it mustn't go on. She thrust her long legs down the bed, and when her toes caught against the iron rail she bit tight on her lower lip and screwed up her eyes and in the bright sparked-off pain patterns in the depth of blackness in front of her lids she saw pictured in vivid detail the tea-table in the Hetheringtons' house. And once again she was overwhelmed with shame about the fork business, until the shame was suddenly flicked away and her eyes sprung wide with the thought, It'll come to nothing, them being chapel.

All along she had known it would come to nothing–what hope was there for a Catholic and a chapelite? It was a greater barrier than a social one. The Hetheringtons might live in the Fifteen Streets, but the gap between her family and them was as wide as between a prop man in the docks and one of the managers living in his big house down Westoe end in Shields. The fact that the four Hetherington men all went to work in collars and ties and that three of the men living in one house were actually in work, whereas her own father–as her mother had insisted she call him–hadn't done a batt for the past seven years, and would have fought shy of it now if he had the chance of it, even this barrier, the difference which meant living with bugs behind the wallpaper or without them, could, with a miracle, have been surmounted, but not even time or death could alter the religious difference. And yet here she was, yarping on to herself about making a mess of using a fruit fork. That's what she did, she told herself heatedly: she never faced up to things, always started worrying about some little thing that didn't matter a damn, trying to cover up the bigger issues, like trying to cover the sky with a blade of grass. If you held the grass or anything else close enough to your eyes you could blot out what was behind it. At least for a time, then your arm got tired, so to speak. She had to face up to things in the end, but it was always in the night that they caught up with her, which was why she was so tired in the morning.

Well, she had known who he was from the word go, hadn't she? When he had stood outside the shop waiting for her she had known he was from the posh house at the end of Camelia Street. Everybody knew the big house at the end of Camelia Street because it wasn't divided into two. It had seven rooms and a brass knocker on the door, and the curtains were always beautifully white.

He had said to her 'Hello', and she had answered 'Hello', while sweat had suddenly burst into her oxters and the palms of her hands.

'I hope you don't mind.' He had stopped, as embarrassed as she was, and then she had answered. 'No, no, not at all', in the swanky tone she tried to adopt at times. She had got it from the people who came into the sweet shop–some talked swanky. But they didn't get many like that, although it was a good-class shop.

He said, 'Can I walk home with you?'

The shop was in Ocean Road in Shields and she always took the tram from the Market Place to Tyne Dock and there changed to the Jarrow tram. In the mornings she usually walked part of the distance to save the fare, but at night, her feet were nearly always swollen with so much standing, and her heavy build didn't make them any better, so she was glad to sit down in the tram. But this first night they walked all the way from Ocean Road to Tyne Dock, then up through the arches, past Simonside Bank, which led up into the country, past the respectable New Buildings flanking the Jarrow Slacks, past the dark jumble of houses built on a rise and called Bogey Hill, and on to the Fifteen Streets. It was a long walk and she really only came to herself as they neared his street, Camelia Street, and she stopped as if she had been pulled to a halt with a rope and said, primly, 'Thank you, but I can see me own way now.' It was such a silly thing to say and she blushed with the stupidity of it, but he smiled and said, 'Can I see you tomorrow night?'

To this she merely nodded shyly.

'The same time?' he said.

'Yes.' She was on the point of moving away when again she was halted, by the fascinating sight of a man raising his hat to her, a trilby hat.

She had tried to walk straight because she knew he was still standing watching her, but her legs were tired, and they felt wonky, just as if she was slightly tipsy.

There were men grouped at the bottom of all the streets past Dudley Street–Dudley Street was the sixth street from the top end. The men looked at her, they always did, but none of them spoke until she came to the corner of their own street. There were about a dozen men here; some were on their hunkers, some leaning against the wall, all with their coats and caps and mufflers on, although the night was stifling. the older ones hailed her, while the younger ones just spoke with their eyes.

'Brought any bullets with you the night, Sarah?'

She smiled, and with a feeling of gaiety answered them, saying, 'There was only a box of chocolates over, and I knew you wouldn't like them so I gave them away to the bairns.'

'Oh, aye!'

'Well, Aa never liked choclates,' said another; 'acid drops is more in me line.'

'Sherbert dips for me.'

'I like suckers, oh! I'm very fond of a sucker.' She was well past them when this remark was made; it came from a man who lived three doors down from her, a nasty man. She heard one of the older men saying, 'That's enough, shut tha' gob.'

The man who had spoken in the pitmatic was Mr Ferris and lived opposite to them. He had often slipped her a ha'penny when she was a bairn. they had no children of their own. She liked Mr Ferris. . . .

So that had been the beginning, only three weeks ago, and every night at half-past eight he had been waiting for her when the shop closed and he had walked her home. He had wanted to take her to the pictures, but she had refused. When at the end of the second week he had again asked her to go to the pictures and she again refused he had seemed puzzled. How could she tell him it was because she felt shabby and hadn't any Sunday things. It was different being met coming from work, you weren't expected to be dressed up then. Then last Saturday night he had asked her if she would come to tea on the Sunday, and she had stayed up late washing and ironing her skirt and blouse.

The odd thing about all this was her father had never mentioned the matter. If he had known that she was seeing a lad of any kind the place would have been raised; he simply went mad if he saw her talking to a lad. He had belted her when she was sixteen because he had seen her coming up the road three nights running with the same lad. None of the lads around the Buildings made up to her–perhaps because she kept herself aloof, but she also knew that they were slightly afraid of Pat Bradley. This had puzzled her in her early years because her stepfather was an undersized, insignificant-looking man, but lately she had come to understand people's fear of him, for there was an innate vicious strength about him that had nothing to do with his stature.

Of one thing she was sure: if he had known about her meeting with David Hetherington she would have heard about it. There were a number of people who had seen her with David, Mrs Ratcliffe next door for one, yet none of them had split on her. She felt a warm feeling towards the whole population of the Fifteen Streets. But the warm feeling fled with the thought. Perhaps the longer he's in the dark the bigger the bust-up there'll be, and that's what they're waiting for. Her father was known as a know-all, and likely a lot of the men were laughing up their sleeves at the way she was hoodwinking him. They would think of it as hoodwinking although she had done nothing on the sly.

Her mother had said last night, 'There'll be murder when he finds out; I would drop it if I were you.' And to this she had answered, 'I will after tomorrow night. He's asked me to tea, I'll tell him then.' Her mother's answer had been, 'My God! And them chapel!'

She turned on her side now and began to pray. 'Holy Mary, Mother of God, pray for us sinners now and at the hour of our death, amen. What am I going to do? Make him turn . . . don't let him be bigoted, Holy Mother. Oh, Queen of Heaven, the ocean star, guide of the wanderer here below.' Her praying trailed away and slowly she turned her face into the straw pillow and pressed her nose until it was pushed to one side and her mouth bit on the rough ticking. Was she mad altogether? She had only known him three weeks and here she was thinking he would ask her to marry him. Yet why had he asked her home? Why was he meeting her every day if there wasn't something in his mind? You didn't ask a girl home unless it meant something. Yet he knew where she came from, he knew she came from the bottom end–in fact the bottom, bottom end, for they lived in the last street, the last habitable street. Beyond, the houses were so dilapidated, so overrun with bugs, that they were only inhabited now and again by flitters, and there was talk of them being pulled down any time. Yes, he knew where she lived, and his mother must know too. She had been afraid of meeting his mother; she hadn't been afraid of meeting his father, or his brother, or his uncle. She wasn't afraid of men as she was of women; not really, except perhaps her father. But his mother had turned out to be . . . well, all right in a way. Cautious; oh yes, very cautious. scrutinising, looking her over from the side, and quizzing in her talk. How long had she worked at Bentons?

Since she was fourteen, she had said; it was her first job.

How long had her father been out of work? What was he when he was in work?

He had been a platelayer, but that was before the War, and then he had been in the Army, but could only get odd jobs since he came out. Work was very scarce. She had said this as if they didn't know, and found the eyes of the three men on her–the father, the uncle, and David. The other son wasn't there. He was married and lived in the next street.

Where did her sister work?

She worked in a café in Shields.

She was glad they didn't ask where the café was.

David sat opposite her through the tea, and every time she became slightly overawed or embarrassed she would look at him. His eyes were always waiting for her. She thought he had the kindest eyes she had ever seen in a man. They were clear grey. They were his best feature, although he had a nice mouth too. All his features were nice, yet they didn't make him good looking. She supposed that was because of his skin. It was rough, with red veins high on the cheeks, like a man who had worked in the blast furnaces all his life. His face was more suited to what she classed a working man than a man who worked in the dock offices. But his voice was not that of a working man. He had a lovely voice; soft, warm, kindly. She liked his voice and his eyes; she liked him altogether.

His father must have looked pretty much the same at David's age, but now his hair, instead of being brown, was wispy grey and he had a twitch in one eye. But he, too, was nice. Then there was the uncle. She had laughed when she was introduce to the uncle. David hadn't called him uncle but Dan, 'This is Dan,' he said. 'He's really my uncle, but he's only six years older than me so why should I call him uncle. And he's a rogue, so you look out for him.'

She had been at home with Dan right away, more than with any of them, even David. Dan wasn't as tall as David, who was close on six feet, but he was broader, much broader, with a big square face. You could call Dan good looking. And from the start she had seen that Dan was what was known as a joker. He could keep the conversation going and make you laugh. And yet there was something about Dan that she couldn't fathom; it was linked up in some way with his sister's attitude towards him, the sister being David's mother. She had noticed right away that Mrs Hetherington's manner towards her brother was different altogether from the manner she used to either her husband or her son. Either she ignored him, or when she was forced to speak, as when she thanked him for passing something across the table to her, she did not look at him and her voice took on a prim sound as if she was displeased, like a teacher's attitude towards an erring pupil. Sarah hadn't realised this fully until now, when she was going over the whole scene in her mind.

But there was one thing she was sure of: all the Hetheringtons were wonderful; and if only David would ask her she would die of happiness.

And so with another prayer to Our Lady to get him to turn, she dropped into fitful, dream-threaded sleep.

Chapter Two

The last customer was a boy about seven years old. He couldn't decide whether he wanted jube-jubes, everlasting strips, or walnut-tray toffee. Sarah said as gently as she could, 'We're closing, hinny; come on, make up your mind.'

The child thought a little longer, then, looking up, he asked, 'Can I have a ha'porth of each of two of them?'

Sarah sighed, 'Which two?'

Again there was some consideration and Sarah raised her eyes from the top of the boy's head to the glass door and to the figure walking slowly past.

As the boy's mouth opened on his decision a voice from the back of the shop called quietly, 'It's time, Sarah.'

'Yes, Mrs Benton.'

She flung the sweets into a bag, then pushed them at the boy, who had the temerity to say, with no small indignation, 'Why, you've put them in the same bag? The jube-jubes'll stick to the taffy.'

'Go on,' she hissed at him now.

Having pushed him out of the door, she stooped quickly and shot the bolt in while keeping her eyes averted from the street beyond.

She was getting into her coat as she said, 'I'm all locked up, Mrs Benton. I'll away then.'

The elderly woman smiled quietly. 'Yes, get yourself away. . . . I wouldn't like to have to pay for his shoe leather.'

The colour flooded up into Sarah's face. She hadn't imagined that Mrs Benton had noticed David.

'Is he a nice boy?'

'Yes, very nice, Mrs Benton.'

'Be a good girl.'

Sarah said nothing to this, only her eyes widened a little as she turned away with her head bent. She felt she should laugh, but she couldn't, for she was slightly annoyed. The admonition hadn't been spoken in a jocular way, as one of their neighbours might have said it, but more broadly, more casually. 'Divn't dee what I wouldn't dee unless ya want the priest after ya.' No, Mrs Benton's words had sounded like a warning and they made her feel hot. And so, when she came out of the side passage and he was standing there facing the alleyway, his first words were, 'You look warm.'

She stood in front of him, smiling widely now, 'I am . . . I've just finished a big deal . . . a shipping order.'

'Yes?' His smile too was wide as he waited.

'That bairn you saw coming out. He couldn't make up his mind how to spend a penny. He wanted jube-jubes, everlasting strips, and walnut toffee. He just couldn't make up his mind.'

'What eventually did he plunge for?'

'A ha'porth of walnut taffy and a ha'porth of jube-jubes, then he went for me because I put them in the same bag.'

Their heads back but their eyes holding, and still laughing, they turned away and walked as one, not touching, yet their bodies joined through the rhythmic swing of their limbs. But at the corner of Fowler Street, where it branched off Ocean Road he stopped and said, 'We'll get the tram here.'

She turned her head quickly towards him. They had done the journey on foot every night since they had first met. It was the only time they had together. She watched his eyes flick down towards her ankles as he said, 'You've done enough standing for one day.'

She had the desire to crouch down, covering her feet with her clothes, as she had done when a child, when they had played mothers and fathers in the back-yard and she had always wanted to be the baby which had occasioned her doubling herself in two. But now she looked down at her ankles and she hated them. They were the only part of her body that she hated; in her opinion they spoilt her. For she could not help but be aware that her body earned her the northern compliment of being 'a strapping lass'. In the morning her ankles were as thin as her wrists, but they always swelled if she stood on her feet for any length of time. With her build she supposed she should have tried for a sitting-down job. As it was, there wasn't even a stool behind the shop counter.

'They get like that with standing.' She didn't want him to think that they were always swollen.

'I know; Dan's swell too.'

Dan, she had been surprised to learn, worked in a grocer's shop in Jarrow. She imagined that he would have worked in the dock offices, seeing that David and his father did. She didn't know where the other son worked; she supposed it was in the dock offices too.

She said, 'But I don't mind walking, they don't pain.'

'Nevertheless we're taking the tram.' his voice sounded firm, nicely firm. 'Here it is; come on.' He took her arm and hurried her across the road.

As they were going up the gangway of the tram he spoke to a workman sitting in the back, saying, 'Hello there, Fred.'

'Hello there, Mr Hetherington.'

The distinction in the form of address pleased Sarah. She felt proud, as if she was bathing in the glorified reflection of a title; the workman had called him Mr Hetherington.

David's hand was on her arm now, pulling her gently back, and he ushered her into the seat in front of the man; then, twisting round, he asked him, 'Did you get it, Fred?'

'No-o.' The words was drawn out, it was a long deep thick syllable. 'There was about thirty waiting for it. It's no good, man; even a bit of influence isn't any good any more.'

'I'm sorry.'

'Oh, don't you worry, Mr Hetherington, man. It was good of you to put me on to it.'

David turned to give the conductor the fares, then he looked at Sarah and said under his breath, 'It's frightful, this business, trying to get a job.'

Sarah didn't catch all he said because of the rumble of the tram-car, but she gauged he was speaking sympathetically about the man. Then he turned again and, looking over his shoulder, said, 'Try Fullers, Fred, first thing in the morning. There might be something doing, you never know. You'll find our John somewhere in the yard.' His voice dropped. 'If you can get a word with him on the quiet, tell him I sent you.'

'Oh, thanks, Mr Hetherington. Thanks, I'll do that. I'll be up afore the lark. Man, this life gets you down.'

'Good luck, Fred.'

'Aye, good luck, that's what we want. And good luck to you, sir.' His eyes flicked to Sarah's profile and back to David, and the jerk of his head was an open compliment. He rose to his feet, jabbed at the bell pull, as the conductor was upstairs, and brought the tram to a stop.

David did not look at her as he now said, 'It gets me down, to see them standing about, rotting away. I remember him as a big man when I first started in the dock office. Now he seems to have shrunk to half his size. It has effect on all of them in the end: it shrivels up something inside of them, I suppose.'

Sarah glanced sharply at him, her face quite grave. She had heard all he had said and somehow she didn't like it; she didn't like to think of him associating with workmen, talking to them as man to man. He was from a different world, from the top end. He worked in an office. She wanted to keep him, at least in her mind, secluded, away from all contact with labourers, riveters, platemen, propmen, trimmers, pitmen, and the like.

And then he said, 'My brother's a foreman joiner, it's a small firm, but he'll set him on if it's at all possible.'

His brother a joiner? This news came in the form of a blow, even with the title foreman before it. She hadn't imagined one of the Hetheringtons working in the docks, actually working among the rough-and-tumble. Oh, she wasn't an upstart, she wasn't, and she didn't want to be an upstart, she didn't. Her mind reiterated the phrase as if she was answering in agitated defence some voice that was spitting scorn at her, and her environment-encumbered mind, being unable to put forward any argument to uphold her snobbishness, ended helplessly. Oh, I just want to get away from it all.

She was looking at her hands encased in thin cotton grey gloves–an outward sign of gentility. And from her hands her gaze dropped to David's feet. He was wearing nice brown shoes, very highly polished. He had worn black ones last night, but then he had been wearing a dark suit. Fancy having different shoes to go with different suits. She had seen him in two different suits besides grey flannels and a tweed coat.

'Have you dropped something?'

'No.' She jerked her head up to him. 'I . . . I was only looking at your shoes.' She hadn't meant to say any such thing.

'Oh . . . the polish?' He brought his lips tightly together and his eyes twinkled as he bounced his head before saying, 'My mother. She polishes all our shoes. You would think she had been trained in the army.'

She answered his smile, but weakly. It was as her mother was so fond of saying . . . you got everything in batches. And it was true in every aspect of life. He had talked to the workman as if he was on the same level as the man. Then he had told her his brother was a fitter, and now he had pricked the illusion of the exclusiveness of his family, by telling her his mother cleaned all their shoes. Why, even her father, as bad and as lazy as he was, cleaned his own shoes.

The tram was rumbling its way down Stanhope Road now, and as it passed the Catholic Church, the church that she had attended from when she first went to school, she bowed her head deeply in obeisance to the Sacred Heart that was ever present on the altar. It was an involuntary, almost an unconscious movement.

That the action had not been lost on David was given to her just after they alighted at the bottom of the dock bank and had crossed the road, beginning the walk through the arches towards East Jarrow.

'Are you a regular attendant at church?' he asked, smiling quietly.

'A regular attendant?' She repeated his phrase as if muttering a foreign language, and then said hastily, 'Yes, yes, I go every Sunday. We have to.'

They walked on in silence for a few minutes before he said, 'I used to go every Sunday too. To chapel, that was.' He smiled, rather apologetically, following this statement.

'Don't you go now?'

'No . . . no. I've never been since I was eighteen.'

There came a lightness to her mind. This could make things easier, oh, so much easier. 'Why?' she asked.

He moved his head slowly. 'I just couldn't stand it any more. The narrowness, the idea that God belonged to the Baptists and he would shoot you down sort of business if you didn't think along the particular lines they laid down appeared mad to me. Of course I didn't see it all in a flash, I had a long time of troubled thinking to go through. But now I think people are quite bats, almost insane, to believe that if there is a God he's there just for them and their particular way of thinking, while the rest of the community–and not only the community but the world–is damned if they don't come in with them.'

Her mind for a moment was devastated. If he thought that about the Baptists what did he think about the Catholics, for the Catholic religion was the only one true religion, and every Catholic knew this and maintained it. They might stay off mass, they might get drunk, the men might knock their wives about, but when they went to confession and their sins were absolved, they knew that they were receiving a privilege given to no one except a Catholic. . . . The devastation moved its dull sickening weight to allow for a ray of brightness. Didn't his attitude make things easier? The very fact that he was no longer a chapelite made the battle half won. But even as she thought this she said, 'But you believe in God?'

'I just don't know.' He shook his head. 'Sometimes I know positively that I don't, at others . . . well, I just don't know. I could cry for the greatness, the simplicity, the naïveness, in Jesus. I could wring his hand for his detestation of the holier than thou's. I could walk beside him as he smiles on the publicans and whores. But I can't see eye to eye with him when he tells me that the slow, slow force that urged a seed into a tree, then compressed it into fuel for firing for man it had not yet conceived–is my Father. But does it matter all that much? Does it matter much?' He was walking close to her now, his face, long and serious, turned towards her, and she did not look at him as she answered quite untruthfully, 'No, no.'

Again they were walking in silence, and now they were on a quiet stretch of the road bordered by high stone walls that ran between Simonside Bank and the Saw Mill, and it was at a spot where no one was in sight that he suddenly took hold of her arm and brought them both to a stop. His hand still holding her, his eyes roamed round her face, and in a way that she termed quaint he said, 'Hello, Sarah.' She had the desire to giggle; it was funny the way he said it, as if they had just met, and her lids began to blink as his eyes slowly picked out her features. It was as if he were detaching them from her face and examining them. When his eyes came to rest on hers again he said, 'What about it, Sarah?'

She didn't know how to answer. She wetted her lips, which were trembling, and, like the fool she told herself she was, she remained dumb, and he went on speaking. 'I've never spoken your name before. We've come up this road twenty-five times. I've kept count–and I've never called you by your name. And tonight is the first time I've touched you, when I helped you on to the bus. You know something, Sarah . . . you're very beautiful.'

'O . . . oh!' it was an inarticulate sound, like a groan.

His eyes flicked from her now up and down the road and then he said softly, 'May I kiss you?'

Still she could make no answering sound, but her whole body spoke for her and the next moment they were close and his lips were on hers, gently, softly, as if afraid of what they were about. It was over in an instant, and then silently again they were walking up the road, their arms rubbing every now and again. Her body felt light, there was no longer any heavy tight pressure around her ankles, she seemed to be afloat. They passed the open space of the Jarrow Slacks. The tide was high and there were children playing on the timbers. They passed the tram sheds. They passed Bogey Hill. And not until they walked up the bank that led to the plateau of the Fifteen Streets did he break the enchanted silence.

'Will you come to Newcastle with me tomorrow night, Sarah, to a show?'

'Ooh!' It was another groan, but a different kind of groan. Go to Newcastle and do a show. That would be living indeed; hitting the high spots. Oh, if only she could say yes. She had her pay in her pocket, eighteen and six; it was good money and she could have been dressed up to the eyes if she had been able to keep at least the eight and six, but no, she had to tip up fourteen shillings each and every week. then there was two shillings out of the remainder for her clothes club. That left half a crown and she wouldn't have had that if she hadn't stuck out for her bus fare each day. If only she could have managed a five-pound club she would have been able to rig herself out. Well, she would get a club. Her chest moved upwards on the decision. She would get a five-pound club and get herself a new coat and shoes. . . . But that wouldn't fix tomorrow. Her chest moved downwards again, and she answered, 'I'm sorry, I can't tomorrow.'

'Why? You said last week it was your early night off this Saturday . . . Sarah.' Again they were standing facing each other, 'There isn't somebody else?'

'Somebody else!' Her voice was high, right up in her head, and she laughed as she repeated, 'Somebody else?' Then, putting her head on one side, she dared joke. 'And where do you think he's been every night for the last three weeks?'

They laughed together, his head back in his characteristic style. And when he was looking at her again he asked, 'Then why won't you come?'

Now her eyes were steady and travelling over his face. It was a good face she was looking into, a kindly, honest face, and as she stared at it, it came to her that this man had no side. The knowledge was warming. She felt wise, even superior, being able to appraise his character. She knew it was because of his lack of side that he was to the workmen one of themselves. That was why he could talk about his mother cleaning their shoes and his brother being a fitter. He had no side. Her revealed knowledge of him supplied her with the courage to touch the front of her coat, lifting it outwards, and say, 'I haven't any clothes.'

'What!' His eyebrows moved up in genuine surprise. Then his long face seemed to crumple into agitated concern and the end of his nose twitched with a rabbit-like movement before he went on, 'Oh, my dear. Why, fancy you worrying about that! I've never even noticed what you've got on.' His features spread outwards again into an amused smile. 'Nobody will ever notice what you're wearing, Sarah. You carry your clothes like . . . well, like someone who doesn't have to have clothes to make her out. You know what I mean,' he finished swiftly.

Her lids were lowered. 'It's nice of you to put it like that, but a girl needs clothes. It does something to you to have nice clothes . . . new clothes.'

'I tell you people will never look at what you're . . . Oh, come on.' He swung her away now, holding on to her, laughing. 'You're coming to Newcastle tomorrow night and the dames in their rabbit skins won't be able to hold a candle to you.'

Her chin was on her chest, her large body was shaking with a gurgle of intense happy laughter. Then abruptly it stopped. She was looking ahead, speaking quietly. 'You know what?'

'No.'

'I think you're the nicest man in the world.'

'Oh, Sarah!' She was about to be pulled to a stop yet once again when she said hurriedly, 'Eeh, no! Look, we're nearing the streets. There's people about.'

She was blushing all over; she hadn't intended to say anything like that, about him being nice. It was a bit forward at this stage, she supposed, like pushing herself, throwing herself on to his neck. But he wouldn't take it like that, he wasn't that kind, and she had meant it–he was the nicest man in the world. And he was a man. He looked a man, not a lad, or a chap; he was a man. She wondered how old he was, he had never said. He appeared about twenty-five or twenty-six. She seemed to have no control over her tongue tonight, for she heard herself asking quite boldly, 'How old are you?'

'What do you think?' There was laughter in his voice again.

She cast her eyes slantwise towards him as if taking a measure of his age, and then she said, 'Twenty-six.'

'Twenty-six? His eyebrows went up. 'Three years out.'

'You're not twenty-nine?'

'No. Are you disappointed? I'm twenty-three.'

No, she wasn't disappointed, but he looked older. She was startled now as he said, 'And you're nineteen.'

'How do you know?'

'Oh, I know when you left school.'

'You do?'

He leant near her and whispered menacingly, 'I've had my eye on you for years, Sarah Bradley.'

Again she was flooded with a happy gurgling feeling, an unusual carefree feeling. Fancy now, he'd had his eye on her for years. . . . But if that was so, why hadn't he come forward sooner? Perhaps because she had never looked at him. Now and again she had passed him on the road but had always averted her gaze, knowing he was from the top end.

As they were passing Camelia Street two women came round the corner, and he said to them, 'Good evening, Mrs Talbot. Good evening, Mrs Francis.'

'Good evening, David,' one of them said, while both of them nodded, with their eyes tight on Sarah.

A coolness touched her warm body. What were they thinking? Oh, she knew what they were thinking: that he was mad. Well–she bridled inside–he wasn't the only one that was mad, she was mad in her own way too.

She stopped at their usual place of parting.

'Why don't you let me walk down with you?'

She looked straight into his eyes. 'Do I need to have to tell you?' It was a relief to be honest. Since she had told him about her clothes she felt she could tell him anything.

'Don't be silly.'

'I'm not being silly, but you know what it's like down there.'

'Well, I'll have to come sometime.'

The coolness was pressed from her body, she was warm again. She dropped her eyes from his.

'I'll call for you tomorrow . . . that's fixed.'

Her head was up. 'No, no. Please, oh please.' She was pleading now. 'Don't come to the door, I'll meet you here.'

He was about to say something when a group of boys who had come tearing down the roadway now raced round them on the pavement, and one of them, as he swung away from a pursuer, grabbed at Sarah's skirt. As she almost overbalanced David's hand went out to steady her, and he cried at the boy, 'Here! Here! Let up on that, will you?'

The boy scrambled back into the road again, but the one who had been doing the chasing stopped in the gutter and peered up at Sarah, and without a preliminary lead-up remarked, 'There's hell going on in your back-yard, Sarah. Yer da's taken the belt to Phyllis. She's been screaming blue murder and he's locked yer ma in the netty.'

Sarah's lips moved without any intention of uttering words. For a moment they were like the lips of a very old woman chewing the cud of unformulated thought; only Sarah's thoughts were not unformulated. In a matter of seconds the faint sweetness of life that she had tasted was smudged out with the picture conjured up by the boy's words. She could not bear to look at David but turned away and with a swing of her body sped from him and raced up the road. Then he was by her side running with her, and she was forced to stop. Gasping, she almost barked at him, 'No, no! Don't come, please. I don't want you to. Don't you see?'

He remained still, saying nothing, and once again she was running past the street corners. There were no men standing at the bottom of her own corner tonight, nor were they in the front street. The street was strangely bare, except for Mrs Young, the neighbour on the right-hand side. She was coming out of her house as Sarah hammered on the front door, and she said quietly, 'I doubt you'll not get in that way, hinny; he's been at it for the last half- hour. You know, something should be done with him. I would go to the Cruelty Inspector, I would an' all, if it wasn't for your ma. He's belted that poor lass within an inch of her life. Sam Ferris just got over the wall in time. He's mad, you know, vicious and mad when the fit takes him. I wouldn't care if he did it in drink, but for a man who's tee-total and acts the way he does there's somethin' radically wrong with him.'

'But what'd she done, Mrs Young?'

'Aw lass, it's none of my business, you'll know soon enough. But I'd go round the back if I was you.'

Running again, Sarah entered the back lane. There were groups gathered together all along its length, the men mostly by themselves, the women likewise. Outside of their back door were four men standing and a woman. The woman turned and said, 'Oh, it's you, Sarah.' And one man, taking hold of her arm, said, 'I wouldn't go in for a while if I was you, lass; let him cool down. Your mother's with him now.'

'He's not all to blame,' another man was addressing her, his head bouncing as if on wires. 'You've got to do something when it comes to that, you know.'

'What are you talking about, Mr Riley? Comes to what? What's happened? . . . Leave go of me.' She turned to the man who was holding her arm, and when he released her the other man said, 'Arabs, to put it in a nutshell.'

'Arabs?' Sarah was aware that she was showing all her teeth, that her lips had moved back from her gums as if the word itself smelt.

'Aye, that's what I said, lass. Young Phyllis's been with an Arab. Now your da's no angel, we all know that, but I would have done the same in his case.'

'No bloody fear you wouldn't; he's a maniac!'

As the woman spoke, Sarah pushed past the group and went through the open back door and up the yard. There was no sound coming from the kitchen, the whole place appeared quiet. She opened the door and stepped into the little square scullery and noted that the tin dish, which usually stood on the cracket behind the door and in which they did the washing up and used for everything that required the use of water, was lying against the wall end up, and that the floor surrounding it was covered with soapy suds. She opened the kitchen door and stepped quietly into the room. Her father was sitting at the corner of the table. His thin sour face looked yellow, and the red marks that always streaked the whites of his eyes seemed to have spread completely over them. They looked a bloodshot blur except for two dark jets pointed at her from his narrowed lids. His short wiry body and equally short legs were held taut; he looked as if he were jointless.

She glanced quickly from him towards her mother, who was standing with her hands gripping the mantelpiece, her head hanging forward, gazing down into the low fire in the bottom of the deep grate between the black-leaded oven and the pan hob. Her mother was a big woman, almost twice the size of her father. She had been bonnie too at one time, with a fine figure and a laughing face, but Sarah hadn't seen her really laugh for years. A thought that she had asked herself countless times she asked again now. Why did she do it . . . marry him? A man ten years younger than herself. Perhaps, as she had told herself before, it was just because he was ten years younger and she had been flattered.

Her words came out on a stammer as she asked, 'W-what's the matter?' She couldn't believe what they had said in the back lane, that Phyllis had been with an Arab. Her father would jump at anything that would give him the excuse to use his belt.

'So you've come in, have you?'

Ignoring his words, she said again, addressing herself pointedly to her mother, 'What's the matter?'

Pat Bradley was on his feet, glaring at her now from his bloodshot eyes. 'You're goin' to make on you know nowt about it, that's what you're going to do, aren't you? There's a pair of you. Oh, aye, there's a pair of you. What she doesn't know you'll put her up to. Not that she needs much coachin'.'

Her mother turned from the fireplace, speaking for the first time, her voice heavy with a dead kind of weariness. She said, 'Go on upstairs, Sarah, and see to Phyllis.'

'She'll go when I give the word.'

'Leave her alone.' Annie Bradley turned on her husband, towering over him, threatening now. 'You've done enough for one night, I've told you. You've gone too far this time. I told you what would happen if you lifted your hand to one of them again, didn't I?' She turned from the staring eyes of the man and said again to Sarah, 'Go on up to Phyllis.'

Sarah turned away slowly. She wanted to go up to Phyllis and yet she didn't want to go, at least not yet. She wanted to face up to this man too, to tell him what would happen if he dared raise his hand to her. She knew that she had been waiting for a long time for this opportunity and praying for the courage to use it, but she obeyed her mother. Moving between the square wooden table and the leather couch, she opened the staircase door and, groping for the rope balustrade, she pulled herself up the almost precipitous staircase. One step across the four-foot square of landing and she was in the bedroom, standing by the bed looking down at Phyllis.

Her sister was lying on her side. Her jumper lay in shreds across her back; there were two rents in her skirt from waistband to hem, and the seat of her bloomers were all black as if she had been dragged around the yard. Sarah brought her face closer to the torn blouse. There was no sign of blood, but, lifting the shreds of material apart, she saw a criss-cross of rising dark-blue weals.

'Oh, Phyllis!' She put her hands gently on her sister's shoulder, but Phyllis did not move or speak, and Sarah said, urgently now, 'Phyllis, sit up. Phyllis, do you hear me? Come on. . . . Phyllis.'

Phyllis moved slowly; then with an effort, as if her body was tied to the bed, she turned on to her hip. Her eyes were closed; her face, except for a dark weal that started at the top of her ear and came down across her cheek to the corner of her mouth, was a sickly white. But Sarah was not looking at her face, she was looking at her breasts, the small undeveloped breasts that Phyllis was for ever trying to enlarge. They were bare and criss-crossed with lines, similar to the one on her face.

'Oh, my God!' Sarah sat down on the edge of the bed and gently enfolded the slight body within her arms, rocking her like a mother with a child. And again she said, 'Oh, my God!' She stayed like this for some time, gently rocking and making sounds that expressed pain; and then she said, 'I've got some Pond's cream; I'll rub it on, Eh?'

Phyllis still did not speak, but when Sarah released her she moved her legs and sat on the edge of the bed. She looked as if all life had been whipped out of her, not a protest left. But this impression was shattered as Sarah went to apply, with gentle fingers, the first dab of cream on to the weal on her sister's cheek, for Phyllis's hand came up and gripped her wrist and in a whisper, cracked and hoarse but laden with a fierce strength, she said, 'One day I'm going to kill him, Sarah.'

Sarah did not reprimand her for the statement, but, sitting close to her, she whispered, 'Why did he do it?'

'He said I'd been with an Arab.' Phyllis's eyes were looking straight into Sarah's.

'But you hadn't, had you? Not an Arab.'

'He said I'd been WITH an Arab . . . not just speaking to one . . . WITH him.'

'But you've never even spoken to an Arab, have you?'

'Of course I have.' Phyllis's eyes did not drop away. 'They come into the café every day, you've got to speak to them.'

'Yes I know, but not outside?'

'Yes, I've spoken to one outside.'

'Oh, Phyllis!'

'Don't say "Oh, Phyllis!" like that. He's a decent enough fellow; in fact he's better than them around these doors, I can tell you that.'

'Oh, Phyllis . . . but . . . but an Arab. You know you'll get your name up. You'll be hounded out of the place. Remember Betty Fuller? You mightn't, but I do. She married one, and when she came back to see her mother, Mrs Baxter emptied the chamber on her out of the upstairs window. I was only about ten, but I remember. The whole neighbourhood was raised.'

'What do I care? Anyway, I hadn't BEEN WITH him and I've only spoken to him twice outside the shop. Once, when I was crossing the ferry, Mr Benito had sent me to North Shields with an order and he was on the ferry and we got talkin', and I can tell you'–her voice now hissed at Sarah with a strength born of anger–'I can tell you he spoke to me better than the lads around this quarter do. He talked just like any Geordie, but he had manners.'

Sarah did not say anything; she was bewildered, amazed. Phyllis talking to an Arab! Everybody knew what happened to girls who went with Arabs; they were ostracised, never again could they come back into the clan. Their families knew them no more–at least not around this quarter, they daren't. Most of the white girls who married Arabs lived in the Arab community in Costerfine Town and East Holborn way. Those who made a break and took houses in other parts of the town only stayed for a short time, the neighbours saw to that.

Even among their own kind Sarah knew that class distinction was strong. The top and the bottom of the Fifteen Streets knew their places; they didn't mix . . . or at least they hadn't until she had broken–or, more correctly, David Hetherington had broken–the hoodoo. But this distinction of class, which took its pattern from the even stronger sense of distinction that prevailed in Jarrow and Shields, even crippled as each town was with unemployment, was nothing to the distinction between a white girl of any class and an Arab.

At this point Phyllis's face screwed up with pain and she pressed her hands gently over her chest; then, turning her head slowly to Sarah, she said, 'You don't believe me?'

'Yes, yes, I do, Phyllis. But tell me, how did he'–she nodded towards the floor–'get to know?'

'It was this afternoon; it was only the second time I'd spoken to him outside, as I told you. I'd just finished and I was comin' up into the market when I thought I would like to bring me ma something home; you know she likes mussels, and so I went to that shop, you know that sells the mussels and the brown bread and beer, and he was inside. He was having a plate of mussels and he asked me if I'd have one. I said no thanks, I'd just come in to take some home, and when I came out he came with me and we walked along the street and up into the market. I couldn't say "You can't walk along of me", could I?' Her eyes, pain-filled yet rebellious, asked the question, and Sarah said, 'No. No, of course not. . . . And that was all?'

'Aye, that was all; atween me and God that was all. But you know something?' Phyllis brought her face to Sarah's. 'It won't be all from now on. You bet your bottom dollar it won't be all. He's done something to me the night, broken something. He's belted me afore but not like the night, and I swear I'll get me own back. An' I know how I'll do it an' all. By God! Aye, I'll get me own back!'

'Oh, Phyllis, you're feelin' bad, don't talk like that.'

'Aye, I'm feelin' bad, I feel awful.' Phyllis now moved her head in a desperate fashion. 'I feel I'm gona die, but I'll not die.' Her head wagged quicker now. 'No, I'll not die, I'll live just to spite him. Oh God.' She joined her hands tightly together. 'Oh God, I'll get out of here and quick. You'll see, you'll see. I'll be gone afore you; you'll see, our Sarah.' She was talking as if Sarah was opposing her. And Sarah said, 'All right, all right, don't excite yourself. Go and lie down; let me put some of the cream on your back.'

Like a child now, Phyllis lay on her stomach, and when Sarah had treated her back she turned over slowly and said, 'I feel bad, Sarah; oh, I do feel bad.'

'You lie still, I'll go and get you something.'

Sarah smiled compassionately down at the slight figure, and her fingers touched the white cheek, the one without the weal.

But when she closed the bedroom door behind her she stood leaning against the wall for a moment. There was in her an overpowering feeling of rage. Such was its strength, it filled her with apprehension, for she had the desire to rush down the stairs, pick up the shaving strap that hung below the little mirror to the side of the fireplace and lash his thin body with it until he cringed for mercy; and she knew she could do it, she knew she was big enough and tough enough to do just that. Then why didn't she? Perhaps because she had never raised her hand to anyone in her life. She tried to force herself to carry out the urge, but all she did was to say, 'Holy Mary, Mother of God.' Then, as she groped her way down to the room below, she ground out at herself, 'You're big and soft. Why don't you do it? If you did he'd never use that belt again.'

There was only her mother in the kitchen, but a signal from her indicated that her father was in the scullery. She said to her, 'I'm going to get the doctor.'

'What's that you say?' The small tousled head came round the scullery door.

'I said I'm going to get a doctor.'

'Be God y'are! You bring a doctor here and he'll be attendin' to two of you; I'll give you a taste of what I've given her. I intend to in any case, me lady. An' if I hadn't come across her the night with her chocolate-coloured fancy man you would have had it first. But it isn't too late.'

'I've told you I'm having no more of it.' Annie had moved towards her husband.

'You save your breath, woman. If you're satisfied to have a couple of tarts for daughters they're not staying under my roof.'

'Well, let them go!' Annie was shouting now.

'They'll go when I'm ready and not afore. But I'm not keeping a roof over a pair of bloody prostitutes.'

Sarah took two rapid steps and she stood leaning forward, gripping the edge of the table as she cried, 'Who you meanin'? You'd better be careful, because I' telling you, after what I've seen upstairs it won't take much for me to turn the tables. You've had it your own way too long, everybody scared to death you've had. Well, it's finished. If you as much as raise your hand to me or anybody else in this house I'll use your belt on you and flay you live I will! I will, I'm telling you!' Sarah was yelling now, almost screaming the words, and her mother was standing to the side of her, pulling her away from the table by the shoulders, as she tried to drown her voice by shouting, 'Give over! Give over! Do you hear me?'

As if she had been galloping down the road, Sarah leaned back, drawing in great gasps of air. And this was the only sound for some moments, then Pat Bradley, pushing the door back to its fullest extent, came into the room. He began talking, but his voice was low, even calm. 'Huh! We're talkin' big now, aren't we, since we're rubbed shoulders with the top end?'

'What about the top end?' Sarah was glaring at him over her mother's shoulders. She watched him saunter casually to the fireplace and stand with his back to it, the palms of his hands pressed against his small buttocks.

'Nothin''. Nothin' at all, if you know where you stand. But when a fellow from Camelia Street picks up someone from the midden end it's not with the idea of turnin' her into a respectable woman. Is it now? Plain thinkin', all round, is it now?'

'Well, you're wrong then.' She was barking at him again. 'You, with your sewer mind, you're wrong then, because I'm going to be married, see . . . SEE!'

She felt her mother's body start, and it acted like an injection on her own. She slumped against the table. My God! What had she said?

There was silence in the kitchen again, until the alarm clock on the mantelpiece gave a rheumaticky whirring sound as it passed the hour.

'Well, well, we're movin' fast, aren't we? What's all the hurry for, eh? You haven't known him a month.'

She was gasping again. He had known all the time? No, no, he couldn't have; he would have been at her before if he had. But somebody had told him.

'Has he put one in your oven already.'

Before she realised what she was doing she had grabbed the teapot from the table. It was only Anna's strength against hers that forced her arm downwards and the big brown china pot fell with a dull thud on to the mat, where the lid rolled off and the tea spewed outwards.

This unusual retaliation coming from his stepdaughter seemed to tell Pat

Bradley that he no longer had any domination over her–not physically, anyway. But he did not rely solely on physical force to gain his ends; he had other methods. And now he put them into action. Buttoning up his coat and pushing the knot of his muffler upwards towards his prominent Adam's apple, he hunched his shoulders and marched towards the scullery door, saying, 'Marriage is it, atween a Catholic and a chapelite? And him in the dock office and his father a boss there an' all. Don't make me laugh. Anyway, there's only one way to find out, and that's to go and ask him, isn't it?' He turned and faced them from the doorway, his thin features splitting into a wheedling grin. 'Will you kindly tell me your intentions towards me daughter, Mr Hetherington . . . sir?' He cut his mimicking short and ended, 'There's no time like the present for gettin' at the truth, is there, me girl?'

As the door banged behind him Sarah held her face tightly between her hands, repeating aloud, 'Oh no. Oh no. Oh no. Oh, my God, no!' Then she was gripping her mother's arms. 'He's going down there . . . stop him! Stop him, will you?'

'It's no use, lass. He may not go; when he gets outside he may think better of it. If I try an' stop him that's the one thing that'll send him pell-mell to their door.'

'Oh no, no no!' Sarah went to the mantelpiece and laid her brow against it. 'I want to die . . . I want to die. Oh God, I want to die.'

'Has he asked you?'

'No, no. I just said that.'

'A . . . aw, lass!'

'Yes, I know–aw, lass!'

'Well, you've cooked your own goose. You shouldn't have said a thing like that, not if the fellow hasn't said anything . . . he hasn't hinted?'

'No, no, not really. Even if he had this would have killed it.' She brought her head slowly up and then, turning and facing her mother, she said dully, 'You've got to get a doctor to Phyllis, she's bad.'

'I'm not gettin' the doctor, lass. If a doctor was to see her it would mean the polis.'

'Well, don't you think it's time somebody took a hand?'

'I don't want no polis here. Anyway, I haven't paid his club for months; I'd have to pay on the nail and I can't. I'll go up and see to her. I'll bathe it in her own water, it's good for bruises.'

Sarah's nose wrinkled in distaste as her lips moved apart. She felt weak, tired and weak; all the verve had gone out of her. What was the use? She looked round the darkening kitchen. Well, she had known it couldn't last, hadn't she? But the shame of it . . . the shame of it. What would he think of her? And his mother and the rest of them? If she could only die.

She stood looking down at her feet, her mind curiously blank now, numbed with pain. Then once again she opened the staircase door and pulled herself slowly up to the landing, and when she entered the bedroom the blind was down and her mother, by the light of a candle, was bathing Phyllis's back with a flannel rag that she was dipping into the chamber.

Chapter Three

The round-faced stark-looking clock on the wall said one minute to twelve. David eyed the man at the end of the long-counter-like desk as he began quietly to clear his allotted portion. First, he closed two notebooks and put them into a drawer; next, he cleaned an ordinary narrow-pointed pen. This he returned to the groove next to the inkwell. The pointer on the clock had moved thirty seconds. Slowly he closed the ledger, screwed up some dirty blotting-paper, and dropped it into a basket where his feet were under the desk. Then, standing up, he pulled down his coat, adjusted his tie, pushed the legs of the stool over the wastepaper basket, then moved towards the man who was still writing in a ledger. The clock struck twelve.

'Will it be all right if I have a word with my father, Mr Batty?'

The man raised his eyes upwards, not towards David, but towards the clock, and his tone was significant as he said, 'Oh, it's twelve.'

The colour deepened around David's cheekbones and his tones were apologetic as he answered, 'I've got a bit of business to do. . . .' His voice trailed off.

'Aw, well, go on along . . . He won't be finished yet.'

This remark, with a stress on the he and a raising of the eyebrows, was a reprimand on clock watching, and as David went along the corridor he wondered what his reaction would be to old Batty if he weren't afraid of losing his job. Very likely the same as it was now, because he hated disturbances, rows, unpleasantness. He wished at times he had a bit of their John in him.

As he neared the door at the end of the corridor it opened and two men, one about his own age, and one well into his fifties, came out. The younger one said, 'Going to the match this afternoon, David?'

'No, not this afternoon, I can't make it.'

When he entered the room that held three desks his father looked up from a ledger in which he was writing and said, 'Hello there. Are you off?'

'Yes.' David stood in front of the desk looking down at his father, and he rubbed his hand across his chin before saying, 'Will you tell Mother that I won't be in for a while, not until about two?'

'You know what she is about spoilt dinners?'

'I can't help it.'

Stanley Hetherington took off his glasses and peered at his son. His eye was twitching rapidly. 'You're going through with it then?' he said.

'Yes. Yes, of course.'

'There's no of course about it, you've been rushed into this. I don't believe you asked that girl to marry you and neither does your mother. In fact, she's positive that you didn't. Bradley's a little snake of a man. I've known him for years; he'll neither work nor want. I knew him when he was in the docks here, a mischief-making little rat if ever there was one, and a toady into the bargain. The only thing he doesn't do is drink, and that makes it worse. You can forgive a man what he does in drink. But there's a bad streak in Bradley. Now look.' He wagged his finger slowly at his son. 'Don't you be driven into anything. . . . Oh, I know.' He closed his eyes and flapped his hand before his face before going on, 'She's a fine looking lass, but if you marry her don't forget you're marrying her family, and is it fair . . . is it fair to your mother?'

'You know what my mother thinks, don't you? This is the lesser of two evils. Don't let's hoodwink ourselves about that.'

'Yes, yes, I suppose so.' The older man dropped his head; then, bringing it up sharply, he demanded, 'There's one thing you won't do, will you; you won't go over?'

'No, I won't go over. Yet I can't see, Father, why that should worry you.'

'My belief or lack of it has nothing to do with this present business really; all I know is, if they get you into the Catholic Church, under whatever pretext, you're finished, you won't be able to call your soul your own. No, my God, you won't.'

'But I'm not . . .'

'Yes, you say that now, but wait till the priests get at you. I've seen some of their tactics, I'm telling you. From all angles you've got to look at this thing with open eyes. She's from a bad home, she's a Catholic. Then there'll be the gossip; there's enough already, for, let's face it, David, to take up with somebody from the bottom end isn't the right thing to do. I can't see it working, although on the surface I must admit she's a nice enough lass, but she's got too many reins tied to her, holding her down to that end!'

'I'm going to marry her.'

Stanley closed his eyes; then, opening them again, he wiped his glasses and put the wires slowly behind his ears before saying, 'Well. there's nothing more to be said, is there?'

'I'm sorry, Father.'

'Look, don't be sorry for hurting me or even your mother, although she's taken this better than ever I imagined . . .' He jerked his head. 'But, as you said, I suppose she's doing it because she can't bear the thought of anything coming of the other business. But it's yourself you've got to think about in this case. Marriage is a long and difficult business no matter which way you take it. You're in love with somebody one minute and you hate their guts the next. . . . Aw, go on. Get yourself away of I'll say too much. Go on.'

David turned and went slowly from the room. He collected his raincoat and his trilby hat and went out of the main door of the dock office, and he stood for a moment on the pavement. The Saturday bustle was all around him; men coming out of the dock gates, those who were fortunate enough to be in work; men going into The Grapes, into The North-Eastern, into one after the other of the bars that lined the street opposite the dock wall and part of the bank that led to the station, the bank which always looked black, black with the figures of men standing against the railings or in groups on the pavement, waiting, waiting, and hoping, some cursing, some even praying to be set on, to get a few shifts in; even one a week would be something to help tide things over and take away the feeling of utter uselessness.

David never stepped on to this pavement but he imbibed this feeling that was sapping the moral fibre of the men of the docks, and of Jarrow, and of the whole Tyne, and many parts of the whole country. But today the feeling, although present, was subordinate. Covering his mind was the thought of Sarah and of getting to her and speaking to her, and comforting her.

He threaded his way across the road to where the tram was halted for its usual five-minute break, and as he went to mount the platform his arm was gripped and he was pulled round on to the road again.

'Where you off to?'

'Oh, I'm just going into Shields.'

'At this time? What about your dinner?'

David stepped back on to the pavement and looked at his brother in silence for a moment. John Hetherington was two inches shorter than David but he was almost twice his breadth. Like his uncles, his face was nearly square, his eyes wide and of a deep brown colour, with a brooding quality in them. His mouth too was wide, as were his nostrils. His nose could be said to mar his face; it forbade the term handsome to be applied to it but made place for the word attractive, or perhaps arresting, for people always gave this man a second look. He now brought his heavy fringed lids together as he said, 'You look under the weather. Feeling off-colour?'

'No, no, I'm all right. I'd better tell you what's happening though. . . .'

As David wetted his lips John said, 'Happening? Aye, well, go on then, but look slippy, I want to catch the tram.'

'I'm going to be married.'

'You're what?' The question was low, easy sounding and full of disbelief. Then his tone changing swiftly, he said under his breath, 'Aw, no! You're not going to be such a bloody soft-headed fool. Man, it'll be suicide. And you know how me mother . . .'

'It's not Eileen.'

'Not Eileen.' The eyes were screwed tighter. 'O . . . h! No?' He thrust his fist out and punched David in the shoulder. 'Not the missy from the bottom end that I've heard about? Why, man, you've only known her a couple of weeks.'

'I've known her longer than that, much longer.' 'Well, well!' John took a deep breath that pushed open his coat, 'Why all the hurry-burry?'

'Look, I've got to go. You'll hear all about it if you call in home . . . at least what happened last night.'

'Aye, aye, I suppose I will. But look here, Davie, don't let yourself be rushed into anything.' John's face was straight now, there was no lightness of any kind in the brown eyes. 'Look, lad, you be warned by me, and I'm speaking from experience. I've never said anything to you or anyone at home before, you know that, but I think you can put two and two together for yourself as far as my case is concerned. You make your bed and, by God, you have to lie on it! There's no truer saying than that in the whole world. Marriage can be hell, sheer bloody unadulterated hell. Oh, aye.' His voice was very low now. 'I know, I know there are wonderful marriages that go on for ten, twenty, thirty, forty, fifty years. You hear about them, in fact you see them; but, you know, you've got to ask yourself, have either of them done a day's thinking in their lives? Most of them are together because of the house and the sticks of furniture; they exist together, but they don't live. You know what most men are? A bread ticket. . . .'

'Look, John, I'll have to go now; I want to catch this tram.' He motioned to where the conductor was mounting the platform. 'I'll see you later.'

'All right, all right.'

They stared at each other a moment longer, then David swung round, leaped on to the platform, and took the stairs two at a time.

When their John started talking nobody could stop him; he could make an issue out of anything. He was always probing and dissecting the whys and wherefores of even the simplest things. . . . But he had just said that marriage was hell. It had been his own marriage he was speaking of sure enough. He hadn't realised that he had felt about it like that. He had known that he and May went at it, but then May had a mind too. There was a pair of them in that way. May argued against politics and strikes and the dole, because, like half the women in the town, she was worried that the next pay-day might be the last.

Sheer bloody unadulterated hell.

He could never imagine his own life like that, not if he married Sarah. . . . Sarah was no May. Yet what about his father saying you could love them one minute. . . . Oh, my God! He wished they would all hold their tongues and let him do what he knew he must do. . . .

Half an hour later he stood gazing into the shop window until there was only one customer left, then he went in.

Sarah saw him as she passed the woman her change and she started visibly, and the woman, turning and looking at David, smiled knowingly to herself.

He stood facing her in the valley between the hills of glass jars. He saw immediately that she looked ill; her eyes, although not red, were puffy, and her face, which he held always in his mind as representing a bright light, looked dull, even brow-beaten. The fact that this girl, this well set-up girl who was going to be his wife–yes, she was going to be his wife–should show an emotion that held the ingredients of intimidation, raised in him a rare and answering emotion of anger; and so his voice sounded stiff to her ears when he said, 'What time do you finish?'

She could not look at him. More than ever now she wanted to die, just to sink through the earth and be swallowed up. Humiliation had stripped her of any small pride she had clung to in desperation to keep herself afloat in the bog of her section of the Fifteen Streets.

'Do you get out for dinner? Sarah, speak to me.'

'One o'clock.' It was a mumble coming from the region of her chest.

He whispered now with gentle insistence: 'Sarah, Sarah, look at me.'

She did not raise her head but turned it aside, and her hands did something with a box, pulling out pieces of crinkled paper and rolling them up into balls.

'It's ten minutes to, I'll wait outside. . . .'

At three minutes to one Mrs Benton came downstairs from her flat above and Sarah, stacking empty boxes in the corner of the back room, said nervously, 'I've got a bit of shopping to do. I'll take me sandwiches and have them in the park the day, if you don't mind.'

Sarah felt Mrs Benton looking down at her. Mrs Benton didn't like serving in the shop. Sarah guessed that she thought it slightly beneath her, her being the owner, and it was rarely that she served the full hour. Very often at a quarter to two she would come into the back room and say, 'There's nothing doing; I'll just pop upstairs. Call me if the bell rings.' Sarah never called her. It was a good job and she wanted to keep it. Not many girls were getting eighteen and six a week and not soiling their hands. Of course a twelve-hour day was a long stretch, but she wasn't grumbling.

Without looking at her employer she knew she was annoyed. Mrs Benton was always annoyed when she didn't speak. Sarah grabbed up her coat and pulled her hat on without looking in the glass, and with a mumbled 'I won't be long' she went out of the side door and into the alley.

She had her head down and she did not stop in her walk as she saw David's legs coming towards her across the pavement but kept on moving down the road towards the sea and the park.

'Don't be like this.' He was walking close to her, his head bent down to hers.

'How should I be?' Her muttered words were not only a question but an answer in themselves.

They went on in silence until they entered the park and found a seat, which was easy, as the place was virtually empty at this time of the day. It was Sarah who spoke first, her head still down, looking at her fingers as they plucked at each other. She said, 'I'm sorry.'

'Sarah, look at me.' He had hold of her hands now, pulling at them with small tugging movements, trying to get her to raise her head, but she wouldn't, and he said, 'I've watched you for years going up and down the road, and I knew from the first night that I stood outside that shop that I was going to marry you. The only thing was I was too blooming shy to get it out, and you know you weren't very helpful.'

'Don't, don't.' The tears were raining down her face now from beneath her closed lids.

'Oh, Sarah, Sarah.' He pulled her forearm against his chest. 'Oh, my dear, my love. Oh, Sarah, dear, don't.' He took out his handkerchief and gently dried her face, all the while murmuring, 'Don't, Sarah, dear. Don't, Sarah, dear.'

'He . . . he said you were t-taken aback. He . . . he . . . said you got the surprise of . . . of your life.' She gasped out the words now as if wanting to be rid of the burden of them.

'Who did? You mean your father said that?'

'Yes.'

'Aye, well, I was taken aback. But just at the sight of him and the way he blurted it out. But I said straight off the bat that I wanted to marry you. I did, Sarah.' He shook her arm once. 'Believe me, I did.'

'Your mother was there an' all.'

'Yes, she was there. She came into the hall.'

Her head dropped lower as she put the question, 'Did he raise the house?'

'No.' David's voice was high. 'No. He was very quiet; in fact, I thought he was most reasonable. If I hadn't heard about him and was meeting him for the first time I would have thought he was a reasonable kind of man altogether. But things get about, you know, even as far as our end.'

'What did you say to him?' She had her head up now and was blinking away the still running tears.

'Well, when I opened the door . . . well, you see it was all so sudden. He said "What's this I hear about you going to marry my daughter?" And quite honestly I couldn't say anything for the moment.' He gripped her hands tightly and once again brought them to his chest. 'He was putting into words something that's never been out of my mind since I met you, but at that moment it was such a surprise I couldn't say anything. And then he said, "Have you asked her?" It was then I sensed there was something wrong–I linked it up with what the boy said he was doing to your sister–so I said to him, "Will you come in?" And when he stood in the hall he repeated, "I asked you a question," and to that I said, "Yes . . . yes, I've asked her to marry me." It was then my mother joined us. He was very civil to her, very polite. He said, "I've just come round because my girl said that your son here asked her to marry him. . . ."'

'And your mother didn't say anything, did she?' Sarah licked the tears from her lips. 'She was so flabbergasted that she didn't say anything, for she knew if you had asked me you would have told her.'

'But listen, listen to me. I told her that I had asked you and that I was going to tell her . . . but later. I told her I had every intention of telling her and then bringing you round this evening for tea.'

'But she didn't believe you?'

'Why do you keep saying that?'

'Oh'–she screwed her body away from him, trying to pull her hands loose from his grip–'I had it all word for word, nothing left out.' She shook her head slowly now and the scene of last night returned to her with all its ignominy; it returned for its hundredth showing in the few hours since it had been enacted. She had been lying in bed with Phyllis when the door had been kicked open and he stood on the threshold yelling into the darkness. 'Surprised to bloody death he was and frightened out of his bloody skin, an' all. Oh yes, yes, he said, he had asked you. . . . But he only said that because . . . because why? Because he knew I'd tell his mother what he'd bloody well been up to, an' I was right. No bloke like him is gonna be taken for a ride up the aisle by the likes of you unless he's gone in by the back door, you big-bellied sod, you!'

The street had been quiet; there was no sound coming from the Youngs' house or from the Ratcliffes', for they were all listening and would be able to hear without any straining of their ears, as would the neighbours down the road. And those who had missed anything would be given it in detail, she knew, before the sun shone without shadow tomorrow.

Eternities of suffering later, when the flesh of her body seemed to have melted with shame and her large frame was twisted with the force of the humiliation that had beaten upon her, she heard the distant chimes of a clock, somewhere in the town, striking three. It was then that Phyllis, her own pain forgotten, her arms about her tightly, whispered. 'Don't let him take the gumption out of you. That's what he's after, to break your spirit, to have you crawl. You know why he's goin' for you, don't you? It's because he wants you himself.'

Her crumpled body had shuddered and straightened itself as if by an electric shock. But Phyllis still held her and went on whispering, fiercely, 'Me ma knows. What you want to do is pack up an' get away. Don't think of how me ma'll manage, he'll have to stump up if there's nobody here. . . . You know something? He had three pounds in the lining of his waistcoat yesterda' mornin'. He must have forgotten it, his waistcoat I mean, and left it on the chair downstairs. I went through the pockets when I was down early, and felt this paper in the lining. He's been running for a bookie this week. I'd like to bet he's got money tucked away somewhere. . . . You stop worryin' about me ma and get yourself out of this, our Sarah, because I'm going to. . . .'

'Sarah, look at me!'

She looked at him, into the eyes that were soft and glowing with love and kindliness, and her heart was sick at what she was losing.

'I love you, Sarah; I love you so much I just can't find words or ways or means of telling you. . . . Now answer me one thing. If when we were going home last night I had asked you to marry me what would you have said? Truthfully, Sarah, what would you have said?'

'I'd . . . I'd have said yes.'

'Because you love me?'

'Yes.'

'Oh, Sarah, that's wonderful, wonderful. You know I just can't understand what you see in me. I've no push, no go.' He smiled. 'If you had fallen for someone like our John it would have been understandable, but me! I'll never be anything. I'm quite content to stay in my little rut until I die . . . that is as long as I have you.'

He was changing the atmosphere, subtly threading it with the description of his own character, making it slightly jocular, ordinary; and under this influence her bones seemed to straighten and the flesh on them fill out again. her whole being was becoming saturated in enervating relief. She wanted to slump forward on to him, lay her head on his shoulder and rest. And then she thought of his mother. She wouldn't be able to face his mother; his father and his uncle, yes, but not his mother. She said now with candour borne of dead hope, 'There's your mother . . . I couldn't face your mother, it's no use.'

'My mother!' He screwed up his face until it looked comical. 'Why, she's the one who understands most. Look, Sarah.' He had her by the shoulders now. 'My mother wants me to marry you; there's a particular reason why she wants me to marry you. I won't tell you it now, but she wants it, in spite of your father.'

'My stepfather.' It was the only thing left she had to be proud of, that there was no blood relation between her and Pat Bradley.

'Your stepfather. I'm glad he's your stepfather. Well, in spite of him and his barging in last night . . . although I maintain he came in quietly and left quietly; but in spite of all this she still wants me to marry you. You know, I think, she's taken to you. She doesn't take to many people. She's what you would term a close woman, reticent, difficult, but she's been a very good mother, and, as I said, she's taken to you. I know her so well, better than my brother; better, I think, than my father, and I can vouch for what I say. Now. . . .' He brought his hands from her shoulders to her cheeks, and, holding them, raised her face towards him. 'We were going to Newcastle tonight, remember? But instead we'll go home. I've told her I'm bringing you, and she's expecting you. I'll meet you when you're finished and we'll go straight there.'

'Oh, David . . . David!' She was leaning against him, her head in his neck, shaking both their bodies with the convulsion of her weeping.

Then once again he was drying her face–under her eyes, round her nose, round her lips. His eyes remained on her lips, fixed as if he had become lost in a dream. Then with a suddenness his hands were clamped to her ears, and when he pulled her face towards his her hat fell backwards on to the grass. And then they were kissing. In the open on a bench in the Marine Park and on a Saturday dinner-time, they were kissing. It was enough to get your name up. You could cry on a bench but not kiss. Something of this ran through her mind. But what did it matter? What odds? What odds? Nothing, nothing in the world mattered at this moment except this man, this man David who wanted her.

Chapter Four

His mother opened the door to them. 'Well, you've got here,' she said. She was smiling faintly.

David pressed Sarah before him up the two steps and into the hall. 'Give me your coat,' he said.

His mother opened the sitting-room door now. She put her head inside; then, withdrawing it, she looked at Sarah. 'There's a fire on; it gets chilly at nights, especially when it's drizzling.'

'Have we kept you waiting?' David was straightening his tie.

'No, no, there're all in the living-room. Tea isn't quite ready yet. Go on in.' She held out her hand and touched Sarah's arm with the tips of her fingers, halting her as she crossed the threshold into the room and adding quietly, 'There'll be plenty of time to talk later.'

When she turned away and walked across the small hall and into the room, from where came a buzz of voices, and the high gleeful shriek of a young child, Sarah, standing stock still, gazed after her. She felt unnerved; she didn't know if it was with relief because the talking had been put off, or because it was to come.

'Don't look so mesmerised.' David was pulling her into the room and towards the couch.

'Oh! If I get over the night I'll live to be a hundred.' It was her first attempt at jocularity, and he pulled her swiftly into his arms and held her tightly for a second. Then, releasing her as quickly, he whispered, 'They'll all be in in a minute.' And as if working along the lines that attack was the best form of defence, he said, 'Would you like to come into the living-room now and get it over with?'

'No, no.' Her tone was low and rapid. 'Give me a breather.'

'Do you mind if I leave you for a minute, then? I . . .'

He seemed hesitant to tell her why he had to leave her. It could be that he had to go to some place like the lavatory, she thought, then dismissed the idea. No, he wanted to have a word with them, or likely with his mother.

'Go on.' She pushed him gently, playfully. 'I've only got to die once.'

He laughed at this. His head back, in spite of his evident nervousness, he laughed. Then, clasping the palms of his hands for a second over her ears, an action of endearment she was to find that had its drawback, as it dimmed her hearing, he whispered, 'We're going to have some times together, Sarah, good times; you were made to laugh, you know.'

He left her on this, and the sound rushed back into her ears again. She sat down on the edge of the couch thinking, I was made to laugh. Funny that; there's been so little laughter in me life. But he's right, I love a good laugh. Fancy him knowing that. She looked round the room. To her eyes it was a beautiful room, beautiful in its arrangement, in its prismatic brightness, and the absence of litter of any kind; not a paper or a book to be seen, nor clothes lying about, not a cap or a coat dropped carelessly. No packets of Woodbines on the mantelpiece. She looked at the gleaming white-painted wooden frame that surrounded the pale-blue tiles. She couldn't see anyone daring to lean a finger on that edifice, except to dust the marble clock and the two pink vases with the pictures on the front of ladies in old-fashioned dress. She turned her head and looked over the back of the couch to the piano. It wasn't cluttered either; it held only two photographs, one at each end. They were both of boys. One of them was David, when about six. His eyes hadn't changed, nor yet his smile. She sat gazing at it with a warmth of feeling that was yet threaded with awe. She was going to marry that boy. She was really going to marry that boy.

Her head jerked away as the door opened and she looked at the man standing just within the room, and he looked at her. He still held the door in his hand, and after a second, when he went to close it, he did so without taking his eyes from her. Then he shook his head as he exclaimed, 'Good Lord! Fancy seeing you.'

Sarah had sidled to her feet. She couldn't remember seeing this man before. She guessed this was John, the brother. But he didn't look at all like David. Just as she was an oversize of a girl, he was certainly an outsize of a man.

'Well, well.' He was standing in front of her, holding out his hand now. 'I'm John, your future brother-in-law.'

His hand was hard, his grip was tight. 'I've seen you going up and down the road for years, but I didn't know it was you our David was after.' He jerked his head to the side. 'Well, I must say he knows when he's on a good thing.'

Sarah hadn't spoken. She was standing smiling weakly, as she thought. It's hard to believe they're brothers. The only thing she recognised as similar in both of them was their voices. Yet even these were different because this man used his words in a way that made his voice seem ordinary, in fact even like the voices of the people from her own end. Although he wasn't broad Geordie there was no refinement in his speech as there was in David's.

He dropped her hand and pointed to the couch and said, 'Sit down and don't look so worried.' The last words brought his chin out and his head and shoulders towards her. He was speaking like a kindly conspirator. 'In a few weeks you'll wonder you ever felt nervous and you'll kick yourself.' He stood looking down at her, his hands on his hips, and he brought the side of his face into his hunched shoulder, which action laid stress on the enquiry, 'You can talk; you're not deaf and dumb, are you?'

'Yes. . . . No.' Now they were laughing.

'I . . . I said to David if I get over the night I'll live to be a hundred.'

He did not answer for some seconds; his broad face took on an expression that puzzled her in its implication of aggressiveness until his words explained it when, bending down to her, his face not more than six inches from hers, he said tersely, 'Look, you set out with the idea that you're not going to be frightened of anybody, in this house or anywhere else. If you think you're going to be frightened you'll be frightened. If you let people put the wind up you you've had it, you're finished.'

'Yes, yes, you're right there.' What else could she say. She could feel the heat from his face. She looked at his mouth. It was well shaped, broad, but not kind like David's. He was better looking in all ways than David, handsome she would say, but he wasn't like David. She was feeling disturbed, nervous under the pressure of his eyes, when the door opened once again and Dan entered.

'Oh, hello there.' He looked past John towards Sarah, and Sarah took in a deep breath and smiled. There came a slackening of her muscles as if she had been relieved from an ordeal and answered, 'Hello.'

'Oh, of course, you two have met before.' John cast his glance between Dan and Sarah, and Dan, tossing his head and winking, said, 'Yes, I've got one up on you there, lad.'

'Mind, I'm going to tell you something.' John was standing on the hearthrug, his back to the fire, his hands rubbing his buttocks, his body bent forward towards her again. 'You look out for him there.' He motioned towards Dan with a sideways tilt of his eyebrows. 'A proper Casanova we've got in this family. It's a fact. He'll be after your blood'

'Enough of that, John, enough of that.'

Sarah saw that Dan's face was slightly flushed and he looked put out, not really annoyed but just a little put out; she could almost have said a little hurt.

'You know he's my uncle?' John's arm went out and gripped Dan around the shoulders and they stood pressed together looking at Sarah.

'He doesn't look old enough to be your uncle.' Sarah looked at Dan as she spoke, and Dan said. 'I don't feel old enough to be their uncle. It's one of these odd situations, I was born late. . . .'

'You said it, chum, you said it.' John rocked them backwards and forwards for a moment until Dan put in laughingly, 'Stop acting the goat, Sarah'll think you're barmy. She knows what I mean.' He nodded towards her. 'I was just a baby when Mary, their mother'–he indicated John–'was married. We were all brought up together, so to speak. Mind you'–his voice dropped to a confidential whisper–'they wouldn't have been my choice of relatives; but there, I didn't have any say in the matter. . . . Davie's all right, but this one. . . .' He tried to pull away from John, and now John's two arms were around him crushing him to his chest, and Dan was crying, 'Leave over, man. Look, you don't want to start a rough-and-tumble. You'll have your mother on us like a ton of bricks; leave o-ver.' With a sudden twisting jerk he freed himself and the two men stood apart, laughing at each other.

'See what I mean?' Dan sat down beside Sarah on the couch. 'Anyone would think by the look of him and the size of him he was grown-up, mature-like, but not him, he's still in the puppy stage.'

'Puppy-stage! That's right, that's right.' John was standing on the hearthrug again, his hands once more behind his back and his expression and tone reverted with a suddenness to what it had been before Dan had entered the room. 'That's funny, that is. Not grown-up! When I'm the only one among the lot of you that sees straight. Davie with his head in the clouds . . . no offence meant, it's a compliment.' His tone was slow and flat, and he accompanied each word with a movement of his head towards Sarah, then went on, 'Father with the spunk beaten out of him.' He looked towards the door, then his eyes moved towards Dan, 'And you not caring a damn except . . .' He stopped abruptly and, screwing up his eyes, asked loudly, 'Why did you set me off?'

'Aw! You don't need much setting off; and Sarah might as well know the worst from the beginning. What do you say, Sarah?'

Sarah turned and looked at the man sitting beside her, and before she answered she thought. This one could be David's brother, there's a kindliness about him. With sudden daring gaiety she replied, in broad Geordie dialect, 'Aa've summed him up, shockin' lot. He'd never get past the dock polis, him.'

This retort was daring in the extreme. She was joking as if with her equals, her equals down at the bottom end. Yet she had never thought of the inhabitants of the bottom end as her equals, and had rarely, if ever, joked with any of the neighbours and never with the men. But if she had done so her remark would have been similar to the one she had just made. And now she was amazed, and a little apprehensive at the reaction to it, for the two men, their heads back–this seemed to be a characteristic of the Hetherington family, to laugh with their heads back–were now filling the room with their laughter, and the sound seemed out of place in the atmosphere of gentility.

'Well, well! And what's all the noise about?' Mary Hetherington came into the room, followed by David and a thin dark young woman with a child in her arms.

'You know what? You've picked a cheeky monkey.' John's arm was out, the finger extended, stabbing in the direction of David, and David's face, with a bright relieved smile, said, not without pride, 'I have?'

'Yes.'

'Well, that's good.' He went and took up his place beside the couch, putting his hand on Sarah's shoulder. Sarah was looking at Mrs Hetherington now; fear and nervousness had leapt back into her system again. She hadn't liked it, coming into the room and finding them all laughing. Perhaps she thought she was being forward. But she was speaking to her now, stiffly.

'This is May, John's wife.' She nodded towards her son. 'And this is their child Paul.' She took the child's hand from its mother's shoulder as she spoke. The introduction had a formal sound and no one moved in the room while it was being made. Then Sarah attempted to rise to her feet, but Dan, heaving himself upwards, said, 'No, no, sit where you are; you come and sit here, May.'

May sat down, the child still in her arms. Neither she nor Sarah had spoken to acknowledge the introduction. The child was between their faces now, gurgling and bouncing, and as Sarah lifted a finger to touch it its plump hands shot out, and with startling suddenness and the power and demoniac tenacity, which in all infants is a contradiction to their helplessness, its fingers entwined themselves in Sarah's hair, dragging and pulling her sideways, bearing her head towards its mother's shoulder.

Although the diversion was painful, Sarah was thankful for it. The attention was on the child and amid cries of, 'Oh, you naughty boy, let go. Naughty Paul. Leave go, you rascal. Would you believe it, isn't he a little beggar?' she was eventually released.

Sarah laughed as she combed the thick waves of her long chestnut hair back into the bun with her fingers. 'It's all right; my sister used to do that. My scalp is tough.'

The baby was now in it's father's arms, kicking its toes into his flat and seemingly unfeeling stomach, and as Sarah looked at him she became aware, as if she had not noticed it at the time, that they were his fingers which had prised the child's hands from her head.

'Well, now, that rumpus is over and we can have tea.' Mary Hetherington threaded her way through her family towards the door, adding as she went into the hall, 'Come on, Father is waiting.'

One after the other they followed her, David coming last, his hand extended, cupping Sarah's elbow. Before her went May, and with the perspicacity that lends itself to intuitiveness Sarah thought, I'm not going to like her, she's sour.

And when they were all seated round the tea-table and she found herself right opposite to May, she said to herself, She looks uppish and discontented. Her eyes moved to John sitting to the right of his wife, the child on his knee, and she thought, What's she got to be discontented about? He seems a nice enough fellow, a bit noisy. And then she's got the child.

It was strange, and Sarah was aware of this, that all during tea her thoughts were on the slight, dark thin girl opposite to her. Her mind was occupied so much with this new acquaintance that for the time being she forgot about Mrs Hetherington; and although she did not fail to notice that Mr Hetherington was very quiet and had hardly spoken to her, she did not worry about it. Perhaps he was always quiet. It was not until they were rising from the table to return once more to the sitting-room that it came to her that John's wife, as she thought of her rather than as May, had not opened her mouth at all during the meal; in fact she hadn't heard her speak at all. And yet nobody had seemed to notice it; nobody had remarked on her silence or pulled her leg about it.

'Let's have a sing-song. Come on, the occasion calls for it.' They were in transit between the living-room and the sitting-room when John, in a loud voice, made this announcement, but his mother's voice came quickly in answer, saying, 'Don't be so rowdy, John.'

'Look . . . my God, it's an occasion. Davie's going to be married. . . . Oh, all right. I'm sorry.'

As John came into the sitting-room, his head lowered, he said in an aside to David, 'I wish she'd put a notice up, No blasphemy, no swearing, then I'd remember.'

David turned to his brother, punching him gently in the back as he said, 'Come on, big fellow, forget about it. She's a bit up. . . .' He pulled himself up abruptly, but not abruptly enough. Sarah knew he was going to say she's a bit upset.

She was again seated on the couch, and once more she was alone with the men. There were present now not only the brother and the uncle but Mr Hetherington. He was sitting to the side of her in an armchair, his hands resting idly on his knees. It was perhaps the idleness conveyed by his motionless hands that made her realise that not one of the men were smoking. That was strange, nearly all men smoked.

A rolling chord of notes brought her body twisting round towards the piano. She was looking at David's back; it was David who was playing, her

David. The thought added dimension to her body.

'Oh, not Chopin, not tonight. Let's have something we can sing to. . . . You don't want Chopin, do you, Sarah?' John's big head was turned towards her, then away again in a second before she would have been called upon to stammer her ignorance of Chopin.

'"Blue Heaven." Come on, let's have "Blue Heaven". Where's the music? That's appropriate: "Happy in my Blue Heaven".' John was singing now in a deep resounding bass voice. 'Here it is, and "All Alone on the Telephone", and "Yacky-hoo-lah, Hicky-doo-lah".'

Sarah wanted to get up and go to the piano. She knew the songs and she could sing them too. She was told she had a decent voice–she would have gone in for a singing competition before this if it hadn't been for her father. But she had better be careful. Yes, she had better be careful. She'd better not sing too loud, or push herself. At this point she thought, I should have asked her if she wanted any help with the washing-up. She leant forwards towards Mr Hetherington and said under the cover of David's playing and John's voice, 'Do you think Mrs Hetherington needs any help with the washing-up?'

For the first time Mr Hetherington smiled at her. He smiled slowly, a considered smile, as if it was the outcome of thought and a decision taken, and he brought his hands from his knees and joined them together as he leant towards her, saying, 'Mrs Hetherington can cope. And don't worry, don't be nervous any more. What has to be will be. I hope you'll be happy and make him happy.'

It was the first time that anyone had made any direct reference to her marrying David. It was in everybody's mind, but they were all doing different things, it would seem, so as not to have to mention it. She looked at the older man, his eye twitching every few seconds, and she had an almost uncontrollable urge to clasp his hands and bring them to her face and cry over them and pour out her thanks to him. She felt gratitude towards him equal to that she had for David. But all she could say was, 'Thank you, thank you, Mr Hetherington.' And then, her voice trembling and her eyes lowered, she finished, 'I'm very grateful.'

'Aw, lass.' He shook his head and his tone conveyed the same meaning as John's had done; it was telling her not to humble herself, not to crawl.

'Come on, up you get.' John's arms came over the couch under her oxters, pushing her upwards. Then, grabbing her hand, he pulled her round towards the piano stool and David, saying, 'Stand yourself there, next to your intended, and raise your voice in joyful song, something soft and harmonious. Come on: "Yacky-hoo-lah, Hicky-doo-lah".'

'Stop your clowning.' It was Dan speaking across David now. 'Go and fetch May in.'

'Aw, May knows the way. And, anyway, we're not speaking. . . . There you are, there you are . . .' John was wagging his finger at Sarah. 'You're being let in on family secrets already: my wife and I are not speaking.'

The music stopped. David's hands became still on the keys, and, turning his head slowly upwards, he looked at his brother and said quietly, 'Stop it,

John, and put the ego under lock and key for tonight, eh?'

Sarah watched the brothers. They were looking at each other, their faces strained, slightly tense. Put the ego under lock and key. What did David mean? What was an ego? Something to do with the way John was carrying on, but what was it? She must get a dictionary; she had always promised herself a dictionary.

'Sorry, let's sing. There . . . he's strapped down.' John's hands made the motion of tying a knot across his chest.

David touched the keys again and then they were singing. John and Dan and even Mr Hetherington. Mr Hetherington was singing with an odd-looking smile on his face as if he were laughing at himself. But Sarah found she could not join her voice to theirs; they were singing 'Blue Heaven' and she was finding it embarrassing.

Just Molly and me and baby makes three,
We're happy in my Blue Heaven.

She had a feeling almost of horror in case John should change the Molly to Sarah, but John was apparently behaving himself. The chorus finished, David's fingers changed the key almost imperceptibly into the ballad 'Parted', and at this her eyes brightened. Oh, she knew 'Parted'–she loved 'Parted'.

Dearest, the night is passing,
Endeth the dream divine,
You must go back to your life,
I must go back to mine.

She forgot her embarrassment. In a moment she was singing softly, as if to herself, and then, when David turned his glance towards her, nodding in approbation and encouragement, she let her voice rise. But not to its full extent; even so, it impressed them. She felt herself glow because of this, her one accomplishment: they liked her voice. She saw Dan signalling to John to stop, but John was already stopping, and when there was only her voice carrying the song she looked from one to the other and her words faltered and died away.

'I can't sing by my . . .'

'Come on, come on,' said John. 'Start again, David. You're going to sing that right through. You've got a voice, my girl.'

'Come on, Sarah, let's hear it right through from the beginning.' David's voice was quiet, even firm. It steadied her. He seemed, when sitting at the piano, masterful, in command as it were. Perhaps that's how he felt; he played beautifully, lovely.

She stood ready to sing, telling herself not to let her voice go . . . to do it gently.

Dearest, the night is passing,
Endeth the dream divine.

She was singing with only part of her mind, analysing the words with the other. She hoped . . . oh, she prayed that her dream divine would never end.

You must go back to your life,
I must go back to mine.

David and she would have no life separate from each other. She would love him until she died, she couldn't help it; even if only out of gratitude she would love him until she died. But she did not feel only grateful to him for wanting her; oh no, she loved him, she loved him because he was David, somebody different.

Back to the joyless duties,
Back to the ceaseless cares;
Living and loving parted,
All through the empty years.
How can I live without you,
How can I let you go,
I whom you love so well, dear.
You whom I worship so . . .
You whom I worship so.

There was a short silence when she finished, and it was Mr Hetherington who broke it. He said, 'Very nice, very nice. You could do things with that voice, you know.'

David was looking at her, not speaking, his eyes tender and proud.

And Dan was looking at her. He was smiling with his head on one side, and he said, 'I would like to hear you let rip.'

But John was not looking at her, nor did he say anything. He was at the fireplace carefully lifting a piece of coal from the scuttle, carefully because one hand was poised underneath the coal in case it fell from the tongs. Sarah had not noticed him moving from the piano, but she did notice that he made no comment on her singing. Well, he can't have thought much of it, she said to herself; then added, he's a funny fellow, I can't really make him out.

'Play "Fur Elise".' Dan was sorting some music on a table by the side of the piano as he spoke, and then the front-door bell rang. 'Aw, who's this now?' His voice held a touch of impatience. It gave Sarah the impression that he was enjoying the present gathering and did not want it extended in any way.

She turned her head towards John. He was standing to the side of the bow window. It was the note of apprehension in his voice that brought her attention to him. He was squinting through the narrow aperture of the curtains looking into the street, and at the same time he was speaking directly to David. 'It's Eileen,' he said, 'and . . . and her mother.' Now his head turned quickly about and he looked over his shoulder to where David had moved from the piano stool to face him.

'Well, what about it? Let them come in, they've got to some time.'

'Not tonight, man.' Now all of them were looking at Dan. His head was still bent over the music. 'Here it is,' he went on as he lifted up a dog-eared doubled sheet and handed it to David, nodding at him. 'Go on, play.'

Whatever all this was about Sarah couldn't understand, but what impinged itself on her notice was that Mr Hetherington was sitting quietly in his chair and he had made no remark whatever. It could have been that he was stone-deaf.

David was now holding the music, and after rolling it backwards he placed it on the stand, manoeuvring it to keep it upright; and while he was doing this there was a movement in the passage and the front door was opened. There filtered into the room an exchange of voices, and then the room door was opened.

Instantly Sarah saw that all the men were disturbed, even Mr Hetherington, for he was now on his feet.

Standing to one side, with the door in her hand, was May, and past her came a short plump woman with fair hair. She was well dressed; as Sarah explained to herself, well put-on. Behind her came a tall girl. She was also fair and she had the most beautiful face that Sarah had ever seen, and it wasn't the first time that she had seen it. She had on occasions seen this girl when coming round the Stanhope Road way, and she had thought, By! She's beautiful, that girl. Her skin was the colour of thick cream and her eyes were the deepest blue of any eyes that Sarah had looked at. Her features were perfect, too perfect. She looked–and Sarah was again colloquially explaining this to herself–the girl looked–too good to be true.

The two visitors were staring at Sarah, but before any remark could be made there appeared behind the girl the tall dominating figure of Mary Hetherington. Her face was flushed, her eyes bright, and her voice had lost the coolness that Sarah associated with this woman's whole demeanour. The tone was now brittle, nervous. She began talking straight away. 'Why, Ellen, I didn't expect you. . . . And you, Eileen, how are you?'

'Oh, I'm very well, Auntie.'

'Well now, well now, you must come into the living-room and have a cup of tea. I was just making a fresh one. I never manage to get a decent cup when I'm looking after this hoard. Oh, by the way, this is Sarah. Sarah Bradley.' Mary Hetherington paused here, took a deep breath, then brought out in slow meaningful tones, 'She's David's young lady; they've become engaged today.'

Sarah was looking at the girl, and the girl was looking at David, and David was now looking at 'Fur Elise'.

'Oo . . . oh!' The sound seemed to be acting in reverse, as if it had started outside the elder woman and was sinking down into the depths of her stomach, for she held her arm across her waist as if in pain. She was looking at Sarah now with a look that made Sarah want to exclaim, Don't take it like that. The woman looked hurt, shocked, and angry, but most of all she looked hurt. Sarah watched her take hold of her daughter's arm and push her past Mrs Hetherington into the passage, and as May went to follow them and close the door, Mr Hetherington, his eye twitching at twice its usual rate, went hastily across the room, and, pulling the almost closed door out of May's grasp, went into the hall, from where the visitor's voice came clearly into the room, saying in broken tones, 'You're cruel, Mary, cruel. You've had everything and you're still not satisfied. You're cruel, cruel.'

As the door closed on the voice John seemed to spring across the room, and pulling it open, he thrust his arm outside, saying, 'Here a minute you.' And in the next second he had pulled May into the room.

'Leave go. What are you playing at?' May jerked her arm from his hand. It was the first time Sarah had heard her voice, and to her surprise it sounded refined.

'Why couldn't you have shown them into the other room?' John was hissing at his wife, his face hanging menacingly above her.

'Why should I?' Her voice was cool, aggravatingly cool. 'They always come in here, don't they?'

'You're a bloody mischief-making little bitch. You're never happy unless . . .'

'Here! Here! John, steady on!'

'Steady on?' John turned his head towards Dan. 'Steady on, you said?'

'Yes, that's what I said, steady on. And keep your domestic differences for your own hearth.'

'Now you're asking something.' May was nodding her head while her eyes stretched themselves into large circles. 'You're asking something, aren't you, Dan? Did you ever know him to use tact or discretion, the big fellow. The great I am.'

Sarah, standing apart, was experiencing a feeling of shock, and the shock in this case could almost be classed as severe. That the Hetherington family, this family from the top end who lived in the best house in the Fifteen Streets, who were the best people among the two thousand or more who filled the houses, that they could quarrel, that one of their members could swear, could even look as if he was going to hit his wife, the wife who appeared as aggravating as any other working man's wife did when having a row, was a shock.

In this moment she saw all the Hetheringtons struggling in the mire beside her, and the effect was distressing in the extreme.

Only one thing was clear in her mind–and her reasoning on this point surprised her. She knew that she understood why John had lost his temper, and she could understand and even condone his attitude towards his wife. She watched him now screw up his eyes as if someone had suddenly thrown acid into them, clench his teeth as if the pain was unbearable, and with his head down, like a charging bull, dash from the room.

'Well! Nice conduct, isn't it?' May looked from Dan to David, then her eyes settling on Sarah, she spoke to her directly for the first time since they had met. 'You want to be thankful there are no two people alike in one family,' she said.

'Oh, May, May.' Dan moved towards her. 'You know what he's like; he'll be over it in no time.'

'Yes, I know what he's like, Dan. And as you say, he'll get over it in no time, but that will make no difference to me.' She tilted her chin on this statement and, turning slowly and deliberately about, she left the room, closing the door behind her, and this with quiet deliberation too.

David turned on the piano stool and, facing Sarah, he bowed his head as he said, 'I'm sorry about all this. I was going to explain it all to you later, but there's been so little time. It's all so very simple, Sarah.'

'It's all right, it's all right. It doesn't matter.'

But it did matter. Again Sarah was feeling afraid. Nothing ever went smooth in life, did it?

'You go into the kitchen, David, and have a word with them, and then you and Sarah take yourselves out for a walk. Go on.' Dan pushed at David's shoulder. 'I'll do the explaining to Sarah.' He laughed here. 'I've an idea I can do it better than you. Go on now.'

'I won't be long.' David, his face tense-looking and sad, touched Sarah's hand, and again she said, 'It's all right.'

'Here, come and sit down.' Dan put the tips of his fingers lightly on her arm and drew her towards the couch, adding, 'And don't look so worried, there's nothing going to happen. Look, I'll make it brief and put you out of your misery.' He smiled again and patted her hand while she waited, sick with anxiety, to hear what he had to say.

'It's just like this. Eileen's always been sweet of Davie, but he's never returned the sentiments, if you follow me, not in the same way. Now her mother wanted to make a match of it. She had her own reasons.' He smiled widely here. 'You see, years ago her and Stan . . . you know, David's father . . .' He nodded towards the kitchen. 'Well, they were as good as promised to each other; nothing in the open or anything like that, but a sort of understanding between them. And then he goes and meets Mary and that was that. But Ellen's a nice woman, a forgiving woman, and over the years the two families have kept in touch, with the precise idea on Ellen's part that Eileen and David should make up for her lost romance. You see the pattern?' He raised his eyebrows at her. 'But then Mary didn't see it like that and she had every reason. And they were good ones, I must say that much, because . . . well'–he wagged his head–'you would know, anyway, sooner or later; but Eileen's father's in Harton, in the mental block. He's had three trips inside these last few years, and Eileen, poor lass, has the curse of fits on her; not very bad, but nevertheless she has them. And she is also cursed, as you've seen for yourself, I'm sure, with a beautiful face. It's out of this world, isn't it? . . . Now, look . . . look. You're not going to cry, are you?'

'No, no.' Sarah swallowed. 'But it's sad, very sad.'

'Yes, it is, I grant you. But you must believe this. Davie had never any intention of marrying her. Yet him being a soft-hearted chap . . . and you know he is soft-hearted, and it's nothing to be ashamed of . . .' Again his eyebrows went up. 'Well, his mother was always a bit afraid that he would sink under the pressure both from Eileen, her mother, and Stan. And now . . . well, she's relieved. But I must tell you that his father doesn't see it in the same way as she does. In fact, I'm sure Stan would have welcomed Davie's match with Eileen. I think at the back of his mind'–he was whispering now–'he thought that in some way it would make up for the dirty trick he had done on Ellen. You know, we're queer cattle, we humans. We'd sacrifice somebody else, our nearest and dearest, to our conscience. Anyway, there's the tale. And David picked for himself, and a very very good choice he's made, I'll say that for him.'

He was smiling at her, and she should have felt warmed by his evident sincerity and the fact that David had never any idea of marrying the girl, but instead she felt afraid because her thoughts were now taken up with Mary Hetherington. . . . That was why she had been welcomed into this higher stratum; why she had been welcomed by this woman who evidently ruled and dominated her family. It was a case of any port in a storm. She thought of the little woman's voice saying, 'You're cruel, Mary, cruel. You've got everything . . .'

If things hadn't happened in such a whirlwind of hurry she would have asked herself before why this woman had stooped from her high perch and welcomed her. But she had the answer now: she was the lesser of two evils. Perhaps his mother had thought too that if she opposed her son's choice he might become more pliable under the silent pressure of his father and the desire of both the girl and her mother. It was as Dan had said.

'Don't look so sad. I've told you there's nothing more to it than that. Come on, smile . . . laugh.' He put his fingers out to touch her cheek but withheld them before they made contact. Then with an embarrassed laugh he withdrew his hand, saying, 'You know, you look the kind of lass that should laugh a lot.'

Everybody thought she should laugh, just because she was big. But he was nice, this young uncle of David's, so nice. He should have been the brother and John the odd man out. She smiled sadly at him now, saying, 'I've never had very much to laugh at.'

'We'll alter all that. You know, before John was married we used to have some good nights in this room. All except Sunday.' He pulled a face. 'David's a fine player, you know. He's passed all his exams and could teach if he liked, but there's nothing in it, he says. And his mother plays the fiddle; she's a grand hand with the fiddle is Mary.'

'Do you play anything?' she asked quietly.

'Me? Oh, yes, yes.' He nodded his head quickly. 'I've got me diploma, first grade; mind you, it took some getting. There was a big do at Morgan's Hall the day it was presented.'

Morgan's Hall! That was at East Jarrow near the New Buildings, a big gaunt empty place. She never knew they presented prizes there. She asked politely, 'What do you play?'

'The comb. But mind'–he held his finger up–'I have a special kind of paper on it.'

She was laughing; her body shaking, her hands pressed over her mouth, and her face turned into the corner of the couch. And Dan was laughing too; lying back, he too was holding his mouth.

'Oh!' Sarah groaned inside. He was funny, dry; he had her believing him.

She slanted her wet eyes towards him and he was looking at her, his face alight.

'We needed that, didn't we?' His whisper was as one pal to another.

At this moment the door opened abruptly and David entered the room with Sarah's hat and coat in his hands. He looked to where she sat wiping her eyes and for a moment a lightness spread over his face and he drew in a long breath as if of relief. Then on a note he attempted to make jocular he said, 'What was it? Dan been telling you about the time he fell in the rain-barrel, or when Father was on the roof and he took the ladder away?'

'No.' Sarah shook her head. 'About him passing the examination for playing the comb.'

'Oh, that's a new one.' David nodded at Dan, then added, 'You are a fool, you know.'

Sarah was in her coat and hat now, and David said, 'We won't bother going into the other room, we'll come back later.'

'Goodnight, Mr . . .' Sarah turned to Dan.

'Plain Dan, Sarah.'

'Goodnight, Dan.'

'Goodnight, Sarah.'

When she reached the front door she heard Dan's voice, soft sounding and careless, call, 'Here a minute, David.' And as she stood waiting she heard him say, his tone changed now, low and earnest, 'Macdonalds are moving from next door, they'll be out before Christmas. It mightn't be the most suitable place, so close, but empty houses up this end are few and far between as you know. I would get things settled as soon as possible, the wind might change at any time, understand?'

'Yes, Dan . . . thanks.'

Out in the dark street he took her arm. It was a firm possessive hold, and when they came to the main road he said, 'You heard what Dan said?'

'Yes.' Her voice was low and she kept her eyes ahead.

'Well?' The pressure tightened on her arm. 'Would you marry me before Christmas, Sarah?'

Her heart began thumping against her ribs, knocking like a small wooden mallet. It checked her answer for some seconds. Then she stopped and, looking fully at him in the dim lamplight, she said, 'I'll marry you any time you like, David.' Then she added. 'Thanks.' The last word had a silly sound. She wondered why she'd had to say it like that; it made her feel cheap, common. She didn't want to feel cheap or common. She thought of what John had said about being afraid of people. But she wasn't afraid of David, only grateful to him, so very grateful.

Chapter Five

Sarah stood just within the kitchen door. She still wore her hat and coat. The kitchen was warm with the heat from a blazing fire piled high in the grate, but she still felt cold, and her body seemed to become stiffer as she looked at the priest, and he at her.

Father O'Malley was seated at one corner of the kitchen table, her father was seated at the opposite corner, and her mother at the corner nearest her. They formed the usual triangle of persuasion. One using threats–her father; one using cool fear-filled reason–the priest; one using the weapon of superstition–not the least strong of the three, her mother.

'Good evening, Sarah.'

'Well, don't stand there as if you were struck. You heard the Father speaking to you.'

'Yes, I heard, I'm not deaf.'

As she glared at Pat Bradley there arose in her, yet again, an acute feeling of hate. She had always hated this man, but the feeling had become stronger during the past weeks during which he had done everything in his power to break up her association with David and the family at the other end. The weapon he used was her religion, and his natural ally was the priest–at least this priest.

Father Bailey, on the other hand, had been understanding, even nice. He had asked her to bring David to see him, and David had gone and told him in a quiet way his reasons for not wishing to become a Catholic. He had pointed out to him that it wasn't a case of changing his religion because he wasn't of any particular denomination, he was an agnostic. She had felt proud that David was able to talk to the priest as he had done, and she felt that Father Bailey liked and respected him. He had said, 'Well, the Bishop, under certain circumstances, gives permission for a mixed marriage . . . they are not popular.' Father Bailey had smiled as he had said this. 'But nevertheless permission is given on the understanding that you will allow the children to be brought up in the Catholic faith.'

Sarah had felt embarrassed at this point, yet had waited eagerly for David's answer. It hadn't come immediately, but when he did speak she had let out a long slow breath, for he had said, 'Well, as I'm no longer speaking for myself on this point . . . It won't be a matter of personal opinion but what Sarah thinks too. I'll leave it to her, Father.'

He had buried deep into her heart when he had called the priest, Father. Oh, David was so reasonable, and Father Bailey was reasonable. . . . Father

O'Malley kept saying that he too was reasonable, but he wasn't–he was adamant, fanatic. By the things he said anyone would think she was marrying a leper.

Yet this same priest spoke civilly to her father simply because he attended Mass every Sunday. It was a wonder, she thought, that the church didn't fall round about his ears. This undersized man who looked what he was: a dirty-minded swine.

'Have you thought over what I said last week, Sarah?'

'Yes, Father.'

'Then you know you can expect no happiness or peace through a mixed marriage.'

Sarah remained silent.

'Can't you answer the Father?'

'Be quiet, Pat.' The priest lifted his hand in temperate admonition, then went on, 'I understand from Father Bailey that this man has no intention of changing his views, now or at any other time.'

Still Sarah did not answer.

'So in that case you must see your position clearly. Surely you cannot contemplate damaging your immortal soul by joining in a union with this man. . . . If you do you will be damned, and your children will be damned, and you will be held responsible. Do you understand that?'

Sarah's throat was swelling, her eyes were widening. All the pores in her body seemed to have taken on separate lives and were rubbing one against the other, jangling her whole being. Looking into the priest's eyes, she saw the loss of her immortal soul. It took the shape of agony brought on by misfortune after misfortune as he had prophesied during the past weeks. If she married David bad luck would dog her. The penance for her crime while she lived would come in the shape of every disaster. . . . But no disaster that her brain could conceive would be equal to the loss of her immortal soul and the immortal souls of her children, so his eyes told her. She turned from their penetrating stare and the eyes of the others and, tearing open the staircase door, she crawled frantically like some wild animal up to her room, there to find Phyllis waiting for her.

'What's the matter? What's he done?'

Sarah turned from her sister and, pressing her hands over her face, leant against the door.

'What is it, Sarah?' Phyllis was tugging at her. 'Look, what did he say?'

The hands still covering her face, Sarah whimpered, 'My immortal soul. . . . He said. . . .'

'Oh, my God!' Phyllis's sharp retort came as if from an older woman. 'Don't be a blasted fool, our Sarah, and let him scare the daylights out of you with that talk. Immortal soul! Tell him he can have your IMMORTAL SOUL, and stick it. . . . Tell him to take my dear father's . . . there's an immortal soul for you. I bet if Father O'Malley hadn't taken up the priesthood he'd have been twin brother to Pat Bradley.'

'Ssh! Don't talk like that, Phyllis, not about the priest.'

'Look, our Sarah,' Phyllis was whispering again. 'I thought you had some guts. You don't mean to tell me you're going to let him get you down, not at this stage.'

'No, no, I'm not.' Sarah sat on the bed and, tearing off her hat, flung it into the corner of the room, repeating, 'No, I'm not! David's not going to turn and that's that. He's even willing to be married in the church, but he's not going to turn. No, they won't get me down.'

'Look, Sarah.' Phyllis was kneeling by Sarah's knees now, gripping her hands, looking up into her face with an urgency that seemed in excess of sisterly interest in this matter. 'Why don't you do what the uncle said, the Dan one? Why don't you get married in the registry office, then there would be neither Baptist chapel as his mother wants, nor the church?'

'I couldn't. . . . No.' Sarah shook her head wearily. 'Not in a registry office; I wouldn't feel married somehow.'

Phyllis pulled herself back on to her haunches and, looking up at Sarah, said, 'You know, our Sarah, you're a big softy; you let people play on your feelings, first one side then the other. When the only one you've got to think about is David. Now I'm telling you, our Sarah, things can happen, things that'll put the kibosh on you marrying him altogether.'

'Nothing'll stop me marrying him. The only thing I want is to be married in church, and he's for it.'

Phyllis looked at Sarah for a long moment now before turning and walking to the window. The paper blind was down but she stared at it as if she were looking through the glass, and her tone was fierce as she whispered, 'I expected you to be married afore this. Now I'm waiting no longer.'

'Afore this?' Sarah repeated in a harsh whisper. 'Well, we've only been going together just over two months. And what do you mean, you can wait no longer?'

Sarah was sitting on the edge of the bed now, her hands gripping the iron frame. Something that she had dreaded but forced down under the pressure of her own particular worries came rushing upwards. 'Our Phyllis! You're not going to do anything silly?'

'It all depends on what you call silly. An' don't say it that way.'

Sarah, getting up, went to Phyllis and pulled her round by the shoulders, peering into her face in the dim light.

'You're not going to live . . .'

'Yes, I am, but I'm goin' to marry him. I could have married him a month ago but I waited thinkin' that you would do something definite, stop being pushed around.'

'But . . . but you can't, our Phyllis. You just can't go down and live among the Arabs.' Sarah couldn't bring herself to say: live with an Arab, marry an Arab.

'Let me tell you somethin'.' Phyllis's voice was quiet now and her words deliberately slow. 'If half of them round these doors were as decent as them Arabs–not all, mind you, not all, I know that, I'm not daft–but taking them singularly and weighing them one against the other, this lot would lose hands down.'

'What's the good of cutting off your nose to spite your face?' Sarah was pleading now. 'You know what it'll mean going down there just to spite him?'

Phyllis shrugged herself from Sarah's hold, then, her voice still quiet, said, 'It was like that at first, but not any more. I like Ali and he can give me a home, and a decent one; they've got money.' She jerked her head up. 'His father runs one of them boarding-houses and Ali helps. It'll be his one day and a lot more besides. His father's a name down there, and they have their own kind of stuckupness. . . . Do you know something? He and some of the others are not very keen about Ali taking up with me. I thought everybody looked upon them as scum. Even from the bottom end here they do; but let me tell you, them Arabs have their own idea of scum, and we from this quarter are pretty well at the top of the list. I've had me eyes opened this last few weeks.'

'He won't let you do it.' Sarah's breast was heaving nearly as much now as when she had scrambled up the stairs a few minutes earlier. 'He'll go to the polis.'

'He can go where the bloody hell he likes. . . .'

'Don't swear, our Phyllis. . . .'

'Well, he can, and as far beyon't because once it's been signed and sealed he can do very little about it–nowt in fact. I was eighteen last week, an' I know him; it'll be such a slap in his dirty face that he won't be able to wipe it off, and he'll want to keep mum about it.'

'Then you are doing it just to hit him.'

'No, I'm not; I've told you. But I can hear him: "Aa'va washed me hands off her, the trollop!" Ooh!' Phyllis lifted her face to the low ceiling, and there was a twisted smile on it as she exclaimed in tones that held even wonder, 'Won't it be lovely to be a trollop and get way from here, and him, and everything?'

Sarah sat down again. She felt sick, really sick as if she could vomit. This was the finish–the finish of her, anyway. Phyllis would go, but she would stay because when David's mother heard that her sister had gone down into Costerfine Town way to live with an Arab–even if she were married to him–that would be the finish.

And Mrs Hetherington had been rather strange lately, cool at times. She, of course, wanted them to be married in the Baptist chapel. Sarah had learned one thing about David's mother during the past weeks. She was a dominant, proud woman, proud of her family, proud of her station in the top end, of living in the best house–the only double house–in the whole place. When this knowledge of her future mother-in-law's character was added to that of her determination not to let David marry the girl Eileen, she appeared super-humanly strong. Sarah knew for certain now that if Mrs Hetherington hadn't been pushed for a substitute at a critical time she herself would never have got across the doorstep.

She swung her body round, straining it forward towards her sister, appealing with every fibre of it as she whispered, 'Wait till I'm settled, Phyllis; aw, wait till I'm settled.'

'I've been waitin', Sarah. I thought the way you started it was all going to happen in a rush, you'd be married and settled afore now. Well, you started like that.' She shook her head at the silent denial from Sarah. 'I can't wait any longer, there's a reason. I'm . . . I'm leavin' here a week come Monday, it's all settled. I'm to be married then.'

'A reason?' Sarah's mouth was hanging open and the lashes of her upper lids were lying flat against the smooth skin of her eyes. 'A reason?' Her voice had sunk into deep emphasis.

'Yes, and it's no good going off the deep end, it's over and done.'

'Oh, my God!'

'Mine too.' This flippant remark would have at one time caused them to giggle helplessly even while Sarah reprimanded Phyllis for treating the name of God with lightness; but now she could only stare at the slight boyish-like figure of her sister. 'How far?' she asked.

'Six or seven weeks. It happened after he gave me the lathering. Ali saw me face and weals sticking up above the top of me blouse and he was kind to me. You know what?' Phyllis shook her head. 'He nearly cried. Can you believe that, he nearly cried. Well, it happened that night, and don't think I'm sorry 'cos I'm not, but you can see I've got to get away. An' you know it'll be just like gettin' out of prison. I've never been inside but I'd like to bet me bottom dollar that this place is ten degrees worse than any prison. D'you know, I've had to come straight up here every night for weeks to get out of his sight, for his hands 'ave been itching to leather me again. He can manage me, you see; even if I kick and tear he can manage me. He couldn't you; that's why he's never started on you, only that once when you first went to work and that lad set you home. But me, I'm smaller than him, something that he can handle in the way he wants, and me mother's let him get away with it. She's putting her foot down now when it's too late 'cos she knows we can both skedaddle. She's as much to blame as he is. She could have managed him with her bulk, but now he's got her as frightened as he thinks he's got me. But he doesn't know he's made a mistake. Oh lad, I wish I could be in two places at once next week when I post them me news. An' you know how I'm goin' to end it?' She cocked her head up defiantly. 'I've been goin' over it in me mind for days. I'm goin' to say, after the bit about me being married, I'm goin' to say, 'You can come to the christenin' if yer like, it'll be in about seven months' time''.'

'Oh, our Phyllis!' Sarah lowered her head in a series of low swings until her chin lay on her breast.

'Listen!' Phyllis had raised her hand. 'He's goin' out. He's likely settin' the priest down the road, and on his way back he'll do a bit of his snooping on the courtin' couples. Oh, I wish some fellow would catch him at it and take him by the legs and swing him face forward against a coal hatch.'

Sarah put her fingers to her lips and stared at the tiny iron grate opposite her. Then, jumping to her feet, she asked, 'What time do you think it is?' She was standing at the foot of the bed buttoning her coat up now.

'About quarter to ten I should say. Where you goin'?'

'To see David. I've got to.'

'You goin' to the house?'

'Yes.'

'What will his mother say?'

'I don't suppose she'll be there. The grandchild . . . John's boy's ill, it's whooping cough, and bad. David said his mother was taking a turn over there tonight, but if she isn't I'll just have to make some excuse, I don't know what yet.' She was gabbling now.

'But how'll you get back . . . in I mean?'

'I'll take the back-door key and get me mother to leave the bolt loose. I'll sleep on the couch until the mornin'.'

'If he finds out he won't let you in.'

'I'll have to risk that; I've got to see David. I can't wait until tomorrow night. I'll go mad.'

'You're goin' to tell him you're going to be married in the Baptist?'

'No, no.' Sarah shook her head violently.

'What, then?'

'Oh, I don't know. I just don't know. I just want to talk to him.'

'An' tell him what a wicked girl you've got for a sister?'

'Aw, our Phyllis, I won't do any such thing, you know I won't.'

'I know you won't, Sarah. You're soft, our Sarah, soft. But go on. Go on and get back as quick as you can, I'll keep awake.'

Down in the kitchen Annie said, 'For God's sake don't make a noise when you come in.' She pulled the big key from the lock of the back door. 'I'll stay down as long as I can.' Then she added, 'What's got into you? Why do you want to go out at this time? Are you going to the top end?'

'Yes.'

'Is it about the priest?'

Sarah hesitated. She would have to give some reason for going, so she nodded abruptly before slipping out of the door.

There was a moon shining, caressing the grey slate roofs of the long street, casting deep shadows over the rows of small windows on one side and lighting them up on the other, showing them as elongated eyes in an elongated face of dirty reddy-brown brick. But the moon was kind. The streets were mellowed. The grimness of the poorer houses was dimmed, and where the streets began to improve the moon lent a touch of enchantment. In Camelia Street everything was bright and gleaming. The houses looked like smiling faces. The bow-windows were glistening eyes and the bath-bricked steps large white teeth sticking out of flushed faces. All the doors in Camelia Street were painted every year.

Sarah stood with her arm raised towards the knocker of number one, and before she grasped it she doubled her hand into a fist and punched her cheek as she asked herself, 'What will I say? How will I begin?'

It seemed to her that the knocker had hardly touched the door when it was pulled open, and there stood Dan.

'Why, Sarah, come in, come in. What are you after at this time of night? David said he had packed you off home because of your . . .' He looked down at her ankles. 'Because you were tired.'

'Is he in, Dan?'

'Yes, yes. He'd have been here waiting on the step if he'd thought you were coming back. Come on, come in.' He pulled her aside so that he could close the door; then, peering at her through the hall light, he whispered, 'Anything wrong?'

She did not answer his question but whispered back, 'Is . . . is his mother in?'

'No, she's over the road. The young 'un is pretty bad. There's only Davie and me in. His dad's over there an' all . . . Come on.'

When Dan opened the living-room door he pushed Sarah before him, saying, 'Look what the moon's flushed up, Davie.'

David was on his feet. 'What's the matter?' He was holding her hands now, looking into her face. 'Is anything wrong?'

'Yes. Can I sit down?'

'Can you sit down!' It was Dan who pressed her into the chair while David still held her hand. 'What is it?' David asked gently.

'Look, I'll be off to bed now, I'll say goodnight.'

'No, no.' Sarah looked up at Dan. Somehow she felt that Dan's cool head, his easy unaffected way of seeing things, might help. 'You might as well know.' She turned her face to David. 'I had to come straight away an' tell you. It's about our Phyllis. I know it's going to make all the difference, but I had to come and tell you. It isn't her fault really, but she's marrying an Arab. . . . A week come Monday.'

When she felt her fingers slide from David's she cried wildly inside herself. 'Oh no! no! Hold me hands.' She turned her eyes from his startled face and looked at Dan. His face too was wearing almost the same expression as David's, and the two men were looking at each other now. David's lips were moving; it was as if he were saying something to Dan yet no sound came.

The thoughts flowing between the two men were like hot wires passing through her body, vibrating pain. She couldn't bear to look at them any more. She wanted to rise from the chair and rush out of the house, but she hadn't the strength; she hadn't even the strength to keep her body upright. It was bending over as if beaten. From her downcast lids she saw David's legs move. He swung a chair round and then his knees were touching hers and there was promise of life when once again her hands were in his and he was asking, 'When did you say she was going to be married?'

'A . . . a week come Monday.' Her voice cracked on the last word and she cleared her throat.

'There's not much time.' Dan had turned another chair round and he too was sitting, almost in a line with David and in front of her. 'Look, Sarah.' David was shaking her hands as if bringing her awake, and he began to talk rapidly, his words crisp, decisive. 'You won't countenance the Baptist chapel, and this business of your church is going to take weeks. There's only one thing for it: the registry office.'

The words jerked Sarah. It was as if the wires had twanged against a patch of fear, disturbing it, sending it flowing in all directions through her body.

'I know you don't want to be married in a registry office, and neither do I, but it's like this, Sarah. Well . . .'

He stopped and closed his eyes, and Dan, putting his hand out and gripping his knee, said, 'I'd better finish for you. It's his mother, Sarah. You know how things are, you're no fool. When this business of your sister's is made public, it isn't only God alone who will know what her reactions will be, we'll all know. She's a very proud woman is Mary, and she can be hard, unmoving. . . . Now, what you've got to do is to create a *fait accompli.'* He smiled here, then went on. 'I mean, you've got to do the trick, get married. The thing is then done, achieved, and she'll have to face it. But, on the other hand, if she gets wind of your sister marrying . . . an Arab . . .' He wagged his hand at Sarah. 'I'm not saying that there aren't decent Arabs . . . they would be bad if they weren't as good as some of the whites; but you know how it's taken, don't you?'

Into the silence David said, 'Will you, Sarah? Will you get married in the registry office?'

Sarah stared into David's eyes. If she didn't marry this man in the registry office she wouldn't get the chance to marry him at all, of that she was certain. Between the pressure of the priest and the power of Mrs Hetherington, David and she would be torn apart, the battle would be too much for them. It mustn't be. Never again would she meet a man of David's standing, not one who would want to marry her. Not one so lacking in side, not one who was the antithesis of his mother, of all proud mothers. But that she would suffer if she was married in a registry office she also knew. . . . Her immortal soul would be in jeopardy, and her actions would make her responsible for the souls of her children–the priest had said. Even so, she must do it. She must marry David, if not in the sight of God, then in the sight of man.

Thinking along these lines, she was surprised that she should openly show the extent of her relief in the way she did, for she cried, 'Yes. Oh yes, David . . . any place . . . any place.'

David pulled her hands up under his chin and held them there, and Dan rose to his feet with the comment, 'Well, now, we'll drink on that, the kettle's on. And don't let's waste any time. How soon can this thing be got through–in the registry office, I mean?'

'About a week.' David was not looking at Dan, he was looking at Sarah.

'Well, if you give the notice in tomorrow you should be able to do the deed in a week to a fortnight. And if you make it a Wednesday I can get the morning off. Look.' He turned round the teapot in his hand. 'I tell you what I'll do. I'll stand the wedding breakfast, eh?'

'Aw, Dan, man, there's no need for that.'

'No need? Of course there's no need, but I'll do it all the same. It'll be a bit of a wedding present. And look.' He came eagerly towards them, the teapot outstretched in the direction of the wall. 'The Macdonalds are moving on Friday, it couldn't be better. Everything will work out. And you can spend your honeymoon doing the place up. You've got a week to come, haven't you?' He now dug the spout of the teapot into David's shoulder, and David smiled up at him without answering. 'Well, there you are, everything fixed.' He was looking at Sarah as he spoke, his voice and manner sweeping away all obstacles. But there was one obstacle it was impossible for him to remove from her path, and it wasn't her religion she was thinking about now, it was Mary Hetherington. Her face straight, she looked at David and said, 'Your mother will never forgive me.'

'Oh yes she will. I'll take the blame.'

She moved her head in small jerks. 'She'll never forgive me. She'll even hate me.'

'Now don't be silly.' Dan was bending over her, his face on a level with David's. He spoke sternly as if to a recalcitrant child. 'That's nonsense. Get the thing done and stop shilly-shallying. I'm glad this has happened, you know, for you could both have gone on between church and chapel, between turning and not turning for the next two years and then finished up'–he straightened his broad shoulders, and spread his arms wide, the teapot still in his hand–'not getting married at all.'

'You're wrong there, Dan. Sarah and me will be married whether it's next week, or next year, or the year after. But for my money it's next week. . . . That's it, isn't it, Sarah?'

She was about to nod when the latch of the back door clicked and they all turned their eyes in the direction of the kitchen.

'What can I say?' She was on her feet whispering.

'Nothing, nothing.' David was patting her hands. 'I brought you in, that's all. We'd just come back.' That meant his mother had been out when he returned home.

When the living-room door opened and John entered their combined sigh brought his gaze from one to the other. 'Aye, aye! What's up here? You all look as if you'd been caught in the act of breaking and entering.'

Dan cast a quick glance at David, wanting to know whether he was going to confide in his brother, and David answered him by looking at John and saying, 'A little crisis has arisen. Good in a way, in fact for my part I'd say splendid. Sarah and I are going to be married next week . . . in the registry office.'

John stared at his brother. 'Sudden!' he said quietly.

'Yes, it is. But things are better that way.'

'Mother know?'

'No, and I don't want her to.'

'Dad?'

'Nor him either. Nobody, only Dan here and you.'

'Do you want a best man?' His lips smiled.

'Would you?' David moved towards him.

'It's as little as I can do.'

'Thanks, John.' David thumped his brother's broad chest without causing him to move in the slightest. 'And Dan's seeing to the breakfast. I couldn't feel happier about it.'

'Well, she doesn't think she's going to get you without taking the rest of us on, does she?' John was looking over David's shoulder, holding Sarah's eyes now. 'She takes one, she takes the lot–the Three Musketeers, one for all and all for one, isn't that it, Dan?'

'You're a fool. Take no heed of him, Sarah,' said Dan.

'Well, we've always hung together, haven't we, against authority . . . politics, religion, and . . . women?' He smiled broadly as he said the last word. Then, coming towards Sarah, he held out his hand. She placed hers in it, and when he covered it with his other large square palm and said gallantly, 'But not–not this one,' she had the strange desire to fall against him, to put her arms around his thick neck and cry and cry and cry and cry.

This feeling, unheralded, springing upon her from nowhere, was as frightening as the hate which had attacked her in the bedroom a short while ago, and again, as on that occasion, she was trembling, every pore in her body was moving. Her breath quickened; her neck swelled and the pain in it became so unbearable that it forced itself up the back of her throat and into her eyes. She closed them tightly to stop the flood escaping, but it was no use.

'Oh! Oh! Don't, Sarah. Aw! What is it? Come now, come now.' Their voices were floating around her, exclaiming, soothing. Their hands were touching her, her arms, her shoulders, her head, patting, patting. Her feelings changed now into panic; she wanted to push them off, all of them, and fly from the house. It was only a momentary feeling; it was gone as quickly as it had come.

Through her blurred vision she put out her hands and grasped those of David. His hands were different altogether from anyone else's. She gripped them and turned her face into his shoulder, and the others melted away.

The room became quiet, there was only David and her. There would always be only David and her. The rage, the fears, the strange emotions, were things of the past. There came upon her spirit a quietness which even the thought of Mary Hetherington or the loss of her immortal soul could not dispel: she had David. Next week she would have him for life and she would know peace.

Chapter Six

'Well, how do you feel?' Dan leant his big head across the table towards Sarah as he whispered the question.

'Fu . . . funny.'

'Not f . . . funny-daft, funny-nice, eh?'

'Stop acting the goat, here's the waiter.' David, the red veins on his cheeks seeming more prominent because his skin was a shade paler, pushed Dan upwards by the shoulder.

The waiter had a bottle in his hand which he presented to Dan as if for him to read the label, saying, 'All right, sir?'

'All right.' Dan nodded. The waiter tore off the lead cap, pulled out the stubby-headed cork and proceeded with practised art to fill the four glasses with the sparkling wine.

When the waiter had departed and they had the glasses in their hands David said under his breath, 'Either you're loopy or you've come into money . . . Champagne! You're daft, man.'

'Drink it up and stop your nattering. . . . Here's to you both.' Dan held out his glass. It was on a level with John's, but John did not speak, he merely inclined his head.

The wine had very little taste, Sarah thought. It's only noticeable effect was the gas which pricked her nostrils. But it was champagne. Fancy her drinking champagne! Oh, Dan was kind. He was a nice man was Dan.

This is the life.' Dan was sitting back in his chair beaming. 'Wednesday morning and me not at work. It's never happened before. Every Wednesday morning at this time'–he looked at his watch–'quarter to twelve, in comes Mrs Flaherty, and we have the same performance, it never varies. If her old man's had the dole or not the programme is as usual. 'What's your ham, the day, Mr Hetherington?' she says. Give her her due, she's about the only one that gives me me title. 'Wan and two, Mrs Flaherty.' I'm very deferential to her; we're both deferential to each other, and she has me talkin' in the Irish as broad as herself.'

Dan was addressing himself solely to Sarah and she was smiling at him. She knew he was doing his stuff to put them at their ease . . . oh, Dan was nice.

'"Wan an' two, Mr Hetherington. Aw, dear God, Aa couldn't go for that, not this smorin'. An' what's your back?"

'"The short is a shillin', Mrs Flaherty, and the long is eightpence."

'"Begod! it gets dearer . . ." And us the cheapest shop in the town, cutting everybody else's throat.' Dan made this quick aside to David, and David choked on his drink.

'"What about a bit of collar, Mrs Flaherty?"

'"Aw, it's always too lean an' it kizzles up in the pan. Like the top of his boots he says it is; he'd throw it at me he would . . . collar!"

'"Well, I've some nice streaky here, now how about that? There, look, that's a nice lean piece, an inch or more running through its middle!"' Dan held out the table napkin and Sarah could believe it was streaky bacon she was looking at. 'I tell you I'm talkin' as thick as she is by this time. And this happens every Wednesday in life.'

They were all laughing now, even John; and with the bubbles from another sip of champagne making her screw up her face, Sarah asked, 'What did she have in the end?'

'Pieces.'

Their laughter turned into a roar and they made individual efforts to stifle it while glancing round the half-empty hotel dining-room. And they were returning to normal when Dan finished laconically, 'Three pennorth.' His accent was exaggerated now into broad Geordie, the inflexion high on the last syllable. They were off again, unrestrained now, and Sarah thought wistfully, Oh, if we could go on like this all day right till the night, just laughing and carrying on.

There was no doubt in her mind that Dan could have kept them laughing for a week, but within the next hour or so she would have to face Mary Hetherington, and the prospect, when she let herself think about it, was terrifying.

The meal began with sole, and when the main course turned out to be duck, and this accompanied by another wine, David, looking at Dan, shook his head reprovingly, 'You shouldn't have gone to this, man.'

'Why not? You mind your own business and tuck in, that's all you've got to do.'

'Don't worry about him throwing his money about.' John was looking at Dan. 'It'll take a little weight out of the stocking leg and he's got stacks of them piled away, and not even Mrs Flaherty could get her big toe into one of them.'

Sarah, laughing with the rest, looked at John and realised that it was the first time he had opened his mouth since they had left the registry office. He looked slightly off-colour, and his manner was not so boisterous as usual. He was not striding ahead as though the world were a football at his feet. That was how she saw John, this brother of David's who was so totally unlike him. Perhaps she thought he was worrying about the child, but the boy was getting better now; or perhaps he'd had another row with his wife.

It wasn't until an hour later, when they stood in King Street, outside the hotel, that she felt she had been given the reason for John's quiet manner and him looking so off-colour.

David had just said, 'I don't know how to thank you, Dan. Do we, Sarah?' And she had shaken her head dumbly.

'Look,' said Dan, 'it's nothing. Anyway, it's only half your wedding present. . . . I'm opening another stocking leg.' He thrust his hand out towards John on this remark.

David too had turned to John, and he asked, 'Where you going? You coming back home?'

'No,' said John, 'I'm off to the Labour Ex. . . .' He bit sharply down on his lip.

'So that's it?' Dan was standing with his chin pulled in. 'I was wondering what was up with you. You're out?' His face was screwed up. 'When did this happen?'

'Aw, my big mouth. I was off me guard. . . . Oh, for over a week.'

'For over a week? And you've never said anything?' David's voice held a reproach. 'Does May know?'

'No, nobody knows; at least they didn't.' John's head was wagging as if it had been snapped at the nape. 'I thought I'd be set on afore this, it's just one of those things.' His head bounced up now. 'Don't start being sorry for me, either of you.' His eyes were round and bright, his face and manner aggressive. 'Look, they're not getting me on the scrap-heap, I'll be in work next week.'

'What happened?' Dan asked quietly. 'I thought it would be the last place to pay off, and you the last one.'

'Well, there was no more orders for boats; big, little, tall, or small.'

'But your place only dealt with small craft. I thought there was still a market for them from the south, and for lifeboats.'

'Aye, well, so did everybody else, but they seem to have all the boats they need in the south. And nobody seems to be getting drowned now as there's fewer ships on the water so nobody wants any more lifeboats. And that's something to be thankful for, isn't it, nobody getting drowned?' He was grinning now, a false grin. 'Look.' He took them all in with a swing of his head. 'Don't let it be on my conscience that I've put a damper on the proceedings. Don't be sorry for me, for God's sake. I'm all right. For weeks ahead, I'm not broke, but I'm not going to let the blasted government get off with anything. No, by God, I'm going to get some dole out of them.'

'You won't get any for a fortnight, anyway; they don't recognise the first week and then there's three days lying on.' Dan was still talking quietly.

'Tell me something I don't know, man. Anyway, I told you I'll be at it again next week and I'll tell them what to do with their dole. But look.' His manner changed abruptly and his voice became serious as he turned to David. 'Don't let on to me mother, mind.'

'No, no, of course not. Although'–David was now smiling wryly from one to the other and his eyes came to rest on Sarah as he finished–'I think it would be really the best time to tell her, for she'll be going at us two so much it'll pass over her head.'

His words were meant to reassure Sarah but they failed, and it was evident to the three men. Dan said briskly, 'It'll be all right, never fear. . . . Well, I'm off to . . . Westoe.' It seemed as if the name had brought a self-consciousness to him, for his laugh was sheepish.

'Go on, you old roué.' Sarah could not understand this remark of John's. She did not know what a roue was but she could gauge that it was something not quite nice, for as Dan looked at her there was a pink tinge under his skin. The next moment he was holding her hand, saying, 'I wish you all the happiness in the world, Sarah.'

'Thanks, Dan.' Her voice had a cracked sound.

'And mind you, you make the best of those three days in Newcastle and when you come back I'll have one room cleaned out at least, if not papered . . . I'll put the big fellow on here.' He grabbed at John's arm. 'You know what he is when he gets started, skull, hair, and white-wash flying . . . God bless you.' The last was soft as a benediction and it was almost too much for Sarah. That is what the priest would have said, God bless you–at least Father Bailey would have said it.

Now John was standing in front of her. He did not touch her, not even to take her hand, but he looked deep into her eyes, past the worried surface of her mind, past the deeper level where lay the love she had for David, down, down, until his gaze reached a depth in her she did not know existed. She did not retreat from the return of the strange feeling, but wide-eyed watched his lids droop, the short black thick lashes creating a shadow on the broad high cheek-bones. She was married and safe, she had nothing to fear from strange feelings or anything else . . . except perhaps David's mother.

'All the best.' It was an ordinary, trite remark, used on such occasions. It was intended to mean everything, it usually meant nothing. Again John repeated this as he now shook hands with David. 'All the best, man,' he said. And David, gripping his shoulder with his free hand, answered, 'Thanks, John, thanks.'

David now took Sarah's arm and turned her about and across the road to where the tram was, the same tram that had carried her part of the way home during all her working days. Now she would use it no more–not as Sarah Bradley, anyway. She was Mrs David Hetherington. She made an effort and forced her shoulders back and lifted her head. What could they do? What could any of them do? Her father, his mother. She was married, legally married. . . .

Dan and John stood still on the pavement watching them until they boarded the tram, then they waved.

'Better them than me.' Dan's voice was low. 'Your mother's going to play merry hell. That lass is going to have a time of it. We'll all have to stand by her. Davie alone won't be able to screen her. You know what your mother is when she gets her fangs in, and she hasn't had a target for a long time. We'll all have to act as a buffer in one way or another , she's too nice to be nooled.'

'I can't see anybody nooling her.' John spoke as he looked ahead to where the tram was disappearing into the distance. 'I mean, I can't see anybody wanting to nool her. And me mother puts up with May.' John now turned and glanced at Dan, a quizzical smile twisting his lips.

'Yes, but May married you, she didn't marry Davie. The truth is, your mother didn't ever have any intention of anybody marrying Davie, at least that's how I figure it. She pretended to accept the lass knowing that the scales were weighed heavily against her, her coming from the bottom end and all that, and she was hoping that the weight would gradually tell on Davie–religion, background, the lot. Of course I might be wrong.'

'You're never very wrong, Dan.'

Dan turned and looked at his nephew. There was six years between them, but this was in no way apparent, they had always looked and felt equal. Dan said now, 'You look off-colour. Are you worrying about being out?'

'No, no, I told you. . . . No, by God.' He turned his head round on his shoulder as if looking at someone behind him. 'No. They're not getting me to rot at the street corner. Don't you worry about me, Dan. I'll fall on me feet, I always have. Now, I'm off. . . . And by the way, thanks for the meal. You went to town, didn't you, and it was decent of you. I thought about making them a dining table and chairs. I can get the wood at cost.'

'Oh, they'd be tickled pink at that; that's a good idea, John.'

'Well, I'll be off. So long, Dan.'

'So long, John. See you the night.'

'Yes, see you the night.'

Dan crossed the road, and John turned the corner and went in the direction of the station, his stride long and quick. He reached the yard and made for the urinal, and there with his body bent double and his hand against the wall he retched.

'You feeling bad, mate?'

John wiped his face with his handkerchief. The sweat was running in rivulets down from his hair. After nodding at the man he said, 'Eating too well . . . duck and champagne.'

'Aye, begod, you'll get sick on duck and champagne these days, on seventeen bob a week. Aye, you'll get sick on that. Sick for the want of a good feed. You all right now?'

The man's reaction to John's remark had been what he had intended, and after he had nodded at him the man went on, 'Duck and champagne. You'd have to be in Parliament to have duck and champagne these days. Even the mayoral banquets wouldn't sport that the day in case the smell got into the streets and sent people mad. Something should be done . . . it'll have to be done.' The man pointed his thin dirty finger at John. 'We'll have to hang together, that's the solution. The bloody unions will have to find out whose side they're on. Why aren't they up in London doing somethin'? There'll be riots afore long, you'll see.'

If the fool didn't shut up he would push him on his back. He turned away from the man and kept his face to the wall, and the voice coming from a distance now said. 'That's it, get it up. It's better out than in, whatever it is.'

Left alone, John again turned and leaned against the wall. 'Get it up,' the man had said. 'Better out than in.' But the man didn't know that he was sick in two ways.

A mixture of sauterne and champagne and duck had been too much for his stomach which had grown accustomed to the dull diets of an indifferent cook. But this was a kind of sickness you could get rid of. He wished to God the other could be vomited up in the same way. What had Dan said? They would all have to act as a buffer between her and his mother. That was funny that was, damned funny, for Dan didn't know that from the minute he had seen her that night in the front room he had wanted to act as a buffer between her and the world.

Before he'd had May he'd had his practice. He knew all about women. From when he was fourteen and looked seventeen, and the lasses had made a bee line for him, he'd had them; he couldn't help but have them, for they had tripped over themselves to get him to touch them. He'd had his first lass when he was fifteen. His mother would have had a seizure if she had known. Yes, he knew all about women, but he had never loved any of them. Wanted them? Oh, aye, wanted them until he couldn't bear himself. Lusted after them was the phrase. He had wanted May but he hadn't loved her, but he had taken her and she had seen that he damned well paid for that bit of frisking. She was the only one, at least to his knowledge, whom, as his mother would have said, he had got with child. Paul had been born prematurely. He had laughed at that. He wondered if the midwife had laughed too. If she had, she hadn't done it in front of him or his mother. Everything that had happened to the child since had been put down to his premature birth. Did a child ever become aware that he had been born of lust and not love? He had told himself that as long as you had the other thing you could live without love. That's what he had told himself. Until the night he had walked into the front room to see the lass their David was going to marry. That night he had said to himself, Don't be a blasted fool, it couldn't happen as quickly as that. But the passing days had proved him wrong. He was known as the big fellow, he liked the title. But the bigger the weight the harder the fall, and by God his fall had been hard.

He pulled himself from the wall and wiped his face, then straightened his hat and buttoned up his coat. Well, it was done. Two hours ago she had become Davie's wife. If it had been anybody else but Davie, Dan even, he would have gone all out, full sails set, and caught her up like a demon of wind, all the magnificent size of her, all her unconscious, unaffected loveliness. He would have cried, To hell, let's get out of here. What did it matter about a wife and a bairn, about a mother who was so stiff-necked with pride and a sense of security it became painful at times for him to look, or listen, to her. He knew that if he had let himself sail before the wind of his passion, Sarah, whether she wanted to or not, would have been borne along with him. But it was Davie she had married, Davie she wanted. Or, did she? . . . Anyway, Davie had wanted her, and the only decent thing that had been in his life had been the love for his brother.

BOOK TWO

Chapter One

Sarah alighted from the tram at the Market Place and made her way to the ferry. Her step was light, for there was no swelling around her ankles. Three men, coming up the bank from the landing, turned their heads towards her and one of them whistled as he winked at her.

Cheeky thing. She moved her body slightly, expressing indignation that she did not feel. That's what new clothes did, she told herself, made men cheeky.

But as she bought her ticket the pleasure that the men's admiration aroused in her vanished, to be replaced with the feeling of being slightly ashamed, slightly anxious and apprehensive.

Before boarding the ferry, she thought, What if she hasn't turned up? Well, I'll only have to come across again. But she said the two-thirty.

She stepped on to the boat and moved quickly around the engine-house, and there in the bows, her back to the rail, stood Phyllis. In a moment they were together, their hads joined, exchanging smiles and gabbled greetings.

'I thought you weren't comin'. You got me letter?'

'Well, I wouldn't be here else, would I?'

'Don't be silly.'

They laughed at each other as they moved back to the rail, and Phyllis, leaning her side against it, examined Sarah, and her verdict was, 'By! You look bonny. I've never seen you look like this. All new things?' She flicked Sarah's coat with her finger.

'Yes.' Sarah smiled shyly. 'I've got two complete rigouts right through.... But never mind me. What about you? Are you in trouble?'

'Trouble?' Phyllis drew her chin in. 'No, no, I'm in no trouble.'

'Oh?' Sarah paused. 'I thought when I got your letter . . .'

'I just wanted to see you. I felt I had to see you. An' I wanted to hear about me mother an' all.'

Phyllis turned and leant her forearms on the rail; and bending over it and looking down to where the water was beginning to froth as the boat moved from the quay, she added, 'I would have come up to see her.' She swung her head quickly up and sideways. 'I'm not afraid of that lot up there. They couldn't do anything to me. I'm not afraid of any of them, but it was him. I didn't want to run into him. You understand?'

Yes, Sarah understood. She, too, looked over the side of the boat, but without leaning her arm on the rail because it was grubby and would soil her new coat. She looked for some time at the waves dashing themselves against the bows before she said, 'I've missed you an' all, Phyllis. I've thought about you nearly all the time. I've wanted to write but didn't know where to. . . . How's things?'

'Oh, fine.' Phyllis now turned her back again to the river, and, supporting herself with her elbows against the rail, she nodded slowly at Sarah as she said, 'An' it's the truth, things are fine, better than I thought. I can hardly believe it, mind.' She flicked her eyes downwards. 'Still, things isn't all jam.'

'He's all right to you?'

'Ali? Oh, Ali's all right? I've got him there.' She twisted the forefinger of her left hand around the little finger of her right. 'I can manage him. Course he's a bit rough at times.' She pulled a knowing face. 'You know what I mean.' Noting Sarah's flushed face she laughed, and said, 'Aw, our Sarah, come off it, man, you're married. . . . An' when we're on, how's things with you? Is he all right?'

Sarah wanted to say wonderful, wonderful, but she felt that her enthusiasm might in some way hurt Phyllis. Yet she seemed happy enough. But still it might, so she answered almost flippantly, 'Oh, you know, could be worse.'

'You've got your own house?'

'Yes, next door. You know, the one I told you about. We've got the kitchen and one bedroom furnished and are getting at the front room now. John, David's brother, is making us some furniture.'

'I thought he was a joiner . . . a boat joiner?'

'He is, but he can do anything with his hands and wood, it's a hobby. And he's got plenty of time now, he's on the dole.'

'On the dole! . . . One of the Hetheringtons out of work?' Phyllis was evidently surprised. 'My! I didn't think it would touch them. Anyway, how you findin' them all?'

'Oh, they're lovely. At least . . .' She pulled a face at Phyllis. 'The male members are.'

'His mother still sticky?'

'Oh, Phyllis.' Sarah now covered her mouth with her hand and closed her eyes for a second. 'I don't think I'll ever forget the day we were married and we went back and told her. Honestly. . . . You know she's a quiet woman, I told you; you wouldn't think she would ever lose her temper, all dignified like, you know. Well, you know something?' She leaned towards her sister, and it was as if they were on the bed again in the back bedroom. 'I thought she was going to hit me, I did, honest. I've never seen anyone get into such a rage. You know how Mrs Cartwell used to go mad and break things around the house and throw them into the yard. Well, she went on just like her. It was an eye-opener. I thought she would be stiff, and cold and on her high-horse, but I never dreamed she'd act like that. I think she shocked David an' all. He looked flabbergasted. He expected her to go off the deep end 'an all but not in that way. It put the damper on our time in Newcastle, and she never spoke to me for a fortnight. I don't think she would have spoken even yet if David hadn't stopped goin in; that made her come round.'

'Is she all right now?'

'She is, on the surface. But you know, Phyllis, somehow I think she'll never forgive me. I've got to be so careful. You see, when David stopped going in, the men started to come into our place, Dan, and John, and even the father; but now that things are all right–at least, as I said, on the surface–they still keep coming in. . . . Oh, I like it.' She smiled at Phyllis. 'It's lovely to have them all there, and Dan's a lad, he keeps us in stiches. But the awful thing is now, she's started to knock through. You see, our kitchen fireplace and their living-rrom fireplace are back to back and she must have heard us all laughing the other night, for there came a rat-tat on the back of the grate. Oh, Mr Hetherington was vexed. I've never seen him so vexed. And you know, one night last week he said to me, "Can I smoke, Sarah?" Just like that, he asked me could he smoke. Do you know where he's got to smoke?'

'In the lav!'

'No. She won't allow it there; he's got to use the shed at the bottom of the yard. She's never let him smoke in the house. That's why David or Dan don't smoke. John does, in his own place. When he asked me I said. "Of course, fancy asking." And when he said to me, "I shan't make a habit of it, only now and again", do you know, I could have cried, Phyllis. I like him, I like him better than I did at first. The twitch in his eyes got on my nerves, but now I don't notice it.'

'Her and Ali's father would make a pair. He tried to put me there.' Phyllis pressed her thumb into the palm of her hand. 'But I let him see just how far he could go. He runs a boardin' house, you know, and he thought he'd got some cheap labour in me, but he found his mistake out. He's as mean as muck. But Ali's got ideas. . . . What d'you think we're going to do, Sarah? . . . Start a shop. Oh, I wish this wasn't comin'.' She patted the front of her coat, and Sarah exclaimed, 'Oh, I'd forgotten. You're not showing, how are you feeling?'

'All right now. I felt lousy at first.'

'But this shop, what kind? Oh, it would be lovely if you could start a shop.'

'Well, it'll be a sort of café. There's money in it, 'cause even if it's only tea and buns people've got to eat. Eeh, the men that's out of work around us, from the boats, it makes you frightened. It's worse down here than our end was, and that was bad enough, God knows. . . . That's why'–her voice was excited–'I'd love a café, 'cos food's the most important thing in life. It is, you know; you've only got to see them looking hungry and you know damn well just how import . . .'

As the ferry bumped against the North Shields pier Phyllis stopped talking, and for the first time looked rather helplessly at Sarah and asked, 'What we going to do? Have you got to get back?'

'No, not until tea-time. Let's go for a walk and have a cup of tea somewhere.'

'Aw, I'd like that.'

In the murky half-light of the December afternoon they walked through the dull streets talking, talking, talking. When in the main thoroughfare they came across a café that looked a . . . bit posh, they went shyly in, and over the elegance of a set tea with toasted tea-cakes and cream buns they laughed and giggled with the excitement of two girls let out on their own for the first time.

It wasn't until the ferry was half-way across the darkened water nearing South Shields again that their chatter trailed away, and they stood silently side by side, their arms touching, looking towards the unseen waterfront picked out with meagre lighting along its jumble-scarred length.

'Look.' Phyllis was fumbling in her bag now. 'I want you to give this to me mother for Christmas.' She handed Sarah two pound notes, and Sarah said, 'All that? Can you afford it?'

'Oh, aye. I look after number one.' The remark sounded as if it came from a woman versed in the ways of handling men, of riddling pockets, of demanding pay packets. But Phyllis wasn't like that; she was still a young girl, at least so she looked to Sarah, a short pink-and-white, doll-faced young girl.

'She'll be grateful for it, Phyllis.'

'Tell her it's for herself, mind. I'd burn it if I thought he'd get his chaps on it. . . . Do you know how much Ali gives me a week, just to run the house with odds and ends, because we mainly feed downstairs?'

Sarah shook her head now.

'Three pounds. He said once we get the café going he'll double it.'

'Three pounds!' Sarah exclaimed.

Three pounds for odds and ends. Why, David's whole wage was only two pounds seventeen and she had thought that marvellous. She said to Phyllis, 'By! You're lucky!'

In the darkness Phyllis turned from her towards the rail, and her voice had a flat far-away sound as she said, 'Yes, yes, I'm lucky. An' I'm all right, Aye, I'm all right.' It was as if she was confirming a statement in her own mind. 'There's only one thing I can't stand.' In the darkness she swung round to Sarah and caught at her hand, and her voice cracked as she said, 'I feel a beast, Sarah, a proper swine 'cos Ali's good. He's better than any of them up there. I know that, I do. But . . . but it turns me stomach up when we walk down King Street or through the market. It's all right in our quarter, it doesn't matter, 'cos there's other white girls there. Some of them's tarts, but one or two's nice. One girl's from High Jarrow. So it doesn't matter there. But going down King Street I want to yell at them . . . people who look at me: "Keep your pity for yoursel', missus!" I want to say. You know something, Sarah? You know the Howards that live in Duxham Street, you know when all the schemozzle was on a few years ago about the girl having a bairn to her brother . . . well, she didn't know whether it was her brother or her father, you remember? Well, you know, I always felt sorry for her and I've always spoken to her on the road when we passed. Well, what do you think the bitch did? We were in the market and she cut me as dead as a doornail. Do you know, I almost threw me basket at her. I was so flaming mad.'

'Oh, Phyllis! Perhaps you imagined it. Oh, our Phyllis!' Sarah's compassion brought the tears into her voice.

'Don't be daft; you don't imagine things like that. An' the others told me they've all had to go through it. But most of 'em can go back and see their folks. . . . Oh, Sarah!' She was holding tightly to Sarah's hands. 'I wish we could be together, or we lived nearer, so I could pop in.'

There was a new kind of pain tearing through Sarah now. She wanted to say wholeheartedly, 'Well, don't you be daft. Come whenever you like; you'll be welcome, you know that.' And if she was speaking for herself Phyllis would be welcome. She would have even let her bring the Arab with her–she couldn't think of the man as Phyllis's husband. But there was David to think of. No, it wasn't David she was thinking about–David had said everybody must do what they felt driven to do. He had added lovingly at this point that he had felt driven to marry her. No, it wasn't David she was thinking about, it was his mother. She had hurt his mother very much, she realised that. Deep within herself she felt guilty. She felt she had forced herself into her family, and Mrs Hetherington fed this impression. So she couldn't make matters worse at this stage by asking her sister into her house. If they hadn't lived next door to David's mother she would have managed it somehow, but asking Phyllis up would be like asking her into the Hetherington's living-room. She couldn't do it–but oh, she wished she could. She gripped Phyllis's hands as she said, 'Look, we'll get together, make a habit of meeting, and I'll bring me mother with me sometime. What do you say?'

'I'd love that. . . . You know, Sarah, you can come to our place if you wouldn't mind. I've the two rooms at the top done nice. You'd be surprised at the things I've got. But . . . but don't come on a Friday.' It was as if Sarah had already accepted the invitation. 'Friday's their Sunday, you know. You wouldn't believe it, you talk about the Catholics being religious . . . Coo! They couldn't hold a candle to Ali's people. His father's a big noise in their kind of church . . . they're Moslems. They're always prayin' all times of the day, you wouldn't believe it, an' yet the old devil–Ali's father, I mean–bleeds his own folk white.' She pushed at Sarah. 'That's funny, isn't it? Bleeding them white! . . . They want me to become a Moslem.'

Sarah was aghast, 'but you're not!'

'No, I'll not. Not that it makes any difference; I was never affected by our church as you were, it just slid off me. Hell fire if you missed mass on Sunday. Who do they think they're kiddin'! You know, Sarah, you learn a lot by mixin' with other people. Still, I'd have to learn a lot more afore I became a Moslem.' She was laughing now and punching Sarah on the arm. And her laughter began to rise until Sarah said, 'Be quiet, our Phyllis, you'll raise the boat.' She wanted to slap her sister to stop her laughing because the sound was painful, it wasn't real laughter; it was the kind of laugh you laugh to stop crying.

As the boat once again bumped against the quay she gripped Phyllis by the arm and together they walked over the gangway and up the rough road to the market-place.

As the clock struck five Sarah exclaimed, 'Eeh! David will be in and he'll wonder what on earth's happened to me. No tea ready.'

'You didn't tell him you were meetin' me?'

'Yes, yes, I did.' Sarah made the lie sound convincing. 'But you know what they are for their tea. There's the tram in, Phyllis, I'd better catch it.'

They stood peering at each other in the dim light; then, their arms around each other, they held together tightly for a moment before turning away without further words. . . .

All the way home Sarah wanted to cry. She kept saying over and over in her mind. Oh, our Phyllis. Oh, our Phyllis.

When she alighted at the bottom of the street there was David standing waiting for her. He came forward at a bound, saying, 'Where on earth have you been? I've been worried stiff. Look, it's quarter to six, the house all in darkness. Where've you been?'

'Oh, I'm sorry I am, David. I'll get your tea directly.'

He had her by the arm hurrying her up the street. 'It's not my tea I'm worrying about, woman.' He shook her. 'You've never been out before and there was no note or anything; I didn't know what to think.'

Sarah suddenly felt warm, wanted . . . she belonged. She dropped her head on to her shoulder and hunched it up against him as she said, 'Don't worry, I'll never run away.'

He patted her cheek before saying, 'But I do worry . . . and about you running away.'

'You're joking.'

'No, no I'm not.'

They were at the front door now. 'But you must be, David.'

'Get yourself in.' He pushed her playfully from behind. Then when the door was closed and they stood in the black darkness of the passage he groped at her and pulling her into his arms, kissed her. It was a long hard kiss, and when he was finished he said, 'Always leave a note, will you?'

'Yes, David.' His deep concern at her absence puzzled her, she couldn't fully understand it. If he had been a little irritable, or chastised her in a jocular way, or even sulked, not that David would ever sulk, but if he had taken any of these attitudes she would have understood it, but that he was really frightened that she wouldn't come back was something that she couldn't take in because it put value on her beyond her worth, at least the worth she placed on herself. Now if the boot were on the other foot and she was concerned about him walking out on her, well, she could have understood that plainly, because she knew that compared to David she was very ignorant. She wondered sometimes how he put up with her ignorance. She was doing her best to improve, she had even asked him to get her books, but she could never see herself conversing with David other than on personal topics. She would never be like May, able to hold her own, even argue with John or Dan about unemployment and politics. Yes, she could have understood it if the boot were on the other foot.

When the gas was lit in the kitchen it showed the fire banked down and almost out, and she hurried forward, saying, 'Eeh! I'll never let this happen again. I don't know what I was thinking about.'

'Don't worry.'

'But I am. And no tea ready for you. The time just flew.' She straightened her back from the fire, and turning to him, said, 'I haven't told you where I've been.'

'It doesn't matter.'

'I've been to see our Phyllis.'

He swung round towards her. 'You've been into Costerfine Town . . . to the house?' His voice held concern again.

'No, no, I got a letter from her by the second post. She asked me to meet her on the ferry. We went across to North Shields. I didn't know whether to tell you or not.' She drooped her head. 'I thought if I did you might stop me, and I wanted to see her because . . . because she's a good girl really. She's not bad, our Phyllis, she's only a child yet.'

'Oh, Sarah.' He was enfolding her again now. 'I wouldn't have stopped you. The only thing is I hate you going around the lower docks and that quarter on your own. It's pretty rough round there, you know, at all times, and'–he pummelled gently round her chin with his fist–'you're an eyecatcher in any port.'

'Oh, David, I'm not. You stretch it.' She laughed, raising her brows at him. 'You forget I've been going back and forwards into Shields since I was fourteen.'

'Perhaps, but you didn't look . . . well . . . like you do now . . . happy. You're more than fetching, Mrs Hetherington, when you're happy.'

'Am I?' She slanted her eyes up to the ceiling as if thinking. 'Well, I'm not to blame, it's all your fault . . . Oh, David. Darlin' . . .'

They sprung apart as if cleaved by a chopper when there came a voice from the backyard and a knocking on the back door. 'Are you in?'

As David withdrew the bolt Sarah applied herself madly to the fire. No fire on, no tea ready . . . his mother would have to come in at this minute.

'I've been round three times this afternoon. You've just got in?'

Sarah turned from the fire. She was still wearing her outdoor coat and she muttered hastily, 'Yes, yes, I was held up.'

'She's been looking round the shops for Christmas boxes, got fascinated with the bargains and forgot the time.'

Mary Hetherington was looking at the table covered with a chenille cloth and no sign of food on it. Then, looking at the fire, she remarked coolly, 'It'll be some time before you'll get anything going on that; the tea's still on the table indoors, you'd better come in and have it.' Then, looking at David she added, 'I suppose you're ready for it with not a bite since dinner-time.' On this she went quietly out.

Sarah and David exchanged glances, and as Sarah saw him make a gesture towards his mother's back that meant refusal she quickly raised her hand, then called, 'We'll be in in a minute.' She pushed at David as she whispered now, 'You go on. I'll just put some sticks on and get it going. I'll follow you.'

'No, no, I'll see to it. I'm not going to be . . .'

She swung him about and pushed him out of the kitchen, saying, 'Go on. Go on.'

When she had closed the door on him she stood with her back to it looking towards the dead fire, but she felt as warm as if it was ablaze and its flames were lapping the heat towards her. If David had to choose between her and his mother there was no doubt which side he would be on. She knew that when a man married the cord was not always cut between him and his mother, and if the wife went to snap it she was in for trouble. But in this case it was his mother who had snapped the cord. Yet there was a part of her that felt sorry about the severance. She didn't want any upset. She didn't want David to have to take sides. She wanted him to want his mother; not as much as he wanted her, but to want her nevertheless. She wanted them all to be happy and jolly together because she was happy. Life was being wonderful to her, and, oh God, she was thankful. As her mind uttered the word God she turned her glance quickly round the kitchen as if to reassure herself she was alone, then, dropping quickly on to her knees by the side of David's chair, she buried her face in her hands and began to pray, asking God, as always, to overlook her past sins and to recognise her marriage. She followed this up with a prayer of thanksgiving, praying in her own way, her words bereft of any supplication. She made no pleas for future happiness, she only thanked God for giving her David.

And as she rose from her knees she thought of Sunday morning and muttered aloud, 'I'll go to Jarrow mass, early. They know nothing about me there.'

Only once since her marriage had she been to Tyne Dock church and she had come out feeling like the scarlet woman herself, and she knew that she couldn't sit under the glaze of Father O'Malley ever again.

She turned down the gas and was about to move out of the kitchen when she stopped and looked around. It had been a funny day. Funny things happened to people, perhaps they always had. But as you got older you became more aware of them. She had been to North Shields with Phyllis and walked countless streets, talking, talking talking. David had met her off the tram and had nearly carried her into the house and had wanted to make love to her in the passage. Her body shivered deliciously at the thought. And then his mother had come in and brought with her bleak condemnation. And just a minute ago she had gone on her knees and prayed. She had never gone on her knees in the day-time before, unless she was in church. . . . Yes, it had been a funny day.

She locked the door leading into the yard, and when she went to open the back door into the lane it was pushed inwards and she was confronted with John's broad back. He swung round towards her, his bulk only discernible in the reflection of the lamp from the bottom of the lane. His body stood within the shadow of the wall, but she could make out the chair he held in front of him.

'I've just finished this one,' he said.

'Oh, I've been out. There was no tea ready. Your mother came round and said we must go in for tea. I've locked up; will I let you in?' She was gabbling.

'Well, I'll only have to take it back, I'm not leaving it in the yard. Don't you want to see it?'

'Oh yes, yes, John.' She rushed back up the yard, unlocked the door and held it open for him, and he moved past her into the kitchen and placed the chair by the side of the table.

'There, what do you think?' He was looking at her.

'Oh, it's lovely.' The words were slow in admiration. 'I've never seen any like it, with a carved back.'

'Sit in it and see how it feels.'

She sat down and moved her ribs into the curve, then wriggled her body in the seat. 'It's lovely, and so comfortable. Oh, thanks, John. But you shouldn't go on wasting your time making these. You've done us the table, that's enough.' She got to her feet and put her hand on the top rail.

'I don't think it's a waste of time.' He was looking at the chair. 'Chairs are the most difficult things to do, more so than a table. A chair knows it's going to be sat on; it's a personal thing, a chair.' He touched its back and moved his fingers across the grained wood to within an inch of hers.

'Nice feel wood, hasn't it? Clean, nothing underhand about wood.'

She looked at him. He was waiting for her eyes. They hadn't been alone together but once since she was married. She felt nervous, even slightly afraid, of what she couldn't say. There came to her the memory of the night when she had wanted to fall on his breast and cry. She moved quickly and said, 'Eeh! I'll have to be getting next door or I'll be in the black books. Are you staying?'

'If you don't mind.' His eyes were still on her.

'Have you had your tea?'

'Yes, I've had my tea, but I'll stay until you come back. I want to have a talk with Davie. But don't let on to the old lady I'm here.' He smiled. 'It wouldn't do, would it?'

She shook her head. They were like conspirators now. She moved towards the door, but felt compelled to turn and look at him again. His eyes never seemed to have left her. She said quietly, 'Thanks for the chairs, John.'

'It's nothing,' he said. As she turned away again his voice came at her. 'You know what I'm going to do when I get me dole this week?' She looked over her shoulder waiting. 'I'm going to get blind drunk. I'm going to bust the lot, every penny, and I'm going to roll in next door and lie on the couch snoring.'

She couldn't laugh. She knew that he wouldn't get drunk on his dole. She knew that he would never lie on his mother's couch snoring, as much as he might want to. He just said these things, he said them to her often, these things, apropos of nothing that had gone before, to hold her attention, to keep her looking at him. At first she had not known how to meet these moods–they were like the tantrums of a precocious child–and she had remained silent and embarrassed on the spate of his words, but on this occasion she put them in their place by saying, 'A raw egg in tea is a very good thing for a hangover.'

She was closing the back gate as she heard his laugh. It was high and mirthless, of the same quality as Phyllis's had been on the ferry.

It had been an odd day.

Chapter Two

'Have you tried Palmer's lately?' said Dan.

'Aye.' John lowered himself further into the couch by letting out a deep breath.

'No good?'

'No good.'

'I thought since the N.S.S. had taken it over things had looked up. I heard they had a number of ships ordered.'

'Aye, they have; and they've got a number of men to do the work and they're sitting tight. They'll drop down dead on the job before they'll take a day off sick, that's what fear will do to you. . . . But, look, don't worry about me, Dan. Stop it, man, will you?' John hoisted himself up straight again. 'You're like an old hen. Isn't he, Sarah?'

Sarah was working at a side table, her arms deep in a batch of dough, mixing, turning, kneading. She looked relaxed, completely at ease. She turned and smiled, not at John in particular but at the three men sitting around the fire. Her eyes coming to rest on David, his long legs stretched out on the fender, her smile widened, and he said to her, 'Are you ready for more water?'

'No, I've got enough, I don't want to drown the miller.'

'You can't kid me,' said Dan, 'you're worried. Why not admit it and stop acting the big fellow. It stands to reason, everybody's worried. Even with the Palmers' little boom on, people are not spending like they used to, they're frightened. And who's to blame them? You know, some of them on the dole are spending as much on groceries as those in work. I had a talk about this to a woman, a Mrs Robinson–she's been a customer of ours for years. She admitted it. She said they were clearing up the rent and clubs and things because when the next bad spell comes they'd be able to run up again. But if they didn't pay up now they'd get short shrift if they ever wanted tick again. And, as she said, you may be sure they'd want it again. It's an awful look-out, you know.'

'Don't.' said John bitterly now. 'It makes me want to go berserk. We're back a hundred years ago, man. There's riots breaking out all over the country, and fellows being jailed. Nothing changed in a hundred years. The men marched from Hebburn and Shields to Jarrow in those days to be at a Trade Union meeting, and what happened? Seven of 'em were sentenced to death. It was changed to transportation. Lads who were God-fearing, peace-loving individuals, Primitive Methodists, but all they and the others wanted to do was to work and eat.'

John was sitting forward now addressing Dan loudly as if this young uncle of his was the cause of all the past and present trouble. 'Young lads under twelve kept at work for twenty-four hours at a stretch they were then.'

'But that was in the pits . . .' Dan began, but was shouted down again by John crying, 'Pits or shipyards or steel mills or pudding mills, what does it matter on a twenty-four-hour stretch? It shouldn't 'ave been tolerated. And it's as bad today in a way. How do they expect a man to live? Twenty-six shillings to keep three of us. Two shillings to keep a child! Did you ever hear anything like it? And if I hadn't been working full time these last years I wouldn't be getting that. How about the poor devils who haven't had thirty contributions on their cards in the last two years or so. I tell you it's a bloody scandal.'

'Look, John, calm down and fight your own battles for the moment. As you stand now you could be off for seventy-four weeks and still get benefit. . . .'

'Seventy-four weeks! My God, man do you want me to land up in the loony bin in the Institution. . . . Look, Dan. Don't you start talking as if they were being kind to me. Every man Jack of us is up afore them every eleven weeks and our money could be stopped like that.' He cracked his thick fingers and the sound was like the meeting of drumsticks. 'There's a clause called "the not genuinely seeking work clause". Have you heard of it?' His voice was sarcastic. 'You want to get into that queue, Dan, and hear just how those boys behind the wire grids with their smug jobs can manoeuvre it.'

'They're not to blame. John. They're just doing their job.'

They all turned and looked at David now. He was speaking quietly, his eyes directed towards the fire. 'Phil Taggart in the Exchange said he would be out of it tomorrow, but it would just mean him standing on the other side of the grid.'

'Phil Taggart!' John's voice was scornful. 'He's just one; you want to see the attitude of most of those swine. They look at you as if you'd just drawled up the wire. "Stand aside." "Come back this afternoon." "What did you say your number was?"' John's voice had taken up a haughty tone. Then it changed abruptly back as he said, 'There'll be riots I tell you, men can only stand so much.'

Yes, there would be riots, If all the men were like John there would be riots all the time, Sarah thought as she turned the dough over for the last time. Lack of work, resulting in enforced idleness, broken only by miles of tramping in search of the elusive job, had taken the spunk out of most of the men. She remembered the men two or three years ago standing at the corners, talking loudly, protest oozing out of them, aggressive against misfortune. Now they still stood at the corners, but they were more quiet, their talk intermittent. Some of them walked slower. Their faces had a pale-yellow tinge. They hoarded Woodbine ends in small tin boxes. Some of them pushed home-made barrows down to the tip at the bottom of Simonside Bank and scraped there for cinders and came around the doors selling them; a shilling they would ask for a barrow-load. She always bought a load. There were six buckets to the barrow. They were burnt-out cinders and wouldn't burn on their own, but they did all right for banking down. One man had called twice last week. He did not ask her to buy the second time, he just stood looking helplessly at her. She hadn't wanted the second load but she had taken it and said, 'Would you like a flat cake? It's just out of the oven?' 'Oh, missis!' was all he had said, but his lips became soft with saliva. It was the first time she had been addressed as'missis', and it made her feel married and very adult.

Then there was David. David worried about the unemployed. He always had apparently, but now his concern was centred around John. He was very fond of John. He didn't agree with half he said and argued with him, but nevertheless she knew from the way he talked that he thought a lot of his elder brother. He said John was the last person on earth who should be out of work, it would do something to him. Unemployment was like a personal insult to a man of his calibre. John, he said, would die protesting. He was made like that. . . .

Tomorrow was New Year's Eve, the last day of nineteen twenty-nine. She had decided to get her baking done tonight so that tomorrow she would only have the cleaning to do. Everything must be polished and shining with an extra brightness to greet the New Year. Everybody everywhere–to her everywhere was a synonym for the North–cleared up for New Year's Day. She wanted to be all done before tea-time because they were going to spend the evening next door. Apparently they had a lot of jollification on New Year's Eve, and also apparently without getting drunk. But this was the one night, she understood, when David's mother allowed wine in the house. Also for this night she brewed a batch of home-brewed beer, the recipe for which she would tell no one, and which had a kick Dan said that was better than any Burton and as good as some whiskies. She was a strange woman was David's mother, Sarah thought, and a frightening woman in some ways. She had decided on one thing: she wouldn't sing tomorrow night, not even if they pressed her, because she knew that her mother-in-law didn't like her to sing–not on her own. She had gone out of the room when she had sang last time. It was 'Where my caravan has rested', and they had all praised her–all except David's mother.

As she put a cloth over the dough David rose from his chair and lifted the heavy earthenware dish down on to the fender. John was still at it; he was thrusting his finger at Dan now and saying, 'We'll be marching from here, you'll see. It's the only way to get things done. The Scots did it last year, they're not the blokes to sit down under injustice. They've been marching and protesting since 1922.'

'The N.U.W.M. got up the national march last year, don't forget that,' said Dan. 'You don't have to be a dour Scot to get things done. They made the Tories consider the "Not genuinely seeking work clause" that you're on about; they didn't get it abolished but they got another year's grace. And it was prophetic that only a few weeks later the Tories were out. . . .'

'Well, for all the good the change has done they might as well have stayed in, for Ramsay Macdonald and Snowdon are still carrying on the same policy; they make my belly heave. Once the Labour Government got in it was going to play hell with a big stick. And it's done bug . . .' On a warning look from David. John just suppressed the adjective and substituted 'damn all' in its place.

The little incident caught at Dan's sense of humour. The heat of the discourse, the added colour that rose to John's face with the suppression of the word bugger, was too much; he put head back and let out a bellow of a laugh.

'You . . . you big stiff!' John's great arm knocked Dan sideways on the couch. 'You can laugh.' But now John's laughter had joined Dan's. And Dan's finger came out and wagged itself in John's face while with the other arm he gripped himself around the waist to ease the pain that his merriment was causing. The next moment the two men were locked together sparring like irrespressible schoolboys.

'Give over, give over, you fools!' David was standing above them. 'You'll break the couch, the pair of you.' He jumped aside as they fell sideways on to the floor and there, locked together, they lay panting and still laughing.

'You pair of fools!' David, himself laughing now, was staring down at them where they both sat with their backs to the seat of the couch, their legs stretched out on the mat.

'That takes us back some years.' John had his head turned to Dan, and Dan, rubbing his wet face with his hand, said, 'By! It does that. We used to have some fun and games, didn't we?' As they hitched themselves back on to the couch, Dan took a fit of coughing which caused him to press his hand across his chest.

David, turning now to where Sarah was rubbing fat into flour preparatory to making pastry, and herself laughing at the antics of these men acting like young lads, said eagerly, 'What about us throwing a bit of a party, eh, Sarah?'

Her hands stopped their rubbing. 'A party! Oh, yes. Oh yes, I'd like that. When?' They were all looking at her. 'What about Thursday?' she said. They continued to look at her but no one spoke. John was the first to look away. He cast his eyes sideways towards Dan and then said on a small laugh, 'Well, what about Thursday?'

Dan got to his feet, pulling his coat straight, saying as he did so, 'Not Thursday, Sarah.'

'Oh no.' She nodded her head. She had forgotten, Dan always went to stay with a friend of his on Thursday. She could understand Dan having lots of friends. She had never seen this friend. Apparently he lived at yon side of Westoe village. Perhaps he had a wife, she didn't know. David hadn't seemed to know much about it when she had asked him about Dan's friend some time ago. Impetuously she said now, 'Why don't you bring your friend along, Dan? Shouldn't he, David?'

Dan's head came up quickly. He had been dusting the legs of his trousers and now his hands were held outwards as if the question had fixed him in one position. There was a look of perplexity on his face, until he turned his gaze full on David and smiled at him. Then, moving towards the scullery door and coming abreast of Sarah, he said quietly, 'Make it Friday and we'll have a night of it.'

When the door closed quietly John turned to David, and speaking below his breath, he said, 'Do you mean to say you haven't told her?'

'I didn't see the need.' There was an unusually sharp note in David's reply.

John turned his head and looked at Sarah now, and she looked at him as he said, 'Well, she's a married woman and she won't faint, and, being Sarah, she'll understand, won't you, Sarah?'

'Understand what?'

'About Dan. You see . . .'

'I'll tell her, John. If it's necessary, I'll tell her.'

'All right, have it your own way, but it would have saved an embarrassing situation if she had known already, wouldn't it? But that's you.' He brought his fist in a quick flick past the end of David's nose. Then he screwed his face up at him and moved across the room. 'Goodnight, Sarah.' His voice was quiet now.

'Goodnight, John.'

When the back door had closed, Sarah, scraping the flour and fat from her hands, looked over her shoulder and asked, 'What was all that about, about Dan? Is there something wrong?'

'Really it's none of our business.'

'Did I put my foot in it in some way?'

'No.' He caught at her floured hand and pulled her towards him, pressing her down into the big leather chair at the side of the fireplace. Then, seated himself on a cracket close to her knee and looking to where the rising dough was pushing against the cloth, he said, 'Dan's got a woman.'

Dan with a woman! Sarah couldn't believe it. Dan the kindly, jocular, nice man, carrying on with a woman! He wasn't the type. She made David look at her as she said, 'I just can't take that in.'

'It's true. But it's his own business; it's Dan's own life and he can do what he likes with it.'

'Yes, yes, I know, David. Yes.' She was quick to agree with him. 'But somehow–well, Dan just doesn't seem . . . Is she married?'

'No.'

'She's not? Well, why doesn't he marry her?'

'It's very difficult to explain.' David took hold of her hand again. 'It sounds a bit fantastic, but you know different people think in different ways and some people think for themselves. Dan does, and apparently this woman does too. She's a widow and as far as I can gather she's glad to be a widow, as she has a pretty rough time during the six years she was married to her husband. He was killed by a lorry and the firm was found to be at fault and she gets a small pension. Perhaps this is a bit of the reason for her independence. Well, anyway, she doesn't want to marry and neither does Dan.'

'Dan doesn't want to marry her?'

'No, nor nobody else. I mean Dan doesn't want to marry anybody. Dan's been serving in a shop since he was twelve. He started running errands then and he's had a sort of education against marriage through listening to women . . . at least that's how he laughingly put it to me. But he just doesn't want to marry. Anyway, he met this woman. How, I don't know, he never told me; I only know that she's got a decent kind of house and that one night in the week, Thursday night–it has never varied over the last four years–he goes and sees her.'

'But your mother . . . ?'

'Oh! There was the devil to pay. Being Dan, he was quite straight about it. But fancy having to tell a thing like that to my mother; imagine the scene; especially when she looked on him almost as a son and not a brother. You see, she had the business of bringing him up when her own mother died. Anyway, he gave her the option; he was quite willing, he said, to go and get lodgings elsewhere. He emphasised to her that he was not going to live with the woman, only see her that one night a week. Lord, he had some pluck. It all sounded fantastic and I can see how my mother thought he was going up the pole. But, anyway, she didn't tell him to get out and take his life of sin with him. And for two reasons. First, she's a saver, and a very careful housekeeper as you have gathered. She's nearly always had twice as much coming in each week as what she's spent. She could teach Micawber a thing or two.'

'Micawber?'

'Oh, he's a character in Dickens. I must get you Dickens, you'll like him. . . . And then there was the fact that if she ordered Dan out he might, although he said he wouldn't, go and live with the woman, whereas if she kept him under her eye she might manage to convert him from his sinful ways. But up to date she hasn't made any impression on him. The atmosphere in the house on a Thursday morning is always painful.'

'But it's fantastic. I can't see . . . well, I can't see Dan doing it. And if he's living with her part of the time what's the difference, why doesn't he live with her all the time?'

'Don't ask me, Sarah, I just don't know. Dan has arranged his life and he has found someone to arrange it with.'

'I liked Dan.'

'Don't say it like that in the past tense, Sarah. Surely this won't stop you going on liking him. Dan's a fine fellow.'

'But it's a bit of a shock. Dan doesn't look . . .'

'You can never tell by people's looks, Sarah. And see here.' He tilted her chin upwards, his voice holding a note which she had never heard before. 'You are not going to make any difference to Dan, I mean in your manner; I wouldn't like that, Sarah.'

'No, no, of course not.' She smiled at him now. 'It was just . . . well, just as I said. I . . . I couldn't see Dan doing anything like that. But don't worry, I'll be the same to him. And why should I make any difference?' She shook her head. 'I've got no room to speak. Look at our Phyllis. And she's nice and all. I've always told you our Phyllis is nice.'

'There you are then.' They were smiling at each other. He leant towards her now. 'And you're nice, too, Mrs Hetherington. Very, very, very nice. Do you know that, Mrs Hetherington.'

The niceness was inside her, she could feel it. David could make her feel that she was nice. She felt a different person when she was with David, soft inside, even refined. Yes, even refined. She had always longed to be refined, to know what to say, to know what to do. She had always felt she would never reach this desired pinnacle, not only because she was ignorant but because she didn't look refined, at least her body didn't, it was too big–the word was voluptuous. She had looked that up in the dictionary David had bought her. He bought it for her the very next day after she had told him she had always wanted a dictionary. He had seemed very pleased that she had wanted a dictionary.

David was looking at her now. She knew the look and she became quiet. She remained quiet when he rose swiftly from the cracket and went and put the bolt in the back door. She hitched her hips to one side and made room for him when he returned, and he lay with his head on her shoulder, his fingers slowly outlining her breasts. Her lips dropped apart; they were trembling slightly and moist. 'I've got the bread to do,' she said in a whisper. 'I've got all my baking to get through.'

He opened her blouse, and, supporting the large cup of her breast on the palm of his hand, he said, 'I wish all men joy because of you.'

She felt more than nice; more than refined, she felt wonderful, honoured, like a queen must feel.

Chapter Three

New Year's Eve was typical, the day being made up of a number of small busy-busy issues leading to the climax. But when Sarah looked back on this particular day she saw that everything she had done had a bearing on what was to come. Like threads of a tapestry, on which was worked the outline pattern of her life, they began to work inwards to the central point.

It was when she finished scrubbing the scullery and had returned to the snug warmth of the kitchen that she thought, I wonder how me mother is. I should slip across, it being New Year's Eve. She'll feel it, being all on her own. And he'll be out this morning, signing on. Yes, I should slip across.

Ten minutes later she locked the scullery door and went down the back-yard and out into the lane. The back lane was clean and empty–you very rarely saw the women of Camelia Street standing gossiping at their back doors; it was a sign of their raised status, that any gossiping they did was over a cup of tea in the afternoon after they had . . . got the men off.

The morning was biting cold; there was a high wind blowing that spoke of snow. Sarah felt she could smell it. She pulled the collar of her new coat up around her ears and kept her gloved hands up under its warmth as she walked. She loved this coat, she had never had anything like it; it was David's Christmas box. He had paid five pounds ten for it. She had played war with him. It was dove grey, trimmed with brown fur, and it fitted her as if it had been made to measure.

Perhaps it was because her life was now spent between the sparkling cleanliness of her mother-in-law's house and her own home, that the streets through which she was now passing seemed dirtier than she had ever noticed them before, and the houses, although the same size as those in Camelia Street except for number one, looked smaller.

There were three men standing at the bottom of Howard Street and they looked at her but seemed shy of acknowledging her, until she remarked breezily, 'By! It's a stinger, isn't it?'

'Aye, aye, it is that. How are you getting on, Sarah?'

'Oh, fine, Mr Prideau.'

'That's the ticket, Sarah. You're looking well . . . Bonny.'

She turned her head as she passed them, smiling widely on them. People were nice, people were kind.

'Happy New Year, Sarah. Happy New Year.'

The combined voices turned her head towards them again and she called back, her mouth wide and laughing, 'Happy New Year to you an' all. Happy New Year.'

Mrs West from number seven was doing her windows, and Mrs Young was doing her step. It was late to do steps this time in the morning; still it was New Year's Eve and all the work was topsy-turvy.

The two women stopped what they were doing and waited for her approach. 'Hello, Sarah. Goin' to see your mother?' Mrs West nodded her head at her.

'Yes.' She nodded back, then turned to Mrs Young. 'Hello, Mrs Young.'

'Hello, Sarah, lass. By! Isn't it cold!'

'Freezing.'

'How's things going?' Mrs West was poking her head forward, speaking in a confidential whisper.

'Oh, fine, Mrs West, fine.'

'You like it up there?'

'I couldn't help but, could I?'

'No, I suppose not. Anyway, I'm glad to see you've fallen on your feet. Your mother can be proud of you, at least.'

Sarah turned from Mrs West again. She would have to say that, digging at their Phyllis. She said quickly, 'How are you keeping, Mrs Young?'

'Fine, lass, fine. But I won't say I wouldn't be better if they were at work. Still, you never know what the New Year'll bring, do you?'

'No, Mrs Young.' Sarah knocked on the front door, and as she heard the steps approaching on the other side she said, 'I wish you a Happy New Year in case I don't see you again.'

'The same to you, lass.'

'A Happy New Year, Mrs West.' She nodded to the other woman.

'The same to you, Sarah. The same to you.'

Annie was surprised to see her, but the light that spread over her face showed her pleasure. 'Why, lass, I didn't expect you across the day.' She spoke as if Sarah was in the habit of visiting every day. She went before her through the front room and into the kitchen, talking quickly. 'I've just made a cup of tea, I must have known you were comin'. I haven't done me baking yet, I was just about to start. Sit down, sit down, lass. By! You're looking well. Is that a new coat? It's bonny . . . a beauty.'

'David bought it for my Christmas box.'

She hadn't seen her mother since three days before Christmas when she had given her Phyllis's money and a pound of her own.

Sarah watched her mother pouring the tea out. Her hands were shaking slightly, and she spilled the tea into the saucers, exclaiming on her awkwardness as she did so. Sarah glanced around the kitchen. Everything looked clean but not with the sparkle of her own house. She said, 'You're all done, I see.'

'Yes. Yes, I thought I might as well get it over with. Yet I ask meself, what for?' Annie sat down suddenly opposite to Sarah. Her hand was still on the teapot. She looked at her daughter for a long moment before saying, 'Oh, I'm glad to see you; I felt the house would be empty all the day. You notice it more on New Year's Eve and I was dreading twelve o'clock. We always sat up, didn't we, me and you and Phyllis, and saw the New Year in. But it'll be different this year.'

Sarah felt a lump rise to her throat. Yes, it would be different for them both. As her mother had said, they had always seen the New Year in; their father never sat up. Not given to drink or merriment of any kind, he saw no point in it. His logic on the matter had always been: It's just another day so why kid yourself? And he had usually left them with this sentiment, but slightly more embellished.

She said to her mother now, 'Are you going to sit up?'

'Well, I always have, lass. It's like a habit. Mrs Young has asked me next door but I don't think I'll go.

'Why not? Go on.'

'I like me own fireside. You know what it is on a New Year's Eve. Everybody should be at their own fireside.'

Sarah hesitated only a moment, then she said, 'Why don't you come across to us? You've never been. You'll have to come some time. Come on.' She leant forward and caught her mother's hands.

'Ooh, no. lass, no, I wouldn't dream of it. I don't know them.'

'But you've met David that once, and you said you liked him.'

'Yes, yes, I do. I think he's a fine fellow. But no, no, no, lass. But mind'– she nodded her head at her daughter–'I'm glad you asked me, and I won't forget it. But don't worry about me.' She straightened herself up in the chair. 'I'm all right now that I've seen you.'

'I tell you what.' Sarah's voice was eager, her attitude like that of an excited child. 'Are you sure you're going to sit up?'

'Yes, lass, yes, I'll sit up.'

'Then I'll come across about half-past twelve and wish you a Happy New Year.' Their hands were joined again. It was as if some great problem had been solved. Their hands still holding, they got to their feet and Sarah said, 'That's what I'll do.'

'But, look, you haven't drunk your tea.'

'Oh no.' Sarah took up the cup.

Oh, I'd love that, lass. Do you think you'd be able to get away?'

'Oh yes. David will run over with me.'

In the middle of the front room Sarah stopped and, turning to her mother, asked quietly, 'But what if he stays up the night, you being on your own?'

'There's very little possibility of that, lass. But if he does, well . . .' She looked around as if searching for a solution. Then she said quickly, 'Well, if he's up or if we're in next door–he was asked an' all and you never know with him–well, if that happens I'll leave the front room blind up. All right?'

'All right.' They nodded at each other then moved towards the door, but there stopped again, and Sarah, looking down at the handle round which her fingers were curved, said, 'I do miss our Phyllis. With everything I've got I still miss seeing our Phyllis. . . . Oh, I'm sorry.' She looked at her mother's bent head. 'I shouldn't have mentioned her again.'

'Aw, lass, I'm glad you did. I think of her all the time. And you know what?' Annie thrust her head forward. 'In the New Year I'm going to start going out, I'm going to take trips into Shields.' She spoke as if Shields was a long distance away instead of three miles to its centre. 'And then I'm going to look in on our Phyllis. I don't care, I'm going to look in on her. He needn't know anything about it. But now and again I'll look in on her.'

'Oh, Mother, I'm glad. Oh, I'm glad of that.'

'Well, something must be done, she can't come up here.'

'No, no, that's true. Oh, I'm glad you're going to see her.' She leant quickly forward and they kissed and clung together, not close, just holding each other's arms. Annie was crying gently now, and Sarah, fumbling with the lock, let herself out and hurried down the street. She felt sad and happy at the same time, and overall a feeling of relief. Her mother was going to see Phyllis and she too was going to see Phyllis. Yes, she would in the New Year on the quiet. She would tell David. Oh yes, she would tell David. He wouldn't stop her, but she must do it on the quiet. His mother would never forgive her if she knew she was going into a house in Costerfine Town. . . .

The second thread was the arrival of Dan through her back door around twelve o'clock, long before his usual dinner hour. His face looked peaked and his voice was husky as he said, 'Oh, I'm glad you're in, Sarah. I wouldn't have known what to do with this except put it in your coalhouse.' He pulled from the inside pocket of his coat a flat flask of whisky. 'It's about the only sure cure for this.' He pointed to his chest. 'It's settling here. If I have this hot and stay by the fire for half an hour or so it'll do the trick. You don't mind?'

'No, no, of course not.' She looked hard at him. But she was not seeing him as the man whose goings-on had shocked her last night in spite of her denial. She did not see him as the man who was keeping a woman, and in a very odd way. He was just Dan, who was nice. She said, 'Sit yourself down, I'll get the fire going. You've had this cold coming on for nearly a week, why haven't you done something about it?'

'Oh, Mary wanted to put me to bed, but I thought I could work it off. I hate to be away from the shop. Young George is all right, he can carry on, but the girl and the lad are new to it. Just started this past month, and Friday and Saturday are our busiest days. But I felt I had to come away this morning, I thought I was going to pass out. I told the old man.'

'You should be in bed.' She was bustling around filling the kettle, bringing in a mug and sugar, putting more coals on the fire. 'Take your coat off,' she said, 'and I'll fill a bottle.' She bent down to the bottom cupboard and brought out a stone water-bottle.

'No, no, Sarah, I'd better not get too hot. I'll be all right. If I'd had a hot whisky going to bed each night it would have done the trick. But you know Mary.' he sighed. 'And yet the stuff she brewed yesterday is more deadly than raw Scotch.'

She was pouring the boiling water on to the generous portion of whisky when the back door opened and a voice called, 'Are you in, Sarah?'

'Yes, yes.' She glanced quickly at Dan. 'It's May.'

'Oh, May's all right.' Dan smiled wearily.

May stood within the kitchen door. She looked smart, yet cool and distant as always. She wrinkled her nose as she said, 'What's this? Whisky?'

'Help yourself,' said Dan, pointing to the bottle. 'I had to get something for this stinking cold.'

'Well, well.' May came and sat down by the table, and, lifting up the bottle, she looked at it. 'I won't say no.' She glanced at Sarah and smiled.

It was rarely May smiled and that was a pity, Sarah thought, because she looked attractive when she smiled. And softer, oh so much softer. She said, 'You really want a drop?'

'Yes, of course. Why not? We often used to have a toddy when we were first married, late at night . . . so the smell wouldn't carry. . . . How you going to get over that, Dan? She'll smell it off you.'

'I brought some mints. . . . Provided for everything.' He smiled weakly.

As Sarah watched May pouring herself out a good measure of the whisky her mind lifted to the room on the other side of the fireplace and it came to her with a strange feeling of sadness that Mary Hetherington was ruling an inaginary world. Within the confines of her four walls she dictated and claimed obedience, and was satisfied, at least apparently, that her family were subject to her. But did she guess, even faintly, that all of them threw off her domination once they crossed the threshold into the street? Dan with his women and his whisky–he likely had his whisky when he was with her; John with May and their toddies at night. This was only a small thing, the bigger issue there was the separate turbulent life that John and his wife led away from the narrow confines of number one. Then there was David. David most of all, she thought, had moved away from his mother's domination. Although he was still nice to her, gentle with her because that was David's nature, there was a part in him that had been set free when he had taken herself from the bottom end and married her. The only one who could not escape was the father. Yet even he tried. Yes, she could see that her mother-in-law was ruling a world that existed only within her own mind, and a part of her was unhappy for the dominant, self-satisfied woman, for this woman who would never like her.

An exclamation from May broke the trend of her thoughts and brought her eyes to the kitchen window and the dark shadow passing it.

'It's the big fellow himself, he must have smelt it.' May sniffed disdainfully, and as John entered the room she looked at her husband and said, 'Altogether like the folks of Shields. Did you smell it?'

John did not answer his wife but looked to where Dan was crouched over the fire. 'You've got it bad,' he said. 'You should be in bed.'

'This'll put me right.' Dan held up the mug.

'It'll do no such thing unless you can sweat it out of you. You'll be a damn sight worse drinking that and then going out into the blast. Have some sense, man; go on, get into bed.'

'Yes, it's the wisest thing,' said May. 'He's right. You should get yourself to bed, Dan.'

'What! On a New Year's Eve and the jollification coming up? What'll they do without me?' He grinned and inclined his head towards the back of the fireplace.

'Aw, you think too much of yourself,' said John. 'You won't be missed as long as there's Davie to play the piano. That's all that she'll want. That's all that'll be necessary.'

Dan, taking the remark the way it was meant, said, 'True, true. But all the same, I'm not going to bed. I've never been to bed on a New Year's Eve yet and I'm not going to start now. And'–his grin widened–'what do you think I am, to miss the home brew and the port at three shillings a bottle, mind you. You must think I'm barmy!'

As they laughed, Dan, thumbing the whisky bottle, said, 'Help yourself; I'm bringing down another later. I've got to have them in flat halves so they won't bulge my coat. You never know, she could have run into me coming round the back way.'

The air of conspiracy was again to the fore. The feeling was always strong when the family were together–outside the parent's home.

May, like a practised hand, threw off the last of her whisky, then, looking up at Sarah, said, 'I just popped over to see if you would have Paul this afternoon. I want to go over to my mother's and it's too cold to take him, crossing the water and all.'

Before Sarah could reply John put in, 'I'll stay with him, I told you.'

'You're doing nothing of the sort, you're coming to my mother's. You never show your face there from one year's end to the other; in fact my family . . .' May now looked from Sarah to Dan. 'My family don't believe I've a husband.'

John's head was lowered in a bull-like attitude. He was biting on his lip but he said nothing.

Sarah said quickly, 'Oh, I'd love to have him, May. Oh yes, leave him with me.'

May rose to her feet. 'Thanks.' She smiled at Sarah. 'He likes coming over here. You wouldn't believe I found him up the back lane the other day. He was crawling on his hands and knees over Mrs Barrett's step. He had gone to the wrong end, but he knew the house was near the end. . . . Come on, big boy.' She pushed her husband sharply on the shoulder. 'Finish that up and get on your feet.' She spoke to him as if he were drunk and incapable; her tone held a deriding note. It made Sarah think, Why does she do it? She could handle him if she didn't use that voice and manner.

She watched John rise to his feet as if obedient to his wife's summons. She could not see the expression in his eyes, for his lids were lowered. He nodded towards Dan, saying abruptly, 'you look after that cold or it'll mean trouble.' Then he followed May out. He had not, Sarah noticed, said one word to her, neither hello nor goodbye. He must be in a state inside, she thought. It wasn't only not having a pay packet; it was, as David said, John needed to work.

Dan was laughing now, and his voice cracking, he said, 'That's a funny remark, you know, and everybody makes it. Take care of that cold, they say, as if it was something tender to be cherished. People say funny things.' Then, turning his body half from the fire, he asked quietly and abruptly, 'David tell you about me last night?'

The suddenness of the question took Sarah aback. She blinked and moved her head, then she made a gesture with one hand as if flapping something aside and answered, 'Yes, yes, Dan, but that's all right.'

'You weren't shocked?'

'No, Dan, no. That's your business. As David says, it's your business.'

'Aye, David says that, but what do you say?'

'Well'–again her hand flapped outwards–'if you want it that way, and it's good for you . . . well then.' She paused and finished inanely, 'It's your life.'

'Yes, it's my life.' He turned towards the fire again. 'And I've arranged it as I want it. Though, let me tell you . . .' His voice was cracking more now. 'Eva wants it like that too. I'm not taking any young lass down, believe me, nor wrecking a home or spoiling a married woman's life. She's a widow, a very quiet sort, and wants no ties no more than I do.'

'All right, all right, Dan, now don't get upset. Look, it's like John said. I should go to bed if I were you.'

'I'll be all right, I'll be all right.' He lay back in the chair holding the stone water-bottle to him and closed his eyes. Sarah stood looking at him. His face looked drawn and weary, but still there was about him an attractiveness. She could understand any woman going for Dan, but she couldn't understand her not wanting to marry him. All the Hetherington men had something about them, in different ways. Yet Dan wasn't a Hetherington, was he? His name was Blyth.

A few minutes later, when the back door opened again and David entered the house, she was scrambling round setting the table. The dinner, a hotpot, was already in the oven. She greeted David in the scullery. They held each other for a moment while they kissed, and then she whispered swiftly, 'Dan's inside. he's not well, he should be in bed. It's his cold.'

When she entered the kitchen with the dish in her hands Dan was saying, 'It's only a cold, don't worry your head. I'm sweating it out. Look, it's running down me. I've got over half an hour before I need to go next door, I'll be all right. Help yourself.' He pointed.

David did not reply. He just continued to look at Dan and shake his head. Then, turning to the table, he picked up the bottle, went to the cupboard and got himself a glass and poured himself out a measure of the whisky.

She hadn't known David drank whisky. Again her thoughts turned towards the woman in the room behind the fireplace, and again she felt sad for her, sad in a strange inexplicable way.

The jollification had begun. It had got on its way around ten o'clock. Beside the family there were additions to the party. Mr and Mrs Riley from number fourteen. Mr Riley was one of the two men who worked under Mr Hetherington. And there was Mrs Riley's sister and her husband who had come down from Hartlepool for the New Year. Then there was Mr and Mrs Ramsay from next door to Sarah. The sitting-room was crowded, and laughter filled the house, and the passage between the front room and the living-room was as busy as Newcastle station.

Already Mary Hetherington had doled out the first taste of her brew, and as usual it had been acclaimed with high praise and requests from the visitors to know the recipe. But, 'Ah! Ah!' said Mary. No one was getting that, it would die with her. No, not even her husband knew how the brew was concocted. Nor did her brother either. Her mother had passed the recipe on to her; men had never had anything to do with it. There was high laughter at this point.

Sarah was in the kitchen beating up tinned salmon with mustard and vinegar to make up another batch of sandwiches; the first lot had vanished quicker than snow under the sun. She lifted her head from her task, her face bright and flushed with happiness, and looked at her mother-in-law who was entering the room. Mary Hetherington's face too was bright and flushed, and for the first time since she had come to know her, Sarah saw her smiling, really smiling. She looked relaxed and happy . . . in her element, as Sarah put it to herself. She said to her, 'These won't be a minute, I've got all the bread buttered.'

'That's good of you, Sarah. May could have given you a hand, but no, May's not like that.' There returned to her face a reflection of the primness that was usual to it, and then it was gone as she asked, 'How did you like my ale?'

'Oh, I thought it was wonderful, lovely. I've never tasted anything like it. I'm not going to ask you how you make it because David said it was a secret, but oh, I wouldn't mind a drop of that every day.'

'No, no.' The tone held laughter. 'It's not for every day, it's just for special occasions. I make it once a year as my mother did, and her mother afore her.

You know, my mother was a farmer's daughter from near Blanchland. Lovely country that, lovely. It was a big farm, quite an estate. She took me once to see it when I was a little girl. She knew lots of country secrets did my mother, and . . . well, my ale is one of them. I could tell anyone what I put in it but they couldn't make it. It's just wheat and barley and hops and horehound, and odds and ends, but it's the quantities and how you use them. It's like cooking; some cooks can turn cream sour.'

As if she had uttered a great witticism they both laughed. Then their laughter stopping suddenly, they looked at each other, and Mary Hetherington said, 'Don't you think it's about time you had a name for me, Sarah?'

Oh! Oh!' Sarah wagged her head in embarrassment. She had always addressed this woman as 'Mrs Hetherington', she had not dared say, 'mother'.

Mary Hetherington turned away and began to transfer mince-pies from a tray on to a plate and her hand moved swiftly and her words kept pace with it as she said, 'Mam would be nice I think, don't you? We can't go on for ever being addressed as 'Mrs Hetherington', can we? Yes, I think Mam will do.' Her hand and her voice halted abruptly and she turned her head and looked at Sarah.

Sarah remained very still as she said softly, 'Yes. Oh yes, I'd like that.' It was as if an honour had been bestowed on her.

And Mary Hetherington, acting in the manner of one who had bestowed the great gift, inclined her head downwards. Then adding one more mince-pie to the plate, she said, 'Well, that's that settled,' and left the kitchen.

Sarah sighed. A smile spread slowly over her happy face; she felt her ears moving backwards with it. Wouldn't David be tickled to death. Oh, his mother . . . Mam . . . should make her brew every week. Oh, she should! She'd had a glass or two, that was evident, she was a different woman the night. Sarah gripped the bowl with her two hands and had the desire to throw it towards the ceiling. Then her body shaking with inward laughter, she applied herself frantically to the sandwiches. It was a lovely New Year's Eve, lovely.

Sarah had become conscious that David had stopped playing the piano some time before she took the two plates of sandwiches into the room. As she pushed at the door with her hip, John, standing behind it, pulled it open and, relieving her of one of the plates, whispered, 'The old man's on his feet.'

Sarah looked to where Mr Hetherington was standing on the hearth rug, his back towards the blazing fire. He had a glass in his hand and was motioning with it down to his subordinate Mr Riley, saying, 'It's true, you'll endorse it, Bill. Hope can be as dead as a doornail, but come this night and it's injected with a spark of life. Even those who have been out for years, the night they'll be thinking next year's bound to be different. Am I right?'

Mr Riley made a deep obeisance with his head. 'Yes, you're right, Stan.' There followed a rustle through the room, then silence again as they all looked towards their host. And Stan went on, 'New Year's Eve, as I said, is not an ending, it's merely a day afore a beginning, a day when you clean inside and out, a day when you see your assets mounting. This affects every man Jack the same up till the moment the clock strikes twelve. You know, nobody, at least no northerner, can be without hope on New Year's Eve; we've proved it again and again, haven't we?'

His thin chin thrust forward, Stan looked around the company and was greeted with, 'Yes, you're right there, Stan. Aye, aye, never a truer word spoken.' And then they waited once again for him to go on as if they were enjoying it.

It seemed to Sarah as if Mr Hetherington was doing a turn. She looked towards David, but he was looking at his father. She looked quickly towards John, and John was looking towards her and he indicated with a swift downward glance the bottles on the sideboard, and Sarah, picking up his meaning, nodded and smiled, then turned to listen to her father-in-law again.

'The North is a separate world, you know, and it breeds a separate kind of man.' Stan was waxing eloquent now. 'Men who are anathema to men of softer tones, to men whose egos are of a normal size and who argue only with knowledge . . . for let's face the facts, we are an aggressive, pig-headed lot. And I say thank God for it. . . . What do you say?'

'Hear hear! Stan. Hear hear! Carry on. Carry on.'

'Well, as I was saying, the Tynesider, right back to Bede, has had to push himself up through the mire for both bread and learning, and always on this particular night he dons the cloak of hope, and throws his head back and looks to the coming year, to the set number of days, days in which he sees himself working hard, eating well, and sleeping soundly. And why not, why not?'

At this point Stan dramatically raised his glass, crying, 'Let's drink to the northerner!' There was a rising to the feet and crys of 'Well spoken, Stan!'

John, turning to Sarah, whispered loudly, 'He should have been in Parliament, he could give Macdonald points. . . . That's if me mother brewed every day.'

Their laughter was lost amidst the noise and chatter now filling the room, and Sarah, looking towards her father-in-law, thought, It's funny to hear him lead off like that. He must think that way all the time. He's like David, or David's like him. They both think alike, but it takes the drink to bring it out. And his eye has hardly twitched at all the night.

'It happens twice a year,' said John, still whispering. 'New Year's Eve and Armistice Day. He generally gets blotto then, on Armistice Day.'

'Really!' This surprised Sarah.

'It's a kind of protest against the War and . . .' He moved his finger unobtrusively towards his eyes.

Sarah couldn't imagine Mr Hetherington getting really drunk, but she remembered back to Armistice Day just a few weeks ago when he had been in bed for two days with a cold. She smiled to herself, and shook her head. Funny the things you didn't know.

'Look, it's three minutes to. Get the glasses filled there, Mary.' Mr Hetherington was addressing his wife as if he was master in his own house, and obediently she went to the sideboard and began refilling the glasses. She looked proud and happy.

Sarah was standing with David now, an arm around each other. They were behind Dan, who was sitting to the side of the fireplace, and they each had a hand on his shoulder. Dan, Sarah thought, was in a bad way, he should be in bed.

David bent down towards Dan, pulling Sarah with him as he said under his breath, 'Why don't you go up, man?'

'I will as soon as it's in.'

Sarah and David raised their heads, then looked at each other and for a moment pressed closer together. The room became full of bustle. Mr Riley, who was to be first-foot, had left by the back door laden with coal and bread–Mary Hetherington had never added a bottle to the ritual as was the rule–and now as many of the company as could manage it were in the passageway.

The ship's hooters were blowing. The church bells were ringing. The whole world outside of the house seemed to be alive with sound. In contrast the house appeared quiet, almost empty for all the voices had died away. Each member of the party was waiting, all touched in this moment with a feeling of awe, touched with the elemental feeling of mystery and of sadness. One woman, Mrs Riley's sister-in-law, was crying quietly. All the expressions were touched with tenderness. It was as if the essence of this quality had been brushed swiftly over them all. Not one of them at this moment held within himself bitterness or anger. Not one of them remembered past grievances. At the death-bed of the year their souls shone out from their eyes.

The wind was blowing high and hard and it brought the first booms from the clock in the centre of the town right to the door itself, and the sound split them apart. The faces returned to normal, mouths opened and cried in different ways: 'It's here. It's here.' As the clock struck for the twelfth time the rapper on the front door banged, and borne in on the wind came Mr Riley.

'Happy New Year. Happy New Year.'

'Happy New Year. Happy New Year.'

They shook hands; they embraced each other, they all pressed back into the sitting-room, still shaking hands, still embracing. Sarah found herself being held by her father-in-law.

'A happy New Year, a happy New Year, Sarah. And I mean that, I mean that.' He leant towards her and his moustache pressed tight against the side of her mouth.

'Happy New Year,' she cried. 'Happy New Year . . . Dad.'

At this Stan let out a bellow of laughter and for a moment they hugged each other. Then she was standing over Dan.

'Don't kiss me unless you want this cold. Happy New Year, Sarah. Oh, that's what I wish you, a very happy New Year. Indeed I do.'

'The same to you, Dan. The same to you.' They were holding hands, shaking them up and down like children.

The three strange men kissed her, great smacks on the side of her cheek.

She stood before May for a moment exclaiming a Happy New Year, then such was the power of this night they leant swiftly to each other and embraced.

And Mary Hetherington kissed her. Her lips touched her cheek, and she said, 'A Happy New Year, Sarah.'

'A Happy New Year, Mam.' Again they laughed together.

People were passing from one to the other, and then she was standing in the passage opposite John.

'A Happy New Year, Sarah.'

'A Happy New Year, John.' They looked at each other, but they did not even touch hands. He smiled, and his smile still held something of the gentleness of the moment before twelve. He said again, 'A very happy New Year.'

When he passed her and went into the room the laughter slid from her face for a moment; she felt slightly disturbed, even slighted. Then, tossing her head up, she almost ran into the living-room. That was John–she never knew how to take him. And now she began whipping up plates of mince-pies, and rice loaf, and bacon and egg tart, on to a large tray. As she turned to leave the room May came into the kitchen, saying, 'Dan wants a strong cup of tea.'

'I'll make it for him in a jiffy.'

'No, you carry on with what you are doing. I'll see to it.' May sounded pleasant, nice. Everybody was nice. . . .

And then it was quarter-to-one.

David was playing the piano. Everybody was singing. Sticking to her decision she had refused to be persuaded to sing alone; nothing must mar the new-found harmony between herself and her mother-in-law. It was at this point she thought, I must slip across now. As she went from the room she whispered quietly to Mary Hetherington, who was still busy at the sideboard, 'I'm just going to slip across to wish me mother a happy New Year.'

'Will you be all right?'

The concern was warming, heartening. She nodded briskly. 'Yes, yes, I'll be all right.'

May was standing near the door and she touched her arm, saying, 'You're not going across there on your own, surely?'

'Oh, I'll be all right, I'm used to it.'

'Well, I wouldn't take a gold watch and go through the streets at this time of the morning.'

'There'll be plenty of people about.'

Oh, everybody was nice. Fancy May being concerned about her.

May followed her into the passage, saying. 'You should have somebody with you. Tell Davie.'

'No, no. It will spoil things, they want him to play. I'll be all right, May, honest.'

'Wait until John comes back, then; he's just gone over to see to the fire, and he's going to look in on old Mrs Watson next door. He won't be long.'

'No, I won't wait, May. I'll be back before you know I'm gone. You see'–she smiled broadly–'I'm used to going about the streets in the dark. I had to do it every night for years coming from work.' She nodded at May, then hurried into the living-room, and from a cupboard under the stairs she took out her coat and wrapped a scarf around her head, then went out of the kitchen door.

It was as she entered the back lane that she bumped into John. He gripped her arm to steady her and peered at her in the dim light from the lamp at the bottom of the lane, saying, 'Where on earth are you off to?'

'Oh . . . oh!' she laughed. It was a nervous laugh. 'I'm just going to run across and wish me mother a happy New Year. I won't be long.'

'You're not going on your own? Where's Davie?'

'He's playing, I didn't want to stop him.'

'Well, you're not going across there on your own at this time of the night, I'll come along with you.'

'No, no.' She was standing stiff, talking stiff. 'I'm all right I tell you. There's no need, I won't be a minute.'

'A minute or half an hour, what do you think I am? What would Davie think if he knew I let you go across the streets, especially at this time, on your own? There'll be drunks all over the place; it doesn't take much to knock them out these days.'

'No, no.' She was protesting now, with her eyes closed.

'All right then . . .' His voice sounded sulky. 'If you don't want me to go with you come back in and get Davie, but I'm not letting you go over there on your own. If anything was to happen to you, what would they say? Fancy him doing that, letting her go across there on New Year's morning by herself.'

Yes, she knew. That's just what they would say. But nothing was going to happen to her and she didn't want him to come with her. She didn't. She didn't. She felt herself jerked around. He had hold of her arm, laughing as he pulled forward, but his voice was gentle, very gentle as he said, 'It's New Year's Day, Sarah, New Year's Day. Everybody's nice to everybody on New Year's Day, remember?'

They met the full force of the wind as they came out of the lane and into the main road.

'By! It's blowing itself in all right. And look at that moon riding up there. It looks as if it's training for the Derby.'

Sarah looked up through the scudding clouds. David said it was the clouds that moved not the moon, at least not quickly. David had learned her lots of thing. . . . Eeh, that was one of the things he had taught her, that nobody can learn you, only yourself. They teach and you learn, David knew more than John, at least about some things, about the nice things. John was eaten up with politics and such. . . . Eeh! The exclamation burst from her now as her hand was gripped and she was forced into a run.

John was running against the wind like a great lolloping bear. She tried to shake herself free, but his grip was like iron, and she could do nothing but run with him.

'We'll race him.' He was yelling like a lad and pointing upwards. He was daft. Mad. They fled past two groups of people all singing, and mingled laughter and song followed them on the wind.

'J-o-h-n . . . stop!' She pressed her body back from him and strained at his hand, and gradually they came to a stop, just three streets from her own. She leant against the wall now, her two hands under her breasts pressing against her ribs. She was gasping and laughing. It was either laugh or get into a temper and this was a New Year's morning.

'You . . . You are a fool, John. You're mad.'

'Perhaps I am. But have you never raced the moon afore?'

She shook her head at him. He was standing with the palm of one hand against the wall, the arm straight; the coat sleeve touched her shoulder. His face, looking upwards, appeared young and boyish. As he turned his head towards her the moon disappeared behind a bank of cloud and she could no longer see his face. As she pulled herself from the wall, she said, 'I'm all out of puff, I've never run like that since I was at school.'

'You've missed something then.' His voice was even now, and his tone ordinary, 'Up to the last few years I used to run every morning before breakfast, I was in the harriers. Six miles sometimes, and more; and then I cycled to work. And on a Sunday a hundred miles with the Cycling Club was nothing. I felt fit in those days.' His voice trailed away and they walked a few steps before he said, 'Is this your street?'

'No, the last one.'

Everything seemed very ordinary. He was David's brother. Why had she made such a fuss about him bringing her over? He was just like a young lad. He might be older than David in years but in his mind he was younger. That was because he did sillier things, and said sillier things; and although at times he was surly, he had, she thought, something of Dan's sense of fun. She turned to him now, saying, 'This is it. Look, I won't be more than five minutes. I won't keep you waiting.'

'Stay as long as you like, I'll do some skipping until you come out.' He lifted his big frame from the ground with a lightness that surprised her and began skipping in an imaginary rope.

'You are daft, you know.' She was laughing freely. Then, 'I won't be long,' she said again, and hurried from him.

When she reached the house and found the blind up she felt a sense of disappointment. Her mother had gone to Mrs Young's then, or perhaps to bed. No, she wouldn't have gone to bed. She must have gone next door to bring the New Year in. There came to her the sound of laughter and voices from the Youngs' kitchen and as she turned away she thought, Well, I'm glad she's having a bit of enjoyment.

'By! That was quick.' John was standing against the wall, not jumping up or down any longer.

'She's not in. She's next door, by the sound of it. Anyway, we'll get back all the sooner.'

She had turned to walk down the road when he said, 'Let's cut down the back end, we'll escape the wind that way. We won't have it in our faces then.'

'All right.'

They went across the road and through Walham Street. 'We can cut through Fanny's Alley here,' he said.

She turned to him, her mouth wide. 'You know Fanny's Alley?'

'Of course! Why do you sound so surprised? I know every bit of the streets.'

'I didn't think you'd know about this end, and Fanny's Alley.'

'Why?' There was a slight argumentative note in his voice now that put her on her guard, and her tone was placating when she answered, 'Oh, well, you know, the top end never came down to the bottom end . . . that was until Davie came for me.' Her voice was soft as she finished speaking.

They had entered a cut between two houses, Fanny's Alley. He went first and they came out on a piece of wind-torn waste ground that had on it a number of corrugated iron huts–the tool sheds of the allotments. They were in the black shadow of the gable-end wall of the last house and the first of the sheds when he turned on her bringing her to a halt, saying fiercely, 'Don't talk like that . . . humble. . . . Why must you eat humble pie all the time? What's the matter with you?'

'What do you mean? What are you on about now?' She sounded both surprised and frightened.

'I'm on about you bending the knee so much. . . .'

'I don't.'

'Yes you do, and you know it. My God! Where do you think you've landed, anyway? In Lord Redhead's or with the Percy family? Look, Sarah, get it into your head that you're still in the Fifteen Streets. We're in the Fifteen Streets . . . we're all in the Fifteen Streets. I tell you it makes me flaming mad to see you acting as if somebody had picked you up out of the gutter. . . . And when you're with my mother . . . oh my God!'

He stopped, and in the darkness she felt his arm going up as he put his hand to his head, and she retreated a step from him. She was shivering inside with a feeling which his words were forcing into life, the feeling that had come unbidden into her body when she had first looked at him. She fought it now in the only way she knew. She said, 'Don't be silly, going on like that; it's the beer you've had.' She laughed nervously.

'Beer! Huh! It might knock them over, but it doesn't touch me. It'll take something stronger than that. I've had very little the night. Look, don't evade the question. I've been wanting to get at you about this for some time. . . . Sarah.'

She felt her body jerk upwards as his hands came down on her shoulders covering them like clamps. 'Don't you realise your worth, woman? They . . . I mean our family isn't bestowing any honour on you; you're doing the honours, if it comes to talking about honours. Aye, you've given them life. You've brought the old man alive. You've made Davie into a man, and you've done something for Dan . . . aye, Dan, who doesn't need any lessons. Don't you know what you've done, woman?' He was shaking her now.

'Don't you know what you've done?' His voice was a hoarse whisper. His words were sending gusts of hot breath over her face. He still had hold of her shoulders, but his elbows were bent now, his body touching hers, but lightly, just their clothes.

'Sarah! Sarah!' The wind was whirling her name about her head. 'You know what you've done to me, don't you? You know it, that's why you've kept out of my way. . . . Oh my God, Sarah.'

'No! No!' She thought she was screaming, but the scream was only inside her. Her words came out on a low hiss. 'No! No!' And then she was lost between his body and the corrugated iron hut. Through the thickness of their clothes she felt him, every inch of him; his knees, his thighs, his belly, his breast, they were all picking out the counterparts in her and she was gasping under the pressure of them.

'No, no, leave go of me. You're mad, mad. . . . David!'

'Aye, David.' His mouth was against her ear; his words dropping into it like molten lead, burning her. 'There's David. You've got no need to remind me there's David. If it wasn't for David I would have tipped you up from the start. Didn't you feel it in the first time we met in the front room? I knew then, in an instant.'

'Let me go! I tell you let me go! What if David found . . .'

'Don't worry, he'll not find out.'

'I'd rather die than hurt David, do you hear? Do you hear?' She was speaking through her teeth. 'Let me go.'

'Just a moment longer. Let's be like this a minute longer. It might have to last a lifetime. Oh, Sarah, Sarah.' His mouth was covering her ear.

She screwed her head into her shoulder and struggled with all her might to free herself from his arms, but he held her fast. As big as she was, he held her as if she were a child. Then with a suddenness that made her feel sick she felt her body go limp against him and she spluttered as she cried, 'I'm happy, I'm happy, leave me be, don't spoil it. I've never been so happy in me life, it's all I want, David and the house. . . . A place of me own.'

'You're not happy. You don't know what it means. Davie rescued you. He was the first plank thrust out to the bottom end and you grabbed it, and now you're breaking your neck with gratitude.'

'I'm not, I'm not.'

'How does he love you, eh? How does he? Gentle, considerate, kindly, as if asking a favour? He doesn't take you, he couldn't.'

'Shut up, you! David's good . . . good.'

'Aye, he's good. Davie's a good fellow, a fine fellow. I'm his brother, Aye, aye, I'm his brother, and I wouldn't hurt him for the world either, so you have it, you needn't worry, but he hasn't got it in him to love you. Not like this . . . and this!' He jerked his loins into her. His mouth almost covered the lower part of her face and for as long as it took her to realise that he was right, every word he had said was right, she submitted to him, and then she was thumping and pushing and kicking his body from hers.

They were standing apart now, breathing like two great animals lost in the wind and darkness, still alone in a world that had been created when she had submitted for an instant to him. It made no difference that there was no contact of flesh, they knew each other as if they had sported stark naked on an open moor.

Then her limbs became weak, all strength left her and she had to lean against the shed again for support. Her whole body was shaking as if with St Vitus' dance. Her bones seemed to be strung on jangling wires. She had no power to move, nor did she want to; she had no urge to get away from him. No desire to run, nor did she wish she were dead, or that he had never been born. The only coherent thought in her turbulent brain was that David must not be hurt.

So close were they at this moment, even spiritually, that he picked up her thought and said, 'Stop worrying.' His tone was flat now. 'Davie won't be hurt. You would never hurt him, not with your sense of gratitude. And I don't want to hurt him either, I've told you. . . . But I'm not in a position to hurt anybody, am I? You don't say "Come fly with me and be my love" when you're on the dole, do you? But everything apart, this is between you and me, so don't worry. Me madness is under lock and key and I'll try to see it doesn't break out again. Not in that way, anyhow. . . .' He groped now and found her hands, and she did not resist him and he said softly and sadly, 'But, by God, how I could have loved you, Sarah.'

When she heard her voice answering him it sounded strange to her, she couldn't recognise herself, for it was a woman who was speaking, speaking the thoughts of a woman, slow and flat, 'It all depends on what you call love. David's kind of love takes in even me feet, and they aren't lovely. They swell and go shapeless and look like big white puddings, but he takes me shoes off and pulls me stockings away from me soles after I've walked back from the docks, or shopping. He's even washed me feet in hot water and soda–you wouldn't do that, would you?'

Except for their heavy breathing, which was caught and whirled away by the wind, there was no sound between them for some minutes, then he said, 'What you talking about? . . . I was talking about loving you.' His voice was hoarse and there was a note of perplexity in it.

'Loving me?' She experienced a weird urge to laugh, long and loud. She was afraid of the feeling. She was afraid of herself altogether at this moment, and she was actually shocked at the rawness of her next words, but still in that slow flat grown-up woman's tone, she said then, 'I know your kind of loving, you'd take me clothes off but not me shoes. . . . Oh, I know, I'm no fool. . . . Leave go me hands.'

She was shaking herself roughly, violently, to try to get away from him when with his voice, urgent and tender, now he appealed to her. 'Don't shut me out, Sarah . . . don't. And don't be frightened of me, ever. I won't do anything, try anything, I promise you. Just let me talk to you now and again and look at you. Give me this much. . . . Say something to me, at times, something kind, Sarah. I need kindness, I do. You just don't know what it's like to be without kindness. And you're kind. The first minute I saw you, I saw your big heart shining from every part of you. . . . You're big, Sarah, in every way. You're big and kind. . . .'

Normality was rushing back into her body, the normality of fear, fear against the softening effect of his pleading. She almost whimpered now, speaking as if to herself. 'If I bring trouble on the house I'll kill myself, I will, I will. I couldn't bear it. . . . Your mother . . .'

It was as if the mention of his mother's name broke the spell, for now he burst out, 'Oh, for God's sake! I've told you to stop being afraid of me mother, and of any of them. I think that's about the only thing that could make me really mad with you. It drives me crazy when I see you bending before them. And when May, the upstart, looks down her nose . . .'

'M . . . ay?' she put in stammering. 'M . . . ay? May looks down her nose at me?'

'Can't you see it? And she's not fit to wipe your shoes. May's a prig; a cold, bloodless prig. She's got as much of a woman in her as Leslie Waters next door, and he doesn't know what he is. But you've only yourself to blame, you're so damned humble . . . humble and kindly. Kindly, that's you, Sarah, when you should be haughty and proud, because you've got something to be proud of. . . . You're beautiful. My God, you're beautiful . . . your face . . . your body . . . everything. . . . Oh, it's all right, don't worry, I'm not going to start again.'

Above her own gasping breath she could hear the quick intake of his as if he were sucking it in and out through his teeth. They stood quiet and without words for some minutes, and then he asked, 'Is it a deal?'

There was another moment of silence before she said, 'What do you mean?'

'That you'll not ignore me, not push me aside as if I didn't matter. I won't ask anything of you, I promise you, and I mean it. . . . Mind, I wouldn't say I'd be talking like this if there wasn't somebody like Davie with a claim on you. but that's the throw of the dice. It is Davie and that's that. . . . Come on.' He pulled her sharply from the support of the shed and, holding her arm, he said softly, 'Stop trembling. You can't go in like that. Come in, walk briskly.' He led her forward, supporting her, and she walked like someone slightly drunk.

They went across the waste land above the bottom ends of the streets until they came to Camelia Street back lane. Neither of them had spoken since they started to walk, but now she halted and with her head down she muttered, 'You'd better go on, I'm going in our house for a minute.'

He went to take her hand again, but she pulled it aside, saying under her breath, 'Don't! My God, don't! Not here. You don't know who's out the night.'

He stood looking at her bent head for not more than a few seconds, then, without further words, he turned abruptly and walked down the back lane.

She stood, with her back arched, leaning against the wind, and not until she heard the dull thud of the back door banging did she go down the lane and through her own back door and up the yard.

Once in the kitchen she didn't light the gas, but, crouching down on the mat beside the fender, rested her arm on the seat of David's chair and, twisting her hands together, she stared into the dying embers of the fire, crying, 'Oh, David! Oh David! Oh, David!' Then jerking herself around she enfolded the chair in her arms as if it was the kindly gentle loving David himself. And her mind kept reiterating, Oh, David! Oh, David! Oh, David! and she told herself that she only wanted David, and David's kind of loving. She didn't want that other kind, not John's kind. No, no, she didn't want that, she didn't.

She became still, quite still, her body and her mind, and in the stillness she recaptured again the moment of terrifying intensity when he had grappled and strained and writhed to answer his body's demands and now she extended it. She could feel them struggling together like two savages, their bodies joined at every possible point, striving towards a climax of unearthly rapture, receiving and inflicting pain that created laughter, and the laughter did not escape from them but flowed back and forth through their beings as if through one body. The chair moved under her across the line and its motion brought her heaving body to stillness again and her mind to the present.

She became aware for the first time since entering the kitchen that they were still singing next door and she turned her face slowly towards the fireplace and whispered aloud, 'I can't help it. It wasn't my fault.' And it was as if in answer Mary Hetherington came walking through the wall and stood before her, saying, as she had done on the day of the wedding, 'A mixed marriage is bad enough, but to have it unsanctified in a registry office . . . Well, I only hope some good will come of it.'

Then she saw her mother-in-law joined by the priest, and Father O'Malley said, 'I told you mixed marriages have their penalties and this is only the beginning.'

Her greatest fear from a mixed marriage had been the loss of her immortal soul, but now even the phrase seemed meaningless. It was something that might or might not happen, something that wouldn't be proven until she was dead. What had come upon her tonight was something of the now–and it was tangible, this thing, this other love.

'No, no, I don't love him.' she was on her feet, speaking her denial aloud. She pressed her hand over her mouth and stood looking through the dark towards the wall. Then, heaving a great sigh that swelled and deflated her body, she said helplessly to herself, 'You'd better get in.'

They'd be wondering next door and they mustn't wonder, they mustn't ask questions. Nothing had happened, nothing ever would. As she had said, she would die rather than hurt David. David had pulled her up out of the mire. . . . All right, what if he was a plank, he was a plank that she was going to cling to all her life. She would manage this thing, this wild-beast thing. She would have to. She straightened her shoulders gulped spittle into her dry mouth, pulled the bolt out of the door, and went into the yard.

Chapter Four

Sarah came quietly down the stairs and into the living-room. Mary Hetherington was sitting in the armchair near the fire, her eyes closed, and as Sarah tiptoed past she opened them and said, 'I'm not asleep.'

'Oh, I thought you might have dropped off. You should, you know, you're worn out. He's asleep now; it seems sound, not like it's been.'

'I've made some tea. Would you like to pour it out, Sarah?'

Sarah poured out two cups of tea and took one to her mother-in-law, then sat near the end of the table drinking hers.

Mary Hetherington sipped at her tea, then, looking down into the cup, she said, 'It's been a time, hasn't it? All that jollification on New Year's Eve and since then we've never stopped running, three weeks of it.' She looked up and towards Sarah, and added, 'You've been very good, Sarah. I don't know what I'd have done without you. May is very little use in sickness, and she hasn't the lifting power of a mouse.'

'Well, I'm about twice her size. And she's been very good with the shopping and getting the medicine and that.' Sarah felt that she had to defend May, as if she owed her something. She didn't like this feeling and the only way she could ease it was to say something nice about May.

'I don't know what we'd have done if John hadn't been off work. Everything has its other side, hasn't it? He's been so good sitting up too, because David and his father couldn't have kept it up. With having to go to work they need their sleep. . . . Ah, well.' She took another sip from her cup. 'He's past the worst but I never thought he'd get over it.'

'Nor did I.' Sarah shook her head. No, she never had thought Dan would get over it. His cold had resulted in double pneumonia and he had at one point seemed almost sure to die.

'Oh!' The cup wobbled in the saucer as Mary Hetherington brought herself upwards in the chair and, leaning towards Sarah, said, 'I'm awfully sorry, I forgot to tell you. I hope it isn't important, but your father called round this morning to see you. It was when you were out.'

'Me–my father!' Sarah screwed her face up in disbelief. 'My father called here?' Her lips were spread wide from her teeth.

'Yes.' Mary Hetherington's voice was soft. 'And he was very nice and civil. He asked if you were in and I told him you had gone out shopping for me. He said he was very sorry to hear about my brother. He asked if he could do anything.'

'My father!'

'Yes, your father. Now you mustn't be vindictive.' Mary Hetherington's Christianity was to the fore at the moment. 'Although I'd be the last person to tell you to encourage him, you mustn't bear malice or bitterness. It's never worth it. As I said, he was very civil and he looked very clean and tidy.'

'Did he say what he wanted?'

'No, no, he didn't say.'

'Perhaps my mother isn't very well?'

'I shouldn't think so. He said he called at the back door once or twice last week but got no reply; he wondered if you were all right.'

Again Sarah's face screwed up, but she said nothing this time. Her father calling on her? What was he after? Likely on the cadge. He was having to stump up his dole now that her mother hadn't got Phyllis's and her own money coming in. Yet he was no fool was her father, he knew the feeling that existed between them. He had never asked her for any money in his life, he had just taken it–that is, everything he could get his hands on. But was it likely that he would come cadging from her now? She couldn't understand it. Still, she would likely know what he was after when he turned up again. She said now, 'I'll take the washing round and put it in soak while there's still light.'

'Now, no, no, Sarah, it's far too much; you've done it for weeks now. I'll get Mrs Watson to come in. She used to, you know.'

'There's no need when I can do it. I'm doing our own, and I'm as strong as a bull, anyway.' She flexed the muscles of her arm and smiled, and Mary Hetherington returned the smile, saying, 'Well, have it your own way.'

Sarah went out of the scullery and down the yard into the washhouse, and, gathering up the dirty linen from the poss tub, made it into a bundle and carried it next door, and placed it in her own washhouse.

In a way, if she could put it like this, she felt grateful to Dan for being ill. It had helped her to be of use to Mary Hetherington, really of use, and it had broken down some of the older woman's reserve. . . . It had also given herself less time to think.

She began now to carry buckets of water from the tap at the bottom of the yard and fill the poss tub, then she placed in the ice-cold water all the white linen, sousing them, with her arms up to the elbows, until they were all wet. They would be ready for her early start in the morning.

The twilight was deepening when she went into the kitchen, but she didn't light the gas straight away, she was practising economy. Over the past three weeks she had learned more of the running of a house from her mother-in-law than she had in all the first weeks of her marriage. Mary Hetherington had unbent enough to give advice, such as, 'You can save so much by doing a thing the right way; you needn't be mean, you know. for instance, if you riddle your cinders every day you'd save a bucket of coal a week, four buckets a month and fifty-two a year. Reckon that up; the saving would buy you something for the house, wouldn't it? And then there's the men's clothes. Now when I buy a new shirt I always cut three inches off the tail straight away. this piece will give you a new collar and cuff facings later on.'

Yes, Sarah was learning a lot, and she had already started to save and with an object in view . . . she was going to get David a second-hand piano. She hadn't told anyone about this, not even David, and certainly not his mother, for she didn't think the purchase would be looked upon favourably; it would mean that David wouldn't be such a frequent visitor next door. Not that she minded him going to his mother's, but she knew that he would like a piano of his own.

But with regards to saving through economy Sarah found it was difficult to economise on food, because she and David went down to Shields Market on a Saturday afternoon. When they had first married it had been a sort of hilarious excursion and they had come back laden. That was, until the day they passed the men standing in the roadway, when one of them, looking at the top-heavy baskets, had remarked with sadness but without envy, 'By! That's a sight for sore eyes. There's not a better sight in the world than a basket laden with grub.'

On that Saturday David had said, 'We mustn't buy so much altogether, we'll just get what we need for the weekend and you can get the rest in the middle of the week.' So she did that, but she found it was dearer buying in bits and pieces.

After she had set the table for the tea she sat down for a moment by the fire, in the now darkening room. She had had little time to sit in the past three weeks and that was just as well. Sometimes she though that what had happened in the wind-maddened first hour of the New Year was a figment of her imagination, and she could at times actually believe this, for neither by look nor sign had John reminded her that he had been party to the madness . . . the instigator of the madness. If there was any noticeable change in his manner towards her it was evident in an unusual gentleness of manner, like the gentleness he used towards Dan, but in Dan's case the gentleness was charged with power, and authority, even to ward off death. John had literally fought with death to keep Dan alive, seeming almost to breathe for him when this became almost as agony. Only once had she seen the old John come rearing through this new gentleness. It was one evening down in the living-room when May said, 'Why don't you put in for a job of male nurse? They're going at Harton, you'd be in your element. They are always wanting them on the mental block. . . .'

When she heard the knock on the front door she thought, Oh dear, somebody selling something again. But she was half through the front room when she remembered Mary Hetherington saying, 'Your father called.' She stopped for a moment. What if it was him?

Her approach to the door was slow, and when she opened it her face was set, almost grim, and it didn't change when she saw Father O'Malley standing below her on the pavement.

'Good afternoon, Sarah.'

'Good afternoon, Father.' They stared at each other.

'Well, aren't you going to ask me in?' This was no jocular request, it was made in the form of a command.

Without answering, Sarah stood aside and the priest moved past her and into the passage, where he waited for her to close the door. She seemed to take some time over this, but when she at last passed him she said, 'Will you come this way, Father. I'll light the gas.'

After the gas plopped and fluttered, then filled the mantle, its rays, through the pink porcelain globe, softened both their expressions. The priest was looking round the room and his gaze moved from the low-backed oak chairs to the legs of the table that had a stretcher joining them; then his hand going slowly out, he turned one of the chairs away from the table and without an invitation sat down.

'You've got this very nice.'

'Thank you, Father,' Sarah remained standing and he looked up at her, saying, 'Sit down, sit down; we'll talk more comfortably then.' He was entirely in command of the situation . . . and her. She could have been the visitor. His features moved into what was for him a smile, but it didn't lessen the agitation that was filling her.

The priest began drumming his fingers in a rhythmic beat on the corner of the table, and he looked at them for a full moment before saying, 'You are going to tell me that you are very happy?'

Her body was stiff, yet her chin trembled as she answered, 'I can say that, Father, and it's true.'

'The days are young yet, your life hasn't begun. It would be disastrous at this stage if you found yourself unhappy.' He paused. 'The awareness of conscience is a slow process.'

'I've got nothing on my conscience, Father.' Her voice was trembling now, her agitation visible.

'Well, that's a matter of opinion, and time will prove which of us is right or wrong. God works in strange ways, sometimes through a series of disasters.' The priest turned towards the fire as if he were actually seeing the events passing before his eyes. 'Sometimes by withholding His hand until the eleventh hour, His ways are strange and it is not for us to question them. . . . But it is our duty . . .' Now his voice was stern and his eyes were riveted on her, and he repeated, 'It is our duty not to bring His wrath upon us, not to aggravate Him too much.'

Sarah swallowed. At least she made an effort, for she felt that she was choking. She felt as she had done when a child, that God was a man who lived up in Newcastle, a big pot of big pots. Someone who could order you, through the medium of the priest, to be condemned to hell. Hell to her then was the blast furnace, the blast furnace that illuminated the sky all over Jarrow when the residue was poured on to the slag heap. That was hell: hell was fire, and hell was in Jarrow, administered from Newcastle . . . such were the narrow boundaries of her world. She had been twelve before she could grope with the fact that hell was not directly connected with Newcastle, nor yet the blast furnace. But she still believed in hell, then, and now, and she still believed it was administered by God. And she still believed that people paid for their sins. But at the same time she knew that she didn't want to believe it, and it wasn't only since she met David that she had kicked against these beliefs. Her rebellion had begun to stir much earlier . . . yet not against her religion. No, it was against Father O'Malley's delivered conception of

God and of his own vindictive power that she had dared set her puny mind.

'Why haven't you been to mass, lately?'

'I have, Father.'

The priest's eyes narrowed. 'I haven't seen you, nor has Father Bailey.'

'I go to Jarrow, first mass.'

'Why to Jarrow? All your life you have attended my church, so why to Jarrow?'

She wetted her lips and cast her eyes downwards but did not lower her head because the thoughts in it tended to thrust her chin out and upwards. She didn't go because of him. She didn't go because they all looked at her. The girls she had gone to school with, their mothers and fathers, they all knew she had married a Protestant; and if that wasn't bad enough, she had got married in a registry office. So to them she wasn't married at all. That's why she didn't go.

'It wouldn't be because you're ashamed of what you've done?'

'No, I'm not ashamed.' She was on her feet now. 'I've got nothing to be ashamed of, Father. I've married a good man, a very good man.'

The priest slowly drew himself upwards; he buttoned the top button of his black coat, took from the pocket his black gloves and put them on before saying, 'You know as well as I do, Sarah, that in the sight of God and His Holy Church you are not married, in fact you are living in sin. . . . Well, I'll leave you with that thought. I'm always in the Presbytery any time you want to see me to make arrangements for the ceremony.' He turned and walked into the dark room, and from there he said, 'Tell your husband I've called.'

She heard him fumbling at the front door, but she could not go to his assistance.

She heard the door open and then close, and slowly she lowered herself into David's chair. 'I'll see you in hell first.' She did not recognise the sound of her own voice; it wasn't a young girl's voice, it was again the voice of a woman, the woman who had spoken to John on New Year's morning. He was cruel, cruel. She was married, she was. He was a pig of a man, a swine. She shuddered at her daring, at the blasphemy of calling a priest a pig, a swine. Well, she didn't care, she didn't care if she was struck down dead this minute . . . he was. He was a priest, a Christian, and he had sat there prophesying disasters, wishing them on her; yes, wishing them on her to prove himself right. . . . The awareness of conscience. . . . God works slowly.

She leaned back in the chair, feeling faint of a sudden. The fight seeped out of her. She felt funny, odd, and she asked herself was she frightened. Yes, she supposed she was. He had the name of being able to put the fear of God into anybody. Yet this was an odd feeling she had, a sickly odd feeling. She found that her stomach was acting in a strange way.

She wished David was in, just to look at him, to feel his hands holding hers, to know that she was secure. She lay with her eyes closed and gradually the feeling passed. It was funny to feel like this, weak . . . she had said to David's mother she felt as strong as a horse. Well, at this moment she felt as weak as a kitten, like a baby. The word brought her sitting straight up in the chair, a great question mark filling the room. She looked round as if for the answer. Then her eyes slowly came to rest on her stomach. She put her two hands across it and stroked it slowly, then whispered aloud, 'Oh . . . oh . . . but I'd better be sure before I say anything. . . . Yes. Yes. I'd better. It might only be fright through him. . . .'

When David came in, even before he changed his shoes or sat down and had a cup of tea, he took her in his arms. He looked at her, he kissed her. Then, holding her at arm's length, he said, 'Hello, Mrs Hetherington.'

It was a game, a playful routine, but it was also something that set their marriage apart from other marriages. Marriages, everybody knew, sank into mundane ordinariness after a wedding. Life became a routine. Even a battleground of wills, of warring temperaments, of hitherto unrevealed personal habits, irritating, maddening personal habits which became obnoxious to the other party. Sarah knew all about marriage from this angle. She had witnessed the process around the doors. She had heard it discussed among women in the kitchen. She had seen it enacted between her mother and father. Their first flush of love had not reached even the pale pink tinted stage before reality had hit them. Terms such as, 'Anybody seen that old cow of mine?' were thought funny and even a sign that a man loved his wife. That's how marriage went in the bottom end. And people and attitudes weren't all that different in the top end. Sarah was coming to this knowledge painfully. The upper stratum was only a bath-bricked step from the lower stratum. John had been right there.

But her marriage was different. She had been married for weeks now and David seemed to get more loving and gentle every day. . . . John had been right there too. . . . Damn John! Damn the priest!

'I said hello, Mrs Hetherington.'

'Hello, Mr Hetherington.' She rubbed her nose against his.

'What's the matter? You look peaked. Are you all right?'

'Yes, yes, I'm fine. Of course, I'm all right.'

'Have you been washing, doing all the lot? I told you last week that you hadn't to do it, Mother can get Mrs Watson. She's had her before. . . .'

She had her fingers over his lips. 'You're wasting your breath; I haven't been washing, I've been sitting most of the afternoon with Dan.'

'Well, that's not good for you either. You've been up there too much. You've got no colour in your face . . . How is he?'

'Oh, much better. He seems to have improved a ton today.'

He turned from her now and, going to his chair and sitting down to change his shoes, he said, 'I want to talk to you, Sarah, about Dan. You know what I told you about his friend . . . the woman down Westoe?' He cast his eyes at her and she nodded. 'Well, he hasn't seen her for over a month, and on New Year's day, as bad as he was feeling, he wrote her a note, but he's received no reply. He wrote another after he got over the crisis, and when he had no reply to that either it dawned on him that they hadn't been posted; my mother just hadn't posted them. Naturally he was worried. He didn't know what she'd be thinking. From what I can gather–he did some talking to me when he wasn't quite himself–things haven't been running too smoothly lately in that direction. Surprisingly, he has asked her to marry him and she won't.

Anyway, to ease his mind I wrote to her and told her what's happened. And I've talked the matter over with John, and he says that she should be allowed to come and see him if she wants to. It would likely get Dan on to his feet quicker than anything, for he's very low at present and it's not like him–he could joke with a gun at his head, could Dan.'

Sarah, her mouth hanging slightly open, said. 'Her come up here? Your mother would go mad.'

'Yes, if she knew, but she needn't. Dan's likely to be confined to the house for weeks yet, so we thought that if Mother could be persuaded to go to the chapel meeting as usual on Wednesday afternoon the woman could come in here, and when mother's gone she could slip next door for half an hour, no one would be any the wiser.'

'But, David, what if your mother didn't go out?'

'Well, that would be just too bad. But look.' He reached out and grabbed her hand. 'There's no need to get worried. We're not planning a bank robbery or anything like that.'

'A bank robbery would be safer. What if she was to find out?'

'But she won't. Nothing will happen if she doesn't go to the chapel meeting, that's all there is about it. But don't you see.' He pulled her towards him. 'It would please Dan, and I want to please Dan. He's a good fellow is Dan. I've always known that, but I didn't realise how much I'd miss him until I thought he was a goner. Come on, come on.' He shook her hands. 'Don't look so frightened. If me mother found out, and she wanted to kill anyone, it would be me or John.'

Sarah looked down at him in silence. She made a small motion with her head but she did not reply, except to herself, and she said, 'No, no, she wouldn't kill either of you, it would be me she would kill.' And the knowledge brought a feeling of dread into her being.

Chapter Five

Sarah liked the woman from the moment she opened the door to her, but at the same time she wondered what Dan saw in her. She was quite well-dressed and she spoke nicely. Her manner was shy, quiet. She had about her a quality of refinement, but the impression she imparted to Sarah almost at once was that she looked nooled. Perhaps this was because she'd had a disastrous marriage, but still, that was over and she had Dan now and Dan wanted to marry her. And there was a timidness about her; she was like–Sarah searched in her mind to describe what the woman was like and, when the thought came to her . . . she looks like a superior mouse. She was pleased with herself because it was an indication that she was learning, that she was picking these things up from David.

The woman's name was Mrs Mount, Eva Mount. Sarah addressed her as

Mrs Mount. She offered her tea and biscuits and tried to make conversation, but it was hard going.

'Are you sure it's convenient?' The woman asked for at least the third time since her arrival, and Sarah assured her that it was, or it would be. 'My husband did explain to you about his mother?' She said this gently.

'Yes, he did.' Mrs Mount's voice was small, high. She spoke in monosyllables most of the time. Only once more did she break away from yes, and no, to ask, 'Dan has told you about me?' And Sarah answered, 'Yes.' And added, 'Dan's nice.'

Following this there was another silence, and Sarah glancing at the clock, said, 'It's half-past two. She's likely gone now, I'll go in and see.'

Mary Hetherington had gone. John was in charge in the bedroom, and when she entered he looked quickly towards her and said, 'All set?'

She nodded, but towards Dan, an older-looking, much thinner Dan now, and he smiled at her and said, 'You're like a lot of conspirators. By! If this was to come out it would be the end of the world.'

'I'll go and get her.' As she turned away John said, 'I'll make myself scarce an' all. I'll go over home for an hour. I'll be back.' He punched the air in the direction of Dan, and for answer Dan smiled weakly, saying, 'Thanks for everything. If ever a war comes they'll make you a general.'

'Roll on a war.' John was coming down the stairs behind Sarah now, and he added, 'That's what we want, a war.'

Sarah wanted to say, 'Don't be silly.' But, as always, she prevented herself from making any retort to John's provocative remarks. She didn't want to get him going in any way, she told herself. Like a dangerous dog, he was better left sleeping.

They were in the living-room now, alone, and as she went to pass him she looked at him because he willed that she should. She was an arm's length from him and for a second or so they stared at each other until he asked quietly, 'Not mad at me any more, Sarah?'

And just as quietly, even gently, she replied, 'No.'

'Good.' He turned abruptly and preceded her into the scullery, and as he opened the door to let her pass he said. 'You'd better tell her to keep it to half an hour, just in case.' And as he closed the door on them he said under his breath, with a laugh that was both sad and bitter, 'The things we do for love.'

Then they went down the yard and parted in the back lane without looking at each other again, but she was trembling. He could always make her tremble.

Almost moving on tiptoe, Sarah led the woman from her house and into Mary Hetherington's. She never thought of her mother-in-law as mam although she now called her by this name; she thought of her as she, or David's mother.

As she opened the kitchen door the very house itself seemed aghast at the act she was perpetrating. She said hastily to the woman, 'Give me your coat and hat. You'll need them when you go out, it's so cold.'

But the woman said, 'I'll keep them on, if you don't mind.'

Without further ado Sarah led the way out of the room and up the stairs.

Then, tapping gently on Dan's door, she went in. She smiled at him, let the woman pass her, then went quickly out and down the stairs again.

As she stood in the living-room looking at the clock her heart began to beat uncomfortably fast. Just supposing what would happen, just supposing she walked in that door at this minute. Just supposing! . . . She gave a violent shake of her head. Why was she so frightened of her mother-in-law? John was right: she shouldn't be frightened of anybody. She was big and strong enough to face ten Mary Hetheringtons, yet . . . She looked at the clock. Only five minutes gone. She wished, oh, she wished somebody would come. Oh, she'd better be careful and state her wishes precisely, else who knew but his mother herself might walk in the door. She wished John would come back. She didn't feel half so afraid when he was about; not of other people anyway, only of him, but that was a different kind of fear.

She filled the kettle and set Dan's tea-tray. She took the chenille cloth off the dining-table and put on the lace-edged one, the second best, and set the table for two.

She looked at the clock again. The woman had been up there twenty minutes. Oh, she wished she had said a quarter of an hour instead of half an hour.

There were two pairs of shoes by the door with mud on them; she cleaned them. The woman had been upstairs now twenty-seven minutes. She gazed up towards the ceiling, and as if her anxiety had prised through the floor she heard footsteps walking towards the bedroom door. She heard it open and close, then she herself moved towards the living-room door. She was two steps from it when the key turned in the front door and she let out an agonised exclamation that was also a prayer. 'Oh God in Heaven!' she groaned.

The woman was on the last stair but one when Mary Hetherington saw her. She had the door in her hand, but she didn't close it. Slowly she pushed it behind her and slowly she walked forward. She brought her eyes for a second from the woman to Sarah's red and agitated face, then looked back towards the woman again.

'Who are you? What are you doing here?'

The woman opened her mouth to speak, then, glancing fearfully at Sarah, she closed it again, and as she did so Mary Hetherington looked over her head towards the top of the stairs and the bedroom. Then, speaking below her breath, in a voice so deep that it seemed to be that of a man's, she growled, 'How dare you! Get out of here.'

'I've done nothing. Wh . . .'

'Get out of here!' Mary Hetherington seemed to leap backwards towards the door and, pulling it wide, she pointed dramatically towards the street.

The little woman, very, very like a mouse now, a trembling pathetic mouse, gave Sarah one piteous glance, then made her exit on the point of a run. As Sarah watched her scrambling ignominiously down the steps into the street, the reason why Dan had taken up with her became clear: it was because the poles of the earth were not more apart than she and his sister. In spite of being brought up under the domination of Mary Hetherington, he had survived and had become a man with a mind of his own, but Mary's dominance had coloured his choice of a woman.

As Sarah watched her mother-in-law come towards her she said to herself, Stand up to her, don't let her frighten you. But the admonition did not prevent her retreating into the living-room, where she stood at the far side of the table not daring to look into the outraged face before her. She had only seen this woman in a temper once before, that was on the day she and David had returned from the registry office, and, as she had told Phyllis, she had been frightening. During that particular scene she had raised her voice–if she had not actually shouted she had talked loudly–but now her voice was not raised, it was very low and it made her much more frightening than any wild burst of temper could.

'You . . . you knew about this, didn't you?'

'No, I didn't.'

'You arranged it.'

'No! No, I didn't.'

'You're a liar . . . a big blowsy, lazy liar.'

The attack widened Sarah's eyes. This was how the women of the bottom end talked. Moreover, this was an attack on her. It had really nothing to do with Dan or the woman, it was directed against her. She felt it. She knew it.

'Dan would never have dared, he knows how far he can go. But you . . . do you know what you've done?' She had her hands flat on the table and the edge of it was pressing her clothes into her thighs, her stomach, surprisingly large for one so thin, was covering inches of the table, and she was leaning at an angle that brought her head and shoulders half-way across it. 'You've wrecked my home, that's what you've done.'

'You don't know what you're talking about. I've done nothing. It wasn't me who . . .'

'Shut up! You could talk until you're black in the face and I'd never believe you. You're sly, cunning . . . using your lumps of flesh. . . . ' She released one white-knuckled hand from the table and flicked it within an inch of Sarah's breasts. 'You don't need any sign outside the door saying "All men welcome", you've just got to show yourself. . . . You–you young hussy–setting your cap for my menfolk! And you've taken them, haven't you . . . my menfolk. That's what you've done. And you meant to, didn't you?'

'I . . . I . . . What are you talking about? You must be mad!' Sarah shook her head slowly. Her mouth hung open and her tongue hung slack on her teeth with amazement.

'Go on, play the innocent, first David and then Dan. Oh, he has his woman on the side but he can't keep away from your kitchen. And then my own husband . . . what did you do to him? Encourage him in. . . . "You can smoke in here, Dad" . . .' She was mimicking Sarah's voice. 'You think I don't know your little game. I wasn't born yesterday. And John, running round making your furniture when he won't knock a nail in for me, or May either.' She took a great intake of breath now. The beads of sweat were ringing her upper lip. She straightened her back, breathed hard again, then with her eyes still riveted in patent hate on Sarah, she went on, 'You should be in Costerfine Town with your sister. There's not a pin to choose between you. I must have been crazy to think that you were the lesser of two evils. Ellen said I'd be paid back, and how true her words have come. But I realised it from the beginning. And it wouldn't have happened if you hadn't sneaked off to the registry office. There are worse things than a taint of insanity. Well, God has punished me. Sure enough. He's punished me. I've lost a good friend in Ellen, I've lost a girl who'd have been a daughter to me, and what have I got? . . . You . . . who've split my family apart.'

'It's not true.' Sarah was standing straight now, her breathing sharp. 'Not a word you've said is true. I've never asked any of them into the house. If they come next door it's not to see me but for a bit of peace, do you hear? Do you hear that? For a bit of peace!' Although she was still trembling, still afraid of this woman, there came to her aid retaliation born of a sense of injustice. This feeling came boiling up in her when dealing with her father, or the priest, and it now enabled her to thrust back at her mother-in-law the truth, the truth that was going to sever their connection for all time. Her voice spitting out the words, she cried, 'And if they do come into my house who's to blame them. What is there for them here?' She flung one arm wide. 'Is there any real comfort or happiness? This isn't a home, it's your show-place, and you're the big boss. Dan is the only one who has kicked over the traces, but it's a wonder to me they're not all regular visitors at Maggie Conaman's. . . . There, you've asked for it, and you've got it. . . . You never intended I should have David, did you? No, you didn't. As you said, it wouldn't have happened if we hadn't sneaked off to the registry office. Well, you were foxed, weren't you? I've got David, and I'm going to keep him, and you can't do a thing about it. Now you've really got something to get your teeth into, so bite hard. You can't hurt me, do you hear? You can't hurt me.'

She turned away from the livid countenance and went out of the house, not rushing, just walking, walking steadily. Although fearful at her temerity and amazed at her daring, she was possessed of the knowledge that she was indeed a woman, all of her and for ever. The girl in her was gone completely.

Maggie Conaman was a notorious character of the docks and Sarah would have denied any knowledge of her existence if the question had been put to her, but now she had used her knowledgeably and thrown her into her mother-in-law's chapel-going sanctimonious teeth.

A few minutes later, as she stood in her own kitchen, her hands above her shoulders gripping the mantlepiece as she stared down into the fire, she seemed to see there her values being melted and reshaped. What were this family, anyway? What were they? They were no better than those at the bottom end. When she thought of . . . the family she was not including the men. There was one figure only who represented the family; her mother-in-law. She had talked and gone on like any woman from Baxter Street or Poltar's Row. And only yesterday she had said one mustn't bear malice or bitterness. That was funny, that was. Anyway, who did she think she was, anyway? WHO? She grabbed at the poker and rammed it into the fire, stirring it vigorously, sending the ash over her shining black-leaded hob. A big, blowsy, lazy liar. She dropped the poker with a clatter on to the hearth, then, throwing herself into David's chair, she turned her face into the corner and began to cry, slow painful tears. There was always someone or something to spoil things, always, always.

'Don't worry yourself.' They both said it at once, John and David. They were standing in front of her and she looked up at them as she said, 'You're wasting your time. She blames me for it all. So let her go on thinking that. You're not going to make things any better by telling her the truth. In fact you'll make them worse.'

'We'll see about that.' David nodded his head down sharply at her. 'Come on.' He beckoned to John. 'This is one thing we can get straightened out and waste no time about it.

'Have your tea first,' she said.

'Tea be damned!'

That was the first time she had heard David say damn; he was very upset for her. As she heard their combined footsteps going down the yard she joined her hands in her lap and sat waiting. Within a matter of minutes she heard the sound of voices, low and muffled coming through the wall.

Five minutes later she raised her eyes towards the kitchen door as she heard the back door open. She was surprised to see John coming in alone. 'I've left him,' he said, jerking his head towards the fireplace, 'pouring buckets of oil on the troubled waters. Not that it will do much good. You were right.' He came close to her, and, bending towards her, his hands cupping his knees, he asked quietly, 'Did you say we should all have gone down to Maggie Conaman's for diversion?'

She dropped her eyes from his and after a moment said, 'Something like that.'

'Good for you.'

She looked up at him. His eyes were twinkling, his face twisted into a wry grin. 'You certainly rent the temple asunder with that salvo. And the funny thing is, you know'–he wagged his finger slowly in front of her face–'many's the time I nearly did just that.'

She lowered her eyes again and looked down at his feet. They were an extra large size. His boots were highly polished; he always took pride in his appearance. She liked that about him; he would never look down and out if he was out of work for ten years, she thought. She was wondering why she was thinking this way at this particular moment when his voice came at her again, saying, 'You know, some people think your church is the last word in domination. Well, it might be, but with it neck and neck at the post are the Baptists, ones like my mother. Humbugs who condemn drinking yet make a brew with a kick in it. . . . Oh, I know I said it didn't affect me, but then I can stand a good deal. . . . You know, I once believed in God. But no smoking, no drinking, no swearing, no taking the Lord's name in vain, no reading books on a Sunday other than . . . the Book; no playing the piano on a Sunday unless hymns, these things changed my opinion pretty early on about God, and chapel, and living the good life. And if they hadn't, the face of the bolster atween her and Dad would have done it in any case.

'What?' She did not quite follow him. 'A bolster?'

'It's a fact. After Davie was born no more of . . . THAT, she said. I wasn't five at the time, but I remember as if it was yesterday, and getting out of bed because something disturbed me, I didn't know what, and opened the bedroom door. There she was standing on the landing in her nightie saying, "I want no more of that." The word THAT stuck in my mind for years. I was about ten when I discovered what THAT was and just turned thirteen when I learned about the bolster. It was the first of Dad's Armistice celebrations. You know, he always gets tight the day before Armistice Day and he told me–he was crying just like a kid–and he told me. "Fighting all through the War," he said; "and I had to come back to the bolster. It's unnatural, isn't it?"'

Sarah lowered her eyes. She felt embarrassed, as if somebody had told her a filthy story. She had never liked filthy stories.

'She's a cruel woman is me mother; narrow, and cruel and, like all such women, bitchy. May is bitchy, but she's not narrow in that way. You know something, Sarah?' He was still bent towards her with his hands on his knees and she looked at him again. 'You've struck a blow for all of us the day. Every single one of us . . . Dan, Dad, Davie, and me. Oh yes . . . and me. For how many times have I wanted to say to her just what you said the day. You know, it's funny. We're known about the doors as a united family, yet each one of us hates her guts in some way . . . aw, don't let it trouble you, don't look so sad. Come on, cheer up. You've stood on your two feet today so you shouldn't look sad.' He took his hands from his knees and bent over her, and his tone dropped to a whisper as he said, 'I worry when you look sad, I do, I do . . . Sarah.' His hand came out to touch her cheek when she pressed herself away from him, saying under her breath, 'No, don't don't. Don't, don't.

'All right.' He straightened up and stood looking down at her for a moment before turning abruptly from her. 'I'll be seeing you,' he said.

She lay back in the chair. Her heart was pounding against her ribs. Why must he do it . . . touch her? Everything would be all right if he didn't touch her. When the beating subsided she thought of what he had said. She had struck a blow for all of them. Yes, she had struck a blow, and smashed the house. Very likely if she had kept her mouth shut this business would have died down and a veneer would have covered the real feelings of them all and they could have gone on with the daily business of living amicably–but never again. The blow she had struck had severed the lives of the two houses; and in her own house there stood David, Dan, and John, with her father-in-law astraddle the wreckage. But standing alone in the rooms of the other house was Mary Hetherington, bereft of her menfolk. This knowledge brought no feeling of triumph to Sarah, only awareness of the hard bitter woman's pain.

Chapter Six

Sarah felt dreadful. She longed to go in to Dan to help as usual, to see to him, but she knew that even if she had the courage to walk up the next yard she would find the door bolted against her.

She had tidied upstairs. She had done her kitchen and dusted the few bits of furniture that were in the front room. She had prepared the dinner far in advance of its time. And now, taking up some socks of David's she sat down near the fire. She didn't feel well–she supposed it was the upset of last night–she felt all to pot. She said to herself, Get up and make yourself a cup of strong coffee–coffee was David's innovation. He liked it. He liked it better than tea. She wasn't very struck on it herself, but David said it bucked you up.

As she snapped off the wool from the sock there was a flick of shadow against the left-hand pane of the kitchen window. This meant there was someone at the back door. She was in the scullery before they knocked, and when she opened the door her mouth did not drop open into a gape of surprise, it clamped closed, her lips losing their full shape in a tight line. 'What do you want?'

'You were always civil, weren't you?'

'I asked you what you want?'

'Just a word.'

Her tongue drew a quick line over her upper lip before she said, 'Get it out then.'

'Well.' He moved from one foot to the other; then rubbed his thumb under his nose and brought his eyebrows close together before saying. 'It's a bit private like, I don't think I'd do me talking out here.'

She stood staring at him. She wanted to bang the door in his face. She remembered that he had been trying to see her before this. Without a word she pulled the door wide to give him plenty of room to pass her, she never liked getting close to him–there was a smell about him, a body smell. Even when he had washed himself down there had still been that smell, a smoky, sweet, funny smell.

In the kitchen she kept her distance from him. She did not ask him to sit down but stood looking at him, waiting. He was looking about him, a smile on his face. When he looked like this she could understand anyone thinking he was a quiet, inoffensive little chap.

'You've got it nice . . . grand. Did well for yourself, didn't you?' He was still smiling as if an approbation. 'I'll sit down a minute, off me legs. I've been to the doctor's with me back . . . I'm on the sick. They stopped me dole.'

So that was it. He had come cadging. He had a nerve. She repeated the words in her mind, slow, deep, and emphatic. By! Yes . . . he had a nerve all right. Then, as she had guessed, it came.

'I was wondering if you could spare me a few bob to tide me over.' He had not said, us over, which would have meant he wanted the money for the house.

Her face was hard, her voice equally so, as she rapped out, 'I haven't any money to give or lend.'

'No?' He shook his head slowly.

'No, not now or any other time.'

'But your man's doing all right, he's got a permanent job. From three pounds five a week they get in the dock office, I understand.'

'It doesn't matter what they get, or what you understand, I've got no money to give you; it takes me all my time to manage. And now you'll have to go, I've got to go out.'

He sighed here, then leant his short body forward until his elbows were resting on his knees, his hands hanging idly downwards, his whole impression one of relaxation. 'It's a pity.' He sounded sorry.

She was puzzled by his reaction. She had expected him to bounce to his feet and tell her what he thought she was, a bloody upstart. Instead he started talking about David.

'Nice fellow, that man of yours. Did he tell you I had a word with him on the road the other day?'

David hadn't told her.

'He asked me how long I'd been out and he gave me a bob.'

Oh, David, David, what a silly thing to do. But that was David.

'I should think he was a chap in a thousand, straight like; no side to him. I was talking to some of them at the dock gates and they said he was the civilist fellow in the office.' He lifted his eyes upwards looking at her under his lids. 'You've been lucky, you know. You fell on your feet. It'd be a pity if you were knocked on your back now, wouldn't it?'

Her brows came together. 'Knocked on me back? What are you getting at? Look.' She did not go near him, but she bent her body towards him. 'I don't know what you're yammering on about or what you're leading up to. I only know one thing: coming from you it won't be any good.'

'Well, it's all how you look at it, isn't it? A thing is good or bad how you look at it, that's what I say. . . . The mother's a bit of tartar.' He jerked his head towards the wall. 'Thinks herself somebody, I hear. Never out of the Baptist chapel they say. Narrow as they come. No understanding. Now our lot can booze and whore and think nowt of it. . . .'

'I'll have none of that talk in my house.'

'Well, I was just explaining, no offence. But you know yourself we're all human, you should know that better than anybody.' He was smiling again, nodding at her now. 'But what a Catholic would laugh off a Baptist would hang you for.'

Sarah was standing straight now, stiff and tall, her hands gripped in front of her waist. There had come upon her a terrible feeling of apprehension. It might only be imagination, she told herself, but the smell from him seemed to be filling the room. She felt faint, sick with it. He was staring at her, not speaking. She told herself not to let him see that she was agitated. That's what he wants, she said. Stand up to him like you did to her yesterday . . . go on. She took a deep breath, then said, 'Look, if you've had your say you'd better go because I'm going out, I've told you.'

When he still did not answer but continued to look at her with his unblinking red eyes she withdrew one hand from the other hand, and, putting them behind her, supported herself against the edge of the table. And as she did so he said quietly, 'It's a pity the big fellow hadn't been single an' all, you'd have had your pick then.'

'W . . . w . . . what?'

'I said . . .'

She was away from the table now, standing over him, shouting, 'I heard what you said.' She glanced at the wall. She would hear her next door if she went on like this. Her voice dropping, she hissed at him, 'Don't think you can frighten me with anything your sewer mind can make up. All David's family come in here, his uncle and his father.'

'Oh?' He turned his eyes up towards her and his voice sounded almost childish. 'I didn't know they all came in, that's nice. But it wasn't that I was meaning. You see. . . .' He pushed his head back as if to get a better view of her. 'About New Year's morning. You know the Collins, me cousins down Bogey Hill way, well, they asked me over for first footin'. I was a bit surprised like but I went, but didn't stay long, and on me way back Aa was took short.' He stopped at this point and Sarah closed her eyes and waited, her breath suspended, her whole life suspended. She waited.

'I went in one of the huts, you know, the end one on the waste lad, and then I heard this coughing. Well, you know, there's always couples around there. I bumped into two or three on me way up, making the best of the New Year's morning. Well, this couple began . . . well, they began to talk. At least he did, an' Aa was a bit surprised like. Well, you see what I mean.'

Sarah, her eyes open now, was pressing herself against the table; then her body, arching itself upwards, shot forward and she was hanging over him and words, each borne on a spurt of rage, came frothing from her mouth. 'You devil! You dirty, evil devil! it was nothing . . . nothing. I tell you it was nothing. Nothing happened.'

'No?' He seemed to be untroubled by her rage, and his voice still held a childish innocent note and he shook his head as if in perplexity.

'You dirty-minded swine!'

'Now, look, Sarah.' He got slowly to his feet. 'I don't want to quarrel with you. There's no reason. An' it wasn't my doings, was it? I just happened to be there, and there I had to stay. You wouldn't have liked me to show me face, now would you? I had to stay put for over ten minutes, you know.'

Oh God! Oh God! Oh God! Sarah bowed her head deeply.

'I couldn't close me ears, that's why I said it was a pity, a pity the big fellow's married, for he seems clean gone on you . . . Mind . . .' He moved his head slowly. 'I don't blame him, but it's awkward, isn't it? It's an awkward situation all round, I mean with your man being such a nice bloke an' his mother being such a tartar an' all that. And then the big fellow's got a bairn, hasn't he, and a wife that's a bit of a spitfire too as far as I can gather. . . .'

'Shut up! Shut your evil mouth. I tell you, nothing happened, noth . . ing, do you hear? Noth . . . ing.' Spurts of frothy saliva came from her mouth with the last word. A voice was going mad inside her now, urging, directing, yelling, Stand up to him. Don't let him get you. Tell him to go to hell and do what he likes. . . . But he wouldn't go to hell. She would, she would be plunged into a living hell. If she hurt David in any way that would be hell. But what she could do was to take the wind out of this slimy devil's sails by telling David what had happened. . . . And turn him against John? No, no. She could never do that. Then she must tell John. . . . What, and have him murder this little reptile! Whatever road she tried to take out of this mess was blocked, she could see that. If she made a move in any direction she'd bring disaster on them all, the disaster that Mary Hetherington had prophesied, that the priest had prophesied. She remembered Father O'Malley's words: God works in strange ways, sometimes through a series of disasters. Her whole being trembled. It was as if he had known what was going to happen, as if he had a hand in the plan.

'I wouldn't take on like that, there's no need to upset yourself. I just thought I'd tell you and put you on your guard like in case you got careless.'

Her eyes were closed again. She could not bear to look at him in case she sprang on him and beat her fists into his face. Her mouth opened twice before she said, with eerie quietness, 'There was nothing happened, he was drunk.'

'Aye, I can believe that. Yes, New Year's morning, lots of funny things happen in drink. Meself, I've always steered clear of it, but there it is. . . . Well, I just thought I'd pop in and tell you an' see if you had a couple of shillings on you. that's all I want, a couple of shillings until you see your way clear . . . anyway, what's five bob a week to keep everybody happy, eh? I ask you now.'

She was going to be sick. She was going to faint. She had never fainted in her life, but she wanted to faint now, to pass right out, for if she didn't she would do something to him, she knew she would.

She found herself at the cupboard next to the fireplace where she kept her bag, and, groping blindly in it, she found her purse, and taking from it a two-shilling piece she threw it with a backward movement on to the table. She heard it bounce twice; then from the corner of her eye she saw him stooping to pick it up from the floor.

'Thanks. Thanks, lass. Now don't worry, there's nothing to worry about. I won't tell your mother so you needn't worry, 'cos it would upset her, you know. She lays great store by your being up this end. It sort of makes up for the other one and the Arab like. There's nobody need know anything about this only you and me . . . and them concerned. . . . Well, so long. Aa'll be seeing you. Aa'll pop over now and again. So long. Aa'll see meself out. Don't you bother.'

When she heard the door close she stood with her back pressed against the cupboard shelves. She would go mad. This would drive her mad. What could she do? She staggered to the table and gripped its edge until her nails broke. Then she was leaning over it, her stomach heaving. It seemed to turn over and rush upwards. The next moment she was standing over the sink vomiting.

She was still sick when David came in at dinner-time. 'What is it?' he said. 'Have you eaten something?'

She hung on to his hands tightly with both of hers, and she made herself smile when she gave him the news, 'I'm going to have a baby I think,' she said.

At two o'clock the following morning Sarah awoke screaming from a nightmare, and when David held her, trying to assure her that she was awake and safe, she grabbed at him. 'I was in the mud. Everybody was in the mud, but they dragged me to the middle. I had it in my mouth and I was choking . . . Oh, David, it was awful, awful. I'm frightened, David.'

'There's nothing to be frightened about, darling; it was only a dream.'

Yes, it was only a dream. Her body slowly unwound against him. 'But it was worse than usual.' She said, 'It was worse than usual, much worse.'

'You've had it before then?'

She nodded against his breast. 'It started with an overdose of cough mixture my mother gave me.' She felt a tremor of laughter go through his body. 'Well, that's put paid to cough mixture.'

They lay silently, their bodies close, breathing almost the same breath, until David whispered, 'Don't let anything frighten you, dreams or anything else. And as long as you've got me I'll see to it that nothing does, not even . . .' He pressed his finger into her backbone and the pressure spelt 'mother'. 'You understand, love?'

Yes, she understood. She also understood that his words meant the exact opposite from what he thought. They meant, for as long as she had him she would know fear, the fear of her little world, her new superior little world exploding.

BOOK THREE

Chapter One

'I think there's going to be a march,' said John.

'Where to?' asked David.

'London, of course.'

'It'll likely be the same as the one in Seaham Harbour when you met Ramsay MacDonald. Tea and soft soap and the promise that Jarrow would be kept in mind. That's three years ago.'

'We'll get results this time or else . . .'

'Or else what?' said David. 'Riots?'

'Aye, if necessary. But they don't want it to be like that; everything's going to be orderly, at least from our end. Ellen's coming with us.'

'Oh, that woman!' May's thin voice broke in on the men. 'My godfathers! You would think she was a priestess; I'm sick of the sound of Ellen Wilkinson's name.'

'Shut up!' John turned on her, spitting the words at her. 'You haven't got the list to lift a hand to help anybody, and you haven't a good word in your belly for those who do.'

May raked John with her cold glance before rising to her feet and saying, almost listlessly 'Lift a hand? You've been lifting hands for years now, the great John the Baptist, and where's it got you? What's it got us?'

'As much as it's got anybody else in this town–a place in the dole queue. If we hadn't fought, you and the likes of you would now be in Harton, that's if you could get in. You'd more likely be lying on the salt grass, as they did not fifty years ago, dying on a bit of sacking.'

'Oh, for God's sake! Let up, will you! I've heard it so often it's got whiskers.' May moved round the table, past Sarah, who sat silently sewing, and made her way towards the staircase door, saying, 'I'll call Paul down.' But before she reached it David spoke to her quietly, 'But he's right, you know, May. If it wasn't for the likes of John here and people like Alfred Rennie and Drummond . . .'

'Oh, David, don't you start . . . please. And tell me something I don't know. I'm sick of listening to the virtues of Drummond and Riley and Rennie and Thompson and the rest. Oh yes, and the Virgin Mary herself, Miss Ellen Wilkinson. But tell me, David. . . .' She stepped back into the room. 'What have they done? All this cafuffling and what have they done?'

Before David could answer John was on his feet crying, 'They just keep men sane, that's all. Keep reminding them that they're men, that they might be down but not bloody well out. They're trying to feed their minds. At least, put into them as much as their depleted systems will allow them to take, so that when we march into London it won't be a band of ignorant numbskulls they'll be talking to, and that's what they take us for down here, a lot of bloody brainless numbskulls. And they're not alone in thinking along those lines, are they, May dear?'

They glared at each other for a moment. But just as May was about to speak John put in quickly, 'You won't come up to the rooms, will you? No, because you'd have to swallow your words. And, what's more, you might learn something. . . . Oh, but you don't need to learn, do you? No, you know it all, don't you? Like them up there. Well, as I said, they'll get an eye-opener when we march in.'

'Da-di-da, da-di-da; tra-le-la-la.' May gave an imitation of blowing a bugle, and as John took a step forward David, catching his arm, said quickly, 'Now then, now then. Stop it, you two.'

'I'll make some tea.' Sarah rose from her chair, and, pushing the little dress she was smocking on to the dresser, went out into the scullery, while John, looking towards May again, said bitterly, 'One of these days I'll land you one and you'll not get up again.'

'Try it on.' She smiled at him as she rolled her head tauntingly on the back of her shoulders. Then, going into the passage, she called upstairs, 'Paul! Paul, do you hear me? Come on. We're going over.'

There was some laughter and chatter from the room above, then a bouncing step on the stairs and a boy of about eight years old followed May into the kitchen. He was tall for his age and thin, and he looked like neither May nor John, but there was a suggestion of his father in his mercurial manner. With a flicking movement of his eyes he looked from his father to David and said, 'You'll never be able to make her spell, Uncle, I bet you won't. She can read long words, but she can't even spell cat.'

'What should I do with her? Bray her?' David made great play of rolling up his shirt-sleeves, and the boy laughed a high tinkling laugh. 'I can see you doing that, Uncle David. But you being a good speller and knowing about words, you'd think she could spell, wouldn't you? She's over five.'

'Yes, you would at that age.' David shook his head sadly at the boy, causing him to laugh again.

May, pushing at her son, now cried, 'Get going. It's a shame to waste two houses between you and her.'

'Aw, let's have a minute, Mam.' The boy swung away from her and went quickly round the table to where John sat moving cardboard letters with his finger.

'You playing Lexicon, Dad?'

'Do as your mother bids you.' John did not raise his eyes.

'You playing Lexicon, Uncle David?'

'Do you want to get shot, Paul Hetherington?' David looked into the boy's grinning face.

'I want to watch you play. Why are you always messing about with letters, Uncle? You should have been a teacher. Have you always messed about with letters, like when you was a young lad?'

'Yes, Paul, always. they've always fascinated me.'

'Did you hear me?'

'Yes, Mam. Just one minute, only one minute. Go on, Uncle Davie.'

David looked at May and shook his head.

'Why do they fascinate you, Uncle Davie?'

'Well, I suppose it's because a few lines differently arranged can tell you so much.'

'But they're not lines, Uncle Davie, they're squibbles and things.'

'No, they all start with lines. Look.' David took from his pocket a piece of string and, cutting it into lengths with his pen-knife, he placed one piece before him, then he bent another in two, and, sticking it in the middle of the first piece, he said, 'There you are, one straight line, another straight line, bent in two, stick them together and you've got K.' The boy nodded and David went on, 'Then you take another straight piece, put it next to the K and you've got I. Now I is the most important letter in the alphabet; it not only means I, it means ME.' David thumped his chest in a number of places. 'It means all of ME. I've always thought the letter I was an amazing letter. You think of that straight line and then you think of what it means . . . you see?'

Paul nodded again, his eyes bright and twinkling.

'Then you want an S, so you take your straight line and you bend it like that . . . there.' He pointed. 'You've got an S.' He did the same again, then said, 'Look, another S, and what have you? Kiss.'

Paul thumped his uncle in the arm and laughed his high laugh. 'Do some more.'

'Oh no you don't. Come on.' May grabbed her son by the collar, swung him round and marched him out of the room.

In the scullery, protesting but still laughing, Paul grabbed at Sarah's skirt as he was hustled past her and cried, 'Goodnight, Aunt Sarah. She's not asleep. I bet you a shillin' she starts howling in a minute.'

'Goodnight, Paul. She'll get her bottom smacked if she does.'

'What you havin' for supper?'

This question brought May to a halt, and, turning towards Sarah, she said, 'Do you know something? I think he's got a tapeworm–I'm serious.' She nodded at Sarah. 'The minute he got in he had a basin of stew left over from the dinner. That was half-past four. When I went next door'–she jerked her head towards the scullery window–'he was sitting up having a full tea with his grandad. Chips . . . the lot. And then I come over here and finds him scoffing again. And look at him.' She shook his collar. 'There's not a peck of flesh on his bones, people think he's starved. I tell you, he's got a tapeworm.'

Sarah smiled. 'Well, he never ails anything, does he?'

'Ail anything? He hasn't got time, he's always eating.' She gave her son another shake, then pushed him out into the yard, saying, 'Goodnight then.'

'Goodnight, May.'

The door had hardly closed behind her when it was opened immediately and May, her face in the aperture, said, 'Tell him to get over home before twelve, will you? I hate to be woken up in the middle of the night.'

She was gone before Sarah could make any retort, but if she had thought of one she would not have been able to voice it. She stood for a moment looking out into the dark yard. What did she mean by that? May knew that she herself went up to bed and left them downstairs talking until all hours. She had likely meant nothing. What could she mean, anyway? But May was deep. No one ever knew what May was thinking, you couldn't get to the bottom of her.

'Mammy! Mammy!' The cry came from almost above her head and she turned and, picking up the tray of tea, went into the kitchen.

David had half risen from his chair. 'I'll see to her,' he said.

'No, it's all right. Leave her to me.'

'She'll keep you going. She'll have you up there until dawn.'

'It's all right.' She put the tray on the corner of the table and went out and up the stairs, and when she entered her daughter's bedroom the child was sitting up in bed waiting for her.

'Paul didn't read me a story, Mammy.'

'Well, he was helping you with your spelling, wasn't he?'

'He wasn't. I was reading to him and when it was his turn Auntie May called.'

'Come on, lie down. What do you want?'

'Oh.' The child snuggled down into the bedclothes. 'Henny-penny and Cocky-locky and the sky is going to fall.'

Sarah pulled a chair towards the bedside, and, reaching out, picked up a thick-backed nursery book from the table. She had no need of the book, she knew the story word for word, but she flipped the pages over until she came to the story of Henny-penny and Cocky-locky going to tell the King the sky was going to fall. But before starting on it she cast a smiling glance down on her daughter and the child smiled back at her. Every now and again during the reading they would do this. Sarah would lift her head and look at the child and they would smile at each other. Almost from the day she was born it had been like that. They would look at each other and smile and become one.

Every time Sarah looked at this child of hers she knew she was the luckiest woman alive, for she not only had the child, she had its father. In this tiny world of hers she had everything, everything to make a woman happy. Was not David one of the few men in work? They had four meals a day, they owed no one, they had everything, everything that made for joy . . . that was David's phrase. He had said to her, 'I just can't understand about you having nerves, honey, you're not built like that. And we have everything, haven't we? Everything that makes for joy. Is there anything you want? Tell me. Tell me, is there anything in the world that I can give?' And then he had added quickly, 'That's a silly question on three pounds fifteen a week.'

On that occasion she had thrown herself into his arms and assured him with all her heart that he had given her the world. Then why had she got nerves? Why had the doctor said she was suffering from nerves? The doctor had said he thought she was worrying about something. . . . What was she worrying about?

Again she had reassured him that she hadn't a worry in the world. Perhaps, she had said, something had happened to her when she was carrying Kathleen, for it was from when she was first pregnant that she had felt this way.

Yes, David remembered it was from the night she had the nightmare, the night following the day she told him about the baby coming.

She came to the end of the story.

'There now, go to sleep.' Sarah closed the book.

'I haven't said my prayers, Mammy.'

'Yes, you have. You said them before you got into bed. You know you did.' She patted the plump cheek, then, bending over, she laid her mouth to it and was imprisoned by two podgy arms.

'Mammy.'

'Yes, darling.'

'Paul says he loves you.'

'Does he? that's nice. I love Paul too.'

'Paul says that when he grows up he's going to have a house with fifteen rooms and a big car.'

'Oh, I'm glad to hear that; we'll have to go and stay with him. . . . Leave go, darling.'

As Sarah disengaged herself Kathleen said, 'I want Nancy, Mammy, to keep me warm.'

'Oh, Nancy's too hard, you might roll on her and hurt yourself. Have Peter, he's soft.'

'He kicks me, Mammy.'

'I'll tell him not to.' Sarah went to the corner of the small room and from a shelf attached to the wall she took from among numerous toys a dilapidated velvet rabbit, and, holding it at arm's length as she walked to the bed, she said, 'If you kick Kathleen, Peter, you'll get your bottom smacked in the morning.' She placed the rabbit in the child's arms, kissed her once again, then saying as she put the light out, 'I'll leave the door open,' she went from the room and down the stairs.

Dan was in the kitchen now, sitting at the table shuffling a set of dominoes. He turned his head at Sarah's entry. 'Hello, there, how's it going?'

'Oh, all right, Dan.'

'Is she asleep?'

'Yes, she'll be off in a minute . . . I hope.' She smiled at him.

'You go to the doctor's today?'

'Yes.'

'What did he say?'

'Oh, nothing fresh, but he gave me a different bottle, it's very bitter.'

'That'll be for your appetite.'

Sarah picked up her sewing from the dresser again and seated herself in

David's leather chair to the side of the fire and continued with the smocking. The dominoes clicked, and the two brothers and their uncle, all looking of a similar age now, played their nightly game. It had become almost a ritual, this gathering together each night from seven o'clock onwards. If, as they sometimes did, David and she went to the pictures, they would find Dan and John sitting at the table on their return. The key was always kept in the wash-house in between the legs of the poss stick which stood in the middle of the poss tub.

And Dan played on a Thursday night too now.

Sometimes they played Lexicon, or cards, but for the most part it was dominoes, and it was seldom that the evening did not end in some form of discussion. That their discourse kept clear of heated argument was due entirely to David's even temper and Dan's humour.

The only reason why David played games, Sarah thought, was to keep his fingers moving, for he missed his piano-playing. She had tried in every way she knew to persuade him to continue his practice, but his answer was always the same. When she was welcome next door he would start practising again. She had learned in her six years of marriage to David he could be stubborn, and it was surprising to her to realise that he could carry this stubbornness to great lengths. She knew that neither Dan nor John would have been so tenacious with regard to his principles. Although David still visited his mother his visits were short and they had become shorter with the years. the reason for this, Sarah knew, was that Mary Hetherington had not taken to her granddaughter. Although David had not put this in actual words, she knew that he was aware of it.

David's voice now brought her attention to the table, and Dan, as he said, 'What's up with you the night, Dan? That's the seventh game you've lost, and you've doubled twice. That means you owe me . . .' He consulted a piece of paper to his hand, then looked up and laughed. 'Four pounds seven-and-sixpence. I'll let you off with the sixpence.'

'Will you have it now or wait till you get it?'

'I'll wait till I get it.'

'Aw.' Dan scraped his chair back from the table, and, lifting his thick hair from his scalp with his spread fingers, he said, 'To tell you the truth, me mind's not on it, it's miles away . . . in the shop.'

'In the shop?' John looked up from shuffling the cards. 'Anything wrong?'

'Well, yes and no. it's like this.' Dan leaned forward, his forearms on the table again, and looked from John to David. 'The old man made a proposition to me today and I don't really know what to do. It's like this. He's up against the wall now, like all the others; four shops have closed in the last month down the street and our books are so full of tick there isn't any margin left. One of the main snags is that some of them when they've any money go elsewhere, down to Shields Market or some such place. I've said to them, "Look, you can have what tick you like as long as you bring your little bit of ready in." Some of them do, but you just can't keep going on the few. Well, he called me upstairs this morning, and there was the wife sitting. I tell you it was awful, but he put it to me plainly. He said he would have to shut up unless he could find a bit of ready to meet the bills. He's a proud old devil you know, but straight as a die. He's got his faults, but he's honest, and there he was, near tears. And the old woman, she was in tears. And he said to me without any palaver, "Well, Dan, what about it? What have you got left of your winnings?" "Well," I said, "I've got just over four hundred."'

Sarah's hands became still, the needle poised, and involuntarily she repeated, 'Four hundred?' And Dan, turning and looking at her, said, 'Yes, from me winnings. You know, out of *John Bull.*' then, jerking his head round to David and shaking it, he muttered, 'Don't tell me you never told Sarah about it?'

'No, I never told her. There was no need. It's years ago you got it. I've never thought about it.'

'That's him.' Dan was looking at Sarah now, smiling. 'Yes, I won six hundred in *John Bull*. . . . Fashions, you know.'

'Really?' Sarah smiled. 'Fashions?'

'Yes, I was a dab hand at fashions. I knew absolutely nothing about them, so I came up. . . . Well, there it is.' He looked at the men again. 'The old boy's offered me a partnership if I'll put me money in the shop. But he warned me, mind, that it might be like throwing it down the sink. If things don't turn in another year, well, we'll be like the others, we'll be shut up. But the other side of it is that if I don't go in with him we'll be shut up in any case and soon, and I'll be out of a job. And if I don't get another I'll have to live on the four hundred, won't I? They won't give me dole with that gold mine in the bank, not likely. So it's really as broad as it's long. What do you say?' He looked from one to the other.

'You could start up on your own on four hundred,' said John.

'Oh no you couldn't except in a huxter's shop; not a place like Campbell's. It's a well-established shop and it's got a licence too, you see. He's had that place thirty-eight years; in 1921 he could have retired, for he was sitting pretty then. And there's another thing that needs thinking about. He said that if we can keep the place going he'll leave it to me, that's if his wife goes before him. If she doesn't, then I'll have to make her an allowance, but in the end it would be mine. . . . It's not to be sneezed at, is it? What do you say, Davie?'

'I think it's worth taking a chance on, Dan, for in the long run you've got nothing to lose. Anyway, you've already made up your mind, haven't you?'

Dan's hand came out and he pushed at Davie, saying, 'Aye, I suppose I have. But I wanted to know what you think.'

'Go ahead,' said Davie. 'And all the luck in the world. You won't sink. I couldn't imagine you ever sinking.'

Shuffling the cards, John put in quietly, 'If you want an errand boy remember charity begins at home, I'm ready any time.'

Sarah, rising from her chair, looked at Dan. 'I'll make a cup of tea, and we'll drink to it,' she said, smiling.

'That's the ticket, Sarah. And look. . . .' He grabbed at her arm. 'When I have me . . . me chain of shops running from Shields Pier to the Swing Bridge in Newcastle, you know what? I'll buy you a car and a mink coat.'

'Thank you very much.' She was laughing now. 'But I'd rather have a wireless set.'

'Oh, but you're getting a wireless set; John's making you a . . .'

'Your big mouth!' John slapped out at Dan, and Dan said, 'Aw, I'm sorry.' He turned to Sarah. 'It was to be a surprise.'

Sarah looked at John. He was dealing out the cards now. She did not say 'Thank you' immediately, but, turning to David, she asked, 'Did you know about this?'

He nodded at her and she said, 'And you let me go on talking about wirelesses. . . . Oh.' She ruffled his hair, then, glancing towards John's still bent head, she said, 'I didn't know you could do wirelesses. Thanks, John.'

'That fellow can do anything,' said Dan, laughing. 'Anything he puts his hand to. He is a blooming genius.'

Sarah's words had sounded grateful, but as she went into the scullery the thought in her mind was, Why had he to be the one to give her things? He had made nearly all their furniture, except for the bed, the couch, and the armchair. And what would May say about this? Very likely nothing, but she would think and look all the more.

As she put the kettle on she found herself feeling sorry for anyone who had to live with May, and she dared now to say to herself, I'm sorry for him. Every day for the past six years she had suffered because of John. There were times when she hated him and her feelings would come out in her attitude towards him. And most of the time she was on her guard in case she would say something to him that would bring comment from David. Yet besides all her submerged feelings concerning him, she was sorry for this big, bustling, bumptious, and frustrated individual. And he was frustrated in so many ways. Unemployment to him was a disease that was eating into the very core of his being, and it wasn't lightened by the fact that his father, his uncle, and his brother were all in jobs. He was the one that could least suffer unemployment. There were times when, seeing him in the depths of depression, she had wanted to put her hand out and touch him, to give him comfort, but the fear that accompanied this desire almost paralysed her body, and she was thankful that it did. There had been one particular occasion during the past few years when she had been grateful, yes grateful that she was being blackmailed because of him; for if anything could prevent her softening towards him it was this weekly trial on her nerves. The situation had arisen when one day John had returned hungry and tired from a fruitless workers' march, to be greeted by May and her barbed tongue. He had come over into the kitchen here–she had been alone in the house and he rarely came in when she was alone now–and with the sadness of an aged man, he had asked, 'Can I rest awhile here, Sarah? I'm dog-beat and May's playing hell.' She had made him a meal, and then he had fallen asleep in David's chair, and it was as he slept that there came on her an almost uncontrollable desire for her hands to touch him. And she had flown upstairs and stayed there until David came in. . . .

As she made the tea she thought, Him always making things for me, David must be blind. Then she attacked the suggestion with, Well, you don't want his eyes opened, do you? Oh, my God! No, no, never that. Rather the nauseating sight of her father, the parting weekly with the precious five shillings, and her visits to the doctor for her nerve tonic. But how much longer could it go on? She could see her nerves as worn wires, and the strength of a wire at its weakest part. What was her weakest part? There was no answer to this, and she mashed the tea and took it into the kitchen to drink to Dan's success.

Chapter Two

Over the years Sarah and Phyllis had met once or twice a month. If the weather was fine they took a ride on the ferry across the river. At other times they would walk down towards the sea. They had never reached the sands, for the time they spent together as the years went on grew shorter. Phyllis had now three children to see to, and Sarah always wanted to get back home to be in when David returned from work. Neither of them visited the other's home. Their homes were rarely mentioned. Sarah's decision, years earlier, had come to nothing. She had too much on her mind.

On this Saturday morning Sarah stood in the shelter of a doorway in the Market Place looking over the stalls in the direction of Waterloo Vale where Phyllis was now living. They, as a rule, never met at the week-ends–week-ends were for the family and was a busy time–but this morning was an exception and it was Sarah who had written to Phyllis making the appointment.

The market was almost deserted except for the stalls and their owners. The cutting wind was carrying on it a thick rain almost like sleet, and it was only early October.

When she saw Phyllis moving rapidly with her light step across the cobbles towards her, she went to meet her. After both exclaiming about the wretchedness of the weather, Phyllis said, 'Let's go in here and sit down.'

'Here' was a working-man's café, and when they had taken their thick cups of dark-looking tea from the counter they sat in the corner of the dismal and almost empty room. After sipping from the steaming cup, Phyllis, holding her hands over it, said, 'Do you know any more? Have you heard anything?'

'No, nothing, only what's in the papers . . . Phyllis.' She leant towards her sister. 'Do you know anything about it?'

'Me?' Phyllis pressed herself against the back of the chair, repeating, 'Me? No. No, I don't, but by God I wish I'd thought of it years ago. Is he going to live?'

'I don't know. I just saw me mother for a minute yesterday. We hadn't got the paper on Thursday night, I knew nothing about it until she came in; she had just come back from the hospital. She said he was in an awful state.'

'Hell's cure to him. He's got what he's been asking for for years. Some bloke likely caught him snooping and beat him up. I only wish the polis hadn't come across him so soon; if he'd lain out all night he might have died from exposure . . . that's what they said in the paper an' all.'

Sarah bowed her head. The feeling of guilt lifted from her for a moment; she hadn't been the only one to think along these lines. But she doubted if Phyllis had prayed for him to die. She herself had prayed every minute since yesterday morning that he wouldn't regain consciousness.

'The paper says his arm's broken and he's got injuries to his head. 'Oh'–Phyllis took another quick sip of her tea–'if anybody's got their deserts he's got his. It said in the paper a pair of binoculars were found near him that he used for bird-watching. My God, that's something . . . bird-watching. Birds all right. You wouldn't think a reporter would be so daft as to put it in. Him! A man like him bird-watching. But me mother told them that. She said she had to say something because of him going round with a spy glass. I wonder where he got the money from to get it because he hasn't got the guts to pinch. But what made you think I'd 'ad a hand in it?'

Sarah's head was lowered. She knew where he had got the money from, only too true she knew. She looked up quickly, saying now, 'Since he was found near Redhead's Docks down East Holborn way I thought . . . well, to tell you the truth, Phyllis, I thought you might know something about it.'

'No, no, I tell you I don't; but mind, if I'd known he was in the habit of coming down that way, take it from me I'd have done something about it. There's one or two blokes down there who'd beat up their mother for a pint. But he chose the wrong place to use his spy glass when he chose Holborn. It's as Ali says, he was likely watching a couple. But somebody was watching him, and they lathered him. And good luck I say, good luck to whoever it was.'

Yes, good luck to whoever it was. She endorsed that, oh, she did. She only wished they had done the job properly. Eeh! If only she could stop thinking like that. . . . She finished her tea, then asked, 'How's the children?'

'Oh, I've got Jimmy in bed again, he never seems well. I've had the doctor. He just says, well, nothing's wrong with him really; give him plenty of fresh air and feed him well, he says. I can do that all right. He gets his grub, he's luckier than some. I thank God for the café every day of me life. Getting things at cost, it means a lot.'

'How is it going now?'

'Oh, just scraping along. In fact hardly that, nobody's got anything.'

'It's worse up in Jarrow.'

'Yes, I know. I went up there the other day. It's dead. I was glad to get back. While I was waiting for a tram there was a fellow talking to a group of them; they all looked as if the smell of a pot of stew would knock them over. But the way this fellow was talking! Like a lawyer. And something he said stuck with me. It isn't very often I listen to the blah-blah-blahing. But it was true what he said. He said Jarrow had been raped and it had given birth to twins, hated twins, hunger and idleness. That's what he said.'

'He's right too, in a way, at least. Only I don't know so much about the idleness. All the men up there are trying to do something. John is for ever helping to organise things. It's funny.' She smiled. 'He said the other day that a lot of the fellows have received an education through being on the dole, and when your stomach isn't full he says you can always think better.'

'I saw him in the market last Saturday afternoon. He was with a woman; she was youngish, but she looked a snipe. Would it be his wife?'

'Yes, that sounds like May.' Sarah nodded. 'Small, thin. And she's a snipe all right, you never know how you have her.'

Sarah now gathered her bag and gloves towards her, saying, 'I'll have to be moving, I've left Paul looking after Kathleen and they'll have the place turned upside-down.'

It wasn't until they were on the pavement that Phyllis turned towards Sarah, saying, 'Are you still wanting a piano for David?'

'Yes. You know I do. But I can't manage the money now.'

'This one's only four pounds. Ali says it's a bargain. You know, he said he'd keep a look-out for you. He takes adverts for the café window, it always helps, and he got this one for the piano. He even went and had a look at it. It's just off Fowler Street and the people are in straits. Ali says it's being given away.'

'But four pounds! I haven't got it, Phyllis. I've got about thirty shillings put by and that's the lot.'

'I could lend it to you. Oh, I'm not on me beam ends, don't you worry. I keep slipping a shilling or two into the old tin. Look, Sarah, you can have it and welcome.'

Sarah looked through the slanting rain over the market place towards St Hilda's Church and she thought that the morning had lightened, her future had lightened. She saw through the rain a space ahead without the dread of the tap on the back door on a Monday morning. Perhaps weeks, months of respite, perhaps a lifetime of release. . . . If he should die. Oh, dear God, let him die. . . . There she was again. It was dreadful to keep going on like this, wishing somebody dead. But he deserved to die; he was wicked, horrible. She felt at times she could embrace a reptile easier than she could look at him. . . . And then there was Phyllis offering to lend her money for the piano. Yes, the morning was lighter.

'Look, will I tell Ali to put five shillings on it, then you could go and have a look at it yourself, eh?'

'Yes, yes, Phyllis.' Sarah was nodding enthusiastically down on Phyllis. 'Yes, I'll come down on Monday, eh? What's the address?'

'Oh, I can't remember it off-hand. It'll be in the shop.' They looked at each other in silence for a moment, then Phyllis asked softly, 'Won't you come round to the house, Sarah? You've never been.'

'You've never asked me.' They smiled shyly at each other.

'It's Seven, Waller Place.'

'Seven, Waller Place. All right, I'll come, Phyllis; I'll come in the afternoon after I've dropped Kathleen into school. About two, eh?'

'About two. But mind, don't expect too much. Although'–Phyllis's chin went up–'I'm not ashamed of our place, I've got no reason to be. It's a damned sight better furnished than some of them at the other side of the town, I can tell you that.'

'I'd love to see it, Phyllis.'

'Well, Monday. So long, Sarah.'

'So long, Phyllis.'

They touched hands quickly, shyly, then went their separate ways, hurrying as if to get rid of their embarrassment.

It was as the tram came to a stop at the top of Stanhope Road that the thought sprang into Sarah's mind: 'I'll pay a visit.' And just as the bell rang for the tram to move on again she jumped off and crossed the road and went down the gentle slope towards the church.

The church was empty and quiet. She blessed herself with holy water from the font, then went down the side aisle, past the pictures of the Stations of the Cross to the front pew before the altar of the Virgin Mary; and as always when she came to this church she felt in a strange way as if she had come home. But she hadn't been in the church for years, and over the past four years she had rarely seen the priest. Father O'Malley had apparently given her up as a bad job, but since Kathleen had started at St Peter and St Paul's school Father Bailey had been to see her twice. He was nice was Father Bailey, and he thought the world of Kathleen.

She began to pray. The Our Father, the Hail Mary. Then she repeated parrot-wise, 'Come Holy Ghost, fill the hearts of thy faithful and kindle in them the fire of thy love. Send forth thy spirit and they shall be created and they shall renew the face of the earth.' All the set prayers of her childhood. And then she was talking to God, talking rapidly, beseechingly, asking Him of His mercy to take her father, to make him die. She bent her back until her buttocks were resting against the seat, and her head bowed on the back of the seat in front of her; her forearms at each side of her head brought her hands clasped above her hat, and she talked to God as if He was before her, as if she was clutching His garments. Take him, O Lord, take him, because I'm frightened. I nearly hit him last week. Take him, O Lord. I can't bear the sight of him, he's evil, I'm afraid of what I might do. I've thought of doing just what this man's done to him. O Lord. I've thought of following him on a dark night, O God forgive me. Take him, Lord; please take him. And for no reason she could think of she found herself now repeating the seven capital or deadly sins. Pride, covetousness, lust, envy, gluttony, anger, and sloth.

'Sarah.'

She sprang back on to the seat, crouching against the pillar to the side of her, staring up at the hand that had touched her shoulder and the face above it.

'Are you all right, Sarah?'

'Y-e-s, Father. Oh, Father, you gave me a fright.'

'I'm sorry, Sarah.' The priest slowly sat down on the edge of the pew a few feet from her and he asked quietly, 'Are you in trouble, Sarah?'

She swallowed and moved her head as if in denial; yet its very action was an affirmative answer, and Father Bailey said, 'What is it? Can I help you? Dry your eyes.'

She fumbled in her bag for her handkerchief and dried her eyes and blew her nose, and then dried the fresh tears that were flowing down her cheeks.

'Is it your husband?'

'Oh no. No!' The denial was emphatic. 'He's wonderful to me, Father. Believe me, no one on earth could be better. No. No.'

'It isn't the child, is it? There can't be anything wrong with Kathleen, I saw her yesterday.'

'No, Father, Kathleen's all right.'

'Wouldn't you like to tell me, Sarah?'

'Oh, Father.' Her whole body slumped against the pillar. Could she tell him. Not a living soul had she uttered a word of the cause of her mental anguish over the past years. Everybody thought she had nerves, and indeed she had nerves now. But oh, the relief to be able to tell someone, to know that someone would understand, and this priest, this good priest, would understand. She wondered why she hadn't thought about it before. But then she remembered she had thought about telling it in confession and dismissed it. She lifted her eyes wearily to his now and asked quietly, 'Could you hear me in confession, Father?'

'Certainly, Sarah.' He held out his hand and raised her to her feet as if she was a sick person, and to him she was a sick person. Then he turned from her and moved out of the pew and up the church towards the confessional box, and he went into one door, and she into the other.

When she was kneeling on the kneeler, her face to the wire mesh, she whispered, 'Will I start as if in confession, Father?'

'Yes, Sarah.' And so she began formally, 'Please, Father, give me your blessing for I have sinned'–this opening had always struck her as comical, for it seemed you were asking the priest to bless you because you had sinned–but not today. She went on, 'It is nearly six years since my last confession. I have only missed Mass a few times but I have never been to Communion or my Easter duties.' She paused here, thinking of all the venal sins she had committed. Bouts of temper. Thinking unkind thoughts. Missing her morning and night prayers. All her small sins she told him, and then she paused again before saying, 'My main sin, Father, is wishing someone dead. It's about this I want to tell you.'

'Go on, Sarah, I'm listening.'

And so she told him. She told him exactly what happened on that New Year's morning, and she told him of the morning her father had visited her and his weekly visits since. Of the five shillings a week she paid him, and of the terror rising in her of late in case she would do him an injury. And lastly she told him of feeling glad, in fact joyful, when she heard he had been beaten into unconsciousness.

When she had finished, the priest made no sound and she remained still, waiting. And then he said a surprising thing, he said, 'Do you love this man, Sarah, your husband's brother?'

'No, no, Father.' Her reply was like rapid fire.

'In no way, Sarah? You haven't encouraged him to take a liberty with you?'

'No, Father, no. I was a little afraid of him because I think I knew what he was feeling.'

'And there was no answering response in you to this feeling?'

She waited before answering, and then said falteringly, 'He's a very attractive man, very virile. He's . . . he's unhappy with his wife, I know. I've felt . . . well, sorry for him at times. At times I wanted . . . I wanted to be kind to him. But no, Father, I've never encouraged him and . . . and I don't love him.' She could not say to the priest that there was some part of her that called to her husband's brother and made her ashamed that this part would rear up like a wild animal at times, and these times usually occurred with the gentle loving of David. It was then that this part of her would long for a different loving, a wild, frenzied, mad loving, a kind of loving she sensed on the New Year's morning when locked in John's embrace. No, she could not say this to the priest because she was only barely conscious of it. The thoughts in your head while your man was loving you, and the thoughts that filled it for the rest of the day and night belonged to two separate beings. But when these two beings attempted to merge, as they sometimes did in the light of day, she was overcome by a feeling she had to flay, and flay it she did. She flayed it with her happiness, the happiness given to her by David. She flayed it with the gratitude she owed to David. She flayed it with the passionate love she had for her child.

The priest was talking now. He was saying, 'You have been very silly, Sarah. You should never have given your father money in the first place.'

'I couldn't help it, Father. I knew he would have told my husband, and although David wouldn't have believed him, not really, it would have caused a difference between him and his brother, and he's very fond of his brother, they are very fond of each other. And then there was his mother. His mother doesn't like me, and I knew that if she heard about this, life would be unbearable for us all. Then there was my sister-in-law, John's wife. She's an odd type of girl. Well, what I mean is, Father, she seems quiet, but she's quarrelsome, hard. You see, I just had to keep my father quiet.'

'When he comes out of hospital–you must stop praying that he won't come out, Sarah, do you hear me?'

'Yes, Father.'

'Well, when he comes out you must tell him that you're going to give him no more money, and if he becomes nasty you must tell him you are going to the police.'

'But, Father!'

'Listen, Sarah. You must tell him that. You must frighten him off. Whether you go to the police or not is up to you, but blackmailing is a serious offence and they'll soon put him in his place. What you've got to realise is that he is undermining your health. You've lost a lot of weight, haven't you?'

'Yes, Father, two stone.'

'Well, you can't go on like that. You know what you should do, but you won't do it. But I feel that your husband should know about this. What I have seen of him he is a very reasonable man. I like him, Sarah.'

'Thank you, Father, but . . . but I couldn't tell him.'

'Well, leave it for a time until your father comes out of hospital, but in the meantime think about it seriously, think about confiding in your husband. Bring him down to me if you like and we'll talk it over.'

'I couldn't, Father. There are too many complications.'

'Well, you must do what you think best. And remember, Sarah, I'm always here if you should need me.'

'Thank you, Father. I feel better now.'

'Make a good act of contrition, Sarah.'

She came out of the confessional box and waited a moment and then the priest joined her; he walked with her to the door of the church and there, taking her hand in his, he said, 'Nothing matters if your conscience is clear. . . . Make that your aim in life, Sarah. Keep your conscience clear.'

'Yes, Father.' She inclined her head towards him. 'Goodbye, Father, and thank you, thank you very much.'

'Goodbye, Sarah.'

She walked quietly down the steps of the church, past the station, and down the Dock Bank. The Bank, as usual, was black with men, some talking in groups, some standing silently against the rails, just looking out of the hungry present into the hungry future. No longer were they on the lookout for the gangers with the hope of being set on a boat, because the gangers, too, were standing staring. Gone from the Bank was that notable measured stride of the burly, proud captains; the noticeable bearing of the arrogant chief engineers. No longer were there strings of coolies shopping on the Bank, their bass bags swelled with fish, their bare knees pointing upwards as their seemingly unbending feet left the ground. The colour, the excitement, had gone from the docks.

Sarah cast her eyes towards the Dock offices as she passed them. David was in there. She knew where he would be sitting, the exact spot, to the right of the main door where you went in, and her glance towards the grimed window next to the door was tender.

David was lucky; he was one of the envied ones, he was in work. As long as the docks were moving at all he was secure, and she was secure. But David didn't give the docks credit for his security, he gave it to Mr Batty. He had once said to her when talking about the office, 'He feel's he's tamed me . . . training me he would call it, so if there is any security in the job at all it's that, just that. He hasn't made life unbearable for me like he has for some. I feel he holds me up to himself as part of his success.'

'And you don't mind?' she had said to him.

'No.' He had smiled at her. 'Why should I? It pleases him and it doesn't hurt me.'

That was David, the gentle way every time. Oh, she thanked God for David. She felt lighter, happier. Why hadn't she gone to Father Bailey before. Oh, she wished she had.

It had stopped raining, so she decided to walk home, it would save the bus fare. She crossed over the road to the path that led under the dock arches. The arches were dark and dismal, the brickwork was as black as a singed bloater, and the water dribbled down the walls in rivulets of slimy green. But the arches left no impression on Sarah; they were part of the dismal whole, unseen, except on rare occasions, because of their familiarity.

The pavement bordered by the actual dock wall curved round by the bottom of Simonside Bank, the Bank which led into . . . the country, to the nice houses and Hedworth Hall and the Robin Hood and places like that. She hadn't been up into the country for years. As she looked up the steep incline of the bank she said to herself, 'I must start and take Kathleen for walks up there, away from the streets.' They could do it on a Sunday afternoon; she would speak to David.

She was turning her gaze away when it was pulled back again. A man had just rounded the bend. He came striding down the road, his step quick and purposeful, and as she watched him raise his hand quickly then break into a run she turned her head away and groaned inside. Oh, no, no, not this morning. Then fear came upon her. She would have to walk all the way home with him. What if her father . . . She closed her eyes. She had forgotten, he was in hospital. The relief scuttled the fear from her being and she turned and looked towards John as he came running up to her.

'Fancy seeing you. . . . Here, give me your bag.' He took the bag from her hand.

'There's nothing in it,' she said.

'No, there's not.' He shook it up and down. 'Well, where've you been then?'

'To see Phyllis.'

'Oh, oh!' He was walking by her side now, suiting his step to hers. 'How is she?'

'Oh, she's fine.'

'I've been up to see Ted Cobber. He lives up near Jarrow cemetery, but I wanted a walk so I came back the country way . . . getting in training. Him and me, we were mates for years. He's a bit cut up, he wasn't picked for the march.'

'Is he oldish?'

'No, no, same age as me about. But he didn't pass the doctor. We all had to go through an examination, you know. It's a wonder that he found two hundred fit among us when you take everything into consideration.' His voice was quiet, and Sarah nodded. 'Yes, it is a wonder,' she said.

They walked in silence for some minutes, and each second of each minute Sarah was aware of the man by her side. It was always like this when she was alone with him. She wanted to break the silence but couldn't, and was relieved when he said, 'I went up to get a loan of his ground sheet; he used to do a lot of cycling at one time and sleep out.'

'But you won't have to sleep out?'

'No. No. It's all been arranged in different town centres and places, but we'll likely have to sleep rough on the boards. But you can use a ground sheet to cover you in the rain, you know.'

He was excited about the march on Monday, the march from Jarrow to London, the march of protest against starvation, and he had talked of nothing else for weeks. She had become almost as familiar with the names of those chiefly concerned as May was. David Reilly, Councillor Paddy Scullion, and Councillor Symonds; Councillor Studdick, the Conservative agent, and Harry Stoddard, his Labour counterpart. She knew that these latter two, political men from opposing sides, had been sent ahead–and together–to prepare the reception for the marchers in places like Harrogate, Leeds, Barnsley, Bedford, Luton, and other towns.

But the name mostly on John's lips was that of Ellen Wilkinson. Sarah had never seen Ellen Wilkinson. She didn't think of her as a woman, not an ordinary, normal woman. A woman who could lead men on a march to London could not be an ordinary, normal woman. In fact any woman who was in Parliament could, of course, not be ordinary. As for being normal, well, women had their place, hadn't they, and it wasn't really their place to yell their heads off among a lot of men in Parliament. So thought Sarah.

But John was quiet now. He was not talking at high speed about the arrangements and the arrangers, those for and those against. He wasn't wanting to wipe the floor with Bishop Hemsley Henson, Bishop of Durham, or worship at the feet of Bishop Gordon of Jarrow–his homage of the latter having nothing to do with the man being a churchman.

As Sarah glanced at him she was surprised at the unusual expression of sadness on his face; she had never seen him looking sad before. Aggressive, bitter, cynical, jolly, rollicking, but never sad. He was looking ahead as he said, 'There's going to be a short service in Christ Church for the marchers afore we leave.'

'Oh, that'll be nice.' Her answer sounded inane, but it was all she could find to say. And then he asked, 'Would you come, Sarah?'

She flashed her eyes towards him. 'To church, you mean?'

'Yes.' He was still looking ahead.

'Yes . . . yes, all right, John. Yes, I'll come. May could call for me. . . .'

'May's not coming, nor is me mother. Neither of them, but for different reasons. My mother wouldn't put her foot inside a church if it meant saving her life, or anybody else's for that matter. As for May, she neither believes in God . . . or man.' He stressed the last word. 'She says it's a lot of damned hypocrisy, the men going to church before the march, for ten to one there hadn't been a man Jack of us inside a church or chapel for years . . . and I suppose she's right in a way. But you know, this isn't just an ordinary march, at least I don't see it that way. They're marching from Scotland and Cumberland, and Yorkshire and Wales, and Durham, but ours is different somehow. Runciman's said that the Government could do nothing for Jarrow, that Jarrow must work out its own salvation–well, that's what we're doing in this march. Some of us might never make it; it's a long way on two feet and mended shoes.' He looked down at his boots, and Sarah looked down at them too. They were newly cobbled. On each boot were two bulging patches of leather, but the boots were shining. As always John was tidy.

There came over her body now a softening, an enervating wave. Again, and almost unconsciously, her body and mind were forgiving him for all the trouble he had caused her. She even forgot for the moment that a short while ago she had knelt in an agony of mental suffering in the church. At this point there came into her mind what she termed a silly thought. I wish I was his mother, she said to herself. She seemed to see inside the big aggressive bulk of him to the everlasting little boy who needed someone to turn to, someone who would always listen to his prattling and who would push the black hair back from his brow as he talked. . . .

'Keep your conscience clear. Make that your aim in life, Sarah. Keep your conscience clear.' The priest's words were loud in her head and she exclaimed to herself, Oh God! But I've done nothing, said nothing. She was throwing denials back at her mind now. It was just that when she was alone with him she felt something, a sympathy; it was nothing else, just a feeling of sympathy. He made her feel like this, as if he wanted her protection. . . . Protection. John needing protection . . . huh! Don't be so daft. She threw scorn at herself. What he wanted was to bear her to the ground and crush her into it with love. Oh, she knew, she knew what John wanted. Her body told her what John wanted, and there she was talking about being a mother to him. She hadn't been honest with the priest . . . Oh, she had, she said; she hadn't thought like this when she was with the priest, it was only when she was alone with John that she thought like this. Oh God, she wished she was home. And why had she said she would go to the church on the Monday morning and neither the one or the other going. She herself had more than one reason why she shouldn't go. It was forbidden that a Catholic should partake of a service in another church; it was a sin, she knew that, yet she had said she would go. And after Father Bailey being so kind to her. Oh, she wished she was home.

They were walking in step silently, both looking ahead. Then John, picking up where he had left off a few minutes earlier, said, 'It's as if every one of us was going on a private mission. Not a man of us but wants everything to be ordered and who wants to thrust the word rabble down the necks of those that say that's what it'll be. I don't think there's been anything so well organised as this march for years. Nothing has come out of the North so well organised, I'd like to swear on that. That petition will be handed over to Parliament by men, not a rabble. And for the few that's against us we've got the majority with us. All Tyneside is behind us, and the Lord Mayor of Newcastle, Alderman Lock, is with us all the way. He's not standing aside and saying every man for himself, Jack. He says, and these are his very words, "Jarrow's troubles are our troubles", and . . . and you know, Sarah'–he turned his face fully towards her now–'what a lot forget is that it's us the day, but it'll be them the morrow if the canker isn't stopped.'

When she didn't answer he waited for a moment before saying, 'Are you all right?'

'Yes, yes. It's just the damp gets into you with all this rain.'

Again he was looking ahead, and again he was silent for a time until he said, 'Have you been to the doctor's this week?'

'Yes.'

'What did he say?'

'Oh, just that I must eat more.' She forced herself to smile at him. 'And I told him I didn't mind losing weight, it was fashionable to be thin.'

He kept his eyes on her now as he asked quietly, 'Sarah, has your worry anything to do with me?' He put out his hand quickly towards her, exclaiming with concern, 'Look . . . look, don't jib away from me like that, I'm not going to take anything up; and I can't do anything, can I?' He moved his head round to indicate the open space of the Slacks and the broad daylight. 'It's only that I get worried at times. Aye, yes, I do.' He nodded his head quickly at her. 'I get worried about you because you never seem to have been right since . . . well . . .' He flung his head round on his shoulders and muttered through his teeth. 'Since that New Year's Eve. If it's about me you are worried you can put your mind at rest, it won't happen again, I've told you. . . . There now.' He swung his head sideways once more. 'Well, is it me that's worrying you . . . I'm asking you?'

She was sweating now; she could feel it running down between her breasts and from her armpits. Never before had she wanted to pour out the truth to him. Hadn't she done enough pouring out for one morning? The distress in her was like froth in a bottle, and she knew that once it was released it would be difficult to stop the flow. One thing was sure: if she told him she would have no more trouble with her father. He would scare the daylights out of him, perhaps finish the job that the other fellow had started. She shivered on the thought. . . . But there was another thing she could be sure of too. If she were to answer his question truthfully they would be drawn together, held together by ties stronger than those they would have created through any physical means. She could not explain to herself this knowledge of John's reaction, except that in fighting her father for her he would unconsciously cloak himself with moral righteousness. Moreover, he would glory in holding some part of her that was not David's.

She made herself aggressive both in voice and manner and used it as a screen behind which to hide as she cried, 'Why must you bring that up? And what makes you imagine you have anything to do with the way I feel? You've got a nerve, you know, John.' Her eyes were blinking, her chin was thrust out at him, and her step became uneven as she quickened it with an effort to move away from him.

'All right, all right.' His voice was calming. 'I only wondered. But don't take on. When you act like that you sound like May.' His voice was still calm.

She paused in her stride. 'I'm not like May.'

'No . . . no, you're not.' He was looking at her, his eyes soft, his whole expression tender. 'I'm sorry, I shouldn't have said that. No, thank God, you're not like May.'

Again they walked in silence. They were approaching the streets now, and when she turned into Camelia Street he turned too. He did not say, 'So long, I'll be seeing you.' Nor did he say. 'You don't mind if I drop in for a moment?' He just accompanied her home.

As they approached the front door they heard high laughter, and after she had knocked on the rapper there came a scurrying through the front room and the door was pulled open. And there stood Paul and Kathleen, their faces bright with careless childhood.

Kathleen was about to cry, 'Oh, Mummy!' when she saw John, then, literally leaving the ground, she jumped from the high step into his arms, shouting, 'Uncle John! Why, Uncle John!' It was as if she hadn't seen him for days.

John walked through the front room with her legs straddled round his waist, his arms supporting her shoulders as her head dangled beyond them.

Paul, walking by Sarah's side into the kitchen, said under his breath, 'We've broken a cup and saucer, Auntie.'

'You didn't.' Kathleen was looking from her upside-down position towards Paul and she waved her arms at him now as she cried, 'You didn't, I did. I threw it at him, Mammy.'

'You what! Let her down, John.'

John, with a lift, planted the child on her feet, and Sarah, looking down at her daughter, said, 'You threw a cup and saucer at Paul? Why did you do that?'

Putting her hands behind her back. Kathleen sauntered towards the fender; then sat down on it before she answered, 'Just 'cos.'

'Never mind just 'cos.' Sarah's voice was stern. She turned to Paul. 'Why did she throw it at you, Paul?'

'He likely deserved it.' John gave his son a gentle push that landed him in David's chair, and the boy, looking at Sarah, said, 'We . . . we were just playin'. I . . . I was teasing her.'

'You weren't, you were telling lies. You were . . . you were.' The little chin was thrust out at Paul. 'He said, Mammy . . .' She looked at Sarah now. 'He said you loved him better than me. So there. That's why I threw the cup and saucer at him. It hit the fender.' She looked down and pointed with her finger towards the brass rail that rimmed the steel fender, and she continued to look at it as she ended, 'And you don't do you?'

'I was only teasing, Auntie.' The boy spoke with his head down, and Sarah turned her eyes away from him, away from her daughter, and away from John. She could not please her daughter by saying, 'Of course I don't,' because that would hurt the boy, and the boy was John's. What she did say was, 'You'll get a skelped behind, me lady, one of these days.'

Then she fell back on the old stand-by that helped her through trying moments and over little obstacles, and big obstacles too. She said, 'I'll make a cup of tea . . . we're froze.'

On the Monday morning Sarah stood outside the Jarrow Town Hall and watched the mayor review the men. Two hundred shabbily dressed, freshly shaved, tidy, thin men. She followed them as they marched to Christ Church, and as they entered a man stopped a boy in front of her from going in by saying, 'It's only the wives and mothers, lad.' For a moment she hesitated, but the man accepted her and she passed into the church and sat in the back row. The Mayor and Corporation were seated at the front, and Bishop Gordon took the service.

Sarah had never been in any but a Catholic church in her life, but she did not find this service strange, as she did not follow it. Her mind was elsewhere, for she was overcome by a feeling of deep sadness. Yet at the same time she was experiencing a sense of exhilaration, and she was wishing that she too could march with them. Oh, she wished she could. Oh, she told herself, she did.

The service over, they filed outside, and John came to her side. He had a groundsheet in a roll slung across his shoulders. He looked big and gaunt, yet he too looked elated.

'Well, this is it.' It sounded like the goodbye of a man going to war. She looked at him, but she could not speak. Sadness had excluded all other feelings. A couple to the right of them were enfolded in each other's arms; all about them people were embracing, wives, mother's, children, all clinging to men as if they were about to march to their deaths.

She should say something, but she could not translate her thoughts into words; her mind was a jumble and full of pain, as was her body. It was a strange pain, unlike anything she had experienced before. As the tears welled into her eyes, John's face moved before her like a reflection beneath rippling water. She heard him saying, softly, 'Sarah, Sarah. Oh, Sarah.' He had hold of her hand now. 'Thanks for coming. You can't believe what it means. Goodbye, Sarah.'

She could not even say his name or bid him goodbye, but her mind, still in a turmoil, was creating a force which was driving something through her body, something that was beyond the voice of conscience, that could not be held in bounds by discretion, discretion that would have enforced propriety. There was only inches between them, yet the distance seemed immense; it was as if she had to leap to reach him, but reach him she did. Her mouth rested against his hard jaw line just to the side of his lips. After a second of hesitation, when she thought he would not touch her, his arms came about her, and he held her in a vice-like grip. Then she was standing shaking and blind among the other women, and he was on the road, somewhere in the ranks.

With the pad of her thumb she swiftly wiped the tears from her cheeks, and over the head of the throng she saw him clearly. He was looking towards her. He did not raise his hand in a last salute, he just looked at her and held her gaze. She watched him turn his head away, and it looked like that of a conqueror.

A small woman to the side of her was crying. She sniffed and blew her nose loudly. 'There they go,' she said; 'the skeletons of Palmers. It'll be fruitless, the march. The shipyard's dead an' it can't never be brought to life again.'

A woman standing behind Sarah said harshly, 'Well they'll have a damned good try. It's a good job everybody doesn't think alike. When that lot gets to London they may look like skeletons, but what they lack in flesh they'll make up for in spirit. By the livin' Harry they will that.'

The little woman, now apparently aiming to make up for her despondency, looked at Sarah, and said, 'But your man'll be all right; he's big and tough looking, he'll stand it. His name's Hetherington, isn't it . . . John? I've heard me son on about him. Have you any bairns?'

Sarah's mind was working now. Like a juggler, it was tossing words here and there. Before she had time to stop herself she said, 'I've one, but he . . . he isn't my husband.'

'No!' There was surprise in the exclamation.

'He's my . . . my brother . . .'

'Oh.' The woman smiled as she put in, 'Aye, Aa should have gathered that, you're both the same build like, big, strappin'.' Her smile became wider.

Sarah turned slowly about. The marchers had disappeared; some of the crowd had moved with them; the people about her were breaking up into groups. She nodded farewell to the little woman, then she found herself confronted by the woman behind her, who was looking at her through narrowed eyes, her whole expression one of close scrutiny, and she stopped Sarah's passage with her voice, saying quietly, 'Aa did washin' for Mrs Hetherington for years, it's the first time. Aa knew she'd a daughter.'

Sarah took a great intake of breath and stammered, 'I didn't mean b-brother, I meant brother-in-law . . . but the woman'–she motioned her head towards the roadway where the little woman was now standing–'she . . . she cut me off.'

'Aw, Aa see. Yes.' The head moved with each word the woman spoke. 'How is Mrs Hetherington these days?'

'Oh, she's quite well.'

'Tell her Hannah was askin' after her.'

'I will . . . goodbye.'

'Goodbye.'

Sarah knew what the woman was thinking as plainly as if she had yelled the words at her. 'Where's his wife then? Why couldn't she come?'

She did not take a bus from the town but kept walking, walking quickly as if this would enable her to get away from the condemning voice in her head which kept reiterating, 'You're mad, you're mad, you're mad, you're mad.' She had walked almost halfway home before she rounded on it. 'But I love David, I do.'

'You proved it, didn't you, to do that in the open in front of everyone, to kiss him in the open.'

'It was nothing. I tell you, it was nothing. He looked so lonely. He is lonely. He hasn't got anybody.'

'That woman thought different; that woman knew he has a wife. . . . And she knows his mother, think of that. You're mad, I tell you, stark staring mad. Now you won't only have your father on your tracks, you'll have the gossips. You could see by the look of her she was a talker.'

Just beyond the Don Bridge she stood for a moment looking down at the slimy banks of the river, between which the narrow stream of dark water made its way to the Tyne. she felt beaten, tired, and her mind was weary, too weary to erect any façade, too weary to cover up for John, or for herself. He's like a magnet, she thought, drawing badness from me body, from some black depths of me.

Father Bailey had said: Keep your conscience clear.

Kind Father Bailey.

But Father O'Malley had said no good ever came out of a mixed marriage.

Clever Father O'Malley.

But what do you say? The question seemed to rise from the black mud lining the river bank, the mud with which she was familiar in her nightmares, the mud which sucked her closer towards its middle each time she dreamed of it. But it was a challenge she could face in the daylight. Yet the voice which answered it was still weary, 'I'll never hurt, David,' it said. 'Never.'

She turned away and walked home, and the journey seemed never ending, like the years ahead.

BOOK FOUR

Chapter One

'This is the best place for you.' David touched Sarah's hair with his fingers as he leaned over the bed. 'If anybody should knock let them knock, I've been in and told Dan that you would be upstairs, and he's going across the road'–he motioned his head in the direction of the window–'to tell our John that you're all locked up for the night. I've got my key, so you stay put. Do you hear?'

She nodded up at him and raised her mouth to his as he bent to kiss her.

When he withdrew his lips from hers he did not straighten up immediately but said, 'Of course, if there's a warning you'll go into the shelter; that's different.'

'Yes, if there's one I'll go in.' She put her hand out now and gripped his arm. 'You'll be careful?'

'I'll be careful.' He smiled down on her. 'But whatever's on, as soon as I go on duty the night becomes as dead as a doornail. I've been firewatching now for two years and never put out as much as a candle. They just don't come my way . . . scared of me that's it.' He straightened up now but did not move from the bed. Instead, he sat down slowly on its edge and, taking her hand in both of his, he looked at her for a long moment before saying, 'I wish I knew what's worrying you.' It seemed almost as if the word scared had prompted this question.

She moved her legs quickly and looked away from him as she answered, 'That's simple. Isn't everybody worried about the War dragging on like this?'

'I don't suppose you would have worried so much if they'd taken me.'

'Oh yes I would.' She was gazing up into his face now. 'I should have gone mad without you.'

'Look, Sarah.' He tapped her hand gently. 'I'm going to ask you something and I don't want you to get annoyed. It isn't the day or yesterday that it's been in my mind, it's been there for a long time, and somehow I've got an idea I'm right, because when our John's on leave you're as edgy as a foal.'

She had actually stopped breathing. She was staring at him, her eyes stretched wide.

'Now tell me, Sarah. Has he ever said anything to you . . . tried anything on?'

'No, no. . . . No.' She was shaking her head rapidly, emphasising the denial of her words.

'Now, now, don't get yourself agitated, it was just an idea I got because, you know, you've never really been nice to our John, you're not snappy by nature.' He touched her cheek lovingly. 'But you've snapped at him, time and again, I've noticed it. And then this week, when he's been on leave, he's never been out of the house. And him drinking like a fish . . . well, I thought . . . perhaps he might have . . .'

'No, David, no.'

'All right, all right. Mind you'–he pointed his finger at her–'I'm very fond of our John, but if I thought he'd ever said a wrong word to you I'd have him on his back as big as he is, and that would be the finish. As brothers go we've been close, very close, but there's some things I wouldn't stand, not from him or anyone else. I was for going for him last night, acting the goat like he did following you round. . . .'

'Don't . . . don't quarrel with him, David, please. It's just that when he's on leave he goes a bit mad. I suppose it's understandable, him being stuck away in the far point of Scotland for months at a time, it . . . it must get him down. He's lonely there, and he's lonely here I think, and May . . . well, she . . .'

'Oh, May! May's the cause of his trouble, if you ask me. She's only got one thought in her head and that's the lad. There'll be trouble in that quarter, you'll see, for, as quiet as Paul is, he's got a will of his own, that boy. And if she brings her ruling hand down too heavy on him . . . Well. Of course the trouble with Paul too is that he's too fond of you. That gets under May's skin; it's evident.' He stopped speaking for a moment and stared at her, his head slightly to the side, his face wearing its usual gentle expression. And then he said softly, 'You've never liked our John, have you, Sarah?'

Her lids flickered just the slightest before she closed her eyes and brought her chin into the deep white flesh of her neck.

'It's all right, it's all right.' His voice was urgent yet consoling. 'I understand. And I'm glad in a way because John's always been a devil with the women. Your know me, don't you? I've never talked about him, or Dan, or their affairs. Dan, as far as I know, had that one woman and that was all, at least to my knowledge, but our John . . . aw, one was never any use to him. But I must say he steadied up after he married May. Then came the hard times afore the war and he hadn't any money to toss around, but since he joined the Air Force, I understand from Dan he's gone the whole hog again and that's why I didn't like the idea of him acting the goat with you, especially as you objected to it, as I could see you did without uttering a word.'

Sarah kept her eyes closed. Up till a moment ago her whole body had been full of fear; now, to it, was added pain. For days she had feared that John, with his boisterous drink-created hilarity, might go too far, might say something that would open David's eyes to this thing that was between them, this undeveloped thing that had been stunted in its growth, but which was nevertheless still alive. Twice during this past week she had thought, if he hurts David he'll cook his own goose, he'll kill whatever is in me for him. But David must not be hurt. She would do anything to save David from hurt, mental hurt. This gentle creature, whose love had lifted her from the mire of the bottom end–this man without fire. This docile man. Docile, even at times to the point of boredom, yet who had brought her love for him almost to the peak of adoration. Nothing or nobody must hurt David, because David was gentle, kind and incapable of hurting any living thing.

Yet there was room in her for pain of a dimension equal to that of the protective fear. It was the pain of degradation and humiliation, as if her body had been assailed. The pain would have been understandable had she been John's wife, or even his woman, and heard he was carrying on with someone else. But as she was neither, why should such news, news of which she was already aware, hurt her so deeply? She couldn't really understand herself.

'Aw, don't be upset.' David was bending over her again, enfolding her in his arms. 'I don't mind how you feel about our John, believe me. In fact, to tell the truth I think I'm glad you feel that way. As long as you love me that's all I care about.'

'Oh, David, David.'

'There now, there now. Look, I've got to go. I should be there now. Old Butler's a stickler for time; that's what comes of being a sergeant in the First War. You know'–he smiled at her–'some of them enjoy it, I know they do.... There now, give us a smile, come on.'

She smiled at him; she put her arms about him and held him fiercely to her; and then they stared at each other for a moment before he pulled himself up from the bed.

'Go to sleep.'

'Goodnight, darling.'

'Goodnight, my love.'

He was at the door when she whispered, 'Look in on Kathleen, will you, and see her blackout's all right? She's a devil with that blind.'

'I will. Goodnight, love.'

Sarah was not asleep when at a quarter-past ten the siren sounded. It lifted her out of bed and to the bedroom door, and, pulling it open, she called quickly, 'Kathleen! Kathleen!' She had begun dressing before its wailing died away. She called again, 'Are you up, Kathleen?'

'Yes, Mam, I'm nearly ready.'

As Sarah hurried to the landing Kathleen came out of her bedroom, dressed in a siren suit and with an eiderdown over her arm. She was tall for fourteen and big-boned. In this way she took after Sarah, but her face held little resemblance as yet to her mother's, or yet her father's. If she resembled anyone it was her grandfather Hetherington, yet the resemblance to Stan stopped here, for her manner, unlike his, was quick, vivacious, even boisterous. She ran down the narrow stairs with the fleetness of a hare, crying up to Sarah behind her, 'I'll get the flask 'cos Uncle Dan will likely come in. Will I bring some cake?'

'Leave that alone'–Sarah's voice sounded unusually sharp–'and get yourself over. I'll see to the flask and things. Go on now.'

'We'll both do it and we'll get there quicker. I'll put the kettle on.' She was flying into the kitchen as if partaking in a game.

'You know what your father said, we haven't to play about. Come on, let's get settled in, I can come in later and get the tea.'

'It won't take a minute. . . . O-oh! Mam.'

The sound that cut off Kathleen's voice was a force that lifted her off her feet and sent her staggering against the wall.

Sarah found herself on the floor by David's chair. She was gripping handfuls of the mat. The house seemed to have stood on its end for a moment and was now settling back. As the gas flickered twice, then went out, she cried, 'Kathleen! Kathleen! Where are you? Are you all right?'

'Yes, yes.' Kathleen's voice was very small. 'It's a bomb somewhere . . . somewhere near, isn't it?'

Sarah pulled herself to her feet. There was cold air coming into the room and she said, 'Be careful, the window's broken. Where are you?' She groped forward until she found Kathleen's hand, and, pulling her towards her, she whispered, 'Let's get into the street.'

The front door was stuck, and as she tried to pull it open it was pushed from the outside and a voice out of the darkness said anxiously, 'Are you all right, Sarah?'

'Yes, Dad. Yes, we're all right. I thought the house was down . . . Where did it drop?'

'It must have been at the bottom end. We . . . we only got the blast.'

'The . . . bottom . . . end?' She repeated the words slowly, separating them. David was at the bottom end, that's where the post was. Her mother was at the bottom end too, but that didn't matter so much. David . . . David was on duty there. She gasped out now, 'Dad! Dad! David . . . he's on duty.'

'I know. Now keep calm, it'll likely not be anywhere near the houses. You go into the shelter . . . or, better still, come into ours.' His hand found her arm. 'Mary'll be glad if you'll come in, I know she will. It's hard for her to give in, she's made like that.'

'Yes, all right, I'll come, but later, Dad. Yes, yes, I'll come in later, but I must see if I can find David . . . he . . .' She stopped talking. A moment ago she hadn't been able to see Stan, and now his face, grey, thin, and pinched, was outlined before her and it was covered with a rosy glow.

'Fire. There's a fire, a big one.' She made to run from him when he caught her by both arms, crying, 'Now be sensible, Sarah; he's got his job to do. Be sensible. Get inside and I'll go and see how things are. Dan's already gone down.'

'No! No! . . . And there's me mother, it might be our street.' She pulled away from him. 'Look, Dad, take Kathleen in, I'll just go and see, I'll be back in a minute.' She grabbed Kathleen and pushed her towards her grandfather.

'But, Mam. . . .'

'Do as you're told and stay where you are.' On this she turned from them and ran round the corner. The red glow was brighter here, shot through with flashes crossing the sky. It showed up the main road and lorries and moving shapes. There was a constant rattle of anti-aircraft fire, and from the distance there came two more dull thuds, heaving pressing thuds. She was half-way to the bottom end when her running was jerked to a stop and a voice said, 'Where are you off to, missis?'

She gasped and her head wobbled back and forwards on her shoulders before she could bring out, 'Howard Street. Me Mother . . . and me husband's on duty.'

'Take it easy, missis. Take it easy; get your breath. . . .' He paused a moment before saying, 'I'm afraid the bottom end's had it; they must have been trying for the factory beyond. Four of the streets are like matchwood, at least as far as I can gather. Best keep away, you'd never get through, any way.'

'But me . . . me . . . hus . . . husband. Hetherington's the name.'

'Oh, Hetherington . . . David. Oh, aye, I know David, missis. Well, look, let me take you back home now, come on.' His voice was gentle and he turned her about, but she jerked away from his hold.

'I've got to see if he's all right; the post is up that way.'

'Look, lass, you couldn't do anything; the place is a shambles, fire and all that, you can see for yourself.' He pointed upwards.

'I've got to go. I must find out. Leave go, please.'

He was gripping her by the shoulders, his voice harsh now. 'They've got their work cut out as it is, getting people out, them that's left. You'll know sooner or later. I only know the post has gone. But that doesn't say your husband's not all right, he could have been any place.'

Perhaps it was because he didn't expect any further resistance that he found himself stumbling back against the wall. Sarah was running like the wind now, gabbling over and over again in her mind, 'David! David! Oh, don't be dead, David!'

She was stopped before she reached Dudley Street or where Dudley Street had once been. There were a group of men frantically pulling hoses from a fire engine, and she fell headlong over a length of hose and on to her face. They picked her up, and one said, 'Steady, missis, steady on. You're going the wrong way; you must get out of this.' Another asked, 'Are you from here?'

She was standing on her feet supported between them; she was shaken with the fall and it rocked her words into a drunken mutter and she stuttered, 'Da . . . vid. I want Da . . . vid . . . my husband. Fi . . . fire-watching. He . . . he was f . . . fire-watching at the post.'

One of the men said something gently to her, but it was lost in the noise of the guns pop-popping overhead.

The older man shouted to someone and a woman came running. 'What is it?' she asked.

'Take her to headquarters.' He lifted Sarah's hand like that of a child towards her and the woman, who scarcely came up to Sarah's shoulder, put her arm around her waist and led her away. And she allowed herself to be led away from the burning tortured jumble of bricks, wood, and bodies. But when they reached the main road she said quietly to the woman, 'I'm going home, I live in Camelia Street.'

The woman still had her arm around Sarah's waist when they reached the front door.

Chapter Two

It was three o'clock the next afternoon when they brought David home. John and Dan carried him in and laid him on the bed, and he still looked alive. He was unmarked except for the brick dust that covered him. They had found him in a pocket of beams. He had not died by being crushed, or by a blow, or yet by fire, he had died from shock. The heart that had stopped him passing for the Army had given up.

Sarah, alone in the room with him, knelt by the bedside. Gently she lifted up his hand, his long thin hand. It felt cool, not cold or clammy. He's not dead, she thought. He could be in a coma; they should do something. If he was dead she would be crying, wouldn't she, and she couldn't cry. She could only keep moaning, Oh, David, David.

Not until she laid her face against his did it get through to her that he was really dead, and with this knowledge was born a strange weird feeling. It worked itself up from the core of her being. She felt its approach even through the subconscious layers of her mind, and when it burst the surface she screwed her eyes tightly shut for a moment against the black light of the startling truth it presented to her. . . . She was relieved, she was glad that David was dead.

Oh, NO! NO! NO!

But yes, she was. Her mind, rocking from the impact of this knowledge, steadied itself and spoke to her with frightening calm reasoning. He'll never be unhappy through you now, it said. It couldn't have gone on; look at last night. There was a rift opening between him and John and because of you. He knew how John felt about you; he never said anything, but he knew. What he didn't know was how you felt. He died thinking you perfect; be glad of that.

Yes, she was glad of that. He had gone on loving her wholeheartedly to his last breath, and that was what she had prayed for, wasn't it? But it couldn't have gone on much longer, not if John had remained in England, and had kept getting leaves. She thought at times lately that she must tell David, she just must tell him why her father came so often when he got no welcome, when she even showed her hate of him. David had known that she gave him money, but he took it for granted that it was to help her mother, and she had not disabused him of this idea.

But now it was all over, the fear and the worry . . . and the love. She would never be loved again as David had loved her, never. Nor would she ever love again as she had loved David. . . . She would never love again, except Kathleen. But that was a different kind of love. In a way she was free. Her mother was dead, her husband was dead . . . and her father was dead.

There came a gentle tapping on the bedroom door. She made no movement or sound, but she knew it was May who had entered the room.

'It's Mam, she's coming up.'

When Mary Hetherington entered the bedroom her eyes went straight to the figure lying on the bed and she moved slowly towards it; she did not look at Sarah or say any word to her.

On the older woman's approach Sarah had moved back from the bed, and now she stood looking towards her mother-in-law. She hadn't looked at her for years, not in the face. Mary Hetherington did not seem much older than on the day they had faced each other across the table in the living-room; the only difference about her was that her face looked sharper and harder. But this woman was David's mother, she would be sorrowing too. She was his mother and had loved him the best–more, oh, much more, than she had loved John, or even her husband, for that matter. She must remember that; she must remember that she was suffering at this moment.

When Mary Hetherington turned from the bed without having touched the figure that lay there, Sarah, making a valiant effort through compassion towards reconciliation, whispered brokenly, 'Will you help me to see to him?'

Mary Hetherington paused and she brought her eyes from space to look at her daughter-in-law, and she kept them on her for a full minute while Sarah waited for her to speak. Then she turned her gaze away and with it her body. She did it with a measured timing that was an insult in itself, and with this timing in her step she went out of the room.

Sarah's lower jaw was trembling. When she tried to control it by clenching her teeth their chattering became loud in her head. It wasn't possible that anyone could keep up hate like that, and particularly at a time like this, but she had, David's mother had. Her face had been full of it. She had looked the picture of fury, as a female god might have looked, a jealous god. . . .

'I'll give you a hand, Sarah.' May's voice was gentle, and Sarah, her throat swelled to bursting, murmured, 'Thank you, but if you don't mind, I'd . . . I'd rather see to him myself.'

'Very well.' May inclined her head, then went out, closing the bedroom door quietly after her, and Sarah set about the task of doing the last service she would ever do for David.

Two hours later Sarah sat in the kitchen; she felt drained and empty, yet filled with grief and still that strange, unwelcome sense of relief. Kathleen was standing on one side of her and Paul on the other. Kathleen was crying and Paul was not far from it. Sarah had hold of Kathleen's hand, and when Paul muttered, 'Oh, Auntie Sarah', she took his also.

The boy bent his willowy length towards her. He looked older than sixteen, he could have been eighteen, even nineteen, and he spoke like a man now as he said under his breath, 'Don't worry, Aunt Sarah, don't worry about anything. I'll see to you, I'll always see to you and Kathleen.' He flicked his eyes to the tear-drenched face of the girl who had always been his playmate. 'You'll neither of you want for anything, I'll see to that, I will.'

Sarah looked at the boy. He was a nice lad, a fine lad. Yes, she could imagine him meaning what he said, at least about Kathleen, because he was more than fond of Kathleen. He had never attempted to hide his feelings in that direction. But youth changed, all that was in the future. She could think of the future at this moment, at least for them, but there was no future for herself; she could see only a wilderness, a vast wilderness, in which she would walk until one day she met up with David again. It was funny how the habit of religion caught up with you when you were amidst death. She realised that the latter thought in her head could have been David speaking. He had said wise things had David.

Oh, David, David. How was she going to bear being alone, for from now on she would be entirely alone. Oh yes, there were the others. John. She shuddered on the name. If only it had been he who had died. And then there was Dan. There would always be Dan. Dan was good and thoughtful and kind. He was like David was Dan, only different, more carefree, more careless, at least about things in general, but so good, oh, so good. Yes, there would always be Dan. And in the background, her father-in-law. But close, close to her there was Kathleen and Paul. Yes, Paul was close to her, closer to her than he was to his own mother. But why was her mind thinking like this, for it didn't matter who she had when she hadn't David.

She heard May's voice now coming from the room. It was low and murmuring. She was talking to Dan and John about something, likely the preparation for the funeral.

There came a knock on the back door and Paul said, 'I'll see who it is.' He hurried away through the scullery and she heard the murmur of voices. Then filling the doorway and pushing into the room were three figures. Two of the men she had not seen before, but the man they were supporting between them was her father, and the sight of him changed her world yet again. As she looked at the dirty, bedraggled, undersized man her body became charged with a force that brought her to her feet and sent the chair spinning backwards across the room. She felt her body and her head swelling into gigantic proportions; she had the idea that her expanding flesh would push the walls apart.

One of the men, looking at her across the kitchen, said, 'They thought he was in the rubble but he just got the blast. He's been wandering about. He says you're his daughter, so we brought . . .'

'GET HIM OUT!'

'But, missis.'

'GET HIM OUT!'

'But he's got no place to go. . . .'

'What is it?' She heard Dan's voice behind her, then she heard John's voice saying, 'My God!' She saw him move forward to her father. 'Well, you were lucky,' he said quietly.

Sarah glared at them, the big figure of John, the small wizened figure of her father. Because of these two men she was thankful, unnaturally thankful that her man was dead. Her body was swelling, swelling; her lungs were pushing her ribs out, there was pain all over her. She screamed again, 'Get him out, I tell you!'

All the faces were turned towards her, and when no one moved, her hand, darted with the swiftness of a panther's paw, grabbed the teapot from the table, and, lifting it high, went to hurl it at the man who had seemingly come back from the dead.

In a flash, almost as swift as that which had enabled her to grab up the teapot, John reached her. With his body pressed against hers, his arms stretched wide, muscle to muscle, they stood outlined like a crooked cross for a second; then, as the teapot crashed to the floor, she heaved the gigantic structure that her body seemed to have become, and, like a wrestler throwing off an opponent, she hurled him from her. This was the second time she had been prevented from hitting her father with a teapot.

She could see the room once more. The two strangers had gone, her father with them. Dan, too, had gone. She could hear his voice from the yard exclaiming angrily, 'You'll just have to find some place but not here. Can't you see?'

There were only May and John left in the kitchen, and Kathleen. Kathleen was crouched in the far corner of the room, fear written all over her. It was the sight of her daughter's fear that seemed to pierce the swelling in her body. She felt herself running down like a deflated balloon as it were, and when she was her normal size again she looked from one to the other, from Kathleen to May, and then to John, and for the first time in her life she hated him, hated him at this moment almost as much as his mother hated her. Groping her way to David's chair, she dropped on to it and, turning her face into the corner, she began to cry, tearing, agonised crying that knew no end.

BOOK FIVE

Chapter One

They left the tennis hut, their shoes and rackets swinging from their hands. They walked down by the wall of the workhouse, down Talbot Road and into Stanhope Road, and they never stopped talking, first one and then the other.

Paul at nineteen was half a head taller than Kathleen. His hair was dark and his eyes brown and his overall expression intense, yet attractive. His body had remained thin; unlike his father, he had no bulk.

Kathleen, on the other hand, had bulk; her body was just a younger edition of her mother's. She was not quite as pretty perhaps as Sarah had been at her age, but happier looking, freer.

Kathleen turned her bright gaze up to Paul now as she said, 'Don't you feel furious about having to do your National Service first? Why don't you go and tell them that you'll do it after you finish at Oxford? Some people do. Renee Patten said her cousin did it.'

'Don't talk dizzy. Renee Patten!' Paul gave an exaggerated sigh, and, turning a solemn countenance towards her, raised his free hand, and in a voice of a bishop intoning a blessing, began, 'My dear child, I do not intend to try to penetrate your dim wits again. After attempting, and having failed on several occasions, to get the facts through your thick skull that my future hangs on a small matter of a small amount of money, small being a comparative word, I am dismayed . . . indeed I am dismayed, dear child. . . .'

As she hit out at him with her racket he skipped aside into the road; then they came together again and went on down the street laughing.

'I know you've got to have money,' Kathleen began once more, stressing each word with deliberation. 'But I meant that if you were to put it to them they would give you the money to go up first and then you could do your National Service after.'

Again Paul sighed, another deep exaggerated sigh, and staring ahead, he said, as if reading from a letter now, 'My dear His Majesty's Forces. You know that I intend to serve you with all my brain and brawn for two years, and in return–I hope – you are going to feed me and fend for me during my stay in a certain celestial city. But would it be too much to ask if you would reverse the process and put off my sojourn with you until I have my fling in the said celestial city, while probing, of course, during the said fling, deeper into English Literature, so that after three years, when I gladly join you, a cross between a neologist and a paleographer–trusting by that time to have achieved this distinction–you will understand how much more valuable I will be to my brothers in the barracks should they ever be lost for words. . . .'

Again Kathleen's racket swung out. 'You think you're clever, don't you? You're swanking all the time. Neologist! Paleographer! I hope when you get to the British Museum they'll stuff you.'

Paul threw his head back and laughed, and in this action he took on a semblance of John.

'Yes, you can laugh, but listen; it's funny, isn't it, about you going in for words all because of Dad.' Her face had a thoughtful look now.

'Yes, it is funny when you come to think about it. And funny isn't the correct word but we'll skip it on this occasion.' He glanced teasingly towards her. But his flippancy didn't bring her to attack him with her tongue or racket, and, picking up her mood, he went on, 'No, I don't suppose I'd ever have thought about words if it hadn't been for Uncle. I remember the first time he told me all words were straight lines. I didn't believe him. Even when he showed me, I didn't believe him, I wanted to argue with him. I suppose it was this feeling that years later made me get that book on Chinese writing. I remember thrusting it under his nose with a triumphant feeling and saying, 'Straighten those out, Uncle David.' He did laugh.'

'It's three years ago,' said Kathleen softly, 'and I still miss him. He was lovely was me Dad.'

They were walking down the bank now towards the church, quiet for the first time since they had left the tennis court, and when they came to the foot of the steps Kathleen stopped and said, 'I'm going to pay a visit.'

'O.K.' He turned with her and walked up the steps.

At the church door Kathleen stopped again and, looking at him, said, 'Do you think you'd better. Me Aunt May will go for you.'

'She's not to know.'

'Well, it's odd but she has ways of finding out. You remember what she said a while ago: she said she could smell the incense off you.'

'That was sheer imagination. Anyway, I've always come in with you and I'm not going to stop now. Come on.' He pushed her forward into the dim porch.

The church was cool after the reflected heat of the pavements. Kathleen led the way down the side aisle to the front pew opposite the Lady altar. This was the pew her mother had always sat in when she came to church as a young girl. She prayed daily that she would one day return to it. She genuflected deeply before she entered the pew, then knelt down and, bowing her head, covered her face unself-consciously with both hands.

Paul had not genuflected; nor did he kneel down, he just sat back on the seat and looked quietly about him. He had told himself a number of times that he didn't quite know what the attraction was about this place. It certainly wasn't the beautiful structure of the church, not yet its interior decoration, for the stencils, to his mind, were horrible. Kathleen said the lads from the club usually did most of the decoration and everybody thought it was lovely; well, it certainly was a matter of opinion. Nor was he attracted by the statues, for they appeared crude to him, glaringly crude except perhaps the face of the Virgin, whose expression, he had the idea, seemed to change from time to time. No, he couldn't quite lay his finger on what drew him to this church. Was it because Kathleen loved it? Perhaps. He glanced towards her, her face still buried in her hands, and a feeling of exquisite tenderness flowed through him. She was lovely was Kathleen; everything about her was lovely, her face, her figure, her simplicity. She tried to be clever–he smiled inwardly–oh, she tried hard, but he hoped she would never be clever because it was that inbred simplicity and her uncluttered way of looking at things that he loved. She was like her mother in that way. His Aunt Sarah had the same qualities, an uncluttered way of thinking. But his Aunt Sarah never tried to be clever. She was one of those women who didn't need to be. He remembered his father saying that. He loved his Aunt Sarah, that's why he loved Kathleen, he supposed, because they were one. He would soon have to speak to his mother about Kathleen, and it wasn't going to be easy. She didn't like Kathleen, nor his Aunt Sarah. Why, he didn't really know. But then she liked so few people, so he supposed it wasn't so strange. But his father would welcome the idea of Kathleen as a daughter, for he thought the world of her. His mother had taunted him once by saying that his father thought more of Kathleen than he did of him, but it didn't matter; he was glad his father loved Kathleen. . . . Yet he was getting away from the question uppermost in his mind, his attraction towards this church. Mr Rogers, his Sixth Form master, had had a pet theory. 'If you cannot control your thinking before you are twenty, then you'll never control it or anything else.'

He looked towards the High Altar. He liked the High Altar. Perhaps this was the main attraction, the High Altar, where, Kathleen had told him a long, long time ago, the priest brought Christ alive every day. He had laughed his head off about that at the time and teased the life out of her, and yet now, when he knew so much more, when for years he had been delving back into the strange history of language, where myths and magic were realities, he laughed no longer. But still he couldn't understand why, with his extended knowledge, the idea of a daily resurrection had become more credible to him. 'As the hart pants after the foundations of water so does my soul pant after thee.' He had read these words in Kathleen's Prayer Book, and as they came to his mind now he felt strangely disturbed, as if he was being hurt by beauty.

Kathleen raised her head, blessed herself, then turned her face towards him and smiled. He rose to his feet and went out of the pew, and she followed him. He paused for a moment as she dipped her fingers into the holy water in the little font, then, watching her bless herself and genuflect again towards the main altar, he pushed open the door and let her pass out.

'Oh, wasn't it cool in there!' She drew in a deep breath, took a flying leap down the first flight of stairs, laughing over her shoulder at him as she cried, 'Oh, I always feel wonderful after I've been into church.'

He took the steps two at a time and caught up with her as she stepped on to the pavement, and they both bumped into Father Bailey.

'There you go, dunching into everybody.' The priest was steadying her, laughing down into her face.

'Oh, I'm sorry . . . I'm sorry, Father.'

'And so you should be, knocking poor old men over, going round wrecking joints.' He now stooped and stroked his knee.

'Wrecking joints?' They repeated the priest's slanging quip on high laughter.

'It's nothing to laugh about.' He wagged his finger at them. 'It's another joint I'm referring to . . . the tennis hut. Who broke the seat, eh? Who broke the back off the garden seat?'

'Oh, Father,' Kathleen put her hand across her mouth, and glanced at Paul 'We were having a bit fun, a bit carry on.'

'A bit carry on!' He nodded at her with mock sternness. 'As far as I can gather there were ten of you having a bit carry on, and I want two shillings from each of you, understood?' He looked from one to the other, and Paul, nodding his head once, replied, 'Understood.' He did not say Father.

As he looked at the young boy the priest's expression changed, the smile which lifted his cheeks up into pouches under his eyes had a seriousness to it. 'I'm to congratulate you, Paul, I understand. Oxford? Now isn't that wonderful . . . a scholarship to Oxford! When do you go up?'

'Oh, not for some time, sir.' The sir came out naturally. 'I've got to do my National Service first.'

'When did you have your interview . . . I mean for Oxford?'

'Oh, before last Christmas.'

The priest nodded. 'You must have done well, you must have impressed them, indeed you must, to have got a scholarship.'

'Oh no, sir.' Paul's eyes narrowed and his mouth took on a humorous twist, and with a facetiousness of youth he went on, 'I was just dead lucky. The English tutor who took the interview happened to be a dialectologist, and, hearing my Geordie twang, he said, 'By, lad, y' just watt Aa'm lukin' for. Aa can de aall the dialects but Aa get stumped wi' the Geordie. By, yo're a God-send, lad!''

They were all laughing again, the priest heartily, and when Father Bailey laughed heartily the tears ran out of his eyes. 'Go on with you. Go on.' He pushed at Paul, then as he dried his eyes he exclaimed, 'Oh, I wonder if you're any good at languages . . . translating? Do you know any Spanish?'

'Spanish? No.' Paul shook his head. 'I'm sorry.'

Father Bailey drew a piece of paper from his inside pocket and, after looking at it, he handed it to Paul, saying, 'Well, take a look at that and see if you can make anything of it.'

Paul took the paper on which was written the following:

Si Senor, Derdago, Forte Lorez Inaro.
Demainte Lorez Demis Trux,
Foolacoos Andens Andux.

Slowly he read aloud, 'Si Senor, Derdago.' Then looking at the priest he said, 'No, sir, I can't make head or tail of it . . . sorry.'

The priest shook his head solemnly. 'Well, if you can't read that it's a poor lookout for you up at Oxford,' and taking the paper from Paul he pointed his finger to each word, translating, as he went, by splitting up the words. And what he read was:

Si Senor, der dey go, forty lorries in a row.
Dem ain't lorries, dem is trucks,
Full of coos and hens and ducks.

Paul and Kathleen looked at each other, then at the priest, then together they let out a howl of laughter, and again the tears ran from the priest's eyes. 'I had you that time . . . the last one's on me.'

'Oh, Father, you old twister!' Kathleen was pointing at the priest, and Paul through his laughter was crying, 'You wait, sir, I'll have my own back on you.'

'Any time, any time.' The priest was moving away from them now, waving his hand at them. 'Goodbye, goodbye.'

'Goodbye, Father.'

'Goodbye.' They called together.

Then, half running, half walking, in their laughter and excitement they went past the station calling to each other as if yards apart, 'Dem ain't lorries, dem is trucks, full of coos and hens and ducks.'

'Isn't Father Bailey lovely?'

'He's all right.' Paul was non-committal, mainly to tease her.

'He's not all right, he's lovely.' She swung her racket at him again in an upward movement, and he caught her arm and they struggled together until of a sudden Kathleen became still, and her face, losing its merriment, she whispered hastily under her breath, 'Give over, there's me grandda behind.'

Letting go of her, Paul glanced casually back up the road, and there, walking as always with his hands in his pockets, was the little man who Kathleen called grandad. Whenever Paul saw this man he would remind himself that there was no blood relation between his Aunt Sarah and Pat Bradley, and he was glad, even relieved. He would have hated to think there was anything of this man in his Aunt Sarah, or Kathleen.

They walked on quickly now, sedately, a space and silence between them. Kathleen said quietly, 'He gives me the creeps.'

'Don't let him worry you.'

'He worries me mother. He's started coming round again. He hasn't been for months. He's been living with his cousins, but they've had a row and now he's in digs and he doesn't like them. He wants to come and live with us.' She glanced towards Paul. 'I think I would die if he lived with us. I couldn't bear him in the house. But, anyway, I needn't worry about that, for me mother can't stand the sight of him. She's warned him time and time again, but he still comes. There's some people think we should have him because we've got room. Betty Lawson said last term when we had a quarrel that everybody knew that my mother was hard because she wouldn't give her own father house room after the blitz that time. The quarrel was nothing to do with Mam or anything else, it was about netball, but she brought that up. So people still think that Mam is hard. She isn't, is she?'

'Aunt Sarah hard? Good lord no. She's too soft, if anything. Don't you take any notice. People only get half of the story, then they make up the other half. Aunt Sarah's got reason to hate his guts because he led her and your Aunt Phyllis a life of it when they were young. Dad told me all about it.'

Kathleen said now, 'Let's get the bus. I want to get home. He might catch up on us. Look! There's one coming in, we'll just make it.'

Simultaneously they began to run, and they caught the bus.

Fifteen minutes later, laughing again, they came up the backyard and burst into the kitchen on Sarah and Phyllis.

'Oh, hello, Aunt Phyllis.'

'Hello, Kathleen pet; been playing tennis?'

'Yes, Aunt Phyllis.' She threw her racket and shoes on to the armchair, and Sarah, turning from the table where she was rolling out pastry, said, 'Now get those off there, Kathleen. I've told you before.'

'O.K., Mam. O.K., Mam.' And picking up the racket and holding it at arm's length and dangling it from her fingers, she asked innocently, 'Where'll I put it, Mam?'

Sarah and Phyllis exchanged glances, and Sarah, trying to suppress a smile, said, 'Wherever you're going to put it you'd better get it there and quick!' She turned round sharply, her hand extended to give her daughter a wallop across the buttocks, but Kathleen, leaping past Paul and towards the scullery, cried, 'Save me! Save me!'

'Save yourself, you're big enough.' With manly indifference Paul sauntered to the hearth and, jerking his head at Phyllis, exclaimed in throaty tones, 'That's telling 'em.' Whereupon Phyllis let out a bellow of a laugh. Sarah too laughed, but as she trimmed the pastry from the edge of a large plate she said without looking at Paul, 'Your mother's been across, Paul. She wondered if you were back.'

'Oh.' The laughter slid from Paul's face and again he said, 'Oh,' then added, 'I'd better be getting over.'

'Where you going?' Kathleen was entering the kitchen again.

'Over home, of course . . . I have one, you know . . . a home.' He thrust his head down to her.

'I didn't say you hadn't, there's nobody arguing with you. I'll come over with you.'

Before Paul could make any reply Sarah put in quietly, 'No, Kathleen, I want you for a moment. Let Paul go over home.'

'But . . .'

'Never mind any buts. Go on, Paul.' She smiled at the boy, and Paul, returning her smile, said, 'Be seeing you.' He made a small swipe with his racket in Kathleen's direction then went out.

'What do you want me for, Mam?'

'Never you mind, that can wait. You haven't been in the house five minutes.'

'Do you want me to do something?'

'No, I just want you to stay put for five minutes.' She turned, and, looking down at her daughter, smiled at her. And Kathleen, as always, returned her smile, but pursing her mouth and grinning now, her expression saying, 'Anything to humour you.'

'Well, I must be off, Sarah.' Phyllis rose to her feet.

'Oh, wait a minute, I'll make a cup of tea before you go.'

'You'll not. I've had two lots of tea since I've been in. You'll drown me in tea. It's a wonder your stomach's not poisoned. How many times do you have it at work?'

'Oh, only twice. In the morning and afternoon break.'

'When are you going back?'

'Monday, I suppose, if he'll sign me off. It seems daft to catch a cold, weather like this, doesn't it? It's sweltering. But they're worse in the summer.'

'Will you be able to come down at the weekend?'

'Yes, I'll likely be at the market; I'll look in.'

'Bring Kathleen with you.' Phyllis looked towards her niece, and added quietly, 'You don't often look in on us. The lads love you to come. Young Dick said to me the other day, why weren't there any girls in our family, and I said to him the doctor thought I could look after boys better; he said me hands are too hard for braying girls with.'

Kathleen just smiled at this quip, she did not laugh, and Phyllis, turning abruptly away, said, 'Here's me for the road. Bye-bye, Kathleen.'

'Bye-bye, Aunt Phyllis.'

Clapping her hands over the board, then drying the remainder of the flour from them on her apron, Sarah followed Phyllis into the passage.

When they reached the door they stood for a moment looking down into the street, and Phyllis said, 'She's bats about Paul, isn't she? How's it going to work out?'

'Oh, it'll take its course.'

'What if they want to get married?'

'I hope they will.'

'You do?'

'Yes, why not?'

The sisters looked at each other, and Phyllis, her head drooping, said, 'Nothing, I suppose. There's not so much pressure against cousins marrying the day.' Then, glancing quickly up, she asked, 'You really want them to?'

'Yes.' Sarah was now staring out into the street. 'It's about the only thing I do want.'

'Why don't you marry again?' Phyllis's voice was gentle. 'You could, you know. You're bonnier now than you were at twenty, being thinner, except for your bust . . . you're stuck with that.' Sarah pushed her and they both laughed. Then Phyllis ended, 'Well, you wouldn't have to go to the factory day in and day out if you did.'

'I prefer the factory.'

'Well, I suppose you know your own road best, like us all.' She paused here before asking, 'How long are you going to keep Kathleen at school?'

'As long as she can stay. She'll never reach Paul's standard. But that doesn't matter; the main thing for her is an education so there won't be so much difference between them.'

'You've got it all cut and dried, haven't you?' Phyllis was smiling her understanding smile. 'Well, that's how it should be. I wish I could do the same for even one of my four, but they haven't a pennorth of brains atween them, except for making money, that is, and Ronnie isn't bad on the piano.' She laughed. 'Oh, they'll make out all right, the money way. You'd think our Jimmy was seventy instead of seventeen. And do you know that it was him who discovered ice-cream?' She pushed her fist into Sarah's arm. 'Yes, ice-cream hadn't been heard of until our Jimmy struck it. Anyway'–her laughter was high now–'he's making money out of it, so good luck to him.'

As Phyllis's loud laugh floated into the street Sarah glanced towards the door that was only a few yards from her own, and she made a warning sign to Phyllis, and Phyllis, clapping her hand over her mouth, drew her head into her shoulders. 'Sorry,' she whispered. Then, looking towards the other door, she asked, 'No sign of a thaw?'

Sarah shook her head. 'I don't want any thaw now.'

'It would drive me round the bend. Do you mean to say she still doesn't open her mouth to you?'

'Not a word, and when we pass in the street she could be blind, she doesn't even see me. But there it is.' Sarah gave a small smile. 'It doesn't matter, it doesn't matter any more. You know, I forget she's there. For days on end I forget she's there.'

'Does the old man still pop in?'

'Oh yes, once or twice a week, mostly at the weekend. And Kathleen goes in and out.'

'If she was mine I wouldn't let her darken the door. If they wouldn't have me they damn well wouldn't have her.'

'No, I would never stop her. After all, she's her grandmother.'

'Well, as I said, better you than me. I couldn't put up with it. I must be off. . . . Well, see you at the Assizes.'

To this macabre but colloquial parting Sarah laughed and replied, 'Yes. See you at the Assizes.' Which saying they were to recall within a matter of hours. 'My love to the boys,' she added softly.

'I'll tell them. So long.'

Going back through the front room, Sarah thought, It's odd what Phyllis thinks she couldn't stand, and her standing the stigma of the Arabs for years and still keeping her flag flying. . . . Phyllis was a good lass. Yes, she was indeed. And she had spunk. By, she had that!

'I'm not going down to Aunt Phyllis's on Saturday, Mam.' Kathleen was waiting for her when she entered the kitchen.

'All right, all right, there's nobody forcing you.' Sarah's tone was tart.

'Well, I can't help it, Mam; I've tried.'

Sarah was at the table again, her back to her daughter and, her voice quiet now, she said, 'I know you can't. We'll not go into it, it's all right.'

Kathleen sat down in what had been David's chair, and she bowed her head as she said, 'I like Aunt Phyllis, I do. She's nice, and she's a good sort . . . but the boys, and Ali . . . Well, somehow . . .'

Sarah turned from the board. 'It's all right, dear.' Her manner was soothing. 'I know how you feel, so don't worry. But all you've got to do is to remember that the boys can't help looking like Arabs and that they're nice boys, they are.'

'I know.' Kathleen was mumbling now. 'But it's since Iris Bannister got to know about it and she told the others. And just before the holidays, just as recently as that, Peggy Crofton, the sneaky little cat, came up to me and said, 'It isn't true, is it, that your auntie lives among the Arabs?' I could have smacked her face. I nearly did.'

'Coloured folk are marrying white folk all the time now and it's only ignorant people who make something out of it. You've got to look at it like that. And those girls ought to be ashamed of themselves. And them with their education an' all.'

'Education!' Kathleen sniffed. 'Iris Bannister lives in Westoe village. Their house–I've seen it–it's not much bigger than this, but because she lives in Westhoe she thinks she's the last word, and she's always telling you about the private school she went to before she came to the High School. Betty Chalmers says it was a potty little place, just a house run by two people, old maids, who hadn't even been teachers, but of course they were very . . . very refeened, and they talked like this.' Kathleen screwed up her nose and lifted her upper lip into a point showing two large white front teeth, and as her mother burst out laughing her face fell into its natural lines again, and she too laughed as she said, 'Betty Chalmers can do it wonderfully, she'd make you scream.'

'Oh, dear, dear.' Sarah, still laughing, shook her head at the tragedies of youth, but when Kathleen, rising from the chair, said, 'I think I'll go across to my Aunt May's for a bit,' Sarah stopped laughing and answered quickly, 'No, I wouldn't. Your Aunt May doesn't see much of Paul and you know he'll be gone soon.'

'Well, that's why . . .'

'But you must think of your Aunt May, Kathleen. . . . Oh'–Sarah tapped her brow with the knuckle of her thumb–'I forgot to tell you. Lorna MacKay called in this morning. She wanted you to go and hear her new record.'

'Oh, bust.'

'But I thought you liked Lorna?'

'I do, I do, but then Michael will likely be in.'

Sarah smiled. 'You used to like Michael, too, at one time.'

'Yes . . . well, I suppose I did. He's all right but he's always asking me to go out now, to the pictures and places.'

'Well, you go to the pictures with Paul, don't you?'

'Yes, I know, but that's different. But that's what he said too: I went to the pictures with Paul.'

'And what did you say to that?' Sarah was smiling quietly as she worked away at the table.

'Oh, I said . . . well . . .' Kathleen paused and gave a hick of a laugh. 'Well, I said, you let me go with Paul because he was my cousin, but you thought I wasn't old enough to go out with him.' Her voice became smothered with suppressed laughter.

'You little monkey!' Sarah was looking at her daughter, her eyes bright. 'Anyway, I would go up and see Lorna.' It was an order put gently over.

'Oh, all right. It'll be an educational afternoon,' she sighed, 'interposed with a running commentary on . . . our Michael.' Here she mimicked Lorna's voice and attitude. 'Our Michael's earning sixteen pounds a week and him only nineteen, and when he gets to the coal face he can make over twenty pounds a week, he can.' She waggled her plump, adolescent body, and Sarah said, 'Now don't be catty.'

'Well, she's always on about the money their Michael's making. Always getting a dig in that Paul won't be making any for years. She even said that her mother said that Paul would be twenty-three before he earned a penny.'

'Did she now?'

'Yes, she did.'

'Well, Paul has got something money can't buy, you tell her that.'

'I have; and I really don't believe that Michael makes sixteen pounds a week, do you?'

'Oh yes, they can make that at the pits now doing overtime. And I shouldn't be surprised that he reaches twenty when he gets to the face. Coal is like gold now. And long may it last for them, they've had it rough long enough.'

'I'd hate to marry a pitman.' Kathleen was sauntering to the door as Sarah said, 'Well, don't.'

'I won't.' And once again they looked at each other and once again they laughed.

'I won't stay long,' said Kathleen.

'There's no need to hurry. If Paul comes over I'll come up and knock for you.'

'You will?' Kathleen's face brightened. 'O.K. Bye-bye.'

'Bye-bye, my dear.'

Paul, Paul, Paul; Paul all the time, waking and sleeping. Would she change? She was only sixteen, she might. But no, Sarah shook her head at the thought. She was held fast. Although Paul did not look like his father, there emanated from him the same virile attraction. No, Kathleen wouldn't change. She prayed to God she wouldn't, anyway, because if she did, well then . . . Sarah's hands became quiet on the board and she looked at the wall opposite. All her efforts, all her self-denial, all her trying to do the right thing would have been in vain, wouldn't it? Still staring at the wall, she saw there the day of her choice. It happened six months ago in this very kitchen. John had been out of the Air Force for eighteen months then and was doing well in his wireless business. That's how he had started, talking about the shop. 'I'm on to something here, Sarah,' he had said. 'You'd never believe the money that's in it. Joe's opening another shop in Wallsend and I'm going to keep on with the Newcastle one and see to the workshops. And if we can get a likely enough fellow we'll open one down here in Shields. Everybody is wireless mad. And you know another thing that's going to boom . . . television. I bet you a shilling before ten years is out everybody'll have a television in their own house.'

'Television? Just what is television?'

'The pictures, that's what it is, the pictures.'

'And in your own house?' She had laughed as one would at a tall story.

He had shaken his head solemnly at her. 'It's a fact, Sarah. Fellows have been working on this long before the War and now they're getting pictures from London. I'm telling you, it's no fairy-tale. And we're in on the ground floor, Joe and me.' He had looked away from her at this point and said, 'That's one good thing that came out of the Air Force anyway, Joe and me stuck in that godforsaken hole planning what we'd do together after the War. Joe was to do the talking and the buying, and I was to do the making, wireless and that, and to see to the production end. And that's how it has worked out. When I think of those years on the dole . . . years . . . my God, it was an eternity! I can't believe this is really happening to us. . . . I've bought a car, Sarah.'

'A car?' Her eyes screwed up at him.

'Yes, a dandy. I got it as a snip. It's second-hand, but it was lying up all through the War. A nineteen thirty-eight Rover, a beautiful job, like a Rolls-Royce, it is, honest.'

'Oh, John.' She had looked at him softly and smiled. She was pleased for him. Success would ease the turbulence in him, part of it at any rate.

He had said then, 'I made plans at the end of the War, Sarah, not only with Joe, with meself. I said, I'll make money, real money, and then I'll buy me out, so to speak, and I'll do what I've longed to do for years.'

Her body had become stiff, rigid, but she had remained silent as he went on, 'I've had enough, a bellyfull if anyone has. I'm not God's gift to woman, I know. Oh, I know, nobody better, but that's over. I've got money now and I'll have a hell of a lot more before I've finished. But I'm determined on one thing . . . May's not going to wallow in it. No, by God, I'll see to that. I'd rather give it to all the whores in the town.'

She had exclaimed aloud at this and he had cut in abruptly saying, 'You don't know what it's been like, Sarah. She's me mother all over, only in a different way. A damned sight worse if you ask me. No, I've made up me mind.'

She had said at this point, in a voice she could scarcely hear herself, 'Aren't you forgetting about Paul?'

'No, I'm not!' he had barked back at her. 'Paul will know where he's going in a few month's time. He'll have to do his National Service, anyway, and once he leaves the house he'll be on his own and my life sentence'll be finished.'

She had looked at him then and stated flatly, 'Paul is in love with Kathleen and she with him.'

His mouth had dropped open and he had gaped at her; for a full minute he had gaped at her before he said, 'But they're just kids; they've been brought up together.'

'It's more than that, at least I think so. Anyway, I'll have to wait and see.'

He had taken a step towards her, crying, 'Look, Sarah!' but with her outstretched hand she had stopped him. She had not touched him, she had just put her arm out towards him, her hand raised vertically.

'I'm waiting,' she said. 'Kathleen is the only thing that matters to me, you've got to know that.'

'I do know it, but I'm willing to take a chance, I'm willing to take what's left.'

She had her head bowed on her chest when she murmured, 'There's time enough for that.'

Again he looked at her for a long, long moment, and then characteristically he spoke the truth. 'There might be for you, but not for me. I'm at the end of my tether, Sarah. I'm made that way. . . . There's got to be somebody. . . . For years and years I've wanted it to be you.'

'I cannot help you,' she said. Her head was still lowered.

At this he had turned and walked out. It had all been comparatively quiet and orderly, the arranging of their future lives.

Sarah brought her attention back to the table. She gathered the scraps of pastry up, pressed them together, then rolled them out. As she lined an oven plate she saw Dan come in from the back lane and her face brightened.

When he entered the kitchen he sniffed, saying, 'Coo! That smells good. What is it?'

'Oh, just odds and ends; they're always hungry.'

'They are? You mean Paul. If you were to be paid for all the food he's eaten here you'd have a tidy sum.'

'Oh, that.' She gave an impatient toss of her head. 'I've got to bake, anyway. She can tuck it away like a young horse an' all.'

'By! It's hot.'

'I'll make you a cup of tea.'

'No, no, I won't be staying a minute.' Yet as he spoke he sat down by the side of the table'

Sarah looked at him. 'But it's Wednesday; you're off, aren't you?'

'The shop's closed.' He nodded at her. 'I'm off that far, but I'm going up again; the old lady wants some rooms turned round.' He bounced his head. 'She's got an idea, and she's working on it. She thinks I can't see it. . . . She wants me to go and live up there.'

'Really!'

'Aye. She's lonely since the old man went. I've known this has been coming for some time, and'–he wagged his finger at Sarah–'it wouldn't be a bad thing, it wouldn't at that, for she's a dear old soul. I'm more than a bit fond of her, and, as she says, the place'll be mine some time. . . . You know.' He rested his elbow on the table and pushed against a glass bottle lying on its side, and Sarah exclaimed quickly, 'Look, you'll get flour all over you.' As she lifted the bottle out of his way, he said, 'That's a cute idea, using a bottle for a rolling-pin. Where'd you find that?'

'Oh, in a magazine. It works an' all. You fill it with cold water and it helps to keep the pastry firm.'

'Well, well, I wonder what next. But as I was saying. You know, Sarah, there's kind people in the world, and those two have been pure gold to me, and not a drop of blood between us. Strangers can be kinder than your own, don't you think?' He did not wait for her to comment on this but went on, 'I did meself a good turn the day I put that four hundred into the business; they've paid me back a thousand-fold. . . . Well, not quite,' he laughed. 'But you know what I mean. And now this changing round of rooms. There's six of them, you know, fine big ones at that, and well furnished. Oh, aye, they've got some nice pieces, and she's been on about making two flats of it for some time now. She keeps saying two people could live here amicably and not get in each other's hair. . . . Poor old soul! I've known what she's been driving at, but I've never let on. You see, it's going to be difficult, I mean leaving next door.'

'Yes.' Sarah nodded down at him. 'That is going to be difficult. I don't think you should do it, Dan; she would be lonely without you.'

Dan stared at her for a moment before saying, 'You know, you're a remarkable woman, Sarah. I've always thought that.'

'Oh, don't make game, Dan. Remarkable, huh! I know just how remarkable I am.' She was nodding her head slowly at him.

'I'm not making game, not on this matter, I'm not. I know what I think. Here you are trying to persuade me not to leave her because you think she would be lonely. She's got Stan, she's got John and May across the way, she's got two grandchildren, and you say she'll be lonely. After the way she's treated you, you can still feel sorry for her.'

'She's not a happy woman . . . inside. That's what I mean. And unhappy people are lonely. We are all lonely in a way, but unhappy people are more lonely.'

'Yes, I suppose you're right there. But there's another thing against it, but I suppose you wouldn't notice. I wouldn't be able to pop in here every day.'

'Oh, I'd noticed that all right, Dan.' She stood with her hands resting on the table, her body leaning towards him. 'I just don't know what I would have done without you, Dan. I've . . . I've never said this before, but I think that at the beginning I would have gone clean off my head, really off my head, if it hadn't been for you. Oh, I know what it would be like if you stopped popping in.'

Dan stared at her, his eyes holding no vestige of humour now. Then, pushing his fingers through his thick greying hair, he rose abruptly and went towards the fireplace and stood looking down into the empty grate. And Sarah stood by the table, her hands moving nervously and without purpose until he said, 'Have you talked to John lately?'

'John?' The name said like that jerked her into stiffness and she twisted her head over her shoulder and looked towards his back. And again she said, 'John?'

'There's going to be a bust-up there and it's a pity? He should let the lad get settled first. Although in a way I don't blame him, he's had it rough since he came back. It was bad enough before the War.'

She watched him turn slowly towards her now and he held her gaze when he spoke, 'He's going to leave May.'

There was a pressure in her throat as if from the point of a bone; the feeling would not allow her to swallow. Yet this was not news to her, she had known it was going to happen.

She heard him say, 'What are you going to do, Sarah?'

'Me? . . . Me?' She moved her head from side to side in one wide startled sweep. 'Nothing, nothing. Why . . . why should I?' She sounded indignant. But she could not keep her eyes on his and her lids dropped over them; then her head moved downwards. She felt him coming towards her, and when he was near he said, 'I'm glad of that, Sarah, I'm glad. I'll tell the old lady that I won't be moving up there, at least not for the present. I'll be going now. So long, Sarah.'

'So long, Dan.'

She waited for him to move, and when he didn't she looked up. She looked into the kindly face of this man—this man who had about him the gentleness of David and the virility of John. It was a strange attractive combination, seeing that he was also the brother of her mother-in-law. When he put out his hand and touched her cheek gently it was as if David had come alive. He turned from her and went out.

As Sarah watched him go down the backyard, pausing to turn off the dripping tap before going into the back lane, she did not think of him, nor yet of John, nor yet of David, but she thought of the woman next door who was mother and sister to these three men, and the words she had once spoken resounded loudly through the kitchen: 'You have taken my menfolk.'

Her head drooped again and she supported her brow with the palm of her hand. Then, blinking rapidly, she said to herself, 'I'll make a cup of tea before I clear.'

As she sat drinking her tea she thought of what the years had done to her, of what loving a number of people had done to her. She had loved David . . . Oh, yes, she had. But she had passioned for John. Without loving him she had wanted him. She realised that. During the first month of her marriage her body had in a way become a university for her natural desire, but she had learned so quickly in this direction that her tutor was left far behind on a plane from which he had not the power to propel himself. David was not ruthless enough, not brutal enough, not selfish enough. John in this particular field would have been all three.

She pulled at the neck of her blouse to give herself air. She felt as if she was going to suffocate, the room was stifling. She rose and went to the window and pushed it further upwards, and as she did so there walked in through the back door the thin wizened figure of her father. He saw her almost at the same moment as she caught sight of him, and to prevent the door being locked in his face he sprinted up the yard.

Breathing heavily, Sarah turned to the table. It was no good rushing into the scullery, he'd be in by now. The next moment his voice came from behind her, not placating as it was once, but surly. 'You would have shut me out, wouldn't you?'

She did not answer him for a moment, and then she said in a voice so unlike her own that it was impossible to imagine herself speaking. 'I've told you not to come here. Can't you take a telling?' But she knew that she became an entirely different being when confronted with this man.

'Aa've got no place else to go, Aa've been turned out.'

'It isn't the first time, you can find other lodgings.'

'Aa can't, not on my money; only place is a hovel.'

'It's of no interest to me where you stay, I've told you before. Now get out.' She still had her back towards him.

'Folks is talkin'. You with a room goin' beggin' and me on the street. You'd see me in the workhouse.'

'Yes, I would.'

'Well, you won't then, I'm comin' here.'

She turned towards him now, her eyes wide. 'You're what? You'll come here over my dead body. You've blackmailed me for years, but now, as I told you before, the only one I was afraid of you hurting has gone. And you can say what you damn well like now, it makes no difference. Go on, get on with it; shout about all you think you know.'

'You're speaking out of turn, you should think a bit afore you open your mouth so wide.' He was speaking slowly, quietly.

She narrowed her eyes at him. She couldn't follow him. What did he mean? What was he alluding to? He had got something else into that warped, twisted mind of his. 'What are you up to now?' she said from between her teeth.

He peered at her through his bleary eyes. There was a trickle of saliva running down one corner of his mouth. He asked again, 'Aa y' goin' to give me that room? You'll be sorry if y' don't, mind. Aa'm tellin' you, you'll be sorry.'

'Get out!' she took a step from the table, a threatening step, but he did not move.

'Y' could handle me if y' liked. It would be worth your while, Aa'm tellin' you.'

'Get out!'

'Aye, aall right then. If y' want it that way, Aa will. An' Aa'll find those two an' tell 'em.'

Her face screwed up. 'Those two? What two? Who you talking about?'

'The bairns.'

'The bairns?' she repeated.

'Aye, that's what Aa said, the bairns. Do Aa need t' name 'em. Aa'll tell 'em they'd better go careful.'

Her face was slowly stretching. She mouthed the word 'careful', but without a sound.

'They were carrying on together down the station bank, rolling about; they're ready to jump into bed any minute, and they can't, can they?' He stared into her wild, startled face. 'Y' mustn't let that happen, must you? It'd be unnatural, wouldn't it? After you given' 'em the same faather an' all . . . Well, didn't you? She was born practically nine months to the minute from one o'clock on that New Year's morning on the waste land, where you and the big fellow were neckin'. An' that's putting it mildly, isn't it? If there'd been nowt in it, do you think you'd have paid up all these years. . . . You had somethin' to hide all right, an' y' still have.'

Once before she had experienced the feeling of her body swelling to explosive point; the feeling was with her again only more intense, more terrible. She felt her rage lift her off her feet. She swung round to the table and grabbed up the first thing that came to hand, which was the rolling-pin bottle filled with water, and she hurled it at him. As he turned his face from the onslaught it caught him full on the temple and he dropped like a stone.

She was standing, her back to the table, hanging on to its edge. She was aware that someone was in the yard, but she didn't know who; her body was still swelling, her head seemed to fill the room. She could feel her eyes stretching to snapping point as she watched the blood flow over the lino. The bigger her body grew, the quieter she became inside, it was as if she was being carried away into a great silence. Even when she saw May burst into the room with Paul by her side she made no sound. She watched May kneeling on the floor, she saw her raise his head up, then put her hand inside his waistcoat. May looked more human in this moment than she had ever seen her before. 'He's dead,' she said.

Sarah knew he was dead. She knew as soon as the bottle had hit him that he had died. She was glad he was dead. Oh, she was glad he was dead. He could never hurt or terrify her again. He could never hurt anyone again. He could never hurt Kathleen now . . . that was the important thing, he could never hurt Kathleen. Kathleen was safe, safe, safe. And Paul too; yes, Paul was safe too. They were both safe.

Chapter Two

Time was only in the mind. David had said that. He had read it some place. He had said how true it was. . . . Time was only in the mind. She herself knew how true it was now, for time had almost ceased to exist for her. Soon she knew that time, as the mind knew it, would end altogether, but it wasn't worrying her. Her mind had rejected time as it had all other things. If it thought about anything clearly it was that it wished . . . it . . . was all over. She wasn't afraid of the end; she had even said so to the priest. At times her mind came back into the present sufficiently to answer questions if it considered they needed answering. When the priest spoke to her of God she almost laughed; the thought of God was ludicrous to her now, really funny. When her mind was on this other plane she was amazed at the credulity of all the people who believed in this thing called God, this thing that had become an . . . it, to her. Her mind admitted to this 'it' being alive, yet at the same time she saw it as inanimate because it was without feeling for the human being. She felt a malicious desire now to bring her thoughts from this far-away plane and hurl them at the priest, hurl 'it' at the priest. But the priest was Father Bailey, and he was kind was Father Bailey. But he kept repeating one thing to her, trying to drag an answer from her, a response. 'You've got to tell them, Sarah,' he kept saying. 'And today. It'll be your last chance. Tell them that he blackmailed you for years. Tell them. Do you hear me, Sarah? Sarah.'

She bowed her head before his pitying gaze. He could do nothing. Being a priest, his tongue was tied. And she would do nothing, because if she opened her mouth she could only tell them half the truth. She could say: My father blackmailed me because he thought I have been with John and I hadn't. But would they believe her? No. No. They would say, those clever ones in the court, they would say, Then why did you pay him to keep silent? And then it would become complicated. She couldn't begin to tell them why at first she paid him to keep silent, it was all too far in the past. Even if she could explain it would bear no weight. She alone knew the thing that would bear weight. Her father had known it and now he was dead. He was dead because he had created it . . . this thing, this thing that she alone knew now and must hide. And it was a lie this thing, the biggest lie of the lot, but nevertheless she must hide it because if she once showed it the light everyone would believe it. There was never smoke without fire, they would say. Yes, yes, that's why she had paid up all the years, they would say. They would look at Kathleen and Paul and remember they had been inseparable since they were babies. They would remember that John loved Kathleen like a father. . . . But, she needn't worry, they wouldn't remember, for they wouldn't hear the lie spoken, the lie that would help her to live. It would die with her. Kathleen would be safe.

The priest went away and the warders came, two of them. One of them had a nice face, she had a kind voice too. She was about Sarah's own age and she took Sarah's hand and patted it before they mounted the steps. But when she sat down beside Sarah her face looked cold and remote. . . .

Sarah looked around the court-room, her head moving slowly as if with an effort. There was Phyllis, her face filled with two great compassion-filled eyes. Dear Phyllis. And next to her was Ali and Jimmy . . . They were nice, Ali and Jimmy.

There was Dan, his eyes waiting for her. Something in her stretched out towards him and said, Don't cry any more; don't cry any more, Dan. And next to him was Kathleen, her face like paste, and her eyes like great dark pools, pools full of pity. The thing inside her stretched out to Kathleen, it leaped to Kathleen and said, 'Oh, my dear, my dear! Don't worry, you'll be all right.' And then there was Paul. Paul's head was down and he was not looking at her, he never looked at her. A voice from the far-away plane cried out to Paul, 'Look at me, Paul, I'm not bad. Please look at me.' But Paul refused to look at her. Next to Paul sat May, and May was looking at her. But what was May thinking? No one ever knew what May was thinking. There was a man sitting next to May but Sarah did not look at him, or say his name to herself, for it was because of him, because he had been born, because the desire of his body was the ruling power in his life, that she was sitting here now. . . . I'll see you at the assizes. . . . I'll see you at the assizes.

Her mind slipped away on to the distant plane again, and from it she heard faintly the voice of the prosecuting counsel, the man who seemed to hate her. He talked as if he had known her from birth and as if she had never done a decent thing in her life. Why was he talking about her like that? He also seemed to hate the nice man who was defending her. He said nasty things to him, spiteful, sarcastic things, and they always referred to her. Her counsel was now speaking to the judge, asking to bring forward another witness. Time passed and then she was looking at a man in the box. She couldn't remember ever having seen him in her life. Of course that was natural because he had just said he lived in Wallsend and she didn't know anybody in Wallsend. He said his name was James Ballast and that his brother had once beaten up the deceased man.

'Why did your brother beat up the deceased man?' asked the nice man.

Because the deceased was always spying on courting couples, the man said. He had been spying on his brother, and his brother laid a trap for him, then beat him up.

'Where is your brother now?' asked the nice man.

'He's dead,' said the man in the box. 'He died in the War.'

The cool voice from the high bench cut through the examination, saying, 'What is all this? This has no bearing on the case at all.'

'I'm just trying to show, my lord,' said the nice man, 'what kind of man the deceased was.'

'We are not here to deal with the dead man's character,' said the cool voice. 'We are here to prove or disprove murder. Why have you raked up such a witness?'

'The man offered himself as a witness, me lord. He thought he could help the accused.'

'And apparently you did too?'

'Yes, me lord.'

People were kind. It was as Dan always kept saying, people were kind . . . all except the prosecuting counsel. He was standing in front of the jury now, telling them how bad she was. He even remembered to tell them about the day after the big raid when she wouldn't give her father shelter and had screamed at him and gone to throw something at him.

People had long memories, May had a long memory. It was she who had told them that bit when she was asked if she had ever seen her raise her hand to her father before. May had a lot in common with the prosecuting counsel.

Then the nice man was talking to the jury. He was telling them what she had gone through in her childhood, how she had feared the deceased, how he had beaten her and her sister. . . . Phyllis had told them all about that, and Phyllis had been fearless. Phyllis wasn't frightened of anybody. She had said to them, 'I always wanted to kill him and many a time I said I would, and I would if I'd got the chance.' The judge had told her to stop talking, and when she wouldn't he had warned her she would be put out of court. He had warned her twice because she was always jumping up and down in her seat.

Now the jury filed out of the benches and went into a room and the warders took her downstairs and the kind one squeezed her shoulder, but she said nothing. They wanted her to eat and drink, but all she wanted was a cup of tea. And then it didn't taste like tea, not her kind of tea.

She sat staring ahead, waiting, her hands joined in her lap. Time passed. She supposed it was hours, she didn't know. Everybody seemed restless. The policeman came and spoke to her; even the stiff-looking ones spoke nicely. Then they went and talked in the passage outside. She heard a voice say, 'Well, he didn't find her insane, did he? And he examined her long enough. She's just withdrawn herself. They do, you know. She'll likely be like that until near the end . . . if there's an end.' 'Ssh!' said somebody else. 'Ssh!' and the voice answered, 'It's all right, she doesn't take it in.'

And then of a sudden they took her upstairs, and there they all were in their places as if there had been no long interval. And one man from the benches stood up and the judge asked him a question, and he said, 'We have found the prisoner guilty of manslaughter, my lord. Because we are agreed that there was no premeditation to kill.'

Her mind began to race now, flying away to reach the plane, the safe plane, where the voice of the judge couldn't follow, but even when she reached it she couldn't shut the voice out. Two sentences came floating to her. One was, 'The jury have agreed your act was unpremeditated.' But for some reason she got the impression that he didn't agree with the jury's verdict. The second sentence was: 'Nevertheless you have killed a man and been found guilty of manslaughter; therefore I sentence you to prison for fifteen years.'

Her mind was shot from the plane and into her head again. She wasn't to die, she wasn't going to die. She was surprised, amazed. Then her mind whimpered, But fifteen years! Fifteen years! Then she heard Phyllis screaming: 'It's monstrous! Cruel! He should've been dead years ago, the swine! I wish I had done it myself, I tell you. Oh, my God! Sarah, Sarah! Fifteen years! God Almighty!' Phyllis's voice trailed away as they pulled her from the court.

Just before she was led downstairs she glanced towards her family. They were all standing as if petrified, looking at her, all with the exception of John. Perhaps it was because he was not looking at her that her eyes went involuntarily to him. His head was bowed deep and his face was covered with his hands.

Chapter Three

The day was dull, the world was dull. Everything was crazy; he was crazy. At times he thought he was going stark staring mad. Everybody had changed since the trial; everybody and everything had changed. . . . But some of them had changed before the trial. Paul had. What was up with the lad? Just look how he was treating Kathleen.

In three rapid strides John was at the window looking down into the yard seeing Kathleen going through the back door and across the lane into her own backyard. Because it was still her own backyard, she had refused to budge. But she was no longer a young girl skipping and gay; she had grown up overnight, as it were, and the transition had left her dazed. She wanted help, comfort, and the one who could give her the most comfort was turning his back on her. Why? Why? Well, he would find out; he would have something to say to that young squirt, he would that.

As he turned from the window about to stalk from the room, Paul entered, and John stood aside and let him reach the fireplace before he started: 'Look, what's the matter with you these days? We've all had a shock, but the one that's troubled most is Kathleen and she needs your help. And what have you done? You've kept clear of her for weeks as if she's got the mange. I don't like it.' John's face screwed up, his lips leaving his teeth. 'I don't like the trait in your character that makes you shy off when you're most needed. Even if your Aunt Sarah has done something wrong, and that's a matter of opinion, you cannot hold Kathleen accountable for it. But that's what you're doing. Every time she walks in the door you go out. Now look here, let's get this straight.'

'I want to talk to you.' Paul's voice was quiet, cold and quiet.

'Then talk. Fire ahead.'

John looked at his son and waited, and when he did not begin he said brusquely, 'What's holding you up? I thought you wanted to . . . ?'

'I'm going to become a priest.'

The silence in the room was like sound amplified; it penetrated through the cries of the children outside in the back lane, through a man calling a boy's name, through the high cry of a baby.

'Say that again.' John's tone sounded ordinary.

'You heard what I said.'

'Aye . . . aye, I thought I did. I thought you said, "I'm going to become a priest." That's what I thought you said.'

'And that is what I said.'

John pulled his chin into his neck, pushing out the flesh that looked tough and thick like a reddy-brown hide. 'You're going to become . . . ? Look, lad, have you gone barmy?'

'No.'

'But you said a priest . . . not a minister, or a curate, but a priest?'

'That's what I said.'

'A Catholic priest?'

'A Catholic priest.'

'You trying to make me do something–hit you, knock you out or something?'

'It won't make any difference what you do.'

'It won't, eh? Get out.' John swung his arm in a half-circle motion indicating the door, but as Paul turned towards it he sprang across the room barring his way, crying, 'No begod! What am I saying? You'll not get out of here until I hear you talk sense. . . . Priest! You going to become a priest. . . . Over my bloody dead body you will. Now sit down.' He pointed to a chair. 'Sit down and let's hear what all this is about.'

The boy moved with seeming quietness towards the chair and sat on its edge and waited; and John, towering over him, demanded, 'Well now, get going. Since when have you had the idea you're going to be a priest?' His voice was sneering.

Paul turned his white face up to his father's. 'Since the day my Aunt Sarah killed her father.'

The answer nonplussed John and it brought his shoulders back and his head up. It brought the lids of his eyes together, and he asked, puzzled, 'But what has that to do with this business? There's no connection that I can see.'

'You can't?'

'No, I can't.'

'I happened to hear what her father said before she hit him.'

'But you said . . . you said you didn't hear anything. You told them in court . . . only a babble of voices, you said.'

'I know what I told them.' Paul now thrust out his arm as if pushing his father aside, and, getting to his feet, he moved a few steps backwards, putting distance between them before he spoke again, 'The old man said Kathleen and I were acting like a courting couple and we shouldn't because . . . because you had fathered us both.'

The telling silence took over again until John whispered, 'I had what?' He brought his hand up to his chin, the forefinger pressing below his lower lip, and as if coming out of a daze he repeated, 'I had what? God Almighty!' With a movement of his leg he flicked the chair across the room, and as it crashed against the fender he cried, 'He said that? Well, let me tell you, son, and I'm swearing it on God's oath, it's a bloody lie . . . a bloody lie. Do you hear!' His voice was high now.

'Yes, I hear, but I also heard the old man remind my Aunt Sarah of the night Kathleen had been conceived. It was on New Year's morning nineteen and thirty on the waste ground. . . . Kathleen's birthday is on the fourth of October.'

John stood as if someone had hit him a resounding blow, a blow that should have felled him to the ground. He swayed slightly, his hand moving now round his face, his eyes blinking; he had difficulty in speaking and when he did his voice had a note of pleading in it. 'Paul . . . listen, Paul boy. It's not true. Your Aunt Sarah and I did stand round there that night, and we talked. We talked because . . . Oh, my God. What does it matter now? I loved your Aunt Sarah, but nothing . . . ever . . . happened between us. You've got to believe me. Your Aunt Sarah's a good woman.'

'If nothing happened, then why did she let her father blackmail her all these years?'

'Blackmail her?' The word sprung John's brows upwards. 'What you saying? Have you gone barmy?'

'No, I've not gone barmy, and you know I haven't. She'd been paying him money for years to keep quiet about that night.'

'Christ alive!' Slowly John turned his gaze from his son, and going towards the fallen chair he picked it up, and when it was righted he sat down, gripping the seat with his hands as if to support himself. His mind in a blinding turmoil, he was seeing a picture which covered the years; Sarah's nerves, her tenseness, her terror of being left alone with him. Aye, she had been terrified, and with what reason! God Almighty! . . . God Almighty! 'Paul.' He put out a shaking hand towards his son, and his lips moved, trying to form the words that would establish his innocence in the boy's mind, but they were ineffective when they came. His tone held no conviction, he was too dazed to be convincing. 'There was nothing, Paul, nothing, nothing, between your Aunt Sarah and me. That swine of a man must have heard us talking that night and held it over her. She loved your Uncle Davie. There was only one person for her, she could see nobody but your Uncle Davie. It was likely because she didn't want trouble, and didn't want to hurt him, that she paid up. But, my God . . . !' His hands dropped to his side. 'My God! What she must have gone through.' Now his voice roughened and strengthened. 'You should have spoken up and told them, it would have helped her.'

'Would it? Would it have helped if they had thought she was carrying on with you and that you were Kathleen's father? Would it have helped her?' Paul's voice was accusing.

John shook his head. 'No, I suppose you're right. But, Paul . . .' He leant well forward from the chair. 'You've got to believe me, and you've got to make things right between you and Kathleen.'

Paul moved to the side of the table and he looked down at it before he said, 'That's over. We were like brother and sister, anyway. We were brought up too close.'

'But you're not brother and sister, or half-brother and sister. You could get married.'

'No.' The boy's voice was so harsh it could have been John himself speaking. The tables seemed to be turned; it was the boy who had the strength and John who was the weaker in this moment. 'I'm going through with this. I know now it was what I wanted to do all along. I was always attracted to the Catholic Church.'

'Oh, my God! Don't talk, boy, don't talk.' John's head was bowed forward, his hands supporting his brow.

'I've got to talk, and now. In six days' time I'll be in the Army. . . . I've been taking a form of instruction from Father Bailey, a very preliminary form. He has told me of all the obstacles that are in my way, so you won't be the only one who will try to put a spoke into the wheel. I've got to convince them that I'm serious. I've got to see the Bishop, Bishop McCormack, and Father Bailey wouldn't make the appointment until I'd told you everything.'

'That's bloody kind of him.' John was rearing now. 'I'll have something to say to this Father Bailey, and one thing will be that you can't do a damn thing about it. I've got the idea that you're under my jurisdiction until you're twenty-one.'

'I know all about that, we've gone into that. You can get a Court Order to prevent me from becoming a priest. You can also prevent me turning a Catholic while I'm a minor, but I'll be twenty-one before I come out of the Army, and until then you or no one else can stop me reading and learning. I'll be getting myself ready. . . .'

'For Christ's sake! Shut up, will you! Be quiet, before I do something to you. . . . And'–he paused–'where does the university come in in all this?'

'I won't be going to Oxford. I can take my degrees while I'm studying. I'll likely go to Ushaw College near Durham.'

John bounced to his feet. He still looked dazed, but he sounded more like himself when he cried, 'Ushaw College, be buggered! I'll see you in hell first before I'll let you go through with this. You're mad. This business had turned your brain. As for those bloody cunning priests, wait till I get my tongue round them . . . and my hands.' He doubled his fist and shook it towards Paul. 'You know something? I'd rather see you dead than let you go through with this. Now get out.' He turned his back on his son and looked into the fire, and Paul moved slowly from the table and went to the door and opened it, and his intake of breath brought John's head round quickly to see May standing in the doorway. There was no need to wonder if she had heard anything; her face told him that there was nothing she hadn't heard; she must have been there all the time.

As Paul hesitated and looked at her she said evenly, in the ice-rimmed tone that was natural to her, 'Go on out, I'll see you later.' Then she went into the room and closed the door.

May stood with her back to the door, not leaning against it; she did not look in need of support, her small compact body was rigid with the white heat of hate. 'So!' she said.

'Aye. So. Well, you heard what he said.'

'Yes, I heard what he said, but I lay no stock on that. I understand my son where you never did. A priest indeed! He means that as a girl would mean it–if she said she was going to be a nun after being let down. I'll see to him presently. It isn't him I want to talk about now, it's you . . . and her!'

John's lips met in a straight line, the corners pulled in as if he was sucking.

'That's it, get ready to do battle. Get ready to lie your way out.'

'I've got no need to lie about anything and I'm not going to, so don't worry your head on that score.'

'Yes, I loved your Aunt Sarah.' She was mimicking his tone now, her face spread into a mirthless leer. Then as if a switch had changed her expression, her face was straight. The muscles tight and her eyes flint-hard as she spat at him, 'There was a pair of you. The big fellow and the big, fat floppy-breasted bitch.'

As she watched him silently writhing, she taunted him, 'Why don't you say something? At least defend her and say she wasn't a floppy-breasted bitch, she was beautiful. Aye, like a sow on her side she was beautiful all right.' She paused again. Then her voice dropping deep into her throat, she muttered, 'There could be another killing this very minute.'

'Aye, there could. So look out, I'm telling you.' His words sounded thick and fuddled as if he were drunk.

'I'm not frightened of you and your bulk, and you know it. . . . To think that all these years, you and her . . . I could spit on you.'

'You're barking up the wrong tree as usual.' John moved his head slowly. 'It's true what I said and I'm not going to deny it. I was in love with her, and still am if you want to know, so coat that with your venom and burn it through. . . . But there's been nothing between us, not a damn thing. That first New Year's Eve I tried to kiss her coming back from her mother's, but that's all that happened–she soon put me in me place. And I'm going to tell you something, right now I'm going to tell you something. If it hadn't been for our Davie the tale would have been different, for I would have taken her–and I could have–and I'd have left you high and dry. Twenty years I've sat like a mute under your tongue, but now it's finished. So you know.'

May was standing within an arm's length of him. She looked up at him, her thin face wearing a twisted smile, and her voice sounded deceptively normal when she said, 'That's where you're wrong, John. Things are only beginning; you forget about Kathleen.'

'You can do nothing there; Kathleen isn't mine.'

'Can you prove it?' The smile slid from her face. 'If you went on your bended knees at this moment I wouldn't believe you, nor would anybody else. You've always been very fond . . . fond, that's a light term for your feeling for Kathleen, isn't it? You liked her better than you did your own son. You've never had much use for Paul, have you? Oh no. But Kathleen looks like her mother, doesn't she, and she takes after you, doesn't she? There's nothing of Davie in her, but you stick out a mile. Helter-skelter, never stay still. That's Kathleen . . . just like her father, eh?'

'I tell you you're barking up the wrong tree.' John's voice, although loud, sounded weary.

'I don't think so. In fact I'm sure I'm not.' May was talking in a conversational tone now. 'If your dear Sarah had nothing to hide, why didn't she bring this all out at the trial; it would have helped her, she would have gained sympathy, a woman who had been blackmailed for years. But no, she was frightened because she knew that if she opened her mouth the cat would be out of the bag. As Paul said, Kathleen's birthday is on the fourth of October. You haven't to do much counting up from the first of January have you?'

'Look!' He was bawling now. 'You can talk until you're sick and you'd still be wrong. I tell you . . .'

'You can tell me nothing. Now you listen to me.' May's tone changed yet again; her face was tight, bitter. 'As I see it, your dear Sarah took a longer stretch than she need have done just to save Kathleen knowing the truth. Well . . . now listen hard, big fellow, because if you make a mistake it'll be a pity. If you think you're going to wait for her coming out you're mistaken, because if you as much as go and visit her, just once, I'll go across that back lane and I'll tell our dear Kathleen who her daddy is. You know, there are more ways of killing a cat than drowning it. And just think how Dan would take this bit of news . . . and your Dad. Oh, you wouldn't care what your mother thought, in fact you'd like to hit your mother with this, but not the other two. Oh no, you'd like to keep their good opinion, wouldn't you? All men together.' She stepped back quickly as John advanced towards her. 'Don't try it,' she said. 'Don't try it, I warn you.'

They stood staring at each other, the hate like molten lead between them. It was May who moved first. She turned from him, showing her disdain by giving him her back, and as she reached the door she looked over her shoulder towards him and said evenly. 'The way business is going we want a better address, don't you think? I'll look for a place down Westhoe in Shields, it's nice down there. And by the way, if you should get the idea into your head to let the business go flat to spite me, remember it would be a pity to think that your dear Sarah had sacrificed herself in vain, wouldn't it?'

When the door had closed on her, John turned slowly and went to the window, and, looking out across the back lane, he gazed down into Sarah's yard, into Sarah's kitchen window, and he said aloud: 'All this because of those few minutes that night. God Almighty! First her going through it, and now me. But I'm not Sarah. How long can I hold out? God Almighty!'

BOOK SIX

Chapter One

It was 1957 and Dan's birthday, and he was fifty-seven years old. He stood appraising himself in the wardrobe mirror. He was still upright and his figure hadn't fattened. He patted his flat tummy–he was too much on his feet to get any flesh on there. His hair, although quite thick, was a grisly grey, and there was no bright twinkle in his eyes now. They had a serious look, as had the whole of his face. He remarked to himself on the seriousness of his expression and thought, You've got to feel light inside. What you feel like inside always tells. But the mirror presented him with a smart, well-set-up man, a prosperous man. But what, he asked himself, was prosperity if there was nobody to share it? Well, things would be different within a week. Yes, the week ahead would be a very telling time. Now he must get going; he did not want to keep Kathleen and the Sunday dinner waiting.

He went out of the bedroom and stepped into a large carpeted hallway. He walked across it and into a sitting-room. It looked an extremely comfortable and well-furnished room. He put a wire guard round the fire, went to the window, and looked down into the main street for a moment. It looked utterly deserted, as a shopping thoroughfare always does on a Sunday. Unconsciously he arranged the velvet curtains; then with one last look round the room he went out into the hall again, took his overcoat out of an oak wardrobe standing near the door, adjusted his trilby hat, and picked up a pair of fur-lined leather gloves from a small table. Going out, he locked the door and descended the carpeted stairs to the street, and there, getting into his car, he drove the two miles to the Fifteen Streets.

There was another car parked outside of the house he now thought of as Kathleen's. He drew up behind it, but when he alighted he did not go into Kathleen's, but went around the corner and into the back door of number one.

Mary Hetherington was setting the table for the dinner. She turned from a sideboard drawer with some cutlery in her hand and, looking casually at Dan, said, 'You're early.'

'Yes, I am a bit. Stan out?'

'He's next door.'

Dan stood with his back to the fire. He held his hat and his gloves in his hand and watched his sister laying three places at the table–May always came over to dinner on a Sunday now.

She went into the scullery next and filled a glass jug with water, and when she returned and set the jug on the corner of the table and straightened the knives again, she said, 'Well?'

'Well, what?'

'Well, what have you arranged? You know what I mean.'

Dan remained silent, looking at this woman as he had looked at her over the years wondering how he ever came from the same source. She was seventy now and still upright–her tightly-laced stays helped here. But there was no help for her face; her skin looked like old Chinese silk that had cracked here and there where it had been folded. Her eyes still held the alert quality; that had never diminished, for it had been fed continuously on bitterness.

'You're not bringing her back here?'

'Where else can she go?'

'I don't care where she goes, you know that, but I'm warning you not to bring her back here.'

'Her home's next door, her daughter is next door, you seem to forget that.'

'I forget nothing, nothing.'

'No, you don't, Mary, you forget nothing. Forgiveness isn't in you, and the odd thing about it is that she had never done a damn thing to you.'

'What! What do you say? And, by the way, I'll thank you not to swear in my house, And as to her not doing a thing to me, how can you stand there and say that? You know she ruined this family. She broke it up.'

'She did no such thing.'

Mary Hetherington drew herself up. 'I'm not going to argue with you, you've always been soft. But I warn you, if you bring that woman next door it will mean trouble. You wouldn't want Kathleen's life to be broken, too, would you?'

'There's no fear of that.'

'Just you wait and see.' She nodded warningly at him. 'They should never have let her out of a sudden like this, she should have been made to do the full fifteen years.'

Dan pulled the rim of his hat through his hands, then, moving from the fireplace, he walked past her. He did not exchange any form of farewell, and he went out, closing the door none too gently.

No sooner had he gone than Mary Hetherington was out of the room and up the stairs and into the back bedroom, and there she stood to the side of the curtain watching him crossing the lane to May's back door. She saw him go up the yard and into the house, and as she stood waiting she glanced at the little clock on the mantelshelf. When he came out she looked at the clock again. He had been in there nearly fifteen minutes. She smiled to herself, a tight, satisfied smile, then went out of the room and down the stairs.

Meals at Kathleen's were never talkative or boisterous affairs. Kathleen had lost the art of laughter ten years ago, but today's meal was even quieter than usual. Dan sat opposite to Kathleen, and to her right sat her husband,

Michael, and to her left, in a high chair and close to her, was a two-year-old baby girl.

Kathleen was nearly twenty-seven but she looked older, she looked a woman well into her thirties. Her face over the years had taken on a resemblance to Sarah's, but she had not Sarah's expression. There was a solemnesss about Kathleen's face now, an innate sadness printed on it. The look had been there for years. At first it had not been permanent; the day it became permanent was the day that Paul had been ordained a priest. That was over three years ago. Three months from that particular day she married Michael MacKay.

Michael, Dan thought, was a good fellow, and in a way Kathleen was lucky. Feeling as she did, and acting at times as if she wasn't aware of anybody, it said a great deal for him that he never lost patience with her. It was well for her that he had loved her for a long time–ever since he was a lad, in fact. At the same time Dan thought it was a bit hard on him.

From the day they had taken Sarah from the house to the magistrates' court at Clervaux Terrace in Jarrow Dan had made it his home and for over six years he had looked after Kathleen, right until the time Michael took over. On that day he had moved to the shop. Braving Mary Hetherington's tongue, he had taken his belongings and gone up to his new home. And now he held pleasant memories of two peaceful years with Mrs Campbell. But since the old lady had died over a year ago he had lived on his own. He didn't like living on his own and he had for some time now been hoping to change this state of affairs. But, like everything else, the outcome of this hope remained to be seen.

The meal over, he sat with Jessica on his knee making her laugh while Kathleen and Michael washed-up the dinner things. Then Michael took the child upstairs to bed, and Kathleen and he were alone together. Having so much to say, they said nothing waiting for the other to make an opening. Kathleen busied herself in putting the room to rights, placing the modern dining chairs, with the different-coloured leather seats, under the table, pushing the G-Plan armchairs into different positions. There was not a piece of the old furniture to be seen throughout the house. The whole place had been re-decorated and re-furnished.

At last Kathleen came and sat down by Dan, and, putting her hands between her knees, she looked at him as she said, 'How do you think it will work out, Uncle Dan?'

'We'll just have to wait and see, Kathleen, that's all.'

'I'm terrified.'

'What is there to be terrified about? She's your mother, remember that, and a good woman. A good woman, Kathleen. I've told you again and again, Sarah is a good woman.'

'If I only didn't believe . . .' Kathleen's head dropped down to her chest.

'But you've got to believe it, Kathleen, because it's the truth, I believe it. I know your Uncle John, I know him inside out. I tell you he almost went on his bended knees to prove it to me. You know he was fond–oh, more than fond of your father; there was a strong tie between them, a strong, strong tie, and your Uncle John admitted that if David hadn't been your father he would have gone off with your mother, but . . . well, he, in his own way . . . well, he loved your father, he couldn't bring himself to hurt him. . . . David was your father, Kathleen.'

She looked at him, saying quietly, 'You know, Uncle Dan, I think I could be happy now if I could just believe it. I've tried, but I keep remembering . . . I keep remembering my Uncle John and . . . and him always being over here, and how he used to look at her . . . and Aunt May's jealousy, and her not liking me.'

'Look, Kathleen, we've been over all this before, it's old ground; but I say again, what your Uncle John felt for your mother we all felt in one way or another. She was a very fetching woman and she didn't go out of her way to attract anybody. She wasn't smart-tongued like your Aunt May, or clever in any way; she was just nice and kind . . . loving, sort of. And then the way she looked . . . you look like her, you know, Kathleen.'

Kathleen was on her feet. 'Don't say that, Uncle Dan.'

'I'm going to say it. And don't take that tone, Kathleen, it's a compliment.'

Kathleen turned from him and walked to the kitchen window, and from there she said, 'About Wednesday–will you pick me up? I'm leaving Jessica with Michael's mother. I'm not telling Grannie I'm going, she'd go mad.'

'I've got it all arranged. I'm picking up your Aunt Phyllis at half-past nine, that should get us there in time.'

Dan was standing behind Kathleen now, with his hand on her shoulder. 'Don't worry, my dear; things are going to turn out all right. Believe me.' His tone was emphatic. 'Just believe me. And try and remember that she'll be in a state too. She's been away for ten years, she'll be changed. She's likely as fearful of coming back as you are of her coming.'

Kathleen did not reply to this, but said, 'That tea. I suppose it's kind of them to want to welcome her back like that, but having a tea in the street and putting flags out, because that's what they'll do down there. You would still think they lived in the ramshackle houses the way they go on. And when me grannie knows she'll be wild . . . wild.'

'Well, there's nothing we can do about that, it's their way of expressing their feelings.'

'But she didn't know hardly any of them from the bottom end, not for years.'

He patted her shoulder, saying, 'It'll all be over this time next week. Everything will have settled down by then. You'll see, you'll see.

'This time next week.' Kathleen muttered the words to herself as she looked up over the chimney-pots and into the sky. She had tried to readjust her life, she had tried to close the wound, but on Wednesday, between her grannie, her Aunt May, and her mother, the wound would not only be torn open again–she would be rent apart.

Chapter Two

Before she had done a month of her sentence Sarah's mind came down from the plane to which it had escaped: time had a different meaning now. She got up with it early in the morning, in the mornings that always seemed like night, and the daytime was broken up into pieces of time; pieces when she ate colourless food, when she walked round a square; when she worked in a laundry; when she ate again, and worked again, and ate again, and then went to bed while it was still day. Nevertheless she longed for this time when she could go to bed, not to sleep or rest but to be by herself.

That was the most difficult thing: getting herself used to time, time being used in a different way from that in which she had used it before. Everything inside was connected with time; everybody was doing time. But she found you can get used to anything; so she got used to using time. She had to, as she had to get used to not being nauseated with the smell, the smell of urine. In the block it permeated the air; even in the laundry, where there was soap and water, the smell still hung around some of the women. She liked few of the women; there was one, but she went out after six years. Her name was Gladys and she had liked reading. She had looked after the library. It was because of her that Sarah got the job helping in the library for an hour after tea. So for over six years she had accepted time. It would be thought she hadn't much choice, yet some didn't accept it, and for them life was a living hell.

But her acceptance ended one visiting day when Dan had said to her from across the table, 'Kathleen is going to get married.' Her heart had come alive at that moment. But she didn't know for how short a time. Kathleen hadn't been to visit her for four months, and she had written her only short, terse letters. She was at work and she couldn't get off, she had a cold. Then Dan, his head bowed, had said, 'I've got to tell you this, Sarah. She's marrying Michael MacKay.'

She had mouthed the name without a sound, then asked gropingly, 'Why, Dan, why?' and he had to say to her:

'Paul has become a priest.'

'A priest!' It was the first time she had heard anything about Paul and the priesthood. She had been hurt sore that he had never been near her, nor yet had written her a scribe of the pen, she couldn't understand it. But then there were lots of things she couldn't understand, such as Kathleen's aloof attitude. Her daughter seemed to have turned against her. . . . This was torture.

Her mind dizzying as it had been wont to do, she asked again, 'But why, Dan why?'

He had been forced to tell her the truth, the truth as Paul thought he had heard it, and, thinking she might as well know the rest, he went on to tell her of John, how he had left May and gone to live in Newcastle. But he did not tell her that he was living with a girl young enough to be his daughter, he couldn't tell her that. Nor that on the day he had broke away from May she gone over to Kathleen's and told her why Paul was becoming a priest. There are things you cannot get the tongue to speak.

But Sarah had not been concerned at what was happening to John or May, she could only think of Kathleen and Paul. Paul a priest! It was unbelievable. Just because he had heard what was said that day, that terrible but fading day. Why was God doing this to her? Perhaps he was answering Father O'Malley's prayer and wreaking more vengeance on her. Perhaps, she thought, it was meant that she should go through all this just so Paul could become a priest. But no. No. She wouldn't like that. She had given up thinking like a Catholic, she was no longer a Catholic. She was no longer anything that was connected with a God. She was just no longer anything. She didn't want to go on. She was finished. Paul a priest! A Protestant, with his mother and father bigots. Paul a priest! And then it had penetrated through her mind, the real reason–half-brother and sister. Oh, Kathleen! Oh, poor, poor Kathleen! It was all crazy . . . mad, mad. Who was causing this to happen, anyway? God? . . . God was mad.

It was from this time that she spent three months in the prison hospital, but she could not die. Her body, although thin and a shadow of its former self, would not give her up. Her mind was ready any moment, and it did its best to force her release, but it failed. And when she left the hospital they did not put her back into the laundry; her time was spent between the sewing-room and the library. And through this change she got to know, and in fact became friendly with a warder called Peters. Her life was now lived on a level plane, orderly, monotonous. Until one day, without any warning, she was told she was going to be released.

It was seven o'clock on a Monday morning when Sarah stood with one foot outside the prison gates. The officer said to her, 'Will you be all right? I think you should have told them it was today.'

Sarah shook her head. 'I would rather it was this way.' She spoke in an undertone as if afraid of disturbing someone.

'Goodbye, Mrs Hetherington, and good luck.' The officer was smiling and holding out her hand, and Sarah took it. 'Thank you,' she said. 'You've been kind.' Then she turned away.

She did not feel the strangeness of being in the open for the first moment because she was thinking. . . . Mrs Hetherington, she was . . . Mrs for the first time in years. She was Mrs. Then she looked across the road. The other side looked far away. When her legs began to tremble she said to herself, It's no different to walking inside, and she kept on. The clothes that she was wearing felt strange, loose, as if she had no body to support them. She looked down at herself. She was so thin now. All except her bust. Her bust hadn't altered so much. The officer had joked with her and said she had a figure like Marilyn Monroe. Were people looking at her? No, no, they weren't. She passed a woman and glanced at her, but the woman was looking ahead. She felt surprised at this. Wasn't there some kind of a stamp on her to tell people where she had come from? When she reached the corner of the road she had the desire to run back and bang on the prison gates. She felt frightened; she was by herself and she hadn't been by herself for a long, long time. She wanted someone near, not to touch, oh no, but just to know that they were near. . . . But yes . . . yes, she did . . . she did want someone to touch, a hand to hold. She had been silly, telling them it was Wednesday she was coming out. She should have told them it was today. But she couldn't face a street tea, anything but face a street tea and a sea of curious faces. She had told the warden that and the warden had understood. Dan said people were kind and this was their way of showing their kindness. Perhaps . . . but she didn't want this kind of kindness. Doubtless they had deluded themselves into thinking that in getting up a street tea and a jollification for her coming home they were doing her a kindness, but what they were really doing was giving themselves a bit of cheap sensation. She was not surprised at her own insight into human nature, for, as the idleness of the dole years ago had turned many a man towards self-education, so had her years of confinement and daily dealing with books tutored her mind a little, at least, to a certain stage of analytical reasoning. It had happened unobtrusively, so unobtrusively that she was unaware of the change. And yet she knew she was different, her way of thinking was different. She felt that she would never know fear as she had known it before; in a way it had overstepped itself. But being afraid, and facing a table full of laughing faces and questing eyes set out in the open street, was a different thing. If it were to rain they would hold it in the factory hall; they were prepared for all contingencies. But wherever it was held they would have provided the opportunity to gape and question. . . . 'What's it like in there, Sarah? What did they do to you? Did you ever get solitary? Come on, woman, open up, you're among friends.' And she was not exaggerating in imagining the trend the reception would take. She knew what some of them at the bottom end were like, and it would doubtless have been these very people who had proposed the welcome home tea, and their every probe would be in good part. Oh yes, everything would be in good part; it was a favourite cover-up for curiosity, the term, good part. And if she didn't take everything in good part, she would be damned. . . . She couldn't have stood it. . . .

The officer had told her the way to the station. She turned right down the street, then left, and left again, across a square, up another street, and there it was, the station. She didn't remember seeing it before, but she must have seen it, at least once, when they brought her here from the magistrates' court in Jarrow. 'You are committed in custody to await trial at Durham Assizes.'

The man at the ticket office said, 'What do you say, missis? Speak up.'

'A single to Newcastle.'

'A single to Newcastle . . . there you are.'

She put the change in her bag. It was funny having a bag hanging from your arm, it felt awkward. She thought people must think how stiffly she held her arm with the bag on it.

She had the carriage to herself all the way to Newcastle, and she did not stand up and walk from one window to the other taking her fill of both views, but sat quietly in the corner, her back straight, her head turned towards the changing scenery. The trees looked bonny, oh so bonny. The sun turned their browning leaves to glittering gold and bronze. She realized she was looking at colour. She had missed colour; oh yes, she had missed colour. She had always kept her home colourful. Cushion covers made from cheap remnants, curtains with patterns on, never Nottingham lace curtains. . . . How would the kitchen look? She turned her mind deliberately from the kitchen, saying to herself, One thing at a time. You'll get the bus outside Newcastle station, it isn't likely that the stop will be changed; and then you'll get off at the corner. . . . One thing at a time.

The bus stop was changed. 'Which part of Jarrow do you want to go?' said a man in a peaked cap.

'The Fifteen Streets,' she said.

'Oh, down that far? Oh well then, you can get either the one that will take you the Robin Hood way, or there's the other that goes straight through the town. The town one, I think, that's the one you want. And it's in, look, over there.'

Sarah thanked him; then boarded the bus, taking a seat right up at the front.

'Which part of the Fifteen Streets do you want?' the conductor asked her. 'It's a long walk if you get off at the wrong end.'

'The . . . top end?' She put this as a question and he replied, 'Oh yes. Well, I'll tell you when to get off.' Evidently he thought of her as someone who didn't know where she was going.

And from Hebburn onwards Sarah saw that she didn't know where she was going. The immediate landscape had changed; the places which she had last seen as open stretches of flat land were now covered with houses, dozens of houses, hundreds of houses. Here and there, she would think to herself, Yes, I remember that; that is the way to the ferry; that is the way to the church near Dee Street. We should be nearing the church bank now, and the park, and the quay corner.

At the quay corner she saw the church of St Paul. It looked so much smaller than she remembered; it looked lost, forgotten. She felt akin to it. Then the bus conductor came up to her and said, 'This is your stop , missis.' She followed him down the bus without looking to see where she was and the next minute she was on the main road. From the pavement she looked up at him puzzled, and he said, 'This is the top end, the top end of the Fifteen Streets. . . . All right?'

She nodded her head slowly at him, and he rang the bell and the bus sped away. But he paused a while to look at her.

She stood looking across the road. He had put her off at the wrong end, he had put her off at the bottom end. But it was a different bottom end from when she had last seen it. Then there had been an open space where the four streets had stood before the night of the raid. Now before her were stretched not only four streets but street after street of new houses all with little gardens in front and bigger gardens behind. She walked slowly across the road, and was at the end of the first street. There was a fancy board supported by two stout wooden pillars at the corner, and on it was written: Churchill Street. She began to walk past the corner of the streets going in the direction the bus had taken. The second street was called Eisenhower Avenue. This was about where they had lived, she thought. The following street was Montgomery Terrace, on and on; Wavell Avenue, Laurence Street, all new streets, all named after men of war. Here and there, there were children playing in back gardens, but except in the distance she saw no adults. Being nearly two o'clock, the men had returned to work and the women were taking it easy for an hour, things seemingly hadn't altered that much. On and on, slowly, towards the top end she went. And then abruptly the new houses ceased and she could see ahead four of the original streets, and the contrast gave her a shock. Like beggars lying at the rich man's gate the four streets lay at the foot of the new estate, and they looked dirty, old, and shrunken. Her step became slower. She knew now why the bus conductor had put her off at the other end of the streets. The situation of the place had turned a complete somersault; the top end had now become the bottom end. Yet among the people in the new houses were those who still thought along the lines of street teas. Places, she realised, could be altered or renewed in a week, a month, a year, but not people. It took the accumulated years of a generation and perhaps another to alter people, turn them from their inbred ways. The Fifteen Streets would be the Fifteen Streets until this generation died, that was certain. It was only the status of the Streets themselves that had turned the somersault.

The sight of Camelia Street staggered her. This was the place she had once invested with royal status. Here she had lived in the glory of exclusiveness. For years she had thanked God at night in her prayers for depositing her at this end.

In the middle of the street two motor-cycles leaned against the kerb, their new brightness forcing its way through the shadow cast by the dismal houses. There were also three cars standing in the roadway, one of them outside her own door–she still thought of it as her own door. The car would be Michael's. Fancy him having a car; fancy anybody who lived here having a car.

She was standing at the door now, her hand half-raised to the knocker. But before she touched it she gripped the front of her coat and shook herself. Now then, steady, steady . . . take it easy, one thing at a time.

When the door opened, there stood Kathleen. Sarah watched her mouth drop into a loose gape, then close on a gasp: 'Wh . . . why,' she stammered. 'I thought . . . What brought you? Who's brought you?' She shook her head wildly, and then, pulling the door further open, she added, 'Come in.'

It was as if she were bidding a stranger enter, and, like a stranger, Sarah walked into what had been her home, for immediately she crossed the threshold the change sprang at her. She would have had to be blind not to take it in in one glance.

Kathleen walked sideways along the little passage through the front room and into the kitchen; she had her hand extended as if for guidance, but she didn't touch her mother.

In the kitchen they stood looking at each other, Kathleen with her hands joined at her throat. The action was painful to Sarah, for it gave away Kathleen's distress.

'You said Wednesday.'

'Yes, yes, I know, Kathleen, but I . . . I couldn't bear them making a tea and all that.'

'Oh.' Kathleen jerked her chin up as if in understanding, and then she said, 'Sit down. Why, sit down.' She pulled a chair hastily forward. It was one of the coloured-seated dining chairs and Sarah looked at it before she sat on it.

'I'll tell Michael. He's on night shift, but he would be getting up shortly.'

'Don't wake him, there's plenty of time.' Sarah was still speaking in that peculiar undertone she had come to use over the years.

'Oh, I'll tell him, I'll tell him.'

Kathleen almost ran from the room and she went up the stairs calling loudly, 'Michael! Michael!'

Sarah listened now to Kathleen's quick steps overhead. She heard the murmur of her speaking rapidly, warningly, and she bowed her head. How was she going to bear it? . . . One thing at a time, one thing at a time. Once today was over it wouldn't be so bad. She reminded herself that she was sitting in her own kitchen, she was home. But was she? She raised her head and looked about her. There wasn't a stick of furniture that she could recognise as hers. She experienced a new kind of pain.

When Kathleen came down the stairs there were footsteps behind her, and Sarah turned her head to look at the man entering the room. He was dressed in trousers and shirt; his sandy hair was ruffled, and his eyes still full of sleep, but she recognised Michael MacKay. He hadn't changed much. He was older of course.

'Well, hello, there,' he said.

'Hello, Michael,' she answered.

'We weren't expecting you the day. You should have told us, coming all that way by yourself.'

He was trying to be kind, not to show his surprise, not to let her see that he was put out in any way. 'Have you had a cup of tea?' he said.

'No, not yet.' She smiled towards Kathleen.

'We'll make one in a jiffy,' he said and went into the scullery.

Yes, Michael was nice. As Dan said, Kathleen could have done a lot worse. But Michael wasn't Paul. . . . Oh, Paul . . . Paul. But she mustn't think of Paul. . . . One thing at a time.

'How's the baby?' she said, looking up at Kathleen.

'Oh, she's fine, she's asleep.' She made for the door again. 'I'll bring her down.'

'Kathleen.' Sarah's voice halted her. 'Don't . . . don't disturb her, there'll be plenty of time.'

'Yes, yes, of course.' After a pause Kathleen came back towards the table, and, standing before her mother, she said, 'Take your hat off . . . take your things off.'

Sarah reached up and slowly she removed her hat. Then, standing up, she took off her coat. As she put her hand up to smooth back her hair in which there was still not a thread of grey Michael entered the kitchen. He had a tray in his hand and he stopped dead for a moment and looked at Sarah. He saw a woman so like his wife that the resemblance startled him. When she'd had her coat and hat on he hadn't seen it so clearly, but now he was seeing them together. It was a strange experience. The only difference was that the older woman had a better figure and a softer face. Yes . . . yes, he had to admit that to himself. Even after all she had gone through, and she must have had a packet, she didn't look hard or bitter. Not that Kathleen looked hard or bitter; but there was a set look about her face that didn't show in her mother's. He sighed and smiled. Things wouldn't be too bad. Better than he'd thought. Now that her mother was out Kathleen might forget about the past. He hoped to God she would, anyway. 'There you are.' He placed the tray on the table. 'Nothing like a cup of char.' As he poured out the tea he looked at Sarah and said, 'We'll have to get your room ready, but that won't take long, it only needs the bed putting up. We can take the cot out any time.'

'But'–Sarah shook her head–'the little boxroom will do me. Don't move anything.'

'There isn't a boxroom any more.' Kathleen was looking at the fire. 'Michael made it into a bathroom.'

'Oh!' Sarah glanced at Michael. 'That's nice. Oh, it's nice to have a bathroom.'

They were sitting, the three of them, drinking their tea when silence attacked them, the awkward horrible silence that yells aloud, and Sarah was just about to break it, she was just about to say, 'Don't worry, I won't be in your way. I'll get a job and then perhaps I'll find a little place of my own.' That is what she was going to say when the back door opened and Kathleen jerked out of her chair as if she had been shot.

There was the sound of steps in the scullery. The kitchen door opened and Mary Hetherington entered the room, and perhaps for the first time in years she was caught off her guard, and it registered on her face which showed utter and blank surprise.

Sarah's heart was beating wildly. This was the moment she had dreaded more so than entering her old home again and the meeting with Kathleen. Yet she had never imagined herself being actually confronted by her mother-in-law. Being passed by her in the street, yes; ignored, yes. At the same time being made vitally aware of her hate and loathing, but she had never imagined her walking into the kitchen like this. She had come in as if she were used to coming in. . . . Yes, undoubtedly she was used to coming in.

Michael, trying to smooth over the tense moment, said, 'Come and sit down, Gran. I've just made some tea. Have a . . .'

Mary Hetherington, indicating with a swift movement of her arm towards him that she wished him to be quiet, he became quiet. His voice trailed away and he looked sharply at his wife, but Kathleen was looking at no one. She had her head down. It looked as if she were rejecting something, something shameful.

'So you've come!' Mary Hetherington's voice was thick, like someone who was gone in drink. 'How soon are you going?'

Sarah did not rise to her feet nor did she made any retort, but she sat, her stomach sick, looking up at this old woman, and she saw that she was old, and her hate was old, but strong still, stronger if anything. Sarah could see it all clearly. This hate-filled woman had taken Kathleen under her wing, not with the desire of protecting her, but of separating her from herself, from contamination with herself. that's how she would think of it.

'Look, Gran.' Michael was tentatively appealing again, and again he was silenced by a more violent wave of the hand now as Mary Hetherington repeated, 'When are you going? I asked you a question.'

Sarah had got out of the habit of talking. You didn't talk in there, you listened, and you only spoke when you were asked a question. She had been asked a question and now she forced herself to answer it. She said softly, 'I've come home. . . .'

Before Sarah's lips settled on the last word Mary Hetherington charged in, crying, 'Home! This is no longer your home. You gave up this home ten years ago.'

Sarah, her voice still level, her words still spoken in that peculiar undertone, said, 'The rent book's still in my name. Dan said . . .'

'Dan said! Dan said!' There was scorn in Mary Hetherington's voice. 'I know what Dan said. What he doesn't know is that Michael had it transferred to his name two years ago. And look round you. Is there a stick of yours here? No, not so much as would fill a matchbox. Your home! Now again I say to you . . . When are you going?'

'Gran . . . Gran, stop it. I tell you, stop it! Leave her alone; it's my affair, our affair.' Kathleen was confronting her grandmother now, swallowing between each word, daring to oppose this woman who had imposed her rule on her.

'You leave this to me, Kathleen. Unless you want your life ruined and Michael in trouble . . . because let me tell you—' The old woman leant towards Kathleen and wagged her finger at her. 'As sure as God's in heaven she'll have Michael. She'll have your husband; no man is safe within a mile of her. They're never too old, they're never too young. I'm speaking from experience.'

Sarah rose to her feet, not hastily; she just rose from the chair, as if she were being pulled up by a mechanical device. She was trembling all over. She had a desire to cry, but she could neither cry nor speak; she could just stand, her hands on the table looking towards this hate-corroded being.

'You don't believe me?' Mary Hetherington lifted her eyes from Kathleen and brought them to Michael. 'I'll bet all I own this moment that within a few weeks, yes, within a few weeks she'll have set her cap at you and you won't know where you are.'

'Now look, Gran, stop talking like that. Let up. There's a limit.' Michael was obviously embarrassed and he wagged his head, his gaze directed towards the floor.

'You want proof . . . I'll give it to you.' The old woman swung round and, snatching at the curtain, lifted it into a loop, and as she did so Kathleen cried, 'No, no, Gran . . . don't bring Aunt May over . . . please!' She went to pull the curtain from her grandmother, but the old woman pushed her aside.

'Far better bring May across than have your home broken up. Leave it alone, I want May here. This woman took your Aunt May's man . . . my son, when she was only married a few weeks to my other son. She takes everything . . . everything with trousers on.'

Years ago Sarah would have thought, She's talking like one of the women at the bottom end; now she could only think, I'll have to go . . . I'll have to go . . . I can't bear it. Something will happen if I don't get out. Oh, my God!

She turned her head wildly now in the direction of the couch where lay her hat, coat, and bag, and then her head was jerked back with startling suddenness to her mother-in-law again. Mary Hetherington was glaring at Kathleen and saying, 'She deprived my son, my David, of fatherhood. I've told you what she did, but you only half believed me. But let May confront her with it; yes, let May con . . .'

'Be quiet! You evil creature . . . be quiet!'

They were all looking at Sarah now. A different Sarah. Not the Sarah that Mary Hetherington remembered, nor the Sarah that Kathleen remembered as her mother, nor yet was there any connection with the Sarah who had sat so timidly before them only a few minutes earlier. The tall, pale, wide-eyed woman before them had a majestic bearing, a towering majestic bearing; there was no aggressiveness in her attitude, yet it held them all still. She stared at her mother-in-law for a full minute in silence before she began to speak again.

Her voice too was different now, the tone strong, the words crisp, yet quiet. 'I'm not going to let you get away with this. Oh no, not with this. From the day we met you've hated me; you've sent your venom and your spleen through that wall there at me'–she pointed–'until the very bricks were tense with the atmosphere you created. You hated me because David loved me; you hated the idea that I could make him happy. Me!' She pressed her finger gently into her breast. 'The scum from the bottom end. That's how you thought of me, wasn't it? And you couldn't bear the thought that I'd brought your favourite son alive; you couldn't bear the thought that in my kitchen your menfolk found peace from your nagging. That's all they came in here for, just to get away from your nagging. They were sick of listening to the gaffer of God.' She did not fire a barbed shaft here by adding, 'That was David's name for you'–but went on, 'From the moment I came into your life, you have tried to ruin me; every bit as much as my father did, you tried . . .'

'How . . . how you can stand there and speak the name of your . . .'

Sarah cut Mary Hetherington's words off with an uplifting movement of her head: 'I dare speak his name. I have paid for what I did . . . I'm free . . . and I dare speak his name. He doesn't trouble my conscience, he never has. Let that horrify you.' She paused for a second before going on. 'But that's beside the point. . . . As I said, there's one thing you're not going to do. You're not going to burn that last lie into my daughter's mind.' Sarah now switched her eyes to Kathleen, and her voice had a ring of command in it. 'Kathleen,' she said, 'listen to me . . . listen closely to me. I never once went with your Uncle John . . . you understand? NEVER ONCE. Not once. . . . Your Uncle John loved me. Once he kissed me, once on New Year's morning, 1930, near the bottom end. I'd been to first-foot my mother. He came over with me because everybody else was joining in the jollification, and he kissed me and we talked. That was all. And my father heard what we talked about. Well, you know all about that part of it. The next time was the morning he marched to London with the hunger marchers. Neither his wife nor his mother would go to see him off; he asked me if I would, and that morning I kissed him . . . on the cheek. That, Kathleen, is the story of the vileness between your Uncle John and me. And that, when you sum it all up, is what I've done time for.'

Kathleen was looking at Sarah, staring up into her face. As they once used to look at each other and laugh, now they were looking at each other, but there was no laughter between them. As Sarah stared into the sad pleading countenance of her daughter she knew that she had to do something to give the seal of truth to her words. Her eyes flicked from Kathleen's face to the wall. There, hanging on it, was a modern version of the picture of the Sacred Heart of Jesus. Like everything else, it was new.

It was the only holy picture in the room; likely it was Michael's choice, for he was a strong Catholic. She had never hung holy pictures in the house during her married life, but she remembered a similar one to this hanging in the kitchen when she was a child. The picture, although in a plain modern frame, held the same face of Christ, the same head and shoulders with the hand across the chest, palm up holding on it his bleeding heart, the blood dripping down through his fingers. She no longer believed in God or Jesus, or in any other symbol of the Catholic Church, but Kathleen did, and always would. With a swift movement she stepped to the wall and, lifting the picture by its string, brought it to Kathleen, and, laying it flat on one hand, she put the fingers of her other hand at the centre of the heart. But before she spoke she turned her eyes from Kathleen and fixed them on Mary Hetherington, and it was to her she said, 'I swear by the Sacred Heart of Jesus that what I have said is true.' Then, looking at Kathleen again, she said. 'David was your father, Kathleen.'

Sarah imagined she saw a cloud lift from Kathleen's face, leaving it a shade lighter. She turned from her now and hung the picture back on the wall. Then once again she looked at her mother-in-law. It was evident that Mary Hetherington had received a setback, but it was also evident that she wasn't beaten, and she showed this by renewing her attack almost immediately. With a deriding mirthless laugh, and addressing no one in particular, she cried, 'Well! You can take that bit of acting for what it's worth, and from where it comes. the Sacred Heart of Jesus . . . Huh! But the Lord isn't mocked. . . . Let me tell you, the mills of God grind slow, but they grind exceedingly small.'

'The mills of God!' Sarah repeated, shaking her head slowly as she looked now almost pityingly at the old woman. 'Though the mills of God grind slowly, yet they grind exceedingly small; though with patience he stands waiting, with exactness grinds he all.' Sarah sensed immediately that her mother-in-law had never heard the second line of the quotation, and in this moment she felt a strange feeling of superiority over her . . . Prison life had done something for her after all. It had introduced her to the library, from where she had gathered a small amount of knowledge, small because her need in this direction was small, for she had never aspired to education—not for herself; all she had aspired to was to talk properly, as she put it to herself, to be able to pass herself. She had always had this desire. Hadn't she longed for a dictionary when she was a girl just so that she could pass herself in conversation?

Her voice held an authoritative note as she repeated now, 'With exactness grinds he all. But not all . . . oh no, because you know what? He'd blind, your miller, blind and vindictive. Indiscriminately doling out pain and agony, that's your God. Well, all I hope is that His groping hands don't find you, for even now I don't wish you your just deserts. I just pity you. I always have, you know. . . .So there, you have it.'

With her bearing upright and dignified, she turned from the bitter face to the couch, and, picking up her coat, she put it on. And as she did so, Kathleen cried, 'Where you going? Oh, Mam, where you going?'

'Don't worry.' She smiled a sad faint smile at her daughter. 'Don't worry,' she said again. She put on her hat and picked up her bag. Then once again she turned, and, looking her mother-in-law straight in the eyes, she held her gaze for a moment before leaving the room. But she had just reached the in-between door when Mary Hetherington's voice sent its last bolt at her: 'And leave our Dan alone,' she cried. 'Him and May's going to be married. He spent enough years looking after you and yours, so let him do what he likes with the remainder of his life. Do that one decent thing at least.'

Her words halted Sarah, but only for a second. She went on through the front room into the passage. But when she reached the door Kathleen was behind her, and her hands on her Mother's shoulders, she turned her round and looked into her face for a moment before enfolding her in her arms, crying through her tears, 'Oh, Mam . . . Mam.'

'There, there. Don't upset yourself.'

'I believe you. I want you to know I believe you.'

Sarah remained quiet, and they clung together for a moment longer.

'Where you going?'

'Down to Phyllis's.'

'Look.' Kathleen was whispering now, her face close to Sarah's. 'We want to get a house away from here. We'll get fixed up, and you can come with us then. I would like it. Oh, I would, I would.'

'We'll see, we'll see. Don't worry.' Sarah opened the door, and Kathleen stood on the top step clinging on to her hand, saying, 'Oh, Mam. Oh, Mam.'

When there came to them from the kitchen the sound of raised voices, Sarah knew that May had arrived. She couldn't face May, she had stood all she could from them all. She knew she was going to break down, but she didn't want to upset Kathleen any more. She said hastily, 'Pop down to your Aunt Phyllis's when you can. Goodbye, my dear. Goodbye, my dear.'

Once again Kathleen had her arms around her; once again they clung together. Then Sarah was walking quickly away.

She could restrain the outlet no longer. When she reached the main road the tears were raining down her face, and she walked with her head down. The road between the Fifteen Streets and the New Buildings at East Jarrow was practically empty, but a woman who had passed her came running back after her, saying, 'What's the matter, lass? Are you in trouble?' Sarah did not look at the woman but shook her head. And the woman, walking by her side now, said, 'Can I help you, hinny?'

She raised her eyes to the woman and managed to say, 'No, thank you.'

As the woman looked at her her face crinkled slowly with recognition. But Sarah stopped her making any exclamation by waving her off with her hand; then she said, 'I'm sorry, just let me be,' and hurried on, leaving the woman standing on the pavement looking after her.

It was as she neared the New Buildings that the car drew up alongside the kerb. Michael had only a coat over his shirt and his hair was still ruffled. He said softly, 'Get in.' And she got in, still with her head bowed, the tears washing down her face.

Michael sat in deep embarrassed silence looking at her before starting the car, then he muttered, 'I'm sorry.' After a short while he asked quietly, 'Do you know the house?'

'It's in Laygate.'

He went through Tyne Dock, cut through the Deans, and they were in Laygate before she spoke again. 'She's an old devil.' He kept his eyes on the road as he spoke. 'I've had a job to keep me tongue meself. She's always trying to dominate Kathleen. I was goin' to try and get a job away last year in one of the Durham pits so we could move, but then things got a bit shaky. They're closing some pits down, so you've got to stay put. But I'll get a place out of it now. I told her afore I left just what I thought about her.'

There was an audible groan inside Sarah now. If Mary Hetherington wanted anything to confirm all she had said, Michael turning on her would have proved how right she had been about her daughter-in-law. She said now under her breath, 'It's the ice-cream café on the right.'

He helped her out of the car, then followed her into the shop.

Behind the counter stood a tall youth with Arab features and a fairish skin. And talking to him was a woman, a shortish, fat woman. She turned at the approach of customers, then her mouth springing open, she cried, 'Sarah! Why, Sarah! The day? You've come the day?' She was round the counter and they were holding each other. With tears running down her cheeks Phyllis kept repeating, 'Sarah! Oh, Sarah!' She held her at arm's length. 'Oh, lass, lass, am I glad to see you!' Becoming aware of the interest of the only two customers in the shop, she cried, 'Come on, away up out of this.' She went to pull Sarah forward; but pausing, she looked at her son, shouting to him as if he was streets away, 'You remember your Aunt Sarah, don't you?'

The young man smiled shyly. 'Yes . . . yes. Hello, Aunt Sarah.'

'Hello. . . .' Sarah didn't remember this one's name, and Phyllis cried, 'He's Joss, the youngest. Look at him, he's twice my size. But come on, come on. . . . Come on, Michael.' Her arm extended, she drew Michael after them towards a door at the end of the long café. And leading the way up the stairs and into a large living-room, expensively if not artistically furnished, she turned again to Sarah. And now like a child she stood in front of her and laid her head on her breast. 'Oh, Sarah, lass! Oh, Sarah!' she said softly.

Sarah was overcome with emotion. Here indeed was a welcome. In the home of her sister who had married an Arab, a man who had always slightly repulsed her. Though Ali had always treated her with kindess, she had never met him but she had thought, How could our Phyllis do it? But she knew that Ali too would welcome her, warmly, sincerely. Life was strange. Oh, indeed, life was strange.

'Here, let me get your things off.' Phyllis was now pulling at Sarah's coat. 'We'll have a slap-up meal the night. I had it all prepared, in me mind that is, for Wednesday. What happened?'

Briefly, Sarah told her.

'Aw well, I see your point.' As Phyllis nodded it was evident to Sarah that she didn't quite see eye to eye with her in the matter of a street party. If Phyllis had spoken the truth she would have said, 'Well, I think it was jolly decent of them to think of such a thing.'

'Sit down, Michael. Sit down. And we'll have a cup of tea. . . . Oh no we won't.' She raised her arm in a Hitler-like salute. 'We'll had something stronger to begin with, we will that.'

'Not for me, thanks all the same.' Michael smiled widely at her. 'I'm driving. And I've got to get back. In fact, I'd better be going. But I'll look in again.' He nodded his head quickly.

'Oh . . . Oh, all right then.' Phyllis didn't detain him, she wanted Sarah to herself.

'I'll be seeing you.' He was speaking to Sarah now in an undertone. 'I'll bring Kathleen down.'

'Will you, Michael? Oh, that's kind of you.'

'The night, if you like.'

'Please. Oh, thanks, Michael, thanks.'

'Don't you worry.' He nodded his head down to her. 'Things'll pan out, you'll see. Now don't you worry.' He stood looking at her sympathetically for a moment before going to the door where Phyllis was waiting. And as he passed her he motioned to her with his head, and Phyllis, picking up the signal, turned to Sarah and said, 'I'll just see him down the stairs in case he breaks his neck. They're a bit dark. Go in the kitchen and get that tea under way. Make yourself busy, for if I know you, you'd rather tea than anything else.'

The sisters smiled at each other. The years seemed to have slipped away. Phyllis went out and closed the door, and Sarah went into the kitchen.

Here again everything was expensive and overcrowded. An outsize fridge, an electric washing machine, an electric food mixer . . . the lot. And Sarah was glad, glad that Phyllis had the things that stood for success.

She had made the tea and had it in the living-room before Phyllis returned. Phyllis's face was straight as she entered the room, and, looking across at Sarah, she said quietly, 'Michael's told me. . . . You just got in about two? God, what a reception!' She came and stood close to Sarah, looking up into her face. 'But, anyway, you'd have likely got it on Wednesday, so it's over you. She's a sod. She's a sod of a woman if ever there's one. Sit down, lass, sit down and let's have a drink.' She pressed Sarah gently into an armchair. 'Will you have a drop of something in yours?' She pointed to the tea.

'No, Phyllis, no. Just a good cup of tea, that's all I want.' She smiled. 'I've longed for a real good cup of tea.'

Phyllis turned from her, and going to a cocktail-cabinet that stood in the corner of the room she brought out a bottle, saying as she did so, 'I could go up there and pulverise that old bitch. I could that, this very minute.' She came back to the table and poured a generous measure of whisky into her own tea. Then, sitting down, she raised her cup to Sarah, saying, 'Here's to us, lass. Here's to us. We'll never be parted again. At least not if I can help it. You can stay here until you die. You can have a job if you want it, or you can leave it alone, it's all up to you. You've got nothing to worry about, not any more.'

'Oh, Phyllis.' Her sister's kindness was almost as painful as her mother-in-law's attack. She said again, 'Oh, Phyllis.'

Phyllis took a long drink from her cup; then, putting it down on the table, she wiped her mouth with the pad of her thumb, and, looking across the room towards the window, she said thoughtfully, 'What I cannot understand is this business about Dan and May. Michael's just told me. I would have thought he had more sense.' She looked towards Sarah. But Sarah's head was bowed; she was staring down into her teacup. Then, lifting the cup to her lips, she took a long drink, as if something warm might soothe the new pain that had entered into her. . . . Dan and May. Well, why not? Dan deserved happiness; Dan had been so good to her; pure gold Dan had been all through. he had been so kind and attentive that she had come to think of Dan as her main support; she had imagined him supporting her, at least morally, through the first strange months of her release. She remembered the time when he had told her that Paul had become a priest and that Kathleen was going to marry Michael. She had given up then, yet all the time a hand had been holding hers . . . Dan's hand, and it was this hand that had pulled her back into existence. Whatever happened there would always be Dan. He had even said those words to her, time and again, time and again. When he had come to visit her he had said in some way, 'You've got me; you'll always have me; I'll always be there, Sarah.'

Phyllis was saying, 'I'm beginning to see the light. She wouldn't give John a divorce, not for years. That lass had three bairns to him; she was likely in a stew in case he'd walk out on her. You could never tell with a bloke like that. But he did try, I'll say that much for him. He tried again and again to get May to agree to a divorce, but she wouldn't bite. But then, just about eighteen months ago, she tells him to go ahead, and early on this year it was went through. And now he's married at last. Aw, Sarah!' Phyllis put her fingers over her mouth and shook her head slowly. 'This doesn't hurt you, does it, to know this?'

'No . . . no, Phyllis. Don't worry. Ten years is a long time; you have time to think in ten years. If you haven't got to worry about eating, or the rent, or firing, or light, you've got to put your mind to work in some way. I set mine the task of straightening up my thinking, and learning not to be afraid of being afraid.'

Phyllis lay back in the corner of the couch and her eyes narrowed as she looked at Sarah. And she said quietly, 'You've changed, you know; you've changed, Sarah.'

'I hope so,' said Sarah.

'Oh, I don't.' Phyllis was bending forward, her hand touching Sarah's knee. And Sarah covered it with her own as she said, 'Come on, it's your turn. Tell me about the family.'

'Oh, you know all about them; I've kept you informed over the years. Things are just the same. They're all set in the cafés. We did think about taking another, but Ali's biding his time; things are not as bright as they were a few years ago, you know. Oh, by the way, Ronnie's in Newcastle with the band this weekend.'

'Oh, is he? I'd love to hear him play.'

'It's funny that, isn't it?' said Phyllis. 'I mean how he became a pianist . . . all through that old four-pound piano. You remember?'

Sarah remembered . . . the day that she had kissed John, before he had marched off to London. And that dinner-time, to take her mind off things, she had told David that she was going down to see a second-hand piano, and to her amazement he had put his foot down and said he was having no piano in the house. 'Don't you see, it will only make matters worse,' he had said as he inclined his head towards the wall. She had written and told Phyllis. And Phyllis had written back to say it was all right, and that, anyway, Ali had bought the piano himself, he thought it would do for the bairn. And it had done for the bairn. Her second eldest son had become a first-class pianist.

'I would never have thought about a piano for meself, or any of us,' went on Phyllis. 'But there, it's fate; we had to have that piano because playing the piano is the only thing Ronnie lives for. . . .'

For the next hour they talked, as they always had done when they were together; they talked until the light went. Phyllis was pulling herself to her feet, saying, 'What about a little light on the subject,' when a voice called from the foot of the stairs, 'Mum! Mum!'

'What is it now?' Phyllis went to the door and, opening it, cried, 'What is it? Can't you manage without me for five minutes?'

'There's someone to see you. It's Mr Blythe.'

'Dan?' Sarah rose to her feet. Of a sudden she felt nervous, uncomfortable. For the first time in her life she didn't want to come face to face with Dan.

Dan paused in the doorway a moment, then came swiftly forward, and, taking her hands in his, said, 'Why, Sarah! You silly lass, you silly lass. You should have told me.'

'It's all right, Dan. It's better this way.'

'Better?' He withdrew his hands from hers and his face became solemn, almost stern. 'Not from what Michael told me on the phone. That woman will go off her head one of these days. . . . But perhaps it's all for the good . . . I mean you coming today, Sarah.'

'Yes, perhaps, Dan.'

He was standing away from her, looking at her now, his attitude slightly uneasy, and Phyllis, quick to sense this, jumped into the awkward breach by exclaiming loudly, 'Well, you'll stay to tea, Dan. Now, I'm not taking no.' She flapped her hand at him, although he had made no sign of refusal to her offer. Then going to the sideboard and taking out a cloth, she spread it over the dining-table, talking all the time.

'Well, this is a get-together, the first of many, I hope . . . and how's business, Dan?'

'Oh, pretty fair, you know, Phyllis, pretty fair.'

He was sitting to the side of Sarah now but not looking at her. He kept his eyes on Phyllis as he talked, and it would seem that the state of business at the moment was all that concerned him. 'We've all been making hay in the last few years, but it looks like the harvest's over. The dole circle's enclosing the Tyne again, I can feel it. I bet you can an' all in your weekly returns.'

'Well yes, you're right there, Dan. I won't say they're as shining as they were a couple of years ago.'

'No. And they won't be for a long time again. A grocer's shop is a money thermometer; I've seen it again and again. And what have we now? Unemployment, getting worse every week. It's bad when it hits the young 'uns, the lads just out of their time. Just the twenties over again: they do their apprenticeships and then they're stood off.'

'Still, you're not in the workhouse yet, Dan.' Phyllis was smiling at him.

And he returned her smile with a laugh. 'No, not yet, Phyllis. On the doorstep, like, looking through the gates as it were, but not quite in.'

They both laughed together, and Phyllis asked now, 'Well, what about a mixed grill? I've got some nice chops and sausages. What about it?'

'Not for me, Phyllis. A cup of tea and a toasted tea-cake. Now I wouldn't turn my nose up at that.'

'How about you, Sarah?'

'I'll just have the same. No grill, Phyllis. Not yet, anyway.'

'Well, you're customers that's easily served. And I bet you don't leave a tip. . . . Mean lot!' In mock indignation she stalked into the kitchen. And they were left alone.

Dan, turning fully round in his chair, now looked at this woman who had never, in his eyes, changed one iota from the first time he had seen her across the tea-table on her first visit to the house.

And Sarah was looking at him, at his kindly face, still handsome, but perhaps not so jolly looking as when he was younger. And the more she looked at him the more she ached inside. She was feeling more lost at this moment than she had done since the prison gates had closed behind her.

'How you feeling?'

'Oh, all right, Dan.'

'You're not. You can't fool me. Look.' He leaned forward and gripped her hands. 'I've something I want to say to you.'

She closed her eyes for a second; then forced herself to open them and look at him and wait. Dan deserved to be happy.

She watched his lips move two or three times before they formed words, and then he was speaking hesitantly.

'I wanted to give you this gradually, not spring it on you. I wanted to do things gently, take perhaps a week over it. Not because I wanted to wait a week. No, but because I wanted to give you time to settle in. Time to think. Not feel you were forced to do anything you didn't want. But now, what Michael told me on the phone has altered everything. I could go up there and slap her mouth for her, I could really. . . . Saying that me and May . . .'

'It's all right, Dan.' She was holding his hands now, and she was looking down at them. 'It's all right, I understand.'

'Oh no you don't. You don't. That's what I'm getting at; that's what I'm trying to say. Look, Sarah, I'd have to be damned hard up for a woman and gone in the head before I'd go within a mile of May. All the way down in the car coming here, you know I really felt frightened. I can see it all now: Mary's plans. And May's an' all. The divorce and everything, after she had sat tight for years. And then her coming up to the shop and wanting to do things upstairs. I cooled her off there, but I still didn't guess, and I kept on going across on a Sunday to have a word with her–I always have since John left. But my God in Heaven! Men are infants! That's all we are, infants. . . . Sarah . . . oh, lass, don't cry.' He put his hand up to her face and wiped away the tears.

'It's all right, Dan, it's all right.'

'Can I go on?'

'Yes, Dan, yes.'

He looked down at their joined hands now, and with his voice scarcely above a whisper, he said, 'I've waited a long time. Every day of ten years I've waited, knowingly waited, knowing what I was going to say to you the minute you came out. I've waited with hope these last ten years. And you might as well know it, I've waited from the first minute I saw you, but without hope. . . . Mary was right about one thing, you know, Sarah: you did take us all. But not from her, because she never had us. . . . Now don't get upset. Aw don't, you could no more help the lot of us coming to you than a flower can help itself opening to the sun. Anyway, I've thought and planned what I would say to you. Sometimes, especially at nights, I got worried. I'm not young any more; I'm ten years older than you; and whereas, as you hardly look–and I mean this, Sarah–with all you've gone through you hardly look a day older than when I first saw you. I could even say you were better looking, if that is possible. Well, what I was going to say to you after you'd got your breath was . . . Will you have me, Sarah?' He waited. Then in a small voice: 'Will you?'

'Dan. Oh, Dan.'

He slipped from his chair on to his knees by her side, and his arms going about her, he waited. 'Will you?'

She nodded slowly.

His head was on her breast now, as Phyllis's had been, and she laid her cheek on his hair. She did not ask herself if she loved Dan; she didn't, not as she had loved David, and again not as she had loved John. But this was a new kind of feeling, a feeling of warmth, of tenderness, a feeling without fear, without worry, a feeling that expressed laughter because she couldn't see herself living with Dan and not laughing.

It was as if Dan had read her thoughts, for he said, 'I'll give you everything I have, Sarah. There'll be no fifty-fifty, you can have all I've got. I've enough money put by to see us out comfortably. I've got enough to enable us to laugh.' He raised his head and looked at her. 'You were made for laughter, Sarah, laughter and jollity. But you've never had it; it's always been damped down one way or another.'

'Oh, Dan . . . Dan.' She was gazing at him, but she could see him only through a thick mist.

'I love you, Sarah.'

The tears still running. She smiled at him.

'And now I'm going to do something I've waited a long time to do.' And on this he bent forward and kissed her. His lips hard and firm; he kissed her full on the mouth. Then, getting to his feet and holding out his hands, he pulled her upwards and into his arms.

Holding close, they looked at each other. Then through her tears Sarah laughed. She laughed haltingly but freely for the first time in years. And she said to him, her voice cracking, 'How's Mrs Flaherty? Is she still alive?' She was giving him a lead to make her laugh, more and more, more and more.

Dan's head was back now, his laughter filling the room. And so he stayed for a moment before bringing it forward again to look at her and say, 'Alive and kicking. Oh, the things I'll tell you about Mrs Flaherty! You'll split your sides.'

But what he said to her now about Mrs Flaherty was: 'You know, over all the years when she was reduced to twopennorth of bacon scraps she would always say, "God's good. Aw, God's good." She hadn't a thing in the world to be thankful for, but always she would say that . . . God's good. Well, here's me. I have everything at this minute to be thankful for, and I say with Mrs Flaherty, God's good.'

No recess in her mind questioned Dan's conception of God, nor yet the God of Mrs Flaherty who had inspired faith even through hunger. Perhaps there were millions of gods. Perhaps every man had his own god, and as he saw him in life so he found him in death. . . . Gods like Mrs Flaherty's, gods like Dan's . . . and David's, who weren't acknowledged, only lived. God's like Father Bailey's. Then there were the gods of Father O'Malley's, and the gods of men like her father, and the gods of the Mary Hetheringtons, and these gods were all blind millers. These were terrible gods, and their followers could be terrible people.

Phyllis came from the kitchen now, crying, 'I couldn't leave the toast. What are you two la . . . ?' She brought herself to a halt and looked at them for a full minute before flinging her arms wide and rushing at them. And as they entwined her in their embrace she lent her head once again on Sarah's breast, and between laughter and tears she too said, 'Aw, lass, God's good. When all's said and done, God's good.'

Though the mills of God grind slowly,
Yet they grind exceeding small;
Though with patience he stands waiting.
With exactness grinds he all.